THE FIRST STAGE OF THEIR JOURNEY WAS BY LAND, TO
MONTEGO BAY

Richard Hughes

A High Wind in Jamaica

(The Innocent Voyage)

Buccaneer Books
Cutchogue, New York

International Standard Book Number: 1-56849-582-x

For ordering information, contact:

Buccaneer Books, Inc.
P.O. Box 168
Cutchogue, N.Y. 11935

(516) 734-5724, Fax (516) 734-7920

>>>>>>>>>>>>>>>>>>>><<<<<<<<<<<<<<<<<<<

Chapter One

ONE of the fruits of Emancipation in the West Indian islands is the number of ruins, either attached to the houses that remain or within a stone's throw of them: ruined slaves' quarters, ruined sugar-grinding houses, ruined boiling houses; often ruined mansions that were too expensive to maintain. Earthquake, fire, rain, and deadlier vegetation, did their work quickly.

One scene is very clear in my mind, in Jamaica. There was a vast stone-built house called Derby Hill (where the Parkers lived). It had been the centre of a very prosperous plantation. With Emancipation, like many others, that went *bung*. The sugar buildings fell down. Bush smothered the cane and guinea-grass. The field-negroes left their cottages in a body, to be somewhere less disturbed by even the possibility of work. Then the house-negroes' quarters burnt down, and the three remaining faithful servants occupied the mansion. The two heiresses of all this, The Misses Parker, grew old; and were by education incapable. And the scene is this: coming to Derby Hill on some business or other, and wading waist-deep in bushes up to the front door, now lashed permanently open by a rank plant. The jalousies of the house had been all torn down, and then supplanted as darkeners, by powerful vines: and out of this crumbling half-vegetable gloom an old negress peered, wrapped in filthy brocade. The two old Miss Parkers lived in bed, for the negroes had taken away all their clothes: they were nearly starved. Drinking-water was brought, in two cracked Worcester cups and three cocoanut shells on a silver salver. Presently one of the heiresses persuaded her tyrants to lend her a print dress, and came and pottered about in the mess half-heartedly: tried to wipe the old blood and feathers of slaughtered chickens from a gilt-and-marble table: tried to talk sensibly: tried to wind an ormolu clock: and then gave it up and mooned away back to bed. Not long after this, I believe, they were both starved altogether to death. Or, if that were hardly possible in so prolific a country, perhaps given ground glass—rumour varied. At any rate, they died.

That is the sort of scene which makes a deep impression on the mind; far deeper than the ordinary, less romantic, every-day thing which shows the real state of an island in the statistical sense. Of course, even in the transition period one only found melodrama like this in rare patches. More truly typical was Ferndale, for instance, an estate about fifteen miles away from Derby Hill. Here only the overseer's house remained: the Big

House had altogether collapsed and been
smothered over. It consisted of a ground
floor of stone, given over to goats and the
children, and a first floor of wood, the inhabited part, reached from outside by a
double flight of wooden steps. When the
earthquakes came the upper part only slid
about a little, and could be jacked back into
position with big levers. The roof was of
shingles: after very dry weather it leaked like
a sieve, and the first few days of the rainy
season would be spent in a perpetual general-
post of beds and other furniture to escape
the drips, until the wood swelled.

The people who lived there at the time I
have in mind were called Bas-Thornton: not
natives of the Island, "Creoles", but a family
from England. Mr. Bas-Thornton had a business of some kind in St. Anne's, and used to
ride there every day on a mule. He had such
long legs that his stunted mount made him
look rather ridiculous: and being quite as

temperamental as a mule himself a quarrel between the two was generally worth watching.

Close to the dwelling were the ruined grinding and boiling houses. These two are never quite cheek by jowl: the grinding house is set on higher ground, with a water-wheel to turn the immense iron vertical rollers. From these the cane juice runs down a wedge-shaped trough to the boiling house, where a negro stands and rinses a little lime-wash into it with a grass brush to make it granulate. Then it is emptied into big cop-per vats, over furnaces burning faggots and *trash*, or squeezed-out cane. "There a few negroes stand, skimming the poppling vats with long-handled copper ladles, while their friends sit round, eating sugar or chewing trash, in a mist of hot vapour." What they skim off oozes across the floor with an admix-ture of a good deal of filth—insects, even rats, and whatever sticks to negroes' feet—

into another basin, thence to be distilled into rum.

This, at any rate, is how it used to be done. I know nothing of modern methods— nor if there are any, never having visited the island since 1860, which is a long time ago now.

But long before that, even, all this was over at Ferndale: the big copper vats were overturned, and up in the grinding house the three great rollers lay about loose. No water reached it: the stream had gone about its own business elsewhere. The Bas-Thornton children used to crawl into the cut-well through the vent, among dead leaves and the wreck of the wheel. There, one day, they found a wild-cat's nest, with the mother away. The kittens were tiny, and Emily tried to carry them home in her pinafore; but they bit and scratched so fiercely, right through her thin frock, that she was very glad—except for pride—that they all escaped but one. This one, Tom, grew up; though he was never really tamed. Later he begat several litters on an old tame cat they had, Kitty Cranbrook; and the only survivor of this progeny, Tabby, became rather a famous cat in his way. (But Tom soon took to the jungle altogether.) Tabby was faithful, and a good swimmer, which he would do for pleasure, sculling around the bathing-pool behind the children, giving an occasional yowl of excitement. Also, he had mortal sport with snakes: would wait for a rattler or a black-snake like a mere mouse: drop on it from a tree or some-where and fight it to death. Once he got bitten, and they all wept bitterly, expecting to see a spectacular death-agony; but he just went off into the bush and probably ate something, for he came back in a few days quite cock-a-hoop and as ready to eat snakes as ever.

Red-headed John's room was full of rats: he used to catch them in big gins, and then

>>>>>>>>>>>>>>>>>>>><<<<<<<<<<<<<<<<<<<
let them go for Tabby to despatch. Once the
cat was so impatient he seized trap and all
and caterwauled off into the night banging
it on the stones and sending up showers of
sparks. Again he returned in a few days,
very sleek and pleased: but John never saw
his trap again.

Another plague of his were the bats, which
also infested his room in hundreds. Mr. Bas-
Thornton could crack a stockwhip, and used
to kill a bat on the wing with it most neatly.
But the din this made in that little box of a
room at midnight was infernal: earsplitting
cracks, and the air already full of the tiny
penetrating squeaks of the vermin.

It was a kind of paradise for English children to come to, whatever it might be for
their parents: especially at that time, when
no one lived in at all a wild way at home.
Here, one had to be a little ahead of the
times: or decadent, whichever you like to call
it. The difference between boys and girls,

for instance, had to be left to look after itself. Long hair would have made the evening search for grass-ticks and nits interminable: Emily and Rachel had their hair cut short, and were allowed to do everything the boys did: to climb trees, swim, and trap animals and birds: they even had two pockets in their frocks.

It was round the bathing pool their life centred, more than the house. Every year, when the rains were over, a dam was built across the stream, so that all through the dry season there was quite a large pool to swim in. There were trees all round: enormous fluffed cotton trees, with coffee trees between their paws, and, in contrast to the general shapeless enormousness of the vegetation, delicate log-wood, and gorgeous red and green peppers: amongst them, the pool was almost completely shaded. Emily and John set tree-springs in them—Lame-foot Sam taught them how. Cut a bendy stick, and tie a string to one end. Then sharpen the other, so that it can impale a fruit as bait. Just at the base of this point flatten it a little, and bore a hole through the flat part. Cut a little peg that will just stick in the mouth of this hole. Then make a loop in the end of the string: bend the stick, as in stringing a bow, till the loop will thread through the little hole, and jam it with the peg, along which the loop should lie spread. Bait the point, and hang it in a tree among the twigs: the bird alights on the peg to peck the fruit, the peg falls out, the loop whips tight round its ankles: then away up out of the water like pink predatory monkeys, and decide by "Eena, deena, dina, do," or some such rigmarole, whether to twist its neck or let it go free—thus the excitement and suspense, both for child and bird, can be prolonged even beyond the moment of capture.

It was only natural that Emily should have great ideas of improving the negroes. They were, of course, Christians, so there was nothing to be done about their morals: nor were they in need of soup, or knitted things; but they were sadly ignorant. After a good deal of negotiation they consented in the end to let her teach Little Jim to read: but she had no success. Also she had a passion for catching house-lizards without their dropping their tails off, which they do when frightened: it wanted endless patience to get them whole and unalarmed into a match box. Catching green grass-lizards was also very delicate. She would sit and whistle, like Orpheus, till they came out of their crannies and showed their emotion by puffing out their pink throats: then, very gently, she would lasso them with a long blade of grass. Her room was full of these and other pets, some alive, others probably dead. She also had tame fairies; and a familiar, or oracle, the White Mouse with an Elastic Tail, who was

→ 11 ←

always ready to settle any point in question, and whose rule was a rule of iron—especially over Rachel, Edward, and Laura, the little ones (or Liddlies, as they came to be known in the family). To Emily, his interpreter, he allowed of course certain privileges: and with John, who was older than Emily, he quite wisely did not interfere.

He was omnipresent: the fairies were more localised, living in a small hole in the hill guarded by two dagger-plants.

The best fun at the bathing-pool was had with a big forked log. John would sit astride the main stem, and the others pushed him about by the two prongs. The little ones, of course, only splashed about the shallow end: but John and Emily dived. John, that is to say, dived properly, head-foremost: Emily only jumped in feet first, stiff as a rod; but she, on the other hand, would go off higher boughs than he would. Once, when she was eight, Mrs. Thornton had thought she was too big to bathe naked any more. The only bathing-dress she could rig was an old cotton nightgown. Emily jumped in as usual: first the balloons of air tipped her upside down, and then the wet cotton wrapped itself round her head and arms and nearly drowned her. After that, decency was let go hang again: it is hardly worth being drowned for: at least, it does not at first sight appear to be.

But once a negro really was drowned in the pool. He had gorged himself full of stolen mangoes: and feeling guilty, thought he might as well cool himself in the forbidden pond as well, and make one repentance cover two crimes. He could not swim, and had only a black child (Little Jim) with him. The cold water and the surfeit brought on an apoplexy: Jim poked at him with a piece of stick a little, and then ran away in a fright. Whether the man died of the apoplexy or the drowning was a point for an inquest; and the doctor, after staying at Ferndale for a week, decided it was from drowning, but that he was full of green mangoes right up to his mouth. The great advantage of this was that no negro would bathe there again, for fear the dead man's "duppy," or ghost, should catch him. So if any black even came near while they were bathing John and Emily would pretend the duppy had grabbed at them, and off he would go, terribly upset. Only one of the negroes at Ferndale had ever actually seen a duppy, but that was quite enough. They cannot be mistaken for living people, because their heads are turned backwards on their shoulders, and they carry a chain: moreover one must never call them duppies to their faces, as it gives them power. This poor man forgot, and called out *"Duppy!"* when he saw it. He got terrible rheumatics.

>>>>>>>>>>>>>>>>>>>>>>><<<<<<<<<<<<<<<<<<<<

Lame-foot Sam was the one who told most stories. He used to sit all day on the stone barbecues where the pimento was dried, digging maggots out of his toes. This seemed at first very horrid to the children, but he seemed quite contented; and when jiggers got under their own skins, and laid their little bags of eggs there, it was not absolutely unpleasant. John used to get quite a sort of thrill from rubbing the place. Sam told them the Anansi stories: Anansi and the Tiger, and how Anansi looked after the Crocodile's nursery, and so on. Also he had a little poem which impressed them very much:

Quacko Sam
Him bery fine man:
Him dance all de dances dat de darkies can:
Him dance de schottische, him dance de Cod Reel:
Him dance ebery kind of dance till him foot-
   bottom peel.

Perhaps that was how old Sam's own afflic-

tion first came about: he was very sociable.
He was *said* to have a great many children.

ii

The stream which fed the bathing-hole ran
into it down a gully through the bush. It
offered an enticing vista for exploring: but
somehow the children did not often go up it
very far. Every stone on the way had to be
overturned, in the hope of finding cray-fish:
or if not, John had to take a sporting gun,
which he bulleted with spoonfuls of water to
shoot humming-birds on the wing—too tiny
frail quarry for any solider projectile. For,
only a few yards up, there was a Frangipani
tree: a mass of brilliant blossom and no
leaves, which was almost hidden in a cloud
of humming-birds so vivid as much to out-
shine the flowers. Writers have often lost
their way trying to explain how brilliant a

jewel the humming-bird is: it cannot be done.

They build their wee woollen nests on the tips of twigs, where no snake can reach them. They are devoted to their eggs, and will not move though you touch them. But they are so delicate the children never did that: they held their breath and stared and stared—and were out-stared.

Somehow, the celestial vividness of this barrier generally arrested them. It was seldom any of them explored further: only once, I think, on a day when Emily was feeling peculiarly irritated.

It was her own tenth birthday. They had frittered away the whole morning in the glass-like gloom of the bathing hole. Now John sat naked on the bank making a wicker trap. In the shallows the small ones rolled and chuckled. Emily, for coolness, sat up to her chin in water, and hundreds of infant fish were tickling with their inquisitive mouth every inch of her body, a sort of expression-less light kissing.

Anyhow she had lately come to hate being touched—but this was abominable. At last, when she could stand it no longer, she clambered out and dressed. Rachel and Laura were too small for a long walk: and the last thing, she felt, that she wanted was to have one of the boys with her: so she stole quietly past John's back, scowling balefully at him for no particular reason. Soon she was out of sight among the bushes.

She pushed on rather fast up the river bed, not taking much notice of things, for about three miles. She had never been so far afield before. Then her attention was caught by a clearing leading down to the water: and here was the source of the river. She caught her breath delightedly: it bubbled up clear and cold, through three distinct springs, under a clump of bamboos, just as a river should: the greatest possible find, and a private discovery of her own. She gave instantaneous inward thanks to God for thinking of such a perfect birthday treat, especially as things had seemed to be going all wrong: and then began to ferret in the limestone sources with the whole length of her arm, among the ferns and cresses.

Hearing a splash, she looked round. Some half dozen strange negro children had come down the clearing to fetch water, and were staring at her in astonishment. Emily stared back. In sudden terror they flung down their calabashes and galloped away up the clearing like hares. Emily followed them: immediately, but with dignity. The clearing narrowed to a path, and the path led in a very short time to a village.

It was all ragged and unkempt, and shrill with voices. There were small one-storey wattle huts dotted about, completely overhung by the most enormous trees. There was no sort of order: they appeared anywhere:

there were no railings, and only one or two of the most terribly starved mangy cattle to keep in or out. In the middle of all was an indeterminate quagmire or muddy pond, where a group of negroes were splashing with geese and ducks.

Emily stared: they stared back. She made a movement towards them: they separated at once into the various huts, and watched her from there. Encouraged by the comfortable feeling of inspiring fright she advanced, and at last found an old creature who would talk: Dis Liberty Hill, dis Black Man's Town. Old-time niggers, dey go fer run from de bushas (overseers), go for live here. De piccanninies, dey neber seen buckras (whites) . . . And so on. It was a refuge, built by runaway slaves, and still inhabited.

And then, that her cup of happiness might be full, some of the bolder children crept out and respectfully offered her flowers—really to get a better look at her pallid face. Her heart bubbled up in her, she swelled with glory: and taking leave with the greatest condescension she trod all the long way home on veritable air, back to her beloved family, back to a birthday cake wreathed with stephanotis, lit with ten candles, and in which it so happened that the sixpenny piece was invariably found in the birthday-person's slice.

iii

This was, fairly typically, the life of an English family in Jamaica. Mostly these only stayed a few years. The Creoles—families who had been in the West Indies for more than one generation—gradually evolved something a little more distinctive. They lost some of the traditional mental mechanism of Europe, and the outlines of a new one began to appear.

There was one such family the Bas-Thorntons were acquainted with, who had a ramshackle estate to the eastward. They invited John and Emily to spend a couple of days with them, but Mrs. Thornton was in two minds about letting them go, lest they should learn bad ways. The children there were a wildish lot, and, in the morning at least, would often run about barefoot like negroes, which is a very important point in a place like Jamaica where the whites have to keep up appearances. They had a governess whose blood was possibly not pure, and who used to beat the children ferociously with a hairbrush. However, the climate at the Fernandez's place was healthy, and also Mrs. Thornton thought it good for them to have some intercourse with other children outside their own family, however undesirable: and she let them go.

It was the afternoon after that birthday, and a long buggy-ride. Both fat John and thin Emily were speechless and solemn with excitement: it was the first visit they had ever paid. Hour after hour the buggy laboured over the uneven road. At last the lane to Exeter, the Fernandez's place, was reached. It was evening, the sun about to do his rapid tropical setting. He was unusually large and red, as if he threatened something peculiar. The lane, or drive, was gorgeous: for the first few hundred yards it was entirely hedged with "seaside grapes", clusters of fruit half-way between a gooseberry and a golden pippin, with here and there the red berries of coffee trees newly planted among the burnt stumps in a clearing, but already neglected. Then, a massive stone gateway in a sort of Colonial-Gothic style. This had to be circumvented: no one had taken the trouble to heave open the heavy gates for years. There was no fence, nor ever had been, so the track simply passed it by.

And beyond the gate an avenue of magnificent cabbage-palms. No tree, not oldest

>>>>>>>>>>>>>>>>>>>>>>>><<<<<<<<<<<<<<<<<<<<
beech nor chestnut, is more spectacular in an avenue: rising a sheer hundred feet with no break in the line before the actual crown of plumes; and palm upon palm, palm upon palm like a heavenly double row of pillars, leading on interminably, till even the huge house was dwarfed into a sort of ultimate mouse-trap.

As they journeyed on between these palms, the sun went suddenly down: darkness flooded up round them out of the ground, retorted to almost immediately by the moon. Presently, shimmering like a ghost, an old blind white donkey stood in their way. Curses did not move him: the driver had to climb down and push him aside. The air was full of the usual tropic din: mosquitoes humming, cicadas trilling, bull-frogs twanging like guitars. That din goes on all night and all day almost: is more insistent, more memorable than the heat itself, even, or the number of things that bite. In the valley beneath the fire-flies came to life; as if at a signal passed along, wave after wave of light swept down the gorge. From a neighbouring hill the cockatoos began their serenade, an orchestration of drunk men laughing against iron girders tossed at each other and sawn up with rusty hack-saws: the most awful noise: but Emily and John, so far as they noticed it at all, found it vaguely exhilarating. Through it could presently be distinguished another sound: a negro praying. They soon came near him: where an orange-tree, loaded with golden fruit, gleamed dark and bright in the moonlight, veiled in the pinpoint scintillation of a thousand fireflies sat the old black saint among the branches, talking loudly, drunkenly, and confidentially with God.

Almost unexpectedly they came on the house, and were whisked straight off to bed. Emily omitted to wash, since there seemed such a hurry, but made up for it by spend-

>>>>>>>>>>>>>>>>>>>>><<<<<<<<<<<<<<<<<<<<<

ing an unusually long time over her prayers. She pressed her eyeballs devoutly with her fingers to make sparks appear, in spite of the slightly sick feeling it always induced: and then, already sound asleep, clambered, I suppose, into bed.

The next day the sun rose as he had set: large, round and red. It was blindingly hot —foreboding. Emily, who woke early in a strange bed, stood at the window, watching the negroes release the hens from the chicken-houses, where they were shut up at night for fear of John-crows. As each bird hopped sleepily out, the black passed his hand over its stomach to see if it meditated an egg that day: if so, it was confined again or it would have gone off and laid in the bush. It was already as hot as an oven. Another black, with eschatological yells and tail-twistings and lassoings, was confining a cow in a kind of pillory, that it might have no opportunity of sitting down while being milked. The

>>>>>>>>>>>>>>>>>>><<<<<<<<<<<<<<<<<<

poor brute's hooves were aching with the heat, its miserable tea-cup of milk fevered in its udder. Even as she stood at the shady win-dow Emily felt as sweaty as if she had been running. The ground was fissured with drought.

Margaret Fernandez, whose room Emily was sharing, slipped out of bed silently and stood beside her, wrinkling the short nose in her pallid face.

"Good morning", said Emily, politely.

"Smells like an earthquake", said Mar-garet, and dressed. Emily remembered the awful story about the governess and the hair-brush: certainly Margaret did not use one for its ordinary purpose, though she had long hair: so it must be true.

Margaret was ready long before Emily, and banged out of the room. Emily followed later, neat and nervous, to find no one. The house was empty. Presently she spied John under a tree, talking to a negro boy. By his off-hand manner Emily guessed he was telling *disproportionate* stories (not *lies*) about the importance of Ferndale, compared with Exeter. She did not call to him, because the house was silent and it was not her place, as guest, to alter anything: so she went out to him. Together they circumnavigated: they found a stable-yard, and negroes preparing ponies, and the Fernandez children, bare-foot even as Rumour had whispered. Emily caught her breath, shocked. Even at that moment a chicken, scuttling across the yard, trod on a scorpion, and tumbled over stark dead as if shot. But it was not so much the danger which upset Emily as the unconventionality.

"Come on," said Margaret: "it's much too hot to stay about here. We'll go down to Exeter Rocks."

The cavalcade mounted: Emily very conscious of her boots, buttoned respectably half-way up her calf. Somebody had food, and

calabashes of water. The ponies evidently
knew the way. The sun was still red and
large: the sky above cloudless, and like blue
glaze poured over white-hot clay: but close to
the ground a dirty grey haze hovered. As
they followed the lane towards the sea they
came to a place where, yesterday, a fair-sized
spring had bubbled up by the roadside.
Now, it was dry. But even as they passed a
kind of gout of water gushed forth: and
then it was dry again, although gurgling inwardly to itself. But the cavalcade were hot,
far too hot to speak to one another: they sat
their ponies as loosely as possible, longing
for the sea.

The morning advanced. The heated air
grew quite easily hotter, as if from some reserve of enormous blaze on which it could
draw at will. Bullocks only shifted their
stinging feet when they could bear the soil
no longer: even the insects were too languor-
ous to pipe, the basking lizards hid them-

selves and panted. It was so still you could have heard the least buzz a mile off. Not a naked fish would willingly move his tail. The ponies advanced because they must: the children ceased even to muse.

They all very nearly jumped out of their skins: for close at hand a crane had trumpeted once desperately. Then the broken silence closed down as flawless as before. They perspired twice as violently with the stimulus. Their pace grew slower and slower. It was no faster than a procession of snails that at last they reached the sea.

Exeter Rocks is a famous place. A bay of the sea, almost a perfect semi-circle, guarded by the reef: shelving white sands to span the few feet from the water to the undercut turf: and then, almost at the mid point, a jutting-out shelf of rocks right into deep water—fathoms deep. And a narrow fissure in the rocks, leading the water into a small pool, or miniature lagoon, right inside their bastion.

>>>>>>>>>>>>>>>>>>>><<<<<<<<<<<<<<<<<<<

There it was, safe from sharks or drowning, that the Fernandez children meant to soak themselves all day, like turtles in a crawl. The water of the bay was as smooth and im-movable as basalt, yet clear as the finest gin: albeit the swell muttered a mile away on the reef. The water within the pool itself could not reasonably be smoother. No sea breeze thought of stirring. No bird trespassed on the inert air.

For a while they had not energy to get into the water, but lay on their faces, looking down, down, down, at the sea-fans and sea-feathers, the scarlet-plumed barnacles and corals, the black and yellow schoolmistress-fish, the rainbow-fish—all that forest of ideal christmas-trees which is a tropical sea-bottom. Then they stood up, giddy and seeing black, and in a trice were floating suspended in water like drowned ones, only their noses above the surface, under the shadow of a rocky ledge.

>>>>>>>>>>>>>>>>>>>>>>><<<<<<<<<<<<<<<<<<<<<

An hour or so after noon they clustered to-gether, puffy from the warm water, in the insufficient shade of a Panama Fern: ate such of the food they had brought as they had appetite for; and drank all the water, wishing for more. Then a very odd thing happened: for even as they sat there they heard the most peculiar sound: a strange, rushing sound that passed overhead like a gale of wind—but not a breath of breeze stirred, *that* was the odd thing: followed by a sharp hissing and hurtling, like a flight of rockets, or gigantic swans—very distant rocs, perhaps—on the wing. They all looked up: but there was nothing at all. The sky was empty and lucid. Long before they were back in the water again all was still. Except that after a while John noticed a sort of tapping, as if someone were gently knocking the outside of a bath you were in. But the bath they were in had no outside, it was solid world. It was funny.

By sunset they were so weak from long

immersion they could barely stand up, and as salted as bacon: but, with some common impulse, just before the sun went down they all left the rocks and went and stood by their clothes, where the ponies were tethered, under some palms. As he sank the sun grew even larger and instead of red was now a sodden purple. Down he went, behind the western horn of the bay, which immediately blackened till its waterline disappeared, and substance and reflection seemed one sharp symmetrical pattern.

Not a breath of breeze even yet ruffled the water: but momentarily it trembled of its own accord, shattering the reflections: then was glassy again. On that the children held their breath, waiting for it to happen.

A school of fish, terrified by some purely submarine event, thrust their heads right out of the water, squattering across the bay in an arrowy rush, dashing up sparkling ripples with the tiny heave of their shoulders: yet after each disturbance all was soon like hardest, dark, thick, glass.

Once things vibrated slightly, like a chair in a concert-room: and again there was that mysterious winging, though there was nothing visible beneath the swollen, iridescent stars.

Then it came. The water of the bay began to ebb away, as if someone had pulled up the plug: a foot or so of sand and coral gleamed for a moment new to the air: then back the sea rushed in miniature rollers which splashed right up to the foot of the palms. Mouthfuls of turf were torn away: and on the far side of the bay a small piece of cliff tumbled into the water: sand and twigs showered down, dew fell from the trees like diamonds: birds and beasts, their tongues at last loosed, screamed and bellowed: the ponies, thought quite unalarmed, lifted up their heads and yelled.

That was all: a few moments. Then silence, with a rapid countermarch, recovered all his rebellious kingdom. Stillness again. The trees moved as little as the pillars of a ruin, each leaf laid sleekly in place. The bubbling foam subsided: the reflections of the stars came out among it as if there could never have been a disturbance, however slight. The naked children too continued to stand motionless beside the quiet ponies, shine on their infantile round paunches.

But as for Emily, it was too much. The earthquake went completely to her head. She began to dance, hopping laboriously from one foot onto another. John caught the infection. He turned head over heels on the damp sand, over and over in an elliptical course till before he knew it he was in the water, and so giddy as hardly to be able to tell up from down.

At that, Emily knew what it was she wanted to do. She scrambled onto a pony and galloped him up and down the beach, trying to bark like a dog. The Fernandez children stared, solemn but not disapproving. John, shaping a course for Cuba, was swimming as if sharks were paring his toe-nails. Emily rode her pony into the sea, and beat and beat him till he swam: and so she followed John towards the reef, yapping herself hoarse.

It must have been fully a hundred yards before they were spent. Then they turned for the shore, John holding on to Emily's leg, puffing and gasping, both a little overdone, their emotion run down. Presently John gasped:

"You shouldn't ride on your bare skin, you'll catch ringworm."

"I don't care if I do," said Emily.

"You would if you did," said John.

"I don't care!" chanted Emily.

It seemed a long way to the shore. When

they reached it the others had dressed and
were preparing to start. Soon the whole
party were on their way home in the dark.
Presently Margaret said:

"So that's that."

No one answered.

"I could smell it was an earthquake coming
when I got up. Didn't I say so, Emily?"

"You and your smells!" said Jimmie Fernandez. "You're always smelling things!"

"She's awfully good at smells," said the
youngest, Harry, proudly, to John. "She can
sort out people's dirty clothes for the wash by
smell: who they belong to."

"She can't really," said Jimmie: "She fakes
it. As if everyone smelt different!"

"I can!"

"Dogs can, anyway," said John.

Emily said nothing. Of course people
smelt different: it didn't need arguing. She
could always tell her own towel from John's.

for instance: or even knew if one of the others had used it. But it just showed what sort of people Creoles were, to *talk* about Smell, in that open way.

"Well, anyhow I said there was going to be an earthquake and there was one," said Margaret.

That was what Emily was waiting for! So it really had been an earthquake (she had not liked to ask, it seemed so ignorant: but now Margaret had said in so many words that it was one).

If ever she went back to England, she could now say to people, *"I have been in an earthquake."*

With that certainty, her soused excitement began to revive. For there was nothing, no adventure from the hands of God or Man, to equal it. Realise that if she had suddenly found she could fly it would not have seemed more miraculous to her. Heaven had played its last, most terrible card; and small Emily had survived, where even grown men (such as Korah, Dathan, and Abiram), had succumbed.

Life seemed suddenly a little empty: for never again could there happen to her anything so dangerous, so sublime.

Meanwhile, Margaret and Jimmie were still arguing:

"Well, there's one thing, there'll be plenty of eggs tomorrow," said Jimmie. "There's nothing like an earthquake for making them lay."

How funny Creoles were! They didn't seem to realise the difference it made to a person's whole after-life to have been in an Earthquake.

When they got home, Martha, the black housemaid, had hard things to say about the sublime cataclysm. She had dusted the drawing-room china only the day before: and now

everything was covered again in a fine penetrating film of dust.

iv

The next morning, Sunday, they went
home. Emily was still so saturated in earthquake as to be dumb. She ate earthquake
and slept earthquake: her fingers and legs
were earthquake. With John, it was ponies.
The earthquake had been fun: but it was the
ponies that mattered. But at present it did
not worry Emily that she was alone in her
sense of proportion. She was too completely
possessed to be able to see anything, or realise
that anyone else pretended to even a self-
delusive fiction of existence.

Their mother met them at the door. She
bubbled questions: John chattered ponies,
but Emily was still tongue-tied. She was,

in her mind, like a child who has eaten too much even to be able to be sick.

Mrs. Thornton got a little worried about her at times. This sort of life was very peaceful, and might be excellent for nervy children like John: but a child like Emily, thought Mrs. Thornton, who is far from nervy, really needs some sort of stimulus and excitement, or there is a danger of her mind going to sleep altogether for ever. This life was too vegetable. Consequently Mrs. Thornton always spoke to Emily in her brightest manner, as if everything was of the greatest possible interest. She had hoped, too, the visit to Exeter might liven her up; but she had come back as silent and expressionless as ever. It had evidently made no impression on her at all.

John marshalled the small ones in the cellar, and round and round they marched, wooden swords at the slope, singing "Onward, Christian Soldiers." Emily did not join them. What did it now matter, that earlier woe, that being a girl she could never when grown up become a real soldier with a real sword? She had been in an Earthquake!

But even the others did not keep it up very long. (Sometimes they would go on for three or four hours.) For, whatever it might have done for Emily's soul, the earthquake had done little to clear the air. It was as hot as ever. In the animal world there seemed some strange commotion, as if they had wind of something. The usual lizards and mosquitoes were still absent: but in their place the earth's most horrid progeny, creatures of darkness, sought the open: land-crabs wandered about aimlessly, angrily twiddling their claws: and the ground seemed almost alive with red ants and cockroaches. Up on the roof the pigeons were gathered, talking to each other fearfully.

The cellar (or rather, ground floor), where

>>>>>>>>>>>>>>>>>>>>>><<<<<<<<<<<<<<<<<<<<<

they were playing, had no communication
with the wooden structure above, but had an
opening of its own under the twin flight of
steps leading to the front door; and there the
children presently gathered in the shadow.
Out in the compound lay one of Mr. Thornton's best handkerchiefs. He must have
dropped it that morning. But none of them
felt the energy to go and retrieve it, out into
the sun. Then, as they stood there, they saw
Lame-foot Sam come limping across the yard.
Seeing the prize, he was about to carry it off.
Suddenly he remembered it was Sunday. He
dropped it like a hot brick, and began to
cover it with sand, exactly where he had
found it.

"Please God, I thieve you tomorrow," he
explained, hopefully: "Please God, you still
there?"

A low mutter of thunder seemed to offer
grudging assent.

"Thank you, Lord," said Sam, bowing to a

low bank of cloud. He hobbled off: but then, not too sure perhaps that Heaven would keep Its promise, changed his mind: snatched up the handkerchief and made off for his cottage. The thunder muttered louder and more angrily: but Sam ignored the warning.

It was the custom that, whenever Mr. Thornton had been to St. Anne's, John and Emily should run out to meet him, and ride back with him, one perched on each of his stirrups.

That Sunday evening they ran out as soon as they saw him coming, in spite of the thunderstorm that by now was clattering over their very heads—and not only over their heads, either, for in the Tropics a thunderstorm is not a remote affair up in the sky, as it is in England, but is all round you: lightning plays ducks and drakes across the water, bounds from tree to tree, bounces about the ground, while the thunder seems to proceed from violent explosions in your own very core.

"Go back! Go back, you damned little fools!" he yelled furiously: "Get into the house!"

They stopped, aghast: and then began to realise that after all it was a storm of more than ordinary violence. They discovered that they were drenched to the skin—must have been the moment they left the house. The lightning kept up a continuous blaze: it was playing about their father's very stirrup-irons; and all of a sudden they realised that he was afraid. They fled to the house, shocked to the heart: and he was in the house almost as soon as they were. Mrs. Thornton rushed out:

"My dear, I'm so glad . . ."

"I've never seen such a storm! Why on earth did you let the children come out?"

"I never dreamt they would be so silly!

And all the time I was thinking—but thank
Heaven you're back!"

"I think the worst is over now."

Perhaps it was; but all through supper the
lightning shone almost without flickering.
And John and Emily could hardly eat: the
memory of that momentary look on their
father's face haunted them.

It was an unpleasant meal altogether. Mrs.
Thornton had prepared for her husband his
"favourite dish"; than which no action could
more annoy a man of whim. In the middle
of it all in burst Sam, ceremony dropped: he
flung the handkerchief angrily on the table
and stumped out.

"What on earth . . . ?" began Mr. Thornton.

But John and Emily knew; and thoroughly
agreed with Sam as to the cause of the storm.
Stealing was bad enough anyway: but on a
Sunday!

Meanwhile, the lightning kept up its play.

The thunder made talking arduous, but no one was anyhow in a mood to chatter. Only thunder was heard, and the hammering of the rain. But suddenly, close under the windows, there burst out the most appalling inhuman shriek of terror.

"Tabby!" cried John, and they all rushed to the window.

But Tabby had already flashed into the house: and behind him was a whole club of wild cats in hot pursuit. John momentarily opened the dining-room door and puss slipped in, dishevelled and panting. Not even then did the brutes desist: what insane fury led these jungle creatures to pursue him into the very house is unimaginable; but there they were, in the passage, caterwauling in concert: and as if at their incantation the thunder awoke anew, and the lightning nullified the meagre table lamp. It was such a din as you could not speak through. Tabby, his fur on end, pranced up and down the room,

his eyes blazing, talking and sometimes ex-
claiming in a tone of voice the children had
never heard him use before, and which made
their blood run cold. He seemed like one
inspired in the presence of Death, he had
gone utterly Delphic: and without in the passage Hell's pandemonium reigned terrifically.

The check could be only a short one. Outside the dining-room door stood the big filter,
and above the door the fanlight was long
since broken. Something black and yelling
flashed through the fanlight, landing clean in
the middle of the supper table, scattering the
forks and spoons and upsetting the lamp.
And another and another—but already
Tabby was through the window and streak-
ing again for the bush. The whole dozen of
those wild cats leapt one after the other from
the top of the filter clean through the fanlight on to the supper table, and away from
there only too hot in his tracks. In a moment

the whole devil-hunt and its hopeless quarry had vanished into the night.

"Oh Tabby, my darling Tabby!" wailed John; while Emily rushed again to the window.

They were gone. The lightning behind the creepers in the jungle lit them up like giant cobwebs; but of Tabby and his pursuers there was nothing to be seen.

John burst into tears, the first time for several years, and flung himself on his mother: Emily stood transfixed at the window, her eyes glued in horror on what she could not, in fact, see: and all of a sudden was sick.

"God, what an evening!" groaned Mr. Bas-Thornton, groping in the darkness for what might be left of their supper.

Shortly after that Sam's hut burst into flames. They saw, from the dining-room, the old negro stagger dramatically out into the darkness. He was throwing stones at the sky.

>>>>>>>>>>>>>>>>>>>>><<<<<<<<<<<<<<<<<<<<<

In a lull they heard him cry: "I gib it back, didn't I? I gib de nasty t'ing back?"

Then there was another blinding flash, and Sam fell where he stood. Mr. Thornton pulled the children roughly back and said something like, "I'll go and see. Keep them from the window."

Then he closed and barred the shutters, and was gone.

John and the little ones kept up a continuous sobbing. Emily wished someone would light a lamp, she wanted to read: it might help her not to think about poor Tabby.

I suppose the wind must have begun to rise some while before this, but now, by the time Mr. Thornton had managed to carry old Sam's body into the house, it was more than a gale. The old man, stiff in the joints as he might have been in life, had gone as limp as a worm. Emily and John slipped unbeknownst into the passage, and were thrilled beyond measure at the way he dangled: they could hardly tear themselves away, and be back in the dining-room, before they should be discovered.

There Mrs. Thornton sat heroically in a chair, her brood all grouped round her, saying the psalms, and the poems of Sir Walter Scott, over by heart. Emily tried to keep her mind off Tabby by going over in her head all the details of her Earthquake. At times the din, the rocketing of the thunder and torrential shriek of the wind, which up to now she had hardly noticed, became so loud as almost to impinge on her inner world: she wished this wretched thunderstorm would hurry up and get over. First, she held an actual performance of the earthquake, went over it direct, as if it was again happening. Then she put it into Oratio Recta, told it as a story, beginning with that magic phrase, "Once I was in an Earthquake." But before long the dramatic element reappeared—this time, the awed comments of her imaginary English audience. When that was done, she put it into the Historical—a Voice, declaring that a girl called Emily was once in an Earthquake. And so on, right through the whole thing a third time.

The horrid fate of poor Tabby appeared suddenly before her eyes, caught her unawares: and she was all but sick again. Even her Earthquake had failed her. Caught by the incubus, her mind struggled frantically to clutch at even the outside world, as an only remaining straw. She tried to fix her interest on every least detail of the scene around her —to count the slats in the shutters, any least detail that was *outward*. So it was that for the first time she really began to notice the weather.

The wind by now was more than redoubled. The shutters were bulging as if tired elephants were leaning against them, and Father was trying to tie the fastening with that handkerchief. But to push against this wind was like pushing against rock. The handkerchief, shutters, everything burst: the rain poured in like the sea into a sinking ship, the wind occupied the room, snatching pictures from the wall, sweeping the table bare. Through the gaping frames the light-ning-lit scene without was visible. The creepers, which before had looked like cob-webs, now streamed up into the sky like new-combed hair. Bushes were lying flat, laid back on the ground as close as a rabbit lays back his ears. Branches were leaping about loose in the sky. The negro huts were clean gone, and the negroes crawling on their stomachs across the compound to gain the shelter of the house. The bouncing rain seemed to cover the ground with a white smoke, a sort of sea in which the blacks wal-lowed like porpoises. One nigger-boy began to roll away: his mother, forgetting caution, rose to her feet: and immediately the fat old beldam was blown clean away, bowling

along across fields and hedgerows like someone in a funny fairy-story, till she fetched up
against a wall and was pinned there, unable
to move. But the others managed to reach
the house, and soon could be heard in the
cellar underneath.

Moreover the very floor began to ripple, as
a loose carpet will ripple on a gusty day:
in opening the cellar door the blacks had let
the wind in, and now for some time they
could not shut it again. The wind, to push
against, was more like a solid block than a
current of air.

Mr. Thornton went round the house—to
see what could be done, he said. He soon
realised that the next thing to go would be
the roof. So he returned to the Niobe-group
in the dining-room. Mrs. Thornton was half
way through *The Lady of the Lake*, the
smaller children listening with rapt attention.
Exasperated, he told them that they would
probably not be alive in half an hour. No

one seemed particularly interested in his news: Mrs. Thornton continued her recitation with faultless memory.

After another couple of cantos the threatened roof went. Fortunately, the wind taking it from inside, most of it was blown clear of the house: but one of the couples collapsed skew-eyed, and was hung up on what was left of the dining-room door—within an ace of hitting John. Emily, to her intense resentment, suddenly felt cold. All at once, she found she had had enough of the storm: it had become intolerable, instead of a welcome distraction.

Mr. Thornton began to look for something to break through the floor. If only he could make a hole in it, he might get his wife and children down into the cellar. Fortunately he did not have to look far: one arm of the fallen couple had already done the work for him. Laura, Rachel, Emily, Edward and John, Mrs. Thornton, and finally Mr. Thornton himself, were passed down into the darkness already thronged with negroes and goats.

With great good sense, Mr. Thornton brought with him from the room above a couple of decanters of Madeira, and everyone had a swig, from Laura to the oldest negro. All the children made the most of this unholy chance, but somehow to Emily the bottle got passed twice, and each time she took a good pull. It was enough, at their age; and while what was left of the house was blown away over their heads, through the lull and the ensuing aerial return match, John, Emily, Edward, Rachel, and Laura, blind drunk, slept in a heap on the cellar floor: a sleep which the appalling fate of Tabby, torn to pieces by those fiends almost under their very eyes, dominated with the easy empire of nightmare.

>>>>>>>>>>>>>>>>>>>><<<<<<<<<<<<<<<<<<<<

Chapter Two

A L L night the water poured through the house floor onto the people sheltering below: but (perhaps owing to the Madeira) it did them no harm. Shortly after the second bout of blowing, however, the rain stopped: and when dawn came Mr. Thornton crept out to assess the damage.

The country was quite unrecognisable, as if it had been swept by a spate. You could hardly tell, geographically speaking, where you were. It is vegetation which gives the character to a tropic landscape, not the shape of the ground: and all the vegetation, for miles, was now pulp. The ground itself had been ploughed up by instantaneous rivers, biting deep into the red earth. The only living thing in sight was a cow: and she had lost both her horns.

The wooden part of the house was nearly all gone. After they had succeeded in reaching shelter, one wall after another had blown down. The furniture was splintered into matchwood. Even the heavy mahogany dining-table, which they loved and had always kept with its legs in little glass baths of oil to defeat the ants, was spirited right away. There were some fragments which might be part of it, or they might not: you could not tell.

Mr. Thornton returned to the cellar and helped his wife out: she was so cramped as hardly to be able to move. They knelt down together and thanked God for not having treated them any worse. Then they stood up and stared about them rather stupidly. It seemed not credible that all this had been done by a current of air. Mr. Thornton patted the atmosphere with his hand. When still, it was so soft, so rare: how could one believe that Motion, itself something impalpable, had lent it a hardness: that this gentle, hind-like Meteor should have last night seized Fat Betsy with the rapacity of a tiger and the lift of a roc, and flung her, as he had seen her flung, across two fair-sized fields?

Mrs. Thornton understood his gesture.

"Remember who is its Prince," she said.

The stable was damaged, though not completely destroyed: and Mr. Thornton's mule was so much hurt he had to tell a negro to cut its throat. The buggy was smashed beyond repair. The only building undamaged was a stone chamber which had been the hospital of the old sugar-estate: so they woke the children, who were feeling ill and beyond words unhappy, and moved into this: where the negroes, with an unexpected energy and kindliness, did everything they could to make them comfortable. It was paved and unlighted: but solid.

The children were bilious for a few days, and inclined to dislike each other: but they accepted the change in their lives practically without noticing it. It is a fact that it takes experience before one can realise what is a catastrophe and what is not. Children have little faculty of distinguishing between disaster and the ordinary course of their lives. If Emily had known this was a *Hurricane,* she would doubtless have been far more impressed, for the word was full of romantic terrors. But it never entered her head: and a thunderstorm, however severe, is after all a commonplace affair. The mere fact that it had done incalculable damage, while the earthquake had done none at all, gave it no right whatever to rival the latter in the hierarchy of cataclysms: an Earthquake is a thing apart. If she was silent, and inclined to brood over some inward terror, it was not the hurricane she was thinking of, it was the death of Tabby. That, at times, seemed a horror beyond all bearing. It was her first intimate contact with death--and a death of violence, too. The death of Old Sam had no such effect: there is after all a vast difference between a negro and a favourite cat.

There was something enjoyable, too, in camping in the hospital: a sort of everlasting picnic in which their parents for once were taking part. Indeed it led them to begin for the first time to regard their parents as rational human beings, with understandable tastes—such as sitting on the floor to eat one's dinner.

It would have surprised Mrs. Thornton very much to have been told that hitherto she had meant practically nothing to her children. She took a keen interest in Psychology (the Art Bablative, Southey calls it). She was full of theories about their upbringing which she had not time to put into effect; but

nevertheless she thought she had a deep understanding of their temperaments and was
the centre of their passionate devotion. Actually, she was congenitally incapable of telling one end of a child from the other. She
was a dumpy little woman—Cornish, I believe. When she was herself a baby she was
so small they carried her about on a cushion
for fear a clumsy human arm might damage
her. She could read when she was two and
a half. Her reading was always serious. Nor
had she been backward in the humaner stud-
ies: her mistresses spoke of her Deportment
as something rarely seen outside the older
Royal Houses: in spite of a figure like a boul-
ster, she could step into a coach like an angel
getting onto a cloud. She was very quick-
tempered.

Mr. Bas-Thornton also had every accom-
plishment, except two: that of primo-geni-
ture, and that of making a living. Either
would have provided for them.

If it would have surprised the mother, it would undoubtedly have surprised the children also to be told how little their parents meant to them. Children seldom have any power of quantitative self-analysis: whatever the facts, they believe as an article of faith that they love Father and Mother first and equally. Actually, the Thornton children had loved Tabby first and foremost in all the world, some of each other second, and hardly noticed their mother's existence more than once a week. Their father they loved a little more: partly owing to the ceremony of riding home on his stirrups.

Jamaica remained, and blossomed anew, its womb being inexhaustible. Mr. and Mrs. Thornton remained, and with patience and tears tried to reconstruct things, in so far as they could be reconstructed. But the danger which their beloved little ones had been through was not a thing to risk again.

Heaven had warned them. The children must go.

Nor was the only danger physical:

"That awful night!" said Mrs. Thornton, once, when discussing their plan of sending them home to school: "Oh my dear, what the poor little things must have suffered! Think how much more acute Fear is to a child! And they were so brave, so English."

"I don't believe they realised it." (He only said that to be contradictious: he could hardly expect it to be taken seriously.)

"You know, I am terribly afraid what permanent, *inward* effect a shock like that may have on them. Have you noticed they never so much as mention it? In England they would at least be safe from dangers of that sort."

Meanwhile, the children, accepting the new life as a matter of course, were thoroughly enjoying it. Most children, on a railway journey, prefer to change at as many stations as possible.

The rebuilding of Ferndale, too, was a matter of absorbing interest. For there is one advantage to these match-box houses—easy gone, easy come: and once begun the work proceeded apace. Mr. Thornton himself led the building gang, employing no end of mechanical devices of his own devising, and it was not long before the day came when he stood with his handsome head emerging through the fast dwindling hole in the new roof, shouting directions to the two black carpenters, who, lying spread-eagle in their check shirts, pinned on shingle after shingle —walling him in, like the victim in some horrid story. At last he had to draw in his head, and where it had been the last few shingles were clapt into place.

An hour later the children had looked their last on Ferndale.

When they had been told they were to go

to England, they had received it as an isolated fact: thrilling in itself, but without any particular causation—for it could hardly be due to the death of the cat, and nothing else of importance had occurred lately.

The first stage of their journey was by land, to Montego Bay: and the notable thing about it was that the borrowed wagonette was drawn not by a pair of horses or a pair of mules, but by one horse and one mule. Whenever the horse wanted to go fast the mule fell asleep in the shafts: and if the driver woke it up it set off at a gallop, which angered the horse. Their progress would have been slow anyhow, as all the roads were washed away.

John was the only one who could remember England. What he remembered was sitting at the top of a flight of stairs, which was fenced off from him by a little gate, playing with a red toy milk-cart: and he knew, without having to look, that in the room on the left Baby Emily was lying in her cot. Emily *said* she could remember something which sounded like a Prospect of the Backs of some Brick Houses at Richmond: but she might have invented it. The others had been born in the Island—Edward, only just.

They all had nevertheless most elaborate ideas about England, built up out of what their parents had told them, and from the books and old magazines they sometimes looked at. Needless to say it was a very Atlantis, a land at the back of the North Wind: and going there was about as exciting as it would be to die and go to Heaven.

John told them all about the top of the stairs for the hundredth time as they drove along; the others listening attentively (as the Believing do to a man remembering his re-incarnations).

Suddenly Emily recalled sitting at a window and seeing a big bird with a beautiful tail. At the same time there had been a horrid screeching going on, or perhaps something else disagreeable—she could not quite remember which sense was offended. It did not occur to her that it was this selfsame bird which had screeched: and anyhow it was all too vague for her to try and describe it. She switched off to wondering how it was possible actually to *sleep* when walking, as the driver said the mule did.

They put up for the night at St. Anne's, and there another notable thing occurred. Their host was a hardened Creole: and at supper he ate Cayenne pepper with a spoon. Not ordinary Cayenne pepper, mind, such as is sold in shops, which is heavily adulterated with logwood; but the far fierier pure original. This indeed was an Event of the first water: none of them ever forgot it.

The desolation through which they drove is indescribable. Tropical scenery is anyhow tedious, prolific, and gross: the greens more or less uniform: great tubular stems

supporting thick leaves: no tree has an outline because it is crushed up against something else—no *room*. In Jamaica this pro-
fusion swarms over the very mountain
ranges: and even the peaks are so numerous
that on the top of one you are surrounded by
others, and can see nothing. There are hundreds of flowers. Then imagine all this lux-
uriance smashed, as with a pestle and mortar
—crushed, pulped, and already growing
again! Mr. Thornton and his wife were
ready to shout with relief when they caught
their first glimpse of the sea, and at last came
out in view of the whole beautiful sweep of
Montego Bay itself.

In the open sea there was a considerable
swell: but within the shelter of the coral
reef, with its pinhole entrance, all was still as
a mirror, where three ships of different sizes
lay at anchor, the whole of each beautiful
machine repeated in the water under it.
Within the Roads lay the Bogue Islands; and

immediately to the left of the islands, in the
low land at the base of the hills, was the
mouth of a small river—swampy, and (Mr.
Thornton informed John) infested with crocodiles. The children had never seen a crocodile, and hoped one might venture as far as
the town, where they presently arrived: but
none did. It was with considerable disap-
pointment that they found they were to go on
board the barque at once; for they still hoped
that round some corner of the street a crocodile might yet appear.

The *Clorinda* had let go her anchor in six
fathoms: the water so clear, and the light so
bright, that as they drew near the reflection
suddenly disappeared, and instead they
found themselves looking right underneath
her and out the other side. The refraction
made her seem as flat-bellied as a turtle, as if
practically all of her were above the surface:
and the anchor on its cable seemed to stream
out flatly, like a downwards kite, twisting and

twining (owing to the undulating surface) in the writhing coral.

This was the only impression Emily retained of going on board the ship: but the ship itself was a strange enough object, requiring all her attention. John was the only one who could remember the journey out at all clearly. Emily thought she could, but was really only remembering her visualisations of what she had been told: in fact, she found that a real ship was totally unlike the thing she thought she remembered.

By some last whim of the captain's the shrouds were being set up—tauter than seemed good to the sailors, who grumbled as they strained the creaking lanyards. John did not envy them, winding away at that handle in the hot sun: but he did envy the chap whose job it was to dip his hand in a great pot of aromatic Stockholm tar, and work it into the dead-eyes. He was tarred up to the elbows: and John itched to be so too.

In a moment the children were scattered all over the ship, smelling here, miaowing, sniffing there, like cats in a new home. Mr. and Mrs. Thornton stood by the main companionway, a little disconsolate at their children's happy preoccupation, a little regretting the lack of proper emotional scene.

"I think they will be happy here, Frederic," said Mrs. Thornton. "I wish we could have afforded to send them by the steamboat: but children find amusement even in discomfort."

Mr. Thornton grunted.

"I wish schools had never been invented!" he suddenly burst out: "They wouldn't then be so indispensable!"

There was a short pause for the logic of this to cross the footlights: then he went on:

"I know what will happen; they'll come away . . . *mugs!* Just ordinary little mugs, like anyone else's brats! I'm dashed if I don't think a hundred hurricanes would be better than that."

Mrs. Thornton shuddered: but she continued bravely:

"You know, I think they were getting almost *too* devoted to us? We have been such
an unrivalled centre of their lives and
thoughts. It doesn't do for minds developing to be completely dependent on one
person."

Captain Marpole's grizzled head emerged
from the scuttle. A sea-dog: clear blue eyes
of a translucent truthworthiness: a merry,
wrinkled, morocco-coloured face: a rumbling
voice.

"He's too good to be true," whispered Mrs.
Thornton.

"Not at all! It's a sophism to imagine
people don't conform to type!" barked Mr.
Thornton. He felt at sixes and sevens.

Captain Marpole certainly looked the ideal
Children's Captain. He would, Mrs. Thornton decided, be careful without being fussy—

for she was all in favour of courageous gymnastics, though glad she would not have to witness them herself. Captain Marpole cast his eyes benignantly over the swarming imps.

"They'll worship him," she whispered to her husband. (She meant, of course, that he would worship them.) It was an important point, this, of the captain: important as the personality of a headmaster.

"So that's the nursery, eh?" said the captain, crushing Mrs. Thornton's hand. She strove to answer, but found her throat undoubtedly paralysed. Even Mr. Thornton's ready tongue was at a loss. He looked hard at the captain, jerked his thumb towards the children, wrestled in his mind with an elaborate speech, and finally enunciated in a small, unlikely voice:

"Smack 'em."

Then the captain had to go about his duties: and for an hour the father and mother sat disconsolately on the main hatch, quite deserted. Even when all was ready for departure it was impossible to muster the flock for a collective good-bye.

Already the tug was fulminating in its gorge: and ashore they must go. Emily and John only had been captured, and stood talking uneasily to their parents, as if to strangers, using only a quarter of their minds. With a rope to be climbed dangling before his very nose, John simply did not know how this delay was to be supported, and lapsed into complete silence.

"Time to go ashore, Ma'am," said the captain: "we must be off now."

Very formally the two generations kissed each other, and said farewell. Indeed the elders were already at the gangway before the meaning of it all dawned in Emily's head. She rushed after her mother, gripped her ample flesh in two strong fists, and sobbed and wept, "Come, too, Mother, oh, do come too!"

Honestly, it had only occurred to her that very moment that this was a *parting*.

"But think what an adventure it will be," said Mrs. Thornton bravely: "much more than if I came too!—You'll have to look after the Liddlies, just as if you were a real grown-up!"

"But I don't want any more adventures!" sobbed Emily: "I've *got* an *Earthquake!*"

Passions were running far too high for anyone to be aware how the final separation took place. The next thing Mrs. Thornton could remember was how tired her arm had been, after waving and waving at that dwindling speck which bore away on the land breeze, hung awhile stationary in the intervening calm, then won the Trade and climbed up into the blue.

Meanwhile, at the rail stood Margaret

Fernandez, who, with her little brother Harry, was going to England by the same boat. No one had come to see them off: and the brown nurse who was accompanying them had gone below the moment she came on board, so as to be ill as quickly as possible. How handsome Mr. Bas-Thornton had looked, with his English distinction! Yet everyone knew he had no money. Her set white face was turned towards the land, her chin quivering at intervals. Slowly the harbour disappeared: the disordered profligacy of the turbulent, intricate mass of hills sank lower in the sky. The occasional white houses, and white puffs of steam and smoke from the sugar-mills, vanished. At last the land, all palely shimmering like the bloom on grapes, settled down into the mirror of emerald and blue.

She wondered whether the Thornton children would prove companionable, or a nui-

sance. They were all younger than she was;
which was a pity.

ii

On the journey back to Ferndale both
father and mother were silent, actuated by
that tug of jealousy against sympathy which
a strong common emotion begets in familiar
rather than passionate companions.

They were above the ordinary sentimen-
talities of grass-bereavement (above choking
over small shoes found in cupboards), but
not above a rather strong dose of the natural
instincts of parenthood, Frederic no less than
his wife.

But when they were nearly home, Mrs.
Thornton began to chuckle to herself:

"Funny little thing, Emily! Did you notice
almost the last thing she said? She said 'I've
got an earthquake.' She must have got it

mixed up in her silly old head with ear-
ache."

There was a long pause: and then she re-
marked again:

"John is so much the most sensitive: he
was absolutely too full to speak."

iii

When they got home it was many days
before they could bring themselves openly to
mention the children. When some reference
had to be made, they spoke round them, in an
uncomfortable way, as if they had died.

But after a few weeks they had a most
welcome surprise. The *Clorinda* was calling
at the Caymans, and taking the Leeward
Passage: and while riding off the Grand
Cayman Emily and John wrote letters, and a
vessel bound for Kingston had taken charge
of them and eventually they reached Fern-

dale. It had not even occurred to either parent that this would be possible.

This was Emily's:

MY DEAR PARENTS,

This ship is full of Turtles. We stopped here and they came out in boats. There is turtles in the saloon under the tables for you to put your feet on, and turtles in the passages and on the deck, and everywhere you go. The captain says we mustn't fall overboard now because his boats are full of turtles too, with water. The sailors bring the others on deck every day to have a wash and when you stand them up they look just as if they had pinafores on. They make such a funny sighing and groaning in the night, at first I thought it was everybody being ill, but you get used to it, it is just like people being ill.

Your loving daughter,
EMILY

And John's:

MY DEAREST PARENTS,

The captain's son Henry is a wonderful chap, he goes up the rigging with his hands alone, he is

ever so strong. He can turn round under a belly-
ing pin without touching the deck, I can't but I
hang from the ratlines by my heels which the
sailors say is very brave, but they don't like Emily
doing it, funny. I hope you are both in excellent
health, one of the sailors has a monkey but its tail
is Sore.

Your affectionate Son,
JOHN

That was the last news they could expect
for many months. The *Clorinda* was not
touching anywhere else. It gave Mrs. Thornton a cold feeling in the stomach to measure
just *how* long. But she argued, logically
enough, that the time must come to an end,
all time does: there is nothing so inexorable
as a ship, plodding away, plodding away, all
over the place, till at last it quite certainly
reaches that small speck on the map which all
the time it had intended to reach. Philo-
sophically speaking, a ship in its port of departure is just as much in its port of arrival:

↦↦↦↦↦↦↦↦↦↦↦↦↦↦↦↤↤↤↤↤↤↤↤↤↤↤↤↤↤↤↤

two point-events differing in time and place, but not in degree of reality. *Ergo,* that first letter from England was as good as written, only not quite . . . legible yet. And the same applied to seeing them. (But here one must stop, for the same argument applied to old age and death, it wouldn't do.)

Yet, a bare fortnight after the arrival of this first budget, still another letter arrived, from Havana. The *Clorinda* had put in there unexpectedly, it appeared: the letter was from Captain Marpole.

"What a dear man he is," said Alice. "He must have known how anxious we would be for every scrap of news."

Captain Marpole's letter was not so terse and vivid as the children's had been; still, for the news it contained, I give it in full:

HAVANA DE CUBA
HONOURED SIR AND MADAM,

I hasten to write to you to relieve you of any uncertainty!

>>>>>>>>>>>>>>>>>>>>>>>><<<<<<<<<<<<<<<<<<<<<<<<

After leaving the Caymans we stood for the Leeward Passage, and sighted the Isle of Pines and False Cape on the morning of the 19th and Cape S. Antonio in the evening, but were prevented from rounding the same by a true Norther, the first of the season, on the 22nd, however, the wind coming round sufficiently we rounded the cape in a lively fashion and stood N½E well away from the Coloradoes which are a dangerous reef lying off this part of the Cuban coast. At six o'clock on the morning of the 23rd there being light airs only I sighted three sail in the North East, evidently merchantmen bound on the same course as ourselves, at the same time a schooner of similar character was observed standing out towards us from the direction of Black Key, and I pointed her out to my mate just before going below, having the wind of us he was within hailing distance by ten in the morning, judge then of our astonishment when he rudely opened ten or twelve disguised gun-ports and unmasked a whole broadside of artillery trained upon us, ordering us at the same time in the most peremptory manner to heave-to or he would sink us instanter. There was nothing to do but to comply although considering the friendly relations at present existing between the English and all other governments my mate was quite at a loss to account for his action, and imagined it due to a mistake which would be speedily explained, we were immediately boarded by about fifty or seventy ruffians of the worst Spanish type, armed with knives and cutlasses, who took possession of the ship and confined me in my cabin and my mate and crew forward while they ransacked the vessel committing every possible excess broaching rum-casks and breaking the necks off wine-bottles and soon a great number of them were lying about the deck in an intoxicated condition, their leader then informed me he was aware I had a considerable sum in specie on board and used *every possible threat which vilainy could devise* to make me disclose its hiding-place, it was useless for me to assure him that beyond the fifty or so pounds they had already discovered I carried none, he grew even more insistent in his demands, declaring that his information was certain, tearing down the paneling in my cabin in his search. He carried off my instruments, my clothes, and all my personal possessions, even taking from me

>>>>>>>>>>>>>>>>>>>>>>><<<<<<<<<<<<<<<<<<<<

the poor Locket in which I was used to carry the portrait of my Wife, and no appeal to his sensibility, tho' I shed tears, would make him return this to him worthless object, he also tore down and carried away the cabin bell-pulls, which could be of no possible use to him and was an act of the most open *piracy,* at length, seeing I was obdurate, he threatened to blow up the ship *and all in it* if I would not yield, he prepared the train and would have proceeded to carry out this devilish threat if I had not in this last extremity, consented.

I come now to the latter part of my tale. The children had taken refuge in the deck-house and had been up to now free from harm, except for a cuff or two and the Degrading Sights they must have witnessed, but no sooner was the specie some five thousand pounds in all mostly my private property and most of our cargo (chiefly rum sugar coffee and arrowroot) removed to the schooner than her captain, in sheer infamous wantonness, had them all brought out from their refuge your own little ones and the two Fernandez children who were also on board and murdered them, every one. That anything so wicked should look

>>>>>>>>>>>>>>>>>>>>><<<<<<<<<<<<<<<<<<<<<

like a man I should not have believed, had I been told, tho' I have lived long and seen all kinds of men, I think he is mad; indeed I am sure of it; and I take Oath that he shall be brought to at least that tithe of justice which is in Human hands, for two days we drifted about in a helpless condition, for our rigging had all been cut, and at last fell in with an American man-of-war, who gave us some assistance, and would have proceeded in pursuit of the miscreants himself had he not most explicit orders to elsewhere. I then put in to the port of Havannah, where I informed the correspondent of Lloyds, the government, and the representative of the *Times* newspaper, and take the opportunity of writing you this melancholy letter before proceeding to England.

There is one point on which you will still feel some anxiety, considering the sex of some of the poor innocents, and on which I am glad to be able to set your minds at rest, the children were taken onto the other vessel in the evening and I am glad to say there done to death *immediately,* and their little bodies cast into the sea, as I saw with great relief with my own eyes. There was no time for what you might fear to have oc-

curred, and this consolation I am glad to be able
to give you.

I have the honour to be
Your obedient servant,
JAS. MARPOLE,
Master, barque *Clorinda*

>>>>>>>>>>>>>>>>>>>>>>><<<<<<<<<<<<<<<<<<<<<

Chapter Three

THE passage from Montego Bay to the
Caymans, where the children had written their letters, is only a matter of a few
hours: indeed, in clear weather one can look
right across from Jamaica to the peak of
Tarquinio in Cuba.

There is no harbour: and the anchorage,
owing to the reefs and ledges, is difficult.
The *Clorinda* brought up off the Grand Cayman, the look-out man in the chains feeling
his way to a white, sandy patch of bottom
which affords the only safe resting-place
there: and causing the anchor to be let go to
windward of it. Luckily, the weather was
fine.

The island, a longish one at the western

>>>>>>>>>>>>>>>>>>>>>><<<<<<<<<<<<<<<<<<<<

end of the group, is low, and covered with
palms. Presently a succession of boats
brought out a quantity of turtles, as Emily
described. The natives also brought parrots
to sell to the sailors: but failed to dispose of
many.

At last, however, the uncomfortable Caymans were left behind, and they set their
course towards the Isle of Pines, a large
island in a gulf of the Cuban coast. One of
the sailors, called Curtis, had once been
wrecked there, and was full of stories about
it. It is a very unpleasant place; sparsely
inhabited, and covered with labyrinthine
woods. The only food available is a kind of
tree. There is also a species of bean which
looks tempting: but it is deadly poison. The
crocodiles, Curtis said, were so fierce they
chased him and his companions into trees:
the only way to escape from them was to
throw them your cap to worry: or if you were
bold, to disable them with a blow of a stick

on the loins. There were also a great many snakes, including a kind of boa.

The current off the Isle of Pines sets strongly to the east: so the *Clorinda* kept close inshore, to cheat it. They passed Cape Corrientes—looking, when first sighted, like two hummocks in the sea: they passed Holandes Point, known as False Cape San Antonio: but were prevented for some time, as Captain Marpole told in his letter, from rounding the true one. For to attempt Cape San Antonio in a Norther is to waste your labour.

They lay-to in sight of that long, low, rocky, treeless promontory in which the great island of Cuba terminates, and waited. They were so close that the fisherman's hut on its southern side was clearly discernible.

For the children, those first few days at sea had flashed by like a kind of prolonged circus. There is no machine invented for sober purposes so well adapted also to play

as the rigging of a ship: and the kindly captain, as Mrs. Thornton had divined, was willing to give them a lot of freedom. First
came the climbing of a few rungs of the ratlines in a sailor's charge: higher each time,
till John attained a gingerly touching of the
yard: then hugged it: then straddled it. Soon,
running up the ratlines and prancing on the
yard (as if it were a mere table-top) had no
further thrill for John or Emily either. (To
go out on the yard was not allowed.)

But when the ratlines had palled, the most
lasting joy undoubtedly lay in that network
of foot-ropes and chains and stays which
spreads out under and on each side of the
bowsprit. Here, familiarity only bred content. Here, in fine weather, one could climb
or be still: stand, sit, hang, swing, or lie: now
this end up, now that: and all with the cream
of the blue sea being whipt up for one's own
especial pleasure, almost within touching distance: and the big white wooden lady

>>>>>>>>>>>>>>>>>>>>><<<<<<<<<<<<<<<<<<

(*Clorinda* herself), bearing the whole vessel so lightly on her back, her knees in the hubble-bubble, her cracks almost filled up with so much painting, vaster than any living lady, as a constant and unannoying companion.

In the midst there was a kind of spear, its haft set against the underside of the bowsprit, its point perpendicularly down towards the water—the dolphin-striker. Here it was that the old monkey (who had the Sore tail) loved to hang, by the mere stub which was all a devouring cancer had left him, chattering to the water. He took no notice of the children, nor they of him: but both parties grew attached to each other, for all that.

—— How small the children all looked, on a ship, when you saw them beside the sailors! It was as if they were a different order of beings! Yet they were living creatures just the same, full of promise.

John, with his downy, freckled face, and general round energeticalness.

>>>>>>>>>>>>>>>>>>>>>><<<<<<<<<<<<<<<<<<<<<

Emily, with her huge palm-leaf hat, and colourless cotton frock tight over her minute impish erect body: her thin, almost expressionless face: her dark grey eyes contracted to escape the blaze, yet shining as it were in spite of themselves: and her really beautiful lips, that looked almost as if they were sculptured.

Margaret Fernandez, taller (as midgets go: she was just thirteen), with her square white face and tangled hair, her elaboratish clothes.

Her little brother *Harry,* by some throwback for all the world like a manikin Spaniard.

And the smaller Thorntons: *Edward,* mouse-coloured, with a general mousy (but pleasing) expression: *Rachel,* with tight short gold curls and a fat pink face (John's colouring watered down): and last of all *Laura,* a queer mite of three with heavy dark eyebrows, and blue eyes, a big head-top and a receding chin—as if the Procreative Spirit was getting a little hysterical by the time it reached her. A silver-age conception, Laura's, decidedly.

When the Norther blew itself out, it soon fell away almost dead calm. The morning they finally rounded Cape San Antonio was hot, blazing hot. But it is never stuffy at sea: there is only this disadvantage, that while on land a shady hat protects you from the sun, at sea nothing can protect you from that second sun which is mirrored upwards from the water, strikes under all defences, and burns the unseasoned skin from all your undersides. Poor John! His throat and chin were a blistered red.

From the point itself there is a whitish bank in two fathoms, bowed from North to North-East. The outer side is clean and steep-to, and in fine weather one can steer along it by eye. It ends in Black Key, a rock standing out of the water like a ship's hull. Beyond that lies a channel, very foul and

>>>>>>>>>>>>>>>>>>>>><<<<<<<<<<<<<<<<<<<<

difficult to navigate: and beyond that again the Coloradoes Reef begins, the first of a long chain of reefs following the coast in a north-easterly direction as far as Honde Bay, two-thirds the way to Havana. Within these reefs lies the intricate Canal de Guaniguanico (of which this channel is the westernmost outlet) with its own rather dubious little ports. But ocean traffic, needless to say, shuns the whole box of tricks: and the *Clorinda* advisedly stood well away to the northward, keeping her course at a gentle amble for the open Atlantic.

John was sitting outside the galley with the sailor called Curtis, who was instructing him in the neat mystery of a Turk's-head. Young Henry Marpole was steering. Emily was messing around—not talking, just being by him.

As for the other sailors, they were all congregated in a ring, up in the bows, so that one saw nothing but their backs. But every now and then a general guffaw, and a sudden surging of the whole group, showed they were up to something or other.

John presently tip-toed forward, to see what it might be. He thrust his bullet-head among their legs, and worked his way in till he had as good a view as the earliest comer.

He found they had got the old monkey, and were filling him up with rum. First they gave him biscuit soaked in it: then they dipped rags in a pannikin of the stuff, and squeezed them into his mouth. Then they tried to make him drink direct; but that he would not do—it only wasted a lot of spirit.

John felt a vague horror at all this: though of course he did not guess the purpose behind it.

The poor brute shivered and chattered, rolled his eyes, spluttered. I suppose it must have been an excruciatingly funny sight. Every now and then he would seem altogether overcome by the spirit. Then one of the sailors would lay him on the top of an old beef barrel—but hey presto, he would be up like lightning, trying to streak through the air over their heads. But he was no bird; they caught him each time, and set to work to dope him again.

As for John, he could no more have left the scene now than Jacko the monkey could.

It was astonishing what a lot of spirit the wizened little brute could absorb. He was drunk, of course: hopelessly, blindly, madly drunk. But he was not paralytic, not even somnolent: and it seemed as if nothing could overcome him. So at last they gave up the attempt. They fetched a wooden box, and cut a notch in the edge. Then they put him on the barrel-top, and clapt the box over him, and after much manoeuvring his gangrenous tail was made to come out through the notch. Anaesthetised or not, the operation on him was to proceed. John stared, transfixed, at that obscene wriggling stump which was all one could see of the animal: and out of the corner of his eye he could see at the same time the uproarious operators, the tar-stained knife.

But the moment the blade touched flesh, with an awful screech the mommet contrived to fling off his cage—leapt on the surgeon's head—leapt from there high in the air—caught the forestay—and in a twinkling was away and up high in the fore-rigging.

Then began the hue and cry. Sixteen men flinging about in lofty acrobatics, all to catch one poor old drunk monkey. For he was drunk as a lord, and sick as a cat. His course varied between wild and hair-raising leaps (a sort of inspired gymnastics), and doleful incompetent reelings on a taut rope which threatened at every moment to catapult him into the sea. But even so they could never quite catch him.

No wonder that all the children, now, stood open-mouthed and open-eyed on the

>>>>>>>>>>>>>>>>>>>><<<<<<<<<<<<<<<<<<<

deck beneath in the sun till their necks nearly broke—*such* a Free Fun Fair and Circus!

And no wonder that on that passenger-schooner which Marpole, before going be·low, had sighted drifting towards them from the direction of the Black Key channel, the ladies had left the shade of the awning and were crowding at the rail, parasols twirling, lorgnettes and opera-glasses in action, all twittering like a cage of linnets. Just too far off to distinguish the tiny quarry, they might well have wondered what sort of a bedlam-vessel of sea-acrobats the light easterly air was bearing them down upon.

They were so interested that presently a boat was hoisted out, and the ladies—and some gentlemen as well—crowded into it.

Poor little Jacko missed his hold at last: fell plump on the deck and broke his neck. That was the end of him—and of the hunt too, of course. The aerial ballet was over, in its middle, with no final tableau. The sailors began, in twos and threes, to slide to the deck.

But the visitors were already on board.

That is how the *Clorinda* really was taken. There was no display of artillery—but then, Captain Marpole could hardly know this, seeing he was below in his bunk at the time. Henry was steering by that sixth sense which only comes into operation when the other five are asleep. The mate and crew had been so intent on what they were doing that the *Flying Dutchman* himself might have laid alongside, for all they cared.

ii

Indeed, the whole manoeuvre was executed so quietly that Captain Marpole never even woke—incredible though this will seem to a seaman. But then, Marpole had begun life as a successful coal merchant.

The mate and crew were bundled into the fo'c'sle (the fox-hole, the children thought it was called), and confined there, the scuttle being secured with a couple of nails.

The children themselves were shepherded, as related, into the deck-house, where the chairs, and perfectly useless pieces of old rope, and broken tools, and dried-up paint-pots were kept, without taking alarm. But the door was immediately shut on them. They had to wait for hours and hours before anything else happened—nearly all day, in fact: and they got very bored, and rather cross.

The actual number of the men who had effected the capture cannot have been more than eight or nine, most of them "women" at that, and not armed—at least with any visible weapon. But a second boatload soon followed them from the schooner. These, for form's sake, were armed with muskets. But there was no possible resistance to fear.

Two long nails through the scuttle can secure any number of men pretty effectually.

With this second boatload came both the captain and the mate. The former was a clumsy great fellow, with a sad, silly face. He was bulky; yet so ill-proportioned one got no impression of power. He was modestly dressed in a drab shore-going suit: he was newly shaven, and his sparse hair was pomaded so that it lay in a few dark ribbons across his baldish head-top. But all this shore-decency of appearance only accentuated his big splodgy brown hands, stained and scarred and corned with his calling. More-over, instead of boots he wore a pair of gigan-tic heel-less slippers in the Moorish manner, which he must have sliced with a knife out of some pair of dead sea-boots. Even his great spreading feet could hardly keep them on, so that he was obliged to walk at the slowest of shuffles, flop-flop along the deck. He stooped, as if always afraid of banging

>>>>>>>>>>>>>>>>>>>>>>>>>>><<<<<<<<<<<<<<<<<<<<<<

his head on something: and carried the backs
of his hands forward, like an orang-outang.

Meanwhile the men set to work methodi-
cally but very quietly to remove the wedges
that held the battens of the hatches, getting
ready to haul up the cargo.

Their leader took several turns up and
down the deck before he seemed able to
make up his mind to the interview: then lowered himself into Marpole's cabin, followed
by his mate.

This mate was a small man: very fair, and
intelligent-looking beside his chief. He was
almost dapper, in a quiet way, in his dress.

They found Captain Marpole even now
only half awake: and the stranger stood for a
moment in silence, nervously twiddling his
cap in his hands. When he spoke at last, it
was with a soft German accent:

"Excuse me," he began, "but would you
have the goodness to lend me a few stores?"

Captain Marpole stared in astonishment,

first at him and then at the much be-painted faces of the "ladies" pressed against his cabin skylight.

"Who the devil are you?" he contrived to ask at last.

"I hold a commission in the Columbian navy." the stranger explained: "and I am in need of a few stores."

(Meanwhile his men had the hatches off, and were preparing to help themselves to everything in the ship.)

Marpole looked him up and down. It was barely conceivable that even the Columbian navy should have such a figure of an officer. Then his eye wandered back to the skylight.

"If you call yourself a man-of-war, Sir, who in Heaven's name are *those?*" As he pointed, the smirking faces hastily retreated.

The stranger blushed.

"They are rather difficult to explain," he admitted ingenuously.

"If you had said *Turkish* navy, that would

have been more reasonable-sounding," said Marpole.

But the stranger did not seem to take the joke. He stood, silent, in a characteristic attitude: rocking himself from foot to foot, and rubbing his cheek on his shoulder.

Suddenly Marpole's ear caught the muffled racketing forward. Almost at the same time a bump that shivered the whole barque told that the schooner had been layed alongside.

"What's that?" he exclaimed. "Is there someone in my hold?"

"Stores . . ." mumbled the stranger.

Marpole up to now had lain growling in his bunk like a dog in its kennel. Now for the first time realising that something serious was afoot he flung himself out and made for the companion way. The little silent fair man tripped him up, and he fell against the table.

"You had much better stay here, yes?" said the big man. "My fellows shall keep a tally, you shall be paid in full for everything we take."

The eyes of the marine coal-merchant gleamed momentarily:

"You'll have to pay for this outrage to a pretty tune!" he growled.

"I will pay you," said the stranger, with a sudden magnificence in his voice, "at the very least five thousand pounds!"

Marpole stared in astonishment.

"I will write you an order on the Columbian government for that amount," the other went on.

Marpole thumped the table, almost speechless:

"D'you think I believe that cock-and-bull story?" he thundered.

Captain Jonsen made no protest.

"Do you realise that you are technically guilty of *piracy*, making a forced requisition on a British ship like this, even if you pay every farthing?"

Still Jonsen made no reply: though the bored expression of his mate was lit up for a moment by a smile.

"You'll pay me in *cash!*" Marpole concluded. Then he went off on a fresh tack: "Though how the devil you got on board without my being called beats me! Where's my mate?"

Jonsen began in a toneless voice, as if by rote: "I will write you an order for five thousand pounds: three thousand for the stores, and two thousand you will give me in money."

"We know you've got specie on board," interjected the little fair mate, speaking for the first time.

"Our information is certain!" declared Jonsen.

Marpole at last went white and began to sweat. It took even Fear an extraordinarily long time to penetrate his thick skull. But he denied that he had any treasure on board.

"Is that your answer?" said Jonsen. He drew a heavy pistol from his side pocket: "If you do not tell us the truth, your life shall pay the forfeit." His voice was peculiarly gentle, and mechanical, as if he did not attach much meaning to what he said: "Do not expect mercy, for this is my profession, and in it I am inured to blood."

A frightful squawking from the deck above told Marpole that his chickens were being moved to new quarters.

In an agony of feeling Marpole told him that he had a wife and children, who would be left destitute if his life was taken.

Jonsen, with a rather perplexed look on his face, put the gun back in his pocket, and the two of them began searching for themselves, at the same time stripping the saloon and cabins of everything they contained: fire-arms, wearing apparel, the bedclothes, and even (as Marpole with a rare touch of accuracy mentioned in his report) the bell-pulls.

Overhead there was a continuous bumping: the rolling of casks, cases, etc.

"Remember," Jonsen went on over his shoulder while he searched, "money cannot recall life, nor in the least avail you when you are dead. If you regard your life in the least, at once acquaint me with the hiding-place, and your life shall be safe."

Marpole's only reply was again to invoke the thought of his wife and children (he was, as a matter of fact, a widower: and his only relative, a niece, would be the better off by his death to the tune of some ten thousand pounds).

But this reiteration seemed to give the mate an idea: and he began to talk to his chief rapidly in a language Marpole had never even heard. For a moment a curious glint came into Jonsen's eye: but soon he was chuckling in the sentimentalest manner, and rubbing his hands.

The mate went on deck to prepare things.

>>>>>>>>>>>>>>>>>>>>><<<<<<<<<<<<<<<<<<<

Marpole had no inkling of what was afoot. The mate went on deck to prepare his plan, whatever it was: and Jonsen busied himself with a last futile search for the hiding-place, in silence.

Presently the mate shouted down to him, and he ordered Marpole on deck.

Poor Marpole groaned. Unloading cargo is inclined to be a messy business anyway: but these visitors had been none too careful. There is no smell in the world worse than when molasses and bilge-water marry: now it was let loose like ten thousand devils. His heart almost broke when he saw the havoc that had been made with the cargo: broken cases, casks, bottles, all about the deck: everything in the greatest confusion: tarpaulins cut to pieces: hatches broken.

From the deck-house came the piercing voice of Laura:

"I want to come out!"

The Spanish ladies seemed to have re-

>>>>>>>>>>>>>>>>>>>><<<<<<<<<<<<<<<<<<<<
turned to the schooner. His own men were
shut up in the fo'c'sle. It was obvious where
all the children were, for Laura was not the
only vociferator. But the only persons to be
seen were six members of the visiting crew,
who stood in a line, facing the deck-house, a
musket a-piece.

It was the little mate who now took charge
of the situation:

"Where is your specie hid, Captain?"

The musketeers having their backs to him,
"Go to the devil!" replied Marpole.

A startling volley rang out: six neat holes
were punctured in the top of the deck-house.

"Hi! Steady there, what are you doing?"
John cried out, indignantly, from within.

"If you refuse to tell us, next time their aim
will be a foot lower."

"You fiends!" cried Marpole.

"Will you tell me?"

"*No!*"

"*Fire!*"

>>>>>>>>>>>>>>>>>>>>>>><<<<<<<<<<<<<<<<<<<

The second row of holes can only have missed the taller children by a few inches.

There was a moment's silence: then a sudden wild shriek from within the deck-house. It was so terrified a sound not their own mothers could have told which throat it came from. One only, though.

The stranger-captain had been slouching about in an agitated way: but at that shriek he turned on Marpole, his face purple with a sudden fury:

"*Now* will you say?"

But Marpole was now completely master of himself. He did not hesitate:

"NO!"

"Next time he gives the order it will be to shoot right through their little bodies!"

So that was what Marpole had meant in his letter by *"every possible threat which vilainy could devise"*!

But even by this he was not to be daunted:

"No, I tell you!"

>>>>>>>>>>>>>>>>>>>>><<<<<<<<<<<<<<<<<<<<

Heroic obstinacy!

But instead of giving the fatal order, Jonsen lifted a paw like a bear's, and banged Marpole's jaw with it. The latter fell to the deck, stunned.

It was then they took the children out of the deck-house.

They were not really much frightened: except Margaret, who did seem to be taking it all to heart rather. Being shot at is so unlike what one expects it to be that one can hardly connect the two ideas enough to have the appropriate emotions, the first few times. It is not half so startling as someone jumping out on you with a *"Boo!"* in the dark, for instance. The boys were crying a little: the girls were hot and cross and hungry.

"What were you doing?" Rachel asked, brightly, of one of the firing-party.

But only the captain and the mate could speak English. The latter, ignoring Rachel's question, explained that they were all to go on board the schooner—"to have some supper," he said.

He had all a sailor's reassuring charm of manner. Under the charge of two Spanish seamen they were helped over the bulwarks onto the smaller vessel, which was just casting off.

There the strange sailors broke open a whole case of crystallised fruits, on which they might turn the edge of their long appetites as much as they would.

When poor stunned Captain Marpole came to his senses, it was to find himself tied to the mainmast. Several handfuls of shavings and splintered wood were piled round his feet, and Jonsen was sprinkling them plentifully with gun-powder—though not perhaps enough, it is true, to "blow up the ship and all in it."

The small fair mate stood at hand in the

gathering dusk with a lighted torch, ready to fire the pyre.

What could a man do in such straits? At that dreadful moment, the old fellow had to admit that he was beaten at last. He told them where his freight-money—some £900—was hidden: and they let him go.

Just as the darkness closed in, the last of the pirates returned to their ship. Not a sound was to be heard of the children: but Marpole guessed that they had been taken there too.

Before releasing his crew he lit a lantern, and began a sort of inventory of what was gone. It was heart-breaking enough: besides the cargo, all his spare sails, cordage, provisions, guns, paint, powder: all his wearing apparel, and that of his mates: all nautical instruments gone, cabin stores—the saloon in fact gutted of everything, not even a knife or spoon left, tea or sugar, nor a second shirt to his back left. Only the children's luggage was left untouched: and the turtles. Their melancholy sighing was the sole sound to be heard.

But it was almost as heart-breaking to see what the pirates had *left:* anything damaged, such worn-out and useless gear as he had been only waiting for some "storm" to wash overboard—not one of these eyesores was missing.

What, in Heaven's name, was the use of an insurance policy? He began to collect the rubbish himself, and dump it over the side.

But Captain Jonsen saw him:

"Hi!" he shouted: "You dirty svindler! I will write to Lloyds and expose you! I will write myself!" He was horribly shocked at the other's dishonesty.

So Marpole had to give it up, for the time at any rate. He took a spike and broke open the fo'c'sle: and as well as the sailors found Margaret's brown nurse. She had hidden

>>>>>>>>>>>>>>>>>>>>>><<<<<<<<<<<<<<<<<<<<
there the whole day, probably from motives
of fright.

iii

You would have thought that supper on
the schooner that night would have been a
hilarious affair.   But, somehow, it was
manqué.

A prize of such value had naturally put the
crew in the best of humours: and a meal
which consisted mainly of crystallised fruit,
followed as an afterthought by bread and
chopped onions served in one enormous com-
munal bowl, eaten on the open deck under
the stars after bed-time, should have done the
same by the children.   But nevertheless both
parties were seized by a sudden, overpowering, and most unexpected fit of shyness.   Consequently no state banquet was ever so formal, or so boring.

I suppose it was the lack of a common language which first generated the infection. The Spanish sailors, used enough to this difficulty, grinned, pointed, and bobbed: but the children retired into a display of good manners which it would certainly have surprised their parents to see. Whereon the sailors became equally formal: and one poor monkeyfied little fellow who by nature belched continually was so be-nudged and be-winked by his companions, and so covered in confusion of his own accord, that presently he went away to eat by himself. Even then, so silent was this revel, he could still be heard faintly belching, half the ship's length away.

Perhaps it would have gone better if the captain and mate had been there, with their English. But they were too busy, looking over the personal belongings they had brought from the barque, sorting out by the light of a lantern anything too easily identifiable and reluctantly committing it to the sea.

It was at the loud splashes made by a couple of empty trunks, stamped in large letters JAS MARPOLE, that they heard a roar of unassumed indignation arise from the neighbouring barque. The two paused in their work, astonished: why should a crew already spoiled of all they possessed take it so hardly, when one heaved a couple of old worthless trunks into the sea?

It was inexplicable.

They continued their task, taking no further notice of the *Clorinda*.

Once supper was over, the social situation became even more awkward. The children stood about, not knowing what to do with their hands, or even their legs: unable to talk to their hosts, and feeling it would be rude to talk to one another: wishing badly that it was time to leave. If only it had been light they could have been happy enough exploring: but in the darkness there was nothing to do, nothing whatever.

The sailors soon found occupations of their own: and the captain and mate, as I have said, were already busy.

Once the sorting was over, however, there was nothing for Jonsen to do except return the children to the barque, and get well clear while the breeze and the darkness lasted.

But on hearing those splashes, Marpole's lively imagination had interpreted them in his own way. They suggested that there was now no reason to wait: indeed, every reason to be gone.

I think he was quite honestly misled.

It was after all but a small slip to say he had "seen with his own eyes" what he had heard with his own ears: and the intention was pious.

He set his men feverishly to work: and when Captain Jonsen looked his way again, the *Clorinda,* with every stitch spread in the starlight, was already half a mile to leeward.

>>>>>>>>>>>>>>>>>>>>><<<<<<<<<<<<<<<<<<<<

To pursue her, right in the track of shipping, was out of the question. Jonsen had to content himself with staring after her through his night-glass.

iv

Captain Jonsen set the little monkeyfied sailor, who had been so mortified earlier in the evening, to clear the schooner's fore-hold. The warps and brooms and fenders it contained were piled to one side, and a sufficiency of bedclothes for the guests was provided from the plunder.

But nothing could now thaw them. They clambered down the ladder and received their blanket apiece in an uncomfortable silence. Jonsen hung about, anxious to be helpful in this matter of getting into beds which were not there, but not knowing how to set about it. So he gave it up at last, and swung himself up through the fore hatch, talking to himself.

The last they saw of him was his fantastic slippers, hanging each from a big toe, outlined against the stars: but it never entered their heads to laugh.

Once, however, the familiar comfort of a blanket under their chins had begun to have its effect, and they were obviously quite alone, a little life did begin to return into these dumb statues.

The darkness was profound, only accentuated by the starlit square of the open hatchway. First the long silence was broken by someone turning over, almost freely. Then presently:

LAURA (*in slow, sepulchral tones*): I don't like this bed.

RACHEL (*ditto*): I do.

LAURA: It's a horrid bed; there isn't any!

EMILY
JOHN } : Sh! Go to sleep!

EDWARD: I smell cockroaches.

EMILY: Sh!

EDWARD (*loudly and hopefully*): They'll bite our nails off, because we haven't washed, and our skin, and our hair, and——

LAURA: There's a cockroach in my bed! Get out!

(*You could hear the brute go zooming away. But* LAURA *was already out too.*)

EMILY: Laura! Go back to bed!

LAURA: I can't when there's a cockroach in it!

JOHN: Get into bed again, you little fool! He's gone long ago!

LAURA: But I expect he has left his wife.

HARRY: They don't have wives, they're wives themselves.

RACHEL: Ow! Laura, stop it! Emily, Laura's walking on me!

EMILY: Lau-*rer!*

LAURA: Well, I must walk on something!

EMILY: Go to sleep!

>>>>>>>>>>>>>>>>>>>>>>>><<<<<<<<<<<<<<<<<<<<<<

(Silence for a while.)

LAURA: I haven't said my prayers.

EMILY: Well, say them lying down.

RACHEL: She mustn't, that's lazy.

JOHN: Shut up, Rachel, she must.

RACHEL: It's wicked! You go to sleep in the middle, then. People who go to sleep in the middle ought to be damned, they ought. Oughtn't they? *(Silence.)* Oughtn't they? *(Still silence.)* Emily, I say, oughtn't they?

JOHN: No!

RACHEL *(dreamily)*: I think there's lots more people ought to be damned than are.

(Silence again.)

HARRY: Marghie. *(Silence.)* Marghie! *(Silence.)*

JOHN: What's up with Marghie? Won't she speak?

(A faint sob is heard.)

HARRY: I don't know.

(Another sob.)

JOHN: Is she often like this?

>>>>>>>>>>>>>>>>>><<<<<<<<<<<<<<<<<

HARRY: She's an awful ass sometimes.

JOHN: Marghie, what's up?

MARGARET (*miserably*): Let me alone!

RACHEL: I believe she's frightened! (*Chants tauntingly.*) Marghie's got the bogies, the bogies, the bogies!

MARGARET (*sobbing out loud*): *Oh* you little fools!

JOHN: Well, what's the matter with you, then?

MARGARET (*after a pause*): I'm older than any of you.

JOHN: Well, *that's* a funny reason to be frightened!

MARGARET: It isn't.

JOHN: It is!

MARGARET (*warming to the argument*): It isn't, I tell you!

JOHN: *It is!*

MARGARET (*smugly*): That's simply because you're all too young to know. . . .

JOHN: Oh, hit her, Emily!

EMILY (*sleepily*) : Hit her yourself.

HARRY: But Marghie, why are we here? (*No answer.*) Emily, why are we here?

EMILY (*indifferently*): I don't know. I expect they just wanted to change us.

HARRY: I expect so. But they never *told* us we were going to be changed.

EMILY: Grown-ups never *do* tell us things.

≫≫≫≫≫≫≫≫≫≫≫≫≫≫≫≫≫≪≪≪≪≪≪≪≪≪≪≪≪≪≪

Chapter Four

THE children all slept late, and all woke at the same moment as if by clockwork. They sat up, and yawned uniformly, and stretched the stiffness out of their legs and backs (they were lying on solid wood, remember).

The schooner was steady, and people tramping about the deck. The main-hold and fore-hold were all one: and from where they were they could see the main-hatch had been opened. The captain appeared through it legs first, and dropped onto the higgledy-piggledy of the *Clorinda's* cargo.

For some time they simply stared at him. He looked uneasy, and was talking to himself as he tapped now this case with his pencil, now that: and presently shouted rather fiercely to people on deck.

"All right, all right," came from above the injured voice of the mate. "There's no such hurry as all that."

On which the captain's mutterings to himself swelled, as if ten people were conversing at once in his chest.

"May we get up yet?" asked Rachel.

Captain Jonsen spun round—he had forgotten their existence.

"Eh?"

"May we get up, please?"

"You can go to the debble." He muttered this so low the children did not hear it. But it was not lost on the mate.

"Hey! Ey! Ey!" he called down, reprovingly.

"Yes! Get up! Go on deck! Here!" The captain viciously set up a short ladder for them to climb through the hatch.

They were greatly astonished to find the

schooner was no longer at sea. Instead, she
was snugly moored against a little wooden
wharf, in a pleasant land-locked bay; with a
pleasant but untidy village, of white wooden
houses with palm-leaf roofs, behind it; and
the tower of a small sandstone church emerging from the abundant greenery. On the
quay were a few well-dressed loungers,
watching the preparations for unloading.
The mate was directing the labours of the
crew, who were rigging the cargo-gaff and
getting ready for a hot morning's work.

The mate nodded cheerfully to the children, but thereafter took no notice of them,
which was rather mortifying. The truth is
that the man was busy.

At the same time there emerged from somewhere aft a collection of the oddest-looking
young men. Margaret decided she had never
seen such beautiful young men before. They
were slim, yet nicely rounded; and dressed in
exquisite clothes (if a trifle thread-bare).

But their faces! Those beautiful olive-tinted
ovals! Those large, black-ringed, soft brown
eyes, those unnaturally carmine lips! They
minced across the deck, chattering to each
other in high-pitched tones, "twittering like a
cage of linnets . . ." and made their way on
shore.

"Who are they?" Emily asked the captain,
who had just re-emerged from below.

"Who are who?" he murmured, absently,
without looking round: "Oh, those?—
Fairies."

"*Hey! Yey! Yey!*" cried the mate, more
disapprovingly than ever.

"*Fairies?*" cried Emily in astonishment.

But Captain Jonsen began to blush. He
went crimson from the nape of his neck to
the bald patches on the top of his head, and
left.

"He is *silly!*" said Emily.

"I wonder if we go onto the land yet," said
Edward.

>>>>>>>>>>>>>>>>>>>>><<<<<<<<<<<<<<<<<<<<

"We'd better wait until we're told, hadn't we, Emily?" said Harry.

"I didn't know England would be like this," said Rachel: "it's very like Jamaica."

"This isn't England," said John, "you stupid!"

"But it must be," said Rachel: "England's where we're going."

"We don't get to England yet," said John: "it must be somewhere we're stopping at, like when we got all those turtles."

"I like stopping at places," said Laura.

"I don't," said Rachel.

"I do, though," pursued Laura.

"Where are those young men gone?" Margaret asked the mate. "Are they coming back?"

"They'll just come back to be paid, after we've sold the cargo," he answered.

"Then they're not living on the ship?" she pursued.

"No, we hired them from Havana."

>>>>>>>>>>>>>>>>>>>>>><<<<<<<<<<<<<<<<<<<<

"But what for?"

He looked at her in surprise: "Why, those are the 'ladies' we had on board, to look like passengers. You didn't think they were real ladies, did you?"

"What, were they dressed up?" asked Emily excitedly: "What fun!"

"I like dressing up," said Laura.

"I don't," said Rachel, "I think it's baby-ish."

"*I* thought they were real ladies," admitted Emily.

"We're a respectable ship's crew, we are," said the mate, a trifle stiffly—and without too good logic, when you come to think of it. "Here, you go on shore and amuse yourselves."

So the children went ashore, holding hands in a long row, and promenaded the town in a formal sort of way. Laura wanted to go off by herself, but the others would not let her: and when they returned the line was still unbroken. They had seen all there was to see, and no one had taken the least notice of them (so far as they were aware), and they wanted to start asking questions again.

It was, then, a charming little sleepy old place, in its way, Santa Lucia: isolated on the forgotten western end of Cuba between Nombre de Dios and the Rio de Puercos: cut off from the open sea by the intricate nature of the channels through the reefs and the banks of Isabella, channels only navigable to the practised and creeping local coasting craft and shunned like poison by bigger traffic: on land isolated by a hundred miles of forest from Havana.

Time was, these little ports of the Canal de Guaniguanico had been pretty prosperous, as bases for pirates: but it was a fleeting prosperity. There came the heroic attack of an American squadron under Captain Allen, in 1823, on the Bay of Sejuapo, their headquarters. From that blow (although it took many years to take full effect) the industry never really recovered: it dwindled and dwindled, like hand-weaving. One could make money much faster in a city like Havana, and with less risk (if less respectably). Piracy had long since ceased to pay, and should have been scrapped years ago: but a vocational tradition will last on a long time after it has ceased to be economic, in a decadent form. Now, Santa Lucia—and piracy—continued to exist because they always had; but for no other reason. Such a haul as the *Clorinda* did not come once in a blue moon. Every year the amount of land under cultivation dwindled, and the pirate schooners were abandoned to rot against the wharves, or ignominiously sold as traders. The young men left for Havana or the United States. The maidens yawned. The local grandees increased in dignity as their numbers and property dwindled: an idyllic, simple-minded country community, oblivious of the outer world and of its own approaching oblivion.

"I don't think I should like to live here," John decided, when they got back to the ship.

Meanwhile the cargo had been unloaded onto the quay: and after the siesta a crowd of about a hundred people gathered round, poking and discussing. The auction was about to begin. Captain Jonsen tramped about rather in the way of everybody, but especially annoying the mate by shouting contrary directions every minute. The latter had a ledger, and a number of labels with numbers on them which he was pasting onto the various bales and packages. The sailors were building a kind of temporary stage—the thing was to be done in style.

Every moment the crowd increased. Because they all talked Spanish it was a pantomime to the children: like puppets acting, not like real people moving and talking. So they discovered what a fascinating game it is to

watch foreigners, whose very simplest words
mean nothing to you, and try and guess what
they are about.

Moreover, these were all such funny-look-
ing people: they moved about as if they were
kings, and spat all the time, and smoked thin
black cigars, the blue smoke of which as-
cended from their enormous hats as from
censers.

At one moment there was a diversion—the
crowd suddenly gaped, and there staggered
onto the stage the whole crew of the schooner
carrying a huge pair of scales: it was always
on the point of being too much for them, and
running suddenly away with them in another
direction.

There were quite a number of ladies in the
crowd—old ones, they seemed to the children. Some were thin and dried up, like
monkeys; but most were fat, and one was
fatter than all of them and treated with the
greatest respect (perhaps for her moustache).

She was the wife of the Chief Magistrate: Señora del Ilustrious Juzgado del Municipal de Santa Lucia, to give her her title. She had a rocking-chair of suitable strength and width, which was carried by a short squinting negro and set in the very middle of the scene, right in front of the platform. There she throned herself: and the negro stood behind her, holding a violet silk sunshade over her head.

No one can doubt that she would immediately become the most noticeable thing in the picture.

She had a powerful bass voice, and when she uttered some jocundity (as she repeatedly did), everyone heard it, however much they were chattering among themselves.

The children, as was their custom, wormed their way without any excess of civility through the crowd and grouped themselves round her throne.

The captain either did not know, or suddenly refused to know, a single word of Spanish: so the auctioneering devolved on the mate. The latter mounted the stage; and with a great assumption of competence, began.

But auctioneering is an art: it is as easy to write a sonnet in a foreign tongue as to conduct a successful auction. One must have at one's command eloquence without a hitch: the faculty of kindling an audience, amusing them, castigating them, converting them, till they rattle out increments as a camp-meeting rattles out Amens: till they totally forget the worth (and even the nature) of the lot, and begin to take a real pride in a long run of bidding—as a champion does in a long break at billiards.

The little Viennese had been to a good school, it is true: for he had once resided in Wales, where one sees auctioneering in its finest flower. In Welsh, or English, or even in his native tongue, he could have acquitted himself fairly well: but in Spanish, just that margin of power was lacking to him. The audience remained stern, cold, critical, bidding grudgingly.

As if this language difficulty were not in itself enough, there sat that overpowering old dame on her throne, distracting with her jokes whatever vestige of attention he might otherwise have managed to arouse.

When the third lot of coffee came to be dealt with, there was even the beginning of a rather nasty row. The children were highly scandalised: they had never seen grown-ups being rude to one another before. The captain had undertaken the weighing: and it was something to do with a habit he had of leaning against the scales while he read them. Being short-sighted, he could see the figures much more clearly like that: but it displeased the buyers, and they had a lot to say about it.

The captain, mortified, wrung his hands, and began to answer them in Danish. They rejoined in Spanish even more stingingly. He stumped off in a sulk: they could all conduct his affairs without him, if they weren't prepared to treat him with a little consideration.

But who would be less partial? The mate, angry, maintained that to elect one of the buyers was equally objectionable.

Thereon an earthquake began in the fat old lady, and gradually gathered enough force to lift her onto her feet. She took John by the shoulders, and pushed him before her to the scales. Then in a few witty, ringing words she suggested her solution—*he* should do the weighing.

The audience were pleased: but as soon as John understood he went very red, and wanted to escape. The rest of the children, on the other hand, were eaten with envy.

"Mayn't I help too?" piped Rachel.

The despairing mate thought he saw just a forlorn hope in this. While John was being

instructed, he gathered the other children:
and out of the heap of miscellaneous clothing
rigged them all out in a sort of fancy dress.
Then he gave them the samples to carry
round, and the sale began anew.

It had now assumed rather the character of
a parochial bazaar. Even the Vicar was present—though less well shaved than he would
have been in England, and cunninger-look-
ing. He was one of the only buyers.

The children thoroughly enjoyed themselves, and minced and pranced and tugged
each other's turbans. But the crowd was a
Latin one, not Nordic: and their endearing
tricks failed altogether to arouse any interest. The sale went worse than ever.

There was only one exception, and that was
the important old lady. Once her attention
had been called (by her own act) to the children, it fixed itself on one of them, on Edward. She drew him to her bosom, like a

mother in melodrama, and with her hairy
mouth gave him three resounding kisses.

Edward could no more have struggled than
if caught by a boa. Moreover, the portentous
woman fascinated him, as if she had been a
boa indeed. He lay in her arms limp, self-
conscious, and dejected: but without active
thought of escape.

And so the business went on: on the one
hand the unheeded drone of the mate, on the
other the great creature still keeping up her
witticisms, still dominating everything: all of
a sudden remembering Edward, and giving
him a couple of kisses like so many bombs:
then forgetting clean all about him: then remembering him again, and hugging him:
then dropping her salts: then nearly dropping
Edward: then suddenly twisting round to
launch a dart into the crowd behind her—
she was the despair of that unhappy auc-
tioneer, who saw lot after lot fall for a tenth
of its value, or even find no bidder at all.

Captain Jonsen, however, had his own idea of how to enliven a parochial bazaar that is proving a frost. He went on board, and mixed several gallons of that potion known in alcoholic circles as Hangman's Blood (which is compounded of rum, gin, brandy, and porter). Innocent (merely beery) as it looks, refreshing as its tastes, it has the property of increasing rather than allaying thirst, and so, once it has made a breach, soon demolishes the whole fort.

This he poured out into mugs, merely remarking that it was a noted English cordial, and gave it to the children to distribute among the crowd.

At once the Cubans began to show more interest in them than when they came bearing samples of arrow-root; and with their popularity their happiness increased, and like rococo Ganymedekins and Hebelettes they darted about the crowd, distributing the enticing poison to all who would.

>>>>>>>>>>>>>>>>>>>><<<<<<<<<<<<<<<<<<<<

When he saw what was on foot, the mate wiped his mouth in despair.

"*Oh* you fool!" he groaned.

But the captain himself was highly pleased with his ruse: kept rubbing his hands, and grinning, and winking.

"That'll liven 'em, eh?"

"Wait and see!" was all the mate let himself say. "You just wait and see!"

"Look at Edward!" said Emily to Margaret in a pause. "It's perfectly sickening!"

It was. The very first mug rendered the fat señora even more motherly. Edward by now was fascinated, was in her power completely. He sat and gazed up in her little black eyes, his own large brown ones glazed with sentiment. He avoided her moustache, it is true: but on her cheek he was returning her kisses earnestly. All this, of course, without the possibility of their exchanging a single word —pure instinct. "With a fork drive Nature out . . ." one would gladly have taken a fork to Nature, on that occasion.

Meanwhile, on the rest of the crowd the liquor was having exactly the effect the mate had foreseen. Instead of stimulating them, it dissolved completely whatever vestiges of attention they were still giving to the sale. He stepped down from the platform—gave it all up in despair. For they had now broken up into little groups, which discussed and argued their own affairs as if they were in a café. He in his turn went on board, and shut himself in his cabin—Captain Jonsen could deal with the mess he had made himself!

But alas! No worse host than Jonsen was ever born: he was utterly incapable of either understanding or controlling a crowd. All he could think of to do was to ply them with more.

For the children, the spectacle was an absorbing one. The whole nature of these people, as they drank, seemed to be changing:

under their very eyes something seemed to be breaking up, like ice melting. Remember that to them this was a pantomime: no word spoken to explain, and so the eyes exercised a peculiar clearness.

It was rather as if the whole crowd had been immersed in water, and something dissolved out of them while the general structure yet remained. The tone of their voices changed, and they began to talk much slower, to move more slowly and elaborately. The expression of their faces became more candid, and yet more mask-like: hiding less, there was also less to hide. Two men even began to fight: but they fought so incompetently it was like a fight in a poetic play. Conversation, which before had a beginning and an end, now grew shapeless and interminable, and the women laughed a lot.

One old gentleman in most respectable clothes settled himself on the dirty ground at full length, with his head in the shade of the throned lady, spread a handkerchief over his face, and went to sleep: three other middle-aged men, holding each other with one hand to establish contact and using the other for emphasis, kept up a continuous clacking talk, that faltered intolerably though never quite stopping—like a very old engine.

A dog ran in and out among them all wagging its tail, but no one kicked it. Presently it found the old gentleman who was asleep on the ground, and began licking his ear excitedly: it had never had such a chance before.

The old lady also had fallen asleep, a little crookedly—she might even have slipped off her chair if her negro had not buttressed her up. Edward got off her, and went and joined the other children rather shamefacedly: but they would not speak to him.

Jonsen looked round him perplexedly. Why had Otto abandoned the sale, now the crowd were all primed and ready? Probably he had some good reason, though. He was an incomprehensible man, that mate: but clever.

The truth is that Captain Jonsen was himself a man with a very weak head for liquor, and so he very seldom touched it, and knew little of the subtler aspects of its effects.

He paced up and down the dusty wharf at his usual slow shuffle, his head sunk forward in wretchedness, occasionally wringing his hands in the naturalest way, and even whimpering. When the priest came up to him confidentially and offered him a price for all that remained unsold he simply shook his head and continued his shuffle.

There was something a little nightmare-like in the whole scene which riveted the children's attention, and was very near the border of frightening them. It was with something of a struggle that at last Margaret said "Let's go on the ship." So they all went

>>>>>>>>>>>>>>>>>>>>>>><<<<<<<<<<<<<<<<<<<<

on board; and feeling a little unprotected even there descended into the hold, which was the safest place because they had already slept in it. They sat down on the kelson without doing or saying much, still with a vague apprehension, till boredom at last eliminated it.

"Oh I *wish* I had brought my paint-box!" said Emily, with a sigh fetched right up from her boots.

ii

That night, after they had all gone to bed, they saw in a half-asleep state a lantern bobbing up and down in the open hatch. It was held by José, the little monkeyfied one (they had already decided he was the nicest of the crew). He was grinning winningly, and beckoning to them.

Emily was too sleepy to move, and so were

Laura and Rachel: so leaving them to lie the others—Margaret, Edward and John—scrambled on deck.

It was mysteriously quiet. Not a sign of the crew, but for José. In the bright starlight the town looked abnormally beautiful: there was music coming from one of the big houses up by the church. José conducted them ashore and up to this house: tiptoed up to the jalousies and signed to them to follow him.

As the light struck his face it became transfigured, so affected was he by the opulence within.

The children craned up to the level of the windows and peered in too, oblivious of the mosquitoes making havoc of their necks.

It was a very grand sight. This was the house of the Chief Magistrate: and he was giving a dinner in honour of Captain Jonsen and his mate. There he sat at the head of the table, in uniform; very stiff, yet his little beard even stiffer than himself. His was the kind of dignity that grows from reserve and stillness, from freezing every minute like game which scents the hunter; while in total contrast to him there sat his wife (the important señora who had made so much of Edward), more impressive easily than her husband, but doing it not by dignity but by that calculated abandon and vulgarity which transcend dignity. Indeed, her flinging about got the greater part of its effect from the very formality of her setting.

When the children arrived at the window she must even have been discussing the size of her own belly: for she suddenly seized the shy hand of the mate, and made him, willy-nilly, feel it, as if to clench an argument.

As for her husband, he did not seem to see her: nor did the servants: she was such a very great lady.

But it was not her, it was the meal which raped José's attention. It was certainly an impressive one. Together on the table were tomato soup, mountain mullet, cray-fish, a huge red-snapper, land-crabs, rice and fried chicken, a young turkey, a small joint of goat-mutton, a wild duck, beefsteak, fried pork, a dish of wild pigeons, sweet potatoes, yuca, wine, and guavas and cream. It was a meal which would take a long time.

Captain Jonsen and the lady appeared to be on excellent terms: he pressing some project on her, and she, without the least loss of amiability, putting it on one side. What they were talking about, of course, the children could not hear. As a matter of fact, it was themselves. Captain Jonsen was trying to get the lady to discuss the disposal of his impromptu nursery: the most reasonable solution being plainly to leave them at Santa Lucia, more or less in her charge. But she was adept at eluding the importunate. It was not till the banquet was over that he realised

>>>>>>>>>>>>>>>>>>>>>>>>><<<<<<<<<<<<<<<<<<<<<

he had failed to make any arrangement whatever.

But long before this, before the dinner was ended and the dance began, the children were tired of the peep-show. So José tiptoed away with them, down to the back streets by the dock. Presently they came to a mysterious door at the bottom of a staircase, with a negro standing as if on guard. But he made no effort to stop them, and, José leading them, they climbed several flights to a large upper room.

The air was one you could hardly push through. The place was crowded with negroes, and a few rather smudgy whites: among whom they recognised most of the rest of the crew of the schooner. At the far end was the most primitive stage you ever saw: there was a cradle on it, and a large star swung on the end of a piece of string. There was to be a Nativity-play—rather early in the season. While the Chief Magistrate enter-

tained the pirate Captain and Mate, the priest
had got this up in honour of the pirate crew.

A Nativity-play, with real cattle.

The whole audience had arrived an hour
early, so as to see the entry of the cow. The
children were just in time for this.

The room was in the upper part of a ware-
house, which had been built, through some
freak of vanity, in the English fashion, several stories high; and was provided with the
usual large door opening onto nothingness,
with a beam-and-tackle over it. Many the
load of gold-dust and arrow-root which must
have once been hoisted into it: now, like most
of the others at Santa Lucia, it had long since
ceased to be used.

But today a new rope had been rove
through the block: and a broad belly-band
put round the waist of the priest's protesting
old cow.

Margaret and Edward lingered timidly
near the top of the stairs; but John, putting

his head down and burrowing like a mole, was not content till he had reached the open doorway. There he stood looking out into the darkness; where he saw a slowly revolving cow treading the air a yard from the sill, while at each revolution a negro reached out to the utmost limit of balance, trying to catch her by the tail and draw her to shore.

John, in his excitement, leant out too far. He lost his balance and fell clear to the ground, forty feet, right on his head.

José gave a cry of alarm, sprang onto the cow's back, and was instantly lowered away —just as if the cinema had already been invented. He must have looked very comic. But what was going on inside him the while it is difficult to know. Such a responsibility does not often fall on an old sailor; and he would probably feel it all the more for that reason. As for the crowd beneath, they made no attempt to touch the body till José had completed his descent: they stood back and let him have a good look at it, and shake it, and so on. But the neck was quite plainly broken.

Margaret and Edward, however, had not any clear idea of what was going on, since they had not actually seen John fall. So they were rather annoyed when two of the schooner's crew appeared and insisted on their coming back to bed at once. They wanted to know where John was: but even more they wanted to know where José was, and why they weren't to be allowed to stay. However they obeyed, in the impossibility of asking questions, and started back to bed.

Just as they were about to go on board the schooner, they heard a huge report on their left, like a cannon. They turned; and looking past the quiet, silver town, with its palm-groves, to the hills behind, they saw a large ball of fire, travelling at a tremendous rate. It was quite close to the ground: and not very far off either—just beyond the Church. It left a wake of the most brilliant blue, green, and purple blobs of light. For a while it hovered: then it burst, and the air was shortly charged with a strong sulphurous smell.

They were all frightened by the meteor, the sailors even more than the children, and hastened on board.

In the small hours, Edward suddenly called Emily in his sleep.

She woke up: "What is it?"

"It's rather cow-catching, isn't it?" he asked anxiously, his eyes tight shut.

"What's the matter?"

He did not answer, so she roused him—or thought she had.

"I only wanted to see if you were a *real* Cow-catching Zomfanelia," he explained in a kind voice: and was immediately deep asleep again.

In the morning they might easily have thought the whole thing a dream, if John's bed had not been so puzzlingly empty.

Yet, as if by some mute flash of understanding, no one commented on his absence. No one questioned Margaret, and she offered no information. Neither then nor thereafter was his name ever mentioned by anybody: and if you had known the children intimately you would never have guessed from them that he had ever existed.

iii

The children's only enemy on board the schooner (which presently put to sea again, with them still on board) was the big white pig. (There was a little black fellow, too.)

He was a pig with no decision of mind. He could never choose a place to lie for himself; but was so ready to follow anyone else's opinion, that whatever position you took up he immediately recognised as the best, the only site: and came and routed you out of it. Seeing how rare shady patches of deck are in a calm, or dry patches in a stiff breeze, this was a most infernal nuisance. One is so defenceless against big pigs when lying on one's back.

The little black one could be a nuisance also, it is true, but that was only from excess of friendliness. He hated to be left out of any party; nay more, he hated lying on inanimate matter, if a living couch was to be found.

On the north beach of Cape San Antonio it is possible to land a boat, if you pick your spot. About fifty yards through the bushes there are a couple of acres of open ground: cross this, and among some sharp coral rocks in the scrub on the far side are two wells, the northernmost the better of the two.

So, being becalmed off the Mangrove Keys

>>>>>>>>>>>>>>>>>>>>>><<<<<<<<<<<<<<<<<<<
one morning, Jonsen sent a boat on shore to
get water.

The heat was extreme. The ropes hung
like dead snakes, the sails as heavy as ill-
sculptured drapery. The iron stanchion of
the awning blistered any hand that touched
it. Where the deck was unsheltered, the
pitch boiled out of the seams. The children
lay gasping together in the small shade, the
little black pig squealing anxiously till he
found a comfortable stomach to settle
down on.

The big white pig had not found them yet.

From the silent shore came an occasional
gun-shot. The water-party were potting
pigeons. The sea was like a smooth pampas
of quick-silver: so steady you could not split
shore from reflection, till the casual collision
of a pelican broke the phantom. The crew
were mending sails, under the awning, with
infinite slowness: all except one negro, who
straddled the bowsprit in his trousers, admir-

ing his own grin in the mirror beneath. The
sun lit an iridescent glimmer on his shoulders: in such a light even a negro could not
be black.

Emily was missing John badly: but the
little black pig snuffled in supreme content,
his snout buried amicably in her arm-pit.

When the boat-load returned, they had
other game besides pigeons and grey land-
crabs. They had stolen a goat from some
lonely fisherman.

It was just as they came up over the side
that the big white pig discovered the party
under the awning, and prepared for the attack. But the goat at that moment bounded
nimbly from the bulwarks: and without even
stopping to look round, swallowed his chin
and charged. He caught the old pig full in
the ribs, knocking his wind out completely.

Then the battle began. The goat charged,
the pig screamed and hustled. Each time the
goat arrived at him the pig yelled as if he was

killed; but each time the goat drew back the pig advanced towards him. The goat, his beard flying like a prophet's, his eyes crimson and his scut as lively as a lamb's at the teat, bounded in, bounded back into the bows for a fresh run: but at each charge his run grew shorter and shorter. The pig was hemming him in.

Suddenly the pig gave a frightful squeal, chiefly in surprise at his own temerity, and pounced. He had got the goat cornered against the windlass; and for a few flashing seconds bit and trampled.

It was a very chastened goat which was presently led off to his quarters: but the children were prepared to love him for ever, for the heroic bangs he had given the old tyrant.

But he was not entirely inhuman, that pig. That same afternoon, he was lying on the hatch eating a banana. The ship's monkey was swinging on a loose tail of rope; and spotting the prize, swung further and further till at last he was able to snatch it from between the pig's very trotters. You would never have thought that the immobile mask of a pig could wear a look of such astonishment, such dismay, such piteous injury.

Chapter Five

WHEN Destiny knocks the first nail in the coffin of a tyrant, it is seldom long before she knocks the last.

It was the very next morning that the schooner, in the lightest of airs, was sidling gently to leeward. The mate was at the wheel, shifting his weight from foot to foot with that rhythmic motion many steersmen affect, the better to get the feel of a finnicky helm; and Edward was teaching the Captain's terrier to beg, on the cabin-top. The mate shouted to him to hang on to something.

"Why?" said Edward.

"*Hang on!*" cried the mate again, spinning the wheel over as fast as he could to bring her into the wind.

The howling squall took her, through his promptness, almost straight in the nose; or it would have carried all away. Edward clung to the skylight. The terrier skidded about alarmedly all over the cabin-top, slipped off onto the deck, and was kicked by a dashing sailor clean through the galley door. But not so that poor big pig, who was taking an airing on deck at the time. Overboard he went, and vanished to windward, his snout (sometimes) sticking up manfully out of the water. God, Who had sent him the goat and the monkey for a sign, now required his soul of him. Overboard, too, went the coops of fowls, three new-washed shirts, and—of all strange things to get washed away—the grindstone.

Up out of his cabin appeared the Captain's shapeless brown head, cursing the mate as if it was *he* who had upset the apple-cart. He came up without his boots, in grey wool socks, and his braces hanging down his back.

>>>>>>>>>>>>>>>>>>>>>>>><<<<<<<<<<<<<<<<<<<<<

"Get below!" muttered the mate furiously: "I can manage her!"

The captain did not, however: still in his socks he came up on deck and took the wheel out of the mate's hand. The latter went a dull brick-red: walked for'ard: then aft again: then went below and shut himself in his cabin.

In a few moments the wind had combed up some quite hearty waves: then it blew their tops off, and so flattened the sea out again, a sea that was black except for little whipt-up fountains of iridescent foam.

"Get my boots!" bellowed Jonsen at Edward.

Edward dashed down the companion with alacrity. It is a great moment, one's first order at sea; especially when it comes in an emergency. He re-appeared with a boot in each hand, and a lurch flung him boots and all at the captain's feet.

"Never carry things in both hands," said the captain, smiling pleasantly.

"Why?" asked Edward.

"Keep one hand to lay hold with."

There was a pause.

"Someday, I will teach you the Three Sovereign Rules of Life." He shook his head meditatively. "They are very wise. But not yet. You are too young."

"Why not?" asked Edward: "When shall I be old enough?"

The captain considered, going over the Rules in his head.

"When you know which is windward and which is leeward, then I will teach you the first rule."

Edward made his way forward, determined to qualify as soon as he possibly could.

When the worst of the squall was over they got the advantage of it, the schooner lying over lissomly and spinning along like a race-horse. The crew were in great spirits—

chaffing the carpenter, who, they declared, had thrown his grindstone overboard as a life-buoy for the pig.

The children were in good spirits also. Their shyness was all gone now. The schooner lying over as she did, her wet deck made a most admirable toboggan-slide; and for half an hour they tobogganed happily on their bottoms from windward to leeward, shrieking with joy, fetching up in the lee scuppers, which were mostly awash, and then climbing from thing to thing to the windward bulwarks raised high in the air, and so all over again.

Throughout that half hour, Jonsen at the wheel said not a single word. But at last his pent-up irritation broke out:

"Hi! You! Stop that!"

They gazed at him in astonishment and disillusion.

There is a period in the relations of children with any new grown-up in charge of them, the period between first acquaintance and the first reproof, which can only be compared to the primordial innocence of Eden. Once a reproof has been administerd, this can never be recovered again.

Jonsen now had done it.

But he was not content with that—he was still bursting with rage:

"Stop it! Stop it, I tell you!"

(They had already done so, of course.)

The whole unreasonableness, the monstrousness of the imposition of these brats on his ship suddenly came over him, and summed itself up in a single symbol:

"If you go and wear holes in your drawers, do you think *I* am going to mend them? Lieber Gott! What do you think I am, eh? What do you think this ship is? What do you think we all are? To mend your drawers for you, eh? *To mend . . . your . . . drawers?*"

There was a pause, while they all stood thunderstruck.

But even now he had not finished:

"Where do you think you'll get new ones, eh?" he asked, in a voice explosive with rage. Then he added, with an insulting coarseness of tone: "And I'll not have you going about my ship without them! See?"

Scarlet to the eyes with outrage they retreated to the bows. They could hardly believe so unspeakable a remark had crossed human lips. They assumed an air of lightness, and talked together in studied loud voices: but their joy was dashed for the day.

So it was that—small as a man's hand—a spectre began to show over their horizon: the suspicion at last that this was *not* all according to plan, that they might even be not wanted. For a while their actions showed the unhappy wariness of the uninvited guest.

Later in the afternoon, Jonsen, who had not spoken again, but looked from time to time acutely miserable, was still at the wheel. The mate had shaved himself and put on shore clothes, as a parable: he now appeared on deck: pretended not to see the captain, but strolled like a passenger up to the children and entered into conversation with them.

"If I'm not fit to steer in foul weather, I'm not fit to steer in fair!" he muttered, but without glancing at the captain. "He can take the helum all day and night, for all the help *I'll* give him!"

The captain appeared equally not to see the mate. He looked quite ready to take both watches till kingdom come.

"If *he*'d been at the wheel when that squall struck us," said the mate under his voice but with biting passion, "he'd have lost the ship! He's no more eye for a squall coming than a sucker-fish! And he knows it, too: that's what makes him go on this way!"

The children did not answer. It shocked them deeply to have to see a grown-up, a should-be Olympian, displaying his feelings. In exact opposition to the witnesses at the Transfiguration, they felt it would have been good for them to be almost anywhere rather than there. He was totally unconscious of their discomfort, however: too self-occupied to notice how they avoided catching his eye.

"Look! There's a steamship!" exclaimed Margaret, with much too bright a brightness.

The mate glowered at it.

"Aye, they'll be the death of us, those steamers," he said. "Every year there's more of them. They'll be using them for men-of-war next, and then where'll we be? Times are bad enough without steamers."

But while he spoke he wore a pre-occupied expression, as if he were more concerned with what was going on at the back of his mind than with what went on in the front.

"Did you ever hear about what happened when the first steamer put to sea in the Gulf of Paria?" he asked, however.

>>>>>>>>>>>>>>>>>>>><<<<<<<<<<<<<<<<<<<<

"No, what?" asked Margaret, with an eagerness that even exceeded the necessities of politeness in its falsity.

"She was built on the Clyde, and sailed over. (Nobody thought of using steam for a long ocean voyage in those days.) The Company thought they ought to make a to-do —to popularise her, so to speak. So the first time she put to sea under her own power, they invited all the big-wigs on board: all the Members of Assembly in Trinidad, and the Governor and his staff, and a Bishop. It was the Bishop what did the trick."

His story died out: he became completely absorbed in watching sidelong the effect of his bravado on the captain.

"Did what?" asked Margaret.

"Ran 'em aground."

"But what did they let him steer for?" asked Edward: "They might have known he couldn't!"

"Edward! How dare you talk about a

Bishop in that rude way!" admonished Rachel.

"It wasn't the steamer he run aground, sonny," said the mate: "it was a poor innocent little devil of a pirate craft, that was just beating up for the Boca Grande in a northerly breeze."

"Good for him!" said Edward: "How did he do it?"

"They were all sea-sick, being on a steamer for the first time: the way she rolls, not like a decent sailing vessel. There wasn't a man who could stay on deck—except the Bishop, and he just thrived on it. So when the poor little pirate cut under her bows, and seen her coming up in the eye of the wind, no sail set, with a cloud of smoke amidships and an old Bishop bung in the middle of the smoke, and her paddles making as much turmoil as a whale trying to scratch a flea in its ear, he just beached his vessel and took to the woods. Never went to sea again, he didn't: started growing cocoa-nuts. But there was one poor fish was in such a hurry he broke his leg, and they came ashore and found him. When he saw the Bishop coming for him he started yelling out it was the Devil."

"O-oh!" gasped Rachel, horror-struck.

"How silly of him," said Edward.

"I don't know so much!" said the mate. "He wasn't too far wrong! Ever since that, they've been the death of our profession, Steam and the Church . . . what with steaming, and what with preaching, and steaming and preaching. . . . Now that's a funny thing," he broke off, suddenly interested by what he was saying: "*Steam* and the *Church!* What have they got in common, eh? Nothing, you'd say: you'd think they'd fight each other cat-and-dog: but no: they're thick as two thieves . . . thick as thieves.—Not like in the days of Parson Audain."

"Who was he?" asked Margaret helpfully.

>>>>>>>>>>>>>>>>>>>>>><<<<<<<<<<<<<<<<<<<<<

"He was a right sort of a parson, he was,
yn wyr iawn! He was Rector of Roseau—
oh, a long time back."

"Here! Come and take this wheel while I
have a spell!" grunted the captain.

"I couldn't well say *how* long back," continued the mate in a loud, unnatural, and now
slightly exultant voice: "Forty years or more."

He began to tell the story of the famous
Rector of Roseau: one of the finest pathetic
preachers of his age, according to contempo-
raries; whose appearance was fine, gentle,
and venerable, and who supplemented his
stipend by owning a small privateer.

"Here! Otto!" called Jonsen.

But the mate had a long recital of the Parson's misfortunes before him: beginning with
the capture of his schooner (while smuggling
negroes to Guadaloupe), by another privateer, from Nevis; and how the Parson went
to Nevis, posted his rival's name on the court-
house door, and stood on guard there with

loaded pistols for three days in the hope the man would come and challenge him.

"What, to fight a *duel?*" asked Harry.

"But wasn't he a clergyman, you said?" asked Emily.

But duels, it appeared, did not come amiss to this priest. He fought thirteen altogether in his life, the mate told them: and on one occasion, while waiting for the seconds to re-load, he went up to his opponent, suggested "just a little something to fill in time, good sir,"—and knocked him flat with his fist.

This time, however, his enemy lay low: so he fitted out a second schooner, and took command of her, weekdays, himself. His first quarry was an apparently harmless Spanish merchantman: but she suddenly opened fourteen masked gun-ports and it was he who had to surrender. All his crew were massacred but himself and his carpen-ter, who hid behind a water-cask all night."

>>>>>>>>>>>>>>>>>>>>><<<<<<<<<<<<<<<<<<<<

"But I don't understand," said Margaret: "was he a pirate?"

"Of course he was!" said Otto the mate.

"Then *why* did you say he was a clergyman?" pursued Emily.

The mate looked as puzzled as she did. "Well, he was Rector of Roseau, wasn't he? And B.A., B.D.?—Anyway, he was rector until the new governor listened to some cockand-bull story against him, and made him resign. He was the best preacher they ever had—he'd have been a bishop one day, if someone hadn't slandered him to the Governor!"

"Otto!" called the captain in a conciliatory voice: "Come over here, I want to speak to you."

But the deaf and exulting mate had plenty of his story still to run: how Audain now turned trader, and took a cargo of corn to San Domingo, and settled there: how he challenged two black generals to a duel, and

shot them both, and Christophe threatened
to hang him if they died. But the parson
(having little faith in Domingan doctors)
escaped by night in an open boat and went to
St. Eustatius. There he found many re-
ligions but no ministers; so he recommenced
clergyman of every kind: in the morning he
celebrated a mass for the Catholics, then a
Lutheran service in Dutch, then Church of
England matins: in the evening he sang
hymns and preached hell-fire to the Method-
ists. Meanwhile his wife, who had more
tranquil tastes lived at Bristol: so he now
married a Dutch widow, resourcefully conducting the ceremony himself.

"But I *don't* understand!" said Emily de-
spairingly: "Was he a real clergyman?"

"Of course he wasn't," said Margaret.

"But he couldn't have married himself
himself if he wasn't," argued Edward:
"Could he?"

The mate heaved a sigh.

"But the English Church aren't like that nowadays," he said: "They're all against us."

"I should think not, indeed!" pronounced Rachel slowly, in a deep indignant voice. "He was a very wicked man!"

"He was a most respectable person," replied the mate severely, "and a *wonderful* pathetic preacher!—You may take it they were chagrined at Roseau, when they heard St. Eustatius had got him!"

Captain Jonsen had lashed the wheel, and came up, his face piteous with distress.

"Otto! Mein Schatz . . . !" he began, laying his great bear's-arm round the mate's neck. Without more ado they went below together, and a sailor came aft unbidden and took the wheel.

Ten minutes later the mate reappeared on deck for a moment, and sought out the children.

"What's the captain been saying to you?"

he asked. "Flashed out at you about something, did he?"

He took their complex, uncomfortable silence for assent.

"Don't you take too much notice of what he says," he went on. "He flashes out like that sometimes; but a minute after he could eat himself, fair eat himself!"

The children stared at him in astonishment: what on earth was he trying to say?

But he seemed to think he had explained his mission fully: turned, and once more went below.

For hours a merry but rather tedious hubble-bubble, suggesting liquor, was heard ascending from the cabin skylight. As evening drew on, the breeze having dropped away almost to a calm, the steersman reported that both Jonsen and Otto were now fast asleep, their heads on each other's shoulders across the cabin table. As he had long for-

→ 181 ←

gotten what the course was, but had been simply steering by the wind, and there was now no wind to steer by, he (the steersman) concluded the wheel could get on very well without him.

The reconciliation of the Captain and the mate deserved to be celebrated by all hands with a blind.

A rum-cask was broached; and the common sailors were soon as unconscious as their betters.

Altogether this was one of the unpleasantest days the children had spent in their lives.

When dawn came, everyone was still pretty incapable, and the neglected vessel drooped uncertainly. Jonsen, still rather unsteady on his feet, his head aching and his mind Napoleonic but muddled, came on deck and looked about him. The sun had come up like a searchlight; but it was about all there was to be seen. No land was anywhere in sight, and the sea and sky seemed very uncertain as to the most becoming place to locate their mutual firmament. It was not till he had looked round and round a fair number of times that he perceived a vessel, up in what by all appearances must be sky, yet not very far distant.

For some little while he could not remember what it is a pirate captain does when he sees a sail, and he felt in no mood to overtax his brain by trying to. But after a time it came back unbidden—one gives chase.

"Give chase!" he ordered solemnly to the morning air; and then went below again and roused the mate, who roused the crew.

No one had the least idea where they were, or what kind of a craft this quarry might be; but such considerations were altogether too complicated for the moment. As the sun parted farther from his reflection a breeze sprung up; so the sails were trimmed after a fashion, and chase was duly given.

In an hour or two, as the air grew clearer,

>>>>>>>>>>>>>>>>>>>><<<<<<<<<<<<<<<<<<<<

it was plain their quarry was a merchant brig, not too heavily laden and making a fair pace: a pace, indeed, which in their incompetently trimmed condition they were finding it pretty difficult to equal. Jonsen shuffled rapidly up and down the deck like a shuttle, passing his woof backwards and forwards through the real business of the ship. He was hugging himself with excitement, trying to evolve some crafty scheme of capture. The chase went on: but noon past, the distance between the two vessels was barely, if at all, lessened. Jonsen, however, was much too optimistic to realise this.

It used to be a common device of pirates when in chase of a vessel to tow behind them a spare topmast, or some other bulky object. This would act as a drogue, or brake: and the pursued, seeing them with all sail set apparently doing their utmost, would underestimate their powers of speed. Then when night fell the pirate would haul the spar on

>>>>>>>>>>>>>>>>>>>>>><<<<<<<<<<<<<<<<<<<<<

board, overtake the other vessel rapidly and catch it unprepared.

There were several reasons why this device was unsuitable to the present occasion. First and most obviously, it was doubtful whether, in their present condition, they were capable of overtaking the brig at all, leaving such handicaps altogether out of consideration. A second was that the brig showed no signs of alarm. She was proceeding on her voyage at her natural pace, quite unaware of the honour they were doing her.

However, Captain Jonsen was nothing if not a crafty man; and during the afternoon he gave orders for a spare spar to be towed behind as I have described. The result was that the schooner lost ground rapidly: and when night fell they were at least a couple of miles further from the brig than they had been at dawn. When night fell, of course, they hauled the spar on board and prepared for the last act. They followed the brig by

compass through the hours of darkness, without catching sight of her. When morning
came, all hands crowded expectantly at the
rail.

But the brig was vanished. The sea was
as bare as an egg.

If they were lost before, now they were
double-lost. Jonsen did not know where he
might be within two hundred miles; and being no sextant-man, but an incurable dead-
reckoner, he had no means of finding out.
This did not worry him very greatly, however, because sooner or later one of two things
might happen: he might catch sight of some
bit of land he recognised, or he might capture some vessel better informed than himself. Meanwhile, since he had no particular
destination, one bit of sea was much the same
to him as another.

The piece he was wandering in, however,
was evidently out of the main track of shipping; for days went by, and weeks, without

his coming even so near to effecting a capture as he had been in the case of the brig.

But Captain Jonsen was not sorry to be
out of the public eye for a while. Before
he had left Santa Lucia, news had reached
him of the *Clorinda* putting in to Havana;
and of the fantastic tale Marpole was telling.
The "twelve masked gun-ports" had amused
him hugely, since he was altogether without
artillery; but when he heard Marpole ac-
cused him of murdering the children—Marpole, that least reputable of skunks—his
anger had broken out in one of its sudden
explosions. For it was unthinkable—during
those first few days—that he would ever
touch a hair of their heads, or even speak
a cross word to them. They were still a sort
of holy novelty, then; it was not till their
shyness had worn off that he had begun to
regret so whole-heartedly the failure of his
attempt to leave them behind with the Chief
Magistrate's wife.

Chapter Six

THE weeks passed in aimless wandering. For the children, the lapse of time acquired once more the texture of a dream: things ceased happening: every inch of the schooner was now as familiar to them as the *Clorinda* had been, or Ferndale: they settled down quietly to grow, as they had done at Ferndale, and as they would have done, had there been time, on the *Clorinda*.

And then an event did occur, to Emily, of considerable importance. She suddenly realised who she was.

There is little reason that one can see why it should not have happened to her five years earlier, or even five later; and none, why it should have come that particular afternoon.

She had been playing houses in a nook right in the bows, behind the windlass (on which she had hung a devil's-claw as a door-knocker); and tiring of it was walking rather aimlessly aft, thinking vaguely about some bees and a fairy queen, when it suddenly flashed into her mind that she was *she.*

She stopped dead, and began looking over all of her person which came within the range of her eyes. She could not see much, except a fore-shortened view of the front of her frock, and her hands when she lifted them for inspection; but it was enough for her to form a rough idea of the little body she suddenly realised to be hers.

She began to laugh, rather mockingly. "Well!" she thought, in effect: "Fancy *you,* of all people, going and getting caught like this!—You can't get out of it now, not for a very long time: you'll have to go through with being a child, and growing up, and getting old, before you'll be quit of this mad prank!"

Determined to avoid any interruption of this highly important occasion, she began to climb the ratlines, on her way to her favourite perch at the masthead. Each time she moved an arm or a leg in this simple action, however, it struck her with fresh amazement to find them obeying her so readily. Memory told her, of course, that they had always done so before: but before, she had never realised how surprising this was.

Once settled on her perch, she began examining the skin of her hands with the utmost care: for it was *hers*. She slipped a shoulder out of the top of her frock; and having peeped in to make sure she really was continuous under her clothes, she shrugged it up to touch her cheek. The contact of her face and the warm bare hollow of her shoulder gave her a comfortable thrill, as if it was the caress of some kind friend. But whether the feeling came to her through her cheek or her shoulder, which was the caresser and which the caressed, that no analysis could tell her.

Once fully convinced of this astonishing fact, that she was now Emily Bas-Thornton (why she inserted the "now" she did not know, for she certainly imagined no trans-migrational nonsense of having been anyone else before), she began seriously to reckon its implications.

First, what agency had so ordered it that out of all the people in the world who she might have been, she was this particular one, this Emily; born in such-and-such a year out of all the years in Time, and encased in this particular rather pleasing little casket of flesh? Had she chosen herself, or had God done it?

At this, another consideration: who was God? She had heard a terrible lot about Him, always: but the question of His identity had been left vague, as much taken for granted as her own. Wasn't she perhaps God, herself? Was it that she was trying to remember? However, the more she tried, the more it eluded her. (How absurd, to disremember such an important point as whether one was God or not!) So she let it slide: perhaps it would come back to her later.

Secondly, why had all this not occurred to her before? She had been alive for over ten years, now, and it had never once entered her head. She felt like a man who suddenly remembers at eleven o'clock at night, sitting in his own arm-chair, that he had accepted an invitation to go out to dinner that night. There is no reason for him to remember it now: but there seems equally little why he should not have remembered it in time to keep his engagement. How could he have sat there all the evening, without being disturbed by the slightest misgiving? How could Emily have gone on being Emily for ten years, without once noticing this apparently obvious fact?

It must not be supposed that she argued it all out in this ordered, but rather long-winded fashion. Each consideration came to her in a momentary flash, quite innocent of words; and in between her mind lazed along, either thinking of nothing or returning to her bees and the fairy queen. If one added up the total of her periods of conscious thought, it would probably reach something between four and five seconds; nearer five, perhaps; but it was spread out over the best part of an hour.

Well then, granted she was Emily, what were the consequences, besides enclosure in that particular little body (which now began on its own account to be aware of a sort of unlocated itch, most probably somewhere on the right thigh), and lodgement behind a particular pair of eyes?

It implied a whole series of circumstances. In the first place, there was her family, a number of brothers and sisters from whom, before, she had never entirely dissociated herself; but now she got such a sudden feeling of being a discrete person that they seemed as separate from her as the ship itself. However, willy-nilly she was almost as tied to them as she was to her body. And then there was this voyage, this ship, this mast round which she had wound her legs. She began to examine it with almost as vivid an illumination as she had studied the skin of her hands. And when she came down from the mast, what would she find at the bottom? There would be Jonsen, and Otto, and the crew: the whole fabric of a daily life which up to now she had accepted as it came, but which now seemed vaguely disquieting. What was going to happen? Were there disasters running about loose, disasters which

>>>>>>>>>>>>>>>>>>>><<<<<<<<<<<<<<<<<<<

her rash marriage to the body of Emily Thornton made her vulnerable to?

A sudden terror struck her: did anyone know? (Know, I mean, that she was someone in particular, Emily—perhaps even God —not just any little girl.) She could not tell why, but the idea terrified her. It would be bad enough if they should discover she was a particular person—but if they should discover she was God! At all costs she must hide *that* from them.—But suppose they knew already, had simply been hiding it from her (as guardians might from an infant king)? In that case, as in the other, the only thing to do was to continue to behave as if she did not know, and so outwit them.

But if she was God, why not turn all the sailors into white mice, or strike Margaret blind, or cure somebody, or do some other Godlike act of the kind? Why should she hide it? She never really asked herself why: but instinct prompted her strongly of the necessity. Of course, there was the element of doubt (suppose she had made a mistake, and the miracle missed fire): but more largely it was the feeling that she would be able to deal with the situation so much better when she was a little older. Once she had declared herself there would be no turning back; it was much better to keep her godhead up her sleeve, for the present.

Grown-ups embark on a life of deception with considerable misgiving, and generally fail. But not so children. A child can hide the most appalling secret without the least effort, and is practically secure against detection. Parents, finding that they see through their child in so many places the child does not know of, seldom realise that, if there is some point the child really gives his mind to hiding, their chances are nil.

So Emily had no misgivings when she determined to preserve her secret, and needed have none.

》》》》》》》》》》》》》》》》》》》》》》《《《《《《《《《《《《《《《《《《《《《

Down below on the deck the smaller children were repeatedly crowding themselves into a huge coil of rope, feigning sleep and then suddenly leaping out with yelps of panic and dancing round it in consternation and dismay. Emily watched them with that impersonal attention one gives to a kaleidoscope. Presently Harry spied her, and gave a hail.

"Emilee-ee! Come down and play House-on-fire!"

At that, her normal interests momentarily revived. Her stomach as it were leaped within her sympathetically toward the game. But it died in her as suddenly: and not only died, but she did not even feel disposed to waste her noble voice on them. She continued to stare without making any reply whatever.

"Come on!" shouted Edward.

"Come and play!" shouted Laura. **"Don't be a pig!"**

Then in the ensuing stillness Rachel's voice floated up:

"Don't call her, Laura, we don't really want her."

ii

But Emily was completely unaffected—only glad that for the present they were all right by themselves. She was already beginning to feel the charge of the party a burden.

It had automatically devolved on her with the defection of Margaret.

It was puzzling, this Margaret business. She could not understand it, and it disturbed her. It dated back really to that night, about a week ago, when she herself had so unaccountably bitten the captain. The memory of her own extraordinary behaviour gave her now quite a little shiver of alarm.

Everybody had been very drunk that night,

>>>>>>>>>>>>>>>>>>>>>><<<<<<<<<<<<<<<<<<<<

and making a terrible racket—it was impossible to get to sleep. So at last Edward had asked her to tell them a story. But she was not feeling "storyable," so they had asked Margaret; all except Rachel, who had begged Margaret not to, because she wanted to think, she said. But Margaret had been very pleased at being asked, and had begun a very stupid story about a princess who had lots and lots of clothes and was always beating her servant for making mistakes and shutting him up in a dark cupboard. The whole story, really, had been nothing but clothes and beating, and Rachel had *begged* her to stop.

In the middle, a sort of rabble of sailors had come down the ladder, very slowly and with much discussion. They stood at the bottom in a knot, swaying a little and all turned inwards on one of their number. It was so dark one could not see who it was. They were urging him to do something—he hanging back.

"Oh, damn it!" he cried in a thick voice: "Bring me a light, I can't see where dey are!"

It was the voice of the captain—but how altered! There was a sort of suppressed excitement in it. Someone lit a lantern and held it up in the middle. Captain Jonsen stood on his legs half like a big sack of flour, half like a waiting tiger.

"What do you want?" Emily had asked kindly.

But Captain Jonsen stood irresolute, shifting his weight from foot to foot as if he was steering.

"You're drunk, aren't you?" Rachel had piped, loudly and disapprovingly.

But it was Margaret who had behaved most queerly. She had gone yellow as cheese, and her eyes large with terror. She was shivering from head to foot as if she had the fever. It was absurd. Then Emily remembered how

>>>>>>>>>>>>>>>>>>>>>>><<<<<<<<<<<<<<<<<<<
stupidly frightened Margaret had been the
very first night on the schooner.

At that moment Jonsen had staggered up
to Emily, and putting one hand under her
chin had begun to stroke her hair with the
other. A sort of blind vertigo seized her:
she caught his thumb and bit it as hard as she
could: then, terrified at her own madness,
dashed across the hold to where the other
children were gathered in a wondering knot.

"What *have* you done!" cried Laura, pushing her away angrily: "Oh you wicked girl,
you've hurt him!"

Jonsen was stamping about, swearing and
sucking his thumb. Edward had produced a
handkerchief, and between them all they had
managed to tie it up. He stood staring at the
bandaged member for a few moments; shook
his head like a wet retriever and retreated on
deck, dang-danging under his breath. Margaret had then been so ill they thought she

must really have caught fever, and they couldn't get any sense out of her at all.

As Emily, with her new-found consciousness, recapitulated the scene, it was like re-reading a story in a book, so little responsibility did she feel for the merely mechanical creature who had bitten the captain's thumb. Nor was she even very interested: it had been queer, but then there was very little in life which didn't seem queer, now.

As for Jonsen, he and Emily had avoided each other ever since, by mutual consent. She indeed had been in Coventry with everybody for biting him; none of the other children would play with her all the next day, and she recognised that she thoroughly deserved it— it was a *mad* thing to have done. And yet Jonsen, in avoiding her, had himself more the air of being ashamed than angry . . . it was unaccountable.

But what interested her even more was the

curious way Margaret had gone on, the next few days.

For some time she had behaved very oddly indeed. At first she seemed exaggeratedly frightened of all the men: but then she had suddenly taken to following them about the deck like a dog—not Jonsen, it is true, but Otto especially. Then suddenly she had departed from them altogether, and taken up her quarters in the cabin.

The curious thing was that now she avoided them all utterly, and spent all her time with the sailors: and the sailors, for their part, seemed to take peculiar pains not only not to let her speak to, but even not to let her be seen by the other children.

Now, they hardly saw her at all: and when they did she seemed so different they hardly recognised her: though where the difference lay it would be hard to say.

Emily, from her perch at the masthead, could just see the girl's head now, through the cabin skylight. Further forward, José had joined the children at their game, and was crawling about on hands and knees with all of them on his back—a fire-engine, of course, such as they had seen in the illustrated magazines from England.

"Emily!" called Harry: "Come and play!"

Down with a rush fell the curtain on all Emily's cogitations. In a second she was once more a happy little animal—*any* happy little animal. She slid down the shrouds like a real sailor, and in no time was directing the fire-fighting operations as imperiously as any other of this brigade of superintendents.

iii

That night in the Parliament of Beds there was raised at last a question which you may well be surprised had not been raised before. Emily had just reduced her family to silence

>>>>>>>>>>>>>>>>>>>>>>><<<<<<<<<<<<<<<<<<<<<

by sheer ferocity, when Harry's rapid, nervous, lisping voice piped up:

"Emily, Emily may I ask you a question
please?"

"Go to sleep!"

There was a moment's whispered confabu-
lation.

"But it's very important, please, and we
all want to know."

"What?"

"Are these people pirates?"

Emily sat bolt upright with astonishment.

"Of course not!"

Harry sounded rather crestfallen.

"I don't know. . . . I just thought they
might. . . ."

"But they *are!*" declared Rachel firmly:
"Margaret told me!"

"Nonsense!" said Emily: "There aren't any
pirates nowadays."

"Margaret said," went on Rachel, "that
time we were shut up on the other ship she

heard one of the sailors calling out pirates
had come on board."

Emily had an inspiration.

"No, you silly, he must have said *pilots*."

"What are pilots?" asked Laura.

"They come on board," explained Emily,
lamely. "Don't you remember that picture
in the dining-room at home, called 'The Pilot
Comes On Board'?"

Laura listened with rapt attention. The explanation of what pilots were was not very
illuminating; but then she did not know what
pirates were either. So you might think the
whole discussion meant very little to her, but
there you would be wrong: the question was
evidently important to the older ones, therefore she gave her whole mind to listening.

The pirate heresy was considerably shaken.
How could they say for certain which word
Margaret had really heard? Rachel changed
sides.

"They can't be pirates," she said: "Pirates are wicked."

"Couldn't we ask them?" Edward persisted.

Emily considered.

"I don't think it would be very polite."

"I'm sure they wouldn't mind," said Edward: "They're awfully decent."

"I think they mightn't like it," said Emily. In her heart she was afraid of the answer; and if they were pirates, it would here again be better to pretend not to know.

"I know!" she said: "Shall I ask the Mouse with the Elastic Tail?"

"Yes, do!" cried Laura. It was months since the oracle had been consulted; but her faith was still perfect.

Emily communed with herself in a series of short squeaks.

"He says they are *Pilots*," she announced.

"Oh," said Edward deeply: and they all went to sleep.

Chapter Seven

EDWARD often thought, as he strode scowling up and down the deck by himself, that this was exactly the life for him. What a lucky boy he was, to have tumbled into it by good fortune, instead of having to run away to sea as most other people did! In spite of the White Mouse's pronouncement (whom secretly he had long ceased to believe in), he had no doubt that this was a pirate vessel; and no doubt either that when presently Jonsen was killed in some furious battle the sailors would unanimously elect him their captain.

The girls were a great nuisance. A ship was no place for them. When he was captain he would have them marooned.

Yet there had been a time when he had wished he was a girl himself. "When I was young," he once confided to the admiring Harry, "I used to think girls were bigger and stronger than boys. Weren't I silly?"

"Yes," said Harry.

Harry did not confide it to Edward, but he also, *now,* wished he was a girl. It was not for the same reason: younger than Edward, he was still at the amorous age; and because he found the company of girls almost magically pleasing, fondly imagined it would be even more so if he were one himself. He was always finding himself, for being a boy, shut out from their most secret councils. Emily of course was too old to count as female in his eyes: but to Rachel and Laura he was indiscriminately devoted. When Edward was captain, he would be mate: and when he imagined this future, it consisted for the most part in rescuing Rachel—or Laura, *n'importe* — from new and complicated dangers.

They were all by now just as much at home on the schooner as they had been in Jamaica. Indeed, nothing very continuous was left of Ferndale for the youngest ones: only a number of luminous pictures of quite unimportant incidents. Emily of course remembered most things, and could put them together. The death of Tabby, for instance: she would never forget that as long as she lived. She could recollect, too, that Ferndale had tumbled down flat. And her Earthquake: she had been in an earthquake, and could remember every detail of *that*. Had it been as a result of the earthquake that Ferndale had tumbled down? That sounded likely. There had been quite a high wind at that time, too. . . . She could remember that they had all been bathing when the earthquake had come, and then had ridden somewhere on ponies. But they had been *in* the house when it fell down: she was pretty sure of that. It was all a little difficult to join up.—Then, when was it she had found that negro village? She could remember with a startling clearness bending down, and feeling among the bamboo roots for the bubbling spring, then looking round and seeing the black children scampering away up the clearing. That must have been years and years ago. But clearer than everything was that awful night when Tabby had stalked up and down the room, his eyes blazing and his fur twitching, his voice melodious with tragedy, until those horrible black shapes had flown in through the fanlight and savaged him out into the bush. The horror of the scene was even increased because it had once or twice come back to her in dreams, and because when she dreamt it (though it seemed the same) there was always some frightful difference. One night (and that was the worst of all) she had rushed out to rescue him, when her darling faithful Tabby had come up to her with the same horrible look on his face the Captain had worn that time she bit his thumb, and had chased her down avenues and avenues and avenues and avenues and avenues of cabbage-palms, with Exeter House at the end of them never getting any nearer however much she ran. She knew, of course, it was not the real Tabby, but a sort of diabolic double: and Margaret had sat up an orange tree jeering at her, gone as black as a negro.

One of the drawbacks of life at sea was the cockroaches. They were winged. They infested the hold, and the smell they made was horrible. One had to put up with them. But one didn't do much washing at sea: and it was a common thing to wake up in the morning and find the brutes had gnawed the quick from under one's nails, or gnawed all the hard skin off the soles of one's feet, so that one could hardly walk. Anything in the least greasy or dirty they set on at once. Buttonholes were their especial delight. One did little washing: fresh water was too valuable, and salt water had practically no effect. From handling tarry ropes and greasy ironwork their hands would have disgraced a slum-child. There is a sailor saying which includes a peck of dirt in the mariner's monthly rations: but the children on the schooner must have often consumed far more.

Not that it was a dirty ship—the fo'c'sle probably was, but the Nordicism of captain and mate kept the rest looking clean enough. But even the cleanest-looking ship is seldom clean to the touch. Their clothes José washed occasionally with his own shirt: and in that climate they were dry again by the morning.

Jamaica had faded into the past. England, to which they had supposed they were going, and of which a very curious picture had formerly been built up in their minds by their parents' constant reference to it, receded again into the mists of myth. They lived in the present, adapted themselves to it, and might have been born in a hammock and christened at a binnacle before they had been there many weeks. They seemed to have no natural fear of heights, and the farther they were above the deck, the happier. On a calm day Edward used to hang by his knees from the crosstrees in order to feel the blood run into his head. The flying-jib, too, which was usually down, made an admirable cocoon for hide-and-seek: one took a firm grip of the hanks and robands, and swathed oneself in the canvas. Once, suspecting Edward was hidden there, instead of going out on the jib-boom to look, the other children cast off the down-haul and then all together gave a great tug at the halyard which nearly pitched him into the sea. The shark myth is greatly exaggerated: it is untrue, for instance, that they can take a leg clean off at the hip—their bite is a tearing one, not a clean cut: and a practised bather can keep them off easily with a

✦✦✦✦✦✦✦✦✦✦✦✦✦✦✦✦✦✦✦✦✦✦✦✦✦✦✦✦✦✦✦✦✦✦✦✦

welt on the nose each time they turn over to strike: [1] but all the same, once overboard there would have been little hope for a small boy like Edward: and a severe wigging they all got for their prank.

Often several of those thick, rubber-like protuberances would follow the vessel for hours—perhaps in the hope of just some such antic.

Sharks were not without their uses, however: it is well known that Catch a Shark Catch a Breeze, so when a breeze was needed the sailors baited a big hook and presently hauled one on board with the winch. The bigger he was, the better breeze was hoped for: and his tail was nailed to the jib-boom. One day they got a great whacking fellow on board, and having cut off his jaw someone heaved it into the ship's latrine (which no one was so lubberly as to use for its proper

[1] The tiger-shark of the South Seas is of course a **very** different cattle.

purpose), and thought no more about it. One wildish night, however, old José did go there, and sat full on that wicked cheval-de-frise. He yelled like a madman: and the crew were better pleased than they had been with any joke that year and even Emily thought if only it had been less improper how funny it would have been. It would certainly have puzzled an archæologist, faced with José's mummy, to guess how he came by those curious scars.

The ship's monkey also added a lot to the ship's merriment. One day some sucker-fish had fixed themselves firmly to the deck, and he undertook to dislodge them. After a few preliminary tugs, he braced three legs and his tail against the deck and lunged like a madman. But they would not budge. The crew were standing round in a ring, and he felt his honour was at stake: somehow, they *must* be removed. So, disgusting though they must have tasted to a vegetarian, he set to and ate them, right down to the sucker, and was loudly applauded.

Edward and Harry often talked over how they would distinguish themselves in the next engagement. Sometimes they would rehearse it: storm the galley with uncouth shouts, or spring into the main rigging and order every one to be thrown into the sea. Once, as they went into battle,

"I am armed with a sword and a pistol!" chanted Edward:

"And I am armed with a key and a half a whist-le!" chanted the more literal Harry.

They took care to hold these rehearsals when the real pirates were out of the way: it was not so much that they feared the criticism of the professional eye, as that it was not yet openly recognised what they were; and all the children shared Emily's instinct that it was better to pretend not to know— a sort of magical belief, at bottom.

Although Laura and Rachel were thrown

together a great deal, and were all one goddess to Harry, their inner lives differed in
almost every respect. It was a matter of prin-
ciple, as will have been noticed, for them
to disagree on every point; but it was a matter of nature too. Rachel had only two activ-
ities. One was domestic. She was never
happy unless surrounded by the full para-
phernalia of a household: she left houses and
families wherever she went. She collected
bits of oakum and the moultings of a worn-
out mop, wrapped them in rags and put them
to sleep in every nook and cranny. *Guai,*
who woke one of her twenty or thirty babies
—worse still, should he clear it away! She
could even summon up maternal feelings for
a marline-spike, and would sit up aloft rocking it in her arms and crooning. The sailors
avoided walking underneath: for such an infant, if dropped from a height, will find its
way through the thickest skull (an accident

which sometimes befalls unpopular cap-
tains).

Further, there was hardly an article of
ship's use, from the windlass to the bosun's
chair, but she had metamorphosed it into
some sort of furniture: a table or a bed or a
lamp or a tea-set: and marked it as her property: and what she had marked as her property no one might touch—if she could prevent it. To parody Hobbes, she claimed as
her own whatever she had mixed her imagination with; and the greater part of her time
was spent in angry or tearful assertions of
her property-rights.

Her other interest was moral. She had an
extraordinary, vivid, simple sense, that child,
of Right and Wrong—it almost amounted to
a precocious ethical genius. Every action,
her own or anyone else's, was immediately
judged good or bad, and uncompromisingly
praised or blamed. She was never in doubt.

To Emily, Conscience meant something

very different. She was still only half aware
of that secret criterion within her: but she
was terrified of it. She had not Rachel's clear
divination: she never knew when she might
offend this inner harpy, Conscience, unwittingly: and lived in terror of those brazen
claws, should she ever let it be hatched from
the egg. When, poor child, she felt its
latent strength stir in its pre-natal sleep, she
forced her mind to other things, and would
not even let herself recognise her fear of it.
But she knew, at the bottom of her heart she
knew, that one day some action of hers would
rouse it, something awful done quite unwittingly would send it raging round her soul
like a whirlwind. She might go weeks together in a happy unconsciousness, she might
have flashes of vision when she knew she was
God Himself: but at the same time she knew,
beyond all doubt, in her innermost being,
that she was damned: that there never had

been anyone as wicked as her since the world began.

Not so Rachel: to her, Conscience was by no means so depressing an affair. It was simply a comfortable mainspring of her life, smooth-working, as pleasant as a healthy appetite. For instance, it was now tacitly admitted that all these men were pirates. That is, they were wicked. It therefore devolved on her to convert them: and she entered on her plans for this without a shadow of either misgiving or reluctance. Her conscience gave her no pain because it never occurred to her as conceivable that she should do anything but follow its dictates, or fail to see them clearly. She would try and convert these people, first: probably they would reform, but if they did not—well, she would send for the police. Since either result was right, it mattered not at all which Circumstance should call for.

So much for Rachel. The inside of Laura

was different indeed: something vast, complicated and nebulous that can hardly be put into language. To take a metaphor from tadpoles, though legs were growing her gills had not yet dropped off. Being nearly four years old she was certainly a child: and children are human (if one allows the term "human" a wide sense): but she had not altogether ceased to be a baby: and babies of course are not human—they are animals, and have a very ancient and ramified culture, as cats have, and fishes, and even snakes: the same in kind as these, but much more complicated and vivid, since babies are, after all, one of the most developed species of the lower vertebrates.

In short, babies have minds which work in terms and categories of their own which cannot be translated into the terms and categories of the human mind.

It is true they look human—but not so human, to be quite fair, as many monkeys.

Subconsciously, too, everyone recognises they are animals—why else do people always laugh when a baby does some action resembling the human, as they would at a Praying Mantis? If the baby was only a less-developed man, there would be nothing funny in it, surely.

Possibly a case might be made out that children are not human either: but I should not accept it. Agreed that their minds are not just more ignorant and stupider than ours, but differ in kind of thinking (are *mad*, in fact) : but one can, by an effort of will and imagination, think like a child at least in a partial degree—and even if one's success is infinitesimal it invalidates the case: while one can no more think like a baby, in the smallest respect, than one can think like a bee.

How then can one begin to describe the inside of Laura, where the child-mind lived in the midst of the familiar relics of the baby-mind, like a Fascist in Rome?

When swimming under water, it is a very sobering thing suddenly to look a large octopus in the face. One never forgets it: one's respect, yet one's feeling of the hopelessness of any real intellectual sympathy. One is soon reduced to mere physical admiration, like any silly painter, of the cow-like tenderness of the eye, of the beautiful and infinitesimal mobility of that large and toothless mouth, which accepts as a matter of course that very water against which you, for your life's sake, must be holding your breath. There he reposes in a fold of rock, apparently weightless in the clear green medium but very large, his long arms, suppler than silk, coiled in repose, or stirring in recognition of your presence. Far above everything is bounded by the surface of the air, like a bright window of glass. Contact with a small baby can conjure at least an echo of that feeling in those who are not obscured by an uprush of maternity to the brain.

Of course it is not really so cut-and-dried as all this; but often the only way of attempting to express the truth is to build it up, like a card-house, of a pack of lies.

It was only in Laura's inner mind, however, that these elaborate vestiges of baby-hood remained: outwardly she appeared fully a child—a rather reserved, odd, and indeed rather captivating one. Her face was not pretty, with its heavy eyebrows and reduced chin: but she had a power of apt movement, the appropriate attitude for every occasion that was most striking. A child who can show her affection for you, for instance, in the very way she plants her feet on the ground, has a liberal gift of that bodily genius called charm. Actually, this particular one was a rare gesture with her: nine-tenths of her life being spent in her own head, she seldom had time to feel at all strongly either for or against people. The feelings she thus expressed were generally of a more impersonal kind, and would have fascinated an admirer of the ballet: and it was all the more remarkable that she had developed a dog-like devotion to the reserved and coarse-looking captain of the pirates.

No one really contends that children have any insight into character: their likings are mostly imaginative, not intuitive. "What do you think I am?" the exasperated ruffian had asked on a famous occasion. One might well ask what Laura thought he was: and there is no means of knowing.

ii

Pigs grow quickly, quicker even than children: and much though the latter altered in the first month on board, the little black porker (whose name by the bye was Thunder) altered even more. He soon grew to such a size one could not possibly allow him

>>>>>>>>>>>>>>>>>>>><<<<<<<<<<<<<<<<<

to lie on one's stomach any more: so, as his friendliness did not diminish, the functions were reversed, and it became a common thing to find one child, or a whole bench of them, sitting on his scaly side. They grew very fond of him indeed (especially Emily), and called him their Dear Love, their Only Dear, their Own True Heart, and other names. But he had only two things he ever said. When his back was being scratched he enunciated an occasional soft and happy grunt; and that same phrase (only in a different tone) had to serve for every other occasion and emotion— except one. When a particularly heavy lot of children sat down on him at once, he uttered the faintest ghost of a little moan, as affecting as the wind in a very distant chimney, as if the air in him was being squeezed out through a pin-hole.

One cannot wish for a more comfortable seat than an acquiescent pig.

＞＞＞＞＞＞＞＞＞＞＞＞＞＞＞＞＞＞＞＞＞＞＞＞＜＜＜＜＜＜＜＜＜＜＜＜＜＜＜＜＜＜＜＜＜

"If I was the Queen," said Emily, "I should most certainly have a pig for a throne."

"Perhaps she has," suggested Harry.

"He *does* like being scratched," she added presently in a very sentimental tone, as she rubbed his scurfy back.

The mate was watching:

"I should think *you'd* like being scratched, if your skin was in that condition!"

"Oh how dis*gust*ing you are!" cried Emily, delighted.

But the idea took root:

"I don't think I should kiss him quite so much if I was you," Emily presently advised Laura, who was lying with her arms tight round his neck and covering his briny snout with kisses from ring to ears.

"My pet! My love!" murmured Laura, by way of indirect protest.

The wily mate had foreseen that some estrangement would be necessary, if they were ever to have fresh pork served without

>>>>>>>>>>>>>>>>>>>>><<<<<<<<<<<<<<<<<<<<

salt tears. He intended this to be the thin
end of the wedge. But alas! Laura's mind
was as humoursome an instrument to play as
the Twenty-three-stringed Lute.

When dinnertime came, the children mustered for their soup and biscuit.

They were not overfed on the schooner:
they were given little that is generally considered wholesome, or to contain vitamines
(unless these lurked in the aforesaid peck of
dirt) : but they seemed none the worse. First
the cook boiled the various non-perishable
vegetables they carried together in a big pot,
for a couple of hours. Then a lump of salt
beef from the cask forward, having been
rinsed in a little fresh water, was added, and
allowed to simmer with the rest till it was
just cooked. Then it was withdrawn, and the
captain and mate ate their soup first and their
meat afterwards, out of plates, like gentlemen. After that, if it was a weekday, the
meat was put to cool on the cabin shelf,

ready to warm up in tomorrow's soup, and the crew and children ate the liquor with biscuit: but if it was Sunday, the captain took the lump of meat and with a benevolent air cut it up in small pieces, as if indeed for a nursery, and mixed it up with the vegetables in the huge wooden bowl out of which crew and children all dipped. It was a very patriarchal way of feeding.

Even at dinner Margaret did not join the others, but ate in the cabin: though there was only two plates on the whole ship. Probably she used the mate's when he had finished.

Laura and Rachel fought that day to tears over a particularly succulent piece of yam. Emily let them. To make those two agree was a task she was wise not to undertake. Besides, she was very busy over her own dinner. Edward managed to silence them however by declaring in a most terrible voice "Shut up or I'll SABRE you!"

Emily's estrangement from the captain had

reached by now a rather uncomfortable stage. When these things are fresh and new the two parties avoid meeting, and all is well: but after some days they are apt to forget, find themselves on the point of chatting and then suddenly remember that they are not on speaking-terms and have to retire in confusion. Nothing can be more uncomfortable for a child. The difficulty of effecting a reconciliation in this case was that both parties felt wholly in the wrong. Each repented the impulse of a momentary insanity, and neither had an inkling the other felt the same: thus each waited for the other to show signs of forgiveness. Moreover, while the captain had far the more serious reason for being ashamed of himself, Emily was naturally far the more sensitive and concerned of the two: so it about balanced. Thus, if Emily rushed blithely up to the captain embracing a flying-fish, caught his eye and slunk round the other side of the galley, he put it down to

a permanent feeling of condemnation and re-
pulsion: blushed a deep purple and stared
stonily at his wrinkling mainsail—and Emily
wondered if he was *never* going to forget
that bitten thumb.

But this afternoon things came to a head.
Laura was trotting about behind him, striking her attitudes. Edward had at last discovered which was windward and which was
leeward, and had come hot-foot to learn the
first of the Sovereign Rules of Life: and
Emily, with one of her wretched lapses of
memory, was all agog at his elbow.

Edward was duly catechised and passed.

"Dis is the first rule," said the captain:
*"Never throw anything to windward except
hot water or ashes."*

Edward's face developed exactly the look
of bewilderment that was intended.

"But *windward* is . . ." he began: "I
mean, wouldn't they blow. . . ." Then he
stopped, wondering if he had got the terms

the right way round after all. Jonsen was delighted at the success of this ancient joke. Emily, trying to stand on one leg, bewildered also, lost her balance and clutched at Jonsen's arm. He looked at her—they all looked at her.

Much the best way of escaping from an embarrassing rencontre, when to walk away would be an impossible strain on the nerves, is to retire in a series of somersaults. Emily immediately started turning head over heels up the deck.

It was very difficult to keep direction, and the giddiness was appalling: but she *must* keep it up till she was out of sight, or die.

Just then Rachel, who was up the main-mast, dropped, for the first time, her marline-spike. She uttered a terrible shriek—for what *she* saw was a baby falling to dash its brains out on the deck.

Jonsen gave an ineffectual little grunt of

alarm—men never can learn to give a full-bodied scream like a woman.

But Emily gave the most desperate yell of all, though several seconds after the other two: for the wicked steel stood quivering in the deck, having gouged a track through her calf on the way. Her wrought-up nerves, and sickening giddiness, joined with the shock and pain to give a heart-rending poignancy to her crying. Jonsen was by her in a second, caught her up, and carried her sobbing miserably down into the cabin. There sat Margaret, bending over some mending, her slim shoulders hunched up, humming softly and feeling deadly ill.

"Get out!" said Jonsen, in a low, brutal voice. Without a word or sign Margaret gathered up her sewing and climbed on deck.

Jonsen smeared some Stockholm tar on a rag, and bound up Emily's leg with more than a little skill, though the tar of course was agonising to her. She had cried herself right out by the time he laid her in his bunk. When she opened her streaming eyes and saw him bending over her, nothing in his clumsy face but concern and an almost overpowering pity, she was so full of joy at being at last forgiven that she reached up her arms and kissed him. He sat down on the locker, rocking himself backwards and forwards gently. Emily dosed for a few minutes: when she woke up he was still there.

"Tell me about when you were little," she said.

Jonsen sat on, silent, trying to project his unwieldy mind back into the past.

"When I was a boy," he said at last, "it wasn't thought lucky to grease your own sea-boots. My Auntie used to grease mine, before we went out with the lugger."

He paused for some time.

"We divided the fish up into six shares—one for the boat, and one for each of us."

That was all. But it was of the greatest

interest to Emily, and she shortly fell asleep again, supremely happy.

So for several days the captain and mate had to share the latter's bunk, Box-and-Cox; Heaven knows what hole Margaret was banished to. The gash in Emily's leg was one which would take some time to heal. To make things worse, the weather became very unsteady: when she was awake she was all right, but if she fell asleep she began to roll about the bunk, and then of course the pain waked her again; which soon reduced her to a feverish and nervous condition, although the leg itself was going on as well as could be expected. The other children of course used to come and see her: but they did not enjoy it much as there was nothing to do down in the cabin, once the novelty of admittance to the Holy Place had worn off. So their visits were perfunctory and short. They must have had a high old time at night, however, by themselves in the forehold, now that the cat was away. They looked like it, too, in the mornings.

Otto used sometimes to come and teach her to make fancy knots, and at the same time pour out his grievances against the captain: though these latter were always received with an uncomfortable silence. Otto was a Viennese by birth, but had stowed away in a Danube barge when he was ten years old, had taken to the sea, and thereafter generally served in English ships. The only place since his childhood where he had ever spent any considerable time on shore was Wales. For some years he had sailed coastwise from the once-promising harbour of Portdinlleyn, which is now practically dead: and so, as well as German, Spanish, and English, could talk Welsh fluently. It was not a long residence, but at an impressionable age; and when he talked to Emily of his past it was mostly of his life as a "boy" on the slate-boats. Captain Jonsen came of a Danish family set-

tled on the Baltic coast, at Lübeck. He too
had spent most of his time on English ships.
How or when he and Otto had first met, or
how they had drifted into the Cuban piracy
business, Emily never discovered. They had
plainly been inseparable for many years. She
preferred letting them ramble on, to asking
questions or trying to fit things together: she
had that sort of mind.

When the knots palled, José sent her a
beautiful crochet-hook he had carved out of
a beef bone: and by pulling threads out of a
piece of sail-cloth she was able to set to work
to crochet doyleys for the cabin table. But
I am afraid that she also drew a lot, till the
whole of the inside of the bunk was soon as
thoroughly scribbled-over as a palæolithic
cave. What the captain would say when he
found out was a consideration best post-
poned. The fun was to find knots, and un-
evennesses in the paint, that looked like something; and then with a pencil make them look

more like it—putting an eye in the walrus, or supplying the rabbit with his missing ear. That is what artists call having a proper feeling for one's material.

Instead of getting better the weather got worse: and the universe soon became a very unstable place indeed: it became almost impossible to crochet. She had to cling on to the side of the bunk all the time, to prevent her leg getting banged.

It was in this inconvenient weather, however, that the pirates chose at last to make another capture. It turned out not a rich one: a small Dutch steamer, taking a consignment of performing animals to one of Mr. Barnum's predecessors. The captain of the steamer, who was conceited in a way that only certain Dutchmen *can* be conceited, gave them a lot of trouble, in spite of the fact that he had practically nothing worth taking. He was a first-class sailor: but he was very fair, and had no neck. In the end they had to tie him up, bring him on board the schooner, and lay him on the cabin floor where Emily could keep an eye on him. He reeked of some particularly nauseous brand of cigars, that made her head swim.

The other children had played quite an important part in the capture. They did far better as a badge of innocuousness than even the "ladies." The steamer (little more than dressed-up sailing vessels they were then), thoroughly disgruntled at the weather, was wallowing about like a porpoise, her decks awash and her funnel over one ear, so to speak: so when a boat put out from the schooner, its departure cheered lustily by Edward, Harry, Rachel and Laura, though his pride might resent it the Dutchman never thought of suspecting this presumable offer of assistance, and let them come on board.

It was then he began to give trouble, and they had to remove him onto the schooner. Their tempers were none too good on finding

>>>>>>>>>>>>>>>>>>>>><<<<<<<<<<<<<<<<<<<<
their booty was a lion, a tiger, two bears and
a lot of monkeys: so it is quite likely they
were none too gentle with him in transit.

The next thing was to discover whether
the *Thelma,* like the *Clorinda,* carried another, a secret cargo of greater value. They
had imprisoned all the crew, now, aft: so one
by one they were brought up on deck and
questioned. But either there was no money
on board, or the crew did not know of it, or
would not tell. Most of them, indeed, appeared frightened enough to have sold their
grandmothers: but some of them simply
laughed at the pirates' bogey-bogey business,
guessing they drew the line at murder in cold
blood, sober.

What was done in each case was the same.
When each man was finished with he was
sent forward and shut in the fo'c'sle: and before bringing another up from aft one of the
pirates would unmercifully belabour a roll of
sail-cloth with a cat-o'-nine-tails while an-

other yelled like the damned. Then a shot was fired in the air, and something thrown overboard to make a splash. All this, of course, was to impress those still down in the cabin awaiting their turns: and the pretence was quite as effective as the reality could have been. But it did no good, since probably there was no treasure to disclose.

There was, however, a plentiful supply of Dutch spirits and liqueurs on board: and these they found a welcome change after so much West Indian rum.

After they had been drinking them for an hour or two Otto had a brilliant idea. Why not give the children a circus? They had begged and begged to be taken onto the steamer to see the animals. Well, why not stage something really magnificent for them —a fight between the lion and the tiger, for instance?

No sooner said than done. The children, and every man who could be spared, came

>>>>>>>>>>>>>>>>>>>>>>><<<<<<<<<<<<<<<<<<<<

onto the steamer, and took up positions at safe heights in the rigging. The cargo-gaff was rigged, the hatch opened, and the two iron cages, with their stale cat-like reek, were hauled up on deck. Then the little Malay keepers, who kept twittering to each other in their windy tones, were made to open them, that the two monarchs of the jungle might come out and do battle.

How they were to be got in again was a question that never occurred to anyone's consideration. Yet it is generally supposed to be easier to let tigers out of cages than to put them back.

In this case however, even when the cages were open, neither of the beasts seemed very anxious to get out. They lay on the floor growling (or groaning) slightly, but making no move except to roll their eyes.

It was very unfortunate for poor Emily that she was missing all this, laid by the leg

in Jonsen's stuffy cabin with the Dutch captain to guard.

When at first they had been left alone together he had tried to speak to her: but
unlike so many Dutchmen he did not know a
word of English. He could just move his
head, and he kept turning his eyes first on a
very sharp knife which some idiot had
dropped in a corner of the cabin floor, then
on Emily. He was asking her to get it for
him, of course.

But Emily was terrified of him. There is
something much more frightening about a
man who is tied up than a man who is not
tied up—I suppose it is the fear he may get
loose.

The feeling of not being able to get out of
the bunk and escape added the true nightmare panic.

Remember that he had no neck, and the
cigar-reek.

At last he must have caught the look of

fear and disgust in her face, where he had expected compassion. He began to act for himself. First gently rocking his bound body
from side to side, he set himself to roll.

Emily screamed for help, beating with her
fist on the bunk: but none came. Even the
sailors who were left on board were out of
ear-shot: they were straining all their attention to see what was happening on the
steamer, that wallowed and heaved seventy
yards away. There, one of the pirates, greatly
daring, had descended to the rail and begun
throwing belaying-pins at the cages, to rouse
their occupants. If the beasts so much as
lashed their tails in response, however, he
would scuttle up any rope like a frightened
mouse. Only the Malay keepers remained
permanently on deck, taking no notice: sitting on their heels in a ring and crooning dis-
cordantly through their noses. Probably they
felt inside much as the lion and tiger did.

After some minutes, however, the pirates

grew bolder. Otto came right up to one cage, and started poking the tiger's ribs with a handspike. But the poor beast was far too sea-sick to be roused even by that. Gradually the whole crowd of the spectators descended onto the deck and stood round, still not unprepared to bolt, while the drunken mate, and even Captain Jonsen (who was perfectly sober), goaded and jeered.

It was not surprising no one heard poor Emily, left alone in the cabin with the terrible Dutchman.

She screamed and screamed: but there was no awakening from *this* nightmare.

By now he had managed to roll himself, in spite of the motion of the vessel, almost within reach of the coveted knife. The veins on his forehead stood out with his exertion and the stricture of his bonds. His fingers were groping, behind his back, for the edge.

Emily, beside herself with terror, suddenly became possessed by the strength of despair.

In spite of the agony it caused her leg she flung herself out of the bunk, and just managed to seize the knife before he could manoeuvre his bound hands within reach of it.

In the course of the next five seconds she had slashed and jabbed at him in a dozen places: then, flinging the knife towards the door, somehow managed to struggle back into the bunk.

The Dutchman, bleeding rapidly, blinded with his own blood, lay still and groaned. Emily, her own wound re-opened and overcome with pain and terror, fainted. The knife, flung wildly, missed its aim and clattered down the steps again onto the cabin floor: and the first witness of the scene was Margaret, who presently peered down from the deck above, her dulled eyes standing out from her small, skull-like face.

As for Jonsen and Otto, unable by other means to rouse the dormant animals, they col-

>>>>>>>>>>>>>>>>>>>>>><<<<<<<<<<<<<<<<<<<<<

lected their men and with big levers managed to tilt the cages, spilling the beasts out onto the deck.

But not even so would they fight—or even show signs of resentment. As they had lain and groaned in their cages, so they now lay and groaned on the deck.

They were small specimens of their kind, and emaciated by travel. Otto with a sudden oath seized the tiger round its middle and hauled it upright on its hind legs: Jonsen did the same by the more top-heavy lion: and so the two principals to the duel faced each other, their heads lolling over the arms of their seconds.

But in the eyes of the tiger a slight ember of consciousness seemed to smoulder. Suddenly it tautened its muscles: a slight effort, yet it burst from the merely human grip of Otto like Samson from the new ropes—nearly dislocated his arms before he had time to let go. Quicker than eye could see it had cuffed him, rending half his face. Tigers are no playthings. Jonsen dropped the huge bulk of the lion on top of it, and escaped with Otto through an open door: while the pirates, tumbling over one another like people in a burning theatre, struggled to get back in the rigging.

The lion rolled clear. The tiger, lurching unsteadily, crept back into its cage. The keening Malays took no notice of the whole scene.

And yet, what a scene it had been!

But now the heroic circus was over. Chastened, bruising one another in their panic, the drunken pirates helped the mate into the first of the two boats, and pulling helter-skelter in the choppy sea, returned to the schooner. One by one they climbed the rail and vaulted on deck.

Sailors have keen noses. They smelt blood at once, and crowded round the companionway, where Margaret still sat, as if numb, on the top step.

Emily lay in the bunk below, her eyes shut —conscious again, but her eyes shut.

The Dutch captain they could see on the floor, stretched in a pool of blood. *"But, Gentlemen, I have a wife and children!"* he suddenly said in Dutch, in a surprised and gentle tone: then died, not so much of any mortal wound as the number of superficial gashes he had received.

It was plainly Margaret who had done it— killed a bound, defenceless man, for no reason at all: and now sat watching him die, with her dull, meaningless stare.

Chapter Eight

THE contempt they already felt for Margaret, their complete lack of pity in her obvious illness and misery, had been in direct proportion to the childhood she had belied.

This crime would have seemed to them grave on the part of a grown man, in its unrelieved wantonness: but done by one of her years, and nurture, it was unspeakable. She was lifted by the arms from the stair where she still sat, and without a moment's hesitation (other than that resulting from too many helping hands) was dropped into the sea.

But yet the expression of her face, as—like the big white pig in the squall—she vanished to windward, left a picture in Otto's mind he never forgot. She was, after all, his affair.

The Dutchman's body was fetched up on deck. Captain Jonsen went below: and once bent over poor little Emily. She screwed up her eyes tighter when she felt his hot breath on her face. She did not open them till everybody had quite gone—and shut them again when presently José came to swab the cabin floor.

The second boat, bringing back the rest of the crew and the four children, almost ran into Margaret before they saw her. She was swimming desperately, but in complete silence: her hair now plastered across her eyes and mouth, now floating out on the water as her head went under. They lifted her into the boat and set her in the stern-sheets with the other children. So it was they found themselves together again.

In her sopping condition, the others naturally gave her elbow-room: but still, she was *among* them. They sat and stared at her, their eyes very wide and serious, but without speaking. Margaret, her teeth chattering with exhaustion, tried ineffectually to wring out the hem of her frock. She did not speak either: but nevertheless it was not long before both she and the other children felt a sort of thaw setting in between them.

As to the oarsmen, they never troubled their heads as to how she came in the water. They supposed she had accidentally slipped over the side: but were not particularly interested, especially as they had their work cut out manoeuvring round to the schooner's lee and clambering on board. There was a tremendous pow-wow going on aft, so that no one noticed them arrive.

Once on board, Margaret went straight forward as of old, climbed down the ladder into the fore-hold, and undressed, the other children watching her every movement with an unfeigned interest. Then she rolled herself in a blanket, and lay down.

They none of them noticed quite how it happened: but in less than half an hour they were all five absorbed in a game of Consequences. Presently one of the crew came, peered down the hatch and then shouted "Yes!" to the rest, and then went away again. But they neither saw nor heard him.

From now on, however, the atmosphere of the schooner suffered a change. A murder is inclined to have this effect, on a small community. As a matter of fact, the Dutch captain's was the first blood to be shed on board, in the course of business at any rate (I will not answer for private quarrels). The way it had been shed left the pirates profoundly shocked, their eyes opened to a depravity of human nature they had not dreamt of: but also it gave them an uncomfortable feeling round the neck. So long as there was only the circus-prank to avenge, no American man-of-war was likely to be despatched in their pursuit: high Naval Authorities shrink naturally from any contact with the ridiculous: but suppose the steamer put into port, and announced the forcible abduction of her captain? Or worse, suppose her mate, with an accursed spy-glass, had seen that captain's bloody body take its last dive? Pursuit would be only too likely.

The plea "It was none of us men did this wicked deed, but one of our young female prisoners," was hardly one which could be submitted to a jury.

Captain Jonsen had discovered from the steamer's log where he was: so he put the schooner about, and set a course for his refuge at Santa Lucia. It was unlikely, he thought, now, that any British man-of-war would still be cruising about the scene of the *Clorinda* episode—they had too much to do: and he had reasons (fairly expensive ones) for not anticipating any molestation from the Spanish authorities. He did not like going home with an empty ship, of course: but that appeared inevitable.

The outward sign of this change in the atmosphere of the schooner was a spontaneous increase in the strictness of discipline. Not a drop of rum was drunk. Watch was kept with the regularity of a line-of-battle ship. The schooner became tidier, more seamanlike in every way.

Thunder was slain and eaten, the next day, without any regard for the feelings of his lovers: indeed, all tenderness towards the children vanished. Even José ceased playing with them. They were treated with a detached severity not wholly divorced from fear —as if these unfortunate men at last realised what diabolic yeast had been introduced into their lump.

So sensible were the children themselves of the change that they even forgot to mourn for Thunder—excepting Laura, whose face burned an angry red for half a day.

>>>>>>>>>>>>>>>>>>>>><<<<<<<<<<<<<<<<<<<·

But the ship's monkey, on the other hand, with no pig now to tease, nearly died of ennui.

ii

The reopening of the wound in her leg made it several days more before Emily was fit to be moved from the cabin. During this time she was much alone. Jonsen and Otto seldom came below, and when they did were too preoccupied to heed her blandishing. She sang, and conversed to herself, almost incessantly; only interrupting herself to beseech these two, with a superfluity of endearments, to pick up her crochet hook, to look at the animal she had built out of her blanket, to tell her a story, to tell her what naughty things they did when they were little—how unlike Emily it was, all this gross bidding for attention! But as a rule they went away again, or went to sleep, without taking the least notice of her.

As well, she told herself, to herself, endless stories: as many as there are in the Arabian Nights, and quite as involved. But the strings of words she used to utter aloud had nothing to do with this: I mean, that when she made a sort of narrative noise (which was often), she did it for the noise's sake: the silent, private formation of sentences and scenes, in one's head, is far preferable for real story-telling. If you had been watching her then, unseen, you could only have told she was doing it by the dramatic expressions of her face, and her restless flexing and tossing— and if she had had the slightest inkling you were there, the audible rigmarole would have started again. (No one, who has private thoughts going on in his own head, is quite sure of their not being overheard unless he is providing something else to occupy foreign ears.)

When she sang, however, it was always wordless: an endless succession of notes, like a bird's, fixed to the first vocable handy, and practically without tune. Not being musical, there was never any reason for her to stop: so one song would often go on for half an hour.

Although José had scrubbed the cabin floor as well as he could, a large stain still remained.

At times she let her mind wander about, quite peacefully, in her memories of Jamaica: a period which now seemed to her very remote, a golden age. How young she must have been! When her imagination grew tired, too, she could recall the Anansi stories Old Sam had told her: and they often proved the point of departure for new ones of her own.

Also she could remember the creepy things he had told her about duppies. How they used to tease the negroes about the supposed duppy at the bathing hole, the duppy of the

drowned man! It gave one an enormous
sense of power, that—not to believe in duppies.

But she found herself taking much less
pleasure in duppies now than she used.

She even once caught herself wondering
what the Dutchman's duppy would look like,
all bloody, with its head turned backwards
on its shoulders and clanking a chain . . . it
was a momentary flash, the way the banished
image of Tabby had come back to her. For
a moment her head reeled: in another she was
far from Jamaica, far from the schooner, far
from duppies, on a golden throne in the re-
motest East.

The other children were no longer allowed
in the cabin to visit her: but when she heard
their feet scampering overhead, she often
conversed with them in loud yells. One of
these yells from above told her:

"Marghie's back, you know."

"O-oh."

＞＞＞＞＞＞＞＞＞＞＞＞＞＞＞＞＞＞＞＞＞＜＜＜＜＜＜＜＜＜＜＜＜＜＜＜＜＜＜

After that Emily was silent for a bit, her beautiful, innocent grey eyes fixed on the ear of a dwarf at the end of her bunk. Only the slight pucker at the top of her nose showed with what intensity she was thinking: and the minute drops of sweat on her temples.

But it was not only when there was some outward occasion, like this, that she suffered acute distress.

Froth as she might, those times of consciousness, which had begun with a moment of such sublime vision, were both growing on her and losing their lustre. They were become sinister. Life threatened to be no longer an incessant, automatic discharge of energy: more and more often, and when least expected, all that would suddenly drop from her, and she would remember that she was *Emily*, who had killed . . . and who was *here* . . . and that Heaven alone knew what was going to happen to the incompetent little thing, by what miracle she was going to keep

>>>>>>>>>>>>>>>>>>>>><<<<<<<<<<<<<<<<<<

her end up. . . . Whenever this happened, her stomach seemed to drop away within her a hundred and fifty feet.

She, like Laura, had one foot each side of a threshold now. As a piece of Nature, she was practically invulnerable. But as *Emily,* she was absolutely naked, tender. It was particularly cruel that this transition should come when so fierce a blast was blowing.

For mark this: anyone in bed, with a blanket up to her chin, is in a measure safe. She might go through abysms of terror; but once these passed, no practical harm had been done. But once she was up and about? Suppose it was at some crisis, some call to action that her Time came on her? What appalling blunder could she fail to make?

Oh why must she grow up? Why, for pity's sake?

Quite apart from these attacks of blind, secret panic, she had other times of an ordinary, very rational anxiety. She was ten and

>>>>>>>>>>>>>>>>>>>>><<<<<<<<<<<<<<<<<<<<<<
a half now. What sort of future lay before
her, what career? (Their mother had im-
planted in them young, as a matter of prin-
ciple, girls and boys alike, the idea that they
would one day have to earn their own liv-
ings.) I say she was ten and a half: but it
seemed such ages since she had come on the
schooner that she thought she was probably
older even than that.—Now this life was full
of interest: but was it, she asked herself, a
really useful education? What did it fit her
for? Plainly, it taught her nothing but to be
a sort of pirate too (what sort of a pirate,
being a girl, was a problem in itself). But
as time slipped by, it became clearer and
clearer that every other life would be impossible for her—indeed, for all of them.

Gone, alas, was any shred of confidence
that she was God. That particular, supreme
career was closed to her. But the conviction
that she was the wickedest person who had
ever been born, this would not die for much

longer. Some appalling Power had determined it: it was no good struggling against it. Had she not already committed the most awful of crimes . . . the most awful of crimes, though, that was not murder, that was the mysterious crime against the Holy Ghost, which dwarfed even murder . . . had she, unwittingly, at some time done this too? She so easily might have, since she did not know what it was. And if that were so, no wonder the pity of Heaven was sealed against her!

So the poor little outcast lay, shivering and sweating under her blanket, her gentle eyes fixed on the ear of the dwarf she had drawn.

But presently she was singing again happily, and hanging right out of the bunk to outline in pencil the brown stain on the floor. A touch here, a touch there, and it was an old market-woman to the life, hobbling along with a bundle on her back! I admit that it staggered even Otto, a bit, when he came in later and saw what she had done.

But when again she lay still on her back, and contemplated the practical difficulties of the life ahead of her (even leaving God and her Soul and all that on one side) she had not the support of Edward's happy optimism: she was old enough to know how helpless she really was. How should she, dependent now for her very life on the kindness of those around her, how could she ever acquire the wit and strength to struggle against them and their kind?

She had developed by this time a rather curious feeling about Jonsen and Otto. In the first place, she had become very fond of them. Children it is true have a way of becoming more or less attached to anyone they are in close contact with: but it was more than that, deeper. She was far fonder of them than she had ever been of her parents, for instance. They, for their part, showed every mild sign consonant with their natures of being fond of her: but how could she *know?*

It would be so easy for adult things like them to dissemble to her, she felt. Suppose they really intended to kill her: they could so easily hide it: they would behave with exactly this same kindness. . . . I suppose it was the reflection of her own instinct for secretiveness?

When she heard the Captain's step on the stairs, it might be that he was bringing her a plate of soup, or it might be that he had come to kill her—suddenly, with no warning change of expression on his amiable face even at the very end.

If that was his intention, there was nothing whatever she could do to hinder him. To scream, struggle, attempt flight—they would be absolutely useless, and—well, a breach of decorum. If he chose to keep up appearances, it behoved her to do so too. If he showed no sign of his intention, she must show no sign of her inkling of it.

That was why, when either of them came

below, she would sing on, smile at him imp-ishly and confidently, actually plague him for notice.

She was a little fonder of Jonsen than of Otto. Ordinarily, any coarseness or mal-formity of adult flesh is in the highest degree repulsive to a child: but the cracks and scars on Jonsen's enormous hands were as inter-esting to her as the valleys on the moon to a boy with a telescope. As he clumsily handled his parallel rulers and dividers, fitting them with infinite care to the marks on his chart, Emily would lie on her side and explore them, give them all names.

Why must she grow up? *Why* couldn't she leave her life always in other people's keeping, to order as if it was no concern of hers?

Most children have something of this feel-ing. With most children it is outweighed: still, they will generally hesitate before tell-ing you they prefer to grow up. But then, most children live secure lives, and have an at least apparently secure future to grow up to. To have already murdered a full-size man, and to have to keep it for ever secret, is not a normal background for the child of ten: to have a Margaret one could not altogether banish from one's thoughts: to see every ordinary avenue of life locked against one, only a violent road, leading to Hell, open.

She was still on the border-line: so often Child still, and nothing but Child . . . it needed little conjuring . . . Anansi and the Blackbird, Genies and golden thrones. . . .

Which is all a rather groping attempt to explain a curious fact: that Emily appeared— indeed *was* rather young for her age: and that this was due to, not in spite of, the adventures she had been through.

But this youngness, it burnt with an intenser flame. She had never yelled so loud at Ferndale, for sheer pleasure in her own

>>>>>>>>>>>>>>>>>>>>><<<<<<<<<<<<<<<<<<<

voice, as now she yelled in the schooner's
cabin, carolling like a larger, fiercer lark.

Neither Jonsen nor Otto were nervous
men; but the din she made sometimes drove
them almost distracted. It was very little use
telling her to shut up: she only remembered
for such a short time. In a minute she was
whispering, in two she was talking, in five
her voice was in full blast.

Jonsen was himself a man who seldom
spoke to anyone. His companionship with
Otto, though devoted, was a singularly silent
one. But when he did speak, he hated not
to be able to make himself heard at all: even
when, as was usual, it was himself he was
talking to.

iii

Otto was at the wheel (there was hardly
one of the crew fit to steer). His lively mind

was occupied with Santa Lucia, and his young lady there. Jonsen slipper-sloppered up and down his side of the deck.

Presently, his interest in his subject waning, Otto's eye was caught by the ship's monkey, which was sporting on its back on the cabin skylight.

That animal, with the same ingenious adaptability to circumstance which has produced the human race, had now solved the playmate question. As a gambler will play left hand against right, so he fought back legs against front. His extraordinary lissomeness made the dissociation most lifelike: he might not have been joined at the waist at all, for all the junction discommoded him. The battle, if good-tempered on both sides, was quite a serious one: now, while his hind feet were doing their best to pick out his eyes, his sharp little teeth closed viciously on his own private parts.

From below the skylight, too, came tears

>>>>>>>>>>>>>>>>>>>>><<<<<<<<<<<<<<<<<<<<

and cries for help that one might easily have taken for real, if they had not been occasionally interrupted by such phrases as "It's no good! I shall cut off your head just the same!"

Captain Jonsen was thinking about a little house in far-off, shadowy Lübeck—with a china stove . . . it didn't do to talk about retiring: above all, one must never say aloud 'this is my last voyage," even addressing oneself. The sea has an ironic way of interpreting it in her own fashion, if you do. Jonsen had seen too many skippers sail on their "last voyage"—and never return.

He felt acutely melancholy, not very far from tears; and presently he went below. He wanted to be alone.

Emily by now was conducting, in her head, a secret conversation with John. She had never done so before: but today he had suddenly presented himself to her imagination. Of course his disappearance was strictly taboo

>>>>>>>>>>>>>>>>>>>>>>><<<<<<<<<<<<<<<<<<<<<

between them: what they chiefly discussed was the building of a magnificent raft, to use in the bathing-hole at Ferndale; just as if they had never left the place.

When she heard the captain's step, so nearly surprising her at it, she blushed a deep red. She felt her cheeks still hot when he arrived. As usual, he did not even glance at her. He plumped down on a seat, put his elbows on the cabin table, his head in his hands, and rocked it rhythmically from side to side.

"Look, Captain!" she insisted. "Do I look pretty like this? Look! *Look!* Look, *do* I look pretty like this?"

For once he raised his head, turned, and considered her at length. She had rolled up her eyes till only the whites showed, and turned her under-lip inside out. With her first finger she was squashing her nose almost level with her cheeks.

≻≻≻≻≻≻≻≻≻≻≻≻≻≻≻≻≻≻≻≻≻≺≺≺≺≺≺≺≺≺≺≺≺≺≺≺≺≺≺≺

"No," he said simply, "you do not." Then he returned to his cogitation.

She stuck out her tongue as well, and waggled it.

"Look!" she went on, "Look!"

But instead of looking at her, he let his eye wander round the cabin. It seemed changed somehow—emasculated: a little girl's bedroom, not a man's cabin. The actual physical changes were tiny: but to a meticulous man, they glared. The whole place smelt of children.

Unable to contain himself, he crammed on his cap and burst up the stairs.

On deck, the others were romping round the binnacle, wildly excited.

"*Damn!*" cried Jonsen at the sight of them, stamping in an ungovernable rage.

Of course his slippers came off, and one of them skiddered up the deck.

What devil entered into Edward I do not know; but the sight was too much for him.

He seized the slipper and rushed off with it, shrieking with delight. Jonsen roared at him: he passed it to Laura, and was soon dancing up and down at the end of the jib-boom. Edward, of all people! The timid, respectful Edward!

Laura could hardly carry the enormous thing: but she clasped it tight in her arms, lowered her head, and with the purposeful air of a rugger-player ran back with it very fast up the deck, apparently straight into Jonsen's arms. At the last moment she dodged him neatly: continued right on past Otto at the wheel, just as serious and just as fast, and forward again on the port side. Jonsen, no quick mover at any time, stood in his socks and roared himself hoarse. Otto was shaking with laughter like a jelly.

This mad intoxication, which had flashed from child to child, now dropped a spark into the crew. They were already peering excitedly from the fo'c'sle hatch, grins struggling with outrage for pride of place: but at this point they broke into a cheer. Then, like the devils in a pantomime, they all sank together through the floor, aghast at themselves, and pulled the scuttle over their heads.

Laura, still hugging the slipper, caught her toe in an eye-bolt and fell full length, set up a yell.

Otto, with a suddenly straight face, ran forward, picked up the slipper and returned it to Jonsen, who put it on. Edward stopped jumping up and down and became frightened.

Jonsen was trembling with rage. He advanced on Edward with an iron belaying pin in his hand.

"Come down from there!" he commanded.

"Don't! Don't! Don't!" cried Edward, not moving. Harry suddenly ran and hid himself in the galley, though he had had no part in it.

With a surprising agility which he rarely

used, Jonsen started out along the bowsprit towards Edward, who did nothing but moan "Don't!" at the sight of that murderous belaying pin. When Jonsen was just on him, however, he swarmed up a stay, helping himself with the iron hanks of the jib.

Jonsen returned to the deck, wringing his hands and angrier than ever. He sent a sailor to the crosstrees to head the boy off and drive him down again.

Indeed, but for an extraordinary diversion, I shudder to think what might have happened to him. But just at this moment there appeared, up the ladder from the children's forehold, Rachel. She wore one of the sailors' shirts, back to front, and reaching to her heels: in her hand, a book. She was singing *"Onward Christian Soldiers"* at the top of her voice. But as soon as she reached the deck she became silent: strutted straight aft, looking neither to right nor left, genuflected to Otto at the wheel and then sat herself down on a wooden bucket.

Everyone, Jonsen included, stood petrified. After a moment of silent prayer she arose, and commenced an inarticulate gabble-gabble which reproduced extraordinarily well the sound of what she used to hear in the little church at St. Anne's, where the whole family went one Sunday in each month.

Rachel's religious revival had begun. It could hardly have been more opportune: who shall say it was not Heaven which had chosen the moment for her?

Otto, entering into the thing at once, rolled up his eyes and spread out his arms, crosswise, against the wheel-house at his back.

Jonsen, rapidly recovering some of his temper, strode up to her. Her imitation was admirable. For a few moments he listened in silence. He wavered: should he laugh? Then what remained of his temper prevailed.

"Rachel!" he rebuked.

>>>>>>>>>>>>>>>>>>>>><<<<<<<<<<<<<<<<<<<

She continued, almost without taking breath, "Gabble-gabble, Bretheren, gabble-gabble."

"I am not a religious man myself," said the captain, "but I will not allow religion to be made a mock of on my ship!"

He caught hold of Rachel.

"Gabble-gabble!" she went on, slightly faster and on a higher note, "Let me alone! Gabble-gabble! Amen! Gabble . . ."

But he sat himself on the bucket, and stretched her over his knee.

"You're a wicked pirate! You'll go to Hell!" she shrieked, breaking at last into the articulate.

Then he began to smack her so hard that she screamed almost as much with pain as with rage.

When at last he set her down her face was swollen and purple. She directed a tornado of punches with her little fists against his

knees, crying "Hell! Hell! Hell!" in a stran-
gulated voice.

He flipped her fists aside with his hand,
and presently she went away, so tired with
crying she could hardly get her breath.

Meanwhile, Laura's behaviour had been
characteristic. When she tripped and fell,
she roared till her bumps ceased hurting.
Then, with no perceptible transition, her con-
vulsions of agony became an attempt to stand
on her head. This she kept up throughout
Edward's flight up the stay, throughout the
electric appearance of Rachel. During the
latter's punishment, having happened to top-
ple in the direction of the mainmast, and
finding her feet against the rack round its
base for belaying the halyards to, she gave a
shove off—she would roll instead. And roll
she did, very rapidly, till she arrived at the
captain's feet. There she lay, all the while
he was smacking Rachel, completely uncon-

cerned, on her back, her knees drawn up to
her chin, humming a little tune.

iv

When Emily returned to the forehold, her
first act was one which greatly complicated
life. As if there was not sea enough already,
outside the ship, she decreed that practically
all the deck was sea also. The main hatch
was an island, of course; and there were
others—chiefly natural excrescences of the
same kind. But all the rest, all the open deck,
could only be safely crossed in a boat, or
swimming.

As to who was in a boat, and who wasn't,
Emily decided that herself. No one ever
knew, till they had asked her. But Laura,
once she had got the main idea into her head,
always swam, whether said to be in a boat or
not—to be on the safe side.

"Isn't she silly?" said Edward, once, when she refused to stop working her arms although they had all told her she was safe on board.

"I expect we were all as silly as that, when we were young," said Harry.

It was a source of consternation to the children that none of the grown-ups would recognise this "sea". The sailors trod carelessly on the deepest oceans, refusing so much as to paddle with their hands. But it was equally irritating to the sailors when the children, either safe on an island or bearing down in a vessel of their own, would scream at them in a tone of complete conviction:

"You're drowning! You're drowning! O-o-oh, look out! You're out of your depth there! The sharks'll eat you!"

"O-oh look! Miguel's sinking! The waves are right over his head!"

That happens to be the one sort of joke sailors can't enjoy. Even though the words were unintelligible, their gist—eked out by

the slightly malicious hints of the mate—was
not. If they steadily refused to swim, they
at least took to crossing themselves fervently
and continuously whenever they had to tra-
verse a piece of open deck. For there was
no way one could be certain that these brats
were not gifted with second sight—*hijos de
puntas!*

What the children were really doing, of
course, was trying out what it would feel like
when they themselves were all grown pirates,
running a joint venture or each with a craft of
his own: and though they never so much as
mentioned piracy in the course of these public
navigations, they talked their heads off about
it at night, now.

Margaret also refused to swim: but they
knew by now it was no good trying to make
her: no good yelling at *her* she was drowning, for all she did at that word was to sit
down and cry. So it became a recognised
convention that Margaret, wherever she

went or whatever she was doing, was on a raft, with a keg of biscuit and a barrel of water, by herself—and could be ignored.

For, since her return, she had become very dull company. That one game of Consequences had been a flash in the pan. For several days after it she had remained in bed, hardly speaking, and inclined to tear strips off her blanket when she was asleep: and even when she was about again, though perfectly amiable—more amiable than before—she refused to join in any game whatever. She seemed happy: but for any imaginative purpose she was useless.

Moreover, she made no attempt to regain the sovereignty to which Emily had succeeded. She never ordered anyone about. There was not even any fun to be got out of baiting her: nothing seemed to ruffle her temper. She was treated sometimes with a good-humoured contempt, sometimes ignored altogether: and it was enough for *her* to say something for it to be automatically voted silly.

Rachel also, for several days after her service, showed no disposition to join with the others either. She preferred to sit about below, sulking, in the hold. From time to time she attempted to pick a hole, with a copper nail she had got hold of, in the bottom of the ship, and so sink it. It was Laura who discovered her purpose, and came hot-foot to Emily with the news. Laura never doubted, any more than Rachel did, that the task was a possible one.

Emily came below, and found her at it. After three days, she had only managed to scratch up one single splinter—partly because she never attacked the same place twice: but both she and Laura expected to see quantities of water come welling through, and rapidly fill the ship. Indeed, though no water had yet appeared, Laura was convinced the ship was already perceptibly lowered as a result of Rachel's efforts.

Laura clasped her hands in expectation, waiting to see what Emily would do in the face of this impending disaster.

"You stupid, *that's* no good!" was all Emily's comment.

Rachel looked at her angrily:

"You leave me alone! I know what I am doing!"

Emily's eyes grew very wide, and danced with a strange light.

"If you talk to me like that, I'll have you hanged from the yard-arm!"

"What's *that?*" asked Rachel sulkily.

"You ought to know which is the yard-arm by now!"

"I don't care!" growled Rachel, and went on scratching with her nail.

Emily picked up a big piece of iron, in a corner, so heavy she could hardly carry it:

>>>>>>>>>>>>>>>>>>>>><<<<<<<<<<<<<<<<<<<<<

"Do you know what I am going to do?" she asked in a strange voice.

At the sound of it Rachel stopped scratching and looked up.

"No," she said, a trifle uneasily.

"I'm going to kill you! I'm turned a pirate, and I'm going to kill you with this sword!"

At the word "sword", the misshapen lump of metal seemed to Rachel to flicker to a sharp, wicked point.

She looked Emily in the eyes, doubtfully. Did she mean it, or was it a game?

As a matter of fact, she had always been a little afraid of Emily. Emily was so huge, so strong, so old (as good as grown up), so cunning! Emily was the cleverest, the most powerful person in the world! The muscles of a giant, the ancient experience of a serpent!—And now, her terrible eyes, with no hint in them of pretence.

Emily glared fixedly, and saw real panic

dawn in Rachel's face. Suddenly the latter turned, and as fast as her short fat legs would carry her began to swarm up the ladder. Emily rang her iron once against it, and Rachel nearly tumbled down again in her haste.

The iron was so big and heavy it took Emily a long time to haul it up on deck. Even when that was done, it greatly impeded her running, so that she and Rachel did three laps round the deck without their distances altering much, cheered boisterously by Edward. Even in her terror Rachel did not forget to work her arms as in breast-stroke. Finally, with a cry of "Oh I can't run any more, my bad leg's hurting!" Emily flung down the iron and dropped panting beside Edward on the main hatch.

"I shall put poison in your dinner!" she shouted cheerfully to Rachel; but the latter retreated behind the windlass and began to nurse with an abandoned devotion the particular brood she had parked there, working herself almost to tears with the depth of her maternal pity for them.

Emily went on chuckling for some time at the memory of her sport.

"What's the matter with you?" asked Edward scornfully, puffing out his chest. He was feeling particularly manly at the moment. "Have you got the giggles?"

"I *like* having the giggles," said Emily disarmingly. "Let's see if we can't all get them. Come on Laura! Harry, come!"

The two smaller ones came obediently. They stared her in the face, attentively and seriously, awaiting the Coming of the God, while she herself broke into louder and louder explosions of laughter. Soon the infection took and they were laughing too, each shriller and more wildly than the other.

"I can't stop! I can't stop!" they cried at intervals.

"Come on Edward! Look me in the face!"

>>>>>>>>>>>>>>>>>>>><<<<<<<<<<<<<<<<<<<·

"I won't!" said Edward.

So she set on him and tickled him, till he was as hysterical as the rest.

"Oh I *do* want to stop, my tummy is hurting so!" complained Harry at last.

"Go away, then," advised Emily in a lucid interval. And so the group presently broke up. But they had all to avoid each other's eye for a long while, if they were not to risk another attack.

It was Laura who was cured the quickest. She suddenly discovered what a beautiful deep cave her arm-pit made, and decided to keep fairies in it in future. For some while she could think of nothing else.

v

Captain Jonsen called suddenly to José to take the wheel, and went below for his telescope. Then, buttressing his hip against the rail, and extending the shade over the object-glass, he stared fixedly at something almost in the eye of the setting sun. Emily, in a gentle mood, wandered up to him, and stood, her side just touching him. Then she began lightly rubbing her cheek on his coat, as a cat does.

Jonsen lowered the glass and tried his naked eye, as if he had more trust in it. Then he explored with the glass once more.

What was that businesslike-looking sail, tall and narrow as a pillar? He swept his eye round the rest of the horizon: it was empty: only that single threatening finger, pointing upwards.

Jonsen had chosen his course with care to avoid all the ordinary tracks of shipping at that time of year. Especially he had chosen it to avoid the routine-passages of the Jamaica Squadron from one British island to another. This—it had no business here: no more than he had himself.

Emily put her arm round his waist and gave it a slight hug.

"What is it?" she said: "Do let me look."

Jonsen said nothing, continuing to stare with concentration.

"*Do* let me look!" said Emily: "I haven't ever looked through a telescope, ever!"

Jonsen abruptly snapped the glass to, and looked down at her. His usually expression-less features were stirred from their roots. He lifted one hand and gently began to stroke her hair.

"Do you love me?" he asked.

"Mm," assented Emily. Later she added, with a wriggle, "You're a darling."

"If it was to help me, would you do something . . . very difficult?"

"Yes but *do* let me have a look through your telescope, because I haven't, not ever, and I do so want to!"

Jonsen gave a weary sigh, and sat down on

the cabin-top. What *on Earth* were children's heads made of, inside?

"Now listen," he said: "I want to talk to you seriously."

"Yes," said Emily, trying to hide her extreme discomfort. Her eye plaintively searched the deck for something to hold it. He pressed her against his knee in an attempt to win her attention.

"If bad, cruel men came and wanted to kill me and take you away, what would you do?"

"Oh how horrid!" said Emily: "Will they?"

"Not if you help me."

It was unbearable. With a sudden leap she was astride his knees, her arms round his neck and her hands pressing the back of his head.

"I wonder if you make a good Cyclops?" she said; and holding his head firmly laid her nose to his nose, her forehead to his forehead, both staring into each other's eyes, an inch

apart, till each saw the other's face grow narrow and two eyes converge to one large,
misty eye in the middle.

"Lovely!" said Emily; "You're just right
for one! Only now one of your eyes has got
loose and is floating up above the other one!"

The sun touched the sea, and for thirty
seconds every detail of the distant man-of-
war was outlined in black against the flame.
But, for the life of him, Jonsen could think of
nothing but that house in quiet Lübeck, with
the green porcelain stove.

>>>>>>>>>>>>>>>>>>>>>>>><<<<<<<<<<<<<<<<<<<<<<<<<

Chapter Nine

THE darkness closed down with its sudden curtain on that minatory finger.

Captain Jonsen remained on deck all night, whether it was his watch or not. It was a hot night, even for those latitudes: and no moon. The suffused brilliance of the stars lit up everything close quite plainly, but showed nothing in the distance. The black masts towered up, clear against the jewelry, which seemed to swing slowly a little to one side, a little to the other, of their tapering points. The sails, the shadows in their curves all diffused away, seemed flat. The halyards and topping-lifts and braces showed here, were invisible there, with an arbitrariness which took from them all meaning as mechanism.

Looking forward with the glowing bin-nacle-light at one's back, the narrow milky deck sloped up to the foreshortened tilt of the bowsprit, which seemed to be trying to point at a single enlarged star just above the hori-zon.

The schooner moved just enough for the sea to divide with a slight rustle on her stem, breaking out into a shower of sparks, which lit up also wherever the water rubbed the ship's side, as if the ocean were a tissue of sensitive nerves; and still twinkled behind in the mere paleness of the wake. Only a faint tang of tar in the nostrils was there to remind one that this was no ivory and ebony fantasia but a machine. For a schooner is in fact one of the most mechanically satisfactory, austere, unornamented engines ever invented by Man.

A few yards off, a shoal of luminous fish shone at different depths.

But a few hundred yards off, one could see nothing! The sea became a steady glittering black, that did not seem to move. Near, one could see so much detail it seemed impossible to believe that there a whole ship might lie invisible: impossible to believe that by no glass, no anxious straining of the eyes, could one ever *see*.

Jonsen strode up and down the lee side of the vessel, so that what breeze there was, collecting in the hollow of the sails, overflowed down onto him in a continuous cool cascade. From time to time he climbed to the foremast head, in spite of the fact that added height could not possibly give added vision: stared into the blank till his eyes ached, and then came down and resumed his restless pacing. A ship with her lights out might creep within a mile of him, and he not know it.

Jonsen was not given to intuitions: but he had now an extraordinary feeling of certainty that somewhere close in that cover of darkness his enemy lay, preparing destruction for him. He strained his ears too: but he could

>>>>>>>>>>>>>>>>>>>>>><<<<<<<<<<<<<<<<<<<<

hear nothing either, except the rustle of the water, the occasional knocking of a loose block.

If only there had been a moon! He remembered another occasion, fifteen years before. The slaver of which he was then second mate was bowling along, the hatches down on her stinking cargo, all canvas spread, when right across the glittering path of the moon a frigate crossed, almost within gun-shot—crossed the light, and disappeared again. Jonsen had realised at once that though the frigate, with the light behind it, was now invisible to them, they, with the moonlight shining full on them, would be perfectly visible to the frigate. The boom of a gun soon proved it. He had wanted to make a blind bolt for it: but his captain, instead, ordered every stitch of sail to be furled: and so they lay all night under their bare poles, not moving of course but (with nothing to reflect the light) grown invisible in their turn. When dawn came the frigate was so far down the wind they had easily shown her a clean pair of heels.

But tonight! There was no friendly moon-track to betray the attacker: nothing but this inner conviction, which grew every moment more certain.

Shortly after midnight he had descended from one of his useless climbs to the mast-head, and stood for a moment by the open forehatch. The warm breath of the children was easily discernible. Margaret was chattering in her sleep—quite loud, but you could not distinguish a single clear word.

Moved by a whim, Jonsen climbed down the ladder into the hold. Below, it was hot as an oven. A zooming winged cockroach cannoned about. The sound of the water, a dry rustle above, was here a pleasant gurgle and plop against the wooden shell; most musical of sounds to a sailor.

Laura lay on her back in the faint light of the open hatch. She had discarded her blanket; and the vest which did duty for a night-gown was rucked right up under her arms. Jonsen wondered how anything so like a frog could ever conceivably grow into the billowy body of a woman. He bent down and attempted to pull down the vest: but at the first touch Laura rolled violently over onto her stomach, then drew her knees up under her, thrusting her pointed rump up at him; and continued to sleep in that position, breathing noisily.

As his eyes got used to the gloom, vague white splodges showed him that most of the children had discarded their dark blankets. But he did not notice Emily, sitting up in the darkness and watching him.

As he turned to go, an experimental smile lit up his face: he bent, and gently flicked Laura's behind with his finger-nail. It collapsed like a burst balloon; but still she went on sleeping, flat on her face now.

Jonsen was still chuckling to himself as he

reached the deck. But there his forebodings returned to him with redoubled force. He could *feel* that man-of-war lying-to in the darkness, biding its time! For the fiftieth time he climbed the ratlines and took his stand at the crosstrees, skinning his eyes.

Presently, looking down, he could just discern the small white figure on the deck which was Emily, hopping and skipping about. But it passed at once out of his mind.

Suddenly his tired eye caught a patch of something darker than the sea. He looked away, then back again, to make sure. It was still there: on the port bow: impossible to make out clearly, though . . . Jonsen slid down the shrouds in a flash, like a prentice. Landing on the deck like a thunderbolt he nearly startled Emily out of her life: she had no idea he was up there. She startled him no less.

"It's so *hot* down there," she began, "I can't sleep ——"

"Get below!" hissed Jonsen furiously: "Don't you dare come up again! And don't let any of the others, till I tell you!"

Emily, thoroughly frightened, tumbled down the ladder as fast as she could and rolled herself in her blanket from head to foot: partly because her bare legs were really a little chilled, but more for comfort. What had she done? What was happening? She was hardly down when feet were heard scurrying across the deck, and the hatches over her head were loosely fitted into place. The darkness was profound, and seemed to be rolling on her. No one was within reach: and she dared not move an inch. Everyone was asleep.

Jonsen called all hands on deck: and in silence they mustered at the rail. The patch was clearly visible now: nearer, and smaller than he had thought at first. They listened for the splash of oars: but it came on in silence.

Suddenly they were upon it, it was grating against the ship's side, slipping astern. It was a dead tree, carried out to sea by some river in spate, and tangled up with weed.

But after that, he kept all hands on deck till dawn. In their new mood, they obeyed him readily enough. For they knew he was not incompetent. He generally did the right thing—it was only the fuss he made in any emergency which gave him the appearance of blundering.

Yet, though there were now so many eyes watching, no further alarm was given.

But the moment the first paleness of dawn glimmered, everyone's nerves tightened to cracking-point. The rapidly increasing light would any moment show them their fate.

It was not till full daylight, however, that Jonsen would let himself be convinced there was absolutely no man-of-war there.

As a matter of fact, its royals had sunk below the horizon less than an hour after he had first sighted it.

ii

But the alarm of that night caused Jonsen at last to make up his mind.

He altered his course: and as before he had designed it to avoid other shipping, now on the contrary it was calculated to run as soon as possible into the very track of the Eastward Bounders.

Otto rubbed his eyes. What had come over the fellow? Did he want revenge for the fright he had had? Was he going to try and cut out a prize right in the thick of the traffic? It would be like Jonsen, that; to put his head in the lion's mouth after trembling at its roar: and Otto's heart warmed towards him. But he asked no questions.

Meanwhile Jonsen went to his cabin,

opened a secret receptacle in his bunk, and took out a job-lot of ships' papers which he had bought from a Havana dealer in such things. *The "John Dodson", of Liverpool, bound for the Seychelles with a cargo of cast-iron pots*—what use was that in these waters? The man had sold him a pup!—Ah, this was better: *"Lizzie Green", of Bristol, bound from Matanzas to Philadelphia in ballast . . .* a funny trip to make in ballast, true: but that was no one's affair but his imaginary owner's. Jonsen made sure all was in order—filled in the blank dates, and so on—then returned the bundle to its hiding place for another occasion. Coming on deck he gave a number of orders.

First, stages were rigged over the bows and stern, and José and a paint-pot went over the rail to add *Lizzie Green* to the many names which from time to time had decorated the schooner's escutcheon. Not content with that, he had it painted on every other appropriate place—the boats, the buckets—it was as well to be thorough. Meanwhile, many of the sails were taken down and new ones bent—or rather old ones, distinctive sails that a man would swear he couldn't have forgotten, if he had ever seen them before. Otto sewed a large patch to the mainsail, where there was no hole. In his zeal Jonsen even considered lowering the yards and rigging her as a pure fore-and-after: but luckily for his sweating crew abandoned the idea.

The master-stroke of his disguise was permanent—that he carried no guns. Guns can be hidden or thrown overboard, it is true: but the grooves they make in the deck cannot, as many a protesting-innocent sea-robber has found to his cost. Jonsen not only had no guns to hide, he had no grooves: any fool could see he had no guns, and never had had any. And who ever heard of a pirate without guns? It was laughable: yet he had proved, again and again, that one could make a capture just as easily without them: and further, that the captured merchantman, in making his report, could generally be counted on to imagine a greater or less display of artillery. Whether it was to save their faces, or pure conservatism—presumption that there must have been guns—nearly every vessel Jonsen had had dealings with had reported masked artillery, manned by "fifty or seventy ruffians of the worst Spanish type."

Of course if he met and was challenged by a man-of-war, he would have to give in without a fight. But then, it never pays to fight a man-of-war anyhow. If he is a big one, he sinks you. If he is some little cock-shell of a cutter, commanded by a fire-eating young officer just into his teens, you sink him—and then there is the devil to pay. Better be sunk outright, than insult the honour of a great nation in that fashion.

When he at last remembered to take the hatches off the children, they were half dead with suffocation. It was hot enough, stuffy enough anyhow down there, only the square opening above for ventilation; but with the hatches even loosely in place it was a Black Hole. Emily had at last dropped asleep, and slept late, through a chain of night-mares: when she did wake in the closed hold, she sat up, then fainted immediately, and fell back, her breath coming in loud snores. Before she came to again she was already sobbing miserably. At that the little ones began to cry too: which sound it was that reminded Jonsen, rather late, to take the hatches off.

He was quite alarmed when he saw them. It was not till they had been out in the morning freshness of the deck for some time that they even summoned up interest in the strange metamorphosis of the schooner that was in progress.

Jonsen looked at them with a troubled eye. They had not indeed the appearance of well cared for children; though he had not noticed this before. They were dirty to a fault: their clothes torn, and mended, if at all, with twine. Their hair was not only uncombed—there was tar in it. They were mostly thin, and a yellowy-brown colour. Only Rachel remained obstinately plump and pink. The scar on Emily's leg was still a blushing purple: and they all were blotched with insect-bites.

Jonsen called José off his painting job: gave him a bucket of fresh water: the mate's (the only) comb: and a pair of scissors. José wondered innocently: they did not look to him particularly dirty. But he did his duty, while they were still too sorry for themselves to object actively, to do anything more than sob weakly when he hurt them. Even when he had finished their toilet, of course, he had not reached the point at which a nurse-maid usually begins.

It was noon before the *Lizzie Green* looked herself—whoever that might be: and a little after noon she was still heading for "Philadelphia" when, hull down on the horizon, two sail were sighted, many miles apart, at about the same minute. Captain Jonsen considered carefully; made his choice, and altered his course so as to fall in with her as soon as might be.

Meanwhile, the crew had no more doubt than Otto had of Jonsen's intention: and the sound of the whetstone floated merrily aft, till each man's knife had an edge that did its master's heart good. I have said that the murder of the Dutch captain had affected the whole character of their piracy. The yeast was working.

Presently the smoke of a large steamer cropped up over the horizon as well. Otto sniffed the breeze. It might hold, or it might not. They were still far from home, and these seas crowded The whole enterprise looked to him pretty desperate.

Jonsen was at his usual shuffle-shuffle, nerv·

ously biting his nails. Suddenly he turned on Otto and called him below. He was plainly very agitated; his cheeks red, his eye wild. He began by plotting himself meticulously on the chart. Then he growled over his shoulder:

"Those children, they must go."

"Aye," said Otto. Then, as Jonsen said no more, he added: "You'll land them at Santa, I take it?"

"No! They must go now. We may never get to Santa."

Otto took a deep breath.

Jonsen turned on him, blustering:

"If we get taken with them, where'll *we* be, eh?"

Otto went white, then red, before he answered.

"You'll have to risk that," he said slowly. "You can't land them no other place."

"Who said I was going to land them?"

"There's nothing else you can do," said Otto stubbornly.

A light of comprehension dawned suddenly in Jonsen's worried face.

"We could sew them up in little bags," he said with a genial smile, "and put them **over** the side."

Otto gave him one quick glance; what he saw was enough to relieve him.

"What are you going to do?" he asked.

"Sew them up in little bags! Sew them up in little bags!" Jonsen affirmed, rubbing his hands together and chuckling, all the latent sentimentality of the man getting the better of him. Then he pushed past Otto and went on deck.

The big brigantine, which he had aimed for at first, was proving a bit too far up the wind for him: so now he took the helm and let the schooner's head down a couple of points, to intercept the steamer instead.

Otto whistled. At last an inkling of what
the captain was at had dawned on him.

iii

As they drew nearer, the children were all
immensely interested: they had never before
seen anything like this big, miraculous tub.
The Dutch steamer, an old-fashioned craft,
had not differed very materially from a sail-
ing-vessel: but this, in form, was already
more like the steamers of our own day. Its
funnel was still tall and narrow, with a kind
of artichoke on top, it is true: but otherwise
it was much the same as you and I are used to.

Jonsen spoke her urgently: and presently
her engines stopped. The *Lizzie Green*
slipped round under her lee. Jonsen had a
boat lowered: then embarked in it himself.
The children and the schooner's crew stood
at the rail in tense excitement: watched a

little ladder lowered from her towering iron side: watched Jonsen, alone, in his dark Sunday suit and the peaked cap of his rank, climb on board. He had timed it nicely: in another hour it would be dark.

He had no easy task. First he had his premeditated fiction to establish, his explanation of how he came by his passengers. Secondly, he had to persuade the captain of the steamship, a stranger, to relieve him, where he had so signally failed to persuade his friend the señora at Santa Lucia.

Otto was not a man to show agitation: but he felt it, none the less. This scheme of Jon's was the foolhardiest thing he had ever heard of: the slightest suspicion, and they were as good as done for.

Jonsen had ordered him, if he guessed anything was wrong, to run.

Meanwhile, the breeze was dropping, and it was still daylight.

Jonsen had vanished into the steamer as into a forest.

Emily was as excited as any of them, pointing out the novel features of this extraordinary vessel. The children still thought it was professional quarry. Edward was openly bragging of what he would do when he had captured it.

"I shall cut the captain's head off and throw it in the water!" he declared aloud.

"S-s-sh!" exclaimed Harry, in a stage whisper.

"Coo! I don't care!" cried Edward, intoxicated with bravado: "Then I shall take out all the gold and keep it for myself."

"I shall sink it!" said Harry, in imitation: then added as an afterthought, "Right to the very bottom!"

Emily fell silent, her peculiarly vivid imagination having the mastery of her. She saw the hold of the steamer, piled with gold and jewels. She saw herself, fighting her way through hordes of hairy sailors, with her bare fists, till only the steamer's captain stood between her and the treasure.

Then it happened! It was as if a small cold voice inside her said suddenly: *"How can you? You're only a little girl!"* She felt herself falling giddily from the heights, shrinking. She was *Emily.*

The awful, blood-covered face of the Dutch captain seemed to threaten her out of the air. She cowered back at the shock. But it was over in a moment.

She looked around her in terror. Did anyone know how defenceless she was? Surely someone must have noticed her. The other children were gibbering in their animal innocence. The sailors, their knives half concealed, grinned at each other or cursed. Otto, his brows knotted, stood with his eyes fixed on the steamer.

She feared everybody, she hated everybody.

Margaret was whispering something to Edward, and he nodded. Again panic seized her. What was Margaret telling him? Had she told everyone? Did they all know? Were they all playing with her, deceiving her by pretending not to know, waiting their own time to burst their revelation on her and punish her in some quite unimaginably awful way?

Had Margaret told? If she crept up behind Margaret now, and pushed her in the sea, might she yet be in time?—But even as she thought it, she seemed to see Margaret rising waist-high out of the waves, telling the whole story to everybody in a calm, dispassionate voice, and climbing back on board.

In another flash she saw the fat, comfortable person of her mother, standing at the door of Ferndale, abusing the cook.

Again her eyes roamed round the sinister reality of the schooner. She suddenly felt sick to death of it all: tired, beyond words

tired. Why must she be chained for ever to
this awful life?   Could she never escape,
never get back to the ordinary life little girls
lead, with their papas and mamas and . . .
birthday cakes?

Otto called her. She went to him obediently; though with a presentiment that it was
to her execution. He turned, and called Margaret too.

She was in a more attentive mood than she
had been the night before with the captain,
Heaven knows! But Otto was too pre-occupied to notice how frightened her eyes were.

Jonsen had no easy task on the steamer: but
Otto did not greatly relish his own. He did
not know how to begin—and everything de-
pended on his success.

"See here," he burst out: "You're going to
England."

Emily shot him a quick glance. "Yes?"
she said at last: her voice showing merely a
polite interest.

>>>>>>>>>>>>>>>>>>>>><<<<<<<<<<<<<<<<<<<<<

"The Captain has gone onto that steamboat, to arrange about it."

"Aren't we staying with you any longer, then?"

"No," said Otto: "you're going home on that steamboat."

"Shan't we see you any more, then?" Emily pursued.

"No," said Otto: "—Well, someday, perhaps."

"Are they all going, or only us two?"

"Why, all of you of course!"

"Oh. I didn't know."

There was an awkward silence, while Otto wondered how to tackle the real problem.

"Had we better go and get ready?" asked Margaret.

"Now listen!" Otto interrupted her. "When you get on board, they'll ask you all about everything. They'll want to know how you got here."

"Are we to tell them?"

Otto was astonished she took his point so readily.

"No," he said. "The Captain and me don't want you to. We want you to keep it a secret, do you see?"

"What *are* we to say, then?" Emily asked.

"Tell them . . . you were captured by pirates, and then . . . they put you ashore at a little port in Cuba ——"

"—Where the Fat Woman was?"

"—Yes. And then we came along, and took you on board our schooner, which was going to America, to save you from the pirates."

"I see," said Emily.

"You'll say that, and keep the . . . other a secret?" Otto asked anxiously.

Emily gave him her peculiar, gentle stare.

"Of course!" she said.

Well, he had done his best: but Otto felt heavy at heart. That little cherub! He didn't believe she could keep a secret for ten seconds.

"Now: do you think you can make the little ones understand?"

"Oh yes, I'll tell them," said Emily easily. She considered for a moment: "I don't suppose they remember much anyway.—Is that all?"

"That's all," said Otto; and they walked away.

"What was he saying?" Margaret asked. "What was it all about?"

"Oh shut up!" said Emily rudely: "It's nothing to do with you!"

But inwardly, she did not know whether she was on her head or her heels. Were they really going to let her escape? Weren't they just tantalising her, meaning to stop her at the last moment? Were they handing her over to strangers, who had come to hang her for murder? Was her mother perhaps on that steamer, come to save her? But she loved

>>>>>>>>>>>>>>>>>>>>><<<<<<<<<<<<<<<<<<<<

Jonsen and Otto: how could she bear to part
with them? The dear, familiar schooner.
. . . All these thoughts in her head at once!
But she dealt firmly enough with the Liddlies:

"Come on!" she said: "We're going on
that steamer."

"Are *we* to do the fighting?" Edward
asked, timorously enough.

"There isn't going to be any fighting," said
Emily.

"Will there be another circus?" asked
Laura.

Then she told them they were to change
ships again.

When Captain Jonsen came back, mopping
the sweat from his polished forehead with a
big cotton handkerchief, he seemed in a terrible hurry. As for the children, they were
so excited they were ready to tumble into the
boat: in such a flurry they nearly tumbled into

the sea instead. *Now* they knew why they had been washed and combed.

It did not seem at first as if there was going to be any difficulty about getting them started. But it was Rachel who began the break-away:

"My babies! My babies!" she shrieked, and began running all over the ship, routing out bits of rag, fuzzy rope-ends, paint-pots . . . her arms were soon full.

"Here, you can't take all that junk!" dissuaded Otto.

"Oh but my darlings, I can't leave you behind!" cried Rachel piteously. Out rushed the cook, just in time to retrieve his ladle— and a battle-royal began.

Naturally, Jonsen was on tenterhooks to be gone. But it was essential they should part on good terms.

José was lifting Laura over the side.

"*Darling* José!" she burst out suddenly, and twined her arms tightly round his neck.

At that Harry and Edward, who were already in the boat, scrambled back on deck. They had forgotten to say goodbye. And so each child said goodbye to each pirate, kissing him and lavishing endearments on him.

"Go on! Go on!" muttered Jonsen impatiently.

Emily flung herself in his arms, sobbing as if her heart would break.

"Don't make me go!" she begged: "Let me stay with you always, always!" She clung tight to the lapels of his coat, hiding her face in his chest: "Oh I *don't* want to go!"

Jonsen was strangely moved: for a moment, almost toyed with the idea.

But the others were already in the boat.

"Come on!" said Otto, "or they'll go without you!"

"Wait! Wait!" shrieked Emily, and was over the side and in the boat in a flash.

Jonsen shook his head confusedly. For this last time, she had him puzzled.

But now, as they rowed across to the

steamer, all the children stood up in the boat, in danger of tumbling out, and cried:

"Goodbye! Goodbye!"

"Adios!" cried the pirates, waving sentimental hands, and guffawing secretly to each other.

"C-c-ome and see us in England!" came Edward's clear treble.

"Yes!" cried Emily: "Come and stay with us! All of you!—*Promise* you'll come and stay with us!"

"All right!" shouted Otto: "We'll come!"

"Come *soon!*"

"My babies!" wailed Rachel, "I've lost 'most all my babies!"

But now they were alongside the steamer: and soon they were mounting a rope ladder to her deck.

What a long way up it was! But at last they were all on board.

The little boat returned to the schooner.

The children never once looked after it.

And well might they forget it! For exciting as it had been to go onto a ship of any kind for the first time, to find themselves on this steamer was infinitely more so. The luxury of it! The white paint! The doors! The windows! The stairs! The brass!—A fairy palace, no: but a mundane wonder of a quite unimagined kind.

But they had little time now to take in the details. All the passengers, wild with curiosity, were gathered round them in a ring. As the dirty, disheveled little mites were handed one by one on board, a gasp went up. The story of the capture of the *Clorinda* by as fiendish a set of buccaneers as any in the past that roamed the same Carribean was well known; and how the little innocents on board her had been taken and tortured to death before the eyes of the impotent captain. To see now face to face the victims of so foul a murder was for them too a thrill of the first water.

The tension was first broken by a beautiful

young lady in a muslin dress. She sank on her knees beside little Harry, and folded him in her delicate arms.

"The little angel!" she murmured: "You poor little man, what horrors you have been through! How will you ever forget them?"

As if that were the signal, all the lady passengers fell on the astonished children and pitied them: while the men, less demonstrative, stood around with lumps in their throats.

Bewildered at first, it was not long before they rose to the occasion—as children generally will, when they find themselves the butt of indiscriminate adoration. Bless you, they were kings and queens! They were so sleepy they could hardly keep their eyes open: but they were not going to bed, not they! They had never been treated like this before. Heaven alone knew how long it would last. Best not waste a minute of it.

It was not long before they ceased even to be surprised, became convinced that it was all their right and due. They were very important people—quite unique.

Only Emily stood apart, shy, answering questions uncomfortably. She did not seem to be able to throw herself into her importance with the same zest as the others.

Even the passengers' children joined in the fuss and admiration: perhaps realising the opportunity which the excitement gave of avoiding their own bed-time. They began to bring (probably not without suggestion) their toys, as offerings to these new gods: and vied with each other in their generosity.

A shy little boy of about her own age, with brown eyes and a nice smile, his long hair brushed smooth as silk, his clothes neat and sweet-smelling, sidled up to Rachel.

"What's your name?" she asked him.

"Harold."

She told him hers.

"How much do you weigh?" he asked her

"I don't know."

"You look rather heavy. May I see if I can lift you?"

"Yes."

He clasped his arms round her stomach from behind, leant back, and staggered a few paces with her. Then he set her down, the friendship cemented.

Emily stood apart; and for some reason, everyone unconsciously respected her reserve. But suddenly something seemed to snap in her heart. She flung herself face-downwards on the deck—not crying, but kicking convulsively. It was a huge great stewardess who picked her up and carried her, still quivering from head to foot, down to a neat, clean cabin. There, soothing and talking to her without ceasing, she undressed her, and washed her with warm water, and put her to bed.

Emily's head felt different to any way it had ever felt before: hardly as if it were her own. It sang, and went round like a wheel, without so much as with your leave or by your leave. But her body, on the other hand, was more than usually sensitive, absorbing the tender, smooth coolness of the sheets, the softness of the mattress, as a thirsty horse sucks up water. Her limbs drank in comfort at every pore: it seemed as if she could never be sated with it. She felt physical peace soaking slowly through to her marrow: and when at last it got there, her head became more quiet and orderly too.

All this while she had hardly heard what was said to her: only a refrain that ran through it all made any impression, *"Those wicked men . . . men . . . nothing but men . . . those cruel men. . . ."*

Men! It was perfectly true that for months and months she had seen nothing but men. To be at last back among other women was heavenly. When the kind stewardess bent over her to kiss her she caught tight hold of her, and buried her face in the warm, soft,

>>>>>>>>>>>>>>>>>><<<<<<<<<<<<<<<<<<
yielding flesh, as if to sink herself in it. Lord,
how unlike the firm, muscular bodies of Jonsen and Otto!

When the stewardess stood up again,
Emily feasted her eyes on her, eyes grown
large and warm and mysterious. The woman's enormous, swelling bosom fascinated
her. Forlornly, she began to pinch her own
thin little chest. Was it conceivable she
would herself ever grow breasts like that—
beautiful, mountainous breasts, that had to
be cased in a sort of cornucopia? Or even
firm little apples, like Margaret's?

Thank God she had not been born a boy!
She was overtaken with a sudden revulsion
against the whole sex of them. From the tips
of her fingers to the tips of her toes she felt
female: one with that exasperating, idiotic
secret communion: initiate of the γυναικεῖον

Suddenly Emily reached up and caught the
stewardess by the head, pulling it down to her
close: began whispering earnestly in her ear.

On the woman's face the first look of incredulity changed to utter stupefaction, from stupefaction to determination.

"My eye!" she said at last: "The cheek of the rascals! The impudence!"

Without another word she slipped out of the cabin. And you may imagine that the steamer captain, when he heard the trick that had been played upon him, was as astonished as she.

For a few moments after she had gone Emily lay staring at nothing, a very curious expression on her face indeed. Then, all of a sudden, she dropped asleep, breathing sweetly and easily.

But she only slept for about ten minutes; and when she woke the cabin door was open, and in it stood Rachel and her little boy friend.

"What do you want?" said Emily forbiddingly.

"Harold has brought his alligator," said Rachel.

Harold stepped forward, and laid the little creature on Emily's coverlet. It was very small: only about six inches long: a yearling: but an exact miniature of its adult self, with the snub nose and round Socratic forehead that distinguish it from the crocodile. It moved jerkily, like a clockwork toy. Harold picked it up by the tail: it spread its paws in the air, and jerked from side to side, more like clockwork than ever. Then he set it down again, and it stood there, its tongueless mouth wide open and its harmless teeth looking like grains of sand-paper, alternately barking and hissing. Harold let it snap at his finger—it was plainly hungry, in the warmth down there. It darted its head so fast you could hardly see it move: but its bite was still so weak as to be painless, even to a child.

Emily drew a deep breath, fascinated.

✦✦

"May I have him for the night?" she asked.

"All right," said Harold: and he and Rachel were summoned away by someone without.

Emily was translated into Heaven. So this was an alligator! She was actually going to sleep with an alligator! She had thought that to anyone who had once been in an earthquake nothing really exciting could happen again: but then, she had not thought of this.

There was once a girl called Emily, who slept with an alligator . . .

In search of greater warmth, the creature high-stepped warily up the bed towards her face. About six inches away it paused, and they looked each other in the eye, those two children.

The eye of an alligator is large, protruding, and of a brilliant yellow, with a slit pupil like a cat's. A cat's eye, to the casual observer, is expressionless: though with attention one can distinguish in it many changes of emotion. But the eye of an alligator is infinitely more stony, and brilliant—reptilian.

What possible meaning could Emily find in such an eye? Yet she lay there, and stared, and stared: and the alligator stared too. If there had been an observer it might have given him a shiver to see them so—well, eye to eye like that.

Presently the beast opened his mouth and hissed again gently. Emily lifted a finger and began to rub the corner of his jaw. The hiss changed to a sound almost like a purr. A thin, filmy lid first covered his eye from the front backwards, then the outer lid closed up from below.

Suddenly he opened his eyes again, and snapped on her finger: then turned and wormed his way into the neck of her nightgown, and crawled down inside, cool and rough against her skin, till he found a place

⭢ 334 ⭠

to rest. It is surprising that she could stand
it, as she did, without flinching.

Alligators are utterly untamable.

iv

From the deck of the schooner, Jonsen
and Otto watched the children climb onto the
steamer: watched their boat return, and the
steamer get under way.

So: it had all gone without a hitch. No
one had suspected his story—a story so simple as to be very nearly the truth.

They were gone.

Jonsen could feel the difference at once:
and it seemed almost as if the schooner could.
A schooner, after all, is a place for *men*. He
stretched himself, and took a deep breath,
feeling that a cloying, enervating influence
was lifted. José was industriously sweeping

>>>>>>>>>>>>>>>>>>>>><<<<<<<<<<<<<<<<<<<<

up some of Rachel's abandoned babies. He
swept them into the lee scuppers. He drew
a bucket of water, and dashed it at them over
the deck. The trap swung open—whew, it
was gone, all that truck!

"Batten down that forehatch!" ordered
Jonsen.

The men all seemed lighter of heart than
they had been for many months: as if the
weight they were relieved of had been enormous. They sang as they worked, and two
friends playfully pummelled each other in
passing—hard. The lean, masculine schooner
shivered and plunged in the freshening evening breeze. A shower of spray for no particular reason suddenly burst over the bows,
swept aft and dashed full in Jonsen's face.
He shook his head like a wet dog, and
grinned.

Rum appeared: and for the first time since
the encounter with the Dutch steamer all the
sailors got bestially drunk, and lay about the

deck, and were sick in the scuppers. José
was belching like a bassoon.

It was dark by then. The breeze dropped
away again. The gaffs clanked aimlessly in
the calm, with the motion of the sea: the
empty sails flapped with reports like cannon,
a hearty applause. Jonsen and Otto themselves remained sober, but they had not the
heart to discipline the crew.

The steamer had long since disappeared
into the dark. The foreboding which had
oppressed Jonsen all the night before was
gone. No intuition told him of Emily's whispering to the stewardess: of the steamer,
shortly after, meeting with a British gunboat:
of the long series of lights flickering between
them. The gunboat, even now, was fast over-
hauling him: but no premonition disturbed
his short peace.

He was tired—as tired as a sailor ever lets
himself be. The last twenty-four hours had

been hard. He went below as soon as his watch was over, and climbed into his bunk.

But he did not, at once, sleep. He lay for a while conning over the step he had taken. It was really very astute. He had returned the children, undoubtedly safe and sound: Marpole would be altogether discredited.

Even to have landed them at Santa Lucia, his first intention, could never have closed the *Clorinda* episode so completely, since the world at large would not have heard of it: and it would have been difficult to produce them, should need arise.

Indeed, it had seemed to be a choice of evils: either he must carry them about always, as a proof that they were alive, or he must land them and lose control of them. In the first case, their presence would certainly connect him with the *Clorinda* piracy of which he might otherwise go unsuspected: in the second, he might be convicted of their murder if he could not produce them.

>>>>>>>>>>>>>>>>>><<<<<<<<<<<<<<<<<<

But this wonderful idea of his, now that he had carried it out successfully, solved both difficulties.

It had been a near thing with that little bitch Margaret, though . . . lucky the second boat had picked her up. . . .

The light from the cabin lamp shone into the bunk, illuminating part of the wall defaced with Emily's puerile drawings. As they caught his eye a frown gathered on his forehead: but as well a sudden twinge affected his heart. He remembered the way she had lain there, ill and helpless. He suddenly found himself remembering at least forty things about her—an overwhelming flood of memories.

The pencil she had used was still among the bedding, and his fingers happened on it. There were still some white spaces not drawn on.

Jonsen could only draw two things: ships, and naked women. He could draw any type

of ship he liked, down to the least detail—
any particular ship he had sailed in, even.
In the same way he could draw voluptuous,
buxom women, also down to the least detail:
in any position, and from any point of view:
from the front, from the back, from the side,
from above, from below: his foreshortening
faultless. But set him to draw any third
thing—even a woman with her clothes on—
and he could not have produced a scribble
that would have been recognisable.

He took the pencil: and before long there
began to appear between Emily's crude uncertain lines round thighs, rounder bellies,
high swelling bosoms, all somewhat in the
manner of Rubens.

At the same time his mind was still occupied with reflections on his own astuteness.
Yes, it had been a near thing with Margaret
—it would have been awkward, if, when he
returned the party, there had been one missing.

A recollection descended on his mind like a cold douche, something he had completely forgotten about till then. His heart sank— as well it might:

"Hey!" he called to Otto on the deck above: "What was the name of that boy who broke his neck at Santa? Jim? Sam? What was he called?"

Otto did not answer, except by a long-drawn-out whistle.

Chapter Ten

EMILY grew quite a lot during the passage to England on the steamer: suddenly shot up, as children will at that age. But she did it without any gawkiness: instead, an actual increase of grace. Her legs and arms, though longer, did not lose any of the nicety of their shape; and her grave face lost none of its attractiveness by being a fraction nearer your own. The only drawback was that she used to get pains in the calves of her legs, now, and sometimes in her back: but those of course did not show. (They were all provided with clothes by a general collection, so it did not matter that she grew out of her old ones.)

She was a nice child: and being a little

less shy than formerly was soon the most popular of all of them. Somehow, no one seemed to care very much for Margaret: old ladies used to shake their heads over her a good deal. At least, anyone could see that Emily had infinitely more sense.

You would never have believed that Edward after a few days washing and combing would look such a little gentleman.

After a short while Rachel threw Harold over, to be uninterrupted in her peculiar habits of parthenogenesis, eased now a little by the many presents of real dolls. But Harold became soon just as firm friends with Laura, young though she was.

Most of the steamer children had made friends with the seamen, and loved to follow them about at their romantic occupations —swabbing decks, and so on. One day, one of these men actually went a short way up the rigging (what little there was), leaving a glow of admiration on the deck below. But all this had no glamour for the Thorntons. Edward and Harry liked best to peer in at the engines: but what Emily liked best was to walk up and down the deck with her arm round the waist of Miss Dawson, the beautiful young lady with the muslin dresses: or stand behind her, while she did little water-colour compositions of toppling waves with wrecks foundering in them, or mounted dried tropical flowers in wreaths round photographs of her uncles and aunts. One day Miss Dawson took her down to her cabin and showed her all her clothes, every single item—it took hours. It was the opening of a new world to Emily.

The Captain sent for Emily, and questioned her: but she added nothing to that first, crucial burst of confidence to the stewardess. She seemed struck dumb—with terror, or something: at least, he could get nothing out of her. So he wisely let her alone. She would probably tell her story in her own time: to her new friend, perhaps. But this she did not do. She would not talk about the schooner, or the pirates, or any-thing concerning them: what she wanted was to listen, to drink in all she could learn about England, where they were really going at last —that wonderfully exotic, romantic place.

Louisa Dawson was quite a wise young person for her years. She saw that Emily did not want to talk about the horrors she had been through: but considered it far better that she should be made to talk than that she should brood over them in secret. So when the days passed and no confidences came she set herself to draw the child out. She had, as everybody has, a pretty clear idea in her own head of what life is like in a pirate vessel. That these little innocents should have come through it alive was miraculous, like the three Hebrews in the fiery furnace.

"Where used you to live, when you were

>>>>>>>>>>>>>>>>>>>>><<<<<<<<<<<<<<<<<<<<

on the schooner?" she asked Emily one day suddenly.

"Oh, in the hold," said Emily nonchalantly. "Is that your Great-uncle *Vaughan*, did you say?"

In the hold. She might have known it. Chained, probably, down there in the darkness like blacks, with rats running over them, fed on bread and water.

"Were you very frightened when there was a battle going on? Did you hear them fighting over your head?"

Emily looked at her with her gentle stare: but kept silence.

Louisa Dawson was very wise, in thus trying to ease the load on the child's mind. But also she was consumed with curiosity. It exasperated her that Emily would not talk.

There were two questions which she particularly wanted to ask. One however seemed insuperably difficult of approach. The other she could not contain:

"Listen, darling," she said, wrapping her arms round Emily: "Did you ever actually see anyone killed?"

Emily stiffened palpably. "Oh no," she said: "Why should we?"

"Didn't you ever even see a body?" she went on: "A dead one?"

"No," said Emily, "There weren't any." She seemed to meditate a while. "There weren't many," she corrected.

"You poor, poor little thing," said Miss Dawson, stroking her forehead.

But though Emily was slow to talk, Edward was not. Suggestion was hardly necessary. He soon saw what he was expected to say. It was also what he wanted to say. All these rehearsals with Harry, these springings into the main rigging, these stormings of the galley . . . they had seemed real enough at the time. Now, he had soon no doubt about them at all. And Harry backed him up.

It was wonderful for Edward that everyone seemed ready to believe what he said. Those who came to him for tales of blood-shed were not sent empty away.

Nor did Rachel contradict him. .The pirates were wicked—deadly wicked, as she had good reason to know. So they had prob-ably done all Edward said: probably when she was not looking.

Miss Dawson did not always press Emily like this: she had too much sense. She spent a good deal of her time simply in tying more firmly the knots of the child's passion for her.

She was ready enough to tell her about England. But how strange it seemed that these humdrum narrations should interest anyone who had seen such romantic, terrible things as Emily had!

She told her all about London, where the traffic was so thick things could hardly pass, where things drove by all day, as if the supply of them would never come to an end. She tried also to describe trains, but Emily could not see, them, somehow: all she could envisage was a steamer like this one, only going on land—but she knew that was not right.

What a wonderful person her Miss Dawson was! What marvels she had seen. Emily had again the feeling she had in the schooner's cabin: how time had slipped by, been wasted. Now she would be eleven in a few months: a great age: and in all that long life, how little of interest or significance had happened to her! There were just two things: her earthquake, of course, and she had slept with an alligator: but what were these compared with the experiences of Miss Dawson, who knew London so well it hardly seemed any longer wonderful to her, who could not even count the number of times she had travelled in a train?

Her Earthquake . . . it was a great possession. Dared she tell Miss Dawson about it? Was it possible that it would raise her a little in Miss Dawson's esteem, show that even she, little Emily, had had experiences? But she never dared. Suppose that to Miss Dawson earthquakes were as familiar as railway trains: the fiasco would be unbearable. As for the alligator, Miss Dawson had told Harold to take it away as if it was a worm.

Sometimes Miss Dawson sat silently fondling Emily, looking now at her, now at the other children at play. How difficult it was to imagine that these happy-looking creatures had been, for months together, in hourly danger of their lives! Why had they not died of fright? She was sure that she would have. Or at least gone stark, staring, raving mad?

She had always wondered how people survived even a moment of danger without dropping dead with fear: but months and months . . . and children. . . . Her head could not swallow it.

As for that other question, how dearly she would have liked to ask it, if only she could have devised a formula delicate enough.

>>>>>>>>>>>>>>>>>>>>><<<<<<<<<<<<<<<<<<<

Meanwhile Emily's passion for her was nearing its crisis; and one day this was provoked. Miss Dawson kissed Emily three times, and told her in future to call her Lulu.

Emily jumped as if shot. Call this goddess by her Christian name? She burnt a glowing vermilion at the very thought. The Christian names of all grown-ups were sacred: something never to be uttered by childish lips: to do so, the most blasphemous disrespect.

For Miss Dawson to tell her to do so, was as embarrassing as if she had seen written up in Church PLEASE SPIT.

Of course if Miss Dawson told her to call her Lulu, at least she must not call her Miss Dawson any more. But say . . . the Other Word aloud, her very lips refused.

And so, for some time by elaborate subterfuges she managed to avoid calling her anything at all. But the difficulty of this in-

creased in geometrical progression: it began
to render all intercourse an intolerable strain.

Before long she was avoiding Miss Dawson.

Miss Dawson was terribly wounded: what
could she have done to offend this strange
child? ("Little Fairy-girl," she used to call
her.) The darling had seemed so fond of
her, but now. . . .

So Miss Dawson used to follow her about
the ship with hurt eyes, and Emily used to
escape from her with scarlet cheeks. They
had never had a real talk, heart to heart,
again, by the time the steamer reached
England.

ii

When the steamer took in her pilot, you
may imagine that her news travelled ashore;
and also, that it quickly reached the *Times*
newspaper.

Mr. and Mrs. Bas-Thornton, after the disaster, unable to bear Jamaica any longer, had sold Ferndale for a song and travelled straight back to England, where Mr. Thornton soon got posts as London dramatic critic to various Colonial newspapers, and manipulated rather remote influence at the Admiralty in the hope of getting a punitive expedition sent against the whole island of Cuba. It was thus the *Times* which, in its quiet way, broke the news to them, the very morning that the steamer docked at Tilbury.

She was a long time doing it, owing to the fog, out of which the gigantic noises of dockland reverberated unintelligibly. Voices shouted things from the quays. Bells ting-a-linged. The children welded themselves into a compact mass facing outwards, an improvised Argus determined to miss nothing whatever. But they could not gather really what anything was about, much less everything.

Miss Dawson had taken charge of them all, meaning to convey them to her Aunt's London house till their relations could be found. So now she took them ashore, and up to the train, into which they climbed.

"What are we getting into this box for?" asked Harry: "Is it going to rain?"

It took Rachel several journeys up and down the steep steps to get all her babies inside.

The fog, which had met them at the mouth of the river, was growing thicker than ever. So they sat there in semi-darkness at first, till a man came and lit the light. It was not very comfortable, and horribly cold: but presently another man came, and put in a big flat thing which was hot: it was full of hot water, Miss Dawson said, and for you to put your feet on.

Even now that she was in a train, Emily could hardly believe it would ever start. She had become quite sure it was not going to when at last it did, jerking along like a shark would on a leash.

Then their powers of observation broke down. For the time they were full. So they played Up-Jenkins riotously all the way to London: and when they arrived hardly noticed it. They were quite loath to get out, and finally did so into as thick a pea-soup fog as London could produce at the tail end of the season. At this they began to wake up again, and jog themselves to remember that this really was *England,* so as not to miss things.

They had just realised that the train had run right inside a sort of enormous house, lit by haloed yellow lights and full of this extraordinary orange-coloured air, when Mrs. Thornton found them.

"Mother!" cried Emily. She had not known she could be so glad to see her. As for Mrs. Thornton, she was far beyond the bounds of hysteria. The little ones held back at first, but soon followed Emily's example, leaping on her and shouting: indeed it looked more like Actæon with his hounds than a mother with her children: their monkey-like little hands tore her clothes in pieces, but she didn't care a hoot. As for their father, he had totally forgotten how much he disliked emotional scenes.

"I slept with an alligator!" Emily was shouting at intervals: "Mother! I've slept with an alligator!"

Margaret stood in the background holding all their parcels. None of her relations had appeared at the station. Mrs. Thornton's eye at last took her in.

"Why, Margaret . . ." she began vaguely.

Margaret smiled and came forward to kiss her.

"Get out!" cried Emily fiercely, punching her in the chest, "She's *my* Mother!"

"Get out!" shouted all the others: "She's *our* Mother!"

Margaret fell back again into the shadows: and Mrs. Thornton was too distracted to be as shocked as she would normally have been.

Mr. Thornton however was just sane enough to take in the situation. "Come on, Margaret!" he said: "Margaret's *my* pal! Let's go and look for a cab!"

He took the girl's arm, bowing his fine shoulders, and walked off with her up the platform.

They found a cab, and brought it to the scene, and they all got in, Mrs. Thornton just remembering to say "How-d'you-do-good-bye" to Miss Dawson.

Packing themselves inside was difficult. It was in the middle of it all that Mrs. Thornton suddenly exclaimed:

"But where's John?"

The children fell immediately silent.

"Where is he?—Wasn't he on the train with you?"

>>>>>>>>>>>>>>>>>>>>>>>><<<<<<<<<<<<<<<<<<<<<<

"No," said Emily, and went as dumb as the rest.

Mrs. Thornton looked from one of them to another.

"John! Where is John?" she asked the world at large, a faint hint of uneasiness beginning to tinge her voice.

It was then that Miss Dawson showed a puzzled face at the window:

"John?" she asked: "Why, who is John?"

iii

The children passed the spring at the house their father had taken in Hammersmith Terrace, on the borders of Chiswick: but Captain Jonsen, Otto, and the crew passed it in Newgate.

They were taken there as soon as the gunboat which apprehended them reached the Thames.

The children's bewilderment lasted. London was not what they had expected, but it was even more astounding. From time to time however they would realise how this or that did chime in with something they had been told, though not at all with the idea that the telling had conjured up. On these occasions they felt something as Saint Matthew must have felt when, after recounting some trivial incident, he adds "That it might be fulfilled which was spoken by the Prophet So-and-so."

"Why look!" exclaimed Edward: "There's only toys in this store!"

"Why, don't you remember . . ." began Emily.

Yes, their Mother had told them, on a visit to their Father's general store in St. Anne's, that in London there were stores which not only sold toys but which sold toys only. At that time, they hardly knew what toys were. A cousin in England had once sent them out

some expensive wax dolls, but even before
the box was opened the wax had melted: consequently the only dolls they had were empty
bottles, which they clothed with bits of rag.
These had another advantage over the wax
kind: you could feed them, poking it into
the neck. If you put in some water too, in a
day or so the food began to digest, visibly.
The bottles with square shoulders they called
He-beasties, and the bottles with round shoulders they called She-beasties.

Their other toys were mostly freakish
sticks, and different kinds of seeds and berries. No wonder it seemed strange to them
to imagine these things in a shop. But the
idea engaged them, nevertheless. Down by
the bathing-hole there were several enormous
cotton-trees, which lift themselves on their
roots right out of the earth, as on stilts, making a big cage. One of these they dubbed
their toy-shop: decorated it up with lace-bark,
and strings of bright-coloured seeds, and

their other toys: then they would go inside and take turns to sell them to each other. So now this was the picture the phrase "toy-shop" evoked in them. No wonder the London kind was a surprise to them, seemed a very far-fetched fulfillment of the prophecy.

The houses in Hammersmith Terrace are tall, roomy, comfortable houses, though not big or aristocratic, with gardens running right down to the river.

It was a shock to them to find how dirty the river was. The litter-strewn mud when the tide was out somehow offended them much less than the sewery water when it was up. At low tide they would often climb down the wall and scrounge about in the mud for things of value to them happily enough. They stank like pole-cats when they came up again. Their father was sensible about dirt. He ordered a tub of water to be kept permanently outside the basement door, in which they must wash before entering the house:

but none of the other children in the Terrace were allowed to play in the mud at all.

Emily did not play in the mud either; it was only the little ones.

Mr. Thornton was generally at a theatre till the small hours; and when he came home used to sit and write, and then he would go out, about dawn, to the post. The children were often awake in time to hear him going to bed. He drank whiskey while he worked, and that helped him to sleep all the morning (they had to be quiet too). But he got up for luncheon, and then he often had battles with their mother about the food. She would try to make him eat it.

All that spring they were an object of wonder to their acquaintances, as they had been on the steamer; and also an object of pity. In the wide world they had become almost national figures: but it was easier to hide this from them then than it would be nowadays. But people—friends—would often come and tell them about the pirates: what wicked men they were, and how cruelly they had mal-treated them. Boys would generally ask to see Emily's scar. These friends were espe-cially sorry for Rachel and Laura, who, as being the youngest, must have suffered most. They used also to tell them about John's heroism, and that he had died for his coun-try just the same as if he had grown up and become a real soldier: that he had shown himself a true English gentleman, like the knights of old were and the martyrs. They were to grow up to be very proud of John, who though still a child had dared to defy these villains and die rather than allow anything to happen to his sisters.

The glorious deeds which Edward would occasionally confess to were still received with an admiration hardly at all tempered with incredulity. He had the intuition, by now, to make them always done in defiance of Jonsen and his crew, not, as formerly, in alliance with or superseding them.

The children listened to all they were told: and according to their ages believed it. Having as yet little sense of contradiction they blended it quite easily in their minds with their own memories; or sometimes it even cast their memories out. Who were they, children, to know better what had happened to them than grown-ups?

Mrs. Thornton was a feeling, but an essentially Christian woman. The death of John was a blow to her from which she would never recover, as indeed the death of all of them had once been. But she taught the children in saying their prayers to thank God for John's noble end and let it always be an example to them: and then she taught them to ask God to forgive the pirates for all their cruelty to them. (She explained to them that God could only do this when they had been properly punished on Earth.) The only one

who could not understand this at all was
Laura—she was after all rather young. She
used the same form of words as the others,
yet contrived to imagine that she was praying to the pirates, not for them; so that it
gradually came about that whenever God was
mentioned in her hearing the face she imagined for Him was Captain Jonsen's.

Once more a phase of their lives was receding into the past, and crystallising into myth.

Emily was too old to say her prayers aloud,
so no one could know whether she put in
the same phrase as the others about the pirates
or not. No one, in point of fact, knew much
what Emily was thinking about anything, at
that time.

iv

One day a cab came for the whole family,
and they drove together right into London.

The cab took them into the Temple: and then they had to walk through twisting passages and up some stairs.

It was a day of full spring, and the large room into which they were ushered faced south. The windows were tall and heavily draped with curtains. After the gloomy stairs it seemed all sunshine and warmth. There was a big fire blazing, and the furniture was massive and comfortable, the dark carpet so thick it clung to their shoes.

A young man was standing in front of the fire when they came in. He was very correctly, indeed beautifully, dressed; and he was very handsome as well, like a prince. He smiled at them all pleasantly, and came forward and talked like an old friend. The suspicious eyes of the Liddlies soon accepted him as such. He gave their parents cake and wine: and then he insisted on the children being allowed a sip too, with some cake, which was very kind of him. The taste of the wine recalled to all of them that blowy night in Jamaica: they had had none since.

Soon some more people arrived. They were Margaret and Harry, with a small, yellow, fanatical-looking aunt. The two lots of children had not seen each other for a long time: so they only said Hullo to each other very perfunctorily. Mr. Mathias, their host, was just as kind to the new arrivals.

Everyone was at great pains to make the visit appear a casual one; but the children all knew more or less that it was nothing of the sort, that something was presently going to happen. However, they could play-act too. Rachel presently climbed onto Mr. Mathias's knee. They all gathered round the fire, Emily sitting bolt upright on a foot-stool, Edward and Laura side by side in a capacious arm-chair.

In the middle of everyone talking there was a pause, and Mr. Thornton, turning to

Emily, said: "Why don't you tell Mr. Mathias about your adventures?"

"Oh yes!" said Mr. Mathias, "Do tell me all about it.—Let me see, you're . . ."

"Emily," whispered Mr. Thornton.

"Age?"

"Ten."

Mr. Mathias reached for a piece of clean paper and a pen.

"What adventures?" asked Emily clearly.

"Well," said Mr. Mathias, "you started for England on a sailing-ship, didn't you? The *Clorinda?*"

"Yes. She was a barque."

"And then what happened?"

She paused before answering.

"There was a monkey," she said judicially.

"A monkey?"

"And a lot of turtles," put in Rachel.

"Tell him about the pirates," prompted Mrs Thornton. Mr. Mathias frowned at her

>>>>>>>>>>>>>>>>>><<<<<<<<<<<<<<<<
slightly: "Let her tell it in her own words,
please."

"Oh yes," said Emily dully, "We were captured by pirates, of course."

Both Edward and Laura sat up at the word,
stiff as spokes.

"Weren't you with them too, Miss Fernandez?" Mr. Mathias asked.

Miss Fernandez! Everyone turned to see
who he could mean. He was looking at
Margaret.

"Me?" she said suddenly, as if waking up.

"Yes, you! Go on!" said her aunt.

"Say yes," prompted Edward: "You were
with us, weren't you?"

"Yes," said Margaret, smiling.

"Then why couldn't you say so?" hectored
Edward.

Mr. Mathias silently noted this curious
treatment of the eldest: and Mrs. Thornton
told Edward he mustn't speak like that.

"Tell us what you remember about the

>>>>>>>>>>>>>>>>>>>>><<<<<<<<<<<<<<<<<<

capture, will you?" he asked, still of Margaret.

"The what?"

"Of how the pirates captured the *Clorinda.*"

She looked round nervously and laughed, but said nothing.

"The monkey was in the rigging, so they just came on the ship," Rachel volunteered.

"Did they—er—fight with the sailors? Did you see them hit anybody? Or threaten anybody?"

"Yes!" cried Edward, and jumped up from his chair, his eyes wide and inspired: *"Bing! Bang! Bong!"* he declared, thumping the seat at each word; then sat down again.

"They didn't," said Emily, "Don't be silly, Edward."

"Bing, bang, bong," he repeated, with less conviction.

>>>>>>>>>>>>>>>>>>>><<<<<<<<<<<<<<<<<

"*Bung!*" contributed Harry to his support, from under the arm of the fanatical aunt.

"Bim-bam, bim-bam," sing-songed Laura, suddenly waking up and starting a tatoo of her own.

"Shut up!" cried Mr. Thornton. "Did you, or did you not, any of you, see them hit anybody?"

"Cut off their heads!" cried Edward, "And throw them in the sea!—Far, far . . ." his eyes became dreamy and sad.

"They didn't hit anybody," said Emily. "There wasn't anyone to hit."

"Then where were all the sailors?" asked Mr. Mathias.

"They were all up the rigging," said Emily.

"I see," said Mr. Mathias. "Er—didn't you say the monkey was in the rigging?"

"He broke his neck," said Rachel. She wrinkled up her nose disgustedly: "He was drunk."

"His tail was rotted," explained Harry.

"Well," said Mr. Mathias, "when they came on board, what did they do?"

There was a general silence.

"Come come! What did they do?—What did they do, Miss Fernandez?"

"I don't know."

"Emily?"

"*I* don't know."

He sat back in despair: "But you saw them!"

"No we didn't," said Emily, "We went in the deck-house."

"And stayed there?"

"We couldn't open the door."

"*Bang-bang-bang!*" Laura s u d d e n l y rapped out.

"Shut up!"

"And then, when they let you out?"

"We went on the schooner."

"Were you frightened?"

"What of?"

>>>>>>>>>>>>>>>>>>>>><<<<<<<<<<<<<<<<<<<

"Well: them."

"Who?"

"The pirates."

"Why should we?"

"They didn't do anything to frighten you?"

"To *frighten* us?"

"Coo! José did belch!" Edward interjected merrily, and began giving an imitation. Mrs. Thornton chid him.

"Now," said Mr. Mathias gravely, "there's something I want you to tell me, Emily. When you were with the pirates, did they ever do anything you didn't like? You know what I mean, something *nasty?*"

"Yes!" cried Rachel, and everyone turned to her. "He talked about drawers," she said in a shocked voice.

"What did he say?"

"He told us once not to toboggan down the deck on them," put in Emily uncomfortably.

"Was that all?"

"He shouldn't have talked about drawers," said Rachel.

"Don't *you* talk about them, then," cried Edward: "Smarty!"

"Miss Fernandez," said the lawyer diffidently, "have you anything to add to that?"

"What?"

"Well . . . what we are talking about."

She looked from one person to another, but said nothing.

"I don't want to press you for details," he said gently, "but did they ever—well, make suggestions to you?"

Emily fixed her glowing eyes on Margaret, catching hers.

"It's no good questioning Margaret," said the aunt morosely; "but it ought to be perfectly clear to you what has happened."

"Then I am afraid I must," said Mr. Mathias. "Another time, perhaps."

Mrs. Thornton had for some while been frowning and pursing her lips, to stop him.

>>>>>>>>>>>>>>>>>>>><<<<<<<<<<<<<<<<<<

"Another time would be much better," she said: and Mr. Mathias turned the examination back to the capture of the *Clorinda*.

But they seemed to have been strangely unobservant of what went on around them, he found.

v

When the others had all gone, Mathias offered Thornton, whom he liked, a cigar: and the two sat together for a while over the fire.

"Well," said Thornton, "Did the interview go as you had expected?"

"Pretty much."

"I noticed you questioned them chiefly about the *Clorinda*. But you have got all the evidence you need on that score, surely?"

"Naturally I did. Anything they affirmed I could check exactly by Marpole's detailed affidavit. I wanted to test their reliability."

"And you found?"

"What I have always known. That I would rather extract information from the devil himself than from a child."

"But what information exactly do you need?"

"Everything. The whole story."

"You know it."

Mathias spoke with a hint of exasperation:

"Do you realise, Thornton, that without considerable help from them we may even fail to get a conviction?"

"What is the difficulty?" asked Thornton, in a peculiar, restrained tone.

"We could get a conviction for piracy of course. But since '37, piracy has ceased to be a hanging offence unless it is accompanied by murder."

"And is the killing of one small boy insufficient to count as murder?" asked Thornton, in the same cold voice.

Mathias looked at him curiously.

"We are able to guess at the probabilities of what happened," he said. "The boy was undoubtedly taken onto the schooner; and now he can't be found. But, strictly speaking, we have no proof that he is dead."

"He may, of course, have swum across the Gulf of Mexico and landed at New Orleans."

Thornton's cigar, as he finished speaking, snapped in two.

"I know this is . . ." began Mathias with professional gentleness, then had the sense to check himself. "I am afraid there is no doubt which we can personally entertain that the lad is dead: but there is a legal doubt: and where there is a legal doubt a jury might well refuse to convict."

"Unless they were carried away by an attack of common sense."

Mathias paused for a moment before asking:

"And the other children have dropped, as

yet, no hint as to what precisely did happen to him?"

"None."

"Their mother has questioned them?"

"Exhaustively."

"Yet they must surely know."

"It is a great pity," said Thornton, deliberately, "that when the pirates decided to kill the child, they did not invite in his sisters to watch."

Mathias was ready to make allowances. He merely shifted his position and cleared his voice.

"Unless we can get definite evidence of murder, either of your boy or the Dutch captain, I am afraid there is a real danger of these men escaping with their lives: though they would of course be transported.—It's all highly unsatisfactory, Thornton," he went on confidentially. "We do not, as lawyers, like aiming at a conviction for piracy alone. It is too vague. The most eminent jurists have

not even yet decided on a satisfactory definition of piracy. I doubt, now, if they ever
will. One school holds that it is any felony
committed on the High Seas. But that definition does little except render the employment
of a separate term otiose. Moreover, it is not
accepted by other schools of thought."

"To the layman, at least, it would seem to
be a queer sort of piracy to commit suicide
in one's cabin, or to perform an illegal operation on the captain's daughter."

"Well, you see the difficulties. Consequently we always prefer to make use of it
simply as a make-weight with another more
serious charge. Captain Kidd, for instance,
was not, strictly speaking, hanged for piracy.
The first count in his indictment, on which
he was condemned, sets forth that he feloni-
ously, intentionally, and with malice afore-
thought hit his own gunner on the head with
a wooden bucket value eightpence. That is
something definite. What *we* need is some-

thing definite. We have not got it. Take the second case, the piracy of the Dutch steamer. We are in the same difficulty there: a man is taken on board the schooner, he disappears. What happened? We can only surmise."

"Isn't there such a thing as turning King's Evidence?"

"Another most unsatisfactory proceeding, to which I should be very loath to have recourse. No, the natural and proper witnesses are the children. There is a kind of beauty in making them, who have suffered so much at the hands of these men, the instruments of justice upon them."

Mathias paused, and looked at Thornton narrowly.

"You haven't been able, in all these weeks, to get the smallest hint from them with regard to the death of Captain Vandervoort either?"

"None."

"Well, is it your impression that they do truly know nothing, or that they have been terrorised into hiding something?"

Thornton gave a gentle sigh, almost of relief.

"No," he said, "I don't think they have been terrorised. But I do think they may know something they won't tell."

"But, why?"

"Because, during the time they were on the schooner, they plainly got very fond of this man Jonsen, and of his lieutenant, the man called Otto."

Mathias was incredulous.

"Is it possible for children to be mistaken in a man's whole nature like that?"

The look of irony on Thornton's face attained an intensity that was almost diabolical.

"I think it is possible," he said, "even for children to make such a mistake."

"But this . . . affection: it is highly improbable."

"It is a fact."

Mathias shrugged. After all, a criminal lawyer is not concerned with facts, he is concerned with probabilities. It is the novelist who is concerned with facts, whose job it is to say what a particular man did do on a particular occasion: the lawyer does not, cannot be expected to go further than to show what the ordinary man would be most likely to do under presumed circumstances.

Mathias, as he conned these paradoxes, smiled a little grimly. It would never do to give utterance to them.

"I think if they know anything I shall be able to find it out," was all he said.

"D'you mean to put them in the box?" Thornton asked suddenly.

"Not all of them, certainly: Heaven forbid! But we shall have to produce one of them at least, I am afraid."

"Which?"

"Well. We had intended it to be the

Fernandez girl. But she seems . . . unsatisfactory?"

"Exactly." Then Thornton added with a
characteristic forward jerk, "She was sane
enough when she left Jamaica.—Though always a bit of a fool."

"Her aunt tells me she seems to have lost
her memory: or a great part of it. No, if I
call her it will simply be to exhibit her condition."

"Then?"

"I think I will call your Emily."

Thornton stood up.

"Well," he said, "you'll have to settle with
her yourself what she's to say. Write it out,
and make her learn it by heart."

"Certainly," said Mathias, looking at his
finger-nails. "I am not in the habit of going
into court unprepared.—It's bad enough having a child in the box anyway," he went on.

Thornton paused at the door.

"—You can never count on them. They

say what they think you want them to say.
And then they say what they think the oppos-
ing counsel wants them to say too—if they
like his face."

Thornton gesticulated—a foreign habit.

"I think I'll take her to Madame Tussaud's
on Thursday afternoon and try my luck,"
ended Mathias: and the two bade each other
goodbye.

vi

Emily enjoyed the wax-works; even though
she did not know that a wax-work of Captain Jonsen, his scowling face bloody and a
knife in his hand, was already in contem-
plation. She got on well with Mr. Mathias.
She felt very grown-up, going out at last
without the little ones endlessly tagging.
Afterwards he took her to a bun-shop in
Baker Street, and tried to persuade her to

pour out his tea for him: but she turned shy at that, and he had in the end to do it for himself.

Mr. Mathias, like Miss Dawson, spent a good deal of his time and energy in courting the child's liking. He was at least sufficiently successful for it to come as a complete surprise to her, when he presently began to throw out questions about the death of Captain Vandervoort. Their studied casualness did not deceive her for a moment. He learnt nothing: but she was hardly home, and his carriage departed, than she was violently sick. Presumably she had eaten too many cream buns. But, as she lay in bed sipping from a tumbler of water in that mood of fatalism which follows on the heels of vomiting, Emily had a lot to think over, as well as an opportunity of doing so without emotion.

Her father was spending a rare evening at home: and now he stood unseen in the shadows of her bedroom, watching her. To his fantastic mind, the little chit seemed the stage of a great tragedy: and while his bowels of compassion yearned towards the child of his loins, his intellect was delighted at the beautiful, the subtle combination of the contending forces which he read into the situation. He was like a powerless stalled audience, which pities unbearably, but would not on any account have missed the play.

But as he stood now watching her, his sensitive eyes communicated to him an emotion which was not pity and was not delight: he realised, with a sudden painful shock, that he was afraid of her!

But surely it was some trick of the candle-light, or of her indisposition, that gave her face momentarily that inhuman, stony, basilisk look?

Just as he was tiptoe-ing from the room, she burst out into a sudden, despairing moan, and leaning half out of her bed began again an ineffectual, painful retching. Thornton persuaded her to drink off her tumbler of water, and then held her hot moist temples between his hands till at last she sank back, exhausted, in a complete passivity, and slipped off to sleep.

There were several other occasions after this when Mr. Mathias took her out on excursions, or simply came and examined her at the house. But still he learnt nothing.

What was in her mind now? I can no longer read Emily's deeper thoughts, or handle their cords. Henceforth we must be content to surmise.

As for Mathias, there was nothing for it but to accept the defeat at her hands, and then explain it away to himself. He ceased to believe that she had anything to hide, because, if she had, he was convinced she could not have hidden it.

But if she could not give him any information, she remained, spectacularly speaking, a most valuable witness. So, as Thornton had suggested, he set his clerk to copy out in his beautiful hand a sort of Shorter Catechism: and this he gave to Emily and told her to learn it.

She took it home and showed it to her mother, who said Mr. Mathias was quite right, she was to learn it. So Emily pinned it to her looking-glass, and learnt the answers to two new questions every morning. Her mother would hear her these with her other lessons, and badgered her a lot for the sing-song way she repeated them. But how can one speak naturally anything learnt by heart, Emily wondered? It is impossible. And Emily knew this catechism backwards and forwards, inside and out, before the day came.

Once more they drove into town: but this time it was to the Central Criminal Court. The crowd outside was enormous, and Emily was bundled in with the greatest rapidity. The building was impressive, and full of policemen, and the longer she had to wait in the little room where they were shown the more nervous she became. Would she remember her piece, or would she forget it? From time to time echoing voices sounded down the corridors, summoning this person or that. Her Mother stayed with her, but her Father only looked in occasionally, when he would give some news to her Mother in a low tone. Emily had her catechism with her, and read it over and over.

Finally a policeman came, and conducted them into the court.

A criminal court is a very curious place. The seat of a ritual quite as elaborate as any religious one, it lacks in itself any impressiveness or symbolism of architecture. A robed judge in court looks like a catholic Bishop would, if he were to celebrate mass in some municipal bath-house. There is nothing to make one aware that here the Real Presence is: the presence of death.

As Emily came into court, past the many men in black gowns writing with their quill pens, she did not at first see judge, jury, or prisoners. Her eye was caught by the face of the Clerk, where he sat below the bench. It was an old and very beautiful face, cultured, unearthly refined. His head laid back, his mouth slightly open, his eyes closed, he was gently sleeping.

That face remained etched on her mind as she was shown her way into the box. Then the Oath, which formed the opening passages of her catechism, was administered; and with its familiar phrases her nervousness vanished, and with complete confidence she sang out her responses to the familiar questions which Mr. Mathias, in fancy dress, was putting to her. But until he had finished she kept her eyes fixed on the rail in front of her, for fear something should confuse her.

At last, however, Mr. Mathias sat down; and Emily began to look around her. High above the sleeping man sat another, with a face even more refined, but wide awake. His voice, when now he spoke a few words to her, was the kindest she had ever heard. Dressed in his strange disguise, toying with a pretty nosegay, he looked like some benign old wizard who spent his magic in doing good.

Beneath her was the table where so many other wigged men were sitting. One was drawing funny faces: but his own was grave. Two more were whispering together.

Now another man was on his feet. He was shorter than Mr. Mathias, and older, and in no way good-looking or even interesting. He in turn began to ask her questions.

He, Watkin, the defending counsel, was no fool. He had not failed to notice that, among all the questions Mathias had put to her, there had been no reference to the death of Captain Vandervoort. That could only mean either that the child knew nothing of it, itself a valuable lacuna in the evidence to establish, or that what she did know was somehow in his clients' favour. Up till now, he had meant to pursue the obvious tactics—question her on the evidence she had already given, perhaps frighten her, at any rate confuse her and make her contradict herself. But anyone, even a jury, could see through that. Nor was there any hope, under any circumstances, of a total acquittal: the most he could hope for was escape from the murder charge.

He suddenly decided to change his whole policy. When he spoke, his voice too was kind (though it lacked perforce the full benign timbre of the judge's). He would make no attempt to confuse her. By his sympathy with her, he hoped for the sympathy, himself, of the court.

His first few questions were of a general nature: and he continued them until her answers were given with complete confidence.

"Now, my dear young lady," he said at last, "There is just one more question I want to ask you: and please answer it loudly and clearly, so that we can all hear. We have been told about the Dutch steamer, which had the animals on board. Now a very horrible thing has been suggested." His voice grew blandly incredulous: "It has been said that a man was taken off the steamer, the captain of it in fact, onto the schooner, and that he was murdered there. Now what I want to ask you is this. Did you see any such thing happen?"

Those who were watching the self-contained Emily saw her turn very white, and begin to tremble. Suddenly she gave a shriek: then after a second's pause she began to sob. Everyone listened in an icy stillness, their hearts in their mouths. Through her tears they heard, they all heard, the words: ". . . He was all lying in his blood . . . he was awful! He . . . he died, he said something and then he *died!*"

That was all that was articulate. Watkin sat down, thunderstruck. The effect on the court could hardly have been greater. As for Mathias, he did not show surprise: he looked more like a man who has digged a pit into which his enemy has fallen.

The judge leant forward and tried to question her: but she only sobbed and screamed. He tried to soothe her: but by now she had become too hysterical for that. She had already, however, said quite enough for the matter in hand: and they let her father come forward and lift her out of the box.

As he stepped down with her she caught sight for the first time of Jonsen and the crew, huddled up together in a sort of pen. But they were much thinner than the last time she had seen them. The terrible look on Jonsen's face as his eye met hers, what was it that it reminded her of?

≻≻≻≻≻≻≻≻≻≻≻≻≻≻≻≻≺≺≺≺≺≺≺≺≺≺≺≺≺≺≺≺

Her father hurried her home. As soon as she was in the cab she became herself again with a surprising rapidity. She began to talk about all she had seen, just as if it had been a party: the man asleep, and the man drawing funny faces, and the man with the bunch of flowers, and had she said her piece properly?

"Captain was there," she said: "Did you see him?"

"What was it all about?" she asked presently: "Why did I have to learn all those questions?"

Mr. Thornton made no attempt to answer her questions: he even shrank back, physically, from touching his child Emily. His mind reeled with the many possibilities. Was it conceivable she was such an idiot as really not to know what it was all about? Could she possibly not know what she had done? He stole a look at her innocent little face, even the tear-stains now gone. What was he to think?

But as if she read his thoughts, he saw a faint cloud gather.

"What are they going to do to Captain?" she asked, a faint hint of anxiety in her voice.

Still he made no answer. In Emily's head the Captain's face, as she had last seen it . . . what was it she was trying to remember?

Suddenly she burst out:

"Father, *what* did happen to Tabby in the end, that dreadful windy night in Jamaica?"

vii

Trials are quickly over, once they begin. It was no time before the judge had condemned these prisoners to death and was trying someone else with the same concentrated, benevolent, individual attention.

Afterwards, a few of the crew were reprieved and transported.

>>>>>>>>>>>>>>>>>>>>>>>>>><<<<<<<<<<<<<<<<<<<<

The night before the execution, Jonsen managed to cut his throat: but they found out in time to bandage him up. He was unconscious by the morning, and had to be carried to the gallows in a chair: indeed, he was finally hanged in it. Otto bent over once and kissed his forehead; but he was completely insensible.

It was the negro cook, however, according to the account in the Times, who figured most prominently. He showed no fear of death himself, and tried to comfort the others.

"We have all come here to die," he said: "*That*" (pointing to the gallows) "was not built for nothing. We shall certainly end our lives in this place: nothing can now save us. But in a few years we should die in any case. In a few years the judge who condemned us, all men now living, will be dead. *You* know that I die innocent: anything I

＞＞＞＞＞＞＞＞＞＞＞＞＞＞＞＞＜＜＜＜＜＜＜＜＜＜＜＜＜＜＜＜

have done, I was forced to do by the rest of you. But I am not sorry. I would rather die now, innocent, than in a few years perhaps guilty of some great crime."

viii

It was a few days later that the term began, and Mr. and Mrs. Thornton took Emily to her new school at Blackheath. While they remained to tea with the head mistress, Emily was introduced to her new playmates.

"Poor little thing," said the mistress, "I hope she will soon forget the terrible things she has been through. I think our girls will have an especially kind corner in their hearts for her."

In another room, Emily with the other new girls was making friends with the older pupils. Looking at that gentle, happy throng of clean innocent faces and soft graceful limbs, listening to the ceaseless, artless babble of chatter rising, perhaps God could have picked out from among them which was Emily: but I am sure that I could not.

For your reading pleasure ...

P.O. Box 393 • Peconic • N.Y. 11958
(516) 734-5650   **Fax (516) 298-1790**

The Complete
Out-Of-Print Book Service

We are an international book search service serving libraries, collectors and book lovers throughout the world.

We would be happy to help you locate that out-of-print title you've been looking for.

Send us your complete want list. We can usually locate a title within two days. At that point, we will notify you and give you a detailed description of the book, and the price. With your approval, and receipt of your check, we will reserve the title and forward it on to you.

1991

WRITING COMPILERS AND INTERPRETERS

An Applied Approach

Ronald Mak

WILEY

John Wiley & Sons, Inc.

New York • Chichester • Brisbane • Toronto • Singapore

To my parents, teachers, students, coworkers, and friends.
I have learned from you all.

In recognition of the importance of preserving what has been written, it is a policy of John Wiley & Sons, Inc. to have books of enduring value published in the United States printed on acid-free paper, and we exert our best efforts to that end.

Library of Congress Cataloging-in-Publication Data

Mak, Ronald, 1953-
    Writing compilers and interpreters : an applied approach / Ronald Mak.
      p. cm.
    Includes index.
    ISBN 0-471-50968-X
    1. Compilers (Computer programs) 2. Interpreters (Computer
programs) 3. IBM Personal Computer—Programming. 4. Pascal
(Computer program language) I. Title.
QA76.76.C65M35 1991
005.4'53—dc20   90-48155

Printed in the United States of America
91 92 10 9 8 7 6 5 4 3 2 1

Preface

This book teaches you how to write compilers and interpreters by *doing*. In this book, we will write a working Pascal interpreter, an interactive symbolic debugger, and a compiler that generates code for a real computer, the 8086 processor of the IBM PC. Along the way, we will also write a set of useful utility programs.

I wrote this book for the practicing programmer who needs to learn how to write a compiler or interpreter but who does not want to study a more traditional theoretical textbook. Whether you are a professional programmer who needs to write a compiler at work, or a personal programmer who wants to write an interpreter for an experimental language you've developed, this book will quickly show you what you need to know.

If you are taking a computer science course on compiler writing, you will also find that this book is a good laboratory text. The programs are all examples of how to apply the theory, and you can make numerous exercises and projects out of improving them.

A skills approach

Writing a compiler or an interpreter is not a simple task. I believe the best way to learn how to do it is to learn the necessary skills first. You can best learn these skills by using them in working programs. This theme runs throughout all the chapters. Each chapter teaches a set of skills, and in the first eight chapters, you see how these skills can be applied in practical utility programs. These programs include a program lister, a source file compactor, a cross-reference generator, an interactive calculator, a syntax checker, and a pretty-printer.

Each chapter's programs also build upon the ones in the previous chapters. When we finally complete our interpreter in Chapter 10, we will have utilized parts from all the programs that came before it. The interactive debugger in Chapter 11 is built on top of the interpreter. The compiler that we complete in Chapter 14 is the culmination of all the previous chapters' skills and programs. The program chart in Figure P-1 shows how the programs are related. This approach enables you to see an interpreter and a compiler evolve in stages. If you study the utility programs in each chapter, you can be certain of your understanding of the skills at each stage before you move on to the next stage.

By design, this book teaches you essentially one way to write a compiler or an interpreter. The techniques that you will see will not always be the best or most efficient ones, just ones that do the job and are easy to learn and understand. I hope that you will be inspired to study more advanced texts and replace some of the routines with better ones. We'll write the code in a modular fashion to make it easier to do just that.

Why learn how to write compilers and interpreters?

As a competent programmer, you can no longer afford not to know something about writing compilers and interpreters. Today's computing environment places strong emphasis on "user-friendly" software. The languages we use to communicate with the computer play a major role in determining just how friendly software is.

After a period of relative inactivity, a revolution is beginning in software science. Recently, we have seen the development of new third generation programming languages such as C++, Modula 2, and Ada. The new object-oriented programming paradigm promises to be as important today for improving programmer productivity as was structured programming yesterday.

Even "non-programmer" developers of applications software have seen advances. So-called fourth generation, or specification, languages enable developers to specify *what* to do, and the software is responsible for deciding *how* to do it. People who have never considered themselves programmers in the traditional sense are now developing sophisticated applications using HyperCard software on the Apple Macintosh, which includes a language called HyperTalk for writing scripts.

As users become more sophisticated, they demand systems with greater flexibility. They are less willing to accept preset, unmodifiable parameters or behavior. One way to satisfy these users is to offer systems that are extensible. This can be achieved with a programming language. A prime example is the use of the PostScript language to program laser printers and control graphical displays.

If you wish to keep abreast of these software advances, you must understand the workings of the language compilers and interpreters. If you wish to make new advances yourself, you must also be able to write your own compilers and interpreters. I hope this book helps.

Organization

This book is organized into three parts. The first part teaches you the basic skills of reading a source program and producing a listing, decomposing the program into tokens (scanning), and analyzing the program based on its syntax (parsing).

FIGURE P-1   The Program Chart.

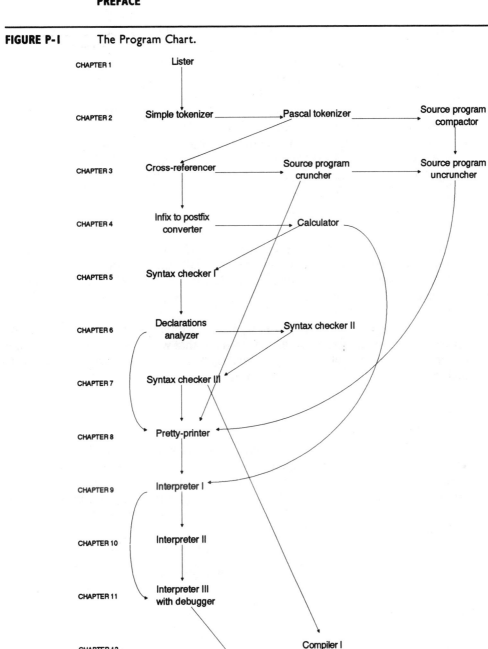

By the second part of the book, you will have built up a sufficient repertoire of skills to write a Pascal interpreter. But we won't stop with merely executing a program. We'll add a symbolic debugger with an interactive command language that allows you to set breakpoints and watchpoints, single-step and trace the flow of the program, and print and modify the values of variables.

In the third part of the book, we'll write a compiler that will translate a Pascal source program into an equivalent 8086 assembly language object program. You will then be able to assemble the compiler's output and run it on an IBM PC-compatible computer. In the very last chapter, we will take a brief look at some advanced concepts that are beyond the scope of this book.

Prerequisites

I assume that you can already program well in C, and that you understand concepts like recursion and data structures, especially stacks, pointers, linked lists, and binary trees. A reading knowledge of Pascal is helpful. You should also have some experience writing and managing large programs consisting of several modules.

We will write all our programs in C, a language that is becoming the standard for writing such systems software. The language that we will interpret and compile is Pascal, a popular language with a relatively simple syntax but which nevertheless contains many important features.

System requirements

All of the C programs in this book were developed with Microsoft's Quick C and Borland's Turbo C development environments. The assembly language programs generated by the compiler can be assembled by Microsoft's Quick Assembler or by Borland's Turbo Assembler. Both the C and assembly language programs can be run on an IBM PC-compatible machine. The C programs should also run with few if any changes on most UNIX systems.

The Pascal source language is acceptable by Microsoft's Quick Pascal compiler and by Borland's Turbo Pascal compiler.

The software disk

You can purchase a high-density 5–1/4 inch floppy disk containing all the programs in this book in source form. Please send a check or money order for $25 plus $2 for shipping and handling (California residents please add your local sales tax) to:

Apropos Logic
4899 Bela Drive
San Jose, CA 95129

Acknowledgments

Bill Gladstone first got me going on this book, and then my editors at Wiley, including Ellen Greenberg, Katherine Schowalter, and Laura Lewin, kept me on track. The technical reviewer my editors provided did an excellent job. The improvements from the first to the second draft are mostly due to his suggestions. Joyce Jackson supervised the final layout.

Several people knew that I was writing a book. My neighbors always asked about it whenever we saw each other. My coworkers often knew it was better not to ask when I wandered the halls in a daze. I hope my friends forgive me for being always too busy.

Special thanks to my good friend who is an excellent cook, house painter, plumber, electrician, and computer repairman. He helped me find more time for writing by pulling me through two house remodelings.

Final thanks go to Freundin, who made sure her master went for a walk every evening, and who was nice to him even though he didn't pay quite enough attention to her.

A final word on bugs

I always got upset whenever I bought a computer book and found bugs in the programs. How can the author do such shoddy work, I would ask myself.

Well, now that I have written a book myself under a tight schedule, I know how that happens. The compiler and the interpreter in this book are complex programs. The ones that I have worked on professionally went through extensive quality assurance testing. Unfortunately, the programs in this book were not tested nearly so thoroughly.

So, the question is not whether there are any bugs left, or even how many. I only hope that they aren't too embarrassing. I apologize in advance for them.

If you find a bug, or if you have a suggestion for an improvement, please write to me.

Contents

PART I

Scanning and Parsing

CHAPTER I

Introduction

1.1 What are compilers and interpreters?

MISSING SEMICOLON. SYNTAX ERROR.

Well, so much for respect for your latest programming masterpiece! We programmers swear and curse at compilers more than just about any other systems software. Yet, they enable us to concentrate more on our algorithms than on the intricacies of machine language. And, as we are often reminded, compilers meticulously check our programs for syntactic correctness.

The main purpose of a compiler and of its close cousin, the interpreter, is to translate a program written in a high-level programming language like Pascal into a form that a computer can understand in order to execute the program. In the context of this translation, the high-level language is the *source language*.

A compiler translates a program written in a high-level language into a low-level language, which can be the assembly language or even the machine language of a particular computer. In the context of this translation, the low-level language is the *object language*. The program that you write in the high-level language is called the *source program*. Its translated version is the *object program*.

Once created, an object program is a separate program in its own right. If it is in machine language, it must be loaded into the computer's memory and then executed. If it is in assembly language, it must first be translated by an assembler to machine language, and then loaded and executed.

On the other hand, an interpreter does not produce an object program. It may translate the source program into an internal intermediate form that it can execute, or it may simply execute the source language statements directly. The net result is that an interpreter translates a program into the actions that the program describes.

1.1.1   Differences between compilers and interpreters

What an interpreter does with a source program is very similar to what you would do if you had to figure it out without a computer. Suppose that you are handed a Pascal program. You first look it over to check for syntax errors. Then, you locate the start of the main program, and you start to execute the statements one at a time by hand. You have a pencil and a scratch pad by your side to keep track of the values of the variables. For example, if you encounter the statement

```
i := j + k
```

you look up the current values of j and k on your scratch pad, add the values, and write down the sum as the new value for i.

An interpreter essentially does what you just did. It is a program that runs on the computer. A Pascal interpreter reads in a Pascal source program, checks it for syntax errors, and executes the source statements one at a time. Using some of its own variables as a scratch pad, the interpreter keeps track of the values of the source program's variables.

A compiler is also a program that runs on the computer. A Pascal compiler reads in a Pascal source program and checks it for syntax errors. But then, instead of executing the source program, it translates the source program into the object program. For example, if a compiler generates an assembly language object program, it translates the same statement into the following assembly statements:

```
mov ax,WORD PTR j
add ax,WORD PTR k
mov WORD PTR i,ax
```

(Of course, if it generates a machine language object program, the output is even more cryptic!)

1.1.2 Advantages and disadvantages of compilers and interpreters

Which is easier to use, a compiler or an interpreter? To execute a source program with an interpreter, you simply feed the source program into the interpreter, and the interpreter takes over to check and execute the program. A compiler, however, checks the source program and then produces an object program. After running the compiler, you need to load the object program into memory in order to execute it. If the compiler generates an assembly language object program, you also must first run an assembler. So, an interpreter definitely has advantages over a compiler when it comes to the effort required to execute a source program.

An interpreter is also more versatile than a compiler. Remember that they are themselves programs, and like any other programs, they can run on different computers. A Pascal interpreter can run on both an IBM PC and an Apple Macintosh and it will execute Pascal source programs on either computer. A compiler, however, generates object programs for a particular computer. Therefore, if you make a Pascal compiler for the PC to run on the Macintosh, it still generates object programs in the assembly language or the machine language of the PC.

What happens if the source program contains a logic error that does not show up until run time, such as an attempt to divide by a variable whose value is zero? Since an interpreter is in control when it is executing a source program, it can stop and indicate the line number of the offending statement and the name of the variable. It can even prompt you for some corrective action (like changing the value of the variable) before resuming execution. The object program generated by a compiler, on the other hand, usually runs by itself. Information from the source program, such as line numbers and names of variables, might not be in the object program. When a runtime error occurs, the program may simply abort, and perhaps print a message containing the address of the offending instruction. It is then up to you to figure out what source statement that address corresponds to, and what variable has the wrong value.

When it comes to debugging, an interpreter is generally the way to go. However, some modern program-development environments now give compilers debugging capabilities almost as good as those of interpreters. You can compile a program and then run it under the control of the environment. If a runtime error occurs, you are given the information and control you need to correct the error. Then, you can either resume the execution of the program, or compile and run it again. Such compilers, though, usually generate extra information or instructions in the object program to keep the environment informed of the current state of the program's execution. This may cause the compiler to generate less efficient code than it otherwise would.

The most important concern may be how *fast* a source program executes. As we saw, an interpreter executes the statements of the source program pretty much the way you would by hand. Each time it executes a statement, it looks it over to figure out what operations the statement says to do. With a compiler, the computer executes a machine language program, either generated directly by the compiler or indirectly via an assembler. Since a computer directly executes a machine language program at top speed, such a program can run ten to 100 times faster than the interpreted source program. A compiler is definitely the winner when it comes to speed. This is certainly true with an optimizing compiler that knows how to generate especially efficient code.

So, we see that compilers and interpreters have advantages and disadvantages. It depends on what aspects of program development and execution we consider. A compromise may be to have both a compiler and an interpreter for the same source language. Then we have the best of both worlds, easy development and fast execution.

That is the ultimate goal of this book. By the time you finish, you will have written a Pascal interpreter with interactive debugging facilities, and a Pascal compiler that generates assembly language object programs.

1.2 Writing compilers and interpreters

Until recently, only the most advanced systems programmers were privy to the arcane art of writing compilers and interpreters. That was part of the mystique of being considered the Grand Guru of the programming department.

That no longer needs to be so! Even though writing a compiler or an interpreter is a complex task, we can tackle it if we start by learning the individual concepts. The best way to learn a concept is to apply it in a program, and once we understand it well, that concept becomes a skill we can use in other programs. That will be our approach: we'll acquire the necessary skills to write compilers and interpreters by writing programs.

Compiler and interpreter concepts deal with operations on source programs. Many of these operations are actually quite useful in their own right. We will write programs that perform these useful operations, so not only will we acquire skills, but we'll also end up with a good set of source program utilities.

1.2.1 The parts of a compiler and an interpreter

To see what we're getting ourselves into, we will first take a high-level overview of what compilers and interpreters are made of. In later chapters, we'll examine these parts in much greater detail. Figure 1-1 shows the parts of a compiler, and Figure 1-2 shows the parts of an interpreter.

The brain of a compiler is its *parser*. The parser knows the *syntax* of the source language, or the "grammar rules" that determine how the source statements are written. Armed with such knowledge, the parser controls the compilation process.

Whenever the parser needs more of the source program to work on, it calls upon the *scanner*. The scanner reads in the source program and breaks it apart into a sequence of *tokens*—numbers, identifiers, operators, etc. It hands them one at a time to the parser whenever the parser calls for the next one.

The parser also knows the *semantics* of the source language. The semantics of a language determine the meaning of its expressions and statements. For example, Pascal's syntax tells us that i + j is a correct way to write an expression. Its semantics tell us that the values of i and j should be added together to obtain a new value.

The parser's knowledge of the source language's syntax allows it to know whenever it has obtained enough tokens from the scanner to form a syntactic entity, such as an expression. Its knowledge of the language's semantics enables it to then call the *code generator* to produce object code that performs the op-

FIGURE I-I   The parts of a compiler.

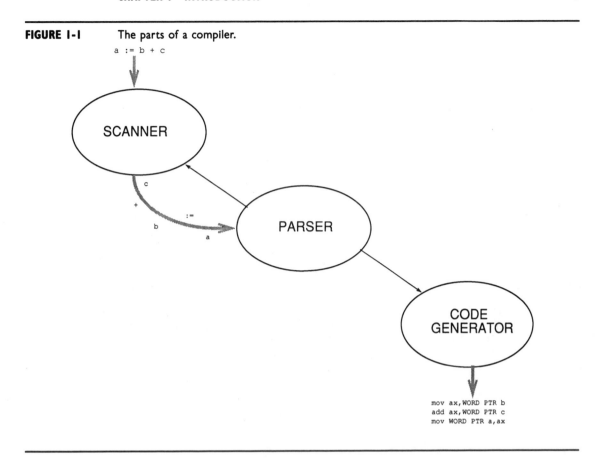

erations specified by the expression. This continues until the entire source program has been read in. The result is an equivalent object program.

An interpreter also has a parser that controls it. Its scanner does the same job as the one in a compiler. However, an interpreter has an *executor* instead of a code generator. For every syntactic entity, the parser calls upon the executor to perform the operations specified by the semantics of the entity. Whenever the source program loops, the parser goes back in the program and reprocesses the statements in the loop. If the program calls a procedure, the parser goes off to process the statements in that procedure until it returns. This continues until the entire program is finished.

In this book, we will write an interpreter and then a compiler. We will develop these programs incrementally—the utility programs in each chapter build upon the ones in previous chapters. In the first part of the book, we will concentrate on the parser and the scanner, which are common to both compilers and interpreters. The first task is one of the scanner: generating a program listing.

FIGURE I-2   The parts of an interpreter.

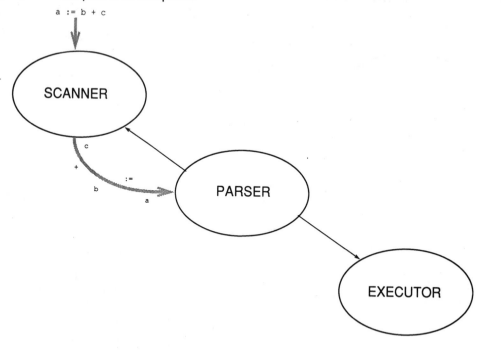

1.3 The program listing

In the rest of this chapter, we will write our first utility program. In doing so, we will develop the following skills:

- open a source file named in the command line
- read the file one line at a time into a source buffer
- print lines with line numbers and page headers

The scanner's main role is to hand tokens over to the parser. Since it reads in the source program, it can also print it out. The printed version is called a *program listing*.

A program listing contains each line of the source program printed on a separate line. Each printed line usually begins with a line number. Each page can have a page header that contains the page number, the name of the source file, and the current date and time.

1.4 Program 1-1: A Source Program Lister

Our first utility program does the scanner's job of listing the source file. Shown in Figure 1-3, this program is also the framework upon which we will build the rest of the scanner in the next chapter.

FIGURE 1-3   A source program lister.

```
/**************************************************************/
/*                                                          */
/*      Program 1-1:  Source File Lister                    */
/*                                                          */
/*      Print the contents of a source file                 */
/*      with line numbers and page headings.                */
/*                                                          */
/*      FILE:       list.c                                  */
/*                                                          */
/*      USAGE:      list sourcefile                         */
/*                                                          */
/*          sourcefile      name of source file to list     */
/*                                                          */
/**************************************************************/

#include <stdio.h>
#include <sys/types.h>
#include <sys/timeb.h>

#define FORM_FEED_CHAR          '\f'

#define MAX_FILE_NAME_LENGTH    32
#define MAX_SOURCE_LINE_LENGTH  256
#define MAX_PRINT_LINE_LENGTH   80
#define MAX_LINES_PER_PAGE      50
#define DATE_STRING_LENGTH      26

typedef enum {
    FALSE, TRUE,
} BOOLEAN;

/*------------------------------------------------*/
/* Globals                                        */
/*------------------------------------------------*/

int line_number = 0;                /* current line number */
int page_number = 0;                /* current page number */
int level       = 0;                /* current nesting level */
int line_count  = MAX_LINES_PER_PAGE;  /* no. lines on current pg */

char source_buffer[MAX_SOURCE_LINE_LENGTH]; /* source file buffer */

char source_name[MAX_FILE_NAME_LENGTH]; /* name of source file */
char date[DATE_STRING_LENGTH];          /* current date and time */

FILE *source_file;

/*------------------------------------------------*/
/* main             Contains the main loop that drives */
/*                  the lister.                   */
/*------------------------------------------------*/

main(argc, argv)
```

```
int argc;
char *argv[];

{
    BOOLEAN get_source_line();

    init_lister(argv[1]);

    /*
    -- Repeatedly call get_source_line to read and print
    -- the next source line until the end of file.
    */
    while (get_source_line());
}

/*------------------------------------------------------------*/
/* init_lister          Initialize the lister globals.     */
/*------------------------------------------------------------*/

init_lister(name)

    char *name;                 /* name of source file */

{
    time_t timer;

    /*
    -- Copy the source file name and open the source file.
    */
    strcpy(source_name, name);
    source_file = fopen(source_name, "r");

    /*
    -- Set the current date and time in the date string.
    */
    time(&timer);
    strcpy(date, asctime(localtime(&timer)));
}

/*------------------------------------------------------------*/
/* get_source_line      Read the next line from the source  */
/*                      file.  If there was one, print it out */
/*                      and return TRUE.  Else at end of file, */
/*                      so return FALSE.                    */
/*------------------------------------------------------------*/

    BOOLEAN
get_source_line()

{
    char print_buffer[MAX_SOURCE_LINE_LENGTH + 9];

    if ((fgets(source_buffer, MAX_SOURCE_LINE_LENGTH,
```

```
                            source_file)) != NULL) {          line_count = 1;
        ++line_number;                                   };

        sprintf(print_buffer, "%4d %d: %s",              if (strlen(line) > MAX_PRINT_LINE_LENGTH)
                    line_number, level, source_buffer);       save_chp = &line[MAX_PRINT_LINE_LENGTH];
        print_line(print_buffer);
                                                         if (save_chp) {
        return(TRUE);                                        save_ch  = *save_chp;
    }                                                        *save_chp = '\0';
    else return(FALSE);                                  }
}
                                                         printf("%s", line);
/*----------------------------------------------*/
/* print_line        Print out a line.  Start a new page if */   if (save_chp) *save_chp = save_ch;
/*                   the current page is full.            */
/*----------------------------------------------*/        }

print_line(line)                                         /*----------------------------------------------------------*/
                                                         /* print_page_header   Print the page header at the top of   */
    char line[];        /* line to be printed */         /*                     the next page.                       */
                                                         /*----------------------------------------------------------*/
{
    char save_ch;                                        print_page_header()
    char *save_chp = NULL;
                                                         {
    if (++line_count > MAX_LINES_PER_PAGE) {                 putchar(FORM_FEED_CHAR);
        print_page_header();                                printf("Page %d   %s   %s\n\n", ++page_number, source_name, date);
                                                         }
```

The basic idea is to read each line from the source file into the buffer named source_buffer and then to print each line to the standard output file. We want each source line to be numbered and each page to have a header. Figure 1-4 shows a sample listing with these features.

FIGURE 1-4   A sample source program listing.

```
Page 1   newton.pas   Mon Jul 09 01:51:57 1990        18 0:      ELSE IF number < 0 THEN BEGIN
                                                      19 0:          writeln('*** ERROR:  number < 0');
 1 0: PROGRAM newton (input, output);                 20 0:      END
 2 0:                                                 21 0:      ELSE BEGIN
 3 0: CONST                                           22 0:          sqroot := sqrt(number);
 4 0:     epsilon = 1e-6;                             23 0:          writeln(number:12:6, sqroot:12:6);
 5 0:                                                 24 0:          writeln;
 6 0: VAR                                             25 0:
 7 0:     number, root, sqroot : real;                26 0:          root := 1;
 8 0:                                                 27 0:          REPEAT
 9 0: BEGIN                                           28 0:              root := (number/root + root)/2;
10 0:     REPEAT                                      29 0:              writeln(root:24:6,
11 0:         writeln;                                30 0:                      100*abs(root - sqroot)/sqroot:12:2,
12 0:         write('Enter new number (0 to quit): ');31 0:                      '%')
13 0:         read(number);                           32 0:          UNTIL abs(number/sqr(root) - 1) < epsilon;
14 0:                                                 33 0:      END
15 0:         IF number = 0 THEN BEGIN                34 0:  UNTIL number = 0
16 0:             writeln(number:12:6, 0.0:12:6);     35 0: END.
17 0:         END
```

The lister utility requires that the name of the source file be in the command line when it is run. In the main routine, we fetch this name as argv[1] and pass it to function init_lister. There, we copy the name into variable source_name, open the source file source_file, and set the date and time string.

In the main routine's while loop, we call boolean function get_source_line repeatedly to read and print source lines. That function returns TRUE if it successfully read and printed a line. If it reached the end of the source file instead, it returns FALSE.

In function get_source_line, we call fgets to fill source_buffer with the contents of the next source line. Variable line_number keeps track of the line number. Variable level is zero for now and the next few chapters. In later chapters, its value will be the current nesting level. We call sprintf to print the source line, along with its line number and level, into print_buffer. We then ship print_buffer off to function print_line to print it.

In function print_line, variable line_count keeps track of how many lines have been printed on the current page. If the number of lines exceeds MAX_LINES_PER_PAGE, we call function print_page_header to skip to the top of the next page and print a page header. In any case, we make sure that the current line will fit on one printed line. If the line is too long, we truncate it before printing it, and then restore it to its original length.

Note the difference between variables line_number and line_count. We initialize line_number to zero and increment it by one for each source line. Its final value is the total number of source lines. line_count counts the number of lines on the current page. We reset it to one for each new page. Initializing it to MAX_LINES_PER_PAGE is a clever trick to force the very first source line to trigger a new page and page header.

Questions and exercises

1. A compiler translates a source program into an equivalent object program. How can we determine that two programs written in two different languages are equivalent for all possible input? Does this uncertainty about compilers make interpreters more desirable?

2. A *cross compiler* runs on one computer but generates object programs written in the machine or assembly language of another computer. How can this be useful?

3. Explain the statement: A computer is an interpreter for its machine language.

4. Modify the lister utility to wrap a long line to the next line instead of truncating it.

CHAPTER 2

Scanning

Now that we've taken care of the scanner's task of producing a source program listing, we can tackle its main business: scanning. In this chapter, we will write a complete scanner to serve us, with only a few changes, throughout the rest of this book.

In order to better understand what a scanner does and how it works, we will write a utility program that uses the scanner. It reads in a Pascal program and then lists the words, numbers, strings, and special symbols that are in the program. Then, to further show how a scanner can be used, we will write another utility program that compacts a source program. In this chapter, we will develop the following skills:

- scan words, numbers, strings, and special characters
- determine the value of a number
- recognize reserved words

We will also begin to organize our code into separate modules. This will make writing the compiler and the interpreter, which are large and complex programs, much more manageable.

2.1 How to scan for tokens

Scanning is going through and breaking up the text of a program into its language components, such as words, numbers, and special symbols. These components are called *tokens*. For example, you can scan the following sentence:

They cried, "54-40 or fight!"

to obtain the following tokens:

word:	They
word:	cried
comma:	,
quotation mark:	"
number:	54
hyphen:	-
number:	40
word:	or
word:	fight
exclamation mark:	!
quotation mark:	"

Now how do you manage to do that? You visually scan the characters of the sentence from left to right. As soon as you have seen enough characters to make up a token, you mentally extract it from the sentence. You begin to recognize the type of token by its first character: If it's a letter, you have a word, and if it's a digit, you have a number. If it is any other character, you have a special symbol. Each time you have extracted a token, you resume scanning the sentence from where you last left off.

The scanner that we'll write will work just like that. To see what is happening in greater detail, we begin with three simple tokens: word, number, and period. A word is made of letters, and a number is made of digits. Suppose you read the following line into the character array source_buffer:

Add 12 and 34.

You want to extract each token in turn from source_buffer and place its characters into the empty character array token_string. This is shown in Figure 2-1.

At the start of a word token, you fetch its first letter and each subsequent letter from source_buffer. You append each letter to the contents of token_string. As soon as you fetch a character that is not a letter, you stop. All the letters in token_string make up the word token.

Similarly, at the start of a number token, you fetch its first digit and each subsequent digit from source_buffer. You append each digit to the contents of token_string. As soon as you fetch a character that is not a digit, you stop. All the digits in token_string make up the number token.

If you have a period, you fetch that character and place it into token_string. You must then fetch the next character.

Once you are done extracting a token, you have the first character after the token. (That is why you fetched the character after a period.) This character tells you that you have finished extracting the token. If the character is a blank, you

FIGURE 2-1   Extracting tokens from source_buffer and placing them into token_string.

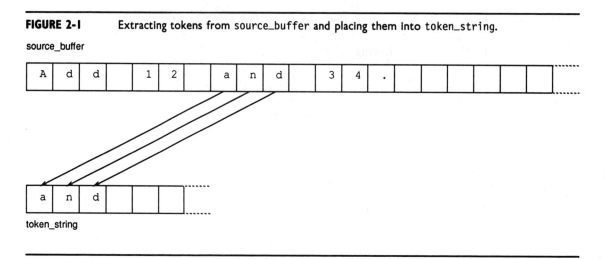

skip it and any subsequent blanks until you are looking again at a nonblank character. This character is the start of the next token.

You extract this next token the same way you extracted the previous one. This process continues until all the tokens have been extracted from the source buffer. Between extracting tokens, you must reset token_string to the empty string to prepare it for the next token.

Let's work this out with the sample input line. Variable bufferp points to a character in source_buffer. Variable ch is the character pointed to by bufferp, that is, ch has the value of *bufferp. You begin with the first nonblank character in the buffer. Since it is the letter A, you extract a word token:

```
source_buffer:  Add 12 and 34.
      bufferp:  ^
           ch:  A
 token_string:  A

source_buffer:  Add 12 and 34.
      bufferp:    ^
           ch:  d
 token_string:  Ad

source_buffer:  Add 12 and 34.
      bufferp:     ^
           ch:  d
 token_string:  Add

source_buffer:  Add 12 and 34.
      bufferp:       ^
           ch:
```

When `bufferp` points to a character that is not a letter, you are done extracting the word token Add. You can now print it out or otherwise process it. Afterwards, you can clear `token_string` and skip `bufferp` up to the next nonblank character. Since that character is the digit 1, you extract a number token:

```
  source_buffer:  Add 12 and 34.
        bufferp:           ^
             ch:  1
   token_string:  1


  source_buffer:  Add 12 and 34.
        bufferp:            ^
             ch:  2
   token_string:  12


  source_buffer:  Add 12 and 34.
        bufferp:             ^
             ch:
```

When `bufferp` points to a character that is not a digit, you are done extracting the number token 12. You can clear `token_string` and skip `bufferp` up to the next nonblank character.

You continue to extract the word token and and the number token 34. Now, `bufferp` points to the period:

```
  source_buffer:  Add 12 and 34.
        bufferp:               ^
             ch:  .
```

Since `ch` is not a blank, no skipping is necessary. Extracting the period token leaves us with the following:

```
   token_string:  .

  source_buffer:  Add 12 and 34.❖
        bufferp:                 ^
             ch:  ❖
```

Here, `bufferp` points to the character after the period which for now, we will represent with ❖.

Following are the basic steps to scanning:

1. Skip any blanks up to the next nonblank character. This character is the first character of the token to extract, and it indicates the token type.

2. Fetch characters of the token up to a character that does not belong. You are done extracting that token.

3. Now you have the first character after the token. Process the token you have just extracted. Then repeat these steps to extract the next token.

2.2 Program 2-1: A Simple Tokenizer

A scanner for Pascal source programs must, of course, recognize Pascal tokens. The Pascal language contains several types of tokens: identifiers, reserved words, numbers, strings, and special symbols. Our first utility program is a simple tokenizer that reads a source file and lists the tokens that it finds. The first version recognizes only words, numbers, and the period, but it provides the foundation upon which we will build the full Pascal scanner in the second version of the tokenizer.

A Pascal word token is made up of a letter followed by any number of letters and digits (including zero). For now, we restrict a number token to a Pascal unsigned integer, which is one or more consecutive digits. (We'll handle signs, decimal points, fractions, and exponents later.) And, we use the rule that an input file must have a period as its last token.

The tokenizer prints its output in the source listing. For example, the following input lines:

```
The sum of 123
and 456 is 579.
```

produce the following listing:

```
1 0: The sum of 123
   >> <WORD>          The
   >> <WORD>          sum
   >> <WORD>          of
   >> <NUMBER>        123
2 0: and 456 is 579.
   >> <WORD>          and
   >> <NUMBER>        456
   >> <WORD>          is
   >> <NUMBER>        579
   >> <PERIOD>        .
```

What is not immediately obvious from the example is that we are not just printing the digits that make up each number, but the number's value. Thus, the simple tokenizer needs to know how to calculate integer values.

As shown in Figure 2-2, the simple tokenizer borrows code from the source program lister in Chapter 1 to initialize itself and to read and print the source file. The other functions make up the rudimentary scanner.

FIGURE 2-2   A simple tokenizer.

```
/*****************************************************************/
/*                                                             */
/*      Program 2-1:  Simple Tokenizer                         */
/*                                                             */
/*      Recognize words, small integers, and the period.       */
/*                                                             */
/*      FILE:        token1.c                                  */
/*                                                             */
/*      USAGE:       token1 sourcefile                         */
/*                                                             */
/*          sourcefile      name of source file to tokenize    */
/*                                                             */
/*****************************************************************/

#include <stdio.h>
#include <math.h>
#include <sys/types.h>
#include <sys/timeb.h>


#define FORM_FEED_CHAR          '\f'
#define EOF_CHAR                '\x7f'

#define MAX_FILE_NAME_LENGTH    32
#define MAX_SOURCE_LINE_LENGTH  256
#define MAX_PRINT_LINE_LENGTH   80
#define MAX_LINES_PER_PAGE      50
#define DATE_STRING_LENGTH      26
#define MAX_TOKEN_STRING_LENGTH MAX_SOURCE_LINE_LENGTH
#define MAX_CODE_BUFFER_SIZE    4096

#define MAX_INTEGER             32767
#define MAX_DIGIT_COUNT         20

typedef enum {
    FALSE, TRUE,
} BOOLEAN;

/*------------------------------------------------------------*/
/*  Character codes                                          */
/*------------------------------------------------------------*/

typedef enum {
    LETTER, DIGIT, SPECIAL, EOF_CODE,
} CHAR_CODE;

/*------------------------------------------------------------*/
/*  Token codes                                              */
/*------------------------------------------------------------*/

typedef enum {
    NO_TOKEN, WORD, NUMBER, PERIOD,
    END_OF_FILE, ERROR,
} TOKEN_CODE;

/*------------------------------------------------------------*/
/*  Token name strings                                       */
/*------------------------------------------------------------*/
```

```
char *symbol_strings[] = {
    "<no token>", "<WORD>", "<NUMBER>", "<PERIOD>",
    "<END OF FILE>", "<ERROR>",
};

/*------------------------------------------------------------*/
/*  Literal structure                                        */
/*------------------------------------------------------------*/

typedef enum {
    INTEGER_LIT, STRING_LIT,
} LITERAL_TYPE;

typedef struct {
    LITERAL_TYPE type;
    union {
        int  integer;
        char string[MAX_SOURCE_LINE_LENGTH];
    } value;
} LITERAL;

/*------------------------------------------------------------*/
/*  Globals                                                  */
/*------------------------------------------------------------*/

char        ch;             /* current input character */
TOKEN_CODE  token;          /* code of current token */
LITERAL     literal;        /* value of literal */
int         buffer_offset;  /* char offset into source buffer */
int         level = 0;      /* current nesting level */
int         line_number = 0; /* current line number */

char source_buffer[MAX_SOURCE_LINE_LENGTH]; /* source file buffer */
char token_string[MAX_TOKEN_STRING_LENGTH]; /* token string */
char *bufferp = source_buffer;         /* source buffer ptr */
char *tokenp  = token_string;          /* token string ptr */

int     digit_count;        /* total no. of digits in number */
BOOLEAN count_error;        /* too many digits in number? */

int page_number = 0;
int line_count  = MAX_LINES_PER_PAGE;  /* no. lines on current pg */

char source_name[MAX_FILE_NAME_LENGTH]; /* name of source file */
char date[DATE_STRING_LENGTH];          /* current date and time */

FILE *source_file;

CHAR_CODE char_table[256];

/*------------------------------------------------------------*/
/*  char_code          Return the character code of ch.      */
/*------------------------------------------------------------*/

#define char_code(ch)   char_table[ch]
```

```
/*------------------------------------------------*/
/*  main              Loop to tokenize source file.        */
/*------------------------------------------------*/

main(argc, argv)

    int  argc;
    char *argv[];

{
    /*
    -- Initialize the scanner.
    */
    init_scanner(argv[1]);

    /*
    -- Repeatedly fetch tokens until a period
    -- or the end of file.
    */
    do {
        get_token();
        if (token == END_OF_FILE) {
            print_line("*** ERROR: Unexpected end of file.\n");
            break;
        }

        print_token();
    } while (token != PERIOD);

    quit_scanner();
}

/*------------------------------------------------*/
/*  print_token       Print a line describing the current  */
/*                    token.                                */
/*------------------------------------------------*/

print_token()

{
    char line[MAX_PRINT_LINE_LENGTH];
    char *symbol_string = symbol_strings[token];

    switch (token) {

        case NUMBER:
            sprintf(line, "    >> %-16s %d\n",
                        symbol_string, literal.value.integer);
            break;

        default:
            sprintf(line, "    >> %-16s %-s\n",
                        symbol_string, token_string);
            break;
    }
    print_line(line);
}

        /*********************************/
        /*                               */
        /*          Initialization       */
        /*                               */
        /*********************************/

/*------------------------------------------------*/
/*  init_scanner      Initialize the scanner globals        */
/*                    and open the source file.             */
```

```
/*------------------------------------------------*/
init_scanner(name)

    char *name;        /* name of source file */

{
    int ch;

    /*
    -- Initialize character table.
    */
    for (ch = 0;   ch < 256;  ++ch) char_table[ch] = SPECIAL;
    for (ch = '0'; ch <= '9'; ++ch) char_table[ch] = DIGIT;
    for (ch = 'A'; ch <= 'Z'; ++ch) char_table[ch] = LETTER;
    for (ch = 'a'; ch <= 'z'; ++ch) char_table[ch] = LETTER;
    char_table[EOF_CHAR] = EOF_CODE;

    init_page_header(name);
    open_source_file(name);
}

/*------------------------------------------------*/
/*  quit_scanner      Terminate the scanner.               */
/*------------------------------------------------*/

quit_scanner()

{
    close_source_file();
}

        /*********************************/
        /*                               */
        /*        Character routines     */
        /*                               */
        /*********************************/

/*------------------------------------------------*/
/*  get_char          Set ch to the next character from the */
/*                    source buffer.                        */
/*------------------------------------------------*/

get_char()

{
    BOOLEAN get_source_line();

    /*
    -- If at end of current source line, read another line.
    -- If at end of file, set ch to the EOF character and return.
    */
    if (*bufferp == '\0') {
        if (! get_source_line()) {
            ch = EOF_CHAR;
            return;
        }
        bufferp = source_buffer;
        buffer_offset = 0;
    }

    ch = *bufferp++;   /* next character in the buffer */

    if ((ch == '\n') || (ch == '\t')) ch = ' ';
}

/*------------------------------------------------*/
/*  skip_blanks       Skip past any blanks at the current   */
```

```
/*                    location in the source buffer.  Set    */
/*                    ch to the next nonblank character.      */
/*----------------------------------------------------------*/

skip_blanks()

{
    while (ch == ' ') get_char();
}

            /********************************/
            /*                              */
            /*        Token routines        */
            /*                              */
            /********************************/

        /* Note that after a token has been extracted, */
        /* ch is the first character after the token.   */

/*----------------------------------------------------------*/
/* get_token        Extract the next token from the source  */
/*                  buffer.                                  */
/*----------------------------------------------------------*/

get_token()

{
    skip_blanks();
    tokenp = token_string;

    switch (char_code(ch)) {
        case LETTER:    get_word();             break;
        case DIGIT:     get_number();           break;
        case EOF_CODE:  token = END_OF_FILE;    break;
        default:        get_special();          break;
    }
}

/*----------------------------------------------------------*/
/* get_word         Extract a word token and set token to   */
/*                  IDENTIFIER.                              */
/*----------------------------------------------------------*/

get_word()

{
    BOOLEAN is_reserved_word();

    /*
    -- Extract the word.
    */
    while ((char_code(ch) == LETTER) || (char_code(ch) == DIGIT)) {
        *tokenp++ = ch;
        get_char();
    }

    *tokenp = '\0';
    token   = WORD;
}

/*----------------------------------------------------------*/
/* get_number       Extract a number token and set literal  */
/*                  to its value.  Set token to NUMBER.     */
/*----------------------------------------------------------*/

get_number()

{
```

```
    int     nvalue      = 0;      /* value of number */
    int     digit_count = 0;      /* total no. of digits in number */
    BOOLEAN count_error = FALSE;  /* too many digits in number? */

    do {
        *tokenp++ = ch;

        if (++digit_count <= MAX_DIGIT_COUNT)
            nvalue = 10*nvalue + (ch - '0');
        else count_error = TRUE;

        get_char();
    } while (char_code(ch) == DIGIT);

    if (count_error) {
        token = ERROR;
        return;
    }

    literal.type          = INTEGER_LIT;
    literal.value.integer = nvalue;
    *tokenp = '\0';
    token   = NUMBER;
}

/*----------------------------------------------------------*/
/* get_special      Extract a special token.  The only      */
/*                  special token we recognize so far is     */
/*                  PERIOD.  All others are ERRORs.          */
/*----------------------------------------------------------*/

get_special()

{
    *tokenp++ = ch;
    token = (ch == '.') ? PERIOD : ERROR;
    get_char();
    *tokenp = '\0';
}

            /********************************/
            /*                              */
            /*      Source file routines    */
            /*                              */
            /********************************/

/*----------------------------------------------------------*/
/* open_source_file   Open the source file and fetch its    */
/*                    first character.                      */
/*----------------------------------------------------------*/

open_source_file(name)

    char *name;       /* name of source file */

{
    if ((name == NULL) ||
        ((source_file = fopen(name, "r")) == NULL)) {
        printf("*** Error:  Failed to open source file.\n");
        exit(-1);
    }

    /*
    -- Fetch the first character.
    */
    bufferp = ""        ;
    get_char();
```

```
}

/*-------------------------------------------------------*/
/* close_source_file   Close the source file.           */
/*-------------------------------------------------------*/

close_source_file()

{
    fclose(source_file);
}


/*-------------------------------------------------------*/
/* get_source_line     Read the next line from the source */
/*                     file.  If there is one, print it out */
/*                     and return TRUE.  Else return FALSE */
/*                     for the end of file.              */
/*-------------------------------------------------------*/

    BOOLEAN
get_source_line()

{
    char print_buffer[MAX_SOURCE_LINE_LENGTH + 9];

    if ((fgets(source_buffer, MAX_SOURCE_LINE_LENGTH,
                            source_file)) != NULL) {
        ++line_number;

        sprintf(print_buffer, "%4d %d: %s",
                        line_number, level, source_buffer);
        print_line(print_buffer);

        return(TRUE);
    }
    else return(FALSE);
}


            /*******************************/
            /*                             */
            /*        Printout routines    */
            /*                             */
            /*******************************/

/*-------------------------------------------------------*/
/* print_line          Print out a line.  Start a new page if */
/*                     the current page is full.         */
/*-------------------------------------------------------*/

print_line(line)

    char line[];        /* line to be printed */

{
```

```
    char save_ch;
    char *save_chp = NULL;

    if (++line_count > MAX_LINES_PER_PAGE) {
        print_page_header();
        line_count = 1;
    };

    if (strlen(line) > MAX_PRINT_LINE_LENGTH)
        save_chp = &line[MAX_PRINT_LINE_LENGTH];

    if (save_chp) {
        save_ch   = *save_chp;
        *save_chp = '\0';
    }

    printf("%s", line);

    if (save_chp) *save_chp = save_ch;
}

/*-------------------------------------------------------*/
/* init_page_header    Initialize the fields of the page  */
/*                     header.                            */
/*-------------------------------------------------------*/

init_page_header(name)

    char *name;         /* name of source file */

{
    time_t timer;

    strncpy(source_name, name, MAX_FILE_NAME_LENGTH - 1);

    /*
    -- Set the current date and time in the date string.
    */
    time(&timer);
    strcpy(date, asctime(localtime(&timer)));
}

/*-------------------------------------------------------*/
/* print_page_header   Print the page header at the top of  */
/*                     the next page.                    */
/*-------------------------------------------------------*/

print_page_header()

{
    putchar(FORM_FEED_CHAR);
    printf("Page %d   %s   %s\n\n", ++page_number, source_name, date);
}
```

The scanner has two important enumeration types. CHAR_CODE defines constants that represent the different types of characters that the scanner can fetch. For now, these are LETTER (the characters A through Z and a through z), DIGIT (the characters 0 through 9), SPECIAL (only the character . for now), and EOF_ CODE (to represent the end of file). TOKEN_CODE defines constants that represent the different types of tokens that the scanner recognizes. For now, these are WORD,

NUMBER, PERIOD, END_OF_FILE, and (when all else fails) ERROR. When indexed by a token code, string array symbol_strings returns the name string of the corresponding token type.

Global variables for the tokenizer include ch (the current character from source_buffer), token (the token code of the current token), and bufferp (which points to characters in source_buffer). Variable token_string contains each token as it is extracted, and variable literal contains the value of literals. Enumeration type LITERAL_TYPE defines the possible literal types. (We only care about integer for now.)

Array char_table maps characters to character codes. Macro char_code indexes into the array with a character to obtain and return the character's code. For example, the value of char_table['a'] is LETTER. char_table is initialized in routine init_scanner.

The main routine's loop is simple. We call function get_token to extract the next token from the source file and function print_token to print it. This happens repeatedly until get_token extracts a period. Since the period token must be the last in the file, it is an error to extract the END_OF_FILE token.

Function print_token obtains the name string of the token from symbol_strings. Then, if the token is a number, we print the value of literal.value.integer. In all other cases, we just print the value of token_string.

As we said before, function init_scanner initializes char_table. We also call function init_page_header to initialize the information in the page header, and function open_source_file to open the source file. Function quit_scanner closes the source file.

Function get_char fetches the next character from source_buffer. We set ch to *bufferp and advance bufferp to the next character. If the last character of the source line has already been fetched from source_buffer (bufferp points to the null character \0), we call function get_source_line to refill the buffer.

In get_char, we take a few liberties with each character we fetch. We set ch to EOF_CHAR if we have reached the end of the file. Since Pascal dictates that we treat the end-of-line and tab characters as blanks, we set ch to a blank if \n or \t is fetched.

The real workhorse of the scanner is routine get_token. We first call function skip_blanks to skip up to the next nonblank character. Then ch is the first character of the next token. Based on this character's code, we call function get_word, get_number, or get_special to extract a word, number, or period token. If we are at the end of the file, we set token to the END_OF_FILE code.

Function get_word works much the same. We repeatedly call get_char to fetch characters and append them to the contents of token_string. We don't stop until we fetch a character that does not belong to the token, one that is not a letter or a digit. When the function returns, ch is the first character after the token.

Routine get_special so far only knows the period. Everything else is an error. After fetching the period, we call get_char so that ch is the first character after the token.

Function get_number not only extracts a number token (an unsigned integer literal for now), but it also calculates the number's value. It is calculated in local variable nvalue, and at the end of the function, we set literal.value.integer to the value.

Each time we call get_number, nvalue is initially zero. To accumulate the value as each digit of the number is fetched from left to right, we multiply nvalue by ten, and then add the numeric value of the digit. For example:

```
            nvalue:   0

     source_buffer:   386
           bufferp:   ^
                ch:   3
            nvalue:   10*0 + 3 = 3

     source_buffer:   386
           bufferp:    ^
                ch:   8
            nvalue:   10*3 + 8 = 38

     source_buffer:   386
           bufferp:     ^
                ch:   6
            nvalue:   10*38 + 6 = 386
```

When the value of ch is a digit, the value of the expression

```
            ch - '0'
```

is the numeric value of the digit. This works because the ASCII codes of the characters '0' through '9' are 48 through 57. If, for example, ch has the value '5', then '5'-'0' is simply 53–48, or five.

We must also guard against an overflow caused by a number with too many digits. Since the maximum integer value is 32767, we define MAX_DIGIT_COUNT to be four. (Of course, in the full scanner, we allow a much greater range of values!) If a number has too many digits, we set local boolean variable count_error to TRUE and stop accumulating the value. Then, after all the digits have been fetched, we set token to ERROR.

Function open_source_file opens the source file. Then, to force get_char to fill the source buffer before attempting to fetch the file's first character, we initialize bufferp to point to the null character in the empty string "". Function close_source_file closes the source file.

Functions get_source_line, print_line, and print_header are taken directly from the lister utility program. Function init_page_header also uses code from that program.

2.3 Modularizing the code

Before beginning the second version of the tokenizer utility, we should prepare to modularize our code by breaking it apart into separate files. We will now create two modules, the scanner module and the error module.

Scanner Module

scanner.h	*n*	Scanner header file
scanner.c	*n*	Scanner routines

Error Module

error.h	*n*	Error header file
error.c	*n*	Error routines

Miscellaneous

common.h	*n*	Common header file

Where: *n*   new file

Each chapter builds upon the organization we will establish here. We may create new modules, add new files to existing modules, or modify existing files.

Figure 2-3 shows file common.h. It defines various constants and the boolean type that we saw in the simple tokenizer. These definitions will be useful throughout the various modules. We also define three memory allocation macros that we will frequently use.

FIGURE 2-3   File common.h.

```
/*************************************************************/
/*                                                           */
/*     C O M M O N   R O U T I N E S   (Header)              */
/*                                                           */
/*     FILE:       common.h                                  */
/*                                                           */
/*     MODULE:     common                                    */
/*                                                           */
/*************************************************************/

#ifndef common_h
#define common_h

#define FORM_FEED_CHAR          '\f'

#define MAX_FILE_NAME_LENGTH    32
```

```
#define MAX_SOURCE_LINE_LENGTH   256
#define MAX_PRINT_LINE_LENGTH    80
#define MAX_LINES_PER_PAGE       50
#define DATE_STRING_LENGTH       26
#define MAX_TOKEN_STRING_LENGTH MAX_SOURCE_LINE_LENGTH
#define MAX_CODE_BUFFER_SIZE     4096
#define MAX_NESTING_LEVEL        16

typedef enum {
    FALSE, TRUE,
} BOOLEAN;

/******************************************/
/*                                        */
/*       Macros for memory allocation     */
/*                                        */
/******************************************/
```

```
#define alloc_struct(type)         (type *) malloc(sizeof(type))       #define alloc_bytes(length)        (char *) malloc(length)
#define alloc_array(type, count)   (type *) malloc(count*sizeof(type))
                                                                       #endif
```

At the beginning of each header file, we test for and define a special pre-processor flag. For example, in common.h, we begin with the following:

```
#ifndef common_h
#define common_h
```

At the end of the file, we have:

```
#endif
```

These flags ensure that whenever all the modules are compiled together, each header file is included only once, since the flag is defined the first time the file is included.

2.4 Program 2-2: A Pascal Tokenizer

Now that you understand how a simple scanner works, we can write the second version of the tokenizer utility. This version uses a scanner that recognizes all Pascal tokens: words (identifiers and reserved words), numbers (integer and real), strings, and all the special symbols.

Figure 2-4 shows the main file of the utility, token2.c. Most of the globals are gone. They've been moved to file scanner.h, and only three are used in the main file: token, token_string, and literal. String array symbol_strings now has entries for all the Pascal tokens. Function print_token now distinguishes between integer and real numbers and it can print string tokens.

FIGURE 2-4   Main file of the Pascal tokenizer.

```
/****************************************************************/     #include <stdio.h>
/*                                                            */       #include "common.h"
/*      Program 2-2:  Pascal Source Tokenizer                 */       #include "error.h"
/*                                                            */       #include "scanner.h"
/*      Recognize Pascal tokens.                              */
/*                                                            */       /*------------------------------------------------------------*/
/*      FILE:       token2.c                                  */       /*  Token name strings                                        */
/*                                                            */       /*------------------------------------------------------------*/
/*      REQUIRES:   Modules error, scanner                    */
/*                                                            */       char *symbol_strings[] = {
/*      USAGE:      token2 sourcefile                         */           "<no token>", "<IDENTIFIER>", "<NUMBER>", "<STRING>",
/*                                                            */           " ", "*", "(", ")", "-", "+", "=", "[", "]", ":", ";",
/*          sourcefile    name of source file to tokenize     */           "<", ">", " ", ".", "/", ":=", "<=", ">=", "<>", "..",
/*                                                            */           "<END OF FILE>", "<ERROR>",
/****************************************************************/           "AND", "ARRAY", "BEGIN", "CASE", "CONST", "DIV", "DO", "DOWNTO",
```

```
    "ELSE", "END", "FILE", "FOR", "FUNCTION", "GOTO", "IF", "IN",
    "LABEL", "MOD", "NIL", "NOT", "OF", "OR", "PACKED", "PROCEDURE",
    "PROGRAM", "RECORD", "REPEAT", "SET", "THEN", "TO", "TYPE",
    "UNTIL", "VAR", "WHILE", "WITH",
};

/*--------------------------------------------------------*/
/*  Externals                                             */
/*--------------------------------------------------------*/

extern TOKEN_CODE token;
extern char       token_string[];
extern LITERAL     literal;

/*--------------------------------------------------------*/
/*  main              Loop to tokenize source file.       */
/*--------------------------------------------------------*/

main(argc, argv)

    int  argc;
    char *argv[];

{
    /*
    -- Initialize the scanner.
    */
    init_scanner(argv[1]);

    /*
    -- Repeatedly fetch tokens until a period
    -- or the end of file.
    */
    do {
        get_token();
        if (token == END_OF_FILE) {
            error(UNEXPECTED_END_OF_FILE);
            break;
        }
```

```
        print_token();
    } while (token != PERIOD);

    quit_scanner();

}

/*--------------------------------------------------------*/
/*  print_token        Print a line describing the current */
/*                     token.                              */
/*--------------------------------------------------------*/

print_token()

{
    char line[MAX_SOURCE_LINE_LENGTH + 32];
    char *symbol_string = symbol_strings[token];

    switch (token) {

        case NUMBER:
            if (literal.type == INTEGER_LIT)
                sprintf(line, "    >> %-16s %d (integer)\n",
                        symbol_string, literal.value.integer);
            else
                sprintf(line, "    >> %-16s %g (real)\n",
                        symbol_string, literal.value.real);
            break;

        case STRING:
            sprintf(line, "    >> %-16s '%-s'\n",
                        symbol_string, literal.value.string);
            break;

        default:
            sprintf(line, "    >> %-16s %-s\n",
                        symbol_string, token_string);
            break;
    }
    print_line(line);

}
```

The Pascal tokenizer works similarly to the simple tokenizer, only smarter. For example, if we give it the Pascal program shown in Figure 2-5, we can expect the output shown in Figure 2-6.

FIGURE 2-5   Sample input file for the Pascal tokenizer.

```
PROGRAM hello (output);

{Write 'Hello, world.' ten times.}

VAR
    i : integer;
```

```
BEGIN {hello}
    FOR i := 1 TO 10 DO BEGIN
        writeln('Hello, world.');
    END;
END {hello}.
```

FIGURE 2-6   Sample output from the Pascal tokenizer.

```
Page 1  hello.pas   Mon Jul 09 23:18:52 1990              >> BEGIN          BEGIN
                                                       9 0:     FOR i := 1 TO 10 DO BEGIN
                                                          >> FOR            FOR
  1 0: PROGRAM hello (output);                            >> <IDENTIFIER>    i
     >> PROGRAM         PROGRAM                           >> :=             :=
     >> <IDENTIFIER>    hello                             >> <NUMBER>        1 (integer)
     >> (              (                                  >> TO             TO
     >> <IDENTIFIER>    output                            >> <NUMBER>        10 (integer)
     >> )              )                                  >> DO             DO
     >> ;              ;                                  >> BEGIN          BEGIN
  2 0:                                                 10 0:        writeln('Hello, world.');
  3 0: {Write 'Hello, world.' ten times.}                >> <IDENTIFIER>    writeln
  4 0:                                                    >> (              (
  5 0: VAR                                                >> <STRING>        'Hello, world.'
     >> VAR             VAR                               >> )              )
  6 0:    i : integer;                                    >> ;              ;
     >> <IDENTIFIER>    i                              11 0:    END;
     >> :              :                                  >> END            END
     >> <IDENTIFIER>    integer                           >> ;              ;
     >> ;              ;                              12 0: END {hello}.
  7 0:                                                    >> END            END
  8 0: BEGIN {hello}                                      >> .              .
```

Figure 2-7 shows file scanner.h. It contains three of the types that were originally defined by the simple tokenizer. We move them to this header file because other modules will use these types. Note that token_code now defines constants for all Pascal tokens. In particular, it defines a separate constant for each reserved word.

FIGURE 2-7   File scanner.h.

```
/****************************************************/      UPARROW, STAR, LPAREN, RPAREN, MINUS, PLUS, EQUAL,
/*                                                */      LBRACKET, RBRACKET, COLON, SEMICOLON, LT, GT, COMMA, PERIOD,
/*      S C A N N E R    (Header)                 */      SLASH, COLONEQUAL, LE, GE, NE, DOTDOT, END_OF_FILE, ERROR,
/*                                                */      AND, ARRAY, BEGIN, CASE, CONST, DIV, DO, DOWNTO, ELSE, END,
/*      FILE:      scanner.h                       */      FFILE, FOR, FUNCTION, GOTO, IF, IN, LABEL, MOD, NIL, NOT,
/*                                                */      OF, OR, PACKED, PROCEDURE, PROGRAM, RECORD, REPEAT, SET,
/*      MODULE:    scanner                         */      THEN, TO, TYPE, UNTIL, VAR, WHILE, WITH,
/*                                                */    } TOKEN_CODE;
/****************************************************/
                                                       /*--------------------------------------------------------*/
#ifndef scanner_h                                      /* Literal structure                                      */
#define scanner_h                                      /*--------------------------------------------------------*/

#include "common.h"                                    typedef enum {
                                                           INTEGER_LIT, REAL_LIT, STRING_LIT,
/*--------------------------------------------------------*/    } LITERAL_TYPE;
/* Token codes                                      */
/*--------------------------------------------------------*/    typedef struct {
                                                           LITERAL_TYPE type;
typedef enum {                                             union {
    NO_TOKEN, IDENTIFIER, NUMBER, STRING,                     int    integer;
```

```
        float real;                                    } LITERAL;
        char  string[MAX_SOURCE_LINE_LENGTH];
    } value;                                           #endif
```

Figure 2-8 shows file scanner.c. Although it retains the structure of the scanner in the simple tokenizer, this version is greatly expanded. The CHAR_CODE enumeration type now defines QUOTE. We now have reserved word tables and several new global variables, buffer_offset, print_flag, and word_string. Note that digit_count and count_error, formerly local variables, are now global.

FIGURE 2-8   File scanner.c.

```
/******************************************************/      RW_STRUCT rw_2[] = {
/*                                                  */          {"do", DO}, {"if", IF}, {"in", IN}, {"of", OF}, {"or", OR},
/*       S C A N N E R                              */          {"to", TO}, {NULL, 0 },
/*                                                  */      };
/*       Scanner for Pascal tokens.                 */
/*                                                  */      RW_STRUCT rw_3[] = {
/*       FILE:     scanner.c                        */          {"and", AND}, {"div", DIV}, {"end", END}, {"for", FOR},
/*                                                  */          {"mod", MOD}, {"nil", NIL}, {"not", NOT}, {"set", SET},
/*       MODULE:   scanner                          */          {"var", VAR}, {NULL , 0 },
/*                                                  */      };
/******************************************************/
                                                             RW_STRUCT rw_4[] = {
#include <stdio.h>                                               {"case", CASE}, {"else", ELSE}, {"file", FFILE},
#include <math.h>                                                {"goto", GOTO}, {"then", THEN}, {"type", TYPE},
#include <sys/types.h>                                           {"with", WITH}, {NULL , 0 },
#include <sys/timeb.h>                                       };
#include "common.h"
#include "error.h"                                           RW_STRUCT rw_5[] = {
#include "scanner.h"                                             {"array", ARRAY}, {"begin", BEGIN}, {"const", CONST},
                                                                 {"label", LABEL}, {"until", UNTIL}, {"while", WHILE},
#define EOF_CHAR          '\x7f'                                 {NULL   , 0   },
#define TAB_SIZE          8                                  };

#define MAX_INTEGER       32767                             RW_STRUCT rw_6[] = {
#define MAX_DIGIT_COUNT   20                                    {"downto", DOWNTO}, {"packed", PACKED}, {"record", RECORD},
#define MAX_EXPONENT      37                                    {"repeat", REPEAT}, {NULL   , 0   },
                                                             };
#define MIN_RESERVED_WORD_LENGTH   2
#define MAX_RESERVED_WORD_LENGTH   9                         RW_STRUCT rw_7[] = {
                                                                {"program", PROGRAM}, {NULL, 0},
/*--------------------------------------------------*/      };
/* Character codes                                  */
/*--------------------------------------------------*/      RW_STRUCT rw_8[] = {
                                                                {"function", FUNCTION}, {NULL, 0},
typedef enum {                                               };
    LETTER, DIGIT, QUOTE, SPECIAL, EOF_CODE,
} CHAR_CODE;                                                  RW_STRUCT rw_9[] = {
                                                                {"procedure", PROCEDURE}, {NULL, 0},
/*--------------------------------------------------*/      };
/* Reserved word tables                             */
/*--------------------------------------------------*/      RW_STRUCT *rw_table[] = {
                                                                NULL, NULL, rw_2, rw_3, rw_4, rw_5, rw_6, rw_7, rw_8, rw_9,
typedef struct {                                             };
    char      *string;
    TOKEN_CODE token_code;                                  /*---------------------------------------------------*/
} RW_STRUCT;                                                 /* Globals                                           */
                                                             /*---------------------------------------------------*/
```

(handwritten annotations: `TAB_SIZE 8` with `4`; `MIN_RESERVED_WORD_LENGTH 2` with `3`; `MAX_RESERVED_WORD_LENGTH 9` with `5`; `Min_opw 1`, `Max_opw 4`)

```
char        ch;              /* current input character */
TOKEN_CODE  token;           /* code of current token */
LITERAL     literal;         /* value of literal */
int         buffer_offset;   /* char offset into source buffer */
int         level = 0;       /* current nesting level */
int         line_number = 0; /* current line number */
BOOLEAN     print_flag = TRUE; /* TRUE to print source lines */

char source_buffer[MAX_SOURCE_LINE_LENGTH]; /* source file buffer */
char token_string[MAX_TOKEN_STRING_LENGTH]; /* token string */
char word_string[MAX_TOKEN_STRING_LENGTH];  /* downshifted */
char *bufferp = source_buffer;              /* source buffer ptr */
char *tokenp  = token_string;               /* token string ptr */

int     digit_count;         /* total no. of digits in number */
BOOLEAN count_error;         /* too many digits in number? */

int page_number = 0;
int line_count  = MAX_LINES_PER_PAGE;   /* no. lines on current pg */

char source_name[MAX_FILE_NAME_LENGTH]; /* name of source file */
char date[DATE_STRING_LENGTH];          /* current date and time */

FILE *source_file;

CHAR_CODE char_table[256];

/*-------------------------------------------------------------*/
/* char_code            Return the character code of ch.       */
/*-------------------------------------------------------------*/

#define char_code(ch)   char_table[ch]

                /*******************************/
                /*                             */
                /*       Initialization        */
                /*                             */
                /*******************************/

/*-------------------------------------------------------------*/
/* init_scanner         Initialize the scanner globals         */
/*                      and open the source file.              */
/*-------------------------------------------------------------*/

init_scanner(name)

    char *name;         /* name of source file */

{
    int ch;

    /*
    -- Initialize character table.
    */
    for (ch = 0;   ch < 256; ++ch) char_table[ch] = SPECIAL;
    for (ch = '0'; ch <= '9'; ++ch) char_table[ch] = DIGIT;
    for (ch = 'A'; ch <= 'Z'; ++ch) char_table[ch] = LETTER;
    for (ch = 'a'; ch <= 'z'; ++ch) char_table[ch] = LETTER;
    char_table['\''] = QUOTE;
    char_table[EOF_CHAR] = EOF_CODE;

    init_page_header(name);
    open_source_file(name);
}

/*-------------------------------------------------------------*/
/* quit_scanner         Terminate the scanner.                 */
```

```
/*-------------------------------------------------------------*/

quit_scanner()

{
    close_source_file();
}

                /*******************************/
                /*                             */
                /*       Character routines     */
                /*                             */
                /*******************************/

/*-------------------------------------------------------------*/
/* get_char             Set ch to the next character from the  */
/*                      source buffer.                         */
/*-------------------------------------------------------------*/

get_char()

{
    BOOLEAN get_source_line();

    /*
    -- If at end of current source line, read another line.
    -- If at end of file, set ch to the EOF character and return.
    */
    if (*bufferp == '\0') {
        if (! get_source_line()) {
            ch = EOF_CHAR;
            return;
        }
        bufferp = source_buffer;
        buffer_offset = 0;
    }

    ch = *bufferp++;    /* next character in the buffer */

    /*
    -- Special character processing:
    --
    --    tab        Increment buffer_offset up to the next
    --               multiple of TAB_SIZE, and replace ch with
    --               a blank.
    --
    --    new-line   Replace ch with a blank.
    --
    --    {          Start of comment:  Skip over comment and
    --               replace it with a blank.
    */
    switch (ch) {

        case '\t': buffer_offset += TAB_SIZE -
                                buffer_offset%TAB_SIZE;
                   ch = ' ';
                   break;

        case '\n': ++buffer_offset;
                   ch = ' ';
                   break;

        case '{': ++buffer_offset;
                  skip_comment();
                  ch = ' ';
                  break;

        default:  ++buffer_offset;
```

```
    }
}

/*------------------------------------------------------------*/
/* skip_comment        Skip over a comment.  Set ch to '}'.  */
/*------------------------------------------------------------*/

skip_comment()

{
    do {
        get_char();
    } while ((ch != '}') && (ch != EOF_CHAR));
}

/*------------------------------------------------------------*/
/* skip_blanks         Skip past any blanks at the current   */
/*                     location in the source buffer.  Set   */
/*                     ch to the next nonblank character.    */
/*------------------------------------------------------------*/

skip_blanks()

{
    while (ch == ' ') get_char();
}

                /*****************************/
                /*                           */
                /*       Token routines      */
                /*                           */
                /*****************************/

        /* Note that after a token has been extracted, */
        /* ch is the first character after the token.  */

/*------------------------------------------------------------*/
/* get_token           Extract the next token from the source */
/*                     buffer.                                */
/*------------------------------------------------------------*/

get_token()

{
    skip_blanks();
    tokenp = token_string;

    switch (char_code(ch)) {
        case LETTER:    get_word();             break;
        case DIGIT:     get_number();           break;
        case QUOTE:     get_string();           break;
        case EOF_CODE:  token = END_OF_FILE;    break;
        default:        get_special();          break;
    }
}

/*------------------------------------------------------------*/
/* get_word            Extract a word token and downshift its */
/*                     characters.  Check if it's a reserved */
/*                     word.  Set token to IDENTIFIER if it's */
/*                     not.                                   */
/*------------------------------------------------------------*/

get_word()

{
    BOOLEAN is_reserved_word();
```

```
    /*
    -- Extract the word.
    */
    while ((char_code(ch) == LETTER) || (char_code(ch) == DIGIT)) {
        *tokenp++ = ch;
        get_char();
    }
    *tokenp = '\0';
    downshift_word();

    if (! is_reserved_word()) token = IDENTIFIER;
}

/*------------------------------------------------------------*/
/* get_number          Extract a number token and set literal */
/*                     to its value.  Set token to NUMBER.    */
/*------------------------------------------------------------*/

get_number()

{
    int     whole_count    = 0;     /* no. digits in whole part */
    int     decimal_offset = 0;     /* no. digits to move decimal */
    char    exponent_sign  = '+';
    int     exponent       = 0;     /* value of exponent */
    float   nvalue         = 0.0;   /* value of number */
    float   evalue         = 0.0;   /* value of exponent */
    BOOLEAN saw_dotdot     = FALSE;  /* TRUE if encounter .. */

    digit_count  = 0;
    count_error  = FALSE;
    token        = NO_TOKEN;

    literal.type = INTEGER_LIT;      /* assume it's an integer */

    /*
    -- Extract the whole part of the number by accumulating
    -- the values of its digits into nvalue.  whole_count keeps
    -- track of the number of digits in this part.
    */
    accumulate_value(&nvalue, INVALID_NUMBER);
    if (token == ERROR) return;
    whole_count = digit_count;

    /*
    -- If the current character is a dot, then either we have a
    -- fraction part or we are seeing the first character of a ..
    -- token.  To find out, we must fetch the next character.
    */
    if (ch == '.') {
        get_char();

        if (ch == '.') {
            /*
            -- We have a .. token.  Back up bufferp so that the
            -- token can be extracted next.
            */
            saw_dotdot = TRUE;
            --bufferp;
        }
        else {
            literal.type = REAL_LIT;
            *tokenp++ = '.';

            /*
            -- We have a fraction part.  Accumulate it into nvalue.
            -- decimal_offset keeps track of how many digits to move
```

```
        -- the decimal point back.
        */
        accumulate_value(&nvalue, INVALID_FRACTION);
        if (token == ERROR) return;
        decimal_offset = whole_count - digit_count;
    }
}

/*
-- Extract the exponent part, if any. There cannot be an
-- exponent part if the .. token has been seen.
*/
if (!saw_dotdot && ((ch == 'E') || (ch == 'e'))) {
    literal.type = REAL_LIT;
    *tokenp++ = ch;
    get_char();

    /*
    -- Fetch the exponent's sign, if any.
    */
    if ((ch == '+') || (ch == '-')) {
        *tokenp++ = exponent_sign = ch;
        get_char();
    }

    /*
    -- Extract the exponent.  Accumulate it into evalue.
    */
    accumulate_value(&evalue, INVALID_EXPONENT);
    if (token == ERROR) return;
    if (exponent_sign == '-') evalue = -evalue;
}

/*
-- Were there too many digits?
*/
if (count_error) {
    error(TOO_MANY_DIGITS);
    token = ERROR;
    return;
}

/*
-- Adjust the number's value using
-- decimal_offset and the exponent.
*/
exponent = evalue + decimal_offset;
if ((exponent + whole_count < -MAX_EXPONENT) ||
    (exponent + whole_count >  MAX_EXPONENT)) {
    error(REAL_OUT_OF_RANGE);
    token = ERROR;
    return;
}
if (exponent != 0) nvalue *= pow(10, exponent);

/*
-- Set the literal's value.
*/
if (literal.type == INTEGER_LIT) {
    if ((nvalue < -MAX_INTEGER) || (nvalue > MAX_INTEGER)) {
        error(INTEGER_OUT_OF_RANGE);
        token = ERROR;
        return;
    }
    literal.value.integer = nvalue;
}
else literal.value.real = nvalue;
```

```
    *tokenp = '\0';
    token   = NUMBER;
}

/*-------------------------------------------------------------*/
/*  get_string          Extract a string token. Set token to  */
/*                       STRING.  Note that the quotes are     */
/*                       stored as part of token_string but not*/
/*                       literal.value.string.                 */
/*-------------------------------------------------------------*/

get_string()

{
    char *sp = literal.value.string;

    *tokenp++ = '\'';
    get_char();

    /*
    --    Extract the string.
    */
    while (ch != EOF_CHAR) {
        /*
        -- Two consecutive single quotes represent
        -- a single quote in the string.
        */
        if (ch == '\'') {
            *tokenp++ = ch;
            get_char();
            if (ch != '\'') break;
        }
        *tokenp++ = ch;
        *sp++     = ch;
        get_char();
    }

    *tokenp      = '\0';
    *sp          = '\0';
    token        = STRING;
    literal.type = STRING_LIT;
}

/*-------------------------------------------------------------*/
/*  get_special         Extract a special token. Most are      */
/*                       single-character. Some are double-     */
/*                       character. Set token appropriately.    */
/*-------------------------------------------------------------*/

get_special()

{
    *tokenp++ = ch;
    switch (ch) {
        case '^':  token = UPARROW;    get_char();  break;
        case '*':  token = STAR;       get_char();  break;
        case '(':  token = LPAREN;     get_char();  break;
        case ')':  token = RPAREN;     get_char();  break;
        case '-':  token = MINUS;      get_char();  break;
        case '+':  token = PLUS;       get_char();  break;
        case '=':  token = EQUAL;      get_char();  break;
        case '[':  token = LBRACKET;   get_char();  break;
        case ']':  token = RBRACKET;   get_char();  break;
        case ';':  token = SEMICOLON;  get_char();  break;
        case ',':  token = COMMA;      get_char();  break;
        case '/':  token = SLASH;      get_char();  break;
```

```
case ':':   get_char();            /* : or := */
            if (ch == '=') {
                *tokenp++ = '=';
                token    = COLONEQUAL;
                get_char();
            }
            else token = COLON;
            break;

case '<':   get_char();            /* < <= or <> */
            if (ch == '=') {
                *tokenp++ = '=';
                token    = LE;
                get_char();
            }
            else if (ch == '>') {
                *tokenp++ = '>';
                token    = NE;
                get_char();
            }
            else token = LT;
            break;

case '>':   get_char();            /* > or >= */
            if (ch == '=') {
                *tokenp++ = '=';
                token    = GE;
                get_char();
            }
            else token = GT;
            break;

case '.':   get_char();            /* . or .. */
            if (ch == '.') {
                *tokenp++ = '.';
                token    = DOTDOT;
                get_char();
            }
            else token = PERIOD;
            break;

default:    token = ERROR;
            get_char();
            break;
    }
    *tokenp = '\0';
}

/*-----------------------------------------------------------*/
/* downshift_word      Copy a word token into word_string    */
/*                     with all letters downshifted.         */
/*-----------------------------------------------------------*/

downshift_word()

{
    int  offset = 'a' - 'A';    /* offset to downshift a letter */
    char *wp    = word_string;
    char *tp    = token_string;

    /*
    -- Copy word into word_string.
    */
    do {
        *wp++ = (*tp >= 'A') && (*tp <= 'Z')    /* if a letter, */
                    ? *tp + offset              /* then downshift */
                    : *tp;                      /* else just copy */
```

```
        ++tp;
    } while (*tp != '\0');

    *wp = '\0';
}

/*-----------------------------------------------------------*/
/* accumulate_value    Extract a number part and accumulate  */
/*                     its value.  Flag the error if the first */
/*                     character is not a digit.             */
/*-----------------------------------------------------------*/

accumulate_value(valuep, error_code)

    float     *valuep;
    ERROR_CODE error_code;

{
    float value = *valuep;

    /*
    -- Error if the first character is not a digit.
    */
    if (char_code(ch) != DIGIT) {
        error(error_code);
        token = ERROR;
        return;
    }

    /*
    -- Accumulate the value as long as the total allowable
    -- number of digits has not been exceeded.
    */
    do {
        *tokenp++ = ch;

        if (++digit_count <= MAX_DIGIT_COUNT)
            value = 10*value + (ch - '0');
        else count_error = TRUE;

        get_char();
    } while (char_code(ch) == DIGIT);

    *valuep = value;
}


/*-----------------------------------------------------------*/
/* is_reserved_word    Check to see if a word token is a     */
/*                     reserved word.  If so, set token      */
/*                     appropriately and return TRUE.  Else, */
/*                     return FALSE.                         */
/*-----------------------------------------------------------*/

    BOOLEAN
is_reserved_word()

{
    int       word_length = strlen(word_string);
    RW_STRUCT *rwp;

    /*
    -- Is it the right length?
    */
    if ((word_length >= MIN_RESERVED_WORD_LENGTH) &&
        (word_length <= MAX_RESERVED_WORD_LENGTH)) {
        /*
```

```
        -- Yes.  Pick the appropriate reserved word list
        -- and check to see if the word is in there.
        */
        for (rwp = rw_table[word_length];
             rwp->string != NULL;
             ++rwp) {
            if (strcmp(word_string, rwp->string) == 0) {
                token = rwp->token_code;
                return(TRUE);            /* yes, a reserved word */
            }
        }
    }

    return(FALSE);                      /* no, it's not */
}

            /*******************************/
            /*                             */
            /*      Source file routines   */
            /*                             */
            /*******************************/

/*---------------------------------------------------------*/
/* open_source_file    Open the source file and fetch its  */
/*                     first character.                    */
/*---------------------------------------------------------*/

open_source_file(name)

    char *name;        /* name of source file */

{
    if ((name == NULL) ||
        ((source_file = fopen(name, "r")) == NULL)) {
        error(FAILED_SOURCE_FILE_OPEN);
        exit(-FAILED_SOURCE_FILE_OPEN);
    }

    /*
    -- Fetch the first character.
    */
    bufferp = ""        ;
    get_char();
}

/*---------------------------------------------------------*/
/* close_source_file   Close the source file.              */
/*---------------------------------------------------------*/

close_source_file()

{
    fclose(source_file);
}

/*---------------------------------------------------------*/
/* get_source_line     Read the next line from the source  */
/*                     file.  If there is one, print it out */
/*                     and return TRUE.  Else return FALSE  */
/*                     for the end of file.                */
/*---------------------------------------------------------*/

    BOOLEAN
get_source_line()

{
    char print_buffer[MAX_SOURCE_LINE_LENGTH + 9];
```

```
    if ((fgets(source_buffer, MAX_SOURCE_LINE_LENGTH,
                                source_file)) != NULL) {
        ++line_number;

        if (print_flag) {
            sprintf(print_buffer, "%4d %d: %s",
                    line_number, level, source_buffer);
            print_line(print_buffer);
        }

        return(TRUE);
    }
    else return(FALSE);
}

            /*******************************/
            /*                             */
            /*      Printout routines      */
            /*                             */
            /*******************************/

/*---------------------------------------------------------*/
/* print_line          Print out a line.  Start a new page if */
/*                     the current page is full.           */
/*---------------------------------------------------------*/

print_line(line)

    char line[];       /* line to be printed */

{
    char save_ch;
    char *save_chp = NULL;

    if (++line_count > MAX_LINES_PER_PAGE) {
        print_page_header();
        line_count = 1;
    };

    if (strlen(line) > MAX_PRINT_LINE_LENGTH) {
        save_chp  = &line[MAX_PRINT_LINE_LENGTH];
        save_ch   = *save_chp;
        *save_chp = '\0';
    }

    printf(line);

    if (save_chp) *save_chp = save_ch;
}

/*---------------------------------------------------------*/
/* init_page_header    Initialize the fields of the page   */
/*                     header.                             */
/*---------------------------------------------------------*/

init_page_header(name)

    char *name;        /* name of source file */

{
    time_t timer;

    strncpy(source_name, name, MAX_FILE_NAME_LENGTH - 1);

    /*
    -- Set the current date and time in the date string.
    */
```

```
    time(&timer);                                          print_page_header()
    strcpy(date, asctime(localtime(&timer)));
}                                                          {
/*-----------------------------------------------------*/     putchar(FORM_FEED_CHAR);
/* print_page_header   Print the page header at the top of  */   printf("Page %d   %s   %s\n\n", ++page_number, source_name, date);
/*                     the next page.                  */   }
/*-----------------------------------------------------*/
```

Functions init_scanner and get_token have small changes. The former now initializes the QUOTE element of char_table, and the latter now calls the new function get_string whenever char_code(ch) is QUOTE. Function get_source_line now does not print the line if print_flag is FALSE.

The rest of the changes to the scanner enable it to scan Pascal programs more intelligently. We will begin with the ability to scan comments.

2.4.1 Comments

In Pascal, a comment is enclosed in curly braces: {This is a comment.} A comment can appear anywhere a blank can appear; in fact, a comment is treated as a single blank. We add this feature to the scanner by making function get_char a bit smarter. Whenever we fetch the character {, we call function skip_comment to skip over a comment, and then we set ch to a blank.

With the comment-smart get_char, the following input lines:

```
{This is a comment
 that spans two lines.}


Two{comments in}{a row}here.
```

produce the following output:

```
1 0: {This is a comment
2 0:  that spans two lines.}
3 0:
4 0: Two{comments in}{a row}here.
   >> <IDENTIFIER>    Two
   >> <IDENTIFIER>    here
   >> .                      .
```

We now also update global variable buffer_offset. When the contents of source_buffer is printed, the value of buffer_offset is the character offset from the beginning of source_buffer to the current character. Thus, we set it to zero each time we read a new source line, and for each non-tab character, we increment

it by one. For each tab character, we bump it up to the next multiple of TAB_
SIZE. Later, we will see how buffer_offset helps us print error messages that
point to the current character when an error occurs.

2.4.2 Identifiers and reserved words

A Pascal word token is either an identifier or a reserved word. Function get_
word now makes this distinction. Your first thought might be to simply list all the
reserved words in a string array:

```
char *reserved_words[] = {"and", "array", "begin", ... };
```

Then, whenever you extract a word token, you can compare the token against
the elements of the string array. If a match is found, the token is a reserved word;
otherwise, it's an identifier.

This would work fine, except Pascal ignores case in its word tokens. Thus,
the scanner must recognize all of the following to be the same identifier:

lastname   LASTNAME   LastName

and all of the following to be the same reserved word:

begin   BEGIN   Begin   BeGiN

The solution to this problem is quite simple. You downshift all the letters of word
tokens to lowercase, and store the downshifted word token in the new global
variable word_string. You can then reliably compare them against a list of downshifted reserved words.

Instead of putting all the reserved words in one string array, you can speed
up the comparisons by grouping the reserved words based on their lengths into
several short arrays. These are the reserved word arrays at the beginning of file
scanner.c. Array rw_table is actually an array of pointers to these lists. For
example, rw_table[5] is a pointer to the list of five-letter reserved words.

In get_word, we extract a word token and store it in token_string, just as
before. But now we call function downshift_word to copy the token into word_
string with all of its letters downshifted. Then, we call the boolean function is_
reserved_word to determine whether or not we have a reserved word. If not, we
set token to IDENTIFIER.

In function is_reserved_word, we use the length of the word token to pick
the current reserved word list from rw_table. If the word is found in the list, we
set token appropriately and return TRUE. Otherwise, we return FALSE.

We saw how the scanner recognizes identifiers and reserved words in Figures
2-5 and 2-6.

2.4.3 Strings

A Pascal scanner must recognize Pascal strings and special symbols. Whenever it fetches a single-quote character, function `get_token` calls function `get_string` to extract a string token. In function `get_string`, we repeatedly fetch characters and append them to `token_string` and to `literal.value.string` until we encounter the other single quote. We include the leading and trailing quote characters in `token_string` but not in `literal.value.string`. (We'll see in a later chapter why it is useful to keep the quote characters.)

In Pascal, two consecutive single quotes represent one single quote in a string: the string `'don''t'` contains the characters don't. Otherwise, one single quote terminates the string. Given the following input:

```
'This is a string.'
'Don''t skip this'.
```

the tokenizer outputs:

```
1 0: 'This is a string.'
  >> <STRING>        'This is a string.'
2 0: 'Don''t skip this'.
  >> <STRING>        'Don't skip this'
  >> .                      .
```

2.4.4 Special symbols

Most of Pascal's special symbol tokens are single character, like + and =. Some are double character, like .. and :=. The double-character special symbols have an extra bit of complexity: the first character looks just like a single-character special symbol token. If the scanner fetches a character that can either be a single-character special symbol or the first character of a double-character special symbol, it must fetch the following character. From this second character, the scanner can tell whether it has a single-character or a double-character special symbol token.

Function `get_special` now knows how to extract all the special symbol tokens. Like the other token extraction functions, it always leaves ch at the first character after the token. Given the following input:

```
+ - : = := < <= <> .
```

the tokenizer outputs:

```
1 0: + - : = := < <= <> .
  >> +                    +
  >> -                    -
```

```
>> :                    :
>> =                    =
>> :=                   :=
>> <                    <
>> <=                   <=
>> <>                   <>
>> .                    .
```

2.4.5 Numbers

Now we are ready to tackle scanning both integer and real numbers. The definition of a Pascal number begins with an *unsigned integer*. An unsigned integer consists of one or more consecutive digits. The simplest form of a number token is an unsigned integer:

3   75   13456

A number token can also be an unsigned integer (the whole part) followed by a fraction part. A fraction part consists of a decimal point followed by an unsigned integer, such as:

123.45   0.967

These numbers have whole parts 123 and 0, and fraction parts .45 and .967, respectively.

A number token can also be a whole part followed by an exponent part. An exponent part consists of the letter E or e followed by an unsigned integer. An optional exponent sign + or - can appear between the letter and the first exponent digit. Examples are:

152e3   2E53   345e-12   7825E+5

Finally, a number token can be a whole part followed by a fraction part *and* an exponent part, in that order:

163.98E7   0.000123e-45

The scanner now limits the number of digits in the number to 20 (see constant MAX_DIGIT_COUNT). Also, the exponent value must be in the range of -37 through $+37$ (see constant MAX_EXPONENT). The specific values we use here depend on how real numbers are represented on a particular computer.

Function get_number is the longest function in the scanner, but it is easy to follow in light of the definition of what a number is and what we have already seen in the simple tokenizer. Note that local variable nvalue is now real and we can accumulate values greater than 9999.

In function get_number, we extract up to three unsigned integers. We always extract the whole part, and we can extract neither, one, or both of the fraction and the exponent parts. For each part, we call function accumulate_value. In this function, we first check that the current character is a digit, and then we accumulate the number's value just as we did before. If the current character is not a digit, we call function error with the error code that was passed in. (Function error will be explained when we discuss how to flag syntax errors.)

After we have accumulated the value of the whole part in nvalue, we set whole_count to the number of digits in that part. We then look for a decimal point. If we find one, we call accumulate_value again to further accumulate the value into nvalue. After this call, we set local variable decimal_offset to the number of places we need to move the decimal point back from the right end of nvalue. decimal_offset is always either zero or a negative value.

For example, suppose get_number is called to extract the number token 386.07. After the first call to accumulate_value to obtain the value of the whole part, the situation is as follows:

```
        nvalue:  386
 decimal_offset:  0

 source_buffer:  386.07
       bufferp:       ^
           ch:  .
```

We call accumulate_value a second time for the fraction part, and then we have the following:

```
        nvalue:  38607
 decimal_offset:  -2

 source_buffer:  386.07❖
       bufferp:         ^
           ch:  ❖
```

We now look for an exponent part. There is one if the current character is an E or an e. The next character after that can be a + or -. If so, we save that character in exponent_sign. We call accumulate_value for the exponent, but this time we use a fresh local variable evalue. If exponent_sign is -, then we negate evalue and we have the following:

```
        nvalue:  38607
 decimal_offset:  -2
        evalue:  -3
```

```
source_buffer:   386.07e-3◆
      bufferp:                ^
           ch:   ◆
```

At this point, we check to see if there were too many digits in the number token. If so, we call function error with the TOO_MANY_DIGITS error code.

Now, to compute the final value of nvalue, we first set local variable exponent to the sum of evalue and decimal_offset. We check to see if we are still within the valid range for exponents, and if so, exponent is the power of ten by which to multiply nvalue. If the number is an integer, we check to see if it is within the valid range of integers. Finally, we set either literal.value.integer or literal.value.real to the value of nvalue.

We have one more thing to consider. Pascal uses the token .. as a subrange specifier, as in the following:

```
TYPE
     teenyears = 11..19;
```

When get_number has fetched the first period, we must fetch another character to see if we have a decimal point or the .. token. If we find a second period, we don't have a fraction part, nor can we have an exponent part. We just back bufferp up to put the second period back, and we are done fetching the digits of the number token. The next time get_token is called, it will extract the .. token. Given the following input:

```
123 -456 12..34 +123.45 -0.00012 .... 0012.3e001
123.4e27 0 000 00000.100000 -123.4567E-27.
```

the tokenizer outputs the following:

```
1 0: 123 -456 12..34 +123.45 -0.00012 .... 0012.3e001
   >> <NUMBER>        123 (integer)
   >> -              -
   >> <NUMBER>        456 (integer)
   >> <NUMBER>        12 (integer)
   >> ..             ..
   >> <NUMBER>        34 (integer)
   >> +              +
   >> <NUMBER>        123.45 (real)
   >> -              -
   >> <NUMBER>        0.00012 (real)
   >> ..             ..
   >> ..             ..
   >> <NUMBER>        123 (real)
```

```
2 0: 123.4e27 0 000 00000.100000 -123.4567E-27.
   >> <NUMBER>            1.234e+029 (real)
   >> <NUMBER>            0 (integer)
   >> <NUMBER>            0 (integer)
   >> <NUMBER>            0.1 (real)
   >> -                   -
   >> <NUMBER>            1.23457e-025 (real)
   >> .                   .
```

2.4.6 Flagging errors

What should the scanner do when it encounters an error? It should print out an error message. A nice touch is to point to the error itself. For example, the following input:

```
123e99 123456 1234567890.123457890e12
1234.56e.
```

should produce the following output:

```
 1 0: 123e99 123456 1234567890.123457890e12
         ^

*** ERROR: Real literal out of range.
   >> <ERROR>             123e99
                ^

*** ERROR: Integer literal out of range.
   >> <ERROR>             123456

                                              ^
*** ERROR: Too many digits.
   >> <ERROR>             1234567890.123457890e12
 2 0: 1234.56e.
          ^

*** ERROR: Invalid exponent.
   >> <ERROR>             1234.56e
   >> .                   .
```

Figures 2-9 and 2-10 show files error.h and error.c of the error module. File error.h defines the maximum number of syntax errors that we will tolerate. It also defines all the syntax error codes that we will use in the rest of the modules.

FIGURE 2-9   File error.h.

```
/******************************************************************/
/*                                                              */
/*        E R R O R   R O U T I N E S   (Header)                */
/*                                                              */
/*        FILE:      error.h                                    */
/*                                                              */
/*        MODULE:    error                                      */
/*                                                              */
/******************************************************************/

#ifndef error_h
#define error_h

#define MAX_SYNTAX_ERRORS 25

/*--------------------------------------------------------------*/
/* Error codes                                                  */
/*--------------------------------------------------------------*/

typedef enum {
    NO_ERROR,
    SYNTAX_ERROR,
    TOO_MANY_SYNTAX_ERRORS,
    FAILED_SOURCE_FILE_OPEN,
    UNEXPECTED_END_OF_FILE,
    INVALID_NUMBER,
    INVALID_FRACTION,
    INVALID_EXPONENT,
    TOO_MANY_DIGITS,
    REAL_OUT_OF_RANGE,
    INTEGER_OUT_OF_RANGE,
    MISSING_RPAREN,
    INVALID_EXPRESSION,
    INVALID_ASSIGNMENT,
    MISSING_IDENTIFIER,
    MISSING_COLONEQUAL,
    UNDEFINED_IDENTIFIER,
    STACK_OVERFLOW,
    INVALID_STATEMENT,
    UNEXPECTED_TOKEN,
    MISSING_SEMICOLON,
    MISSING_DO,
    MISSING_UNTIL,
    MISSING_THEN,
    INVALID_FOR_CONTROL,
    MISSING_OF,
    INVALID_CONSTANT,
    MISSING_CONSTANT,
    MISSING_COLON,
    MISSING_END,
    MISSING_TO_OR_DOWNTO,
    REDEFINED_IDENTIFIER,
    MISSING_EQUAL,
    INVALID_TYPE,
    NOT_A_TYPE_IDENTIFIER,
    INVALID_SUBRANGE_TYPE,
    NOT_A_CONSTANT_IDENTIFIER,
    MISSING_DOTDOT,
    INCOMPATIBLE_TYPES,
    INVALID_TARGET,
    INVALID_IDENTIFIER_USAGE,
    INCOMPATIBLE_ASSIGNMENT,
    MIN_GT_MAX,
    MISSING_LBRACKET,
    MISSING_RBRACKET,
    INVALID_INDEX_TYPE,
    MISSING_BEGIN,
    MISSING_PERIOD,
    TOO_MANY_SUBSCRIPTS,
    INVALID_FIELD,
    NESTING_TOO_DEEP,
    MISSING_PROGRAM,
    ALREADY_FORWARDED,
    WRONG_NUMBER_OF_PARMS,
    INVALID_VAR_PARM,
    NOT_A_RECORD_VARIABLE,
    MISSING_VARIABLE,
    CODE_SEGMENT_OVERFLOW,
    UNIMPLEMENTED_FEATURE,
} ERROR_CODE;

#endif
```

FIGURE 2-10   File error.c.

```
/******************************************************************/
/*                                                              */
/*        E R R O R   R O U T I N E S                           */
/*                                                              */
/*        Error messages and routines to print them.            */
/*                                                              */
/*        FILE:      error.c                                    */
/*                                                              */
/*        MODULE:    error                                      */
/*                                                              */
/******************************************************************/

#include <stdio.h>
#include "common.h"
#include "error.h"

/*--------------------------------------------------------------*/
/* Externals                                                    */
/*--------------------------------------------------------------*/

extern char     *tokenp;
extern BOOLEAN  print_flag;
extern char     source_buffer[];
extern char     *bufferp;

/*--------------------------------------------------------------*/
/* Error messages    Keyed to enumeration type ERROR_CODE       */
/*                   in file error.h.                           */
/*--------------------------------------------------------------*/

char *error_messages[] = {
```

```
"No error",                                              "Unimplemented feature",
"Syntax error",                                      };
"Too many syntax errors",
"Failed to open source file",          /*--------------------------------------------------------*/
"Unexpected end of file",              /* Globals                                                */
"Invalid number",                      /*--------------------------------------------------------*/
"Invalid fraction",
"Invalid exponent",                    int error_count = 0;    /* number of syntax errors */
"Too many digits",
"Real literal out of range",                       /*********************************/
"Integer literal out of range",                    /*                               */
"Missing right parenthesis",                       /*        Error routines         */
"Invalid expression",                              /*                               */
"Invalid assignment statement",                    /*********************************/
"Missing identifier",
"Missing := ",                         /*--------------------------------------------------------*/
"Undefined identifier",                /* error              Print an arrow under the error and then */
"Stack overflow",                      /*                    print the error message.               */
"Invalid statement",                   /*--------------------------------------------------------*/
"Unexpected token",
"Missing ; ",                          error(code)
"Missing DO",
"Missing UNTIL",                           ERROR_CODE code;    /* error code */
"Missing THEN",
"Invalid FOR control variable",        {
"Missing OF",                              extern int buffer_offset;
"Invalid constant",                        char message_buffer[MAX_PRINT_LINE_LENGTH];
"Missing constant",                        char *message = error_messages[code];
"Missing : ",                              int  offset   = buffer_offset - 2;
"Missing END",
"Missing TO or DOWNTO",                     /*
"Redefined identifier",                     -- Print the arrow pointing to the token just scanned.
"Missing = ",                               */
"Invalid type",                            if (print_flag) offset += 8;
"Not a type identifier",                   sprintf(message_buffer, "%*s^\n", offset, " ");
"Invalid subrangetype",                    if (print_flag) print_line(message_buffer);
"Not a constant identifier",               else            printf(message_buffer);
"Missing .. ",
"Incompatible types",                       /*
"Invalid assignment target",                -- Print the error message.
"Invalid identifier usage",                 */
"Incompatible assignment",                 sprintf(message_buffer, " *** ERROR: %s.\n", message);
"Min limit greater than max limit",        if (print_flag) print_line(message_buffer);
"Missing [ ",                              else            printf(message_buffer);
"Missing ] ",
"Invalid index type",                      *tokenp = '\0';
"Missing BEGIN",                           ++error_count;
"Missing period",
"Too many subscripts",                     if (error_count > MAX_SYNTAX_ERRORS) {
"Invalid field",                               sprintf(message_buffer,
"Nesting too deep",                                "Too many syntax errors.  Aborted.\n");
"Missing PROGRAM",                             if (print_flag) print_line(message_buffer);
"Already specified in FORWARD",                else            printf(message_buffer);
"Wrong number of actual parameters",
"Invalid VAR parameter",                       exit(-TOO_MANY_SYNTAX_ERRORS);
"Not a record variable",                   }
"Missing variable",                    }
"Code segment overflow",
```

In file error.c, string array error_message contains the messages that correspond to the error codes. In function error, we index into this array with an
error code. We use global variable buffer_offset to print an arrow under the end

of the last token we scanned, which is the token that caused the error. We then print the error message.

If we have too many errors, we simply abort. Of course, this is just the sort of action that drives programmers crazy about compilers. We put this in as a last resort and hope that it does not occur often.

2.5 Program 2-3: A Source Program Compactor

The tokenizer utility calls the scanner to provide it with tokens, just like a compiler or an interpreter. To demonstrate that you have indeed written a good general-purpose Pascal scanner, here is another utility to use it.

Pascal programs are written to be read by people, with line breaks, blanks, indentation, and comments to improve readability. But suppose you want to save disk space, even at the expense of readability. You can then store a compacted version of the Pascal source file with all comments and unnecessary blanks removed. Line breaks only serve to keep line lengths at, say, 80 characters or less. For example, the following Pascal program:

```
PROGRAM hello (output);

{Write 'Hello, world.' ten times.}

VAR
    i : integer;

BEGIN {hello}
    FOR i := 1 TO 10 DO BEGIN
        writeln ('Hello, world.');
    END;
END {hello}.
```

can be compacted to:

```
PROGRAM hello(output);VAR i:integer;BEGIN FOR i:=1 TO 10 DO BEGIN
writeln('Hello, world.');END;END.
```

The output is a compacted Pascal program that can still be correctly compiled by a Pascal compiler. As far as the Pascal compiler is concerned, the two versions are equivalent. In fact, the Pascal scanner would process the compacted version faster!

Note how all the comments and unnecessary blanks are removed. Wherever a blank is still required, only one is used. One blank is required between two words, between two numbers, or between a word and a number. No blank is required between a word and a special symbol, or between a number and a special symbol. Any blanks in a string are not removed.

The source compactor utility uses the Pascal scanner to read in a Pascal source program and outputs a compacted version. We depend on the scanner to read the source file, and we call get_token each time we want the next token. We set the scanner's print_flag to FALSE so that the compactor does not produce a listing.

The compactor needs to classify each token it obtains from the scanner as a *delimiter* or a *nondelimiter*. A delimiter is a token that establishes a boundary for itself and any adjacent token. Thus, a special symbol is a delimiter. In the expression alpha*pi, it is clear that there are three tokens. Words and numbers are not delimiters. The identifier alpha and the number 3 cannot be written together; alpha3 is scanned as a single identifier token. In Pascal, blanks, tabs, and line breaks also serve as delimiters. The compactor defines an enumeration type as follows:

```
typedef enum {
     DELIMITER, NONDELIMITER,
} TOKEN_CLASS;
```

We call function token_class to return the class of the current token. All special symbols and strings are in class DELIMITER. All other tokens (identifiers, reserved words, and numbers) are in class NONDELIMITER. Global variable token_class records the class of the current token.

Figure 2-11 shows the main file of the compactor utility, compact.c. The scanner has done most of the work. We call the scanner to extract tokens which we then output. We keep track of the class of current token and that of the previous token. If the previous token and the current token are both nondelimiters, we output a blank between them. In all other cases, we can output the current token adjacent to the previous one. See routines append_blank and append_token.

FIGURE 2-11   A source program compactor.

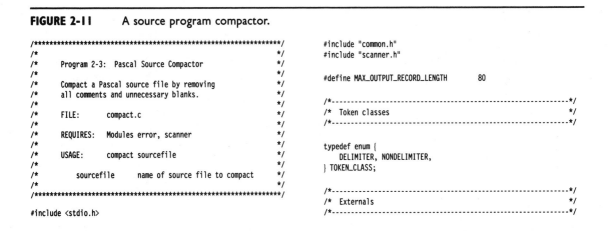

```
/**************************************************/
/*                                                */
/*      Program 2-3:  Pascal Source Compactor     */
/*                                                */
/*      Compact a Pascal source file by removing  */
/*      all comments and unnecessary blanks.      */
/*                                                */
/*      FILE:      compact.c                       */
/*                                                */
/*      REQUIRES:  Modules error, scanner          */
/*                                                */
/*      USAGE:     compact sourcefile              */
/*                                                */
/*         sourcefile    name of source file to compact */
/*                                                */
/**************************************************/

#include <stdio.h>
```

```
#include "common.h"
#include "scanner.h"

#define MAX_OUTPUT_RECORD_LENGTH        80


/*----------------------------------------------*/
/* Token classes                                */
/*----------------------------------------------*/

typedef enum {
     DELIMITER, NONDELIMITER,
} TOKEN_CLASS;

/*----------------------------------------------*/
/* Externals                                    */
/*----------------------------------------------*/
```

```
extern TOKEN_CODE token;
extern char       token_string[];
extern BOOLEAN     print_flag;

/*------------------------------------------------------------*/
/*  Globals                                                   */
/*------------------------------------------------------------*/

int   record_length;         /* length of output record */
char *recp;                  /* pointer into output record */

char output_record[MAX_OUTPUT_RECORD_LENGTH];

/*------------------------------------------------------------*/
/*  main              Loop to process tokens.                 */
/*------------------------------------------------------------*/

main(argc, argv)

    int  argc;
    char *argv[];

{

    TOKEN_CLASS class;         /* current token class */
    TOKEN_CLASS prev_class;    /* previous token class */
    TOKEN_CLASS token_class();

    /*
    -- Initialize the scanner.
    */
    print_flag = FALSE;
    init_scanner(argv[1]);

    /*
    -- Initialize the compactor.
    */
    prev_class = DELIMITER;
    recp = output_record;
    *recp = '\0';
    record_length = 0;

    /*
    -- Repeatedly process tokens until a period
    -- or the end of file.
    */
    do {
        get_token();
        if (token == END_OF_FILE) break;
        class = token_class();

        /*
        -- Append a blank only if two adjacent nondelimiters.
        -- Then append the token string.
        */
        if ((prev_class == NONDELIMITER) && (class == NONDELIMITER))
            append_blank();
        append_token();

        prev_class = class;
    } while (token != PERIOD);

    /*
    -- Flush the last output record if it is partially filled.
    */
    if (record_length > 0) flush_output_record();

    quit_scanner();
```

```
}

/*------------------------------------------------------------*/
/*  token_class        Return the class of the current token. */
/*------------------------------------------------------------*/

    TOKEN_CLASS
token_class()

{
    /*
    -- Nondelimiters: identifiers, numbers, and reserved words
    -- Delimiters:    strings and special symbols
    */
    switch (token) {

    case IDENTIFIER:
    case NUMBER:
        return(NONDELIMITER);

    default:
        return(token < AND ? DELIMITER : NONDELIMITER);
    }
}

/*------------------------------------------------------------*/
/*  append_blank       Append a blank to the output record,   */
/*                     or flush the record if it is full.     */
/*------------------------------------------------------------*/

append_blank()

{
    if (++record_length == MAX_OUTPUT_RECORD_LENGTH - 1)
        flush_output_record();
    else strcat(output_record, " ");
}

/*------------------------------------------------------------*/
/*  append_token       Append the token string to the output  */
/*                     record if it fits.  If not, flush the   */
/*                     current record and append the string    */
/*                     to append to the new record.            */
/*------------------------------------------------------------*/

append_token()

{
    int token_length;          /* length of token string */

    token_length = strlen(token_string);
    if (record_length + token_length
                   >= MAX_OUTPUT_RECORD_LENGTH - 1)
        flush_output_record();

    strcat(output_record, token_string);
    record_length += token_length;
}

/*------------------------------------------------------------*/
/*  flush_output_record           Flush the current output    */
/*                                record.                     */
/*------------------------------------------------------------*/

flush_output_record()
```

```
{                                                          *recp = '\0';
    printf("%s\n", output_record);                          record_length = 0;
    recp = output_record;                                  }
```

This compactor has a maximum output record length of 80 characters. To fill each output record as much as possible, we start a new output record only when the current token cannot fit in the current output record. In function flush_output_record, we write out the current record and start a new one. It is also called at the very end of the program to write out the last record.

Questions and exercises

1. Suppose the syntax rules of Pascal stated that a comment is to be completely ignored. Then, if the source contains:

   al{comment}pha 123{another}45

   the scanner would extract the word token alpha and the number token 12345. What changes would need to be made to function get_char to implement this rule?

2. Number tokens in Pascal are all represented as unsigned values. How does our scanner process input like -3?

3. The final calculation in routine get_number may be time consuming.

   nvalue *= pow(10, exponent)

   Rewrite the routine to avoid such a calculation.

CHAPTER 3

The Symbol Table

Compilers and interpreters build and maintain a data structure used throughout the translation process. This structure is commonly called the *symbol table*, and it is where all the information about a source program's identifiers are kept.

Maintaining a well-organized symbol table is an important skill for all compiler writers. As a compiler or an interpreter parses a source program, it relies on the symbol table to provide information about each identifier. It must be able to access and update existing information and enter new information quickly and efficiently. Otherwise, the translation process is slowed, or worse, it produces incorrect results.

In this chapter, we will write three utility programs to develop our symbol table skills. These skills enable us to:

- create a symbol table organized as a binary tree
- search for and update information in the symbol table

The first program generates a cross-reference listing by keeping line number information in the symbol table. The second program uses the symbol table to keep track of identifiers as it crunches a source program into a compressed form. The third program restores a crunched program.

3.1 Symbol table entries and operations

What information about an identifier is kept in the symbol table? Any information that is useful! Information about an identifier is stored as an *entry* in the table.

Such information typically includes the identifier's name string, its type, and how it is defined.

No matter what information a symbol table keeps about each identifier or how it is organized, certain operations are fundamental. You *enter* information about an identifier into the table by creating an entry. You *search* the table to look up an identifier's entry and make available the information stored there. You can then *update* the entry to modify the stored information.

There can be only one entry per identifier in a symbol table. Therefore, for each identifier, you first search the table to see if it already has an entry, and if so, you just access or update that entry. Otherwise, you must create a new entry.

In order to maintain the modularity of our code, we will keep the symbol table routines in their own files. In this chapter, we will introduce the new symbol table module.

Scanner Module

scanner.h	*u*	Scanner header file
scanner.c	*u*	Scanner routines

Symbol Table Module

symtab.h	*n*	Symbol table header file
symtab.c	*n*	Symbol table routines

Error Module

error.h	*u*	Error header file
error.c	*u*	Error routines

Miscellaneous

common.h	*u*	Common header file

Where: *u* file unchanged from the previous chapter
       n new file

3.2 Binary tree organization

How should you organize the symbol table? You can choose from many different data structures, such as arrays, linked lists, trees, and hash tables. The most common operations that are performed on a symbol table are creating new entries and searching for existing entries. You also want the entries to be sorted alphabetically to aid searching. These operations can be done very efficiently if you organize a symbol table as a binary tree, and then the functions to do the operations are not hard to write. Figure 3-1 shows a small symbol table organized as a binary tree.

FIGURE 3-1   A symbol table organized as a binary tree. To keep the node diagrams simple, we show the name string inside the name field. Actually, the name field points to the name string.

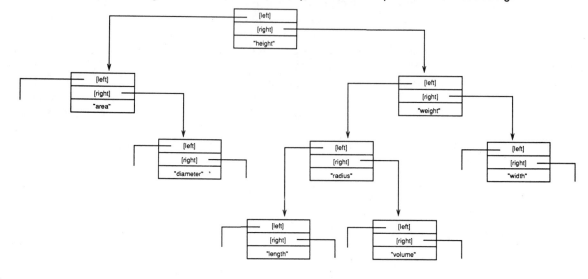

Each entry of the symbol table is stored as a node of the binary tree. Each node contains a pointer to the identifier's name string and pointers to its left and right subtrees. At any given node, that node's left subtree is either empty or contains nodes whose name strings are alphabetically less than the given node's name string. The given node's right subtree is either empty or contains nodes whose name strings are alphabetically greater than the given node's name string.

Figure 3-2 shows the header file symtab.h. The definition of a symbol table entry, SYMTAB_NODE, reflects this structure. Besides the left and right subtree and name string pointers, the structure contains other fields that will be useful in later chapters. Field level will be the nesting level of the identifier, and field label_index will be used by the compiler to emit an assembly-language reference to the identifier. Field info is "wild," as we will see later, we can use this field whenever necessary to point to any information specific to a particular utility program.

FIGURE 3-2   File symtab.h.

```
/***************************************************************/
/*                                                             */
/*     S Y M B O L   T A B L E   (Header)                      */
/*                                                             */
/*     FILE:     symtab.h                                      */
/*                                                             */
/*     MODULE:   symbol table                                  */
/*                                                             */
/***************************************************************/

#ifndef symtab_h
```

```
#define symtab_h

#include "common.h"

/*------------------------------------------------------------*/
/* Value structure                                            */
/*------------------------------------------------------------*/

typedef union {
    int    integer;
```

```
        float  real;
        char   character;
        char   *stringp;
    } VALUE;

    /*------------------------------------------------------------*/
    /* Definition structure                                    */
    /*------------------------------------------------------------*/

    typedef enum {
        UNDEFINED,
        CONST_DEFN, TYPE_DEFN, VAR_DEFN, FIELD_DEFN,
        VALPARM_DEFN, VARPARM_DEFN,
        PROG_DEFN, PROC_DEFN, FUNC_DEFN,
    } DEFN_KEY;

    typedef enum {
        DECLARED, FORWARD,
        READ, READLN, WRITE, WRITELN,
        ABS, ARCTAN, CHR, COS, EOFF, EOLN, EXP, LN, ODD, ORD,
        PRED, ROUND, SIN, SQR, SQRT, SUCC, TRUNC,
    } ROUTINE_KEY;

    typedef struct {
        DEFN_KEY key;
        union {
            struct {
                VALUE value;
            } constant;

            struct {
                ROUTINE_KEY    key;
                int            parm_count;
                int            total_parm_size;
                int            total_local_size;
```

```
                struct symtab_node *parms;
                struct symtab_node *locals;
                struct symtab_node *local_symtab;
                char               *code_segment;
            } routine;

            struct {
                int                offset;
                struct symtab_node *record_idp;
            } data;
        } info;
    } DEFN_STRUCT;

    /*------------------------------------------------------------*/
    /* Symbol table node                                       */
    /*------------------------------------------------------------*/

    typedef struct symtab_node {
        struct symtab_node *left, *right;  /* ptrs to subtrees */
        struct symtab_node *next;          /* for chaining nodes */
        char               *name;          /* name string */
        char               *info;          /* ptr to generic info */
        DEFN_STRUCT        defn;           /* definition struct */
        int                level;          /* nesting level */
        int                label_index;    /* index for code label */
    } SYMTAB_NODE, *SYMTAB_NODE_PTR;

    /*------------------------------------------------------------*/
    /* Functions                                               */
    /*------------------------------------------------------------*/

    SYMTAB_NODE_PTR search_symtab();
    SYMTAB_NODE_PTR enter_symtab();

    #endif
```

Field defn is a structure of type DEFN_STRUCT. This substructure contains more information when an identifier is defined to be the name of a constant, procedure, function, variable, or parameter. We will see how this information is entered in Chapters 6 and 7.

The DEFN_KEY enumeration type defines constants that specify how an identifier is defined. An identifier is either undefined, or it is the name of a constant, type, variable, record field, value parameter, VAR (reference) parameter, program, procedure, or function. We will set the defn.key field of a symbol table node to the identifier's definition key.

The ROUTINE_KEY enumeration type defines constants that represent the programmer-defined or standard Pascal procedures and functions. Starting in Chapter 7, we will set the defn.info.routine.key field of a symbol table node when the identifier is the name of a procedure or function.

Once we see how to parse Pascal constant definitions, we will enter the value of a constant identifier into the defn.info.constant.value field of the identifier's symbol table node. The field type is defined by the VALUE union type, which is similar to the LITERAL type of the scanner.

An identifier's type is a major piece of information that is missing. We will modify symtab.h to include type information when we see how to parse declarations in Chapter 6.

Figure 3-3 shows file symtab.c, which contains the symbol table functions. There are only two functions, one to search the symbol table, and another one to enter information into it.

FIGURE 3-3   File symtab.c.

```
/**************************************************************/
/*                                                            */
/*      S Y M B O L   T A B L E                               */
/*                                                            */
/*      Symbol table routines.                                */
/*                                                            */
/*      FILE:       symtab.c                                  */
/*                                                            */
/*      MODULE:     symbol table                              */
/*                                                            */
/**************************************************************/

#include <stdio.h>
#include "common.h"
#include "error.h"
#include "symtab.h"

/*-----------------------------------------------------------*/
/* Globals                                                   */
/*-----------------------------------------------------------*/

SYMTAB_NODE_PTR symtab_root = NULL;     /* symbol table root */

/*-----------------------------------------------------------*/
/* search_symtab     Search for a name in the symbol table.  */
/*                   Return a pointer of the entry if found, */
/*                   or NULL if not.                         */
/*-----------------------------------------------------------*/

    SYMTAB_NODE_PTR
search_symtab(name, np)

    char            *name;      /* name to search for */
    SYMTAB_NODE_PTR np;         /* ptr to symtab root */

{
    int cmp;

    /*
    -- Loop to check each node.  Return if the node matches,
    -- else continue search down the left or right subtree.
    */
    while (np != NULL) {
        cmp = strcmp(name, np->name);
        if (cmp == 0) return(np);               /* found */
        np = cmp < 0 ? np->left : np->right;    /* continue search */
    }

    return(NULL);                               /* not found */
}

/*-----------------------------------------------------------*/
/* enter_symtab      Enter a name into the symbol table,     */
/*                   and return a pointer to the new entry.  */
/*-----------------------------------------------------------*/

    SYMTAB_NODE_PTR
enter_symtab(name, npp)

    char            *name;      /* name to enter */
    SYMTAB_NODE_PTR *npp;       /* ptr to ptr to symtab root */

{
    int             cmp;        /* result of strcmp *.
    SYMTAB_NODE_PTR new_nodep;  /* ptr to new entry */
    SYMTAB_NODE_PTR np;         /* ptr to node to test */

    /*
    -- Create the new node for the name.
    */
    new_nodep = alloc_struct(SYMTAB_NODE);
    new_nodep->name = alloc_bytes(strlen(name) + 1);
    strcpy(new_nodep->name, name);
    new_nodep->left = new_nodep->right = new_nodep->next = NULL;
    new_nodep->info = NULL;
    new_nodep->defn.key = UNDEFINED;
    new_nodep->level = new_nodep->label_index = 0;

    /*
    -- Loop to search for the insertion point.
    */
    while ((np = *npp) != NULL) {
        cmp = strcmp(name, np->name);
        npp = cmp < 0 ? &(np->left) : &(np->right);
    }

    *npp = new_nodep;                           /* replace */
    return(new_nodep);
}
```

A complete compiler or interpreter has more than just one symbol table. During the translation process, there is a symbol table for the source program's global identifiers and a separate symbol table for the local identifiers of each procedure and function. Until Chapter 7, we will have a single symbol table. Global variable symtab_root points to the root of the symbol table tree. We initialize it to NULL, since the table starts out empty.

Whenever we need to search for an identifier's symbol table node, we pass function search_symtab a pointer to the identifier's name string and a pointer to the root node of the symbol table to search. Until Chapter 7, the value of the second parameter will be the value of symtab_root.

In the while loop of search_symtab, we first check the node pointed to by np. If the names match, we have found the node, so we return the pointer to that node. However, if the name we are searching for is less than the node's name, we set np to point to the node's left subtree. Or, if our name is greater, we set np to point to the node's right subtree. At the top of the loop, we check again. If np becomes NULL, that is, the search went off the bottom of the tree, the name was not in the symbol table and we return NULL.

Whenever we need to create a new symbol table node for an identifier, we pass function enter_symtab a pointer to the identifier's name string and a *pointer to a pointer* to the root of the symbol table. Until Chapter 7, the value of the second parameter will be &symtab_root. We use a pointer to a pointer because inserting a node causes a pointer itself to be changed.

FIGURE 3-4   Inserting a new node into the symbol table. Variable npp is a pointer to a pointer to a symbol table node. Here, it points to the NULL link that will be replaced by the pointer to the new node. Also shown are the three previous node pointers that npp pointed to during the search for the correct insertion point.

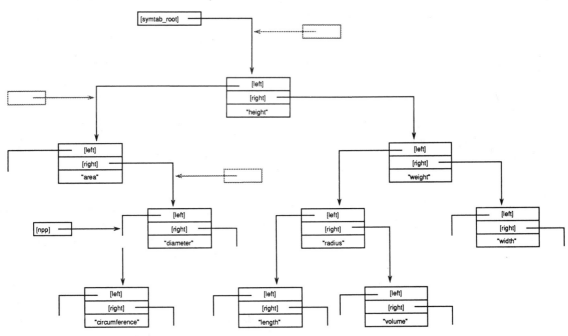

In enter_symtab, we first allocate and initialize a new node. We set the info field to NULL, and since we will not be using them until later chapters, we set the level and label_index fields to zero. We also set the defn.key field to UNDEFINED. Eventually, we will reset this field to another DEFN_KEY value.

Then, as in function search_symtab, we search the binary tree to find where to insert the new node. We find the proper entry point when npp points to a NULL pointer. This is shown in Figure 3-4. We replace the NULL pointer with a pointer to the new node, and we return that pointer.

We have seen how a symbol table can be organized and maintained. Next, we will see how some utility programs can use it. These programs will give us insight into how compilers and interpreters use symbol tables.

3.3 Program 3-1: A Cross-Referencer

A *cross-reference* listing of a source program is an alphabetical listing of all the identifiers that appear in the program. As shown in Figure 3-5, alongside each identifier's name are the source line numbers that contain the identifier. This is useful for tracking where each identifier is used.

FIGURE 3-5   A sample cross-reference listing.

```
Page 1   hello.pas   Mon Jul 09 03:45:59 1990                    12 0: END {hello}.

                                                         Cross-Reference
  1 0: PROGRAM hello (output);                           ---------------
  2 0:
  3 0: {Write 'Hello, world.' ten times.}                hello          1
  4 0:
  5 0: VAR                                                i              6   9
  6 0:     i : integer;
  7 0:                                                    integer        6
  8 0: BEGIN {hello}
  9 0:     FOR i := 1 TO 10 DO BEGIN                      output         1
 10 0:        writeln('Hello, world.');
 11 0:     END;                                           writeln       10
```

Our cross-referencer utility program is built upon the scanner, symbol table, and error modules. The first time the scanner extracts a particular identifier, it is entered into the symbol table along with its line number. Each subsequent time the scanner extracts that same identifier, its node is updated to include the current line number. We use the info field to point to a linked list of line numbers. As soon as the entire program has been scanned, all the identifier names and their line numbers are printed in alphabetical order.

Figure 3-6 shows the main file of the utility xref.c. In the main routine, the scanner loop goes around once for each token until the scanner extracts a period. For each identifier, we call function search_symtab to search the symbol table for the identifier's node. If it is not found, this must be the first time it is used, so we call function enter_symtab to create a node for it. Then, whether the node was newly-created or found, we call function record_line_number to record the current line number in the entry. When the scanner loop terminates, we call print_xref to print the cross-reference listing.

FIGURE 3-6   File xref.c.

```
/****************************************************************/
/*                                                              */
/*      Program 3-1:  Pascal Cross-Referencer                   */
/*                                                              */
/*      List all identifiers alphabetically each with the line  */
/*      numbers of the lines that reference it.                 */
/*                                                              */
/*      FILE:      xref.c                                       */
/*                                                              */
/*      REQUIRES:  Modules symbol table, scanner, error         */
/*                                                              */
/*      USAGE:     xref sourcefile                              */
/*                                                              */
/*          sourcefile     name of source file to cross-ref     */
/*                                                              */
/****************************************************************/

#include <stdio.h>
#include "common.h"
#include "scanner.h"
#include "symtab.h"

#define MAX_LINENUMS_PER_LINE   10

/*--------------------------------------------------------------*/
/* Line number item and list header                            */
/*--------------------------------------------------------------*/

typedef struct linenum_item {
    struct linenum_item *next;          /* ptr to next item */
    int                 line_number;
} LINENUM_ITEM, *LINENUM_ITEM_PTR;

typedef struct {
    LINENUM_ITEM_PTR first_linenum, last_linenum;
} LINENUM_HEADER, *LINENUM_HEADER_PTR;

/*--------------------------------------------------------------*/
/* Externals                                                   */
/*--------------------------------------------------------------*/

extern int        line_number;
extern TOKEN_CODE token;
extern char       word_string[];

extern SYMTAB_NODE_PTR symtab_root;

/*--------------------------------------------------------------*/
/* main              Loop to process identifiers.  Then         */
/*                   print the cross-reference listing.         */
/*--------------------------------------------------------------*/

main(argc, argv)
```

```
int  argc;
char *argv[];

{
    SYMTAB_NODE_PTR np;          /* ptr to symtab entry */
    LINENUM_HEADER_PTR hp;       /* ptr to line item list header */

    init_scanner(argv[1]);

    /*
    -- Repeatedly process tokens until a period
    -- or the end of file.
    */
    do {
        get_token();
        if (token == END_OF_FILE) break;

        if (token == IDENTIFIER) {
            /*
            -- Enter each identifier into the symbol table
            -- if it isn't already in there, and record the
            -- current line number in the symbol table entry.
            */
            np = search_symtab(word_string, symtab_root);
            if (np == NULL) {
                np = enter_symtab(word_string, &symtab_root);
                hp = alloc_struct(LINENUM_HEADER);
                hp->first_linenum = hp->last_linenum = NULL;
                np->info = (char *) hp;
            }
            record_line_number(np, line_number);
        }

    } while (token != PERIOD);

    /*
    -- Print out the cross-reference listing.
    */
    printf("\n\nCross-Reference");
    printf(  "\n--------------\n");
    print_xref(symtab_root);

    quit_scanner();
}

/*--------------------------------------------------------------*/
/* record_line_number  Record a line number into the symbol     */
/*                     table entry.                             */
/*--------------------------------------------------------------*/

record_line_number(np, number)

    SYMTAB_NODE_PTR np;          /* ptr to symtab entry */
```

```
       int              number;      /* line number */            {

{                                                                      int n;
                                                                       LINENUM_ITEM_PTR ip;        /* ptr to line item */
       LINENUM_ITEM_PTR   ip;        /* ptr to line item */            LINENUM_HEADER_PTR hp;       /* ptr to line item list header */
       LINENUM_HEADER_PTR hp;        /* ptr to line item list header */
                                                                       if (np == NULL) return;
       /*
       --  Create a new line number item ...                          /*
       */                                                             --  First, print the left subtree.
       ip = alloc_struct(LINENUM_ITEM);                               */
       ip->line_number = number;                                      print_xref(np->left);
       ip->next = NULL;
                                                                       /*
                                                                       --  Then, print the root of the subtree
       /*                                                             --  with at most MAX_LINENUMS_PER_LINE.
       --  ... and link it to the end of the list                     */
       --  for this symbol table entry.                               printf("\n%-16s   ", np->name);
       */                                                             n = strlen(np->name) > 16 ? 0 : MAX_LINENUMS_PER_LINE;
       hp = (LINENUM_HEADER_PTR) np->info;                            hp = (LINENUM_HEADER_PTR) np->info;
       if (hp->first_linenum == NULL)                                 for (ip = hp->first_linenum; ip != NULL; ip = ip->next) {
           hp->first_linenum = hp->last_linenum = ip;                     if (n == 0) {
       else {                                                                 printf("\n%-16s   ", " ");
           (hp->last_linenum)->next = ip;                                     n = MAX_LINENUMS_PER_LINE;
           hp->last_linenum = ip;                                          }
       }                                                                  printf(" %4d", ip->line_number);
}                                                                          --n;
                                                                       };
/*----------------------------------------------------------*/         printf("\n");
/*  print_xref         Print the names and line numbers in    */
/*                     alphabetical order.                     */      /*
/*----------------------------------------------------------*/         --  Finally, print the right subtree.
                                                                       */
print_xref(np)                                                         print_xref(np->right);

       SYMTAB_NODE_PTR np;       /* ptr to subtree */             }
```

Line numbers for an identifier are stored in a linked list of LINENUM_ITEM structures. The LINENUM_HEADER structure points to the head and tail items in the list. We use the info field of each identifier's node to point to this header structure. We pass to function record_line_number a pointer to a symbol table node and a line number. There, we create a line number item for the line number, and then we append the item at the end of the node's linked list of items.

Recursive function print_xref does an *inorder traversal* of the symbol table tree in order to print the names alphabetically. We pass to it a pointer to the root node. First, the function calls itself for the node's left subtree. Then the node's name followed by the list of line numbers is printed. At most MAX_LINENUMS_PER_ LINE numbers are printed per line, and multiple lines are printed, if necessary. Finally, print_xref calls itself again for the node's right subtree.

So, with our existing scanner module and a simple symbol table module, we have written a utility program that performs quite adequately.

3.4 Program 3-2: A Source Program Cruncher

In Chapter 2, we wrote a compactor utility program that made Pascal source files smaller by squeezing out comments and all unnecessary blanks. We will now write a source program cruncher that reduces the file size even more by replacing tokens with byte-sized codes. This utility program not only shows another use of a symbol table, but it also prepares us for writing our interpreter. Starting in Chapter 8, we will use this crunched form as the interpreter's intermediate form.

A crunched program is no longer readable by either humans or by Pascal compilers and interpreters. Therefore, we will follow with an uncruncher utility to render a crunched source program back to a form readable by the compilers and interpreters.

Where do you get the byte codes? In file scanner.h of the scanner module, we defined the enumeration type TOKEN_CODE. The values of the enumeration constants will be the byte codes! You can replace, for example, the reserved word token BEGIN with the value of the enumeration constant BEGIN. The TOKEN_CODE constants are small integers.

What about an identifier? You can replace it with the value of the enumeration constant IDENTIFIER, but you also need to indicate which identifier. That is where the symbol table comes into play. Following each IDENTIFIER byte code, you place another code to indicate which symbol table entry represents the identifier. You do the same for the NUMBER and STRING byte codes, which means that you will enter number and string tokens into the symbol table too.

Our cruncher utility makes two passes over the source file—in other words, it reads the source file twice. During the first pass, we build the symbol table and then output the crunched symbol table entries to the crunch file. During the second pass, we crunch the source program and output it to the crunch file after the symbol table.

Figure 3-7 shows the main file of the cruncher utility program, crunch.c. It expects the first argument in the command line, argv[1], to be the name of the input source file, and the second argument, argv[2], to be the name of the output crunch file.

FIGURE 3-7   File crunch.c.

```
/******************************************************************/
/*                                                              */
/*      Program 3-2: Pascal Source Cruncher                     */
/*                                                              */
/*      Crunch a Pascal source file.  It can be restored later  */
/*      with the uncruncher utility.                            */
/*                                                              */
/*      FILE:       crunch.c                                    */
/*                                                              */
/*      REQUIRES:   Modules symbol table, scanner, error        */
/*                                                              */
/*      USAGE:      crunch sourcefile crunchfile                */
/*                                                              */
/*          sourcefile      [input] source file to crunch       */
/*                                                              */
/*          crunchfile      [output] crunch file                */
/*                                                              */
/******************************************************************/

#include <stdio.h>

#include "common.h"
#include "scanner.h"
#include "symtab.h"

/*--------------------------------------------------------------*/
/*  Externals                                                   */
/*--------------------------------------------------------------*/

extern TOKEN_CODE       token;
extern char             token_string[];
extern char             word_string[];
extern BOOLEAN          print_flag;

extern SYMTAB_NODE_PTR symtab_root;

/*--------------------------------------------------------------*/
/*  Globals                                                     */
/*--------------------------------------------------------------*/

short index = 0;        /* symtab entry index */
```

```
FILE  *crunch_file;

/*-------------------------------------------------------*/
/* Main program          Crunch a source file in two passes    */
/*                        over the file.                        */
/*-------------------------------------------------------*/

main(argc, argv)

    int argc;
    char *argv[];

{
    /*
    -- Initialize the scanner.
    */
    print_flag = FALSE;
    init_scanner(argv[1]);

    /*
    -- Pass 1.
    */
    do_pass_1();
    close_source_file();

    /*
    -- Open the crunch file and output the crunched
    -- symbol table.
    */
    crunch_file = fopen(argv[2], "wb");
    if (crunch_file == NULL) {
        fprintf(stderr, "*** ERROR: Failed to open crunch file.\n");
        exit(-2);
    }
    fwrite(&index, sizeof(short), 1, crunch_file);
    output_crunched_symtab(symtab_root);

    /*
    -- Pass 2.
    */
    open_source_file(argv[1]);
    do_pass_2();

    fclose(crunch_file);
    quit_scanner();
}

/*-------------------------------------------------------*/
/* do_pass_1          Pass 1: Read the source file to build   */
/*                          the symbol table.                 */
/*-------------------------------------------------------*/

do_pass_1()

{
    SYMTAB_NODE_PTR np;          /* ptr to symtab node */

    /*
    -- Repeatedly process tokens until a period
    -- or the end of file.
    */
    do {
        get_token();
        if (token == END_OF_FILE) break;

        /*
        -- Enter each identifier, number, or string into
```

```
        -- the symbol table if it isn't already in there.
        */
        switch (token) {

            case IDENTIFIER:
                if ((np = search_symtab(word_string, symtab_root))
                        == NULL) {
                    np = enter_symtab(word_string, &symtab_root);
                    np->info = (char *) index++;
                }
                break;

            case NUMBER:
            case STRING:
                if ((np = search_symtab(token_string, symtab_root))
                        == NULL) {
                    np = enter_symtab(token_string, &symtab_root);
                    np->info = (char *) index++;
                }
                break;

            default:
                break;
        }

    } while (token != PERIOD);
}

/*-------------------------------------------------------*/
/* do_pass_2          Pass 2: Reread the source file to       */
/*                          output the crunched program.      */
/*-------------------------------------------------------*/

do_pass_2()

{
    SYMTAB_NODE_PTR np;          /* ptr to symtab node */

    /*
    -- Repeatedly process tokens until a period
    -- or the end of file.
    */
    do {
        get_token();
        if (token == END_OF_FILE) break;

        output_crunched_token();
    } while (token != PERIOD);
}

/*-------------------------------------------------------*/
/* output_crunched_symtab      Output a crunched symbol table */
/*                             in alphabetical order.         */
/*-------------------------------------------------------*/

output_crunched_symtab(np)

    SYMTAB_NODE_PTR np;          /* ptr to symtab subtree */

{
    char length;                 /* byte-sized string length */

    if (np == NULL) return;

    /*
    -- First, crunch the left subtree.
    */
```

```
    output_crunched_symtab(np->left);

    /*
    -- Then, crunch the root of the subtree.
    */
    length = strlen(np->name) + 1;
    index  = (short) np->info;
    fwrite(&index,  sizeof(short), 1, crunch_file);
    fwrite(&length, 1,             1, crunch_file);
    fwrite(np->name,length,        1, crunch_file);

    /*
    -- Finally, crunch the right subtree.
    */
    output_crunched_symtab(np->right);
}

/*----------------------------------------------------------*/
/* output_crunched_token      Output a token record.        */
/*----------------------------------------------------------*/

output_crunched_token()

{
    SYMTAB_NODE_PTR np;               /* ptr to symtab node */
    char            token_code = token; /* byte-sized token code */

    /*
    -- Write the token code.
    */
    fwrite(&token_code, 1, 1, crunch_file);

    /*
    -- If it's an identifier, number, or string,
    -- look up the symbol table entry and write
    -- the entry index.
    */
    switch (token) {

        case IDENTIFIER:
            np = search_symtab(word_string, symtab_root);
            index = (short) np->info;
            fwrite(&index, sizeof(short), 1, crunch_file);
            break;

        case NUMBER:
        case STRING:
            np = search_symtab(token_string, symtab_root);
            index = (short) np->info;
            fwrite(&index, sizeof(short), 1, crunch_file);
            break;

        default:
            break;
    }
}
```

In the main routine, we call functions do_pass_1 and do_pass_2. After the first pass, we open the crunch file and write the number of symbol table entries to the file. Then, we call function output_crunched_symtab to write out the crunched symbol table. In between passes, we close and reopen the source file so that the second pass rereads the source program.

Function do_pass_1 reads the source file the first time to build the symbol table. In this utility, not only do we enter identifier names into the symbol table, but also number and string tokens.

Each time we create a new symbol table node, we set the info field to the value of global variable index. We initialize index to zero, and increment it after each new symbol table node, so that each node has a unique value. We will use this value during the second pass. For example, if the node for identifier gamma has the index value five, then whenever gamma appears in the source program, we will write the value of the enumeration constant IDENTIFIER followed by five to the crunch file. The final first pass value of index is the number of symbol table entries.

Function do_pass_2 reads the source file a second time. We call function output_crunched_token for each token to crunch and output it to the crunch file.

Recursive function output_crunched_symtab does an inorder traversal of the binary tree to output the nodes alphabetically. For each node, we write the index value from the info field, the length of the name string, and the name string itself. Note that we write only as much of the string as necessary.

In function output_crunched_token, we write a byte-sized token code to the crunch file for each token. The value is that of the appropriate TOKEN_CODE enumeration constant. For an identifier, number, or string, we also look up the symbol table node and write the index value from the node's `info` field to the crunch file.

   After two passes over the source file, the cruncher utility has written a crunch file consisting of a crunched representation of the source program's symbol table followed by a crunched representation of the source program itself. To uncrunch the source file, we need the uncruncher utility.

3.5 Program 3-3: A Source Program Uncruncher

The uncruncher utility shown in Figure 3-8 uncrunches a crunched Pascal source file to a form acceptable by a compiler or an interpreter. The format of an uncrunched program is similar to the output of the compactor utility we wrote in the previous chapter.

FIGURE 3-8   The uncruncher utility program.

```
/****************************************************************/
/*                                                              */
/*      Program 3-3:  Pascal Source Uncruncher                  */
/*                                                              */
/*      Uncrunch a crunched Pascal source file.                 */
/*                                                              */
/*      FILE:      uncrunch.c                                   */
/*                                                              */
/*      USAGE:     uncrunch crunchfile                          */
/*                                                              */
/*          crunchfile      file to uncrunch, as created by     */
/*                          the cruncher utility                */
/*                                                              */
/****************************************************************/

#include <stdio.h>
#include "common.h"
#include "scanner.h"

#define MAX_OUTPUT_RECORD_LENGTH       80

/*--------------------------------------------------------------*/
/* Token classes                                                */
/*--------------------------------------------------------------*/

typedef enum {
    DELIMITER, NONDELIMITER,
} TOKEN_CLASS;

/*--------------------------------------------------------------*/
/* Globals                                                      */
/*--------------------------------------------------------------*/

FILE *crunch_file;
char token_string[MAX_TOKEN_STRING_LENGTH];
char output_record[MAX_OUTPUT_RECORD_LENGTH];

TOKEN_CODE ctoken;                /* current token from crunch file*/
int     record_length;            /* length of output record */
```

```
char      *recp;            /* pointer into output record */
char      **symtab_strings;  /* array of symtab strings */

char *symbol_strings[] = {
    "<no token>", "<IDENTIFIER>", "<NUMBER>", "<STRING>",
    "^", "*", "(", ")", "-", "+", "=", "[", "]", ":", ";",
    "<", ">", ",", ".", "/", ":=", "<=", ">=", "<>", "..",
    "<END OF FILE>", "<ERROR>",
    "AND", "ARRAY", "BEGIN", "CASE", "CONST", "DIV", "DO", "DOWNTO",
    "ELSE", "END", "FILE", "FOR", "FUNCTION", "GOTO", "IF", "IN",
    "LABEL", "MOD", "NIL", "NOT", "OF", "OR", "PACKED", "PROCEDURE",
    "PROGRAM", "RECORD", "REPEAT", "SET", "THEN", "TO", "TYPE",
    "UNTIL", "VAR", "WHILE", "WITH",
};

TOKEN_CLASS token_class();

/*--------------------------------------------------------------*/
/* Main program       Uncrunch a source file.                   */
/*--------------------------------------------------------------*/

main(argc, argv)

    int  argc;
    char *argv[];

{
    TOKEN_CLASS class;            /* current token class */
    TOKEN_CLASS prev_class;       /* previous token class */

    /*
    -- Open the crunch file.
    */
    crunch_file = fopen(argv[1], "rb");
    if (crunch_file == NULL) {
        printf("*** Error: Failed to open crunch file.\n");
        exit(-2);
    }

    /*
```

```
    --   Initialize the uncruncher.
    */
    prev_class = DELIMITER;
    recp  = output_record;
    *recp = '\0';
    record_length = 0;

    /*
    --   Read the crunched symbol table.
    */
    read_crunched_symtab();

    /*
    --   Repeatedly process tokens until a period
    --   or the end of file.
    */
    do {
        get_ctoken();
        if (ctoken == END_OF_FILE) break;
        class = token_class();

        /*
        --   Append a blank only if two adjacent nondelimiters.
        --   Then append the token string.
        */
        if ((prev_class == NONDELIMITER) && (class == NONDELIMITER))
            append_blank();
        append_token();

        prev_class = class;
    } while (ctoken != PERIOD);

    /*
    --   Flush the last output record if it is partially filled.
    */
    if (record_length > 0) flush_output_record();
}

/*------------------------------------------------------------*/
/*   read_crunched_symtab       Read the crunched symbol table  */
/*                              and build an array of its name  */
/*                              strings.                        */
/*------------------------------------------------------------*/

read_crunched_symtab()

{
    short count;        /* number of symtab entries */
    short index;        /* symtab entry index */
    char  length;       /* length of name string, incl. '\0' */

    /*
    --   Read the count of symbol table entries and
    --   allocate that many elements for the array.
    */
    fread(&count, sizeof(short), 1, crunch_file);
    symtab_strings = (char **) alloc_bytes(count*sizeof(char *));

    /*
    --   Read each symbol table entry (array index, string length,
    --   and string). Set the array element.
    */
    do {
        fread(&index, sizeof(short), 1, crunch_file);
        fread(&length, sizeof(char), 1, crunch_file);

        symtab_strings[index] = alloc_bytes(length);
```

```
        fread(symtab_strings[index], length, 1, crunch_file);
    } while (--count > 0);
}

/*------------------------------------------------------------*/
/*   get_ctoken          Read the next token code from the    */
/*                       crunch file. Uncrunch the token into */
/*                       token _string with a lookup in the   */
/*                       symbol table name strings array or in */
/*                       the symbol strings array.            */
/*------------------------------------------------------------*/

get_ctoken()

{
    /*
    --   Read the crunched token code.
    */
    fread(&ctoken, sizeof(char), 1, crunch_file);

    /*
    --   Identifier, number, and string tokens:  Look up in the
    --   symbol table name strings array.  All other tokens:  Look
    --   up in the symbol strings array.
    */
    switch (ctoken) {

        case IDENTIFIER:
        case NUMBER:
        case STRING:   {
            short index;            /* symtab strings index */

            fread(&index, sizeof(short), 1, crunch_file);
            strcpy(token_string, symtab_strings[index]);
            break;
        }

        default:
            strcpy(token_string, symbol_strings[ctoken]);
            break;
    }
}

/*------------------------------------------------------------*/
/*   token_class        Return the class of the current token. */
/*------------------------------------------------------------*/

    TOKEN_CLASS
token_class()

{
    /*
    --   Nondelimiters: identifiers, numbers, and reserved words
    --   Delimiters:    strings and special symbols
    */
    switch (ctoken) {

        case IDENTIFIER:
        case NUMBER:
            return(NONDELIMITER);

        default:
            return(ctoken < AND ? DELIMITER : NONDELIMITER);
    }
}

/*------------------------------------------------------------*/
/*   append_blank        Append a blank to the output record, */
```

```
/*                       or flush the record if it is full.    */
/*-----------------------------------------------------------*/

append_blank()

{
    if (++record_length == MAX_OUTPUT_RECORD_LENGTH - 1)
        flush_output_record();
    else strcat(output_record, " ");
}

/*-----------------------------------------------------------*/
/*  append_token      Append the token string to the output  */
/*                    record if it fits.  If not, flush the   */
/*                    current record and append the string    */
/*                    to append to the new record.            */
/*-----------------------------------------------------------*/

append_token()

{
    int token_length;          /* length of token string */
```

```
    token_length = strlen(token_string);
    if (record_length + token_length
                        >= MAX_OUTPUT_RECORD_LENGTH - 1)
        flush_output_record();

    strcat(output_record, token_string);
    record_length += token_length;
}

/*-----------------------------------------------------------*/
/*  flush_output_record       Flush the current output        */
/*                            record.                         */
/*-----------------------------------------------------------*/

flush_output_record()

{
    printf("%s\n", output_record);
    recp = output_record;
    *recp = '\0';
    record_length = 0;
}
```

The uncruncher borrows the TOKEN_CLASS structure from the compactor. Global variable symtab_strings points to a string array that contains the name strings from the crunched symbol table. This array is allocated and filled in function read_crunched_symtab. String array symbol_strings maps token codes back to their token strings.

The main routine expects the name of the crunch file to be the first command line argument, argv[1]. We open the crunch file, initialize some global variables, and then call function read_crunched_symtab to read the crunched symbol table. The rest of the routine is essentially a copy of the main routine of the compactor: we write token strings with or without a blank in between.

Function read_crunched_symtab reads the crunched symbol table and places the name strings into string array symtab_strings. We first read the number of symbol table entries and then allocate the symbol_strings array large enough to hold that many name strings.

In the cruncher utility, we entered identifier, number, and string tokens into the symbol table. When we crunched each node, we wrote the node's index value followed by the length of the node's name string and then the string itself. Now, when we read it back in, the index value determines which element of symtab_strings to use. For example, if the index value for identifier gamma is five, we set symtab_strings[5] to point to the string "gamma".

Back in the main routine, we call function get_ctoken in a loop to extract tokens from the crunch file. In that function, we read the next value of ctoken from the crunch file. If ctoken is IDENTIFIER, NUMBER, or STRING, we also read the symbol table index and use it to obtain the token string from array symtab_strings, which we copy into token_string. For any other token code, we use the code itself to obtain the token string from array symbol_strings.

Functions token_class, append_blank, append_token, and flush_output_record are all from the compactor utility.

The output of the uncruncher utility is virtually the same as what the compactor utility produced. It can be processed by a Pascal compiler or an interpreter, but not easily read by humans. In Chapter 7, we will write a "pretty-printer" utility that will take any source file, including output from the compactor and uncruncher utilities, and reprint it in a neatly-indented format.

Questions and exercises

1. Functions search_symtab and enter_symtab are *interface routines* of the symbol table module. Reimplement the symbol table as a hash table and rewrite these two functions.

2. If an identifier appears more than once in a source line, the line number appears more than once for that identifier in the cross-reference listing. Fix the cross-referencer so that a line number appears once at most for each identifier.

3. Rewrite the cruncher utility to make only one pass over the source file.

4. One difference between the output of the compactor utility and that of the uncruncher utility is how case is preserved. The compactor preserves the case of identifier name strings and reserved words, while the uncruncher downshifts all name strings and writes all reserved words in uppercase. Rewrite the cruncher and uncruncher utilities to preserve case.

CHAPTER 4

Parsing Expressions

Every programming language has a syntax, the set of "grammar rules" that specify how statements and expressions in that language are correctly written. A language's syntax plays a vital role for a compiler and an interpreter. Pascal compilers and interpreters must know Pascal's syntax in order to translate Pascal programs.

The part of a compiler or an interpreter that knows the source language's syntax is the parser. The parser controls the translation process since it analyzes the source program based on the syntax. It calls the scanner routines to give it tokens, and it calls the symbol table routines to enter and search for identifiers. When a compiler's parser has recognized a syntactic entity, such as an arithmetic expression, it calls the code generator routines to emit the appropriate object code. Similarly, an interpreter's parser calls the executor routines to perform the appropriate operations.

The rest of the chapters in the first part of this book are about parsing. This chapter begins with parsing expressions. We will write two utility programs to develop parsing skills that enable us to:

- write parsing routines based on syntax diagrams
- parse expressions
- interpret expressions

The first program parses simple arithmetic expressions in order to translate them into postfix form. The second program is a calculator for Pascal expressions. It also gives us a preview of interpreting, the topic of the second part of this book.

4.1 Syntax diagrams

Before you can write a parser, you need to be able to describe the source language's syntax. There are several ways to do this, but Pascal's relatively simple syntax lends itself well to *syntax diagrams*. These are graphical representations of the syntax rules.

In Chapter 2, we used a written description of a Pascal number. Figure 4-1 shows the same description using syntax diagrams. For example, the first diagram states that a digit is any of the characters 0 through 9. Figure 4-2 shows the syntax diagram for an identifier. In the diagrams, you follow the lines from left to right, and sometimes, as in the diagram for an unsigned integer, you have a loop. You can also have alternate paths, as in the diagram for a number. Rounded boxes enclose literal text (although case variations are not shown), and square boxes enclose elements that are defined by other diagrams. Not all the details of the syntax rules are shown by the syntax diagrams. For example, the diagram for an unsigned integer does not indicate the maximum number of allowable digits.

We will design our parser so that its structure mirrors the syntax diagrams. Thus, the diagrams not only describe the source language's syntax, but they also help us write the parser. The diagrams representing the lowest-level syntactic

FIGURE 4-1   Syntax diagrams for a number.

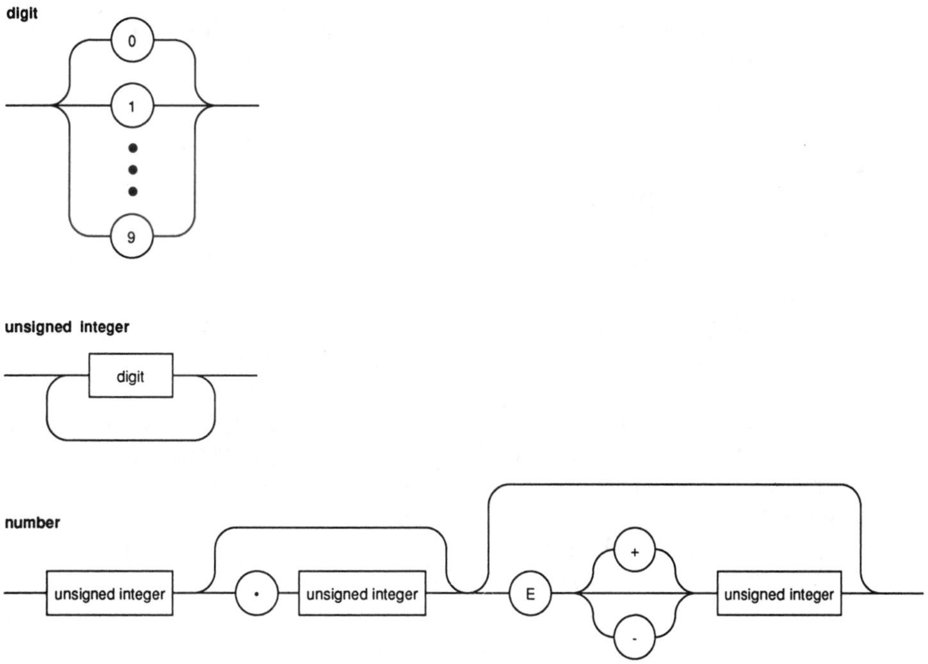

FIGURE 4-2   Syntax diagram for an identifier.

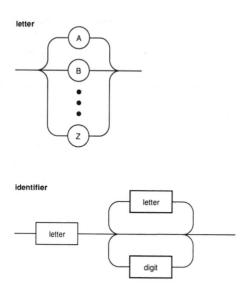

---

entities, like identifier and number tokens, help us write the scanner. In Chapter 15, we will discuss other ways to describe a language's syntax and other ways to write a parser.

4.2 Simple expressions

We begin our work on an expression parser by considering simple expressions. Figure 4-3 shows the syntax diagrams which we will use to design the parser. The names *simple expression*, *term*, and *factor* are descriptive but are otherwise arbitrary. Such labels are often also used as the names of routines in the parser.

The first diagram states that an expression is a simple expression. (We will deal with the complete Pascal expression syntax later.) The second diagram states that a simple expression is either a single term, or several terms separated by + or - operators. The third diagram states that a term is either a single factor, or several factors separated by * or / operators. The fourth diagram states that a factor is either an identifier, a number, or a parenthesized expression.

Together, these diagrams show how the definitions are nested: expressions are simple expressions, simple expressions are made up of terms, and terms are made up of factors. Expressions are also defined recursively, since a factor can contain an expression. The way the diagrams refer to each other reflects Pascal's operator precedence rules: * and / have higher precedence (bind more tightly) than + and

FIGURE 4-3   Syntax diagram for a simple expression.

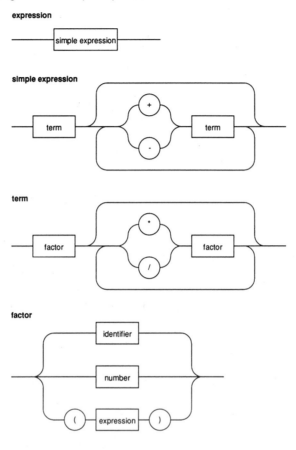

-, and parenthesized subexpressions are evaluated independently. (This will be more obvious when we write the parser.)

Figure 4-4 shows how some sample expressions can be decomposed based on the syntax diagrams. Our first utility program shows how a parser can be written from these diagrams.

4.3 Program 4-1: Infix to Postfix Converter

In both Pascal and normal algebraic notation, expressions are written in *infix* notation, where the operators are in between the operands. For example, a + b.

In *postfix* notation, operators are written after their operands, as in a b +. This notation, also called *Reverse Polish Notation*, or *RPN*, was popularized by

FIGURE 4-4   Decomposing an expression into its parts.

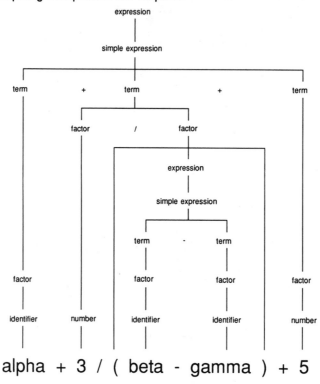

Hewlett-Packard's scientific pocket calculators. It is useful when performing calculations based on a stack. Reading a postfix expression from left to right, each operand pushes its value onto the stack. Each binary operator pops off the top two values, performs the operation on them, and pushes the resulting value back onto the stack. A unary operator pops off the top value, operates on it, and pushes the new value back onto the stack. The following is a more complicated infix expression:

$$((-17 + 49)/4 - 2*3)*(9 - 3 + 2)$$

When converted to postfix, it becomes:

$$17 \text{ neg } 49 + 4 / 2 3 * - 9 3 - 2 + *$$

(We represent the unary - operator as neg to distinguish it from the binary subtraction operator.) We preserve the order of the operands, but we reorder the operators according to the precedence rules. No parentheses are necessary. In the following example, a postfix expression is evaluated on a stack. The stack is shown horizontally: its bottom is at the left, represented by the marker |, and its top is at the right.

Operation	Stack
push 17	| 17
neg	| -17
push 49	| -17 49
+	| 32
push 4	| 32 4
/	| 8
push 2	| 8 2
push 3	| 8 2 3
*	| 8 6
-	| 2
push 9	| 2 9
push 3	| 2 9 3
-	| 2 6
push 2	| 2 6 2
+	| 2 8
*	| 16

Our first utility program, postfix.c, shown in Figure 4-5, converts simple infix expressions to postfix. Its parser follows closely the syntax diagrams of Figure 4-3. Figure 4-6 shows sample output. The program assumes that the expressions are separated by semicolons and that the final expression is terminated by a period.

FIGURE 4-5   File postfix.c.

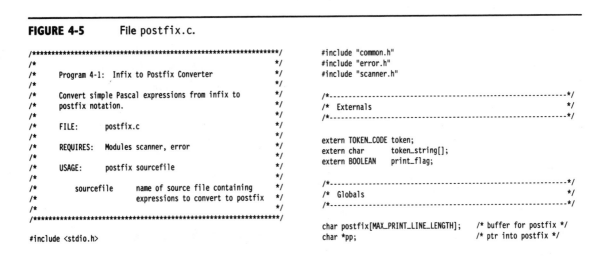

```
/****************************************************************/        #include "common.h"
/*                                                            */          #include "error.h"
/*      Program 4-1:  Infix to Postfix Converter              */          #include "scanner.h"
/*                                                            */
/*      Convert simple Pascal expressions from infix to       */          /*----------------------------------------------------------*/
/*      postfix notation.                                     */          /* Externals                                                */
/*                                                            */          /*----------------------------------------------------------*/
/*      FILE:      postfix.c                                  */
/*                                                            */          extern TOKEN_CODE token;
/*      REQUIRES:  Modules scanner, error                     */          extern char       token_string[];
/*                                                            */          extern BOOLEAN     print_flag;
/*      USAGE:     postfix sourcefile                         */
/*                                                            */          /*----------------------------------------------------------*/
/*          sourcefile     name of source file containing     */          /* Globals                                                  */
/*                         expressions to convert to postfix  */          /*----------------------------------------------------------*/
/*                                                            */
/****************************************************************/         char postfix[MAX_PRINT_LINE_LENGTH];   /* buffer for postfix */
                                                                          char *pp;                               /* ptr into postfix */
#include <stdio.h>
```

```
/*-----------------------------------------------*/
/* main                Contains the main loop that drives    */
/*                     the conversion by calling expression  */
/*                     each time through the loop.           */
/*-----------------------------------------------*/

main(argc, argv)

    int  argc;
    char *argv[];

{
    /*
    -- Initialize the scanner.
    */
    init_scanner(argv[1]);

    /*
    -- Repeatedly call expression until a period
    -- or the end of file.
    */
    do {
        strcpy(postfix, ">> ");
        pp = postfix + strlen(postfix);

        get_token();
        expression();

        output_postfix("\n");
        print_line(postfix);

        /*
        -- After an expression, there should be a semicolon,
        -- a period, or the end of file.  If not, skip tokens
        -- until there is such a token.
        */
        while ((token != SEMICOLON) && (token != PERIOD) &&
               (token != END_OF_FILE)) {
            error(INVALID_EXPRESSION);
            get_token();
        }
    } while ((token != PERIOD) && (token != END_OF_FILE));
}

/*-----------------------------------------------*/
/* expression          Process an expression, which is just a */
/*                     simple expression.                     */
/*-----------------------------------------------*/

expression()

{
    simple_expression();
}

/*-----------------------------------------------*/
/* simple_expression   Process a simple expression consisting */
/*                     of terms separated by + or - operators. */
/*-----------------------------------------------*/

simple_expression()

{
    TOKEN_CODE op;            /* an operator token */
    char      *op_string;     /* an operator token string */

    term();
```

```
    /*
    -- Loop to process subsequent terms
    -- separated by operators.
    */
    while ((token == PLUS) || (token == MINUS)) {
        op = token;     /* remember operator */

        get_token();
        term();         /* subsequent term */

        switch (op) {
            case PLUS:  op_string = "+";        break;
            case MINUS: op_string = "-";        break;
        }
        output_postfix(op_string);      /* output operator */
    }
}

/*-----------------------------------------------*/
/* term                Process a term consisting of factors  */
/*                     separated by * or / operators.        */
/*-----------------------------------------------*/

term()

{
    TOKEN_CODE op;            /* an operator token */
    char      *op_string;     /* an operator token string */

    factor();

    /*
    -- Loop to process subsequent factors
    -- separated by operators.
    */
    while ((token == STAR) || (token == SLASH)) {
        op = token;     /* remember operator */

        get_token();
        factor();       /* subsequent factor */

        switch (op) {
            case STAR:  op_string = "*";        break;
            case SLASH: op_string = "/";        break;
        }
        output_postfix(op_string);      /* output operator */
    }
}

/*-----------------------------------------------*/
/* factor              Process a factor, which is an identi-  */
/*                     fier, a number, or a parenthesized     */
/*                     subexpression.                         */
/*-----------------------------------------------*/

factor()

{
    if ((token == IDENTIFIER) || (token == NUMBER)) {
        output_postfix(token_string);
        get_token();
    }
    else if (token == LPAREN) {
        get_token();
        expression();   /* recursive call for subexpression */

        if (token == RPAREN) get_token();
```

```
        else            error(MISSING_RPAREN);
    }
    else error(INVALID_EXPRESSION);
}


/*----------------------------------------------------------*/
/* output_postfix    Append the string preceded by a blank  */
/*                   to the postfix buffer.                 */
/*----------------------------------------------------------*/
```

```
output_postfix(string)

    char *string;

{
    *pp++ = ' ';
    *pp   = '\0';
    strcat(pp, string);
    pp += strlen(string);
}
```

FIGURE 4-6   Sample output from the infix to postfix converter.

```
Page 1   postfix.in   Mon Jul 09 23:34:54 1990          2 0: ((a + b)*c)/(d - e*f) + 3.14159;
                                                        >>  a b + c * d e f * - / 3.14159 +
                                                         3 0: a + b + c.
    1 0: alpha + beta;                                  >>  a b + c +
>>  alpha beta +
```

We see our familiar scanner loop in the main routine. Each time through the loop, we call function get_token to extract the first token of an expression, and then we call function expression to process it. At the end of an expression, we look for a semicolon, period, or the end of the file. We flag any other tokens as errors.

In function expression, we call function simple_expression, because an expression is just a simple expression. In function simple_expression, we call function term to process the first term. We then begin a loop where we look for either a + or a - operator, and when found, we call term again. Function term parses a term and outputs it in postfix, so we must call function output_postfix to output either a + or a - after whatever term wrote.

Function term is similar to simple_expression, except it calls function factor and looks for * and / operators. Function factor parses a factor and outputs it in postfix, so we must call function output_postfix to output either a * or a / after whatever factor wrote.

In function factor, if we see an identifier or a number, we output it by calling output_postfix. If we find a left parenthesis, we make a recursive call to function expression to output the subexpression in postfix, and then we expect to see a right parenthesis. If we don't it's an error.

Notice that whenever we call expression, simple_expression, term, or factor, we already have the first token of the expression, simple expression, term, or factor. In each function, we consume tokens until we get one that does not belong to the function. This is analogous to the scanner functions: each time we call function get_word, variable ch already has the first letter of the word, and when get_word returns, ch has the first character after the word.

Now that we have seen how to write a parser for simple expressions, we are ready to tackle nearly complete Pascal expressions.

FIGURE 4-7   Syntax diagrams for (nearly complete) Pascal expressions.

expression

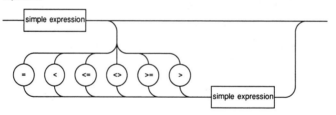

simple expression

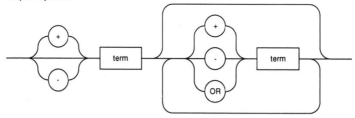

term

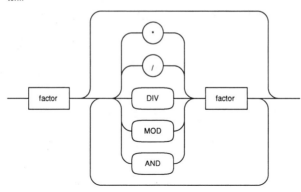

factor

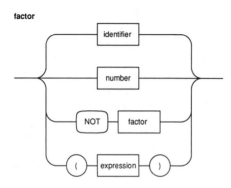

4.4 Pascal expressions

Figure 4-7 shows the syntax diagrams for nearly complete Pascal expressions. We now define an expression to be either a simple expression, or a simple expression followed by a relational operator and then another simple expression. (We won't be doing Pascal's set type in this book, so we leave out the IN operator.)

The complete set of operators now appears in the definitions of simple expression and term. We can have a unary + or - operator before a term, and the definition of factor includes the unary NOT operator. Missing for now are fully-specified variables (with subscripts, pointers, etc.), strings, and function calls. (We'll get to these in later chapters.)

Our latest syntax diagrams implement the full Pascal operator precedence table:

Precedence	Operators
1 (highest)	NOT
2	* / DIV MOD AND
3	+ - OR
4 (lowest)	= < > <> <= >=

4.5 Program 4-2: Calculator

The infix to postfix converter is very much like a compiler since it translates source infix expressions into "object code" for an RPN calculator. Our next utility program is an interpreter that actually performs the stack-based operations specified by infix expressions.

This calculator utility program interprets a language consisting entirely of assignment statements. These statements contain variables that correspond to the calculator's registers. We will keep track of the variables and their values in the symbol table.

Figure 4-8 shows the main file of the calculator, calc.c, which is similar to the infix to postfix converter. The major differences are the addition of the stack, which we implement as an array, and the functions assignment_statement, push, and pop. Function expression now handles relational operators, and function simple_expression now looks for a unary + or - operator before the first term. Function factor now handles a unary NOT and calls itself recursively if it finds one.

FIGURE 4-8   File calc.c.

```
/****************************************************************/
/*                                                              */
/*      Program 4-2:  Calculator                                */
/*                                                              */
/*      Interpret Pascal assignment statements with simple      */
/*      variables.  An assignment to "output" prints the value  */
/*      of the expression.                                      */
/*                                                              */
/*      FILE:      calc.c                                       */
/*                                                              */
/*      REQUIRES:  Modules symbol table, scanner, error         */
/*                                                              */
/*      USAGE:     calc sourcefile                              */
/*                                                              */
/*         sourcefile     name of source file containing        */
/*                        assignment statements to interpret    */
/*                                                              */
/****************************************************************/

#include <stdio.h>
#include "common.h"
#include "error.h"
#include "scanner.h"
#include "symtab.h"

#define STACK_SIZE 32

/*------------------------------------------------------------*/
/* Externals                                                  */
/*------------------------------------------------------------*/

extern TOKEN_CODE token;
extern char       token_string[];
extern char       word_string[];
extern LITERAL    literal;
extern BOOLEAN    print_flag;

extern SYMTAB_NODE_PTR symtab_root;

/*------------------------------------------------------------*/
/* Globals                                                    */
/*------------------------------------------------------------*/

float stack[STACK_SIZE];        /* evaluation stack */
float *tos = stack;             /* top of stack pointer */

/*------------------------------------------------------------*/
/* pop              Return the value popped off the stack.  */
/*------------------------------------------------------------*/

#define pop()        *tos--

/*------------------------------------------------------------*/
/* main             Contains the main loop that drives       */
/*                  the interpretation by calling            */
/*                  assignment_statement each time through   */
/*                  the loop.                                 */
/*------------------------------------------------------------*/

main(argc, argv)

    int  argc;
    char *argv[];
```

```
{
    /*
    -- Initialize the scanner.
    */
    init_scanner(argv[1]);

    get_token();

    /*
    -- Repeatedly call assignment_statement
    -- until a period or the end of file.
    */
    do {
        if (token == IDENTIFIER) assignment_statement();

        /*
        -- After a statement, there should be a semicolon,
        -- a period, or the end of file.  If not, skip tokens
        -- until there is such a token.
        */
        while ((token != SEMICOLON) && (token != PERIOD) &&
               (token != END_OF_FILE)) {
            error(INVALID_ASSIGNMENT);
            get_token();
        }

        /*
        -- Skip any trailing semicolons.
        */
        while (token == SEMICOLON) get_token();

    } while ((token != PERIOD) && (token != END_OF_FILE));
}

/*------------------------------------------------------------*/
/* assignment_statement      Process an assignment statement */
/*                           consisting of:                  */
/*                                                           */
/*                           identifier := expression        */
/*------------------------------------------------------------*/

assignment_statement()

{
    SYMTAB_NODE_PTR np;            /* ptr to symtab node */
    float           *vp;           /* ptr to value */
    BOOLEAN         output_flag;   /* TRUE if assign to "output" */

    /*
    -- Look for the identifier.
    */
    if (token != IDENTIFIER) {
        error(MISSING_IDENTIFIER);
        return;
    }

    /*
    -- Enter the identifier into the symbol table
    -- unless it is "output".
    */
    output_flag = strcmp(word_string, "output") == 0;
    if (!output_flag) {
        if ((np = search_symtab(word_string, symtab_root)) == NULL) {
            np = enter_symtab(word_string, &symtab_root);
```

```
        np->defn.key = VAR_DEFN;
    }
}
/*
-- Look for the := .
*/
get_token();
if (token != COLONEQUAL) {
    error(MISSING_COLONEQUAL);
    return;
}
get_token();

/*
-- Process the expression.
*/
expression();

/*
-- Assign the expression value to the identifier.  If
-- the identifer is "output", print the value instead.
*/
if (output_flag) printf(">> output: %0.6g\n", pop());
else {
    vp = alloc_struct(float);
    *vp = pop();
    np->info = (char *) vp;
}
}

/*-------------------------------------------------------------*/
/* expression        Process an expression consisting of a     */
/*                   simple expression optionally followed     */
/*                   by a relational operator and a second     */
/*                   simple expression.                        */
/*-------------------------------------------------------------*/

expression()

{
    TOKEN_CODE op;                      /* an operator token */
    float     operand_1, operand_2;     /* operand values */

    simple_expression();

    /*
    -- If there is a relational operator, remember it and
    -- process the second simple expression.
    */
    if ((token == EQUAL) || (token == LT) || (token == GT) ||
        (token == NE)    || (token == LE) || (token == GE)) {
        op = token;             /* remember operator */

        get_token();
        simple_expression();    /* second simple expression */
        /*
        -- Pop off the operand values ...
        */
        operand_2 = pop();
        operand_1 = pop();

        /*
        -- ... and perform the operation, leaving the
        -- value on top of the stack.
        */
        switch (op) {
            case EQUAL:
```

```
                push(operand_1 == operand_2 ? 1.0 : 0.0);
                break;

            case LT:
                push(operand_1 < operand_2 ? 1.0 : 0.0);
                break;

            case GT:
                push(operand_1 > operand_2 ? 1.0 : 0.0);
                break;

            case NE:
                push(operand_1 != operand_2 ? 1.0 : 0.0);
                break;

            case LE:
                push(operand_1 <= operand_2 ? 1.0 : 0.0);
                break;

            case GE:
                push(operand_1 >= operand_2 ? 1.0 : 0.0);
                break;
        }
    }
}

/*-------------------------------------------------------------*/
/* simple_expression   Process a simple expression consisting  */
/*                     of terms separated by +, -, or OR       */
/*                     operators.  There may be a unary + or - */
/*                     before the first term.                  */
/*-------------------------------------------------------------*/

simple_expression()

{
    TOKEN_CODE op;                      /* an operator token */
    TOKEN_CODE unary_op = PLUS;         /* a unary operator token */
    float     operand_1, operand_2;     /* operand values */

    /*
    -- If there is a unary + or -, remember it.
    */
    if ((token == PLUS) || (token == MINUS)) {
        unary_op = token;
        get_token();
    }

    term();

    /*
    -- If there was a unary -, negate the top of stack value.
    */
    if (unary_op == MINUS) *tos = -(*tos);

    /*
    -- Loop to process subsequent terms
    -- separated by operators.
    */
    while ((token == PLUS) || (token == MINUS) || (token == OR)) {
        op = token;     /* remember operator */

        get_token();
        term();         /* subsequent term */

        /*
        -- Pop off the operand values ...
```

```
    */
    operand_2 = pop();
    operand_1 = pop();

    /*
    -- ... and perform the operation, leaving the
    -- value on top of the stack.
    */
    switch (op) {
        case PLUS:  push(operand_1 + operand_2);    break;
        case MINUS: push(operand_1 - operand_2);    break;

        case OR:
            push((operand_1 != 0.0) || (operand_2 != 0.0)
                    ? 1.0 : 0.0);
            break;
    }
}
}
```

```
/*-------------------------------------------------------*/
/*  term            Process a term consisting of factors  */
/*                  separated by *, /, DIV, MOD, or AND   */
/*                  operators.                            */
/*-------------------------------------------------------*/

term()

{
    TOKEN_CODE op;                  /* an operator token */
    float       operand_1, operand_2;  /* operand values */

    factor();

    /*
    -- Loop to process subsequent factors
    -- separated by operators.
    */
    while ((token == STAR) || (token == SLASH) || (token == DIV) ||
           (token == MOD)  || (token == AND)) {
        op = token;     /* remember operator */

        get_token();
        factor();/* subsequent factor */

        /*
        -- Pop off the operand values ...
        */
        operand_2 = pop();
        operand_1 = pop();

        /*
        -- ... and perform the operation, leaving the
        -- value on top of the stack.  Push 0.0 instead of
        -- dividing by zero.
        */
        switch (op) {
            case STAR:
                push(operand_1 * operand_2);
                break;

            case SLASH:
                if (operand_2 != 0.0) push(operand_1/operand_2);
                else {
                    printf("*** Warning:  division by zero.\n");
                    push(0.0);
                }
```

```
                break;

            case DIV:
                if (operand_2 != 0.0)
                    push((float) (  ((int) operand_1)
                                    / ((int) operand_2)));
                else {
                    printf("*** Warning:  division by zero.\n");
                    push(0.0);
                }
                break;

            case MOD:
                if (operand_2 != 0.0)
                    push((float) (  ((int) operand_1)
                                    % ((int) operand_2)));
                else {
                    printf("*** Warning:  division by zero.\n");
                    push(0.0);
                }
                break;

            case AND:
                push((operand_1 != 0.0) && (operand_2 != 0.0)
                        ? 1.0 : 0.0);
                break;
        }
    }
}
```

```
/*-------------------------------------------------------------*/
/*  factor              Process a factor, which is an identi-   */
/*                      fier, a number, NOT followed by a fac-  */
/*                      tor, or a parenthesized subexpression.  */
/*-------------------------------------------------------------*/

factor()

{
    SYMTAB_NODE_PTR np;             /* ptr to symtab node */

    switch (token) {

        case IDENTIFIER:
            /*
            -- Push the identifier's value, or 0.0 if
            -- the identifier is undefined.
            */
            np = search_symtab(word_string, symtab_root);
            if (np != NULL) push(*((float *) np->info));
            else {
                error(UNDEFINED_IDENTIFIER);
                push(0.0);
            }

            get_token();
            break;

        case NUMBER:
            /*
            -- Push the number's value.  If the number is an
            -- integer, first convert its value to real.
            */
            push(literal.type == INTEGER_LIT
                    ? (float) literal.value.integer
                    : literal.value.real);

            get_token();
```

```
        break;                                                          break;
                                                                    }
    case NOT:                                                   }
        get_token();
        factor();                                       /*-------------------------------------------------------*/
        *tos = *tos == 0.0 ? 1.0 : 0.0;    /* NOT tos */  /* push           Push a value onto the stack.        */
        break;                                          /*-------------------------------------------------------*/

    case LPAREN:                                        push(value)
        get_token();
        expression();                                       float value;

        if (token == RPAREN) get_token();               {
        else                error(MISSING_RPAREN);          if (tos >= &stack[STACK_SIZE]) {
                                                                error(STACK_OVERFLOW);
        break;                                                  return;
                                                            }
    default:
        error(INVALID_EXPRESSION);                          *++tos = value;
                                                        }
```

Input to the calculator is a sequence of Pascal-like assignment statements. The statements are separated by semicolons, and a period marks the end of the input. An assignment statement is a simple variable (an identifier) followed by := and then by an expression. The appearance of a variable before a := effectively "defines" that variable, and when the statement is executed, the variable is assigned the value of the expression. Using an undefined variable in an expression is an error.

We store a variable's value in the variable identifier's symbol table node. We allocate enough memory to hold a float value, and then we point the node's info field to the value. Whenever a value is assigned to the special variable output, we print that value. Figure 4-9 shows sample output.

FIGURE 4-9   Sample output from the calculator.

```
Page 1   calc.in   Mon Jul 09 23:41:16 1990         >> output: 514.622
                                                      9 0: root := (number/root + root)/2;  output := root;
                                                    >> output: 261.291
  1 0: {Square root of 4096 by Newton's algorithm.}  10 0: root := (number/root + root)/2;  output := root;
  2 0:                                              >> output: 138.483
  3 0: number := 4096;                               11 0: root := (number/root + root)/2;  output := root;
  4 0: root := 1;                                   >> output: 84.0305
  5 0:                                               12 0: root := (number/root + root)/2;  output := root;
  6 0: root := (number/root + root)/2;  output := root;  >> output: 66.3874
>> output: 2048.5                                    13 0: root := (number/root + root)/2;  output := root;
  7 0: root := (number/root + root)/2;  output := root;  >> output: 64.0429
>> output: 1025.25                                   14 0: root := (number/root + root)/2;  output := root;
  8 0: root := (number/root + root)/2;  output := root;  >> output: 64
```

We will not see how to process Pascal type declarations until Chapter 6, so for now, we make do with only the real type. The calculator converts all integer values to real, and uses 0.0 and 1.0 to represent the boolean values false and true, respectively.

Variable tos points to the value at the top of the stack. Function push pushes a value onto the stack by incrementing tos. Function pop returns the value pointed to by tos and then decrements tos.

In the scanner loop of the main routine, we call function assignment_statement to process assignment statements. Each time we call the function, we already have the first token. So in that function, we check if this token is an identifier, and if not, we flag the error and return. Otherwise, unless it is output, we enter the identifier's name into the symbol table if it isn't already in there. We then look for a := and call function expression. At the end of the function, we check if the identifier was output, and if so, we print its value.

In function expression, if there is a relational operator, we pop the two top operand values off of the stack into variables operand_1 and operand_2. We perform the appropriate relational operation and push the result (either 0.0 or 1.0) back onto the stack.

Functions simple_expression and term are similar. For each operator, we pop the top two values off of the stack into operand_1 and operand_2, perform the appropriate operation on those values, and then push the result back onto the stack. In term, to perform the Pascal integer operations DIV and MOD, we first convert the operand values to int, perform the operation, and then convert the result back to float. We also check for an attempt to divide by zero.

If you compare function term of the infix to postfix converter to the corresponding function of the calculator, you can clearly see the difference between a compiler and an interpreter. Function term of the converter (the compiler) outputs code to push two operand values onto the stack, and then it outputs an operator like *. The function in the calculator (the interpreter) actually performs the multiplication on the two values and pushes the product back onto the stack. A compiler *outputs code* to perform an operation, while an interpreter *performs the operation*.

In function factor, we obtain the value of a variable from its symbol table entry, and then we push it onto the stack. We flag an UNDEFINED_IDENTIFIER error if the variable is not in the symbol table, which means the variable was never assigned a value. We push a number's value onto the stack. If the number is an integer, we first convert it to real. For the NOT operator, we call the function recursively, and then we invert the value at the top of stack by replacing a 0.0 value by 1.0, or a nonzero value by 0.0. Finally, we handle a parenthesized expression as before with a recursive call to function expression.

So now we know how to parse assignment statements and expressions. In the next chapter, we will see how to parse the Pascal control statements.

Questions and exercises

1. Trace the function calls of the parser by hand as it converts an expression from infix to postfix.

2. At what point in an expression does the parser detect a missing right parenthesis?

3. The parser does very primitive error checking in the lowest-level function factor. Can better error checking (and recovery from errors) be done in the higher-level functions?

4. Explain how the Pascal operator precedence rules are incorporated in the parser.

5. Pascal has only four operator precedence levels.

   a. Explain why the following expression is incorrect:

      a = b AND c > d

   b. Trace the function calls of the parser as it converts the expression to postfix.

   c. How can Pascal's operator precedence table be modified to have the expressions make sense? How would the expression parser be modified?

6. Is it possible to have an empty expression? What about an empty statement? How does the parser code allow or disallow an empty syntactic construct?

7. Describe the conditions which would cause a stack overflow. Give an example of a statement that causes a stack overflow.

8. Should the parser check for a stack underflow?

9. Extend the calculator program to handle a small set of function calls, such as sqrt and sin.

CHAPTER 5

Parsing Statements

Every Pascal compiler or interpreter checks the source program for syntactic correctness. It flags any errors that it finds with an error message, and only when there are no errors does it output object code or execute the program. Most programmers must sadly admit that their compilers or interpreters do syntax checking more than anything else.

So, a very important task of any parser is syntax checking. In this chapter, we will write a syntax checker to develop the skills to:

- parse Pascal statements
- flag syntax errors in the listing

A syntax checker is a utility program that only does syntax checking. Our first version will only check Pascal statements and expressions. In later chapters, we will write versions that can check other parts of a source program.

5.1 Error reporting and recovery

Programmers are prone to making syntax errors, so it is important to consider how errors are handled. For each syntax error a compiler or an interpreter encounters in the source program, it should:

1. Pinpoint the location of the error.

2. Print a descriptive error message.

3. Recover from the error.

So far, we are taking care of the first two steps by printing an arrow that points to the error and an error message under the erroneous line. The third step is much more difficult. You generally do not generate or execute code if there is even one syntax error. However, you want the parser to continue syntax checking in a meaningful way. So what can a compiler or an interpreter do when it encounters an error?

- It can terminate, crash, or hang; in other words, no recovery is attempted. Thus, at most one syntax error can be uncovered per run.
- It can become hopelessly lost, but still attempt to process the rest of the source program while printing reams of irrelevant error messages. Here, too, there is no error recovery, but the parser does not admit it.
- It can skip tokens until it reaches something that it recognizes. The parser resynchronizes itself at that point and then continues syntax checking as though nothing happened.

The first two options are clearly undesirable. To implement the third option, the parser must look for *synchronization points* after each error. A synchronization point is a location in the source program where syntax checking can be reliably restarted. Ideally, you find such a point as soon after the error as possible.

In this chapter, we begin the parser module. Error reporting and recovery will be a strong theme in the module's routines.

5.2 The parser module

In Chapter 4, we wrote a Pascal expression parser as part of a calculator utility program. Those parsing routines will now be part of the new parser module:

Parser Module

parser.h	*n*	Parser header file
stmt.c	*n*	Parse statements
expr.c	*n*	Parse expressions

Scanner Module

scanner.h	*u*	Scanner header file
scanner.c	*c*	Scanner routines

Symbol Table Module

symtab.h	*u*	Symbol table header file
symtab.c	*u*	Symbol table routines

Error Module

`error.h`	*u*	Error header file
`error.c`	*u*	Error routines

Miscellaneous

`common.h`	*u*	Common header file

Where: *u* file unchanged from the previous chapter
       c file changed from the previous chapter
      n new file

The changes to file `scanner.c` add new error handling functions. File `expr.c` contains the expression parsing functions from Chapter 4, and file `stmt.c` contains new parsing functions for statements. File `parser.h` is their header file. We will examine each of the new or changed files.

5.3 Parsing Pascal statements with error handling

Figure 5-1 shows the syntax diagrams for the Pascal statements. Note how the first diagram shows that a statement can be empty. Just as we did with expressions, we will design our statement parser from the syntax diagrams.

With the aid of these diagrams, we can understand the changes in file `scanner.c`. First, we define several global token lists:

```
TOKEN_CODE []                       = {BEGIN, CASE, FOR, IF, REPEAT,
                                        WHILE, IDENTIFIER, 0};

TOKEN_CODE statement_end_list[]     = {SEMICOLON, END, ELSE, UNTIL,
                                        END_OF_FILE, 0};

TOKEN_CODE declaration_start_list[] = {CONST, TYPE, VAR, PROCEDURE,
                                        FUNCTION, 0};
```

The `statement_start_list` lists the tokens that can start a statement, and the `statement_end_list` lists the tokens that can end a statement. The `declaration_start_list` lists the tokens that can start a declaration. We will save this list for Chapter 6, where we parse declarations. A zero terminates each token list. (This explains why we were careful to have a dummy zero value in the `TOKEN_CODE` enumeration type in file `scanner.h`.)

Figure 5-2 shows two new functions in `scanner.c` that use the token lists. Whenever we call boolean function `token_in`, we pass it a token list. If the current token is in the (nonempty) token list, we return `TRUE`. Otherwise, we return `FALSE`.

FIGURE 5-1 Syntax diagrams for Pascal statements.

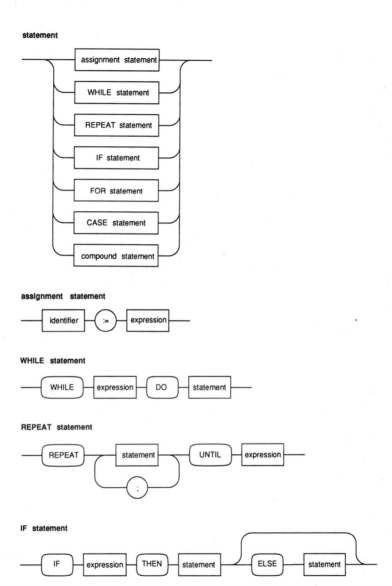

FIGURE 5-1   Continued

FOR statement

CASE statement

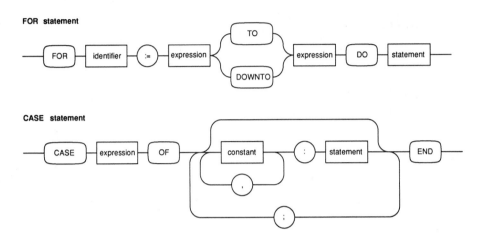

compound statement

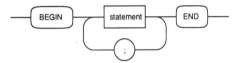

constant

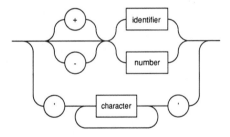

FIGURE 5-2   Functions token_in and synchronize in file scanner.c.

```
/*-----------------------------------------------------------*/       {
/* token_in        Return TRUE if the current token is in  */            TOKEN_CODE *tokenp;
/*                 the token list, else return FALSE.       */
/*-----------------------------------------------------------*/            if (token_list == NULL) return(FALSE);

    BOOLEAN                                                             for (tokenp = &token_list[0]; *tokenp; ++tokenp) {
token_in(token_list)                                                       if (token == *tokenp) return(TRUE);
                                                                       }
    TOKEN_CODE token_list[];                                           return(FALSE);
```

```
}                                                                             (! token_in(token_list3));

/*---------------------------------------------*/             if (error_flag) {
/*  synchronize        If the current token is not in one of  */                 error(token == END_OF_FILE ? UNEXPECTED_END_OF_FILE
/*                     the token lists, flag it as an error.  */                                             : UNEXPECTED_TOKEN);
/*                     Then skip tokens until one that is in  */
/*                     one of the token lists.               */                 /*
/*---------------------------------------------*/                                -- Skip tokens to resynchronize.
                                                                                 */
synchronize(token_list1, token_list2, token_list3)                              while ((! token_in(token_list1)) &&
                                                                                       (! token_in(token_list2)) &&
    TOKEN_CODE token_list1[], token_list2[], token_list3[];                            (! token_in(token_list3)) &&
                                                                                       (token != END_OF_FILE))
{                                                                                    get_token();
    BOOLEAN error_flag = (! token_in(token_list1)) &&                           }
                         (! token_in(token_list2)) &&                    }
```

We call function synchronize whenever we need to check for a syntax error and then resynchronize the parser. We pass it up to three token lists (any of them can be empty). If the current token is not in any of them, we flag an UNEXPECTED_ TOKEN error. Then, to resynchronize, we repeatedly call get_token to skip tokens until we find a token that is in one of the lists.

We will use function synchronize to do most of our error handling. During parsing, whenever we need to do an error check, we call synchronize to make sure we are looking at a correct token. If not, we flag the error and resynchronize the parser.

Header file parser.h, shown in Figure 5-3, contains two macros, if_token_ get and if_token_get_else_error, that represent two very common code sequences in the parser. We call the second macro whenever we are looking for a specific token. Like function synchronize, it flags an error if the current token is not the one we expect, but the macro does not skip tokens.

FIGURE 5-3   File parser.h.

```
/******************************************************/          /******************************/
/*                                                    */          /*                          */
/*     P A R S I N G   R O U T I N E S  (Header)      */          /*     Macros for parsing   */
/*                                                    */          /*                          */
/*     FILE:      parser.h                            */          /******************************/
/*                                                    */
/*     MODULE:    parser                              */          /*----------------------------------------*/
/*                                                    */          /*  if_token_get              If token equals token_code, get */
/******************************************************/          /*                            the next token.                 */
                                                                   /*----------------------------------------*/
#ifndef parser_h
#define parser_h                                                  #define if_token_get(token_code)                \
                                                                      if (token == token_code) get_token()
#include "common.h"
#include "symtab.h"                                               /*----------------------------------------*/
                                                                   /*  if_token_get_else_error   If token equals token_code, get */
```

```
/*                              the next token, else error.    */
/*----------------------------------------------------------*/

#define if_token_get_else_error(token_code, error_code) \
```

```
if (token == token_code) get_token();                \
else                     error(error_code)

#endif
```

Now look at the parsing routines in file `stmt.c`, shown in Figure 5-4. Like the expression parsing functions, when we call each function we already have the first token of the statement. Function `statement` uses this token to call the appropriate parsing function.

FIGURE 5-4   File `stmt.c`.

```
/**************************************************************/
/*                                                        */
/*      S T A T E M E N T   P A R S E R                   */
/*                                                        */
/*      Parsing routines for statements.                  */
/*                                                        */
/*      FILE:       stmt.c                                */
/*                                                        */
/*      MODULE:     parser                                */
/*                                                        */
/**************************************************************/

#include <stdio.h>
#include "common.h"
#include "error.h"
#include "scanner.h"
#include "symtab.h"
#include "parser.h"

/*----------------------------------------------------------*/
/* Externals                                                */
/*----------------------------------------------------------*/

extern TOKEN_CODE token;
extern LITERAL    literal;
extern TOKEN_CODE statement_start_list[], statement_end_list[];

/*----------------------------------------------------------*/
/* statement            Process a statement by calling the  */
/*                      appropriate parsing routine based on */
/*                      the statement's first token.        */
/*----------------------------------------------------------*/

statement()

{
    /*
    -- Call the appropriate routine based on the first
    -- token of the statement.
    */
    switch (token) {

        case IDENTIFIER:    assignment_statement(); break;
        case REPEAT:        repeat_statement();    break;
        case WHILE:         while_statement();     break;
        case IF:            if_statement();        break;
        case FOR:           for_statement();       break;
        case CASE:          case_statement();      break;
```

```
        case BEGIN:         compound_statement();  break;
    }

    /*
    -- Error synchronization:  Only a semicolon, END, ELSE, or
    --                         UNTIL may follow a statement.
    --                         Check for a missing semicolon.
    */
    synchronize(statement_end_list, statement_start_list, NULL);
    if (token_in(statement_start_list)) error(MISSING_SEMICOLON);
}

/*----------------------------------------------------------*/
/* assignment_statement     Process an assignment statement: */
/*                                                          */
/*                          <id> := <expr>                  */
/*----------------------------------------------------------*/

assignment_statement()

{
    get_token();
    if_token_get_else_error(COLONEQUAL, MISSING_COLONEQUAL);

    expression();
}

/*----------------------------------------------------------*/
/* repeat_statement     Process a REPEAT statement:          */
/*                                                          */
/*                      REPEAT <stmt-list> UNTIL <expr>     */
/*----------------------------------------------------------*/

repeat_statement()

{
    /*
    -- <stmt-list>
    */
    get_token();
    do {
        statement();
        while (token == SEMICOLON) get_token();
    } while (token_in(statement_start_list));

    if_token_get_else_error(UNTIL, MISSING_UNTIL);
    expression();
```

```
}

/*-----------------------------------------------------------*/
/* while_statement     Process a WHILE statement:        */
/*                                                       */
/*                          WHILE <expr> DO <stmt>       */
/*-----------------------------------------------------------*/

while_statement()

{
    get_token();
    expression();

    if_token_get_else_error(DO, MISSING_DO);
    statement();
}

/*-----------------------------------------------------------*/
/* if_statement        Process an IF statement:          */
/*                                                       */
/*                          IF <expr> THEN <stmt>        */
/*                                                       */
/*                or:                                    */
/*                                                       */
/*                          IF <expr> THEN <stmt> ELSE <stmt> */
/*-----------------------------------------------------------*/

if_statement()

{
    get_token();
    expression();

    if_token_get_else_error(THEN, MISSING_THEN);
    statement();

    /*
    -- ELSE branch?
    */
    if (token == ELSE) {
        get_token();
        statement();
    }
}

/*-----------------------------------------------------------*/
/* for_statement       Process a FOR statement:          */
/*                                                       */
/*                          FOR <id> := <expr> TO|DOWNTO <expr> */
/*                          DO <stmt>                    */
/*-----------------------------------------------------------*/

for_statement()

{
    get_token();
    if_token_get_else_error(IDENTIFIER, MISSING_IDENTIFIER);

    if_token_get_else_error(COLONEQUAL, MISSING_COLONEQUAL);
    expression();

    if ((token == TO) || (token == DOWNTO)) get_token();
    else error(MISSING_TO_OR_DOWNTO);

    expression();
    if_token_get_else_error(DO, MISSING_DO);
```

```
    statement();
}

/*-----------------------------------------------------------*/
/* case_statement      Process a CASE statement:         */
/*                                                       */
/*                          CASE <expr> OF               */
/*                              <case-branch> ;          */
/*                              ...                      */
/*                          END                          */
/*-----------------------------------------------------------*/

TOKEN_CODE follow_expr_list[]      = {OF, SEMICOLON, 0};

TOKEN_CODE case_label_start_list[] = {IDENTIFIER, NUMBER, PLUS,
                                      MINUS, STRING, 0};

case_statement()

{
    BOOLEAN another_branch;

    get_token();
    expression();

    /*
    -- Error synchronization:  Should be OF
    */
    synchronize(follow_expr_list, case_label_start_list, NULL);
    if_token_get_else_error(OF, MISSING_OF);

    /*
    -- Loop to process CASE branches.
    */
    another_branch = token_in(case_label_start_list);
    while (another_branch) {
        if (token_in(case_label_start_list)) case_branch();

        if (token == SEMICOLON) {
            get_token();
            another_branch = TRUE;
        }
        else if (token_in(case_label_start_list)) {
            error(MISSING_SEMICOLON);
            another_branch = TRUE;
        }
        else another_branch = FALSE;
    }

    if_token_get_else_error(END, MISSING_END);
}

/*-----------------------------------------------------------*/
/* case_branch         Process a CASE branch:            */
/*                                                       */
/*                          <case-label-list> : <stmt>   */
/*-----------------------------------------------------------*/

TOKEN_CODE follow_case_label_list[] = {COLON, SEMICOLON, 0};

case_branch()

{
    BOOLEAN another_label;

    /*
    -- <case-label-list>
```

```
        */
        do {
            case_label();

            get_token();
            if (token == COMMA) {
                get_token();
                if (token_in(case_label_start_list)) another_label = TRUE;
                else {
                    error(MISSING_CONSTANT);
                    another_label = FALSE;
                }
            }
            else another_label = FALSE;
        } while (another_label);

        /*
        -- Error synchronization:  Should be :
        */
        synchronize(follow_case_label_list, statement_start_list, NULL);
        if_token_get_else_error(COLON, MISSING_COLON);

        statement();
}

/*------------------------------------------------------------*/
/* case_label              Process a CASE label and return a  */
/*                         pointer to its type structure.     */
/*------------------------------------------------------------*/

case_label()

{
    TOKEN_CODE sign       = PLUS;       /* unary + or - sign */
    BOOLEAN    saw_sign = FALSE;        /* TRUE iff unary sign */

    /*
    -- Unary + or - sign.
    */
    if ((token == PLUS) || (token == MINUS)) {
        sign      = token;
        saw_sign = TRUE;
        get_token();
    }
```

```
    /*
    -- Number or identifier.
    */
    if ((token == NUMBER) || (token == IDENTIFIER)) return;

    /*
    -- String constant:  Character type only.
    */
    else if (token == STRING) {
        if (saw_sign) error(INVALID_CONSTANT);

        if (strlen(literal.value.string) != 1)
            error(INVALID_CONSTANT);
    }
}

/*------------------------------------------------------------*/
/* compound_statement       Process a compound statement:     */
/*                                                            */
/*                          BEGIN <stmt-list> END             */
/*------------------------------------------------------------*/

compound_statement()

{
    /*
    -- <stmt-list>
    */
    get_token();
    do {
        statement();
        while (token == SEMICOLON) get_token();
        if (token == END) break;

        /*
        -- Error synchronization:  Should be at the start of the
        --                         next statement.
        */
        synchronize(statement_start_list, NULL, NULL);
    } while (token_in(statement_start_list));

    if_token_get_else_error(END, MISSING_END);
}
```

When we return from a parsing function to function statement, we have just parsed a statement, and so we are looking at the first token after the statement. We expect that token to be one of the statement ending tokens (a semicolon, END, ELSE, or UNTIL), and to be sure, we call function synchronize, passing both statement_end_list and statement_start_list. We pass the first list because we want to resynchronize at the end of a statement. We pass the second list in case a statement ending token is missing, so then we want to resynchronize at the beginning of the next statement. The token_in(statement_start_list) test checks for and flags a MISSING_SEMICOLON error.

5.3.1 Assignment statement

Function `assignment_statement` is a simplified version of the one in the calculator utility. Since we are only checking syntax, we no longer make calls to the symbol table routines.

5.3.2 WHILE and REPEAT statements

Function `while_statement` is a straightforward transcription of the corresponding syntax diagram. Function `repeat_statement` is similar, but it processes a statement list consisting of one or more statements separated by semicolons. In its outer loop, we parse each statement in the statement list, and we stay in the loop if, after each statement, we see the start of the next statement. We consume the semicolon(s) after the statement in the inner loop.

5.3.3 IF and FOR statements

Pascal syntax supports two forms of the IF statement, one with an ELSE branch and one without. In function `if_statement`, we look for the reserved word token ELSE after processing the statement of the THEN branch. If there is an ELSE, we parse the statement of the ELSE branch.

One potential problem with IF statements is that of the "dangling ELSE." We will explore this further in the questions and exercises at the end of this chapter.

Function `for_statement` is another straightforward transcription of the corresponding syntax diagram.

5.3.4 CASE statement

The CASE statement has the most complex syntax of all the Pascal statements. We need to define two token lists, `follow_expr_list` and `case_label_start_list`, which are the list of the tokens that can follow the CASE expression and the list of the tokens that can start a CASE branch label:

```
TOKEN_CODE follow_expr_list[]      = {OF, SEMICOLON, 0};

TOKEN_CODE case_label_start_list[] = {IDENTIFIER, NUMBER, PLUS,
                                      MINUS, STRING, 0};
```

In function `case_statement`, we first parse the CASE expression. We next call `synchronize` to look for the OF, passing both `follow_expr_list` and `case_label_start_list`. We want to resynchronize at the OF, but if the OF is missing, we will resynchronize at the start of the first CASE label.

Then, as long as we're looking at the start of a CASE label, we call function `case_branch` to parse a CASE branch. After each CASE branch, we look for a semicolon. If we see one, we loop again to parse the next CASE branch. If we find the start of the next CASE label instead, we flag the MISSING_SEMICOLON error and loop again. If there is any other token, we assume that we are done and exit the loop. We finish with a check for the END.

In function case_branch, we parse a CASE branch that consists of a CASE label list followed by a colon and the branch statement. We define the token list follow_case_label_list to be the list of tokens that can follow the label list:

```
TOKEN_CODE follow_case_label_list[] = {COLON, SEMICOLON, 0};
```

We call function case_label to parse each label. After the last label, we call synchronize, passing both follow_case_label_list and statement_start_list. We want to resynchronize at the colon, but if it is missing, we will settle for the start of the next branch statement.

In function case_label, we parse a CASE label list that consists of one or more constants (numbers, identifiers, or characters) separated by commas. A unary + or - sign can come before a number or an identifier. Note that we do not as yet verify that an identifier is the name of a constant.

5.3.5 Compound statement

In Pascal, a compound statement is a statement list of one or more statements separated by semicolons. The reserved word token BEGIN precedes the statement list, and the reserved word token END follows it. In the outer loop of function compound_statement, we call function statement to parse each statement in the list, and then in the inner loop we consume any semicolons after the statement. If the current token is END, we break out of the outer loop. Otherwise, we call synchronize to make sure we're looking at the start of the next statement instead of one of the other statement ending tokens ELSE or UNTIL. We loop again if we are indeed at the start of the next statement. Outside the loop, we finish by verifying that we have the END.

5.3.6 Expressions

Figure 5-5 shows the other file in the parser module, expr.c. It contains the expression parsing functions from the calculator utility program in Chapter 4. Since we are no longer interpreting the expressions, the stack operations are gone, and function factor no longer makes calls to the symbol table routines. We also take advantage of function token_in and define several new token lists, rel_op_list, add_op_list, and mult_op_list:

```
TOKEN_CODE rel_op_list[]  = {LT, LE, EQUAL, NE, GE, GT, 0};
TOKEN_CODE add_op_list[]  = {PLUS, MINUS, OR, 0};
TOKEN_CODE mult_op_list[] = {STAR, SLASH, DIV, MOD, AND, 0};
```

FIGURE 5-5   File expr.c.

```
/****************************************************************/
/*                                                            */
/*      E X P R E S S I O N   P A R S E R                      */
/*                                                            */
/*      Parsing routines for expressions.                     */
/*                                                            */
/*      FILE:       expr.c                                    */
/*                                                            */
/*      MODULE:     parser                                    */
/*                                                            */
/****************************************************************/

#include <stdio.h>
#include "common.h"
#include "error.h"
#include "scanner.h"
#include "parser.h"

/*------------------------------------------------------------*/
/* Externals                                                  */
/*------------------------------------------------------------*/

extern TOKEN_CODE token;
extern char       word_string[];

/*------------------------------------------------------------*/
/* expression      Process an expression consisting of a      */
/*                 simple expression optionally followed      */
/*                 by a relational operator and a second      */
/*                 simple expression.                         */
/*------------------------------------------------------------*/

TOKEN_CODE rel_op_list[] = {LT, LE, EQUAL, NE, GE, GT, 0};

expression()

{
    TOKEN_CODE op;              /* an operator token */

    simple_expression();        /* first simple expr */

    /*
    -- If there is a relational operator, remember it and
    -- process the second simple expression.
    */
    if (token_in(rel_op_list)) {
        op = token;             /* remember operator */

        get_token();
        simple_expression();    /* 2nd simple expr */
    }
}

/*------------------------------------------------------------*/
/* simple_expression  Process a simple expression consisting  */
/*                    of terms separated by +, -, or OR       */
/*                    operators.  There may be a unary + or - */
/*                    before the first term.                  */
/*------------------------------------------------------------*/

TOKEN_CODE add_op_list[] = {PLUS, MINUS, OR, 0};

simple_expression()
```

```
{
    TOKEN_CODE op;                  /* an operator token */
    TOKEN_CODE unary_op = PLUS;     /* a unary operator token */

    /*
    -- If there is a unary + or -, remember it.
    */
    if ((token == PLUS) || (token == MINUS)) {
        unary_op = token;
        get_token();
    }

    term();            /* first term */

    /*
    -- Loop to process subsequent terms separated by operators.
    */
    while (token_in(add_op_list)) {
        op = token;        /* remember operator */

        get_token();
        term();            /* subsequent term */
    }
}

/*------------------------------------------------------------*/
/* term                  Process a term consisting of factors */
/*                       separated by *, /, DIV, MOD, or AND  */
/*                       operators.                           */
/*------------------------------------------------------------*/

TOKEN_CODE mult_op_list[] = {STAR, SLASH, DIV, MOD, AND, 0};

term()

{
    TOKEN_CODE op;      /* an operator token */

    factor();           /* first factor */

    /*
    -- Loop to process subsequent factors
    -- separated by operators.
    */
    while (token_in(mult_op_list)) {
        op = token;        /* remember operator */

        get_token();
        factor();          /* subsequent factor */
    }
}

/*------------------------------------------------------------*/
/* factor               Process a factor, which is a variable, */
/*                      a number, NOT followed by a factor, or */
/*                      a parenthesized subexpression.        */
/*------------------------------------------------------------*/

factor()

{
    switch (token) {

        case IDENTIFIER:
```

```
            get_token();                                                    break;
            break;
                                                            case LPAREN:
    case NUMBER:                                                get_token();
        get_token();                                            expression();
        break;
                                                                if_token_get_else_error(RPAREN, MISSING_RPAREN);
    case STRING:                                                break;
        get_token();
        break;                                              default:
                                                                error(INVALID_EXPRESSION);
    case NOT:                                                   break;
        get_token();                                    }
        factor();
                                                    }
```

5.4 Program 5-1: Pascal Syntax Checker I

Now that we have all the statement parsing routines, we can put them all together
into the first version of our syntax checking utility program. The main file,
syntax1.c, is shown in Figure 5-6. We initialize the scanner, extract the first token,
and then call function statement to parse a statement, which can be a compound
statement. After parsing the statement, we look for the end of file and we print
a summary showing the number of source lines read and the number of syntax
errors. Figure 5-7 shows sample output.

FIGURE 5-6   File syntax1.c.

```
/*****************************************************************/   extern int        error_count;
/*                                                             */
/*      Program 5-1:  Syntax Checker I                         */    /*-------------------------------------------------------------*/
/*                                                             */    /* Globals                                                     */
/*      Check the syntax of Pascal statements.                 */    /*-------------------------------------------------------------*/
/*                                                             */
/*      FILE:     syntax1.c                                    */    char buffer[MAX_PRINT_LINE_LENGTH];
/*                                                             */
/*      REQUIRES: Modules parser, symbol table, scanner,       */    /*-------------------------------------------------------------*/
/*                      error                                  */    /* main                 Initialize the scanner and call the    */
/*                                                             */    /*                      statement routine.                     */
/*      USAGE:    syntax1 sourcefile                           */    /*-------------------------------------------------------------*/
/*                                                             */
/*      sourcefile     name of source file containing          */    main(argc, argv)
/*                     statements to be checked                */
/*                                                             */        int  argc;
/*****************************************************************/       char *argv[];

#include <stdio.h>                                              {
#include "common.h"                                                 /*
#include "error.h"                                                  -- Initialize the scanner.
#include "scanner.h"                                                */
                                                                    init_scanner(argv[1]);
/*-------------------------------------------------------------*/
/* Externals                                                   */    /*
/*-------------------------------------------------------------*/    -- Parse a statement.
                                                                    */
extern TOKEN_CODE token;                                            get_token();
extern int        line_number;                                      statement();
```

```
/*
-- Look for the end of file.
*/
while (token != END_OF_FILE) {
    error(UNEXPECTED_TOKEN);
    get_token();
}

quit_scanner();

/*
-- Print the parser's summary.
```

```
*/
print_line("\n");
print_line("\n");
sprintf(buffer, "%20d Source lines.\n", line_number);
print_line(buffer);
sprintf(buffer, "%20d Source errors.\n", error_count);
print_line(buffer);

if (error_count == 0) exit(0);
else                  exit(-SYNTAX_ERROR);
}
```

FIGURE 5-7   Sample output from the syntax checker I.

```
Page 1   syntax1.in   Tue Jul 10 00:15:58 1990

  1 0: BEGIN
  2 0:     alpha := beta - gamma;
  3 0:
  4 0:     IF alpha <> theta THEN BEGIN
  5 0:         area := length*width
  6 0:         volume := area*height + ;
                              ^
*** ERROR: Missing ; .
                                        ^
*** ERROR: Invalid expression.
  7 0:     END
  8 0:     ELSE x := ((a - b/c) MOD f;

*** ERROR: Missing right parenthesis.
  9 0:
 10 0:     CASE switch OF
```

```
 11 0:         one, 2, three: z := -123.45;
 12 0:
 13 0:         four, -'5':  BEGIN
                      ^
*** ERROR: Invalid constant.
 14 0:             n := n + 1;
 15 0:             k := k - 1;
 16 0:         END
 17 0:     END
 18 0:
          ^
*** ERROR: Unexpected end of file.

*** ERROR: Missing END.


                    18 Source lines.
                     6 Source errors.
```

5.5 Type checking

A statement that follows the syntax rules as described by the syntax diagrams is not necessarily correct. For example, the diagrams do not indicate type. Type checking must wait until we can parse declarations, which we will do in the next chapter. Nevertheless, the syntax checker is useful for flagging some of the most common errors.

Questions and exercises

1. In Pascal, a compound statement can appear anywhere a simple statement appears. Explain how the statement parsing routines support this rule.

2. *Dangling* ELSE. In the following, the THEN branch of one IF statement contains

another IF statement. The question is, to which IF statement does the ELSE branch belong?

IF a = b THEN IF c = d THEN a := c ELSE a := d

In Pascal, the ELSE always belongs to the IF immediately preceding it, so in the above example, it belongs to the second IF. Explain how function if_statement supports this rule. Does the syntax diagram for the IF statement support this rule?

3. Can the syntax checker guarantee that the expression in an IF statement evaluates to a boolean value? How does it handle a CASE label like 3.2?

4. *Empty statements.* An empty statement is any semicolon not preceded by a statement. For example,

BEGIN ; ; END

contains two empty statements. How does our syntax checker handle empty statements?

5. Functions repeat_statement and compound_statement both contain inner loops to consume semicolons between the statements of the statement list. Why not put that loop instead at the end of function statement to consume semicolons after every statement?

6. In some languages like C, the semicolon is a statement terminator, not a separator. How would the statement parsing routines be modified to support such a rule?

7. In some languages like Ada, compound statements are bracketed by statement keywords. For example:

```
IF i < 0 THEN
    i := -i;
    n := n + 1;
END IF;
```

```
IF count > limit THEN
    error_number := 101;
    count := 0;
ELSE
    circumference := 2*pi*r;
    area := pi*r*r;
END IF;
```

```
WHILE count <= limit LOOP
    i := i + 1;
    j := j - 1;
END LOOP;
```

Discuss what general changes are necessary to the statement parsing routines to support such a rule, and whether or not such a rule leads to simpler parsing routines.

8. In FORTRAN, blanks between tokens are not only ignored, but they are unnecessary! For example, the following statement:

```
DO 10 I = 1, 25
```

can also be correctly written as:

```
DO10I=1,25
```

Describe the difficulties of writing a scanner and a parser for FORTRAN. Compare how the previous statement is scanned and parsed with the following statement:

```
DO10I=1.25
```

At what point do the scanner and parser distinguish between the two statements? What sort of backtracking is necessary?

(Cynical compiler writers have said that FORTRAN is a language that must be parsed before it can be scanned.)

CHAPTER 6

Parsing Declarations

Now that we can parse Pascal statements, we are ready to tackle the declarations that precede them in a program: constant definitions, type definitions, and variable declarations. In this chapter, we'll do more than just syntax checking. We will also perform the semantic actions of building the symbol table structures to represent the information in the declarations.

As in the previous chapters, we will develop the necessary skills by writing utility programs. These skills will enable us to:

- parse and analyze Pascal declarations
- enter declaration information into the symbol table
- perform type checking

The first program is a Pascal declarations analyzer that parses declarations, enters the information into the symbol table, and writes out a description of each declaration based on the symbol table information. The second program builds upon the syntax checker of the previous chapter. Not only will this version check the syntax of declarations and statements, but it also will do type checking.

6.1 Pascal declarations

Figure 6-1 shows the syntax diagrams for the Pascal declarations that you will parse. Declarations consist of three parts: constant definition, type definition, and variable declaration. Each part is optional, but they must be in that order, and each part is separated by a semicolon. In this book, you will not do statement label declarations, packed types, pointer types, set types, or variant record types. These constructs are explored in the questions and exercises at the end of this chapter.

The constant definition part consists of the reserved word CONST followed by a list of constant definitions separated by semicolons. Each definition consists of an identifier followed by an equal sign and then a constant. The constant may be a number or a string, or a previously defined constant identifier. A unary + or

FIGURE 6-1   Syntax diagrams for Pascal declarations.

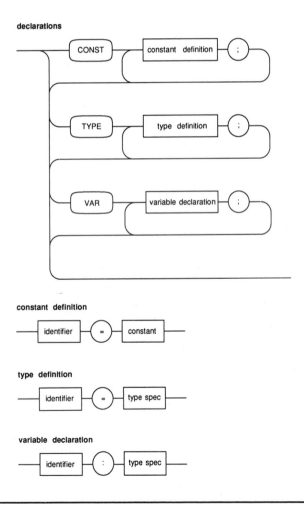

FIGURE 6-1   Continued

type spec

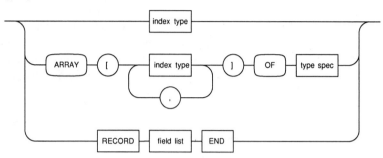

index type

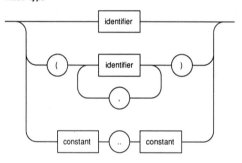

field list

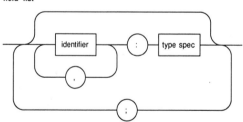

variable declaration

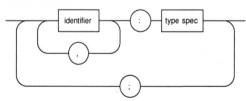

- sign may come before a numeric constant or a constant identifier whose value is a number.

The type definition part consists of the reserved word TYPE followed by a list of type definitions separated by semicolons. Each definition consists of an identifier followed by an equal sign and then a type specification. The specification can be for an enumeration type, a subrange type, an array type, or a record type, or it can simply be a previously-defined type identifier.

The variable declaration part consists of the reserved word VAR followed by a list of variable declarations separated by semicolons. Each declaration consists of a list of identifiers separated by commas, a colon, and then a type specification.

Pascal allows you to define named and unnamed types. The following example defines two names types, the subrange type teens and the array type list. There are also two unnamed types, the subrange type of the values 1..10 and the enumeration type with the values north, south, east, and west.

```
TYPE
    teens = 11..19;
    list  = ARRAY [1..10] OF real;

VAR
    direction : (north, south, east, west);
```

6.2 Changes to the modules

We need to change the parser and symbol table modules to add the ability to parse declarations. Foremost is the addition of the new file decl.c to the parser module:

Parser Module

parser.h	c	Parser header file
stmt.c	c	Parse statements
expr.c	c	Parse expressions
decl.c	n	Parse declarations

Scanner Module

scanner.h	u	Scanner header file
scanner.c	u	Scanner routines

Symbol Table Module

symtab.h	c	Symbol table header file
symtab.c	c	Symbol table routines

Error Module

error.h	*u*	Error header file
error.c	*u*	Error routines

Miscellaneous

common.h	*u*	Common header file

Where: *u* file unchanged from the previous chapter
  c file changed from the previous chapter
  n new file

New file decl.c contains the routines to parse declarations. We add type checking to the routines in stmt.c and expr.c, and we change symtab.h and symtab.c to add type information to the symbol table. Finally, we make changes to parser.h that are related to type checking.

6.3 Symbol table changes

The key to success in parsing declarations is to design good data structures to represent all the information, and then to build these structures as each declaration is parsed. You should not be too surprised that in order for a compiler or an interpreter to be able to parse data structures it must itself be able to create and manipulate its own data structures!

6.3.1 Symbol table structures and macros

The symbol table that we have built so far contains no type information about each identifier. Figure 6-2 shows the new version of file symtab.h. The new structure type TYPE_STRUCT stores type information about each identifier. The SYMTAB_NODE structure now has a TYPE_STRUCT_PTR field typep that points to a TYPE_STRUCT structure that is allocated for each identifier's symbol table node.

FIGURE 6-2   File symtab.h.

```
/*****************************************************************/      #include "common.h"
/*                                                             */
/*      S Y M B O L   T A B L E   (Header)                     */        /*-------------------------------------------------------------*/
/*                                                             */        /* Value structure                                           */
/*      FILE:       symtab.h                                   */        /*-------------------------------------------------------------*/
/*                                                             */
/*      MODULE:     symbol table                               */        typedef union {
/*                                                             */            int    integer;
/*****************************************************************/            float  real;
                                                                            char   character;
#ifndef symtab_h                                                            char   *stringp;
#define symtab_h                                                        } VALUE;
```

```
/*---------------------------------------------------------*/
/*  Definition structure                                   */
/*---------------------------------------------------------*/

typedef enum {
    UNDEFINED,
    CONST_DEFN, TYPE_DEFN, VAR_DEFN, FIELD_DEFN,
    VALPARM_DEFN, VARPARM_DEFN,
    PROG_DEFN, PROC_DEFN, FUNC_DEFN,
} DEFN_KEY;

typedef enum {
    DECLARED, FORWARD,
    READ, READLN, WRITE, WRITELN,
    ABS, ARCTAN, CHR, COS, EOFF, EOLN, EXP, LN, ODD, ORD,
    PRED, ROUND, SIN, SQR, SQRT, SUCC, TRUNC,
} ROUTINE_KEY;

typedef struct {
    DEFN_KEY key;
    union {
        struct {
            VALUE value;
        } constant;

        struct {
            ROUTINE_KEY       key;
            int               parm_count;
            int               total_parm_size;
            int               total_local_size;
            struct symtab_node *parms;
            struct symtab_node *locals;
            struct symtab_node *local_symtab;
            char              *code_segment;
        } routine;

        struct {
            int               offset;
            struct symtab_node *record_idp;
        } data;
    } info;
} DEFN_STRUCT;

/*---------------------------------------------------------*/
/*  Type structure                                         */
/*---------------------------------------------------------*/

typedef enum {
    NO_FORM,
    SCALAR_FORM, ENUM_FORM, SUBRANGE_FORM,
    ARRAY_FORM, RECORD_FORM,
} TYPE_FORM;

typedef struct type_struct {
    TYPE_FORM         form;
    int               size;
    struct symtab_node *type_idp;
    union {
        struct {
            struct symtab_node *const_idp;
            int               max;
        } enumeration;

        struct {
            struct type_struct *range_typep;
            int               min, max;
        } subrange;
```

```
        struct {
            struct type_struct *index_typep, *elmt_typep;
            int               min_index, max_index;
            int               elmt_count;
        } array;

        struct {
            struct symtab_node *field_symtab;
        } record;
    } info;
} TYPE_STRUCT, *TYPE_STRUCT_PTR;

/*---------------------------------------------------------*/
/*  Symbol table node                                      */
/*---------------------------------------------------------*/

typedef struct symtab_node {
    struct symtab_node *left, *right;  /* ptrs to subtrees */
    struct symtab_node *next;          /* for chaining nodes */
    char              *name;           /* name string */
    char              *info;           /* ptr to generic info */
    DEFN_STRUCT       defn;            /* definition struct */
    TYPE_STRUCT_PTR   typep;           /* ptr to type struct */
    int               level;           /* nesting level */
    int               label_index;     /* index for code label */
} SYMTAB_NODE, *SYMTAB_NODE_PTR;

/*---------------------------------------------------------*/
/*  Functions                                              */
/*---------------------------------------------------------*/

SYMTAB_NODE_PTR search_symtab();
SYMTAB_NODE_PTR enter_symtab();
TYPE_STRUCT_PTR make_string_typep();

         /***************************************/
         /*                                     */
         /*    Macros to search symbol tables   */
         /*                                     */
         /***************************************/

/*---------------------------------------------------------*/
/*  search_this_symtab          Search the given symbol    */
/*                              table for the current id   */
/*                              name.  Set a pointer to the */
/*                              entry if found, else to    */
/*                              NULL.                       */
/*---------------------------------------------------------*/

#define search_this_symtab(idp, this_symtab)              \
    idp = search_symtab(word_string, this_symtab)

/*---------------------------------------------------------*/
/*  search_all_symtab           Search the local symbol    */
/*                              table for the current id   */
/*                              name.  Set a pointer to the */
/*                              entry if found, else to    */
/*                              NULL.                       */
/*---------------------------------------------------------*/

#define search_all_symtab(idp)                            \
    idp = search_symtab(word_string, symtab_root)

/*---------------------------------------------------------*/
/*  enter_local_symtab          Enter the current id name  */
/*                              into the local symbol      */
/*                              table, and set a pointer   */
```

```
/*                              to the entry.        */
/*---------------------------------------------------*/


#define enter_local_symtab(idp)                      \
    idp = enter_symtab(word_string, &symtab_root)


/*---------------------------------------------------*/
/*  enter_name_local_symtab      Enter the given name into  */
/*                               the local symbol table, and */
/*                               set a pointer to the entry. */
/*---------------------------------------------------*/


#define enter_name_local_symtab(idp, name)           \
    idp = enter_symtab(name, &symtab_root)


/*---------------------------------------------------*/
/*  search_and_find_all_symtab   Search the local symbol    */
/*                               table for the current id    */
/*                               name. If not found, ID      */
/*                               UNDEFINED error, and enter  */
/*                               into the local symbol table.*/
/*                               Set a pointer to the entry. */
/*---------------------------------------------------*/


#define search_and_find_all_symtab(idp)              \
    if ((idp = search_symtab(word_string,            \
                      symtab_root)) == NULL) {        \
        error(UNDEFINED_IDENTIFIER);                  \
        idp = enter_symtab(word_string, &symtab_root); \
        idp->defn.key = UNDEFINED;                    \
        idp->typep = &dummy_type;                     \
    }
```

```
/*---------------------------------------------------------*/
/*  search_and_enter_local_symtab    Search the local symbol  */
/*                                   table for the current id */
/*                                   name.  Enter the name if */
/*                                   it is not already in there, */
/*                                   else ID REDEFINED error. */
/*                                   Set a pointer to the entry. */
/*---------------------------------------------------------*/


#define search_and_enter_local_symtab(idp)           \
    if ((idp = search_symtab(word_string,            \
                        symtab_root)) == NULL) {      \
        idp = enter_symtab(word_string, &symtab_root); \
    }                                                \
    else error(REDEFINED_IDENTIFIER)


/*---------------------------------------------------------*/
/*  search_and_enter_this_symtab     Search the given symbol  */
/*                                   table for the current id */
/*                                   name.  Enter the name if */
/*                                   it is not already in there, */
/*                                   else ID REDEFINED error. */
/*                                   Set a pointer to the entry. */
/*---------------------------------------------------------*/


#define search_and_enter_this_symtab(idp, this_symtab) \
    if ((idp = search_symtab(word_string,            \
                        this_symtab)) == NULL) {      \
        idp = enter_symtab(word_string, &this_symtab); \
    }                                                \
    else error(REDEFINED_IDENTIFIER)

#endif
```

The new enumeration type TYPE_FORM represents the forms of a Pascal type: scalar, enumeration, subrange, array, or record. We set field form of TYPE_STRUCT to one of these constants and field size to the size in bytes of a variable of the type. If the type is named, we point field type_idp to the identifier symbol table node. Otherwise, for an unnamed type, we set the field to NULL. We store particular information for each Pascal type form in the union field info.

We keep information about an enumeration type in info.enumeration. Field const_idp points to the linked list of symbol table nodes for the enumeration constant identifiers, and field max is the maximum enumeration value.

A subrange type uses info.subrange. Field range_typep points to the type structure that represents the range type, and fields min and max are the minimum and maximum values of the subrange.

We store various pieces of information about an array type in info.array. Fields index_typep and elmt_typep point to the type structures that represent the array's index type and element type. Fields min_index and max_index are the minimum and maximum index values, and field elmt_count is the number of elements. Finally, info.record uses field field_symtab to point to a private symbol table for a record type's field identifiers.

Figure 6-3 shows the symbol table nodes and type structures for various type definitions. The multidimensional array type is especially interesting. Both of the following result in the same data structures:

FIGURE 6-3   Symbol table nodes and type structures for sample type definitions. Again, we draw the name strings inside of, instead of pointed to by, the name field of the symbol table nodes.

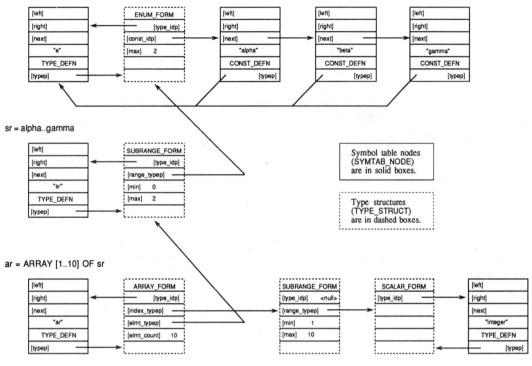

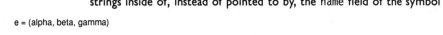

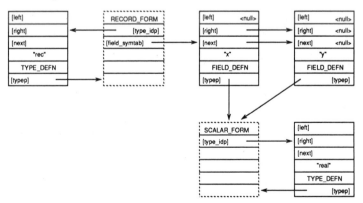

```
ARRAY [1..10, 3..7] OF integer

ARRAY [1..10] OF ARRAY [3..7] OF integer
```

Figure 6-4 shows these structures.

File symtab.h now contains several macros that represent common code sequences for manipulating the symbol table. Their names may not all be meaningful right now; until now, we have used only one symbol table. In this chapter, we will create a private symbol table for each record type, and beginning in the next chapter, we will also create a separate symbol table for each procedure and function. We choose the macro names with all this in mind. In later chapters, we will rewrite some of the macros, but the calls to these macros will not need to change.

We call macro search_this_symtab to search a particular symbol table for the current identifier name in word_string. If we find it, we point idp to the symbol table node. Otherwise, we set idp to NULL. We call macro search_all_ symtab to search all the symbol tables for the current identifier name. For now, we only search the one symbol table pointed to by symtab_root.

FIGURE 6-4   Two equivalent specifications for a multidimensional array type.

ar2 = ARRAY [1..10, 3..7] OF integer
ar2 = ARRAY [1..10] OF ARRAY [3..7] OF integer

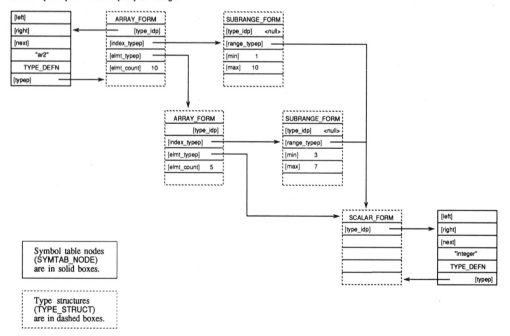

We call macro `enter_local_symtab` to enter the current identifier name into the local symbol table and to point `idp` to the new node. For now, the local symbol table is simply the one symbol table pointed to by `symtab_root`. We call macro `enter_name_local_symtab` to enter a particular name into the local symbol table.

Whenever we call macro `search_and_find_all_symtab`, we expect to find the current identifier name. If we find it, we point `idp` to the symbol table node. Otherwise, we flag the `UNDEFINED_IDENTIFIER` error, enter the name into the local symbol table, and initialize the new node's `defn.key` and `typep` fields to `UNDEFINED` and `dummy_type` (explained later). For now, the only symbol table we will work with is the one pointed to by `symtab_root`.

Whenever we call macro `search_and_enter_local_symtab`, we expect *not* to find the current identifier name. If the name is not in there, we enter it. Otherwise, we flag the `REDEFINED_IDENTIFIER` error. In either case, we point `idp` to the node. For now, the local symbol table is the one pointed to by `symtab_root`. Macro `search_and_enter_this_symtab` is similar, except we use a particular symbol table.

6.3.2 Initializing the symbol table

Pascal has four predefined types, `integer`, `real`, `boolean`, and `char`. Type `boolean` is an enumeration type with constant identifiers `false` and `true`. We must enter all this information into the symbol table before parsing a program.

Figure 6-5 shows the new file `symtab.c`. There are several new global variables. The four pointer variables `integer_typep`, `real_typep`, `boolean_typep`, and `char_typep` point to type structures representing the predefined types. Structure `dummy_type` initializes some symbol table nodes and represents certain errors that the parser will detect.

FIGURE 6-5   File `symtab.c`.

```
/****************************************************************/
/*                                                              */
/*       S Y M B O L   T A B L E                                */
/*                                                              */
/*       Symbol table routines.                                 */
/*                                                              */
/*       FILE:      symtab.c                                    */
/*                                                              */
/*       MODULE:    symbol table                                */
/*                                                              */
/****************************************************************/

#include <stdio.h>
#include "common.h"
#include "error.h"
#include "symtab.h"

/*--------------------------------------------------------------*/
/* Globals                                                      */
/*--------------------------------------------------------------*/

SYMTAB_NODE_PTR symtab_root = NULL;    /* symbol table root */
```

```
TYPE_STRUCT_PTR integer_typep, real_typep,      /* predefined types */
                boolean_typep, char_typep;

TYPE_STRUCT dummy_type = {       /* for erroneous type definitions */
    NO_FORM,        /* form */
    0,              /* size */
    NULL            /* type_idp */
};

/*--------------------------------------------------------------*/
/* search_symtab       Search for a name in the symbol table.  */
/*                     Return a pointer of the entry if found, */
/*                     or NULL if not.                         */
/*--------------------------------------------------------------*/

      SYMTAB_NODE_PTR
search_symtab(name, np)

      char          *name;      /* name to search for */
      SYMTAB_NODE_PTR np;       /* ptr to symtab root */

{
```

```
    int cmp;

    /*
    -- Loop to check each node.  Return if the node matches,
    -- else continue search down the left or right subtree.
    */
    while (np != NULL) {
        cmp = strcmp(name, np->name);
        if (cmp == 0) return(np);           /* found */
        np = cmp < 0 ? np->left : np->right;   /* continue search */
    }

    return(NULL);                           /* not found */
}

/*--------------------------------------------------------------*/
/*  enter_symtab       Enter a name into the symbol table,      */
/*                     and return a pointer to the new entry.   */
/*--------------------------------------------------------------*/

    SYMTAB_NODE_PTR
enter_symtab(name, npp)

    char            *name;      /* name to enter */
    SYMTAB_NODE_PTR *npp;       /* ptr to ptr to symtab root */

{
    int             cmp;        /* result of strcmp */
    SYMTAB_NODE_PTR new_nodep;  /* ptr to new entry */
    SYMTAB_NODE_PTR np;         /* ptr to node to test */

    /*
    -- Create the new node for the name.
    */
    new_nodep = alloc_struct(SYMTAB_NODE);
    new_nodep->name = alloc_bytes(strlen(name) + 1);
    strcpy(new_nodep->name, name);
    new_nodep->left = new_nodep->right = new_nodep->next = NULL;
    new_nodep->info = NULL;
    new_nodep->defn.key = UNDEFINED;
    new_nodep->typep = NULL;
    new_nodep->level = new_nodep->label_index = 0;

    /*
    -- Loop to search for the insertion point.
    */
    while ((np = *npp) != NULL) {
        cmp = strcmp(name, np->name);
        npp = cmp < 0 ? &(np->left) : &(np->right);
    }

    *npp = new_nodep;                       /* replace */
    return(new_nodep);
}

/*--------------------------------------------------------------*/
/*  init_symtab        Initialize the symbol table with         */
/*                     predefined identifiers and types,        */
/*                     and routines.                            */
/*--------------------------------------------------------------*/

init_symtab()

{
    SYMTAB_NODE_PTR integer_idp, real_idp, boolean_idp, char_idp,
                    false_idp, true_idp;

    enter_name_local_symtab(integer_idp, "integer");
    enter_name_local_symtab(real_idp,    "real");
    enter_name_local_symtab(boolean_idp, "boolean");
    enter_name_local_symtab(char_idp,    "char");
    enter_name_local_symtab(false_idp,   "false");
    enter_name_local_symtab(true_idp,    "true");

    integer_typep = alloc_struct(TYPE_STRUCT);
    real_typep    = alloc_struct(TYPE_STRUCT);
    boolean_typep = alloc_struct(TYPE_STRUCT);
    char_typep    = alloc_struct(TYPE_STRUCT);

    integer_idp->defn.key    = TYPE_DEFN;
    integer_idp->typep       = integer_typep;
    integer_typep->form      = SCALAR_FORM;
    integer_typep->size      = sizeof(int);
    integer_typep->type_idp  = integer_idp;

    real_idp->defn.key       = TYPE_DEFN;
    real_idp->typep          = real_typep;
    real_typep->form         = SCALAR_FORM;
    real_typep->size         = sizeof(float);
    real_typep->type_idp     = real_idp;

    boolean_idp->defn.key    = TYPE_DEFN;
    boolean_idp->typep       = boolean_typep;
    boolean_typep->form      = ENUM_FORM;
    boolean_typep->size      = sizeof(int);
    boolean_typep->type_idp  = boolean_idp;

    boolean_typep->info.enumeration.max = 1;
    boolean_idp->typep->info.enumeration.const_idp = false_idp;
    false_idp->defn.key = CONST_DEFN;
    false_idp->defn.info.constant.value.integer = 0;
    false_idp->typep = boolean_typep;

    false_idp->next = true_idp;
    true_idp->defn.key = CONST_DEFN;
    true_idp->defn.info.constant.value.integer = 1;
    true_idp->typep = boolean_typep;

    char_idp->defn.key   = TYPE_DEFN;
    char_idp->typep      = char_typep;
    char_typep->form     = SCALAR_FORM;
    char_typep->size     = sizeof(char);
    char_typep->type_idp = char_idp;
}
```

In the new function init_symtab, we enter the predefined type names integer, real, boolean, and char, along with false and true, into the symbol table,
and then we allocate type structures for the four predefined types. We finish by
initializing various fields of the symbol table nodes and type structures. We also

chain the nodes for false and true off of the type structure for boolean by pointing boolean_typep->info.enumeration.const_idp to false_idp, and then pointing false_idp->next to true_idp.

6.4 Program 6-1: A Pascal Declarations Analyzer

The routines in file decl.c will be much easier to understand if you can examine the data structures that it builds for each declaration. Therefore, we will study them in the context of the declarations analyzer utility program.

When the parser processes type declarations, it checks the declarations for syntactic correctness. It must also perform the semantic actions of building the data structures and entering the appropriate information into the symbol table. A logical way for a declarations analyzer to work is to examine these data structures and symbol table entries and print out the information in the source listing right after each declaration.

Figure 6-6 shows the main file of the analyzer analyze.c. String arrays defn_ names and form_names contain names that correspond to the DEFN_KEY and TYPE_ FORM enumeration constants. We will write out these names in the analysis.

FIGURE 6-6   File analyze.c.

```
/*****************************************************************/
/*                                                               */
/*      Program 6-1:  Declarations Analyzer                      */
/*                                                               */
/*      Analyze Pascal constant definitions, type definitions,   */
/*      and variable declarations.                               */
/*                                                               */
/*      FILE:      analyze.c                                     */
/*                                                               */
/*      REQUIRES:  Modules symbol table, scanner, error          */
/*                                                               */
/*                 File decl.c                                   */
/*                                                               */
/*      FLAGS:     Macro flag "analyze" must be defined          */
/*                                                               */
/*      USAGE:     analyze sourcefile                            */
/*                                                               */
/*        sourcefile      name of source file containing         */
/*                        declarations to be analyzed            */
/*                                                               */
/*****************************************************************/

#include <stdio.h>
#include "common.h"
#include "error.h"
#include "scanner.h"
#include "symtab.h"

/*-----------------------------------------------------------*/
/* Externals                                                 */
/*-----------------------------------------------------------*/

extern TYPE_STRUCT_PTR integer_typep, real_typep,
```

```
                                        boolean_typep, char_typep;

extern TOKEN_CODE token;
extern int        line_number, error_count;

extern TYPE_STRUCT dummy_type;

/*-----------------------------------------------------------*/
/* Globals                                                   */
/*-----------------------------------------------------------*/

char buffer[MAX_PRINT_LINE_LENGTH];

char *defn_names[] = {"undefined",
                      "constant", "type", "variable",
                      "field", "procedure", "function"};

char *form_names[] = {"no form",
                      "scalar", "enum", "subrange",
                      "array", "record"};

/*-----------------------------------------------------------*/
/* main                Initialize the scanner and the symbol */
/*                     table, and then call the declarations */
/*                     routine.                              */
/*-----------------------------------------------------------*/

main(argc, argv)

    int  argc;
    char *argv[];

{
```

```
SYMTAB_NODE_PTR program_idp;          /* artificial program id */

/*
-- Initialize the scanner and the symbol table.
*/
init_scanner(argv[1]);
init_symtab();

/*
-- Create an artifical program id node.
*/
program_idp = alloc_struct(SYMTAB_NODE);
program_idp->defn.key = PROG_DEFN;
program_idp->defn.info.routine.key = DECLARED;
program_idp->defn.info.routine.parm_count = 0;
program_idp->defn.info.routine.total_parm_size = 0;
program_idp->defn.info.routine.total_local_size = 0;
program_idp->typep = &dummy_type;
program_idp->label_index = 0;

/*
-- Parse declarations.
*/
get_token();
declarations(program_idp);

/*
-- Look for the end of file.
*/
while (token != END_OF_FILE) {
    error(UNEXPECTED_TOKEN);
    get_token();
}

quit_scanner();

/*
-- Print summary.
*/
print_line("\n");
print_line("\n");
sprintf(buffer, "%20d Source lines.\n", line_number);
print_line(buffer);
sprintf(buffer, "%20d Source errors.\n", error_count);
print_line(buffer);

exit(0);
}
```

```
/*************************/
/*                       */
/*        Analysis       */
/*                       */
/*************************/
```

```
/*-----------------------------------------------------------*/
/* analyze_const_defn      Analyze a constant definition.    */
/*-----------------------------------------------------------*/

analyze_const_defn(idp)

    SYMTAB_NODE_PTR idp;        /* constant id */

{
    char *bp;

    /*
```

```
    -- The constant's name ...
    */
    sprintf(buffer, ">> id = %s\n", idp->name);
    print_line(buffer);

    /*
    -- ... definition and value ...
    */
    sprintf(buffer, ">>    defn = %s, value = ",
                    defn_names[idp->defn.key]);
    bp = buffer + strlen(buffer);

    if ((idp->typep == integer_typep) ||
        (idp->typep->form == ENUM_FORM))
        sprintf(bp, "%d\n",
                idp->defn.info.constant.value.integer);
    else if (idp->typep == real_typep)
        sprintf(bp, "%g\n",
                idp->defn.info.constant.value.real);
    else if (idp->typep == char_typep)
        sprintf(bp, "'%c'\n",
                idp->defn.info.constant.value.character);
    else if (idp->typep->form == ARRAY_FORM)
        sprintf(bp, "'%s'\n",
                idp->defn.info.constant.value.stringp);

    print_line(buffer);

    /*
    -- ... and type.  (Don't try to re-analyze an
    -- enumeration type, or an infinite loop will occur.)
    */
    if (idp->typep->form != ENUM_FORM)
        analyze_type(idp->typep, FALSE);
}
```

```
/*-----------------------------------------------------------*/
/* analyze_type_defn      Analyze a type definition.         */
/*-----------------------------------------------------------*/

analyze_type_defn(idp)

    SYMTAB_NODE_PTR idp;        /* type id */

{
    char *bp;

    /*
    -- The type's name, definition ...
    */
    sprintf(buffer, ">> id = %s\n", idp->name);
    print_line(buffer);

    sprintf(buffer, ">>    defn = %s\n",
                    defn_names[idp->defn.key]);
    print_line(buffer);

    /*
    -- ... and type.
    */
    analyze_type(idp->typep, TRUE);
}
```

```
/*-----------------------------------------------------------*/
/* analyze_type           Analyze a type by calling the      */
/*                        appropriate type analysis routine. */
/*-----------------------------------------------------------*/
```

```
analyze_type(tp, verbose_flag)

    TYPE_STRUCT_PTR tp;          /* ptr to type structure */
    BOOLEAN verbose_flag;        /* TRUE for verbose analysis */

{
    char *bp;

    if (tp == NULL) return;

    /*
    -- The form, byte size, and, if named, its type id.
    */
    sprintf(buffer, ">>    form = %s, size = %d bytes, type id = ",
                    form_names[tp->form], tp->size);
    bp = buffer + strlen(buffer);

    if (tp->type_idp != NULL)
        sprintf(bp, "%s\n", tp->type_idp->name);
    else {
        sprintf(bp, "<unnamed type>\n");
        verbose_flag = TRUE;
    }
    print_line(buffer);

    /*
    -- Call the appropriate type analysis routine.
    */
    switch (tp->form) {
        case ENUM_FORM:
            analyze_enum_type(tp, verbose_flag);
            break;

        case SUBRANGE_FORM:
            analyze_subrange_type(tp, verbose_flag);
            break;

        case ARRAY_FORM:
            analyze_array_type(tp, verbose_flag);
            break;

        case RECORD_FORM:
            analyze_record_type(tp, verbose_flag);
            break;
    }
}

/*------------------------------------------------------------*/
/* analyze_enum_type       Analyze an enumeration type.      */
/*------------------------------------------------------------*/

analyze_enum_type(tp, verbose_flag)

    TYPE_STRUCT_PTR tp;          /* ptr to type structure */
    BOOLEAN verbose_flag;        /* TRUE for verbose analysis */

{
    SYMTAB_NODE_PTR idp;

    if (!verbose_flag) return;

    /*
    -- Loop to analyze each enumeration constant
    -- as a constant definition.
    */
    print_line(">>    --- Enum Constants ---\n");
    for (idp = tp->info.enumeration.const_idp;
```

```
                            idp != NULL;
                            idp = idp->next) analyze_const_defn(idp);
}

/*------------------------------------------------------------*/
/* analyze_subrange_type        Analyze a subrange type.     */
/*------------------------------------------------------------*/

analyze_subrange_type(tp, verbose_flag)

    TYPE_STRUCT_PTR tp;          /* ptr to type structure */
    BOOLEAN verbose_flag;        /* TRUE for verbose analysis */

{
    if (!verbose_flag) return;

    sprintf(buffer, ">>    min value = %d, max value = %d\n",
                    tp->info.subrange.min,
                    tp->info.subrange.max);
    print_line(buffer);

    print_line(">>    --- Range Type ---\n");
    analyze_type(tp->info.subrange.range_typep, FALSE);
}

/*------------------------------------------------------------*/
/* analyze_array_type      Analyze an array type.            */
/*------------------------------------------------------------*/

analyze_array_type(tp, verbose_flag)

    TYPE_STRUCT_PTR tp;          /* ptr to type structure */
    BOOLEAN verbose_flag;        /* TRUE for verbose analysis */

{
    if (!verbose_flag) return;

    sprintf(buffer, ">>    element count = %d\n",
                    tp->info.array.elmt_count);
    print_line(buffer);

    print_line(">>    --- INDEX TYPE ---\n");
    analyze_type(tp->info.array.index_typep, FALSE);

    print_line(">>    --- ELEMENT TYPE ---\n");
    analyze_type(tp->info.array.elmt_typep, FALSE);
}

/*------------------------------------------------------------*/
/* analyze_record_type     Analyze a record type.           */
/*------------------------------------------------------------*/

analyze_record_type(tp, verbose_flag)

    TYPE_STRUCT_PTR tp;          /* ptr to type structure */
    BOOLEAN verbose_flag;        /* TRUE for verbose analysis */

{
    SYMTAB_NODE_PTR idp;

    if (!verbose_flag) return;

    /*
    -- Loop to analyze each record field
    -- as a variable declaration.
    */
    print_line(">>    --- Fields ---\n");
```

```
    for (idp = tp->info.record.field_symtab;                    {
         idp != NULL;                                               sprintf(buffer, ">> id = %s\n", idp->name);
         idp = idp->next) analyze_var_decl(idp);                    print_line(buffer);
}
                                                                    sprintf(buffer, ">>    defn = %s, offset = %d\n",
/*----------------------------------------------------------*/                  defn_names[idp->defn.key],
/* analyze_var_decl        Analyze a variable declaration.   */                 idp->defn.info.data.offset);
/*----------------------------------------------------------*/           print_line(buffer);

analyze_var_decl(idp)
                                                                    analyze_type(idp->typep, FALSE);
    SYMTAB_NODE_PTR idp;       /* variable id */              }
```

In the main routine, we initialize both the scanner and the symbol table, and then allocate and initialize a dummy symbol table node for the program identifier. This node is needed by function declaration, since the declarations parser will hang information off of this node. In the next chapter, we will actually enter nodes into the symbol table for the program identifier and for each procedure and function identifier.

We call function declarations to parse and analyze declarations. Afterwards, we quit the scanner and print our usual statistics.

All of the analysis routines follow the main routine. We will examine each one in the following sections. We'll first see how to analyze the symbol table and type structure information, and then how the routines in file decl.c build these structures. Figure 6-7 shows a sample input file, and Figure 6-8 shows the listing output of the declarations analyzer.

FIGURE 6-7   Sample input file for the declarations analyzer.

```
CONST                                      ar3 = ARRAY [(fee, fye, foe, fum), ten..hundred] OF
    ten       = 10;                                  ARRAY [ee] OF boolean;
    hundred   = 100;                       ar4 = ARRAY [boolean, 'm'..'r'] OF char;
    maxlength = 80;
    pi        = 3.1415626;                 rec = RECORD
    ch        = 'x';                                 i  : integer;
    hello     = 'Hello, world.';                     x  : real;
                                                     ch : char;
TYPE                                               END;
    e  = (alpha, beta, gamma);
    ee = e;                                VAR
    sr = alpha..gamma;                         length, width : integer;
    cr = 'a'..ch;                              radius, circumference : real;
                                               b         : boolean;
    ar  = ARRAY [1..ten] OF integer;           letter : 'a'..'z';
    ar1 = ARRAY [1..10] OF integer;            buffer : ARRAY [1..maxlength] OF char;
    ar2 = ARRAY [e, sr] OF real;               table  : ARRAY [ee, 1..5] OF rec;
```

FIGURE 6-8   Sample output from the declarations analyzer.

Page 1   analyze.in   Tue Jul 10 02:15:49 1990


```
  1 0: CONST
  2 0:    ten      = 10;
>> id = ten
>>    defn = constant, value = 10
>>    form = scalar, size = 2 bytes, type id = integer
  3 0:    hundred  = 100;
>> id = hundred
>>    defn = constant, value = 100
>>    form = scalar, size = 2 bytes, type id = integer
  4 0:    maxlength = 80;
>> id = maxlength
>>    defn = constant, value = 80
>>    form = scalar, size = 2 bytes, type id = integer
  5 0:    pi       = 3.1415626;
>> id = pi
>>    defn = constant, value = 3.14156
>>    form = scalar, size = 4 bytes, type id = real
  6 0:    ch       = 'x';
>> id = ch
>>    defn = constant, value = 'x'
>>    form = scalar, size = 1 bytes, type id = char
  7 0:    hello    = 'Hello, world.';
>> id = hello
>>    defn = constant, value = 'Hello, world.'
>>    form = array, size = 13 bytes, type id = <unnamed type>
>>    element count = 13
>>    --- INDEX TYPE ---
>>    form = subrange, size = 2 bytes, type id = <unnamed type>
>>    min value = 1, max value = 13
>>    --- Range Type ---
>>    form = scalar, size = 2 bytes, type id = integer
>>    --- ELEMENT TYPE ---
>>    form = scalar, size = 1 bytes, type id = char
  8 0:
  9 0: TYPE
 10 0:    e = (alpha, beta, gamma);
>> id = e
>>    defn = type
>>    form = enum, size = 2 bytes, type id = e
>>    --- Enum Constants ---
>> id = alpha
>>    defn = constant, value = 0
>> id = beta
>>    defn = constant, value = 1
>> id = gamma
>>    defn = constant, value = 2
 11 0:    ee = e;
>> id = ee
>>    defn = type
>>    form = enum, size = 2 bytes, type id = e
```

Page 2   analyze.in   Tue Jul 10 02:15:49 1990

```
>>    --- Enum Constants ---
>> id = alpha
>>    defn = constant, value = 0
>> id = beta
>>    defn = constant, value = 1
```

```
>> id = gamma
>>    defn = constant, value = 2
 12 0:    sr = alpha..gamma;
>> id = sr
>>    defn = type
>>    form = subrange, size = 2 bytes, type id = sr
>>    min value = 0, max value = 2
>>    --- Range Type ---
>>    form = enum, size = 2 bytes, type id = e
 13 0:    cr = 'a'..ch;
>> id = cr
>>    defn = type
>>    form = subrange, size = 1 bytes, type id = cr
>>    min value = 97, max value = 120
>>    --- Range Type ---
>>    form = scalar, size = 1 bytes, type id = char
 14 0:
 15 0:    ar = ARRAY [1..ten] OF integer;
>> id = ar
>>    defn = type
>>    form = array, size = 20 bytes, type id = ar
>>    element count = 10
>>    --- INDEX TYPE ---
>>    form = subrange, size = 2 bytes, type id = <unnamed type>
>>    min value = 1, max value = 10
>>    --- Range Type ---
>>    form = scalar, size = 2 bytes, type id = integer
>>    --- ELEMENT TYPE ---
>>    form = scalar, size = 2 bytes, type id = integer
 16 0:    ar1 = ARRAY [1..10] OF integer;
>> id = ar1
>>    defn = type
>>    form = array, size = 20 bytes, type id = ar1
>>    element count = 10
>>    --- INDEX TYPE ---
>>    form = subrange, size = 2 bytes, type id = <unnamed type>
>>    min value = 1, max value = 10
>>    --- Range Type ---
>>    form = scalar, size = 2 bytes, type id = integer
>>    --- ELEMENT TYPE ---
>>    form = scalar, size = 2 bytes, type id = integer
 17 0:    ar2 = ARRAY [e, sr] OF real;
>> id = ar2
>>    defn = type
>>    form = array, size = 36 bytes, type id = ar2
```

Page 3   analyze.in   Tue Jul 10 02:15:49 1990

```
>>    element count = 3
>>    --- INDEX TYPE ---
>>    form = enum, size = 2 bytes, type id = e
>>    --- ELEMENT TYPE ---
>>    form = array, size = 12 bytes, type id = <unnamed type>
>>    element count = 3
>>    --- INDEX TYPE ---
>>    form = subrange, size = 2 bytes, type id = sr
>>    --- ELEMENT TYPE ---
>>    form = scalar, size = 4 bytes, type id = real
 18 0:    ar3 = ARRAY [(fee, fye, foe, fum), ten..hundred] OF
 19 0:            ARRAY [ee] OF boolean;
>> id = ar3
```

```
>>    defn = type
>>    form = array, size = 2184 bytes, type id = ar3
>>    element count = 4
>>    --- INDEX TYPE ---
>>    form = enum, size = 2 bytes, type id = <unnamed type>
>>    --- Enum Constants ---
>> id = fee
>>    defn = constant, value = 0
>> id = fye
>>    defn = constant, value = 1
>> id = foe
>>    defn = constant, value = 2
>> id = fum
>>    defn = constant, value = 3
>>    --- ELEMENT TYPE ---
>>    form = array, size = 546 bytes, type id = <unnamed type>
>>    element count = 91
>>    --- INDEX TYPE ---
>>    form = subrange, size = 2 bytes, type id = <unnamed type>
>>    min value = 10, max value = 100
>>    --- Range Type ---
>>    form = scalar, size = 2 bytes, type id = integer
>>    --- ELEMENT TYPE ---
>>    form = array, size = 6 bytes, type id = <unnamed type>
>>    element count = 3
>>    --- INDEX TYPE ---
>>    form = enum, size = 2 bytes, type id = e
>>    --- ELEMENT TYPE ---
>>    form = enum, size = 2 bytes, type id = boolean
 20 0:    ar4 = ARRAY [boolean, 'm'..'r'] OF char;
>> id = ar4
>>    defn = type
>>    form = array, size = 12 bytes, type id = ar4
>>    element count = 2
>>    --- INDEX TYPE ---
>>    form = enum, size = 2 bytes, type id = boolean
>>    --- ELEMENT TYPE ---
```

Page 4   analyze.in   Tue Jul 10 02:15:49 1990

```
>>    form = array, size = 6 bytes, type id = <unnamed type>
>>    element count = 6
>>    --- INDEX TYPE ---
>>    form = subrange, size = 1 bytes, type id = <unnamed type>
>>    min value = 109, max value = 114
>>    --- Range Type ---
>>    form = scalar, size = 1 bytes, type id = char
>>    --- ELEMENT TYPE ---
>>    form = scalar, size = 1 bytes, type id = char
 21 0:
 22 0:    rec = RECORD
 23 0:            i  : integer;
 24 0:            x  : real;
 25 0:            ch : char;
 26 0:         END;
>> id = rec
>>    defn = type
>>    form = record, size = 7 bytes, type id = rec
>>    --- Fields ---
>> id = i
>>    defn = field, offset = 0
>>    form = scalar, size = 2 bytes, type id = integer
>> id = x
>>    defn = field, offset = 2
```

```
>>    form = scalar, size = 4 bytes, type id = real
>> id = ch
>>    defn = field, offset = 6
>>    form = scalar, size = 1 bytes, type id = char
 27 0:
 28 0: VAR
 29 0:    length, width : integer;
>> id = length
>>    defn = variable, offset = 0
>>    form = scalar, size = 2 bytes, type id = integer
>> id = width
>>    defn = variable, offset = 1
>>    form = scalar, size = 2 bytes, type id = integer
 30 0:    radius, circumference : real;
>> id = radius
>>    defn = variable, offset = 2
>>    form = scalar, size = 4 bytes, type id = real
>> id = circumference
>>    defn = variable, offset = 3
>>    form = scalar, size = 4 bytes, type id = real
 31 0:    b     : boolean;
>> id = b
>>    defn = variable, offset = 4
>>    form = enum, size = 2 bytes, type id = boolean
 32 0:    letter : 'a'..'z';
>> id = letter
```

Page 5   analyze.in   Tue Jul 10 02:15:49 1990

```
>>    defn = variable, offset = 5
>>    form = subrange, size = 1 bytes, type id = <unnamed type>
>>    min value = 97, max value = 122
>>    --- Range Type ---
>>    form = scalar, size = 1 bytes, type id = char
 33 0:    buffer : ARRAY [1..maxlength] OF char;
>> id = buffer
>>    defn = variable, offset = 6
>>    form = array, size = 80 bytes, type id = <unnamed type>
>>    element count = 80
>>    --- INDEX TYPE ---
>>    form = subrange, size = 2 bytes, type id = <unnamed type>
>>    min value = 1, max value = 80
>>    --- Range Type ---
>>    form = scalar, size = 2 bytes, type id = integer
>>    --- ELEMENT TYPE ---
>>    form = scalar, size = 1 bytes, type id = char
 34 0:    table  : ARRAY [ee, 1..5] OF rec;
>> id = table
>>    defn = variable, offset = 7
>>    form = array, size = 105 bytes, type id = <unnamed type>
>>    element count = 3
>>    --- INDEX TYPE ---
>>    form = enum, size = 2 bytes, type id = e
>>    --- ELEMENT TYPE ---
>>    form = array, size = 35 bytes, type id = <unnamed type>
>>    element count = 5
>>    --- INDEX TYPE ---
>>    form = subrange, size = 2 bytes, type id = <unnamed type>
>>    min value = 1, max value = 5
>>    --- Range Type ---
>>    form = scalar, size = 2 bytes, type id = integer
>>    --- ELEMENT TYPE ---
```

```
>>    form = record, size = 7 bytes, type id = rec                35 Source lines.
   35 0:                                                           0 Source errors.
```

6.4.1 Analyzing constant definitions

Function `analyze_const_defn` analyzes a constant definition. The analysis includes the constant identifier's name and definition, the constant's value, and the form, size, and identifier of the constant's type. For example, the following definition:

$$pi = 3.1415626$$

produces:

```
>> id = pi
>>    defn = constant, value = 3.14156
>>    form = scalar, size = 4 bytes, type id = real
```

For a string constant, some further information about the array type is desirable. For example, the definition:

$$hello = \text{'Hello, world.'}$$

produces:

```
>> id = hello
>>    defn = constant, value = 'Hello, world.'
>>    form = array, size = 13 bytes, type id = <unnamed type>
>>    element count = 13
>>    --- INDEX TYPE ---
>>    form = subrange, size = 2 bytes, type id = <unnamed type>
>>    min value = 1, max value = 13
>>    --- Range Type ---
>>    form = scalar, size = 2 bytes, type id = integer
>>    --- ELEMENT TYPE ---
>>    form = scalar, size = 1 bytes, type id = char
```

We print the first two lines containing the constant's name, definition, and value in function `analyze_const_defn`. We print the information about the constant's type in function `analyze_type`.

6.4.2 Analyzing type definitions

The analysis of a type definition consists of the type identifier's name and definition, and the type's form, size, and identifier. An enumeration type includes the name, definition, and value of each enumeration constant identifier. A subrange type includes information about the range type along with the minimum and maximum values. An array type includes information about the index and element types. A record type includes information about each field identifier. Finally, a type that is defined to be equivalent to a previously-defined type includes information about the previously-defined type.

We analyze a type definition in function `analyze_type_defn` by printing the type identifier's name and definition, and then we call function `analyze_type` to print the rest of the information, such as a type's form, size, and the type identifier's name. The first argument is a pointer to the type structure to analyze. The second argument is `verbose_flag`, which controls the amount of information we print. We will use the general rule that we print all type information whenever a new type is being defined, including unnamed types. Otherwise, we print a shorter version of the information. We call the appropriate analysis routine based on the type's form.

We analyze an enumeration type in function `analyze_enum_type`. We run down the list of the symbol table nodes of the enumeration constant identifiers hanging off of `tp->info.enumeration.const_idp`. For each identifier, we print the identifier's name, definition, and constant value. For example, the type definition:

```
e  =  (alpha, beta, gamma)
```

produces:

```
>> id = e
>>    defn = type
>>    form = enum, size = 2 bytes, type id = e
>>    --- Enum Constants ---
>> id = alpha
>>    defn = constant, value = 0
>> id = beta
>>    defn = constant, value = 1
>> id = gamma
>>    defn = constant, value = 2
```

We call function `analyze_subrange_type` to analyze a subrange type. We print the subrange type's minimum and maximum values, and then recursively call function `analyze_type` to analyze the range type. For example, the type definition:

```
sr = alpha..gamma
```

produces:

```
>> id = sr
>>    defn = type
```

```
>>      form = subrange, size = 2 bytes, type id = sr
>>      min value = 0, max value = 2
>>      --- Range Type ---
>>      form = enum, size = 2 bytes, type id = e
```

Note that the range type identifier name e is that of the previously-defined enumeration type.

In function analyze_array_type, we analyze an array type. We first print the array's element count, and then recursively call function analyze_type twice, first to analyze the index type and then to analyze the element type. For example, the following type definition:

$$ar1 = ARRAY\ [1..10]\ OF\ integer$$

produces:

```
>> id = ar1
>>      defn = type
>>      form = array, size = 20 bytes, type id = ar1
>>      element count = 10
>>      --- INDEX TYPE ---
>>      form = subrange, size = 2 bytes, type id = <unnamed type>
>>      min value = 1, max value = 10
>>      --- Range Type ---
>>      form = scalar, size = 2 bytes, type id = integer
>>      --- ELEMENT TYPE ---
>>      form = scalar, size = 2 bytes, type id = integer
```

Finally, we use function analyze_record_type, to analyze a record type. We run down the list of the symbol table nodes of the field identifiers hanging off of tp->info.record.field_symtab. For each identifier, we call function analyze_var_decl. For example, the type definition:

```
rec = RECORD
            i  : integer;
            x  : real;
            ch : char;
        END;
```

produces:

```
>> id = rec
>>      defn = type
>>      form = record, size = 7 bytes, type id = rec
```

```
>>      --- Fields ---
>> id = i
>>    defn = field, offset = 0
>>    form = scalar, size = 2 bytes, type id = integer
>> id = x
>>    defn = field, offset = 2
>>    form = scalar, size = 4 bytes, type id = real
>> id = ch
>>    defn = field, offset = 6
>>    form = scalar, size = 1 bytes, type id = char
```

6.4.3 Analyzing variable declarations

Function analyze_var_decl analyzes a record field or a variable declaration. We print the identifier's name and definition, and then call function analyze_type to analyze the identifier's type. For example, the declaration:

b : boolean

produces:

```
>> id = b
>>    defn = variable, offset = 4
>>    form = enum, size = 2 bytes, type id = boolean
```

6.4.4 Parsing declarations

Figure 6-9 shows file decl.c, which contains the declaration parsing routines that build the type structures and enter the symbol table information that we have been analyzing.

FIGURE 6-9   File decl.c.

```
/*****************************************************************/     #include "parser.h"
/*                                                             */
/*      D E C L A R A T I O N   P A R S E R                    */     /*-------------------------------------------------------------*/
/*                                                             */     /* Externals                                                 */
/*      Parsing routines for delarations.                      */     /*-------------------------------------------------------------*/
/*                                                             */
/*      FILE:     decl.c                                       */     extern TOKEN_CODE        token;
/*                                                             */     extern char              word_string[];
/*      MODULE:   parser                                       */     extern LITERAL           literal;
/*                                                             */
/*****************************************************************/     extern SYMTAB_NODE_PTR   symtab_root;

#include <stdio.h>
#include "common.h"                                                    extern TYPE_STRUCT_PTR   integer_typep, real_typep,
#include "error.h"                                                                              boolean_typep, char_typep;
#include "scanner.h"
#include "symtab.h"                                                    extern TYPE_STRUCT       dummy_type;
```

```
extern TOKEN_CODE         declaration_start_list[],
                          statement_start_list[];


/*------------------------------------------------------*/
/*  Forwards                                            */
/*------------------------------------------------------*/

TYPE_STRUCT_PTR do_type(),
                identifier_type(), enumeration_type(),
                subrange_type(), array_type(), record_type();


/*------------------------------------------------------*/
/*  declarations       Call the routines to process constant  */
/*                     definitions, type definitions, variable */
/*                     declarations, procedure definitions,    */
/*                     and function definitions.               */
/*------------------------------------------------------*/

declarations(rtn_idp)

    SYMTAB_NODE_PTR rtn_idp;      /* id of program or routine */

{

    if (token == CONST) {
        get_token();
        const_definitions();
    }

    if (token == TYPE) {
        get_token();
        type_definitions();
    }

    if (token == VAR) {
        get_token();
        var_declarations(rtn_idp);
    }
}


            /************************/
            /*                      */
            /*      Constants       */
            /*                      */
            /************************/


/*------------------------------------------------------*/
/*  const_definitions   Process constant definitions:   */
/*                                                       */
/*                      <id> = <constant>                */
/*------------------------------------------------------*/

TOKEN_CODE follow_declaration_list[] = {SEMICOLON, IDENTIFIER,
                                        END_OF_FILE, 0};

const_definitions()

{

    SYMTAB_NODE_PTR const_idp;        /* constant id */

    /*
    -- Loop to process definitions separated by semicolons.
    */
    while (token == IDENTIFIER) {
        search_and_enter_local_symtab(const_idp);
        const_idp->defn.key = CONST_DEFN;

        get_token();
```

```
        if_token_get_else_error(EQUAL, MISSING_EQUAL);

        /*
        -- Process the constant.
        */
        do_const(const_idp);
        analyze_const_defn(const_idp);

        /*
        -- Error synchronization:  Should be ;
        */
        synchronize(follow_declaration_list,
                    declaration_start_list, statement_start_list);
        if_token_get(SEMICOLON);
        else if (token_in(declaration_start_list) ||
                 token_in(statement_start_list))
            error(MISSING_SEMICOLON);
    }
}


/*------------------------------------------------------*/
/*  do_const           Process the constant of a constant  */
/*                     definition.                          */
/*------------------------------------------------------*/

do_const(const_idp)

    SYMTAB_NODE_PTR const_idp;          /* constant id */

{

    TOKEN_CODE      sign    = PLUS;     /* unary + or - sign */
    BOOLEAN         saw_sign = FALSE;   /* TRUE iff unary sign */

    /*
    -- Unary + or - sign.
    */
    if ((token == PLUS) || (token == MINUS)) {
        sign     = token;
        saw_sign = TRUE;
        get_token();
    }

    /*
    -- Numeric constant:  Integer or real type.
    */
    if (token == NUMBER) {
        if (literal.type == INTEGER_LIT) {
            const_idp->defn.info.constant.value.integer =
                sign == PLUS ? literal.value.integer
                             : -literal.value.integer;
            const_idp->typep = integer_typep;
        }
        else {
            const_idp->defn.info.constant.value.real =
                sign == PLUS ? literal.value.real
                             : -literal.value.real;
            const_idp->typep = real_typep;
        }
    }

    /*
    -- Identifier constant:  Integer, real, character, enumeration,
    --                       or string (character array) type.
    */
    else if (token == IDENTIFIER) {
        SYMTAB_NODE_PTR idp;

        search_all_symtab(idp);
```

```
        if (idp == NULL)
            error(UNDEFINED_IDENTIFIER);
        else if (idp->defn.key != CONST_DEFN)
            error(NOT_A_CONSTANT_IDENTIFIER);

        else if (idp->typep == integer_typep) {
            const_idp->defn.info.constant.value.integer =
                sign == PLUS ?  idp->defn.info.constant.value.integer
                             : -idp->defn.info.constant.value.integer;
            const_idp->typep = integer_typep;
        }
        else if (idp->typep == real_typep) {
            const_idp->defn.info.constant.value.real =
                sign == PLUS ?  idp->defn.info.constant.value.real
                             : -idp->defn.info.constant.value.real;
            const_idp->typep = real_typep;
        }
        else if (idp->typep == char_typep) {
            if (saw_sign) error(INVALID_CONSTANT);

            const_idp->defn.info.constant.value.character =
                        idp->defn.info.constant.value.character;
            const_idp->typep = char_typep;
        }
        else if (idp->typep->form == ENUM_FORM) {
            if (saw_sign) error(INVALID_CONSTANT);

            const_idp->defn.info.constant.value.integer =
                        idp->defn.info.constant.value.integer;
            const_idp->typep = idp->typep;
        }
        else if (idp->typep->form == ARRAY_FORM) {
            if (saw_sign) error(INVALID_CONSTANT);

            const_idp->defn.info.constant.value.stringp =
                        idp->defn.info.constant.value.stringp;
            const_idp->typep = idp->typep;
        }
    }

    /*
    -- String constant:  Character or string (character array) type.
    */
    else if (token == STRING) {
        if (saw_sign) error(INVALID_CONSTANT);

        if (strlen(literal.value.string) == 1) {
            const_idp->defn.info.constant.value.character =
                                    literal.value.string[0];
            const_idp->typep = char_typep;
        }
        else {
            int length = strlen(literal.value.string);

            const_idp->defn.info.constant.value.stringp =
                                alloc_bytes(length + 1);
            strcpy(const_idp->defn.info.constant.value.stringp,
                literal.value.string);
            const_idp->typep = make_string_typep(length);
        }
    }

    else {
        const_idp->typep = &dummy_type;
        error(INVALID_CONSTANT);
    }
}
```

```
        get_token();
}

                    /************************/
                    /*                      */
                    /*        Types         */
                    /*                      */
                    /************************/

/*----------------------------------------------------------------*/
/*  type_definitions     Process type definitions:               */
/*                                                                */
/*                       <id> = <type>                            */
/*----------------------------------------------------------------*/

type_definitions()

{
    SYMTAB_NODE_PTR type_idp;          /* type id */

    /*
    -- Loop to process definitions separated by semicolons.
    */
    while (token == IDENTIFIER) {
        search_and_enter_local_symtab(type_idp);
        type_idp->defn.key = TYPE_DEFN;

        get_token();
        if_token_get_else_error(EQUAL, MISSING_EQUAL);

        /*
        -- Process the type specification.
        */
        type_idp->typep = do_type();
        if (type_idp->typep->type_idp == NULL)
            type_idp->typep->type_idp = type_idp;

        analyze_type_defn(type_idp);

        /*
        -- Error synchronization:  Should be ;
        */
        synchronize(follow_declaration_list,
                declaration_start_list, statement_start_list);
        if_token_get(SEMICOLON);
        else if (token_in(declaration_start_list) ||
                token_in(statement_start_list))
            error(MISSING_SEMICOLON);
    }
}

/*----------------------------------------------------------------*/
/*  do_type              Process a type specification.  Call the */
/*                       functions that make a type structure    */
/*                       and return a pointer to it.             */
/*----------------------------------------------------------------*/

    TYPE_STRUCT_PTR
do_type()

{
    switch (token) {
        case IDENTIFIER: {
            SYMTAB_NODE_PTR idp;

            search_all_symtab(idp);

            if (idp == NULL) {
```

```
                error(UNDEFINED_IDENTIFIER);
                return(&dummy_type);
            }
            else if (idp->defn.key == TYPE_DEFN)
                return(identifier_type(idp));
            else if (idp->defn.key == CONST_DEFN)
                return(subrange_type(idp));
            else {
                error(NOT_A_TYPE_IDENTIFIER);
                return(&dummy_type);
            }
        }

        case LPAREN:    return(enumeration_type());
        case ARRAY:     return(array_type());
        case RECORD:    return(record_type());

        case PLUS:
        case MINUS:
        case NUMBER:
        case STRING:    return(subrange_type(NULL));

        default:        error(INVALID_TYPE);
                        return(&dummy_type);
    }
}

/*------------------------------------------------------*/
/* identifier_type     Process an identifier type, i.e., the  */
/*                     identifier on the right side of a type */
/*                     equate, and return a pointer to its    */
/*                     type structure.                        */
/*------------------------------------------------------*/

    TYPE_STRUCT_PTR
identifier_type(idp)

    SYMTAB_NODE_PTR idp;        /* type id */

{
    TYPE_STRUCT_PTR tp = NULL;

    tp = idp->typep;
    get_token();

    return(tp);
}

/*------------------------------------------------------*/
/* enumeration_type    Process an enumeration type:      */
/*                                                       */
/*                     ( <id1>, <id2>, ..., <idn> )      */
/*                                                       */
/*                     Make a type structure and return a */
/*                     pointer to it.                     */
/*------------------------------------------------------*/

    TYPE_STRUCT_PTR
enumeration_type()

{
    SYMTAB_NODE_PTR const_idp;          /* constant id */
    SYMTAB_NODE_PTR last_idp   = NULL;  /* last constant id */
    TYPE_STRUCT_PTR tp         = alloc_struct(TYPE_STRUCT);
    int             const_value = -1;   /* constant value */

    tp->form    = ENUM_FORM;
```

```
    tp->size    = sizeof(int);
    tp->type_idp = NULL;

    get_token();

    /*
    -- Loop to process list of identifiers.
    */
    while (token == IDENTIFIER) {
        search_and_enter_local_symtab(const_idp);
        const_idp->defn.key = CONST_DEFN;
        const_idp->defn.info.constant.value.integer = ++const_value;
        const_idp->typep = tp;

        /*
        -- Link constant ids together.
        */
        if (last_idp == NULL)
            tp->info.enumeration.const_idp = last_idp = const_idp;
        else {
            last_idp->next = const_idp;
            last_idp = const_idp;
        }

        get_token();
        if_token_get(COMMA);
    }

    if_token_get_else_error(RPAREN, MISSING_RPAREN);

    tp->info.enumeration.max = const_value;
    return(tp);
}

/*------------------------------------------------------*/
/* subrange_type       Process a subrange type:          */
/*                                                       */
/*                     <min-const> .. <max-const>        */
/*                                                       */
/*                     Make a type structure and return a */
/*                     pointer to it.                     */
/*------------------------------------------------------*/

TOKEN_CODE follow_min_limit_list[] = {DOTDOT, IDENTIFIER, PLUS, MINUS,
                                      NUMBER, STRING, SEMICOLON,
                                      END_OF_FILE, 0};

    TYPE_STRUCT_PTR
subrange_type(min_idp)

    SYMTAB_NODE_PTR min_idp;    /* min limit const id */

{
    TYPE_STRUCT_PTR max_typep;  /* type of max limit */
    TYPE_STRUCT_PTR tp = alloc_struct(TYPE_STRUCT);

    tp->form    = SUBRANGE_FORM;
    tp->type_idp = NULL;

    /*
    -- Minimum constant.
    */
    get_subrange_limit(min_idp,
                &(tp->info.subrange.min),
                &(tp->info.subrange.range_typep));

    /*
```

```
        --  Error synchronization:  Should be ..
        */
        synchronize(follow_min_limit_list, NULL, NULL);
        if_token_get(DOTDOT);
        else if (token_in(follow_min_limit_list) ||
                    token_in(declaration_start_list) ||
                    token_in(statement_start_list))
            error(MISSING_DOTDOT);

        /*
        --  Maximum constant.
        */
        get_subrange_limit(NULL, &(tp->info.subrange.max), &max_typep);

        /*
        --  Check limits.
        */
        if (max_typep == tp->info.subrange.range_typep) {
            if (tp->info.subrange.min > tp->info.subrange.max)
                error(MIN_GT_MAX);
        }
        else error(INCOMPATIBLE_TYPES);

        tp->size = max_typep == char_typep ? sizeof(char) : sizeof(int);
        return(tp);
}

/*-------------------------------------------------------*/
/*  get_subrange_limit  Process the minimum and maximum limits  */
/*                      of a subrange type.                     */
/*-------------------------------------------------------*/

get_subrange_limit(minmax_idp, minmaxp, typepp)

    SYMTAB_NODE_PTR minmax_idp; /* min const id */
    int             *minmaxp;   /* where to store min or max value */
    TYPE_STRUCT_PTR *typepp;    /* where to store ptr to type struct */

{
    SYMTAB_NODE_PTR idp       = minmax_idp;
    TOKEN_CODE      sign      = PLUS;    /* unary + or - sign */
    BOOLEAN         saw_sign  = FALSE;   /* TRUE iff unary sign */

    /*
    --  Unary + or - sign.
    */
    if ((token == PLUS) || (token == MINUS)) {
        sign     = token;
        saw_sign = TRUE;
        get_token();
    }

    /*
    --  Numeric limit:  Integer type only.
    */
    if (token == NUMBER) {
        if (literal.type == INTEGER_LIT) {
            *typepp  = integer_typep;
            *minmaxp = (sign == PLUS) ?  literal.value.integer
                                      : -literal.value.integer;
        }
        else error(INVALID_SUBRANGE_TYPE);
    }

    /*
    --  Identifier limit:  Value must be integer or character.
    */
```

```
    else if (token == IDENTIFIER) {
        if (idp == NULL) search_all_symtab(idp);

        if (idp == NULL)
            error(UNDEFINED_IDENTIFIER);
        else if (idp->typep == real_typep)
            error(INVALID_SUBRANGE_TYPE);
        else if (idp->defn.key == CONST_DEFN) {
            *typepp  = idp->typep;
            if (idp->typep == char_typep) {
                if (saw_sign) error(INVALID_CONSTANT);
                *minmaxp = idp->defn.info.constant.value.character;
            }
            else if (idp->typep == integer_typep) {
                *minmaxp = idp->defn.info.constant.value.integer;
                if (sign == MINUS) *minmaxp = -(*minmaxp);
            }
            else /* enumeration constant */ {
                if (saw_sign) error(INVALID_CONSTANT);
                *minmaxp = idp->defn.info.constant.value.integer;
            }
        }
        else error(NOT_A_CONSTANT_IDENTIFIER);
    }

    /*
    --  String limit:  Character type only.
    */
    else if (token == STRING) {
        if (saw_sign) error(INVALID_CONSTANT);
        *typepp  = char_typep;
        *minmaxp = literal.value.string[0];

        if (strlen(literal.value.string) != 1)
            error(INVALID_SUBRANGE_TYPE);
    }

    else error(MISSING_CONSTANT);

    get_token();
}

/*-------------------------------------------------------------*/
/*  array_type          Process an array type:                 */
/*                                                             */
/*                          ARRAY [<index-type-list>]          */
/*                          OF <elmt-type>                      */
/*                                                             */
/*                      Make a type structure and return a     */
/*                      pointer to it.                          */
/*-------------------------------------------------------------*/

TOKEN_CODE follow_dimension_list[] = {COMMA, RBRACKET, OF,
                                      SEMICOLON, END_OF_FILE, 0};

TOKEN_CODE index_type_start_list[] = {IDENTIFIER, NUMBER, STRING,
                                      LPAREN, MINUS, PLUS, 0};

TOKEN_CODE follow_indexes_list[]   = {OF, IDENTIFIER, LPAREN, ARRAY,
                                      RECORD, PLUS, MINUS, NUMBER,
                                      STRING, SEMICOLON, END_OF_FILE,
                                      0};

    TYPE_STRUCT_PTR
array_type()

{
```

```
TYPE_STRUCT_PTR tp        = alloc_struct(TYPE_STRUCT);
TYPE_STRUCT_PTR index_tp;              /* index type */
TYPE_STRUCT_PTR elmt_tp = tp;          /* element type */
int array_size();

get_token();
if (token != LBRACKET) error(MISSING_LBRACKET);

/*
-- Loop to process index type list.  For each
-- type in the list after the first, create an
-- array element type.
*/
do {
    get_token();

    if (token_in(index_type_start_list)) {
        elmt_tp->form     = ARRAY_FORM;
        elmt_tp->size     = 0;
        elmt_tp->type_idp = NULL;
        elmt_tp->info.array.index_typep = index_tp = do_type();

        switch (index_tp->form) {
            case ENUM_FORM:
                elmt_tp->info.array.elmt_count =
                        index_tp->info.enumeration.max + 1;
                elmt_tp->info.array.min_index = 0;
                elmt_tp->info.array.max_index =
                        index_tp->info.enumeration.max;
                break;

            case SUBRANGE_FORM:
                elmt_tp->info.array.elmt_count =
                        index_tp->info.subrange.max -
                            index_tp->info.subrange.min + 1;
                elmt_tp->info.array.min_index =
                        index_tp->info.subrange.min;
                elmt_tp->info.array.max_index =
                        index_tp->info.subrange.max;
                break;

            default:
                elmt_tp->form     = NO_FORM;
                elmt_tp->size     = 0;
                elmt_tp->type_idp = NULL;
                elmt_tp->info.array.index_typep = &dummy_type;
                error(INVALID_INDEX_TYPE);
                break;
        }
    }
    else {
        elmt_tp->form     = NO_FORM;
        elmt_tp->size     = 0;
        elmt_tp->type_idp = NULL;
        elmt_tp->info.array.index_typep = &dummy_type;
        error(INVALID_INDEX_TYPE);
    }

    /*
    -- Error synchronization:  Should be , or ]
    */
    synchronize(follow_dimension_list, NULL, NULL);

    /*
    -- Create an array element type.
    */
    if (token == COMMA) elmt_tp = elmt_tp->info.array.elmt_typep =
```

```
                                   alloc_struct(TYPE_STRUCT);
} while (token == COMMA);

if_token_get_else_error(RBRACKET, MISSING_RBRACKET);

/*
-- Error synchronization:  Should be OF
*/
synchronize(follow_indexes_list,
            declaration_start_list, statement_start_list);
if_token_get_else_error(OF, MISSING_OF);

/*
-- Element type.
*/
elmt_tp->info.array.elmt_typep = do_type();

tp->size = array_size(tp);
return(tp);
}

/*------------------------------------------------------------*/
/*  record_type        Process a record type:                 */
/*                                                            */
/*                         RECORD                              */
/*                             <id-list> : <type> ;            */
/*                                 ...                         */
/*                         END                                 */
/*                                                            */
/*                      Make a type structure and return a     */
/*                      pointer to it.                         */
/*------------------------------------------------------------*/

    TYPE_STRUCT_PTR
record_type()

{
    TYPE_STRUCT_PTR record_tp = alloc_struct(TYPE_STRUCT);

    record_tp->form     = RECORD_FORM;
    record_tp->type_idp = NULL;
    record_tp->info.record.field_symtab = NULL;

    get_token();
    var_or_field_declarations(NULL, record_tp, 0);

    if_token_get_else_error(END, MISSING_END);
    return(record_tp);
}

/*------------------------------------------------------------*/
/*  make_string_typep  Make a type structure for a string of  */
/*                     the given length, and return a pointer  */
/*                     to it.                                  */
/*------------------------------------------------------------*/

    TYPE_STRUCT_PTR
make_string_typep(length)

    int length;                /* string length */

{
    TYPE_STRUCT_PTR string_tp = alloc_struct(TYPE_STRUCT);
    TYPE_STRUCT_PTR index_tp  = alloc_struct(TYPE_STRUCT);

    /*
    -- Array type.
```

```
          */
     string_tp->form      = ARRAY_FORM;
     string_tp->size      = length;
     string_tp->type_idp  = NULL;
     string_tp->info.array.index_typep = index_tp;
     string_tp->info.array.elmt_typep  = char_typep;
     string_tp->info.array.elmt_count  = length;

     /*
     -- Subrange index type.
     */
     index_tp->form      = SUBRANGE_FORM;
     index_tp->size      = sizeof(int);
     index_tp->type_idp  = NULL;
     index_tp->info.subrange.range_typep = integer_typep;
     index_tp->info.subrange.min = 1;
     index_tp->info.subrange.max = length;

     return(string_tp);
}

/*------------------------------------------------------------*/
/*  array_size         Return the size in bytes of an array   */
/*                     type by recursively calculating the    */
/*                     size of each dimension.                */
/*------------------------------------------------------------*/

     int
array_size(tp)

     TYPE_STRUCT_PTR tp;       /* ptr to array type structure */

{
     if (tp->info.array.elmt_typep->size == 0)
        tp->info.array.elmt_typep->size =
                        array_size(tp->info.array.elmt_typep);

     tp->size = tp->info.array.elmt_count *
                tp->info.array.elmt_typep->size;

     return(tp->size);
}

               /***********************/
               /*                     */
               /*       Variables     */
               /*                     */
               /***********************/

/*------------------------------------------------------------*/
/*  var_declarations   Process variable declarations:         */
/*                                                            */
/*                     <id-list> : <type>                     */
/*------------------------------------------------------------*/

var_declarations(rtn_idp)

     SYMTAB_NODE_PTR rtn_idp;   /* id of program or routine */

{
     var_or_field_declarations(rtn_idp, NULL, 0);
}

/*------------------------------------------------------------*/
/*  var_or_field_declarations   Process variable declarations  */
/*                              or record field definitions.   */
/*                              All ids declared with the same  */
```

```
/*                              type are linked together into   */
/*                              a sublist, and all the sublists  */
/*                              are then linked together.        */
/*------------------------------------------------------------*/

TOKEN_CODE follow_variables_list[] = {SEMICOLON, IDENTIFIER,
                                      END_OF_FILE, 0};

TOKEN_CODE follow_fields_list[]    = {SEMICOLON, END, IDENTIFIER,
                                      END_OF_FILE, 0};

var_or_field_declarations(rtn_idp, record_tp, offset)

     SYMTAB_NODE_PTR rtn_idp;
     TYPE_STRUCT_PTR record_tp;
     int             offset;

{

     SYMTAB_NODE_PTR idp, first_idp, last_idp;   /* variable or
                                                     field ids */
     SYMTAB_NODE_PTR prev_last_idp = NULL;       /* last id of list */
     TYPE_STRUCT_PTR tp;                         /* type */
     BOOLEAN var_flag = (rtn_idp != NULL);       /* TRUE: variables */
                                                 /* FALSE: fields */

     int size;
     int total_size = 0;

     /*
     -- Loop to process sublist, each of a type.
     */
     while (token == IDENTIFIER) {
        first_idp = NULL;

        /*
        -- Loop process each variable or field id in a sublist.
        */
        while (token == IDENTIFIER) {
           if (var_flag) {
              search_and_enter_local_symtab(idp);
              idp->defn.key = VAR_DEFN;
           }
           else {
              search_and_enter_this_symtab
                  (idp, record_tp->info.record.field_symtab);
              idp->defn.key = FIELD_DEFN;
           }
           idp->label_index = 0;

           /*
           -- Link ids together into a sublist.
           */
           if (first_idp == NULL) {
              first_idp = last_idp = idp;
              if (var_flag &&
                  (rtn_idp->defn.info.routine.locals == NULL))
                 rtn_idp->defn.info.routine.locals = idp;
           }
           else {
              last_idp->next = idp;
              last_idp = idp;
           }

           get_token();
           if_token_get(COMMA);
        }

        /*
```

```
--  Process the sublist's type.                          /*
*/                                                       --  Link this sublist to the previous sublist.
if_token_get_else_error(COLON, MISSING_COLON);           */
tp = do_type();                                          if (prev_last_idp != NULL) prev_last_idp->next = first_idp;
size = tp->size;                                         prev_last_idp = last_idp;

/*                                                       /*
--  Assign the offset and the type to all variable or field    --  Error synchronization:  Should be ; for variable
--  ids in the sublist.                                  --                          declaration, or ; or END for
*/                                                       --                          record type definition.
for (idp = first_idp; idp != NULL; idp = idp->next) {    */
    idp->typep = tp;                                     synchronize(var_flag ? follow_variables_list
                                                                             : follow_fields_list,
    if (var_flag) {                                               declaration_start_list, statement_start_list);
        total_size += size;                              if_token_get(SEMICOLON);
        idp->defn.info.data.offset = offset++;           else if (var_flag && ((token_in(declaration_start_list)) ||
        analyze_var_decl(idp);                                                  (token_in(statement_start_list))))
    }                                                        error(MISSING_SEMICOLON);
                                                     }
    else   /* record fields */ {
        idp->defn.info.data.offset = offset;         if (var_flag)
        offset += size;                                  rtn_idp->defn.info.routine.total_local_size = total_size;
    }                                                else
}                                                        record_tp->size = offset;
}                                                    }
```

We called function declarations from the main routine of the declarations analyzer. In it, we successively look for constant definitions, type definitions, and variable declarations, and, as necessary, we call functions const_definitions, type_definitions, and var_declarations. We passed declarations a pointer to the dummy symbol table node for the program identifier. In the next chapter, we will pass in a pointer to the actual symbol table node for the program identifier or for the identifier of a procedure or a function. We pass this pointer on to the other functions.

6.4.5 Parsing constants

We parse constant definitions in function const_definitions, where we loop once for each definition. We first enter the identifier into the symbol table as a constant identifier. Next, we look for the equal sign before we call function do_const to parse the constant, and then we call function analyze_const_defn to analyze the symbol table node and its type structure. After all that, we call function synchronize to resynchronize the parser either at the end of the declaration, at the beginning of the next declaration, or at the beginning of the first statement, in that order of preference. We also check for a missing semicolon.

We do the work of parsing the constant in function do_const. We pass it a pointer to the constant identifier's symbol table node. After taking care of any unary + or - sign, we expect to see either a number, an identifier, or a string. We enter the constant value into the symbol table node in field defn.info.constant. value.

If the constant is numeric, we get the constant value from the scanner's `literal` variable. We set the constant identifier's `typep` field to point to the type structure of either the predefined integer or real type.

If the constant is an identifier, we search the symbol table for the identifier, which must already be defined to be a constant. We obtain the identifier's value from its symbol table node. The value may be integer, real, character, enumeration, or string (character array) type. We also set field `typep` of the constant identifier being defined to point to the type structure of the already-defined identifier.

If the constant is a string, we first check if the string length is one. If so, we have a character constant. We get the character from `literal`, and we set the constant identifier's `typep` field to point to the type structure of the predefined character type.

If the string length is greater than one, we make a copy of the string and make `defn.info.constant.value.stringp` point to the copy. We then call function `make_string_typep` to create an unnamed character array type. (We'll look at this function later.)

6.4.6 Parsing type definitions

We parse type definitions in function `type_definitions`, where we loop once for each definition. We first enter the identifier into the symbol table as a type identifier. Next, we look for the equal sign before we call function `do_type` to parse the type specification, and then we call function `analyze_type_defn` to analyze the symbol table node and its type structure. After all that, we call function `synchronize` to resynchronize the parser either at the end of the declaration, at the beginning of the next declaration, or at the beginning of the first statement. We conclude with a check for a missing semicolon.

6.4.7 Parsing type specifications

Function `do_type` parses a type specification for both named and unnamed types. In it, we call the appropriate parsing function based on the current token, and we return a pointer to a type structure.

If the first token of a type specification is an identifier, we need to check further. We look up the identifier, and if it is an enumeration constant, it must be the lower limit of a subrange type. Otherwise, it must be a previously-defined type identifier.

6.4.8 Parsing identifier types

We call function `identifier_type` when a type specification is simply a previously-defined type identifier. We return a pointer to the type structure of the identifier.

6.4.9 Parsing enumeration and subrange types

We call function `enumeration_type` to parse an enumeration type specification. First, we allocate a new type structure and set the `form` field to `ENUM_FORM`. We then loop to parse the enumeration constants. We assign each constant identifier its value and enter it into the symbol table. We link the symbol table nodes together via their `next` fields. We point the type structure's `info.enumeration.const_idp` field to the head of this list, and we set its `info.enumeration.max` field to the value of the last enumeration constant. We return a pointer to the type structure.

In function `subrange_type`, we parse a subrange type specification. First, we allocate a new type structure and set the `form` field to `SUBRANGE_FORM`. We call function `get_subrange_limit` twice, first to parse the minimum limit and then to parse the upper limit of the subrange. After the first call, we call function `synchronize` to resynchronize the parser at the `..` token or, if it is missing, at the start of the maximum limit. After the second call, we check to make sure that the types of the minimum and maximum values are the same, and that the maximum value is indeed greater than the minimum value. We store both values and the range type into the type structure, and then we return a pointer to the structure.

A subrange limit may be an integer or character literal, or a constant identifier whose value is an integer or character. We call function `get_subrange_limit` to parse each limit of a subrange type. If a limit is a number, we make sure it is an integer and get its value from the scanner's `literal`. If it is an identifier, we look it up to make sure it is already defined as a constant, and we get the constant value from the symbol table node. Finally, if it is a string, we check that it is a character, and we get its value from `literal`.

6.4.10 Parsing array types

We call function `array_type` to parse an array type specification. First, we allocate a new type structure and set variable `elmt_tp` to point to this structure. We then loop once per index specification.

In the simple case of a single-dimensional array, we execute the index loop only once. At the top of the loop, the token list `index_type_start_list` verifies the start of an index type. We set the array type structure's `form` field to `ARRAY_FORM`. We call function `do_type` to parse the index type, and we point the `info.array.index_typep` field to the index type structure. Then, the `elmt_count`, `min_index`, and `max_index` fields are set according to the index type. After parsing the index, we call function `synchronize` to resynchronize the parser at the comma or `]` token.

Outside the index loop, we check for a missing `]` token, and then call `synchronize` again. We want to resynchronize the parser at the `OF`, but if `OF` is missing, we can resynchronize at the start of the element type specification, at the start of the next declaration, or at the start of the first statement. Finally, we call `do_type` to parse the element type, and we point the `info.array.elmt_typep` field to the element type structure.

For a multiple-dimensional array, there can be an index specification for each dimension between the pair of brackets. We need to chain together array type structures, as we saw in Figure 6-4. At the bottom of the loop, we check for a comma. If there is one, another index specification must follow. We allocate new type structure, and we point both `elmt_tp` and the `elmt_typep` field of the previous type structure to it. At the top of the next execution of the loop, we set the structure's `form` field to `ARRAY_FORM`. Thus, we create a linked list of array type structures, one structure for each dimension. After the loop, we call `do_type` again to parse the element type, and we point the `info.array.elmt_typep` field of the last dimension to the element type structure.

To conclude, we call function `array_size` (explained below) to calculate the byte size of the array. We then return a pointer to the first (or only) array type structure.

6.4.11 Parsing record types

Function `record_type` parses a record type specification. We allocate a new type structure and set the `form` field to `RECORD_FORM`. The `info.record.field_symtab` field of a record type structure points to a private symbol table that contains the record's field identifiers. They are kept in a private symbol table and not in the global symbol table because of the scope of a field identifier. A field identifier can have the same name as that of a global variable or of another record type's field. (The concept of scope is further explained in the next chapter.)

We call function `var_or_field_declarations`, passing a pointer to the record type structure. This function parses both record field and variable declarations. For a record type, it enters the field identifiers into the record type's private symbol table. Afterwards, we check for the `END`, and then we return a pointer to the record type structure.

6.4.12 Creating string types

We call function `make_string_typep` whenever we need to create a type structure to represent an unnamed string type of a given length. In Pascal, a string type is a one-dimensional array of `char`. The index type is the subrange of integers from one through the length. We return a pointer to the string type structure.

6.4.13 Sizes of array variables

Function `array_size` calculates the number of bytes of an array. We call the function recursively for each array element, and then the size of each dimension is the element size times the element count.

6.4.14 Parsing record field and variable declarations

We parse record field or variable declarations in function `var_or_field_declarations`. We call this function from `record_type` to parse field declarations, and from `var_declarations` to parse variable declarations.

A declaration consists of a sublist of one or more identifiers separated by commas, a colon, and then a type specification. We parse one or more declarations separated by semicolons in the outer while loop. We parse the identifiers in a sublist in the inner while loop.

In the inner while loop, each identifier is entered into the symbol table. If we are parsing variables, we use the local symbol table and set the defn.key field to VAR_DEFN. Otherwise, we are parsing record fields, so we use the record type's private symbol table and set the defn.key field to FIELD_DEFN. We link the symbol table nodes together into a sublist via their next fields.

We also chain the sublists together into one list and set the defn.info.routine.locals field of the symbol table node to point to it. This is the node of the program, procedure, or function identifier. In this chapter, it is only the dummy program identifier node.

After the last identifier in a sublist, we look for the colon, and then we call function do_type, which parses the type specification and returns a type structure.

In the for loop, we set the typep field of each node in the sublist to point to the type structure. We calculate the total size of the all the fields or variables being declared, and also set the defn.info.data.offset field of each node. (This offset field will be useful in later chapters.) Note that the offset increments by one for variables, but that it increments by the size of each field for record fields.

Now that we are at the end of a declaration, we call function synchronize to resynchronize the parser. We want to resynchronize at the point just after the declaration (whether variables or record fields), at the start of the next declaration, or at the start of the first statement. We then check for a missing semicolon.

Finally, we need to set the size fields. If we are parsing variables, we set the defn.info.routine.total_local_size field of the symbol table node of the program, procedure, or function identifier. (In this chapter, the dummy program identifier node.) Otherwise, we set the size field of the record type structure.

6.4.15 A final detail

Figure 6-10 shows a new version of file parser.h. At the end of the file, we now have several new macro definitions. These macros have the same names as the analysis functions that we call from file decl.c, and each macro is defined to be the empty string. (The names analyze_routine_header and analyze_block will be useful in Chapter 8.) The idea is to conditionally remove the calls to the analysis routines when we do *not* want declarations analyzed. Since we bracket the macro definitions with #ifndef analyze and #endif, the function calls are left in only if we set the macro flag analyze before the macro definitions. We need to do this for the declarations analyzer. One way is to insert the following line: #define analyze before the #ifndef analyze line. Another way is the set the flag with a command-line option when we invoke the C compiler: /Danalyze

We add a new enumeration type USE whose enumeration constants indicate how a variable is used in a statement, whether it is part of an expression, the

FIGURE 6-10   File parser.h.

```
/*****************************************************/
/*                                                   */
/*      P A R S I N G   R O U T I N E S   (Header)   */
/*                                                   */
/*      FILE:      parser.h                          */
/*                                                   */
/*      MODULE:    parser                            */
/*                                                   */
/*****************************************************/

#ifndef parser_h
#define parser_h

#include "common.h"
#include "symtab.h"

/*-------------------------------------------------*/
/* Uses of a variable                              */
/*-------------------------------------------------*/

typedef enum {
    EXPR_USE, TARGET_USE, VARPARM_USE,
} USE;

/*-------------------------------------------------*/
/* Functions                                       */
/*-------------------------------------------------*/

TYPE_STRUCT_PTR expression();
TYPE_STRUCT_PTR variable();
TYPE_STRUCT_PTR routine_call();
TYPE_STRUCT_PTR base_type();
BOOLEAN        is_assign_type_compatible();

            /*******************************/
            /*                             */
            /*      Macros for parsing     */
            /*                             */
```

```
            /*******************************/

/*---------------------------------------------------*/
/* if_token_get            If token equals token_code, get */
/*                         the next token.           */
/*---------------------------------------------------*/

#define if_token_get(token_code)                   \
    if (token == token_code) get_token()

/*---------------------------------------------------*/
/* if_token_get_else_error    If token equals token_code, get */
/*                            the next token, else error.    */
/*---------------------------------------------------*/

#define if_token_get_else_error(token_code, error_code) \
    if (token == token_code) get_token();           \
    else                     error(error_code)

/*---------------------------------------------------*/
/* Analysis routine calls    Unless the following statements */
/*                           are preceded by        */
/*                                                   */
/*                                 #define analyze   */
/*                                                   */
/*                           calls to the analysis routines */
/*                           are not compiled.       */
/*---------------------------------------------------*/

#ifndef analyze
#define analyze_const_defn(idp)
#define analyze_var_decl(idp)
#define analyze_type_defn(idp)
#define analyze_routine_header(idp)
#define analyze_block(idp)
#endif

#endif
```

target of an assignment, or passed as a VAR parameter. This type will be used in the next utility program. We also specify the return types of functions expression, variable, routine_call, base_type, and is_assign_type_compatible. These, too, are needed by the next utility program.

6.5 Type checking

Now that we have seen how it parses declarations, we need the parser to perform the semantic action of type checking. Type checking verifies that a program uses types correctly. Three common type checks are:

1. Expressions: whether or not the operands of an operator are of the correct type. For example, the arithmetic operator + requires integer or real operands, and the boolean operator AND requires boolean operands.

2. Assignments: whether or not an expression value of one type can be assigned to a variable of a different type. For example, it is legal to assign an integer value to a real variable, but not vice versa.

3. Statements: whether or not an expression that appears in a statement is of the correct type. For example, the expression in an IF statement must be boolean.

We now add type checking to the parser module. We will see how this checking works with the new version of the Pascal syntax checker utility program.

6.6 Program 6-2: Pascal Syntax Checker II

Our second utility program builds upon the syntax checker of the previous chapter and the declarations analyzer. Not only does it check the syntax of both declarations and statements, but it also performs the three types checks specified above.

Figure 6-11 shows the main file `syntax2.c`. In the main routine, we initialize the scanner and the symbol table, and then call function `block`. In `block`, we call function `declarations` to parse declarations, and then call function `compound_statement` to parse a compound statement. Figure 6-12 shows the syntax diagram for a block.

FIGURE 6-11   File `syntax2.c`.

```
/***************************************************************/        extern TOKEN_CODE token;
/*                                                           */          extern int        line_number, error_count;
/*      Program 6-2:  Pascal Syntax Checker II               */
/*                                                           */          extern TYPE_STRUCT dummy_type;
/*      Check the syntax of Pascal declarations and          */
/*      statements.  Perform type checking.                  */          /*------------------------------------------------------*/
/*                                                           */          /* Globals                                              */
/*      FILE:     syntax2.c                                  */          /*------------------------------------------------------*/
/*                                                           */
/*      REQUIRES: Modules parser, symbol table, scanner,     */          char buffer[MAX_PRINT_LINE_LENGTH];
/*                error                                      */
/*                                                           */          /*------------------------------------------------------*/
/*      USAGE:    syntax2 sourcefile                         */          /* main             Initialize the scanner and call the */
/*                                                           */          /*                  statement routine.                  */
/*        sourcefile    name of source file containing       */          /*------------------------------------------------------*/
/*                      statements to be checked             */
/*                                                           */          main(argc, argv)
/***************************************************************/
                                                                             int argc;
#include <stdio.h>                                                           char *argv[];
#include "common.h"
#include "error.h"                                                        {
#include "scanner.h"                                                          SYMTAB_NODE_PTR program_idp;      /* artificial program id */
#include "parser.h"
                                                                             /*
/*------------------------------------------------------*/                   -- Initialize the scanner and the symbol table.
/* Externals                                            */
/*------------------------------------------------------*/
```

```
*/
init_scanner(argv[1]);
init_symtab();

/*
-- Create an artifical program id node.
*/
program_idp = alloc_struct(SYMTAB_NODE);
program_idp->defn.key = PROG_DEFN;
program_idp->defn.info.routine.key = DECLARED;
program_idp->defn.info.routine.parm_count = 0;
program_idp->defn.info.routine.total_parm_size = 0;
program_idp->defn.info.routine.total_local_size = 0;
program_idp->typep = &dummy_type;
program_idp->label_index = 0;

/*
-- Parse a block.
*/
get_token();
block(program_idp);

/*
-- Look for the end of file.
*/
while (token != END_OF_FILE) {
    error(UNEXPECTED_TOKEN);
    get_token();
}

quit_scanner();

/*
-- Print the parser's summary.
*/
```

```
    print_line("\n");
    print_line("\n");
    sprintf(buffer, "%20d Source lines.\n", line_number);
    print_line(buffer);
    sprintf(buffer, "%20d Source errors.\n", error_count);
    print_line(buffer);

    if (error_count == 0) exit(0);
    else                  exit(-SYNTAX_ERROR);
}

/*-------------------------------------------------------------*/
/*  block               Process a block, which consists of     */
/*                      declarations followed by a compound     */
/*                      statement.                              */
/*-------------------------------------------------------------*/

TOKEN_CODE follow_decls_list[] = {SEMICOLON, BEGIN, END_OF_FILE, 0};

block(rtn_idp)

    SYMTAB_NODE_PTR rtn_idp;    /* id of program or routine */

{
    extern BOOLEAN block_flag;

    declarations(rtn_idp);

    /*
    -- Error synchronization:  Should be ;
    */
    synchronize(follow_decls_list, NULL, NULL);
    if (token != BEGIN) error(MISSING_BEGIN);

    compound_statement();
}
```

FIGURE 6-12   Syntax diagram for a block.

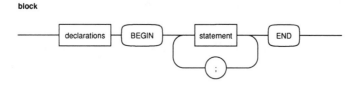

We can use the same file decl.c from the declarations analyzer. Since we do not want to analyze the declarations, we must *not* set the analyze macro flag in file parser.h.

We check the types of expressions and variables in file expr.c, and of statements in file stmt.c. Figure 6-13 shows the new version of file expr.c, and Figure 6-14 shows the new version of file stmt.c.

FIGURE 6-13   File expr.c.

```
/****************************************************************/
/*                                                              */
/*      E X P R E S S I O N   P A R S E R                       */
/*                                                              */
/*      Parsing routines for expressions.                       */
/*                                                              */
/*      FILE:       expr.c                                      */
/*                                                              */
/*      MODULE:     parser                                      */
/*                                                              */
/****************************************************************/

#include <stdio.h>
#include "common.h"
#include "error.h"
#include "scanner.h"
#include "symtab.h"
#include "parser.h"

/*--------------------------------------------------------------*/
/*  Externals                                                   */
/*--------------------------------------------------------------*/

extern TOKEN_CODE  token;
extern char        word_string[];
extern LITERAL     literal;

extern SYMTAB_NODE_PTR symtab_root;

extern TYPE_STRUCT_PTR  integer_typep, real_typep,
                        boolean_typep, char_typep;

extern TYPE_STRUCT      dummy_type;

/*--------------------------------------------------------------*/
/*  Forwards                                                    */
/*--------------------------------------------------------------*/

TYPE_STRUCT_PTR expression(), simple_expression(), term(), factor(),
                function_call();

/*--------------------------------------------------------------*/
/*  integer_operands    TRUE if both operands are integer,      */
/*                      else FALSE.                             */
/*--------------------------------------------------------------*/

#define integer_operands(tp1, tp2)  ((tp1 == integer_typep) && \
                                     (tp2 == integer_typep))

/*--------------------------------------------------------------*/
/*  real_operands       TRUE if at least one or both operands   */
/*                      are real (and the other integer), else  */
/*                      FALSE.                                  */
/*--------------------------------------------------------------*/

#define real_operands(tp1, tp2) (((tp1 == real_typep) &&       \
                                  ((tp2 == real_typep) ||      \
                                   (tp2 == integer_typep)))    \
                                 ||                            \
                                 ((tp2 == real_typep) &&       \
                                  ((tp1 == real_typep) ||      \
                                   (tp1 == integer_typep))))

/*--------------------------------------------------------------*/
/*  boolean_operands    TRUE if both operands are boolean       */
```

```
/*                      else FALSE.                             */
/*--------------------------------------------------------------*/

#define boolean_operands(tp1, pt2)  ((tp1 == boolean_typep) && \
                                     (tp2 == boolean_typep))

/*--------------------------------------------------------------*/
/*  expression          Process an expression consisting of a   */
/*                      simple expression optionally followed   */
/*                      by a relational operator and a second   */
/*                      simple expression.  Return a pointer to */
/*                      the type structure.                     */
/*--------------------------------------------------------------*/

TOKEN_CODE rel_op_list[] = {LT, LE, EQUAL, NE, GE, GT, 0};

    TYPE_STRUCT_PTR
expression()

{
    TOKEN_CODE op;                      /* an operator token */
    TYPE_STRUCT_PTR result_tp, tp2;

    result_tp = simple_expression();    /* first simple expr */

    /*
    -- If there is a relational operator, remember it and
    -- process the second simple expression.
    */
    if (token_in(rel_op_list)) {
        op = token;                     /* remember operator */
        result_tp = base_type(result_tp);

        get_token();
        tp2 = base_type(simple_expression());   /* 2nd simple expr */

        check_rel_op_types(result_tp, tp2);
        result_tp = boolean_typep;
    }

    return(result_tp);
}

/*--------------------------------------------------------------*/
/*  simple_expression   Process a simple expression consisting  */
/*                      of terms separated by +, -, or OR       */
/*                      operators.  There may be a unary + or - */
/*                      before the first term.  Return a        */
/*                      pointer to the type structure.          */
/*--------------------------------------------------------------*/

TOKEN_CODE add_op_list[] = {PLUS, MINUS, OR, 0};

    TYPE_STRUCT_PTR
simple_expression()

{
    TOKEN_CODE op;                      /* an operator token */
    BOOLEAN    saw_unary_op = FALSE;    /* TRUE iff unary operator */
    TOKEN_CODE unary_op = PLUS;         /* a unary operator token */
    TYPE_STRUCT_PTR result_tp, tp2;

    /*
    -- If there is a unary + or -, remember it.
```

```
*/
if ((token == PLUS) || (token == MINUS)) {
    unary_op = token;
    saw_unary_op = TRUE;
    get_token();
}

result_tp = term();        /* first term */

/*
-- If there was a unary operator, check that the term
-- is integer or real.  Negate the top of stack if it
-- was a unary - either with the NEG instruction or by
-- calling FLOAT_NEGATE.
*/
if (saw_unary_op &&
    (base_type(result_tp) != integer_typep) &&
    (result_tp != real_typep)) error(INCOMPATIBLE_TYPES);

/*
-- Loop to process subsequent terms separated by operators.
*/
while (token_in(add_op_list)) {
    op = token;                 /* remember operator */
    result_tp = base_type(result_tp);

    get_token();
    tp2 = base_type(term());    /* subsequent term */

    switch (op) {

        case PLUS:
        case MINUS: {
            /*
            -- integer <op> integer => integer
            */
            if (integer_operands(result_tp, tp2))
                result_tp = integer_typep;

            /*
            -- Both operands are real, or one is real and the
            -- other is integer.  The result is real.
            */
            else if (real_operands(result_tp, tp2))
                result_tp = real_typep;

            else {
            error(INCOMPATIBLE_TYPES);
                result_tp = &dummy_type;
            }

            break;
        }

        case OR: {
            /*
            -- boolean OR boolean => boolean
            */
            if (! boolean_operands(result_tp, tp2))
                error(INCOMPATIBLE_TYPES);

            result_tp = boolean_typep;
            break;
        }
    }
}

return(result_tp);
```

```
}

/*------------------------------------------------------------*/
/*  term               Process a term consisting of factors   */
/*                     separated by *, /, DIV, MOD, or AND     */
/*                     operators.  Return a pointer to the     */
/*                     type structure.                         */
/*------------------------------------------------------------*/

TOKEN_CODE mult_op_list[] = {STAR, SLASH, DIV, MOD, AND, 0};

    TYPE_STRUCT_PTR
term()

{
    TOKEN_CODE op;                      /* an operator token */
    TYPE_STRUCT_PTR result_tp, tp2;

    result_tp = factor();               /* first factor */

    /*
    -- Loop to process subsequent factors
    -- separated by operators.
    */
    while (token_in(mult_op_list)) {
        op = token;                     /* remember operator */
        result_tp = base_type(result_tp);

        get_token();
        tp2 = base_type(factor());      /* subsequent factor */

        switch (op) {

            case STAR: {
                /*
                -- Both operands are integer.
                */
                if (integer_operands(result_tp, tp2))
                    result_tp = integer_typep;

                /*
                -- Both operands are real, or one is real and the
                -- other is integer.  The result is real.
                */
                else if (real_operands(result_tp, tp2))
                    result_tp = real_typep;

                else {
                    error(INCOMPATIBLE_TYPES);
                    result_tp = &dummy_type;
                }

                break;
            }

            case SLASH: {
                /*
                -- Both operands are real, or both are integer, or
                -- one is real and the other is integer.  The result
                -- is real.
                */
                if ((! real_operands(result_tp, tp2)) &&
                    (! integer_operands(result_tp, tp2)))
                    error(INCOMPATIBLE_TYPES);

                result_tp = real_typep;
                break;
```

```
            }

        case DIV:
        case MOD: {
            /*
            --  integer <op> integer => integer
            */
            if (! integer_operands(result_tp, tp2))
                error(INCOMPATIBLE_TYPES);

            result_tp = integer_typep;
            break;
        }

        case AND: {
            /*
            --  boolean AND boolean => boolean
            */
            if (! boolean_operands(result_tp, tp2))
                error(INCOMPATIBLE_TYPES);

            result_tp = boolean_typep;
            break;
        }
    }
}

    return(result_tp);
}

/*-------------------------------------------------------------*/
/*  factor          Process a factor, which is a variable,  */
/*                  a number, NOT followed by a factor, or  */
/*                  a parenthesized subexpression.  Return  */
/*                  a pointer to the type structure.        */
/*-------------------------------------------------------------*/

    TYPE_STRUCT_PTR
factor()

{
    TYPE_STRUCT_PTR tp;

    switch (token) {

        case IDENTIFIER: {
            SYMTAB_NODE_PTR idp;

            search_and_find_all_symtab(idp);

            if (idp->defn.key == CONST_DEFN) {
                get_token();
                tp = idp->typep;
            }
            else tp = variable(idp, EXPR_USE);

            break;
        }

        case NUMBER:
            tp = literal.type == INTEGER_LIT
                    ? integer_typep
                    : real_typep;
            get_token();
            break;

        case STRING: {
```

```
            int length = strlen(literal.value.string);

            tp = length == 1 ? char_typep
                             : make_string_typep(length);
            get_token();
            break;
        }

        case NOT:
            get_token();
            tp = factor();
            break;

        case LPAREN:
            get_token();
            tp = expression();

            if_token_get_else_error(RPAREN, MISSING_RPAREN);
            break;

        default:
            error(INVALID_EXPRESSION);
            tp = &dummy_type;
            break;
    }

    return(tp);
}

/*-------------------------------------------------------------*/
/*  variable        Process a variable, which can be a     */
/*                  simple identifier, an array identifier */
/*                  with subscripts, or a record identifier */
/*                  with fields.                           */
/*-------------------------------------------------------------*/

    TYPE_STRUCT_PTR
variable(var_idp, use)

    SYMTAB_NODE_PTR var_idp;    /* variable id */
    USE             use;        /* how variable is used */

{
    TYPE_STRUCT_PTR tp           = var_idp->typep;
    DEFN_KEY        defn_key     = var_idp->defn.key;
    TYPE_STRUCT_PTR array_subscript_list();
    TYPE_STRUCT_PTR record_field();

    /*
    --  Check the variable's definition.
    */
    switch (defn_key) {
        case VAR_DEFN:
        case VALPARM_DEFN:
        case VARPARM_DEFN:
        case FUNC_DEFN:
        case UNDEFINED:  break;          /* OK */

        default: {                       /* error */
            tp = &dummy_type;
            error(INVALID_IDENTIFIER_USAGE);
        }
    }

    get_token();

    /*
```

```
    -- Subscripts and/or field designators?
    */
    while ((token == LBRACKET) || (token == PERIOD)) {
        tp = token == LBRACKET ? array_subscript_list(tp)
                               : record_field(tp);
    }

    return(tp);
}

/*------------------------------------------------------*/
/*  array_subscript_list    Process a list of subscripts   */
/*                          following an array identifier:  */
/*                                                          */
/*                              [ <expr> , <expr> , ... ]   */
/*------------------------------------------------------*/

    TYPE_STRUCT_PTR
array_subscript_list(tp)

    TYPE_STRUCT_PTR tp;

{
    TYPE_STRUCT_PTR   index_tp, elmt_tp, ss_tp;
    extern TOKEN_CODE statement_end_list[];

    /*
    -- Loop to process a subscript list.
    */
    do {
        if (tp->form == ARRAY_FORM) {
            index_tp = tp->info.array.index_typep;
            elmt_tp  = tp->info.array.elmt_typep;

            get_token();
            ss_tp = expression();

            /*
            -- The subscript expression must be assignment type
            -- compatible with the corresponding subscript type.
            */
            if (!is_assign_type_compatible(index_tp, ss_tp))
                error(INCOMPATIBLE_TYPES);

            tp = elmt_tp;
        }
        else {
            error(TOO_MANY_SUBSCRIPTS);
            while ((token != RBRACKET) &&
                    (! token_in(statement_end_list)))
                get_token();
        }
    } while (token == COMMA);

    if_token_get_else_error(RBRACKET, MISSING_RBRACKET);
    return(tp);
}

/*------------------------------------------------------*/
/*  record_field             Process a field designation   */
/*                           following a record identifier: */
/*                                                          */
/*                               . <field-variable>         */
/*------------------------------------------------------*/

    TYPE_STRUCT_PTR
record_field(tp)
```

```
    TYPE_STRUCT_PTR tp;

{
    SYMTAB_NODE_PTR field_idp;

    get_token();

    if ((token == IDENTIFIER) && (tp->form == RECORD_FORM)) {
        search_this_symtab(field_idp,
                           tp->info.record.field_symtab);

        get_token();

        if (field_idp != NULL) return(field_idp->typep);
        else {
            error(INVALID_FIELD);
            return(&dummy_type);
        }
    }
    else {
        get_token();
        error(INVALID_FIELD);
        return(&dummy_type);
    }
}


            /*******************************/
            /*                             */
            /*        Type compatibility   */
            /*                             */
            /*******************************/

/*------------------------------------------------------------*/
/*  check_rel_op_types   Check the operand types for a rela-   */
/*                       tional operator.                      */
/*------------------------------------------------------------*/

check_rel_op_types(tp1, tp2)

    TYPE_STRUCT_PTR tp1, tp2;          /* operand types */

{
    /*
    -- Two identical scalar or enumeration types.
    */
    if (  (tp1 == tp2)
       && ((tp1->form == SCALAR_FORM) || (tp1->form == ENUM_FORM)))
        return;

    /*
    -- One integer and one real.
    */
    if (  ((tp1 == integer_typep) && (tp2 == real_typep))
       || ((tp2 == integer_typep) && (tp1 == real_typep))) return;

    /*
    -- Two strings of the same length.
    */
    if ((tp1->form == ARRAY_FORM) &&
        (tp2->form == ARRAY_FORM) &&
        (tp1->info.array.elmt_typep == char_typep) &&
        (tp2->info.array.elmt_typep == char_typep) &&
        (tp1->info.array.elmt_count ==
                         tp2->info.array.elmt_count)) return;

    error(INCOMPATIBLE_TYPES);
}
```

```
/*------------------------------------------------------*/
/*  is_assign_type_compatible  Return TRUE iff a value of type */
/*                             tp1 can be assigned to a vari- */
/*                             able of type tp1.             */
/*------------------------------------------------------*/

    BOOLEAN
is_assign_type_compatible(tp1, tp2)

    TYPE_STRUCT_PTR tp1, tp2;

{
    tp1 = base_type(tp1);
    tp2 = base_type(tp2);

    if (tp1 == tp2) return(TRUE);

    /*
    -- real := integer
    */
    if ((tp1 == real_typep) && (tp2 == integer_typep)) return(TRUE);

    /*
    -- string1 := string2 of the same length
    */
```

```
    if ((tp1->form == ARRAY_FORM) &&
        (tp2->form == ARRAY_FORM) &&
        (tp1->info.array.elmt_typep == char_typep) &&
        (tp2->info.array.elmt_typep == char_typep) &&
        (tp1->info.array.elmt_count ==
                    tp2->info.array.elmt_count)) return(TRUE);

    return(FALSE);

}

/*------------------------------------------------------*/
/*  base_type          Return the range type of a subrange */
/*                     type.                              */
/*------------------------------------------------------*/

    TYPE_STRUCT_PTR
base_type(tp)

    TYPE_STRUCT_PTR tp;

{
    return((tp->form == SUBRANGE_FORM)
                ? tp->info.subrange.range_typep
                : tp);
}
```

FIGURE 6-14   File stmt.c.

```
/*************************************************************/
/*                                                         */
/*        S T A T E M E N T   P A R S E R                  */
/*                                                         */
/*    Parsing routines for statements.                     */
/*                                                         */
/*    FILE:      stmt.c                                    */
/*                                                         */
/*    MODULE:    parser                                    */
/*                                                         */
/*************************************************************/

#include <stdio.h>
#include "common.h"
#include "error.h"
#include "scanner.h"
#include "symtab.h"
#include "parser.h"

/*------------------------------------------------------*/
/*  Externals                                            */
/*------------------------------------------------------*/

extern TOKEN_CODE       token;
extern char             word_string[];
extern LITERAL          literal;
extern TOKEN_CODE       statement_start_list[], statement_end_list[];

extern SYMTAB_NODE_PTR  symtab_root;

extern TYPE_STRUCT_PTR  integer_typep, real_typep,
                        boolean_typep, char_typep;

extern TYPE_STRUCT      dummy_type;
```

```
/*------------------------------------------------------*/
/*  statement          Process a statement by calling the */
/*                     appropriate parsing routine based on */
/*                     the statement's first token.       */
/*------------------------------------------------------*/

statement()

{
    /*
    -- Call the appropriate routine based on the first
    -- token of the statement.
    */
    switch (token) {

        case IDENTIFIER: {
            SYMTAB_NODE_PTR idp;

            /*
            -- Assignment statement.
            */
            search_and_find_all_symtab(idp);
            assignment_statement(idp);

            break;
        }

        case REPEAT:    repeat_statement();    break;
        case WHILE:     while_statement();     break;
        case IF:        if_statement();        break;
        case FOR:       for_statement();       break;
        case CASE:      case_statement();      break;
        case BEGIN:     compound_statement();  break;
    }
```

```
    /*
    -- Error synchronization:  Only a semicolon, END, ELSE, or
    --                         UNTIL may follow a statement.
    --                         Check for a missing semicolon.
    */
    synchronize(statement_end_list, statement_start_list, NULL);
    if (token_in(statement_start_list)) error(MISSING_SEMICOLON);
}

/*-------------------------------------------------------------*/
/*  assignment_statement    Process an assignment statement:   */
/*                                                             */
/*                          <id> := <expr>                    */
/*-------------------------------------------------------------*/

assignment_statement(var_idp)

    SYMTAB_NODE_PTR var_idp;           /* target variable id */

{
    TYPE_STRUCT_PTR var_tp, expr_tp;   /* types of var and expr */

    var_tp = variable(var_idp, TARGET_USE);
    if_token_get_else_error(COLONEQUAL, MISSING_COLONEQUAL);

    expr_tp = expression();

    if (! is_assign_type_compatible(var_tp, expr_tp))
        error(INCOMPATIBLE_ASSIGNMENT);
}

/*-------------------------------------------------------------*/
/*  repeat_statement    Process a REPEAT statement:            */
/*                                                             */
/*                      REPEAT <stmt-list> UNTIL <expr>        */
/*-------------------------------------------------------------*/

repeat_statement()

{
    TYPE_STRUCT_PTR expr_tp;

    /*
    -- <stmt-list>
    */
    get_token();
    do {
        statement();
        while (token == SEMICOLON) get_token();
    } while (token_in(statement_start_list));

    if_token_get_else_error(UNTIL, MISSING_UNTIL);

    expr_tp = expression();
    if (expr_tp != boolean_typep) error(INCOMPATIBLE_TYPES);
}

/*-------------------------------------------------------------*/
/*  while_statement    Process a WHILE statement:              */
/*                                                             */
/*                      WHILE <expr> DO <stmt>                 */
/*-------------------------------------------------------------*/

while_statement()

{
    TYPE_STRUCT_PTR expr_tp;
```

```
    get_token();

    expr_tp = expression();
    if (expr_tp != boolean_typep) error(INCOMPATIBLE_TYPES);

    if_token_get_else_error(DO, MISSING_DO);
    statement();
}

/*-------------------------------------------------------------*/
/*  if_statement         Process an IF statement:              */
/*                                                             */
/*                       IF <expr> THEN <stmt>                 */
/*                                                             */
/*                       or:                                   */
/*                                                             */
/*                       IF <expr> THEN <stmt> ELSE <stmt>     */
/*-------------------------------------------------------------*/

if_statement()

{
    TYPE_STRUCT_PTR expr_tp;

    get_token();

    expr_tp = expression();
    if (expr_tp != boolean_typep) error(INCOMPATIBLE_TYPES);

    if_token_get_else_error(THEN, MISSING_THEN);
    statement();

    /*
    -- ELSE branch?
    */
    if (token == ELSE) {
        get_token();
        statement();
    }
}

/*-------------------------------------------------------------*/
/*  for_statement        Process a FOR statement:              */
/*                                                             */
/*                       FOR <id> := <expr> TO|DOWNTO <expr>   */
/*                          DO <stmt>                          */
/*-------------------------------------------------------------*/

for_statement()

{
    SYMTAB_NODE_PTR for_idp;
    TYPE_STRUCT_PTR for_tp, expr_tp;

    get_token();

    if (token == IDENTIFIER) {
        search_and_find_all_symtab(for_idp);

        for_tp = base_type(for_idp->typep);
        get_token();

        if ((for_tp != integer_typep) &&
            (for_tp != char_typep) &&
            (for_tp->form != ENUM_FORM)) error(INCOMPATIBLE_TYPES);
    }
    else {
```

```
        error(IDENTIFIER, MISSING_IDENTIFIER);
        for_tp = &dummy_type;
    }

    if_token_get_else_error(COLONEQUAL, MISSING_COLONEQUAL);

    expr_tp = expression();
    if (! is_assign_type_compatible(for_tp, expr_tp))
        error(INCOMPATIBLE_TYPES);

    if ((token == TO) || (token == DOWNTO)) get_token();
    else error(MISSING_TO_OR_DOWNTO);

    expr_tp = expression();
    if (! is_assign_type_compatible(for_tp, expr_tp))
        error(INCOMPATIBLE_TYPES);

    if_token_get_else_error(DO, MISSING_DO);
    statement();
}

/*------------------------------------------------------------*/
/* case_statement      Process a CASE statement:              */
/*                                                            */
/*                          CASE <expr> OF                    */
/*                              <case-branch> ;               */
/*                                  ...                       */
/*                              END                           */
/*------------------------------------------------------------*/

TOKEN_CODE follow_expr_list[]       = {OF, SEMICOLON, 0};

TOKEN_CODE case_label_start_list[] = {IDENTIFIER, NUMBER, PLUS,
                                      MINUS, STRING, 0};

case_statement()

{
    BOOLEAN         another_branch;
    TYPE_STRUCT_PTR expr_tp;
    TYPE_STRUCT_PTR case_label();

    get_token();
    expr_tp = expression();

    if (   ((expr_tp->form != SCALAR_FORM) &&
            (expr_tp->form != ENUM_FORM) &&
            (expr_tp->form != SUBRANGE_FORM))
        || (expr_tp == real_typep)) error(INCOMPATIBLE_TYPES);

    /*
    -- Error synchronization:  Should be OF
    */
    synchronize(follow_expr_list, case_label_start_list, NULL);
    if_token_get_else_error(OF, MISSING_OF);

    /*
    -- Loop to process CASE branches.
    */
    another_branch = token_in(case_label_start_list);
    while (another_branch) {
        if (token_in(case_label_start_list)) case_branch(expr_tp);

        if (token == SEMICOLON) {
            get_token();
            another_branch = TRUE;
        }
```

```
        else if (token_in(case_label_start_list)) {
            error(MISSING_SEMICOLON);
            another_branch = TRUE;
        }
        else another_branch = FALSE;
    }

    if_token_get_else_error(END, MISSING_END);
}

/*------------------------------------------------------------*/
/* case_branch              Process a CASE branch:            */
/*                                                            */
/*                      <case-label-list> : <stmt>            */
/*------------------------------------------------------------*/

TOKEN_CODE follow_case_label_list[] = {COLON, SEMICOLON, 0};

case_branch(expr_tp)

    TYPE_STRUCT_PTR expr_tp;           /* type of CASE expression */

{
    BOOLEAN         another_label;
    TYPE_STRUCT_PTR label_tp;
    TYPE_STRUCT_PTR case_label();

    /*
    -- <case-label-list>
    */
    do {
        label_tp = case_label();
        if (expr_tp != label_tp) error(INCOMPATIBLE_TYPES);

        get_token();
        if (token == COMMA) {
            get_token();
            if (token_in(case_label_start_list)) another_label = TRUE;
            else {
                error(MISSING_CONSTANT);
                another_label = FALSE;
            }
        }
        else another_label = FALSE;
    } while (another_label);

    /*
    -- Error synchronization:  Should be :
    */
    synchronize(follow_case_label_list, statement_start_list, NULL);
    if_token_get_else_error(COLON, MISSING_COLON);

    statement();
}

/*------------------------------------------------------------*/
/* case_label              Process a CASE label and return a  */
/*                         pointer to its type structure.     */
/*------------------------------------------------------------*/

    TYPE_STRUCT_PTR
case_label()

{
    TOKEN_CODE      sign      = PLUS;   /* unary + or - sign */
    BOOLEAN         saw_sign = FALSE;   /* TRUE iff unary sign */
    TYPE_STRUCT_PTR label_tp;
```

```
/*
-- Unary + or - sign.
*/
if ((token == PLUS) || (token == MINUS)) {
    sign      = token;
    saw_sign = TRUE;
    get_token();
}

/*
-- Numeric constant:  Integer type only.
*/
if (token == NUMBER) {
    if (literal.type == REAL_LIT) error(INVALID_CONSTANT);
    return(integer_typep);
}

/*
-- Identifier constant:  Integer, character, or enumeration
--                       types only.
*/
else if (token == IDENTIFIER) {
    SYMTAB_NODE_PTR idp;

    search_all_symtab(idp);

    if (idp == NULL) {
        error(UNDEFINED_IDENTIFIER);
        return(&dummy_type);
    }

    else if (idp->defn.key != CONST_DEFN) {
        error(NOT_A_CONSTANT_IDENTIFIER);
        return(&dummy_type);
    }

    else if (idp->typep == integer_typep)
        return(integer_typep);

    else if (idp->typep == char_typep) {
        if (saw_sign) error(INVALID_CONSTANT);
        return(char_typep);
    }

    else if (idp->typep->form == ENUM_FORM) {
        if (saw_sign) error(INVALID_CONSTANT);
        return(idp->typep);
    }
```

```
    else return(&dummy_type);
}

/*
-- String constant:  Character type only.
*/
else if (token == STRING) {
    if (saw_sign) error(INVALID_CONSTANT);

    if (strlen(literal.value.string) == 1) return(char_typep);
    else {
        error(INVALID_CONSTANT);
        return(&dummy_type);
    }
}

else {
    error(INVALID_CONSTANT);
    return(&dummy_type);
}
}

/*-------------------------------------------------------------*/
/*  compound_statement      Process a compound statement:      */
/*                                                             */
/*                          BEGIN <stmt-list> END              */
/*-------------------------------------------------------------*/

compound_statement()

{
    /*
    -- <stmt-list>
    */
    get_token();
    do {
        statement();
        while (token == SEMICOLON) get_token();
        if (token == END) break;

        /*
        -- Error synchronization:  Should be at the start of the
        --                         next statement.
        */
        synchronize(statement_start_list, NULL, NULL);
    } while (token_in(statement_start_list));

    if_token_get_else_error(END, MISSING_END);
}
```

Figure 6-15 shows the output from running the syntax checker on a source file containing syntax and type errors.

FIGURE 6-15   Sample output from the syntax checker II.

```
Page 1  syntax2.in  Tue Jul 10 00:53:14 1990


  1 0: CONST
  2 0:    ten  = 10;
  3 0:    pi   = 3.14159.26;
                        ^
```

```
*** ERROR: Unexpected token.
  4 0:    ch   = 'x';
  5 0:    hello  'Hello, world.';
                              ^
*** ERROR: Missing = .
  6 0:
  7 0: TYPE
```

```
 8 0:     e = (alpha, beta, gamma);
 9 0:     ee = e;
10 0:     sr = alpha..gamma
11 0:     cr = 'a'..ch;
                 ^
```

*** ERROR: Missing ; .
```
12 0:
13 0:     ar1 = ARRAY [1..ten] OF integer;
14 0:     ar2 = ARRAY [e, sr OF real;
                              ^
```

*** ERROR: Missing] .
```
15 0:     ar3 = ARRAY [(fee, fye, foe, fum), sr] ARRAY [ee] boolean;
```

*** ERROR: Missing OF.

*** ERROR: Missing OF.
```
16 0:
17 0:     rec = RECORD
18 0:            i, j, k : integer;
19 0:            x  : real;
20 0:            ch : char;
21 0:            a    ARRAY [sr] OF e;
                                ^
```

*** ERROR: Missing : .
```
22 0:          END;
23 0:
24 0: VAR
25 0:     radius, circumference : real;
26 0:     b    : boolean;
27 0:     letter : 'a'..'z'
28 0:     greek  : e;
                ^
```

*** ERROR: Missing ; .
```
29 0:     list   : ar1;
30 0:     a2     : ar2;
31 0:     a3     : ar3;
```

```
32 0:     thing : rec;
33 0:
34 0: BEGIN
```

Page 2   syntax2.in   Tue Jul 10 00:53:14 1990

```
35 0:     radius := (circumference/pi/2;
                                       ^
```

*** ERROR: Missing right parenthesis.
```
36 0:     b := ten*radius >= thing.x;
37 0:     greek := thing.a[beta];
38 0:     a2[alpha, gamma] := a2[beta][alpha];
39 0:     b := a3[foe, alpha, beta] - pi;
                                       ^
```

*** ERROR: Incompatible types.

*** ERROR: Incompatible assignment.
```
40 0:     a3[fye] := a3[7];
```

*** ERROR: Incompatible types.
```
41 0:     thing.what := list[ten, 7, 3];
                  ^
```

*** ERROR: Invalid field.
                                 ^
*** ERROR: Too many subscripts.
                                       ^
*** ERROR: Incompatible assignment.
```
42 0: END
```

```
              42 Source lines.
              15 Source errors.
```

6.6.1 Type checking expressions

In order to type check an expression, we need to know the types of its constituent parts. In file expr.c, we modify the expression parsing functions expression, simple_expression, term, and factor so that each "returns a type"; actually, each function returns pointer to a type structure. In function expression, for example, we return the type of the expression we just parsed.

We add three new macros to check the types of operands. Macro integer_operands and boolean_operands each returns TRUE only if both operands are integer or both are boolean, respectively. Macro real_operands returns TRUE if both operands are real, or if one is real and the other integer.

If we parse only one simple expression in function expression, we return the type of that simple expression. If there is a second simple expression, we return the boolean type. We call function check_rel_op_types to check the types of the operand pairs. We also call function base_type.

In function check_rel_op_typep, we verify the correctness of the two operand types of a relational operator. We check whether both operands have the same scalar or enumeration type, whether one is integer and the other real, or whether both are strings with the same length. If necessary, we flag the INCOMPATIBLE_ TYPES error. In function base_type, we simply return the type that is passed in, or the range type of a subrange type.

If we parse only one term in function simple_expression, we return the type of that term. Otherwise, we update the result type as we parse each subsequent term. If the operator is OR, both operands must be boolean, and the result type is boolean. If both operands are integers, the result type is integer, or if both are real, or one is real and the other is integer, the result type is real.

Function term is similar to simple_expression. We return the type of the factor if there is only a single factor. Otherwise, we update the result type as we parse each subsequent factor. If the operator is DIV or MOD, both operands must be integer, and the result type is integer. If the operator is /, each operand can be either integer or real, and the result type is real. If the operator is AND, both operands must be boolean, and the result type is boolean. If both operands are integer, the result type is integer, or if both are real, or one is real and the other is integer, the result type is real.

Function factor now returns the type of each factor. If the factor is a constant identifier, we return its type. For any other identifier, we call function variable, which returns a type. If the factor is a number, we return either integer or real. If it is a character, we return the character type. If it is string, we call function make_string_typep which returns a string type.

If the token is NOT, we return the type from a recursive call to factor. For a parenthesized expression, we return the type from a recursive call to expression.

6.6.2 Type checking variables

There is a new function variable, in which we parse a variable and return its type. The variable can be a simple identifier, it can be an array variable with subscripts, or a record variable with fields. Whenever we call this function, we pass it a pointer to the variable identifier's symbol table node and the variable's usage. When factor calls variable, the usage is always EXPR_USE, since the variable is used in an expression. We first check the identifier's definition to make sure that we are not using it incorrectly, such as a type identifier in an expression.

A Pascal variable can have a sequence of zero or more subscripts and fields. We parse subscripts and fields in a while loop, where we call functions array_ subscript_list and record_field as appropriate. Each call updates the result type structure pointer tp, which we had initialized to point to the type structure of the variable identifier.

In function array_subscript_list, we loop to parse a list of subscripts between one set of brackets. Argument tp starts out pointing to the type structure of the array identifier. Each time through the loop, we check tp to make sure it is pointing to an array type structure. If so, we call function expression to parse the subscript expression, and then we call is_assignment_compatible to make sure that the type of the subscript is assignment compatible with the corresponding index type. (Assignment compatibility is explained below.) Then, we move tp down to point to the element type structure.

Once we are out of the while loop, tp points to the type structure of an element in the last dimension of the variable. This is the type of the subscripted variable, and it is what we return.

In function record_field, we first make sure that we have a record type and that the current token is an identifier. If so, we look up the identifier in the record type's private symbol table. If we find it there, we return the type of the field identifier.

6.6.3 Assignment compatibility

In Pascal, one type is assignment compatible with another type if an expression of the first type can be assigned to a variable of the second type. We check for assignment compatibility in assignment statements, of course, but also in other places like subscript expressions. Boolean function is_assign_type_compatible is where we make this check. Two types are assignment compatible if they are the same type, or two string types with the same length. We can also assign an integer to a real (but not the other way around). We return TRUE or FALSE, accordingly.

6.6.4 Type checking statements

Now we will see how the statement parsing routines in file stmt.c do type checking. In function assignment_statement, we call function is_assign_type_compatible. In functions while_statement, repeat_statement, and if_statement, we check to make sure that their expressions are boolean.

In function for_statement, we check that the control variable is a scalar but not a real, and we call is_assign_type_compatible twice to check that the initial and final expressions are assignment compatible with the control variable.

In function case_statement, we check that the expression is a scalar but not a real, and in function case_branch, we check that each label is of the same type as the expression. Function case_label now returns the type of the label it parsed.

Now that we can parse declarations and statements, and do type checking, all that remains are procedures and functions. We tackle them in the next chapter.

Questions and exercises

1. *Statement label declarations.* Write the routines to parse statement label declarations. Statement labels can be stored either in the symbol table or in a separate table.

2. *Pointer types and undefined type identifiers.* Write the routines to parse pointer types. Note that it is possible in Pascal to declare a pointer type that points

to a type that is defined later or to a type that is still being defined. For example:

```
TYPE
    recptr = ^rec;
    rec = RECORD
                reclink : ^rec;
                ...
          END;
```

When parsing the definition of recptr, identifier rec is still undefined. When parsing field reclink, the definition of identifier rec is not yet complete. This is the only situation where Pascal allows the use of an undefined identifier. The parser needs to keep track of each such use. When the identifier is finally defined, the parser then must go back and "fix up" each of the previous uses.

3. *Variant records.* Redesign the TYPE_STRUCT for variant records. The structure must keep track of which field, if any, is the tag field, and which fields belong to each value of the tag field type. Write the routines to parse record types that may or may not contain a variant part.

4. *Packed types.* Pascal defines a packed type to be functionally equivalent to an unpacked type, except that a packed type may use less memory. Modify the type parsing routines to accept the reserved word PACKED but otherwise ignore it.

5. *Set types.* Redesign the TYPE_STRUCT for Pascal set types. Write the routines to parse set type specifications, set operations, and set constructors.

6. Extend the cross-referencer utility program from Chapter 3 so that it also prints type information about each identifier.

7. The complete type compatibility rules of Pascal are a bit more complex than we implemented. Look up the complete rules, and rewrite expr.c and stmt.c to implement them.

CHAPTER 7

Parsing Programs, Procedures, and Functions

We can now complete the parser module! In this chapter, we complete the syntax checker from Chapters 5 and 6 to enable it to check the syntax of an entire Pascal program. With this program, we will develop the skills to:

- parse programs, procedures, and functions
- handle scope and nested procedures and functions
- parse calls to both declared and standard procedures and functions

7.1 Changes to the modules

You need to change the parser and symbol table modules. Parser files `routine.c` and `standard.c` are new.

Parser Module

`parser.h`	*u*	Parser header file
`routine.c`	*n*	Parse programs, procedures, and functions
`standard.c`	*n*	Parse standard procedures and functions
`stmt.c`	*c*	Parse statements
`expr.c`	*c*	Parse expressions
`decl.c`	*c*	Parse declarations

Scanner Module

scanner.h	*u*	Scanner header file
scanner.c	*u*	Scanner routines

Symbol Table Module

symtab.h	*c*	Symbol table header file
symtab.c	*c*	Symbol table routines

Error Module

error.h	*u*	Error header file
error.c	*u*	Error routines

Miscellaneous

common.h	*u*	Common header file

Where: *u*   file unchanged from the previous chapter
        c   file changed from the previous chapter
        n   new file

File routine.c contains routines to parse programs, procedures, and functions. File standard.c contains routines to parse the standard predefined procedures and functions like read and sqrt. Change symtab.h and symtab.c to accommodate more than one symbol table and to initialize the global table with the names of the standard procedures and functions.

7.2 Program headers

In the previous chapters we have seen how to parse declarations and statements. When we say that we are going to parse programs, procedures, and functions, we really mean we're going to parse their headers and deal with the concept of scope.

Figure 7-1 shows the syntax diagram for a program. As before, our new parsing routines are based on these diagrams. File routine.c is shown in Figure 7-2. In its first two functions, program and program_header, we parse a program and its program header, respectively.

FIGURE 7-1   Syntax diagram for a program.

program

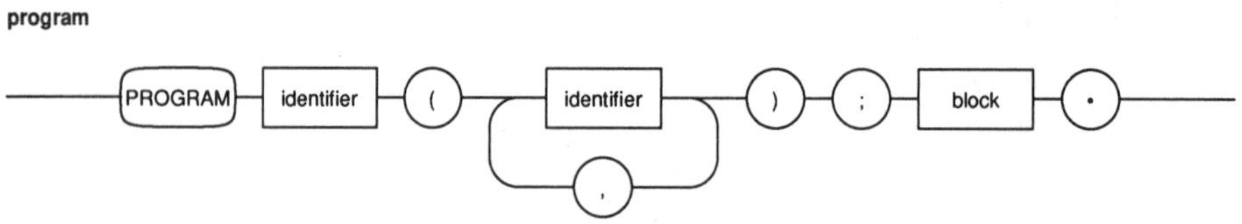

FIGURE 7-2   File routine.c.

```
/********************************************************************/
/*                                                                  */
/*      R O U T I N E   P A R S E R                                 */
/*                                                                  */
/*      Parsing routines for programs and declared                 */
/*      procedures and functions.                                  */
/*                                                                  */
/*      FILE:     routine.c                                         */
/*                                                                  */
/*      MODULE:   parser                                            */
/*                                                                  */
/********************************************************************/

#include <stdio.h>
#include "common.h"
#include "error.h"
#include "scanner.h"
#include "symtab.h"
#include "parser.h"

/*------------------------------------------------------------*/
/* Externals                                                  */
/*------------------------------------------------------------*/

extern int              line_number;
extern int              error_count;

extern TOKEN_CODE       token;
extern char             word_string[];
extern SYMTAB_NODE_PTR  symtab_display[];
extern int              level;

extern TYPE_STRUCT      dummy_type;

extern TOKEN_CODE       statement_start_list[],
                        statement_end_list[],
                        declaration_start_list[];

/*------------------------------------------------------------*/
/* Globals                                                    */
/*------------------------------------------------------------*/

char buffer[MAX_PRINT_LINE_LENGTH];

/*------------------------------------------------------------*/
/* Forwards                                                   */
/*------------------------------------------------------------*/

SYMTAB_NODE_PTR formal_parm_list();
SYMTAB_NODE_PTR program_header(), procedure_header(),
                function_header();

/*------------------------------------------------------------*/
/* program      Process a program:                            */
/*                                                            */
/*                    <program-header> ; <block> .            */
/*------------------------------------------------------------*/

TOKEN_CODE follow_header_list[] = {SEMICOLON, END_OF_FILE, 0};

program()

{
    SYMTAB_NODE_PTR program_idp;        /* program id */
```

```
    /*
    --              PARSE THE PROGRAM
    --
    --
    -- Intialize the symbol table.
    */
    init_symtab();

    /*
    -- Begin parsing with the program header.
    */
    program_idp = program_header();

    /*
    -- Error synchronization:  Should be ;
    */
    synchronize(follow_header_list,
                declaration_start_list, statement_start_list);
    if_token_get(SEMICOLON);
    else if (token_in(declaration_start_list) ||
             token_in(statement_start_list))
        error(MISSING_SEMICOLON);

    analyze_routine_header(program_idp);

    /*
    -- Parse the program's block.
    */
    program_idp->defn.info.routine.locals = NULL;
    block(program_idp);

    program_idp->defn.info.routine.local_symtab = exit_scope();
    program_idp->defn.info.routine.code_segment = NULL;
    analyze_block(program_idp->defn.info.routine.code_segment);

    if_token_get_else_error(PERIOD, MISSING_PERIOD);

    /*
    -- Look for the end of file.
    */
    while (token != END_OF_FILE) {
        error(UNEXPECTED_TOKEN);
        get_token();
    }

    quit_scanner();

    /*
    -- Print the parser's summary.
    */
    print_line("\n");
    print_line("\n");
    sprintf(buffer, "%20d Source lines.\n", line_number);
    print_line(buffer);
    sprintf(buffer, "%20d Source errors.\n", error_count);
    print_line(buffer);

    if (error_count == 0) exit(0);
    else                  exit(-SYNTAX_ERROR);
}

/*------------------------------------------------------------*/
/* program_header      Process a program header:              */
/*                                                            */
```

```
/*                       PROGRAM <id> ( <id-list> )        */
/*                                                         */
/*                    Return a pointer to the program id   */
/*                    node.                                 */
/*---------------------------------------------------------*/

TOKEN_CODE follow_prog_id_list[] = {LPAREN, SEMICOLON,
                                    END_OF_FILE, 0};

TOKEN_CODE follow_parms_list[]  = {RPAREN, SEMICOLON,
                                    END_OF_FILE, 0};

    SYMTAB_NODE_PTR
program_header()

{
    SYMTAB_NODE_PTR program_idp;        /* program id */
    SYMTAB_NODE_PTR parm_idp;           /* parm id */
    SYMTAB_NODE_PTR prev_parm_idp = NULL;

    if_token_get_else_error(PROGRAM, MISSING_PROGRAM);

    if (token == IDENTIFIER) {
        search_and_enter_local_symtab(program_idp);
        program_idp->defn.key = PROG_DEFN;
        program_idp->defn.info.routine.key = DECLARED;
        program_idp->defn.info.routine.parm_count = 0;
        program_idp->defn.info.routine.total_parm_size = 0;
        program_idp->defn.info.routine.total_local_size = 0;
        program_idp->typep = &dummy_type;
        program_idp->label_index = 0;
        get_token();
    }
    else error(MISSING_IDENTIFIER);

    /*
    -- Error synchronization:  Should be ( or ;
    */
    synchronize(follow_prog_id_list,
                declaration_start_list, statement_start_list);

    enter_scope(NULL);

    /*
    -- Program parameters.
    */
    if (token == LPAREN) {
        /*
        -- <id-list>
        */
        do {
            get_token();
            if (token == IDENTIFIER) {
                search_and_enter_local_symtab(parm_idp);
                parm_idp->defn.key = VARPARM_DEFN;
                parm_idp->typep = &dummy_type;
                get_token();

                /*
                -- Link program parm ids together.
                */
                if (prev_parm_idp == NULL)
                    program_idp->defn.info.routine.parms =
                                prev_parm_idp = parm_idp;
                else {
                    prev_parm_idp->next = parm_idp;
                    prev_parm_idp = parm_idp;
```

```
                }
            }
            else error(MISSING_IDENTIFIER);
        } while (token == COMMA);

        /*
        -- Error synchronization:  Should be )
        */
        synchronize(follow_parms_list,
                    declaration_start_list, statement_start_list);
        if_token_get_else_error(RPAREN, MISSING_RPAREN);
    }

    return(program_idp);
}

/*---------------------------------------------------------*/
/* routine            Call the appropriate routine to process */
/*                    a procedure or function definition:  */
/*                                                         */
/*                    <routine-header> ; <block>           */
/*---------------------------------------------------------*/

routine()

{
    SYMTAB_NODE_PTR rtn_idp;    /* routine id */

    rtn_idp = (token == PROCEDURE) ? procedure_header()
                                   : function_header();

    /*
    -- Error synchronization:  Should be ;
    */
    synchronize(follow_header_list,
                declaration_start_list, statement_start_list);
    if_token_get(SEMICOLON);
    else if (token_in(declaration_start_list) ||
             token_in(statement_start_list))
        error(MISSING_SEMICOLON);

    /*
    -- <block> or FORWARD.
    */
    if (strcmp(word_string, "forward") != 0) {
        rtn_idp->defn.info.routine.key = DECLARED;
        analyze_routine_header(rtn_idp);

        rtn_idp->defn.info.routine.locals = NULL;
        block(rtn_idp);

        rtn_idp->defn.info.routine.code_segment = NULL;
        analyze_block(rtn_idp->defn.info.routine.code_segment);
    }
    else {
        get_token();
        rtn_idp->defn.info.routine.key = FORWARD;
        analyze_routine_header(rtn_idp);
    }

    rtn_idp->defn.info.routine.local_symtab = exit_scope();
}

/*---------------------------------------------------------*/
/* procedure_header   Process a procedure header:          */
/*                                                         */
/*                    PROCEDURE <id>                       */
```

```
/*                                              */
/*                  or:                         */
/*                                              */
/*                PROCEDURE <id> ( <parm-list> ) */
/*                                              */
/*              Return a pointer to the procedure id */
/*              node.                           */
/*--------------------------------------------------*/

TOKEN_CODE follow_proc_id_list[] = {LPAREN, SEMICOLON,
                        END_OF_FILE, 0};

    SYMTAB_NODE_PTR
procedure_header()

{
    SYMTAB_NODE_PTR proc_idp;        /* procedure id */
    SYMTAB_NODE_PTR parm_listp;      /* formal parm list */
    int             parm_count;
    int             total_parm_size;
    BOOLEAN         forward_flag = FALSE;   /* TRUE iff forwarded */

    get_token();

    /*
    -- If the procedure identifier has already been
    -- declared in this scope, it must be a forward.
    */
    if (token == IDENTIFIER) {
        search_local_symtab(proc_idp);
        if (proc_idp == NULL) {
            enter_local_symtab(proc_idp);
            proc_idp->defn.key = PROC_DEFN;
            proc_idp->defn.info.routine.total_local_size = 0;
            proc_idp->typep = &dummy_type;
            proc_idp->label_index = 0;
        }
        else if ((proc_idp->defn.key == PROC_DEFN) &&
                (proc_idp->defn.info.routine.key == FORWARD))
            forward_flag = TRUE;
        else error(REDEFINED_IDENTIFIER);

        get_token();
    }
    else error(MISSING_IDENTIFIER);

    /*
    -- Error synchronization:  Should be ( or ;
    */
    synchronize(follow_proc_id_list,
            declaration_start_list, statement_start_list);

    enter_scope(NULL);

    /*
    -- Optional formal parameters.  If there was a forward,
    -- there must not be any parameters here (but parse them
    -- anyway for error recovery).
    */
    if (token == LPAREN) {
        parm_listp = formal_parm_list(&parm_count, &total_parm_size);

        if (forward_flag) error(ALREADY_FORWARDED);
        else {
            proc_idp->defn.info.routine.parm_count = parm_count;
            proc_idp->defn.info.routine.total_parm_size =
                                        total_parm_size;
```

```
            proc_idp->defn.info.routine.parms = parm_listp;
        }
    }
    else if (!forward_flag) {
        proc_idp->defn.info.routine.parm_count = 0;
        proc_idp->defn.info.routine.total_parm_size = 0;
        proc_idp->defn.info.routine.parms = NULL;
    }

    proc_idp->typep = NULL;
    return(proc_idp);
}

/*--------------------------------------------------------*/
/*  function_header    Process a function header:         */
/*                                                        */
/*              FUNCTION <id> : <type-id>                 */
/*                                                        */
/*                  or:                                   */
/*                                                        */
/*              FUNCTION <id> ( <parm-list> )             */
/*                            : <type-id>                 */
/*                                                        */
/*              Return a pointer to the function id       */
/*              node.                                     */
/*--------------------------------------------------------*/

TOKEN_CODE follow_func_id_list[] = {LPAREN, COLON, SEMICOLON,
                        END_OF_FILE, 0};

    SYMTAB_NODE_PTR
function_header()

{
    SYMTAB_NODE_PTR func_idp, type_idp;   /* func and type ids*/
    SYMTAB_NODE_PTR parm_listp;           /* formal parm list */
    int             parm_count;
    int             total_parm_size;
    BOOLEAN         forward_flag = FALSE;  /* TRUE iff forwarded */

    get_token();

    /*
    -- If the function identifier has already been
    -- declared in this scope, it must be a forward.
    */
    if (token == IDENTIFIER) {
        search_local_symtab(func_idp);
        if (func_idp == NULL) {
            enter_local_symtab(func_idp);
            func_idp->defn.key = FUNC_DEFN;
            func_idp->defn.info.routine.total_local_size = 0;
            func_idp->typep = &dummy_type;
            func_idp->label_index = 0;
        }
        else if ((func_idp->defn.key == FUNC_DEFN) &&
                (func_idp->defn.info.routine.key == FORWARD))
            forward_flag = TRUE;
        else error(REDEFINED_IDENTIFIER);

        get_token();
    }
    else error(MISSING_IDENTIFIER);

    /*
    -- Error synchronization:  Should be ( or : or ;
    */
```

```
    synchronize(follow_func_id_list,
              declaration_start_list, statement_start_list);

    enter_scope(NULL);

    /*
    -- Optional formal parameters.  If there was a forward,
    -- there must not be any parameters here (but parse them
    -- anyway for error recovery).
    */
    if (token == LPAREN) {
        parm_listp = formal_parm_list(&parm_count, &total_parm_size);

        if (forward_flag) error(ALREADY_FORWARDED);
        else {
            func_idp->defn.info.routine.parm_count = parm_count;
            func_idp->defn.info.routine.total_parm_size =
                                         total_parm_size;
            func_idp->defn.info.routine.parms = parm_listp;
        }
    }
    else if (!forward_flag) {
        func_idp->defn.info.routine.parm_count = 0;
        func_idp->defn.info.routine.total_parm_size = 0;
        func_idp->defn.info.routine.parms = NULL;
    }

    /*
    -- Function type.  If there was a forward,
    -- there must not be a type here (but parse it
    -- anyway for error recovery).
    */
    if (!forward_flag || (token == COLON)) {
        if_token_get_else_error(COLON, MISSING_COLON);

        if (token == IDENTIFIER) {
            search_and_find_all_symtab(type_idp);
            if (type_idp->defn.key != TYPE_DEFN) error(INVALID_TYPE);
            if (!forward_flag) func_idp->typep = type_idp->typep;
            get_token();
        }
        else {
            error(MISSING_IDENTIFIER);
            func_idp->typep = &dummy_type;
        }

        if (forward_flag) error(ALREADY_FORWARDED);
    }

    return(func_idp);
}

/*-----------------------------------------------------*/
/*  formal_parm_list    Process a formal parameter list:  */
/*                                                     */
/*                      ( VAR <id-list> : <type> ;     */
/*                        <id-list> : <type> ;         */
/*                        ... )                         */
/*                                                     */
/*                      Return a pointer to the head of the  */
/*                      parameter id list.              */
/*-----------------------------------------------------*/

    SYMTAB_NODE_PTR
formal_parm_list(countp, total_sizep)

    int *countp;        /* ptr to count of parameters */
```

```
    int *total_sizep;   /* ptr to total byte size of parameters */

{
    SYMTAB_NODE_PTR parm_idp, first_idp, last_idp;   /* parm ids */
    SYMTAB_NODE_PTR prev_last_idp = NULL;        /* last id of list */
    SYMTAB_NODE_PTR parm_listp = NULL;           /* parm list */
    SYMTAB_NODE_PTR type_idp;                    /* type id */
    TYPE_STRUCT_PTR parm_tp;                     /* parm type */
    DEFN_KEY       parm_defn;                    /* parm definition */
    int            parm_count = 0;               /* count of parms */
    int            parm_offset = 0;

    get_token();

    /*
    -- Loop to process parameter declarations separated by ;
    */
    while ((token == IDENTIFIER) || (token == VAR)) {
        first_idp = NULL;

        /*
        -- VAR parms?
        */
        if (token == VAR) {
            parm_defn = VARPARM_DEFN;
            get_token();
        }
        else parm_defn = VALPARM_DEFN;

        /*
        -- <id list>
        */
        while (token == IDENTIFIER) {
            search_and_enter_local_symtab(parm_idp);
            parm_idp->defn.key   = parm_defn;
            parm_idp->label_index = 0;
            ++parm_count;

            if (parm_listp == NULL) parm_listp = parm_idp;

            /*
            -- Link parm ids together.
            */
            if (first_idp == NULL)
                first_idp = last_idp = parm_idp;
            else {
                last_idp->next = parm_idp;
                last_idp = parm_idp;
            }

            get_token();
            if_token_get(COMMA);
        }

        if_token_get_else_error(COLON, MISSING_COLON);

        if (token == IDENTIFIER) {
            search_and_find_all_symtab(type_idp);
            if (type_idp->defn.key != TYPE_DEFN) error(INVALID_TYPE);
            parm_tp = type_idp->typep;
            get_token();
        }
        else {
            error(MISSING_IDENTIFIER);
            parm_tp = &dummy_type;
        }

        /*
```

```
        --  Assign the offset and the type to all parm ids
        --  in the sublist.
        */
        for (parm_idp = first_idp;
             parm_idp != NULL;
             parm_idp = parm_idp->next) {
            parm_idp->typep = parm_tp;
            parm_idp->defn.info.data.offset = parm_offset++;
        }

        /*
        --  Link this list to the list of all parm ids.
        */
        if (prev_last_idp != NULL) prev_last_idp->next = first_idp;
        prev_last_idp = last_idp;

        /*
        --  Error synchronization:  Should be ; or )
        */
        synchronize(follow_parms_list, NULL, NULL);
        if_token_get(SEMICOLON);
    }

    if_token_get_else_error(RPAREN, MISSING_RPAREN);
    *countp = parm_count;
    *total_sizep = parm_offset;

    return(parm_listp);
}

/*----------------------------------------------------------*/
/*  routine_call          Process a call to a declared or    */
/*                        a standard procedure or function.  */
/*                        Return a pointer to the type       */
/*                        structure of the call.             */
/*----------------------------------------------------------*/

    TYPE_STRUCT_PTR
routine_call(rtn_idp, parm_check_flag)

    SYMTAB_NODE_PTR rtn_idp;            /* routine id */
    BOOLEAN         parm_check_flag;    /* if TRUE check parms */

{
    TYPE_STRUCT_PTR declared_routine_call(), standard_routine_call();

    if ((rtn_idp->defn.info.routine.key == DECLARED) ||
        (rtn_idp->defn.info.routine.key == FORWARD) ||
        !parm_check_flag)
        return(declared_routine_call(rtn_idp, parm_check_flag));
    else
        return(standard_routine_call(rtn_idp));
}

/*----------------------------------------------------------*/
/*  declared_routine_call  Process a call to a declared      */
/*                         procedure or function:            */
/*                                                           */
/*                                  <id>                     */
/*                                                           */
/*                         or:                               */
/*                                                           */
/*                                  <id> ( <parm-list> )     */
/*                                                           */
/*                         The actual parameters are checked */
/*                         against the formal parameters for */
/*                         type and number.  Return a pointer */
```

```
/*                              to the type structure of the call.  */
/*----------------------------------------------------------*/

    TYPE_STRUCT_PTR
declared_routine_call(rtn_idp, parm_check_flag)

    SYMTAB_NODE_PTR rtn_idp;            /* routine id */
    BOOLEAN         parm_check_flag;    /* if TRUE check parms */

{
    actual_parm_list(rtn_idp, parm_check_flag);
    return(rtn_idp->defn.key == PROC_DEFN ? NULL : rtn_idp->typep);
}

/*----------------------------------------------------------*/
/*  actual_parm_list    Process an actual parameter list:    */
/*                                                           */
/*                            ( <expr-list> )                */
/*----------------------------------------------------------*/

TOKEN_CODE follow_parm_list[] = {COMMA, RPAREN, 0};

actual_parm_list(rtn_idp, parm_check_flag)

    SYMTAB_NODE_PTR rtn_idp;            /* routine id */
    BOOLEAN         parm_check_flag;    /* if TRUE check parms */

{
    SYMTAB_NODE_PTR formal_parm_idp;
    DEFN_KEY        formal_parm_defn;
    TYPE_STRUCT_PTR formal_parm_tp, actual_parm_tp;

    if (parm_check_flag)
        formal_parm_idp = rtn_idp->defn.info.routine.parms;

    if (token == LPAREN) {
        /*
        --  Loop to process actual parameter expressions.
        */
        do {
            /*
            --  Obtain info about the corresponding formal parm.
            */
            if (parm_check_flag && (formal_parm_idp != NULL)) {
                formal_parm_defn = formal_parm_idp->defn.key;
                formal_parm_tp   = formal_parm_idp->typep;
            }

            get_token();

            /*
            --  Formal value parm:  Actual parm's type must be
            --                      assignment compatible with
            --                      formal parm's type.  Actual
            --                      parm can be an expression.
            */
            if ((formal_parm_idp == NULL) ||
                (formal_parm_defn == VALPARM_DEFN) ||
                !parm_check_flag) {
                actual_parm_tp = expression();
                if (parm_check_flag && (formal_parm_idp != NULL) &&
                    (! is_assign_type_compatible(formal_parm_tp,
                                                 actual_parm_tp)))
                    error(INCOMPATIBLE_TYPES);
            }

            /*
```

```
   -- Formal VAR parm:  Actual parm's type must be the same
   --                   as formal parm type.  Actual parm
   --                   must be a variable.
   */
   else /* formal_parm_defn == VARPARM_DEFN */ {
       if (token == IDENTIFIER) {
           SYMTAB_NODE_PTR idp;

           search_and_find_all_symtab(idp);
           actual_parm_tp = variable(idp, VARPARM_USE);

           if (formal_parm_tp != actual_parm_tp)
               error(INCOMPATIBLE_TYPES);
       }
       else {
           /*
           -- Not a variable:  Parse an expression anyway
           --                  for error recovery.
           */
           actual_parm_tp = expression();
           error(INVALID_VAR_PARM);
       }
   }

   /*
   -- Check if there are more actual parms
   -- than formal parms.
   */
   if (parm_check_flag) {
       if (formal_parm_idp == NULL)
           error(WRONG_NUMBER_OF_PARMS);
       else formal_parm_idp = formal_parm_idp->next;
   }

   /*
   -- Error synchronization:  Should be , or )
   */
           synchronize(follow_parm_list, statement_end_list, NULL);

       } while (token == COMMA);

       if_token_get_else_error(RPAREN, MISSING_RPAREN);
   }

   /*
   -- Check if there are fewer actual parms than formal parms.
   */
   if (parm_check_flag && (formal_parm_idp != NULL))
       error(WRONG_NUMBER_OF_PARMS);
}

/*------------------------------------------------------------*/
/* block            Process a block, which consists of        */
/*                  declarations followed by a compound        */
/*                  statement.                                  */
/*------------------------------------------------------------*/

TOKEN_CODE follow_decls_list[] = {SEMICOLON, BEGIN, END_OF_FILE, 0};

block(rtn_idp)

    SYMTAB_NODE_PTR rtn_idp;    /* id of program or routine */

{
    declarations(rtn_idp);

    /*
    -- Error synchronization:  Should be ;
    */
    synchronize(follow_decls_list, NULL, NULL);
    if (token != BEGIN) error(MISSING_BEGIN);

    compound_statement();
}
```

In function program, we first initialize the symbol table. Next, we call function program_header, which parses the header and returns a pointer to the symbol table node of the program identifier. We then call function synchronize and check for a missing semicolon. We want to resynchronize the parser either at the end of the header, at the start of the declarations, or at the start of the first statement, in that order of preference.

In this chapter, ignore the call to analyze_routine_header and to analyze_block (we do *not* define the analyze macro flag in file parser.h). These calls will be useful in the next chapter.

Now we are ready to parse the program's block. We call function block, passing it a pointer to the program identifier's symbol table node. As we saw in the previous chapter, we will enter information into this node when we parse the block's declarations. We'll see what the call to exit_scope does later, and we'll use the defn.info.routine.code_segment field starting in the next chapter. For now, we set the field to NULL. After parsing the program's block, we look for the period and then the end of the file. We finish by quitting the scanner and then printing the statistics.

We parse the program header in function program_header. We enter the program identifier into the local symbol table and initialize the fields of the node. Then, we call function synchronize to resynchronize the parser at the point just after the identifier or at the start of the next declaration or first statement. We call routine enter_scope, which, like exit_scope, is explained later. We enter each program parameter identifier into the local symbol table, and we link the nodes together and hang them off of the defn.info.routine.parms field of the program identifier's symbol table node.

To conclude, we call synchronize and check for a missing right parenthesis. We want to resynchronize the parser either at the end of the parameter list or at the start of the next declaration or first statement.

7.3 Procedure and function declarations

Pascal procedures and functions are declared at the end of a block's declarations. Figure 7-3 shows the complete syntax diagram for declarations. The diagram

FIGURE 7-3   Syntax diagram for declarations.

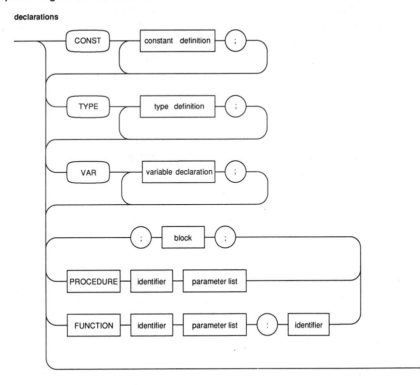

shows that a procedure or function consists of a header followed by a semicolon, a block, and then another semicolon. Since each procedure or function itself contains a block, they can be nested. Nested routines introduce the problem of dealing with the local variable's scopes.

7.3.1 Scope and the symbol table display stack

The *scope* of a variable is the part of the program where that variable can be used. Pascal allows the same *identifier* in a program to name different *variables* as long the variables are in different scopes. A variable's scope includes every part of the program where its identifier can be used to refer to that particular variable. The scope rules prevent any confusion regarding which variable an identifier refers to.

Not only variables, but any object with a name has a scope. Thus, we can speak of the scope of a constant, type, parameter, procedure, function, or even a program. For example, suppose we declare a global integer variable i in a program that has no procedures or functions. The scope of the variable is the entire program, since we can use identifier i throughout to refer to that integer variable. Now suppose we add a function f to the program, and in f, we declare a local real variable i. The scope of the local real variable i is limited to the function, and now the scope of the global integer variable i is only the part of the program outside of the function. Within f, identifier i refers to the local real variable, and outside f, it refers to the global integer variable.

Since the function is nested within the program, we can say that the scope of its local variables is nested within the scope of the program's global variables. If the function contains a procedure p1 that declares a local character variable i, the scope of the procedure's local variables (including the character i) is nested within the scope of the function's local variables.

So how does scope affect how a parser handles an identifier? Whenever a parser encounters a variable's identifier in the body of a procedure or function, it wants to know which variable the identifier refers to. The parser first checks the variables declared locally by that routine (the local scope). If it cannot find the identifier there, the parser then checks the next enclosing scope. The search continues outward within enclosing scopes towards the outermost, global scope. If the search is successful within any scope, the search stops and the parser uses that declaration. This declaration also hides any other declarations with the same identifier that may appear in any more outer scopes. (In the above example, identifier i within procedure p1 refers to the local character variable, not the real variable of function f or the global integer variable.) Only if the identifier is not found within all enclosing scopes should the parser flag it as undefined. Figure 7-4 shows how a parser can flag scope errors.

FIGURE 7-4   Flagging scope errors.

```
Page 1   scope.pas   Tue Jul 10 03:15:22 1990          30 3:
                                                        31 3:            i := 1;  j := 2;  k := 3;
                                                                          ^
    1 0: PROGRAM scope (input, output);           *** ERROR: Incompatible assignment.
    2 1:
    3 1: VAR                                       *** ERROR: Incompatible assignment.
    4 1:     i, j, k : integer;                     32 3:        END {p2};
    5 1:                                            33 2:
    6 1: FUNCTION f (j : boolean) : real;          34 2:        BEGIN {p1}
    7 2:                                            35 2:           i := 'z';   {local of p1}
    8 2:     VAR                                    36 2:           j := 7;     {parm  of p1}
    9 2:         i : real;                          37 2:           k := 9;     {global}
   10 2:                                            38 2:
   11 2:     BEGIN {f}                              39 2:           i := 1;  j := 2;  k := 3;
   12 2:        i := 1.0;    {local of f}                                  ^
   13 2:        j := false;  {parm  of f}          *** ERROR: Incompatible assignment.
   14 2:        k := 3;      {global}               40 2:        END {p1};
   15 2:                                            41 1:
   16 2:        i := 1;  j := 2;  k := 3;           42 1:
                             ^
*** ERROR: Incompatible assignment.
   17 2:     END {f};
   18 1:                                           Page 2   scope.pas   Tue Jul 10 03:15:22 1990
   19 1: PROCEDURE p1 (j : integer);
   20 2:                                            43 1: BEGIN {scope}
   21 2:     VAR                                    44 1:    i := 1;  {global}
   22 2:         i : char;                          45 1:    j := 2;  {global}
   23 2:                                            46 1:    k := 3;  {global}
   24 2:     PROCEDURE p2 (k : boolean);           47 1: END {scope}.
   25 3:                                            48 0:
   26 3:        BEGIN {p2}
   27 3:           i := 'x';   {local of p1}
   28 3:           j := 5;     {parm  of p1}                      48 Source lines.
   29 3:           k := true;  {parm  of p2}                       4 Source errors.
```

Until now, each of our utility programs has gotten by with a single symbol table. This will no longer suffice, since, as you have seen, an identifier like i can appear in several scopes and refer to different variables. To parse a Pascal program, you need multiple symbol tables: one to contain the global identifiers and one for each procedure and function to contain its local identifiers. In the previous chapter, we saw how the type structure for a record type points field info.record.field_symtab to a private symbol table for the field identifiers. Similarly, each symbol table node for a procedure or function identifier points field defn.info.routine.local_symtab to a private symbol table for the routine's local identifiers.

The best way for the parser to use the private routine symbol tables is to keep them on a stack, with the global symbol table at the bottom and the current routine's symbol table on top. Each time you parse a procedure or function, you push its (initially empty) symbol table onto the top, and when you are finished with the routine, you pop off its symbol table. Then, whenever you search for an identifier, you start with the symbol table at the top of the stack. If the identifier is not found there, the identifier is not defined in the current scope. You look in the next enclosing scope by searching the symbol table just below the top one. This process continues until you find the identifier or until you have searched all the symbol tables on the stack. Each time you move down the symbol table stack, you are in effect searching the next enclosing scope.

This symbol table stack is called a *display*. You increment the *current nesting level* each time the parser enters a routine, and you decrement it as the parser leaves the routine. The nesting level of a program's globals is one. Thus, the globals and the top-level procedures and functions are called level-1 variables and routines. Level zero is reserved for the predefined identifiers such as integer, boolean, true, and false. If you implement the display stack as an array, then you can use the level numbers to index into the array.

To implement a display, we need to make changes throughout files symtab.h and symtab.c. Figure 7-5 shows the new version of symtab.c.

FIGURE 7-5   File symtab.c.

```
/*******************************************************/
/*                                                     */
/*      S Y M B O L   T A B L E                        */
/*                                                     */
/*      Symbol table routines.                         */
/*                                                     */
/*      FILE:       symtab.c                            */
/*                                                     */
/*      MODULE:     symbol table                       */
/*                                                     */
/*******************************************************/

#include <stdio.h>
#include "common.h"
#include "error.h"
#include "symtab.h"

/*----------------------------------------------------*/
/* Externals                                          */
/*----------------------------------------------------*/

extern int level;

/*----------------------------------------------------*/
/* Globals                                            */
/*----------------------------------------------------*/

SYMTAB_NODE_PTR symtab_display[MAX_NESTING_LEVEL];

TYPE_STRUCT_PTR integer_typep, real_typep,      /* predefined types */
                boolean_typep, char_typep;

TYPE_STRUCT dummy_type = {         /* for erroneous type definitions */
    NO_FORM,        /* form */
    0,              /* size */
    NULL            /* type_idp */
};

/*----------------------------------------------------*/
/* search_symtab      Search for a name in the symbol table. */
/*                    Return a pointer of the entry if found, */
```

```
/*                    or NULL if not.                  */
/*----------------------------------------------------*/

SYMTAB_NODE_PTR
search_symtab(name, np)

    char            *name;      /* name to search for */
    SYMTAB_NODE_PTR np;         /* ptr to symtab root */

{
    int cmp;

    /*
    -- Loop to check each node.  Return if the node matches,
    -- else continue search down the left or right subtree.
    */
    while (np != NULL) {
        cmp = strcmp(name, np->name);
        if (cmp == 0) return(np);                   /* found */
        np = cmp < 0 ? np->left : np->right;        /* continue search */
    }

    return(NULL);                                   /* not found */
}

/*----------------------------------------------------*/
/* search_symtab_display   Search all the symbol tables in the */
/*                         symbol table display for a name.    */
/*                         Return a pointer to the entry if    */
/*                         found, or NULL if not.              */
/*----------------------------------------------------*/

SYMTAB_NODE_PTR
search_symtab_display(name)

    char *name;                 /* name to search for */

{
    short i;
    SYMTAB_NODE_PTR np;         /* ptr to symtab node */

    for (i = level; i >= 0; --i) {
```

```
        np = search_symtab(name, symtab_display[i]);
        if (np != NULL) return(np);
    }

    return(NULL);
}

/*--------------------------------------------------------*/
/*  enter_symtab       Enter a name into the symbol table, */
/*                     and return a pointer to the new entry. */
/*--------------------------------------------------------*/

    SYMTAB_NODE_PTR
enter_symtab(name, npp)

    char            *name;      /* name to enter */
    SYMTAB_NODE_PTR *npp;       /* ptr to ptr to symtab root */

{
    int             cmp;        /* result of strcmp */
    SYMTAB_NODE_PTR new_nodep;  /* ptr to new entry */
    SYMTAB_NODE_PTR np;         /* ptr to node to test */

    /*
    -- Create the new node for the name.
    */
    new_nodep = alloc_struct(SYMTAB_NODE);
    new_nodep->name = alloc_bytes(strlen(name) + 1);
    strcpy(new_nodep->name, name);
    new_nodep->left = new_nodep->right = new_nodep->next = NULL;
    new_nodep->info = NULL;
    new_nodep->defn.key = UNDEFINED;
    new_nodep->typep = NULL;
    new_nodep->level = level;
    new_nodep->label_index = 0;

    /*
    -- Loop to search for the insertion point.
    */
    while ((np = *npp) != NULL) {
        cmp = strcmp(name, np->name);
        npp = cmp < 0 ? &(np->left) : &(np->right);
    }

    *npp = new_nodep;                   /* replace */
    return(new_nodep);
}

/*--------------------------------------------------------*/
/*  init_symtab        Initialize the symbol table with    */
/*                     predefined identifiers and types,   */
/*                     and routines.                       */
/*--------------------------------------------------------*/

init_symtab()

{
    SYMTAB_NODE_PTR integer_idp, real_idp, boolean_idp, char_idp,
                    false_idp, true_idp;

    /*
    -- Initialize the level-0 symbol table.
    */
    symtab_display[0] = NULL;

    enter_name_local_symtab(integer_idp, "integer");
    enter_name_local_symtab(real_idp,    "real");
```

```
    enter_name_local_symtab(boolean_idp, "boolean");
    enter_name_local_symtab(char_idp,    "char");
    enter_name_local_symtab(false_idp,   "false");
    enter_name_local_symtab(true_idp,    "true");

    integer_typep = alloc_struct(TYPE_STRUCT);
    real_typep    = alloc_struct(TYPE_STRUCT);
    boolean_typep = alloc_struct(TYPE_STRUCT);
    char_typep    = alloc_struct(TYPE_STRUCT);

    integer_idp->defn.key   = TYPE_DEFN;
    integer_idp->typep      = integer_typep;
    integer_typep->form     = SCALAR_FORM;
    integer_typep->size     = sizeof(int);
    integer_typep->type_idp = integer_idp;

    real_idp->defn.key   = TYPE_DEFN;
    real_idp->typep      = real_typep;
    real_typep->form     = SCALAR_FORM;
    real_typep->size     = sizeof(float);
    real_typep->type_idp = real_idp;

    boolean_idp->defn.key   = TYPE_DEFN;
    boolean_idp->typep      = boolean_typep;
    boolean_typep->form     = ENUM_FORM;
    boolean_typep->size     = sizeof(int);
    boolean_typep->type_idp = boolean_idp;

    boolean_typep->info.enumeration.max = 1;
    boolean_typep->info.enumeration.const_idp = false_idp;
    false_idp->defn.key = CONST_DEFN;
    false_idp->defn.info.constant.value.integer = 0;
    false_idp->typep = boolean_typep;

    false_idp->next = true_idp;
    true_idp->defn.key = CONST_DEFN;
    true_idp->defn.info.constant.value.integer = 1;
    true_idp->typep = boolean_typep;

    char_idp->defn.key   = TYPE_DEFN;
    char_idp->typep      = char_typep;
    char_typep->form     = SCALAR_FORM;
    char_typep->size     = sizeof(char);
    char_typep->type_idp = char_idp;

    enter_standard_routine("read",    READ,    PROC_DEFN);
    enter_standard_routine("readln",  READLN,  PROC_DEFN);
    enter_standard_routine("write",   WRITE,   PROC_DEFN);
    enter_standard_routine("writeln", WRITELN, PROC_DEFN);

    enter_standard_routine("abs",     ABS,     FUNC_DEFN);
    enter_standard_routine("arctan",  ARCTAN,  FUNC_DEFN);
    enter_standard_routine("chr",     CHR,     FUNC_DEFN);
    enter_standard_routine("cos",     COS,     FUNC_DEFN);
    enter_standard_routine("eof",     EOFF,    FUNC_DEFN);
    enter_standard_routine("eoln",    EOLN,    FUNC_DEFN);
    enter_standard_routine("exp",     EXP,     FUNC_DEFN);
    enter_standard_routine("ln",      LN,      FUNC_DEFN);
    enter_standard_routine("odd",     ODD,     FUNC_DEFN);
    enter_standard_routine("ord",     ORD,     FUNC_DEFN);
    enter_standard_routine("pred",    PRED,    FUNC_DEFN);
    enter_standard_routine("round",   ROUND,   FUNC_DEFN);
    enter_standard_routine("sin",     SIN,     FUNC_DEFN);
    enter_standard_routine("sqr",     SQR,     FUNC_DEFN);
    enter_standard_routine("sqrt",    SQRT,    FUNC_DEFN);
    enter_standard_routine("succ",    SUCC,    FUNC_DEFN);
```

```
    enter_standard_routine("trunc",    TRUNC,        FUNC_DEFN);
}

/*--------------------------------------------------------*/
/*  enter_standard_routine    Enter a standard procedure or  */
/*                            function identifier into the   */
/*                            symbol table.                  */
/*--------------------------------------------------------*/

enter_standard_routine(name, routine_key, defn_key)

    char       *name;          /* name string */
    ROUTINE_KEY routine_key;
    DEFN_KEY    defn_key;

{
    SYMTAB_NODE_PTR rtn_idp = enter_name_local_symtab(rtn_idp, name);

    rtn_idp->defn.key                     = defn_key;
    rtn_idp->defn.info.routine.key        = routine_key;
    rtn_idp->defn.info.routine.parms      = NULL;
    rtn_idp->defn.info.routine.local_symtab = NULL;
    rtn_idp->typep                        = NULL;
}

/*--------------------------------------------------------*/
/*  enter_scope        Enter a new nesting level by creating  */
/*                     a new scope.  Push the given symbol    */
/*                     table onto the display stack.          */
/*--------------------------------------------------------*/
```

```
enter_scope(symtab_root)

    SYMTAB_NODE_PTR symtab_root;

{
    if (++level >= MAX_NESTING_LEVEL) {
        error(NESTING_TOO_DEEP);
        exit(-NESTING_TOO_DEEP);
    }

    symtab_display[level] = symtab_root;
}

/*--------------------------------------------------------------*/
/*  exit_scope        Exit the current nesting level by         */
/*                    closing the current scope.  Pop the       */
/*                    current symbol table off the display      */
/*                    stack and return a pointer to it.         */
/*--------------------------------------------------------------*/

    SYMTAB_NODE_PTR
exit_scope()

{
    SYMTAB_NODE_PTR symtab_root = symtab_display[level--];

    return(symtab_root);
}
```

Now we reference the scanner variable level. (Up until now, it had always been zero.) In function enter_symtab, we set field level to the current value of variable level:

$$new\_nodep\text{->}level = level;$$

and we replace the declaration of symtab_root with:

$$SYMTAB\_NODE\_PTR\ symtab\_display[MAX\_NESTING\_LEVEL];$$

From now on, instead of having just one active symbol table, you will have several pointed to by elements of symtab_display. The local symbol table is pointed to by symtab_display[level]. Also, symtab_display[1] points to the table containing the program's global identifier, and symtab_display[0] points to the table containing the predefined identifiers. In the new function search_symtab_display, we search all the active symbol tables pointed to by elements of the display stack from top to bottom.

We call function enter_scope whenever we start to parse a program, procedure, or function. (For example, we previously called it from function program_header.) We increment level and push the pointer to program's or routine's private symbol table onto the display stack.

Conversely, we call function exit_scope whenever we finish parsing a program, procedure, or function. We decrement level to pop the display stack, and we return the pointer to the symbol table that was popped off. This table now contains all the local identifiers, so after we return, we can set the defn.info.routine.local_symtab field of the program or routine identifier's symbol table node to the pointer.

We will look at the rest of the changes in file symtab.c later when we discuss the standard procedures and functions. We will use this version of the file throughout the rest of this book.

Figure 7-6 shows the new version of file symtab.h, which we will also use from now on. Several of the symbol table macros are changed. They must now distinguish between searching just the local symbol table and searching the display stack.

FIGURE 7-6   File symtab.h.

```
/******************************************************************/
/*                                                                */
/*      S Y M B O L   T A B L E   (Header)                        */
/*                                                                */
/*      FILE:       symtab.h                                      */
/*                                                                */
/*      MODULE:     symbol table                                  */
/*                                                                */
/******************************************************************/

#ifndef symtab_h
#define symtab_h

#include "common.h"

/*----------------------------------------------------*/
/*  Value structure                                   */
/*----------------------------------------------------*/

typedef union {
    int     integer;
    float   real;
    char    character;
    char    *stringp;
} VALUE;

/*----------------------------------------------------*/
/*  Definition structure                              */
/*----------------------------------------------------*/

typedef enum {
    UNDEFINED,
    CONST_DEFN, TYPE_DEFN, VAR_DEFN, FIELD_DEFN,
    VALPARM_DEFN, VARPARM_DEFN,
    PROG_DEFN, PROC_DEFN, FUNC_DEFN,
} DEFN_KEY;

typedef enum {
    DECLARED, FORWARD,
    READ, READLN, WRITE, WRITELN,
    ABS, ARCTAN, CHR, COS, EOFF, EOLN, EXP, LN, ODD, ORD,
    PRED, ROUND, SIN, SQR, SQRT, SUCC, TRUNC,
} ROUTINE_KEY;

typedef struct {
```

```
    DEFN_KEY key;
    union {
        struct {
            VALUE value;
        } constant;

        struct {
            ROUTINE_KEY         key;
            int                 parm_count;
            int                 total_parm_size;
            int                 total_local_size;
            struct symtab_node *parms;
            struct symtab_node *locals;
            struct symtab_node *local_symtab;
            char               *code_segment;
        } routine;

        struct {
            int                 offset;
            struct symtab_node *record_idp;
        } data;
    } info;
} DEFN_STRUCT;

/*----------------------------------------------------------*/
/*  Type structure                                          */
/*----------------------------------------------------------*/

typedef enum {
    NO_FORM,
    SCALAR_FORM, ENUM_FORM, SUBRANGE_FORM,
    ARRAY_FORM, RECORD_FORM,
} TYPE_FORM;

typedef struct type_struct {
    TYPE_FORM           form;
    int                 size;
    struct symtab_node *type_idp;
    union {
        struct {
            struct symtab_node *const_idp;
            int                 max;
        } enumeration;

        struct {
```

```
        struct type_struct *range_typep;
        int                 min, max;
    } subrange;

    struct {
        struct type_struct *index_typep, *elmt_typep;
        int                 min_index, max_index;
        int                 elmt_count;
    } array;

    struct {
        struct symtab_node *field_symtab;
    } record;
} info;
} TYPE_STRUCT, *TYPE_STRUCT_PTR;

/*------------------------------------------------*/
/* Symbol table node                              */
/*------------------------------------------------*/

typedef struct symtab_node {
    struct symtab_node *left, *right;  /* ptrs to subtrees */
    struct symtab_node *next;          /* for chaining nodes */
    char                *name;         /* name string */
    char                *info;         /* ptr to generic info */
    DEFN_STRUCT         defn;          /* definition struct */
    TYPE_STRUCT_PTR     typep;         /* ptr to type struct */
    int                 level;         /* nesting level */
    int                 label_index;   /* index for code label */
} SYMTAB_NODE, *SYMTAB_NODE_PTR;

/*------------------------------------------------*/
/* Functions                                      */
/*------------------------------------------------*/

SYMTAB_NODE_PTR search_symtab();
SYMTAB_NODE_PTR search_symtab_display();
SYMTAB_NODE_PTR enter_symtab();
SYMTAB_NODE_PTR exit_scope();
TYPE_STRUCT_PTR make_string_typep();

        /**************************************/
        /*                                    */
        /*     Macros to search symbol tables */
        /*                                    */
        /**************************************/

/*------------------------------------------------*/
/* search_local_symtab        Search the local symbol    */
/*                            table for the current id    */
/*                            name. Set a pointer to the  */
/*                            entry if found, else to     */
/*                            NULL.                        */
/*------------------------------------------------*/

#define search_local_symtab(idp)                            \
    idp = search_symtab(word_string, symtab_display[level])

/*------------------------------------------------*/
/* search_this_symtab        Search the given symbol      */
/*                           table for the current id      */
/*                           name. Set a pointer to the   */
/*                           entry if found, else to      */
/*                           NULL.                         */
/*------------------------------------------------*/

#define search_this_symtab(idp, this_symtab)               \
    idp = search_symtab(word_string, this_symtab)
```

```
/*------------------------------------------------*/
/* search_all_symtab          Search the symbol table    */
/*                            display for the current id  */
/*                            name. Set a pointer to the  */
/*                            entry if found, else to     */
/*                            NULL.                        */
/*------------------------------------------------*/
#define search_all_symtab(idp)                              \
    idp = search_symtab_display(word_string)


/*------------------------------------------------*/
/* enter_local_symtab         Enter the current id name   */
/*                            into the local symbol       */
/*                            table, and set a pointer    */
/*                            to the entry.                */
/*------------------------------------------------*/

#define enter_local_symtab(idp)                             \
    idp = enter_symtab(word_string, &symtab_display[level])


/*------------------------------------------------*/
/* enter_name_local_symtab    Enter the given name into   */
/*                            the local symbol table, and */
/*                            set a pointer to the entry. */
/*------------------------------------------------*/

#define enter_name_local_symtab(idp, name)                 \
    idp = enter_symtab(name, &symtab_display[level])


/*------------------------------------------------*/
/* search_and_find_all_symtab  Search the symbol table    */
/*                             display for the current id */
/*                             name. If not found, ID     */
/*                             UNDEFINED error, and enter */
/*                             into the local symbol table.*/
/*                             Set a pointer to the entry. */
/*------------------------------------------------*/

#define search_and_find_all_symtab(idp)                               \
    if ((idp = search_symtab_display(word_string)) == NULL) {         \
        error(UNDEFINED_IDENTIFIER);                                  \
        idp = enter_symtab(word_string, &symtab_display[level]);      \
        idp->defn.key = UNDEFINED;                                    \
        idp->typep = &dummy_type;                                     \
    }


/*------------------------------------------------*/
/* search_and_enter_local_symtab   Search the local symbol */
/*                                 table for the current id */
/*                                 name. Enter the name if  */
/*                                 it is not already in there, */
/*                                 else ID REDEFINED error.  */
/*                                 Set a pointer to the entry. */
/*------------------------------------------------*/

#define search_and_enter_local_symtab(idp)                            \
    if ((idp = search_symtab(word_string,                             \
                             symtab_display[level])) == NULL) {       \
        idp = enter_symtab(word_string, &symtab_display[level]);      \
    }                                                                 \
    else error(REDEFINED_IDENTIFIER)


/*------------------------------------------------*/
/* search_and_enter_this_symtab   Search the given symbol */
/*                                table for the current id */
/*                                name. Enter the name if  */
/*                                it is not already in there, */
```

```
/*                            else ID REDEFINED error.   */                              this_symtab)) == NULL) {            \
/*                            Set a pointer to the entry. */            idp = enter_symtab(word_string, &this_symtab);       \
/*-------------------------------------------------------*/          }                                                      \
                                                                     else error(REDEFINED_IDENTIFIER)
#define search_and_enter_this_symtab(idp, this_symtab)         \
    if ((idp = search_symtab(word_string,                      \     #endif
```

Macro `search_local_symtab` is new. We call it to search the local symbol table pointed to by `symtab_display[level]`. Macro `search_all_symtab` now calls function `search_symtab_display` to search the display stack. Macros `enter_local_symtab` and `enter_name_local_symtab` now use the local symbol table pointed to by `symtab_display[level]`.

Macro `search_and_find_all_symtab` now calls function `search_symtab_display` to search the display stack. Macro `search_and_enter_local_symtab` searches the local symbol table pointed to by `symtab_display[level]`. Both macros now enter into the local symbol table.

Macros `search_this_symtab` and `search_and_enter_this_symtab` have not changed.

So from now on, whenever we parse the definition of a new identifier in file `decl.c`, we call `search_and_enter_local_symtab` to make sure the identifier is not already defined in the local scope. Whenever we parse an identifier in an expression, we call `search_and_find_all_symtab` to make sure the identifier is defined in the local or any enclosing scope.

7.3.2 Procedure and function headers

As we have seen, Pascal procedures and functions are declared in the declarations part of a block. Figure 7-7 shows a new version of function `declarations` in file `decl.c`. In the `while` loop, we call function `routine` (in file `routine.c`) to parse a procedure or a function. After parsing each routine, we call function `synchronize` and check for a missing semicolon. We want to resynchronize the parser at the point just after the routine or at the start of the next declaration or first statement. In file `decl.c`, we must also replace the line:

```
extern SYMTAB_NODE_PTR  symtab_root;
```

with the following lines:

```
extern SYMTAB_NODE_PTR  symtab_display[];
extern int              level;
```

FIGURE 7-7   Function declarations in file decl.c.

```
/*-----------------------------------------------------------*/
/*  declarations        Call the routines to process constant  */
/*                      definitions, type definitions, variable */
/*                      declarations, procedure definitions,    */
/*                      and function definitions.               */
/*-----------------------------------------------------------*/

TOKEN_CODE follow_routine_list[] = {SEMICOLON, END_OF_FILE, 0};

declarations(rtn_idp)

    SYMTAB_NODE_PTR rtn_idp;    /* id of program or routine */

{
    if (token == CONST) {
        get_token();
        const_definitions();
    }

    if (token == TYPE) {
        get_token();
        type_definitions();
    }
```

```
    if (token == VAR) {
        get_token();
        var_declarations(rtn_idp);
    }

    /*
    -- Loop to process routine (procedure and function)
    -- definitions.
    */
    while ((token == PROCEDURE) || (token == FUNCTION)) {
        routine();

        /*
        -- Error synchronization:  Should be ;
        */
        synchronize(follow_routine_list,
                    declaration_start_list, statement_start_list);
        if_token_get(SEMICOLON);
        else if (token_in(declaration_start_list) ||
                 token_in(statement_start_list))
            error(MISSING_SEMICOLON);
    }
}
```

In function routine, we call either function procedure_header or function_header to parse the header. Following the header, we call synchronize and check for a missing semicolon. We want to resynchronize the parser at the point just after the identifier or at the start of the next declaration or first statement.

Then, we parse either the routine's block or the identifier forward. We set the defn.info.routine.key field of the routine identifier's symbol table node either to DECLARED or to FORWARD. If we are declaring the routine, we call function block to parse its block. (Ignore the calls to functions analyze_routine_header and analyze_block.) We conclude with a call to function exit_scope and set the local_symtab field. The routine's private symbol table now contains all of its local identifiers.

In function procedure_header, we first parse the procedure identifier. If the identifier is not already in the local symbol table, we enter it and initialize the node's defn.key field to PROC_DEFN. If the identifier is already in there, it has been previously defined within the same scope. We check whether this previous definition was a forward procedure declaration.

We next call function synchronize to resynchronize the parser at the point after the procedure identifier or at the start of the next declaration or first statement. Then, we call function enter_scope to create the procedure's scope by pushing its private symbol table (initially empty) onto the display stack.

If there is a left parenthesis, we call function formal_parm_list, which parses the formal parameters and returns a pointer to a linked list of symbol table nodes for the parameter identifiers. The function also sets the parameter count and their total byte size. We check to make sure we have not redeclared the parameters if there was a forward declaration. We initialize the parm_count, total_parm_size, and parms fields of the procedure identifier's symbol table node.

If we do not find a formal parameter list, and there was no forward declaration, then the procedure has no parameters. If there was a forward declaration, then we have already parsed the parameters (if any) and initialized the symbol table node fields.

Function function_header is similar, except that we also parse the function type identifier. If there was a forward declaration for the function, neither the formal parameters nor the function type should be redeclared.

7.3.3 Formal parameter lists

In function formal_parm_list, we parse the formal parameter list in a procedure or a function header, and we return a pointer to the linked list of symbol table nodes for the parameter identifiers. Figure 7-8 shows the syntax diagram.

This function is similar to function var_or_field_declarations in file decl.c. We link the symbol table nodes for the parameter identifiers together as we enter them into the local symbol table at the top of the display stack, which is the routine's private symbol table. We set the node's defn.key field to either VARPARM_DEFN or VALPARM_DEFN, depending on whether or not VAR headed the declaration.

We enter all of a routine's local identifiers, including those of its formal parameters and local variables, into its private symbol table, which the defn.info.routine.local_symtab field of its symbol table node points to. As we saw in Chapter 3, the symbol table nodes are linked together into a binary tree via their left and right fields.

In function formal_parm_list, we also link the nodes for parameter identifiers together into a linear linked list via their next fields, and the routine node's parms field points to the head of this list. In file decl.c, we link the nodes for the routine's local variable identifiers together in function var_or_field_declarations, and the routine node's locals field points to the head of this list. Thus, there can be two separate linked lists among the nodes in a routine's private symbol table. We will see how the formal parameter list is useful when we parse actual arguments,

FIGURE 7-8   Syntax diagram for a formal parameter list.

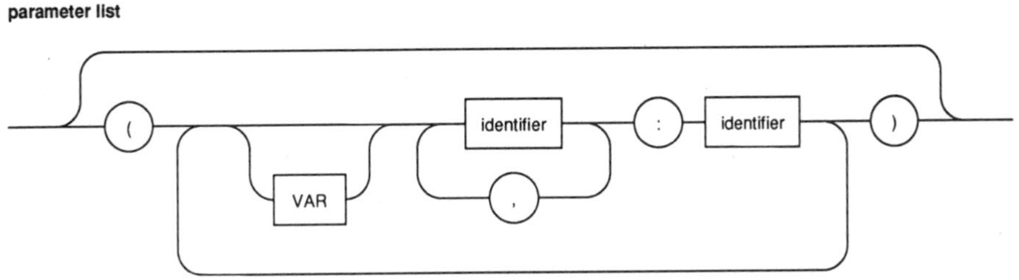

FIGURE 7-9   Syntax diagrams for procedure and function calls.

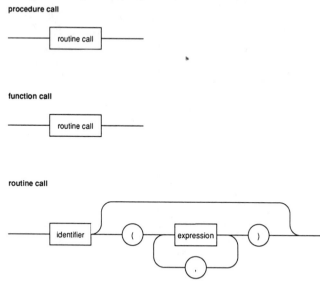

FIGURE 7-10   Syntax diagram for a Pascal statement.

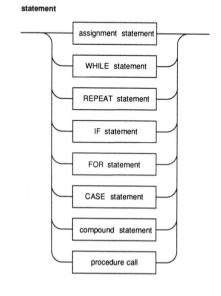

FIGURE 7-11   Syntax diagram for a factor.

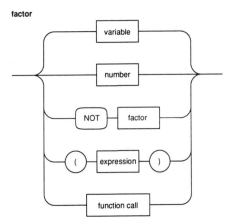

and see how the local variable list is used in later chapters. The offset and total parameter size calculations will become significant in Chapter 9.

7.4 Procedure and function calls

You can see from the syntax diagrams in Figure 7-9 that procedure calls and function calls are syntactically similar. In Figure 7-10, the complete syntax diagram for a Pascal statement shows a procedure call is by itself a statement, and in Figure 7-11, the complete syntax diagram for a factor shows that a function call is a factor.

Figure 7-12 shows the new version of function statement in file stmt.c. If we parse an identifier that leads off a statement, we must check the defn.key field of the identifier's symbol table node to decide whether the statement is an assignment statement or a procedure call. We call function routine_call (in file routine.c) to parse a procedure call.

FIGURE 7-12   Function statement in file stmt.c.

```
/*-----------------------------------------------------------*/        -- Call the appropriate routine based on the first
/* statement        Process a statement by calling the    */           -- token of the statement.
/*                  appropriate parsing routine based on  */           */
/*                  the statement's first token.          */           switch (token) {
/*-----------------------------------------------------------*/
                                                                           case IDENTIFIER: {
statement()                                                                    SYMTAB_NODE_PTR idp;

{                                                                              /*
     /*                                                                        -- Assignment statement or procedure call?
```

```
        */
        search_and_find_all_symtab(idp);

        if (idp->defn.key == PROC_DEFN) {
            get_token();
            routine_call(idp, TRUE);
        }
        else assignment_statement(idp);

        break;
    }

    case REPEAT:    repeat_statement();    break;
    case WHILE:     while_statement();     break;
```

```
    case IF:        if_statement();         break;
    case FOR:       for_statement();        break;
    case CASE:      case_statement();       break;
    case BEGIN:     compound_statement();   break;
    }

    /*
    -- Error synchronization:  Only a semicolon, END, ELSE, or
    --                         UNTIL may follow a statement.
    --                         Check for a missing semicolon.
    */
    synchronize(statement_end_list, statement_start_list, NULL);
    if (token_in(statement_start_list)) error(MISSING_SEMICOLON);
}
```

Figure 7-13 shows the new version function factor in file expr.c. If we parse an identifier, we must also consider the case that we have a function call. If so, we call routine_call to parse it. (For error handling, if we have a procedure identifier, we go ahead and parse the parameter list.)

FIGURE 7-13   Function factor in file expr.c.

```
/*------------------------------------------------------------*/
/* factor              Process a factor, which is an variable, */
/*                     a number, NOT followed by a factor, or  */
/*                     a parenthesized subexpression.  Return  */
/*                     a pointer to the type structure.        */
/*------------------------------------------------------------*/

    TYPE_STRUCT_PTR
factor()

{
    TYPE_STRUCT_PTR tp;

    switch (token) {

        case IDENTIFIER: {
            SYMTAB_NODE_PTR idp;

            search_and_find_all_symtab(idp);

            switch (idp->defn.key) {

                case FUNC_DEFN:
                    get_token();
                    tp = routine_call(idp, TRUE);
                    break;

                case PROC_DEFN:
                    error(INVALID_IDENTIFIER_USAGE);
                    get_token();
                    actual_parm_list(idp, FALSE);
                    tp = &dummy_type;
                    break;

                case CONST_DEFN:
                    get_token();
                    tp = idp->typep;
```

```
                    break;

                default:
                    tp = variable(idp, EXPR_USE);
                    break;
            }

            break;
        }

        case NUMBER:
            tp = literal.type == INTEGER_LIT
                    ? integer_typep
                    : real_typep;
            get_token();
            break;

        case STRING: {
            int length = strlen(literal.value.string);

            tp = length == 1 ? char_typep
                             : make_string_typep(length);
            get_token();
            break;
        }

        case NOT:
            get_token();
            tp = factor();
            break;

        case LPAREN:
            get_token();
            tp = expression();

            if_token_get_else_error(RPAREN, MISSING_RPAREN);
            break;
```

```
    default:
        error(INVALID_EXPRESSION);
        tp = &dummy_type;
        break;
    }

    return(tp);
}
```

In both files `stmt.c` and `expr.c`, we must replace the line:

```
extern SYMTAB_NODE_PTR  symtab_root;
```

with the following lines:

```
extern SYMTAB_NODE_PTR  symtab_display[];
extern int              level;
```

Back in file `routine.c`, function `routine_call` parses procedure calls and function calls. We check the `defn.info.routine.key` field of the routine identifier's symbol table node to determine whether a call is to a declared (programmer-written) routine or to a standard predefined routine. We call function `declared_routine_call` for the former and function `standard_routine_call` (in file `standard.c`) for the latter, and return the type returned by either of these functions.

Function `declared_routine_call` parses a call to a declared procedure or function. We call function `actual_parm_list` to parse the actual parameter list. Then, for a function call, we return the function's type, and for a procedure call, we return `NULL`.

In function `actual_parm_list`, we parse the actual parameters and check each parameter's type against the type of the corresponding formal parameter. We also check that the number of parameters is correct. We do neither of these checks if `parm_check_flag` is FALSE, which is the case if we called the routine to parse an actual parameter list for error recovery (such as parsing a procedure call in a factor). We obtain the list of the symbol table nodes of the formal parameters from the `defn.info.routine.parms` field of the routine's symbol table node. After parsing each actual parameter, we call function `synchronize` to resynchronize the parser at the comma or right parenthesis, or at the end of the statement.

An actual parameter corresponding to a formal value parameter may be an expression, and its type must be assignment compatible with that of the formal. An actual parameter corresponding to a formal VAR parameter must be a variable, and its type must be the same as that of the formal. In the latter case, if we find an expression, we parse it anyway for error recovery.

The final function in file `routine.c` is `block`, which we take from the main file of the syntax checker in the previous chapter.

7.5 Standard procedures and functions

The standard predefined procedures and functions need special treatment from the parser, since some of them have a variable number of actual parameters of mixed types, and the type of the return value of some of the functions depends on the type of the actual parameter. write and writeln have especially peculiar actual parameters.

We must first enter information about the routines into the level-0 symbol table (the one pointed to by symtab_display[0]). We do this in the new version of function init_symtab and the new function enter_standard_routine in file symtab.c (see Figure 7-5).

File standard.c, shown in Figure 7-14, contains the routines to parse calls to the standard procedures and functions. In function standard_routine_call, we test the defn.info.routine.key field of the standard routine identifier's symbol table node to determine which function to call. We then return the type of a standard function, or NULL if the call was to a standard procedure.

FIGURE 7-14   File standard.c.

```
/*****************************************************************/
/*                                                               */
/*      S T A N D A R D   R O U T I N E   P A R S E R            */
/*                                                               */
/*      Parsing routines for calls to standard procedures and    */
/*      functions.                                               */
/*                                                               */
/*      FILE:       standard.c                                   */
/*                                                               */
/*      MODULE:     parser                                       */
/*                                                               */
/*****************************************************************/

#include <stdio.h>
#include "common.h"
#include "error.h"
#include "scanner.h"
#include "symtab.h"
#include "parser.h"

#define DEFAULT_NUMERIC_FIELD_WIDTH    10
#define DEFAULT_PRECISION               2

/*--------------------------------------------------------------*/
/* Externals                                                    */
/*--------------------------------------------------------------*/

extern TOKEN_CODE       token;
extern char             word_string[];
extern SYMTAB_NODE_PTR  symtab_display[];
extern int              level;
extern TYPE_STRUCT      dummy_type;

extern TYPE_STRUCT_PTR  integer_typep, real_typep,
                        boolean_typep, char_typep;

extern TOKEN_CODE       follow_parm_list[];
```

```
extern TOKEN_CODE       statement_end_list[];

/*--------------------------------------------------------------*/
/* Forwards                                                     */
/*--------------------------------------------------------------*/

TYPE_STRUCT_PTR eof_eoln(), abs_sqr(),
                arctan_cos_exp_ln_sin_sqrt(),
                pred_succ(), chr(), odd(), ord(),
                round_trunc();

/*--------------------------------------------------------------*/
/* standard_routine_call   Process a call to a standard         */
/*                         procedure or function.  Return a     */
/*                         pointer to the type structure of     */
/*                         the call.                            */
/*--------------------------------------------------------------*/

    TYPE_STRUCT_PTR
standard_routine_call(rtn_idp)

    SYMTAB_NODE_PTR rtn_idp;          /* routine id */

{
    switch (rtn_idp->defn.info.routine.key) {

        case READ:
        case READLN:    read_readln(rtn_idp);    return(NULL);

        case WRITE:
        case WRITELN:   write_writeln(rtn_idp);  return(NULL);

        case EOFF:
        case EOLN:      return(eof_eoln(rtn_idp));

        case ABS:
        case SQR:       return(abs_sqr());
```

```
        case ARCTAN:
        case COS:
        case EXP:
        case LN:
        case SIN:
        case SQRT:        return(arctan_cos_exp_ln_sin_sqrt());

        case PRED:
        case SUCC:        return(pred_succ());

        case CHR:         return(chr());
        case ODD:         return(odd());
        case ORD:         return(ord());

        case ROUND:
        case TRUNC:       return(round_trunc());
    }
}

/*------------------------------------------------------------*/
/*  read_readln              Process a call to read or readln.  */
/*------------------------------------------------------------*/

read_readln(rtn_idp)

    SYMTAB_NODE_PTR rtn_idp;              /* routine id */

{
    TYPE_STRUCT_PTR actual_parm_tp;       /* actual parm type */

    /*
    -- Parameters are optional for readln.
    */
    if (token == LPAREN) {
        /*
        -- <id-list>
        */
        do {
            get_token();

            /*
            -- Actual parms must be variables (but parse
            -- an expression anyway for error recovery).
            */
            if (token == IDENTIFIER) {
                SYMTAB_NODE_PTR idp;

                search_and_find_all_symtab(idp);
                actual_parm_tp = base_type(variable(idp,
                                           VARPARM_USE));

                if (actual_parm_tp->form != SCALAR_FORM)
                    error(INCOMPATIBLE_TYPES);
            }
            else {
                actual_parm_tp = expression();
                error(INVALID_VAR_PARM);
            }

            /*
            -- Error synchronization:  Should be , or )
            */
            synchronize(follow_parm_list, statement_end_list, NULL);

        } while (token == COMMA);

        if_token_get_else_error(RPAREN, MISSING_RPAREN);
```

```
    }
    else if (rtn_idp->defn.info.routine.key == READ)
        error(WRONG_NUMBER_OF_PARMS);
}

/*------------------------------------------------------------*/
/*  write_writeln           Process a call to write or writeln. */
/*                          Each actual parameter can be:       */
/*                                                              */
/*                          <expr>                              */
/*                                                              */
/*                          or:                                 */
/*                                                              */
/*                          <epxr> : <expr>                     */
/*                                                              */
/*                          or:                                 */
/*                                                              */
/*                          <expr> : <expr> : <expr>            */
/*------------------------------------------------------------*/

write_writeln(rtn_idp)

    SYMTAB_NODE_PTR rtn_idp;              /* routine id */

{
    TYPE_STRUCT_PTR actual_parm_tp;       /* actual parm type */
    TYPE_STRUCT_PTR field_width_tp, precision_tp;

    /*
    -- Parameters are optional for writeln.
    */
    if (token == LPAREN) {
        do {
            /*
            -- Value <expr>
            */
            get_token();
            actual_parm_tp = base_type(expression());

            if ((actual_parm_tp->form != SCALAR_FORM) &&
                (actual_parm_tp != boolean_typep) &&
                ((actual_parm_tp->form != ARRAY_FORM) ||
                 (actual_parm_tp->info.array.elmt_typep !=
                                        char_typep)))
                error(INVALID_EXPRESSION);

            /*
            -- Optional field width <expr>
            */
            if (token == COLON) {
                get_token();
                field_width_tp = base_type(expression());

                if (field_width_tp != integer_typep)
                    error(INCOMPATIBLE_TYPES);

                /*
                -- Optional precision <expr>
                */
                if (token == COLON) {
                    get_token();
                    precision_tp = base_type(expression());

                    if (precision_tp != integer_typep)
                        error(INCOMPATIBLE_TYPES);
                }
            }
```

```
                    /*
                    -- Error synchronization:  Should be , or )
                    */
                    synchronize(follow_parm_list, statement_end_list, NULL);

            } while (token == COMMA);

            if_token_get_else_error(RPAREN, MISSING_RPAREN);
        }
        else if (rtn_idp->defn.info.routine.key == WRITE)
            error(WRONG_NUMBER_OF_PARMS);
}

/*-----------------------------------------------------------*/
/*  eof_eoln              Process a call to eof or to eoln.  */
/*                        No parameters => boolean result.   */
/*-----------------------------------------------------------*/

    TYPE_STRUCT_PTR
eof_eoln(rtn_idp)

    SYMTAB_NODE_PTR rtn_idp;            /* routine id */

{
    if (token == LPAREN) {
        error(WRONG_NUMBER_OF_PARMS);
        actual_parm_list(rtn_idp, FALSE);
    }

    return(boolean_typep);
}

/*-----------------------------------------------------------*/
/*  abs_sqr               Process a call to abs or to sqr.   */
/*                        integer parm => integer result     */
/*                        real parm    => real result        */
/*-----------------------------------------------------------*/

    TYPE_STRUCT_PTR
abs_sqr()

{
    TYPE_STRUCT_PTR parm_tp;            /* actual parameter type */
    TYPE_STRUCT_PTR result_tp;          /* result type */

    if (token == LPAREN) {
        get_token();
        parm_tp = base_type(expression());

        if ((parm_tp != integer_typep) && (parm_tp != real_typep)) {
            error(INCOMPATIBLE_TYPES);
            result_tp = real_typep;
        }
        else result_tp = parm_tp;

        if_token_get_else_error(RPAREN, MISSING_RPAREN);
    }
    else error(WRONG_NUMBER_OF_PARMS);

    return(result_tp);
}

/*-----------------------------------------------------------*/
/*  arctan_cos_exp_ln_sin_sqrt  Process a call to arctan, cos, */
/*                          exp, ln, sin, or sqrt.           */
/*                          integer parm => real result      */
/*                          real_parm    => real result      */
/*-----------------------------------------------------------*/
```

```
    TYPE_STRUCT_PTR
arctan_cos_exp_ln_sin_sqrt()

{
    TYPE_STRUCT_PTR parm_tp;            /* actual parameter type */

    if (token == LPAREN) {
        get_token();
        parm_tp = base_type(expression());

        if ((parm_tp != integer_typep) && (parm_tp != real_typep))
            error(INCOMPATIBLE_TYPES);

        if_token_get_else_error(RPAREN, MISSING_RPAREN);
    }
    else error(WRONG_NUMBER_OF_PARMS);

    return(real_typep);
}

/*-----------------------------------------------------------*/
/*  pred_succ             Process a call to pred or succ.    */
/*                        integer parm => integer result     */
/*                        enum parm   => enum result         */
/*-----------------------------------------------------------*/

    TYPE_STRUCT_PTR
pred_succ()

{
    TYPE_STRUCT_PTR parm_tp;            /* actual parameter type */
    TYPE_STRUCT_PTR result_tp;          /* result type */

    if (token == LPAREN) {
        get_token();
        parm_tp = base_type(expression());

        if ((parm_tp != integer_typep) &&
            (parm_tp->form != ENUM_FORM)) {
            error(INCOMPATIBLE_TYPES);
            result_tp = integer_typep;
        }
        else result_tp = parm_tp;

        if_token_get_else_error(RPAREN, MISSING_RPAREN);
    }
    else error(WRONG_NUMBER_OF_PARMS);

    return(result_tp);
}

/*-----------------------------------------------------------*/
/*  chr                   Process a call to chr.             */
/*                        integer parm => character result   */
/*-----------------------------------------------------------*/

    TYPE_STRUCT_PTR
chr()

{
    TYPE_STRUCT_PTR parm_tp;            /* actual parameter type */

    if (token == LPAREN) {
        get_token();
        parm_tp = base_type(expression());

        if (parm_tp != integer_typep) error(INCOMPATIBLE_TYPES);
        if_token_get_else_error(RPAREN, MISSING_RPAREN);
```

```
    }
    else error(WRONG_NUMBER_OF_PARMS);

    return(char_typep);
}

/*-------------------------------------------------*/
/* odd                       Process a call to odd.        */
/*                           integer parm => boolean result */
/*-------------------------------------------------*/

    TYPE_STRUCT_PTR
odd()

{
    TYPE_STRUCT_PTR parm_tp;            /* actual parameter type */

    if (token == LPAREN) {
        get_token();
        parm_tp = base_type(expression());

        if (parm_tp != integer_typep) error(INCOMPATIBLE_TYPES);
        if_token_get_else_error(RPAREN, MISSING_RPAREN);
    }
    else error(WRONG_NUMBER_OF_PARMS);

    return(boolean_typep);
}

/*-------------------------------------------------*/
/* ord                       Process a call to ord.        */
/*                           enumeration parm => integer result */
/*-------------------------------------------------*/

    TYPE_STRUCT_PTR
ord()
```

```
{
    TYPE_STRUCT_PTR parm_tp;            /* actual parameter type */

    if (token == LPAREN) {
        get_token();
        parm_tp = base_type(expression());

        if (parm_tp->form != ENUM_FORM) error(INCOMPATIBLE_TYPES);
        if_token_get_else_error(RPAREN, MISSING_RPAREN);
    }
    else error(WRONG_NUMBER_OF_PARMS);

    return(integer_typep);
}

/*-------------------------------------------------*/
/* round_trunc               Process a call to round or trunc. */
/*                           real parm => integer result   */
/*-------------------------------------------------*/

    TYPE_STRUCT_PTR
round_trunc()

{
    TYPE_STRUCT_PTR parm_tp;            /* actual parameter type */

    if (token == LPAREN) {
        get_token();
        parm_tp = base_type(expression());

        if (parm_tp != real_typep) error(INCOMPATIBLE_TYPES);
        if_token_get_else_error(RPAREN, MISSING_RPAREN);
    }
    else error(WRONG_NUMBER_OF_PARMS);

    return(integer_typep);
}
```

In function read_readln, we parse calls to procedures read and readln. The actual parameters must be variables. We parse calls to procedures write and writeln in function write_writeln. The actual parameters may be expressions, and each parameter may be followed by field width and precision designators, which we check to make sure they are integers.

Function eof_eoln parses calls to the parameterless functions eof and eoln and returns the boolean type. Function abs_sqr parses calls to the single-parameter functions abs and sqr and returns the integer type if the actual parameter is an integer, and the real type if the actual parameter is real.

In function arctan_cos_exp_ln_sin_sqrt, we parse calls to the single-parameter functions arctan, cos, exp, ln, sin, and sqrt. We return the real type, but the actual parameter may be integer or real.

We parse calls to the single-parameter functions pred and succ in function pred_succ, and we return the enumeration type of the actual parameter. In function chr, we parse calls to the single-parameter function chr. We return the character type, but the actual parameter must be integer. In function odd, we parse calls to the single-parameter function odd. We return the boolean type, but the actual parameter must be integer. Finally, in function ord, we parse calls to the single-parameter function ord. We return the integer type, but the actual parameter must be of an enumeration type.

7.6 The FOR statement

Figure 7-15 shows the new version of function for_statement in file stmt.c. We now have a stricter test on the control variable. It must be a local variable or formal parameter, but not a VAR parameter.

FIGURE 7-15   Function for_statement in file stmt.c.

```
/*-----------------------------------------------------------*/
/* for_statement      Process a FOR statement:              */
/*                                                           */
/*                         FOR <id> := <expr> TO|DOWNTO <expr> */
/*                         DO <stmt>                         */
/*-----------------------------------------------------------*/

for_statement()

{
    SYMTAB_NODE_PTR for_idp;
    TYPE_STRUCT_PTR for_tp, expr_tp;

    get_token();

    if (token == IDENTIFIER) {
        search_and_find_all_symtab(for_idp);

        if ((for_idp->level != level) ||
            (for_idp->defn.key != VAR_DEFN))
            error(INVALID_FOR_CONTROL);

        for_tp = base_type(for_idp->typep);
        get_token();

        if ((for_tp != integer_typep) &&
            (for_tp != char_typep) &&
            (for_tp->form != ENUM_FORM)) error(INCOMPATIBLE_TYPES);
    }
    else {
        error(IDENTIFIER, MISSING_IDENTIFIER);
        for_tp = &dummy_type;
    }

    if_token_get_else_error(COLONEQUAL, MISSING_COLONEQUAL);

    expr_tp = expression();
    if (! is_assign_type_compatible(for_tp, expr_tp))
        error(INCOMPATIBLE_TYPES);

    if ((token == TO) || (token == DOWNTO)) get_token();
    else error(MISSING_TO_OR_DOWNTO);

    expr_tp = expression();
    if (! is_assign_type_compatible(for_tp, expr_tp))
        error(INCOMPATIBLE_TYPES);

    if_token_get_else_error(DO, MISSING_DO);
    statement();
}
```

7.7 Program 7-1: Pascal Syntax Checker III

At last, we can put everything together into the third and final version of our syntax checker. Figure 7-16 shows the main file of this utility program, syntax3.c. It initializes the symbol table, fetches the first token, and calls function program.

FIGURE 7-16   File syntax3.c.

```
/*****************************************************************/
/*                                                              */
/*       Program 7-1:  Pascal Syntax Checker III                */
/*                                                              */
/*       Read and check the syntax of a Pascal program.         */
/*                                                              */
/*       FILE:       syntax3.c                                  */
/*                                                              */
/*       REQUIRES:   Modules parser, symbol table, scanner,     */
/*                               error                          */
/*                                                              */
/*       USAGE:      syntax3 sourcefile                         */
/*                                                              */
/*          sourcefile     name of source file containing       */
/*                         the program to be checked            */
/*                                                              */
/*****************************************************************/

#include <stdio.h>
#include "common.h"
#include "error.h"
#include "scanner.h"
#include "parser.h"
```

```
/*--------------------------------------------------------------*/
/*  main              Initialize the scanner and call the       */
/*                    statement routine.                        */
/*--------------------------------------------------------------*/

main(argc, argv)

    int argc;
    char *argv[];

{
    /*
    -- Initialize the scanner.
    */
    init_scanner(argv[1]);

    /*
    -- Process a program.
    */
    get_token();
    program();
}
```

This syntax checker can check an entire Pascal program. We saw some sample output from this program in Figure 7-4. Figure 7-17 shows more output that illustrates some of the error checking that it is capable of performing. This program is the foundation for both the interpreter that we will write in the next part of this book, and for the compiler that we will write in the last part of the book.

FIGURE 7-17   Sample output from the syntax checker III.

```
Page 1   rtn.pas   Tue Jul 10 03:13:36 1990

   1 0: PROGRAM rtn(input, output);
   2 1:
   3 1:    VAR
   4 1:        i, j, k    : integer;
   5 1:        p, z       : real;
   6 1:        ch, letter : char;
   7 1:
   8 1:    FUNCTION func(VAR ch : char) : real;
   9 2:        forward;
  10 1:
  11 1:    PROCEDURE proc(b      : boolean;
  12 2:                   VAR x  : real;
  13 2:                   y      : real);
  14 2:
  15 2:        CONST
  16 2:            n = 5;
  17 2:
  18 2:        VAR
  19 2:            p, q : boolean;
  20 2:
  21 2:        BEGIN
```

```
  22 2:            p := x + z - n*func(letter);
                                        ^
*** ERROR: Incompatible assignment.
  23 2:            proc(ch);
                        ^
*** ERROR: Incompatible types.
                                ^
*** ERROR: Wrong number of actual parameters.
  24 2:        END;
  25 1:
  26 1:    FUNCTION func(i : integer) : boolean;
                                       ^
*** ERROR: Already specified in FORWARD.
                                                ^
*** ERROR: Already specified in FORWARD.
  27 2:
  28 2:        TYPE
  29 2:            stooge = (larry, moe, curly);
  30 2:
  31 2:        VAR
  32 2:            s, t : stooge;
  33 2:
  34 2:        BEGIN
  35 2:            s := pred(t);
```

```
36 2:              proc(s = t, p, j DIV k);
37 2:              func(letter) := 'xyz';

*** ERROR: Unexpected token.
                                    ^


Page 2   rtn.pas   Tue Jul 10 03:13:36 1990


*** ERROR: Incompatible assignment.
38 2:              func := round(3.14) - trunc(3);
                                              ^
*** ERROR: Incompatible types.
39 2:         END;
40 1:
41 1:    BEGIN
```

```
42 1:         j := -3;
43 1:         proc(false, 4.5*z, z);

*** ERROR: Invalid VAR parameter.
44 1:         z := 3.14 + func(ch, 123) - func + func(p) + func(-3);
                                     ^
*** ERROR: Wrong number of actual parameters.
                                                            ^
*** ERROR: Wrong number of actual parameters.

*** ERROR: Incompatible types.
                                                                    ^
*** ERROR: Invalid VAR parameter.
45 1:    END.


        45 Source lines.
        13 Source errors.
```

Questions and exercises

1. In functions program_header, procedure_header, and function_header, we call function enter_scope *after* we parse the program or routine identifier and *before* we parse the formal parameters and the block. What does this say about the scopes of these elements?

2. Error recovery in function actual_parm_list is awkward if an expression is passed as a VAR parameter, and the expression begins with a variable. Improve the error recovery in the function.

3. Modify the symbol table and its initialization routines so that the symbol table contains enough useful information about the standard procedures and functions so that calls to them can be parsed more like calls to the declared routines.

4. Upgrade the cross-referencer utility program to list the name of the procedure or function in which each identifier is defined.

5. Write a call chart generator utility program that parses an entire source program and then produces a chart showing, for each procedure and function, which routines call it and which routines it calls. Show the line number of each call.

PART II

Interpreting

CHAPTER 8

An Intermediate Form for Interpretation

In the first part of this book, we wrote a scanner, a parser, and a utility program that can check an entire Pascal program for syntax errors. In the second part of the book, we will build upon our previous programs to write a Pascal interpreter. In this chapter, we see how to translate a source program into an intermediate form that can be interpreted. In the next two chapters, we will write a fully working Pascal interpreter, and in Chapter 11, we will add an interactive debugger.

In this chapter, we will write a pretty-printer utility program to develop our skills to manipulate a source program in its intermediate form. These skills will enable us to:

- convert a Pascal source program into an intermediate form
- interpret the intermediate code to reconstruct the source program

The pretty-printer will work by first translating the source program into the intermediate form. Then, like an interpreter, it will read the intermediate code. Instead of executing it, however, it will reconstruct the source program and write it back out in a neatly-indented format.

8.1 The need for an intermediate form

The calculator utility program in Chapter 4 interpreted expressions and assignment statements directly from the source program—it did the semantic actions as soon as it parsed each statement and expression. Such a scheme is adequate for an interactive calculator that interprets each statement and expression only once, and when speed is not so important.

Speed is more important when interpreting a program. A program can have loops and procedures and functions, so that some statements can be executed many times. It is no longer a good idea to interpret directly from the source, since doing so means that if a statement is in a loop, then each time the interpreter executes the statement it must rescan and reparse the statement and do a symbol table lookup for each identifier in the statement.

The prime motivation for an intermediate form is to do all of the scanning, most of the parsing, and all of symbol table lookups only once. As the interpreter parses the source program, it translates it to this form. The intermediate code for a source statement contains a byte code for each token and a pointer to the symbol table node of each identifier. The scanner provides the token codes, and the parser obtains the symbol table pointers from the symbol table routines as it parses each identifier. We have already seen how all this is happens in our syntax checker.

Therefore, when the interpreter executes a program in the intermediate form, it does not need to do any scanning or symbol table lookups. If an interpreter only executes programs that have no syntax errors, then when it is parsing the intermediate code during execution, it does not need to do any time-consuming syntax and type checking.

You can use a very simple intermediate form for our interpreter, namely, one similar to the crunched form produced by the cruncher utility program in Chapter 3. You only need to convert the executable statements of the source program to this form. As we have done before, you will convert all the declarations into information for the symbol table. Indeed, the symbol table node for each program, procedure, or function identifier will point to a "code segment" containing the intermediate code from the routine's statements.

Other intermediate forms are possible. We will explore some of these in the questions and exercises at the end of the chapter.

8.2 Changes to the modules

We require only a few changes to our modules to generate the intermediate code. There are no new files.

Parser Module

parser.h	*u*	Parser header file
routine.c	*c*	Parse programs, procedures, and functions
standard.c	*u*	Parse standard procedures and functions
stmt.c	*c*	Parse statements
expr.c	*c*	Parse expressions
decl.c	*u*	Parse declarations

Scanner Module

scanner.h	*u*	Scanner header file
scanner.c	*c*	Scanner routines

Symbol Table Module

symtab.h	*u*	Symbol table header file
symtab.c	*u*	Symbol table routines

Error Module

error.h	*u*	Error header file
error.c	*u*	Error routines

Miscellaneous

common.h	*u*	Common header file

Where: *u*   file unchanged from the previous chapter
          c   file changed from the previous chapter

We make a small change to file scanner.c to cause it to output a token code to the intermediate form. We make a few changes to stmt.c and expr.c to enter number and string tokens into the symbol table and to output symbol table pointers to the intermediate form. Finally, we change routine.c to create code segments.

8.3 Program 8-1: A Pascal Source Pretty-Printer

You will see how to translate a source program to its intermediate form in the context of a pretty-printer utility program. This program will also show you how to read the intermediate code. Most of the code for writing and reading the intermediate code will show up in the interpreter.

A pretty-printer reads a source program and rewrites it in a "pretty" format. The rewritten source strictly follows certain coding conventions that govern how to indent statements. Such a utility program is surprisingly easy to write, given all the programs we have written and the skills we have acquired. The output of our pretty-printer may not win any awards for aesthetics, but it does format programs in a consistent manner. The questions and exercises at the end of this chapter will suggest improvements.

You can pretty-print declarations (constant definitions, type definitions, variable declarations, and program, procedure, and function headers) by reconstructing them from information in the symbol table. You can translate a routine's executable statements into the intermediate form and store them in a code segment that you allocate for each routine. You can then pretty-print the statements by reconstructing the statements from the intermediate code. You can continue to pretty-print only while there are no syntax errors.

Besides the modules listed, the pretty-printer has several other files:

pprint.h	header file
pprint.c	main file
ppdecl.c	pretty-print declarations
ppstmt.c	pretty-print statements and expressions

Figure 8-1 shows file pprint.c. In the main routine, we set the scanner variable print_flag to FALSE (since we don't want the usual listing), initialize the scanner, and call routine program to pretty-print the source program.

FIGURE 8-1   File pprint.c.

```
/******************************************************************/
/*                                                                */
/*      Program 8-1:  Pascal Pretty Printer                       */
/*                                                                */
/*      Read and check the syntax of a Pascal program,            */
/*      and then print it out in a nicely-indented format.        */
/*                                                                */
/*      FILE:       pprint.c                                      */
/*                                                                */
/*      REQUIRES:   Modules parser, symbol table, scanner,        */
/*                      error                                     */
/*                                                                */
/*                  Files ppdecl.c, ppstmt.c                      */
/*                                                                */
/*      FLAGS:      Macro flag "analyze" must be defined          */
/*                                                                */
/*      USAGE:      pprint sourcefile                             */
/*                                                                */
/*          sourcefile    name of source file containing          */
/*                        the program to be pretty-printed        */
/*                                                                */
/******************************************************************/

#include <stdio.h>
#include "common.h"
#include "error.h"
#include "scanner.h"
#include "parser.h"
#include "pprint.h"

/*--------------------------------------------------------*/
/* Externals                                              */
/*--------------------------------------------------------*/

extern BOOLEAN print_flag;

/*--------------------------------------------------------*/
/* Globals                                                */
/*--------------------------------------------------------*/

char *code_buffer;              /* code buffer */
char *code_bufferp;             /* code buffer ptr */
char *code_segmentp;            /* code segment ptr */
char *code_segment_limit;       /* end of code segment */
```

```
TOKEN_CODE ctoken;                      /* token from code segment */

char pprint_buffer[MAX_PRINT_LINE_LENGTH];   /* print buffer */
int  left_margin = 0;                        /* margin in buffer */

/*--------------------------------------------------------*/
/* main            Initialize the scanner and call        */
/*                 routine program.                       */
/*--------------------------------------------------------*/

main(argc, argv)

    int  argc;
    char *argv[];

{
    /*
    -- Initialize the scanner.
    */
    print_flag = FALSE;
    init_scanner(argv[1]);

    /*
    -- Process a program.
    */
    get_token();
    program();
    quit_scanner();
}

/*--------------------------------------------------------*/
/* emit            Emit a string to the print buffer.     */
/*--------------------------------------------------------*/

emit(string)

    char *string;

{
    int buffer_length = strlen(pprint_buffer);
    int string_length = strlen(string);

    if (buffer_length + string_length >= MAX_PRINT_LINE_LENGTH - 1) {
```

```
        flush();                                            else
        indent();                                               pprint_buffer[0] = '\0';
    }                                                   }

    strcat(pprint_buffer, string);              /*-----------------------------------------------------------*/
}                                               /*  flush              Print the print buffer if there is   */
                                                /*                     anything in it.                       */
/*-----------------------------------------------*/      /*-----------------------------------------------------------*/
/*  indent         Indent left_margin spaces in the print */
/*                 buffer.                             */      flush()
/*-----------------------------------------------*/

indent()                                        {
                                                    if (pprint_buffer[0] != '\0') {
{                                                       printf("%s\n", pprint_buffer);
    if (left_margin > 0)                                pprint_buffer[0] = '\0';
        sprintf(pprint_buffer, "%*s", left_margin, " ");    }
                                                }
```

We have two new global variables. We construct lines of the pretty-printed program in pprint_buffer before we print them. We keep the current position of the left margin of a pretty-printed line in left_margin. When left_margin is zero, there is no indentation, and when it is four, the line is indented four spaces from the left.

We call function emit to append a string to the end of whatever is already in pprint_buffer. If the string would cause the line to be too long, we print the contents of pprint_buffer and indent the next line by the same amount. In effect, we wrap long lines.

In function indent, we add the correct number of spaces to the beginning of pprint_buffer. We call function flush to print the contents of pprint_buffer if it is not empty.

~~~ 8-2 shows the header file pprint.h. It contains several useful macros. dvance_left_margin and retreat_left_margin move the left margin for-back by indent_size spaces. Macro set_left_margin remembers the position of the left margin and then sets the left margin to the current sition. Macro reset_left_margin puts the left margin back to the re-ed position.

```
int.h.

/********************************/        #define retreat_left_margin() if ((left_margin -= indent_size) < 0) \
                        */                                              left_margin = 0;
                        */
                        */
/********************************/        #define set_left_margin(m)    {m = left_margin; \
                                                                left_margin = strlen(pprint_buffer);}

eft_margin += indent_size              #define reset_left_margin(m)  left_margin = m
```

8.3.1 Pretty-printing declarations

You can pretty-print each declaration just after you have parsed it and entered its information into the symbol table. You can then pretty-print by analyzing the symbol table information, just as you did for the declarations analyzer in Chapter 6. Therefore, you must reactivate the calls to the functions analyze_const_defn, analyze_type_defn, and analyze_var_decl in file decl.c. As explained in Chapter 6, we accomplish this by making sure the analyze macro flag is defined for file parser.h. Of course, we will write new versions of these functions, along with two new ones, analyze_routine_header and analyze_block.

Figure 8-3 shows the new version of function program, and Figure 8-4 shows the new version of function routine, both in file routine.c. Both functions contain similar calls for pretty-printing. In program, we call function analyze_routine_header (we ignored this call in the previous chapter) to pretty-print the program header. We call function block to parse the program's block. As we will see later, when we are parsing a block's declarations, we pretty-print them, and when we parse a block's statements, we translate them into the internal form.

FIGURE 8-3   Function program in file routine.c.

```
/*----------------------------------------------------*/
/* program       Process a program:                   */
/*                                                     */
/*                    <program-header> ; <block> .     */
/*----------------------------------------------------*/

TOKEN_CODE follow_header_list[] = {SEMICOLON, END_OF_FILE, 0};

program()

{
    SYMTAB_NODE_PTR program_idp;        /* program id */

    /*
    --                  PARSE THE PROGRAM
    --
    --
    -- Intialize the symbol table and then allocate
    -- the code buffer.
    */
    init_symtab();
    code_buffer  = alloc_bytes(MAX_CODE_BUFFER_SIZE);
    code_bufferp = code_buffer;

    /*
    -- Begin parsing with the program header.
    */
    program_idp = program_header();

    /*
    -- Error synchronization:  Should be ;
    */
```

```
    synchronize(follow_header_list,
                declaration_start_list, statement_start_list);
    if_token_get(SEMICOLON);
    else if (token_in(declaration_start_list) ||
             token_in(statement_start_list))
        error(MISSING_SEMICOLON);

    analyze_routine_header(program_idp);

    /*
    -- Parse the program's block.
    */
    program_idp->defn.info.routine.locals = NULL;
    block(program_idp);

    program_idp->defn.info.routine.local_symtab = exit_scope();
    program_idp->defn.info.routine.code_segment =create_code_segment();
    analyze_block(program_idp->defn.info.routine.code_segment);

    if_token_get_else_error(PERIOD, MISSING_PERIOD);

    /*
    -- Look for the end of file.
    */
    while (token != END_OF_FILE) {
        error(UNEXPECTED_TOKEN);
        get_token();
    }

    quit_scanner();
    free(code_buffer);
    exit(0);
}
```

FIGURE 8-4   Function `routine` in file `routine.c`.

```
/*---------------------------------------------------------*/
/* routine          Call the appropriate routine to process */
/*                  a procedure or function definition:    */
/*                                                         */
/*                  <routine-header> ; <block>             */
/*---------------------------------------------------------*/

routine()

{
    SYMTAB_NODE_PTR rtn_idp;    /* routine id */

    rtn_idp = (token == PROCEDURE) ? procedure_header()
                                   : function_header();

    /*
    -- Error synchronization:  Should be ;
    */
    synchronize(follow_header_list,
            declaration_start_list, statement_start_list);
    if_token_get(SEMICOLON);
    else if (token_in(declaration_start_list) ||
            token_in(statement_start_list))
```

```
        error(MISSING_SEMICOLON);

    /*
    -- <block> or FORWARD.
    */
    if (strcmp(word_string, "forward") != 0) {
        rtn_idp->defn.info.routine.key = DECLARED;
        analyze_routine_header(rtn_idp);

        rtn_idp->defn.info.routine.locals = NULL;
        block(rtn_idp);

        rtn_idp->defn.info.routine.code_segment = create_code_segment();
        analyze_block(rtn_idp->defn.info.routine.code_segment);
    }
    else {
        get_token();
        rtn_idp->defn.info.routine.key = FORWARD;
        analyze_routine_header(rtn_idp);
    }

    rtn_idp->defn.info.routine.local_symtab = exit_scope();
}
```

We then call function `create_code_segment`, which allocates a code segment for the program, fills it with the intermediate code from the block's statements, and returns a pointer to a code segment. We point field `defn.info.routine.code_segment` of the program identifier's symbol table node to the code segment. Finally, we call function `analyze_block` (which we also ignored in the previous chapter) to pretty-print the statements. File `ppdecl.c`, shown in Figure 8-5, contains the functions to pretty-print declarations.

FIGURE 8-5   File `ppdecl.c`.

```
/************************************************************/
/*                                                         */
/*      Pretty-print declarations and program, procedure, and */
/*      function headers.                                  */
/*                                                         */
/*      FILE:       ppdecl.c                               */
/*                                                         */
/************************************************************/

#include <stdio.h>
#include "common.h"
#include "symtab.h"
#include "pprint.h"
```

```
/*---------------------------------------------------------*/
/* Externals                                               */
/*---------------------------------------------------------*/

extern TYPE_STRUCT_PTR integer_typep, real_typep,
                       boolean_typep, char_typep;

extern char pprint_buffer[];
extern int  left_margin;
extern int  error_count;

/*---------------------------------------------------------*/
/* Globals                                                 */
/*---------------------------------------------------------*/
```

```
char string[MAX_PRINT_LINE_LENGTH];      /* buffer for literals */
BOOLEAN const_flag, type_flag, var_flag; /* TRUE if keywords
                                            already printed */


/*----------------------------------------------------------*/
/* analyze_routine_header  Pretty-print a program, procedure, */
/*                         or function header:              */
/*                                                          */
/*                          PROGRAM <id> (<parms>);         */
/*                          PROCEDURE <id> (<parms>);       */
/*                          FUNCTION <id> (<parms>) : <id>  */
/*----------------------------------------------------------*/

analyze_routine_header(rtn_idp)

    SYMTAB_NODE_PTR rtn_idp;

{
    int             save_left_margin;  /* current left margin */
    DEFN_KEY        common_key;        /* defn of parm sublist */
    TYPE_STRUCT_PTR common_tp;         /* type of parm sublist */
    SYMTAB_NODE_PTR parm_idp = rtn_idp->defn.info.routine.parms;

    if (error_count > 0) return;
    const_flag = type_flag = var_flag = FALSE;

    emit(" ");
    flush();
    indent();

    switch (rtn_idp->defn.key) {
        case PROG_DEFN: emit("PROGRAM ");   break;
        case PROC_DEFN: emit("PROCEDURE "); break;
        case FUNC_DEFN: emit("FUNCTION ");  break;
    }

    emit(rtn_idp->name);

    /*
    -- Print the formal parameters if there are any
    -- and the routine was not previously forwarded.
    */
    if ((parm_idp != NULL) &&
        (! (BOOLEAN) rtn_idp->info)) {
        BOOLEAN sublist_done;

        emit(" (");
        set_left_margin(save_left_margin);

        /*
        -- Loop to print the parameter sublists.
        */
        do {
            common_key = parm_idp->defn.key;
            common_tp = parm_idp->typep;
            if ((rtn_idp->defn.key != PROG_DEFN) &&
                (common_key == VARPARM_DEFN)) emit("VAR ");
            emit(parm_idp->name);

            /*
            -- Loop to print the parameters in a sublist.
            */
            do {
                parm_idp = parm_idp->next;
                sublist_done = ((parm_idp == NULL) ||
                                (parm_idp->defn.key != common_key) ||
                                (parm_idp->typep != common_tp));
```

```
                if (!sublist_done) {
                    emit(", ");
                    emit(parm_idp->name);
                }
            } while (!sublist_done);

            if (rtn_idp->defn.key != PROG_DEFN) {
                emit(" : ");
                print_type(common_tp, FALSE);
            }

            if (parm_idp != NULL) {
                emit(";");
                flush();
                indent();
            }
        } while (parm_idp != NULL);

        emit(")");

        if (rtn_idp->defn.key == FUNC_DEFN) {
            emit(" : ");
            print_type(rtn_idp->typep, FALSE);
        }

        reset_left_margin(save_left_margin);
    }

    emit(";");
    flush();

    /*
    -- Print a forward declaration.
    */
    if (rtn_idp->defn.info.routine.key == FORWARD) {
        rtn_idp->info = (char *) TRUE;

        advance_left_margin();
        indent();
        emit("FORWARD;");
        flush();
        retreat_left_margin();
    }

    else advance_left_margin();
}

/*----------------------------------------------------------*/
/* declaration_keyword     Print the keyword CONST, TYPE, or */
/*                         VAR in string if flag is FALSE.  */
/*                         Each keyword is printed at most   */
/*                         once per block.                   */
/*----------------------------------------------------------*/

declaration_keyword(flag, string)

    BOOLEAN *flag;      /* TRUE if keyword already printed */
    char    *string;    /* keyword */

{
    if (! *flag) {
        emit(" ");
        flush();

        indent();
        emit(string);
        flush();
```

```
        *flag = TRUE;
    }
}

/*----------------------------------------------*/
/* analyze_const_defn    Pretty-print a constant definition: */
/*                                              */
/*                      CONST                   */
/*                              <id> = <literal>; */
/*----------------------------------------------*/

analyze_const_defn(const_idp)

    SYMTAB_NODE_PTR const_idp;              /* constant id */

{
    TYPE_STRUCT_PTR const_tp = const_idp->typep;  /* constant type */

    if (error_count > 0) return;

    declaration_keyword(&const_flag, "CONST");
    advance_left_margin();

    indent();
    emit(const_idp->name);
    emit(" = ");

    if (const_tp->form == ARRAY_FORM) {         /* string */
        emit("'");
        emit(const_idp->defn.info.constant.value.stringp);
        emit("'");
    }
    else if (const_tp == integer_typep) {
        sprintf(string, "%d",
                const_idp->defn.info.constant.value.integer);
        emit(string);
    }
    else if (const_tp == real_typep) {
        sprintf(string, "%g",
                const_idp->defn.info.constant.value.real);
        emit(string);
    }
    else if (const_tp == char_typep) {
        sprintf(string, "'%c'",
                const_idp->defn.info.constant.value.character);
        emit(string);
    }

    emit(";");
    flush();
    retreat_left_margin();
}

/*----------------------------------------------*/
/* analyze_type_defn     Pretty-print a type definition: */
/*                                              */
/*                      TYPE                    */
/*                              <id> = <type>;  */
/*----------------------------------------------*/

analyze_type_defn(type_idp)

    SYMTAB_NODE_PTR type_idp;               /* type id */

{
    if (error_count > 0) return;

    declaration_keyword(&type_flag, "TYPE");
```

```
    advance_left_margin();

    indent();
    emit(type_idp->name);
    emit(" = ");

    print_type(type_idp->typep,
               type_idp == type_idp->typep->type_idp);
    emit(";");
    flush();
    retreat_left_margin();
}

/*----------------------------------------------------*/
/* print_type              Pretty-print a type.       */
/*----------------------------------------------------*/

print_type(tp, defn_flag)

    TYPE_STRUCT_PTR tp;          /* type */
    BOOLEAN         defn_flag;   /* TRUE if named definition */

{
    /*
    -- Identifier type.
    */
    if (!defn_flag && (tp->type_idp != NULL))
        emit(tp->type_idp->name);

    /*
    -- Other type.
    */
    else switch (tp->form) {
        case ENUM_FORM:      print_enum_type(tp);      break;
        case SUBRANGE_FORM:  print_subrange_type(tp);  break;
        case ARRAY_FORM:     print_array_type(tp);     break;
        case RECORD_FORM:    print_record_type(tp);    break;
    }
}

/*----------------------------------------------------*/
/* print_enum_type         Pretty-print an enumeration type: */
/*                                                    */
/*                      (<id1>, <id2>, ..., <idn>)    */
/*----------------------------------------------------*/

print_enum_type(tp)

    TYPE_STRUCT_PTR tp;          /* type */

{
    SYMTAB_NODE_PTR idp = tp->info.enumeration.const_idp;

    emit("(");

    /*
    -- Loop to print the enumeration constant id list.
    */
    while (idp != NULL) {
        emit(idp->name);
        idp = idp->next;
        if (idp != NULL) emit(", ");
    }

    emit(")");
}
```

```
/*----------------------------------------------------------*/
/*  print_subrange_type      Pretty-print a subrange type:  */
/*                                                          */
/*                           (<const1>..<const2>)           */
/*----------------------------------------------------------*/

print_subrange_type(tp)

    TYPE_STRUCT_PTR tp;          /* type */

{
    print_subrange_limit(tp->info.subrange.min,
                         tp->info.subrange.range_typep);
    emit("..");
    print_subrange_limit(tp->info.subrange.max,
                         tp->info.subrange.range_typep);
}


/*----------------------------------------------------------*/
/*  print_subrange_limit     Pretty-print a subrange constant */
/*                           limit.                         */
/*----------------------------------------------------------*/

print_subrange_limit(limit, range_tp)

    int            limit;
    TYPE_STRUCT_PTR range_tp;

{
    if (range_tp == integer_typep) {
        sprintf(string, "%d", limit);
        emit(string);
    }
    else if (range_tp == char_typep) {
        sprintf(string, "'%c'", limit);
        emit(string);
    }
    else if (range_tp->form == ENUM_FORM) {
        SYMTAB_NODE_PTR idp = range_tp->info.enumeration.const_idp;

        while (limit-- > 0) idp = idp->next;
        emit(idp->name);
    }
}

/*----------------------------------------------------------*/
/*  print_array_type         Pretty-print an array type:   */
/*                                                          */
/*                           ARRAY [<type>] OF             */
/*                           ARRAY [<type>] OF <type>       */
/*----------------------------------------------------------*/

print_array_type(tp)

    TYPE_STRUCT_PTR tp;               /* type */

{
    int            save_left_margin;  /* current left margin */
    TYPE_STRUCT_PTR index_tp = tp->info.array.index_typep;
    TYPE_STRUCT_PTR elmt_tp  = tp->info.array.elmt_typep;

    set_left_margin(save_left_margin);

    emit("ARRAY [");
    print_type(index_tp, FALSE);
    emit("] OF ");

    if (elmt_tp->type_idp != NULL) print_type(elmt_tp, FALSE);
```

```
    else {
        flush();

        /*
        -- Cascade multidimensional array definitions.
        */
        advance_left_margin();
        indent();
        print_type(elmt_tp, FALSE);
    }

    reset_left_margin(save_left_margin);
}

/*----------------------------------------------------------*/
/*  print_record_type        Pretty-print a record type:   */
/*                                                          */
/*                           RECORD                         */
/*                               <field-list1> : <type>;    */
/*                               <field-list2> : <type>     */
/*                           END                            */
/*----------------------------------------------------------*/

print_record_type(tp)

    TYPE_STRUCT_PTR tp;

{
    int            save_left_margin;     /* current left margin */
    BOOLEAN        sublist_done;         /* TRUE iff done */
    SYMTAB_NODE_PTR field_idp = tp->info.record.field_symtab;
    TYPE_STRUCT_PTR common_tp;           /* type of field sublist */

    set_left_margin(save_left_margin);

    emit("RECORD");
    flush();
    advance_left_margin();

    /*
    -- Loop to print field sublists.
    */
    while (field_idp != NULL) {
        indent();
        emit(field_idp->name);
        common_tp = field_idp->typep;

        /*
        -- Loop to print fields of a sublist.
        */
        do {
            field_idp = field_idp->next;
            sublist_done = ((field_idp == NULL) ||
                           (field_idp->typep != common_tp));
            if (!sublist_done) {
                emit(", ");
                emit(field_idp->name);
            }
        } while (!sublist_done);

        emit(" : ");
        print_type(common_tp, FALSE);
        emit(";");
        flush();
    }

    retreat_left_margin();
```

```
    indent();                                              return;
    emit("END");                                       }
    reset_left_margin(save_left_margin);          else done_var_idp = var_idp->next;
}
                                                  declaration_keyword(&var_flag, "VAR");
/*-------------------------------------------*/    advance_left_margin();
/*  analyze_var_decl   Pretty-print a variable declaration: */
/*                                           */    indent();
/*                  VAR                      */    emit(var_idp->name);
/*                     <id> : <type>;        */    common_tp = var_idp->typep;
/*-------------------------------------------*/
                                                  /*
analyze_var_decl(var_idp)                          -- Loop to print the variables in a sublist.
                                                   */
    SYMTAB_NODE_PTR var_idp;      /* variable id */  do {
                                                       var_idp = var_idp->next;
{                                                      sublist_done = (var_idp == NULL);
    TYPE_STRUCT_PTR common_tp;    /* type of id sublist */   if (!sublist_done) {
    BOOLEAN       sublist_done;   /* TRUE iff sublist done */    emit(", ");
    static SYMTAB_NODE_PTR done_var_idp = NULL;  /* id already          emit(var_idp->name);
                                        printed */        }
                                                   } while (!sublist_done);
    if (error_count > 0) return;
                                                  emit(" : ");
    /*                                             print_type(common_tp, FALSE);
    -- If this variable is part of a sublist that has  emit(";");
    -- already been printed, don't print it again.  flush();
    */
    if (var_idp == done_var_idp) {                 retreat_left_margin();
        done_var_idp = var_idp->next;          }
```

We pretty-print routine (program, procedure, and function) headers in function analyze_routine_header. We print each header using the current left margin. We print the entire header on one line if there are no formal parameters, if there was a previous forward declaration for the routine, or if the formal parameter lists consists of only one sublist (the parameters all have the same definition and type). This is a "virtual" line, since function emit wraps long lines. Otherwise, we print each parameter sublist on a new line, and we indent the subsequent lines so that they line up just after the opening left parenthesis. If the routine is a function and there wasn't a previous forward declaration for it, we print the function type after the closing right parenthesis. Some examples are:

```
FUNCTION func (VAR ch : char) : real;

PROCEDURE proc (b : boolean;
                VAR x, xx : real;
                y, yy : real);
```

If the header is a forward declaration, we print forward on the line below the header, and indent it from the left margin. Otherwise, we advance the left margin to prepare for pretty-printing the routine's declarations and statements.

We also initialize the global boolean flags const_flag, type_flag, and var_flag to FALSE. These flags make sure that we print the reserved words CONST,

TYPE, and VAR only once for each set of a routine's local declarations. Later, we will call function declaration_keyword to emit one of these reserved words and pass it the corresponding flag to set to TRUE.

We print constant definitions in function analyze_const_defn. Before the first definition, we call declaration_keyword to print CONST on a separate line using the current left margin. We use sprintf to format each constant value. We print definitions on separate lines that we indent from CONST. For example:

```
CONST
    ten = 10;
    pi = 3.14156;
    ch = 'x';
    hello = "Hello, world.";
```

Function analyze_type_defn prints type definitions. Before the first definition, we call declaration_keyword to print TYPE on a separate line using the current left margin. We then print the definitions on the following lines, starting each definition on a new line and indenting it from TYPE. We emit the type identifier followed by =, and then we call function print_type to pretty-print the type specification.

In function print_type, we first check if the type is simply the identifier of a previously-defined type. If so, we emit that identifier. Otherwise, we call the appropriate function to print the type specification.

We print an enumeration type specification on a single line in function print_enum_type. In function print_subrange_type, we print a subrange type specification on a single line, and we call function print_subrange_limit to print each limit of the subrange.

Function print_array_type prints an array type specification. We call print_type recursively to print each index and element type. We print a single-dimensional array type on one line, and multidimensional array types on several lines, one per dimension. We indent the second dimension from the beginning of the ARRAY of the first dimension, and we indent each subsequent dimension similarly from the previous one.

We print a record type specification in function print_record_type. We emit RECORD, print each field sublist starting on a new line, and then call function print_type recursively to print the field type. We indent all the field sublist lines from RECORD. After the last field sublist line, we emit END on a separate line and line it up under RECORD. Examples of pretty-printed type definitions are:

```
TYPE
    e = (alpha, beta, gamma);
    ee = e;
    sr = alpha..gamma;
    cr = 'a'..'x';
    ar1 = ARRAY [1..10] OF integer;
```

```
        ar2 = ARRAY [e] OF
                    ARRAY [sr] OF real;
        ar3 = ARRAY [(fee, fye, foe, fum)] OF
                    ARRAY [sr] OF
                        ARRAY [e] OF boolean;
        rec = RECORD
                i, j, k : integer;
                x : real;
                ch : char;
                a : ARRAY [sr] OF e;
            END;
```

   We call function `analyze_var_decl` to print a variable declaration. Before the first definition, we call `declaration_keyword` to print VAR on a separate line using the current left margin. We then print the declarations on the following lines, starting each declaration on a new line and indenting it from VAR.

   We call this function once per variable identifier from function `var_or_field_declarations` in file `decl.c`, but we want to print a sublist of variables of the same type on one line. Therefore, when we call `analyze_var_decl` for an identifier, we print not only that identifier, but all the subsequent identifiers in the linked sublist. To prevent us from printing an identifier in a sublist again, we point static variable `done_var_idp` to each identifier. Each time we call the function, we move `done_var_idp` to the next identifier in the sublist. If the identifier we pass to the function is the same as the one `done_var_idp` points to, we do not print it. Since `done_var_idp` is NULL for the first identifier of a sublist, we do print that identifier and the rest of the sublist. We call `print_type` recursively to print the type. Examples of pretty-printed variable declarations are:

```
VAR
    radius, circumference : real;
    b : boolean;
    letter : 'a'..'z';
    greek : e;
    list : ar1;
```

8.3.2 Pretty-printing statements and expressions

   As we discussed before, we only convert the executable statements of a routine's block to the intermediate form. The scanner does most of the work of converting a statement's tokens into byte-sized codes, so we need to tell the scanner when it is scanning the statements. We use a new scanner global, which we now must declare and initialize at the beginning of file `scanner.c`:

```
BOOLEAN block_flag = FALSE;
```

This flag will be TRUE only when we are parsing the statements of a block.

Figure 8-6 shows the new version of function block in file routine.c. We set block_flag to TRUE just before we parse the block's compound statement, and we reset it to FALSE afterwards. We also call function crunch_token to convert the reserved word token BEGIN. (We'll look at this function later.)

FIGURE 8-6   Function block in file routine.c.

```
/*-----------------------------------------------------*/          declarations(rtn_idp);
/*  block            Process a block, which consists of    */
/*                   declarations followed by a compound    */     /*
/*                   statement.                             */     -- Error synchronization:  Should be ;
/*-----------------------------------------------------*/          */
                                                                   synchronize(follow_decls_list, NULL, NULL);
TOKEN_CODE follow_decls_list[] = {SEMICOLON, BEGIN, END_OF_FILE, 0};    if (token != BEGIN) error(MISSING_BEGIN);

block(rtn_idp)                                                     crunch_token();

    SYMTAB_NODE_PTR rtn_idp;      /* id of program or routine */   block_flag = TRUE;
                                                                   compound_statement();
{                                                                  block_flag = FALSE;
    extern BOOLEAN block_flag;                                 }
```

In the new version of function get_token in file scanner.c shown in Figure 8-7, we test block_flag to decide whether or not to call crunch_token to convert the current token.

FIGURE 8-7   Function get_token in file scanner.c.

```
/*-----------------------------------------------------*/          case DIGIT:    get_number();        break;
/*  get_token        Extract the next token from the source  */    case QUOTE:    get_string();        break;
/*                   buffer.                               */      case EOF_CODE: token = END_OF_FILE;  break;
/*-----------------------------------------------------*/          default:       get_special();       break;
                                                                   }
get_token()
                                                                   /*
{                                                                  -- For the interpreter:  While parsing a block, crunch
    skip_blanks();                                                 -- the token code and append it to the code buffer.
    tokenp = token_string;                                         */
                                                                   if (block_flag) crunch_token();
    switch (char_code(ch)) {                                   }
        case LETTER:   get_word();          break;
```

Back in Chapter 3, the cruncher utility program entered not only identifiers, but also number and string tokens into the symbol table. We need to do that again here, except that we also enter the literal values. For a number, we set the symbol table node's defn.info.constant.value field to the literal value. We make a copy of a literal string and point the node's info field to the copy. We also set the node's typep field.

When we convert an IDENTIFIER, NUMBER, or STRING token, we want to follow the token code by a pointer to the symbol table node of the token. In this chapter, the pretty-printer only uses the token string from the node's name field. Starting in the next chapter, the literal value will also be useful.

In several functions of the parser module, we now call function crunch_symtab_node_ptr right after we do a symbol table lookup or entry of an identifier, number, or string token. Figures 8-8, 8-9, and 8-10 show new versions of functions statement, for_statement, and case_label, respectively, in file stmt.c. Figures 8-11 and 8-12 show new versions of functions factor and variable, respectively, in file expr.c.

FIGURE 8-8   Function statement in file stmt.c.

```
/*--------------------------------------------------------*/
/*  statement        Process a statement by calling the   */
/*                    appropriate parsing routine based on */
/*                    the statement's first token.         */
/*--------------------------------------------------------*/

statement()

{
    /*
    -- Call the appropriate routine based on the first
    -- token of the statement.
    */
    switch (token) {

        case IDENTIFIER: {
            SYMTAB_NODE_PTR idp;

            /*
            -- Assignment statement or procedure call?
            */
            search_and_find_all_symtab(idp);

            if (idp->defn.key == PROC_DEFN) {
                crunch_symtab_node_ptr(idp);
                get_token();
                routine_call(idp, TRUE);
            }
            else assignment_statement(idp);

            break;
        }

        case REPEAT:    repeat_statement();     break;
        case WHILE:     while_statement();      break;
        case IF:        if_statement();         break;
        case FOR:       for_statement();        break;
        case CASE:      case_statement();       break;
        case BEGIN:     compound_statement();   break;

    }

    /*
    -- Error synchronization:  Only a semicolon, END, ELSE, or
    --                         UNTIL may follow a statement.
    --                         Check for a missing semicolon.
    */
    synchronize(statement_end_list, statement_start_list, NULL);
    if (token_in(statement_start_list)) error(MISSING_SEMICOLON);
}
```

FIGURE 8-9   Function for_statement in file stmt.c.

```
/*--------------------------------------------------------*/
/*  for_statement     Process a FOR statement:            */
/*                                                         */
/*                       FOR <id> := <expr> TO|DOWNTO <expr> */
/*                       DO <stmt>                         */
/*--------------------------------------------------------*/

for_statement()

{
    SYMTAB_NODE_PTR for_idp;
    TYPE_STRUCT_PTR for_tp, expr_tp;

    get_token();

    if (token == IDENTIFIER) {
        search_and_find_all_symtab(for_idp);
        crunch_symtab_node_ptr(for_idp);

        if ((for_idp->level != level) ||
            (for_idp->defn.key != VAR_DEFN))
            error(INVALID_FOR_CONTROL);

        for_tp = base_type(for_idp->typep);
        get_token();

        if ((for_tp != integer_typep) &&
            (for_tp != char_typep) &&
```

```
            (for_tp->form != ENUM_FORM)) error(INCOMPATIBLE_TYPES);
    }
    else {
        error(IDENTIFIER, MISSING_IDENTIFIER);
        for_tp = &dummy_type;
    }

    if_token_get_else_error(COLONEQUAL, MISSING_COLONEQUAL);

    expr_tp = expression();
    if (! is_assign_type_compatible(for_tp, expr_tp))
```

```
            error(INCOMPATIBLE_TYPES);

    if ((token == TO) || (token == DOWNTO)) get_token();
    else error(MISSING_TO_OR_DOWNTO);

    expr_tp = expression();
    if (! is_assign_type_compatible(for_tp, expr_tp))
        error(INCOMPATIBLE_TYPES);

    if_token_get_else_error(DO, MISSING_DO);
    statement();
}
```

FIGURE 8-10   Function case_label in file stmt.c.

```
/*----------------------------------------------------------*/
/*  case_label            Process a CASE label and return a  */
/*                        pointer to its type structure.     */
/*----------------------------------------------------------*/

    TYPE_STRUCT_PTR
case_label()

{
    TOKEN_CODE      sign      = PLUS;    /* unary + or - sign */
    BOOLEAN         saw_sign = FALSE;   /* TRUE iff unary sign */
    TYPE_STRUCT_PTR label_tp;

    /*
    -- Unary + or - sign.
    */
    if ((token == PLUS) || (token == MINUS)) {
        sign     = token;
        saw_sign = TRUE;
        get_token();
    }

    /*
    -- Numeric constant:  Integer type only.
    */
    if (token == NUMBER) {
        SYMTAB_NODE_PTR np = search_symtab(token_string,
                                           symtab_display[1]);

        if (np == NULL) np = enter_symtab(token_string,
                                          symtab_display[1]);
        crunch_symtab_node_ptr(np);

        if (literal.type == REAL_LIT) error(INVALID_CONSTANT);
        return(integer_typep);
    }

    /*
    -- Identifier constant:  Integer, character, or enumeration
    --                       types only.
    */
    else if (token == IDENTIFIER) {
        SYMTAB_NODE_PTR idp;

        search_all_symtab(idp);
        crunch_symtab_node_ptr(idp);

        if (idp == NULL) {
```

```
            error(UNDEFINED_IDENTIFIER);
            return(&dummy_type);
        }

        else if (idp->defn.key != CONST_DEFN) {
            error(NOT_A_CONSTANT_IDENTIFIER);
            return(&dummy_type);
        }

        else if (idp->typep == integer_typep)
            return(integer_typep);

        else if (idp->typep == char_typep) {
            if (saw_sign) error(INVALID_CONSTANT);
            return(char_typep);
        }

        else if (idp->typep->form == ENUM_FORM) {
            if (saw_sign) error(INVALID_CONSTANT);
            return(idp->typep);
        }

        else return(&dummy_type);
    }

    /*
    -- String constant:  Character type only.
    */
    else if (token == STRING) {
        SYMTAB_NODE_PTR np = search_symtab(token_string,
                                           symtab_display[1]);

        if (np == NULL) np = enter_symtab(token_string,
                                          symtab_display[1]);
        crunch_symtab_node_ptr(np);

        if (saw_sign) error(INVALID_CONSTANT);

        if (strlen(literal.value.string) == 1) return(char_typep);
        else {
            error(INVALID_CONSTANT);
            return(&dummy_type);
        }
    }

    else {
```

```
        error(INVALID_CONSTANT);
        return(&dummy_type);
    }
}
```

FIGURE 8-11   Function `factor` in file `expr.c`.

```
/*--------------------------------------------------------------*/
/* factor              Process a factor, which is a variable,  */
/*                     a number, NOT followed by a factor, or  */
/*                     a parenthesized subexpression.  Return   */
/*                     a pointer to the type structure.         */
/*--------------------------------------------------------------*/

    TYPE_STRUCT_PTR
factor()

{
    TYPE_STRUCT_PTR tp;

    switch (token) {

        case IDENTIFIER: {
            SYMTAB_NODE_PTR idp;

            search_and_find_all_symtab(idp);

            switch (idp->defn.key) {

                case FUNC_DEFN:
                    crunch_symtab_node_ptr(idp);
                    get_token();
                    tp = routine_call(idp, TRUE);
                    break;

                case PROC_DEFN:
                    error(INVALID_IDENTIFIER_USAGE);
                    get_token();
                    actual_parm_list(idp, FALSE);
                    tp = &dummy_type;
                    break;

                case CONST_DEFN:
                    crunch_symtab_node_ptr(idp);
                    get_token();
                    tp = idp->typep;
                    break;

                default:
                    tp = variable(idp, EXPR_USE);
                    break;
            }

            break;
        }

        case NUMBER: {
            SYMTAB_NODE_PTR np;

            np = search_symtab(token_string, symtab_display[1]);
            if (np == NULL) np = enter_symtab(token_string,
                                        symtab_display[1]);
```

```
            if (literal.type == INTEGER_LIT) {
                tp = np->typep = integer_typep;
                np->defn.info.constant.value.integer =
                    literal.value.integer;
            }
            else {  /* literal.type == REAL_LIT */
                tp = np->typep = real_typep;
                np->defn.info.constant.value.real =
                    literal.value.real;
            }

            crunch_symtab_node_ptr(np);
            get_token();

            break;
        }

        case STRING: {
            SYMTAB_NODE_PTR np;
            int          length = strlen(literal.value.string);

            np = search_symtab(token_string, symtab_display[1]);
            if (np == NULL) np = enter_symtab(token_string,
                                        symtab_display[1]);

            if (length == 1) {
                np->defn.info.constant.value.character =
                    literal.value.string[0];
                tp = char_typep;
            }
            else {
                np->typep = tp = make_string_typep(length);
                np->info  = alloc_bytes(length + 1);
                strcpy(np->info, literal.value.string);
            }

            crunch_symtab_node_ptr(np);

            get_token();
            break;
        }

        case NOT:
            get_token();
            tp = factor();
            break;

        case LPAREN:
            get_token();
            tp = expression();

            if_token_get_else_error(RPAREN, MISSING_RPAREN);
            break;

        default:
```

```
            error(INVALID_EXPRESSION);
            tp = &dummy_type;
            break;
    }

    return(tp);
}
```

FIGURE 8-12   Function `variable` in file `expr.c`.

```
/*----------------------------------------------------------*/
/*  variable           Process a variable, which can be a    */
/*                      simple identifier, an array identifier */
/*                      with subscripts, or a record identifier */
/*                      with fields.                          */
/*----------------------------------------------------------*/

    TYPE_STRUCT_PTR
variable(var_idp, use)

    SYMTAB_NODE_PTR var_idp;    /* variable id */
    USE             use;        /* how variable is used */

{
    TYPE_STRUCT_PTR tp          = var_idp->typep;
    DEFN_KEY        defn_key    = var_idp->defn.key;
    TYPE_STRUCT_PTR array_subscript_list();
    TYPE_STRUCT_PTR record_field();

    crunch_symtab_node_ptr(var_idp);

    /*
    -- Check the variable's definition.
    */
    switch (defn_key) {
        case VAR_DEFN:
        case VALPARM_DEFN:
        case VARPARM_DEFN:
        case FUNC_DEFN:
```

```
        case UNDEFINED: break;      /* OK */

        default: {                  /* error */
            tp = &dummy_type;
            error(INVALID_IDENTIFIER_USAGE);
        }
    }

    get_token();

    /*
    -- There must not be a parameter list, but if there is one,
    -- parse it anyway for error recovery.
    */
    if (token == LPAREN) {
        error(UNEXPECTED_TOKEN);
        actual_parm_list(var_idp, FALSE);
        return(tp);
    }

    /*
    -- Subscripts and/or field designators?
    */
    while ((token == LBRACKET) || (token == PERIOD)) {
        tp = token == LBRACKET ? array_subscript_list(tp)
                               : record_field(tp);
    }

    return(tp);
}
```

We manipulate the intermediate form to pretty-print the statements and expressions in file `ppstmt.c`, shown in Figure 8-13. There, we see again the string array `symbol_strings`.

FIGURE 8-13   File `ppstmt.c`.

```
/****************************************************************/
/*                                                              */
/*      Pretty-print statements.                                */
/*                                                              */
/*      FILE:       ppstmt.c                                    */
/*                                                              */
/****************************************************************/

#include <stdio.h>
```

```
#include "common.h"
#include "error.h"
#include "symtab.h"
#include "scanner.h"
#include "pprint.h"

#define MAX_CODE_BUFFER_SIZE 4096
```

```
/*------------------------------------------------------*/
/*  Externals                                           */
/*------------------------------------------------------*/

extern TOKEN_CODE token;
extern TOKEN_CODE ctoken;

extern int  left_margin;
extern char pprint_buffer[];
extern int  error_count;

extern char *code_buffer;
extern char *code_bufferp;
extern char *code_segmentp;
extern char *code_segment_limit;

/*------------------------------------------------------*/
/*  Globals                                             */
/*------------------------------------------------------*/

char *symbol_strings[] = {
    "<no token>", "<IDENTIFIER>", "<NUMBER>", "<STRING>",
    "^", "*", "(", ")", "-", "+", "=", "[", "]", ":", ";",
    "<", ">", ",", ".", "/", ":=", "<=", ">=", "<>", "..",
    "<END OF FILE>", "<ERROR>",
    "AND", "ARRAY", "BEGIN", "CASE", "CONST", "DIV", "DO", "DOWNTO",
    "ELSE", "END", "FILE", "FOR", "FUNCTION", "GOTO", "IF", "IN",
    "LABEL", "MOD", "NIL", "NOT", "OF", "OR", "PACKED", "PROCEDURE",
    "PROGRAM", "RECORD", "REPEAT", "SET", "THEN", "TO", "TYPE",
    "UNTIL", "VAR", "WHILE", "WITH",
};

            /*******************************/
            /*                             */
            /*      Code segment routines  */
            /*                             */
            /*******************************/

/*------------------------------------------------------*/
/*  crunch_token      Append the token code to the code  */
/*                    buffer.  Called by the scanner routine */
/*                    get_token only while parsing a block.  */
/*------------------------------------------------------*/

crunch_token()

{
    char token_code = token;    /* byte-sized token code */

    if (code_bufferp >= code_buffer + MAX_CODE_BUFFER_SIZE) {
        error(CODE_SEGMENT_OVERFLOW);
        exit(-CODE_SEGMENT_OVERFLOW);
    }
    else *code_bufferp++ = token_code;
}

/*------------------------------------------------------*/
/*  crunch_symtab_node_ptr    Append a symbol table node */
/*                            pointer to the code buffer. */
/*------------------------------------------------------*/

crunch_symtab_node_ptr(np)

    SYMTAB_NODE_PTR np;        /* pointer to append */

{
    SYMTAB_NODE_PTR *npp = (SYMTAB_NODE_PTR *) code_bufferp;
```

```
    if (code_bufferp >= code_buffer + MAX_CODE_BUFFER_SIZE
                        - sizeof(SYMTAB_NODE_PTR)) {
        error(CODE_SEGMENT_OVERFLOW);
        exit(-CODE_SEGMENT_OVERFLOW);
    }
    else {
        *npp = np;
        code_bufferp += sizeof(SYMTAB_NODE_PTR);
    }
}

/*------------------------------------------------------*/
/*  create_code_segment    Create a code segment and copy in */
/*                         the contents of the code buffer. */
/*                         Reset the code buffer pointer.   */
/*                         Return a pointer to the segment. */
/*------------------------------------------------------*/

    char *
create_code_segment()

{
    char *code_segment = alloc_bytes(code_bufferp - code_buffer);

    code_segment_limit = code_segment + (code_bufferp - code_buffer);
    code_bufferp       = code_buffer;
    code_segmentp      = code_segment;

    /*
    -- Copy in the contents of the code buffer.
    */
    while (code_segmentp != code_segment_limit)
        *code_segmentp++ = *code_bufferp++;

    code_bufferp = code_buffer;          /* reset code buffer ptr */
    return(code_segment);
}

/*------------------------------------------------------*/
/*  get_ctoken         Extract the next token code from the */
/*                     current code segment.                */
/*------------------------------------------------------*/

#define get_ctoken()    ctoken = *code_segmentp++

/*------------------------------------------------------*/
/*  get_symtab_cptr    Extract a symbol table node pointer */
/*                     from the current code segment and    */
/*                     return it.                           */
/*------------------------------------------------------*/

    SYMTAB_NODE_PTR
get_symtab_cptr()

{
    SYMTAB_NODE_PTR np;
    SYMTAB_NODE_PTR *npp = (SYMTAB_NODE_PTR *) code_segmentp;

    np = *npp;
    code_segmentp += sizeof(SYMTAB_NODE_PTR);
    return(np);
}

            /*****************************************/
            /*                                       */
            /*      Pretty-printing routines         */
            /*                                       */
```

```
                    /*****************************************/
```

```
/*------------------------------------------------------*/
/*   analyze_block        Pretty-print the code segment of  */
/*                        a block.                          */
/*------------------------------------------------------*/

analyze_block(code_segment)

    char *code_segment;

{
    if (error_count > 0) return;

    code_segmentp = code_segment;
    emit(" ");
    flush();

    get_ctoken();
    print_statement();        /* should be a compound statement */
    retreat_left_margin();

    /*
    -- Output any trailing semicolons or period.
    */
    while (code_segmentp <= code_segment_limit) {
        indent();
        emit(symbol_strings[token]);
        flush();
        get_ctoken();
    }
}
```

```
/*------------------------------------------------------*/
/*   print_statement      Call the appropriate statement printing */
/*                        routine.                           */
/*------------------------------------------------------*/

print_statement()

{
    indent();

    switch (ctoken) {
        case IDENTIFIER:  print_assign_or_call_statement();  break;
        case BEGIN:       print_compound_statement();        break;
        case CASE:        print_case_statement();            break;
        case FOR:         print_for_statement();             break;
        case IF:          print_if_statement();              break;
        case REPEAT:      print_repeat_statement();          break;
        case WHILE:       print_while_statement();           break;
    }

    while (ctoken == SEMICOLON) {
        emit(";");
        get_ctoken();
    }

    flush();
}
```

```
/*------------------------------------------------------*/
/*   print_assign_or_call_statement       Pretty-print an assign-  */
/*                                         ment or procedure call  */
/*                                         statement:              */
/*                                                                 */
/*                                         <variable> := <expr>    */
```

```
/*                             <id>(<parm-list)        */
/*------------------------------------------------------*/

print_assign_or_call_statement()

{
    print_identifier();

    if (ctoken == COLONEQUAL) {
        emit(" := ");
        get_ctoken();
        print_expression();
    }
}
```

```
/*------------------------------------------------------*/
/*   print_compound_statement    Pretty-print a compound  */
/*                                statement:               */
/*                                                         */
/*                                BEGIN                    */
/*                                    <stmt-list>          */
/*                                END                      */
/*------------------------------------------------------*/

print_compound_statement()

{
    emit("BEGIN");
    flush();
    advance_left_margin();

    get_ctoken();
    while (ctoken != END) print_statement();

    retreat_left_margin();
    indent();
    emit("END");
    get_ctoken();
}
```

```
/*------------------------------------------------------*/
/*   print_case_statement        Pretty-print a CASE statement:  */
/*                                                               */
/*                                CASE <expr> OF                 */
/*                                    <const-list> : <stmt>      */
/*                                    ...                        */
/*                                END                            */
/*------------------------------------------------------*/

print_case_statement()

{
    emit("CASE ");

    get_ctoken();
    print_expression();
    emit(" OF ");
    flush();
    advance_left_margin();

    get_ctoken();

    /*
    -- Loop to print CASE branches.
    */
    do {
        indent();
```

```
        /*
        -- Loop to print each constant
        -- in the constant list.
        */
        do {
            print_expression();
            if (ctoken == COMMA) {
                emit(", ");
                get_ctoken();
            }
        } while (ctoken != COLON);

        emit(":");
        flush();
        advance_left_margin();

        get_ctoken();
        print_statement();
        retreat_left_margin();
    } while (ctoken != END);

    retreat_left_margin();
    indent();
    emit("END");
    get_ctoken();
}

/*-----------------------------------------------------*/
/* print_for_statement    Pretty print a FOR statement:  */
/*                                                       */
/*                        FOR <id> := <expr> TO|DOWNTO   */
/*                        <expr> DO <stmt>               */
/*-----------------------------------------------------*/

print_for_statement()

{
    emit("FOR ");

    get_ctoken();
    print_identifier();
    emit(" := ");

    get_ctoken();
    print_expression();
    emit(ctoken == TO ? " TO " : " DOWNTO ");

    get_ctoken();
    print_expression();
    emit(" DO ");
    flush();

    advance_left_margin();
    get_ctoken();
    print_statement();
    retreat_left_margin();
}

/*-----------------------------------------------------*/
/* print_if_statement      Pretty-print an IF statement: */
/*                                                       */
/*                        IF <expr> THEN                 */
/*                              <stmt>                    */
/*                                                       */
/*                        IF <expr> THEN                 */
/*                              <stmt>                    */
/*                        ELSE                           */
```

```
/*                              <stmt>                  */
/*-----------------------------------------------------*/

print_if_statement()

{
    emit("IF ");

    get_ctoken();
    print_expression();
    emit(" THEN");
    flush();

    advance_left_margin();
    get_ctoken();
    print_statement();
    retreat_left_margin();

    if (ctoken == ELSE) {
        indent();
        emit("ELSE");
        flush();

        advance_left_margin();
        get_ctoken();
        print_statement();
        retreat_left_margin();
    }
}

/*-----------------------------------------------------*/
/* print_repeat_statement     Pretty-print a REPEAT     */
/*                            statement:                */
/*                                                      */
/*                            REPEAT                    */
/*                               <stmt-list>            */
/*                            UNTIL <expr>              */
/*-----------------------------------------------------*/

print_repeat_statement()

{
    emit("REPEAT");
    flush();
    advance_left_margin();

    get_ctoken();
    while (ctoken != UNTIL) print_statement();

    retreat_left_margin();
    indent();
    emit("UNTIL ");

    get_ctoken();
    print_expression();
}

/*-----------------------------------------------------*/
/* print_while_statement     Pretty-print a WHILE statement: */
/*                                                      */
/*                            WHILE <expr> DO           */
/*                               <stmt>                 */
/*-----------------------------------------------------*/

print_while_statement()

{
```

```
        emit("WHILE ");

        get_ctoken();
        print_expression();

        emit(" DO");
        flush();
        advance_left_margin();

        get_ctoken();
        print_statement();
        retreat_left_margin();
}


/*------------------------------------------------------------*/
/*  print_expression          Pretty-print an expression.     */
/*------------------------------------------------------------*/

print_expression()

{
    BOOLEAN done = FALSE;       /* TRUE at end of expression */

    do {
        switch (ctoken) {
            case IDENTIFIER:   print_identifier();          break;
            case NUMBER:       print_number();              break;
            case STRING:       print_string();              break;

            case PLUS:      emit("+");       get_ctoken();  break;
            case MINUS:     emit("-");       get_ctoken();  break;
            case STAR:      emit("*");       get_ctoken();  break;
            case SLASH:     emit("/");       get_ctoken();  break;
            case DIV:       emit(" DIV ");   get_ctoken();  break;
            case MOD:       emit(" MOD ");   get_ctoken();  break;
            case AND:       emit(" AND ");   get_ctoken();  break;
            case OR:        emit(" OR ");    get_ctoken();  break;
            case EQUAL:     emit(" = ");     get_ctoken();  break;
            case NE:        emit(" <> ");    get_ctoken();  break;
            case LT:        emit(" < ");     get_ctoken();  break;
            case LE:        emit(" <= ");    get_ctoken();  break;
            case GT:        emit(" > ");     get_ctoken();  break;
            case GE:        emit(" >= ");    get_ctoken();  break;
            case NOT:       emit("NOT ");    get_ctoken();  break;

            case LPAREN:
                emit("(");
                get_ctoken();
                print_expression();
                emit(")");
                get_ctoken();
                break;

            default:
                done = TRUE;
                break;
        }
    } while (!done);
}


/*------------------------------------------------------------*/
/*  print_identifier     Pretty-print an identifier, which    */
/*                       can be a variable or a procedure      */
/*                       or function call.                     */
/*------------------------------------------------------------*/

print_identifier()

{
    SYMTAB_NODE_PTR idp = get_symtab_cptr();

    emit(idp->name);
    get_ctoken();

    /*
    -- Loop to print any following modifiers.
    */
    while ((ctoken == LBRACKET) || (ctoken == LPAREN) ||
           (ctoken == PERIOD)) {
        /*
        -- Subscripts or actual parameters.
        */
        if ((ctoken == LBRACKET) || (ctoken == LPAREN)) {
            emit(ctoken == LBRACKET ? "[" : "(");
            get_ctoken();
            while ((ctoken != RBRACKET) && (ctoken != RPAREN)) {
                print_expression();
                while (ctoken == COLON) {
                    emit(":");
                    get_ctoken();
                    print_expression();
                }
                if (ctoken == COMMA) {
                    emit(", ");
                    get_ctoken();
                }
            }
            emit(ctoken == RBRACKET ? "]" : ")");
            get_ctoken();
        }

        /*
        -- Record fields.
        */
        else /* ctoken == DOT */ {
            emit(".");
            get_ctoken();
            print_identifier();
        }
    }
}


/*------------------------------------------------------------*/
/*  print_number                 Pretty-print a number.       */
/*------------------------------------------------------------*/

print_number()

{
    SYMTAB_NODE_PTR idp = get_symtab_cptr();

    emit(idp->name);
    get_ctoken();
}


/*------------------------------------------------------------*/
/*  print_string                 Pretty-print a string.       */
/*------------------------------------------------------------*/

print_string()
```

```
{
    SYMTAB_NODE_PTR idp = get_symtab_cptr();
    emit(idp->name);
    get_ctoken();
}
```

Global variable code_buffer contains a block's executable statements in their intermediate form. We reuse this buffer for every block, but after we are done parsing a block (as we saw in functions program and routine), we call function create_code_segment to copy the contents of the code buffer into the routine's code segment. Global pointer variables code_bufferp and code_segmentp point into the code buffer and the code segment, respectively, and code_segment_limit points to the end of the code segment. Global TOKEN_CODE variable ctoken is similar to variable token, except that its value is obtained from the intermediate code in the current code segment.

In functions crunch_token and crunch_symtab_node_ptr, we append a token code and a pointer to a symbol table node to the code buffer, after first checking for an overflow. The byte-sized token code is from the scanner's TOKEN_CODE enumeration type.

As we saw earlier, we call function create_code_segment after we have already parsed and converted a block. We allocate a code segment and copy the contents of the code buffer into the segment. We then reset the code buffer pointer to the beginning and return the pointer to the code segment.

We call macro get_ctoken to set ctoken to the next token code in the current code segment. We call function get_symtab_cptr to retrieve a pointer to a symbol table node.

In function analyze_block, we print the compound statement of a block by calling function print_statement. Afterwards, since we are at the end of a routine, we call retreat_left_margin. We then simply emit any remaining tokens (usually a semicolon or the final period). In function print_statement, we call the appropriate pretty-printing function for the statement, and then we emit any trailing semicolons.

We print an assignment statement or a procedure call in function print_assign_or_call_statement. We call function print_identifier, and then, for an assignment statement, we emit := and call function print_expression.

In function print_compound_statement, we print a compound statement using the format:

```
BEGIN
    <stmt-1>;
    <stmt-2>;
    ...
    <stmt-n>
END
```

In function `print_case_statement`, we print a CASE statement using the format:

```
CASE <expr> OF
    <label-list-1> : <stmt-1>;
    <label-list-2> : <stmt-2>;
    ...
    <label-list-n> : <stmt-n>
END
```

In function `print_for_statement`, we print a FOR statement using the format:

```
FOR <id> := <expr-1> TO <expr-2> DO
    <stmt>
```

(The TO may instead be DOWNTO.)

In function `print_if_statement`, we print an IF statement using either the format:

```
IF <expr> THEN
    <stmt>
```

or the format:

```
IF <expr> THEN
    <stmt-1>
ELSE
    <stmt-2>
```

In function `print_repeat_statement`, we print a REPEAT statement using the format:

```
REPEAT
    <stmt-1>;
    <stmt-2>;
    ...
    <stmt-n>
UNTIL <expr>
```

Finally, in function `print_while_statement`, we print a WHILE statement using the format:

```
WHILE <expr> DO
    <stmt>
```

We print an expression in function print_expression. We simply loop to retrieve tokens from the current code segment that belong to an expression and emit each one. Whenever we retrieve a left parenthesis, we call the function recursively.

In function print_identifier, we print an identifier and any following modifiers, such as array subscripts, record field designators, and actual parameter lists. We call function get_symtab_cptr to retrieve the pointer to the identifier's symbol table node. Here, we also print the field width and precision designators of the actual arguments for calls to write and writeln.

We print a number and a string, respectively, in functions print_number and print_string. In both functions, we call get_symtab_cptr to retrieve the pointer to the token's symbol table node so that we can get back the token string.

The pretty-printer has done almost all of the work of translating a source program into an intermediate form for the interpreter. Figure 8-14 shows sample output. Now we're ready to start executing!

FIGURE 8-14   Sample output from the pretty-printer.

```
PROGRAM graph (output);                                             BEGIN
                                                                        write(' ':n, '*');
    CONST                                                               IF h-n-1 > 0 THEN
        d = 0.0625;                                                         write(' ':h-n-1);
        s = 32;                                                         writeln('|')
        h = 34;                                                     END
        c = 6.28318;                                            ELSE
        lim = 32;                                                   IF n > h THEN
                                                                        BEGIN
    VAR                                                                     write(' ':h, '|');
        x, y : real;                                                        IF n-h-1 > 0 THEN
        i, n : integer;                                                         write(' ':n-h-1);
                                                                            writeln('*')
    BEGIN                                                               END
        i := 0;                                                     ELSE
        WHILE i <= lim DO                                               writeln(' ':n, '*');
            BEGIN                                                   i := i+1;
                x := d*i;                                       END;
                y := exp(-x)*sin(c*x);
                n := round(s*y)+h;                      END
                IF n < h THEN                                   .
```

Questions and exercises

1. Make the pretty-printer smarter about when to use more than one line. For example, on a single line, it should be able to print the following IF statement:

                                IF p THEN a := b

2. Why is it necessary for function `print_expression` to call itself recursively when it encounters a left parenthesis? Why not simply print parentheses like the other expression tokens?

3. The scanner removes all comments. Implement a reasonable algorithm for pretty-printing comments.

4. When two types are equated, as in:

```
TYPE type1 = type2
```

then, wherever type2 is used in the source program, the pretty-printer replaces it with type1. Fix this problem.

5. Experiment with other intermediate forms, such as a tree-structured form.

CHAPTER 9

Interpreting Procedures, Functions, and Assignment Statements

In this chapter, we finally begin to write the executor module of the interpreter. We will be able to execute assignment statements and calls to procedures and functions, and we'll see how the interpreter manages the resources in its runtime environment. Above all, we will lay a good foundation for the next chapter, where we'll complete the interpreter and then be able to execute entire Pascal programs.

To help us understand how the interpreter executes statements and manages resources, the executor routines in this chapter will print out tracing information as the interpreter executes each statement, fetches and stores data, and enters and exits procedures and functions. In this chapter, we will develop the skills to:

- maintain the runtime stack
- execute procedure and function calls
- execute expressions and assignment statements
- flag runtime errors
- print runtime tracing information

9.1 The runtime stack

In the previous chapters, you saw how to manage various resources like the symbol table and the code segments. When an interpreter executes a program, it manages another major resource, the runtime stack. You were first introduced to this resource by the calculator in Chapter 4.

While the interpreter executes a program, the stack does more than merely provide a place to evaluate expressions. As we will see, at any point during the execution of a program, the stack represents a "snapshot" of the state of the program. The stack contains information about which procedures and functions have been called, their return addresses, the current values of all the parameters and local variables, and which of these values are currently accessible.

9.1.1   Allocating parameters and local variables

In our calculator, we used the runtime stack to store intermediate values as we evaluated an expression. We kept the current value of each variable in its symbol table node. This won't do for a Pascal interpreter because you can call procedures and functions recursively. When you call a procedure recursively, the old set of values for its parameters and local variables must be stored to make way for the new set of values. This new set of values becomes current and is used during the recursive execution of the procedure, while the old set of values is unavailable. When the recursive call returns, the new set of values must be discarded and the old set of values must again become current and available.

It makes sense to keep the current values of parameters and local variables not in the symbol table, but on the runtime stack. Whenever you call a procedure or a function, you can allocate space on top of the stack to store the values. Then when you return from the routine, you pop the values off. If the call is recursive, you allocate a new set of values on top of the old set, and when you return from the call, you pop off those values to uncover the old values. So now, the symbol table node for a parameter or local variable keeps track of where its current value is stored on the stack.

In this scheme, you can consider the global variables to be local to the program itself, so you allocate their values at the bottom of the stack when you start to execute the program.

One further note. We will assume that the stack items for our interpreter's runtime stack are all one size. Each item can contain an integer, real, character, or enumeration value, or an address. Whenever we want to allocate an array or record value, we allocate space for that variable's data area elsewhere and place a pointer to the data area on the stack.

9.1.2 Stack frames

So now you have two uses for the runtime stack: to store the current values of the parameters and local variables of a routine while it is executing, and to store the intermediate results when you evaluate an expression. An interpreter also uses its runtime stack to keep track of where to return to and (for functions) the return values. It also keeps information on the stack that enables it to legitimately access nonlocal values according to Pascal's scope rules. All this information, except for the intermediate results, is arranged in *stack frames*.

You allocate a stack frame for the program itself at the bottom of the runtime stack when you first begin to execute the program. Then you allocate a stack frame on top of the stack each time you call a procedure or function. You can then use the stack space above the topmost stack frame for keeping intermediate results when you evaluate an expression.

Figure 9-1 shows the interpreter's stack frame. The first item is at the *stack frame base*, and it is for the return value of a function. (Procedures allocate the return value item for consistency but do not use it.) This is followed by items for a static link, a dynamic link, and the return address. These four items make up the *stack frame header*. Above the header, you allocate items to store the current value for each of the routine's parameters, and on top of that you allocate items for the values of each of its local variables. The static and dynamic links point back to previous stack frames. (We will explain these links later.)

A routine's stack frame contains the current set of values for its parameters and local variables. If you call a routine recursively, you allocate a new stack frame for each call, and the current set of values is in its topmost stack frame.

The number of items in each stack frame header is constant. The number of parameters and the number of local variables of a procedure or function never

---

FIGURE 9-1   The interpreter's stack frame. The top four items constitute the stack frame header.

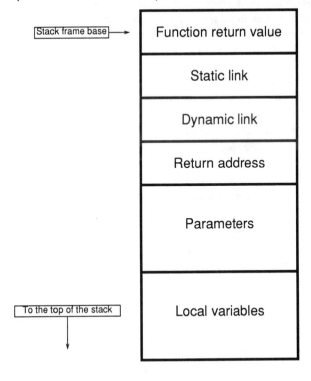

changes. Therefore, if each time you allocate a stack frame for a routine, you allocate the items for the parameters and local variables in the same order (which is reasonable to do), then the offset from the stack frame base to a particular parameter or local variable is always the same. You can store this offset in the symbol table entry so that you can always access the current value of any parameter or local variable. You just get its offset from the symbol table, and the value is in the stack item at that offset from the base of the routine's current stack frame. Figure 9-2 shows the stack frame for a procedure that has several parameters and local variables.

9.1.3 Dynamic links

The dynamic link of a stack frame simply points back to the base of the previous stack frame. In other words, the stack frame of a routine points back to the stack frame of its caller.

When you return from a procedure or a function, the dynamic link enables you to restore the stack to its state when the routine was called. You can pop off the routine's stack frame, so that the stack frame of the caller is again on top.

FIGURE 9-2   The stack frame for a procedure with two parameters p1 and p2, and three local variables i, j, and k. The stack items are all the same size, and the item for each parameter and variable is always at the same offset from the stack frame base. For example, the item for this procedure's local variable i is always at offset +6 from the base.

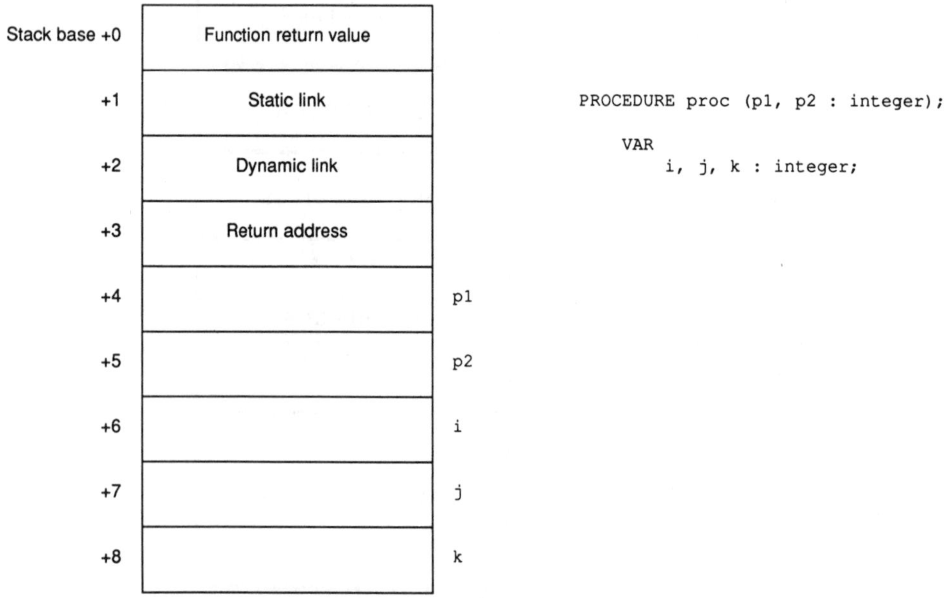

Stack base +0	Function return value
+1	Static link
+2	Dynamic link
+3	Return address
+4	p1
+5	p2
+6	i
+7	j
+8	k

```
PROCEDURE proc (p1, p2 : integer);

    VAR
        i, j, k : integer;
```

When you return from a procedure, you simply reset the top of stack pointer to the item just below the procedure's stack frame base. This puts the pointer back to where it was just before the call. When you return from a function, you reset the top of stack pointer to the item at the base of the function's stack frame. This has the effect of pushing the function return value onto the stack for the caller to use.

9.1.4 Static links

The static link of a routine's stack frame points back to the base of the stack frame of the routine that it is immediately contained in. For example, suppose procedure p1 contains procedure p2 in the source program, and p2 is currently executing. Then, the static link of p2's stack frame points back to the base of p1's stack frame. Thus, while the dynamic links are determined by who *calls* whom at runtime, the static links are determined by who *contains* whom in the source program.

Figure 9-3 shows a program with a nontrivial nesting structure. Figure 9-4 shows how the dynamic and static links change as the program's procedures and functions call each other. As you can see, the dynamic links (drawn on the left) always point back to the stack frame of the caller. The static links are more interesting to watch.

FIGURE 9-3   The outline of a program with nested procedures and functions.

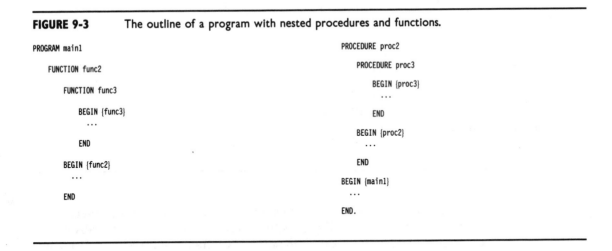

In Figure 9-4a, when main calls proc2, proc2's static link points back to main's stack frame, since main immediately contains proc2. Similarly, in Figure 9-4b, when proc2 calls proc3, proc3's static link points back to proc2's stack frame, since proc2 immediately contains proc3. Suppose proc3 recursively calls itself. Then, as in Figure 9-4c, the static link in proc3's new stack frame also points back to proc2's stack frame.

FIGURE 9-4   How the runtime stack changes during the execution of the program shown in Figure 9-3. In each stack diagram, we draw the dynamic links on the left and the static links on the right. Each link actually points to the base of a previous stack frame. The stack grows downward in this figure, so the top of the stack is at the bottom of each diagram.

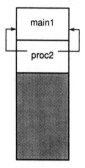

a. main1 > proc2

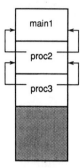

b. main1 > proc2 > proc3

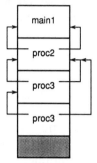

c. main1 > proc2 > proc3 > proc3

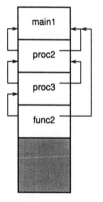

d. main1 > proc2 > proc3 > func2

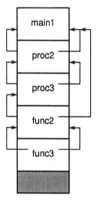

e. main1 > proc2 > proc3 > func2 > func3

When proc3 returns from the recursive call, the runtime stack resets to its previous state, as we saw in Figure 9-4b. In Figure 9-4d, proc3 then calls func2, and func2's static link points back to main's stack frame, since main immediately contains func2. Finally, in Figure 9-4e, when func2 calls func3, func3's static link points back to func2's stack frame, since func2 immediately contains func3.

That is a bit of work to keep track of the static links, and what are they good for? The static links enable us to access nonlocal values. In Figure 9-4e, you are executing func3. Certainly, you can access func3's parameter and local variable values, since they are all allocated in func3's stack frame. If you follow the static link back to func2's stack frame, you can also access func2's values. Then if you follow the static link from func2's stack frame back to main's stack frame, you can access main's values. However, from func3, you cannot access any of proc3's or proc2's values. If you look again at Figure 9-3, you see that you are following Pascal's scope rules. Similarly, in Figure 9-4c, from proc3's second invocation, you cannot access the values from its first invocation.

So, you see that accessing nonlocal values is slower than accessing local values, since you have to follow static links to get to them. How much slower depends on how many links you follow.

9.2 Organization of the interpreter

Now we are ready to start writing the routines to do all this. Let's start with a look at the overall organization our interpreter thus far.

Parser Module

parser.h	*u*	Parser header file
routine.c	*c*	Parse programs, procedures, and functions
standard.c	*u*	Parse standard procedures and functions
decl.c	*c*	Parse declarations
stmt.c	*c*	Parse statements
expr.c	*u*	Parse expressions

Scanner Module

scanner.h	*u*	Scanner header file
scanner.c	*u*	Scanner routines

Symbol Table Module

symtab.h	*u*	Symbol table header file
symtab.c	*u*	Symbol table routines

Executor Module

exec.h	*n*	Executor header file
executil.c	*n*	Executor utility routines
execstmt.c	*n*	Execute statements
execexpr.c	*n*	Execute expressions

Error Module

error.h	*c*	Error header file
error.c	*c*	Error routines

Miscellaneous

common.h	*c*	Common header file

Where: *u* file unchanged from the previous chapter
        c file changed from the previous chapter
        n new file

We make a small change in file decl.c to calculate the runtime stack offsets for local variables, and a few changes in stmt.c to add new information to the intermediate form. We change routine.c to calculate stack offsets for parameters and to start the program execution. We add runtime error handling to error.h and error.c. The executor module files are all new. We add two new constants to file common.h:

```
#define MAX_STACK_SIZE          1024
#define STACK_FRAME_HEADER_SIZE 4
```

The first constant is the size (in stack items) of the runtime stack that we will allocate before executing the program. The second constant is the size of the stack frame header. We also define a new type:

```
typedef char *ADDRESS;
```

9.2.1 Runtime error handling

Up until now, the error module has handled only syntax errors that we detect during parsing. An interpreter, as it executes a program, must also detect runtime errors. In file error.h, we add the following enumeration type that represents the runtime errors that our interpreter will be able to detect:

```
typedef enum {
    RUNTIME_STACK_OVERFLOW,
    VALUE_OUT_OF_RANGE,
    INVALID_CASE_VALUE,
    DIVISION_BY_ZERO,
    INVALID_FUNCTION_ARGUMENT,
    UNIMPLEMENTED_RUNTIME_FEATURE,
} RUNTIME_ERROR_CODE;
```

Then, of course, we need to add the corresponding string array to file error.c:

```
char *runtime_error_messages[] = {
    "Runtime stack overflow",
    "Value out of range",
    "Invalid CASE expression value",
    "Division by zero",
```

```
                    "Invalid standard function argument",
                              "Unimplemented runtime feature",
                    };
```

Figure 9-5 shows a new function `runtime_error` in `error.c`, which routines in the executor module call to flag runtime errors. The two variables `exec_line_number` and `exec_stmt_count` are defined in the executor module, and they are the line number of the last statement executed (the one that caused the error) and the number of statements executed, respectively. In this version of `runtime_error`, a runtime error aborts the program execution. When we write our debugger in Chapter 11, a new version will enable us to interactively correct the error.

FIGURE 9-5   Function `runtime_error` in file `error.c`.

```
/*-------------------------------------------------------*/      char      *message = runtime_error_messages[code];
/* runtime_error      Print a runtime error message and then  */  extern int  exec_line_number;
/*                    abort the program execution.         */   extern long exec_stmt_count;
/*-------------------------------------------------------*/
                                                                 printf("\n*** RUNTIME ERROR in line %d: %s\n",
runtime_error(code)                                                      exec_line_number, message);
                                                                 printf("\nUnsuccessful completion.  %ld statements executed.\n\n",
    ERROR_CODE code;     /* error code */                               exec_stmt_count);
                                                                 exit(-code);
{                                                            }
```

9.2.2 Symbol table changes

Figure 9-6 shows the new version of function `var_declarations` in file `decl.c`. When `var_declarations` calls `var_or_field_declarations`, the third parameter is the runtime stack offset value for the first local variable. This value is the value of STACK_FRAME_HEADER_SIZE plus the number of formal parameters, as shown in Figure 9-2. We recall that when function `record_type` calls `var_or_field_dec-larations`, it passes zero as the initial offset value.

FIGURE 9-6   Function `var_declarations` in file `decl.c`.

```
/*-------------------------------------------------------*/      SYMTAB_NODE_PTR rtn_idp;    /* id of program or routine */
/* var_declarations    Process variable declarations:     */
/*                                                         */   {
/*                    <id-list> : <type>                   */       var_or_field_declarations(rtn_idp, NULL,
/*-------------------------------------------------------*/                              STACK_FRAME_HEADER_SIZE
                                                                                        + rtn_idp->defn.info.routine
                                                                                          .parm_count);
var_declarations(rtn_idp)                                    }
```

Now the reason for the offset field in the symbol table nodes becomes clear. For record fields, the offsets are byte offsets from the beginning of the record. Therefore, we increment parameter offset each time by the size of each field. For variables, the offsets are stack item offsets from the stack frame base, and since the stack items are all one size, we increment offset each time by one.

Figure 9-7 shows a new version of function formal_parm_list in file routine.c, which contains two small changes. We now initialize parm_offset to STACK_FRAME_HEADER_SIZE, since that is the offset of the first parameter (again, see Figure 9-2). As before, we assign the offset to the symbol table node for each parameter, and we increment offset by one each time. The other change is near the end of the function. The total size (in stack items) of all the formal parameters is the final offset value minus STACK_FRAME_HEADER_SIZE.

FIGURE 9-7   Function formal_parm_list in file routine.c.

```
/*----------------------------------------------------------*/
/*  formal_parm_list    Process a formal parameter list:    */
/*                                                          */
/*                      ( VAR <id-list> : <type> ;          */
/*                        <id-list> : <type> ;              */
/*                        ... )                             */
/*                                                          */
/*                      Return a pointer to the head of the */
/*                      parameter id list.                  */
/*----------------------------------------------------------*/

    SYMTAB_NODE_PTR
formal_parm_list(countp, total_sizep)

    int *countp;        /* ptr to count of parameters */
    int *total_sizep;   /* ptr to total byte size of parameters */

{
    SYMTAB_NODE_PTR parm_idp, first_idp, last_idp;   /* parm ids */
    SYMTAB_NODE_PTR prev_last_idp = NULL;       /* last id of list */
    SYMTAB_NODE_PTR parm_listp = NULL;          /* parm list */
    SYMTAB_NODE_PTR type_idp;                   /* type id */
    TYPE_STRUCT_PTR parm_tp;                    /* parm type */
    DEFN_KEY        parm_defn;                  /* parm definition */
    int             parm_count = 0;             /* count of parms */
    int             parm_offset = STACK_FRAME_HEADER_SIZE;

    get_token();

    /*
    -- Loop to process parameter declarations separated by ;
    */
    while ((token == IDENTIFIER) || (token == VAR)) {
        first_idp = NULL;

        /*
        -- VAR parms?
        */
        if (token == VAR) {
            parm_defn = VARPARM_DEFN;
            get_token();
        }
        else parm_defn = VALPARM_DEFN;
```

```
    /*
    -- <id list>
    */
    while (token == IDENTIFIER) {
        search_and_enter_local_symtab(parm_idp);
        parm_idp->defn.key   = parm_defn;
        parm_idp->label_index = 0;
        ++parm_count;

        if (parm_listp == NULL) parm_listp = parm_idp;

        /*
        -- Link parm ids together.
        */
        if (first_idp == NULL)
            first_idp = last_idp = parm_idp;
        else {
            last_idp->next = parm_idp;
            last_idp = parm_idp;
        }

        get_token();
        if_token_get(COMMA);
    }

    if_token_get_else_error(COLON, MISSING_COLON);

    if (token == IDENTIFIER) {
        search_and_find_all_symtab(type_idp);
        if (type_idp->defn.key != TYPE_DEFN) error(INVALID_TYPE);
        parm_tp = type_idp->typep;
        get_token();
    }
    else {
        error(MISSING_IDENTIFIER);
        parm_tp = &dummy_type;
    }

    /*
    -- Assign the offset and the type to all parm ids
    -- in the sublist.
    */
    for (parm_idp = first_idp;
         parm_idp != NULL;
```

```
        parm_idp = parm_idp->next) {              -- Error synchronization:  Should be ; or )
        parm_idp->typep = parm_tp;             */
        parm_idp->defn.info.data.offset = parm_offset++;    synchronize(follow_parms_list, NULL, NULL);
    }                                                  if_token_get(SEMICOLON);
                                                   }
    /*
    -- Link this list to the list of all parm ids.    if_token_get_else_error(RPAREN, MISSING_RPAREN);
    */                                             *countp = parm_count;
    if (prev_last_idp != NULL) prev_last_idp->next = first_idp;    *total_sizep = parm_offset - STACK_FRAME_HEADER_SIZE;
    prev_last_idp = last_idp;

    /*                                             return(parm_listp);

                                                 }
```

9.2.3 The runtime stack routines

Figure 9-8 shows the header file exec.h of the new executor module. We define
two structures for the runtime stack. Union STACK_ITEM shows that each stack
item is either an integer, a real, a byte, or an address. Structure STACK_FRAME_
HEADER represents the items that make up the stack frame header.

FIGURE 9-8   File exec.h.

```
/*****************************************************************/    /*-----------------------------------------------------------*/
/*                                                          */
/*        E X E C U T O R     (Header)                      */    SYMTAB_NODE_PTR get_symtab_cptr();
/*                                                          */    int             get_statement_cmarker();
/*    FILE:      exec.h                                     */    TYPE_STRUCT_PTR exec_routine_call();
/*                                                          */    TYPE_STRUCT_PTR exec_expression(), exec_variable();
/*    MODULE:    executor                                   */
/*                                                          */             /***********************/
/*****************************************************************/         /*                     */
                                                                           /*      Macros         */
#ifndef exec_h                                                             /*                     */
#define exec_h                                                             /***********************/

#include "common.h"                                               /*-----------------------------------------------------------*/
                                                                  /*  get_ctoken     Extract the next token code from the    */
#define STATEMENT_MARKER 0x70                                     /*                 current code segment.                   */
                                                                  /*-----------------------------------------------------------*/
/*-----------------------------------------------------*/
/*  Runtime stack                                    */        #define get_ctoken()    ctoken = *code_segmentp++
/*-----------------------------------------------------*/
                                                                  /*-----------------------------------------------------------*/
typedef union {                                                   /*  pop            Pop the runtime stack.                  */
    int     integer;                                              /*-----------------------------------------------------------*/
    float   real;
    char    byte;                                                 #define pop()           --tos
    ADDRESS address;
} STACK_ITEM, *STACK_ITEM_PTR;                                    /*-----------------------------------------------------------*/
                                                                  /*  Tracing routine calls    Unless the following statements */
typedef struct {                                                  /*                           are preceded by                 */
    STACK_ITEM function_value;                                    /*                                                           */
    STACK_ITEM static_link;                                       /*                                  #define trace             */
    STACK_ITEM dynamic_link;                                      /*                                                           */
    STACK_ITEM return_address;                                    /*                           calls to the tracing routines   */
} *STACK_FRAME_HEADER_PTR;                                        /*                           are not compiled.               */
                                                                  /*-----------------------------------------------------------*/
/*-----------------------------------------------------*/
/*  Functions                                        */        #ifndef trace
```

```
#define trace_routine_entry(idp)
#define trace_routine_exit(idp)
#define trace_statement_execution()
#define trace_data_store(idp, idp_tp, targetp, target_tp)
```

```
#define trace_data_fetch(idp, tp, datap)
#endif


#endif
```

The significance of the STATEMENT_MARKER constant is explained later. Macros get_ctoken and pop are from the pretty-printer in Chapter 8 and the calculator in Chapter 4, respectively. We will explain the tracing macros at the end of this chapter.

Most of the routines that manipulate the runtime stack are in file executil.c, shown in Figure 9-9. Several important new global variables are declared in this file, namely, the runtime stack, the top of stack pointer tos, and the pointer to the current stack frame base stack_frame_basep. An important old global variable is code_segmentp, which points to a location in the code segment. During program execution, it points to the current token in the intermediate code.

FIGURE 9-9   File executil.c.

```
/****************************************************************/
/*                                                              */
/*          E X E C U T O R   U T I L I T I E S                 */
/*                                                              */
/*          Utility routines for the executor module.           */
/*                                                              */
/*          FILE:       executil.c                              */
/*                                                              */
/*          MODULE:     executor                                */
/*                                                              */
/****************************************************************/

#include <stdio.h>
#include "common.h"
#include "error.h"
#include "symtab.h"
#include "scanner.h"
#include "exec.h"

/*----------------------------------------------------------*/
/* Externals                                                */
/*----------------------------------------------------------*/

extern TOKEN_CODE token;
extern int       line_number;
extern int       level;

extern TYPE_STRUCT_PTR integer_typep, real_typep,
                       boolean_typep, char_typep;

/*----------------------------------------------------------*/
/* Globals                                                  */
/*----------------------------------------------------------*/

char *code_buffer;          /* code buffer */
char *code_bufferp;         /* code buffer ptr */
char *code_segmentp;        /* code segment ptr */
char *code_segment_limit;   /* end of code segment */
char *statement_startp;     /* ptr to start of stmt */
```

```
TOKEN_CODE     ctoken;            /* token from code segment */
int            exec_line_number;  /* no. of line executed */
long           exec_stmt_count = 0; /* count of stmts executed */

STACK_ITEM     *stack;            /* runtime stack */
STACK_ITEM_PTR tos;               /* ptr to runtime stack top */
STACK_ITEM_PTR stack_frame_basep; /* ptr to stack frame base */

             /********************************/
             /*                              */
             /*      Code segment routines   */
             /*                              */
             /********************************/

/*----------------------------------------------------------*/
/* crunch_token       Append the token code to the code     */
/*                    buffer.  Called by the scanner routine */
/*                    get_token only while parsing a block.  */
/*----------------------------------------------------------*/

crunch_token()

{
    char token_code = token;     /* byte-sized token code */

    if (code_bufferp >= code_buffer + MAX_CODE_BUFFER_SIZE) {
        error(CODE_SEGMENT_OVERFLOW);
        exit(-CODE_SEGMENT_OVERFLOW);
    }
    else *code_bufferp++ = token_code;
}


/*----------------------------------------------------------*/
/* crunch_symtab_node_ptr     Append a symbol table node    */
/*                            pointer to the code buffer.    */
/*----------------------------------------------------------*/

crunch_symtab_node_ptr(np)
```

```
    SYMTAB_NODE_PTR np;          /* pointer to append */

{
    SYMTAB_NODE_PTR *npp = (SYMTAB_NODE_PTR *) code_bufferp;

    if (code_bufferp >= code_buffer + MAX_CODE_BUFFER_SIZE
                                - sizeof(SYMTAB_NODE_PTR)) {
        error(CODE_SEGMENT_OVERFLOW);
        exit(-CODE_SEGMENT_OVERFLOW);
    }
    else {
        *npp = np;
        code_bufferp += sizeof(SYMTAB_NODE_PTR);
    }
}

/*------------------------------------------------------*/
/* crunch_statement_marker    Append a statement marker to  */
/*                            the code buffer.              */
/*------------------------------------------------------*/

crunch_statement_marker()

{
    if (code_bufferp >= code_buffer + MAX_CODE_BUFFER_SIZE
                                - sizeof(int)) {
        error(CODE_SEGMENT_OVERFLOW);
        exit(-CODE_SEGMENT_OVERFLOW);
    }
    else {
        char save_code = *(--code_bufferp);

        *code_bufferp++ = STATEMENT_MARKER;
        *((int *) code_bufferp) = line_number;
        code_bufferp += sizeof(int);
        *code_bufferp++ = save_code;
    }
}

/*------------------------------------------------------*/
/* create_code_segment    Create a code segment and copy in   */
/*                        the contents of the code buffer.    */
/*                        Reset the code buffer pointer.      */
/*                        Return a pointer to the segment.    */
/*------------------------------------------------------*/

    char *
create_code_segment()

{
    char *code_segment = alloc_bytes(code_bufferp - code_buffer);

    code_segment_limit = code_segment + (code_bufferp - code_buffer);
    code_bufferp      = code_buffer;
    code_segmentp     = code_segment;

    /*
    -- Copy in the contents of the code buffer.
    */
    while (code_segmentp != code_segment_limit)
        *code_segmentp++ = *code_bufferp++;

    code_bufferp = code_buffer;         /* reset code buffer ptr */
    return(code_segment);
}

/*------------------------------------------------------*/
/* get_symtab_cptr    Extract a symbol table node pointer   */
```

```
/*                      from the current code segment and       */
/*                      return it.                              */
/*------------------------------------------------------*/

    SYMTAB_NODE_PTR
get_symtab_cptr()

{
    SYMTAB_NODE_PTR np;
    SYMTAB_NODE_PTR *npp = (SYMTAB_NODE_PTR *) code_segmentp;

    np = *npp;
    code_segmentp += sizeof(SYMTAB_NODE_PTR);
    return(np);
}

/*------------------------------------------------------*/
/* get_statement_cmarker    Extract a statement marker from the */
/*                          current code segment and return its */
/*                          statement line number.             */
/*------------------------------------------------------*/

    int
get_statement_cmarker()

{
    int line_num;

    if (ctoken == STATEMENT_MARKER) {
        line_num = *((int *) code_segmentp);
        code_segmentp += sizeof(int);
    }

    return(line_num);
}

                /********************************/
                /*                            */
                /*       Executor utilities    */
                /*                            */
                /********************************/

/*------------------------------------------------------*/
/* push_integer      Push an integer onto the runtime stack. */
/*------------------------------------------------------*/

push_integer(item_value)

    int item_value;

{
    STACK_ITEM_PTR itemp = ++tos;

    if (itemp >= &stack[MAX_STACK_SIZE])
        runtime_error(RUNTIME_STACK_OVERFLOW);

    itemp->integer = item_value;
}

/*------------------------------------------------------*/
/* push_real          Push a real onto the runtime stack.    */
/*------------------------------------------------------*/

push_real(item_value)

    float item_value;
```

```
{
    STACK_ITEM_PTR itemp = ++tos;

    if (itemp >= &stack[MAX_STACK_SIZE])
        runtime_error(RUNTIME_STACK_OVERFLOW);

    itemp->real = item_value;
}

/*-----------------------------------------------------*/
/* push_byte          Push a byte onto the runtime stack.   */
/*-----------------------------------------------------*/

push_byte(item_value)

    char item_value;

{
    STACK_ITEM_PTR itemp = ++tos;

    if (itemp >= &stack[MAX_STACK_SIZE])
        runtime_error(RUNTIME_STACK_OVERFLOW);

    itemp->byte = item_value;
}

/*-----------------------------------------------------*/
/* push_address       Push an address onto the runtime stack. */
/*-----------------------------------------------------*/

push_address(address)

    ADDRESS address;

{
    STACK_ITEM_PTR itemp = ++tos;

    if (itemp >= &stack[MAX_STACK_SIZE])
        runtime_error(RUNTIME_STACK_OVERFLOW);

    itemp->address = address;
}

/*-----------------------------------------------------*/
/* execute            Execute a routine's code segment.     */
/*-----------------------------------------------------*/

execute(rtn_idp)

    SYMTAB_NODE_PTR rtn_idp;

{
    routine_entry(rtn_idp);

    get_ctoken();
    exec_statement();

    routine_exit(rtn_idp);
}

/*-----------------------------------------------------*/
/* routine_entry      Point to the new routine's code       */
/*                    segment, and allocate its locals.     */
/*-----------------------------------------------------*/

routine_entry(rtn_idp)
```

```
    SYMTAB_NODE_PTR rtn_idp;     /* new routine's id */

{
    SYMTAB_NODE_PTR var_idp;     /* local variable id */

    trace_routine_entry(rtn_idp);

    /*
    -- Switch to the new code segment.
    */
    code_segmentp = rtn_idp->defn.info.routine.code_segment;

    /*
    -- Allocate local variables.
    */
    for (var_idp = rtn_idp->defn.info.routine.locals;
         var_idp != NULL;
         var_idp = var_idp->next) alloc_local(var_idp->typep);
}

/*-----------------------------------------------------*/
/* routine_exit       Deallocate the routine's parameters and */
/*                    locals.  Cut off its stack frame, and   */
/*                    return to the caller's code segment.    */
/*-----------------------------------------------------*/

routine_exit(rtn_idp)

    SYMTAB_NODE_PTR rtn_idp;        /* exiting routine's id */

{
    SYMTAB_NODE_PTR      idp;       /* variable or parm id */
    STACK_FRAME_HEADER_PTR hp;      /* ptr to stack frame header */

    trace_routine_exit(rtn_idp);

    /*
    -- Deallocate parameters and local variables.
    */
    for (idp = rtn_idp->defn.info.routine.parms;
         idp != NULL;
         idp = idp->next) free_data(idp);
    for (idp = rtn_idp->defn.info.routine.locals;
         idp != NULL;
         idp = idp->next) free_data(idp);

    /*
    -- Pop off the stack frame and return to the
    -- caller's code segment.
    */
    hp = (STACK_FRAME_HEADER_PTR) stack_frame_basep;
    code_segmentp = hp->return_address.address;
    tos = (rtn_idp->defn.key == PROC_DEFN)
              ? stack_frame_basep - 1
              : stack_frame_basep;
    stack_frame_basep = (STACK_ITEM_PTR) hp->dynamic_link.address;
}

/*-----------------------------------------------------*/
/* push_stack_frame_header    Allocate the callee routine's  */
/*                            stack frame.                   */
/*-----------------------------------------------------*/

push_stack_frame_header(old_level, new_level)

    int old_level, new_level;  /* levels of caller and callee */

{
```

```
STACK_FRAME_HEADER_PTR hp;

push_integer(0);                            /* return value */
hp = (STACK_FRAME_HEADER_PTR) stack_frame_basep;

/*
-- Static link.
*/
if (new_level == old_level + 1) {
    /*
    -- Calling a routine nested within the caller:
    -- Push pointer to caller's stack frame.
    */
    push_address(hp);
}
else if (new_level == old_level) {
    /*
    -- Calling another routine at the same level:
    -- Push pointer to stack frame of common parent.
    */
    push_address(hp->static_link.address);
}
else  /* new_level < old_level */  {
    /*
    -- Calling a routine at a lesser level (nested less deeply):
    -- Push pointer to stack frame of nearest common ancestor.
    */
    int delta = old_level - new_level;

    while (delta-- >= 0)
        hp = (STACK_FRAME_HEADER_PTR) hp->static_link.address;
    push_address(hp);
}

push_address(stack_frame_basep);            /* dynamic link */
push_address(0);    /* return address to be filled in later */
}

/*-------------------------------------------------------------*/
/*  alloc_local       Allocate a local variable on the stack.  */
/*-------------------------------------------------------------*/

alloc_local(tp)

    TYPE_STRUCT_PTR tp;     /* ptr to type of variable */

{
    if      (tp == integer_typep) push_integer(0);
```

```
    else if (tp == real_typep)    push_real(0.0);
    else if (tp == boolean_typep) push_byte(0);
    else if (tp == char_typep)    push_byte(0);

    else switch (tp->form) {
        case ENUM_FORM:
            push_integer(0);
            break;

        case SUBRANGE_FORM:
            alloc_local(tp->info.subrange.range_typep);
            break;

        case ARRAY_FORM: {
            char *ptr = alloc_bytes(tp->size);

            push_address((ADDRESS) ptr);
            break;
        }

        case RECORD_FORM: {
            char *ptr = alloc_bytes(tp->size);

            push_address((ADDRESS) ptr);
            break;
        }
    }
}

/*-------------------------------------------------------------*/
/*  free_data         Deallocate the data area of an array     */
/*                    or record local variable or value        */
/*                    parameter.                                */
/*-------------------------------------------------------------*/

free_data(idp)

    SYMTAB_NODE_PTR idp;                /* parm or variable id */

{
    STACK_ITEM_PTR  itemp;              /* ptr to stack item */
    TYPE_STRUCT_PTR tp = idp->typep;    /* ptr to id's type */

    if (   ((tp->form == ARRAY_FORM) || (tp->form == RECORD_FORM))
        && (idp->defn.key != VARPARM_DEFN)) {
        itemp = stack_frame_basep + idp->defn.info.data.offset;
        free(itemp->address);
    }
}
```

You can recognize several of the file's functions from the pretty-printer. New functions include push_integer, push_real, push_byte, and push_address, each of which pushes a stack item of a given type onto the runtime stack. In each function, we first check for a stack overflow, and we call runtime_error if one occurs. The other functions in the file are explained later.

9.3 Interpreting procedure and function calls

Now we are ready to write more of the executor module and to start executing source programs!

9.3.1 Executing programs, procedures, and functions

At the beginning of file routine.c, we must add:

```
#include "exec.h"
```

We also need:

```
extern int          line_number;
extern int          error_count;
extern long         exec_stmt_count;

extern STACK_ITEM       *stack;
extern STACK_ITEM_PTR   tos;
extern STACK_ITEM_PTR   stack_frame_basep;
```

Figure 9-10 shows a new version of routine program in routine.c. We first parse the Pascal source program, as before. With the modifications to the scanner and parser that we made in the previous chapter, we also create code segments containing intermediate code. Now, if there are no syntax errors, we want to execute the source program.

FIGURE 9-10   Function program in file routine.c.

```
/*----------------------------------------------------------*/
/* program      Process a program:                          */
/*                                                          */
/*                <program-header> ; <block> .              */
/*----------------------------------------------------------*/

TOKEN_CODE follow_header_list[] = {SEMICOLON, END_OF_FILE, 0};

program()

{
    SYMTAB_NODE_PTR program_idp;        /* program id */

    /*
    --                PARSE THE PROGRAM
    --
    --
    -- Intialize the symbol table and then allocate
    -- the code buffer.
    */
    init_symtab();
    code_buffer  = alloc_bytes(MAX_CODE_BUFFER_SIZE);
    code_bufferp = code_buffer;

    /*
    -- Begin parsing with the program header.
    */
    program_idp = program_header();

    /*
    -- Error synchronization:  Should be ;
```

```
    */
    synchronize(follow_header_list,
                declaration_start_list, statement_start_list);
    if_token_get(SEMICOLON);
    else if (token_in(declaration_start_list) ||
             token_in(statement_start_list))
        error(MISSING_SEMICOLON);

    analyze_routine_header(program_idp);

    /*
    -- Parse the program's block.
    */
    program_idp->defn.info.routine.locals = NULL;
    block(program_idp);

    program_idp->defn.info.routine.local_symtab = exit_scope();
    program_idp->defn.info.routine.code_segment = create_code_segment();
    analyze_block(program_idp->defn.info.routine.code_segment);

    if_token_get_else_error(PERIOD, MISSING_PERIOD);

    /*
    -- Look for the end of file.
    */
    while (token != END_OF_FILE) {
        error(UNEXPECTED_TOKEN);
        get_token();
    }

    quit_scanner();
```

```
free(code_buffer);

/*
-- Print the parser's summary.
*/
print_line("\n");
print_line("\n");
sprintf(buffer, "%20d Source lines.\n", line_number);
print_line(buffer);
sprintf(buffer, "%20d Source errors.\n", error_count);
print_line(buffer);

if (error_count > 0) exit(-SYNTAX_ERROR);
else                 printf("%c\n", FORM_FEED_CHAR);

/*
--                  EXECUTE THE PROGRAM
--
--
-- Allocate the runtime stack.
*/
stack = alloc_array(STACK_ITEM, MAX_STACK_SIZE);
```

```
    stack_frame_basep = tos = stack;

    /*
    -- Initialize the program's stack frame.
    */
    level = 1;
    stack_frame_basep = tos + 1;
    push_integer(0);       /* function return value */
    push_address(NULL);    /* static link */
    push_address(NULL);    /* dynamic link */
    push_address(NULL);    /* return address */

    /*
    -- Go!
    */
    execute(program_idp);

    free(stack);
    printf("\n\nSuccessful completion.  %ld statements executed.\n\n",
           exec_stmt_count);
    exit(0);
}
```

We begin to execute the source program by allocating the runtime stack. Then, we initialize stack_frame_basep and tos to point to the bottom of the stack. We set level to one, the nesting level of the program's global variables, and then we allocate the program's stack frame header at the bottom of the stack.

We call function execute to execute the source program, passing a pointer to the program identifier's symbol table node. This important function, which we will examine later, can execute the Pascal main program, a procedure, or a function. Like our pretty-printer, it works with the intermediate code in a code segment.

9.3.2 Calling a Pascal procedure or function

Before we study further how we execute a Pascal procedure or function, you need to see how to call such a routine. In the following description, we'll use the term "callee" to refer to the called procedure or function to distinguish it from its caller. First, you allocate the callee's new stack frame on top of the runtime stack (first the stack header, then the parameters followed by the local variables), and then you execute the callee's statements. When you are ready to return to the caller, you pop off the new stack frame.

Figure 9-11 shows file execstmt.c of the executor module. This file is analogous to file stmt.c of the parser module.

FIGURE 9-11   File execstmt.c.

```
/**************************************************************/
/*                                                            */
/*       S T A T E M E N T   E X E C U T O R                  */
/*                                                            */
/*       Execution routines for statements.                  */
/*                                                            */
/*       FILE:       execstmt.c                               */
/*                                                            */
/*       MODULE:     executor                                 */
/*                                                            */
/**************************************************************/

#include <stdio.h>
#include "common.h"
#include "error.h"
#include "symtab.h"
#include "scanner.h"
#include "parser.h"
#include "exec.h"

/*----------------------------------------------------------*/
/* Externals                                                */
/*----------------------------------------------------------*/

extern int          level;
extern int          exec_line_number;
extern long         exec_stmt_count;

extern char         *code_segmentp;
extern char         *statement_startp;
extern TOKEN_CODE   ctoken;

extern STACK_ITEM     *stack;
extern STACK_ITEM_PTR tos;
extern STACK_ITEM_PTR stack_frame_basep;

extern TYPE_STRUCT_PTR integer_typep, real_typep,
                       boolean_typep, char_typep;

/*----------------------------------------------------------*/
/* exec_statement      Execute a statement by calling the   */
/*                     appropriate execution routine.       */
/*----------------------------------------------------------*/

exec_statement()

{
    if (ctoken == STATEMENT_MARKER) {
        exec_line_number = get_statement_cmarker();
        ++exec_stmt_count;

        statement_startp = code_segmentp;
        trace_statement_execution();
        get_ctoken();
    }

    switch (ctoken) {

        case IDENTIFIER: {
            SYMTAB_NODE_PTR idp = get_symtab_cptr();

            if (idp->defn.key == PROC_DEFN)
                exec_routine_call(idp);
            else
```

```
                exec_assignment_statement(idp);

                break;
        }

        case BEGIN:    exec_compound_statement();     break;
        case END:      break;

        default:  runtime_error(UNIMPLEMENTED_RUNTIME_FEATURE);
    }

    while (ctoken == SEMICOLON) get_ctoken();
}

/*----------------------------------------------------------*/
/* exec_assignment_statement      Execute an assignment     */
/*                                statement.                */
/*----------------------------------------------------------*/

exec_assignment_statement(idp)

    SYMTAB_NODE_PTR idp;          /* target variable id */

{
    STACK_ITEM_PTR  targetp;      /* ptr to assignment target */
    TYPE_STRUCT_PTR target_tp, base_target_tp, expr_tp;

    /*
    -- Assignment to function id:  Target is the first item of
    --                             the appropriate stack frame.
    */

    if (idp->defn.key == FUNC_DEFN) {
        STACK_FRAME_HEADER_PTR hp;
        int                    delta;   /* difference in levels */

        hp    = (STACK_FRAME_HEADER_PTR) stack_frame_basep;
        delta = level - idp->level - 1;
        while (delta-- > 0)
            hp = (STACK_FRAME_HEADER_PTR) hp->static_link.address;

        targetp = (STACK_ITEM_PTR) hp;
        target_tp = idp->typep;
        get_ctoken();
    }

    /*
    -- Assignment to variable:  Routine exec_variable leaves the
    --                          target address on top of stack.
    */
    else {
        target_tp = exec_variable(idp, TARGET_USE);
        targetp  = (STACK_ITEM_PTR) tos->address;

        pop();            /* pop off target address */
    }

    base_target_tp = base_type(target_tp);

    /*
    -- Routine exec_expression leaves the expression value
    -- on top of stack.
    */
    get_ctoken();
```

```
expr_tp = exec_expression();

/*
-- Do the assignment.
*/
if ((target_tp == real_typep) &&
    (base_type(expr_tp) == integer_typep)) {
    /*
    -- real := integer
    */
    targetp->real = tos->integer;
}
else if ((target_tp->form == ARRAY_FORM) ||
         (target_tp->form == RECORD_FORM)) {
    /*
    -- array  := array
    -- record := record
    */
    char *ptr1 = (char *) targetp;
    char *ptr2 = tos->address;
    int size = target_tp->size;

    while (size--) *ptr1++ = *ptr2++;
}
else if ((base_target_tp == integer_typep) ||
         (target_tp->form == ENUM_FORM)) {
    /*
    -- Range check assignment to integer
    -- or enumeration subrange.
    */
    if (   (target_tp->form == SUBRANGE_FORM)
        && ((tos->integer < target_tp->info.subrange.min) ||
            (tos->integer > target_tp->info.subrange.max)))
        runtime_error(VALUE_OUT_OF_RANGE);
    /*
    -- integer     := integer
    -- enumeration := enumeration
    */
    targetp->integer = tos->integer;
}
else if (base_target_tp == char_typep) {
    /*
    -- Range check assigment to character subrange.
    */
    if (   (target_tp->form == SUBRANGE_FORM)
        && ((tos->byte < target_tp->info.subrange.min) ||
            (tos->byte > target_tp->info.subrange.max)))
        runtime_error(VALUE_OUT_OF_RANGE);
    /*
    -- character := character
    */
    targetp->byte = tos->byte;
}
else {
    /*
    -- real := real
    */
    targetp->real = tos->real;
}

pop();      /* pop off expression value */

trace_data_store(idp, idp->typep, targetp, target_tp);
}

/*-----------------------------------------------------------*/
/* exec_routine_call          Execute a procedure or function */
```

```
/*                               call.  Return a pointer to the */
/*                               type structure.               */
/*-----------------------------------------------------------*/

    TYPE_STRUCT_PTR
exec_routine_call(rtn_idp)

    SYMTAB_NODE_PTR rtn_idp;    /* routine id */

{
    TYPE_STRUCT_PTR exec_declared_routine_call();
    TYPE_STRUCT_PTR exec_standard_routine_call();

    if (rtn_idp->defn.info.routine.key == DECLARED)
        return(exec_declared_routine_call(rtn_idp));
    else
        return(exec_standard_routine_call(rtn_idp));
}

/*-----------------------------------------------------------*/
/* exec_declared_routine_call     Execute a call to a         */
/*                                declared procedure or       */
/*                                function.  Return a pointer */
/*                                to the type structure.      */
/*-----------------------------------------------------------*/

    TYPE_STRUCT_PTR
exec_declared_routine_call(rtn_idp)

    SYMTAB_NODE_PTR rtn_idp;                /* routine id */

{
    int old_level = level;               /* level of caller */
    int new_level = rtn_idp->level + 1;  /* level of callee */
    STACK_ITEM_PTR new_stack_frame_basep;
    STACK_FRAME_HEADER_PTR hp;           /* ptr to frame header */

    /*
    -- Set up stack frame of callee.
    */
    new_stack_frame_basep = tos + 1;
    push_stack_frame_header(old_level, new_level);

    /*
    -- Push parameter values onto the stack.
    */
    get_ctoken();
    if (ctoken == LPAREN) {
        exec_actual_parms(rtn_idp);
        get_ctoken();   /* token after ) */
    }

    /*
    -- Set the return address in the new stack frame,
    -- and execute the callee.
    */
    level = new_level;
    stack_frame_basep = new_stack_frame_basep;
    hp = (STACK_FRAME_HEADER_PTR) stack_frame_basep;
    hp->return_address.address = code_segmentp - 1;
    execute(rtn_idp);

    /*
    -- Return from callee.
    */
    level = old_level;
    get_ctoken();       /* first token after return */
```

```
        return(rtn_idp->defn.key == PROC_DEFN ? NULL : rtn_idp->typep);
}


/*------------------------------------------------------------*/
/* exec_standard_routine_call    Execute a call to a          */
/*                               standard procedure or        */
/*                               function.                    */
/*------------------------------------------------------------*/

    TYPE_STRUCT_PTR
exec_standard_routine_call(rtn_idp)

    SYMTAB_NODE_PTR rtn_idp;    /* routine id */

{
    runtime_error(UNIMPLEMENTED_RUNTIME_FEATURE);
}


/*------------------------------------------------------------*/
/* exec_actual_parms          Push the values of the actual   */
/*                            parameters onto the stack.      */
/*------------------------------------------------------------*/

exec_actual_parms(rtn_idp)

    SYMTAB_NODE_PTR rtn_idp;        /* id of callee routine */

{
    SYMTAB_NODE_PTR formal_idp;    /* formal parm id */
    TYPE_STRUCT_PTR formal_tp, actual_tp;

    /*
    -- Loop to execute actual parameters.
    */
    for (formal_idp = rtn_idp->defn.info.routine.parms;
         formal_idp != NULL;
         formal_idp = formal_idp->next) {

        formal_tp = formal_idp->typep;
        get_ctoken();

        /*
        -- Value parameter.
        */
        if (formal_idp->defn.key == VALPARM_DEFN) {
            actual_tp = exec_expression();

            /*
            -- Range check for a subrange formal parameter.
            */
            if (formal_tp->form == SUBRANGE_FORM) {
                TYPE_STRUCT_PTR base_formal_tp = base_type(formal_tp);
                int             value;

                value = ((base_formal_tp == integer_typep) ||
```

```
                         (base_formal_tp->form == ENUM_FORM))
                            ? tos->integer
                            : tos->byte;

                if ((value < formal_tp->info.subrange.min) ||
                    (value > formal_tp->info.subrange.max)) {
                    runtime_error(VALUE_OUT_OF_RANGE);
                }
            }

            /*
            -- real formal := integer actual
            */
            else if ((formal_tp == real_typep) &&
                     (base_type(actual_tp) == integer_typep)) {
                tos->real = tos->integer;
            }

            /*
            -- Formal parm is array or record:  Make a copy.
            */
            if ((formal_tp->form == ARRAY_FORM) ||
                (formal_tp->form == RECORD_FORM)) {
                int  size      = formal_tp->size;
                char *ptr1     = alloc_bytes(size);
                char *ptr2     = tos->address;
                char *save_ptr = ptr1;

                while (size--) *ptr1++ = *ptr2++;
                tos->address = save_ptr;
            }
        }

        /*
        -- VAR parameter.
        */
        else {
            SYMTAB_NODE_PTR idp = get_symtab_cptr();

            exec_variable(idp, VARPARM_USE);
        }
    }
}


/*------------------------------------------------------------*/
/* exec_compound_statement    Execute a compound statement.   */
/*------------------------------------------------------------*/

exec_compound_statement()

{
    get_ctoken();
    while (ctoken != END) exec_statement();
    get_ctoken();
}
```

In function exec_statement, we look at the first token of a statement to determine what kind of statement it is. In this chapter, we only know about compound statements, assignment statements, and procedure calls. (STATEMENT_MARKER is explained later.) We call function exec_routine_call if the statement is a procedure call. There, we call either function exec_declared_routine_call or exec_standard_routine_call depending on whether the Pascal routine is programmer-written or standard. Since we won't handle the predefined standard routines until the next chapter, exec_standard_routine_call simply calls runtime_error.

Function exec_declared_routine_call sets up the stack for a Pascal procedure or function call. We set old_level to the current nesting level, which is the level of the caller's parameters and local variables. We set new_level to the nesting level of the parameters and local variables of the callee. Remember that the nesting level of a routine's parameter and local variable identifiers is one greater than the level of the routine's identifier. We also set new_stack_frame_basep to point to the runtime stack item that is one above the top of stack.

Next, we call function push_stack_frame_header to push the stack frame header for the callee onto the stack. We call function exec_actual_parms repeatedly to push the actual parameters (if any) onto the stack on top of the new stack frame header.

Then, we set level and stack_frame_basep to their new values, and we also set the return address into the new stack frame. Now we can call function execute, passing a pointer to the symbol table node of the callee's procedure or function identifier.

Function push_stack_frame_header is defined in file executil.c. We call it from exec_declared_routine_call to push the stack frame header for the callee onto the stack. We first push zero as a placeholder for the return value. Then, we compare the values of old_level (of the caller) and new_level (of the callee) to figure out what to push for the static link.

If new_level equals old_level + 1, then the callee is immediately contained by the caller, so the static link is simply a pointer to the base of the caller's stack frame. (This is still the value of stack_frame_basep, since we haven't yet updated it.)

If new_level equals old_level, then both the caller and the callee are immediately contained by the same routine. The static link is a copy of the caller's static link.

Finally, if new_level is less than old_level, the callee is less deeply nested than the caller. (You see this situation in Figure 9-4d.) The static link must point to the stack frame of the routine that immediately contains the callee. We get to the base of that stack frame by starting with the caller's stack frame and following (old_level - new_level + 1) static links, since each link we follow takes us back one nesting level.

On top of the static link, we push the dynamic link onto the stack. It simply points back to the base of the caller's stack frame. We conclude by pushing another zero, this time as a placeholder for the return address. As we saw before, we set the return address into the stack frame header shortly afterwards in function exec_declared_routine_call. We also saw in that function, that we call function exec_actual_parms to push the values of any actual parameters onto the stack on top of the new stack frame header. In that function, we loop over the formal parameter list of the callee.

For each formal value parameter, we call function exec_expression to push the actual parameter's value onto the stack. If the formal parameter is of a subrange type, we do a runtime range check to make sure the value is not outside of the range. If the formal parameter is real but the actual parameter value is integer, we convert the integer value to real. If the formal parameter is an array or a record, exec_expression leaves a pointer on top of the stack that points to the actual parameter's array or record value. We make a copy of the value and change the pointer at the top of the stack to point to the copy. (We will examine function exec_expression later when we look at how to execute expressions.)

For each formal VAR parameter, we call function exec_variable, passing the VARPARM_USE usage code (from file parser.h), to push the address of the actual parameter (which the parser has guaranteed to be a variable) onto the stack.

We have already seen how, in file executil.c, we call function execute to execute the main program, a procedure, or a function. From there, we call function routine_entry, where we complete the callee's stack frame by calling function alloc_local to allocate the local variables on the stack on top of the allocation for the parameters. We call function trace_routine_entry to print tracing information about entering a Pascal procedure or a function.

In function alloc_local, we call either function push_integer, push_real, or push_byte to push a zero for a scalar or enumeration local variable. We call alloc_local recursively for the range type of a subrange variable. If the local variable is an array or a record, we call alloc_bytes to allocate memory for it, and then we call push_address to push its address onto the stack.

Finally, back in execute, we extract the first token (which should be BEGIN) from the callee's code segment and call routine exec_statement to execute the statements in the callee's block. When we are done doing that, we call function routine_exit.

Let's review the steps involved in calling a Pascal procedure or function:

1. Allocate the callee's stack frame header (done in function push_stack_frame_header).

2. Push the actual arguments onto the stack (exec_actual_parms).

3. Update level and stack_frame_basep (exec_declared_routine_call).

4. Allocate the callee's local variables on the stack (routine_entry).

5. Execute the callee's statements (execute).

9.3.3 Returning from a Pascal procedure or function

Returning from the callee to the caller is simple: You deallocate the callee's parameters and variables, pop off its stack frame, and then resume execution of the caller at the return address.

As soon as the callee's statements are done being executed, function exec_statement returns to function execute. We call function routine_exit, and then call function `trace_routine_exit` to print any tracing information about leaving a Pascal procedure or function. Next, we call function `free_data` to deallocate any memory that we had allocated (in function `exec_actual_parms`) for array and record value parameters, and to deallocate any memory that we had allocated (when function `routine_entry` called `alloc_local`) for any local array and record variables. We set `code_segmentp` to the return address. We pop off the callee's stack frame by resetting `tos` to point to the stack item below the callee's stack frame base if the callee was a procedure, or to the item at the stack frame base (the return value) if the callee was a function. Finally, we use the dynamic link to reset `stack_frame_basep` to point to the base of the caller's stack frame, and then we return to execute.

From function execute, we return to `exec_declared_routine_call` and we are done executing the callee. So now, the stack is back to the way it was (except that a function return value may be on top), and `code_segmentp` points to where we left off in the code segment. We restore `level`, fetch the token from the code segment, and return either the function type if the callee was a function, or NULL if it was a procedure.

Let's review the steps involved in returning from a Pascal procedure or function:

1. Deallocate the callee's local variables and value parameters that are arrays or records (done in function `routine_exit`).

2. Reset `code_segmentp` to the return address, pop off the callee's stack frame (but leave a function return value on top), and reset `stack_frame_basep` to point to the base of the caller's stack frame (`routine_exit`).

3. Restore `level` and resume execution of the caller (`exec_declared_routine_call`).

9.4 Interpreting statements and expressions

Now that you have seen how an interpreter calls and returns from a Pascal procedure or function, you may wonder how it executes the callee's statements. The remaining routines of this chapter's executor module execute assignment statements, compound statements, and expressions.

9.4.1 Statement markers

In function `exec_statement`, we test for a STATEMENT_MARKER. Each statement marker in the intermediate form marks the beginning of the code of a statement, and it also contains the statement's source line number. A statement marker enables us to update `exec_line_number` and `exec_stmt_count`, and to call function `trace_statement_execution` to print statement tracing information, as we'll see later. As shown in Figure 9-12, we first add statement markers to the code buffer in function statement in file stmt.c. We also have to add the following to the beginning of stmt.c:

```
#include "exec.h"
```

FIGURE 9-12   Function statement in file stmt.c.

```
/*-------------------------------------------------------*/            crunch_symtab_node_ptr(idp);
/*  statement          Process a statement by calling the   */        get_token();
/*                     appropriate parsing routine based on */        routine_call(idp, TRUE);
/*                     the statement's first token.         */    }
/*-------------------------------------------------------*/        else assignment_statement(idp);

statement()                                                           break;
                                                              }
{
    if (token != BEGIN) crunch_statement_marker();            case REPEAT:    repeat_statement();     break;
                                                              case WHILE:     while_statement();      break;
    /*                                                        case IF:        if_statement();         break;
    -- Call the appropriate routine based on the first        case FOR:       for_statement();        break;
    -- token of the statement.                                case CASE:      case_statement();       break;
    */                                                        case BEGIN:     compound_statement();   break;
    switch (token) {                                      }

        case IDENTIFIER: {                                /*
            SYMTAB_NODE_PTR idp;                           -- Error synchronization:  Only a semicolon, END, ELSE, or
                                                           --                         UNTIL may follow a statement.
            /*                                             --                         Check for a missing semicolon.
            -- Assignment statement or procedure call?     */
            */                                            synchronize(statement_end_list, statement_start_list, NULL);
            search_and_find_all_symtab(idp);              if (token_in(statement_start_list)) error(MISSING_SEMICOLON);

            if (idp->defn.key == PROC_DEFN) {         }
```

Function crunch_statement_marker is in file executil.c. We append the statement marker code followed by the current line number to the code buffer. Whenever we call crunch_statement_marker, the first token code of the statement has already been appended to the code buffer, so we must move it after the line number. Later, we call function get_statement_cmarker to retrieve the line number from the code buffer.

9.4.2 Executing assignment statements

Function exec_assignment_statement in file execstmt.c executes assignment statements. We first point targetp to the target of the assignment. The target may be a stack item or a component within a data area allocated for an array or record.

If the assignment is to a function identifier, then we point targetp to the bottom item (the return value) of the function's stack frame. If the assignment statement is not in that function's block (we are assigning a value to a function that contains the current routine), we must follow static links to find the appropriate stack frame.

Otherwise, we call function exec_variable, passing the TARGET_USE usage code, to evaluate and push the addresss of the target onto the stack. We set targetp to this address before we pop it off. We call function exec_expression to evaluate and push the value of the expression onto the stack, and then we can do the assignment.

If the expression value is integer and the target is integer, we convert the value to real. If the target is of an enumeration or a subrange type, we do a runtime range check to make sure the value is not outside of the range.

If the expression evaluates to an array or a record, exec_expression leaves a pointer on top of the stack that points to the value. In this case, targetp must be pointing to a data area that was allocated (when function routine_entry calls alloc_local) for the target array or record. We copy the array or record value. Finally, we call function trace_data_store to print tracing information about storing a value into a variable.

9.4.3 Executing compound statements

Function exec_compound_statement in file execstmt.c executes compound statements. We simply loop and call function exec_statement until we encounter the END token that matches the BEGIN token.

9.4.4 Executing expressions

Figure 9-13 shows file execexpr.c of the executor module. It contains the functions to execute expressions, and is analogous to file expr.c of the parser module. The functions may also remind you of the ones in the calculator utility program of Chapter 4. The main difference is that now the values on the stack may be of several types. The parser guarantees us, however, that there are no type incompatibilities in the expressions.

FIGURE 9-13   File execexpr.c.

```
/******************************************************************/          #include "exec.h"
/*                                                              */
/*      E X P R E S S I O N   E X E C U T O R                   */          /*------------------------------------------------------------*/
/*                                                              */          /* Externals                                                 */
/*      Execution routines for expressions.                     */          /*------------------------------------------------------------*/
/*                                                              */
/*      FILE:       execexpr.c                                  */          extern int          level;
/*                                                              */
/*      MODULE:     executor                                    */          extern char         *code_segmentp;
/*                                                              */          extern TOKEN_CODE   ctoken;
/******************************************************************/
                                                                            extern STACK_ITEM       *stack;
#include <stdio.h>                                                          extern STACK_ITEM_PTR tos;
#include "common.h"                                                         extern STACK_ITEM_PTR stack_frame_basep;
#include "error.h"
#include "symtab.h"                                                         extern TYPE_STRUCT_PTR integer_typep, real_typep,
#include "scanner.h"                                                                               boolean_typep, char_typep;
#include "parser.h"
```

```
/*------------------------------------------------------------*/
/* Forwards                                                   */
/*------------------------------------------------------------*/

TYPE_STRUCT_PTR exec_expression(), exec_simple_expression(),
                exec_term(), exec_factor(),
                exec_constant(), exec_variable(),
                exec_subscripts(), exec_field();

/*------------------------------------------------------------*/
/* exec_expression     Execute an expression consisting of a  */
/*                     simple expression optionally followed  */
/*                     by a relational operator and a second  */
/*                     simple expression.  Return a pointer to*/
/*                     the type structure.                    */
/*------------------------------------------------------------*/

    TYPE_STRUCT_PTR
exec_expression()

{
    STACK_ITEM_PTR   operandp1, operandp2;    /* ptrs to operands */
    TYPE_STRUCT_PTR  result_tp, tp2;          /* ptrs to types */
    TOKEN_CODE       op;                      /* an operator token */
    BOOLEAN          result;

    result_tp = exec_simple_expression();   /* first simple expr */

    /*
    -- If there is a relational operator, remember it and
    -- process the second simple expression.
    */
    if ((ctoken == EQUAL) || (ctoken == LT) || (ctoken == GT) ||
        (ctoken == NE)    || (ctoken == LE) || (ctoken == GE)) {
        op = ctoken;                          /* remember operator */
        result_tp = base_type(result_tp);

        get_ctoken();
        tp2 = base_type(exec_simple_expression()); /* 2nd simp expr */

        operandp1 = tos - 1;
        operandp2 = tos;

        /*
        -- Both operands are integer, boolean, or enumeration.
        */
        if (   ((result_tp == integer_typep) &&
                (tp2       == integer_typep))
            || (result_tp->form == ENUM_FORM)) {
            switch (op) {
                case EQUAL:
                    result = operandp1->integer == operandp2->integer;
                    break;

                case LT:
                    result = operandp1->integer <  operandp2->integer;
                    break;

                case GT:
                    result = operandp1->integer >  operandp2->integer;
                    break;

                case NE:
                    result = operandp1->integer != operandp2->integer;
                    break;

                case LE:
                    result = operandp1->integer <= operandp2->integer;
                    break;

                case GE:
                    result = operandp1->integer >= operandp2->integer;
                    break;
            }
        }

        /*
        -- Both operands are character.
        */
        else if (result_tp == char_typep) {
            switch (op) {
                case EQUAL:
                    result = operandp1->byte == operandp2->byte;
                    break;

                case LT:
                    result = operandp1->byte <  operandp2->byte;
                    break;

                case GT:
                    result = operandp1->byte >  operandp2->byte;
                    break;

                case NE:
                    result = operandp1->byte != operandp2->byte;
                    break;

                case LE:
                    result = operandp1->byte <= operandp2->byte;
                    break;

                case GE:
                    result = operandp1->byte >= operandp2->byte;
                    break;
            }
        }

        /*
        -- Both operands are real, or one is real and the other
        -- is integer.  Convert the integer operand to real.
        */
        else if ((result_tp == real_typep) ||
                 (tp2        == real_typep)) {
            promote_operands_to_real(operandp1, result_tp,
                                     operandp2, tp2);

            switch (op) {
                case EQUAL:
                    result = operandp1->real == operandp2->real;
                    break;

                case LT:
                    result = operandp1->real <  operandp2->real;
                    break;

                case GT:
                    result = operandp1->real >  operandp2->real;
                    break;

                case NE:
                    result = operandp1->real != operandp2->real;
                    break;

                case LE:
```

```
                result = operandp1->real <= operandp2->real;
                break;

            case GE:
                result = operandp1->real >= operandp2->real;
                break;
        }
    }

    /*
    -- Both operands are strings.
    */
    else if ((result_tp->form == ARRAY_FORM) &&
             (result_tp->info.array.elmt_typep == char_typep)) {
        int cmp = strncmp(operandp1->address, operandp2->address,
                          result_tp->info.array.elmt_count);

        result = (    (    (cmp < 0)
                        && (   (op == NE)
                            || (op == LE)
                            || (op == LT)))
                   || (    (cmp == 0)
                        && (   (op == EQUAL)
                            || (op == LE)
                            || (op == GE)))
                   || (    (cmp > 0)
                        && (   (op == NE)
                            || (op == GE)
                            || (op == GT))));
    }

    /*
    -- Replace the two operands on the stack with the result.
    */
    operandp1->integer = result ? 1 : 0;
    pop();

    result_tp = boolean_typep;
    }

    return(result_tp);
}

/*----------------------------------------------------------*/
/* exec_simple_expression  Execute a simple expression      */
/*                         consisting of terms separated by +, */
/*                         -, or OR operators.  There may be */
/*                         a unary + or - before the first   */
/*                         term.  Return a pointer to the    */
/*                         type structure.                   */
/*----------------------------------------------------------*/

    TYPE_STRUCT_PTR
exec_simple_expression()

{
    STACK_ITEM_PTR operandp1, operandp2;   /* ptrs to operands */
    TYPE_STRUCT_PTR result_tp, tp2;        /* ptrs to types */
    TOKEN_CODE op;                         /* an operator token */
    TOKEN_CODE unary_op = PLUS;            /* unary operator token */

    /*
    -- If there is a unary + or -, remember it.
    */
    if ((ctoken == PLUS) || (ctoken == MINUS)) {
        unary_op = ctoken;
        get_ctoken();
```

```
    }

    result_tp = exec_term();    /* first term */

    /*
    -- If there was a unary -, negate the top of stack
    */
    if (unary_op == MINUS) {
        if (result_tp == integer_typep) tos->integer = -tos->integer;
        else                            tos->real    = -tos->real;
    }

    /*
    -- Loop to process subsequent terms
    -- separated by operators.
    */
    while ((ctoken == PLUS) || (ctoken == MINUS) || (ctoken == OR)) {
        op = ctoken;                    /* remember operator */
        result_tp = base_type(result_tp);

        get_ctoken();
        tp2 = base_type(exec_term());   /* subsequent term */

        operandp1 = tos - 1;
        operandp2 = tos;

        /*
        -- OR
        */
        if (op == OR) {
            operandp1->integer = operandp1->integer ||
                                 operandp2->integer;
            result_tp = boolean_typep;
        }

        /*
        -- + or -
        --
        -- Both operands are integer.
        */
        else if ((result_tp == integer_typep) &&
                 (tp2        == integer_typep)) {
            operandp1->integer = (op == PLUS)
                ? operandp1->integer + operandp2->integer
                : operandp1->integer - operandp2->integer;
            result_tp = integer_typep;
        }

        /*
        -- Both operands are real, or one is real and the other
        -- is integer.  Convert the integer operand to real.
        */
        else {
            promote_operands_to_real(operandp1, result_tp,
                                     operandp2, tp2);

            operandp1->real = (op == PLUS)
                ? operandp1->real + operandp2->real
                : operandp1->real - operandp2->real;
            result_tp = real_typep;
        }

        pop();  /* pop off the second operand */
    }

    return(result_tp);
}
```

```
/*------------------------------------------------------------*/
/*  exec_term          Execute a term consisting of factors   */
/*                     separated by *, /, DIV, MOD, or AND     */
/*                     operators.  Return a pointer to the     */
/*                     type structure.                         */
/*------------------------------------------------------------*/

    TYPE_STRUCT_PTR
exec_term()

{
    STACK_ITEM_PTR operandp1, operandp2;    /* ptrs to operands */
    TYPE_STRUCT_PTR result_tp, tp2;         /* ptrs to types */
    TOKEN_CODE op;                          /* an operator token */

    result_tp = exec_factor();   /* first factor */

    /*
    -- Loop to process subsequent factors
    -- separated by operators.
    */
    while ((ctoken == STAR) || (ctoken == SLASH) || (ctoken == DIV) ||
           (ctoken == MOD)  || (ctoken == AND)) {
        op = ctoken;                        /* remember operator */
        result_tp = base_type(result_tp);

        get_ctoken();
        tp2 = base_type(exec_factor());     /* subsequent factor */

        operandp1 = tos - 1;
        operandp2 = tos;

        /*
        -- AND
        */
        if (op == AND) {
            operandp1->integer = operandp1->integer &&
                                 operandp2->integer;
            result_tp = boolean_typep;
        }

        /*
        -- *, /, DIV, or MOD
        */
        else switch (op) {

            case STAR:
                /*
                -- Both operands are integer.
                */
                if (   (result_tp == integer_typep)
                    && (tp2       == integer_typep)) {
                    operandp1->integer =
                        operandp1->integer * operandp2->integer;
                    result_tp = integer_typep;
                }

                /*
                -- Both operands are real, or one is real and the
                -- other is integer.  Convert the integer operand
                -- to real.
                */
                else {
                    promote_operands_to_real(operandp1, result_tp,
                                             operandp2, tp2);

                    operandp1->real =
                        operandp1->real * operandp2->real;
                    result_tp = real_typep;
                }
                break;

            case SLASH:
                /*
                -- Both operands are real, or one is real and the
                -- other is integer.  Convert the integer operand
                -- to real.
                */
                promote_operands_to_real(operandp1, result_tp,
                                         operandp2, tp2);

                if (operandp2->real == 0.0)
                    runtime_error(DIVISION_BY_ZERO);
                else
                    operandp1->real = operandp1->real/operandp2->real;

                result_tp = real_typep;
                break;

            case DIV:
            case MOD:
                /*
                -- Both operands are integer.
                */
                if (operandp2->integer == 0)
                    runtime_error(DIVISION_BY_ZERO);
                else
                    operandp1->integer = (op == DIV)
                        ? operandp1->integer / operandp2->integer
                        : operandp1->integer % operandp2->integer;

                result_tp = integer_typep;
                break;
        }

        pop();  /* pop off the second operand */
    }

    return(result_tp);
}

/*------------------------------------------------------------*/
/*  exec_factor        Execute a factor, which is a variable,  */
/*                     a number, NOT followed by a factor, or  */
/*                     a parenthesized subexpression.  Return  */
/*                     a pointer to the type structure.        */
/*------------------------------------------------------------*/

    TYPE_STRUCT_PTR
exec_factor()

{
    TYPE_STRUCT_PTR result_tp;          /* type pointer */

    switch (ctoken) {

        case IDENTIFIER: {
            SYMTAB_NODE_PTR idp = get_symtab_cptr();

            /*
            -- Function call or constant or variable.
            */
            if (idp->defn.key == FUNC_DEFN)
                result_tp = exec_routine_call(idp);
```

```
            else if (idp->defn.key == CONST_DEFN)                              }
                result_tp = exec_constant(idp);
            else                                                        return(result_tp);
                result_tp = exec_variable(idp, EXPR_USE);           }

            break;                                                /*------------------------------------------------------------*/
    }                                                             /* exec_constant    Push the value of a non-string constant */
                                                                  /*                  identifier, or the address of the value */
    case NUMBER: {                                                /*                  of a string constant identifier onto   */
        SYMTAB_NODE_PTR np = get_symtab_cptr();                   /*                  the stack.  Return a pointer to the    */
                                                                  /*                  type structure.                       */
                                                                  /*------------------------------------------------------------*/
        /*
        -- Obtain the integer or real value from the                  TYPE_STRUCT_PTR
        -- symbol table entry and push it onto the stack.         exec_constant(idp)
        */
        if (np->typep == integer_typep) {                             SYMTAB_NODE_PTR idp;        /* constant id */
            push_integer(np->defn.info.constant.value.integer);
            result_tp = integer_typep;                            {
        }
        else {                                                        TYPE_STRUCT_PTR tp = idp->typep;
            push_real(np->defn.info.constant.value.real);
            result_tp = real_typep;                                   if ((base_type(tp) == integer_typep) || (tp->form == ENUM_FORM))
        }                                                                 push_integer(idp->defn.info.constant.value.integer);
                                                                      else if (tp == real_typep)
        get_ctoken();                                                     push_real(idp->defn.info.constant.value.real);
        break;                                                        else if (tp == char_typep)
    }                                                                     push_integer(idp->defn.info.constant.value.integer);
                                                                      else if (tp->form == ARRAY_FORM)
    case STRING: {                                                        push_address(idp->defn.info.constant.value.stringp);
        SYMTAB_NODE_PTR np     = get_symtab_cptr();
        int             length = strlen(np->name);                    trace_data_fetch(idp, tp, tos);
                                                                      get_ctoken();
        /*
        -- Obtain the character or string from the symbol             return(tp);
        -- table entry.  Note that the quotes were included,
        -- so the string lengths need to be decreased by 2.     }
        */
        if (length > 3) {                                         /*------------------------------------------------------------*/
            /*                                                    /* exec_variable    Push either the variable's address or   */
            -- String: Push its address onto the stack.           /*                  its value onto the stack.  Return a     */
            */                                                    /*                  pointer to the type structure.          */
            push_address(np->info);                               /*------------------------------------------------------------*/
            result_tp = np->typep;
        }                                                             TYPE_STRUCT_PTR
        else {                                                    exec_variable(idp, use)
            /*
            -- Character: Push its value onto the stack.              SYMTAB_NODE_PTR idp;      /* variable id */
            */                                                        USE             use;     /* how variable is used */
            push_byte(np->name[1]);
            result_tp = char_typep;                               {
        }                                                             int             delta;        /* difference in levels */
                                                                      TYPE_STRUCT_PTR tp = idp->typep;
        get_ctoken();                                                 TYPE_STRUCT_PTR base_tp;
        break;                                                        STACK_ITEM_PTR  datap;        /* ptr to data area */
    }                                                                 STACK_FRAME_HEADER_PTR hp;

    case NOT:                                                         /*
        get_ctoken();                                                 -- Point to the variable's stack item.  If the variable's level
        result_tp = exec_factor();                                    -- is less than the current level, follow the static links to
        tos->integer = 1 - tos->integer;   /* 0 => 1, 1 => 0 */       -- the appropriate stack frame base.
        break;                                                        */
                                                                      hp = (STACK_FRAME_HEADER_PTR) stack_frame_basep;
    case LPAREN:                                                      delta = level - idp->level;
        get_ctoken();                                                 while (delta-- > 0)
        result_tp = exec_expression();                                    hp = (STACK_FRAME_HEADER_PTR) hp->static_link.address;
        get_ctoken();       /* token after ) */                       datap = (STACK_ITEM_PTR) hp + idp->defn.info.data.offset;
        break;
                                                                      /*
```

```
    -- If a scalar or enumeration VAR parm, that item
    -- points to the actual item.
    */
    if ((idp->defn.key == VARPARM_DEFN) &&
        (tp->form != ARRAY_FORM) &&
        (tp->form != RECORD_FORM))
        datap = (STACK_ITEM_PTR) datap->address;

    /*
    -- Push the address of the variable's data area.
    */
    if ((tp->form == ARRAY_FORM) ||
        (tp->form == RECORD_FORM))
        push_address((ADDRESS) datap->address);
    else
        push_address((ADDRESS) datap);

    /*
    -- If there are subscripts or field designators,
    -- modify the address to point to the array element
    -- record field.
    */
    get_ctoken();
    while ((ctoken == LBRACKET) || (ctoken == PERIOD)) {
        if      (ctoken == LBRACKET) tp = exec_subscripts(tp);
        else if (ctoken == PERIOD)   tp = exec_field();
    }

    base_tp = base_type(tp);

    /*
    -- Leave the modified address on top of the stack if:
    --      it is an assignment target, or
    --      it represents a parameter passed by reference, or
    --      it is the address of an array or record.
    -- Otherwise, replace the address with the value that it
    -- points to.
    */
    if ((use != TARGET_USE) && (use != VARPARM_USE) &&
        (tp->form != ARRAY_FORM) && (tp->form != RECORD_FORM)) {

        if ((base_tp == integer_typep) || (tp->form == ENUM_FORM))
            tos->integer = *((int *) tos->address);
        else if (base_tp == char_typep)
            tos->byte = *((char *) tos->address);
        else
            tos->real = *((float *) tos->address);
    }

    if ((use != TARGET_USE) && (use != VARPARM_USE))
        trace_data_fetch(idp, tp,
                        (tp->form == ARRAY_FORM) ||
                        (tp->form == RECORD_FORM)
                           ? tos->address
                           : tos);

    return(tp);
}

/*------------------------------------------------------------*/
/* exec_subscripts     Execute subscripts to modify the array */
/*                     data area address on the top of the    */
/*                     stack.  Return a pointer to the type of */
/*                     the array element.                     */
/*------------------------------------------------------------*/

    TYPE_STRUCT_PTR
```

```
exec_subscripts(tp)

    TYPE_STRUCT_PTR tp;          /* ptr to type structure */

{
    int subscript_value;

    /*
    -- Loop to execute bracketed subscripts.
    */
    while (ctoken == LBRACKET) {
        /*
        -- Loop to execute a subscript list.
        */
        do {
            get_ctoken();
            exec_expression();

            subscript_value = tos->integer;
            pop();

            /*
            -- Range check.
            */
            if ((subscript_value < tp->info.array.min_index) ||
                (subscript_value > tp->info.array.max_index))
                runtime_error(VALUE_OUT_OF_RANGE);

            /*
            -- Modify the data area address.
            */
            tos->address +=
                (subscript_value - tp->info.array.min_index) *
                                 tp->info.array.elmt_typep->size;

            if (ctoken == COMMA) tp = tp->info.array.elmt_typep;
        } while (ctoken == COMMA);

        get_ctoken();
        if (ctoken == LBRACKET) tp = tp->info.array.elmt_typep;
    }

    return(tp->info.array.elmt_typep);
}

/*------------------------------------------------------------*/
/* exec_field           Execute a field designator to modify  */
/*                       the record data area address on the  */
/*                       top of the stack.  Return a pointer to*/
/*                       the type of the record field.        */
/*------------------------------------------------------------*/

    TYPE_STRUCT_PTR
exec_field()

{
    SYMTAB_NODE_PTR field_idp;

    get_ctoken();
    field_idp = get_symtab_cptr();

    tos->address += field_idp->defn.info.data.offset;

    get_ctoken();
    return(field_idp->typep);
}
```

```
/*-------------------------------------------------------*/
/* promote_operands_to_real    If either operand is integer,  */
/*                              convert it to real.           */
/*-------------------------------------------------------*/

promote_operands_to_real(operandp1, tp1, operandp2, tp2)

    STACK_ITEM_PTR  operandp1, operandp2;   /* ptrs to operands */
```

```
    TYPE_STRUCT_PTR tp1, tp2;           /* ptrs to types */

{
    if (tp1 == integer_typep) operandp1->real = operandp1->integer;
    if (tp2 == integer_typep) operandp2->real = operandp2->integer;
}
```

In function `exec_expression`, we execute an expression to evaluate it and leave the result value on the top of the stack. We also return the type (that is, a pointer to the type structure) of the result. We can compare two integer, two real, two character (byte), or two string values, and we compare two enumeration values as integers. Before we compare two real values or an integer value to a real value, we call function `promote_operands_to_real`, where we check both operands and convert any integer value to real.

Function `exec_simple_expression` executes a simple expression and leaves the result value on the top of the stack. For the OR operator, we operate on two boolean values. For the + and - operators, we operate on two integer values. We call `promote_operands_to_real` before we operate on the values if both are real, or if one is integer and the other is real. We return the type of the result.

We execute a term in function `exec_term` and leave the result value on the top of the stack. For the AND operator, we operate on two boolean values. For the * operator, we operate on two integer values. We call `promote_operands_to_real` before we operate on the values if both are real, or if one is integer and the other is real. For the / operator, we operate on integer or real values, but we call `promote_operands_to_real` first to convert any integer values to real. We only operate on two integer values for the DIV and MOD operators. We return the type of the result.

Function `exec_factor` executes a factor and leaves the result value on the top of the stack, and then returns its type. If the factor is an identifier, a number, or a string, we call function `get_symtab_cptr` to retrieve the pointer to its symbol table node. If it's an identifier, we check the node's `defn.key` field to decide whether to call function `exec_routine_call` (to execute a function call), `exec_constant`, or `exec_variable`. If the factor is a number, we push the value in the node's `defn.info.constant.value` field. We call either function `push_integer` or `push_real`.

If the factor is a string, we obtain the string that the node's `info` field points to, and we check its length. If the string is a single character, we call function `push_byte`. Otherwise, we call `push_address` to push the address of the string.

In function `exec_constant`, we push the value that we obtain from the symbol table, and then we return its type.

9.4.5 Evaluating variables

Function `exec_variable` pushes either the value or the address of a variable or a formal parameter onto the runtime stack. Whether we push a value or an address depends on the type of the variable or parameter and how it is used. We also return the type of the variable or parameter. In the following description, anything we say about a variable also applies to a formal parameter, unless we say otherwise.

We first compare level to the variable's level and point hp to the appropriate stack frame. We want datap to point to the stack item that was allocated for the variable, so we point it to the item that is the variable's stack offset away from the base of the stack frame.

If we are evaluating a VAR parameter that is a scalar or an enumeration, datap now points to the stack item that contains the address of the actual stack item. We set datap to datap->address to point it to the actual stack item.

Next, we want to push the address of the variable's data. If the variable is a scalar, datap points to the stack item containing the variable's value so we just push the value of datap. If the variable is an array or variable, the stack item that datap points to contains the *address* of the variable's data area (which we allocated in function alloc_local) so we push the value of datap->address.

So now we have the address of the variable's data on top of the stack. If the variable is subscripted, we call function exec_subscripts to modify that address. If the variable is a record field, we call function exec_field to modify the address.

Then it is time to decide whether to leave the address on top of the stack or to replace the address with the value that it points to. We leave the address alone if the variable is used as the target of an assignment statement (usage is TARGET_USE), if it is being passed as an actual parameter that corresponds to a formal VAR parameter (usage is VARPARM_USE), or if the variable is an array or record. In all other cases, we replace the address with the value. Finally, we call function trace_data_fetch to print tracing information about fetching the value of a variable.

Note that we never put array and record values on the stack. Instead, we always put the address of the data area on the stack. (That's what function alloc_local does too.)

In function exec_subscripts, we loop to execute array subscript expressions to modify the array data address that is on top of the stack. To modify the address for each subscript, we first subtract the array's minimum subscript value from the subscript expression value, multiply this by the element size, and add the product to the address. We also do a range check of the subscript value. After the last subscript, we return the type of the array element.

We modify the record data address that is on top of the stack in function exec_field by adding the field's byte offset. Then we return the type of the record field.

9.4.6 Range checking

Range checking is a runtime error check that is possible because of Pascal's subrange types. This check ensures that a value is not outside the permissible range of values.

You have seen three places where we do a range check. One is in function exec_assignment_statement to check the assignment of a value to a subrange variable. Another is in exec_actual_parms to check the value of an actual parameter against a formal subrange parameter. The third is in function exec_subscripts to check a subscript value against the index subrange.

9.5 Program 9-1: Pascal Interpreter I

Now we are all set to put everything together into an interpreter that can parse and execute Pascal programs that consist of procedures and functions, calls to these routines, and assignment statements.

Figure 9-14 shows the main file of the interpreter run1.c. The main routine is the same as ones we have seen before, but there are also the runtime tracing routines.

FIGURE 9-14   File run1.c.

```
/*****************************************************************/
/*                                                               */
/*       Program 9-1:  Pascal Interpreter I                      */
/*                                                               */
/*       Interpret assignement statements in procedures          */
/*       and functions.                                          */
/*                                                               */
/*       FILE:      run1.c                                       */
/*                                                               */
/*       REQUIRES:  Modules parser, symbol table, scanner,       */
/*                          executor, error                      */
/*                                                               */
/*       FLAGS:     Macro flag "trace" must be defined           */
/*                                                               */
/*       USAGE:     run1 sourcefile                              */
/*                                                               */
/*          sourcefile      name of source file containing       */
/*                          the statements to interpret          */
/*                                                               */
/*****************************************************************/

#include <stdio.h>
#include "symtab.h"
#include "exec.h"

/*--------------------------------------------------------*/
/* Externals                                              */
/*--------------------------------------------------------*/

extern int exec_line_number;

extern TYPE_STRUCT_PTR integer_typep, real_typep,
                       boolean_typep, char_typep;

/*--------------------------------------------------------*/
/* main                 Initialize the scanner and call   */
/*                      routine program.                  */
/*--------------------------------------------------------*/

main(argc, argv)

    int  argc;
```

```
    char *argv[];

{
    /*
    -- Initialize the scanner.
    */
    init_scanner(argv[1]);

    /*
    -- Process a program.
    */
    get_token();
    program();
}

/*----------------------------------------------------------*/
/* trace_routine_entry        Trace the entry into a routine. */
/*----------------------------------------------------------*/

trace_routine_entry(idp)

    SYMTAB_NODE_PTR idp;        /* routine id */

{
    printf(">> Entering routine %s\n", idp->name);
}

/*----------------------------------------------------------*/
/* trace_routine_exit         Trace the exit from a routine. */
/*----------------------------------------------------------*/

trace_routine_exit(idp)

    SYMTAB_NODE_PTR idp;        /* routine id */

{
    printf(">> Exiting routine %s\n", idp->name);
}

/*----------------------------------------------------------*/
/* trace_statement_execution  Trace the execution of a       */
```

```
/*                          statement.                   */
/*-------------------------------------------------------*/

trace_statement_execution()

{
    printf(">>  Stmt %d\n", exec_line_number);
}

/*-------------------------------------------------------*/
/*  trace_data_store          Trace the storing of data into */
/*                            a variable.                 */
/*-------------------------------------------------------*/

trace_data_store(idp, idp_tp, targetp, target_tp)

    SYMTAB_NODE_PTR idp;           /* id of target variable */
    TYPE_STRUCT_PTR idp_tp;        /* ptr to id's type */
    STACK_ITEM_PTR  targetp;       /* ptr to target location */
    TYPE_STRUCT_PTR target_tp;     /* ptr to target's type */

{
    printf(">>  %s", idp->name);
    if      (idp_tp->form == ARRAY_FORM)  printf("[*]");
    else if (idp_tp->form == RECORD_FORM) printf(".*");
    print_data_value(targetp, target_tp, ":=");
}

/*-------------------------------------------------------*/
/*  trace_data_fetch          Trace the fetching of data from */
/*                            a variable.                 */
/*-------------------------------------------------------*/

trace_data_fetch(idp, tp, datap)

    SYMTAB_NODE_PTR idp;           /* id of target variable */
    TYPE_STRUCT_PTR tp;            /* ptr to id's type */
    STACK_ITEM_PTR  datap;         /* ptr to data */

{
    printf(">>  %s", idp->name);
    if      (tp->form == ARRAY_FORM)  printf("[*]");
    else if (tp->form == RECORD_FORM) printf(".*");
    print_data_value(datap, tp, "=");
}
```

```
/*-------------------------------------------------------*/
/*  print_data_value          Print a data value.        */
/*-------------------------------------------------------*/

print_data_value(datap, tp, str)

    STACK_ITEM_PTR  datap;         /* ptr to data value to print */
    TYPE_STRUCT_PTR tp;            /* ptr to type of stack item */
    char            *str;          /* " = " or " := " */

{
    /*
    -- Reduce a subrange type to its range type.
    -- Convert a non-boolean enumeration type to integer.
    */
    if (tp->form == SUBRANGE_FORM)
        tp = tp->info.subrange.range_typep;
    if ((tp->form == ENUM_FORM) && (tp != boolean_typep))
        tp = integer_typep;

    if (tp == integer_typep)
        printf(" %s %d\n", str, datap->integer);
    else if (tp == real_typep)
        printf(" %s %0.6g\n", str, datap->real);
    else if (tp == boolean_typep)
        printf(" %s %s\n", str, datap->integer == 1
                                 ? "true" : "false");
    else if (tp == char_typep)
        printf(" %s '%c'\n", str, datap->byte);

    else if (tp->form == ARRAY_FORM) {
        if (tp->info.array.elmt_typep == char_typep) {
            char *chp = (char *) datap;
            int  size = tp->info.array.elmt_count;

            printf(" %s '", str);
            while (size--) printf("%c", *chp++);
            printf("'\n");
        }
        else printf(" %s <array>\n", str);
    }
    else if (tp->form == RECORD_FORM)
        printf(" %s <record>\n", str);
}
```

We call function trace_routine_entry from function routine_entry, and function trace_routine_exit from routine_exit. In both tracing functions, we print the name of the procedure or function. We call function trace_statement_ execution from exec_statement. There, we print the line number of the statement that we are about to execute.

We call function trace_data_fetch from functions exec_constant and exec_ variable, and function trace_data_store from exec_assignment_statement. In both tracing functions, we print the name of the constant or variable identifier and the value that we fetch or store. If the variable is an array, we print [*] after its name, and if it's a record, we print .* . We call function print_data_value to print the value. It prints either a scalar value, a string value, or, for arrays and records, <array> or <record>.

In Chapter 10, we will want to remove the calls to the tracing routines. In file exec.h, we see that the calls are left in only if we first define the macro flag trace. This is similar to the macro flag analyze that we defined in Chapter 6 for the declarations analyzer and in Chapter 8 for the pretty-printer. We will define trace again in Chapter 11 for the debugger.

Figure 9-15 shows sample interpreter output from a Pascal program containing various assignment statements. Figure 9-16 shows the effect of value and VAR parameters. Figure 9-17 shows output from nested procedures and functions. Figure 9-18 shows a runtime range error.

FIGURE 9-15   Sample interpreter output from a Pascal program containing various assignment statements.

```
Page 1   assign.pas   Wed Jul 11 00:15:10 1990

    1 0: PROGRAM assign (output);
    2 1:
    3 1: CONST
    4 1:     ten = 10;
    5 1:     pi = 3.14159;
    6 1:
    7 1: TYPE
    8 1:     subrange = 5..ten;
    9 1:     enum = (zero, one, two, three, four, five);
   10 1:     arr = ARRAY [enum] OF real;
   11 1:     rec = RECORD
   12 1:                i : integer;
   13 1:                z : RECORD
   14 1:                        x : real;
   15 1:                        al : arr;
   16 1:                    END;
   17 1:           END;
   18 1:     arc = ARRAY [12..15] OF rec;
   19 1:
   20 1: VAR
   21 1:     i, j, k : subrange;
   22 1:     el, e2  : enum;
   23 1:     x, y, z : real;
   24 1:     p, q     : boolean;
   25 1:     ch       : char;
   26 1:     r        : rec;
   27 1:     a        : arc;
   28 1:     string1, string2 : ARRAY [1..ten] OF char;
   29 1:
   30 1: BEGIN
   31 1:     i := 7;
   32 1:     j := ten DIV 2;
   33 1:     k := 4*(i - j);
   34 1:     el := three;
   35 1:     e2 := el;
   36 1:     x := pi/7.2;
   37 1:     y := x + 3;
   38 1:     z := x - ten + y;
   39 1:     p := true;
   40 1:     q := NOT (x = y) AND p;
   41 1:
   42 1:     r.i := 7;
   43 1:     r.z.x := 3.14;
   44 1:     r.z.al[two] := +2.2;
   45 1:     i := r.i;
```

```
   46 1:     x := r.z.x;
   47 1:     x := r.z.al[two];
   48 1:
   49 1:     a[14].i := 7;
   50 1:     a[14].z.x := 3.14;


Page 2   assign.pas   Wed Jul 11 00:15:10 1990

   51 1:     a[14].z.al[two] := +2.2;
   52 1:     i := a[14].i;
   53 1:     x := a[14].z.x;
   54 1:     x := a[14].z.al[two];
   55 1:
   56 1:     ch := 'x';
   57 1:     string1 := 'Hello, you';
   58 1:     string2 := string1;
   59 1:     p := string1 = string2;
   60 1:     string1[ten] := ch;
   61 1:     ch := string1[1];
   62 1:     p := string1 = string2;
   63 1:     p := string1 > string2;
   64 1: END.
   65 0:
   66 0:


                           66 Source lines.
                            0 Source errors.


   >> Entering routine assign
   >>   Stmt 31
   >>     i := 7
   >>   Stmt 32
   >>     ten = 10
   >>     j := 5
   >>   Stmt 33
   >>     i = 7
   >>     j = 5
   >>     k := 8
   >>   Stmt 34
   >>     three = 3
   >>     el := 3
   >>   Stmt 35
```

```
>>  e1 = 3
>>  e2 := 3
>>  Stmt 36
>>  pi = 3.14159
>>  x := 0.436332
>>  Stmt 37
>>  x = 0.436332
>>  y := 3.43633
>>  Stmt 38
>>  x = 0.436332
>>  ten = 10
>>  y = 3.43633
>>  z := -6.12734
>>  Stmt 39
>>  true = true
>>  p := true
>>  Stmt 40
>>  x = 0.436332
>>  y = 3.43633
>>  p = true
>>  q := true
>>  Stmt 42
>>  r.* := 7
>>  Stmt 43
>>  r.* := 3.14
>>  Stmt 44
>>  two = 2
>>  r.* := 2.2
>>  Stmt 45
>>  r = 7
>>  i := 7
>>  Stmt 46
>>  r = 3.14
>>  x := 3.14
>>  Stmt 47
>>  two = 2
>>  r = 2.2
>>  x := 2.2
>>  Stmt 49
>>  a[*] := 7
>>  Stmt 50
>>  a[*] := 3.14
>>  Stmt 51
```

```
>>  two = 2
>>  a[*] := 2.2
>>  Stmt 52
>>  a = 7
>>  i := 7
>>  Stmt 53
>>  a = 3.14
>>  x := 3.14
>>  Stmt 54
>>  two = 2
>>  a = 2.2
>>  x := 2.2
>>  Stmt 56
>>  ch := 'x'
>>  Stmt 57
>>  string1[*] := 'Hello, you'
>>  Stmt 58
>>  string1[*] = 'Hello, you'
>>  string2[*] := 'Hello, you'
>>  Stmt 59
>>  string1[*] = 'Hello, you'
>>  string2[*] = 'Hello, you'
>>  p := true
>>  Stmt 60
>>  ten = 10
>>  ch = 'x'
>>  string1[*] := 'x'
>>  Stmt 61
>>  string1 = 'H'
>>  ch := 'H'
>>  Stmt 62
>>  string1[*] = 'Hello, yox'
>>  string2[*] = 'Hello, you'
>>  p := false
>>  Stmt 63
>>  string1[*] = 'Hello, yox'
>>  string2[*] = 'Hello, you'
>>  p := true
>> Exiting routine assign


Successful completion.  30 statements executed.
```

FIGURE 9-16   Sample interpreter output showing the effects of value and VAR parameters.

```
Page 1   arrparms.pas   Wed Jul 11 00:15:43 1990


 1 0: PROGRAM arrparms (output);
 2 1:
 3 1: TYPE
 4 1:    matrix = ARRAY [1..2, 1..3] OF integer;
 5 1:
 6 1: VAR
 7 1:    i      : integer;
 8 1:    m1, m2 : matrix;
 9 1:
10 1: PROCEDURE proc2 (    pm1 : matrix;
11 2:                  VAR pm2 : matrix);
12 2:
13 2:    VAR
```

```
14 2:        j : integer;
15 2:
16 2:    PROCEDURE proc3 (    ppm1 : matrix;
17 3:                     VAR ppm2 : matrix);
18 3:
19 3:        VAR
20 3:            j : integer;
21 3:
22 3:        BEGIN
23 3:            ppm1[1,1] := 99;    {99}
24 3:            ppm2[1,1] := -99;   {-99}
25 3:            j := ppm1[1,1];     {99}
26 3:            j := ppm2[1,1];     {-99}
27 3:            j := m1[1,1];       {11}
28 3:            j := m2[1,1];       {-99}
29 3:        END;
```

```
30 2:
31 2:      BEGIN
32 2:          pm1[2,2] := 77;        {77}
33 2:          pm2[2,2] := -77;       {-77}
34 2:          j := pm1[2,2];         {77}
35 2:          j := pm2[2,2];         {-77}
36 2:          j := m1[2,2];          {22}
37 2:          j := m2[2,2];          {-77}
38 2:
39 2:          proc3(pm1, pm2);
40 2:      END;
41 1:
42 1: BEGIN
43 1:      m1[1,1] := 11;  m1[1,2] := 12;  m1[1,3] := 13;
44 1:      m1[2,1] := 21;  m1[2,2] := 22;  m1[2,3] := 23;
45 1:
46 1:      m2[1,1] := -11;  m2[1,2] := -12;  m2[1,3] := -13;
47 1:      m2[2,1] := -21;  m2[2,2] := -22;  m2[2,3] := -23;
48 1:
49 1:      i := m1[1,1];          {11}
50 1:      i := m2[1,1];          {-11}
```

Page 2   arrparms.pas   Wed Jul 11 00:15:43 1990

```
51 1:      i := m1[2,2];          {22}
52 1:      i := m2[2,2];          {-22}
53 1:
54 1:      proc2(m1, m2);
55 1:
56 1:      i := m1[1,1];          {11}
57 1:      i := m2[1,1];          {-99}
58 1:      i := m1[2,2];          {22}
59 1:      i := m2[2,2];          {-77}
60 1: END.
61 0:
```

```
            61 Source lines.
             0 Source errors.
```

```
>> Entering routine arrparms
>>   Stmt 43
>>     m1[*] := 11
>>   Stmt 43
>>     m1[*] := 12
>>   Stmt 43
>>     m1[*] := 13
>>   Stmt 44
>>     m1[*] := 21
>>   Stmt 44
>>     m1[*] := 22
>>   Stmt 44
>>     m1[*] := 23
>>   Stmt 46
>>     m2[*] := -11
>>   Stmt 46
>>     m2[*] := -12
>>   Stmt 46
>>     m2[*] := -13
```

```
>>   Stmt 47
>>     m2[*] := -21
>>   Stmt 47
>>     m2[*] := -22
>>   Stmt 47
>>     m2[*] := -23
>>   Stmt 49
>>     m1 = 11
>>     i := 11
>>   Stmt 50
>>     m2 = -11
>>     i := -11
>>   Stmt 51
>>     m1 = 22
>>     i := 22
>>   Stmt 52
>>     m2 = -22
>>     i := -22
>>   Stmt 54
>>     m1[*] = <array>
>> Entering routine proc2
>>   Stmt 32
>>     pm1[*] := 77
>>   Stmt 33
>>     pm2[*] := -77
>>   Stmt 34
>>     pm1 = 77
>>     j := 77
>>   Stmt 35
>>     pm2 = -77
>>     j := -77
>>   Stmt 36
>>     m1 = 22
>>     j := 22
>>   Stmt 37
>>     m2 = -77
>>     j := -77
>>   Stmt 39
>>     pm1[*] = <array>
>> Entering routine proc3
>>   Stmt 23
>>     ppm1[*] := 99
>>   Stmt 24
>>     ppm2[*] := -99
>>   Stmt 25
>>     ppm1 = 99
>>     j := 99
>>   Stmt 26
>>     ppm2 = -99
>>     j := -99
>>   Stmt 27
>>     m1 = 11
>>     j := 11
>>   Stmt 28
>>     m2 = -99
>>     j := -99
>> Exiting routine proc3
>> Exiting routine proc2
>>   Stmt 56
>>     m1 = 11
>>     i := 11
>>   Stmt 57
>>     m2 = -99
>>     i := -99
```

```
>>  Stmt 58                              >>   i := -77
>>    m1 = 22                            >> Exiting routine arrparms
>>    i := 22
>>  Stmt 59
>>    m2 = -77                           Successful completion.  34 statements executed.
```

FIGURE 9-17   Sample interpreter output from nested procedures and functions.

Page 1   nested.pas   Wed Jul 11 00:16:25 1990   Page 2   nested.pas   Wed Jul 11 00:16:25 1990

```
 1 0: PROGRAM main1 (output);                    51 1:         i := 1;      {1}
 2 1:                                            52 1:         proc2;
 3 1:    VAR                                     53 1:         j := i;      {1}
 4 1:        i, j : integer;                     54 1:    END.
 5 1:                                            55 0:
 6 1:    FUNCTION func2 : integer;               56 0:
 7 2:                                            57 0:
 8 2:        VAR
 9 2:            i, j : integer;
10 2:
11 2:        FUNCTION func3 : integer;
12 3:                                                        57 Source lines.
13 3:            VAR                                          0 Source errors.
14 3:                i, j : integer;
15 3:
16 3:            BEGIN
17 3:                i := 123;      {123}        >> Entering routine main1
18 3:                func3 := 0;    {0}          >>  Stmt 51
19 3:                j := i;        {123}        >>    i := 1
20 3:            END;                            >>  Stmt 52
21 2:                                            >> Entering routine proc2
22 2:        BEGIN                               >>  Stmt 45
23 2:            i := 12;           {12}         >>    i := -12
24 2:            func2 := func3;    {0}          >>  Stmt 46
25 2:            j := i;            {12}         >> Entering routine proc3
26 2:        END;                                >>  Stmt 39
27 1:                                            >>    i := -123
28 1:    PROCEDURE proc2;                        >>  Stmt 40
29 2:                                            >> Entering routine func2
30 2:        VAR                                 >>  Stmt 23
31 2:            i, j : integer;                 >>    i := 12
32 2:                                            >>  Stmt 24
33 2:        PROCEDURE proc3;                    >> Entering routine func3
34 3:                                            >>  Stmt 17
35 3:            VAR                             >>    i := 123
36 3:                i, j : integer;             >>  Stmt 18
37 3:                                            >>    func3 := 0
38 3:            BEGIN                           >>  Stmt 19
39 3:                i := -123;     {-123}       >>    i = 123
40 3:                j := func2;    {0}          >>    j := 123
41 3:                j := i;        {-123}       >> Exiting routine func3
42 3:            END;                            >>    func2 := 0
43 2:                                            >>  Stmt 25
44 2:        BEGIN                               >>    i = 12
45 2:            i := -12;     {-12}             >>    j := 12
46 2:            proc3;                          >> Exiting routine func2
47 2:            j := i;       {-12}             >>    j := 0
48 2:        END;                                >>  Stmt 41
49 1:                                            >>    i = -123
50 1:    BEGIN                                   >>    j := -123
                                                 >> Exiting routine proc3
                                                 >>  Stmt 47
                                                 >>    i = -12
```

```
>>   j := -12
>> Exiting routine proc2
>>   Stmt 53
>>   i = 1
>>   j := 1
>> Exiting routine main1


Successful completion.  15 statements executed.
```

FIGURE 9-18   Sample interpreter output showing a runtime range error.

```
Page 1   range1.pas   Wed Jul 11 00:16:48 1990                              13 Source lines.
                                                                             0 Source errors.

 1 0: PROGRAM range1 (output);
 2 1:
 3 1: VAR
 4 1:     i : 1..10;                                    >> Entering routine range1
 5 1:     j : integer;                                  >> Stmt 8
 6 1:                                                   >>   j := 0
 7 1: BEGIN                                             >> Stmt 9
 8 1:     j := 0;                                       >>   j = 0
 9 1:     i := j;       {range error!}
10 1: END.                                              *** RUNTIME ERROR in line 9: Value out of range
11 0:
12 0:                                                   Unsuccessful completion.  2 statements executed.
13 0:
```

In the next chapter, we will complete this interpreter so that it can execute all Pascal statements and the standard predefined procedures and functions.

Questions and exercises

1. Experiment with different stack frame formats. Try allocating array and record data on the stack.

2. In most Pascal programs, we make many references to the program's global variables. We allocate them at the bottom of the runtime stack and if we are in a deeply-nested procedure or function we must follow several static links to get to a global value. Improve this situation by taking advantage of the fact that we know the global values are on the bottom of the stack.

3. Improve the data fetch and store tracing routines to print the values of subscripts and the names of record fields.

4. Improve the parser to do range checking while it is parsing constants and literals.

CHAPTER 10

Interpreting Control Statements

In this chapter, we will complete the executor module by adding execution routines for Pascal control statements and predefined standard procedures and functions. When we finish, we will have reached a major milestone: a fully functional Pascal interpreter. Then in the next chapter, we will enhance the interpreter further by adding interactive debugging capabilities. This chapter develops the skills to:

- use address markers to support executing control statements
- execute calls to the standard procedures and functions
- interpret entire Pascal programs

10.1 Interpreter organization

To execute Pascal control statements, we need to add new files execstmt.c and execstd.c to the executor module, and change several old files.

Parser Module

parser.h	*u*	Parser header file
routine.c	*u*	Parse programs, procedures, and functions
standard.c	*u*	Parse standard procedures and functions
decl.c	*u*	Parse declarations

stmt.c	*c*	Parse statements
expr.c	*u*	Parse expressions

Scanner Module

scanner.h	*u*	Scanner header file
scanner.c	*u*	Scanner routines

Symbol Table Module

symtab.h	*u*	Symbol table header file
symtab.c	*u*	Symbol table routines

Executor Module

exec.h	*c*	Executor header file
executil.c	*c*	Executor utility routines
execstmt.c	*c*	Execute statements
execexpr.c	*u*	Execute expressions
execstd.c	*n*	Execute standard procedures and functions

Error Module

error.h	*u*	Error header file
error.c	*u*	Error routines

Miscellaneous

common.h	*u*	Common header file

Where: *u* file unchanged from the previous chapter
        c file changed from the previous chapter
        n new file

File execstmt.c contains the routines to execute control statements, and ex-ecstd.c contains the routines to execute calls to the standard procedures and functions. We add a few new support routines in executil.c. In stmt.c, we modify some of the statement parsing routines to insert address markers into the code buffer. In file exec.h, we add the new constant:

```
#define ADDRESS_MARKER   0x71
```

and the function types:

```
char *crunch_address_marker();
char *fixup_address_marker();
char *get_address_cmarker();
int  get_cinteger();
char *get_caddress();
```

10.2 Executing control statements

The interpreter executes Pascal control statements in essentially the same way that it executes expressions, assignment statements, and calls to procedure and function. As we saw in Chapter 9, the interpreter extracts tokens from the current code segment and then decides what to do based on what the tokens are.

Control statements require a bit more work. For example, you may need to skip part of the intermediate code for an IF statement, and you need to repeatedly execute the intermediate code for a REPEAT statement. We will see later what we can add to the intermediate code to make skipping and looping more efficient.

Figure 10-1 shows a new version of function exec_statement in file execstmt.c. Depending on the value of ctoken, the function can now call the appropriate function to execute the various control statements. Figure 10-2 shows these new functions.

FIGURE 10-1   Function exec_statement in file execstmt.c.

```
/*----------------------------------------------*/              exec_routine_call(idp);
/* exec_statement    Execute a statement by calling the  */       else
/*                   appropriate execution routine.      */         exec_assignment_statement(idp);
/*----------------------------------------------*/
                                                                  break;
exec_statement()                                              }

{                                                            case BEGIN:   exec_compound_statement();  break;
   if (ctoken == STATEMENT_MARKER) {                         case CASE:    exec_case_statement();      break;
       exec_line_number = get_statement_cmarker();           case FOR:     exec_for_statement();       break;
       ++exec_stmt_count;                                    case IF:      exec_if_statement();        break;
                                                             case REPEAT:  exec_repeat_statement();    break;
       statement_startp = code_segmentp;                     case WHILE:   exec_while_statement();     break;
       trace_statement_execution();
       get_ctoken();                                         case SEMICOLON:
   }                                                         case END:
                                                             case ELSE:
   switch (ctoken) {                                         case UNTIL:                               break;

       case IDENTIFIER: {                                    default:  runtime_error(UNIMPLEMENTED_RUNTIME_FEATURE);
           SYMTAB_NODE_PTR idp = get_symtab_cptr();          }

           if (idp->defn.key == PROC_DEFN)               while (ctoken == SEMICOLON) get_ctoken();

                                                         }
```

FIGURE 10-2   Functions in file execstmt.c that execute the Pascal control statements.

```
/*----------------------------------------------*/        exec_case_statement()
/* exec_case_statement    Execute a CASE statement:  */
/*                                                   */
/*                                                   */    {
/*                    CASE <expr> OF                 */       int    case_expr_value;      /* CASE expr value */
/*                        <case-branch> ;            */       int    case_label_count;     /* CASE label count */
/*                        ...                        */       int    case_label_value;     /* CASE label value */
/*                        END                        */       char   *branch_table_location;  /* branch table addr */
/*----------------------------------------------*/           char   *case_branch_location;   /* CASE branch addr */
```

```
    TYPE_STRUCT_PTR case_expr_tp;              /* CASE expr type */
    BOOLEAN         done = FALSE;


    get_ctoken();        /* token after CASE */
    branch_table_location = get_address_cmarker();


    /*
    -- Evaluate the CASE expression.
    */
    get_ctoken();
    case_expr_tp = exec_expression();
    case_expr_value = (case_expr_tp == integer_typep) ||
                      (case_expr_tp->form == ENUM_FORM)
                          ? tos->integer
                          : tos->byte;
    pop();       /* expression value */


    /*
    -- Search the branch table for the expression value.
    */
    code_segmentp = branch_table_location;
    get_ctoken();
    case_label_count = get_cinteger();
    while (!done && case_label_count--) {
        case_label_value    = get_cinteger();
        case_branch_location = get_caddress();
        done = case_label_value == case_expr_value;
    }


    /*
    -- If found, go to the appropriate CASE branch.
    */
    if (case_label_count >= 0) {
        code_segmentp = case_branch_location;
        get_ctoken();
        exec_statement();

        code_segmentp = get_address_cmarker();
        get_ctoken();
    }
    else runtime_error(INVALID_CASE_VALUE);
}

/*-------------------------------------------------------------*/
/* exec_for_statement      Execute a FOR statement:           */
/*                                                             */
/*                             FOR <id> := <expr>              */
/*                             TO|DOWNTO <expr>                */
/*                             DO <stmt>                       */
/*-------------------------------------------------------------*/

exec_for_statement()

{
    SYMTAB_NODE_PTR control_idp;         /* control var id */
    TYPE_STRUCT_PTR control_tp;          /* control var type */
    STACK_ITEM_PTR  targetp;             /* ptr to control target */
    char            *loop_start_location; /* addr of start of loop */
    char            *loop_end_location;   /* addr of end of loop */
    int             control_value;        /* value of control var */
    int             initial_value, final_value, delta_value;

    get_ctoken();        /* token after FOR */
    loop_end_location = get_address_cmarker();

    /*
    -- Get the address of the control variable's stack item.
```

```
    */
    get_ctoken();
    control_idp = get_symtab_cptr();
    control_tp  = exec_variable(control_idp, TARGET_USE);
    targetp     = (STACK_ITEM_PTR) tos->address;
    pop();       /* control variable address */


    /*
    -- Evaluate the initial expression.
    */
    get_ctoken();
    exec_expression();
    initial_value = (control_tp == integer_typep)
                        ? tos->integer
                        : tos->byte;
    pop();       /* initial value */

    delta_value = (ctoken == TO) ? 1 : -1;

    /*
    -- Evaluate the final expression.
    */
    get_ctoken();
    exec_expression();
    final_value = (control_tp == integer_typep)
                        ? tos->integer
                        : tos->byte;
    pop();       /* final value */

    loop_start_location = code_segmentp;
    control_value = initial_value;


    /*
    -- Execute the FOR loop.
    */
    while (  ((delta_value == 1) &&
              (control_value <= final_value))
          || ((delta_value == -1) &&
              (control_value >= final_value))) {
        if (control_tp == integer_typep)
            targetp->integer = control_value;
        else
            targetp->byte = control_value;

        get_ctoken();           /* token after DO */
        exec_statement();

        control_value += delta_value;
        code_segmentp = loop_start_location;
    }

    code_segmentp = loop_end_location;
    get_ctoken();        /* token after FOR statement */
}

/*-------------------------------------------------------------*/
/* exec_if_statement    Execute an IF statement:              */
/*                                                             */
/*                            IF <expr> THEN <stmt>            */
/*                                                             */
/*                            or:                              */
/*                                                             */
/*                            IF <expr> THEN <stmt> ELSE <stmt> */
/*-------------------------------------------------------------*/

exec_if_statement()

{
```

```
char          *false_location;   /* address of false branch */
BOOLEAN       test;

get_ctoken();        /* token after IF */
false_location = get_address_cmarker();

/*
-- Evaluate the boolean expression.
*/
get_ctoken();
exec_expression();
test = tos->integer == 1;
pop();       /* boolean value */

if (test) {
    /*
    -- True:  Execute the true branch.
    */
    get_ctoken();   /* token after THEN */
    exec_statement();

    if (ctoken == ELSE) {
        get_ctoken();                 /* token after ELSE */
        code_segmentp = get_address_cmarker();
        get_ctoken();                 /* token after false stmt */
    }
}
else {
    /*
    -- False:  Execute the false branch if there is one.
    */
    code_segmentp = false_location;
    get_ctoken();

    if (ctoken == ELSE) {
        get_ctoken();                 /* token after ELSE */
        get_address_cmarker();        /* skip address marker */

        get_ctoken();
        exec_statement();
    }
}
}

/*------------------------------------------------------------*/
/* exec_repeat_statement      Execute a REPEAT statement:     */
/*                                                            */
/*                            REPEAT <stmt-list>              */
/*                            UNTIL <expr>                    */
/*------------------------------------------------------------*/

exec_repeat_statement()

{
    char *loop_start_location = code_segmentp;  /* addr of
                                                   loop start */

    do {
        get_ctoken();        /* token after REPEAT */
```

```
    /*
    -- Execute the statement list.
    */
    do {
        exec_statement();
    } while (ctoken != UNTIL);

    /*
    -- Evaluate the boolean expression.
    */
    get_ctoken();
    exec_expression();
    if (tos->integer == 0) code_segmentp = loop_start_location;
    pop();            /* boolean value */
} while (code_segmentp == loop_start_location);
}

/*------------------------------------------------------------*/
/* exec_while_statement       Process a WHILE statement:      */
/*                                                            */
/*                            WHILE <expr> DO <stmt>          */
/*------------------------------------------------------------*/

exec_while_statement()

{
    char    *loop_end_location;      /* addr of end of loop */
    char    *test_location;          /* addr of boolean expr */
    BOOLEAN loop_done = FALSE;

    get_ctoken();        /* token after WHILE */
    loop_end_location = get_address_cmarker();
    test_location     = code_segmentp;

    do {
        /*
        -- Evaluate the boolean expression.
        */
        get_ctoken();
        exec_expression();
        if (tos->integer == 0) {
            code_segmentp = loop_end_location;
            loop_done = TRUE;
        }
        pop();           /* boolean value */

        /*
        -- If true, execute the statement.
        */
        if (!loop_done) {
            get_ctoken();
            exec_statement();
            code_segmentp = test_location;
        }
    } while (!loop_done);

    get_ctoken();        /* token after WHILE statement */
}
```

10.2.1 Executing the REPEAT statement

We begin with the simplest control statement, the REPEAT statement. Figure 10-3 shows the intermediate *code diagram* for the statement. A code diagram is similar to a syntax diagram, except that it represents how the parser lays out the intermediate code in the code buffer (which we later copy into a code segment where we execute it). The code starts with the single token (represented with an oval) for REPEAT, which is then followed by all the intermediate code (represented by a rectangle) for the statements in the statement list. After that comes the single token for UNTIL followed by the intermediate code for the boolean expression.

FIGURE 10-3   The intermediate code diagram for the REPEAT statement.

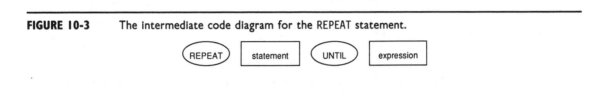

When we call the new function exec_repeat_statement in file execstmt.c, the code segment pointer code_segmentp points to the first token code of the first statement in the statement list. Since this statement list is in a loop, we point loop_start_location to this token. We call function exec_statement to execute each statement in the list, and then we call exec_expression to evaluate the boolean expression. If the expression value is zero (false), we must execute the statement list again, so we reset code_segmentp to the value of loop_start_location. Otherwise, we leave code_segmentp pointing to the first token after the REPEAT statement.

10.2.2 Executing the WHILE statement with an address marker

Figure 10-4 shows the intermediate code diagram for the WHILE statement that represents what the parser has been producing up until now. As with the REPEAT statement, you need to remember the location of the first token after the WHILE token. This is the start of the boolean expression, which you evaluate before each time through the loop.

FIGURE 10-4   The original intermediate code diagram for the WHILE statement.

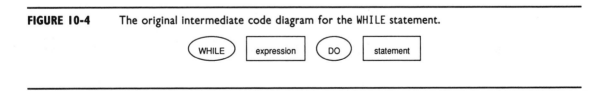

If the expression is true, you execute the statement part, loop back, and re-evaluate the expression. But what happens if the expression is false? You can imagine going into a "skipping mode," when you extract statements from the code segment but do not execute them. Then, you must go back into "execution mode" when you reach the first statement after the WHILE statement.

A cleaner and much more efficient solution is to place an *address marker* into the intermediate code, as shown in Figure 10-5. The addresss marker points to the first token after the WHILE statement, which is where you want to go if the boolean expression is false.

FIGURE 10-5   The intermediate code diagram for the WHILE statement with an address marker.

The parser emits these address markers into the intermediate code in the code buffer. Figure 10-6 shows new versions of some of the statement parsing functions in file stmt.c. In the new version of function while_statement, we call function crunch_address_marker to insert the address marker into the code buffer after the WHILE token. Function crunch_address_marker is one of several new functions in file executil.c that insert new information into the code buffer. They are all shown in Figure 10-7.

FIGURE 10-6   Control statement parsing functions in file stmt.c that insert address markers into the intermediate code.

```
/*--------------------------------------------------------*/
/* while_statement     Process a WHILE statement:         */
/*                                                        */
/*                         WHILE <expr> DO <stmt>         */
/*--------------------------------------------------------*/

while_statement()

{
    TYPE_STRUCT_PTR expr_tp;
    char            *loop_end_location;

    get_token();
    loop_end_location = crunch_address_marker(NULL);

    expr_tp = expression();
    if (expr_tp != boolean_typep) error(INCOMPATIBLE_TYPES);

    if_token_get_else_error(DO, MISSING_DO);
    statement();

    fixup_address_marker(loop_end_location);
}
```

```
/*--------------------------------------------------------------*/
/* if_statement       Process an IF statement:                  */
/*                                                              */
/*                       IF <expr> THEN <stmt>                  */
/*                                                              */
/*                         or:                                  */
/*                                                              */
/*                       IF <expr> THEN <stmt> ELSE <stmt>      */
/*--------------------------------------------------------------*/

if_statement()

{
    TYPE_STRUCT_PTR expr_tp;
    char            *false_location;
    char            *if_end_location;

    get_token();
    false_location = crunch_address_marker(NULL);

    expr_tp = expression();
    if (expr_tp != boolean_typep) error(INCOMPATIBLE_TYPES);

    if_token_get_else_error(THEN, MISSING_THEN);
```

```
        statement();

        fixup_address_marker(false_location);

        /*
        -- ELSE branch?
        */
        if (token == ELSE) {
            get_token();
            if_end_location = crunch_address_marker(NULL);

            statement();

            fixup_address_marker(if_end_location);
        }
    }

    /*-----------------------------------------------------------*/
    /*  for_statement        Process a FOR statement:            */
    /*                                                           */
    /*                       FOR <id> := <expr> TO|DOWNTO <expr> */
    /*                       DO <stmt>                           */
    /*-----------------------------------------------------------*/

    for_statement()

    {
        SYMTAB_NODE_PTR for_idp;
        TYPE_STRUCT_PTR for_tp, expr_tp;
        char           *loop_end_location;

        get_token();
        loop_end_location = crunch_address_marker(NULL);

        if (token == IDENTIFIER) {
            search_and_find_all_symtab(for_idp);
            crunch_symtab_node_ptr(for_idp);

            if ((for_idp->level != level) ||
                (for_idp->defn.key != VAR_DEFN))
                error(INVALID_FOR_CONTROL);

            for_tp = base_type(for_idp->typep);
            get_token();

            if ((for_tp != integer_typep) &&
                (for_tp != char_typep) &&
                (for_tp->form != ENUM_FORM)) error(INCOMPATIBLE_TYPES);
        }
        else {
            error(IDENTIFIER, MISSING_IDENTIFIER);
            for_tp = &dummy_type;
        }

        if_token_get_else_error(COLONEQUAL, MISSING_COLONEQUAL);

        expr_tp = expression();
        if (! is_assign_type_compatible(for_tp, expr_tp))
            error(INCOMPATIBLE_TYPES);

        if ((token == TO) || (token == DOWNTO)) get_token();
        else error(MISSING_TO_OR_DOWNTO);

        expr_tp = expression();
        if (! is_assign_type_compatible(for_tp, expr_tp))
            error(INCOMPATIBLE_TYPES);
```

```
        if_token_get_else_error(DO, MISSING_DO);
        statement();

        fixup_address_marker(loop_end_location);
    }

    /*-----------------------------------------------------------*/
    /*  CASE statement globals                                   */
    /*-----------------------------------------------------------*/

    typedef struct case_item {
        int             label_value;
        char            *branch_location;
        struct case_item *next;
    } CASE_ITEM, *CASE_ITEM_PTR;

    CASE_ITEM_PTR case_item_head, case_item_tail;
    int           case_label_count;

    /*-----------------------------------------------------------*/
    /*  case_statement       Process a CASE statement:           */
    /*                                                           */
    /*                       CASE <expr> OF                      */
    /*                           <case-branch> ;                 */
    /*                           ...                             */
    /*                       END                                 */
    /*-----------------------------------------------------------*/

    TOKEN_CODE follow_expr_list[]     = {OF, SEMICOLON, 0};

    TOKEN_CODE case_label_start_list[] = {IDENTIFIER, NUMBER, PLUS,
                                          MINUS, STRING, 0};

    case_statement()

    {
        BOOLEAN         another_branch;
        TYPE_STRUCT_PTR expr_tp;
        TYPE_STRUCT_PTR case_label();
        CASE_ITEM_PTR   case_itemp, next_case_itemp;
        char            *branch_table_location;
        char            *case_end_chain = NULL;

        /*
        -- Initializations for the branch table.
        */
        get_token();
        branch_table_location = crunch_address_marker(NULL);
        case_item_head = case_item_tail = NULL;
        case_label_count = 0;

        expr_tp = expression();

        if (  ((expr_tp->form != SCALAR_FORM) &&
               (expr_tp->form != ENUM_FORM) &&
               (expr_tp->form != SUBRANGE_FORM))
           || (expr_tp == real_typep)) error(INCOMPATIBLE_TYPES);

        /*
        -- Error synchronization:  Should be OF
        */
        synchronize(follow_expr_list, case_label_start_list, NULL);
        if_token_get_else_error(OF, MISSING_OF);

        /*
        -- Loop to process CASE branches.
        */
```

```
    another_branch = token_in(case_label_start_list);
    while (another_branch) {
        if (token_in(case_label_start_list)) case_branch(expr_tp);

        /*
        -- Link another address marker at the end of
        -- the CASE branch to point to the end of
        -- the CASE statement.
        */
        case_end_chain = crunch_address_marker(case_end_chain);

        if (token == SEMICOLON) {
            get_token();
            another_branch = TRUE;
        }
        else if (token_in(case_label_start_list)) {
            error(MISSING_SEMICOLON);
            another_branch = TRUE;
        }
        else another_branch = FALSE;
    }

    /*
    -- Emit the branch table.
    */
    fixup_address_marker(branch_table_location);
    crunch_integer(case_label_count);
    case_itemp = case_item_head;
    while (case_itemp != NULL) {
        crunch_integer(case_itemp->label_value);
        crunch_offset(case_itemp->branch_location);
        next_case_itemp = case_itemp->next;
        free(case_itemp);
        case_itemp = next_case_itemp;
    }

    if_token_get_else_error(END, MISSING_END);

    /*
    -- Patch the CASE branch address markers.
    */
    while (case_end_chain != NULL)
        case_end_chain = fixup_address_marker(case_end_chain);
}

/*-----------------------------------------------------------*/
/* case_branch            Process a CASE branch:             */
/*                                                           */
/*                        <case-label-list> : <stmt>         */
/*-----------------------------------------------------------*/

TOKEN_CODE follow_case_label_list[] = {COLON, SEMICOLON, 0};

case_branch(expr_tp)

    TYPE_STRUCT_PTR expr_tp;        /* type of CASE expression */

{
    BOOLEAN         another_label;
    TYPE_STRUCT_PTR label_tp;
    CASE_ITEM_PTR   case_itemp;
    CASE_ITEM_PTR   old_case_item_tail = case_item_tail;
    TYPE_STRUCT_PTR case_label();

    /*
    -- <case-label-list>
    */
```

```
    do {
        label_tp = case_label();
        if (expr_tp != label_tp) error(INCOMPATIBLE_TYPES);

        get_token();
        if (token == COMMA) {
            get_token();
            if (token_in(case_label_start_list)) another_label = TRUE;
            else {
                error(MISSING_CONSTANT);
                another_label = FALSE;
            }
        }
        else another_label = FALSE;
    } while (another_label);

    /*
    -- Error synchronization:  Should be :
    */
    synchronize(follow_case_label_list, statement_start_list, NULL);
    if_token_get_else_error(COLON, MISSING_COLON);

    /*
    -- Loop to fill in the branch_location field of
    -- each CASE_ITEM item for this branch.
    */
    case_itemp = old_case_item_tail == NULL
                        ? case_item_head
                        : old_case_item_tail->next;
    while (case_itemp != NULL) {
        case_itemp->branch_location = code_bufferp;
        case_itemp = case_itemp->next;
    }

    statement();
}

/*-----------------------------------------------------------*/
/* case_label            Process a CASE label and return a   */
/*                       pointer to its type structure.      */
/*-----------------------------------------------------------*/

    TYPE_STRUCT_PTR
case_label()

{
    TOKEN_CODE      sign     = PLUS;   /* unary + or - sign */
    BOOLEAN         saw_sign = FALSE;  /* TRUE iff unary sign */
    TYPE_STRUCT_PTR label_tp;
    CASE_ITEM_PTR   case_itemp = alloc_struct(CASE_ITEM);

    /*
    -- Link in a CASE_ITEM item for this label.
    */
    if (case_item_head != NULL) {
        case_item_tail->next = case_itemp;
        case_item_tail = case_itemp;
    }
    else {
        case_item_head = case_item_tail = case_itemp;
    }
    case_itemp->next = NULL;
    ++case_label_count;

    /*
    -- Unary + or - sign.
    */
```

```
    if ((token == PLUS) || (token == MINUS)) {
        sign     = token;
        saw_sign = TRUE;
        get_token();
    }

    /*
    -- Numeric constant:  Integer type only.
    */
    if (token == NUMBER) {
        SYMTAB_NODE_PTR np = search_symtab(token_string,
                                   symtab_display[1]);

        if (np == NULL) np = enter_symtab(token_string,
                                   symtab_display[1]);
        crunch_symtab_node_ptr(np);

        if (literal.type == INTEGER_LIT)
            case_itemp->label_value = sign == PLUS
                            ? literal.value.integer
                            : -literal.value.integer;
        else error(INVALID_CONSTANT);
        return(integer_typep);
    }

    /*
    -- Identifier constant:  Integer, character, or enumeration
    --                       types only.
    */
    else if (token == IDENTIFIER) {
        SYMTAB_NODE_PTR idp;

        search_all_symtab(idp);
        crunch_symtab_node_ptr(idp);

        if (idp == NULL) {
            error(UNDEFINED_IDENTIFIER);
            return(&dummy_type);
        }

        else if (idp->defn.key != CONST_DEFN) {
            error(NOT_A_CONSTANT_IDENTIFIER);
            return(&dummy_type);
        }

        else if (idp->typep == integer_typep) {
            case_itemp->label_value = sign == PLUS
                            ? idp->defn.info.constant
                                      .value.integer
                            : -idp->defn.info.constant
                                      .value.integer;
            return(integer_typep);
        }

        else if (idp->typep == char_typep) {
            if (saw_sign) error(INVALID_CONSTANT);
            case_itemp->label_value = idp->defn.info.constant
                                      .value.character;
            return(char_typep);
        }

        else if (idp->typep->form == ENUM_FORM) {
            if (saw_sign) error(INVALID_CONSTANT);
            case_itemp->label_value = idp->defn.info.constant
                                      .value.integer;
            return(idp->typep);
        }

        else return(&dummy_type);
    }

    /*
    -- String constant:  Character type only.
    */
    else if (token == STRING) {
        SYMTAB_NODE_PTR np = search_symtab(token_string,
                                   symtab_display[1]);

        if (np == NULL) np = enter_symtab(token_string,
                                   symtab_display[1]);
        crunch_symtab_node_ptr(np);

        if (saw_sign) error(INVALID_CONSTANT);

        if (strlen(literal.value.string) == 1) {
            case_itemp->label_value = literal.value.string[0];
            return(char_typep);
        }
        else {
            error(INVALID_CONSTANT);
            return(&dummy_type);
        }
    }

    else {
        error(INVALID_CONSTANT);
        return(&dummy_type);
    }
}
```

FIGURE 10-7   Functions in file `executil.c` that insert new information into the code buffer.

```
/*--------------------------------------------------------*/       {
/* crunch_address_marker     Append a code address to the */           char *save_code_bufferp;
/*                           code buffer.  Return the     */
/*                           addesss of the address.      */           if (code_bufferp >= code_buffer + MAX_CODE_BUFFER_SIZE
/*--------------------------------------------------------*/                                   - sizeof(ADDRESS)) {
                                                                           error(CODE_SEGMENT_OVERFLOW);
    char *                                                                 exit(-CODE_SEGMENT_OVERFLOW);
crunch_address_marker(address)                                         }
                                                                       else {
    ADDRESS address;    /* address value to append */
```

```
        char save_code = *(--code_bufferp);

        *code_bufferp++ = ADDRESS_MARKER;
        save_code_bufferp = code_bufferp;
        *((ADDRESS *) code_bufferp) = address;
        code_bufferp += sizeof(ADDRESS);
        *code_bufferp++ = save_code;

        return(save_code_bufferp);
    }
}

/*------------------------------------------------*/
/*  fixup_address_marker      Fix up an address marker with  */
/*                            the offset from the address    */
/*                            marker to the current code     */
/*                            buffer address.  Return the old */
/*                            value of the address marker.   */
/*------------------------------------------------*/

    char *
fixup_address_marker(address)

    ADDRESS address;     /* address of address marker to be fixed up */

{
    char *old_address = *((ADDRESS *) address);

    *((int *) address) = code_bufferp - address;
    return(old_address);
}

/*------------------------------------------------*/
/*  crunch_integer    Append an integer value to the code    */
/*                    buffer.                                 */
/*------------------------------------------------*/

crunch_integer(value)
```

```
    int value;          /* value to append */

{
    if (code_bufferp >= code_buffer + MAX_CODE_BUFFER_SIZE
                                        - sizeof(int)) {
        error(CODE_SEGMENT_OVERFLOW);
        exit(-CODE_SEGMENT_OVERFLOW);
    }
    else {
        *((int *) code_bufferp) = value;
        code_bufferp += sizeof(int);
    }
}

/*------------------------------------------------*/
/*  crunch_offset     Append an integer value to the code    */
/*                    that represents the offset from the    */
/*                    given address to the current code      */
/*                    buffer address.                        */
/*------------------------------------------------*/

crunch_offset(address)

    ADDRESS address;     /* address from which to offset */

{
    if (code_bufferp >= code_buffer + MAX_CODE_BUFFER_SIZE
                                        - sizeof(int)) {
        error(CODE_SEGMENT_OVERFLOW);
        exit(-CODE_SEGMENT_OVERFLOW);
    }
    else {
        *((int *) code_bufferp) = address - code_bufferp;
        code_bufferp += sizeof(int);
    }
}
```

Function crunch_address_marker is similar to function crunch_statement_marker. When we call this function, we pass it an address of a location in the code buffer. First, we insert the ADDRESS_MARKER code followed by the address value into the code buffer behind the last token code. Then we return the code buffer address of that address value.

In function while_statement, when we first call crunch_address_marker, we do not yet know the address of the end of the WHILE statement. Therefore, we pass NULL so the address marker is initially just a place holder. We store the address of this NULL value in loop_end_location. Later, when we finish parsing the WHILE statement, we pass loop_end_location to function fixup_address_marker to patch the address marker with the current code buffer address, which by then is the address of the first token after the WHILE statement.

So what should function fixup_address_marker do? Your first thought might be that it should just replace the placeholder NULL value with the current code buffer address. Then, you should have the intermediate code shown in Figure 10-5, with the address marker containing the address of the first token in the code buffer after the WHILE statement. Unfortunately, that won't work. You execute the intermediate code after it has been copied into a code segment, not in the code buffer. So, what you want is a code *segment* address. To solve this dilemma, you can calculate the byte offset between the address of the placeholder NULL value and the current code buffer address, and then you replace the NULL value with this offset. Later, when you are executing the intermediate code, you can calculate the code segment address by adding the offset to the current code segment address.

When we are finished in fixup_address_marker, we return the previous value of the address marker. Only parser function case_statement uses this value, so most of the time we ignore it.

Figure 10-8 shows the other new functions in file executil.c, the ones that retrieve the new information from the code segment. One new function is get_address_cmarker, which we call when we encounter an address marker in a code segment as we are executing a statement. It extracts the offset from the code segment, adds the current code segment address, and then subtracts one to calculate the desired code segment address. Subtracting one compensates for the fact that code_segmentp always points one byte ahead of the current token in ctoken. We return the address.

FIGURE 10-8   Functions in file executil.c that retrieve the new information from a code segment.

```
/*------------------------------------------------------*/
/* get_address_cmarker     Extract an address marker from the  */
/*                         current code segment.  Add its      */
/*                         offset value to the code segment    */
/*                         address and return the new address. */
/*------------------------------------------------------*/

    char *
get_address_cmarker()

{
    ADDRESS address;      /* address to return */

    if (ctoken == ADDRESS_MARKER) {
        address = *((int *) code_segmentp) + code_segmentp - 1;
        code_segmentp += sizeof(ADDRESS);
    }

    return(address);
}

/*------------------------------------------------------*/
/* get_cinteger      Extract an integer value from the  */
/*                   current code segment and return the */
/*                   value.                              */
/*------------------------------------------------------*/

    int
```

```
get_cinteger()

{
    int value;           /* value to extract and return */

    value = *((int *) code_segmentp);
    code_segmentp += sizeof(int);

    return(value);
}

/*------------------------------------------------------*/
/* get_caddress      Extract an offset from the current code */
/*                   segment and add it to the code segment  */
/*                   address.  Return the new address.       */
/*------------------------------------------------------*/

    char *
get_caddress()

{
    ADDRESS address;      /* address to return */

    address = *((int *) code_segmentp) + code_segmentp - 1;
    code_segmentp += sizeof(int);

    return(address);
}
```

In the new function exec_while_statement, we call get_address_cmarker to obtain the address of the first token after the WHILE statement, and we store this address in loop_end_location. Then we store the address of the first token of the boolean expression in test_location. We call exec_expression to evaluate the expression.

If the expression is false, we set code_segmentp to the value of loop_end_ location to point it to the first token after the WHILE statement, and we are done. Otherwise, if the expression is true, we call exec_statement to execute the statement part. Afterwards, we reset code_segmentp to the value of test_location in order to loop back and re-evaluate the boolean expression.

10.2.3 Executing the FOR statement

Figure 10-9 shows the intermediate code diagram for the FOR statement. Like the WHILE statement, an address marker points to the first token after the statement.

FIGURE 10-9   The intermediate code diagram for the FOR statement.

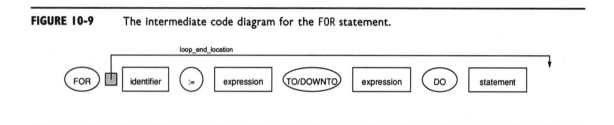

In the new version of function for_statement, we point loop_end_location to the first token after the statement. We create an address marker at the beginning and patch it at the end.

In the new function exec_for_statement, we first call get_address_cmarker to obtain the address of the first token after the FOR statement and store the address in loop_end_location. Next, we call exec_variable, passing usage code TARGET_USE, to obtain the address of the stack item of the control variable. We then evaluate the initial and final expressions with calls to exec_expression. In the while loop, we check and set the value of the control variable, call exec_ statement to execute the statement part, and increment or decrement the control variable. Once we reach the final value, we set code_segmentp to the value of loop_end_location. We leave the control variable with the final value.

10.2.4 Executing the IF statement

Figures 10-10 and 10-11 show the intermediate code diagrams of the IF statement without and with the ELSE part, respectively. The former requires one address marker, and the latter requires two.

FIGURE 10-10   The intermediate code diagram for the IF statement without the ELSE part.

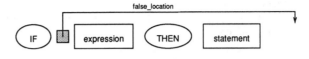

FIGURE 10-11   The intermediate code diagram for the IF statement with the ELSE part.

In the new version of function if_statement, we create an addresss marker at the beginning and store its address in false_location. After we have parsed the THEN part, we patch the address marker. Thus, the false_location address marker either points to the first token after the IF statement if there is no ELSE part (Figure 10-10), or to the ELSE token if there is an ELSE part (Figure 10-11).

If there is an ELSE part, we insert an address marker after the ELSE token, and we store its address in if_end_location. We patch this address marker after we've parsed the ELSE part. Thus, the if_end_location marker points to the first token after the IF statement.

In the new function exec_if_statement, we first call get_address_cmarker to obtain the address of the end of the THEN part and store the address in false_location. Then, we call exec_expression to evaluate the boolean expression.

If the expression is true, we call exec_statement to execute the THEN part. If the next token is not ELSE we are done, since there is no ELSE part and code_segmentp now points to the first token after the IF statement. However, if the next token is ELSE then we must call get_address_cmarker to point code_segmentp to the first token after the ELSE part, and then we are done.

If the boolean expression is false, we set code_segmentp to false_location. If the token at that location is not ELSE then we are done, since there is no ELSE part, and code_segmentp now points to the first token after the IF statement. If the token is ELSE, the function must call get_address_cmarker to skip over the address marker after the ELSE. code_segmentp then points to the first token of the ELSE part. We call exec_statement to execute that statement, and then we are done.

10.2.5 Executing the CASE statement

The CASE statement is the most challenging Pascal control statement. Figure 10-12 shows the intermediate code diagram for a sample statement. At the beginning, just after the CASE token, an address marker points to the CASE *branch table* which is located just after the last CASE branch. At the end of each CASE branch, an address marker points to the first token after the CASE statement.

The branch table begins with the number of entries in the table. There is one entry per CASE label. Each entry consists of the value of its label and the address of the first token of the branch statement corresponding to that label value. We output the branch table to the code buffer after the code for the last branch statement because not until then do we know the addresses of all the branch statements.

We insert these addresss markers and output the branch table in the new version of function case_statement. We need to patch all the address markers at the ends of the CASE branches with the address of the first token after the CASE statement, so we need to keep track of the address markers. We do this by linking the address markers themselves together. Figure 10-13 shows how each address marker initially points to the previous one. At the end of the CASE statement, we

---

FIGURE 10-12   The intermediate code diagram for a sample CASE statement.

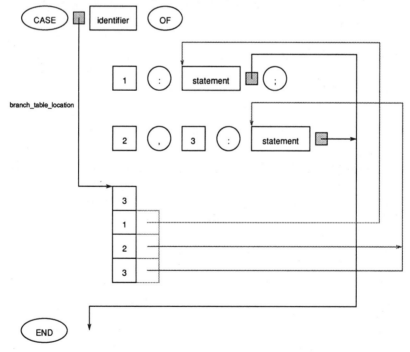

FIGURE 10-13   How each address marker for a CASE statement initially points to the previous one.

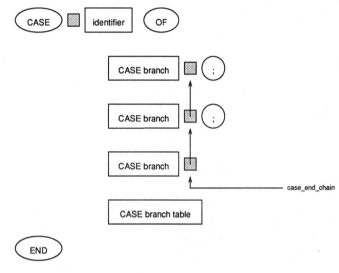

merely run down this list and patch each address marker to point to the first token after the statement.

We keep the data for the branch table in a separate linked list of CASE_ITEM items. We build the list in functions case_branch and case_label, and at the end of function case_statement, we run down the list to emit the branch table.

In case_statement, we begin by creating an address marker and storing its address in branch_table_location. We patch this address marker after we've parsed the last CASE branch. Then we emit the branch table.

We also create an address marker after we have parsed each CASE branch. We link them together by passing the address of the previous marker to crunch_address_marker, and we point case_end_chain to the head of the list. At the end of the CASE statement, we call fixup_address_marker in a loop that runs down the linked list. This is the only call to fixup_address_marker that makes use of the function's return value.

In function case_label, we increment case_label_count and allocate a CASE_ITEM item for each CASE label, which we then link to the end of the list. The new global variables case_item_head and case_item_tail point to the head and tail of this list. We set the label_value field and return to function case_branch.

Back in case_branch, after parsing the colon, we point the branch_location field of each of the branch items to the first token of the CASE branch statement.

When we emit the branch table in function case_statement we call two new functions in file emitutil.c, functions crunch_integer and crunch_offset. Whenever we call crunch_integer, we pass an integer which we append to the code buffer. Whenever we call crunch_offset, we pass a code buffer address. We compute the offset between that address and the current code buffer address, and we append the offset to the code buffer. So each branch table entry contains the offset between the offset itself and the start of the branch statement.

We also have new functions get_cinteger and get_caddress in file execu-til.c. Function get_cinteger extracts and returns an integer value from the current code segment. In function get_caddress, we return a code segment address that we calculate by extracting an offset value from the code segment, adding the current code segment address, and then subtracting one (to compensate for code_segmentp being one byte ahead of ctoken).

In the new function exec_case_statement, we first call function get_address_cmarker to obtain the address of the branch table, which we store in branch_table_location. We call exec_expression to evaluate the expression, and we store the value in case_expr_value.

We set code_segmentp to the value of branch_table_location to jump down to the branch table. We call get_cinteger to obtain the number of branch table entries. Then in a while loop, we call get_cinteger and get_caddress to obtain the CASE label value and the address of the corresponding CASE branch statement.

We compare case_expr_value to the label value of each branch table entry. If there is a match, we set code_segmentp to the corresponding branch statement address and call exec_statement to execute the branch statement at that address. After we execute the branch statement, we call get_address_cmarker to set code_segmentp to the address of the first token after the CASE statement, and we are done. If there was no match, we abort the program execution with the INVALID_CASE_VALUE error.

10.3 Executing calls to standard procedures and functions

Now we can execute all the Pascal control statements. To complete our interpreter, we need to execute calls to Pascal's standard predefined procedures and functions.

Figure 10-14 shows the new file execstd.c of the executor module. Its routines are analogous to those in file standard.c of the parser module.

FIGURE 10-14   File execstd.c.

```
/*****************************************************/        #include "common.h"
/*                                                   */        #include "error.h"
/*    S T A N D A R D   R O U T I N E   E X E C U T O R   */   #include "symtab.h"
/*                                                   */        #include "scanner.h"
/*    Execution routines for statements.             */        #include "parser.h"
/*                                                   */        #include "exec.h"
/*    FILE:      execstd.c                            */
/*                                                   */        #define EOF_CHAR                  '\x7f'
/*    MODULE:    executor                             */
/*                                                   */        #define DEFAULT_NUMERIC_FIELD_WIDTH   10
/*****************************************************/        #define DEFAULT_PRECISION             2

#include <stdio.h>                                             /*----------------------------------------------------*/
#include <math.h>                                              /* Externals                                          */
                                                               /*----------------------------------------------------*/
```

```
extern int          level;
extern int          exec_line_number;

extern char         *code_segmentp;
extern TOKEN_CODE   ctoken;

extern STACK_ITEM    *stack;
extern STACK_ITEM_PTR tos;
extern STACK_ITEM_PTR stack_frame_basep;
extern STACK_ITEM_PTR stack_display[];

extern TYPE_STRUCT_PTR integer_typep, real_typep,
                       boolean_typep, char_typep;

/*-------------------------------------------------------------*/
/* Forwards                                                    */
/*-------------------------------------------------------------*/

TYPE_STRUCT_PTR exec_eof_eoln(), exec_abs_sqr(),
                exec_arctan_cos_exp_ln_sin_sqrt(),
                exec_pred_succ(), exec_chr(),
                exec_odd(), exec_ord(), exec_round_trunc();

/*-------------------------------------------------------------*/
/* Globals                                                     */
/*-------------------------------------------------------------*/

BOOLEAN eof_flag = FALSE;

/*-------------------------------------------------------------*/
/* exec_standard_routine_call  Execute a call to a standard    */
/*                             procedure or function. Return   */
/*                             a pointer to the type structure */
/*                             of the call.                    */
/*-------------------------------------------------------------*/

    TYPE_STRUCT_PTR
exec_standard_routine_call(rtn_idp)

    SYMTAB_NODE_PTR rtn_idp;          /* routine id */

{
    switch (rtn_idp->defn.info.routine.key) {

        case READ:
        case READLN:    exec_read_readln(rtn_idp);    return(NULL);

        case WRITE:
        case WRITELN:   exec_write_writeln(rtn_idp);   return(NULL);

        case EOFF:
        case EOLN:      return(exec_eof_eoln(rtn_idp));

        case ABS:
        case SQR:       return(exec_abs_sqr(rtn_idp));

        case ARCTAN:
        case COS:
        case EXP:
        case LN:
        case SIN:
        case SQRT:      return(exec_arctan_cos_exp_ln_sin_sqrt
                                    (rtn_idp));

        case PRED:
        case SUCC:      return(exec_pred_succ(rtn_idp));
```

```
        case CHR:       return(exec_chr());
        case ODD:       return(exec_odd());
        case ORD:       return(exec_ord());

        case ROUND:
        case TRUNC:     return(exec_round_trunc(rtn_idp));
    }
}

/*-------------------------------------------------------------*/
/* exec_read_readln       Execute a call to read or readln.  */
/*-------------------------------------------------------------*/

exec_read_readln(rtn_idp)

    SYMTAB_NODE_PTR rtn_idp;          /* routine id */

{
    SYMTAB_NODE_PTR parm_idp;        /* parm id */
    TYPE_STRUCT_PTR parm_tp;         /* parm type */
    STACK_ITEM_PTR  targetp;         /* ptr to read target */

    /*
    -- Parameters are optional for readln.
    */
    get_ctoken();
    if (ctoken == LPAREN) {
        /*
        -- <id-list>
        */
        do {
            get_ctoken();
            parm_idp = get_symtab_cptr();
            parm_tp  = base_type(exec_variable(parm_idp,
                                        VARPARM_USE));
            targetp = (STACK_ITEM_PTR) tos->address;

            pop();      /* pop off address */

            if (parm_tp == integer_typep)
                scanf("%d", &targetp->integer);
            else if (parm_tp == real_typep)
                scanf("%g", &targetp->real);

            else if (parm_tp == char_typep) {
                scanf("%c", &targetp->byte);
                if (eof_flag ||
                    (targetp->byte == '\n')) targetp->byte = ' ';
            }

            trace_data_store(parm_idp, parm_idp->typep,
                             targetp, parm_tp);
        } while (ctoken == COMMA);

        get_ctoken();   /* token after ) */
    }

    if (rtn_idp->defn.info.routine.key == READLN) {
        char ch;

        do {
            ch = getchar();
        } while(!eof_flag && (ch != '\n'));
    }
}

/*-------------------------------------------------------------*/
/* exec_write_writeln     Execute a call to write or writeln. */
```

```
/*                    Each actual parameter can be:     */
/*                                                       */
/*                      <expr>                           */
/*                                                       */
/*                    or:                                */
/*                                                       */
/*                      <epxr> : <expr>                  */
/*                                                       */
/*                    or:                                */
/*                                                       */
/*                      <expr> : <expr> : <ex >          */
/*------------------------------------------ ----------*/


exec_write_writeln(rtn_idp)

    SYMTAB_NODE_PTR rtn_idp;            /* routine id */

{
    TYPE_STRUCT_PTR parm_tp;            /* parm type */
    int             field_width;
    int             precision;

    /*
    -- Parameters are optional for writeln.
    */
    get_ctoken();
    if (ctoken == LPAREN) {
        do {
            /*
            -- Push value
            */
            get_ctoken();
            parm_tp = base_type(exec_expression());

            if (parm_tp == integer_typep)
                field_width = DEFAULT_NUMERIC_FIELD_WIDTH;
            else if (parm_tp == real_typep) {
                field_width = DEFAULT_NUMERIC_FIELD_WIDTH;
                precision   = DEFAULT_PRECISION;
            }
            else field_width = 0;

            /*
            -- Optional field width <expr>
            */
            if (ctoken == COLON) {
                get_ctoken();
                exec_expression();
                field_width = tos->integer;
                pop();          /* pop off field width */

                /*
                -- Optional decimal places <expr>
                */
                if (ctoken == COLON) {
                    get_ctoken();
                    exec_expression();
                    precision = tos->integer;
                    pop();      /* pop off precision */
                }
            }

            /*
            -- Write value
            */
            if (parm_tp == integer_typep)
                printf("%*d", field_width, tos->integer);
```

```
            else if (parm_tp == real_typep)
                printf("%*.*f", field_width, precision, tos->real);
            else if (parm_tp == boolean_typep)
                printf("%*s", field_width, tos->integer == 1
                                            ? "TRUE" : "FALSE");
            else if (parm_tp == char_typep)
                printf("%*c", field_width, tos->byte);

            else if (parm_tp->form == ARRAY_FORM) {
                char buffer[MAX_SOURCE_LINE_LENGTH];

                strncpy(buffer, tos->address,
                                parm_tp->info.array.elmt_count);
                buffer[parm_tp->info.array.elmt_count] = '\0';
                printf("%*s", -field_width, buffer);
            }

            pop();      /* pop off value */
        } while (ctoken == COMMA);

        get_ctoken();   /* token after ) */
    }

    if (rtn_idp->defn.info.routine.key == WRITELN) putchar('\n');
}

/*-----------------------------------------------------------*/
/* exec_eof_eoln        Execute a call to eof or to eoln.   */
/*                      No parameters => boolean result.    */
/*-----------------------------------------------------------*/

    TYPE_STRUCT_PTR
exec_eof_eoln(rtn_idp)

    SYMTAB_NODE_PTR rtn_idp;            /* routine id */

{
    char ch = getchar();

    switch (rtn_idp->defn.info.routine.key) {

        case EOFF:
            if (eof_flag || feof(stdin)) {
                eof_flag = TRUE;
                push_integer(1);
            }
            else {
                push_integer(0);
                ungetc(ch, stdin);
            }
            break;

        case EOLN:
            if (eof_flag || feof(stdin)) {
                eof_flag = TRUE;
                push_integer(1);
            }
            else {
                push_integer(ch == '\n' ? 1 : 0);
                ungetc(ch, stdin);
            }
            break;
    }

    get_ctoken();       /* token after function name */
    return(boolean_typep);
}
```

```
/*----------------------------------------------------------*/
/* exec_abs_sqr            Execute a call to abs or to sqr.  */
/*                         integer parm => integer result    */
/*                         real parm    => real result       */
/*----------------------------------------------------------*/

    TYPE_STRUCT_PTR
exec_abs_sqr(rtn_idp)

    SYMTAB_NODE_PTR rtn_idp;          /* routine id */

{
    TYPE_STRUCT_PTR parm_tp;          /* actual parameter type */
    TYPE_STRUCT_PTR result_tp;        /* result type */

    get_ctoken();        /* ( */
    get_ctoken();
    parm_tp = base_type(exec_expression());

    if (parm_tp == integer_typep) {
        tos->integer = rtn_idp->defn.info.routine.key == ABS
                       ? abs(tos->integer)
                       : tos->integer * tos->integer;
        result_tp = integer_typep;
    }
    else {
        tos->real = rtn_idp->defn.info.routine.key == ABS
                    ? fabs(tos->real)
                    : tos->real * tos->real;
        result_tp = real_typep;
    }

    get_ctoken();        /* token after ) */
    return(result_tp);
}


/*----------------------------------------------------------*/
/* exec_arctan_cos_exp_ln_sin_sqrt Execute a call to arctan, */
/*                         cos, exp, ln, sin, or sqrt.       */
/*                         integer parm => real result       */
/*                         real_parm    => real result       */
/*----------------------------------------------------------*/

    TYPE_STRUCT_PTR
exec_arctan_cos_exp_ln_sin_sqrt(rtn_idp)

    SYMTAB_NODE_PTR rtn_idp;          /* routine id */

{
    TYPE_STRUCT_PTR parm_tp;          /* actual parameter type */
    int            code = rtn_idp->defn.info.routine.key;

    get_ctoken();        /* ( */
    get_ctoken();
    parm_tp = base_type(exec_expression());
    if (parm_tp == integer_typep) tos->real = tos->integer;

    if (   ((code == LN)  && (tos->real <= 0.0))
        || ((code == SQRT) && (tos->real < 0.0)))
        runtime_error(INVALID_FUNCTION_ARGUMENT);
    else {
        switch (rtn_idp->defn.info.routine.key) {
            case ARCTAN:  tos->real = atan(tos->real);   break;
            case COS:     tos->real = cos(tos->real);    break;
            case EXP:     tos->real = exp(tos->real);    break;
            case LN:      tos->real = log(tos->real);    break;
            case SIN:     tos->real = sin(tos->real);    break;
```

```
            case SQRT:    tos->real = sqrt(tos->real);   break;
        }
    }

    get_ctoken();        /* token after ) */
    return(real_typep);
}


/*----------------------------------------------------------*/
/* exec_pred_succ          Execute a call to pred or succ.   */
/*                         integer parm => integer result    */
/*                         enum parm    => enum result       */
/*----------------------------------------------------------*/

    TYPE_STRUCT_PTR
exec_pred_succ(rtn_idp)

    SYMTAB_NODE_PTR rtn_idp;          /* routine id */

{
    TYPE_STRUCT_PTR parm_tp;          /* actual parameter type */

    get_ctoken();        /* ( */
    get_ctoken();
    parm_tp = base_type(exec_expression());

    tos->integer = rtn_idp->defn.info.routine.key == PRED
                   ? --tos->integer
                   : ++tos->integer;

    get_ctoken();        /* token after ) */
    return(parm_tp);
}


/*----------------------------------------------------------*/
/* exec_chr                Execute a call to chr.            */
/*                         integer parm => character result  */
/*----------------------------------------------------------*/

    TYPE_STRUCT_PTR
exec_chr()

{
    get_ctoken();        /* ( */
    get_ctoken();
    exec_expression();

    tos->byte = tos->integer;

    get_ctoken();        /* token after ) */
    return(char_typep);
}


/*----------------------------------------------------------*/
/* exec_odd                Execute a call to odd.            */
/*                         integer parm => boolean result    */
/*----------------------------------------------------------*/

    TYPE_STRUCT_PTR
exec_odd()

{
    get_ctoken();        /* ( */
    get_ctoken();
    exec_expression();

    tos->integer &= 1;
```

```
    get_ctoken();        /* token after ) */
    return(boolean_typep);
}

/*-----------------------------------------------------*/
/* exec_ord              Execute a call to ord.         */
/*                       enumeration parm => integer result */
/*-----------------------------------------------------*/

    TYPE_STRUCT_PTR
exec_ord()

{
    get_ctoken();        /* ( */
    get_ctoken();
    exec_expression();

    get_ctoken();        /* token after ) */
    return(integer_typep);
}

/*-----------------------------------------------------*/
/* exec_round_trunc      Execute a call to round or trunc. */
```

```
/*                       real parm => integer result    */
/*-----------------------------------------------------*/

    TYPE_STRUCT_PTR
exec_round_trunc(rtn_idp)

    SYMTAB_NODE_PTR rtn_idp;            /* routine id */

{
    get_ctoken();        /* ( */
    get_ctoken();
    exec_expression();

    if (rtn_idp->defn.info.routine.key == ROUND) {
        tos->integer = tos->real > 0.0
                       ? (int) (tos->real + 0.5)
                       : (int) (tos->real - 0.5);
    }
    else tos->integer = (int) tos->real;

    get_ctoken();        /* token after ) */
    return(integer_typep);
}
```

In function exec_standard_routine_call, we call the appropriate execution function based on the defn.info.routine.key field of the symbol table node of the standard routine's identifier. We return either NULL for a standard procedure, or the type of a standard function.

We execute the standard Pascal procedures read and readln in function exec_read_readln. We call exec_variable, passing usage code VARPARM_USE, to obtain the address of each actual parameter's stack item to read into, and then we call scanf to read in the value. If we are reading a character variable and eof_flag is TRUE or the character we read is a carriage return, we use the blank character instead. Ignore the call to trace_data_store. (Macro flag trace is *undefined* in file exec.h.)

After we have read all the variables in the parameter list, if the standard procedure is readln, we skip input characters until we read the carriage return character or we reach the end of the input file.

In function exec_write_writeln, we execute the standard Pascal procedures write and writeln. We call exec_expression to evaluate each actual parameter expression and to evaluate any field width and precision expressions. We then call printf to output the value in the appropriate format. If the value is a string, we must first copy the string into a buffer and then append the null character. After we have written all the values in the parameter list, if the standard procedure is writeln, we output a carriage return.

We execute the standard Pascal functions eof and eoln in function exec_eof_eoln. First we try to read a single character. For eof, if the end-of-file condition is true we push one (true) onto the stack; otherwise, we push zero (false). For eoln, if the end-of-file condition is true or if the character we read is a carriage return we push one; otherwise, we push zero. Then, unless the end-of-file condition is true, we put the character we read back into the input stream so that the next read or readln will get it. We return a pointer to the boolean type structure.

You can see that the remaining functions are straightforward. They execute the rest of the standard predefined Pascal functions and return the appropriate types. Function exec_arctan_cos_exp_ln_sin_sqrt always requires a real parameter value, so it first converts an integer parameter value to real. It also checks this value for ln and sqrt.

10.4 Program 10-1: Pascal Interpreter II

Figure 10-15 shows the main file for our interpreter, run2.c. The interpreter can parse and execute complete Pascal programs written according to our syntax diagrams.

FIGURE 10-15   File run2.c.

```
/*****************************************************************/
/*                                                               */
/*      Program 10-1:  Pascal Interpreter II                     */
/*                                                               */
/*      Interpret a Pascal program.                              */
/*                                                               */
/*      FILE:      run2.c                                        */
/*                                                               */
/*      REQUIRES:  Modules parser, symbol table, scanner,        */
/*                          executor, error                      */
/*                                                               */
/*      USAGE:     run2 sourcefile                               */
/*                                                               */
/*         sourcefile    name of source file containing          */
/*                        the Pascal program to interpret        */
/*                                                               */
/*****************************************************************/

#include <stdio.h>
#include "symtab.h"
#include "exec.h"


/*-----------------------------------------------*/
/* Externals                                     */
/*-----------------------------------------------*/
```

```
extern TYPE_STRUCT_PTR integer_typep, real_typep,
                        boolean_typep, char_typep;

/*---------------------------------------------------------*/
/* main               Initialize the scanner and call      */
/*                     routine program.                    */
/*---------------------------------------------------------*/

main(argc, argv)

    int argc;
    char *argv[];

{
    /*
    -- Initialize the scanner.
    */
    init_scanner(argv[1]);

    /*
    -- Process a program.
    */
    get_token();
    program();
}
```

In the next chapter, we will add interactive debugging capabilities to the interpreter.

Questions and exercises

1. Modify function exec_case_statement so that if the value of the CASE expression is not among the CASE labels, execution resumes with the statement after the CASE statement.

2. Under certain conditions, the CASE branch table can be more efficient if it is not searched linearly but instead is indexed by the value of the CASE expression. Under what conditions is this true?

3. Modify the pretty-printer of Chapter 8 to skip over statement markers, address markers, and branch tables in a code segment.

CHAPTER 11

Interactive Debugging

One of the greatest benefits of using an interpreter is how well it supports interactive debugging. You have already seen how an interpreter retains full control as it executes a source program, and how it maintains the runtime resources. You would indeed have a very powerful tool for program development if you could interact with the interpreter as it executes a program.

In this chapter, we take the Pascal interpreter we completed in the previous chapter and develop it further by adding an interactive debugger. With this debugger, you will be able to monitor the interpreter as it executes a program by setting breakpoints, watching the values of variables, printing the values of arbitrary expressions, assigning new values to variables, tracing, and executing statements in single-step mode. In this chapter, you will develop the skills to:

- monitor the execution of a Pascal program
- manipulate the program's resources that are maintained by the interpreter
- interpret a simple interactive debugger command language

11.1 Source-level debugging

Two types of software debuggers are used by programmers, *machine-level* and *source-level*. Machine-level debuggers allow you to debug a program at a low level that is close to the machine language. With such a debugger, you can execute a program one machine instruction at a time and monitor such activity as data moving in and out of the machine registers. Machine-level debuggers may have little or no knowledge of the statements or data structures of the original source program. They are often used to debug compiled programs.

Source-level debuggers, on the other hand, allow you to debug at the same level as the high-level language the program is written in. It knows about the statements and data structures of the language, and when you use one, you can think in terms of the programming language, not the machine instructions. A Pascal source-level debugger, for example, allows you to execute a program a statement at a time and monitor the values of the program's variables. You refer to the statements by their line numbers and to variables by their names (hence, source-level debuggers are also called *symbolic debuggers*). Source-level debuggers are often used to debug interpreted programs, although source-level debugging of compiled programs is possible if the compiler can generate special debugging information along with the machine code.

The rest of this chapter shows how we can build a credible source-level debugger on top of the interpreter we completed in the previous chapter. As you will see, we only need to add some debugging routines to the executor module.

11.1.1 Debugger command language

Our debugger will be interactive, so we must implement a command language. Examples of commands you can give to the debugger are "Set a breakpoint at line 17" and "Show me the current value of `table[index].word`."

A command language can range in sophistication from one with a very simple and rigid format to one that is as flexible and expressive as a programming language. For our debugger, we will implement a command language that is simple and yet retains a Pascal flavor. It has a small vocabulary of commands, but it uses Pascal syntax for variables, expressions, and assignment statements. Like Pascal, it is insensitive to whether you use uppercase or lowercase letters. Figure 11-1 shows a sample interactive session using the debugger command language.

FIGURE 11-1   A sample session with the interactive debugger.

```
C:\BOOK\CHAP11>run3 newton.pas


Page 1   newton.pas   Tue Feb 13 00:35:56 1990

  1  0: PROGRAM newton (input, output);
  2  1:
  3  1: CONST
  4  1:     epsilon = 1e-6;
  5  1:
  6  1: VAR
  7  1:     number, root, sqroot : real;
  8  1:
  9  1: BEGIN
 10  1:     REPEAT
```

```
 11  1:         writeln;
 12  1:         write('Enter new number (0 to quit): ');
 13  1:         read(number);
 14  1:
 15  1:         IF number = 0 THEN BEGIN
 16  1:             writeln(number:12:6, 0.0:12:6);
 17  1:         END
 18  1:         ELSE IF number < 0 THEN BEGIN
 19  1:             writeln('*** ERROR: number < 0');
 20  1:         END
 21  1:         ELSE BEGIN
 22  1:             sqroot := sqrt(number);
 23  1:             writeln(number:12:6, sqroot:12:6);
 24  1:             writeln;

 26  1:             root := 1;
 27  1:             REPEAT
```

```
28 1:                   root := (number/root + root)/2;
29 1:                   writeln(root:24:6,
30 1:                         100*abs(root - sqroot)/sqroot:12:2,
31 1:                         '%')
32 1:               UNTIL abs(number/sqr(root) - 1) < epsilon;
33 1:          END
34 1:      UNTIL number = 0
35 1: END.
```

```
                  35 Source lines.
                   0 Source errors.
```

Command? break 15

Command?

Enter new number (0 to quit): 9

Breakpoint
At 15: IF number = 0

Command?
    9.000000   3.000000

                5.000000   66.67%
                3.400000   13.33%
                3.023530   0.78%
                3.000092   0.00%
                3.000000   0.00%

Enter new number (0 to quit): 12

Breakpoint
At 15: IF number = 0

Command? assign number := 16

Command? show sqrt(number)
    4

Command? show pi/number
            ^
 *** ERROR: Undefined identifier.
               ^
 *** ERROR: Incompatible types.

Command? where

At 15: IF number = 0

Command? step

Command?

At 15: IF number = 0

Command?

At 18: IF number < 0

Command?

At 22: sqroot := sqrt (number)

Command?

At 23: writeln (number : 12 : 6 , sqroot : 12 : 6)
    16.000000   4.000000

Command?

At 24: writeln

Command?

At 26: root := 1

Command? unstep

Command? trace

Command?
<27><28><29>   8.500000   112.50%
<28><29>   5.191176   29.78%
<28><29>   4.136665   3.42%
<28><29>   4.002257   0.06%
<28><29>   4.000000   0.00%
<11>
<12>Enter new number (0 to quit): <13>36

Breakpoint
At 15: IF number = 0

Command? untrace

Command? store root

Command? watch
Variables being watched:
            root   (store)

Command? break
Statement breakpoints at:
    15

Command?
    36.000000   6.000000

At 26: Store root := 1

At 28: Store root := 18.5
                18.500000   208.33%

At 28: Store root := 10.2229729
                10.222973   70.38%

At 28: Store root := 6.87222672
                 6.872227   14.54%

At 28: Store root := 6.05535173
                 6.055352   0.92%
```
```

```
At 28:  Store root := 6.00025272                    Breakpoint
                6.000253       0.00%                 At  15: IF number = 0

At 28:  Store root := 6                              Command? kill
                6.000000       0.00%                 Program killed.

Enter new number (0 to quit): 0
```

11.1.2 Breakpoints

A breakpoint is a special tag placed on an executable statement that tells the debugger to temporarily halt the execution of the program just before that statement is to be executed. When the debugger reaches a statement with a breakpoint, it prints the statement's line number followed by the text of the statement, and then it reads a debugging command.

Command: break *number*

Place a breakpoint at the statement beginning on line *number*. For example, break 14. If there are several statements that begin on that line, place a breakpoint at each one of them.

Command: break

Print the line numbers of all the breakpoints.

Command: unbreak *number*

Remove the breakpoint from the statement beginning on line *number*. For example, unbreak 14. If several statements begin on that line, remove all their breakpoints.

Command: unbreak

Remove all breakpoints from all statements.

11.1.3 Statement and routine tracing

Tracing program execution enables you to know which statements and which procedures and functions have been executed, and in what order. Our debugger traces statements by printing the line number of each statement just before executing that statement. It traces procedures and functions by printing a message that a routine has just been entered or is just about to be exited.

Command: trace

Turn on statement tracing.

Command: `untrace`

Turn off statement tracing.

Command: `entry`

Turn on tracing of procedure and function entries.

Command: `unentry`

Turn off tracing of procedure and function entries.

Command: `exit`

Turn on tracing of procedure and function exits.

Command: `unexit`

Turn off tracing of procedure and function exits.

11.1.4 Single-stepping

Single-stepping is running the program one statement at a time. When the debugger executes a program in single-step mode, it operates as though a breakpoint were placed at every statement. Thus, you have an opportunity to enter a debugger command before each statement is executed.

Command: `step`

Turn on single-stepping.

Command: `unstep`

Turn off single-stepping.

The debugger does not allow single-stepping and tracing both to be turned on at the same time. Turning one on automatically turns the other one off.

During single-stepping mode, the debugger prints out the current line number and the text of the statement it is about to execute.

11.1.5 Watching variables

Chapter 9 introduced the useful feature of printing the value of a variable each time it is used (a data fetch) and its new value each time it is assigned one (a data store). The debugger allows you to turn this feature on and off for individual variables. You can watch data fetches, data stores, or both.

Command: `fetch` *variable*
               `store` *variable*
               `watch` *variable*

You can print each data fetch, or each data store, or both fetches and stores of *variable*, respectively. The variable may only be an identifier; it may not be followed by any subscripts or field designators. If you watch an array or record identifier, then you watch all of its elements or fields.

Examples: `fetch alpha`
                  `store beta`
                  `watch gamma`

Command: `watch`
Print the names of all the variables being watched.

Command: `unwatch` *variable*
Remove the watch from *variable*. For example, `unwatch beta`.

Command: `unwatch`
Remove the watches from all the variables.

Whenever you enter an identifier, the debugger checks to make sure that it is a validly defined identifier. It makes this check in the current scope context of the program. In other words, when you enter a `watch` command, the debugger has stopped program execution before a certain statement. Any identifier that you enter must be valid for the program at that point.

11.1.6 Evaluating expressions

A very useful feature of the debugger is printing the value of an arbitrary Pascal expression. The debugger checks the expression both for syntactic correctness and to ensure that all its identifiers are valid with respect to the current program context.

Command: `show` *expression*
Print the value of *expression*.

Examples: `show table[index].word`
                  `show (1.0 - sqrt(rho))/(pi*sqr(sigma))`

11.1.7 Assigning values to variables

When you are debugging a program, you may want to change the value of a variable. You can use the command language to do this with a standard Pascal assignment statement, which the debugger checks for validity.

Command: `assign` *variable* `:=` *expression*

Here, *variable* is any valid Pascal variable, and it may be followed by subscripts and field designators. The *expression* is, as before, any valid Pascal expression.

Example: `assign table[3].count := table[3].count + 1`

11.1.8 Where am I?

Sometimes, especially during an intensive debugging session, you can forget where you are in the program.

Command: `where`

Print the line number followed by the text of the statement to be executed next.

11.1.9 Killing the program

The `kill` command terminates the program execution.

Command: `kill`

11.2 Debugger organization

Since we have created a new command language, someone must parse, syntax check, and execute the commands. Yet despite all this, adding interactive debugging capabilities to our interpreter is actually quite straightforward. Because we kept the command language simple, syntax checking will not be a problem. As for parsing and executing, we simply make use of the interpreter's existing modules!

This chapter adds only one new file, `debug.c`, to the executor module, and modifies files `routine.c` and `error.c`.

Parser Module

parser.h	*u*	Parser header file
routine.c	*c*	Parse programs, procedures, and functions
standard.c	*u*	Parse standard procedures and functions
decl.c	*u*	Parse declarations
stmt.c	*u*	Parse statements
expr.c	*u*	Parse expressions

Scanner Module

scanner.h	*u*	Scanner header file
scanner.c	*u*	Scanner routines

Symbol Table Module

symtab.h	*u*	Symbol table header file
symtab.c	*u*	Symbol table routines

Executor Module

exec.h	*u*	Executor header file
executil.c	*u*	Executor utility routines
execstmt.c	*u*	Execute statements
execexpr.c	*u*	Execute expressions
execstd.c	*u*	Execute standard procedures and functions
debug.c	*n*	Interactive debugger

Error Module

error.h	*u*	Error header file
error.c	*c*	Error routines

Miscellaneous

common.h	*u*	Common header file

Where: *u*   file unchanged from the previous chapter
        c   file changed from the previous chapter
        n   new file

Once again, we will need to activate the calls to the tracing routines that we used in the first version of the interpreter that we wrote in Chapter 9. Therefore, we must make sure that the trace macro flag is *defined* for file exec.h.

11.3 Debugger implementation

In file routine.c, we make one simple change near the end of function program to initialize the debugger. Just before it calls function execute, we add the lines:

```
/*
-- Initialize the debugger.
*/
init_debugger();
```

Figure 11-2 shows the new file, debug.c, of the executor module. It contains all of the routines that make up the interactive debugger.

FIGURE II-2 File debug.c.

```
/**************************************************************/
/*                                                          */
/*        I N T E R A C T I V E   D E B U G G E R           */
/*                                                          */
/*        Interactive debugging routines.                   */
/*                                                          */
/*        FILE:      debug.c                                */
/*                                                          */
/*        MODULE:    executor                               */
/*                                                          */
/**************************************************************/

#include <stdio.h>
#include "common.h"
#include "error.h"
#include "scanner.h"
#include "symtab.h"
#include "exec.h"

#define MAX_BREAKS      16
#define MAX_WATCHES     16
#define COMMAND_QUERY   "Command? "

/*----------------------------------------------------------*/
/* Externals                                                */
/*----------------------------------------------------------*/

extern TYPE_STRUCT_PTR  integer_typep, real_typep,
                        boolean_typep, char_typep;

extern TYPE_STRUCT      dummy_type;

extern int              level;
extern SYMTAB_NODE_PTR  symtab_display[];
extern STACK_ITEM_PTR   tos;

extern int      line_number;
extern int      buffer_offset;
extern BOOLEAN  print_flag;

extern char     *code_segmentp;
extern char     *statement_startp;
extern int      ctoken;
extern int      exec_line_number;
extern int      error_count;

extern char     *bufferp;
extern char     ch;
extern char     source_buffer[];
extern char     word_string[];
extern int      token;
extern LITERAL  literal;
extern BOOLEAN  block_flag;

extern char     *code_buffer;
extern char     *code_bufferp;
extern char     *code_segmentp;

/*----------------------------------------------------------*/
/* Globals                                                  */
/*----------------------------------------------------------*/

FILE    *console;
```

```
BOOLEAN debugger_command_flag,  /* TRUE during debug command */
        halt_flag,              /* TRUE to pause for debug command */
        trace_flag,             /* TRUE to trace statement */
        step_flag,              /* TRUE to single-step */
        entry_flag,             /* TRUE to trace routine entry */
        exit_flag;              /* TRUE to trace routine exit */

int     break_count;                    /* count of breakpoints */
int     break_list[MAX_BREAKS];         /* list of breakpoints */

int             watch_count;            /* count of watches */
SYMTAB_NODE_PTR watch_list[MAX_WATCHES]; /* list of watches */

typedef struct {                        /* watch structure */
    SYMTAB_NODE_PTR watch_idp;          /* id node watched variable */
    BOOLEAN         store_flag;         /* TRUE to trace stores */
    BOOLEAN         fetch_flag;         /* TRUE to trace fetches */
} WATCH_STRUCT, *WATCH_STRUCT_PTR;

char *symbol_strings[] = {
    "<no token>", "<IDENTIFIER>", "<NUMBER>", "<STRING>",
    "^", "*", "(", ")", "-", "+", "=", "[", "]", ":", ";",
    "<", ">", ",", ".", "/", ":=", "<=", ">=", "<>", "..",
    "<END OF FILE>", "<ERROR>",
    "AND", "ARRAY", "BEGIN", "CASE", "CONST", "DIV", "DO", "DOWNTO",
    "ELSE", "END", "FILE", "FOR", "FUNCTION", "GOTO", "IF", "IN",
    "LABEL", "MOD", "NIL", "NOT", "OF", "OR", "PACKED", "PROCEDURE",
    "PROGRAM", "RECORD", "REPEAT", "SET", "THEN", "TO", "TYPE",
    "UNTIL", "VAR", "WHILE", "WITH",
};

/*----------------------------------------------------------*/
/* init_debugger      Initialize the interactive debugger.  */
/*----------------------------------------------------------*/

init_debugger()

{
    int i;

    /*
    -- Initialize the debugger's globals.
    */
    console = fopen("CON", "r");
    code_buffer = alloc_bytes(MAX_SOURCE_LINE_LENGTH + 1);

    print_flag = FALSE;
    halt_flag  = block_flag = TRUE;
    debugger_command_flag = trace_flag = step_flag
                          = entry_flag = exit_flag
                          = FALSE;

    break_count = 0;
    for (i = 0; i < MAX_BREAKS; ++i) break_list[i] = 0;

    watch_count = 0;
    for (i = 0; i < MAX_WATCHES; ++i) watch_list[i] = NULL;
}

/*----------------------------------------------------------*/
/* read_debugger_command    Read and process a debugging    */
/*                          command typed in by the user.   */
/*----------------------------------------------------------*/
```

```
read_debugger_command()

{
    BOOLEAN done = FALSE;

    debugger_command_flag = TRUE;

    do {
        printf("\n%s", COMMAND_QUERY);

        /*
        -- Read in a debugging command and replace the
        -- final \n\0 with ;;\0
        */
        bufferp = fgets(source_buffer, MAX_SOURCE_LINE_LENGTH,
                        console);
        strcpy(&source_buffer[strlen(source_buffer) - 1], ";;");

        ch = *bufferp++;
        buffer_offset = sizeof(COMMAND_QUERY);
        code_bufferp  = code_buffer;
        error_count   = 0;

        get_token();

        /*
        -- Process the command.
        */
        switch (token) {
            case SEMICOLON:    done = TRUE;                 break;
            case IDENTIFIER:   execute_debugger_command(); break;
        }

        if (token != SEMICOLON) error(UNEXPECTED_TOKEN);
    } while (!done);

    debugger_command_flag = FALSE;
}

/*-----------------------------------------------------------*/
/* execute_debugger_command       Execute a debugger command. */
/*-----------------------------------------------------------*/

execute_debugger_command()

{
    WATCH_STRUCT_PTR wp;
    WATCH_STRUCT_PTR allocate_watch();

    if (strcmp(word_string, "trace") == 0) {
        trace_flag = TRUE;
        step_flag  = FALSE;
        get_token();
    }
    else if (strcmp(word_string, "untrace") == 0) {
        trace_flag = FALSE;
        get_token();
    }

    else if (strcmp(word_string, "step") == 0) {
        step_flag = TRUE;
        trace_flag = FALSE;
        get_token();
    }
    else if (strcmp(word_string, "unstep") == 0) {
        step_flag = FALSE;
        get_token();
```

```
    }
    else if (strcmp(word_string, "break") == 0)
        set_breakpoint();
    else if (strcmp(word_string, "unbreak") == 0)
        remove_breakpoint();

    else if (strcmp(word_string, "entry") == 0) {
        entry_flag = TRUE;
        get_token();
    }
    else if (strcmp(word_string, "unentry") == 0) {
        entry_flag = FALSE;
        get_token();
    }

    else if (strcmp(word_string, "exit") == 0) {
        exit_flag = TRUE;
        get_token();
    }
    else if (strcmp(word_string, "unexit") == 0) {
        exit_flag = FALSE;
        get_token();
    }

    else if (strcmp(word_string, "watch") == 0) {
        wp = allocate_watch();
        if (wp != NULL) {
            wp->store_flag = TRUE;
            wp->fetch_flag = TRUE;
        }
    }
    else if (strcmp(word_string, "unwatch") == 0)
        remove_watch();

    else if (strcmp(word_string, "store") == 0) {
        wp = allocate_watch();
        if (wp != NULL) wp->store_flag = TRUE;
    }
    else if (strcmp(word_string, "fetch") == 0) {
        wp = allocate_watch();
        if (wp != NULL) wp->fetch_flag = TRUE;
    }

    else if (strcmp(word_string, "show") == 0)
        show_value();
    else if (strcmp(word_string, "assign") == 0)
        assign_variable();

    else if (strcmp(word_string, "where") == 0) {
        print_statement();
        get_token();
    }
    else if (strcmp(word_string, "kill") == 0) {
        printf("Program killed.\n");
        exit(0);
    }
}
```

```
                    /********************************/
                    /*                              */
                    /*        Tracing routines      */
                    /*                              */
                    /********************************/

/*-----------------------------------------------------------*/
/* trace_statement_execution   Called just before the        */
```

```
/*                          execution of each statement.   */
/*----------------------------------------------------------*/

trace_statement_execution()

{
    if (break_count > 0) {
        int i;

        /*
        -- Check if the statement is a breakpoint.
        */
        for (i = 0; i < break_count; ++i) {
            if (exec_line_number == break_list[i]) {
                printf("\nBreakpoint");
                print_statement();
                halt_flag = TRUE;
                break;
            }
        }
    }

    /*
    -- Pause if necessary to read a debugger command.
    */
    if (halt_flag) {
        read_debugger_command();
        halt_flag = step_flag;
    }

    /*
    -- If single-stepping, print the current statement.
    -- If tracing, print the current line number.
    */
    if (step_flag)  print_statement();
    if (trace_flag) print_line_number();
}

/*----------------------------------------------------------*/
/* trace_routine_entry       Called upon entry into a       */
/*                           procedure or a function.       */
/*----------------------------------------------------------*/

trace_routine_entry(idp)

    SYMTAB_NODE_PTR idp;       /* routine id */

{
    if (entry_flag) printf("\nEntering %s\n", idp->name);
}

/*----------------------------------------------------------*/
/* trace_routine_exit        Called upon exit from a        */
/*                           procedure or a function.       */
/*----------------------------------------------------------*/

trace_routine_exit(idp)

    SYMTAB_NODE_PTR idp;       /* routine id */

{
    if (exit_flag) printf("\nExiting %s\n", idp->name);
}

/*----------------------------------------------------------*/
/* trace_data_store          Called just before a variable  */
/*                           is stored into.                */
/*----------------------------------------------------------*/
```

```
trace_data_store(idp, idp_tp, targetp, target_tp)

    SYMTAB_NODE_PTR idp;        /* id of target variable */
    TYPE_STRUCT_PTR idp_tp;     /* ptr to id's type */
    STACK_ITEM_PTR  targetp;    /* ptr to target location */
    TYPE_STRUCT_PTR target_tp;  /* ptr to target's type */

{
    /*
    -- Check if the variable is being watched for stores.
    */
    if ((idp->info != NULL) &&
        ((WATCH_STRUCT_PTR) idp->info)->store_flag) {
        printf("\nAt %d:  Store %s", exec_line_number, idp->name);
        if      (idp_tp->form == ARRAY_FORM)  printf("[*]");
        else if (idp_tp->form == RECORD_FORM) printf(".*");
        print_data_value(targetp, target_tp, ":=");
    }
}

/*----------------------------------------------------------*/
/* trace_data_fetch          Called just before a variable  */
/*                           is fetched from.               */
/*----------------------------------------------------------*/

trace_data_fetch(idp, tp, datap)

    SYMTAB_NODE_PTR idp;       /* id of target variable */
    TYPE_STRUCT_PTR tp;        /* ptr to id's type */
    STACK_ITEM_PTR  datap;     /* ptr to data */

{

    TYPE_STRUCT_PTR idp_tp = idp->typep;

    /*
    -- Check if the variable is being watched for fetches.
    */
    if (   (idp->info != NULL)
        && ((WATCH_STRUCT_PTR) idp->info)->fetch_flag) {
        printf("\nAt %d:  Fetch %s", exec_line_number, idp->name);
        if      (idp_tp-> form == ARRAY_FORM)  printf("[*]");
        else if (idp_tp->form == RECORD_FORM) printf(".*");
        print_data_value(datap, tp, "=");
    }
}

        /********************************/
        /*                          */
        /*       Printing routines  */
        /*                          */
        /********************************/

/*----------------------------------------------------------*/
/* print_statement           Uncrunch and print a statement. */
/*----------------------------------------------------------*/

print_statement()

{
    int     tk;                /* token code */
    BOOLEAN done = FALSE;
    char    *csp = statement_startp;

    printf("\nAt %3d:", exec_line_number);

    do {
        switch (tk = *csp++) {
```

```
            case SEMICOLON:
            case END:
            case ELSE:
            case THEN:
            case UNTIL:
            case BEGIN:
            case OF:
            case STATEMENT_MARKER:      done = TRUE;
                                        break;

            default:
                done = FALSE;

                switch (tk) {

                    case ADDRESS_MARKER:
                        csp += sizeof(ADDRESS);
                        break;

                    case IDENTIFIER:
                    case NUMBER:
                    case STRING: {
                        SYMTAB_NODE_PTR np = *((SYMTAB_NODE_PTR *) csp);

                        printf(" %s", np->name);
                        csp += sizeof(SYMTAB_NODE_PTR);
                        break;
                    }

                    default:
                        printf(" %s", symbol_strings[tk]);
                        break;
                }
        }
    } while (!done);

    printf("\n");
}

/*-----------------------------------------------------*/
/*  print_line_number        Print the current line number.  */
/*-----------------------------------------------------*/

print_line_number()

{
    printf("<%d>", exec_line_number);
}

/*-----------------------------------------------------*/
/*  print_data_value         Print a data value.        */
/*-----------------------------------------------------*/

print_data_value(datap, tp, str)

    STACK_ITEM_PTR  datap;      /* ptr to data value to print */
    TYPE_STRUCT_PTR tp;         /* ptr to type of stack item */
    char            *str;       /* " = " or " := " */

{
    /*
    -- Reduce a subrange type to its range type.
    -- Convert a non-boolean enumeration type to integer.
    */
    if (tp->form == SUBRANGE_FORM)
        tp = tp->info.subrange.range_typep;
    if ((tp->form == ENUM_FORM) && (tp != boolean_typep))
```

```
        tp = integer_typep;

    if (tp == integer_typep)
        printf(" %s %d\n", str, datap->integer);
    else if (tp == real_typep)
        printf(" %s %0.6g\n", str, datap->real);
    else if (tp == boolean_typep)
        printf(" %s %s\n", str, datap->integer == 1 ? "true"
                                                     : "false");
    else if (tp == char_typep)
        printf(" %s '%c'\n", str, datap->byte);
    else if (tp->form == ARRAY_FORM) {
        if (tp->info.array.elmt_typep == char_typep) {
            char *chp = (char *) datap;
            int  size = tp->info.array.elmt_count;

            printf(" %s '", str);
            while (size--) printf("%c", *chp++);
            printf("'\n");
        }
        else printf(" %s <array>\n", str);
    }
    else if (tp->form == RECORD_FORM)
        printf(" %s <record>\n", str);
}

        /****************************************/
        /*                                      */
        /*      Breakpoints and watches         */
        /*                                      */
        /****************************************/

/*-----------------------------------------------------*/
/*  set_breakpoint     Set a breakpoint, or print all   */
/*                     breakpoints in the break list.   */
/*-----------------------------------------------------*/

set_breakpoint()

{
    get_token();

    switch (token) {

        case SEMICOLON: {
            /*
            -- No line number:  List all breakpoints.
            */
            int i;

            printf("Statement breakpoints at:\n");

            for (i = 0; i < break_count; ++i)
                printf("%5d\n", break_list[i]);

            break;
        }

        case NUMBER: {
            /*
            -- Set a breakpoint by appending it to
            -- the break list.
            */
            int number;

            if (literal.type == INTEGER_LIT) {
                number = literal.value.integer;
```

```
            if ((number > 0) && (number <= line_number)) {
                if (break_count < MAX_BREAKS) {
                    break_list[break_count] = number;
                    ++break_count;
                }
                else printf("Break list is full.\n");
            }
            else error(VALUE_OUT_OF_RANGE);
        }
        else error(UNEXPECTED_TOKEN);

        get_token();
        break;
    }
}
}

/*------------------------------------------------------------*/
/* remove_breakpoint   Remove a specific breakpoint, or remove */
/*                     all breakpoints.                        */
/*------------------------------------------------------------*/

remove_breakpoint()

{
    int i, j, number;

    get_token();

    switch (token) {

        case SEMICOLON: {
            /*
            -- No line number:  Remove all breakpoints.
            */
            for (i = 0; i < break_count; ++i) break_list[i] = 0;
            break_count = 0;
            break;
        }

        case NUMBER: {
            /*
            -- Remove a breakpoint from the break list.
            -- Move the following breakpoints up one in the
            -- list to fill in the gap.
            */
            if (literal.type == INTEGER_LIT) {
                number = literal.value.integer;
                if (number > 0) {
                    for (i = 0; i < break_count; ++i) {
                        if (break_list[i] == number) {
                            break_list[i] = 0;
                            --break_count;

                            for (j = i; j < break_count; ++j)
                                break_list[j] = break_list[j+1];

                            break;
                        }
                    }
                }
                else error(VALUE_OUT_OF_RANGE);
            }

            get_token();
            break;
        }
```

```
    }
}

/*------------------------------------------------------------*/
/* allocate_watch     Return a pointer to a watch structure,  */
/*                    or print all variables being watched.   */
/*------------------------------------------------------------*/

    WATCH_STRUCT_PTR
allocate_watch()

{
    int             i;
    SYMTAB_NODE_PTR idp;
    WATCH_STRUCT_PTR wp;

    get_token();

    switch (token) {

        case SEMICOLON: {
            /*
            -- No variable:  Print all variables being watched.
            */
            printf("Variables being watched:\n");

            for (i = 0; i < watch_count; ++i) {
                idp = watch_list[i];
                if (idp != NULL) {
                    wp = (WATCH_STRUCT_PTR) idp->info;
                    printf ("%16s   ", idp->name);
                    if (wp->store_flag) printf(" (store)");
                    if (wp->fetch_flag) printf(" (fetch)");
                    printf("\n");
                }
            }

            return(NULL);
        }

        case IDENTIFIER: {
            search_and_find_all_symtab(idp);
            get_token();

            switch (idp->defn.key) {

                case UNDEFINED:
                    return(NULL);

                case CONST_DEFN:
                case VAR_DEFN:
                case FIELD_DEFN:
                case VALPARM_DEFN:
                case VARPARM_DEFN: {
                    /*
                    -- Return a pointer to the variable's watch
                    -- structure if it is already being watched.
                    -- Otherwise, allocate and return a pointer
                    -- to a new watch structure.
                    */
                    if (idp->info != NULL)
                        return((WATCH_STRUCT_PTR) idp->info);
                    else if (watch_count < MAX_WATCHES) {
                        wp = alloc_struct(WATCH_STRUCT);
                        wp->store_flag = FALSE;
                        wp->fetch_flag = FALSE;

                        idp->info = (char *) wp;
```

```
                    watch_list[watch_count] = idp;
                    ++watch_count;

                    return(wp);
                }
                else {
                    printf("Watch list is full.\n");
                    return(NULL);
                }
            }

            default: {
                error(INVALID_IDENTIFIER_USAGE);
                return(NULL);
            }
        }
    }
}
```

```
/*----------------------------------------------------------*/
/*  remove_watch          Remove a specific variable from being  */
/*                        watched, or remove all variables from  */
/*                        the watch list.                        */
/*----------------------------------------------------------*/

remove_watch()

{
    int             i, j;
    SYMTAB_NODE_PTR idp;
    WATCH_STRUCT_PTR wp;

    get_token();

    switch (token) {

        case SEMICOLON: {
            /*
            -- No variable:  Remove all variables from watch list.
            */
            for (i = 0; i < watch_count; ++i) {
                if ((idp = watch_list[i]) != NULL) {
                    wp = (WATCH_STRUCT_PTR) idp->info;
                    watch_list[i] = NULL;
                    idp->info = NULL;
                    free(wp);
                }
            }
            watch_count = 0;
            break;
        }

        case IDENTIFIER: {
            /*
            -- Remove a variable from the watch list.
            -- Move the following watches up one in the
            -- list to fill in the gap.
            */
            search_and_find_all_symtab(idp);
            get_token();

            if ((idp != NULL) && (idp->info != NULL)) {
                wp = (WATCH_STRUCT_PTR) idp->info;
                for (i = 0; i < watch_count; ++i) {
                    if (watch_list[i] == idp) {
                        watch_list[i] = NULL;
```

```
                        idp->info = NULL;
                        free(wp);
                        --watch_count;

                        for (j = i; j < watch_count; ++j)
                            watch_list[j] = watch_list[j+1];

                        break;
                    }
                }
            }
            break;
        }
    }
}
```

```
/*********************************/
/*                               */
/*        Show and assign        */
/*                               */
/*********************************/
```

```
/*----------------------------------------------------------*/
/*  show_value            Print the value of an expression.      */
/*----------------------------------------------------------*/

show_value()

{
    get_token();

    switch (token) {

        case SEMICOLON: {
            error(INVALID_EXPRESSION);
            break;
        }

        default: {
            /*
            -- First parse, then execute the expression
            -- from the code buffer.
            */
            TYPE_STRUCT_PTR expression();
            TYPE_STRUCT_PTR tp         = expression();    /* parse */
            char *save_code_segmentp = code_segmentp;
            int   save_ctoken        = ctoken;

            if (error_count > 0) break;

            /*
            -- Switch to the code buffer.
            */
            code_segmentp = code_buffer + 1;
            get_ctoken();
            exec_expression();                            /* execute */

            /*
            -- Print, then pop off the value.
            */
            if ((tp->form == ARRAY_FORM) ||
                (tp->form == RECORD_FORM))
                print_data_value(tos->address, tp, " ");
            else
                print_data_value(tos, tp, " ");

            pop();
```

```
        /*
        -- Resume the code segment.
        */
        code_segmentp = save_code_segmentp;
        ctoken = save_ctoken;
        break;
    }
  }
}

/*----------------------------------------------------------*/
/* assign_variable      Execute an assignment statement.    */
/*----------------------------------------------------------*/

assign_variable()

{
    get_token();

    switch (token) {

        case SEMICOLON: {
            error(MISSING_VARIABLE);
            break;
        }

        case IDENTIFIER: {
            /*
```

```
        -- First parse, then execute the assignment statement
        -- from the code buffer.
        */
        SYMTAB_NODE_PTR idp;
        char *save_code_segmentp = code_segmentp;
        int  save_ctoken         = ctoken;

        search_and_find_all_symtab(idp);

        assignment_statement(idp);          /* parse */
        if (error_count > 0) break;

        /*
        -- Switch to the code buffer.
        */
        code_segmentp = code_buffer + 1;
        get_ctoken();
        idp = get_symtab_cptr();
        exec_assignment_statement(idp);      /* execute */

        /*
        -- Resume the code segment.
        */
        code_segmentp = save_code_segmentp;
        ctoken = save_ctoken;
        break;
    }
  }
}
```

Function init_debugger initializes the debugger. We open the console from which we will read the debugger commands, and we allocate a new code_buffer to store the commands in their intermediate form. Then we initialize break_list and watch_list, which will keep track of breakpoints and watched variables, respectively.

11.3.1 Tracing

The key to running a program under control of the debugger is function trace_statement_execution. As we first saw in Chapter 9, this function is called by function exec_statement in file execstmt.c just before each statement is executed. In its new version, it allows the debugger to assume control before each statement.

In trace_statement_execution, we first check to see if the statement is in the break_list. If so, we print the statement by calling function print_statement and set halt_flag to TRUE. Whenever halt_flag is TRUE, we read a debugger command. We then reset halt_flag to the value of step_flag, which is set by the step and unstep commands. Finally, we call function print_statement if step_flag is TRUE, or function print_line_number if trace_flag is TRUE. trace_flag is set by the trace and untrace commands.

Functions trace_routine_entry and trace_routine_exit are called by functions routine_entry and routine_exit, respectively, in file executil.c (as we saw in Chapter 9). We print their messages if entry_flag and exit_flag are TRUE. These flags are set by the entry and exit debugger commands.

We have already seen calls to function `trace_data_store` from function `exec_assignment_statement` in file `execstmt.c` and from function `exec_read_readln` in file `execstd.c`, and calls to function `trace_data_fetch` from functions `exec_constant` and `exec_variable` in file `execexpr.c`.

Variables that we want to watch have a watch structure pointed to by the `info` field of their identifier's symbol table node. This is done by the `fetch`, `store`, `watch`, and `unwatch` debugger commands. Function `trace_data_store` prints only if the `store_flag` of the watch structure is TRUE, and function `trace_data_fetch` prints only if the structure's `fetch_flag` is TRUE.

11.3.2 Printing

Function `print_statement` "uncrunches" a statement from its intermediate form with the aid of the string array `symbol_strings`. This is an operation that we have seen several times in previous utility programs. This version is very simple; we make no attempt to make the output pretty. We do know to skip over any address markers, however.

Function `print_line_number` prints the current line number during statement tracing. Function `print_data_value` is the same function we first saw in Chapter 9.

11.3.3 Reading and interpreting debugger commands

Function `read_debugger_command` prompts for and reads a debugger command from the console. Since we read the command into the scanner's `source_buffer`, we can let our existing scanner module do the scanning.

We replace the line feed character \n with two semicolons to mark the end of the command. Two are necessary because after `get_token` has gotten the first semicolon, the second one keeps the scanner from trying to read another source line.

We reset `code_bufferp` to point to the beginning of the `code_buffer`, which will contain the current debugger command in its intermediate form. We decide what to do based on the first token of the command. An empty command causes the debugger to resume executing the source program.

Note that boolean variable `debugger_command_flag` is TRUE only during the execution of function `read_debugger_command`. We will see later how function `runtime_error` uses this flag.

Function `execute_debugger_command` executes the debugger command. We decide what to do based on the command keyword.

11.3.4 Breakpoints and watches

Function `set_breakpoint` executes the break command. If the command does not include a line number, we print the line numbers in the `break_list`. If there is a line number, we append the number to the end of the `break_list`. We check to see if the line number is positive and not greater than the number of the last program line. We do not check, however, that an executable statement starts on the line with that number.

Function remove_breakpoint executes the unbreak command. If there is no line number in the command, we clear the break_list. If there is a line number, we remove that line number from the break_list, and move any following numbers in the list up to fill in the gap. This makes searching the break_list faster in function trace_statement_execution.

We call function allocate_watch for the fetch, store, or watch debugger command. If the command does not include a variable identifier, we print the identifiers in the watch_list, along with whether each variable is being watched for fetches, stores, or both.

If the command does include a variable identifier, we search the symbol table for the identifier. We do this with the current state of the symbol table display so the current scope context is maintained. If the identifier is already being watched, we return a pointer to its watch structure. Otherwise, we add the variable to the watch_list, allocate a new watch structure, and return a pointer to it.

Function remove_watch executes the unwatch debugger command. If there was no variable identifier in the command, we clear the watch_list. Otherwise, we look up the identifier, remove it from the watch_list, and then fill in the gap.

II.3.5 Expressions and assignments

Function show_value executes the show debugger command. Since we must parse, check, and evaluate a Pascal expression, we make use of existing functions in the interpreter. First, we call the parser function expression to parse and check the expression, and then we call the executor function exec_expression to execute it. But before making this latter call, we temporarily divert code_segmentp to point to the code_buffer, so that exec_expression executes the debugger command's intermediate code in the code buffer instead of the Pascal routine's intermediate code in the current code segment. The expression value is left on top of the runtime stack, where we can print it and then pop it off. At the end, we reset code_segmentp to point into the current code segment so the program execution can resume from where it was halted.

Function assign_variable executes the assign debugger command. Again, we make use of existing interpreter functions. We call the parser function assignment_statement to parse and check the assignment, and then we call the executor function exec_assignment_statement to execute the intermediate code in the code_buffer.

II.3.6 Runtime error handling

As we saw in Chapter 10, whenever the interpreter encounters a runtime error, it calls function runtime_error which then prints an error message and terminates the program execution. With an interactive debugger, a more reasonable action is to halt the program execution and then read a debugger command. You may be able to correct or repair the error before resuming program execution.

Figure 11-3 shows a new version of function `runtime_error` in file `error.c`. Normally, it calls `read_debugger_command`. However, if `debugger_command_flag` is TRUE, that means that the runtime error was caused by a debugger command, not by the program. In that case, the debugger will itself prompt for and read another command.

FIGURE 11-3   Function `runtime_error` in file `error.c`.

```
/*------------------------------------------------------------*/
/*  runtime_error       Print a runtime error message and then */
/*                      abort the program execution.          */
/*------------------------------------------------------------*/

runtime_error(code)

    ERROR_CODE code;    /* error code */

{
    char        *message = runtime_error_messages[code];
```

```
    extern int      exec_line_number;
    extern BOOLEAN  debugger_command_flag;

    if (debugger_command_flag) printf("%s\n", message);
    else {
        printf("\n*** RUNTIME ERROR in line %d: %s\n",
               exec_line_number, message);
        read_debugger_command();
    }
}
```

11.4 Program 11-1: Interactive Debugger

Figure 11-4 shows the main file, `run3.c`, of the interactive Pascal debugger. This debugger is the culmination of all the programs we have written so far.

FIGURE 11-4   File `run3.c`.

```
/*****************************************************************/
/*                                                             */
/*  Program 11-1:  Interactive Pascal Debugger                 */
/*                                                             */
/*  Interpret a Pascal program under the control of an         */
/*  interactive debugger.                                      */
/*                                                             */
/*  FILE:       run3.c                                         */
/*                                                             */
/*  REQUIRES:   Modules parser, symbol table, scanner,         */
/*                      executor, error                        */
/*                                                             */
/*  FLAGS:      Macro flag "trace" must be defined             */
/*                                                             */
/*  USAGE:      run3 sourcefile                                */
/*                                                             */
/*      sourcefile      name of source file containing         */
/*                      the Pascal program to interpret        */
/*                                                             */
/*****************************************************************/
```

```
#include <stdio.h>

/*------------------------------------------------------------*/
/*  main               Initialize the scanner and call        */
/*                     routine program.                        */
/*------------------------------------------------------------*/

main(argc, argv)

    int argc;
    char *argv[];

{
    /*
    -- Initialize the scanner.
    */
    init_scanner(argv[1]);
```

```
/*                                                    get_token();
-- Process a program.                                 program();
*/                                              }
```

The next chapter begins the third and final part of this book, where we write a Pascal compiler.

Questions and exercises

1. *Execution profiler.* An execution profiler is a very useful tool to use if you want to rewrite a program to make it run faster. A profiler keeps track of how many times each statement has executed, and when the program is finished, it prints this information. Then, you can tell where the program spends most of its time, and you can concentrate on rewriting just those parts. Modify the debugger to maintain and print profiling information.

2. *Conditional breakpoints.* The breakpoints implemented in this chapter are unconditional: the debugger always halts the program execution whenever it encounters one. A conditional breakpoint has a boolean expression attached to it. When the debugger encounters such a breakpoint, it evaluates the expression and halts the execution only if the expression is true. For example, the following debugger command can set a conditional breakpoint:

```
break 14 if number > 7
```

   Implement conditional breakpoints.

3. Rewrite the variable tracing routines to enable a specific array element or a specific record field to be watched. Implement conditional watches. For example:

```
watch table[index].count if index > 100
```

4. *Nonlocal references.* Examine the following program fragment:

```
PROGRAM example (input, output);
    VAR i : integer;

    PROCEDURE proc;
        VAR i : real;

        FUNCTION func : real;
            VAR i : char;
```

```
                        BEGIN {func}
                            {*** BREAKPOINT HERE ***}
                        END {func};

                    BEGIN {proc}
                        {call func}
                    END {proc};

                BEGIN {example}
                    {call proc}
                END {example}.
```

At the breakpoint, three variables named i are active: the global integer i, the real i local to proc, and the character i local to func. The debugger command language implemented in this chapter only allows access to the character i. Implement the ability for the debugger to access the other nonlocal variables named i. For example, the new command language notation might be:

```
                    example'i
                      proc'i
                example'proc'i
```

where the first references the integer i and the second and third both reference the real i.

5. *Call stack.* Sometimes, you want to know more than just where you are in the program, but you also want to know how you got there. As you know, the interpreter's runtime stack contains information about who called whom. Implement a debugger command that prints the current list of calls. Do you need to add more information into each stack frame?

6. Design and implement a better debugger command language. Will you still be able to parse and execute this language using the existing functions?

PART III

Compiling

CHAPTER 12

Emitting 8086 Assembly Language Code

In the third part of the book, we will write a compiler for Pascal programs. This chapter sets the stage with overviews of the 8086 processor architecture and assembly language. We examine both the new code module, which emits the object code, and a runtime library. In the next chapter, we will modify the parser module to make calls to the code module in order to compile procedures, functions, and assignment statements. Then, in Chapter 14, we will complete the compiler so that it can compile entire Pascal programs.

Our compiler will translate a Pascal source program into assembly language code instead of directly into machine language code. Thus, our object language is assembly language. In order for us to see what the compiler is generating, we must be able to read what it emits. Reading assembly code is much easier than deciphering a hexadecimal dump of machine code. Also, an assembler does much useful work. The individual bits of a machine language instruction must be set correctly. Besides the actual code itself, the machine code file must contain various tables and other pieces of information to allow the code to be loaded into memory for execution. Producing a machine language file is difficult, and the assembler does a very nice job for us.

12.1 The 8086 processor architecture

We start with a brief look at the architecture of the 8086 processor. We will examine the processor only enough for us to write the compiler, not in any great detail or thoroughness. This simplified overview also applies to the 80286 and the 80386 processors. Our compiler does not generate code that relies on any features unique to either the 80286 or the 80386.

12.1.1 Machine registers and memory

As shown in Figure 12-1, the 8086 processor has several hardware registers. The 16-bit general-purpose registers are named AX, BX, CX, and DX. Register AX (accumulator) is used for most arithmetic and logic operations. Register DX (data) can also participate in these operations. Register BX (base) is used to contain an address in order to access memory indirectly. Register CX (count) is used as a counter in certain iterative instructions.

FIGURE 12-1   Registers of the 8086 processor.

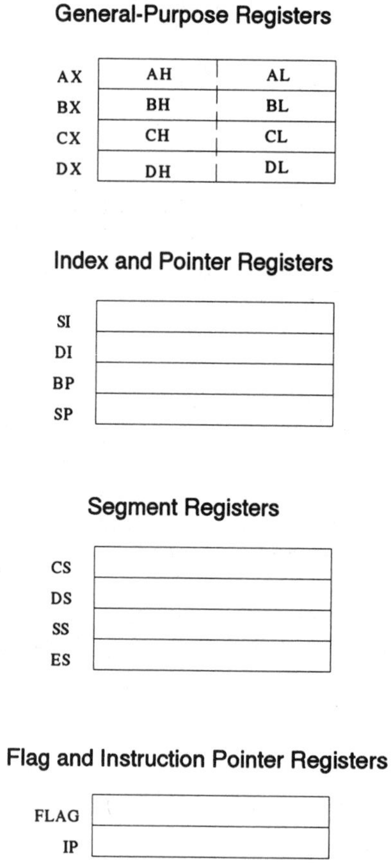

General-Purpose Registers

AX	AH	AL
BX	BH	BL
CX	CH	CL
DX	DH	DL

Index and Pointer Registers

SI	
DI	
BP	
SP	

Segment Registers

CS	
DS	
SS	
ES	

Flag and Instruction Pointer Registers

FLAG	
IP	

Each of the general-purpose registers can also be used as two separate 8-bit registers. For example, you can use the AX register as register AH (A-high) and register AL (A-low).

The index and pointer registers are SI, DI, BP, and SP. Registers SI (source index) and DI (destination index) point to bytes in the source and destination areas of memory for certain string and block operations, such as a string compare and a block move. Register BP (base pointer) points to the current stack frame. Register SP (stack pointer) points to the top of the stack.

The segment registers are CS (code segment), DS (data segment), SS (stack segment), and ES (extra segment). These registers point to the start of the various memory segments.

The IP (instruction pointer) register points to the current instruction. You cannot access it directly from a program; it is implicitly set as instructions are executed. The flag register contains 1-bit flags that record the status of certain conditions, such as the result of a comparison. Conditional jump instructions are affected by bits in the flag register.

A word in memory is 16 bits wide, and a doubleword is 32. The 8086 stores word and doubleword data in memory with their bytes in reversed order. In Figure 12-2, the hexadecimal word value at the memory location labeled WORD is 1234. The hexadecimal doubleword value at the memory location labeled DWORD is 89ABCDEF. Thus, the high-order half of the doubleword value is at DWORD+2.

A word value is usually loaded into register AX to be operated upon, and sometimes into register DX. A doubleword value is loaded into registers with its high-order half in DX and its low-order half in AX (known as the DX:AX register pair). A byte value is usually loaded into register AL.

12.1.2 Code and data segments

The 8086 processor supports a segmented memory architecture. The segment registers point to the start of segments, each one of which can be up to 64K bytes. Segments are a particularly complex feature of the 8086. To keep things simple for our compiler, we use only two segments, a code segment and a data segment, as shown in Figure 12-3. We make the stack segment the same as the data segment

---

FIGURE 12-2   Data are stored in memory with their bytes in reverse order. In the first example, WORD is the address of the word value 1234 (hexadecimal). In the second example, DWORD is the address of the doubleword value 89ABCDEF (hexadecimal). DWORD+2 is the address of the high-order half.

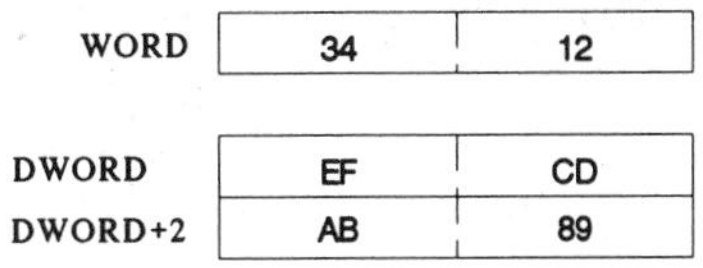

FIGURE 12-3   The code and data segments. The stack segment is the same as the data segment, and the stack grows upward from the bottom of the segment. (These diagrams are drawn so that the lowest address of the segment is at the top.)

Register IP points to the current instruction. Register SP points to the top of the stack, and register BP points to the current stack frame.

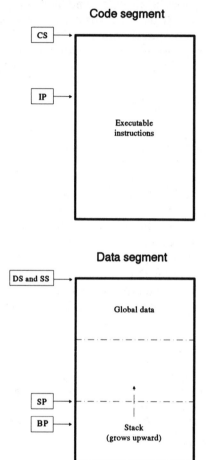

by setting DS and SS to the same value. Our compiler makes very limited use of ES, but when it does, it also sets it to the value of DS.

We allocate global data in the data segment starting from the segment's lowest address and the stack starting at the segment's highest address. Since we drew the segments in the figure with their lowest addresses at the top, the stack begins at the bottom of the data segment and grows upwards to the lower addresses. Register SP always points to the topmost word of the stack. Only word values can be pushed and popped, so pushing a doubleword value onto the stack requires two pushes, first the high-order half followed by the low-order half.

12.1.3 The runtime stack

Just like the software stack of our interpreter, the runtime stack maintained by the 8086 processor is used to store both intermediate results during expression evaluation and the stack frames of active routines.

Figure 12-4 shows the stack frame that is standard for the most popular Pascal compilers on the IBM PC, such as those by Microsoft and Borland. It has the same components as the stack frame we used in our interpreter, only arranged differently. Also, the stack frame base pointer register BP actually points to a word within the frame, instead of to the base of the frame. Thus, both positive and negative offsets off of register BP are needed to access all the items of the stack frame.

FIGURE 12-4   Stack frames from Pascal procedures and functions. These diagrams assume that each routine has two word-sized parameters and two word-sized local variables. Remember that the stack grows upward in these diagrams.

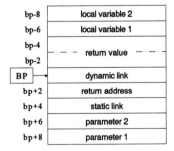

Procedure Stack Frame

bp-4	local variable 2
bp-2	local variable 1
BP →	dynamic link
bp+2	return address
bp+4	static link
bp+6	parameter 2
bp+8	parameter 1

Function Stack Frame

bp-8	local variable 2
bp-6	local variable 1
bp-4	— — return value — —
bp-2	
BP →	dynamic link
bp+2	return address
bp+4	static link
bp+6	parameter 2
bp+8	parameter 1

Because the stack grows towards the lower address of the data segment, pushing values onto the stack decreases the top of stack pointer register SP, and popping values off increases SP.

12.2 The 8086 assembly language

The instruction set of a processor is largely determined by the processor's architecture. Assembly language is one step above the machine language, and there is a one-to-one correspondence between assembly instructions and the machine language instructions.

12.2.1 Assembly language instructions

The following is a list of the instructions that the compiler generates, along with a brief description of each.

mov	*destination,source*	Move a word or a byte from *source* to *destination*.
rep	movsb	Move a block of contiguous bytes. The source address is in register SI, and the destination address is in register DI. The number of bytes to move is in register CX.
lea	*destination,source*	Load the effective address of *source* into *destination*.
cmp	*value1,value2*	Compare *value1* to *value2*.
repe	cmpsb	Compare *string1* to *string2*. The source (*string1*) address is in register SI, and the destination (*string2*) address is in register DI. The number of bytes to compare is in register CX.
push	*source*	Push the *source* word onto the stack.
pop	*destination*	Pop a word from the stack into *destination*.
not	*destination*	*destination* = ~*destination*
and	*destination,source*	*destination* = *destination* & *source*
or	*destination,source*	*destination* = *destination*	*source*
add	*destination,source*	*destination* = *destination* + *source*
sub	*destination,source*	*destination* = *destination* − *source*
imul	*source*	DX:AX = AX * *source*
idiv	*source*	AX = DX:AX / *source* DX = DX:AX % *source*

call *target*	Call routine *target*.
ret *n*	Return from the current routine and cut the stack back by *n* bytes (by adding *n* to register SP).
jmp *target*	Unconditional jump to *target*.
jl *target*	Jump to *target* if $<$
jle *target*	Jump to *target* if $<=$
je *target*	Jump to *target* if $==$
jne *target*	Jump to *target* if $!=$
jge *target*	Jump to *target* if $>=$
jg *target*	Jump to *target* if $>$

12.2.2 Assembly language operands

An operand of an assembly instruction is either a memory reference, a register, or an immediate value. In an instruction that requires two operands, at most one of the operands can be a memory reference. A memory reference can either be direct, or it can be indirect through register BX or register BP. The data that are referenced are either bytes or words. The compiler always generates the type operator BYTE PTR or WORD PTR before a memory reference to indicate the type of the operand. Some examples are:

mov ax,3	Move the immediate value 3 into register AX.
mov ax,dx	Move the contents of register DX into register AX.
mov ax,WORD PTR avg mov dx,WORD PTR avg+2	Move the doubleword real value at the memory location labelled avg directly into registers AX (low-order half) and DX (high-order half).
mov al,BYTE PTR [bx]	Move the byte data pointed to by register BX (indirect reference) into register AL.
mov dx,WORD PTR [bp+8]	Move into register DX the word data located 8 bytes from the location pointed to by register BP (based on the stack frame format, this is a parameter passed to a routine).

12.3 Using a runtime library

Some operations, such as input and output, real arthmetic, and the standard Pascal functions, are difficult for the compiler to generate code to do. You can take care of such operations with a runtime library. The compiler then generates calls to the library routines whenever necessary. After you assemble the compiler's output, you must link and load the library routines along with the assembled code.

Since the runtime library is separate from the compiler, you have several options for how you can write its routines. In an actual development environment, these routines should be as small and fast as possible, so you would probably write them in C or assembly language.

For our compiler, we will strive instead for simplicity. Figure 12-5 shows file paslib.c, which contains all of our runtime library routines written as C functions. We also make use of C library functions such as printf which, unfortunately, will cause the final object code to be larger than it otherwise would be. Using C functions also introduces a few other perverse features.

FIGURE 12-5   File paslib.c.

```
/*****************************************************/
/*                                                 */
/*     P A S C A L   R U N T I M E   L I B R A R Y   */
/*                                                 */
/*                                                 */
/*     Note that all formal parameters are reversed to */
/*     accomodate the Pascal calling convention of the */
/*     compiled code.                              */
/*                                                 */
/*     All floating point parameters are passed in as longs */
/*     to bypass unwanted type conversions. Floating point */
/*     function values are also returned as longs. */
/*                                                 */
/*****************************************************/

#include <stdio.h>
#include <math.h>

#define MAX_SOURCE_LINE_LENGTH  256

typedef enum {
    FALSE, TRUE
} BOOLEAN;

union {
    float real;
    long  dword;
} value;

/*-----------------------------------------------*/
/* Globals                                       */
/*-----------------------------------------------*/

BOOLEAN eof_flag  = FALSE;
BOOLEAN eoln_flag = FALSE;

/*-----------------------------------------------*/
/* main            The main routine, which calls */
/*                 pascal_main, the "main" of the compiled */
/*                 program.                       */
/*-----------------------------------------------*/

main(argc, argv)

    int  argc;
```

```
    char *argv[];

{
    pascal_main();
    exit(0);
}

        /********************************/
        /*                            */
        /*        Read routines       */
        /*                            */
        /********************************/

/*-----------------------------------------------*/
/* read_integer       Read an integer value.     */
/*-----------------------------------------------*/

        int
read_integer()

{
    int i;

    scanf("%d", &i);
    return(i);
}

/*-----------------------------------------------*/
/* read_real          Read a real value.         */
/*-----------------------------------------------*/

        long
read_real()

{
    scanf("%g", &value.real);
    return(value.dword);
}

/*-----------------------------------------------*/
/* read_char          Read a character value.    */
/*-----------------------------------------------*/

        char
read_char()

{
```

```
    char ch;

    scanf("%c", &ch);
    if (eof_flag || (ch == '\n')) ch = ' ';

    return(ch);
}
/*---------------------------------------------------------*/
/* read_line         Skip the rest of the input record.   */
/*---------------------------------------------------------*/

read_line()

{
    char ch;

    do {
        ch = getchar();
    } while(!eof_flag && (ch != '\n'));
}
```

```
                /*******************************/
                /*                             */
                /*        Write routines       */
                /*                             */
                /*******************************/
```

```
/*----------------------------------------------------------*/
/* write_integer        Write an integer value.            */
/*----------------------------------------------------------*/

write_integer(field_width, i)

    int i;
    int field_width;

{
    printf("%*d", field_width, i);
}
```

```
/*----------------------------------------------------------*/
/* write_real        Write a real value.                   */
/*----------------------------------------------------------*/

write_real(precision, field_width, i)

    long i;
    int  field_width;
    int  precision;

{
    value.dword = i;
    printf("%*.*f", field_width, precision, value.real);
}
```

```
/*----------------------------------------------------------*/
/* write_boolean        Write a boolean value.             */
/*----------------------------------------------------------*/

write_boolean(field_width, b)

    int b;
    int field_width;

{
    printf("%*s", field_width, b == 0 ? "FALSE" : "TRUE");
}
```

```
}
/*----------------------------------------------------------*/
/* write_char        Write a character value.              */
/*----------------------------------------------------------*/

write_char(field_width, ch)

    int ch;
    int field_width;


{
    printf("%*c", field_width, ch);
}
```

```
/*----------------------------------------------------------*/
/* write_string        Write a string value.               */
/*----------------------------------------------------------*/

write_string(length, field_width, value)

    char *value;
    int  field_width;
    int  length;

{
    char buffer[MAX_SOURCE_LINE_LENGTH];

    strncpy(buffer, value, length);
    buffer[length] = '\0';

    printf("%*s", -field_width, buffer);
}
```

```
/*----------------------------------------------------------*/
/* write_line        Write a carriage return.              */
/*----------------------------------------------------------*/

write_line()

{
    putchar('\n');
}
```

```
                /*******************************/
                /*                             */
                /*        Other I/O routines   */
                /*                             */
                /*******************************/
```

```
/*----------------------------------------------------------*/
/* std_end_of_file    Return 1 if at end of file, else 0.  */
/*----------------------------------------------------------*/

    BOOLEAN
std_end_of_file()

{
    char ch = getchar();

    if (eof_flag || feof(stdin)) eof_flag = TRUE;
    else                         ungetc(ch, stdin);

    return(eof_flag);
}
```

```
/*-------------------------------------------------*/
/*  std_end_of_line      Return 1 if at end of line, else 0.    */
/*-------------------------------------------------*/

    BOOLEAN
std_end_of_line()

{
    char ch = getchar();

    if (eof_flag || feof(stdin))
        eoln_flag = eof_flag = TRUE;
    else {
        eoln_flag = ch == '\n';
        ungetc(ch, stdin);
    }

    return(eoln_flag);
}

            /*********************************************/
            /*                                           */
            /*      Floating point arithmetic routines   */
            /*                                           */
            /*********************************************/

/*-------------------------------------------------*/
/*  float_negate        Return the negated value.          */
/*-------------------------------------------------*/

    long
float_negate(i)

    long i;

{
    value.dword = i;

    value.real = -value.real;
    return(value.dword);
}

/*-------------------------------------------------*/
/*  float_add           Return the sum x + y.              */
/*-------------------------------------------------*/

    long
float_add(j, i)

    long i, j;

{
    float x, y;

    value.dword = i;  x = value.real;
    value.dword = j;  y = value.real;

    value.real = x + y;
    return(value.dword);
}

/*-------------------------------------------------*/
/*  float_subtract      Return the difference x - y.       */
/*-------------------------------------------------*/

    long
float_subtract(j, i)
```

```
    long i, j;

{
    float x, y;

    value.dword = i;  x = value.real;
    value.dword = j;  y = value.real;

    value.real = x - y;
    return(value.dword);
}

/*--------------------------------------------------------------*/
/*  float_multiply       Return the product x*y.               */
/*--------------------------------------------------------------*/

    long
float_multiply(j, i)

    long i, j;

{
    float x, y;

    value.dword = i;  x = value.real;
    value.dword = j;  y = value.real;

    value.real = x*y;
    return(value.dword);
}

/*--------------------------------------------------------------*/
/*  float_divide         Return the quotient x/y.             */
/*--------------------------------------------------------------*/

    long
float_divide(j, i)

    long i, j;

{
    float x, y;

    value.dword = i;  x = value.real;
    value.dword = j;  y = value.real;

    value.real = x/y;
    return(value.dword);
}

/* ------------------------------------------------------------ */
/*  float_convert        Convert an integer value to real and  */
/*                       return the converted value.           */
/*--------------------------------------------------------------*/

    long
float_convert(i)

    int i;

{
    value.real = i;
    return(value.dword);
}

/*--------------------------------------------------------------*/
/*  float_compare        Return -1 if x < y                    */
```

```
/*                         0 if x == y               */
/*                         +1 if x >  y              */
/*-------------------------------------------------*/

float_compare(j, i)

    long i, j;

{
    int   comp;
    float x, y;

    value.dword = i;  x = value.real;
    value.dword = j;  y = value.real;

    if (x < y)         comp = -1;
    else if (x == y)   comp =  0;
    else               comp = +1;

    return(comp);
}

        /***********************************************/
        /*                                             */
        /*      Standard floating point functions      */
        /*                                             */
        /***********************************************/

/*-------------------------------------------------*/
/*  std_abs           Return abs of parameter.      */
/*-------------------------------------------------*/

    long
std_abs(i)

    long i;

{
    value.dword = i;

    value.real = fabs(value.real);
    return(value.dword);
}

/*-------------------------------------------------*/
/*  std_arctan        Return arctan of parameter.   */
/*-------------------------------------------------*/

    long
std_arctan(i)

    long i;

{
    value.dword = i;

    value.real = atan(value.real);
    return(value.dword);
}

/*-------------------------------------------------*/
/*  std_cos           Return cos of parameter.      */
/*-------------------------------------------------*/

    long
std_cos(i)
```

```
    long i;

{
    value.dword = i;

    value.real = cos(value.real);
    return(value.dword);
}

/*-------------------------------------------------*/
/*  std_exp           Return exp of parameter.      */
/*-------------------------------------------------*/

    long
std_exp(i)

    long i;

{
    value.dword = i;

    value.real = exp(value.real);
    return(value.dword);
}

/*-------------------------------------------------*/
/*  std_ln            Return ln of parameter.       */
/*-------------------------------------------------*/

    long
std_ln(i)

    long i;

{
    value.dword = i;

    value.real = log(value.real);
    return(value.dword);
}

/*-------------------------------------------------*/
/*  std_sin           Return sin of parameter.      */
/*-------------------------------------------------*/

    long
std_sin(i)

    long i;

{
    value.dword = i;

    value.real = sin(value.real);
    return(value.dword);
}

/*-------------------------------------------------*/
/*  std_sqrt          Return sqrt of parameter.     */
/*-------------------------------------------------*/

    long
std_sqrt(i)

    long i;

{
```

```
    value.dword = i;

    value.real = sqrt(value.real);
    return(value.dword);
}

/*------------------------------------------------------*/
/* std_round           Return round of parameter.      */
/*------------------------------------------------------*/

    int
std_round(i)

    long i;

{
    value.dword = i;

    value.dword = (int) (value.real + 0.5);
```

```
        return((int) value.dword);
    }

/*------------------------------------------------------*/
/* std_trunc            Return trunc of parameter.      */
/*------------------------------------------------------*/

    int
std_trunc(i)

    long i;

{
    value.dword = i;

    value.dword = (int) value.real;
    return((int) value.dword);
}
```

The library routines that have more than one formal parameter point out a major difference between how C routines and Pascal routines expect their parameters. Pascal routines expect parameters to be pushed onto the stack in the order that they are written in the source program, so that the last parameter value is on top of the others on the stack. C functions expect the parameters to be pushed in reverse order, so that the first parameter value is on top of the others.

You can get around this difference with a kludge: simply list the formal parameters of the library routines in reverse order. This way, the compiler can use the same code module routines to emit code to pass parameters both to Pascal routines and to the library routines.

Another difference between C and Pascal routines is the code to return from a routine. (This is explained in the next chapter.)

A library function that takes real parameters must receive them as long integers, and one that returns a real value must return it as a long integer. When the C compiler compiles a function with real parameters or that returns a real value, it generates code that expects the caller to convert these real values to a form suitable for a numeric coprocessor or for floating-point emulation routines. This is beyond the scope of these chapters, so we bypass these conversions by dealing only with integers.

Finally, to simplify matters further. we compile the main routine of the Pascal source program as though it were a procedure, and we always give it the name pascal_main. Then, one of the library routines is the main routine that calls pascal_main. Starting the execution of a compiled Pascal program with a main routine written in C ensures us that the various initializations required by C functions are done. Then, the library routines will work properly when they are called by the compiled Pascal program.

Functions read_integer, read_real, read_char, and read_line are extracted from the runtime library of the interpreter (function exec_read_readln in file execstd.c). Functions std_end_of_file and std_end_of_line are also taken from the interpreter (function exec_eof_eoln).

The functions to execute the standard functions are std_abs, std_arctan, std_cos, std_exp, std_ln, std_sin, std_sqrt, and std_trunc. Each function contains a call to the corresponding function in the C library.

12.4 The code module

Now that we have had our overview of the 8086 architecture and its assembly language, we can examine some of the files and routines of the new code module. As we will see in the next two chapters, these routines are called from the parser module to emit assembly code as the compiler parses a Pascal program.

Code Module

code.h	*n*	Code generator header file
emitasm.c	*n*	Emit assembly language statements

Where: *n*   new file

Figure 12-6 shows the new header file code.h. It defines various useful constants, types, and macros used by the code generation routines.

FIGURE 12-6   File code.h.

```
/****************************************************************/
/*                                                            */
/*      C O D E   G E N E R A T O R    (Header)               */
/*                                                            */
/*      FILE:    code.h                                       */
/*                                                            */
/*      MODULE:    code                                       */
/*                                                            */
/****************************************************************/

#ifndef code_h
#define code_h

#include "common.h"

/*------------------------------------------------------------*/
/* Assembly label prefixes                                    */
/*------------------------------------------------------------*/

#define STMT_LABEL_PREFIX      "$L"
#define FLOAT_LABEL_PREFIX     "$F"
#define STRING_LABEL_PREFIX    "$S"

/*------------------------------------------------------------*/
/* Names of library routines                                  */
/*------------------------------------------------------------*/

#define FLOAT_NEGATE     "_float_negate"
#define FLOAT_ADD        "_float_add"
#define FLOAT_SUBTRACT   "_float_subtract"
#define FLOAT_MULTIPLY   "_float_multiply"
```

```
#define FLOAT_DIVIDE     "_float_divide"
#define FLOAT_COMPARE    "_float_compare"
#define FLOAT_CONVERT    "_float_convert"

#define WRITE_INTEGER    "_write_integer"
#define WRITE_REAL       "_write_real"
#define WRITE_BOOLEAN    "_write_boolean"
#define WRITE_CHAR       "_write_char"
#define WRITE_STRING     "_write_string"
#define WRITE_LINE       "_write_line"

#define READ_INTEGER     "_read_integer"
#define READ_REAL        "_read_real"
#define READ_CHAR        "_read_char"
#define READ_LINE        "_read_line"

#define STD_END_OF_FILE  "_std_end_of_file"
#define STD_END_OF_LINE  "_std_end_of_line"

#define STD_ABS          "_std_abs"

#define STD_ARCTAN       "_std_arctan"
#define STD_COS          "_std_cos"
#define STD_EXP          "_std_exp"
#define STD_LN           "_std_ln"
#define STD_SIN          "_std_sin"
#define STD_SQRT         "_std_sqrt"

#define STD_ROUND        "_std_round"
#define STD_TRUNC        "_std_trunc"
```

```
/*-----------------------------------------------------*/
/* Stack frame                                         */
/*-----------------------------------------------------*/

#define PROC_LOCALS_STACK_FRAME_OFFSET   0
#define FUNC_LOCALS_STACK_FRAME_OFFSET  -4
#define PARAMETERS_STACK_FRAME_OFFSET   +6

#define STATIC_LINK          "$STATIC_LINK"        /* EQU <bp+4> */
#define RETURN_VALUE         "$RETURN_VALUE"       /* EQU <bp-4> */
#define HIGH_RETURN_VALUE    "$HIGH_RETURN_VALUE"  /* EQU <bp-2> */

/*-----------------------------------------------------*/
/* Registers and instruction op codes                  */
/*-----------------------------------------------------*/

typedef enum {
    AX, AH, AL, BX, BH, BL, CX, CH, CL, DX, DH, DL,
    CS, DS, ES, SS, SP, BP, SI, DI,
} REGISTER;

typedef enum {
    MOVE, MOVE_BLOCK, LOAD_ADDRESS, EXCHANGE,
    COMPARE, COMPARE_STRINGS, POP, PUSH, AND_BITS, OR_BITS, XOR_BITS,
    NEGATE, INCREMENT, DECREMENT, ADD, SUBTRACT, MULTIPLY, DIVIDE,
    CLEAR_DIRECTION, CALL, RETURN,
    JUMP, JUMP_LT, JUMP_LE, JUMP_EQ, JUMP_NE, JUMP_GE, JUMP_GT,
} INSTRUCTION;

        /**********************************************/
        /*                                            */
        /*        Macros to emit assembly statements  */
        /*                                            */
        /**********************************************/

/*-----------------------------------------------------*/
/* emit            Emit a no-operand instruction.      */
/*-----------------------------------------------------*/

#define emit(opcode)                              \
{                                                 \
    operator(opcode);                             \
    fprintf(code_file, "%s\n", asm_buffer);       \
    asm_bufferp = asm_buffer;                     \
}

/*-----------------------------------------------------*/
/* emit_1          Emit a one-operand instruction.     */
/*-----------------------------------------------------*/

#define emit_1(opcode, operand1)                  \
{                                                 \
    operator(opcode);                             \
    *asm_bufferp++ = '\t';                        \
    operand1;                                     \
    fprintf(code_file, "%s\n", asm_buffer);       \
    asm_bufferp = asm_buffer;                     \
}

/*-----------------------------------------------------*/
/* emit_2          Emit a two-operand instruction.     */
/*-----------------------------------------------------*/

#define emit_2(opcode, operand1, operand2)        \
{                                                 \
    operator(opcode);                             \
    *asm_bufferp++ = '\t';                        \
    operand1;                                     \
    *asm_bufferp++ = ',';                         \
    operand2;                                     \
    fprintf(code_file, "%s\n", asm_buffer);       \
    asm_bufferp = asm_buffer;                     \
}

/*-----------------------------------------------------*/
/* emit_label          Emit a statement label.         */
/*-----------------------------------------------------*/

#define emit_label(prefix, index)    fprintf(code_file, \
                                "%s_%03d:\n",            \
                                prefix, index);

/*-----------------------------------------------------*/
/* advance_asm_bufferp    Advance asm_bufferp to the end */
/*                        of the assembly statement.    */
/*-----------------------------------------------------*/

#define advance_asm_bufferp()    while (*asm_bufferp != '\0') \
                                     ++asm_bufferp;

/*-----------------------------------------------------*/
/* new_label_index            Return a new label index. */
/*-----------------------------------------------------*/

#define new_label_index()        ++label_index

#endif
```

The constants STMT_LABEL_PREFIX, FLOAT_LABEL_PREFIX, and STRING_LABEL_ PREFIX are prefixes for labels in the assembly code. For example, $L_007 is a statement label and $S_014 is a string label.

Next, we define constants that represent the names of the library routines in paslib.c. By convention, we preface the names of external routines in assembly language programs with an underscore.

We then define several constants for the stack frame. As we will see in the next chapter, constants PROC_LOCALS_STACK_FRAME_OFFSET, FUNC_LOCALS_STACK_ FRAME_OFFSET, and PARAMETERS_STACK_FRAME_OFFSET will be used as initial offset values in function var_declarations, of file decl.c, and in function formal_parm_ list, of file routine.c. The constants STATIC_LINK, RETURN_VALUE, and HIGH_RE-TURN_VALUE define assembly code labels that will be equated in the object program to items in the stack frame.

Type REGISTER defines enumeration constants for the machine's registers. Type INSTRUCTION defines enumeration constants for the assembly language instructions that the compiler can generate.

Macros emit, emit_1, and emit_2 are called by the code module to write assembly language instructions with zero, one, or two operands, respectively, into the character buffer asm_buffer. Variable asm_bufferp points into this buffer. (asm_buffer and asm_bufferp are defined in file emitasm.c.) Parameter opcode must be one of the INSTRUCTION constants. (We will see later that function operator writes the instruction mnemonic into asm_buffer.)

Parameters operand1 and operand2 must be calls to functions that write into asm_buffer. (These functions are also defined in file emitasm.c.) emit_1 and emit_2 place a tab between parts of the instruction. Each macro prints the complete instruction in asm_buffer to the object code file and points asm_bufferp to the beginning of the buffer. (We will see examples of macros emit, emit_1, and emit_2 later.)

Macro emit_label writes a statement label to the object code file. A statement label consists of a prefix followed by an underscore, an index, and a colon. For example, $L_003: Macro advance_asm_bufferp advances asm_bufferp to the end of the contents of asm_buffer so that *asm_bufferp is the null character. Macro new_label_index returns a label index by incrementing label_index, defined in file emitasm.c. Figure 12-7 shows the new file emitasm.c, which contains functions that write parts of an assembly language statement, such as a label or an operand, to asm_buffer.

FIGURE 12-7   File emitasm.c.

```
/******************************************************/
/*                                                    */
/*      E M I T   A S S E M B L Y   S T A T E M E N T S   */
/*                                                    */
/*      Routines for generating and emitting          */
/*      language statements.                          */
/*                                                    */
/*      FILE:       emitasm.c                          */
/*                                                    */
/*      MODULE:     code                               */
/*                                                    */
/******************************************************/

#include <stdio.h>
#include "symtab.h"
#include "code.h"


/*--------------------------------------------------*/
/* Globals                                          */
/*--------------------------------------------------*/

int label_index = 0;
```

```
char asm_buffer[MAX_PRINT_LINE_LENGTH];    /* assembly stmt buffer */
char *asm_bufferp = asm_buffer;            /* ptr into asm buffer */

char *register_strings[] = {
    "ax", "ah", "al", "bx", "bh", "bl", "cx", "ch", "cl",
    "dx", "dh", "dl", "cs", "ds", "es", "ss",
    "sp", "bp", "si", "di",
};

char *instruction_strings[] = {
    "mov", "rep\tmovsb", "lea", "xchg", "cmp", "repe\tcmpsb",
    "pop", "push", "and", "or", "xor",
    "neg", "inc", "dec", "add", "sub", "imul", "idiv",
    "cld", "call", "ret",
    "jmp", "jl", "jle", "je", "jne", "jge", "jg",
};


/*********************************************/
/*                                           */
/*      Write parts of assembly statements    */
/*                                           */
/*********************************************/
```

```
/*-----------------------------------------*/
/*  label              Write a generic label constructed from  */
/*                     the prefix and the label index.         */
/*                                                             */
/*                     Example:      $L_007                    */
/*-----------------------------------------*/

label(prefix, index)

    char *prefix;
    int index;

{
    sprintf(asm_bufferp, "%s_%03d", prefix, index);
    advance_asm_bufferp();
}


/*-----------------------------------------*/
/*  word_label         Write a word label constructed from     */
/*                     the prefix and the label index.         */
/*                                                             */
/*                     Example:      WORD PTR $F_007           */
/*-----------------------------------------*/

word_label(prefix, index)

    char *prefix;
    int  index;

{
    sprintf(asm_bufferp, "WORD PTR %s_%03d", prefix, index);
    advance_asm_bufferp();
}


/*-----------------------------------------*/
/*  high_dword_label   Write a word label constructed from     */
/*                     the prefix and the label index and      */
/*                     offset by 2 to point to the high word   */
/*                     of a double word.                       */
/*                                                             */
/*                     Example:      WORD PTR $F_007+2         */
/*-----------------------------------------*/

high_dword_label(prefix, index)

    char *prefix;
    int index;

{
    sprintf(asm_bufferp, "WORD PTR %s_%03d+2", prefix, index);
    advance_asm_bufferp();
}


/*-----------------------------------------*/
/*  reg                Write a register name. Example: ax      */
/*-----------------------------------------*/

reg(r)

    REGISTER r;

{
    sprintf(asm_bufferp, "%s", register_strings[r]);
    advance_asm_bufferp();
}
```

```
/*-----------------------------------------*/
/*  operator           Write an opcode. Example: add          */
/*-----------------------------------------*/

operator(opcode)

    INSTRUCTION opcode;

{
    sprintf(asm_bufferp, "\t%s", instruction_strings[opcode]);
    advance_asm_bufferp();
}


/*-----------------------------------------*/
/*  byte               Write a byte label constructed from     */
/*                     the id name and its label index.        */
/*                                                             */
/*                     Example:      BYTE_PTR ch_007           */
/*-----------------------------------------*/

byte(idp)

    SYMTAB_NODE_PTR idp;

{
    sprintf(asm_bufferp, "BYTE PTR %s_%03d",
                          idp->name, idp->label_index);
    advance_asm_bufferp();
}


/*-----------------------------------------*/
/*  byte_indirect      Write an indirect reference to a byte    */
/*                     via a register.                         */
/*                                                             */
/*                     Example:      BYTE PTR [bx]             */
/*-----------------------------------------*/

byte_indirect(r)

    REGISTER r;

{
    sprintf(asm_bufferp, "BYTE PTR [%s]", register_strings[r]);
    advance_asm_bufferp();
}


/*-----------------------------------------*/
/*  word               Write a word label constructed from     */
/*                     the id name and its label index.        */
/*                                                             */
/*                     Example:      WORD_PTR sum_007          */
/*-----------------------------------------*/

word(idp)

    SYMTAB_NODE_PTR idp;

{
    sprintf(asm_bufferp, "WORD PTR %s_%03d",
                          idp->name, idp->label_index);
    advance_asm_bufferp();
}


/*-----------------------------------------*/
/*  high_dword         Write a word label constructed from     */
/*                     the id name and its label index and     */
/*                     offset by 2 to point to the high word   */
```

```
/*                      of a double word.                      */
/*                                                             */
/*                      Example:     WORD_PTR sum_007+2        */
/*-------------------------------------------------------------*/

high_dword(idp)

    SYMTAB_NODE_PTR idp;

{
    sprintf(asm_bufferp, "WORD PTR %s_%03d+2",
                         idp->name, idp->label_index);
    advance_asm_bufferp();
}

/*-------------------------------------------------------------*/
/*  word_indirect        Write an indirect reference to a word */
/*                       via a register.                       */
/*                                                             */
/*                       Example:     WORD PTR [bx]            */
/*-------------------------------------------------------------*/

word_indirect(r)

    REGISTER r;

{
    sprintf(asm_bufferp, "WORD PTR [%s]", register_strings[r]);
    advance_asm_bufferp();
}

/*-------------------------------------------------------------*/
/*  high_dword_indirect   Write an indirect reference to the   */
/*                        high word of a double word via a     */
/*                        register.                            */
/*                                                             */
/*                        Example:     WORD PTR [bx+2]         */
/*-------------------------------------------------------------*/

high_dword_indirect(r)

    REGISTER r;

{
    sprintf(asm_bufferp, "WORD PTR [%s+2]", register_strings[r]);
    advance_asm_bufferp();
}

/*-------------------------------------------------------------*/
/*  tagged_name          Write an id name tagged with the id's */
/*                       label index.                          */
/*                                                             */
```

```
/*                      Example:     x_007                    */
/*-------------------------------------------------------------*/

tagged_name(idp)

    SYMTAB_NODE_PTR idp;

{
    sprintf(asm_bufferp, "%s_%03d", idp->name, idp->label_index);
    advance_asm_bufferp();
}

/*-------------------------------------------------------------*/
/*  name_lit             Write a literal name.                 */
/*                                                             */
/*                       Example:     _float_convert           */
/*-------------------------------------------------------------*/

name_lit(name)

    char *name;

{
    sprintf(asm_bufferp, "%s", name);
    advance_asm_bufferp();
}

/*-------------------------------------------------------------*/
/*  integer_lit          Write an integer as a string.        */
/*-------------------------------------------------------------*/

integer_lit(n)

    int n;

{
    sprintf(asm_bufferp, "%d", n);
    advance_asm_bufferp();
}

/*-------------------------------------------------------------*/
/*  char_lit             Write a character surrounded by single*/
/*                       quotes.                               */
/*-------------------------------------------------------------*/

char_lit(ch)

    char ch;

{
    sprintf(asm_bufferp, "'%c'", ch);
    advance_asm_bufferp();
}
```

First, we initialize `label_index`, which we use to create assembly language labels. We declare `asm_buffer`, the buffer for an assembly language statement, and `asm_bufferp`, a pointer into the buffer. The string arrays `register_strings` and `instruction_strings` correspond to the enumeration types REGISTER and IN-STRUCTION.

Whenever we emit references to memory data, we can use names derived from the original names in the Pascal source program to make it easier for us to read the generated code. Because assembly programs do not have the scope rules of Pascal, we must tag each name in the generated code with a unique integer. We store this integer in the `label_index` field of the identifier's symbol table node.

For example, suppose a procedure in a Pascal program has a local variable count, and a function in the same program also has a local variable count. When we compile the Pascal program into assembly language, we can use names like `count_007` and `count_014`.

Function `label` writes a label consisting of a label prefix, an underscore, and a label index, such as `$L_003`. Function `word_label` is similar, except that we also add `WORD PTR` before the label, such as `WORD PTR $F_009`. Such a label is used as an instruction operand. Function `high_dword_label` writes a label for the high-order half of a doubleword, such as `WORD PTR $F_009+2`.

Function `reg` simply writes a register name from `register_strings`, such as ax, and function `operator` writes an instruction mnemonic from `instruction_strings`.

Function `byte` writes a label to a byte value. This label is used as an instruction operand and consists of a name from the Pascal source tagged with a label index, such as `BYTE PTR ch_014`. Function `byte_indirect` writes an indirect reference to byte data, such as `BYTE PTR [bx]`. Functions `word` and `word_indirect` are similar, except that they use `WORD_PTR`. Function `high_dword` writes a label that references the high-order half of a doubleword, such as `WORD PTR sum_017+2`. Function `high_dword_indirect` writes an indirect reference to the high-order half of a doubleword, such as `WORD PTR [bx+2]`.

Function `tagged_name` writes a name from the Pascal source tagged with its label index, such as `x_021`. Function `literal_name` writes the name without a tag. Finally, functions `integer_lit` and `char_lit` write integers and characters as strings. Examples are -453 and 'x'.

Now for some examples of how we use macros `emit`, `emit_1`, and `emit_2` with the functions in file `emitasm.c`. The macro call `emit(RETURN);` writes the assembly instruction ret to the code file. The macro call `emit_1(PUSH, reg(AX));` writes push ax and the macro call `emit_2(MOVE, reg(AX), word(var_idp));` writes mov ax,WORD PTR gamma_003 if we assume that var_idp->name is gamma and var_idp->label_index is 3.

Questions and exercises

1. Calling C runtime library functions in file `paslib.c` causes our final executable files to be large, since portions of the C runtime library end up being linked with our programs. Rewrite `paslib.c` so that it does not call any C library functions.

CHAPTER 13

Compiling Procedures, Functions, and Assignment Statements

In this chapter and the next one, we will write a compiler based on the work we have done so far. The previous chapter introduced some of the routines of the code module that emit assembly language code. We now look at the remaining files and routines of the code module and add calls from the parser module.

Many of the things we considered and did in the interpreter carry over to the compiler. For example, we still check types and perform type conversions in expressions. The difference is that instead of actually performing some of these operations, we now generate the code to perform them. So even though the compiler does not have an executor module, many of that module's semantic actions reappear in the parser module.

Another difference between our interpreter and our compiler is that the compiler does its job with only one pass over the source code. It does not use an intermediate form, which is another reason we make calls to the code generation routines directly from the parser module. We will take a brief look at multipass compilers in Chapter 15.

Our interpreter operated on an idealized stack machine architecture that it maintained within itself. Our compiler, on the other hand, generates code for an actual IBM PC, that is, for the 8086 processor. We therefore must deal with the processor's features and idiosyncrasies.

In this chapter, we write the parts of the compiler to generate code for procedures, functions, and assignment statements. We will complete the compiler in the next chapter. This chapter develops the skills to:

• compile calls and returns and assignment statements

- make calls from the parser to code generation routines
- generate calls to a runtime library

This chapter covers much ground in detail; however, it is not as complex as it may seem. Keep in mind that the code the compiler emits for Pascal statements is designed to do what the interpreter did at run time for the same statements.

13.1 Organization of the compiler

The syntax checker we wrote in Chapter 7 is the basis for the compiler. You can also compare it to the interpreter: it lacks the executor module but gains the code module that we began in the previous chapter.

Parser Module

parser.h	*c*	Parser header file
routine.c	*c*	Parse programs, procedures, and functions
standard.c	*c*	Parse standard procedures and functions
decl.c	*c*	Parse declarations
stmt.c	*c*	Parse statements
expr.c	*c*	Parse expressions

Scanner Module

scanner.h	*u*	Scanner header file
scanner.c	*c*	Scanner routines

Symbol Table Module

symtab.h	*u*	Symbol table header file
symtab.c	*u*	Symbol table routines

Code Module

code.h	*u*	Code generator header file
emitasm.c	*u*	Emit assembly language statements
emitcode.c	*n*	Emit sequences of assembly code

Error Module

error.h	*c*	Error header file
error.c	*c*	Error routines

Miscellaneous

common.h	*c*	Common header file

Where: *u*   file unchanged from the previous chapter
        c   file changed from the previous chapter
        n   new file

We modify the parser module to make calls to the code generation routines. Files error.h and error.c revert to the way they were in Chapter 7. We no longer need all the runtime error messages and routines that were used by the interpreter's executor module. File common.h also reverts to what it was in Chapter 7.

In Figure 13-1, the routines of the new file emitcode.c emit sequences of assembly code. We will examine each function later.

FIGURE 13-1   File emitcode.c.

```
/****************************************************************/
/*                                                              */
/*      E M I T   C O D E   S E Q U E N C E S                   */
/*                                                              */
/*      Routines for emitting standard                         */
/*      assembly code sequences.                                */
/*                                                              */
/*      FILE:       emitcode.c                                  */
/*                                                              */
/*      MODULE:     code                                        */
/*                                                              */
/****************************************************************/

#include <stdio.h>
#include "symtab.h"
#include "code.h"

/*------------------------------------------------------------*/
/* Externals                                                  */
/*------------------------------------------------------------*/

extern TYPE_STRUCT_PTR  integer_typep, real_typep,
                        boolean_typep, char_typep;

extern int level;

extern char     asm_buffer[];
extern char     *asm_bufferp;
extern FILE     *code_file;

/*------------------------------------------------------------*/
/* Globals                                                    */
/*------------------------------------------------------------*/

SYMTAB_NODE_PTR  float_literal_list  = NULL;
SYMTAB_NODE_PTR  string_literal_list = NULL;

            /************************************/
            /*                                  */
            /*      Emit prologues and epilogues */
            /*                                  */
            /************************************/

/*------------------------------------------------------------*/
/* emit_program_prologue      Emit the program prologue.      */
/*------------------------------------------------------------*/
```

```
emit_program_prologue()

{
    fprintf(code_file, "\tDOSSEG\n");
    fprintf(code_file, "\t.MODEL  small\n");
    fprintf(code_file, "\t.STACK  1024\n");
    fprintf(code_file, "\n");
    fprintf(code_file, "\t.CODE\n");
    fprintf(code_file, "\n");
    fprintf(code_file, "\tPUBLIC\t_pascal_main\n");
    fprintf(code_file, "\tINCLUDE\tpasextrn.inc\n");
    fprintf(code_file, "\n");

    /*
    -- Equates for stack frame components.
    */
    fprintf(code_file, "%s\t\tEQU\t<WORD PTR [bp+4]>\n",
                        STATIC_LINK);
    fprintf(code_file, "%s\t\tEQU\t<WORD PTR [bp-4]>\n",
                        RETURN_VALUE);
    fprintf(code_file, "%s\tEQU\t<WORD PTR [bp-2]>\n",
                        HIGH_RETURN_VALUE);
    fprintf(code_file, "\n");
}

/*------------------------------------------------------------*/
/* emit_program_epilogue      Emit the program epilogue,      */
/*                            which includes the data         */
/*                            segment.                        */
/*------------------------------------------------------------*/

emit_program_epilogue(prog_idp)

    SYMTAB_NODE_PTR prog_idp;    /* id of program */

{
    SYMTAB_NODE_PTR np;
    int             i, length;

    fprintf(code_file, "\n");
    fprintf(code_file, "\t.DATA\n");
    fprintf(code_file, "\n");

    /*
    -- Emit declarations for the program's global variables.
    */
    for (np = prog_idp->defn.info.routine.locals;
```

```
        np != NULL;
        np = np->next) {
    fprintf(code_file, "%s_%03d\t", np->name, np->label_index);
    if (np->typep == char_typep)
        fprintf(code_file, "DB\t0\n");
    else if (np->typep == real_typep)
        fprintf(code_file, "DD\t0.0\n");
    else if (np->typep->form == ARRAY_FORM)
        fprintf(code_file, "DB\t%d DUP(0)\n", np->typep->size);
    else if (np->typep->form == RECORD_FORM)
        fprintf(code_file, "DB\t%d DUP(0)\n", np->typep->size);
    else
        fprintf(code_file, "DW\t0\n");
}

/*
-- Emit declarations for the program's floating point literals.
*/
for (np = float_literal_list; np != NULL; np = np->next)
    fprintf(code_file, "%s_%03d\tDD\t%e\n", FLOAT_LABEL_PREFIX,
            np->label_index,
            np->defn.info.constant.value.real);

/*
-- Emit declarations for the program's string literals.
*/
for (np = string_literal_list; np != NULL; np = np->next) {
    fprintf(code_file, "%s_%03d\tDB\t\"", STRING_LABEL_PREFIX,
            np->label_index);

    length = strlen(np->name) - 2;
    for (i = 1; i <= length; ++i) fputc(np->name[i], code_file);

    fprintf(code_file, "\"\n");
}

fprintf(code_file, "\n");
fprintf(code_file, "\tEND\n");
}

/*------------------------------------------------------------*/
/* emit_main_prologue         Emit the prologue for the main  */
/*                            routine _pascal_main.           */
/*------------------------------------------------------------*/

emit_main_prologue()

{
    fprintf(code_file, "\n");
    fprintf(code_file, "_pascal_main\tPROC\n");
    fprintf(code_file, "\n");

    emit_1(PUSH, reg(BP));          /* dynamic link */
    emit_2(MOVE, reg(BP), reg(SP)); /* new stack frame base */
}

/*------------------------------------------------------------*/
/* emit_main_epilogue         Emit the epilogue for the main  */
/*                            routine _pascal_main.           */
/*------------------------------------------------------------*/

emit_main_epilogue()

{
    emit_1(POP, reg(BP));       /* restore caller's stack frame */
    emit(RETURN);               /* return */

    fprintf(code_file, "\n");
```

```
    fprintf(code_file, "_pascal_main\tENDP\n");
}

/*------------------------------------------------------------*/
/* emit_routine_prologue        Emit the prologue for a proce- */
/*                              dure or a function.            */
/*------  ----------------------------------------------------*/

emit_routine_prologue(rtn_idp)

    SYMTAB_NODE_PTR rtn_idp;

{
    fprintf(code_file, "\n");
    fprintf(code_file, "%s_%03d\tPROC\n",
                rtn_idp->name, rtn_idp->label_index);
    fprintf(code_file, "\n");

    emit_1(PUSH, reg(BP));          /* dynamic link */
    emit_2(MOVE, reg(BP), reg(SP)); /* new stack frame base */

    /*
    -- Allocate stack space for a function's return value.
    */
    if (rtn_idp->defn.key == FUNC_DEFN) emit_2(SUBTRACT, reg(SP),
                                            integer_lit(4));

    /*
    -- Allocate stack space for the local variables.
    */
    if (rtn_idp->defn.info.routine.total_local_size > 0)
        emit_2(SUBTRACT, reg(SP),
                integer_lit(rtn_idp->defn.info.routine
                                .total_local_size));
}

/*------------------------------------------------------------*/
/* emit_routine_epilogue        Emit the epilogue for a proce- */
/*                              dure or a function.            */
/*------------------------------------------------------------*/

emit_routine_epilogue(rtn_idp)

    SYMTAB_NODE_PTR rtn_idp;

{
    /*
    -- Load a function's return value into the ax or dx:ax registers.
    */
    if (rtn_idp->defn.key == FUNC_DEFN) {
        emit_2(MOVE, reg(AX), name_lit(RETURN_VALUE));
        if (rtn_idp->typep == real_typep)
            emit_2(MOVE, reg(DX), name_lit(HIGH_RETURN_VALUE));
    }

    emit_2(MOVE, reg(SP), reg(BP)); /* cut back to caller's stack */
    emit_1(POP, reg(BP));           /* restore caller's stack frame */

    emit_1(RETURN, integer_lit(rtn_idp->defn.info.routine
                                .total_parm_size + 2));
                                /* return and cut back stack */

    fprintf(code_file, "\n");
    fprintf(code_file, "%s_%03d\tENDP\n",
                rtn_idp->name, rtn_idp->label_index);
}
```

```
/*******************************/
/*                             */
/*       Emit equates and data */
/*                             */
/*******************************/
```

```
/*---------------------------------------------------------*/
/* emit_declarations    Emit the parameter and local variable */
/*                      declarations for a procedure or a     */
/*                      function.                             */
/*---------------------------------------------------------*/

emit_declarations(rtn_idp)

    SYMTAB_NODE_PTR rtn_idp;

{
    SYMTAB_NODE_PTR parm_idp = rtn_idp->defn.info.routine.parms;
    SYMTAB_NODE_PTR var_idp  = rtn_idp->defn.info.routine.locals;

    fprintf(code_file, "\n");

    /*
    -- Parameters.
    */
    while (parm_idp != NULL) {
        emit_text_equate(parm_idp);
        parm_idp = parm_idp->next;
    }

    /*
    -- Local variables.
    */
    while (var_idp != NULL) {
        emit_text_equate(var_idp);
        var_idp = var_idp->next;
    }
}
```

```
/*---------------------------------------------------------*/
/* emit_numeric_equate    Emit a numeric equate for a field */
/*                        id and its offset.                */
/*                                                          */
/*                        Example:   field_007 EQU 3        */
/*---------------------------------------------------------*/

emit_numeric_equate(idp)

    SYMTAB_NODE_PTR idp;

{
    fprintf(code_file, "%s_%03d\tEQU\t%d\n",
                       idp->name, idp->label_index,
                       idp->defn.info.data.offset);
}
```

```
/*---------------------------------------------------------*/
/* emit_numeric_equate    Emit a numeric equate for a para- */
/*                        meter or a local variable id and  */
/*                        its stack frame offset.           */
/*                                                          */
/*                        Examples:  parm_007  EQU <bp+6>   */
/*                                   var_008   EQU <bp-10>  */
/*                                   dword_010 EQU <bp-14>  */
/*                                   dword_010h EQU <bp-14+2> */
/*---------------------------------------------------------*/

emit_text_equate(idp)
```

```
    SYMTAB_NODE_PTR idp;

{
    char *name       = idp->name;
    int  label_index = idp->label_index;
    int  offset      = idp->defn.info.data.offset;

    if (idp->typep == char_typep)
        fprintf(code_file, "%s_%03d\tEQU\t<BYTE PTR [bp%+d]>\n",
                           name, label_index, offset);
    else if (idp->typep == real_typep)
        fprintf(code_file, "%s_%03d\tEQU\t<WORD PTR [bp%+d]>\n",
                           name, label_index, offset);
    else
        fprintf(code_file, "%s_%03d\tEQU\t<WORD PTR [bp%+d]>\n",
                           name, label_index, offset);
}
```

```
/*******************************/
/*                             */
/*       Emit loads and pushes */
/*                             */
/*******************************/
```

```
/*---------------------------------------------------------*/
/* emit_load_value       Emit code to load a scalar value   */
/*                       into AX or DX:AX.                  */
/*---------------------------------------------------------*/

emit_load_value(var_idp, var_tp)

    SYMTAB_NODE_PTR var_idp;
    TYPE_STRUCT_PTR var_tp;

{
    int     var_level  = var_idp->level;
    BOOLEAN varparm_flag = var_idp->defn.key == VARPARM_DEFN;

    if (varparm_flag) {
        /*
        -- VAR formal parameter.
        -- AX or DX:AX = value the address points to
        */
        emit_2(MOVE, reg(BX), word(var_idp));
        if (var_tp == char_typep) {
            emit_2(SUBTRACT, reg(AX), reg(AX));
            emit_2(MOVE, reg(AL), byte_indirect(BX));
        }
        else if (var_tp == real_typep) {
            emit_2(MOVE, reg(AX), word_indirect(BX));
            emit_2(MOVE, reg(AX), high_dword_indirect(BX));
        }
        else emit_2(MOVE, reg(AX), word_indirect(BX));
    }
    else if ((var_level == level) || (var_level == 1)) {
        /*
        -- Global or local parameter or variable:
        -- AX or DX:AX = value
        */
        if (var_tp == char_typep) {
            emit_2(SUBTRACT, reg(AX), reg(AX));
            emit_2(MOVE, reg(AL), byte(var_idp));
        }
        else if (var_tp == real_typep) {
            emit_2(MOVE, reg(AX), word(var_idp));
            emit_2(MOVE, reg(DX), high_dword(var_idp));
```

```
        }
        else emit_2(MOVE, reg(AX), word(var_idp));
    }
    else   /* var_level < level */ {
        /*
        -- Nonlocal parameter or variable.
        -- First locate the appropriate stack frame, then:
        -- AX or DX:AX = value
        */
        int lev = var_level;

        emit_2(MOVE, reg(BX), reg(BP));
        do {
            emit_2(MOVE, reg(BP), name_lit(STATIC_LINK));
        } while (++lev < level);

        if (var_tp == char_typep) {
            emit_2(SUBTRACT, reg(AX), reg(AX));
            emit_2(MOVE, reg(AL), byte(var_idp));
        }
        else if (var_tp == real_typep) {
            emit_2(MOVE, reg(AX), word(var_idp));
            emit_2(MOVE, reg(DX), high_dword(var_idp));
        }
        else emit_2(MOVE, reg(AX), word(var_idp));

        emit_2(MOVE, reg(BP), reg(BX));
    }
}
```

```
/*------------------------------------------------------*/
/* emit_push_operand    Emit code to push a scalar operand */
/*                      value onto the stack.           */
/*------------------------------------------------------*/

emit_push_operand(tp)

    TYPE_STRUCT_PTR tp;

{
    if ((tp->form == ARRAY_FORM) || (tp->form == RECORD_FORM)) return;

    if (tp == real_typep) emit_1(PUSH, reg(DX));
    emit_1(PUSH, reg(AX));
}
```

```
/*------------------------------------------------------*/
/* emit_push_address   Emit code to push an address onto the */
/*                     stack.                           */
/*------------------------------------------------------*/

emit_push_address(var_idp)

    SYMTAB_NODE_PTR var_idp;

{
    int     var_level    = var_idp->level;
    BOOLEAN varparm_flag = var_idp->defn.key == VARPARM_DEFN;

    if ((var_level == level) || (var_level == 1))
        emit_2(varparm_flag ? MOVE : LOAD_ADDRESS,
            reg(AX), word(var_idp))

    else   /* var_level < level */ {
        int lev = var_level;

        emit_2(MOVE, reg(BX), reg(BP));
```

```
        do {
            emit_2(MOVE, reg(BP), name_lit(STATIC_LINK));
        } while (++lev < level);
        emit_2(varparm_flag ? MOVE : LOAD_ADDRESS,
            reg(AX), word(var_idp));
        emit_2(MOVE, reg(BP), reg(BX));
    }

    emit_1(PUSH, reg(AX));
}
```

```
/*------------------------------------------------------*/
/* emit_push_return_value_address        Emit code to push the */
/*                                       address of the function */
/*                                       return value in the */
/*                                       stack frame.   */
/*------------------------------------------------------*/

emit_push_return_value_address(var_idp)

    SYMTAB_NODE_PTR var_idp;


{
    int lev = var_idp->level + 1;

    if (lev < level) {
        /*
        -- Find the appropriate stack frame.
        */
        emit_2(MOVE, reg(BX), reg(BP));
        do {
            emit_2(MOVE, reg(BP), name_lit(STATIC_LINK));
        } while (++lev < level);
        emit_2(LOAD_ADDRESS, reg(AX), name_lit(RETURN_VALUE));
        emit_2(MOVE, reg(BP), reg(BX));
    }
    else emit_2(LOAD_ADDRESS, reg(AX), name_lit(RETURN_VALUE));

    emit_1(PUSH, reg(AX));
}
```

```
/****************************************/
/*                                      */
/*      Emit miscellaneous code         */
/*                                      */
/****************************************/
```

```
/*------------------------------------------------------*/
/* emit_promote_to_real        Emit code to convert integer */
/*                             operands to real.        */
/*------------------------------------------------------*/

emit_promote_to_real(tp1, tp2)

    TYPE_STRUCT_PTR tp1, tp2;

{
    if (tp2 == integer_typep) {
        emit_1(CALL, name_lit(FLOAT_CONVERT));
        emit_2(ADD,  reg(SP), integer_lit(2));
        emit_1(PUSH, reg(DX));
        emit_1(PUSH, reg(AX));                    /* ???_1 real_2 */
    }

    if (tp1 == integer_typep) {
        emit_1(POP,  reg(AX));
        emit_1(POP,  reg(DX));
```

```
emit_1(POP,  reg(BX));                                                emit_1(POP,  reg(BX));
emit_1(PUSH, reg(DX));                                                emit_1(POP,  reg(CX));
emit_1(PUSH, reg(AX));                                                emit_1(PUSH, reg(DX));
emit_1(PUSH, reg(BX));              /* real_2 integer_1 */            emit_1(PUSH, reg(AX));
                                                                      emit_1(PUSH, reg(CX));
                                                                      emit_1(PUSH, reg(BX));              /* real_1 real_2 */
emit_1(CALL, name_lit(FLOAT_CONVERT));                            }
emit_2(ADD,  reg(SP), integer_lit(2));  /* real_2 real_1 */    }
```

Figure 13-2 shows the new version of function get_source_line in file scanner.c. This version outputs each source line to the object code file code_file as an assembly language comment line. This will help us match the emitted code with the original source lines.

FIGURE 13-2   Function get_source_line in file scanner.c.

```
/*---------------------------------------------------*/                                   source_file)) != NULL) {
/*  get_source_line   Read the next line from the source   */            ++line_number;
/*                    file.  If there is one, print it out  */
/*                    and return TRUE.  Else return FALSE   */            if (print_flag) {
/*                    for the end of file.                  */                sprintf(print_buffer, "%4d %d: %s",
/*---------------------------------------------------*/                                    line_number, level, source_buffer);
                                                                             print_line(print_buffer);
    BOOLEAN                                                               }
get_source_line()

{                                                                        fprintf(code_file, "; %4d: %s", line_number, source_buffer);
    char print_buffer[MAX_SOURCE_LINE_LENGTH + 9];                       return(TRUE);
    extern FILE *code_file;                                          }
                                                                     else return(FALSE);
    if ((fgets(source_buffer, MAX_SOURCE_LINE_LENGTH,                }
```

13.2 Procedures and functions

In the previous chapter, we saw how the functions in file emitasm.c emit assembly statements. Now we will look at the code the compiler actually generates for Pascal procedures and functions.

13.2.1 Managing the runtime stack

Like the interpreter, the code generated by the compiler must manage the runtime stack during calls to and returns from Pascal procedures and functions. The only significant difference is the stack frame format, as we saw in Figure 12-4. To call a procedure or function, the *caller* must perform these steps:

1. Push the actual parameter values onto the stack. The last parameter value ends up on top of the stack.

2. Push the static link onto the stack.

3. Push the return address onto the stack.

   Then, the *callee* must perform these steps:

4. Push the dynamic link onto the stack.

5. Set register BP to point to the callee's stack frame.

6. Function only: Allocate space on top of the stack for the return value.

7. Allocate space on top of the stack for local variables.

   Just before the callee returns to its caller, it must perform these steps:

8. Function only: Load the return value from the stack frame into register AX or the DX:AX register pair.

9. Cut the stack back to remove the callee's local variables and, for a function, the return value.

10. Use the dynamic link to restore register BP to point to the caller's stack frame.

11. Pop off the return address.

12. Cut the stack back to remove the actual parameters and the static link.

We will refer to these steps by number when we describe the code emitted by the compiler.

13.2.2 Memory data and symbol table changes

In the previous chapter, you saw that parameters and local variables are allocated on the runtime stack, just as they were in the interpreter. The code generated by the compiler has one major difference: the program's global variables are allocated in the data segment instead of at the bottom of the stack. We do this for efficiency, since data allocated in the data segment can be accessed directly, whereas data allocated on the stack must be accessed indirectly through register BP.

You also saw how the compiler uses names taken from the Pascal source when it generates assembly code. These names are tagged with a label index. For example, variable length in the Pascal program becomes length_009 in the assembly code, assuming a label index value of 9. We store the label index in the label_ index field of the identifier's symbol table node. Figure 13-3 shows a new version of routine var_or_field_declarations in file decl.c. This version calls macro new_label_index in file emitasm.c to assign a unique label index to each identifier.

FIGURE 13-3   Function var_or_field_declarations in file decl.c.

```
/*--------------------------------------------------------*/     /*                             a sublist, and all the sublists */
/* var_or_field_declarations   Process variable declarations  */  /*                             are then linked together.    */
/*                             or record field definitions.   */  /*--------------------------------------------------------*/
/*                             All ids declared with the same */
/*                             type are linked together into  */  TOKEN_CODE follow_variables_list[] = {SEMICOLON, IDENTIFIER,
```

```
                                  END_OF_FILE, 0};

TOKEN_CODE follow_fields_list[]    = {SEMICOLON, END, IDENTIFIER,
                                      END_OF_FILE, 0};

var_or_field_declarations(rtn_idp, record_tp, offset)

    SYMTAB_NODE_PTR rtn_idp;
    TYPE_STRUCT_PTR record_tp;
    int             offset;

{
    SYMTAB_NODE_PTR idp, first_idp, last_idp;   /* variable or
                                                    field ids */
    SYMTAB_NODE_PTR prev_last_idp = NULL;        /* last id of list */
    TYPE_STRUCT_PTR tp;                          /* type */
    BOOLEAN var_flag = (rtn_idp != NULL);        /* TRUE: variables */
                                                 /* FALSE: fields */
    int size;
    int total_size = 0;

    /*
    -- Loop to process sublist, each of a type.
    */
    while (token == IDENTIFIER) {
        first_idp = NULL;

        /*
        -- Loop process each variable or field id in a sublist.
        */
        while (token == IDENTIFIER) {
            if (var_flag) {
                search_and_enter_local_symtab(idp);
                idp->defn.key = VAR_DEFN;
            }
            else {
                search_and_enter_this_symtab
                    (idp, record_tp->info.record.field_symtab);
                idp->defn.key = FIELD_DEFN;
            }
            idp->label_index = new_label_index();

            /*
            -- Link ids together into a sublist.
            */
            if (first_idp == NULL) {
                first_idp = last_idp = idp;
                if (var_flag &&
                    (rtn_idp->defn.info.routine.locals == NULL))
                    rtn_idp->defn.info.routine.locals = idp;
            }
            else {
                last_idp->next = idp;
                last_idp = idp;
            }

            get_token();
            if_token_get(COMMA);
        }
```

```
        /*
        -- Process the sublist's type.
        */
        if_token_get_else_error(COLON, MISSING_COLON);
        tp = do_type();
        size = tp->size;
        if (size & 1) ++size;    /* round up to even */

        /*
        -- Assign the offset and the type to all variable or field
        -- ids in the sublist.
        */
        for (idp = first_idp; idp != NULL; idp = idp->next) {
            idp->typep = tp;

            if (var_flag) {
                offset -= size;
                total_size += size;
                idp->defn.info.data.offset = offset;
                analyze_var_decl(idp);
            }

            else   /* record fields */ {
                idp->defn.info.data.offset = offset;
                offset += size;

                /*
                -- Emit numeric equate for the field id's
                -- name and offset.
                */
                emit_numeric_equate(idp);
            }
        }

        /*
        -- Link this sublist to the previous sublist.
        */
        if (prev_last_idp != NULL) prev_last_idp->next = first_idp;
        prev_last_idp = last_idp;

        /*
        -- Error synchronization:  Should be ; for variable
        --                         declaration, or ; or END for
        --                         record type definition.
        */
        synchronize(var_flag ? follow_variables_list
                             : follow_fields_list,
                    declaration_start_list, statement_start_list);
        if_token_get(SEMICOLON);
        else if (var_flag && ((token_in(declaration_start_list)) ||
                              (token_in(statement_start_list))))
            error(MISSING_SEMICOLON);
    }

    if (var_flag)
        rtn_idp->defn.info.routine.total_local_size = total_size;
    else
        record_tp->size = offset;
}
```

Function `var_or_field_declarations` allocates stack offsets for local variables differently from how they were allocated for the interpreter. For the compiled
code, the offsets must be negative (see Figure 12-4). We decrement variable offset

each time by the size of the variable. As always, we keep track of the total byte size of all the local variables in total_size, and at the end, we set this value in the total_local_size field of the symbol table node of the procedure or function identifier.

For each record field, var_or_field_declarations calls function emit_numeric_equate in file emitcode.c to equate the tagged field name with its offset. As we will see later, these names are used in the generated code to calculate record field addresses. For example, the record definition:

```
RECORD
    i : integer;
    x : real;
    b : boolean;
END
```

results in the equates:

```
i_003 EQU 0
x_004 EQU 2
b_005 EQU 6
```

The new version of routine var_declarations in file decl.c (shown in Figure 13-4) now passes a different initial offset value depending on whether the Pascal routine is a procedure or a function. As we saw in Chapter 12, a function allocates two words on the stack frame for its return value.

FIGURE 13-4   Function var_declarations in file decl.c.

```
/*-----------------------------------------------------*/        SYMTAB_NODE_PTR rtn_idp;    /* id of program or routine */
/* var_declarations    Process variable declarations:  */
/*                                                      */        {
/*                      <id-list> : <type>              */            var_or_field_declarations(rtn_idp, NULL,
/*-----------------------------------------------------*/                                       rtn_idp->defn.key == PROC_DEFN
                                                                                               ? PROC_LOCALS_STACK_FRAME_OFFSET
                                                                                               : FUNC_LOCALS_STACK_FRAME_OFFSET);
var_declarations(rtn_idp)                                        }
```

Figure 13-5 shows a new version of function formal_parm_list in file routine.c. We access formal parameter values with positive offsets from the stack frame location pointed to by register BP (see Figure 12-4). However, we must assign the offsets in reverse order, the last parameter gets the smallest offset, and the first parameter gets the largest offset.

FIGURE 13-5   Function formal_parm_list in file routine.c.

```
/*--------------------------------------------------------*/
/* formal_parm_list    Process a formal parameter list:   */
/*                                                         */
/*                        ( VAR <id-list> : <type> ;       */
/*                          <id-list> : <type> ;           */
/*                          ... )                          */
/*                                                         */
/*                      Return a pointer to the head of the */
/*                      parameter id list.                 */
/*--------------------------------------------------------*/

    SYMTAB_NODE_PTR
formal_parm_list(countp, total_sizep)

    int *countp;        /* ptr to count of parameters */
    int *total_sizep;   /* ptr to total byte size of parameters */

{
    SYMTAB_NODE_PTR parm_idp, first_idp, last_idp;    /* parm ids */
    SYMTAB_NODE_PTR prev_last_idp = NULL;       /* last id of list */
    SYMTAB_NODE_PTR parm_listp = NULL;          /* parm list */
    SYMTAB_NODE_PTR type_idp;                   /* type id */
    TYPE_STRUCT_PTR parm_tp;                    /* parm type */
    DEFN_KEY        parm_defn;                  /* parm definition */
    int             parm_count = 0;             /* count of parms */
    int             parm_offset = PARAMETERS_STACK_FRAME_OFFSET;

    get_token();

    /*
    -- Loop to process parameter declarations separated by ;
    */
    while ((token == IDENTIFIER) || (token == VAR)) {
        first_idp = NULL;

        /*
        -- VAR parms?
        */
        if (token == VAR) {
            parm_defn = VARPARM_DEFN;
            get_token();
        }
        else parm_defn = VALPARM_DEFN;

        /*
        -- <id list>
        */
        while (token == IDENTIFIER) {
            search_and_enter_local_symtab(parm_idp);
            parm_idp->defn.key     = parm_defn;
            parm_idp->label_index = new_label_index();
            ++parm_count;

            if (parm_listp == NULL) parm_listp = parm_idp;

            /*
            -- Link parm ids together.
            */

            if (first_idp == NULL)
                first_idp = last_idp = parm_idp;
            else {
                last_idp->next = parm_idp;
                last_idp = parm_idp;
            }

            get_token();
            if_token_get(COMMA);
        }

        if_token_get_else_error(COLON, MISSING_COLON);

        if (token == IDENTIFIER) {
            search_and_find_all_symtab(type_idp);
            if (type_idp->defn.key != TYPE_DEFN) error(INVALID_TYPE);
            parm_tp = type_idp->typep;
            get_token();
        }
        else {
            error(MISSING_IDENTIFIER);
            parm_tp = &dummy_type;
        }

        /*
        -- Assign the type to all parm ids in the sublist.
        */
        for (parm_idp = first_idp;
             parm_idp != NULL;
             parm_idp = parm_idp->next) parm_idp->typep = parm_tp;

        /*
        -- Link this list to the list of all parm ids.
        */
        if (prev_last_idp != NULL) prev_last_idp->next = first_idp;
        prev_last_idp = last_idp;

        /*
        -- Error synchronization:  Should be ; or )
        */
        synchronize(follow_parms_list, NULL, NULL);
        if_token_get(SEMICOLON);
    }

    /*
    -- Assign the offset to all parm ids in reverse order.
    */
    reverse_list(&parm_listp);
    for (parm_idp = parm_listp;
         parm_idp != NULL;
         parm_idp = parm_idp->next) {
        parm_idp->defn.info.data.offset = parm_offset;
        parm_offset += parm_idp->defn.key == VALPARM_DEFN
                            ? parm_idp->typep->size
                            : sizeof(char *);
        if (parm_offset & 1) ++parm_offset;   /* round up to even */
    }
```

```
reverse_list(&parm_listp);                              *total_sizep = parm_offset - PARAMETERS_STACK_FRAME_OFFSET;

if_token_get_else_error(RPAREN, MISSING_RPAREN);         return(parm_listp);
*countp = parm_count;                                  }
```

To assign the offsets, we first call function `reverse_list` to reverse the order of the formal parameter list. We increment variable `offset` by the size of each parameter. Then we call `reverse_list` a second time to restore the original order of the parameter list. This new function is also defined in `routine.c`, and it is shown in Figure 13-6.

FIGURE 13-6   Function `reverse_list` in file `routine.c`.

```
/*-----------------------------------------------------------*/           --  Reverse the list in place.
/* reverse_list       Reverse a list of symbol table nodes.  */            */
/*-----------------------------------------------------------*/           while (thisp != NULL) {
                                                                              nextp = thisp->next;
reverse_list(listpp)                                                          thisp->next = prevp;
                                                                              prevp = thisp;
    SYMTAB_NODE_PTR *listpp;     /* ptr to ptr to node list head */           thisp = nextp;
                                                                          }
{
    SYMTAB_NODE_PTR prevp = NULL;                                         /*
    SYMTAB_NODE_PTR thisp = *listpp;                                      --  Point to the new head (former tail) of the list.
    SYMTAB_NODE_PTR nextp;                                                */
                                                                          *listpp = prevp;
    /*                                                                }
```

As before, we keep track of the total byte size of all the formal parameters in function `formal_parm_list`. Functions `procedure_header` and `function_header` set this value in the `total_parm_size` field of the symbol table node for the procedure or function identifier.

13.2.3 Program prologue and epilogue code

The new version of function `program` in file `routine.c` is shown in Figure 13-7. We call function `emit_program_prologue`, defined in file `emitcode.c`, which emits the following directives that appear at the start of every assembly program produced by the compiler:

```
DOSSEG
.MODEL  small
.STACK  1024


.CODE
```

```
PUBLIC    _pascal_main
INCLUDE   pasextrn.inc

$STATIC_LINK          EQU   <WORD PTR [bp+4]>
$RETURN_VALUE         EQU   <WORD PTR [bp-4]>
$HIGH_RETURN_VALUE    EQU   <WORD PTR [bp-2]>
```

FIGURE 13-7   Function program in file routine.c.

```
/*-----------------------------------------------------------*/
/* program       Process a program:                          */
/*                                                           */
/*                      <program-header> ; <block> .         */
/*-----------------------------------------------------------*/

TOKEN_CODE follow_header_list[] = {SEMICOLON, END_OF_FILE, 0};

program()

{
    SYMTAB_NODE_PTR program_idp;        /* program id */

    /*
    -- Intialize the symbol table and then emit
    -- the program prologue code.
    */
    init_symtab();
    emit_program_prologue();

    /*
    -- Begin parsing with the program header.
    */
    program_idp = program_header();

    /*
    -- Error synchronization:  Should be ;
    */
    synchronize(follow_header_list,
                declaration_start_list, statement_start_list);
    if_token_get(SEMICOLON);
    else if (token_in(declaration_start_list) ||
             token_in(statement_start_list))
        error(MISSING_SEMICOLON);

    analyze_routine_header(program_idp);

    /*
    -- Parse the program's block.
    */
    program_idp->defn.info.routine.locals = NULL;
    block(program_idp);
    program_idp->defn.info.routine.local_symtab = exit_scope();

    if_token_get_else_error(PERIOD, MISSING_PERIOD);

    /*
    -- Emit the main routine's epilogue code
    -- followed by the program's epilogue code.
    */
    emit_main_epilogue();
    emit_program_epilogue(program_idp);

    /*
    -- Look for the end of file.
    */
    while (token != END_OF_FILE) {
        error(UNEXPECTED_TOKEN);
        get_token();
    }

    quit_scanner();

    /*
    -- Print the parser's summary.
    */
    print_line("\n");
    print_line("\n");
    sprintf(buffer, "%20d Source lines.\n", line_number);
    print_line(buffer);
    sprintf(buffer, "%20d Source errors.\n", error_count);
    print_line(buffer);

    if (error_count == 0) exit(0);
    else                  exit(-SYNTAX_ERROR);
}
```

These directives give the assembler useful information. DOSSEG tells the assembler to place the segments in the object file in the conventional order, and .MODEL specifies that the program will use the "small" memory model, which is one code segment and one data segment (see Figure 12-3). The size of the stack at bottom of the data segment is specified by .STACK while .CODE specifies the start of the code segment. PUBLIC makes the name _pascal_main available to the main library routine (by convention, the assembler adds an underscore in front of each public name). INCLUDE is similar to #include in a C program; it causes the file pasextrn.inc to be included. Each EQU directive is similar to a #define in a C program and the < and > are string delimiters. These statements give names to certain components of the stack frame.

File pasextrn.inc, shown in Figure 13-8, contains EXTRN directives. Each specifies that a library routine is defined elsewhere.

FIGURE 13-8   File pasextrn.inc.

```
EXTRN   _float_negate:PROC          EXTRN   _read_char:PROC
EXTRN   _float_add:PROC             EXTRN   _read_line:PROC
EXTRN   _float_subtract:PROC
EXTRN   _float_multiply:PROC        EXTRN   _std_end_of_file:PROC
EXTRN   _float_divide:PROC          EXTRN   _std_end_of_line:PROC
EXTRN   _float_compare:PROC
EXTRN   _float_convert:PROC         EXTRN   _std_abs:PROC

EXTRN   _write_integer:PROC         EXTRN   _std_arctan:PROC
EXTRN   _write_real:PROC            EXTRN   _std_cos:PROC
EXTRN   _write_boolean:PROC         EXTRN   _std_exp:PROC
EXTRN   _write_char:PROC            EXTRN   _std_ln:PROC
EXTRN   _write_string:PROC          EXTRN   _std_sin:PROC
EXTRN   _write_line:PROC            EXTRN   _std_sqrt:PROC

EXTRN   _read_integer:PROC          EXTRN   _std_round:PROC
EXTRN   _read_real:PROC             EXTRN   _std_trunc:PROC
```

Near the end of function program, we call function emit_program_epilogue, defined in file emitcode.c, where we emit code that appears at the end of every assembly program produced by the compiler. The first line of the code is the directive .DATA which specifies the start of the data segment. Then, we emit the declarations for the program's global variables. Examples of scalar declarations are:

```
ch_012    DB 0
sides_015 DW 0
beta_017  DD 0.0
```

These declare a character, integer, and a real value, respectively. We initialize all values to 0 or 0.0. Following is an example of an array or record declaration which declares a block of 144 bytes, all initialized to 0:

```
vector_020  DB 144 DUP(0)
```

The program epilogue code also declares any floating point and string literals that appeared in the Pascal program. These literals must be declared in the data segment because floating point and string literals cannot be used as immediate operands to assembly instructions. As we will see later, these literals must be entered into the symbol table just like in the interpreter. All the floating point literal symbol table entries are linked together, and pointer variable float_lit-eral_list, declared in file emitcode.c, points to the head of this list. Similarly, the string literal symbol table entries are linked together, and pointer variable string_literal_list points to the head of the list. So after emitting the global variable declarations, we emit the declarations for any floating point and string literals. Examples of such declarations are:

```
$F_021   DD   3.141590e+000
$S_026   DB   "Hello, world."
```

Recall that in file code.h (see Figure 12-6), we defined the label prefixes for floating point literals and for string literals to be $F and $S, respectively.

13.2.4 Main routine prologue and epilogue code

Figure 13-9 shows a new version of function block in file routine.c. For the main Pascal routine, we call function emit_main_prologue. Function program (Figure 13-7) also calls function emit_main_epilogue. These new routines are defined in file emitcode.c and emit the prologue and epilogue code for the main Pascal routine.

FIGURE 13-9   Function block in file routine.c.

```
/*-------------------------------------------------------*/
/* block          Process a block, which consists of     */
/*                declarations followed by a compound     */
/*                statement.                              */
/*-------------------------------------------------------*/

TOKEN_CODE follow_decls_list[] = {SEMICOLON, BEGIN, END_OF_FILE, 0};

block(rtn_idp)

    SYMTAB_NODE_PTR rtn_idp;    /* id of program or routine */

{
    extern BOOLEAN block_flag;

    declarations(rtn_idp);

    /*
```

```
    -- Emit the prologue code for the main routine
    -- or for a procedure or function.
    */
    if (rtn_idp->defn.key == PROG_DEFN)
        emit_main_prologue();
    else
        emit_routine_prologue(rtn_idp);

    /*
    -- Error synchronization:  Should be ;
    */
    synchronize(follow_decls_list, NULL, NULL);
    if (token != BEGIN) error(MISSING_BEGIN);

    block_flag = TRUE;
    compound_statement();
    block_flag = FALSE;
}
```

The prologue code consists of the following:

```
_pascal_main PROC

             push bp
             mov  bp,sp
```

The push bp pushes the dynamic link onto the stack, and the mov bp,sp points register BP to the new stack frame (steps 4 and 5 of 13.2.1 Managing the runtime stack). Since the global variables are allocated in the data segment, no data are allocated on the stack for the Pascal main routine (step 7).

The epilogue code consists of the following:

```
pop bp
ret


_pascal_main   ENDP
```

The pop bp restores register BP (step 10) to point to the caller's stack frame (that of routine main in the runtime library). ret pops off the return address (step 11). The other steps are not necessary for the main Pascal routine.

13.2.5 Procedure and function prologue and epilogue code

Function block calls function emit_routine_prologue for a Pascal procedure or function. In the new version of function routine in file routine.c (shown in Figure 13-10), we call function emit_routine_epilogue at the end. These new routines are defined in file emitcode.c and emit the prologue and epilogue code, respectively, for Pascal routines.

FIGURE 13-10   Function routine in file routine.c.

```
/*------------------------------------------------------*/        /*
/* routine           Call the appropriate routine to process */     -- <block> or FORWARD.
/*                   a procedure or function definition:   */       */
/*                                                      */          if (strcmp(word_string, "forward") != 0) {
/*                   <routine-header> ; <block>        */               rtn_idp->defn.info.routine.key = DECLARED;
/*------------------------------------------------------*/              analyze_routine_header(rtn_idp);

routine()                                                               rtn_idp->defn.info.routine.locals = NULL;
                                                                        block(rtn_idp);
{                                                                   }
    SYMTAB_NODE_PTR rtn_idp;      /* routine id */                  else {
                                                                        get_token();
    rtn_idp = (token == PROCEDURE) ? procedure_header()                 rtn_idp->defn.info.routine.key = FORWARD;
                                   : function_header();                 analyze_routine_header(rtn_idp);

    /*                                                              }
    -- Error synchronization:  Should be ;
    */                                                              /*
    synchronize(follow_header_list,                                 -- Exit the current scope and emit the
            declaration_start_list, statement_start_list);          -- routine's epilogue code.
    if_token_get(SEMICOLON);                                        */
    else if (token_in(declaration_start_list) ||                    rtn_idp->defn.info.routine.local_symtab = exit_scope();
            token_in(statement_start_list))                         emit_routine_epilogue(rtn_idp);
        error(MISSING_SEMICOLON);                               }
```

The prologue code for a Pascal function consists of the following:

```
push bp
mov  bp,sp
sub  sp,4
sub  sp,var_size
```

The push bp pushes the dynamic link onto the stack, and the mov bp,sp points register BP to the new stack frame (steps 4 and 5). The sub sp,4 allocates stack space for the return value (step 6), and the sub sp, var_size allocates stack space for the local variables (step 7). The total byte size of all of the function's local variables is var_size. The prologue code for a Pascal procedure is similar, except we do not emit the sub sp,4.

The epilogue code for a Pascal function consists of:

```
mov  ax,$RETURN_VALUE
mov  sp,bp
pop  bp
ret  parm_size+2
```

The mov ax,$RETURN_VALUE moves the return value into register AX (step 8). ($RETURN_VALUE was equated to WORD PTR [bp-4] in the program prologue.) If the function returns a real value, that statement is followed by mov dx,$HIGH_RETURN_ VALUE (equated to WORD PTR [bp-2]) to move the high-order half of the return value into register DX. The mov sp,bp cuts the stack back to remove the function's local variables and the return value (step 9). The pop bp retrieves the dynamic link and restores register BP to point to the caller's stack frame (step 10). Finally, the ret parm_size+2 pops off the return address (step 11) and cuts the stack back by parm_size+2 bytes to remove the static link and the actual parameters (step 12). parm_size is the total byte size of all of the function's formal parameters. (Of course, the ret instruction also causes a return to the caller.)

The epilogue code for a Pascal procedure is similar, except we do not emit mov ax,$RETURN_VALUE or mov dx,$HIGH_RETURN_VALUE.

13.2.6 Declarations

In order to make the generated assembly code easier to read, the compiler emits text equates for all of a Pascal procedure's or function's formal parameters and local variables, which are allocated in the stack frame. For example, if a procedure has formal parameters p1 and p2 (both type integer) and local variable var (type real), the compiler emits:

```
p1_008   EQU <WORD PTR [bp+8]>
p2_009   EQU <WORD PTR [bp+6]>
var_010  EQU <WORD PTR [bp-4]>
```

The compiler then uses the tagged names in the generated code.

These equates are emitted by function `emit_declarations`, defined in file `emitcode.c`. This function calls function `emit_text_equate`, defined in the same file. Figure 13-11 shows a new version of function `declarations` in file `decl.c`. It makes a call to `emit_declarations` after it has parsed a routine's variable declarations.

FIGURE 13-11   Function `declarations` in file `decl.c`.

```
/*--------------------------------------------------*/
/*  declarations        Call the routines to process constant  */
/*                      definitions, type definitions, variable */
/*                      declarations, procedure definitions,    */
/*                      and function definitions.               */
/*--------------------------------------------------*/

TOKEN_CODE follow_routine_list[] = {SEMICOLON, END_OF_FILE, 0};

declarations(rtn_idp)

    SYMTAB_NODE_PTR rtn_idp;     /* id of program or routine */

{
    if (token == CONST) {
        get_token();
        const_definitions();
    }

    if (token == TYPE) {
        get_token();
        type_definitions();
    }

    if (token == VAR) {
        get_token();
        var_declarations(rtn_idp);
    }

    /*
    -- Emit declarations for parameters and local variables.
    */
    if (rtn_idp->defn.key != PROG_DEFN) emit_declarations(rtn_idp);

    /*
    -- Loop to process routine (procedure and function)
    -- definitions.
    */
    while ((token == PROCEDURE) || (token == FUNCTION)) {
        routine();

        /*
        -- Error synchronization:  Should be ;
        */
        synchronize(follow_routine_list,
                    declaration_start_list, statement_start_list);
        if_token_get(SEMICOLON);
        else if (token_in(declaration_start_list) ||
                 token_in(statement_start_list))
            error(MISSING_SEMICOLON);
    }
}
```

Note that in the case of nested Pascal routines, we emit the declarations for all of the routines together before any of their executable code. This does not cause any problems for the assembler.

13.2.7 Calls to procedures and functions

Now we will look at the code the compiler generates to call a Pascal procedure or function. We emit this code in functions `declared_routine_call` and `actual_parm_list` in file `routine.c`. Figures 13-12 and 13-13 show new versions of these functions.

FIGURE 13-12 Function `declared_routine_call` in file routine.c.

```
/*------------------------------------------------*/
/* declared_routine_call  Process a call to a declared    */
/*                        procedure or function:          */
/*                                                        */
/*                            <id>                        */
/*                                                        */
/*                            or:                         */
/*                                                        */
/*                            <id> ( <parm-list> )        */
/*                                                        */
/*                        The actual parameters are checked */
/*                        against the formal parameters for */
/*                        type and number.  Return a pointer */
/*                        to the type structure of the call. */
/*------------------------------------------------*/

    TYPE_STRUCT_PTR
declared_routine_call(rtn_idp, parm_check_flag)

    SYMTAB_NODE_PTR rtn_idp;           /* routine id */
    BOOLEAN         parm_check_flag;   /* if TRUE check parms */

{
    int old_level = level;             /* level of caller */
    int new_level = rtn_idp->level + 1; /* level of callee */

    actual_parm_list(rtn_idp, parm_check_flag);

    /*
    -- Push the static link onto the stack.
    */
```

```
    if (new_level == old_level + 1) {
        /*
        -- Calling a routine nested within the caller:
        -- Push pointer to caller's stack frame.
        */
        emit_1(PUSH, reg(BP));
    }
    else if (new_level == old_level) {
        /*
        -- Calling another routine at the same level:
        -- Push pointer to stack frame of common parent.
        */
        emit_1(PUSH, name_lit(STATIC_LINK));
    }
    else  /* new_level < old_level */  {
        /*
        -- Calling a routine at a lesser level (nested less deeply):
        -- Push pointer to stack frame of nearest common ancestor.
        */
        int lev;

        emit_2(MOVE, reg(BX), reg(BP));
        for (lev = old_level; lev >= new_level; --lev)
            emit_2(MOVE, reg(BP), name_lit(STATIC_LINK));
        emit_1(PUSH, reg(BP));
        emit_2(MOVE, reg(BP), reg(BX));
    }

    emit_1(CALL, tagged_name(rtn_idp));

    return(rtn_idp->defn.key == PROC_DEFN ? NULL : rtn_idp->typep);
}
```

FIGURE 13-13 Function `actual_parm_list` in file routine.c.

```
/*------------------------------------------------*/
/* actual_parm_list   Process an actual parameter list:   */
/*                                                        */
/*                        ( <expr-list> )                 */
/*------------------------------------------------*/

TOKEN_CODE follow_parm_list[] = {COMMA, RPAREN, 0};

actual_parm_list(rtn_idp, parm_check_flag)

    SYMTAB_NODE_PTR rtn_idp;           /* routine id */
    BOOLEAN         parm_check_flag;   /* if TRUE check parms */

{
    SYMTAB_NODE_PTR formal_parm_idp;
    DEFN_KEY        formal_parm_defn;
    TYPE_STRUCT_PTR formal_parm_tp, actual_parm_tp;

    if (parm_check_flag)
        formal_parm_idp = rtn_idp->defn.info.routine.parms;

    if (token == LPAREN) {
        /*
        -- Loop to process actual parameter expressions.
```

```
        */
        do {
            /*
            -- Obtain info about the corresponding formal parm.
            */
            if (parm_check_flag && (formal_parm_idp != NULL)) {
                formal_parm_defn = formal_parm_idp->defn.key;
                formal_parm_tp   = formal_parm_idp->typep;
            }

            get_token();

            /*
            -- Check the actual parm's type against the formal parm.
            -- An actual parm's type must be the same as the type of
            -- a formal VAR parm and assignment compatible with the
            -- type of a formal value parm.
            */
            if ((formal_parm_idp == NULL) ||
                (formal_parm_defn == VALPARM_DEFN) ||
                !parm_check_flag) {
                actual_parm_tp = expression();
                if (parm_check_flag && (formal_parm_idp != NULL) &&
                    (! is_assign_type_compatible(formal_parm_tp,
```

```
                                   actual_parm_tp)))
       error(INCOMPATIBLE_TYPES);

   /*
   -- Push the argument value onto the stack.
   */
   if (formal_parm_tp == real_typep) {
       /*
       -- Real formal parm.
       */
       if (actual_parm_tp == integer_typep) {
           emit_1(PUSH, reg(AX));
           emit_1(CALL, name_lit(FLOAT_CONVERT));
           emit_2(ADD,  reg(SP), integer_lit(2));
       }
       emit_1(PUSH, reg(DX));
       emit_1(PUSH, reg(AX));
   }
   else if ((actual_parm_tp->form == ARRAY_FORM) ||
            (actual_parm_tp->form == RECORD_FORM)) {

       /*
       -- Block move onto the stack.
       */
       int size = actual_parm_tp->size;
       int offset = size%2 == 0 ? size : size + 1;

       emit(CLEAR_DIRECTION);
       emit_1(POP,  reg(SI));
       emit_2(SUBTRACT, reg(SP), integer_lit(offset));
       emit_2(MOVE, reg(DI), reg(SP));
       emit_2(MOVE, reg(CX), integer_lit(size));
       emit_2(MOVE, reg(AX), reg(DS));
       emit_2(MOVE, reg(ES), reg(AX));
       emit(MOVE_BLOCK);
   }
   else {
       emit_1(PUSH, reg(AX));
   }
}
else  /* formal_parm_defn == VARPARM_DEFN */  {
```

```
           if (token == IDENTIFIER) {
               SYMTAB_NODE_PTR idp;

               search_and_find_all_symtab(idp);
               actual_parm_tp = variable(idp, VARPARM_USE);

               if (formal_parm_tp != actual_parm_tp)
                   error(INCOMPATIBLE_TYPES);
           }
           else {
               actual_parm_tp = expression();
               error(INVALID_VAR_PARM);
           }
       }

       /*
       -- Check if there are more actual parms
       -- than formal parms.
       */
       if (parm_check_flag) {
           if (formal_parm_idp == NULL)
               error(WRONG_NUMBER_OF_PARMS);
           else formal_parm_idp = formal_parm_idp->next;
       }

       /*
       -- Error synchronization:  Should be , or )
       */
       synchronize(follow_parm_list, statement_end_list, NULL);

   } while (token == COMMA);

   if_token_get_else_error(RPAREN, MISSING_RPAREN);
}

/*
-- Check if there are fewer actual parms than formal parms.
*/
if (parm_check_flag && (formal_parm_idp != NULL))
    error(WRONG_NUMBER_OF_PARMS);
```

First, declared_routine_call calls actual_parm_list, where we handle the actual parameters of a call (step 1). As we did in the interpreter, we call function expression to process each actual parameter passed by value, and function variable to process each actual parameter passed by reference (corresponding to a formal VAR parameter). These two functions are defined in file expr.c and we will examine them in detail later. All you need to know for now is that function expression generates code that leaves a scalar word value in register AX, a scalar doubleword value in the DX:AX register pair, or the address of an array or record value on the top of the runtime stack. Function variable, when called with VARPARM_USE, always generates code that leaves the address of the variable on top of the stack.

In function actual_parm_list, we want to emit code that pushes the value of a parameter passed by value. Therefore, after calling expression, we emit the assembly instruction push ax if the expression type is integer, enumeration, or character. Or, if the expression type and the formal parameter type are real, we emit:

```
push dx
push ax
```

to push the high-order half of the doubleword followed by the low-order half. If the expression type is integer but the formal parameter type is real, we must emit code to convert the expression value. Therefore, we emit:

```
push ax
call _float_convert
add  sp,2
push dx
push ax
```

Library function _float_convert is defined in paslib.c. And note the add sp,2. C functions, by convention, do not remove the actual parameters off of the stack; it is the responsibility of the caller. A static link is not pushed onto the stack when calling a C routine.

If the parameter value is an array or a record, the emitted code must allocate and make a copy of the value on the stack. We first obtain the byte size of the value and store this in variable size. Since only words are ever pushed or allocated on the stack, we set variable offset to the smallest even number of bytes that can contain the value. The following code pops off the address of the value and copies the value onto the stack:

```
cld                    ; clear direction flag
pop   si               ; SI = source address
sub   sp,offset        ; allocate stack space
mov   di,sp            ; DI = destination address
mov   cx,size          ; CX = number of bytes to move
mov   ax,ds            ; AX = DS
mov   es,ax            ; ES = AX
rep   movsb            ; block move
```

cld clears the direction flag to indicate that the block move is to proceed forward. Registers SI and DI are set to point the source and destination, respectively. The source address is popped off the stack, and the destination is space allocated on the stack by subtracting the value of *offset* from register SP (remember that the stack grows towards lower addresses). Register CX is set to *size*, the number of consecutive bytes to move (actually, copy).

Register SI normally points to a location in the "extra" segment. We get around this by setting register ES to point to the data segment. The 8086 processor does not allow the contents of register DS to be moved directly into register ES, so the generated code uses register AX as an intermediary. Finally, rep movsb does a block move.

After function actual_parm_list returns to function declared_routine_call, we emit code to push the static link onto the stack (step 2). This code will do what the interpreter did. If the callee is nested in the caller (the nesting level of the callee is one greater than the level of the caller), the static link must point to the caller's stack frame: push bp.

If the callee is at the same nesting level as the caller routine (both routines have the same parent routine), the static link must point to the parent's stack frame: push $STATIC_LINK.

In all other cases (the nesting level of the callee routine is less than the level of the caller routine), the code must search the chain of static links to find the one that points to the nearest common ancestor routine of the caller and the callee. As we saw in the interpreter, this ancestor is the parent of the callee, and its stack frame pointer is found by following old_level - new_level + 1 static links. For example, if the caller is at level 5 and the callee is at level 3, the ancestor must be at level 2, and the code to push a pointer to its stack frame is:

```
mov    bx,bp                    ; save current BP in BX
mov    bp,$STATIC_LINK          ; BP -> level 4 stack frame
mov    bp,$STATIC_LINK          ; BP -> level 3 stack frame
mov    bp,$STATIC_LINK          ; BP -> level 2 stack frame
push   bp                       ; push static link
mov    bp,bx                    ; restore current BP
```

Finally, we emit code to push the return address onto the stack (step 3). The call instruction automatically does this, for example: call proc_032.

13.3 Assignment statements

Now that we have code to enter and exit procedures and functions, we can look at the code to execute the statements contained in these routines. Figure 13-14 shows the new version of file stmt.c. In this chapter, the only statements the compiler can handle are procedure calls, assignment statements, and compound statements. (We will tackle the other statements in the next chapter.)

FIGURE 13-14   File stmt.c.

```
/*****************************************************************/     /*      MODULE:     parser                                     */
/*                                                             */      /*                                                           */
/*     S T A T E M E N T   P A R S E R                         */      /*****************************************************************/
/*                                                             */
/*     Parsing routines for statements.                        */      #include <stdio.h>
/*                                                             */      #include "common.h"
/*     FILE:      stmt.c                                       */      #include "error.h"
/*                                                             */      #include "scanner.h"
```

```
#include "symtab.h"
#include "parser.h"
#include "code.h"

/*------------------------------------------------------------*/
/* Externals                                                  */
/*------------------------------------------------------------*/

extern TOKEN_CODE       token;
extern char             word_string[];
extern LITERAL          literal;
extern TOKEN_CODE       statement_start_list[], statement_end_list[];

extern SYMTAB_NODE_PTR  symtab_display[];
extern int              level;

extern TYPE_STRUCT_PTR  integer_typep, real_typep,
                        boolean_typep, char_typep;

extern TYPE_STRUCT      dummy_type;

extern int              label_index;
extern char             asm_buffer[];
extern char             *asm_bufferp;
extern FILE             *code_file;

/*------------------------------------------------------------*/
/* statement            Process a statement by calling the    */
/*                      appropriate parsing routine based on  */
/*                      the statement's first token.          */
/*------------------------------------------------------------*/

statement()

{
    /*
    -- Call the appropriate routine based on the first
    -- token of the statement.
    */
    switch (token) {

        case IDENTIFIER: {
            SYMTAB_NODE_PTR idp;

            /*
            -- Assignment statement or procedure call?
            */
            search_and_find_all_symtab(idp);

            if (idp->defn.key == PROC_DEFN) {
                get_token();
                routine_call(idp, TRUE);
            }
            else assignment_statement(idp);

            break;
        }

        case BEGIN:     compound_statement();  break;

        case WHILE:
        case REPEAT:
        case IF:
        case FOR:
        case CASE: {
            error(UNIMPLEMENTED_FEATURE);
            exit(-UNIMPLEMENTED_FEATURE);
```

```
        }
    }

    /*
    -- Error synchronization: Only a semicolon, END, ELSE, or
    --                        UNTIL may follow a statement.
    --                        Check for a missing semicolon.
    */
    synchronize(statement_end_list, statement_start_list, NULL);
    if (token_in(statement_start_list)) error(MISSING_SEMICOLON);
}

/*------------------------------------------------------------*/
/* assignment_statement    Process an assignment statement:   */
/*                                                            */
/*                            <id> := <expr>                  */
/*------------------------------------------------------------*/

assignment_statement(var_idp)

    SYMTAB_NODE_PTR var_idp;            /* target variable id */

{
    TYPE_STRUCT_PTR var_tp, expr_tp;   /* types of var and expr */
    BOOLEAN         stacked_flag;      /* TRUE iff target address
                                          was pushed on stack */

    var_tp = variable(var_idp, TARGET_USE);
    stacked_flag = (var_idp->defn.key == VARPARM_DEFN) ||
                   (var_idp->defn.key == FUNC_DEFN) ||
                   (var_idp->typep->form == ARRAY_FORM) ||
                   (var_idp->typep->form == RECORD_FORM) ||
                   ((var_idp->level > 1) && (var_idp->level < level));

    if_token_get_else_error(COLONEQUAL, MISSING_COLONEQUAL);
    expr_tp = expression();

    if (! is_assign_type_compatible(var_tp, expr_tp))
        error(INCOMPATIBLE_ASSIGNMENT);

    var_tp  = base_type(var_tp);
    expr_tp = base_type(expr_tp);

    /*
    -- Emit code to do the assignment.
    */
    if (var_tp == char_typep) {
        /*
        -- char := char
        */
        if (stacked_flag) {
            emit_1(POP, reg(BX));
            emit_2(MOVE, byte_indirect(BX), reg(AL));
        }
        else emit_2(MOVE, byte(var_idp), reg(AL));
    }
    else if (var_tp == real_typep) {
        /*
        -- real := ...
        */
        if (expr_tp == integer_typep) {
            /*
            -- ... integer
            */
            emit_1(PUSH, reg(AX));
            emit_1(CALL, name_lit(FLOAT_CONVERT));
            emit_2(ADD, reg(SP), integer_lit(2));
```

```
    }
    /*
    -- ... real
    */
    if (stacked_flag) {
        emit_1(POP, reg(BX));
        emit_2(MOVE, word_indirect(BX), reg(AX));
        emit_2(MOVE, high_dword_indirect(BX), reg(DX));
    }
    else {
        emit_2(MOVE, word(var_idp), reg(AX));
        emit_2(MOVE, high_dword(var_idp), reg(DX));
    }
}
else if ((var_tp->form == ARRAY_FORM) ||
         (var_tp->form == RECORD_FORM)) {
    /*
    -- array  := array
    -- record := record
    */
    emit_2(MOVE, reg(CX), integer_lit(var_tp->size));
    emit_1(POP,  reg(SI));
    emit_1(POP,  reg(DI));
    emit_2(MOVE, reg(AX), reg(DS));
    emit_2(MOVE, reg(ES), reg(AX));
    emit(CLEAR_DIRECTION);
    emit(MOVE_BLOCK);
}
else {
    /*
    -- integer := integer
    -- enum    := enum
    */
    if (stacked_flag) {
```

```
                emit_1(POP, reg(BX));
                emit_2(MOVE, word_indirect(BX), reg(AX));
            }
            else emit_2(MOVE, word(var_idp), reg(AX));
    }
}


/*------------------------------------------------------------*/
/*  compound_statement       Process a compound statement:    */
/*                                                            */
/*                            BEGIN <stmt-list> END           */
/*------------------------------------------------------------*/

compound_statement()

{
    /*
    -- <stmt-list>
    */
    get_token();
    do {
        statement();
        while (token == SEMICOLON) get_token();
        if (token == END) break;

        /*
        -- Error synchronization:  Should be at the start of the
        --                         next statement.
        */
        synchronize(statement_start_list, NULL, NULL);
    } while (token_in(statement_start_list));

    if_token_get_else_error(END, MISSING_END);
}
```

The compiler-generated code for an assignment statement behaves very similarly to how the interpreter executed an assignment statement. We emit the code in function assignment_statement, which calls function variable for the assignment target, and function expression for the expression.

When the interpreter called function variable with TARGET_USE, the function pushed the address of the assignment target onto the stack. The code generated by the compiler does the same, except when the assignment target is one of the following:

- a simple global scalar variable (one that is not subscripted or a record field)
- a simple local scalar variable
- a simple local value parameter

In these cases, function expression emits code to leave the scalar value in register AX or in the DX:AX register pair, and this value can be moved directly into the target. For example:

```
mov  WORD PTR width_011,ax
```

assigns a word value. We do this to make the object code a bit more efficient. In all other cases, function `variable` generates code to push the target address onto the stack. Then, for example:

```
pop  bx
mov  WORD PTR [bx],ax
```

moves a word value to the target.

In function `assignment_statement`, boolean variable `stacked_flag` is TRUE whenever the target address is pushed onto the stack, and FALSE otherwise. The following are examples of the code we emit for a direct assignment when `stacked_flag` is FALSE:

```
mov  BYTE PTR ch_003,al

mov  WORD_PTR count_007,ax

mov  WORD_PTR average_009,ax
mov  WORD_PTR average_009+2,dx
```

These statements assign a byte (character), a word (integer or enumeration), and a doubleword (real), respectively.

If an integer value is assigned to a real target, an example of the code we emit is:

```
push ax
call _float_convert
add  sp,2
mov  WORD PTR average_009,ax
mov  WORD PTR average_009+2,dx
```

If the target address is on the stack (`stacked_flag` is TRUE), examples of the code we emit are:

```
pop  bx
mov  BYTE PTR [bx],al

pop  bx
mov  WORD PTR [bx],ax

pop  bx
mov  WORD PTR [bx],ax
mov  WORD PTR [bx+2],dx
```

```
push ax
call _float_convert
add  sp,2
pop  bx
mov  WORD PTR [bx],ax
mov  WORD PTR [bx+2],dx
```

These statements assign a byte (character), a word (integer or enumeration), a doubleword (real), and a real value converted from an integer value, respectively.

If the expression value is an array or a record, an example of the code we emit is:

```
mov cx,size         ; CX = number of bytes to move
pop si              ; SI = source address
pop di              ; DI = destination address
mov ax,ds           ; AX = DS
mov es,ax           ; ES = AX
cld                 ; clear direction flag
rep movsb           ; block move
```

where *size* is the structure size in bytes.

13.4 Expressions

Figure 13-15 shows the new version of file expr.c. Routines in this file now call the code generation routines to emit code that evaluates expressions.

FIGURE 13-15   File expr.c.

```
*/****************************************************/
/*                                                  */
/*      E X P R E S S I O N   P A R S E R            */
/*                                                  */
/*      Parsing routines for expressions.            */
/*                                                  */
/*      FILE:      expr.c                            */
/*                                                  */
/*      MODULE:    parser                            */
/*                                                  */
/*****************************************************/

#include <stdio.h>
#include "common.h"
#include "error.h"
#include "scanner.h"
#include "symtab.h"
#include "parser.h"
#include "code.h"

/*-----------------------------------------------*/
/* Externals                                      */
/*-----------------------------------------------*/
```

```
extern TOKEN_CODE token;
extern char        token_string[];
extern char        word_string[];
extern LITERAL     literal;

extern SYMTAB_NODE_PTR symtab_display[];
extern int             level;

extern TYPE_STRUCT_PTR integer_typep, real_typep,
                       boolean_typep, char_typep;

extern TYPE_STRUCT     dummy_type;

extern SYMTAB_NODE_PTR float_literal_list;
extern SYMTAB_NODE_PTR string_literal_list;

extern int             label_index;
extern char            asm_buffer[];
extern char            *asm_bufferp;
extern FILE            *code_file;
```

```
/*----------------------------------------------------------*/
/*  Forwards                                                */
/*----------------------------------------------------------*/

TYPE_STRUCT_PTR expression(), simple_expression(), term(), factor(),
               constant_identifier(), function_call();

TYPE_STRUCT_PTR float_literal(), string_literal();

/*----------------------------------------------------------*/
/*  integer_operands    TRUE if both operands are integer,  */
/*                       else FALSE.                         */
/*----------------------------------------------------------*/

#define integer_operands(tp1, tp2)  ((tp1 == integer_typep) && \
                                     (tp2 == integer_typep))

/*----------------------------------------------------------*/
/*  real_operands       TRUE if at least one or both operands */
/*                       are real (and the other integer), else */
/*                       FALSE.                              */
/*----------------------------------------------------------*/

#define real_operands(tp1, tp2) (((tp1 == real_typep) &&      \
                                   ((tp2 == real_typep) ||     \
                                    (tp2 == integer_typep)))   \
                                  ||                           \
                                  ((tp2 == real_typep) &&      \
                                   ((tp1 == real_typep) ||     \
                                    (tp1 == integer_typep))))

/*----------------------------------------------------------*/
/*  boolean_operands    TRUE if both operands are boolean   */
/*                       else FALSE.                         */
/*----------------------------------------------------------*/

#define boolean_operands(tp1, pt2)  ((tp1 == boolean_typep) && \
                                     (tp2 == boolean_typep))

/*----------------------------------------------------------*/
/*  expression          Process an expression consisting of a */
/*                       simple expression optionally followed */
/*                       by a relational operator and a second */
/*                       simple expression.  Return a pointer to */
/*                       the type structure.                 */
/*----------------------------------------------------------*/

TOKEN_CODE rel_op_list[] = {LT, LE, EQUAL, NE, GE, GT, 0};

    TYPE_STRUCT_PTR
expression()

{
    TOKEN_CODE      op;              /* an operator token */
    TYPE_STRUCT_PTR result_tp, tp2;
    int             jump_label_index;  /* jump target label index */
    INSTRUCTION     jump_opcode;       /* opcode for cond. jump */

    result_tp = simple_expression();   /* first simple expr */

    /*
    -- If there is a relational operator, remember it and
    -- process the second simple expression.
    */
    if (token_in(rel_op_list)) {
        op = token;                  /* remember operator */

        result_tp = base_type(result_tp);
```

```
    emit_push_operand(result_tp);

    get_token();
    tp2 = base_type(simple_expression());   /* 2nd simple expr */

    check_rel_op_types(result_tp, tp2);

    /*
    -- Both operands are integer, character, boolean, or
    -- the same enumeration type.  Compare DX (operand 1)
    -- to AX (operand 2).
    */
    if (integer_operands(result_tp, tp2) ||
        (result_tp == char_typep) ||
        (result_tp->form == ENUM_FORM)) {
        emit_1(POP, reg(DX));
        emit_2(COMPARE, reg(DX), reg(AX));
    }

    /*
    -- Both operands are real, or one is real and the other
    -- is integer.  Convert the integer operand to real.
    -- Call FLOAT_COMPARE to do the comparison, which returns
    -- -1 (less), 0 (equal), or +1 (greater).
    */
    else if ((result_tp == real_typep) || (tp2 == real_typep)) {
        emit_push_operand(tp2);
        emit_promote_to_real(result_tp, tp2);

        emit_1(CALL, name_lit(FLOAT_COMPARE));
        emit_2(ADD, reg(SP), integer_lit(8));
        emit_2(COMPARE, reg(AX), integer_lit(0));
    }

    /*
    -- Both operands are strings.  Compare the string pointed
    -- to by SI (operand 1) to the string pointed to by DI
    -- (operand 2).
    */
    else if (result_tp->form == ARRAY_FORM) {
        emit_1(POP,  reg(DI));
        emit_1(POP,  reg(SI));
        emit_2(MOVE, reg(AX), reg(DS));
        emit_2(MOVE, reg(ES), reg(AX));
        emit(CLEAR_DIRECTION);
        emit_2(MOVE, reg(CX),
               integer_lit(result_tp->info.array.elmt_count));
        emit(COMPARE_STRINGS);
    }

    emit_2(MOVE, reg(AX), integer_lit(1));  /* default: load 1 */

    switch (op) {
        case LT:    jump_opcode = JUMP_LT;  break;
        case LE:    jump_opcode = JUMP_LE;  break;
        case EQUAL: jump_opcode = JUMP_EQ;  break;
        case NE:    jump_opcode = JUMP_NE;  break;
        case GE:    jump_opcode = JUMP_GE;  break;
        case GT:    jump_opcode = JUMP_GT;  break;
    }

    jump_label_index = new_label_index();
    emit_1(jump_opcode, label(STMT_LABEL_PREFIX,
           jump_label_index));

    emit_2(SUBTRACT, reg(AX), reg(AX));     /* load 0 if false */
    emit_label(STMT_LABEL_PREFIX, jump_label_index);
```

```
        result_tp = boolean_typep;
    }

    return(result_tp);
}

/*------------------------------------------------------------*/
/* simple_expression    Process a simple expression consisting */
/*                      of terms separated by +, -, or OR      */
/*                      operators.  There may be a unary + or - */
/*                      before the first term.  Return a       */
/*                      pointer to the type structure.         */
/*------------------------------------------------------------*/

TOKEN_CODE add_op_list[] = {PLUS, MINUS, OR, 0};

    TYPE_STRUCT_PTR
simple_expression()

{
    TOKEN_CODE op;                        /* an operator token */
    BOOLEAN    saw_unary_op = FALSE;      /* TRUE iff unary operator */
    TOKEN_CODE unary_op = PLUS;           /* a unary operator token */
    TYPE_STRUCT_PTR result_tp, tp2;

    /*
    -- If there is a unary + or -, remember it.
    */
    if ((token == PLUS) || (token == MINUS)) {
        unary_op = token;
        saw_unary_op = TRUE;
        get_token();
    }

    result_tp = term();        /* first term */

    /*
    -- If there was a unary operator, check that the term
    -- is integer or real.  Negate the top of stack if it
    -- was a unary - either with the NEG instruction or by
    -- calling FLOAT_NEGATE.
    */
    if (saw_unary_op) {
        if (base_type(result_tp) == integer_typep) {
            if (unary_op == MINUS) emit_1(NEGATE, reg(AX));
        }
        else if (result_tp == real_typep) {
            if (unary_op == MINUS) {
                emit_push_operand(result_tp);
                emit_1(CALL, name_lit(FLOAT_NEGATE));
                emit_2(ADD, reg(SP), integer_lit(4));
            }
        }
        else error(INCOMPATIBLE_TYPES);
    }

    /*
    -- Loop to process subsequent terms separated by operators.
    */
    while (token_in(add_op_list)) {
        op = token;                       /* remember operator */

        result_tp = base_type(result_tp);
        emit_push_operand(result_tp);

        get_token();
        tp2 = base_type(term());          /* subsequent term */

        switch (op) {

            case PLUS:
            case MINUS: {
                /*
                -- integer <op> integer => integer
                -- AX = AX +|- DX
                */
                if (integer_operands(result_tp, tp2)) {
                    emit_1(POP, reg(DX));
                    if (op == PLUS) emit_2(ADD, reg(AX), reg(DX))
                    else {
                        emit_2(SUBTRACT, reg(DX), reg(AX));
                        emit_2(MOVE, reg(AX), reg(DX));
                    }
                    result_tp = integer_typep;
                }

                /*
                -- Both operands are real, or one is real and the
                -- other is integer.  Convert the integer operand
                -- to real.  The result is real.  Call FLOAT_ADD or
                -- FLOAT_SUBTRACT.
                */
                else if (real_operands(result_tp, tp2)) {
                    emit_push_operand(tp2);
                    emit_promote_to_real(result_tp, tp2);

                    emit_1(CALL, name_lit(op == PLUS
                                              ? FLOAT_ADD
                                              : FLOAT_SUBTRACT));
                    emit_2(ADD, reg(SP), integer_lit(8));

                    result_tp = real_typep;
                }

                else {
                    error(INCOMPATIBLE_TYPES);
                    result_tp = &dummy_type;
                }

                break;
            }

            case OR: {
                /*
                -- boolean OR boolean => boolean
                -- AX = AX OR DX
                */
                if (boolean_operands(result_tp, tp2)) {
                    emit_1(POP, reg(DX));
                    emit_2(OR_BITS, reg(AX), reg(DX));
                }
                else error(INCOMPATIBLE_TYPES);

                result_tp = boolean_typep;
                break;
            }
        }
    }

    return(result_tp);
}

/*------------------------------------------------------------*/
/* term             Process a term consisting of factors      */
/*                  separated by *, /, DIV, MOD, or AND        */
```

```
/*                   operators.  Return a pointer to the      */
/*                   type structure.                          */
/*----------------------------------------------------------*/

TOKEN_CODE mult_op_list[] = {STAR, SLASH, DIV, MOD, AND, 0};

    TYPE_STRUCT_PTR
term()

{
    TOKEN_CODE op;                      /* an operator token */
    TYPE_STRUCT_PTR result_tp, tp2;

    result_tp = factor();              /* first factor */

    /*
    -- Loop to process subsequent factors
    -- separated by operators.
    */
    while (token_in(mult_op_list)) {
        op = token;                     /* remember operator */

        result_tp = base_type(result_tp);
        emit_push_operand(result_tp);

        get_token();
        tp2 = base_type(factor());      /* subsequent factor */

        switch (op) {

            case STAR: {
                /*
                -- Both operands are integer.
                -- AX = AX*DX
                */
                if (integer_operands(result_tp, tp2)) {
                    emit_1(POP, reg(DX));
                    emit_1(MULTIPLY, reg(DX));

                    result_tp = integer_typep;
                }

                /*
                -- Both operands are real, or one is real and the
                -- other is integer.  Convert the integer operand
                -- to real.  The result is real.
                -- Call FLOAT_MULTIPLY.
                */
                else if (real_operands(result_tp, tp2)) {
                    emit_push_operand(tp2);
                    emit_promote_to_real(result_tp, tp2);

                    emit_1(CALL, name_lit(FLOAT_MULTIPLY));
                    emit_2(ADD, reg(SP), integer_lit(8));

                    result_tp = real_typep;
                }

                else {
                    error(INCOMPATIBLE_TYPES);
                    result_tp = &dummy_type;
                }

                break;
            }

            case SLASH: {
```

```
                /*
                -- Both operands are real, or both are integer, or
                -- one is real and the other is integer.  Convert
                -- any integer operand to real.  The result is real.
                -- Call FLOAT_DIVIDE.
                */
                if (real_operands(result_tp, tp2) ||
                        integer_operands(result_tp, tp2)) {
                    emit_push_operand(tp2);
                    emit_promote_to_real(result_tp, tp2);

                    emit_1(CALL, name_lit(FLOAT_DIVIDE));
                    emit_2(ADD, reg(SP), integer_lit(8));
                }
                else error(INCOMPATIBLE_TYPES);

                result_tp = real_typep;
                break;
            }

            case DIV:
            case MOD: {
                /*
                -- integer <op> integer => integer
                -- AX = AX IDIV CX
                */
                if (integer_operands(result_tp, tp2)) {
                    emit_2(MOVE, reg(CX), reg(AX));
                    emit_1(POP, reg(AX));
                    emit_2(SUBTRACT, reg(DX), reg(DX));
                    emit_1(DIVIDE, reg(CX));
                    if (op == MOD) emit_2(MOVE, reg(AX), reg(DX));
                }
                else error(INCOMPATIBLE_TYPES);

                result_tp = integer_typep;
                break;
            }

            case AND: {
                /*
                -- boolean AND boolean => boolean
                -- AX = AX AND DX
                */
                if (boolean_operands(result_tp, tp2)) {
                    emit_1(POP, reg(DX));
                    emit_2(AND_BITS, reg(AX), reg(DX));
                }
                else error(INCOMPATIBLE_TYPES);

                result_tp = boolean_typep;
                break;
            }
        }
    }

    return(result_tp);
}

/*----------------------------------------------------------*/
/*  factor              Process a factor, which is a variable,  */
/*                      a number, NOT followed by a factor, or  */
/*                      a parenthesized subexpression.  Return  */
/*                      a pointer to the type structure.        */
/*----------------------------------------------------------*/

    TYPE_STRUCT_PTR
```

```
factor()

{
    TYPE_STRUCT_PTR tp;

    switch (token) {

        case IDENTIFIER: {
            SYMTAB_NODE_PTR idp;

            search_and_find_all_symtab(idp);

            switch (idp->defn.key) {

                case FUNC_DEFN:
                    get_token();
                    tp = routine_call(idp, TRUE);
                    break;

                case PROC_DEFN:
                    error(INVALID_IDENTIFIER_USAGE);
                    get_token();
                    actual_parm_list(idp, FALSE);
                    tp = &dummy_type;
                    break;

                case CONST_DEFN:
                    tp = constant_identifier(idp);
                    break;

                default:
                    tp = variable(idp, EXPR_USE);
                    break;
            }

            break;
        }

        case NUMBER: {
            if (literal.type == INTEGER_LIT) {
                /*
                -- AX = value
                */
                emit_2(MOVE, reg(AX),
                        integer_lit(literal.value.integer));
                tp = integer_typep;
            }

            else { /* literal.type == REAL_LIT */
                /*
                -- DX:AX = value
                */
                tp = float_literal(token_string, literal.value.real);
            }

            get_token();
            break;
        }

        case STRING: {
            int length = strlen(literal.value.string);

            if (length == 1) {
                /*
                -- AH = 0
                -- AL = value
                */
```

```
                emit_2(MOVE, reg(AX),
                        char_lit(literal.value.string[0]));
                tp = char_typep;
            }
            else {
                /*
                -- AX = address of string
                */
                tp = string_literal(literal.value.string, length);
            }

            get_token();
            break;
        }

        case NOT:
            /*
            -- AX = NOT AX
            */
            get_token();
            tp = factor();
            emit_2(XOR_BITS, reg(AX), integer_lit(1));
            break;

        case LPAREN:
            get_token();
            tp = expression();

            if_token_get_else_error(RPAREN, MISSING_RPAREN);
            break;

        default:
            error(INVALID_EXPRESSION);
            tp = &dummy_type;
            break;
    }

    return(tp);
}

/*----------------------------------------------------------*/
/* float_literal      Process a floating point literal.     */
/*----------------------------------------------------------*/

TYPE_STRUCT_PTR
float_literal(string, value)

    char  string[];
    float value;

{
    SYMTAB_NODE_PTR np = search_symtab(string, symtab_display[1]);

    /*
    -- Enter the literal into the symbol table
    -- if it isn't already in there.
    */
    if (np == NULL) {
        np = enter_symtab(string, symtab_display[1]);
        np->defn.key = CONST_DEFN;
        np->defn.info.constant.value.real  = value;
        np->label_index = new_label_index();
        np->next = float_literal_list;
        float_literal_list = np;
    }

    /*
```

```
    --  DX:AX = value
    */
    emit_2(MOVE, reg(AX), word_label(FLOAT_LABEL_PREFIX,
                            np->label_index));
    emit_2(MOVE, reg(DX), high_dword_label(FLOAT_LABEL_PREFIX,
                                np->label_index));

    return(real_typep);
}

/*------------------------------------------------------------*/
/*  string_literal      Process a string_literal.           */
/*------------------------------------------------------------*/

    TYPE_STRUCT_PTR
string_literal(string, length)

    char string[];
    int  length;

{
    SYMTAB_NODE_PTR np;
    TYPE_STRUCT_PTR tp = make_string_typep(length);
    char            buffer[MAX_SOURCE_LINE_LENGTH];

    sprintf(buffer, "'%s'", string);
    np = search_symtab(buffer, symtab_display[1]);

    /*
    -- Enter the literal into the symbol table
    -- if it isn't already in there.
    */
    if (np == NULL) {
        np = enter_symtab(buffer, symtab_display[1]);
        np->defn.key = CONST_DEFN;
        np->label_index = new_label_index();
        np->next = string_literal_list;
        string_literal_list = np;
    }

    /*
    -- AX = address of string
    */
    emit_2(LOAD_ADDRESS, reg(AX),
          word_label(STRING_LABEL_PREFIX, np->label_index));
    emit_1(PUSH, reg(AX));
    return(tp);
}

/*------------------------------------------------------------*/
/*  constant_identifier     Process a constant identifier.  */
/*------------------------------------------------------------*/

    TYPE_STRUCT_PTR
constant_identifier(idp)

    SYMTAB_NODE_PTR idp;             /* id of constant */

{
    TYPE_STRUCT_PTR tp = idp->typep;    /* type of constant */

    get_token();

    if ((tp == integer_typep) || (tp->form == ENUM_FORM)) {
        /*
        -- AX = value
        */
```

```
        emit_2(MOVE, reg(AX),
               integer_lit(idp->defn.info.constant.value.integer));
    }
    else if (tp == char_typep) {
        /*
        -- AX = value
        */
        emit_2(MOVE, reg(AX),
               char_lit(idp->defn.info.constant.value.character));
    }
    else if (tp == real_typep) {
        /*
        -- Create a literal and then call float_literal.
        */
        float value = idp->defn.info.constant.value.real;
        char  string[MAX_SOURCE_LINE_LENGTH];

        sprintf(string, "%e", value);
        float_literal(string, value);
    }
    else /* string constant */ {
        string_literal(idp->defn.info.constant.value.stringp,
                  strlen(idp->defn.info.constant.value.stringp));
    }

    return(tp);
}

/*------------------------------------------------------------*/
/*  variable          Process a variable, which can be a     */
/*                    simple identifier, an array identifier */
/*                    with subscripts, or a record identifier */
/*                    with fields.                           */
/*------------------------------------------------------------*/

    TYPE_STRUCT_PTR
variable(var_idp, use)

    SYMTAB_NODE_PTR var_idp;    /* variable id */
    USE             use;        /* how variable is used */

{
    TYPE_STRUCT_PTR tp         = var_idp->typep;
    DEFN_KEY        defn_key   = var_idp->defn.key;
    BOOLEAN         varparm_flag = defn_key == VARPARM_DEFN;
    TYPE_STRUCT_PTR array_subscript_list();
    TYPE_STRUCT_PTR record_field();

    /*
    -- Check the variable's definition.
    */
    switch (defn_key) {
        case VAR_DEFN:
        case VALPARM_DEFN:
        case VARPARM_DEFN:
        case FUNC_DEFN:
        case UNDEFINED: break;       /* OK */

        default: {                    /* error */
            tp = &dummy_type;
            error(INVALID_IDENTIFIER_USAGE);
        }
    }

    get_token();

    /*
```

```
--  There must not be a parameter list, but if there is one,
--  parse it anyway for error recovery.
*/
if (token == LPAREN) {
    error(UNEXPECTED_TOKEN);
    actual_parm_list(var_idp, FALSE);
    return(tp);
}


/*
--  Subscripts and/or field designators?
*/
if ((token == LBRACKET) || (token == PERIOD)) {
    /*
    --  Push the address of the array or record onto the
    --  stack, where it is then modified by code generated
    --  in array_subscript_list and record_field.
    */
    emit_push_address(var_idp);

    while ((token == LBRACKET) || (token == PERIOD)) {
        tp = token == LBRACKET ? array_subscript_list(tp)
                               : record_field(tp);
    }

    /*
    --  Leave the modified address on top of the stack if:
    --      it is an assignment target, or
    --      it represents a parameter passed by reference, or
    --      it is the address of an array or record.
    --  Otherwise, load AX with the value that the modified
    --  address points to.
    */
    if ((use != TARGET_USE) && (use != VARPARM_USE) &&
        (tp->form != ARRAY_FORM) && tp->form != RECORD_FORM)) {
        emit_1(POP, reg(BX));
        if (tp == char_typep) {
            emit_2(SUBTRACT, reg(AX), reg(AX));
            emit_2(MOVE, reg(AL), byte_indirect(BX));
        }
        else if (tp == real_typep) {
            emit_2(MOVE, reg(AX), word_indirect(BX));
            emit_2(MOVE, reg(DX), high_dword_indirect(BX));
        }
        else emit_2(MOVE, reg(AX), word_indirect(BX));
    }
}

else if (use == TARGET_USE) {
    /*
    --  Push the address of an assignment target onto the stack,
    --  unless it is a local or global scalar parameter or
    --  variable.
    */
    if (defn_key == FUNC_DEFN)
        emit_push_return_value_address(var_idp);
    else if (varparm_flag || (tp->form == ARRAY_FORM) ||
            (tp->form == RECORD_FORM) ||
            ((var_idp->level > 1) && (var_idp->level < level)))
        emit_push_address(var_idp);
}
else if (use == VARPARM_USE) {
    /*
    --  Push the address of a variable
    --  being passed as a VAR parameter.
    */
    emit_push_address(var_idp);
```

```
    }
    else if ((tp->form == ARRAY_FORM) || (tp->form == RECORD_FORM)) {
        /*
        --  Push the address of an array or record value.
        */
        emit_push_address(var_idp);
    }
    else {
        /*
        --  AX = scalar value
        */
        emit_load_value(var_idp, base_type(tp));
    }

    return(tp);
}

/*-----------------------------------------------------------*/
/*  array_subscript_list      Process a list of subscripts   */
/*                            following an array identifier:  */
/*                                                            */
/*                                 [ <expr> , <expr> , ... ]  */
/*-----------------------------------------------------------*/

    TYPE_STRUCT_PTR
array_subscript_list(tp)

    TYPE_STRUCT_PTR tp;


{
    TYPE_STRUCT_PTR   index_tp, elmt_tp, ss_tp;
    int               min_index, elmt_size;
    extern TOKEN_CODE statement_end_list[];

    /*
    --  Loop to process a subscript list.
    */
    do {
        if (tp->form == ARRAY_FORM) {
            index_tp = tp->info.array.index_typep;
            elmt_tp  = tp->info.array.elmt_typep;

            get_token();
            ss_tp = expression();

            /*
            --  The subscript expression must be assignment type
            --  compatible with the corresponding subscript type.
            */
            if (!is_assign_type_compatible(index_tp, ss_tp))
                error(INCOMPATIBLE_TYPES);

            min_index = tp->info.array.min_index;
            elmt_size = tp->info.array.elmt_typep->size;

            /*
            --  Convert the subscript into an offset by subracting
            --  the mininum index from it and then multiplying the
            --  result by the element size.  Add the offset to the
            --  address at the top of the stack.
            */
            if (min_index != 0) emit_2(SUBTRACT, reg(AX),
                                       integer_lit(min_index));
            if (elmt_size > 1) {
                emit_2(MOVE, reg(DX), integer_lit(elmt_size));
                emit_1(MULTIPLY, reg(DX));
            }
```

```
            emit_1(POP,  reg(DX));
            emit_2(ADD,  reg(DX), reg(AX));
            emit_1(PUSH, reg(DX));

            tp = elmt_tp;
        }
        else {
            error(TOO_MANY_SUBSCRIPTS);
            while ((token != RBRACKET) &&
                    (! token_in(statement_end_list)))
                get_token();
        }
    } while (token == COMMA);

    if_token_get_else_error(RBRACKET, MISSING_RBRACKET);
    return(tp);
}

/*-----------------------------------------------------------*/
/* record_field               Process a field designation    */
/*                            following a record identifier:  */
/*                                                            */
/*                                    . <field-variable>      */
/*-----------------------------------------------------------*/

    TYPE_STRUCT_PTR
record_field(tp)

    TYPE_STRUCT_PTR tp;

{
    SYMTAB_NODE_PTR field_idp;

    get_token();

    if ((token == IDENTIFIER) && (tp->form == RECORD_FORM)) {
        search_this_symtab(field_idp,
                        tp->info.record.field_symtab);
        get_token();

        /*
        -- Add the field's offset (using the numeric equate)
        -- to the address at the top of the stack.
        */
        if (field_idp != NULL) {
            emit_1(POP, reg(AX));
            emit_2(ADD, reg(AX), tagged_name(field_idp));
            emit_1(PUSH, reg(AX));
            return(field_idp->typep);
        }
        else {
            error(INVALID_FIELD);
            return(&dummy_type);
        }
    }
    else {
        get_token();
        error(INVALID_FIELD);
        return(&dummy_type);
    }
}
```

```
              /*********************************/
              /*                               */
              /*       Type compatibility      */
              /*                               */
              /*********************************/
```

```
/*-----------------------------------------------------------*/
/* check_rel_op_types  Check the operand types for a rela-   */
/*                         tional operator.                  */
/*-----------------------------------------------------------*/

check_rel_op_types(tp1, tp2)

    TYPE_STRUCT_PTR tp1, tp2;          /* operand types */

{
    /*
    -- Two identical scalar or enumeration types.
    */
    if (   (tp1 == tp2)
        && ((tp1->form == SCALAR_FORM) || (tp1->form == ENUM_FORM)))
        return;

    /*
    -- One integer and one real.
    */
    if (   ((tp1 == integer_typep) && (tp2 == real_typep))
        || ((tp2 == integer_typep) && (tp1 == real_typep))) return;

    /*
    -- Two strings of the same length.
    */
    if ((tp1->form == ARRAY_FORM) &&
        (tp2->form == ARRAY_FORM) &&
        (tp1->info.array.elmt_typep == char_typep) &&
        (tp2->info.array.elmt_typep == char_typep) &&
        (tp1->info.array.elmt_count ==
                    tp2->info.array.elmt_count)) return;

    error(INCOMPATIBLE_TYPES);
}

/*-----------------------------------------------------------*/
/* is_assign_type_compatible   Return TRUE iff a value of type */
/*                             tp1 can be assigned to a vari-  */
/*                             able of type tp1.               */
/*-----------------------------------------------------------*/

    BOOLEAN
is_assign_type_compatible(tp1, tp2)

    TYPE_STRUCT_PTR tp1, tp2;

{
    tp1 = base_type(tp1);
    tp2 = base_type(tp2);

    if (tp1 == tp2) return(TRUE);

    /*
    -- real := integer
    */
    if ((tp1 == real_typep) && (tp2 == integer_typep)) return(TRUE);

    /*
    -- string1 := string2 of the same length
    */
    if ((tp1->form == ARRAY_FORM) &&
        (tp2->form == ARRAY_FORM) &&
        (tp1->info.array.elmt_typep == char_typep) &&
        (tp2->info.array.elmt_typep == char_typep) &&
        (tp1->info.array.elmt_count ==
                    tp2->info.array.elmt_count)) return(TRUE);
```

```
    return(FALSE);                                          base_type(tp)
}
                                                                TYPE_STRUCT_PTR tp;

/*----------------------------------------------*/
/* base_type        Return the range type of a subrange */       {
/*                  type.                        */
/*----------------------------------------------*/                   return((tp->form == SUBRANGE_FORM)
                                                                        ? tp->info.subrange.range_typep
    TYPE_STRUCT_PTR                                                      : tp);

                                                                }
```

The emitted code, when executed, always leaves scalar values in register AX or in the DX:AX register pair. Array or record values are always allocated on top of the stack. Addresses, such as for assignment targets or the address of variables being passed by reference, are pushed onto the stack.

13.4.1 Variables

Function variable emits code to process a variable. It handles several cases. If the variable is subscripted or followed by a field name, we first call function emit_push_address (defined in file emitcode.c). It emits code to push the address of the variable onto the stack. Next, we call functions array_subscript_list and record_field to emit code that modifies this address. Then, if the variable is not an assignment target and the value that is being accessed is a scalar, we emit code to load the value into register AX or the DX:AX register pair:

```
pop   bx                 ; BX = modified address
sub   ax,ax              ; AX = 0
mov   al,BYTE PTR [bx]   ; AL = character
```

(loads a character value into register AL)

```
pop   bx                 ; BX = modified address
mov   ax,WORD PTR [bx]   ; AX = low-order half
mov   dx,WORD PTR [bx+2] ; DX = high-order half
```

(loads a real value into the DX:AX register pair)

```
pop   bx                 ; BX = modified address
mov   ax,WORD PTR [bx]   ; AX = value
```

(loads an integer or enumeration value into register AX).

If the variable is an assignment target, we emit code to push the variable's address onto the stack, unless the variable matches one of the three cases described for assignment targets. If we are assigning a value to a Pascal function, we call function emit_push_return_value to emit code to push the address of the return value slot in the appropriate stack frame. Otherwise, we call function emit_push_ address to emit code to push the address of the variable. These code-emitting functions are all defined in file emitcode.c and are described later.

If the variable is being passed by reference to a Pascal procedure or function (the corresponding formal parameter is a VAR parameter), or if the variable is an array or a record, we call function emit_push_address to emit code to push its address onto the stack.

Finally, if the variable is a simple scalar, we call function emit_load_value to load the value into register AX or into the DX:AX register pair.

Function array_subscript_list emits code to calculate the byte offset represented by a subscript value, and adds this offset to the address on top of the stack. This calculation is similar to the one done by the interpreter. We first call function expression which emits code to evaluate a subscript expression and leave the value in register AX. Then we emit the code:

```
sub   ax,min          ; subtract minimum subscript value
mov   dx,size         ; DX = dimension size
imul  dx              ; AX = offset
pop   dx              ; DX = array address
add   dx,ax           ; DX = address + offset
push  dx              ; push modified address
```

where *min* is the minimum subscript value for its dimension, and *size* is the size in bytes of that dimension. We do not emit the initial sub instruction if *min* is zero.

Function record_field emits code to simply add the field's offset to the address on top of the stack. The code uses the tagged equate name of the field, for example:

```
pop   ax              ; AX = record address
add   ax,x_004        ; AX = address + offset
push  ax              ; push modified address
```

where x_004 is the name that was equated (by code emitted by function var_or_field_declarations) to its numeric offset.

File emitcode.c (see Figure 13-1) defines several functions that emit code to push and load values and addresses. (We saw previously how we call some of them.)

Function emit_load_value emits code to load the value of a variable into register AX or into the DX:AX register pair. If the variable is global or local, the code is simple:

```
sub   ax,ax
mov   al,BYTE PTR ch_016    ; AX = character value

mov   ax,WORD PTR ip_021    ; AX = integer value
```

```
mov   ax,WORD PTR d_025
mov   dx,WORD PTR d_025+2          ; DX:AX = real value
```

If the variable is nonglobal and nonlocal (it is declared in an enclosing procedure or function), the emitted code must establish the appropriate stack frame before loading the value. This is done by following the static links from the current stack frame up to the appropriate one. The number of links to follow is the difference between the current nesting level and the level of the variable. For example, the code to load the integer value of a variable declared in the current routine's "grandparent" (two nesting levels lower) is:

```
mov   bx,bp                        ; save current BP in BX
mov   bp,$STATIC_LINK              ; BP -> parent's stack frame
mov   bp,$STATIC_LINK              ; BP -> grandparent's stack frame
mov   ax,WORD PTR rows_026         ; AX = integer value
mov   bp,bx                        ; restore current BP
```

where $STATIC_LINK is equated in the program prologue to WORD PTR [bp+4].

Finally, if the variable is a formal VAR parameter, we must access the value indirectly though the parameter's address value. For example:

```
mov   bx,WORD PTR parm_029         ; BX = address of value
mov   ax,WORD PTR [bx]             ; AX = integer value
```

Function emit_push_address emits code to push a variable's address onto the stack. If the variable is global or local, an example of the emitted code is:

```
lea   ax,WORD PTR i_030            ; AX = address
push ax                            ; push address
```

If the variable is nonglobal and nonlocal, we must follow the static links up to the appropriate stack frame. For example:

```
mov   bx,bp                        ; save current BP in BX
mov   bp,$STATIC_LINK              ; BP -> parent's stack frame
lea   ax,WORD PTR k_031            ; AX = address
mov   bp,bx                        ; restore current BP
push ax                            ; push address
```

If the variable is actually a formal VAR parameter, its value is an address. In that case, the emitted code is the same, except that the lea instruction is replaced by a mov instruction.

Function emit_push_return_value_address emits code to push the address of the function return value slot in the appropriate stack frame. If the value of the current function is being set, the code is simply:

```
lea   ax,$RETURN_VALUE          ; AX = address
push  ax                        ; push address
```

where $RETURN_VALUE is equated in the program prologue to WORD PTR [bp-4].
However, if the value of an enclosing function is being set, the code must follow
static links up to the appropriate stack frame, for example:

```
mov   bx,bp                     ; save current BP in BX
mov   bp,$STATIC_LINK           ; BP -> parent's stack frame
mov   bp,$STATIC_LINK           ; BP -> grandparent's stack frame
lea   ax,$RETURN_VALUE          ; AX = address
mov   bp,bx                     ; restore current BP
push  ax                        ; push address
```

13.4.2 Arithmetic and logical operations

The remaining functions in file expr.c parse expressions and emit code to evaluate
them. Each of the functions emits code to leave either a scalar value in register
AX or in the DX:AX register pair, or an address on top of the stack. Functions
expression, simple_expression, and term each calls emit_push_operand to emit
code to push a scalar operand onto the stack before emitting code to evaluate a
subsequent operand.

Function expression emits code to do a comparison. If the operands are
integer, character, boolean, or other enumeration, we emit:

```
pop   dx                        ; DX = operand 1 value
cmp   dx,ax                     ; compare DX to AX
```

If the operands are real, or real and integer, we call function emit_push_
operand to push the current operand value onto the stack (so both operands are
on the stack). We also call function promote_operands_to_real to convert any
integer operand to real, and then we emit:

```
call  _float_compare
add   sp,8                      ; pop off operands
cmp   ax,0                      ; check result of float compare
```

where _float_compare is a library routine (see Figure 12-5) that returns 0 if the
two operands are equal, −1 if the first operand is less than the second operand,
or 1 if the first operand is greater than the second operand.

If the operands are two strings, both string addresses are on the stack, and
so we emit:

```
pop   di                        ; DI = string 2 address
pop   si                        ; SI = string 1 address
```

```
        mov   ax,ds                  ; AX = DS
        mov   es,ax                  ; ES = AX
        cld                          ; clear direction flag
        mov   cx,length              ; CX = string length
        repe  cmpsb                  ; compare strings
```

where *length* is the string length. Following any of the those code sequences, we then emit:

```
        mov   ax,1                   ; AX = TRUE (1)
        jump  $L_nnn
        sub   ax,ax                  ; AX = FALSE (0)
$L_nnn:
```

where *jump* is either jl, jle, je, jne, jge, or jg, depending on whether the comparison operator in the Pascal source was <, <=, =, <>, >, or >=, respectively, and *nnn* is the label index.

Function simple_expression emits the code:

```
        neg   ax
```

to negate an integer value that was preceded by a unary minus. If a real value must be negated, we call function push_operand to push the value onto the stack, and then we emit:

```
        call  _float_negate
        add   sp,4                   ; pop off operand
```

to call the library routine to negate the value.

With integer operands and the + operator, we emit:

```
        pop   dx                     ; DX = operand 1 value
        add   ax,dx                  ; AX = AX + DX
```

If the operator is -, we emit instead:

```
        pop   dx                     ; DX = operand 1 value
        sub   dx,ax                  ; DX = DX - AX
        mov   ax,dx                  ; AX = DX
```

With real operands, or integer and real operands, and the + operator, we call emit_push_operand to push the current operand value onto the stack (so both operands are on the stack). Next, we call function promote_operands_to_real to convert any integer operand to real, and then we emit:

```
        call  _float_add
        add   sp,8                      ; pop off operands
```

to call the library routine to do the addition. If the operator is -, we emit a call to _float_subtract instead. Finally, if the operator is OR, we emit:

```
        pop   dx                        ; DX = operand 1 value
        or    ax,dx                     ; AX = AX|DX
```

With integer operands and the * operator, function term emits the code:

```
        pop   dx                        ; DX = operand 1 value
        imul  dx                        ; DX:AX = AX * DX
```

Subsequent code ignores the value in register DX, so if the product exceeds one word in size, an incorrect value is used. (An exercise at the end of this chapter suggests runtime error checking.) If the operator is div, we emit:

```
        mov   cx,ax                     ; CX = operand 2 value
        pop   ax                        ; AX = operand 1 value
        sub   dx,dx                     ; DX = 0
        idiv  cx                        ; AX = DX:AX / CX
```

If the operator is mod, we follow the previous code sequence with:

```
        mov   ax,dx                     ; AX = DX:AX % CX
```

With real operands, or integer and real operands, and the * operator, we call emit_push_operand to push the current operand value onto the stack (so both operands are on the stack). Next, we call function promote_operands_to_real to convert any integer operand to real, and then we emit:

```
        call  _float_multiply
        add   sp,8                      ; pop off operands
```

to call the library routine to multiply. If the operator is /, we emit a call to _float_divide instead. Finally, if the operator is AND, we emit:

```
        pop   dx                        ; DX = operand 1 value
        and   ax,dx                     ; AX = AX & DX
```

Function factor emits the following code for an integer literal:

```
        mov   ax,n                      ; AX = n
```

where n is the literal. If the literal is a character, we emit:

```
mov   ax,'c'                      ; AX = character value
```

where *c* is the literal. If the literal is a real number, we call function float_literal, and if the literal is a string, we call function string_literal.

In function float_literal, we enter the token string into the symbol table, assign a label index to the entry, and link the entry to the list headed by pointer variable float_literal_list. We then emit:

```
mov   ax,WORD PTR $F_nnn          ; AX = low-order half
mov   dx,WORD PTR $F_nnn+2        ; DX = high-order half
```

where *nnn* is the label index. As described, $F_*nnn* will be declared in the data segment as part of the program epilogue.

Similarly, in function string_literal, we enter the token string into the symbol table, assign a label index to the entry, and link the entry to the list headed by pointer variable string_literal_list. We then emit:

```
lea   ax,$S_nnn                   ; AX = address of string
push ax                           ; push address
```

where *nnn* is the label index. $S_*nnn* will also be declared in the data segment as part of the program epilogue.

We call function constant_identifier if the operand is a constant identifier. If the constant is an integer, constant_identifier simply emits:

```
mov   ax,n                        ; AX = n
```

where *n* is the integer. If the constant is a real number or a string, we write the value into a string buffer and call function float_literal or string_literal, respectively.

For the NOT operator, we emit:

```
not   ax                          ; AX = ˜AX
```

Function promote_operands_to_real ensures that both stacked operands of a real-valued operation are real. If the second operand (the one on top) is integer, we emit the following code to convert it to real:

```
call _float_convert
add   sp,2                        ; pop off operands
push dx                           ; push high-order half
push ax                           ; push low-order half
```

The code is a bit more complicated if the first operand is integer, since the second operand is on top of it:

```
pop   ax
pop   dx                      ; DX:AX = operand 2
pop   bx                      ; BX = operand 1
push  dx
push  ax                      ; push operand 2
push  bx                      ; push operand 1
call  _float_convert
add   sp,2                    ; pop off operands
pop   bx
pop   cx                      ; BX:CX = operand 2
push  dx
push  ax                      ; push operand 1 (now real)
push  cx
push  bx                      ; push operand 2
```

13.5 write and writeln

If we are to test the code, the compiler needs to be able to emit code to write out values. Therefore, we modify function write_writeln in file standard.c to emit code for write and writeln (Figure 13-16).

FIGURE 13-16   File standard.c.

```
/*****************************************************************/
/*                                                               */
/*         S T A N D A R D   R O U T I N E   P A R S E R         */
/*                                                               */
/*     Parsing routines for calls to standard procedures and     */
/*     functions.·                                               */
/*                                                               */
/*     FILE:      standard.c                                     */
/*                                                               */
/*     MODULE:    parser                                         */
/*                                                               */
/*****************************************************************/

#include <stdio.h>
#include "common.h"
#include "error.h"
#include "scanner.h"
#include "symtab.h"
#include "parser.h"
#include "code.h"

#define DEFAULT_NUMERIC_FIELD_WIDTH   10
#define DEFAULT_PRECISION             2

/*--------------------------------------------------------------*/
/* Externals                                                    */
/*--------------------------------------------------------------*/

extern TOKEN_CODE    token;
extern char          word_string[];
```

```
extern SYMTAB_NODE_PTR  symtab_display[];
extern int              level;
extern TYPE_STRUCT      dummy_type;

extern TYPE_STRUCT_PTR  integer_typep, real_typep,
                        boolean_typep, char_typep;

extern int              label_index;
extern char             asm_buffer[];
extern char             *asm_bufferp;
extern FILE             *code_file;

extern TOKEN_CODE       follow_parm_list[];
extern TOKEN_CODE       statement_end_list[];

/*--------------------------------------------------------------*/
/* Forwards                                                     */
/*--------------------------------------------------------------*/

TYPE_STRUCT_PTR eof_eoln(), abs_sqr(),
                arctan_cos_exp_ln_sin_sqrt(),
                pred_succ(), chr(), odd(), ord(),
                round_trunc();

/*--------------------------------------------------------------*/
/* standard_routine_call   Process a call to a standard         */
/*                         procedure or function.  Return a     */
/*                         pointer to the type structure of     */
/*                         the call.                            */
/*--------------------------------------------------------------*/
```

```
                TYPE_STRUCT_PTR
        standard_routine_call(rtn_idp)

            SYMTAB_NODE_PTR rtn_idp;            /* routine id */


        {
            switch (rtn_idp->defn.info.routine.key) {

                case WRITE:
                case WRITELN:   write_writeln(rtn_idp);      return(NULL);

                default:
                    error(UNIMPLEMENTED_FEATURE);
                    exit(-UNIMPLEMENTED_FEATURE);
            }
        }


        /*-----------------------------------------------------*/
        /* write_writeln         Process a call to write or writeln. */
        /*                       Each actual parameter can be:       */
        /*                                                           */
        /*                                <expr>                     */
        /*                                                           */
        /*                       or:                                 */
        /*                                                           */
        /*                                <epxr> : <expr>            */
        /*                                                           */
        /*                       or:                                 */
        /*                                                           */
        /*                                <expr> : <expr> : <expr>   */
        /*-----------------------------------------------------*/

        write_writeln(rtn_idp)

            SYMTAB_NODE_PTR rtn_idp;            /* routine id */


        {
            TYPE_STRUCT_PTR actual_parm_tp;      /* actual parm type */
            TYPE_STRUCT_PTR field_width_tp, precision_tp;

            /*
            -- Parameters are optional for writeln.
            */
            if (token == LPAREN) {
                do {
                    /*
                    -- Value <expr>
                    */
                    get_token();
                    actual_parm_tp = base_type(expression());

                    /*
                    -- Push the scalar value to be written onto the stack.
                    -- A string value is already on the stack.
                    */
                    if (actual_parm_tp->form != ARRAY_FORM)
                        emit_push_operand(actual_parm_tp);

                    if ((actual_parm_tp->form != SCALAR_FORM) &&
                        (actual_parm_tp != boolean_typep) &&
                        ((actual_parm_tp->form != ARRAY_FORM) ||
                         (actual_parm_tp->info.array.elmt_typep !=
                                                    char_typep)))
                        error(INVALID_EXPRESSION);

                    /*
                    -- Optional field width <expr>
```

```
                    -- Push onto the stack.
                    */
                    if (token == COLON) {
                        get_token();
                        field_width_tp = base_type(expression());
                        emit_1(PUSH, reg(AX));

                        if (field_width_tp != integer_typep)
                            error(INCOMPATIBLE_TYPES);

                        /*
                        -- Optional precision <expr>
                        -- Push onto the stack if the value to be printed
                        -- is of type real.
                        */
                        if (token == COLON) {
                            get_token();
                            precision_tp = base_type(expression());

                            if (actual_parm_tp == real_typep)
                                emit_1(PUSH, reg(AX));

                            if (precision_tp != integer_typep)
                                error(INCOMPATIBLE_TYPES);
                        }
                        else if (actual_parm_tp == real_typep) {
                            emit_2(MOVE, reg(AX),
                                   integer_lit(DEFAULT_PRECISION));
                            emit_1(PUSH, reg(AX));
                        }
                    }
                    else {
                        if (actual_parm_tp == integer_typep) {
                            emit_2(MOVE, reg(AX),
                                   integer_lit(DEFAULT_NUMERIC_FIELD_WIDTH));
                            emit_1(PUSH, reg(AX));
                        }
                        else if (actual_parm_tp == real_typep) {
                            emit_2(MOVE, reg(AX),
                                   integer_lit(DEFAULT_NUMERIC_FIELD_WIDTH));
                            emit_1(PUSH, reg(AX));
                            emit_2(MOVE, reg(AX),
                                   integer_lit(DEFAULT_PRECISION));
                            emit_1(PUSH, reg(AX));
                        }
                        else {
                            emit_2(MOVE, reg(AX), integer_lit(0));
                            emit_1(PUSH, reg(AX));
                        }
                    }

                    if (actual_parm_tp == integer_typep) {
                        emit_1(CALL, name_lit(WRITE_INTEGER));
                        emit_2(ADD, reg(SP), integer_lit(4));
                    }
                    else if (actual_parm_tp == real_typep) {
                        emit_1(CALL, name_lit(WRITE_REAL));
                        emit_2(ADD, reg(SP), integer_lit(8));
                    }
                    else if (actual_parm_tp == boolean_typep) {
                        emit_1(CALL, name_lit(WRITE_BOOLEAN));
                        emit_2(ADD, reg(SP), integer_lit(4));
                    }
                    else if (actual_parm_tp == char_typep) {
                        emit_1(CALL, name_lit(WRITE_CHAR));
                        emit_2(ADD, reg(SP), integer_lit(4));
                    }
```

```
else /* string */ {                                              -- Error synchronization:  Should be , or )
   /*                                                             */
   -- Push the string length onto the stack.                     synchronize(follow_parm_list, statement_end_list, NULL);
   */
   emit_2(MOVE, reg(AX),                                        } while (token == COMMA);
           integer_lit(actual_parm_tp->info.array
                                     .elmt_count));               if_token_get_else_error(RPAREN, MISSING_RPAREN);
                                                               }
   emit_1(PUSH, reg(AX));                                 else if (rtn_idp->defn.info.routine.key == WRITE)
   emit_1(CALL, name_lit(WRITE_STRING));                      error(WRONG_NUMBER_OF_PARMS);
   emit_2(ADD, reg(SP), integer_lit(6));
}                                                          if (rtn_idp->defn.info.routine.key == WRITELN)
                                                               emit_1(CALL, name_lit(WRITE_LINE));
/*                                                         }
```

In function write_writeln, we first call function expression and then function push_operand to emit code that pushes a value onto the stack. If there is a field width specifier, we call expression to emit code to evaluate it and then emit push ax to push the value onto the stack. If there is a precision specifier, write_writeln calls expression to emit code to evaluate it, but emits the push ax only if the value to be written is real. If any of the field width or precision specifiers are missing, we emit code that pushes default values (based on the type of the value to be written) onto the stack. We then emit calls to the runtime library routines for an integer, real, boolean, character, or string value to be written, respectively:

```
call _write_integer
add  sp,4                    ; pop off parameters

call _write_real
add  sp,8                    ; pop off parameters

call _write_boolean
add  sp,4                    ; pop off parameters

call _write_char
add  sp,4                    ; pop off parameters

mov  ax,length
push ax                      ; push string length

call _write_string
add  sp,6                    ; pop off parameters
```

Note that the length of the string is passed to _write_string. This is necessary because Pascal strings are not null-terminated. If the call was to writeln, we emit:

```
call _write_line
```

13.6 Program 13-1: Pascal Compiler I

Figure 13-17 shows file compile1.c, the main file of the compiler for this chapter. Before calling function program, we open the code file code_file for the emitted assembly language code.

FIGURE 13-17   File compile1.c.

```
/****************************************************************/
/*                                                              */
/*      Program 13-1:  Pascal Compiler I                        */
/*                                                              */
/*      Compile assignement statements in procedures            */
/*      and functions.                                          */
/*                                                              */
/*      FILE:       compile1.c                                  */
/*                                                              */
/*      REQUIRES:   Modules parser, symbol table, scanner,      */
/*                       code, error                            */
/*                                                              */
/*      USAGE:      compile1 sourcefile objectfile              */
/*                                                              */
/*          sourcefile      [input] source file containing the  */
/*                              the statements to compile        */
/*                                                              */
/*          objectfile      [output] object file to contain the */
/*                              generated assembly code          */
/*                                                              */
/****************************************************************/

#include <stdio.h>

/*------------------------------------------------------------*/
/* Globals                                                    */
/*------------------------------------------------------------*/

FILE *code_file;    /* ASCII file for the emitted assembly code */
```

```
/*------------------------------------------------------------*/
/* main              Initialize the scanner and call          */
/*                   routine program.                         */
/*------------------------------------------------------------*/

main(argc, argv)

    int  argc;
    char *argv[];

{
    /*
    -- Open the code file.  If no code file name was given,
    -- use the standard output file.
    */
    code_file = (argc == 3) ? fopen(argv[2], "w")
                            : stdout;

    /*
    -- Initialize the scanner.
    */
    init_scanner(argv[1]);

    /*
    -- Process a program.
    */
    get_token();
    program();
}
```

Figure 13-18 shows a simple Pascal program, and Figure 13-19 shows the emitted assembly code. In the next chapter, we will complete the compiler by generating code for Pascal control statements and calls to the remaining standard procedures and functions.

FIGURE 13-18   A sample Pascal program to be compiled.

```
PROGRAM simple (output);

    VAR
        n : integer;
        x : real;

    PROCEDURE proc (i : integer; VAR j : integer);

        FUNCTION func (y : real) : real;

        BEGIN {func}
            j := 5;
            func := i + y + 0.5;
        END {func};

        BEGIN {proc}
            j := i DIV 2;
            writeln('In proc, the value of j is', j:3);
```

```
        x := func(3.14);                                    writeln('In simple, the value of n is', n:3);
        writeln('In proc, the value of j is', j:3);         proc(7, n);
    END (proc);                                             writeln('In simple, the value of n is', n:3,
                                                                    ' and the value of x is', x:8:4);
  BEGIN (simple)                                        END (simple).
    n := 1;
```

FIGURE 13-19   Assembly language object file generated by the compiler for the sample program in Figure 13-18.

```
;    1: PROGRAM simple (output);                                 mov     ax,WORD PTR y_008
         DOSSEG                                                  mov     dx,WORD PTR y_008+2
         .MODEL  small                                          push    dx
         .STACK  1024                                           push    ax
                                                                pop     ax
         .CODE                                                  pop     dx
                                                                pop     bx
         PUBLIC  _pascal_main                                   push    dx
         INCLUDE pasextrn.inc                                   push    ax
                                                                push    bx
$STATIC_LINK         EQU     <WORD PTR [bp+4]>                  call    _float_convert
$RETURN_VALUE        EQU     <WORD PTR [bp-4]>                  add     sp,2
$HIGH_RETURN_VALUE   EQU     <WORD PTR [bp-2]>                  pop     bx
                                                                pop     cx
;    2:                                                         push    dx
;    3:     VAR                                                 push    ax
;    4:         n : integer;                                    push    cx
;    5:         x : real;                                       push    bx
;    6:                                                         call    float_add
;    7:     PROCEDURE proc (i : integer; VAR j : integer);      add     sp,8
;    8:                                                         push    dx
;    9:         FUNCTION func (y : real) : real;                push    ax
                                                                mov     ax,WORD PTR $F_009
i_005   EQU     <WORD PTR [bp+8]>                               mov     dx,WORD PTR $F_009+2
j_006   EQU     <WORD PTR [bp+6]>                               push    dx
;   10:                                                         push    ax
;   11:             BEGIN (func)                                call    _float_add
                                                                add     sp,8
y_008   EQU     <WORD PTR [bp+6]>                               pop     bx
                                                                mov     WORD PTR [bx],ax
func_007        PROC                                            mov     WORD PTR [bx+2],dx
                                                            ;   14:             END (func);
        push    bp                                              mov     ax,$RETURN_VALUE
        mov     bp,sp                                           mov     dx,$HIGH_RETURN_VALUE
        sub     sp,4                                            mov     sp,bp
;   12:                 j := 5;                                 pop     bp
        mov     bx,bp                                           ret     6
        mov     bp,$STATIC_LINK
        mov     ax,WORD PTR j_006                       func_007        ENDP
        mov     bp,bx                                   ;   15:
        push    ax                                      ;   16:         BEGIN (proc)
        mov     ax,5
        pop     bx                                      proc_004        PROC
        mov     WORD PTR [bx],ax
;   13:                 func := i + y + 0.5;                    push    bp
        lea     ax,$RETURN_VALUE                                mov     bp,sp
        push    ax                                      ;   17:             j := i DIV 2;
        mov     bx,bp                                           mov     ax,WORD PTR j_006
        mov     bp,$STATIC_LINK                                 push    ax
        mov     ax,WORD PTR i_005                               mov     ax,WORD PTR i_005
        mov     bp,bx                                           push    ax
        push    ax                                              mov     ax,2
```

```
              mov     cx,ax
              pop     ax
              sub     dx,dx
              idiv    cx
              pop     bx
              mov     WORD PTR [bx],ax
;   18:               writeln('In proc, the value of j is', j:3);
              lea     ax,WORD PTR $S_010
              push    ax
              mov     ax,0
              push    ax
              mov     ax,26
              push    ax
              call    _write_string
              add     sp,6
              mov     bx,WORD PTR j_006
              mov     ax,WORD PTR [bx]
              push    ax
              mov     ax,3
              push    ax
              call    _write_integer
              add     sp,4
              call    _write_line
;   19:               x := func(3.14);
              mov     ax,WORD PTR $F_011
              mov     dx,WORD PTR $F_011+2
              push    dx
              push    ax
              push    bp
              call    func_007
              mov     WORD PTR x_003,ax
              mov     WORD PTR x_003+2,dx
;   20:               writeln('In proc, the value of j is', j:3);
              lea     ax,WORD PTR $S_010
              push    ax
              mov     ax,0
              push    ax
              mov     ax,26
              push    ax
              call    _write_string
              add     sp,6
              mov     bx,WORD PTR j_006
              mov     ax,WORD PTR [bx]
              push    ax
              mov     ax,3
              push    ax
              call    _write_integer
              add     sp,4
              call    _write_line
;   21:         END {proc};
              mov     sp,bp
              pop     bp
              ret     6


proc_004      ENDP
;   22:
;   23:     BEGIN {simple}

_pascal_main  PROC

              push    bp
              mov     bp,sp
;   24:         n := 1;
              mov     ax,1
              mov     WORD PTR n_002,ax
;   25:         writeln('In simple, the value of n is', n:3);
              lea     ax,WORD PTR $S_012
```

```
              push    ax
              mov     ax,0
              push    ax
              mov     ax,28
              push    ax
              call    _write_string
              add     sp,6
              mov     ax,WORD PTR n_002
              push    ax
              mov     ax,3
              push    ax
              call    _write_integer
              add     sp,4
              call    _write_line
;   26:         proc(7, n);
              mov     ax,7
              push    ax
              lea     ax,WORD PTR n_002
              push    ax
              push    bp
              call    proc_004
;   27:         writeln('In simple, the value of n is', n:3,
              lea     ax,WORD PTR $S_012
              push    ax
              mov     ax,0
              push    ax
              mov     ax,28
              push    ax
              call    _write_string
              add     sp,6
              mov     ax,WORD PTR n_002
              push    ax
              mov     ax,3
              push    ax
              call    _write_integer
              add     sp,4
;   28:                 ' and the value of x is', x:8:4);
              lea     ax,WORD PTR $S_013
              push    ax
              mov     ax,0
              push    ax
              mov     ax,22
              push    ax
              call    _write_string
              add     sp,6
              mov     ax,WORD PTR x_003
              mov     dx,WORD PTR x_003+2
              push    dx
              push    ax
              mov     ax,8
              push    ax
              mov     ax,4
              push    ax
              call    _write_real
              add     sp,8
              call    _write_line
;   29:   END {simple}.
;   30:
;   31:
              pop     bp
              ret


_pascal_main  ENDP

              .DATA

n_002   DW      0
```

```
x_003    DD     0.0                                    $S_012   DB     "In simple, the value of n is"
$F_011   DD     3.140000e+000                          $S_010   DB     "In proc, the value of j is"
$F_009   DD     5.000000e-001
$S_013   DB     " and the value of x is"                        END
```

Questions and exercises

1. The interpreter performed several runtime checks, such as checking for values out of range and division by zero. Modify the compiler so that it emits code to do these checks.

2. There are circumstances where the compiler generates unnecessary instructions. For example, for the Pascal statement: n := 7, the compiler currently emits:

```
mov   ax,7
mov   WORD PTR n_011,ax
```

A better code sequence is simply:

```
mov   WORD PTR n_011,7
```

Find and eliminate as many unnecessary instructions as possible. (More advanced methods of reducing the amount of emitted code are discussed in Chapter 15, where we look at optimization.)

CHAPTER 14

Compiling Control Statements

We can now complete our compiler by adding more calls from the statement parsing routines to the code generation routines. This enables the compiler to generate assembly language code for the Pascal control statements and for calls to the standard procedures and functions. With the experience we gained from implementing the interpreter, the work necessary to complete the compiler and the runtime library is quite straightforward. This chapter develops the skills to:

- emit assembly language code for Pascal control statements
- emit assembly language code for calls to standard Pascal procedures and functions
- compile entire Pascal programs

14.1 Organization of the compiler

We change two files from the previous chapter, stmt.c and standard.c. We modify file stmt.c to compile the control statements, and standard.c to compile calls to the standard procedures and functions.

Parser Module

parser.h	*u*	Parser header file
routine.c	*u*	Parse programs, procedures, and functions

standard.c	*c*	Parse standard procedures and functions
decl.c	*u*	Parse declarations
stmt.c	*c*	Parse statements
expr.c	*u*	Parse expressions

Scanner Module

| scanner.h | *u* | Scanner header file |
| scanner.c | *u* | Scanner routines |

Symbol Table Module

| symtab.h | *u* | Symbol table header file |
| symtab.c | *u* | Symbol table routines |

Code Module

code.h	*u*	Code generator header file
emitasm.c	*u*	Emit assembly language statements
emitcode.c	*u*	Emit sequences of assembly code

Error Module

| error.h | *u* | Error header file |
| error.c | *u* | Error routines |

Miscellaneous

| common.h | *u* | Common header file |

Where: *u*   file unchanged from the previous chapter
         c   file changed from the previous chapter

14.2 Emitting code for the control statements

In Chapter 10, we introduced code diagrams to show how the intermediate code for each statement is laid out. In this chapter, we use code diagrams to show what assembly language code is generated for each statement. We also use *annotated syntax diagrams* to show when the parser emits each statement of the assembly code.

The new complete version of file stmt.c, shown in Figure 14-1, can now generate code for the Pascal control statements.

FIGURE 14-1   File stmt.c.

```
/****************************************************************/
/*                                                              */
/*          S T A T E M E N T   P A R S E R                     */
/*                                                              */
/*          Parsing routines for statements.                   */
/*                                                              */
/*          FILE:       stmt.c                                  */
/*                                                              */
/*          MODULE:     parser                                  */
/*                                                              */
/****************************************************************/

#include <stdio.h>
#include "common.h"
#include "error.h"
#include "scanner.h"
#include "symtab.h"
#include "parser.h"
#include "code.h"


/*------------------------------------------------------------*/
/* Externals                                                  */
/*------------------------------------------------------------*/

extern TOKEN_CODE       token;
extern char             word_string[];
extern LITERAL          literal;
extern TOKEN_CODE       statement_start_list[], statement_end_list[];

extern SYMTAB_NODE_PTR  symtab_display[];
extern int              level;

extern TYPE_STRUCT_PTR  integer_typep, real_typep,
                        boolean_typep, char_typep;

extern TYPE_STRUCT      dummy_type;

extern int              label_index;
extern char             asm_buffer[];
extern char             *asm_bufferp;
extern FILE             *code_file;


/*------------------------------------------------------------*/
/* statement         Process a statement by calling the       */
/*                   appropriate parsing routine based on      */
/*                   the statement's first token.              */
/*------------------------------------------------------------*/

statement()

{
    /*
    -- Call the appropriate routine based on the first
    -- token of the statement.
    */
    switch (token) {

        case IDENTIFIER: {
            SYMTAB_NODE_PTR idp;

            /*
            -- Assignment statement or procedure call?
            */
            search_and_find_all_symtab(idp);
```

```
            if (idp->defn.key == PROC_DEFN) {
                get_token();
                routine_call(idp, TRUE);
            }
            else assignment_statement(idp);

            break;
        }

        case REPEAT:  repeat_statement();    break;
        case WHILE:   while_statement();     break;
        case IF:      if_statement();        break;
        case FOR:     for_statement();       break;
        case CASE:    case_statement();      break;
        case BEGIN:   compound_statement();  break;
    }

    /*
    -- Error synchronization: Only a semicolon, END, ELSE, or
    --                        UNTIL may follow a statement.
    --                        Check for a missing semicolon.
    */
    synchronize(statement_end_list, statement_start_list, NULL);
    if (token_in(statement_start_list)) error(MISSING_SEMICOLON);
}

/*------------------------------------------------------------*/
/* assignment_statement    Process an assignment statement:   */
/*                                                            */
/*                              <id> := <expr>                */
/*------------------------------------------------------------*/

assignment_statement(var_idp)

    SYMTAB_NODE_PTR var_idp;            /* target variable id */

{
    TYPE_STRUCT_PTR var_tp, expr_tp;    /* types of var and expr */
    BOOLEAN         stacked_flag;       /* TRUE iff target address
                                           was pushed on stack */

    var_tp = variable(var_idp, TARGET_USE);
    stacked_flag = (var_idp->defn.key == VARPARM_DEFN) ||
                   (var_idp->defn.key == FUNC_DEFN) ||
                   (var_idp->typep->form == ARRAY_FORM) ||
                   (var_idp->typep->form == RECORD_FORM) ||
                   ((var_idp->level > 1) && (var_idp->level < level));

    if_token_get_else_error(COLONEQUAL, MISSING_COLONEQUAL);
    expr_tp = expression();

    if (! is_assign_type_compatible(var_tp, expr_tp))
        error(INCOMPATIBLE_ASSIGNMENT);

    var_tp  = base_type(var_tp);
    expr_tp = base_type(expr_tp);

    /*
    -- Emit code to do the assignment.
    */
    if (var_tp == char_typep) {
        /*
        -- char := char
        */
```

```
        if (stacked_flag) {
            emit_1(POP, reg(BX));
            emit_2(MOVE, byte_indirect(BX), reg(AL));
        }
        else emit_2(MOVE, byte(var_idp), reg(AL));
    }
    else if (var_tp == real_typep) {
        /*
        -- real := ...
        */
        if (expr_tp == integer_typep) {
            /*
            -- ... integer
            */
            emit_1(PUSH, reg(AX));
            emit_1(CALL, name_lit(FLOAT_CONVERT));
            emit_2(ADD, reg(SP), integer_lit(2));
        }
        /*
        -- ... real
        */
        if (stacked_flag) {
            emit_1(POP, reg(BX));
            emit_2(MOVE, word_indirect(BX), reg(AX));
            emit_2(MOVE, high_dword_indirect(BX), reg(DX));
        }
        else {
            emit_2(MOVE, word(var_idp), reg(AX));
            emit_2(MOVE, high_dword(var_idp), reg(DX));
        }
    }
    else if ((var_tp->form == ARRAY_FORM) ||
             (var_tp->form == RECORD_FORM)) {
        /*
        -- array  := array
        -- record := record
        */
        emit_2(MOVE, reg(CX), integer_lit(var_tp->size));
        emit_1(POP, reg(SI));
        emit_1(POP, reg(DI));
        emit_2(MOVE, reg(AX), reg(DS));
        emit_2(MOVE, reg(ES), reg(AX));
        emit(CLEAR_DIRECTION);
        emit(MOVE_BLOCK);
    }
    else {
        /*
        -- integer := integer
        -- enum    := enum
        */
        if (stacked_flag) {
            emit_1(POP, reg(BX));
            emit_2(MOVE, word_indirect(BX), reg(AX));
        }
        else emit_2(MOVE, word(var_idp), reg(AX));
    }
}

/*----------------------------------------------------------*/
/* repeat_statement    Process a REPEAT statement:          */
/*                                                          */
/*                     REPEAT <stmt-list> UNTIL <expr>      */
/*----------------------------------------------------------*/

repeat_statement()

{
```

```
    TYPE_STRUCT_PTR expr_tp;
    int             loop_begin_labelx = new_label_index();
    int             loop_exit_labelx  = new_label_index();

    emit_label(STMT_LABEL_PREFIX, loop_begin_labelx);

    /*
    -- <stmt-list>
    */
    get_token();
    do {
        statement();
        while (token == SEMICOLON) get_token();
    } while (token_in(statement_start_list));

    if_token_get_else_error(UNTIL, MISSING_UNTIL);

    expr_tp = expression();
    if (expr_tp != boolean_typep) error(INCOMPATIBLE_TYPES);

    emit_2(COMPARE, reg(AX), integer_lit(1));
    emit_1(JUMP_EQ, label(STMT_LABEL_PREFIX, loop_exit_labelx));
    emit_1(JUMP, label(STMT_LABEL_PREFIX, loop_begin_labelx));
    emit_label(STMT_LABEL_PREFIX, loop_exit_labelx);
}

/*----------------------------------------------------------*/
/* while_statement     Process a WHILE statement:           */
/*                                                          */
/*                     WHILE <expr> DO <stmt>               */
/*----------------------------------------------------------*/

while_statement()

{
    TYPE_STRUCT_PTR expr_tp;
    int             loop_test_labelx = new_label_index();
    int             loop_stmt_labelx = new_label_index();
    int             loop_exit_labelx = new_label_index();

    emit_label(STMT_LABEL_PREFIX, loop_test_labelx);

    get_token();
    expr_tp = expression();
    if (expr_tp != boolean_typep) error(INCOMPATIBLE_TYPES);

    emit_2(COMPARE, reg(AX), integer_lit(1));
    emit_1(JUMP_EQ, label(STMT_LABEL_PREFIX, loop_stmt_labelx));
    emit_1(JUMP, label(STMT_LABEL_PREFIX, loop_exit_labelx));
    emit_label(STMT_LABEL_PREFIX, loop_stmt_labelx);

    if_token_get_else_error(DO, MISSING_DO);
    statement();

    emit_1(JUMP, label(STMT_LABEL_PREFIX, loop_test_labelx));
    emit_label(STMT_LABEL_PREFIX, loop_exit_labelx);
}

/*----------------------------------------------------------*/
/* if_statement        Process an IF statement:             */
/*                                                          */
/*                     IF <expr> THEN <stmt>                */
/*                                                          */
/*                         or:                              */
/*                                                          */
/*                     IF <expr> THEN <stmt> ELSE <stmt>    */
/*----------------------------------------------------------*/
```

```
if_statement()

{
    TYPE_STRUCT_PTR expr_tp;
    int         true_labelx  = new_label_index();
    int         false_labelx = new_label_index();
    int         if_end_labelx;

    get_token();
    expr_tp = expression();
    if (expr_tp != boolean_typep) error(INCOMPATIBLE_TYPES);

    emit_2(COMPARE, reg(AX), integer_lit(1));
    emit_1(JUMP_EQ, label(STMT_LABEL_PREFIX, true_labelx));
    emit_1(JUMP,    label(STMT_LABEL_PREFIX, false_labelx));
    emit_label(STMT_LABEL_PREFIX, true_labelx);

    if_token_get_else_error(THEN, MISSING_THEN);
    statement();

    /*
    -- ELSE branch?
    */
    if (token == ELSE) {
        if_end_labelx = new_label_index();
        emit_1(JUMP, label(STMT_LABEL_PREFIX, if_end_labelx));
        emit_label(STMT_LABEL_PREFIX, false_labelx);

        get_token();
        statement();

        emit_label(STMT_LABEL_PREFIX, if_end_labelx);
    }
    else emit_label(STMT_LABEL_PREFIX, false_labelx);
}

/*------------------------------------------------------------*/
/*  for_statement       Process a FOR statement:              */
/*                                                            */
/*                       FOR <id> := <expr> TO|DOWNTO <expr>  */
/*                       DO <stmt>                            */
/*------------------------------------------------------------*/

for_statement()

{
    SYMTAB_NODE_PTR for_idp;
    TYPE_STRUCT_PTR for_tp, expr_tp;
    BOOLEAN         to_flag;
    int             loop_test_labelx = new_label_index();
    int             loop_stmt_labelx = new_label_index();
    int             loop_exit_labelx = new_label_index();

    get_token();
    if (token == IDENTIFIER) {
        search_and_find_all_symtab(for_idp);
        if ((for_idp->level != level) ||
            (for_idp->defn.key != VAR_DEFN))
            error(INVALID_FOR_CONTROL);

        for_tp = base_type(for_idp->typep);
        get_token();

        if ((for_tp != integer_typep) &&
            (for_tp != char_typep) &&
            (for_tp->form != ENUM_FORM)) error(INCOMPATIBLE_TYPES);
    }
    else {
        error(IDENTIFIER, MISSING_IDENTIFIER);
        for_tp = &dummy_type;
    }

    if_token_get_else_error(COLONEQUAL, MISSING_COLONEQUAL);

    expr_tp = expression();
    if (! is_assign_type_compatible(for_tp, expr_tp))
        error(INCOMPATIBLE_TYPES);

    if (for_tp == char_typep) emit_2(MOVE, byte(for_idp), reg(AL))
    else                      emit_2(MOVE, word(for_idp), reg(AX))

    if ((token == TO) || (token == DOWNTO)) {
        to_flag = (token == TO);
        get_token();
    }
    else error(MISSING_TO_OR_DOWNTO);

    emit_label(STMT_LABEL_PREFIX, loop_test_labelx);

    expr_tp = expression();
    if (! is_assign_type_compatible(for_tp, expr_tp))
        error(INCOMPATIBLE_TYPES);

    if (for_tp == char_typep) emit_2(COMPARE, byte(for_idp), reg(AL))
    else                      emit_2(COMPARE, word(for_idp), reg(AX))
    emit_1(to_flag ? JUMP_LE : JUMP_GE,
           label(STMT_LABEL_PREFIX, loop_stmt_labelx));
    emit_1(JUMP, label(STMT_LABEL_PREFIX, loop_exit_labelx));
    emit_label(STMT_LABEL_PREFIX, loop_stmt_labelx);

    if_token_get_else_error(DO, MISSING_DO);
    statement();

    emit_1(to_flag ? INCREMENT : DECREMENT,
           for_tp == char_typep ? byte(for_idp) : word(for_idp));
    emit_1(JUMP, label(STMT_LABEL_PREFIX, loop_test_labelx));

    emit_label(STMT_LABEL_PREFIX, loop_exit_labelx);
    emit_1(to_flag ? DECREMENT : INCREMENT,
           for_tp == char_typep ? byte(for_idp) : word(for_idp));
}

/*------------------------------------------------------------*/
/*  case_statement      Process a CASE statement:             */
/*                                                            */
/*                       CASE <expr> OF                       */
/*                           <case-branch> ;                  */
/*                           ...                              */
/*                           END                              */
/*------------------------------------------------------------*/

TOKEN_CODE follow_expr_list[]      = {OF, SEMICOLON, 0};

TOKEN_CODE case_label_start_list[] = {IDENTIFIER, NUMBER, PLUS,
                                      MINUS, STRING, 0};

case_statement()

{
    BOOLEAN         another_branch;
    int             case_end_labelx = new_label_index();
    TYPE_STRUCT_PTR expr_tp;

    get_token();
```

```
    expr_tp = expression();

    if (   ((expr_tp->form != SCALAR_FORM) &&
            (expr_tp->form != ENUM_FORM) &&
            (expr_tp->form != SUBRANGE_FORM))
         || (expr_tp == real_typep)) error(INCOMPATIBLE_TYPES);

    /*
    -- Error synchronization:  Should be OF
    */
    synchronize(follow_expr_list, case_label_start_list, NULL);
    if_token_get_else_error(OF, MISSING_OF);

    /*
    -- Loop to process CASE branches.
    */
    another_branch = token_in(case_label_start_list);
    while (another_branch) {
        if (token_in(case_label_start_list))
            case_branch(expr_tp, case_end_labelx);

        if (token == SEMICOLON) {
            get_token();
            another_branch = TRUE;
        }
        else if (token_in(case_label_start_list)) {
            error(MISSING_SEMICOLON);
            another_branch = TRUE;
        }
        else another_branch = FALSE;
    }

    if_token_get_else_error(END, MISSING_END);
    emit_label(STMT_LABEL_PREFIX, case_end_labelx);
}

/*------------------------------------------------------------*/
/* case_branch              Process a CASE branch:            */
/*                                                            */
/*                          <case-label-list> : <stmt>        */
/*------------------------------------------------------------*/

TOKEN_CODE follow_case_label_list[] = {COLON, SEMICOLON, 0};

case_branch(expr_tp, case_end_labelx)

    TYPE_STRUCT_PTR expr_tp;          /* type of CASE expression */
    int             case_end_labelx;  /* CASE end label index */

{
    BOOLEAN         another_label;
    int             next_test_labelx;
    int             branch_stmt_labelx = new_label_index();
    TYPE_STRUCT_PTR label_tp;
    TYPE_STRUCT_PTR case_label();

    /*
    -- <case-label-list>
    */
    do {
        next_test_labelx = new_label_index();

        label_tp = case_label();
        if (expr_tp != label_tp) error(INCOMPATIBLE_TYPES);

        emit_1(JUMP_NE, label(STMT_LABEL_PREFIX, next_test_labelx));

        get_token();
```

```
        if (token == COMMA) {
            get_token();
            emit_1(JUMP, label(STMT_LABEL_PREFIX, branch_stmt_labelx));

            if (token_in(case_label_start_list)) {
                emit_label(STMT_LABEL_PREFIX, next_test_labelx);
                another_label = TRUE;
            }
            else {
                error(MISSING_CONSTANT);
                another_label = FALSE;
            }
        }
        else another_label = FALSE;
    } while (another_label);

    /*
    -- Error synchronization:  Should be :
    */
    synchronize(follow_case_label_list, statement_start_list, NULL);
    if_token_get_else_error(COLON, MISSING_COLON);

    emit_label(STMT_LABEL_PREFIX, branch_stmt_labelx);
    statement();

    emit_1(JUMP, label(STMT_LABEL_PREFIX, case_end_labelx));
    emit_label(STMT_LABEL_PREFIX, next_test_labelx);
}

/*------------------------------------------------------------*/
/* case_label               Process a CASE label and return a */
/*                          pointer to its type structure.    */
/*------------------------------------------------------------*/

    TYPE_STRUCT_PTR
case_label()

{
    TOKEN_CODE sign      = PLUS;       /* unary + or - sign */
    BOOLEAN    saw_sign = FALSE;       /* TRUE iff unary sign */

    /*
    -- Unary + or - sign.
    */
    if ((token == PLUS) || (token == MINUS)) {
        sign     = token;
        saw_sign = TRUE;
        get_token();
    }

    /*
    -- Numeric constant:  Integer type only.
    */
    if (token == NUMBER) {
        if (literal.type == INTEGER_LIT)
            emit_2(COMPARE, reg(AX),
                   integer_lit(sign == PLUS
                                   ? literal.value.integer
                                   : -literal.value.integer))
        else error(INVALID_CONSTANT);

        return(integer_typep);
    }

    /*
    -- Identifier constant:  Integer, character, or enumeration
    --                       types only.
```

```
*/
else if (token == IDENTIFIER) {
    SYMTAB_NODE_PTR idp;

    search_all_symtab(idp);

    if (idp == NULL) {
        error(UNDEFINED_IDENTIFIER);
        return(&dummy_type);
    }

    else if (idp->defn.key != CONST_DEFN) {
        error(NOT_A_CONSTANT_IDENTIFIER);
        return(&dummy_type);
    }

    else if (idp->typep == integer_typep) {
        emit_2(COMPARE, reg(AX),
                integer_lit(sign == PLUS
                      ? idp->defn.info.constant
                                .value.integer
                      : -idp->defn.info.constant
                                .value.integer));
        return(integer_typep);
    }

    else if (idp->typep == char_typep) {
        if (saw_sign) error(INVALID_CONSTANT);
        emit_2(COMPARE, reg(AL),
                    char_lit(idp->defn.info.constant
                                .value.character));
        return(char_typep);
    }

    else if (idp->typep->form == ENUM_FORM) {
        if (saw_sign) error(INVALID_CONSTANT);
        emit_2(COMPARE, reg(AX),
                    integer_lit(idp->defn.info.constant
                                .value.integer));
        return(idp->typep);
    }

    else return(&dummy_type);
}

/*
-- String constant:  Character type only.
```

```
*/
else if (token == STRING) {
    if (saw_sign) error(INVALID_CONSTANT);

    if (strlen(literal.value.string) == 1) {
        emit_2(COMPARE, reg(AL), char_lit(literal.value.string[0]));
        return(char_typep);
    }
    else {
        error(INVALID_CONSTANT);
        return(&dummy_type);
    }
}

else {
    error(INVALID_CONSTANT);
    return(&dummy_type);
}
}

/*----------------------------------------------------------*/
/*  compound_statement      Process a compound statement:   */
/*                                                          */
/*                           BEGIN <stmt-list> END          */
/*----------------------------------------------------------*/

compound_statement()

{
    /*
    -- <stmt-list>
    */
    get_token();
    do {
        statement();
        while (token == SEMICOLON) get_token();
        if (token == END) break;

        /*
        -- Error synchronization:  Should be at the start of the
        --                          next statement.
        */
        synchronize(statement_start_list, NULL, NULL);
    } while (token_in(statement_start_list));

    if_token_get_else_error(END, MISSING_END);
}
```

14.2.1 The REPEAT statement

Figure 14-2 shows the annotated syntax diagram and the code diagram for the REPEAT statement. The syntax diagram shows when during the parse of the statement each assembly statement is emitted.

Function repeat_statement generates this code. We first create two statement labels, one with index loop_begin_labelx to mark the beginning of the code for the statements in the loop, and one with index loop_exit_labelx to mark the exit point of the loop. Then we call function statement to emit code for each statement in the loop.

FIGURE 14-2   Annotated syntax diagram and code diagram for the REPEAT statement.

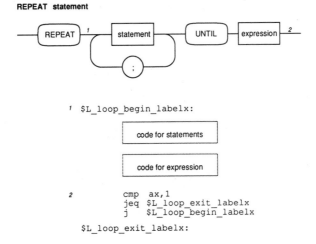

<pre>
¹ $L_loop_begin_labelx:

                    ┌─────────────────────────┐
                    │   code for statements │
                    └─────────────────────────┘

                    ┌─────────────────────────┐
                    │   code for expression │
                    └─────────────────────────┘

    2   cmp ax,1
                    jeq $L_loop_exit_labelx
                    j $L_loop_begin_labelx

                $L_loop_exit_labelx:
</pre>

After the last statement, we call function expression to emit code to evaluate the boolean expression. We then emit the code to test the expression value and to jump based on whether the value is true or false.

We emit the testing code shown in the code diagram instead of the following code, which needs only one label:

```
cmp  ax,1
jne  $L_loop_begin_labelx
```

The reason is one of the idiosyncrasies of the 8086 machine architecture. The conditional jump instruction cannot jump 128 or more bytes, while the unconditional jump can jump to any location in the code segment. Thus, the code will fail unless all the code for the statements in the loop is less than 128 bytes long.

Figure 14-3 shows the code generated for a short Pascal program containing a simple REPEAT statement.

FIGURE 14-3   Assembly code generated for a short Pascal program containing a simple REPEAT statement.

```
;   1: PROGRAM exrepeat (output);          $RETURN_VALUE        EQU   <WORD PTR [bp-4]>
    DOSSEG                                 $HIGH_RETURN_VALUE   EQU   <WORD PTR [bp-2]>
    .MODEL  small
    .STACK  1024                       ;   2:
                                       ;   3: VAR
    .CODE                              ;   4:      i : integer;
                                       ;   5:
    PUBLIC  _pascal_main               ;   6: BEGIN
    INCLUDE pasextrn.inc

$STATIC_LINK      EQU   <WORD PTR [bp+4]>      _pascal_main   PROC
```

```
        push    bp                                  mov     ax,0
        mov     bp,sp                               pop     dx
;   7:      i := 10;                                cmp     dx,ax
        mov     ax,10                               mov     ax,1
        mov     WORD PTR i_002,ax                   jle     $L_005
;   8:      REPEAT                                  sub     ax,ax
$L_003:                                     $L_005:
;   9:      writeln(i);                             cmp     ax,1
        mov     ax,WORD PTR i_002                   je      $L_004
        push    ax                                  jmp     $L_003
        mov     ax,10                       $L_004:
        push    ax                          ;   12: END.
        call    _write_integer              ;   13:
        add     sp,4                        ;   14:
        call    _write_line
;   10:     i := i - 1;
        mov     ax,WORD PTR i_002                   pop     bp
        push    ax                                  ret
        mov     ax,1
        pop     dx                          _pascal_main    ENDP
        sub     dx,ax
        mov     ax,dx                               .DATA
        mov     WORD PTR i_002,ax
;   11:     UNTIL i <= 0;               i_002   DW      0
        mov     ax,WORD PTR i_002
        push    ax                                  END
```

14.2.2 The WHILE statement

Figure 14-4 shows the annotated syntax diagram and the code diagram for the WHILE statement, as emitted by function while_statement. We create three state-

FIGURE 14-4   Annotated syntax diagram and code diagram for the WHILE statement.

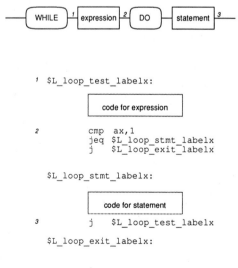

ment labels, one with index loop_stmt_labelx to mark the code for the statement in the loop, one with index loop_exit_labelx to mark the exit point of the loop, and one with index loop_test_labelx to mark the code for the boolean expression.

We first call expression to emit code to evaluate the boolean expression. We next emit code to test the expression value and to jump based on whether the value is true or false, and then we call statement to emit code for the statement in the loop.

The code generated for a short Pascal program containing a simple WHILE statement is shown in Figure 14-5.

FIGURE 14-5 Assembly code generated for a short Pascal program containing a simple WHILE statement.

```
;   1: PROGRAM exwhile (output);          $L_006:
    DOSSEG                                        cmp     ax,1
    .MODEL  small                                 je      $L_004
    .STACK  1024                                  jmp     $L_005
                                          $L_004:
    .CODE                                 ;   9:         writeln(i);
                                                  mov     ax,WORD PTR i_002
    PUBLIC  _pascal_main                          push    ax
    INCLUDE pasextrn.inc                          mov     ax,10
                                                  push    ax
$STATIC_LINK       EQU    <WORD PTR [bp+4]>       call    _write_integer
$RETURN_VALUE      EQU    <WORD PTR [bp-4]>       add     sp,4
$HIGH_RETURN_VALUE EQU    <WORD PTR [bp-2]>       call    _write_line
                                          ;  10:         i := i + 1;
;   2:                                            mov     ax,WORD PTR i_002
;   3: VAR                                        push    ax
;   4:     i : integer;                           mov     ax,1
;   5:                                            pop     dx
;   6: BEGIN                                      add     ax,dx
                                                  mov     WORD PTR i_002,ax
_pascal_main    PROC                      ;  11:     END;
                                                  jmp     $L_003
    push    bp                            $L_005:
    mov     bp,sp                         ;  12: END.
;   7:     i := 1;                        ;  13:
    mov     ax,1                          ;  14:
    mov     WORD PTR i_002,ax
;   8:     WHILE i <= 10 DO BEGIN                 pop     bp
$L_003:                                           ret
    mov     ax,WORD PTR i_002
    push    ax                            _pascal_main    ENDP
    mov     ax,10
    pop     dx                                    .DATA
    cmp     dx,ax
    mov     ax,1                          i_002   DW      0
    jle     $L_006
    sub     ax,ax                                 END
```

14.2.3 The IF statement

Figure 14-6 shows the annotated syntax diagram and the code diagram for the IF statement, as emitted by function if_statement. We first create two statement labels, one with index `true_labelx` to jump to when the boolean expression is true, and one with index `false_labelx` to jump to when the boolean expression is false. We call `expression` to emit code to evaluate the boolean expression, `statement` to emit code for the true branch statement and, if necessary, `statement` again to emit code for the false branch statement.

FIGURE 14-6   Annotated syntax diagram and code diagram for the IF statement.

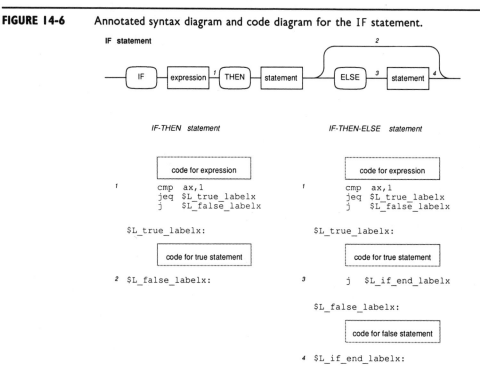

If the IF statement does not have an ELSE branch, the `false_labelx` label marks the code for the statement after the IF statement. If there is an ELSE branch, we create a third label with index `if_end_labelx` to mark the end of the IF statement and emit an unconditional j instruction to jump to that label after the code for the true branch statement. Then, the `false_labelx` label marks the code for the ELSE branch statement. The code generated for a short Pascal program containing simple IF statements is shown in Figure 14-7.

FIGURE 14-7   Assembly code generated for a short Pascal program containing simple IF statements.

```
;   1: PROGRAM exif (output);
       DOSSEG
```
```
.MODEL  small
.STACK  1024
```

```
        .CODE

        PUBLIC  _pascal_main
        INCLUDE pasextrn.inc

$STATIC_LINK          EQU     <WORD PTR [bp+4]>
$RETURN_VALUE         EQU     <WORD PTR [bp-4]>
$HIGH_RETURN_VALUE    EQU     <WORD PTR [bp-2]>

;   2:
;   3: CONST
;   4:    one = 1;
;   5:    two = 2;
;   6:
;   7: BEGIN


_pascal_main    PROC

        push    bp
        mov     bp,sp
;   8:    IF one <> two THEN writeln('true');
        mov     ax,1
        push    ax
        mov     ax,2
        pop     dx
        cmp     dx,ax
        mov     ax,1
        jne     $L_004
        sub     ax,ax
$L_004:
        cmp     ax,1
        je      $L_002
        jmp     $L_003
$L_002:
        lea     ax,WORD PTR $S_005
        push    ax
        mov     ax,0
        push    ax
        mov     ax,4
        push    ax
        call    _write_string
        add     sp,6
        call    _write_line
$L_003:
;   9:    IF one = two THEN writeln('true');
        mov     ax,1
        push    ax
        mov     ax,2
        pop     dx
        cmp     dx,ax
        mov     ax,1
        je      $L_008
        sub     ax,ax
$L_008:
        cmp     ax,1
        je      $L_006
        jmp     $L_007
$L_006:
        lea     ax,WORD PTR $S_005
        push    ax
        mov     ax,0
        push    ax
        mov     ax,4
        push    ax
        call    _write_string
        add     sp,6
        call    _write_line
```

```
$L_007:
;  10:
;  11:    IF one <> two THEN writeln('true')
        mov     ax,1
        push    ax
        mov     ax,2
        pop     dx
        cmp     dx,ax
        mov     ax,1
        jne     $L_011
        sub     ax,ax
$L_011:
        cmp     ax,1
        je      $L_009
        jmp     $L_010
$L_009:
        lea     ax,WORD PTR $S_005
        push    ax
        mov     ax,0
        push    ax
        mov     ax,4
        push    ax
        call    _write_string
        add     sp,6
;  12:            ELSE writeln('false');
        call    _write_line
        jmp     $L_012
$L_010:
        lea     ax,WORD PTR $S_013
        push    ax
        mov     ax,0
        push    ax
        mov     ax,5
        push    ax
        call    _write_string
        add     sp,6
        call    _write_line
$L_012:
;  13:    IF one = two THEN writeln('true')
        mov     ax,1
        push    ax
        mov     ax,2
        pop     dx
        cmp     dx,ax
        mov     ax,1
        je      $L_016
        sub     ax,ax
$L_016:
        cmp     ax,1
        je      $L_014
        jmp     $L_015
$L_014:
        lea     ax,WORD PTR $S_005
        push    ax
        mov     ax,0
        push    ax
        mov     ax,4
        push    ax
        call    _write_string
        add     sp,6
;  14:            ELSE writeln('false');
        call    _write_line
        jmp     $L_017
$L_015:
        lea     ax,WORD PTR $S_013
        push    ax
        mov     ax,0
```

```
    push    ax                                          ret
    mov     ax,5
    push    ax                          _pascal_main    ENDP
    call    _write_string
    add     sp,6                                .DATA
    call    _write_line
$L_017:                                 $S_013  DB      "false"
;   15: END.                            $S_005  DB      "true"
;   16:
                                                END
    pop     bp
```

14.2.4 The FOR statement

Figure 14-8 shows the annotated syntax diagram and the code diagram for the FOR statement, as emitted by function for_statement. We first create three statement labels, one with index loop_test_labelx to mark the code to test the control variable, one with index loop_stmt_labelx to mark the code for the statement in the loop, and one with index loop_exit_labelx to mark the exit point of the loop.

FIGURE 14-8   Annotated syntax diagram and code diagram for the FOR statement.

FOR statement

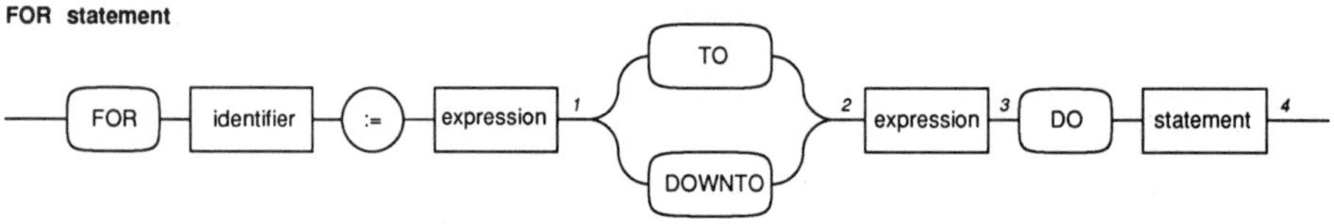

FOR-TO statement

```
            code for initial expression
    1           mov  WORD PTR control_var,ax
    2   $L_loop_test_labelx:
            code for final expression
    3           cmp  WORD PTR control_var,ax
                jle  $L_loop_stmt_labelx
                j    $L_loop_exit_labelx
        $L_loop_stmt_labelx:
            code for statement
    4           inc  WORD PTR control_var
                j    $L_loop_test_labelx
        $L_loop_exit_labelx:
                dec  WORD PTR control_var
```

FOR-DOWNTO statement

```
            code for initial expression
    1           mov  WORD PTR control_var,ax
    2   $L_loop_test_labelx:
            code for final expression
    3           cmp  WORD PTR control_var,ax
                jge  $L_loop_stmt_labelx
                j    $L_loop_exit_labelx
        $L_loop_stmt_labelx:
            code for statement
    4           dec  WORD PTR control_var
                j    $L_loop_test_labelx
        $L_loop_exit_labelx:
                inc  WORD PTR control_var
```

We call expression to emit code to evaluate the initial value expression, and then we emit the appropriate mov instruction to assign the byte or word value to the control variable. We call expression again to emit code to evaluate the final value expression. Then we emit code to compare the control variable's value to the final expression value, followed by code to jump based on the comparison. We emit either a jle or a jge instruction to jump to the code for the statement in the loop depending on whether we saw a TO or DOWNTO, respectively. We follow the jle or jge with an unconditional j instruction to jump to the exit label.

We call function statement to emit code for the statement in the loop. Afterwards, we emit either the inc or the dec instruction to increment or decrement the control variable's value, depending on whether there was a TO or a DOWNTO, respectively.

The code generated for a short Pascal program containing simple FOR statements is shown in Figure 14-9.

FIGURE 14-9   Assembly code generated for a short Pascal program containing simple FOR statements.

```
;   1: PROGRAM exfor (output);                                add    sp,6
        DOSSEG                                                mov    ax,WORD PTR i_002
        .MODEL  small                                         push   ax
        .STACK  1024                                          mov    ax,0
                                                              push   ax
        .CODE                                                 call   _write_integer
                                                              add    sp,4
        PUBLIC  _pascal_main                                  call   _write_line
        INCLUDE pasextrn.inc                                  inc    WORD PTR i_002
                                                              jmp    $L_004
$STATIC_LINK        EQU    <WORD PTR [bp+4]>         $L_006:
$RETURN_VALUE       EQU    <WORD PTR [bp-4]>                  dec    WORD PTR i_002
$HIGH_RETURN_VALUE  EQU    <WORD PTR [bp-2]>         ;   9:   writeln;
                                                              call   _write_line
;   2:                                              ;  10:    FOR i := 5 DOWNTO 1 DO writeln('i = ', i:0);
;   3: VAR                                                    mov    ax,5
;   4:    i : integer;                                        mov    WORD PTR i_002,ax
;   5:    ch : char;                                $L_008:
;   6:                                                        mov    ax,1
;   7: BEGIN                                                  cmp    WORD PTR i_002,ax
                                                              jge    $L_009
_pascal_main    PROC                                          jmp    $L_010
                                                    $L_009:
        push    bp                                            lea    ax,WORD PTR $S_007
        mov     bp,sp                                         push   ax
;   8:    FOR i := 1 TO 5 DO writeln('i = ', i:0);            mov    ax,0
        mov     ax,1                                          push   ax
        mov     WORD PTR i_002,ax                             mov    ax,4
$L_004:                                                       push   ax
        mov     ax,5                                          call   _write_string
        cmp     WORD PTR i_002,ax                             add    sp,6
        jle     $L_005                                        mov    ax,WORD PTR i_002
        jmp     $L_006                                        push   ax
$L_005:                                                       mov    ax,0
        lea     ax,WORD PTR $S_007                            push   ax
        push    ax                                            call   _write_integer
        mov     ax,0                                          add    sp,4
        push    ax                                            call   _write_line
        mov     ax,4                                          dec    WORD PTR i_002
        push    ax                                            jmp    $L_008
        call    _write_string                       $L_010:
```

```
        inc     WORD PTR i_002                                      push    ax
;   11:      writeln;                                               call    _write_char
        call    _write_line                                         add     sp,4
;   12:      FOR ch := 'a' TO 'e' DO writeln('ch = ', ch:0);        call    _write_line
        mov     ax,'a'                                              inc     BYTE PTR ch_003
        mov     BYTE PTR ch_003,al                                  jmp     $L_011
$L_011:                                                     $L_013:
        mov     ax,'e'                                              dec     BYTE PTR ch_003
        cmp     BYTE PTR ch_003,al                          ;   13: END.
        jle     $L_012
        jmp     $L_013                                              pop     bp
$L_012:                                                             ret
        lea     ax,WORD PTR $S_014
        push    ax                                          _pascal_main    ENDP
        mov     ax,0
        push    ax                                                  .DATA
        mov     ax,5
        push    ax                                          i_002   DW      0
        call    _write_string                               ch_003  DB      0
        add     sp,6                                        $S_014  DB      "ch = "
        sub     ax,ax                                       $S_007  DB      "i = "
        mov     al,BYTE PTR ch_003
        push    ax                                                  END
        mov     ax,0
```

14.2.5 The CASE statement

Figure 14-10 shows the annotated syntax diagram and the code diagram for the CASE statement, as emitted by functions case_statement, case_branch, and case_label.

In function case_statement, we create one label with index case_end_labelx to mark the end of the CASE statement. We call expression to evaluate the CASE expression. Then for each CASE branch, we call function case_branch, passing case_end_labelx.

We emit the rest of the code in functions case_branch and case_label. Unlike the interpreter, this code executes the CASE statement as if it were a series of IF statements.

In case_branch, we first create a label with index branch_stmt_labelx to mark the code for the CASE branch statement. Then for each CASE label, we create a label with index next_test_labelx to mark the code to test the next CASE label value. We call case_label, which emits the appropriate cmp instruction to test the label value. We then emit a jne instruction to jump upon inequality to the code to test the next CASE label value. If there is another CASE label in the same CASE branch, we emit an unconditional j instruction to jump to the code for the CASE branch statement, and follow this with the next_test_labelx label that marks the code to test the next CASE label value.

After the last (or only) label of the CASE branch, we emit the branch_stmt_labelx label marking the CASE branch statement, and then we call statement to emit code for that statement. We then emit an unconditional j instruction to jump to the label that was passed from case_branch which marks the end of the CASE statement. Finally, we emit the next_test_labelx label marking the code to test the next CASE label (which, if there is one, is in the next CASE branch).

FIGURE 14-10 Annotated syntax diagram and code diagram for the CASE statement.

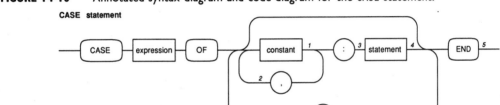

CASE statement

```
                                                                        code for expression

    1                            cmp  ax,constant_1
                                 jne  $L_next_test_labelx_1
    2                            j    $L_branch_stmt_labelx_1


        $L_next_test_labelx_1:


    1                                cmp  ax,constant_2
                                     jne  $L_next_test_labelx_2


    3   $L_branch_stmt_labelx_1:                              3   $L_branch_stmt_labelx_2:


            code for branch statement 1                           code for branch statement 2


    4                            j    $L_case_end_labelx        4              j    $L_case_end_labelx


        $L_next_test_labelx_2:                                    $L_next_test_labelx_3:


    1                                cmp  ax,constant_3        5   $L_case_end_labelx:
                                     jne  $L_next_test_labelx_3
```

The code generated for a short Pascal program containing a simple CASE statement is shown in Figure 14-11.

FIGURE 14-11 Assembly code generated for a short Pascal program containing a simple CASE statement.

```
;    1: PROGRAM excase (output);                    ;    5:
        DOSSEG                                       ;    6: VAR
        .MODEL  small                                ;    7:      i  : integer;
        .STACK  1024                                 ;    8:      ch : char;
                                                     ;    9:
        .CODE                                        ;   10: BEGIN

        PUBLIC  _pascal_main                         _pascal_main    PROC
        INCLUDE pasextrn.inc
                                                                     push  bp
$STATIC_LINK          EQU   <WORD PTR [bp+4]>                        mov   bp,sp
$RETURN_VALUE         EQU   <WORD PTR [bp-4]>        ;   11:     FOR i := 1 TO 9 DO BEGIN
$HIGH_RETURN_VALUE    EQU   <WORD PTR [bp-2]>                        mov   ax,1
                                                                     mov   WORD PTR i_002,ax
;    2:                                              $L_004:
;    3: CONST                                                        mov   ax,9
;    4:     six = 6;                                                 cmp   WORD PTR i_002,ax
```

```
          jle     $L_005
          jmp     $L_006
$L_005:
;   12:            write(i, ' : ');
          mov     ax,WORD PTR i_002
          push    ax
          mov     ax,10
          push    ax
          call    _write_integer
          add     sp,4
          lea     ax,WORD PTR $S_007
          push    ax
          mov     ax,0
          push    ax
          mov     ax,3
          push    ax
          call    _write_string
          add     sp,6
;   13:            CASE i OF
          mov     ax,WORD PTR i_002
;   14:                1:    writeln('one');
          cmp     ax,1
          jne     $L_010
$L_009:
          lea     ax,WORD PTR $S_011
          push    ax
          mov     ax,0
          push    ax
          mov     ax,3
          push    ax
          call    _write_string
          add     sp,6
          call    _write_line
          jmp     $L_008
$L_010:
;   15:                2:    writeln('two');
          cmp     ax,2
          jne     $L_013
$L_012:
          lea     ax,WORD PTR $S_014
          push    ax
          mov     ax,0
          push    ax
          mov     ax,3
          push    ax
          call    _write_string
          add     sp,6
          call    _write_line
          jmp     $L_008
$L_013:
;   16:                3:    writeln('three');
          cmp     ax,3
          jne     $L_016
$L_015:
          lea     ax,WORD PTR $S_017
          push    ax
          mov     ax,0
          push    ax
          mov     ax,5
          push    ax
          call    _write_string
          add     sp,6
          call    _write_line
          jmp     $L_008
$L_016:
;   17:              5,7,4:  writeln('four, five, or seven');
          cmp     ax,5
```

```
          jne     $L_019
          jmp     $L_018
$L_019:
          cmp     ax,7
          jne     $L_020
          jmp     $L_018
$L_020:
          cmp     ax,4
          jne     $L_021
$L_018:
          lea     ax,WORD PTR $S_022
          push    ax
          mov     ax,0
          push    ax
          mov     ax,20
          push    ax
          call    _write_string
          add     sp,6
          call    _write_line
          jmp     $L_008
$L_021:
;   18:              six:    writeln('six');
          cmp     ax,6
          jne     $L_024
$L_023:
          lea     ax,WORD PTR $S_025
          push    ax
          mov     ax,0
          push    ax
          mov     ax,3
          push    ax
          call    _write_string
          add     sp,6
          call    _write_line
          jmp     $L_008
$L_024:
;   19:                8:    writeln('eight');
          cmp     ax,8
          jne     $L_027
$L_026:
          lea     ax,WORD PTR $S_028
          push    ax
          mov     ax,0
          push    ax
          mov     ax,5
          push    ax
          call    _write_string
          add     sp,6
          call    _write_line
          jmp     $L_008
$L_027:
;   20:                9:    writeln('nine');
          cmp     ax,9
          jne     $L_030
$L_029:
          lea     ax,WORD PTR $S_031
          push    ax
          mov     ax,0
          push    ax
          mov     ax,4
          push    ax
          call    _write_string
          add     sp,6
          call    _write_line
          jmp     $L_008
$L_030:
;   21:            END;
```

```
$L_008:                                         i_002    DW    0
;   22:     END;                                 ch_003   DB    0
        inc    WORD PTR i_002                    $S_031   DB    "nine"
        jmp    $L_004                            $S_028   DB    "eight"
$L_006:                                          $S_025   DB    "six"
        dec    WORD PTR i_002                    $S_022   DB    "four, five, or seven"
;   23: END.                                     $S_017   DB    "three"
                                                 $S_014   DB    "two"
        pop    bp                                $S_011   DB    "one"
        ret                                      $S_007   DB    " : "

_pascal_main    ENDP

        .DATA                                             END
```

14.3 Calling the runtime library routines

Figure 14-12 shows the new complete version of file standard.c, which emits calls to the library routines. Function write_writeln was described in Chapter 13.

FIGURE 14-12   File standard.c.

```
/***************************************************************/
/*                                                             */
/*        S T A N D A R D   R O U T I N E   P A R S E R        */
/*                                                             */
/*      Parsing routines for calls to standard procedures and  */
/*      functions.                                             */
/*                                                             */
/*      FILE:       standard.c                                 */
/*                                                             */
/*      MODULE:     parser                                     */
/*                                                             */
/***************************************************************/

#include <stdio.h>
#include "common.h"
#include "error.h"
#include "scanner.h"
#include "symtab.h"
#include "parser.h"
#include "code.h"

#define DEFAULT_NUMERIC_FIELD_WIDTH    10
#define DEFAULT_PRECISION              2

/*-----------------------------------------------------------*/
/* Externals                                                 */
/*-----------------------------------------------------------*/

extern TOKEN_CODE     token;
extern char           word_string[];
extern SYMTAB_NODE_PTR symtab_display[];
extern int            level;
extern TYPE_STRUCT    dummy_type;

extern TYPE_STRUCT_PTR integer_typep, real_typep,
```

```
                       boolean_typep, char_typep;

extern int            label_index;
extern char           asm_buffer[];
extern char           *asm_bufferp;
extern FILE           *code_file;

extern TOKEN_CODE     follow_parm_list[];
extern TOKEN_CODE     statement_end_list[];

/*-----------------------------------------------------------*/
/* Forwards                                                  */
/*-----------------------------------------------------------*/

TYPE_STRUCT_PTR eof_eoln(), abs_sqr(),
                arctan_cos_exp_ln_sin_sqrt(),
                pred_succ(), chr(), odd(), ord(),
                round_trunc();

/*-----------------------------------------------------------*/
/* standard_routine_call   Process a call to a standard      */
/*                         procedure or function. Return a   */
/*                         pointer to the type structure of  */
/*                         the call.                         */
/*-----------------------------------------------------------*/

    TYPE_STRUCT_PTR
standard_routine_call(rtn_idp)

    SYMTAB_NODE_PTR rtn_idp;           /* routine id */

{
    switch (rtn_idp->defn.info.routine.key) {

        case READ:
```

```
        case READLN:     read_readln(rtn_idp);        return(NULL);

        case WRITE:
        case WRITELN:     write_writeln(rtn_idp);      return(NULL);

        case EOFF:
        case EOLN:        return(eof_eoln(rtn_idp));

        case ABS:
        case SQR:         return(abs_sqr(rtn_idp));

        case ARCTAN:
        case COS:
        case EXP:
        case LN:
        case SIN:
        case SQRT:        return(arctan_cos_exp_ln_sin_sqrt(rtn_idp));

        case PRED:
        case SUCC:        return(pred_succ(rtn_idp));

        case CHR:         return(chr());
        case ODD:         return(odd());
        case ORD:         return(ord());

        case ROUND:
        case TRUNC:       return(round_trunc(rtn_idp));
    }
}

/*----------------------------------------------------------*/
/* read_readln          Process a call to read or readln.   */
/*----------------------------------------------------------*/

read_readln(rtn_idp)

    SYMTAB_NODE_PTR rtn_idp;            /* routine id */

{
    TYPE_STRUCT_PTR actual_parm_tp;     /* actual parm type */

    /*
    -- Parameters are optional for readln.
    */
    if (token == LPAREN) {
        /*
        -- <id-list>
        */
        do {
            get_token();

            /*
            -- Actual parms must be variables (but parse
            -- an expression anyway for error recovery).
            */
            if (token == IDENTIFIER) {
                SYMTAB_NODE_PTR idp;

                search_and_find_all_symtab(idp);
                actual_parm_tp = base_type(variable(idp,
                                            VARPARM_USE));

                if (actual_parm_tp->form != SCALAR_FORM)
                    error(INCOMPATIBLE_TYPES);
                else if (actual_parm_tp == integer_typep) {
                    emit_1(CALL, name_lit(READ_INTEGER));
                    emit_1(POP, reg(BX));
```

```
                    emit_2(MOVE, word_indirect(BX), reg(AX));
                }
                else if (actual_parm_tp == real_typep) {
                    emit_1(CALL, name_lit(READ_REAL));
                    emit_1(POP,  reg(BX));
                    emit_2(MOVE, word_indirect(BX), reg(AX));
                    emit_2(MOVE, high_dword_indirect(BX), reg(DX));
                }
                else if (actual_parm_tp == char_typep) {
                    emit_1(CALL, name_lit(READ_CHAR));
                    emit_1(POP,  reg(BX));
                    emit_2(MOVE, byte_indirect(BX), reg(AL));
                }
            }
            else {
                actual_parm_tp = expression();
                error(INVALID_VAR_PARM);
            }

            /*
            -- Error synchronization:  Should be , or )
            */
            synchronize(follow_parm_list, statement_end_list, NULL);

        } while (token == COMMA);

        if_token_get_else_error(RPAREN, MISSING_RPAREN);
    }
    else if (rtn_idp->defn.info.routine.key == READ)
        error(WRONG_NUMBER_OF_PARMS);

    if (rtn_idp->defn.info.routine.key == READLN)
        emit_1(CALL, name_lit(READ_LINE));
}

/*----------------------------------------------------------*/
/* write_writeln        Process a call to write or writeln. */
/*                      Each actual parameter can be:       */
/*                                                          */
/*                          <expr>                          */
/*                                                          */
/*                      or:                                 */
/*                                                          */
/*                          <epxr> : <expr>                 */
/*                                                          */
/*                      or:                                 */
/*                                                          */
/*                          <expr> : <expr> : <expr>        */
/*----------------------------------------------------------*/

write_writeln(rtn_idp)

    SYMTAB_NODE_PTR rtn_idp;            /* routine id */

{
    TYPE_STRUCT_PTR actual_parm_tp;     /* actual parm type */
    TYPE_STRUCT_PTR field_width_tp, precision_tp;

    /*
    -- Parameters are optional for writeln.
    */
    if (token == LPAREN) {
        do {
            /*
            -- Value <expr>
            */
            get_token();
```

```
actual_parm_tp = base_type(expression());

/*
-- Push the scalar value to be written onto the stack.
-- A string value is already on the stack.
*/
if (actual_parm_tp->form != ARRAY_FORM)
    emit_push_operand(actual_parm_tp);

if ((actual_parm_tp->form != SCALAR_FORM) &&
    (actual_parm_tp != boolean_typep) &&
    ((actual_parm_tp->form != ARRAY_FORM) ||
     (actual_parm_tp->info.array.elmt_typep !=
                                    char_typep)))
    error(INVALID_EXPRESSION);

/*
-- Optional field width <expr>
-- Push onto the stack.
*/
if (token == COLON) {
    get_token();
    field_width_tp = base_type(expression());
    emit_1(PUSH, reg(AX));

    if (field_width_tp != integer_typep)
        error(INCOMPATIBLE_TYPES);

    /*
    -- Optional precision <expr>
    -- Push onto the stack if the value to be printed
    -- is of type real.
    */
    if (token == COLON) {
        get_token();
        precision_tp = base_type(expression());

        if (actual_parm_tp == real_typep)
            emit_1(PUSH, reg(AX));

        if (precision_tp != integer_typep)
            error(INCOMPATIBLE_TYPES);
    }
    else if (actual_parm_tp == real_typep) {
        emit_2(MOVE, reg(AX),
               integer_lit(DEFAULT_PRECISION));
        emit_1(PUSH, reg(AX));
    }
}
else {
    if (actual_parm_tp == integer_typep) {
        emit_2(MOVE, reg(AX),
               integer_lit(DEFAULT_NUMERIC_FIELD_WIDTH));
        emit_1(PUSH, reg(AX));
    }
    else if (actual_parm_tp == real_typep) {
        emit_2(MOVE, reg(AX),
               integer_lit(DEFAULT_NUMERIC_FIELD_WIDTH));
        emit_1(PUSH, reg(AX));
        emit_2(MOVE, reg(AX),
               integer_lit(DEFAULT_PRECISION));
        emit_1(PUSH, reg(AX));
    }
    else {
        emit_2(MOVE, reg(AX), integer_lit(0));
        emit_1(PUSH, reg(AX));
    }
}
```

```
}

    if (actual_parm_tp == integer_typep) {
        emit_1(CALL, name_lit(WRITE_INTEGER));
        emit_2(ADD, reg(SP), integer_lit(4));
    }
    else if (actual_parm_tp == real_typep) {
        emit_1(CALL, name_lit(WRITE_REAL));
        emit_2(ADD, reg(SP), integer_lit(8));
    }
    else if (actual_parm_tp == boolean_typep) {
        emit_1(CALL, name_lit(WRITE_BOOLEAN));
        emit_2(ADD, reg(SP), integer_lit(4));
    }
    else if (actual_parm_tp == char_typep) {
        emit_1(CALL, name_lit(WRITE_CHAR));
        emit_2(ADD, reg(SP), integer_lit(4));
    }
    else  /* string */ {
        /*
        -- Push the string length onto the stack.
        */
        emit_2(MOVE, reg(AX),
               integer_lit(actual_parm_tp->info.array
                                       .elmt_count));

        emit_1(PUSH, reg(AX));
        emit_1(CALL, name_lit(WRITE_STRING));
        emit_2(ADD, reg(SP), integer_lit(6));
    }

    /*
    -- Error synchronization:  Should be , or )
    */
    synchronize(follow_parm_list, statement_end_list, NULL);

    } while (token == COMMA);

    if_token_get_else_error(RPAREN, MISSING_RPAREN);
}
else if (rtn_idp->defn.info.routine.key == WRITE)
    error(WRONG_NUMBER_OF_PARMS);

if (rtn_idp->defn.info.routine.key == WRITELN)
    emit_1(CALL, name_lit(WRITE_LINE));
}

/*------------------------------------------------------------*/
/*  eof_eoln               Process a call to eof or to eoln.  */
/*                         No parameters => boolean result.   */
/*------------------------------------------------------------*/

    TYPE_STRUCT_PTR
eof_eoln(rtn_idp)

    SYMTAB_NODE_PTR rtn_idp;            /* routine id */

{
    if (token == LPAREN) {
        error(WRONG_NUMBER_OF_PARMS);
        actual_parm_list(rtn_idp, FALSE);
    }

    emit_1(CALL, name_lit(rtn_idp->defn.info.routine.key == EOFF
                          ? STD_END_OF_FILE
                          : STD_END_OF_LINE));

    return(boolean_typep);
```

```
}


/*-----------------------------------------------------------*/
/*  abs_sqr                    Process a call to abs or to sqr.   */
/*                             integer parm => integer result     */
/*                             real parm   => real result         */
/*-----------------------------------------------------------*/

    TYPE_STRUCT_PTR
abs_sqr(rtn_idp)

    SYMTAB_NODE_PTR rtn_idp;             /* routine id */

{

    TYPE_STRUCT_PTR parm_tp;             /* actual parameter type */
    TYPE_STRUCT_PTR result_tp;           /* result type */

    if (token == LPAREN) {
        get_token();
        parm_tp = base_type(expression());

        if ((parm_tp != integer_typep) && (parm_tp != real_typep)) {
            error(INCOMPATIBLE_TYPES);
            result_tp = real_typep;
        }
        else result_tp = parm_tp;

        if_token_get_else_error(RPAREN, MISSING_RPAREN);
    }
    else error(WRONG_NUMBER_OF_PARMS);

    switch (rtn_idp->defn.info.routine.key) {

        case ABS:
            if (parm_tp == integer_typep) {
                int nonnegative_labelx = new_label_index();

                emit_2(COMPARE, reg(AX), integer_lit(0));
                emit_1(JUMP_GE, label(STMT_LABEL_PREFIX,
                                      nonnegative_labelx));
                emit_1(NEGATE, reg(AX));
                emit_label(STMT_LABEL_PREFIX, nonnegative_labelx);
            }
            else {
                emit_push_operand(parm_tp);
                emit_1(CALL, name_lit(STD_ABS));
                emit_2(ADD, reg(SP), integer_lit(4));
            }
            break;

        case SQR:
            if (parm_tp == integer_typep) {
                emit_2(MOVE, reg(DX), reg(AX));
                emit_1(MULTIPLY, reg(DX));
            }
            else {
                emit_push_operand(parm_tp);
                emit_push_operand(parm_tp);
                emit_1(CALL, name_lit(FLOAT_MULTIPLY));
                emit_2(ADD, reg(SP), integer_lit(8));
            }
            break;
    }

    return(result_tp);
}
```

```
/*-----------------------------------------------------------*/
/* arctan_cos_exp_ln_sin_sqrt  Process a call to arctan, cos, */
/*                             exp, ln, sin, or sqrt.          */
/*                             integer parm => real result     */
/*                             real_parm   => real result      */
/*-----------------------------------------------------------*/

    TYPE_STRUCT_PTR
arctan_cos_exp_ln_sin_sqrt(rtn_idp)

    SYMTAB_NODE_PTR rtn_idp;             /* routine id */

{

    TYPE_STRUCT_PTR parm_tp;             /* actual parameter type */
    char           *std_func_name;      /* name of standard func */

    if (token == LPAREN) {
        get_token();
        parm_tp = base_type(expression());

        if ((parm_tp != integer_typep) && (parm_tp != real_typep))
            error(INCOMPATIBLE_TYPES);

        if_token_get_else_error(RPAREN, MISSING_RPAREN);
    }
    else error(WRONG_NUMBER_OF_PARMS);

    if (parm_tp == integer_typep) {
        emit_1(PUSH, reg(AX));
        emit_1(CALL, name_lit(FLOAT_CONVERT));
        emit_2(ADD, reg(SP), integer_lit(2));
    }

    emit_push_operand(real_typep);

    switch (rtn_idp->defn.info.routine.key) {
        case ARCTAN:    std_func_name = STD_ARCTAN;    break;
        case COS:       std_func_name = STD_COS;       break;
        case EXP:       std_func_name = STD_EXP;       break;
        case LN:        std_func_name = STD_LN;        break;
        case SIN:       std_func_name = STD_SIN;       break;
        case SQRT:      std_func_name = STD_SQRT;      break;
    }

    emit_1(CALL, name_lit(std_func_name));
    emit_2(ADD, reg(SP), integer_lit(4));

    return(real_typep);
}

/*-----------------------------------------------------------*/
/* pred_succ                   Process a call to pred or succ.  */
/*                             integer parm => integer result   */
/*                             enum parm   => enum result       */
/*-----------------------------------------------------------*/

    TYPE_STRUCT_PTR
pred_succ(rtn_idp)

    SYMTAB_NODE_PTR rtn_idp;             /* routine id */

{
    TYPE_STRUCT_PTR parm_tp;             /* actual parameter type */
    TYPE_STRUCT_PTR result_tp;           /* result type */

    if (token == LPAREN) {
        get_token();
```

```
    parm_tp = base_type(expression());

    if ((parm_tp != integer_typep) &&
        (parm_tp->form != ENUM_FORM)) {
        error(INCOMPATIBLE_TYPES);
        result_tp = integer_typep;
    }
    else result_tp = parm_tp;

    if_token_get_else_error(RPAREN, MISSING_RPAREN);
    }
    else error(WRONG_NUMBER_OF_PARMS);

    emit_1(rtn_idp->defn.info.routine.key == PRED
            ? DECREMENT : INCREMENT,
        reg(AX));

    return(result_tp);
}

/*------------------------------------------------------------*/
/* chr                      Process a call to chr.          */
/*                          integer parm => character result */
/*------------------------------------------------------------*/

    TYPE_STRUCT_PTR
chr()

{
    TYPE_STRUCT_PTR parm_tp;        /* actual parameter type */

    if (token == LPAREN) {
        get_token();
        parm_tp = base_type(expression());

        if (parm_tp != integer_typep) error(INCOMPATIBLE_TYPES);
        if_token_get_else_error(RPAREN, MISSING_RPAREN);
    }
    else error(WRONG_NUMBER_OF_PARMS);

    return(char_typep);
}

/*------------------------------------------------------------*/
/* odd                      Process a call to odd.          */
/*                          integer parm => boolean result  */
/*------------------------------------------------------------*/

    TYPE_STRUCT_PTR
odd()

{
    TYPE_STRUCT_PTR parm_tp;        /* actual parameter type */

    if (token == LPAREN) {
        get_token();
        parm_tp = base_type(expression());

        if (parm_tp != integer_typep) error(INCOMPATIBLE_TYPES);
        if_token_get_else_error(RPAREN, MISSING_RPAREN);
```

```
    }
    else error(WRONG_NUMBER_OF_PARMS);

    emit_2(AND_BITS, reg(AX), integer_lit(1));
    return(boolean_typep);
}

/*------------------------------------------------------------*/
/* ord                      Process a call to ord.          */
/*                          enumeration parm => integer result */
/*------------------------------------------------------------*/

    TYPE_STRUCT_PTR
ord()

{
    TYPE_STRUCT_PTR parm_tp;        /* actual parameter type */

    if (token == LPAREN) {
        get_token();
        parm_tp = base_type(expression());

        if (parm_tp->form != ENUM_FORM) error(INCOMPATIBLE_TYPES);
        if_token_get_else_error(RPAREN, MISSING_RPAREN);
    }
    else error(WRONG_NUMBER_OF_PARMS);

    return(integer_typep);
}

/*------------------------------------------------------------*/
/* round_trunc              Process a call to round or trunc. */
/*                          real parm => integer result     */
/*------------------------------------------------------------*/

    TYPE_STRUCT_PTR
round_trunc(rtn_idp)

    SYMTAB_NODE_PTR rtn_idp;        /* routine id */

{
    TYPE_STRUCT_PTR parm_tp;        /* actual parameter type */

    if (token == LPAREN) {
        get_token();
        parm_tp = base_type(expression());

        if (parm_tp != real_typep) error(INCOMPATIBLE_TYPES);
        if_token_get_else_error(RPAREN, MISSING_RPAREN);
    }
    else error(WRONG_NUMBER_OF_PARMS);

    emit_push_operand(parm_tp);
    emit_1(CALL, name_lit(rtn_idp->defn.info.routine.key == ROUND
                            ? STD_ROUND : STD_TRUNC));
    emit_2(ADD, reg(SP), integer_lit(4));

    return(integer_typep);
}
```

Function read_readln calls function variable, which emits code that leaves the address of the actual parameter of read or readln on top of the stack. Then, depending on the type of the parameter, we emit a call to the library function read_integer, read_real, or read_char. These routines leave the value that was read in register AX, in register pair DX:AX, or in register AL, respectively. We emit code to pop the address of the actual parameter into register BX and then move the value that was read indirectly into the parameter. Finally, if we saw readln, we emit a call to the library function read_line.

Function eof_eoln emits a call either to the library function std_end_of_file or to the library function std_end_of_line.

Each of the remaining library functions for the standard Pascal functions first calls function expression to emit code to evaluate the actual parameter expression. Some of them then emit more instructions to operate on the expression value in register AX or register pair DX:AX.

In function abs_sqr, if the actual parameter for abs is integer, we create a label with index nonnegative_labelx for the nonnegative case and emit the inline code:

```
        cmp   ax,0                          ; is it negative?
        jge   $L_nonnegative_labelx         ; no
        neg   ax                            ; yes, so negate
$L_nonnegative_labelx:
```

Otherwise, if the parameter is real, we emit:

```
        push dx
        push ax
        call _std_abs
        add  sp,4
```

If the actual parameter for sqr is integer, we emit inline code to multiply the parameter value by itself:

```
        mov   dx,ax
        imul  dx                            ; AX := AX * AX
```

If the actual parameter is real, we emit:

```
        push dx
        push ax                             ; factor on stack
        push dx
        push ax                             ; factor again on stack
        call _float_multiply
        add  sp,8                           ; DX:AX := factor * factor
```

In function arctan_cos_exp_ln_sin_sqrt, if the parameter is integer, we emit code to convert the value to real:

```
    push ax
    call _float_convert
    add  sp,2
```

Then we emit code to call the appropriate library function:

```
    push dx
    push ax
    call routine
    add  sp,4
```

where *routine* is either _std_arctan, _std_cos, _std_exp, _std_ln, _std_sin, or _std_sqrt.

Function pred_succ emits either an inc or a dec instruction to increment or decrement the expression value in register AX by 1, depending on whether we saw succ or pred.

Functions chr and ord do not emit any more code beyond what expression emits, since the Pascal functions chr and ord do not change the expression value.

Function odd simply emits:

```
    and ax,1
```

When executed, this instruction leaves either a 1 (true) or 0 (false) in register AX, depending on whether the expression value was odd or even.

Finally, function round_trunc emits:

```
    push dx
    push ax
    call routine
    add  sp,4
```

where *routine* is either _std_round or _std_trunc, depending on whether the Pascal function was round or trunc.

14.4 Program 14-1: Pascal Compiler II

Figure 14-13 shows the main file of this chapter's program, a Pascal compiler. Figure 14-14 shows a sample Pascal program, and Figure 14-15 shows the assembly language code emitted by the compiler.

FIGURE 14-13   File compile2.c.

```
/****************************************************************/
/*                                                            */
/*      Program 14-1:  Pascal Compiler II                     */
/*                                                            */
/*      Compile Pascal programs.                              */
/*                                                            */
/*      FILE:       compile2.c                                */
/*                                                            */
/*      REQUIRES:   Modules parser, symbol table, scanner,    */
/*                      code, error                           */
/*                                                            */
/*      USAGE:      compile2 sourcefile objectfile            */
/*                                                            */
/*          sourcefile    [input] source file containing the  */
/*                                the statements to compile   */
/*                                                            */
/*          objectfile    [output] object file to contain the */
/*                                generated assembly code     */
/*                                                            */
/****************************************************************/

#include <stdio.h>

/*------------------------------------------------------------*/
/* Globals                                                    */
/*------------------------------------------------------------*/

FILE *code_file;    /* ASCII file for the emitted assembly code */
```

```
/*----------------------------------------------------------*/
/*   main              Initialize the scanner and call      */
/*                     routine program.                      */
/*----------------------------------------------------------*/

main(argc, argv)

    int  argc;
    char *argv[];

{
    /*
    -- Open the code file.  If no code file name was given,
    -- use the standard output file.
    */
    code_file = (argc == 3) ? fopen(argv[2], "w")
                            : stdout;

    /*
    -- Initialize the scanner.
    */
    init_scanner(argv[1]);

    /*
    -- Process a program.
    */
    get_token();
    program();
}
```

FIGURE 14-14   A sample Pascal program to be compiled.

```
PROGRAM newton (input, output);

CONST
    epsilon = 1e-6;

VAR
    number, root, sqroot : real;

BEGIN
    REPEAT
        writeln;
        write('Enter new number (0 to quit): ');
        read(number);

        IF number = 0 THEN BEGIN
            writeln(number:12:6, 0.0:12:6);
        END
```

```
        ELSE IF number < 0 THEN BEGIN
            writeln('*** ERROR:  number < 0');
        END
        ELSE BEGIN
            sqroot := sqrt(number);
            writeln(number:12:6, sqroot:12:6);
            writeln;

            root := 1;
            REPEAT
                root := (number/root + root)/2;
                writeln(root:24:6,
                        100*abs(root - sqroot)/sqroot:12:2,
                        '%')
            UNTIL abs(number/sqr(root) - 1) < epsilon;
        END
    UNTIL number = 0
END.
```

FIGURE 14-15   Assembly language object file generated by the compiler for the sample program in Figure 14-14.

```
;    1: PROGRAM newton (input, output);
     DOSSEG
     .MODEL  small
     .STACK  1024

     .CODE

     PUBLIC  _pascal_main
     INCLUDE pasextrn.inc

$STATIC_LINK        EQU    <WORD PTR [bp+4]>
$RETURN_VALUE       EQU    <WORD PTR [bp-4]>
$HIGH_RETURN_VALUE  EQU    <WORD PTR [bp-2]>

;    2:
;    3: CONST
;    4:    epsilon = 1e-6;
;    5:
;    6: VAR
;    7:    number, root, sqroot : real;
;    8:
;    9: BEGIN

_pascal_main    PROC

     push    bp
     mov     bp,sp
;   10:    REPEAT
$L_005:
;   11:        writeln;
     call    _write_line
;   12:        write('Enter new number (0 to quit): ');
     lea     ax,WORD PTR $S_007
     push    ax
     mov     ax,0
     push    ax
     mov     ax,30
     push    ax
     call    _write_string
     add     sp,6
;   13:        read(number);
     lea     ax,WORD PTR number_002
     push    ax
     call    _read_real
     pop     bx
     mov     WORD PTR [bx],ax
     mov     WORD PTR [bx+2],dx
;   14:
;   15:        IF number = 0 THEN BEGIN
     mov     ax,WORD PTR number_002
     mov     dx,WORD PTR number_002+2
     push    dx
     push    ax
     mov     ax,0
     push    ax
     call    _float_convert
     add     sp,2
     push    dx
     push    ax
     call    _float_compare
     add     sp,8
     cmp     ax,0
     mov     ax,1
```

```
     je      $L_010
     sub     ax,ax
$L_010:
     cmp     ax,1
     je      $L_008
     jmp     $L_009
$L_008:
;   16:            writeln(number:12:6, 0.0:12:6);
     mov     ax,WORD PTR number_002
     mov     dx,WORD PTR number_002+2
     push    dx
     push    ax
     mov     ax,12
     push    ax
     mov     ax,6
     push    ax
     call    _write_real
     add     sp,8
     mov     ax,WORD PTR $F_011
     mov     dx,WORD PTR $F_011+2
     push    dx
     push    ax
     mov     ax,12
     push    ax
     mov     ax,6
     push    ax
     call    _write_real
     add     sp,8
     call    _write_line
;   17:        END
;   18:        ELSE IF number < 0 THEN BEGIN
     jmp     $L_012
$L_009:
     mov     ax,WORD PTR number_002
     mov     dx,WORD PTR number_002+2
     push    dx
     push    ax
     mov     ax,0
     push    ax
     call    _float_convert
     add     sp,2
     push    dx
     push    ax
     call    _float_compare
     add     sp,8
     cmp     ax,0
     mov     ax,1
     jl      $L_015
     sub     ax,ax
$L_015:
     cmp     ax,1
     je      $L_013
     jmp     $L_014
$L_013:
;   19:            writeln('*** ERROR: number < 0');
     lea     ax,WORD PTR $S_016
     push    ax
     mov     ax,0
     push    ax
     mov     ax,22
     push    ax
     call    _write_string
```

```
        add     sp,6
        call    _write_line
;  20:          END
;  21:          ELSE BEGIN
        jmp     $L_017
$L_014:
;  22:              sqroot := sqrt(number);
        mov     ax,WORD PTR number_002
        mov     dx,WORD PTR number_002+2
        push    dx
        push    ax
        call    _std_sqrt
        add     sp,4
        mov     WORD PTR sqroot_004,ax
        mov     WORD PTR sqroot_004+2,dx
;  23:              writeln(number:12:6, sqroot:12:6);
        mov     ax,WORD PTR number_002
        mov     dx,WORD PTR number_002+2
        push    dx
        push    ax
        mov     ax,12
        push    ax
        mov     ax,6
        push    ax
        call    _write_real
        add     sp,8
        mov     ax,WORD PTR sqroot_004
        mov     dx,WORD PTR sqroot_004+2
        push    dx
        push    ax
        mov     ax,12
        push    ax
        mov     ax,6
        push    ax
        call    _write_real
        add     sp,8
        call    _write_line
;  24:          writeln;
        call    _write_line
;  25:
;  26:              root := 1;
        mov     ax,1
        push    ax
        call    _float_convert
        add     sp,2
        mov     WORD PTR root_003,ax
        mov     WORD PTR root_003+2,dx
;  27:          REPEAT
$L_018:
;  28:                  root := (number/root + root)/2;
        mov     ax,WORD PTR number_002
        mov     dx,WORD PTR number_002+2
        push    dx
        push    ax
        mov     ax,WORD PTR root_003
        mov     dx,WORD PTR root_003+2
        push    dx
        push    ax
        call    _float_divide
        add     sp,8
        push    dx
        push    ax
        mov     ax,WORD PTR root_003
        mov     dx,WORD PTR root_003+2
        push    dx
        push    ax
        call    _float_add
```

```
        add     sp,8
        push    dx
        push    ax
        mov     ax,2
        push    ax
        call    _float_convert
        add     sp,2
        push    dx
        push    ax
        call    _float_divide
        add     sp,8
        mov     WORD PTR root_003,ax
        mov     WORD PTR root_003+2,dx
;  29:              writeln(root:24:6,
        mov     ax,WORD PTR root_003
        mov     dx,WORD PTR root_003+2
        push    dx
        push    ax
        mov     ax,24
        push    ax
        mov     ax,6
        push    ax
        call    _write_real
        add     sp,8
;  30:                      100*abs(root - sqroot)/sqroot:12:2,
        mov     ax,100
        push    ax
        mov     ax,WORD PTR root_003
        mov     dx,WORD PTR root_003+2
        push    dx
        push    ax
        mov     ax,WORD PTR sqroot_004
        mov     dx,WORD PTR sqroot_004+2
        push    dx
        push    ax
        call    _float_subtract
        add     sp,8
        push    dx
        push    ax
        call    _std_abs
        add     sp,4
        push    dx
        push    ax
        pop     ax
        pop     dx
        pop     bx
        push    dx
        push    ax
        push    bx
        call    _float_convert
        add     sp,2
        pop     bx
        pop     cx
        push    dx
        push    ax
        push    cx
        push    bx
        call    _float_multiply
        add     sp,8
        push    dx
        push    ax
        mov     ax,WORD PTR sqroot_004
        mov     dx,WORD PTR sqroot_004+2
        push    dx
        push    ax
        call    _float_divide
        add     sp,8
```

```
            push    dx                                              add     sp,8
            push    ax                                              cmp     ax,0
            mov     ax,12                                           mov     ax,1
            push    ax                                              jl      $L_021
            mov     ax,2                                            sub     ax,ax
            push    ax                                      $L_021:
            call    _write_real                                     cmp     ax,1
            add     sp,8                                            je      $L_019
;   31:                              '%')                           jmp     $L_018
            mov     ax,'%'                                  $L_019:
            push    ax                                      ;   33:         END
            mov     ax,0                                    ;   34:     UNTIL number = 0
            push    ax                                      $L_017:
            call    _write_char                             $L_012:
            add     sp,4                                            mov     ax,WORD PTR number_002
;   32:              UNTIL abs(number/sqr(root) - 1) < epsilon;     mov     dx,WORD PTR number_002+2
            call    _write_line                                     push    dx
            mov     ax,WORD PTR number_002                          push    ax
            mov     dx,WORD PTR number_002+2                        mov     ax,0
            push    dx                                      ;   35: END.
            push    ax                                              push    ax
            mov     ax,WORD PTR root_003                            call    _float_convert
            mov     dx,WORD PTR root_003+2                          add     sp,2
            push    dx                                              push    dx
            push    ax                                              push    ax
            push    dx                                              call    _float_compare
            push    ax                                              add     sp,8
            call    _float_multiply                                 cmp     ax,0
            add     sp,8                                            mov     ax,1
            push    dx                                              je      $L_022
            push    ax                                              sub     ax,ax
            call    _float_divide                           $L_022:
            add     sp,8                                            cmp     ax,1
            push    dx                                              je      $L_006
            push    ax                                              jmp     $L_005
            mov     ax,1                                    $L_006:
            push    ax
            call    _float_convert                                  pop     bp
            add     sp,2                                            ret
            push    dx
            push    ax                                      _pascal_main    ENDP
            call    _float_subtract
            add     sp,8                                            .DATA
            push    dx
            push    ax                                      number_002  DD      0.0
            call    _std_abs                                root_003    DD      0.0
            add     sp,4                                    sqroot_004  DD      0.0
            push    dx                                      $F_020  DD  1.000000e-006
            push    ax                                      $F_011  DD  0.000000e+000
            mov     ax,WORD PTR $F_020                      $S_016  DB  "*** ERROR:  number < 0"
            mov     dx,WORD PTR $F_020+2                    $S_007  DB  "Enter new number (0 to quit): "
            push    dx
            push    ax                                              END
            call    _float_compare
```

And so, we have reached the second major milestone of this book—a complete,
working Pascal compiler. In the next and final chapter of this book, we will briefly
look at some advanced topics.

Questions and exercises

1. The code generated for the FOR statement re-evaluates the final expression each time before executing the loop statement. According to the Pascal semantics, both the initial and final expressions should be evaluated only once each time the FOR statement is executed. Modify the generated code accordingly.

2. The interpreter caught the runtime error of the value of a CASE expression not being one of the CASE labels. Modify the generated CASE statement code to make this check.

3. Modify the runtime library code to check for errors such as an attempt to divide by zero.

4. The code to evaluate the boolean expression of a REPEAT, a WHILE, or an IF statement goes through the step of leaving a 0 (false) or a 1 (true) in register AX. Modify the generated code to eliminate this step whenever possible.

CHAPTER 15

Advanced Concepts: An Overview

In this book, we have written a working interpreter, an interactive debugger, and a compiler. These are major accomplishments, and yet, we have examined only the basic concepts of writing compilers and interpreters. This chapter contains a brief overview of some of the advanced concepts that you will encounter if you plan to study and do more work in this field.

15.1 BNF

In this book, we used graphical syntax diagrams to represent the grammar of the source language. A common textual notation is the Backus-Naur Form, or BNF. As an example, we will use this notation to describe the syntax of Pascal expressions.

BNF is a *metalanguage*, a language used to describe another language. Each statement of the metalanguage is called a *production rule*. Compare the following two rules to the first syntax diagram in Figure 4-7:

```
<expression> ::=  <simple expression>
                  | <simple expression> <rel op>
                      <simple expression>

<rel op> ::=  = | < | <= | <> | >= | >
```

The first rule states that an expression is either a single simple expression or two simple expressions separated by a relational operator. The second rules states that a relational operator is one of the six tokens that are listed.

The symbols ::= and | are *metasymbols*. They belong to the BNF metalanguage and not to the Pascal source language. (When the same symbol belongs to both languages, a different font or face can be used to distinguish one use from another.) The metasymbol ::= separates the left-hand side of a rule (a nonterminal symbol) from its right-hand side (the definition). The metasymbol | separates alternate forms in a definition.

In BNF, *nonterminal symbols* are enclosed by the angle brackets < and >. These are symbols that are defined by other rules. *Terminal symbols* are tokens such as >= and IF. In the syntax diagrams, rectangular boxes represent the nonterminal symbols, and rounded boxes represent the terminal symbols. A simple expression is defined by the rules:

```
<simple expression> ::= <term> | <sign> <term>
                      | <simple expression> <add op> <term>

<sign>    ::= - | +

<add op> ::= - | + | OR
```

These rules state that a simple expression is one or more terms separated by adding operators. The first term is optionally preceded by a sign. A sign is either - or +, and an adding operator is either -, +, or the reserved word OR. Notice how BNF uses recursion to specify repetition, in this case multiple terms separated by adding operators. We can now give the rules for a term, a factor, and a (simple) variable:

```
<term>    ::= <factor> | <term> <mult op> <factor>

<mult op> ::= * | / | DIV | MOD | AND

<factor>  ::= <variable> | <unsigned constant>
            | <function call> | NOT <factor>
            | ( <expression> )

<variable> ::= <identifier>
```

We'll see one of the advantages of using a textual notation like BNF later when we discuss *compiler compilers*.

15.2 Top-down vs. bottom-up parsing

The parser we wrote in this book uses a top-down parsing method known as *recursive descent*. With this method, the parser starts at the topmost nonterminal symbol of the grammar. In our BNF example, that would be <expression>. The parser then proceeds to work its way down to the terminal symbols, such as <expression> to <simple expression> to <term> to <factor> to NOT.

Another way to understand this is to look at the *parse tree* for an expression, as shown in Figure 15-1. The parser starts at the top of the tree and, in effect, constructs the tree downwards to the terminal symbols at the leaves.

You know that a recursive descent parser is implemented by writing a routine to recognize each nonterminal symbol, as defined by the production rule (or syntax diagram) for the symbol. Each routine can contain (possibly recursive) calls to routines to recognize any nonterminal symbols in the definition. You write semantic actions in these routines.

The advantages of a recursive descent parser are that it is easy to write, and once written, it is easy to read and understand. The main disadvantage is that it tends to be large and slow. If the grammar contains many nonterminal symbols, the parser contains many routines. Routine calls and returns can be relatively slow operations.

Another type of parser uses a bottom-up parsing method and is called a *shift-reduce* parser. This parser starts with the terminal symbols and works its way up to the topmost nonterminal symbol. In effect, it starts with the terminal symbols at the bottom of the parse tree and constructs the tree upwards to the topmost nonterminal symbol.

A shift-reduce parser works with a parse stack. The parse stack starts out empty, and during the parse, it contains nonterminal and terminal symbols that

FIGURE 15-1   The parse tree for the expression a + b/c.

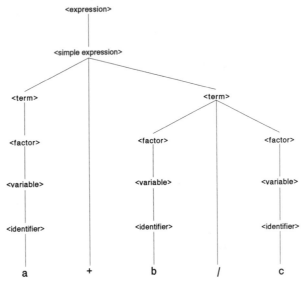

have already been parsed. Each time a token (terminal symbol) is obtained by the scanner, the parser shifts (pushes) the token onto the parse stack. At various times, based on the symbols on top of the stack and the next input token, the parser determines that the symbols on the top of the stack match the right-hand side of a production rule. The matching symbols are then popped off and reduced (replaced) by the nonterminal symbol at the left-hand side of the matching rule. As soon as the stack is reduced to the topmost nonterminal symbol, the parser accepts the input as being syntactically correct.

For example, here is how a shift-reduce parser recognizes the Pascal expression a + b/c. The stack is written horizontally with its bottom at the left, represented by the marker |, and its top at the right. We also show the remaining input at each step with the leftmost token being the next one to be read by the scanner.

꙳ Stack	Input	Action
꙳	a + b/c	shift
꙳ a	+ b/c	reduce
꙳ <identifier>	+ b/c	reduce
꙳ <variable>	+ b/c	reduce
꙳ <factor>	+ b/c	reduce
꙳ <term>	+ b/c	shift
꙳ <term> +	b/c	shift
꙳ <term> + b	/c	reduce
꙳ <term> + <identifier>	/c	reduce
꙳ <term> + <variable>	/c	reduce
꙳ <term> + <factor>	/c	shift
꙳ <term> + <factor> /	c	shift
꙳ <term> + <factor> / c		reduce
꙳ <term> + <factor> / <identifier>		reduce
꙳ <term> + <factor> / <variable>		reduce
꙳ <term> + <factor> / <factor>		reduce
꙳ <term> + <term>		reduce
꙳ <simple expression>		reduce
꙳ <expression>		

A shift-reduce parser uses a parse table which is derived from the grammar. This table determines whether the next action is to shift, reduce, accept, or signal a syntax error. Any semantic actions can also be encoded into this table.

15.3 Compiler compilers

One of the advantages of using a textual metalanguage is that we can feed the description of the syntax of a source language into a *compiler compiler*. A compiler

compiler reads and compiles a syntax description and then generates all or part of a compiler for the source language.

A well-known compiler compiler is Yacc (Yet another compiler-compiler). It reads a syntax description written in a language similar to BNF and generates a shift-reduce parser for the source language. For example, if we described all of Pascal's syntax and fed that into Yacc, it would generate a parser for Pascal. This parser is in the form of a C program. To perform any semantic actions during parsing, we write sequences of C code to perform these operations, and embed these code sequences in the syntax description. When Yacc generates the parser, it includes these code sequences.

For example, suppose we want to write an interpreter for a very simple language consisting of a single expression that has only the add and subtract operators. The following syntax description, along with the embedded semantic code, can be fed into Yacc:

```
%token NUMBER
%left  '+' '-'


expression : expression '+' expression  { $$ = $1 + $3; }
           | expression '-' expression  { $$ = $1 - $3; }
           | '(' expression ')'         { $$ = $2; }
           | NUMBER                      { $$ = $1; }
           ;
```

This description states that NUMBER is a token returned by the scanner, and that the operators + and - are left-associative. In the definition of expression, expression is a nonterminal symbol, and +, -, (,), and NUMBER are terminal symbols. Note that the metasymbol : is used instead of the ::= metasymbol of BNF and that a semicolon terminates each production rule.

Each alternate form in the right-hand side of a rule can have semantic actions attached to it. The C code to perform the semantic actions are enclosed in the { and } braces. Within this code, $$ represents the value of the production rule, and $n represents the value of the nth element of the form. For example, the first semantic action says that the value of parsing and executing an expression plus another expression is the value of the first expression plus the value of the second expression (which is the third element of the form). The fourth semantic action says that whenever the scanner fetches a NUMBER token, the scanner must also specify the token's value (by setting the special variable yylval which is supplied by Yacc).

When Yacc compiles this description, it produces a C routine named yyparse to parse and evaluate an expression. This parser includes the parse stack, a value stack, the parse table, and the semantic code. Within the semantic code, the $$ and $n are replaced by references to the value stack to obtain the appropriate values. The parser calls the scanner, which must be named yylex, whenever it needs the next input token. When it detects a syntax error, the parser calls an error routine named yyerror.

To complete the compiler we must write a C main program that calls yyparse. We must also write the scanner yylex and the error routine yyerror.

A companion to Yacc is Lex, which generates a lexical analyser (a scanner) named yylex. Thus, Yacc and Lex are designed to work together. Lex reads a textual description of the tokens of the source language in order to generate the scanner.

15.4 Intermediate forms for compilers

Our interpreter used an intermediate form to represent the source program, and it executed the program in this form. The intermediate form had a simple linear structure that was interspersed with address markers that pointed off to other parts of the form. Our compiler did not use an intermediate form at all.

There are, however, advantages for a compiler to translate the source program first to an intermediate form. A well-designed intermediate form gives the compiler an opportunity to analyze the program in order to generate better code. When an entire routine (or a substantial portion of a routine) of the source program is available in memory in its intermediate form, the compiler can look at each expression and statement within a greater context. By first examining several parts of an expression or statement, the compiler can generate more optimal code. (We will see examples of this later).

Figure 15-2 shows a tree-structured intermediate form for several Pascal statements. This form can also be used by an interpreter for execution.

15.5 Code optimization

As great a challenge it is for a compiler to generate *correct* code, that is often not enough. You may also want the compiler to generate *optimal* code. Code can be optimal in terms of time (execute as quickly as possible), space (be as small as possible), or both.

A one-pass compiler, such as the one we have written, is not always able to generate optimal code. This is because the parser sees so little of the program at one time, only one or two tokens. For example, for the Pascal assignment statement:

```
count := count + 1
```

our compiler generates code similar to:

```
mov  ax,WORD PTR count
push ax
```

FIGURE 15-2   Tree-structured intermediate forms.

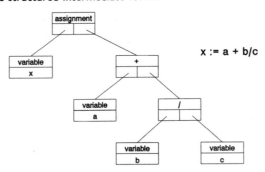

x := a + b/c

REPEAT
  a := a*3.14
UNTIL a > 6.28e23

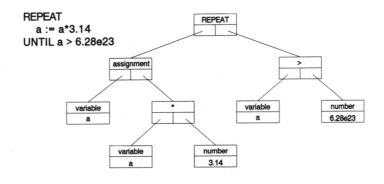

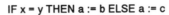
IF x = y THEN a := b ELSE a := c

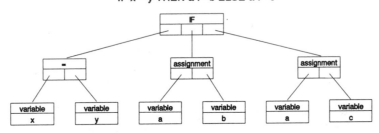

```
mov   ax,1
pop   dx
add   ax,dx
mov   WORD PTR count,ax
```

This is generic code for an addition that the compiler generates for any addition.

However, if the compiler first translated the statement into an intermediate form and then analyzed the entire statement, it would be able to detect that the constant value 1 is added to the variable count, and that the sum is assigned to the same variable. Such a compiler would then be able to generate much more optimal code:

```
inc count
```

This is an example of a local optimization that results from analyzing a small portion of the intermediate form, such as an expression or a statement.

Global optimization requires analysis of larger portions of the intermediate form. Examples of global optimizations include:

- *Dead code elimination.* The compiler simply does not generate code for source statements that can never be reached during execution.
- *In-line calls.* Sometimes when a procedure or a function is short, the expense of a call and a return can be eliminated if the code for the routine itself is inserted in the place of the call.
- *Common subexpressions.* The same subexpression may appear several times in an expression, for example:

```
z := a*(p - q) + b*(p - q) + c*(p - q)
```

To optimize this expression, the compiler can compile the assignment statement as though it were the following two statements:

```
x := p - q;
z := a*x + b*x + c*x
```

It might even be able to compile the second assignment statement as follows:

```
z := x*(a + b + c)
```

to save the cost of two multiplies.

- *Loop-invariant expressions.* An expression in a loop may evaluate to the same value each time through the loop. The compiler can recognize this and move the invariant expression outside of the loop. For example, if the value of limit in the following WHILE loop is not changed within the loop:

```
WHILE i < limit - 1 DO ...
```

the statement can be compiled as though it were written:

```
x := limit - 1;
WHILE i < x DO ...
```

- *Register allocation.* Unlike the 8086 architecture, some machine architectures offer a number of general-purpose registers that can all participate equally in expression evaluation. For faster execution, the compiler generates code that leaves values in the registers as long as possible to save on moves to and from memory. Of course, the compiler must then keep track of which values are in which registers during runtime.

Although optimization is generally desirable, no compiler must ever change the semantics of a program. Rather than risk computing an answer incorrectly (albeit more quickly), most compilers are conservative when it comes to elaborate optimization techniques.

15.6 Common front ends and back ends

Although high-level languages may differ greatly in syntax, they are often alike in semantics. For example, C and Pascal have FOR statements, and FORTRAN has the DO statement. At runtime, these statements behave very similarly.

One of the most efficient ways to write compilers for different languages is to have the compilers share as much as possible. If we design an intermediate form that can represent source programs written in C, Pascal, and FORTRAN, then we only need to write a single compiler "back end" consisting of the optimization and code generation modules. Each language would have its own compiler "front end" consisting of a scanner and a parser. Each front end scans and parses source programs written in the corresponding high-level language and translates the programs to the common intermediate form. Then the common back end takes over to generate the target code.

This scheme also works if we need to write compilers for one source language but for several machine architectures. In this case, we have a single front end but a different back end for each architecture.

15.7 Where to go from here

You may have noticed that we wrote our interpreter and compiler in a very modular fashion. That means that you can substitute routines that work differently but perform the same tasks. For example, you may want to replace the scanner with a faster one, or the parser with one that works bottom-up. The concepts in this chapter might give you some ideas of what you can do to improve what we have written. You should be able to study and understand a more advanced textbook on compiler writing and learn some of the theory behind these concepts.

Of course, you can write a compiler for some high-level language other than Pascal, or improve an existing compiler. A more ambitious project is to invent a new language and then write a compiler or an interpreter (or both) for it.

Whatever it is you want to do from here, go for it!

APPENDIX A

This appendix contains listings of all the source files of the Pascal interpreter with the interactive debugger, as written in Chapter 11.

FIGURE A-1   parser.h

```
/***********************************************************/        /********************************/
/*                                                         */        /*-----------------------------------------------------------*/
/*      P A R S I N G   R O U T I N E S   (Header)         */        /*  if_token_get              If token equals token_code, get */
/*                                                         */        /*                            the next token.                 */
/*      FILE:      parser.h                                */        /*-----------------------------------------------------------*/
/*                                                         */
/*      MODULE:    parser                                  */        #define if_token_get(token_code)                      \
/*                                                         */            if (token == token_code) get_token()
/***********************************************************/
                                                                     /*-----------------------------------------------------------*/
#ifndef parser_h                                                     /*  if_token_get_else_error    If token equals token_code, get */
#define parser_h                                                     /*                             the next token, else error.    */
                                                                     /*-----------------------------------------------------------*/
#include "common.h"
#include "symtab.h"                                                  #define if_token_get_else_error(token_code, error_code) \
                                                                         if (token == token_code) get_token();          \
/*-----------------------------------------------------------*/          else                   error(error_code)
/*  Uses of a variable                                       */
/*-----------------------------------------------------------*/      /*-----------------------------------------------------------*/
                                                                     /*  Analysis routine calls    Unless the following statements */
typedef enum {                                                       /*                            are preceded by                 */
    EXPR_USE, TARGET_USE, VARPARM_USE,                               /*                                                            */
} USE;                                                               /*                                     #define analyze          */
                                                                     /*                                                            */
/*-----------------------------------------------------------*/      /*                            calls to the analysis routines  */
/*  Functions                                                */      /*                            are not compiled.               */
/*-----------------------------------------------------------*/      /*-----------------------------------------------------------*/

TYPE_STRUCT_PTR expression();                                        #ifndef analyze
TYPE_STRUCT_PTR variable();                                          #define analyze_const_defn(idp)
TYPE_STRUCT_PTR routine_call();                                      #define analyze_var_decl(idp)
TYPE_STRUCT_PTR base_type();                                         #define analyze_type_defn(idp)
BOOLEAN         is_assign_type_compatible();                         #define analyze_routine_header(idp)
                                                                     #define analyze_block(idp)
            /********************************/                       #endif
            /*                              */
            /*      Macros for parsing      */                       #endif
            /*                              */
```

FIGURE A-2   routine.c

```
/***********************************************************/        #include "parser.h"
/*                                                         */        #include "exec.h"
/*      R O U T I N E   P A R S E R                        */
/*                                                         */        /*-----------------------------------------------------------*/
/*      Parsing routines for programs and declared         */        /*  Externals                                                */
/*      procedures and functions.                          */        /*-----------------------------------------------------------*/
/*                                                         */
/*      FILE:      routine.c                               */        extern int           line_number;
/*                                                         */        extern int           error_count;
/*      MODULE:    parser                                  */        extern long          exec_stmt_count;
/*                                                         */
/***********************************************************/        extern TOKEN_CODE    token;
                                                                     extern char          word_string[];
#include <stdio.h>                                                   extern SYMTAB_NODE_PTR symtab_display[];
#include "common.h"                                                  extern int           level;
#include "error.h"
#include "scanner.h"                                                 extern TYPE_STRUCT   dummy_type;
#include "symtab.h"
```

```
extern char             *code_buffer;
extern char             *code_bufferp;
extern STACK_ITEM       *stack;
extern STACK_ITEM_PTR   tos;
extern STACK_ITEM_PTR   stack_frame_basep;

extern TOKEN_CODE       statement_start_list[],
                        statement_end_list[],
                        declaration_start_list[];

/*-------------------------------------------------------*/
/* Globals                                               */
/*-------------------------------------------------------*/

char buffer[MAX_PRINT_LINE_LENGTH];

/*-------------------------------------------------------*/
/* Forwards                                              */
/*-------------------------------------------------------*/

SYMTAB_NODE_PTR formal_parm_list();
SYMTAB_NODE_PTR program_header(), procedure_header(),
                function_header();
char            *create_code_segment();

/*-------------------------------------------------------*/
/* program       Process a program:                      */
/*                                                       */
/*                 <program-header> ; <block> .          */
/*-------------------------------------------------------*/

TOKEN_CODE follow_header_list[] = {SEMICOLON, END_OF_FILE, 0};

program()

{
    SYMTAB_NODE_PTR program_idp;        /* program id */

    /*
    --              PARSE THE PROGRAM
    --
    --
    -- Intialize the symbol table and then allocate
    -- the code buffer.
    */
    init_symtab();
    code_buffer  = alloc_bytes(MAX_CODE_BUFFER_SIZE);
    code_bufferp = code_buffer;

    /*
    -- Begin parsing with the program header.
    */
    program_idp = program_header();

    /*
    -- Error synchronization:  Should be ;
    */
    synchronize(follow_header_list,
                declaration_start_list, statement_start_list);
    if_token_get(SEMICOLON);
    else if (token_in(declaration_start_list) ||
             token_in(statement_start_list))
        error(MISSING_SEMICOLON);

    analyze_routine_header(program_idp);

    /*
```

```
    -- Parse the program's block.
    */
    program_idp->defn.info.routine.locals = NULL;
    block(program_idp);

    program_idp->defn.info.routine.local_symtab = exit_scope();
    program_idp->defn.info.routine.code_segment = create_code_segment();
    analyze_block(program_idp->defn.info.routine.code_segment);

    if_token_get_else_error(PERIOD, MISSING_PERIOD);

    /*
    -- Look for the end of file.
    */
    while (token != END_OF_FILE) {
        error(UNEXPECTED_TOKEN);
        get_token();
    }

    quit_scanner();
    free(code_buffer);

    /*
    -- Print the parser's summary.
    */
    print_line("\n");
    print_line("\n");
    sprintf(buffer, "%20d Source lines.\n", line_number);
    print_line(buffer);
    sprintf(buffer, "%20d Source errors.\n", error_count);
    print_line(buffer);

    if (error_count > 0) exit(-SYNTAX_ERROR);
    else                 printf("%c\n", FORM_FEED_CHAR);

    /*
    --
    --              EXECUTE THE PROGRAM
    --
    --
    -- Allocate the runtime stack.
    */
    stack = alloc_array(STACK_ITEM, MAX_STACK_SIZE);
    stack_frame_basep = tos = stack;

    /*
    -- Initialize the program's stack frame.
    */
    level = 1;
    stack_frame_basep = tos + 1;
    push_integer(0);        /* function return value */
    push_address(NULL);     /* static link */
    push_address(NULL);     /* dynamic link */
    push_address(NULL);     /* return address */

    /*
    -- Initialize the debugger.
    */
    init_debugger();

    /*
    -- Go!
    */
    execute(program_idp);

    free(stack);
    printf("\n\nSuccessful completion.  %ld statements executed.\n\n",
           exec_stmt_count);
```

```
    exit(0);
}

/*------------------------------------------------------*/
/*  program_header      Process a program header:        */
/*                                                        */
/*                      PROGRAM <id> ( <id-list> )        */
/*                                                        */
/*                      Return a pointer to the program id */
/*                      node.                             */
/*------------------------------------------------------*/

TOKEN_CODE follow_prog_id_list[] = {LPAREN, SEMICOLON,
                                    END_OF_FILE, 0};

TOKEN_CODE follow_parms_list[]   = {RPAREN, SEMICOLON,
                                    END_OF_FILE, 0};

    SYMTAB_NODE_PTR
program_header()

{
    SYMTAB_NODE_PTR program_idp;        /* program id */
    SYMTAB_NODE_PTR parm_idp;           /* parm id */
    SYMTAB_NODE_PTR prev_parm_idp = NULL;

    if_token_get_else_error(PROGRAM, MISSING_PROGRAM);

    if (token == IDENTIFIER) {
        search_and_enter_local_symtab(program_idp);
        program_idp->defn.key = PROG_DEFN;
        program_idp->defn.info.routine.key = DECLARED;
        program_idp->defn.info.routine.parm_count = 0;
        program_idp->defn.info.routine.total_parm_size = 0;
        program_idp->defn.info.routine.total_local_size = 0;
        program_idp->typep = &dummy_type;
        program_idp->label_index = 0;
        get_token();
    }
    else error(MISSING_IDENTIFIER);

    /*
    -- Error synchronization:  Should be ( or ;
    */
    synchronize(follow_prog_id_list,
                declaration_start_list, statement_start_list);

    enter_scope(NULL);

    /*
    -- Program parameters.
    */
    if (token == LPAREN) {
        /*
        -- <id-list>
        */
        do {
            get_token();
            if (token == IDENTIFIER) {
                search_and_enter_local_symtab(parm_idp);
                parm_idp->defn.key = VARPARM_DEFN;
                parm_idp->typep = &dummy_type;
                get_token();

                /*
                -- Link program parm ids together.
                */
```

```
                if (prev_parm_idp == NULL)
                    program_idp->defn.info.routine.parms =
                                    prev_parm_idp = parm_idp;
                else {
                    prev_parm_idp->next = parm_idp;
                    prev_parm_idp = parm_idp;
                }
            }
            else error(MISSING_IDENTIFIER);
        } while (token == COMMA);

        /*
        -- Error synchronization:  Should be )
        */
        synchronize(follow_parms_list,
                    declaration_start_list, statement_start_list);
        if_token_get_else_error(RPAREN, MISSING_RPAREN);
    }
    else program_idp->defn.info.routine.parms = NULL;

    return(program_idp);
}

/*------------------------------------------------------*/
/*  routine            Call the appropriate routine to process */
/*                     a procedure or function definition: */
/*                                                        */
/*                     <routine-header> ; <block>         */
/*------------------------------------------------------*/

routine()

{
    SYMTAB_NODE_PTR rtn_idp;    /* routine id */

    rtn_idp = (token == PROCEDURE) ? procedure_header()
                                   : function_header();

    /*
    -- Error synchronization:  Should be ;
    */
    synchronize(follow_header_list,
                declaration_start_list, statement_start_list);
    if_token_get(SEMICOLON);
    else if (token_in(declaration_start_list) ||
             token_in(statement_start_list))
        error(MISSING_SEMICOLON);

    /*
    -- <block> or FORWARD.
    */
    if (strcmp(word_string, "forward") != 0) {
        rtn_idp->defn.info.routine.key = DECLARED;
        analyze_routine_header(rtn_idp);

        rtn_idp->defn.info.routine.locals = NULL;
        block(rtn_idp);

        rtn_idp->defn.info.routine.code_segment = create_code_segment();
        analyze_block(rtn_idp->defn.info.routine.code_segment);
    }
    else {
        get_token();
        rtn_idp->defn.info.routine.key = FORWARD;
        analyze_routine_header(rtn_idp);
    }

    rtn_idp->defn.info.routine.local_symtab = exit_scope();
```

```
}

/*------------------------------------------------------*/
/*  procedure_header    Process a procedure header:     */
/*                                                      */
/*                           PROCEDURE <id>             */
/*                                                      */
/*                      or:                             */
/*                                                      */
/*                           PROCEDURE <id> ( <parm-list> )  */
/*                                                      */
/*                      Return a pointer to the procedure id */
/*                      node.                           */
/*------------------------------------------------------*/

TOKEN_CODE follow_proc_id_list[] = {LPAREN, SEMICOLON,
                                    END_OF_FILE, 0};

    SYMTAB_NODE_PTR
procedure_header()

{
    SYMTAB_NODE_PTR proc_idp;          /* procedure id */
    SYMTAB_NODE_PTR parm_listp;        /* formal parm list */
    int             parm_count;
    int             total_parm_size;
    BOOLEAN         forward_flag = FALSE;  /* TRUE iff forwarded */

    get_token();

    /*
    -- If the procedure identifier has already been
    -- declared in this scope, it must be a forward.
    */
    if (token == IDENTIFIER) {
        search_local_symtab(proc_idp);
        if (proc_idp == NULL) {
            enter_local_symtab(proc_idp);
            proc_idp->defn.key = PROC_DEFN;
            proc_idp->defn.info.routine.total_local_size = 0;
            proc_idp->typep = &dummy_type;
            proc_idp->label_index = 0;
        }
        else if ((proc_idp->defn.key == PROC_DEFN) &&
                 (proc_idp->defn.info.routine.key == FORWARD))
            forward_flag = TRUE;
        else error(REDEFINED_IDENTIFIER);

        get_token();
    }
    else error(MISSING_IDENTIFIER);

    /*
    -- Error synchronization:  Should be ( or ;
    */
    synchronize(follow_proc_id_list,
                declaration_start_list, statement_start_list);

    enter_scope(NULL);

    /*
    -- Optional formal parameters.  If there was a forward,
    -- there must not be any parameters here (but parse them
    -- anyway for error recovery).
    */
    if (token == LPAREN) {
        parm_listp = formal_parm_list(&parm_count, &total_parm_size);
```

```
        if (forward_flag) error(ALREADY_FORWARDED);
        else {
            proc_idp->defn.info.routine.parm_count = parm_count;
            proc_idp->defn.info.routine.total_parm_size =
                                              total_parm_size;
            proc_idp->defn.info.routine.parms = parm_listp;
        }
    }
    else if (!forward_flag) {
        proc_idp->defn.info.routine.parm_count = 0;
        proc_idp->defn.info.routine.total_parm_size = 0;
        proc_idp->defn.info.routine.parms = NULL;
    }

    proc_idp->typep = NULL;
    return(proc_idp);
}

/*------------------------------------------------------*/
/*  function_header     Process a function header:      */
/*                                                      */
/*                    FUNCTION <id> : <type-id>         */
/*                                                      */
/*                      or:                             */
/*                                                      */
/*                    FUNCTION <id> ( <parm-list> )     */
/*                                     : <type-id>      */
/*                                                      */
/*                    Return a pointer to the function id */
/*                    node.                             */
/*------------------------------------------------------*/

TOKEN_CODE follow_func_id_list[] = {LPAREN, COLON, SEMICOLON,
                                    END_OF_FILE, 0};

    SYMTAB_NODE_PTR
function_header()

{
    SYMTAB_NODE_PTR func_idp, type_idp;    /* func and type ids */
    SYMTAB_NODE_PTR parm_listp;            /* formal parm list */
    int             parm_count;
    int             total_parm_size;
    BOOLEAN         forward_flag = FALSE;  /* TRUE iff forwarded */

    get_token();

    /*
    -- If the function identifier has already been
    -- declared in this scope, it must be a forward.
    */
    if (token == IDENTIFIER) {
        search_local_symtab(func_idp);
        if (func_idp == NULL) {
            enter_local_symtab(func_idp);
            func_idp->defn.key = FUNC_DEFN;
            func_idp->defn.info.routine.total_local_size = 0;
            func_idp->typep = &dummy_type;
            func_idp->label_index = 0;
        }
        else if ((func_idp->defn.key == FUNC_DEFN) &&
                 (func_idp->defn.info.routine.key == FORWARD))
            forward_flag = TRUE;
        else error(REDEFINED_IDENTIFIER);

        get_token();
    }
```

```
        else error(MISSING_IDENTIFIER);

        /*
        -- Error synchronization:  Should be ( or : or ;
        */
        synchronize(follow_func_id_list,
                    declaration_start_list, statement_start_list);

        enter_scope(NULL);

        /*
        -- Optional formal parameters.  If there was a forward,
        -- there must not be any parameters here (but parse them
        -- anyway for error recovery).
        */
        if (token == LPAREN) {
            parm_listp = formal_parm_list(&parm_count, &total_parm_size);

            if (forward_flag) error(ALREADY_FORWARDED);
            else {
                func_idp->defn.info.routine.parm_count = parm_count;
                func_idp->defn.info.routine.total_parm_size =
                                                total_parm_size;
                func_idp->defn.info.routine.parms = parm_listp;
            }
        }
        else if (!forward_flag) {
            func_idp->defn.info.routine.parm_count = 0;
            func_idp->defn.info.routine.total_parm_size = 0;
            func_idp->defn.info.routine.parms = NULL;
        }

        /*
        -- Function type.  If there was a forward,
        -- there must not be a type here (but parse it
        -- anyway for error recovery).
        */
        if (!forward_flag || (token == COLON)) {
            if_token_get_else_error(COLON, MISSING_COLON);

            if (token == IDENTIFIER) {
                search_and_find_all_symtab(type_idp);
                if (type_idp->defn.key != TYPE_DEFN) error(INVALID_TYPE);
                if (!forward_flag) func_idp->typep = type_idp->typep;
                get_token();
            }
            else {
                error(MISSING_IDENTIFIER);
                func_idp->typep = &dummy_type;
            }

            if (forward_flag) error(ALREADY_FORWARDED);
        }

    return(func_idp);
}

/*------------------------------------------------------*/
/* formal_parm_list   Process a formal parameter list:  */
/*                                                      */
/*                        ( VAR <id-list> : <type> ;    */
/*                          <id-list> : <type> ;        */
/*                          ... )                       */
/*                                                      */
/*                      Return a pointer to the head of the */
/*                      parameter id list.              */
/*------------------------------------------------------*/
```

```
    SYMTAB_NODE_PTR
formal_parm_list(countp, total_sizep)

    int *countp;        /* ptr to count of parameters */
    int *total_sizep;   /* ptr to total byte size of parameters */

{
    SYMTAB_NODE_PTR parm_idp, first_idp, last_idp;   /* parm ids */
    SYMTAB_NODE_PTR prev_last_idp = NULL;       /* last id of list */
    SYMTAB_NODE_PTR parm_listp = NULL;          /* parm list */
    SYMTAB_NODE_PTR type_idp;                   /* type id */
    TYPE_STRUCT_PTR parm_tp;                     /* parm type */
    DEFN_KEY        parm_defn;                   /* parm definition */
    int             parm_count = 0;              /* count of parms */
    int             parm_offset = STACK_FRAME_HEADER_SIZE;

    get_token();

    /*
    -- Loop to process parameter declarations separated by ;
    */
    while ((token == IDENTIFIER) || (token == VAR)) {
        first_idp = NULL;

        /*
        -- VAR parms?
        */
        if (token == VAR) {
            parm_defn = VARPARM_DEFN;
            get_token();
        }
        else parm_defn = VALPARM_DEFN;

        /*
        -- <id list>
        */
        while (token == IDENTIFIER) {
            search_and_enter_local_symtab(parm_idp);
            parm_idp->defn.key   = parm_defn;
            parm_idp->label_index = 0;
            ++parm_count;

            if (parm_listp == NULL) parm_listp = parm_idp;

            /*
            -- Link parm ids together.
            */
            if (first_idp == NULL)
                first_idp = last_idp = parm_idp;
            else {
                last_idp->next = parm_idp;
                last_idp = parm_idp;
            }

            get_token();
            if_token_get(COMMA);
        }

        if_token_get_else_error(COLON, MISSING_COLON);

        if (token == IDENTIFIER) {
            search_and_find_all_symtab(type_idp);
            if (type_idp->defn.key != TYPE_DEFN) error(INVALID_TYPE);
            parm_tp = type_idp->typep;
            get_token();
        }
        else {
```

```
            error(MISSING_IDENTIFIER);
            parm_tp = &dummy_type;
    }

    /*
    -- Assign the offset and the type to all parm ids
    -- in the sublist.
    */
    for (parm_idp = first_idp;
         parm_idp != NULL;
         parm_idp = parm_idp->next) {
        parm_idp->typep = parm_tp;
        parm_idp->defn.info.data.offset = parm_offset++;
    }

    /*
    -- Link this list to the list of all parm ids.
    */
    if (prev_last_idp != NULL) prev_last_idp->next = first_idp;
    prev_last_idp = last_idp;

    /*
    -- Error synchronization:  Should be ; or )
    */
    synchronize(follow_parms_list, NULL, NULL);
    if_token_get(SEMICOLON);
}

    if_token_get_else_error(RPAREN, MISSING_RPAREN);
    *countp = parm_count;
    *total_sizep = parm_offset - STACK_FRAME_HEADER_SIZE;

    return(parm_listp);
}

/*------------------------------------------------------------*/
/*  routine_call        Process a call to a declared or       */
/*                      a standard procedure or function.     */
/*                      Return a pointer to the type          */
/*                      structure of the call.                */
/*------------------------------------------------------------*/

    TYPE_STRUCT_PTR
routine_call(rtn_idp, parm_check_flag)

    SYMTAB_NODE_PTR rtn_idp;              /* routine id */
    BOOLEAN         parm_check_flag;      /* if TRUE check parms */

{
    TYPE_STRUCT_PTR declared_routine_call(), standard_routine_call();

    if ((rtn_idp->defn.info.routine.key == DECLARED) ||
        (rtn_idp->defn.info.routine.key == FORWARD) ||
        !parm_check_flag)
        return(declared_routine_call(rtn_idp, parm_check_flag));
    else
        return(standard_routine_call(rtn_idp));
}

/*------------------------------------------------------------*/
/*  declared_routine_call  Process a call to a declared       */
/*                         procedure or function:             */
/*                                                            */
/*                              <id>                          */
/*                                                            */
/*                         or:                                */
/*                                                            */
/*                              <id> ( <parm-list> )          */
```

```
/*                                                          */
/*              The actual parameters are checked            */
/*              against the formal parameters for            */
/*              type and number.  Return a pointer            */
/*              to the type structure of the call.            */
/*------------------------------------------------------------*/

    TYPE_STRUCT_PTR
declared_routine_call(rtn_idp, parm_check_flag)

    SYMTAB_NODE_PTR rtn_idp;              /* routine id */
    BOOLEAN         parm_check_flag;      /* if TRUE check parms */

{
    actual_parm_list(rtn_idp, parm_check_flag);
    return(rtn_idp->defn.key == PROC_DEFN ? NULL : rtn_idp->typep);
}

/*------------------------------------------------------------*/
/*  actual_parm_list    Process an actual parameter list:     */
/*                                                            */
/*                          ( <expr-list> )                   */
/*------------------------------------------------------------*/

TOKEN_CODE follow_parm_list[] = {COMMA, RPAREN, 0};

actual_parm_list(rtn_idp, parm_check_flag)

    SYMTAB_NODE_PTR rtn_idp;              /* routine id */
    BOOLEAN         parm_check_flag;      /* if TRUE check parms */

{
    SYMTAB_NODE_PTR formal_parm_idp;
    DEFN_KEY        formal_parm_defn;
    TYPE_STRUCT_PTR formal_parm_tp, actual_parm_tp;

    if (parm_check_flag)
        formal_parm_idp = rtn_idp->defn.info.routine.parms;

    if (token == LPAREN) {
        /*
        -- Loop to process actual parameter expressions.
        */
        do {
            /*
            -- Obtain info about the corresponding formal parm.
            */
            if (parm_check_flag && (formal_parm_idp != NULL)) {
                formal_parm_defn = formal_parm_idp->defn.key;
                formal_parm_tp   = formal_parm_idp->typep;
            }

            get_token();

            /*
            -- Formal value parm:  Actual parm's type must be
            --                     assignment compatible with
            --                     formal parm's type.  Actual
            --                     parm can be an expression.
            */
            if ((formal_parm_idp == NULL) ||
                (formal_parm_defn == VALPARM_DEFN) ||
                !parm_check_flag) {
                actual_parm_tp = expression();
                if (parm_check_flag && (formal_parm_idp != NULL) &&
                    (! is_assign_type_compatible(formal_parm_tp,
                                                 actual_parm_tp)))
```

```
                error(INCOMPATIBLE_TYPES);
    }

    /*
    -- Formal VAR parm:  Actual parm's type must be the same
    --                   as formal parm type.  Actual parm
    --                   must be a variable.
    */
    else  /* formal_parm_defn == VARPARM_DEFN */  {
        if (token == IDENTIFIER) {
            SYMTAB_NODE_PTR idp;

            search_and_find_all_symtab(idp);
            actual_parm_tp = variable(idp, VARPARM_USE);

            if (formal_parm_tp != actual_parm_tp)
                error(INCOMPATIBLE_TYPES);
        }
        else {
            /*
            -- Not a variable:  Parse an expression anyway
            --                   for error recovery.
            */
            actual_parm_tp = expression();
            error(INVALID_VAR_PARM);
        }
    }

    /*
    -- Check if there are more actual parms
    -- than formal parms.
    */
    if (parm_check_flag) {
        if (formal_parm_idp == NULL)
            error(WRONG_NUMBER_OF_PARMS);
        else formal_parm_idp = formal_parm_idp->next;
    }

    /*
    -- Error synchronization:  Should be , or )
    */
    synchronize(follow_parm_list, statement_end_list, NULL);
```

```
        } while (token == COMMA);

        if_token_get_else_error(RPAREN, MISSING_RPAREN);
    }

    /*
    -- Check if there are fewer actual parms than formal parms.
    */
    if (parm_check_flag && (formal_parm_idp != NULL))
        error(WRONG_NUMBER_OF_PARMS);
}

/*-------------------------------------------------------------*/
/*  block                Process a block, which consists of    */
/*                       declarations followed by a compound   */
/*                       statement.                            */
/*-------------------------------------------------------------*/

TOKEN_CODE follow_decls_list[] = {SEMICOLON, BEGIN, END_OF_FILE, 0};

block(rtn_idp)

    SYMTAB_NODE_PTR rtn_idp;      /* id of program or routine */

{
    extern BOOLEAN block_flag;

    declarations(rtn_idp);

    /*
    -- Error synchronization:  Should be ;
    */
    synchronize(follow_decls_list, NULL, NULL);
    if (token != BEGIN) error(MISSING_BEGIN);

    crunch_token();

    block_flag = TRUE;
    compound_statement();
    block_flag = FALSE;
}
```

FIGURE A-3   standard.c

```
/***************************************************************/
/*                                                             */
/*      S T A N D A R D   R O U T I N E   P A R S E R          */
/*                                                             */
/*      Parsing routines for calls to standard procedures and  */
/*      functions.                                             */
/*                                                             */
/*      FILE:      standard.c                                  */
/*                                                             */
/*      MODULE:    parser                                      */
/*                                                             */
/***************************************************************/

#include <stdio.h>
#include "common.h"
#include "error.h"
#include "scanner.h"
```

```
#include "symtab.h"
#include "parser.h"

#define DEFAULT_NUMERIC_FIELD_WIDTH    10
#define DEFAULT_PRECISION               2

/*-------------------------------------------------------------*/
/*  Externals                                                  */
/*-------------------------------------------------------------*/

extern TOKEN_CODE       token;
extern char             word_string[];
extern SYMTAB_NODE_PTR  symtab_display[];
extern int              level;
extern TYPE_STRUCT      dummy_type;

extern TYPE_STRUCT_PTR  integer_typep, real_typep,
```

```
                                boolean_typep, char_typep;

extern TOKEN_CODE       follow_parm_list[];
extern TOKEN_CODE       statement_end_list[];

/*--------------------------------------------------------*/
/* Forwards                                               */
/*--------------------------------------------------------*/

TYPE_STRUCT_PTR eof_eoln(), abs_sqr(),
                arctan_cos_exp_ln_sin_sqrt(),
                pred_succ(), chr(), odd(), ord(),
                round_trunc();

/*--------------------------------------------------------*/
/* standard_routine_call  Process a call to a standard    */
/*                        procedure or function. Return a */
/*                        pointer to the type structure of*/
/*                        the call.                       */
/*--------------------------------------------------------*/

    TYPE_STRUCT_PTR
standard_routine_call(rtn_idp)

    SYMTAB_NODE_PTR rtn_idp;          /* routine id */

{
    switch (rtn_idp->defn.info.routine.key) {

        case READ:
        case READLN:    read_readln(rtn_idp);        return(NULL);

        case WRITE:
        case WRITELN:   write_writeln(rtn_idp);      return(NULL);

        case EOFF:
        case EOLN:      return(eof_eoln(rtn_idp));

        case ABS:
        case SQR:       return(abs_sqr());

        case ARCTAN:
        case COS:
        case EXP:
        case LN:
        case SIN:
        case SQRT:      return(arctan_cos_exp_ln_sin_sqrt());

        case PRED:
        case SUCC:      return(pred_succ());

        case CHR:       return(chr());
        case ODD:       return(odd());
        case ORD:       return(ord());

        case ROUND:
        case TRUNC:     return(round_trunc());
    }
}

/*--------------------------------------------------------*/
/* read_readln            Process a call to read or readln. */
/*--------------------------------------------------------*/

read_readln(rtn_idp)

    SYMTAB_NODE_PTR rtn_idp;          /* routine id */
```

```
{
    TYPE_STRUCT_PTR actual_parm_tp;       /* actual parm type */

    /*
    -- Parameters are optional for readln.
    */
    if (token == LPAREN) {
        /*
        -- <id-list>
        */
        do {
            get_token();

            /*
            -- Actual parms must be variables (but parse
            -- an expression anyway for error recovery).
            */
            if (token == IDENTIFIER) {
                SYMTAB_NODE_PTR idp;

                search_and_find_all_symtab(idp);
                actual_parm_tp = base_type(variable(idp,
                                          VARPARM_USE));

                if (actual_parm_tp->form != SCALAR_FORM)
                    error(INCOMPATIBLE_TYPES);
            }
            else {
                actual_parm_tp = expression();
                error(INVALID_VAR_PARM);
            }

            /*
            -- Error synchronization:  Should be , or )
            */
            synchronize(follow_parm_list, statement_end_list, NULL);

        } while (token == COMMA);

        if_token_get_else_error(RPAREN, MISSING_RPAREN);
    }
    else if (rtn_idp->defn.info.routine.key == READ)
        error(WRONG_NUMBER_OF_PARMS);
}

/*--------------------------------------------------------*/
/* write_writeln         Process a call to write or writeln. */
/*                       Each actual parameter can be:       */
/*                                                           */
/*                            <expr>                         */
/*                                                           */
/*                       or:                                 */
/*                                                           */
/*                            <epxr> : <expr>                */
/*                                                           */
/*                       or:                                 */
/*                                                           */
/*                            <expr> : <expr> : <expr>       */
/*--------------------------------------------------------*/

write_writeln(rtn_idp)

    SYMTAB_NODE_PTR rtn_idp;          /* routine id */

{
    TYPE_STRUCT_PTR actual_parm_tp;       /* actual parm type */
    TYPE_STRUCT_PTR field_width_tp, precision_tp;
```

```
    /*
    -- Parameters are optional for writeln.
    */
    if (token == LPAREN) {
        do {
            /*
            -- Value <expr>
            */
            get_token();
            actual_parm_tp = base_type(expression());

            if ((actual_parm_tp->form != SCALAR_FORM) &&
                (actual_parm_tp != boolean_typep) &&
                ((actual_parm_tp->form != ARRAY_FORM) ||
                 (actual_parm_tp->info.array.elmt_typep !=
                                            char_typep)))
                error(INVALID_EXPRESSION);

            /*
            -- Optional field width <expr>
            */
            if (token == COLON) {
                get_token();
                field_width_tp = base_type(expression());

                if (field_width_tp != integer_typep)
                    error(INCOMPATIBLE_TYPES);

                /*
                -- Optional precision <expr>
                */
                if (token == COLON) {
                    get_token();
                    precision_tp = base_type(expression());

                    if (precision_tp != integer_typep)
                        error(INCOMPATIBLE_TYPES);
                }
            }

            /*
            -- Error synchronization:  Should be , or )
            */
            synchronize(follow_parm_list, statement_end_list, NULL);

        } while (token == COMMA);

        if_token_get_else_error(RPAREN, MISSING_RPAREN);
    }
    else if (rtn_idp->defn.info.routine.key == WRITE)
        error(WRONG_NUMBER_OF_PARMS);
}

/*------------------------------------------------------------*/
/* eof_eoln                   Process a call to eof or to eoln.  */
/*                            No parameters => boolean result.   */
/*------------------------------------------------------------*/

    TYPE_STRUCT_PTR
eof_eoln(rtn_idp)

    SYMTAB_NODE_PTR rtn_idp;           /* routine id */

{
    if (token == LPAREN) {
        error(WRONG_NUMBER_OF_PARMS);
        actual_parm_list(rtn_idp, FALSE);
```

```
    }
    return(boolean_typep);
}

/*------------------------------------------------------------*/
/* abs_sqr              Process a call to abs or to sqr.  */
/*                      integer parm => integer result    */
/*                      real parm    => real result       */
/*------------------------------------------------------------*/

    TYPE_STRUCT_PTR
abs_sqr()

{
    TYPE_STRUCT_PTR parm_tp;           /* actual parameter type */
    TYPE_STRUCT_PTR result_tp;         /* result type */

    if (token == LPAREN) {
        get_token();
        parm_tp = base_type(expression());

        if ((parm_tp != integer_typep) && (parm_tp != real_typep)) {
            error(INCOMPATIBLE_TYPES);
            result_tp = real_typep;
        }
        else result_tp = parm_tp;

        if_token_get_else_error(RPAREN, MISSING_RPAREN);
    }
    else error(WRONG_NUMBER_OF_PARMS);

    return(result_tp);
}

/*------------------------------------------------------------*/
/* arctan_cos_exp_ln_sin_sqrt  Process a call to arctan, cos,  */
/*                      exp, ln, sin, or sqrt.            */
/*                      integer parm => real result       */
/*                      real_parm    => real result       */
/*------------------------------------------------------------*/

    TYPE_STRUCT_PTR
arctan_cos_exp_ln_sin_sqrt()

{
    TYPE_STRUCT_PTR parm_tp;           /* actual parameter type */

    if (token == LPAREN) {
        get_token();
        parm_tp = base_type(expression());

        if ((parm_tp != integer_typep) && (parm_tp != real_typep))
            error(INCOMPATIBLE_TYPES);

        if_token_get_else_error(RPAREN, MISSING_RPAREN);
    }
    else error(WRONG_NUMBER_OF_PARMS);

    return(real_typep);
}

/*------------------------------------------------------------*/
/* pred_succ            Process a call to pred or succ.   */
/*                      integer parm => integer result    */
/*                      enum parm    => enum result        */
/*------------------------------------------------------------*/
```

```
    TYPE_STRUCT_PTR
pred_succ()

{
    TYPE_STRUCT_PTR parm_tp;           /* actual parameter type */
    TYPE_STRUCT_PTR result_tp;         /* result type */

    if (token == LPAREN) {
        get_token();
        parm_tp = base_type(expression());

        if ((parm_tp != integer_typep) &&
            (parm_tp->form != ENUM_FORM)) {
            error(INCOMPATIBLE_TYPES);
            result_tp = integer_typep;
        }
        else result_tp = parm_tp;

        if_token_get_else_error(RPAREN, MISSING_RPAREN);
    }
    else error(WRONG_NUMBER_OF_PARMS);

    return(result_tp);
}

/*------------------------------------------------------------*/
/* chr                     Process a call to chr.          */
/*                         integer parm => character result */
/*------------------------------------------------------------*/

    TYPE_STRUCT_PTR
chr()

{
    TYPE_STRUCT_PTR parm_tp;           /* actual parameter type */

    if (token == LPAREN) {
        get_token();
        parm_tp = base_type(expression());

        if (parm_tp != integer_typep) error(INCOMPATIBLE_TYPES);
        if_token_get_else_error(RPAREN, MISSING_RPAREN);
    }
    else error(WRONG_NUMBER_OF_PARMS);

    return(char_typep);
}

/*------------------------------------------------------------*/
/* odd                     Process a call to odd.          */
/*                         integer parm => boolean result   */
/*------------------------------------------------------------*/

    TYPE_STRUCT_PTR
odd()

{
    TYPE_STRUCT_PTR parm_tp;           /* actual parameter type */
```

```
    if (token == LPAREN) {
        get_token();
        parm_tp = base_type(expression());

        if (parm_tp != integer_typep) error(INCOMPATIBLE_TYPES);
        if_token_get_else_error(RPAREN, MISSING_RPAREN);
    }
    else error(WRONG_NUMBER_OF_PARMS);

    return(boolean_typep);
}

/*------------------------------------------------------------*/
/* ord                     Process a call to ord.          */
/*                         enumeration parm => integer result */
/*------------------------------------------------------------*/

    TYPE_STRUCT_PTR
ord()

{
    TYPE_STRUCT_PTR parm_tp;           /* actual parameter type */

    if (token == LPAREN) {
        get_token();
        parm_tp = base_type(expression());

        if (parm_tp->form != ENUM_FORM) error(INCOMPATIBLE_TYPES);
        if_token_get_else_error(RPAREN, MISSING_RPAREN);
    }
    else error(WRONG_NUMBER_OF_PARMS);

    return(integer_typep);
}

/*------------------------------------------------------------*/
/* round_trunc             Process a call to round or trunc. */
/*                         real parm => integer result      */
/*------------------------------------------------------------*/

    TYPE_STRUCT_PTR
round_trunc()

{
    TYPE_STRUCT_PTR parm_tp;           /* actual parameter type */

    if (token == LPAREN) {
        get_token();
        parm_tp = base_type(expression());

        if (parm_tp != real_typep) error(INCOMPATIBLE_TYPES);
        if_token_get_else_error(RPAREN, MISSING_RPAREN);
    }
    else error(WRONG_NUMBER_OF_PARMS);

    return(integer_typep);
}
```

FIGURE A-4 decl.c

```
/*****************************************************************/
/*                                                               */
/*        D E C L A R A T I O N   P A R S E R                    */
/*                                                               */
/*        Parsing routines for delarations.                      */
/*                                                               */
/*        FILE:     decl.c                                       */
/*                                                               */
/*        MODULE:   parser                                       */
/*                                                               */
/*****************************************************************/

#include <stdio.h>
#include "common.h"
#include "error.h"
#include "scanner.h"
#include "symtab.h"
#include "parser.h"


/*--------------------------------------------------------------*/
/* Externals                                                    */
/*--------------------------------------------------------------*/

extern TOKEN_CODE       token;
extern char             word_string[];
extern LITERAL          literal;

extern SYMTAB_NODE_PTR  symtab_display[];
extern int              level;

extern TYPE_STRUCT_PTR  integer_typep, real_typep,
                        boolean_typep, char_typep;

extern TYPE_STRUCT      dummy_type;

extern TOKEN_CODE       declaration_start_list[],
                        statement_start_list[];

/*--------------------------------------------------------------*/
/* Forwards                                                     */
/*--------------------------------------------------------------*/

TYPE_STRUCT_PTR do_type(),
                identifier_type(), enumeration_type(),
                subrange_type(), array_type(), record_type();

/*--------------------------------------------------------------*/
/* declarations      Call the routines to process constant      */
/*                   definitions, type definitions, variable    */
/*                   declarations, procedure definitions,       */
/*                   and function definitions.                  */
/*--------------------------------------------------------------*/

TOKEN_CODE follow_routine_list[] = {SEMICOLON, END_OF_FILE, 0};

declarations(rtn_idp)

    SYMTAB_NODE_PTR rtn_idp;    /* id of program or routine */

{
    if (token == CONST) {
        get_token();
        const_definitions();
    }
```

```
    if (token == TYPE) {
        get_token();
        type_definitions();
    }

    if (token == VAR) {
        get_token();
        var_declarations(rtn_idp);
    }

    /*
    -- Loop to process routine (procedure and function)
    -- definitions.
    */
    while ((token == PROCEDURE) || (token == FUNCTION)) {
        routine();

        /*
        -- Error synchronization:  Should be ;
        */
        synchronize(follow_routine_list,
                    declaration_start_list, statement_start_list);
        if_token_get(SEMICOLON);
        else if (token_in(declaration_start_list) ||
                 token_in(statement_start_list))
            error(MISSING_SEMICOLON);
    }
}


            /*************************/
            /*                       */
            /*        Constants      */
            /*                       */
            /*************************/

/*--------------------------------------------------------------*/
/* const_definitions    Process constant definitions:          */
/*                                                              */
/*                          <id> = <constant>                  */
/*--------------------------------------------------------------*/

TOKEN_CODE follow_declaration_list[] = {SEMICOLON, IDENTIFIER,
                                        END_OF_FILE, 0};

const_definitions()

{
    SYMTAB_NODE_PTR const_idp;          /* constant id */

    /*
    -- Loop to process definitions separated by semicolons.
    */
    while (token == IDENTIFIER) {
        search_and_enter_local_symtab(const_idp);
        const_idp->defn.key = CONST_DEFN;

        get_token();
        if_token_get_else_error(EQUAL, MISSING_EQUAL);

        /*
        -- Process the constant.
        */
        do_const(const_idp);
        analyze_const_defn(const_idp);
```

```
    /*
    -- Error synchronization:  Should be ;
    */
    synchronize(follow_declaration_list,
        .           declaration_start_list, statement_start_list);
    if_token_get(SEMICOLON);
    else if (token_in(declaration_start_list) ||
            token_in(statement_start_list))
        error(MISSING_SEMICOLON);
    }
}


/*------------------------------------------------------------*/
/* do_const              Process the constant of a constant   */
/*                       definition.                          */
/*------------------------------------------------------------*/

do_const(const_idp)

    SYMTAB_NODE_PTR const_idp;          /* constant id */

{
    TOKEN_CODE      sign     = PLUS;     /* unary + or - sign */
    BOOLEAN         saw_sign = FALSE;    /* TRUE iff unary sign */

    /*
    -- Unary + or - sign.
    */
    if ((token == PLUS) || (token == MINUS)) {
        sign     = token;
        saw_sign = TRUE;
        get_token();
    }

    /*
    -- Numeric constant:  Integer or real type.
    */
    if (token == NUMBER) {
        if (literal.type == INTEGER_LIT) {
            const_idp->defn.info.constant.value.integer =
                sign == PLUS ? literal.value.integer
                             : -literal.value.integer;
            const_idp->typep = integer_typep;
        }
        else {
            const_idp->defn.info.constant.value.real =
                sign == PLUS ? literal.value.real
                             : -literal.value.real;
            const_idp->typep = real_typep;
        }
    }

    /*
    -- Identifier constant:  Integer, real, character, enumeration,
    --                       or string (character array) type.
    */
    else if (token == IDENTIFIER) {
        SYMTAB_NODE_PTR idp;

        search_all_symtab(idp);

        if (idp == NULL)
            error(UNDEFINED_IDENTIFIER);
        else if (idp->defn.key != CONST_DEFN)
            error(NOT_A_CONSTANT_IDENTIFIER);

        else if (idp->typep == integer_typep) {
```

```
            const_idp->defn.info.constant.value.integer =
                sign == PLUS ? idp->defn.info.constant.value.integer
                             : -idp->defn.info.constant.value.integer;
            const_idp->typep = integer_typep;
        }
        else if (idp->typep == real_typep) {
            const_idp->defn.info.constant.value.real =
                sign == PLUS ? idp->defn.info.constant.value.real
                             : -idp->defn.info.constant.value.real;
            const_idp->typep = real_typep;
        }
        else if (idp->typep == char_typep) {
            if (saw_sign) error(INVALID_CONSTANT);

            const_idp->defn.info.constant.value.character =
                            idp->defn.info.constant.value.character;
            const_idp->typep = char_typep;
        }
        else if (idp->typep->form == ENUM_FORM) {
            if (saw_sign) error(INVALID_CONSTANT);

            const_idp->defn.info.constant.value.integer =
                            idp->defn.info.constant.value.integer;
            const_idp->typep = idp->typep;
        }
        else if (idp->typep->form == ARRAY_FORM) {
            if (saw_sign) error(INVALID_CONSTANT);

            const_idp->defn.info.constant.value.stringp =
                            idp->defn.info.constant.value.stringp;
            const_idp->typep = idp->typep;
        }
    }

    /*
    -- String constant:  Character or string (character array) type.
    */
    else if (token == STRING) {
        if (saw_sign) error(INVALID_CONSTANT);

        if (strlen(literal.value.string) == 1) {
            const_idp->defn.info.constant.value.character =
                                        literal.value.string[0];
            const_idp->typep = char_typep;
        }
        else {
            int length = strlen(literal.value.string);

            const_idp->defn.info.constant.value.stringp =
                                alloc_bytes(length + 1);
            strcpy(const_idp->defn.info.constant.value.stringp,
                    literal.value.string);
            const_idp->typep = make_string_typep(length);
        }
    }

    else {
        const_idp->typep = &dummy_type;
        error(INVALID_CONSTANT);
    }

    get_token();
}


            /**************************/
            /*                        */
            /*         Types          */
```

```
                        /*                    */
                        /************************/

/*----------------------------------------------------------*/
/*   type_definitions     Process type definitions:         */
/*                                                          */
/*                        <id> = <type>                     */
/*----------------------------------------------------------*/

type_definitions()

{
    SYMTAB_NODE_PTR type_idp;         /* type id */

    /*
    -- Loop to process definitions separated by semicolons.
    */
    while (token == IDENTIFIER) {
        search_and_enter_local_symtab(type_idp);
        type_idp->defn.key = TYPE_DEFN;

        get_token();
        if_token_get_else_error(EQUAL, MISSING_EQUAL);

        /*
        -- Process the type specification.
        */
        type_idp->typep = do_type();
        if (type_idp->typep->type_idp == NULL)
            type_idp->typep->type_idp = type_idp;

        analyze_type_defn(type_idp);

        /*
        -- Error synchronization:  Should be ;
        */
        synchronize(follow_declaration_list,
                declaration_start_list, statement_start_list);
        if_token_get(SEMICOLON);
        else if (token_in(declaration_start_list) ||
                token_in(statement_start_list))
            error(MISSING_SEMICOLON);
    }
}

/*----------------------------------------------------------*/
/*   do_type              Process a type specification.  Call the */
/*                        functions that make a type structure    */
/*                        and return a pointer to it.             */
/*----------------------------------------------------------*/

    TYPE_STRUCT_PTR
do_type()

{
    switch (token) {
        case IDENTIFIER: {
            SYMTAB_NODE_PTR idp;

            search_all_symtab(idp);

            if (idp == NULL) {
                error(UNDEFINED_IDENTIFIER);
                return(&dummy_type);
            }
            else if (idp->defn.key == TYPE_DEFN)
                return(identifier_type(idp));
```

```
            else if (idp->defn.key == CONST_DEFN)
                return(subrange_type(idp));
            else {
                error(NOT_A_TYPE_IDENTIFIER);
                return(&dummy_type);
            }
        }

        case LPAREN:    return(enumeration_type());
        case ARRAY:     return(array_type());
        case RECORD:    return(record_type());

        case PLUS:
        case MINUS:
        case NUMBER:
        case STRING:    return(subrange_type(NULL));

        default:        error(INVALID_TYPE);
                        return(&dummy_type);
    }
}

/*----------------------------------------------------------*/
/*   identifier_type      Process an identifier type, i.e., the  */
/*                        identifier on the right side of a type */
/*                        equate, and return a pointer to its    */
/*                        type structure.                        */
/*----------------------------------------------------------*/

    TYPE_STRUCT_PTR
identifier_type(idp)

    SYMTAB_NODE_PTR idp;        /* type id */

{
    TYPE_STRUCT_PTR tp = NULL;

    tp = idp->typep;
    get_token();

    return(tp);
}

/*----------------------------------------------------------*/
/*   enumeration_type      Process an enumeration type:          */
/*                                                               */
/*                         ( <id1>, <id2>, ..., <idn> )          */
/*                                                               */
/*                         Make a type structure and return a    */
/*                         pointer to it.                        */
/*----------------------------------------------------------*/

    TYPE_STRUCT_PTR
enumeration_type()

{
    SYMTAB_NODE_PTR const_idp;           /* constant id */
    SYMTAB_NODE_PTR last_idp    = NULL;  /* last constant id */
    TYPE_STRUCT_PTR tp          = alloc_struct(TYPE_STRUCT);
    int             const_value = -1;    /* constant value */

    tp->form     = ENUM_FORM;
    tp->size     = sizeof(int);
    tp->type_idp = NULL;

    get_token();

    /*
```

```
    -- Loop to process list of identifiers.
    */
    while (token == IDENTIFIER) {
        search_and_enter_local_symtab(const_idp);
        const_idp->defn.key = CONST_DEFN;
        const_idp->defn.info.constant.value.integer = ++const_value;
        const_idp->typep = tp;

        /*
        -- Link constant ids together.
        */
        if (last_idp == NULL)
            tp->info.enumeration.const_idp = last_idp = const_idp;
        else {
            last_idp->next = const_idp;
            last_idp = const_idp;
        }

        get_token();
        if_token_get(COMMA);
    }

    if_token_get_else_error(RPAREN, MISSING_RPAREN);

    tp->info.enumeration.max = const_value;
    return(tp);
}

/*------------------------------------------------------------*/
/*  subrange_type        Process a subrange type:            */
/*                                                           */
/*                       <min-const> .. <max-const>          */
/*                                                           */
/*                       Make a type structure and return a  */
/*                       pointer to it.                      */
/*------------------------------------------------------------*/

TOKEN_CODE follow_min_limit_list[] = {DOTDOT, IDENTIFIER, PLUS, MINUS,
                                      NUMBER, STRING, SEMICOLON,
                                      END_OF_FILE, 0};

    TYPE_STRUCT_PTR
subrange_type(min_idp)

    SYMTAB_NODE_PTR min_idp;    /* min limit const id */

{
    TYPE_STRUCT_PTR max_typep;  /* type of max limit */
    TYPE_STRUCT_PTR tp = alloc_struct(TYPE_STRUCT);

    tp->form     = SUBRANGE_FORM;
    tp->type_idp = NULL;

    /*
    -- Minimum constant.
    */
    get_subrange_limit(min_idp,
                       &(tp->info.subrange.min),
                       &(tp->info.subrange.range_typep));

    /*
    -- Error synchronization:  Should be ..
    */
    synchronize(follow_min_limit_list, NULL, NULL);
    if_token_get(DOTDOT);
    else if (token_in(follow_min_limit_list) ||
            token_in(declaration_start_list) ||
```

```
        token_in(statement_start_list))
        error(MISSING_DOTDOT);

    /*
    -- Maximum constant.
    */
    get_subrange_limit(NULL, &(tp->info.subrange.max), &max_typep);

    /*
    -- Check limits.
    */
    if (max_typep == tp->info.subrange.range_typep) {
        if (tp->info.subrange.min > tp->info.subrange.max)
            error(MIN_GT_MAX);
    }
    else error(INCOMPATIBLE_TYPES);

    tp->size = max_typep == char_typep ? sizeof(char) : sizeof(int);
    return(tp);
}

/*------------------------------------------------------------*/
/*  get_subrange_limit  Process the minimum and maximum limits  */
/*                      of a subrange type.                   */
/*------------------------------------------------------------*/

get_subrange_limit(minmax_idp, minmaxp, typepp)

    SYMTAB_NODE_PTR minmax_idp; /* min const id */
    int             *minmaxp;   /* where to store min or max value */
    TYPE_STRUCT_PTR *typepp;    /* where to store ptr to type struct */

{
    SYMTAB_NODE_PTR idp      = minmax_idp;
    TOKEN_CODE      sign     = PLUS;    /* unary + or - sign */
    BOOLEAN         saw_sign = FALSE;   /* TRUE iff unary sign */

    /*
    -- Unary + or - sign.
    */
    if ((token == PLUS) || (token == MINUS)) {
        sign     = token;
        saw_sign = TRUE;
        get_token();
    }

    /*
    -- Numeric limit:  Integer type only.
    */
    if (token == NUMBER) {
        if (literal.type == INTEGER_LIT) {
            *typepp  = integer_typep;
            *minmaxp = (sign == PLUS) ? literal.value.integer
                                      : -literal.value.integer;
        }
        else error(INVALID_SUBRANGE_TYPE);
    }

    /*
    -- Identifier limit:  Value must be integer or character.
    */
    else if (token == IDENTIFIER) {
        if (idp == NULL) search_all_symtab(idp);

        if (idp == NULL)
            error(UNDEFINED_IDENTIFIER);
        else if (idp->typep == real_typep)
```

```
                error(INVALID_SUBRANGE_TYPE);
        else if (idp->defn.key == CONST_DEFN) {
            *typepp = idp->typep;
            if (idp->typep == char_typep) {
                if (saw_sign) error(INVALID_CONSTANT);
                *minmaxp = idp->defn.info.constant.value.character;
            }
            else if (idp->typep == integer_typep) {
                *minmaxp = idp->defn.info.constant.value.integer;
                if (sign == MINUS) *minmaxp = -(*minmaxp);
            }
            else /* enumeration constant */ {
                if (saw_sign) error(INVALID_CONSTANT);
                *minmaxp = idp->defn.info.constant.value.integer;
            }
        }
        else error(NOT_A_CONSTANT_IDENTIFIER);
    }

    /*
    -- String limit:  Character type only.
    */
    else if (token == STRING) {
        if (saw_sign) error(INVALID_CONSTANT);
        *typepp = char_typep;
        *minmaxp = literal.value.string[0];

        if (strlen(literal.value.string) != 1)
            error(INVALID_SUBRANGE_TYPE);
    }

    else error(MISSING_CONSTANT);

    get_token();
}

/*--------------------------------------------------------*/
/*  array_type          Process an array type:           */
/*                                                        */
/*                          ARRAY [<index-type-list>]     */
/*                          OF <elmt-type>                */
/*                                                        */
/*                          Make a type structure and return a   */
/*                          pointer to it.                */
/*--------------------------------------------------------*/

TOKEN_CODE follow_dimension_list[] = {COMMA, RBRACKET, OF,
                                      SEMICOLON, END_OF_FILE, 0};

TOKEN_CODE index_type_start_list[] = {IDENTIFIER, NUMBER, STRING,
                                      LPAREN, MINUS, PLUS, 0};

TOKEN_CODE follow_indexes_list[]   = {OF, IDENTIFIER, LPAREN, ARRAY,
                                      RECORD, PLUS, MINUS, NUMBER,
                                      STRING, SEMICOLON, END_OF_FILE,
                                      0};

    TYPE_STRUCT_PTR
array_type()

{
    TYPE_STRUCT_PTR tp      = alloc_struct(TYPE_STRUCT);
    TYPE_STRUCT_PTR index_tp;            /* index type */
    TYPE_STRUCT_PTR elmt_tp = tp;        /* element type */
    int array_size();

    get_token();
```

```
    if (token != LBRACKET) error(MISSING_LBRACKET);

    /*
    -- Loop to process index type list.  For each
    -- type in the list after the first, create an
    -- array element type.
    */
    do {
        get_token();

        if (token_in(index_type_start_list)) {
            elmt_tp->form    = ARRAY_FORM;
            elmt_tp->size    = 0;
            elmt_tp->type_idp = NULL;
            elmt_tp->info.array.index_typep = index_tp = do_type();

            switch (index_tp->form) {
                case ENUM_FORM:
                    elmt_tp->info.array.elmt_count =
                                index_tp->info.enumeration.max + 1;
                    elmt_tp->info.array.min_index = 0;
                    elmt_tp->info.array.max_index =
                                index_tp->info.enumeration.max;
                    break;

                case SUBRANGE_FORM:
                    elmt_tp->info.array.elmt_count =
                                index_tp->info.subrange.max -
                                    index_tp->info.subrange.min + 1;
                    elmt_tp->info.array.min_index =
                                index_tp->info.subrange.min;
                    elmt_tp->info.array.max_index =
                                index_tp->info.subrange.max;
                    break;

                default:
                    elmt_tp->form     = NO_FORM;
                    elmt_tp->size     = 0;
                    elmt_tp->type_idp = NULL;
                    elmt_tp->info.array.index_typep = &dummy_type;
                    error(INVALID_INDEX_TYPE);
                    break;
            }
        }
        else {
            elmt_tp->form    = NO_FORM;
            elmt_tp->size    = 0;
            elmt_tp->type_idp = NULL;
            elmt_tp->info.array.index_typep = &dummy_type;
            error(INVALID_INDEX_TYPE);
        }

        /*
        -- Error synchronization:  Should be , or ]
        */
        synchronize(follow_dimension_list, NULL, NULL);

        /*
        -- Create an array element type.
        */
        if (token == COMMA) elmt_tp = elmt_tp->info.array.elmt_typep =
                            alloc_struct(TYPE_STRUCT);
    } while (token == COMMA);

    if_token_get_else_error(RBRACKET, MISSING_RBRACKET);

    /*
```

```
        --  Error synchronization:  Should be OF
        */
        synchronize(follow_indexes_list,
                    declaration_start_list, statement_start_list);
        if_token_get_else_error(OF, MISSING_OF);

        /*
        --  Element type.
        */
        elmt_tp->info.array.elmt_typep = do_type();

        tp->size = array_size(tp);
        return(tp);
}


/*-------------------------------------------------------*/
/*  record_type        Process a record type:           */
/*                                                       */
/*                          RECORD                       */
/*                              <id-list> : <type> ;     */
/*                              ...                      */
/*                          END                          */
/*                                                       */
/*                      Make a type structure and return a */
/*                      pointer to it.                   */
/*-------------------------------------------------------*/

    TYPE_STRUCT_PTR
record_type()

{
    TYPE_STRUCT_PTR record_tp = alloc_struct(TYPE_STRUCT);

    record_tp->form       = RECORD_FORM;
    record_tp->type_idp = NULL;
    record_tp->info.record.field_symtab = NULL;

    get_token();
    var_or_field_declarations(NULL, record_tp, 0);

    if_token_get_else_error(END, MISSING_END);
    return(record_tp);
}


/*-------------------------------------------------------*/
/*  make_string_typep   Make a type structure for a string of */
/*                      the given length, and return a pointer */
/*                      to it.                           */
/*-------------------------------------------------------*/

    TYPE_STRUCT_PTR
make_string_typep(length)

    int length;                 /* string length */

{
    TYPE_STRUCT_PTR string_tp = alloc_struct(TYPE_STRUCT);
    TYPE_STRUCT_PTR index_tp  = alloc_struct(TYPE_STRUCT);

    /*
    --  Array type.
    */
    string_tp->form       = ARRAY_FORM;
    string_tp->size       = length;
    string_tp->type_idp = NULL;
    string_tp->info.array.index_typep = index_tp;
    string_tp->info.array.elmt_typep  = char_typep;
```

```
        string_tp->info.array.elmt_count = length;

        /*
        --  Subrange index type.
        */
        index_tp->form       = SUBRANGE_FORM;
        index_tp->size       = sizeof(int);
        index_tp->type_idp = NULL;
        index_tp->info.subrange.range_typep = integer_typep;
        index_tp->info.subrange.min = 1;
        index_tp->info.subrange.max = length;

        return(string_tp);
}


/*-------------------------------------------------------*/
/*  array_size          Return the size in bytes of an array */
/*                      type by recursively calculating the */
/*                      size of each dimension.          */
/*-------------------------------------------------------*/

    int
array_size(tp)

    TYPE_STRUCT_PTR tp;         /* ptr to array type structure */

{
    if (tp->info.array.elmt_typep->size == 0)
        tp->info.array.elmt_typep->size =
                            array_size(tp->info.array.elmt_typep);

    tp->size = tp->info.array.elmt_count *
                tp->info.array.elmt_typep->size;

    return(tp->size);
}


                /*********************/
                /*                   */
                /*      Variables    */
                /*                   */
                /*********************/


/*-------------------------------------------------------*/
/*  var_declarations    Process variable declarations:   */
/*                                                       */
/*                          <id-list> : <type>           */
/*-------------------------------------------------------*/

var_declarations(rtn_idp)

    SYMTAB_NODE_PTR rtn_idp;     /* id of program or routine */

{
    var_or_field_declarations(rtn_idp, NULL,
                              STACK_FRAME_HEADER_SIZE
                                + rtn_idp->defn.info.routine
                                            .parm_count);
}

/*-------------------------------------------------------*/
/*  var_or_field_declarations  Process variable declarations */
/*                      or record field definitions.     */
/*                      All ids declared with the same   */
/*                      type are linked together into    */
/*                      a sublist, and all the sublists  */
/*                      are then linked together.        */
/*-------------------------------------------------------*/
```

```
TOKEN_CODE follow_variables_list[] = {SEMICOLON, IDENTIFIER,
                                      END_OF_FILE, 0};

TOKEN_CODE follow_fields_list[]    = {SEMICOLON, END, IDENTIFIER,
                                      END_OF_FILE, 0};

var_or_field_declarations(rtn_idp, record_tp, offset)

    SYMTAB_NODE_PTR rtn_idp;
    TYPE_STRUCT_PTR record_tp;
    int             offset;

{
    SYMTAB_NODE_PTR idp, first_idp, last_idp;  /* variable or
                                                   field ids */
    SYMTAB_NODE_PTR prev_last_idp = NULL;      /* last id of list */
    TYPE_STRUCT_PTR tp;                        /* type */
    BOOLEAN var_flag = (rtn_idp != NULL);      /* TRUE:  variables */
                                               /* FALSE: fields */
    int size;
    int total_size = 0;

    /*
    -- Loop to process sublist, each of a type.
    */
    while (token == IDENTIFIER) {
        first_idp = NULL;

        /*
        -- Loop process each variable or field id in a sublist.
        */
        while (token == IDENTIFIER) {
            if (var_flag) {
                search_and_enter_local_symtab(idp);
                idp->defn.key = VAR_DEFN;
            }
            else {
                search_and_enter_this_symtab
                    (idp, record_tp->info.record.field_symtab);
                idp->defn.key = FIELD_DEFN;
            }
            idp->label_index = 0;

            /*
            -- Link ids together into a sublist.
            */
            if (first_idp == NULL) {
                first_idp = last_idp = idp;
                if (var_flag &&
                    (rtn_idp->defn.info.routine.locals == NULL))
                    rtn_idp->defn.info.routine.locals = idp;
            }
            else {
                last_idp->next = idp;
                last_idp = idp;
            }
```

```
            get_token();
            if_token_get(COMMA);
        }

        /*
        -- Process the sublist's type.
        */
        if_token_get_else_error(COLON, MISSING_COLON);
        tp = do_type();
        size = tp->size;

        /*
        -- Assign the offset and the type to all variable or field
        -- ids in the sublist.
        */
        for (idp = first_idp; idp != NULL; idp = idp->next) {
            idp->typep = tp;

            if (var_flag) {
                total_size += size;
                idp->defn.info.data.offset = offset++;
                analyze_var_decl(idp);
            }

            else   /* record fields */ {
                idp->defn.info.data.offset = offset;
                offset += size;
            }
        }

        /*
        -- Link this sublist to the previous sublist.
        */
        if (prev_last_idp != NULL) prev_last_idp->next = first_idp;
        prev_last_idp = last_idp;

        /*
        -- Error synchronization:  Should be ; for variable
        --                         declaration, or ; or END for
        --                         record type definition.
        */
        synchronize(var_flag ? follow_variables_list
                             : follow_fields_list,
                    declaration_start_list, statement_start_list);
        if_token_get(SEMICOLON);
        else if (var_flag && ((token_in(declaration_start_list)) ||
                              (token_in(statement_start_list))))
            error(MISSING_SEMICOLON);
    }

    if (var_flag)
        rtn_idp->defn.info.routine.total_local_size = total_size;
    else
        record_tp->size = offset;
}
```

FIGURE A-5   stmt.c

```
/****************************************************************/     /*    S T A T E M E N T   P A R S E R                 */
/*                                                       */     /*                                                   */
                                                               /*    Parsing routines for statements.               */
```

```
/*                                          */
/*    FILE:       stmt.c                     */
/*                                          */
/*    MODULE:     parser                     */
/*                                          */
/*****************************************************************/

#include <stdio.h>
#include "common.h"
#include "error.h"
#include "scanner.h"
#include "symtab.h"
#include "parser.h"
#include "exec.h"

/*--------------------------------------------------------*/
/* Externals                                              */
/*--------------------------------------------------------*/

extern TOKEN_CODE       token;
extern char             token_string[];
extern char             word_string[];
extern LITERAL          literal;
extern TOKEN_CODE       statement_start_list[], statement_end_list[];

extern SYMTAB_NODE_PTR  symtab_display[];
extern int              level;
extern char             *code_bufferp;

extern TYPE_STRUCT_PTR  integer_typep, real_typep,
                        boolean_typep, char_typep;
extern TYPE_STRUCT      dummy_type;

/*--------------------------------------------------------*/
/* statement            Process a statement by calling the   */
/*                      appropriate parsing routine based on */
/*                      the statement's first token.         */
/*--------------------------------------------------------*/

statement()

{
    if (token != BEGIN) crunch_statement_marker();

    /*
    -- Call the appropriate routine based on the first
    -- token of the statement.
    */
    switch (token) {

        case IDENTIFIER: {
            SYMTAB_NODE_PTR idp;

            /*
            -- Assignment statement or procedure call?
            */
            search_and_find_all_symtab(idp);

            if (idp->defn.key == PROC_DEFN) {
                crunch_symtab_node_ptr(idp);
                get_token();
                routine_call(idp, TRUE);
            }
            else assignment_statement(idp);

            break;
        }
```

```
        case REPEAT:    repeat_statement();     break;
        case WHILE:     while_statement();      break;
        case IF:        if_statement();         break;
        case FOR:       for_statement();        break;
        case CASE:      case_statement();       break;
        case BEGIN:     compound_statement();   break;
    }

    /*
    -- Error synchronization:  Only a semicolon, END, ELSE, or
    --                         UNTIL may follow a statement.
    --                         Check for a missing semicolon.
    */
    synchronize(statement_end_list, NULL, NULL);
    if (token_in(statement_start_list)) error(MISSING_SEMICOLON);
}

/*--------------------------------------------------------*/
/* assignment_statement     Process an assignment statement: */
/*                                                           */
/*                          <id> := <expr>                   */
/*--------------------------------------------------------*/

assignment_statement(var_idp)

    SYMTAB_NODE_PTR var_idp;            /* target variable id */

{
    TYPE_STRUCT_PTR var_tp, expr_tp;    /* types of var and expr */

    var_tp = variable(var_idp, TARGET_USE);
    if_token_get_else_error(COLONEQUAL, MISSING_COLONEQUAL);

    expr_tp = expression();

    if (! is_assign_type_compatible(var_tp, expr_tp))
        error(INCOMPATIBLE_ASSIGNMENT);
}

/*--------------------------------------------------------*/
/* repeat_statement     Process a REPEAT statement:         */
/*                                                          */
/*                      REPEAT <stmt-list> UNTIL <expr>      */
/*--------------------------------------------------------*/

repeat_statement()

{
    TYPE_STRUCT_PTR expr_tp;

    /*
    -- <stmt-list>
    */
    get_token();
    do {
        statement();
        while (token == SEMICOLON) get_token();
    } while (token_in(statement_start_list));

    if_token_get_else_error(UNTIL, MISSING_UNTIL);

    expr_tp = expression();
    if (expr_tp != boolean_typep) error(INCOMPATIBLE_TYPES);
}

/*--------------------------------------------------------*/
/* while_statement      Process a WHILE statement:          */
```

```
/*                                                    */
/*                      WHILE <expr> DO <stmt>         */
/*--------------------------------------------------*/

while_statement()

{
    TYPE_STRUCT_PTR expr_tp;
    char            *loop_end_location;

    get_token();
    loop_end_location = crunch_address_marker(NULL);

    expr_tp = expression();
    if (expr_tp != boolean_typep) error(INCOMPATIBLE_TYPES);

    if_token_get_else_error(DO, MISSING_DO);
    statement();

    fixup_address_marker(loop_end_location);
}

/*--------------------------------------------------*/
/*  if_statement      Process an IF statement:        */
/*                                                    */
/*                      IF <expr> THEN <stmt>          */
/*                                                    */
/*                      or:                            */
/*                                                    */
/*                      IF <expr> THEN <stmt> ELSE <stmt> */
/*--------------------------------------------------*/

if_statement()

{
    TYPE_STRUCT_PTR expr_tp;
    char            *false_location;
    char            *if_end_location;

    get_token();
    false_location = crunch_address_marker(NULL);

    expr_tp = expression();
    if (expr_tp != boolean_typep) error(INCOMPATIBLE_TYPES);

    if_token_get_else_error(THEN, MISSING_THEN);
    statement();

    fixup_address_marker(false_location);

    /*
    -- ELSE branch?
    */
    if (token == ELSE) {
        get_token();
        if_end_location = crunch_address_marker(NULL);

        statement();

        fixup_address_marker(if_end_location);
    }
}

/*--------------------------------------------------*/
/*  for_statement     Process a FOR statement:        */
/*                                                    */
/*                      FOR <id> := <expr> TO|DOWNTO <expr> */
```

```
/*                      DO <stmt>                      */
/*--------------------------------------------------*/

for_statement()

{
    SYMTAB_NODE_PTR for_idp;
    TYPE_STRUCT_PTR for_tp, expr_tp;
    char            *loop_end_location;

    get_token();
    loop_end_location = crunch_address_marker(NULL);

    if (token == IDENTIFIER) {
        search_and_find_all_symtab(for_idp);
        crunch_symtab_node_ptr(for_idp);

        if ((for_idp->level != level) ||
            (for_idp->defn.key != VAR_DEFN))
            error(INVALID_FOR_CONTROL);

        for_tp = base_type(for_idp->typep);
        get_token();

        if ((for_tp != integer_typep) &&
            (for_tp != char_typep) &&
            (for_tp->form != ENUM_FORM)) error(INCOMPATIBLE_TYPES);
    }
    else {
        error(IDENTIFIER, MISSING_IDENTIFIER);
        for_tp = &dummy_type;
    }

    if_token_get_else_error(COLONEQUAL, MISSING_COLONEQUAL);

    expr_tp = expression();
    if (! is_assign_type_compatible(for_tp, expr_tp))
        error(INCOMPATIBLE_TYPES);

    if ((token == TO) || (token == DOWNTO)) get_token();
    else error(MISSING_TO_OR_DOWNTO);

    expr_tp = expression();
    if (! is_assign_type_compatible(for_tp, expr_tp))
        error(INCOMPATIBLE_TYPES);

    if_token_get_else_error(DO, MISSING_DO);
    statement();

    fixup_address_marker(loop_end_location);
}

/*--------------------------------------------------*/
/* CASE statement globals                             */
/*--------------------------------------------------*/

typedef struct case_item {
    int             label_value;
    char            *branch_location;
    struct case_item *next;
} CASE_ITEM, *CASE_ITEM_PTR;

CASE_ITEM_PTR case_item_head, case_item_tail;
int           case_label_count;

/*--------------------------------------------------*/
/*  case_statement    Process a CASE statement:       */
```

```
/*                                              */
/*                  CASE <expr> OF              */
/*                     <case-branch> ;          */
/*                        ...                    */
/*                     END                       */
/*----------------------------------------------*/

TOKEN_CODE follow_expr_list[]     = {OF, SEMICOLON, 0};

TOKEN_CODE case_label_start_list[] = {IDENTIFIER, NUMBER, PLUS,
                                      MINUS, STRING, 0};


case_statement()

{
    BOOLEAN         another_branch;
    TYPE_STRUCT_PTR expr_tp;
    TYPE_STRUCT_PTR case_label();
    CASE_ITEM_PTR   case_itemp, next_case_itemp;
    char            *branch_table_location;
    char            *case_end_chain = NULL;

    /*
    -- Initializations for the branch table.
    */
    get_token();
    branch_table_location = crunch_address_marker(NULL);
    case_item_head = case_item_tail = NULL;
    case_label_count = 0;

    expr_tp = expression();

    if (   ((expr_tp->form != SCALAR_FORM) &&
            (expr_tp->form != ENUM_FORM) &&
            (expr_tp->form != SUBRANGE_FORM))
        || (expr_tp == real_typep)) error(INCOMPATIBLE_TYPES);

    /*
    -- Error synchronization:  Should be OF
    */
    synchronize(follow_expr_list, case_label_start_list, NULL);
    if_token_get_else_error(OF, MISSING_OF);

    /*
    -- Loop to process CASE branches.
    */
    another_branch = token_in(case_label_start_list);
    while (another_branch) {
        if (token_in(case_label_start_list)) case_branch(expr_tp);

        /*
        -- Link another address marker at the end of
        -- the CASE branch to point to the end of
        -- the CASE statement.
        */
        case_end_chain = crunch_address_marker(case_end_chain);

        if (token == SEMICOLON) {
            get_token();
            another_branch = TRUE;
        }
        else if (token_in(case_label_start_list)) {
            error(MISSING_SEMICOLON);
            another_branch = TRUE;
        }
        else another_branch = FALSE;
    }
```

```
    /*
    -- Emit the branch table.
    */
    fixup_address_marker(branch_table_location);
    crunch_integer(case_label_count);
    case_itemp = case_item_head;
    while (case_itemp != NULL) {
        crunch_integer(case_itemp->label_value);
        crunch_offset(case_itemp->branch_location);
        next_case_itemp = case_itemp->next;
        free(case_itemp);
        case_itemp = next_case_itemp;
    }

    if_token_get_else_error(END, MISSING_END);

    /*
    -- Patch the CASE branch address markers.
    */
    while (case_end_chain != NULL)
        case_end_chain = fixup_address_marker(case_end_chain);
}

/*----------------------------------------------*/
/* case_branch          Process a CASE branch:  */
/*                                              */
/*                  <case-label-list> : <stmt>  */
/*----------------------------------------------*/

TOKEN_CODE follow_case_label_list[] = {COLON, SEMICOLON, 0};

case_branch(expr_tp)

    TYPE_STRUCT_PTR expr_tp;          /* type of CASE expression */

{
    BOOLEAN         another_label;
    TYPE_STRUCT_PTR label_tp;
    CASE_ITEM_PTR   case_itemp;
    CASE_ITEM_PTR   old_case_item_tail = case_item_tail;
    TYPE_STRUCT_PTR case_label();

    /*
    -- <case-label-list>
    */
    do {
        label_tp = case_label();
        if (expr_tp != label_tp) error(INCOMPATIBLE_TYPES);

        get_token();
        if (token == COMMA) {
            get_token();
            if (token_in(case_label_start_list)) another_label = TRUE;
            else {
                error(MISSING_CONSTANT);
                another_label = FALSE;
            }
        }
        else another_label = FALSE;
    } while (another_label);

    /*
    -- Error synchronization:  Should be :
    */
    synchronize(follow_case_label_list, statement_start_list, NULL);
    if_token_get_else_error(COLON, MISSING_COLON);

    /*
```

```
    --  Loop to fill in the branch_location field of
    --  each CASE_ITEM item for this branch.
    */
    case_itemp = old_case_item_tail == NULL
                    ? case_item_head
                    : old_case_item_tail->next;
    while (case_itemp != NULL) {
        case_itemp->branch_location = code_bufferp;
        case_itemp = case_itemp->next;
    }

    statement();
}

/*----------------------------------------------------------*/
/*  case_label           Process a CASE label and return a  */
/*                        pointer to its type structure.    */
/*----------------------------------------------------------*/

    TYPE_STRUCT_PTR
case_label()

{
    TOKEN_CODE      sign     = PLUS;    /* unary + or - sign */
    BOOLEAN         saw_sign = FALSE;   /* TRUE iff unary sign */
    TYPE_STRUCT_PTR label_tp;
    CASE_ITEM_PTR   case_itemp = alloc_struct(CASE_ITEM);

    /*
    --  Link in a CASE_ITEM item for this label.
    */
    if (case_item_head != NULL) {
        case_item_tail->next = case_itemp;
        case_item_tail = case_itemp;
    }
    else {
        case_item_head = case_item_tail = case_itemp;
    }
    case_itemp->next = NULL;
    ++case_label_count;

    /*
    --  Unary + or - sign.
    */
    if ((token == PLUS) || (token == MINUS)) {
        sign     = token;
        saw_sign = TRUE;
        get_token();
    }

    /*
    --  Numeric constant:  Integer type only.
    */
    if (token == NUMBER) {
        SYMTAB_NODE_PTR np = search_symtab(token_string,
                                        symtab_display[1]);

        if (np == NULL) np = enter_symtab(token_string,
                                        symtab_display[1]);
        crunch_symtab_node_ptr(np);

        if (literal.type == INTEGER_LIT)
            case_itemp->label_value = sign == PLUS
                                    ? literal.value.integer
                                    : -literal.value.integer;
        else error(INVALID_CONSTANT);
        return(integer_typep);
```

```
    }
    /*
    --  Identifier constant:  Integer, character, or enumeration
    --                        types only.
    */
    else if (token == IDENTIFIER) {
        SYMTAB_NODE_PTR idp;

        search_all_symtab(idp);
        crunch_symtab_node_ptr(idp);

        if (idp == NULL) {
            error(UNDEFINED_IDENTIFIER);
            return(&dummy_type);
        }

        else if (idp->defn.key != CONST_DEFN) {
            error(NOT_A_CONSTANT_IDENTIFIER);
            return(&dummy_type);
        }

        else if (idp->typep == integer_typep) {
            case_itemp->label_value = sign == PLUS
                                    ? idp->defn.info.constant
                                          .value.integer
                                    : -idp->defn.info.constant
                                          .value.integer;
            return(integer_typep);
        }

        else if (idp->typep == char_typep) {
            if (saw_sign) error(INVALID_CONSTANT);
            case_itemp->label_value = idp->defn.info.constant
                                        .value.character;
            return(char_typep);
        }

        else if (idp->typep->form == ENUM_FORM) {
            if (saw_sign) error(INVALID_CONSTANT);
            case_itemp->label_value = idp->defn.info.constant
                                        .value.integer;
            return(idp->typep);
        }

        else return(&dummy_type);
    }

    /*
    --  String constant:  Character type only.
    */
    else if (token == STRING) {
        SYMTAB_NODE_PTR np = search_symtab(token_string,
                                        symtab_display[1]);

        if (np == NULL) np = enter_symtab(token_string,
                                        symtab_display[1]);
        crunch_symtab_node_ptr(np);

        if (saw_sign) error(INVALID_CONSTANT);

        if (strlen(literal.value.string) == 1) {
            case_itemp->label_value = literal.value.string[0];
            return(char_typep);
        }
        else {
            error(INVALID_CONSTANT);
```

```
        return(&dummy_type);
    }
}

else {
    error(INVALID_CONSTANT);
    return(&dummy_type);
}
}

/*------------------------------------------------------*/
/* compound_statement    Process a compound statement:  */
/*                                                      */
/*                       BEGIN <stmt-list> END          */
/*------------------------------------------------------*/

compound_statement()

{
```

```
/*
-- <stmt-list>
*/
get_token();
do {
    statement();
    while (token == SEMICOLON) get_token();
    if (token == END) break;

    /*
    -- Error synchronization:  Should be at the start of the
    --                         next statement.
    */
    synchronize(statement_start_list, NULL, NULL);
} while (token_in(statement_start_list));

if_token_get_else_error(END, MISSING_END);
}
```

FIGURE A-6   expr.c

```
/******************************************************/
/*                                                    */
/*      E X P R E S S I O N   P A R S E R             */
/*                                                    */
/*      Parsing routines for expressions.             */
/*                                                    */
/*      FILE:       expr.c                             */
/*                                                    */
/*      MODULE:     parser                             */
/*                                                    */
/******************************************************/

#include <stdio.h>
#include "common.h"
#include "error.h"
#include "scanner.h"
#include "symtab.h"
#include "parser.h"

/*------------------------------------------------------*/
/* Externals                                            */
/*------------------------------------------------------*/

extern TOKEN_CODE token;
extern char       token_string[];
extern char       word_string[];
extern LITERAL    literal;

extern SYMTAB_NODE_PTR symtab_display[];
extern int             level;

extern TYPE_STRUCT_PTR integer_typep, real_typep,
                       boolean_typep, char_typep;

extern TYPE_STRUCT     dummy_type;

/*------------------------------------------------------*/
/* Forwards                                             */
/*------------------------------------------------------*/

TYPE_STRUCT_PTR expression(), simple_expression(), term(), factor(),
```

```
            function_call();

/*------------------------------------------------------*/
/* integer_operands    TRUE if both operands are integer, */
/*                     else FALSE.                       */
/*------------------------------------------------------*/

#define integer_operands(tp1, tp2)  ((tp1 == integer_typep) && \
                                     (tp2 == integer_typep))


/*------------------------------------------------------*/
/* real_operands       TRUE if at least one or both operands */
/*                     operands are real (and the other  */
/*                     integer), else FALSE.             */
/*------------------------------------------------------*/

#define real_operands(tp1, tp2) (((tp1 == real_typep) &&      \
                                 ((tp2 == real_typep) ||      \
                                  (tp2 == integer_typep)))    \
                                         ||                   \
                                 ((tp2 == real_typep) &&      \
                                 ((tp1 == real_typep) ||      \
                                  (tp1 == integer_typep))))

/*------------------------------------------------------*/
/* boolean_operands    TRUE if both operands are boolean */
/*                     else FALSE.                       */
/*------------------------------------------------------*/

#define boolean_operands(tp1, pt2)  ((tp1 == boolean_typep) && \
                                     (tp2 == boolean_typep))

/*------------------------------------------------------*/
/* expression          Process an expression consisting of a */
/*                     simple expression optionally followed */
/*                     by a relational operator and a second */
/*                     simple expression.  Return a pointer to */
/*                     the type structure.               */
/*------------------------------------------------------*/

TOKEN_CODE rel_op_list[] = {LT, LE, EQUAL, NE, GE, GT, 0};
```

```
    TYPE_STRUCT_PTR
expression()

{
    TOKEN_CODE op;                      /* an operator token */
    TYPE_STRUCT_PTR result_tp, tp2;

    result_tp = simple_expression();    /* first simple expr */

    /*
    -- If there is a relational operator, remember it and
    -- process the second simple expression.
    */
    if (token_in(rel_op_list)) {
        op = token;                     /* remember operator */
        result_tp = base_type(result_tp);

        get_token();
        tp2 = base_type(simple_expression());   /* 2nd simple expr */

        check_rel_op_types(result_tp, tp2);
        result_tp = boolean_typep;
    }

    return(result_tp);
}

/*-----------------------------------------------------------*/
/* simple_expression   Process a simple expression consisting */
/*                     of terms separated by +, -, or OR      */
/*                     operators.  There may be a unary + or - */
/*                     before the first term.  Return a       */
/*                     pointer to the type structure.         */
/*-----------------------------------------------------------*/

TOKEN_CODE add_op_list[] = {PLUS, MINUS, OR, 0};

    TYPE_STRUCT_PTR
simple_expression()

{
    TOKEN_CODE op;                      /* an operator token */
    BOOLEAN    saw_unary_op = FALSE;    /* TRUE iff unary operator */
    TOKEN_CODE unary_op = PLUS;         /* a unary operator token */
    TYPE_STRUCT_PTR result_tp, tp2;

    /*
    -- If there is a unary + or -, remember it.
    */
    if ((token == PLUS) || (token == MINUS)) {
        unary_op = token;
        saw_unary_op = TRUE;
        get_token();
    }

    result_tp = term();         /* first term */

    /*
    -- If there was a unary operator, check that the term
    -- is integer or real.  Negate the top of stack if it
    -- was a unary - either with the NEG instruction or by
    -- calling FLOAT_NEGATE.
    */
    if (saw_unary_op &&
        (base_type(result_tp) != integer_typep) &&
        (result_tp != real_typep)) error(INCOMPATIBLE_TYPES);

    /*
```

```
    -- Loop to process subsequent terms separated by operators.
    */
    while (token_in(add_op_list)) {
        op = token;                     /* remember operator */
        result_tp = base_type(result_tp);

        get_token();
        tp2 = base_type(term());        /* subsequent term */

        switch (op) {

            case PLUS:
            case MINUS: {
                /*
                -- integer <op> integer => integer
                */
                if (integer_operands(result_tp, tp2))
                    result_tp = integer_typep;

                /*
                -- Both operands are real, or one is real and the
                -- other is integer.  The result is real.
                */
                else if (real_operands(result_tp, tp2))
                    result_tp = real_typep;

                else {
                    error(INCOMPATIBLE_TYPES);
                    result_tp = &dummy_type;
                }

                break;
            }

            case OR: {
                /*
                -- boolean OR boolean => boolean
                */
                if (! boolean_operands(result_tp, tp2))
                    error(INCOMPATIBLE_TYPES);

                result_tp = boolean_typep;
                break;
            }
        }
    }

    return(result_tp);
}

/*-----------------------------------------------------------*/
/* term                Process a term consisting of factors  */
/*                     separated by *, /, DIV, MOD, or AND    */
/*                     operators.  Return a pointer to the    */
/*                     type structure.                        */
/*-----------------------------------------------------------*/

TOKEN_CODE mult_op_list[] = {STAR, SLASH, DIV, MOD, AND, 0};

    TYPE_STRUCT_PTR
term()

{
    TOKEN_CODE op;                      /* an operator token */
    TYPE_STRUCT_PTR result_tp, tp2;

    result_tp = factor();               /* first factor */
```

```
/*
-- Loop to process subsequent factors
-- separated by operators.
*/
while (token_in(mult_op_list)) {
    op = token;                        /* remember operator */
    result_tp = base_type(result_tp);

    get_token();
    tp2 = base_type(factor());         /* subsequent factor */

    switch (op) {

        case STAR: {
            /*
            -- Both operands are integer.
            */
            if (integer_operands(result_tp, tp2))
                result_tp = integer_typep;

            /*
            -- Both operands are real, or one is real and the
            -- other is integer.  The result is real.
            */
            else if (real_operands(result_tp, tp2))
                result_tp = real_typep;

            else {
                error(INCOMPATIBLE_TYPES);
                result_tp = &dummy_type;
            }

            break;
        }

        case SLASH: {
            /*
            -- Both operands are real, or both are integer, or
            -- one is real and the other is integer.  The result
            -- is real.
            */
            if ((! real_operands(result_tp, tp2)) &&
                (! integer_operands(result_tp, tp2)))
                error(INCOMPATIBLE_TYPES);

            result_tp = real_typep;
            break;
        }

        case DIV:
        case MOD: {
            /*
            -- integer <op> integer => integer
            */
            if (! integer_operands(result_tp, tp2))
                error(INCOMPATIBLE_TYPES);

            result_tp = integer_typep;
            break;
        }

        case AND: {
            /*
            -- boolean AND boolean => boolean
            */
            if (! boolean_operands(result_tp, tp2))
                error(INCOMPATIBLE_TYPES);
```

```
                result_tp = boolean_typep;
                break;
            }
        }
    }

    return(result_tp);
}

/*------------------------------------------------------------*/
/* factor              Process a factor, which is an variable, */
/*                     a number, NOT followed by a factor, or  */
/*                     a parenthesized subexpression.  Return  */
/*                     a pointer to the type structure.        */
/*------------------------------------------------------------*/

    TYPE_STRUCT_PTR
factor()

{
    TYPE_STRUCT_PTR tp;

    switch (token) {

        case IDENTIFIER: {
            SYMTAB_NODE_PTR idp;

            search_and_find_all_symtab(idp);

            switch (idp->defn.key) {

                case FUNC_DEFN:
                    crunch_symtab_node_ptr(idp);
                    get_token();
                    tp = routine_call(idp, TRUE);
                    break;

                case PROC_DEFN:
                    error(INVALID_IDENTIFIER_USAGE);
                    get_token();
                    actual_parm_list(idp, FALSE);
                    tp = &dummy_type;
                    break;

                case CONST_DEFN:
                    crunch_symtab_node_ptr(idp);
                    get_token();
                    tp = idp->typep;
                    break;

                default:
                    tp = variable(idp, EXPR_USE);
                    break;
            }

            break;
        }

        case NUMBER: {
            SYMTAB_NODE_PTR np;

            np = search_symtab(token_string, symtab_display[1]);
            if (np == NULL) np = enter_symtab(token_string,
                                              symtab_display[1]);

            if (literal.type == INTEGER_LIT) {
                tp = np->typep = integer_typep;
```

```
                np->defn.info.constant.value.integer =
                    literal.value.integer;
            }
            else {   /* literal.type == REAL_LIT */
                tp = np->typep = real_typep;
                np->defn.info.constant.value.real =
                    literal.value.real;
            }

            crunch_symtab_node_ptr(np);
            get_token();

            break;
        }

        case STRING: {
            SYMTAB_NODE_PTR np;
            int             length = strlen(literal.value.string);

            np = search_symtab(token_string, symtab_display[1]);
            if (np == NULL) np = enter_symtab(token_string,
                                        symtab_display[1]);

            if (length == 1) {
                np->defn.info.constant.value.character =
                    literal.value.string[0];
                tp = char_typep;
            }
            else {
                np->typep = tp = make_string_typep(length);
                np->info  = alloc_bytes(length + 1);
                strcpy(np->info, literal.value.string);
            }

            crunch_symtab_node_ptr(np);

            get_token();
            break;
        }

        case NOT:
            get_token();
            tp = factor();
            break;

        case LPAREN:
            get_token();
            tp = expression();

            if_token_get_else_error(RPAREN, MISSING_RPAREN);
            break;

        default:
            error(INVALID_EXPRESSION);
            tp = &dummy_type;
            break;
    }

    return(tp);
}

/*-----------------------------------------------------------*/
/* variable          Process a variable, which can be a      */
/*                   simple identifier, an array identifier  */
/*                   with subscripts, or a record identifier */
/*                   with fields.                            */
/*-----------------------------------------------------------*/
```

```
    TYPE_STRUCT_PTR
variable(var_idp, use)

    SYMTAB_NODE_PTR var_idp;    /* variable id */
    USE             use;        /* how variable is used */

{
    TYPE_STRUCT_PTR tp        = var_idp->typep;
    DEFN_KEY        defn_key  = var_idp->defn.key;
    TYPE_STRUCT_PTR array_subscript_list();
    TYPE_STRUCT_PTR record_field();

    crunch_symtab_node_ptr(var_idp);

    /*
    -- Check the variable's definition.
    */
    switch (defn_key) {
        case VAR_DEFN:
        case VALPARM_DEFN:
        case VARPARM_DEFN:
        case FUNC_DEFN:
        case UNDEFINED:  break;        /* OK */

        default: {                     /* error */
            tp = &dummy_type;
            error(INVALID_IDENTIFIER_USAGE);
        }
    }

    get_token();

    /*
    -- There must not be a parameter list, but if there is one,
    -- parse it anyway for error recovery.
    */
    if (token == LPAREN) {
        error(UNEXPECTED_TOKEN);
        actual_parm_list(var_idp, FALSE);
        return(tp);
    }

    /*
    -- Subscripts and/or field designators?
    */
    while ((token == LBRACKET) || (token == PERIOD)) {
        tp = token == LBRACKET ? array_subscript_list(tp)
                               : record_field(tp);
    }

    return(tp);
}

/*-----------------------------------------------------------*/
/* array_subscript_list        Process a list of subscripts  */
/*                             following an array identifier: */
/*                                                           */
/*                                 [ <expr> , <expr> , ... ] */
/*-----------------------------------------------------------*/

    TYPE_STRUCT_PTR
array_subscript_list(tp)

    TYPE_STRUCT_PTR tp;

{
    TYPE_STRUCT_PTR   index_tp, elmt_tp, ss_tp;
```

```
extern TOKEN_CODE statement_end_list[];

/*
-- Loop to process a subscript list.
*/
do {
    if (tp->form == ARRAY_FORM) {
        index_tp = tp->info.array.index_typep;
        elmt_tp  = tp->info.array.elmt_typep;

        get_token();
        ss_tp = expression();

        /*
        -- The subscript expression must be assignment type
        -- compatible with the corresponding subscript type.
        */
        if (!is_assign_type_compatible(index_tp, ss_tp))
            error(INCOMPATIBLE_TYPES);

        tp = elmt_tp;
    }
    else {
        error(TOO_MANY_SUBSCRIPTS);
        while ((token != RBRACKET) &&
               (! token_in(statement_end_list)))
            get_token();
    }
} while (token == COMMA);

if_token_get_else_error(RBRACKET, MISSING_RBRACKET);
return(tp);
}

/*------------------------------------------------------------*/
/* record_field              Process a field designation      */
/*                           following a record identifier:   */
/*                                                            */
/*                                  . <field-variable>        */
/*------------------------------------------------------------*/

    TYPE_STRUCT_PTR
record_field(tp)

    TYPE_STRUCT_PTR tp;

{
    SYMTAB_NODE_PTR field_idp;

    get_token();

    if ((token == IDENTIFIER) && (tp->form == RECORD_FORM)) {
        search_this_symtab(field_idp,
                           tp->info.record.field_symtab);

        crunch_symtab_node_ptr(field_idp);
        get_token();

        if (field_idp != NULL) return(field_idp->typep);
        else {
            error(INVALID_FIELD);
            return(&dummy_type);
        }
    }
    else {
        get_token();
        error(INVALID_FIELD);
```

```
        return(&dummy_type);
    }
}

                /********************************/
                /*                              */
                /*      Type compatibility      */
                /*                              */
                /********************************/

/*------------------------------------------------------------*/
/* check_rel_op_types  Check the operand types for a rela-    */
/*                     tional operator.                       */
/*------------------------------------------------------------*/

check_rel_op_types(tp1, tp2)

    TYPE_STRUCT_PTR tp1, tp2;          /* operand types */

{
    /*
    -- Two identical scalar or enumeration types.
    */
    if (   (tp1 == tp2)
        && ((tp1->form == SCALAR_FORM) || (tp1->form == ENUM_FORM)))
        return;

    /*
    -- One integer and one real.
    */
    if (   ((tp1 == integer_typep) && (tp2 == real_typep))
        || ((tp2 == integer_typep) && (tp1 == real_typep))) return;

    /*
    -- Two strings of the same length.
    */
    if ((tp1->form == ARRAY_FORM) &&
        (tp2->form == ARRAY_FORM) &&
        (tp1->info.array.elmt_typep == char_typep) &&
        (tp2->info.array.elmt_typep == char_typep) &&
        (tp1->info.array.elmt_count ==
                    tp2->info.array.elmt_count)) return;

    error(INCOMPATIBLE_TYPES);
}

/*------------------------------------------------------------*/
/* is_assign_type_compatible   Return TRUE iff a value of type */
/*                             tp1 can be assigned to a vari-  */
/*                             able of type tp1.               */
/*------------------------------------------------------------*/

    BOOLEAN
is_assign_type_compatible(tp1, tp2)

    TYPE_STRUCT_PTR tp1, tp2;

{
    tp1 = base_type(tp1);
    tp2 = base_type(tp2);

    if (tp1 == tp2) return(TRUE);

    /*
    -- real := integer
    */
    if ((tp1 == real_typep) && (tp2 == integer_typep)) return(TRUE);
```

```
    /*
    -- string1 := string2 of the same length
    */
    if ((tp1->form == ARRAY_FORM) &&
        (tp2->form == ARRAY_FORM) &&
        (tp1->info.array.elmt_typep == char_typep) &&
        (tp2->info.array.elmt_typep == char_typep) &&
        (tp1->info.array.elmt_count ==
                      tp2->info.array.elmt_count)) return(TRUE);

    return(FALSE);
}

/*-------------------------------------------------------------*/
/* base_type          Return the range type of a subrange     */
```

```
/*                   type.                                    */
/*-------------------------------------------------------------*/

    TYPE_STRUCT_PTR
base_type(tp)

    TYPE_STRUCT_PTR tp;

{
    return((tp->form == SUBRANGE_FORM)
                ? tp->info.subrange.range_typep
                : tp);
}
```

FIGURE A-7   scanner.h

```
/****************************************************************/
/*                                                              */
/*      S C A N N E R   (Header)                                */
/*                                                              */
/*      FILE:      scanner.h                                    */
/*                                                              */
/*      MODULE:    scanner                                      */
/*                                                              */
/****************************************************************/

#ifndef scanner_h
#define scanner_h

#include "common.h"

/*-------------------------------------------------------------*/
/* Token codes                                                 */
/*-------------------------------------------------------------*/

typedef enum {
    NO_TOKEN, IDENTIFIER, NUMBER, STRING,
    UPARROW, STAR, LPAREN, RPAREN, MINUS, PLUS, EQUAL,
    LBRACKET, RBRACKET, COLON, SEMICOLON, LT, GT, COMMA, PERIOD,
    SLASH, COLONEQUAL, LE, GE, NE, DOTDOT, END_OF_FILE, ERROR,
    AND, ARRAY, BEGIN, CASE, CONST, DIV, DO, DOWNTO, ELSE, END,
    FFILE, FOR, FUNCTION, GOTO, IF, IN, LABEL, MOD, NIL, NOT,
    OF, OR, PACKED, PROCEDURE, PROGRAM, RECORD, REPEAT, SET,
```

```
    THEN, TO, TYPE, UNTIL, VAR, WHILE, WITH,
} TOKEN_CODE;

/*-------------------------------------------------------------*/
/* Literal structure                                           */
/*-------------------------------------------------------------*/

typedef enum {
    INTEGER_LIT, REAL_LIT, STRING_LIT,
} LITERAL_TYPE;

typedef struct {
    LITERAL_TYPE type;
    union {
        int    integer;
        float  real;
        char   string[MAX_SOURCE_LINE_LENGTH];
    } value;
} LITERAL;

/*-------------------------------------------------------------*/
/* Functions                                                   */
/*-------------------------------------------------------------*/

BOOLEAN token_in();

#endif
```

FIGURE A-8   scanner.c

```
/****************************************************************/
/*                                                              */
/*      S C A N N E R                                           */
/*                                                              */
/*      Scanner for Pascal tokens.                              */
/*                                                              */
/*      FILE:      scanner.c                                    */
/*                                                              */
```

```
/*      MODULE:    scanner                                      */
/*                                                              */
/****************************************************************/

#include <stdio.h>
#include <math.h>
#include <sys/types.h>
#include <sys/timeb.h>
```

```
#include "common.h"
#include "error.h"
#include "scanner.h"

#define EOF_CHAR          '\x7f'
#define TAB_SIZE          8

#define MAX_INTEGER       32767
#define MAX_DIGIT_COUNT   20
#define MAX_EXPONENT      37

#define MIN_RESERVED_WORD_LENGTH   2
#define MAX_RESERVED_WORD_LENGTH   9

/*------------------------------------------------------------*/
/* Character codes                                            */
/*------------------------------------------------------------*/

typedef enum {
    LETTER, DIGIT, QUOTE, SPECIAL, EOF_CODE,
} CHAR_CODE;

/*------------------------------------------------------------*/
/* Reserved word tables                                       */
/*------------------------------------------------------------*/

typedef struct {
    char      *string;
    TOKEN_CODE token_code;
} RW_STRUCT;

RW_STRUCT rw_2[] = {
    {"do", DO}, {"if", IF}, {"in", IN}, {"of", OF}, {"or", OR},
    {"to", TO}, {NULL, 0 },
};

RW_STRUCT rw_3[] = {
    {"and", AND}, {"div", DIV}, {"end", END}, {"for", FOR},
    {"mod", MOD}, {"nil", NIL}, {"not", NOT}, {"set", SET},
    {"var", VAR}, {NULL , 0 },
};

RW_STRUCT rw_4[] = {
    {"case", CASE}, {"else", ELSE}, {"file", FFILE},
    {"goto", GOTO}, {"then", THEN}, {"type", TYPE},
    {"with", WITH}, {NULL , 0   },
};

RW_STRUCT rw_5[] = {
    {"array", ARRAY}, {"begin", BEGIN}, {"const", CONST},
    {"label", LABEL}, {"until", UNTIL}, {"while", WHILE},
    {NULL   , 0   },
};

RW_STRUCT rw_6[] = {
    {"downto", DOWNTO}, {"packed", PACKED}, {"record", RECORD},
    {"repeat", REPEAT}, {NULL    , 0      },
};

RW_STRUCT rw_7[] = {
    {"program", PROGRAM}, {NULL, 0},
};

RW_STRUCT rw_8[] = {
    {"function", FUNCTION}, {NULL, 0},
};

RW_STRUCT rw_9[] = {
```

```
    {"procedure", PROCEDURE}, {NULL, 0},
};

RW_STRUCT *rw_table[] = {
    NULL, NULL, rw_2, rw_3, rw_4, rw_5, rw_6, rw_7, rw_8, rw_9,
};

/*------------------------------------------------------------*/
/* Token lists                                                */
/*------------------------------------------------------------*/

TOKEN_CODE statement_start_list[]  = {BEGIN, CASE, FOR, IF, REPEAT,
                                      WHILE, IDENTIFIER, 0};

TOKEN_CODE statement_end_list[]    = {SEMICOLON, END, ELSE, UNTIL,
                                      END_OF_FILE, 0};

TOKEN_CODE declaration_start_list[] = {CONST, TYPE, VAR, PROCEDURE,
                                      FUNCTION, 0};

/*------------------------------------------------------------*/
/* Globals                                                    */
/*------------------------------------------------------------*/

char      ch;                /* current input character */
TOKEN_CODE token;            /* code of current token */
LITERAL   literal;           /* value of literal */
int       buffer_offset;     /* char offset into source buffer */
int       level = 0;         /* current nesting level */
int       line_number = 0;   /* current line number */
BOOLEAN   print_flag = TRUE; /* TRUE to print source lines */
BOOLEAN   block_flag = FALSE; /* TRUE only when parsing a block */

char source_buffer[MAX_SOURCE_LINE_LENGTH]; /* source file buffer */
char token_string[MAX_TOKEN_STRING_LENGTH]; /* token string */
char word_string[MAX_TOKEN_STRING_LENGTH];  /* downshifted */
char *bufferp = source_buffer;              /* source buffer ptr */
char *tokenp = token_string;                /* token string ptr */

int     digit_count;         /* total no. of digits in number */
BOOLEAN count_error;         /* too many digits in number? */

int page_number = 0;
int line_count = MAX_LINES_PER_PAGE;   /* no. lines on current pg */

char source_name[MAX_FILE_NAME_LENGTH]; /* name of source file */
char date[DATE_STRING_LENGTH];          /* current date and time */

FILE *source_file;

CHAR_CODE char_table[256];

/*------------------------------------------------------------*/
/* char_code          Return the character code of ch.        */
/*------------------------------------------------------------*/

#define char_code(ch)   char_table[ch]

             /*******************************/
             /*                             */
             /*        Initialization       */
             /*                             */
             /*******************************/

/*------------------------------------------------------------*/
/* init_scanner       Initialize the scanner globals          */
/*                    and open the source file.               */
```

```
/*------------------------------------------------------------*/

init_scanner(name)

    char *name;        /* name of source file */

{
    int ch;

    /*
    -- Initialize character table.
    */
    for (ch = 0;   ch < 256;  ++ch) char_table[ch] = SPECIAL;
    for (ch = '0'; ch <= '9'; ++ch) char_table[ch] = DIGIT;
    for (ch = 'A'; ch <= 'Z'; ++ch) char_table[ch] = LETTER;
    for (ch = 'a'; ch <= 'z'; ++ch) char_table[ch] = LETTER;
    char_table['\''] = QUOTE;
    char_table[EOF_CHAR] = EOF_CODE;

    init_page_header(name);
    open_source_file(name);
}

/*------------------------------------------------------------*/
/* quit_scanner       Terminate the scanner.              */
/*------------------------------------------------------------*/

quit_scanner()

{
    close_source_file();
}

            /*********************************/
            /*                               */
            /*      Character routines       */
            /*                               */
            /*********************************/

/*------------------------------------------------------------*/
/* get_char        Set ch to the next character from the  */
/*                 source buffer.                         */
/*------------------------------------------------------------*/

get_char()

{
    BOOLEAN get_source_line();

    /*
    -- If at end of current source line, read another line.
    -- If at end of file, set ch to the EOF character and return.
    */
    if (*bufferp == '\0') {
        if (! get_source_line()) {
            ch = EOF_CHAR;
            return;
        }
        bufferp = source_buffer;
        buffer_offset = 0;
    }

    ch = *bufferp++;     /* next character in the buffer */

    /*
    -- Special character processing:
    --
```

```
    --      tab        Increment buffer_offset up to the next
    --                 multiple of TAB_SIZE, and replace ch with
    --                 a blank.
    --
    --      new-line   Replace ch with a blank.
    --
    --      {          Start of comment:  Skip over comment and
    --                 replace it with a blank.
    */
    switch (ch) {

        case '\t':  buffer_offset += TAB_SIZE -
                                buffer_offset%TAB_SIZE;
                    ch = ' ';
                    break;

        case '\n':  ++buffer_offset;
                    ch = ' ';
                    break;

        case '{':   ++buffer_offset;
                    skip_comment();
                    ch = ' ';
                    break;

        default:    ++buffer_offset;
    }
}

/*------------------------------------------------------------*/
/* skip_comment      Skip over a comment.  Set ch to '}'.  */
/*------------------------------------------------------------*/

skip_comment()

{
    do {
        get_char();
    } while ((ch != '}') && (ch != EOF_CHAR));
}

/*------------------------------------------------------------*/
/* skip_blanks       Skip past any blanks at the current    */
/*                   location in the source buffer.  Set    */
/*                   ch to the next nonblank character.     */
/*------------------------------------------------------------*/

skip_blanks()

{
    while (ch == ' ') get_char();
}

            /*********************************/
            /*                               */
            /*        Token routines         */
            /*                               */
            /*********************************/

    /* Note that after a token has been extracted, */
    /* ch is the first character after the token.  */

/*------------------------------------------------------------*/
/* get_token        Extract the next token from the source */
/*                  buffer.                                */
/*------------------------------------------------------------*/

get_token()
```

```
{
    skip_blanks();
    tokenp = token_string;

    switch (char_code(ch)) {
        case LETTER:    get_word();          break;
        case DIGIT:     get_number();        break;
        case QUOTE:     get_string();        break;
        case EOF_CODE:  token = END_OF_FILE; break;
        default:        get_special();       break;
    }

    /*
    -- For the interpreter:  While parsing a block, crunch
    -- the token code and append it to the code buffer.
    */
    if (block_flag) crunch_token();
}

/*-------------------------------------------------------------*/
/*  get_word          Extract a word token and downshift its  */
/*                     characters.  Check if it's a reserved   */
/*                     word.  Set token to IDENTIFIER if it's  */
/*                     not.                                     */
/*-------------------------------------------------------------*/

get_word()

{
    BOOLEAN is_reserved_word();

    /*
    -- Extract the word.
    */
    while ((char_code(ch) == LETTER) || (char_code(ch) == DIGIT)) {
        *tokenp++ = ch;
        get_char();
    }
    *tokenp = '\0';
    downshift_word();

    if (! is_reserved_word()) token = IDENTIFIER;
}

/*-------------------------------------------------------------*/
/*  get_number        Extract a number token and set literal   */
/*                    to its value.  Set token to NUMBER.      */
/*-------------------------------------------------------------*/

get_number()

{
    int     whole_count    = 0;     /* no. digits in whole part */
    int     decimal_offset = 0;     /* no. digits to move decimal */
    char    exponent_sign  = '+';
    int     exponent       = 0;     /* value of exponent */
    float   nvalue         = 0.0;   /* value of number */
    float   evalue         = 0.0;   /* value of exponent */
    BOOLEAN saw_dotdot     = FALSE; /* TRUE if encounter .. */

    digit_count  = 0;
    count_error  = FALSE;
    token        = NO_TOKEN;

    literal.type = INTEGER_LIT;     /* assume it's an integer */

    /*
```

```
    -- Extract the whole part of the number by accumulating
    -- the values of its digits into nvalue.  whole_count keeps
    -- track of the number of digits in this part.
    */
    accumulate_value(&nvalue, INVALID_NUMBER);
    if (token == ERROR) return;
    whole_count = digit_count;

    /*
    -- If the current character is a dot, then either we have a
    -- fraction part or we are seeing the first character of a ..
    -- token.  To find out, we must fetch the next character.
    */
    if (ch == '.') {
        get_char();

        if (ch == '.') {
            /*
            -- We have a .. token.  Back up bufferp so that the
            -- token can be extracted next.
            */
            saw_dotdot = TRUE;
            --bufferp;
        }
        else {
            literal.type = REAL_LIT;
            *tokenp++ = '.';

            /*
            -- We have a fraction part.  Accumulate it into nvalue.
            -- decimal_offset keeps track of how many digits to move
            -- the decimal point back.
            */
            accumulate_value(&nvalue, INVALID_FRACTION);
            if (token == ERROR) return;
            decimal_offset = whole_count - digit_count;
        }
    }

    /*
    -- Extract the exponent part, if any. There cannot be an
    -- exponent part if the .. token has been seen.
    */
    if (!saw_dotdot && ((ch == 'E') || (ch == 'e'))) {
        literal.type = REAL_LIT;
        *tokenp++ = ch;
        get_char();

        /*
        -- Fetch the exponent's sign, if any.
        */
        if ((ch == '+') || (ch == '-')) {
            *tokenp++ = exponent_sign = ch;
            get_char();
        }

        /*
        -- Extract the exponent.  Accumulate it into evalue.
        */
        accumulate_value(&evalue, INVALID_EXPONENT);
        if (token == ERROR) return;
        if (exponent_sign == '-') evalue = -evalue;
    }

    /*
    -- Were there too many digits?
    */
```

```
if (count_error) {
    error(TOO_MANY_DIGITS);
    token = ERROR;
    return;
}

/*
-- Adjust the number's value using
-- decimal_offset and the exponent.
*/
exponent = evalue + decimal_offset;
if ((exponent + whole_count < -MAX_EXPONENT) ||
    (exponent + whole_count > MAX_EXPONENT)) {
    error(REAL_OUT_OF_RANGE);
    token = ERROR;
    return;
}
if (exponent != 0) nvalue *= pow(10, exponent);

/*
-- Set the literal's value.
*/
if (literal.type == INTEGER_LIT) {
    if ((nvalue < -MAX_INTEGER) || (nvalue > MAX_INTEGER)) {
        error(INTEGER_OUT_OF_RANGE);
        token = ERROR;
        return;
    }
    literal.value.integer = nvalue;
}
else literal.value.real = nvalue;

*tokenp = '\0';
token   = NUMBER;
}

/*-----------------------------------------------------*/
/*  get_string          Extract a string token.  Set token to  */
/*                       STRING.  Note that the quotes are      */
/*                       stored as part of token_string but not */
/*                       literal.value.string.                  */
/*-----------------------------------------------------*/

get_string()

{
    char *sp = literal.value.string;

    *tokenp++ = '\'';
    get_char();

    /*
    --   Extract the string.
    */
    while (ch != EOF_CHAR) {
        /*
        -- Two consecutive single quotes represent
        -- a single quote in the string.
        */
        if (ch == '\'') {
            *tokenp++ = ch;
            get_char();
            if (ch != '\'') break;
        }
        *tokenp++ = ch;
        *sp++     = ch;
        get_char();
```

```
    }

    *tokenp      = '\0';
    *sp          = '\0';
    token        = STRING;
    literal.type = STRING_LIT;
}

/*-----------------------------------------------------*/
/*  get_special          Extract a special token.  Most are   */
/*                        single-character.  Some are double-  */
/*                        character.  Set token appropriately. */
/*-----------------------------------------------------*/

get_special()

{
    *tokenp++ = ch;
    switch (ch) {
        case '^': token = UPARROW;   get_char();  break;
        case '*': token = STAR;      get_char();  break;
        case '(': token = LPAREN;    get_char();  break;
        case ')': token = RPAREN;    get_char();  break;
        case '-': token = MINUS;     get_char();  break;
        case '+': token = PLUS;      get_char();  break;
        case '=': token = EQUAL;     get_char();  break;
        case '[': token = LBRACKET;  get_char();  break;
        case ']': token = RBRACKET;  get_char();  break;
        case ';': token = SEMICOLON; get_char();  break;
        case ',': token = COMMA;     get_char();  break;
        case '/': token = SLASH;     get_char();  break;

        case ':': get_char();          /* : or := */
                  if (ch == '=') {
                      *tokenp++ = '=';
                      token     = COLONEQUAL;
                      get_char();
                  }
                  else token = COLON;
                  break;

        case '<': get_char();          /* < or <= or <> */
                  if (ch == '=') {
                      *tokenp++ = '=';
                      token     = LE;
                      get_char();
                  }
                  else if (ch == '>') {
                      *tokenp++ = '>';
                      token     = NE;
                      get_char();
                  }
                  else token = LT;
                  break;

        case '>': get_char();          /* > or >= */
                  if (ch == '=') {
                      *tokenp++ = '=';
                      token     = GE;
                      get_char();
                  }
                  else token = GT;
                  break;

        case '.': get_char();          /* . or .. */
                  if (ch == '.') {
                      *tokenp++ = '.';
```

```
                     token    = DOTDOT;                              if (++digit_count <= MAX_DIGIT_COUNT)
                     get_char();                                         value = 10*value + (ch - '0');
                  }                                                  else count_error = TRUE;
                  else token = PERIOD;
                  break;                                             get_char();
                                                            } while (char_code(ch) == DIGIT);
        default:   token = ERROR;
                   get_char();                               *valuep = value;
                   break;                               }
        }
    *tokenp = '\0';
}
                                                            /*****************************/
                                                            /*                           */
/*-------------------------------------------------*/        /*      Token testers        */
/* downshift_word    Copy a word token into word_string  */  /*                           */
/*                   with all letters downshifted.      */   /*****************************/
/*-------------------------------------------------*/

downshift_word()                                            /*-------------------------------------------------*/
                                                            /* token_in          Return TRUE if the current token is in */
{                                                           /*                   the token list, else return FALSE.    */
    int offset = 'a' - 'A';    /* offset to downshift a letter */   /*-------------------------------------------------*/
    char *wp  = word_string;
    char *tp  = token_string;                                   BOOLEAN
                                                            token_in(token_list)
    /*
    -- Copy word into word_string.                              TOKEN_CODE token_list[];
    */
    do {                                                    {
        *wp++ = (*tp >= 'A') && (*tp <= 'Z')   /* if a letter, */    TOKEN_CODE *tokenp;
                ? *tp + offset                 /* then downshift */
                : *tp;                         /* else just copy */   if (token_list == NULL) return(FALSE);
        ++tp;
    } while (*tp != '\0');                                      for (tokenp = &token_list[0]; *tokenp; ++tokenp) {
                                                                   if (token == *tokenp) return(TRUE);
    *wp = '\0';                                                 }
}
                                                                return(FALSE);
                                                            }
/*-------------------------------------------------*/
/* accumulate_value    Extract a number part and accumulate  */  /*-------------------------------------------------*/
/*                     its value. Flag the error if the first */  /* synchronize     If the current token is not in one of */
/*                     character is not a digit.              */  /*                 the token lists, flag it as an error. */
/*-------------------------------------------------*/            /*                 Then skip tokens until one that is in */
                                                                /*                 one of the token lists.              */
accumulate_value(valuep, error_code)                            /*-------------------------------------------------*/

    float      *valuep;                                     synchronize(token_list1, token_list2, token_list3)
    ERROR_CODE error_code;
                                                                TOKEN_CODE token_list1[], token_list2[], token_list3[];
{
    float value = *valuep;                                  {
                                                                BOOLEAN error_flag = (! token_in(token_list1)) &&
    /*                                                                              (! token_in(token_list2)) &&
    -- Error if the first character is not a digit.                                 (! token_in(token_list3)));
    */
    if (char_code(ch) != DIGIT) {                               if (error_flag) {
        error(error_code);                                          error(token == END_OF_FILE ? UNEXPECTED_END_OF_FILE
        token = ERROR;                                                                          : UNEXPECTED_TOKEN);
        return;
    }                                                               /*
                                                                    -- Skip tokens to resynchronize.
    /*                                                              */
    -- Accumulate the value as long as the total allowable          while ((! token_in(token_list1)) &&
    -- number of digits has not been exceeded.                             (! token_in(token_list2)) &&
    */                                                                     (! token_in(token_list3)) &&
    do {                                                                   (token != END_OF_FILE))
        *tokenp++ = ch;                                                 get_token();
                                                                }
```

```
}

/*----------------------------------------------------------*/
/* is_reserved_word       Check to see if a word token is a  */
/*                        reserved word.  If so, set token   */
/*                        appropriately and return TRUE.  Else, */
/*                        return FALSE.                      */
/*----------------------------------------------------------*/

    BOOLEAN
is_reserved_word()

{
    int        word_length = strlen(word_string);
    RW_STRUCT *rwp;

    /*
    -- Is it the right length?
    */
    if ((word_length >= MIN_RESERVED_WORD_LENGTH) &&
        (word_length <= MAX_RESERVED_WORD_LENGTH)) {
        /*
        -- Yes.  Pick the appropriate reserved word list
        -- and check to see if the word is in there.
        */
        for (rwp = rw_table[word_length];
             rwp->string != NULL;
             ++rwp) {
            if (strcmp(word_string, rwp->string) == 0) {
                token = rwp->token_code;
                return(TRUE);            /* yes, a reserved word */
            }
        }
    }

    return(FALSE);                       /* no, it's not */
}


              /*******************************/
              /*                             */
              /*      Source file routines   */
              /*                             */
              /*******************************/

/*----------------------------------------------------------*/
/* open_source_file       Open the source file and fetch its */
/*                        first character.                   */
/*----------------------------------------------------------*/

open_source_file(name)

    char *name;         /* name of source file */

{
    if ((name == NULL) ||
        ((source_file = fopen(name, "r")) == NULL)) {
        error(FAILED_SOURCE_FILE_OPEN);
        exit(-FAILED_SOURCE_FILE_OPEN);
    }

    /*
    -- Fetch the first character.
    */
    bufferp = ""      ;
    get_char();
}
```

```
/*----------------------------------------------------------*/
/* close_source_file  Close the source file.                */
/*----------------------------------------------------------*/

close_source_file()

{
    fclose(source_file);
}

/*----------------------------------------------------------*/
/* get_source_line       Read the next line from the source  */
/*                       file.  If there is one, print it out */
/*                       and return TRUE.  Else return FALSE  */
/*                       for the end of file.                */
/*----------------------------------------------------------*/

    BOOLEAN
get_source_line()

{
    char print_buffer[MAX_SOURCE_LINE_LENGTH + 9];

    if ((fgets(source_buffer, MAX_SOURCE_LINE_LENGTH,
                            source_file)) != NULL) {
        ++line_number;

        if (print_flag) {
            sprintf(print_buffer, "%4d %d: %s",
                        line_number, level, source_buffer);
            print_line(print_buffer);
        }

        return(TRUE);
    }
    else return(FALSE);
}


              /*******************************/
              /*                             */
              /*      Printout routines      */
              /*                             */
              /*******************************/

/*----------------------------------------------------------*/
/* print_line           Print out a line.  Start a new page if */
/*                      the current page is full.            */
/*----------------------------------------------------------*/

print_line(line)

    char line[];        /* line to be printed */

{
    char save_ch;
    char *save_chp = NULL;

    if (++line_count > MAX_LINES_PER_PAGE) {
        print_page_header();
        line_count = 1;
    };

    if (strlen(line) > MAX_PRINT_LINE_LENGTH) {
        save_chp  = &line[MAX_PRINT_LINE_LENGTH];
        save_ch   = *save_chp;
        *save_chp = '\0';
    }
```

```
    printf("%s", line);                                        /*
                                                               -- Set the current date and time in the date string.
    if (save_chp) *save_chp = save_ch;                         */
}                                                              time(&timer);
                                                               strcpy(date, asctime(localtime(&timer)));
/*-------------------------------------------------*/      }
/* init_page_header    Initialize the fields of the page */
/*                     header.                           */   /*-------------------------------------------------*/
/*-------------------------------------------------*/      /* print_page_header  Print the page header at the top of */
                                                             /*                   the next page.                      */
init_page_header(name)                                       /*-------------------------------------------------*/

    char *name;        /* name of source file */             print_page_header()

{                                                            {
    time_t timer;                                                putchar(FORM_FEED_CHAR);
                                                                 printf("Page %d   %s   %s\n\n", ++page_number, source_name, date);
    strncpy(source_name, name, MAX_FILE_NAME_LENGTH - 1);    }
```

FIGURE A-9   symtab.h

```
/*****************************************************************/
/*                                                               */
/*        S Y M B O L   T A B L E   (Header)                     */
/*                                                               */
/*     FILE:      symtab.h                                       */
/*                                                               */
/*     MODULE:    symbol table                                   */
/*                                                               */
/*****************************************************************/

#ifndef symtab_h
#define symtab_h

#include "common.h"

/*-------------------------------------------------*/
/* Value structure                                 */
/*-------------------------------------------------*/

typedef union {
    int   integer;
    float real;
    char  character;
    char  *stringp;
} VALUE;

/*-------------------------------------------------*/
/* Definition structure                            */
/*-------------------------------------------------*/

typedef enum {
    UNDEFINED,
    CONST_DEFN, TYPE_DEFN, VAR_DEFN, FIELD_DEFN,
    VALPARM_DEFN, VARPARM_DEFN,
    PROG_DEFN, PROC_DEFN, FUNC_DEFN,
} DEFN_KEY;

typedef enum {
    DECLARED, FORWARD,
    READ, READLN, WRITE, WRITELN,
    ABS, ARCTAN, CHR, COS, EOFF, EOLN, EXP, LN, ODD, ORD,
    PRED, ROUND, SIN, SQR, SQRT, SUCC, TRUNC,
} ROUTINE_KEY;

typedef struct {
    DEFN_KEY key;
    union {
        struct {
            VALUE value;
        } constant;

        struct {
            ROUTINE_KEY        key;
            int                parm_count;
            int                total_parm_size;
            int                total_local_size;
            struct symtab_node *parms;
            struct symtab_node *locals;
            struct symtab_node *local_symtab;
            char               *code_segment;
        } routine;

        struct {
            int                offset;
            struct symtab_node *record_idp;
        } data;
    } info;
} DEFN_STRUCT;

/*-------------------------------------------------*/
/* Type structure                                  */
/*-------------------------------------------------*/

typedef enum {
    NO_FORM,
    SCALAR_FORM, ENUM_FORM, SUBRANGE_FORM,
    ARRAY_FORM, RECORD_FORM,
} TYPE_FORM;

typedef struct type_struct {
    TYPE_FORM       form;
    int             size;
```

```
    struct symtab_node *type_idp;
    union {
        struct {
            struct symtab_node *const_idp;
            int              max;
        } enumeration;

        struct {
            struct type_struct *range_typep;
            int              min, max;
        } subrange;

        struct {
            struct type_struct *index_typep, *elmt_typep;
            int              min_index, max_index;
            int              elmt_count;
        } array;

        struct {
            struct symtab_node *field_symtab;
        } record;
    } info;
} TYPE_STRUCT, *TYPE_STRUCT_PTR;

/*------------------------------------------------------*/
/* Symbol table node                                    */
/*------------------------------------------------------*/

typedef struct symtab_node {
    struct symtab_node *left, *right;   /* ptrs to subtrees */
    struct symtab_node *next;           /* for chaining nodes */
    char               *name;           /* name string */
    char               *info;           /* ptr to generic info */
    DEFN_STRUCT        defn;            /* definition struct */
    TYPE_STRUCT_PTR    typep;           /* ptr to type struct */
    int                level;           /* nesting level */
    int                label_index;     /* index for code label */
} SYMTAB_NODE, *SYMTAB_NODE_PTR;

/*------------------------------------------------------*/
/* Functions                                            */
/*------------------------------------------------------*/

SYMTAB_NODE_PTR search_symtab();
SYMTAB_NODE_PTR search_symtab_display();
SYMTAB_NODE_PTR enter_symtab();
SYMTAB_NODE_PTR exit_scope();
TYPE_STRUCT_PTR make_string_typep();

        /**************************************/
        /*                                    */
        /*    Macros to search symbol tables  */
        /*                                    */
        /**************************************/

/*------------------------------------------------------*/
/* search_local_symtab         Search the local symbol  */
/*                             table for the current id */
/*                             name.  Set a pointer to the */
/*                             entry if found, else to  */
/*                             NULL.                    */
/*------------------------------------------------------*/

#define search_local_symtab(idp)                          \
    idp = search_symtab(word_string, symtab_display[level])

/*------------------------------------------------------*/
/* search_this_symtab          Search the given symbol  */
```

```
/*                             table for the current id */
/*                             name. Set a pointer to the */
/*                             entry if found, else to  */
/*                             NULL.                    */
/*------------------------------------------------------*/

#define search_this_symtab(idp, this_symtab)              \
    idp = search_symtab(word_string, this_symtab)

/*------------------------------------------------------*/
/* search_all_symtab           Search the symbol table  */
/*                             display for the current id */
/*                             name.  Set a pointer to the */
/*                             entry if found, else to  */
/*                             NULL.                    */
/*------------------------------------------------------*/

#define search_all_symtab(idp)                            \
    idp = search_symtab_display(word_string)

/*------------------------------------------------------*/
/* enter_local_symtab          Enter the current id name */
/*                             into the local symbol    */
/*                             table, and set a pointer */
/*                             to the entry.            */
/*------------------------------------------------------*/

#define enter_local_symtab(idp)                           \
    idp = enter_symtab(word_string, &symtab_display[level])

/*------------------------------------------------------*/
/* enter_name_local_symtab     Enter the given name into */
/*                             the local symbol table, and */
/*                             set a pointer to the entry. */
/*------------------------------------------------------*/

#define enter_name_local_symtab(idp, name)                \
    idp = enter_symtab(name, &symtab_display[level])

/*------------------------------------------------------*/
/* search_and_find_all_symtab  Search the symbol table  */
/*                             display for the current id */
/*                             name.  If not found, ID   */
/*                             UNDEFINED error, and enter */
/*                             into the local symbol table.*/
/*                             Set a pointer to the entry. */
/*------------------------------------------------------*/

#define search_and_find_all_symtab(idp)                            \
    if ((idp = search_symtab_display(word_string)) == NULL) {      \
        error(UNDEFINED_IDENTIFIER);                               \
        idp = enter_symtab(word_string, &symtab_display[level]);   \
        idp->defn.key = UNDEFINED;                                 \
        idp->typep = &dummy_type;                                  \
    }

/*------------------------------------------------------*/
/* search_and_enter_local_symtab  Search the local symbol */
/*                             table for the current id  */
/*                             name.  Enter the name if  */
/*                             it is not already in there, */
/*                             else ID REDEFINED error.  */
/*                             Set a pointer to the entry. */
/*------------------------------------------------------*/

#define search_and_enter_local_symtab(idp)                \
    if ((idp = search_symtab(word_string,                 \
                 symtab_display[level])) == NULL) {  \
```

```
        idp = enter_symtab(word_string, &symtab_display[level]);\
    }                                                            \
    else error(REDEFINED_IDENTIFIER)

/*--------------------------------------------------------------*/
/*  search_and_enter_this_symtab    Search the given symbol    */
/*                                  table for the current id   */
/*                                  name.  Enter the name if    */
/*                                  it is not already in there, */
/*                                  else ID REDEFINED error.    */
/*                                  Set a pointer to the entry. */
```

```
/*--------------------------------------------------------------*/

#define search_and_enter_this_symtab(idp, this_symtab)          \
    if ((idp = search_symtab(word_string,                       \
                             this_symtab)) == NULL) {           \
        idp = enter_symtab(word_string, &this_symtab);          \
    }                                                           \
    else error(REDEFINED_IDENTIFIER)

#endif
```

FIGURE A-10   symtab.c

```
/****************************************************************/
/*                                                              */
/*        S Y M B O L   T A B L E                               */
/*                                                              */
/*        Symbol table routines.                                */
/*                                                              */
/*        FILE:       symtab.c                                  */
/*                                                              */
/*        MODULE:     symbol table                              */
/*                                                              */
/****************************************************************/

#include <stdio.h>
#include "common.h"
#include "error.h"
#include "symtab.h"

/*--------------------------------------------------------------*/
/*  Externals                                                   */
/*--------------------------------------------------------------*/

extern int level;

/*--------------------------------------------------------------*/
/*  Globals                                                     */
/*--------------------------------------------------------------*/

SYMTAB_NODE_PTR symtab_display[MAX_NESTING_LEVEL];

TYPE_STRUCT_PTR integer_typep, real_typep,      /* predefined types */
                boolean_typep, char_typep;

TYPE_STRUCT dummy_type = {       /* for erroneous type definitions */
    NO_FORM,        /* form */
    0,              /* size */
    NULL            /* type_idp */
};

/*--------------------------------------------------------------*/
/*  search_symtab      Search for a name in the symbol table.  */
/*                     Return a pointer of the entry if found, */
/*                     or NULL if not.                          */
/*--------------------------------------------------------------*/

    SYMTAB_NODE_PTR
search_symtab(name, np)

    char        *name;      /* name to search for */
```

```
    SYMTAB_NODE_PTR np;         /* ptr to symtab root */

{
    int cmp;

    /*
    -- Loop to check each node.  Return if the node matches,
    -- else continue search down the left or right subtree.
    */
    while (np != NULL) {
        cmp = strcmp(name, np->name);
        if (cmp == 0) return(np);               /* found */
        np = cmp < 0 ? np->left : np->right;    /* continue search */
    }

    return(NULL);                               /* not found */
}

/*--------------------------------------------------------------*/
/*  search_symtab_display   Search all the symbol tables in the */
/*                          symbol table display for a name.    */
/*                          Return a pointer to the entry if    */
/*                          found, or NULL if not.              */
/*--------------------------------------------------------------*/

    SYMTAB_NODE_PTR
search_symtab_display(name)

    char *name;                 /* name to search for */

{
    short i;
    SYMTAB_NODE_PTR np;         /* ptr to symtab node */

    for (i = level; i >= 0; --i) {
        np = search_symtab(name, symtab_display[i]);
        if (np != NULL) return(np);
    }

    return(NULL);
}

/*--------------------------------------------------------------*/
/*  enter_symtab       Enter a name into the symbol table,     */
/*                     and return a pointer to the new entry.  */
/*--------------------------------------------------------------*/

    SYMTAB_NODE_PTR
```

```
enter_symtab(name, npp)

    char          *name;       /* name to enter */
    SYMTAB_NODE_PTR *npp;       /* ptr to ptr to symtab root */

{
    int           cmp;         /* result of strcmp */
    SYMTAB_NODE_PTR new_nodep; /* ptr to new entry */
    SYMTAB_NODE_PTR np;        /* ptr to node to test */

    /*
    -- Create the new node for the name.
    */
    new_nodep = alloc_struct(SYMTAB_NODE);
    new_nodep->name = alloc_bytes(strlen(name) + 1);
    strcpy(new_nodep->name, name);
    new_nodep->left = new_nodep->right = new_nodep->next = NULL;
    new_nodep->info = NULL;
    new_nodep->defn.key = UNDEFINED;
    new_nodep->typep = NULL;
    new_nodep->level = level;
    new_nodep->label_index = 0;

    /*
    -- Loop to search for the insertion point.
    */
    while ((np = *npp) != NULL) {
        cmp = strcmp(name, np->name);
        npp = cmp < 0 ? &(np->left) : &(np->right);
    }

    *npp = new_nodep;                      /* replace */
    return(new_nodep);
}

/*------------------------------------------------------------*/
/*  init_symtab        Initialize the symbol table with       */
/*                     predefined identifiers and types,      */
/*                     and routines.                          */
/*------------------------------------------------------------*/

init_symtab()

{
    SYMTAB_NODE_PTR integer_idp, real_idp, boolean_idp, char_idp,
                    false_idp, true_idp;

    /*
    -- Initialize the level-0 symbol table.
    */
    symtab_display[0] = NULL;

    enter_name_local_symtab(integer_idp, "integer");
    enter_name_local_symtab(real_idp,    "real");
    enter_name_local_symtab(boolean_idp, "boolean");
    enter_name_local_symtab(char_idp,    "char");
    enter_name_local_symtab(false_idp,   "false");
    enter_name_local_symtab(true_idp,    "true");

    integer_typep = alloc_struct(TYPE_STRUCT);
    real_typep    = alloc_struct(TYPE_STRUCT);
    boolean_typep = alloc_struct(TYPE_STRUCT);
    char_typep    = alloc_struct(TYPE_STRUCT);

    integer_idp->defn.key   = TYPE_DEFN;
    integer_idp->typep      = integer_typep;
    integer_typep->form     = SCALAR_FORM;
```

```
    integer_typep->size     = sizeof(int);
    integer_typep->type_idp = integer_idp;

    real_idp->defn.key      = TYPE_DEFN;
    real_idp->typep         = real_typep;
    real_typep->form        = SCALAR_FORM;
    real_typep->size        = sizeof(float);
    real_typep->type_idp    = real_idp;

    boolean_idp->defn.key   = TYPE_DEFN;
    boolean_idp->typep      = boolean_typep;
    boolean_typep->form     = ENUM_FORM;
    boolean_typep->size     = sizeof(int);
    boolean_typep->type_idp = boolean_idp;

    boolean_typep->info.enumeration.max = 1;
    boolean_idp->typep->info.enumeration.const_idp = false_idp;
    false_idp->defn.key = CONST_DEFN;
    false_idp->defn.info.constant.value.integer = 0;
    false_idp->typep = boolean_typep;

    false_idp->next = true_idp;
    true_idp->defn.key = CONST_DEFN;
    true_idp->defn.info.constant.value.integer = 1;
    true_idp->typep = boolean_typep;

    char_idp->defn.key   = TYPE_DEFN;
    char_idp->typep      = char_typep;
    char_typep->form     = SCALAR_FORM;
    char_typep->size     = sizeof(char);
    char_typep->type_idp = char_idp;

    enter_standard_routine("read",    READ,    PROC_DEFN);
    enter_standard_routine("readln",  READLN,  PROC_DEFN);
    enter_standard_routine("write",   WRITE,   PROC_DEFN);
    enter_standard_routine("writeln", WRITELN, PROC_DEFN);

    enter_standard_routine("abs",     ABS,     FUNC_DEFN);
    enter_standard_routine("arctan",  ARCTAN,  FUNC_DEFN);
    enter_standard_routine("chr",     CHR,     FUNC_DEFN);
    enter_standard_routine("cos",     COS,     FUNC_DEFN);
    enter_standard_routine("eof",     EOFF,    FUNC_DEFN);
    enter_standard_routine("eoln",    EOLN,    FUNC_DEFN);
    enter_standard_routine("exp",     EXP,     FUNC_DEFN);
    enter_standard_routine("ln",      LN,      FUNC_DEFN);
    enter_standard_routine("odd",     ODD,     FUNC_DEFN);
    enter_standard_routine("ord",     ORD,     FUNC_DEFN);
    enter_standard_routine("pred",    PRED,    FUNC_DEFN);
    enter_standard_routine("round",   ROUND,   FUNC_DEFN);
    enter_standard_routine("sin",     SIN,     FUNC_DEFN);
    enter_standard_routine("sqr",     SQR,     FUNC_DEFN);
    enter_standard_routine("sqrt",    SQRT,    FUNC_DEFN);
    enter_standard_routine("succ",    SUCC,    FUNC_DEFN);
    enter_standard_routine("trunc",   TRUNC,   FUNC_DEFN);
}

/*------------------------------------------------------------*/
/*  enter_standard_routine    Enter a standard procedure or   */
/*                            function identifier into the    */
/*                            symbol table.                   */
/*------------------------------------------------------------*/

enter_standard_routine(name, routine_key, defn_key)

    char          *name;         /* name string */
    ROUTINE_KEY   routine_key;
    DEFN_KEY      defn_key;
```

```
{
    SYMTAB_NODE_PTR rtn_idp = enter_name_local_symtab(rtn_idp, name);

    rtn_idp->defn.key                    = defn_key;
    rtn_idp->defn.info.routine.key       = routine_key;
    rtn_idp->defn.info.routine.parms     = NULL;
    rtn_idp->defn.info.routine.local_symtab = NULL;
    rtn_idp->typep                       = NULL;
}

/*-------------------------------------------------------------*/
/*  enter_scope          Enter a new nesting level by creating */
/*                       a new scope.  Push the given symbol   */
/*                       table onto the display stack.         */
/*-------------------------------------------------------------*/

enter_scope(symtab_root)

    SYMTAB_NODE_PTR symtab_root;

{
    if (++level >= MAX_NESTING_LEVEL) {
```

```
        error(NESTING_TOO_DEEP);
        exit(-NESTING_TOO_DEEP);
    }

    symtab_display[level] = symtab_root;
}

/*-------------------------------------------------------------*/
/*  exit_scope           Exit the current nesting level by     */
/*                       closing the current scope.  Pop the   */
/*                       current symbol table off the display  */
/*                       stack and return a pointer to it.     */
/*-------------------------------------------------------------*/

    SYMTAB_NODE_PTR
exit_scope()

{
    SYMTAB_NODE_PTR symtab_root = symtab_display[level--];

    return(symtab_root);
}
```

FIGURE A-11   exec.h

```
/****************************************************************/
/*                                                            */
/*        E X E C U T O R    (Header)                         */
/*                                                            */
/*    FILE:       exec.h                                      */
/*                                                            */
/*    MODULE:     executor                                    */
/*                                                            */
/****************************************************************/

#ifndef exec_h
#define exec_h

#include "common.h"

#define STATEMENT_MARKER 0x70
#define ADDRESS_MARKER   0x71

/*-------------------------------------------------------------*/
/*  Runtime stack                                              */
/*-------------------------------------------------------------*/

typedef union {
    int     integer;
    float   real;
    char    byte;
    ADDRESS address;
} STACK_ITEM, *STACK_ITEM_PTR;

typedef struct {
    STACK_ITEM function_value;
    STACK_ITEM static_link;
    STACK_ITEM dynamic_link;
    STACK_ITEM return_address;
} *STACK_FRAME_HEADER_PTR;
```

```
/*-------------------------------------------------------------*/
/*  Functions                                                  */
/*-------------------------------------------------------------*/

SYMTAB_NODE_PTR get_symtab_cptr();
TYPE_STRUCT_PTR exec_routine_call();
TYPE_STRUCT_PTR exec_expression(), exec_variable();
char            *crunch_address_marker();
char            *fixup_address_marker();
int             get_statement_cmarker();
char            *get_address_cmarker();
int             get_cinteger();
char            *get_caddress();

                /***********************/
                /*                   */
                /*      Macros       */
                /*                   */
                /***********************/

/*-------------------------------------------------------------*/
/*  get_ctoken           Extract the next token code from the  */
/*                       current code segment.                 */
/*-------------------------------------------------------------*/

#define get_ctoken()     ctoken = *code_segmentp++

/*-------------------------------------------------------------*/
/*  pop                  Pop the runtime stack.                */
/*-------------------------------------------------------------*/

#define pop()            --tos

/*-------------------------------------------------------------*/
/*  Tracing routine calls       Unless the following statements */
/*                              are preceded by                 */
/*                                                             */
```

```
/*                                                */        /*                                        */
/*                                                */        /*****************************/
/*                    calls to the tracing routines    */
/*                    are not compiled.                */        /*----------------------------------------------*/
/*--------------------------------------------------*/        /*  crunch_token     Append the token code to the code    */
                                                              /*                   buffer.  Called by the scanner routine   */
#ifndef trace                                                 /*                   get_token only while parsing a block.   */
#define trace_routine_entry(idp)                              /*----------------------------------------------*/
```

```
#define trace_routine_exit(idp)
#define trace_statement_execution()
#define trace_data_store(idp, idp_tp, targetp, target_tp)
#define trace_data_fetch(idp, tp, datap)
#endif


#endif
```

FIGURE A-12   executil.c

```
/********************************************************/
/*                                                */
/*        E X E C U T O R   U T I L I T I E S     */
/*                                                */
/*        Utility routines for the executor module.   */
/*                                                */
/*        FILE:        executil.c                 */
/*                                                */
/*        MODULE:      executor                   */
/*                                                */
/********************************************************/

#include <stdio.h>
#include "common.h"
#include "error.h"
#include "symtab.h"
#include "scanner.h"
#include "exec.h"


/*----------------------------------------------*/
/* Externals                                    */
/*----------------------------------------------*/

extern TOKEN_CODE token;
extern int        line_number;
extern int        level;

extern TYPE_STRUCT_PTR integer_typep, real_typep,
                  boolean_typep, char_typep;


/*----------------------------------------------*/
/* Globals                                      */
/*----------------------------------------------*/

char *code_buffer;              /* code buffer */
char *code_bufferp;             /* code buffer ptr */
char *code_segmentp;            /* code segment ptr */
char *code_segment_limit;       /* end of code segment */
char *statement_startp;         /* ptr to start of stmt */

TOKEN_CODE   ctoken;            /* token from code segment */
int          exec_line_number;  /* no. of line executed */
long         exec_stmt_count = 0;  /* count of stmts executed */

STACK_ITEM      *stack;         /* runtime stack */
STACK_ITEM_PTR  tos;            /* ptr to runtime stack top */
STACK_ITEM_PTR  stack_frame_basep;  /* ptr to stack frame base */

        /*****************************/
        /*                   */
        /*     Code segment routines   */
```

```
crunch_token()

{
    char token_code = token;    /* byte-sized token code */

    if (code_bufferp >= code_buffer + MAX_CODE_BUFFER_SIZE) {
        error(CODE_SEGMENT_OVERFLOW);
        exit(-CODE_SEGMENT_OVERFLOW);
    }
    else *code_bufferp++ = token_code;
}


/*----------------------------------------------*/
/* crunch_symtab_node_ptr     Append a symbol table node   */
/*                            pointer to the code buffer.  */
/*----------------------------------------------*/

crunch_symtab_node_ptr(np)

    SYMTAB_NODE_PTR np;         /* pointer to append */

{
    SYMTAB_NODE_PTR *npp = (SYMTAB_NODE_PTR *) code_bufferp;

    if (code_bufferp >= code_buffer + MAX_CODE_BUFFER_SIZE
                            - sizeof(SYMTAB_NODE_PTR)) {
        error(CODE_SEGMENT_OVERFLOW);
        exit(-CODE_SEGMENT_OVERFLOW);
    }
    else {
        *npp = np;
        code_bufferp += sizeof(SYMTAB_NODE_PTR);
    }
}


/*----------------------------------------------*/
/* crunch_statement_marker    Append a statement marker to  */
/*                            the code buffer.              */
/*----------------------------------------------*/

crunch_statement_marker()

{
```

```
        if (code_bufferp >= code_buffer + MAX_CODE_BUFFER_SIZE
                                      - sizeof(int)) {
            error(CODE_SEGMENT_OVERFLOW);
            exit(-CODE_SEGMENT_OVERFLOW);
        }
        else {
            char save_code = *(--code_bufferp);

            *code_bufferp++ = STATEMENT_MARKER;
            *((int *) code_bufferp) = line_number;
            code_bufferp += sizeof(int);
            *code_bufferp++ = save_code;
        }
}

/*------------------------------------------------------*/
/*  crunch_address_marker     Append a code address to the   */
/*                            code buffer.  Return the       */
/*                            addesss of the address.        */
/*------------------------------------------------------*/

    char *
crunch_address_marker(address)

    ADDRESS address;    /* address value to append */

{
    char *save_code_bufferp;

    if (code_bufferp >= code_buffer + MAX_CODE_BUFFER_SIZE
                                  - sizeof(ADDRESS)) {
        error(CODE_SEGMENT_OVERFLOW);
        exit(-CODE_SEGMENT_OVERFLOW);
    }
    else {
        char save_code = *(--code_bufferp);

        *code_bufferp++ = ADDRESS_MARKER;
        save_code_bufferp = code_bufferp;
        *((ADDRESS *) code_bufferp) = address;
        code_bufferp += sizeof(ADDRESS);
        *code_bufferp++ = save_code;

        return(save_code_bufferp);
    }
}

/*------------------------------------------------------*/
/*  fixup_address_marker      Fix up an address marker with  */
/*                            the offset from the address    */
/*                            marker to the current code     */
/*                            buffer address.  Return the old */
/*                            value of the address marker.   */
/*------------------------------------------------------*/

    char *
fixup_address_marker(address)

    ADDRESS address;    /* address of address marker to be fixed up */

{
    char *old_address = *((ADDRESS *) address);

    *((int *) address) = code_bufferp - address;
    return(old_address);
}
```

```
/*------------------------------------------------------*/
/*  crunch_integer      Append an integer value to the code  */
/*                      buffer.                               */
/*------------------------------------------------------*/

crunch_integer(value)

    int value;          /* value to append */

{
    if (code_bufferp >= code_buffer + MAX_CODE_BUFFER_SIZE
                                  - sizeof(int)) {
        error(CODE_SEGMENT_OVERFLOW);
        exit(-CODE_SEGMENT_OVERFLOW);
    }
    else {
        *((int *) code_bufferp) = value;
        code_bufferp += sizeof(int);
    }
}

/*------------------------------------------------------*/
/*  crunch_offset       Append an integer value to the code  */
/*                      that represents the offset from the  */
/*                      given address to the current code    */
/*                      buffer address.                      */
/*------------------------------------------------------*/

crunch_offset(address)

    ADDRESS address;    /* address from which to offset */

{
    if (code_bufferp >= code_buffer + MAX_CODE_BUFFER_SIZE
                                  - sizeof(int)) {
        error(CODE_SEGMENT_OVERFLOW);
        exit(-CODE_SEGMENT_OVERFLOW);
    }
    else {
        *((int *) code_bufferp) = address - code_bufferp;
        code_bufferp += sizeof(int);
    }
}

/*------------------------------------------------------*/
/*  create_code_segment    Create a code segment and copy in */
/*                         the contents of the code buffer.  */
/*                         Reset the code buffer pointer.    */
/*                         Return a pointer to the segment.  */
/*------------------------------------------------------*/

    char *
create_code_segment()

{
    char *code_segment = alloc_bytes(code_bufferp - code_buffer);

    code_segment_limit = code_segment + (code_bufferp - code_buffer);
    code_bufferp       = code_buffer;
    code_segmentp      = code_segment;

    /*
    -- Copy in the contents of the code buffer.
    */
    while (code_segmentp != code_segment_limit)
        *code_segmentp++ = *code_bufferp++;

    code_bufferp = code_buffer;              /* reset code buffer ptr */
```

```
    return(code_segment);
}

/*-----------------------------------------------------------*/
/* get_symtab_cptr     Extract a symbol table node pointer   */
/*                     from the current code segment and     */
/*                     return it.                            */
/*-----------------------------------------------------------*/

    SYMTAB_NODE_PTR
get_symtab_cptr()

{
    SYMTAB_NODE_PTR np;
    SYMTAB_NODE_PTR *npp = (SYMTAB_NODE_PTR *) code_segmentp;

    np = *npp;
    code_segmentp += sizeof(SYMTAB_NODE_PTR);
    return(np);
}

/*-----------------------------------------------------------*/
/* get_statement_cmarker   Extract a statement marker from the */
/*                         current code segment and return its */
/*                         statement line number.            */
/*-----------------------------------------------------------*/

    int
get_statement_cmarker()

{
    int line_num;

    if (ctoken == STATEMENT_MARKER) {
        line_num = *((int *) code_segmentp);
        code_segmentp += sizeof(int);
    }

    return(line_num);
}

/*-----------------------------------------------------------*/
/* get_address_cmarker   Extract an address marker from the  */
/*                       current code segment. Add its       */
/*                       offset value to the code segment    */
/*                       address and return the new address. */
/*-----------------------------------------------------------*/

    char *
get_address_cmarker()

{
    ADDRESS address;    /* address to return */

    if (ctoken == ADDRESS_MARKER) {
        address = *((int *) code_segmentp) + code_segmentp - 1;
        code_segmentp += sizeof(ADDRESS);
    }

    return(address);
}

/*-----------------------------------------------------------*/
/* get_cinteger         Extract an integer value from the    */
/*                      current code segment and return the  */
/*                      value.                               */
/*-----------------------------------------------------------*/
```

```
    int
get_cinteger()

{
    int value;          /* value to extract and return */

    value = *((int *) code_segmentp);
    code_segmentp += sizeof(int);

    return(value);
}

/*-----------------------------------------------------------*/
/* get_caddress         Extract an offset from the current code */
/*                      segment and add it to the code segment */
/*                      address.  Return the new address.    */
/*-----------------------------------------------------------*/

    char *
get_caddress()

{
    ADDRESS address;    /* address to return */

    address = *((int *) code_segmentp) + code_segmentp - 1;
    code_segmentp += sizeof(int);

    return(address);
}

            /********************************/
            /*                              */
            /*       Executor utilities     */
            /*                              */
            /********************************/

/*-----------------------------------------------------------*/
/* push_integer        Push an integer onto the runtime stack. */
/*-----------------------------------------------------------*/

push_integer(item_value)

    int item_value;

{
    STACK_ITEM_PTR itemp = ++tos;

    if (itemp >= &stack[MAX_STACK_SIZE])
        runtime_error(RUNTIME_STACK_OVERFLOW);

    itemp->integer = item_value;
}

/*-----------------------------------------------------------*/
/* push_real           Push a real onto the runtime stack.   */
/*-----------------------------------------------------------*/

push_real(item_value)

    float item_value;

{
    STACK_ITEM_PTR itemp = ++tos;

    if (itemp >= &stack[MAX_STACK_SIZE])
        runtime_error(RUNTIME_STACK_OVERFLOW);
```

```
        itemp->real = item_value;
}

/*-------------------------------------------------------*/
/* push_byte        Push a byte onto the runtime stack.  */
/*-------------------------------------------------------*/

push_byte(item_value)

    char item_value;

{
    STACK_ITEM_PTR itemp = ++tos;

    if (itemp >= &stack[MAX_STACK_SIZE])
        runtime_error(RUNTIME_STACK_OVERFLOW);

    itemp->byte = item_value;
}

/*-------------------------------------------------------*/
/* push_address     Push an address onto the runtime stack. */
/*-------------------------------------------------------*/

push_address(address)

    ADDRESS address;

{
    STACK_ITEM_PTR itemp = ++tos;

    if (itemp >= &stack[MAX_STACK_SIZE])
        runtime_error(RUNTIME_STACK_OVERFLOW);

    itemp->address = address;
}

/*-------------------------------------------------------*/
/* execute          Execute a routine's code segment.   */
/*-------------------------------------------------------*/

execute(rtn_idp)

    SYMTAB_NODE_PTR rtn_idp;

{
    routine_entry(rtn_idp);

    get_ctoken();
    exec_statement();

    routine_exit(rtn_idp);
}

/*-------------------------------------------------------*/
/* routine_entry    Point to the new routine's code     */
/*                  segment, and allocate its locals.    */
/*-------------------------------------------------------*/

routine_entry(rtn_idp)

    SYMTAB_NODE_PTR rtn_idp;        /* new routine's id */

{
    SYMTAB_NODE_PTR var_idp;        /* local variable id */

    trace_routine_entry(rtn_idp);
```

```
    /*
    -- Switch to the new code segment.
    */
    code_segmentp = rtn_idp->defn.info.routine.code_segment;

    /*
    -- Allocate local variables.
    */
    for (var_idp = rtn_idp->defn.info.routine.locals;
         var_idp != NULL;
         var_idp = var_idp->next) alloc_local(var_idp->typep);
}

/*-------------------------------------------------------*/
/* routine_exit     Deallocate the routine's parameters and */
/*                  locals.  Cut off its stack frame, and */
/*                  return to the caller's code segment. */
/*-------------------------------------------------------*/

routine_exit(rtn_idp)

    SYMTAB_NODE_PTR rtn_idp;        /* exiting routine's id */

{
    SYMTAB_NODE_PTR       idp;      /* variable or parm id */
    STACK_FRAME_HEADER_PTR hp;      /* ptr to stack frame header */

    trace_routine_exit(rtn_idp);

    /*
    -- Deallocate parameters and local variables.
    */
    for (idp = rtn_idp->defn.info.routine.parms;
         idp != NULL;
         idp = idp->next) free_data(idp);
    for (idp = rtn_idp->defn.info.routine.locals;
         idp != NULL;
         idp = idp->next) free_data(idp);

    /*
    -- Pop off the stack frame and return to the
    -- caller's code segment.
    */
    hp = (STACK_FRAME_HEADER_PTR) stack_frame_basep;
    code_segmentp = hp->return_address.address;
    tos = (rtn_idp->defn.key == PROC_DEFN)
              ? stack_frame_basep - 1
              : stack_frame_basep;
    stack_frame_basep = (STACK_ITEM_PTR) hp->dynamic_link.address;
}

/*-------------------------------------------------------*/
/* push_stack_frame_header   Allocate the callee routine's */
/*                           stack frame.                */
/*-------------------------------------------------------*/

push_stack_frame_header(old_level, new_level)

    int old_level, new_level;   /* levels of caller and callee */

{
    STACK_FRAME_HEADER_PTR hp;

    push_integer(0);                        /* return value */
    hp = (STACK_FRAME_HEADER_PTR) stack_frame_basep;

    /*
```

```
        --  Static link.
        */
        if (new_level == old_level + 1) {
            /*
            --  Calling a routine nested within the caller:
            --  Push pointer to caller's stack frame.
            */
            push_address(hp);
        }
        else if (new_level == old_level) {
            /*
            --  Calling another routine at the same level:
            --  Push pointer to stack frame of common parent.
            */
            push_address(hp->static_link.address);
        }
        else /* new_level < old_level */ {
            /*
            --  Calling a routine at a lesser level (nested less deeply):
            --  Push pointer to stack frame of nearest common ancestor.
            */
            int delta = old_level - new_level;

            while (delta-- >= 0)
                hp = (STACK_FRAME_HEADER_PTR) hp->static_link.address;
            push_address(hp);
        }

    push_address(stack_frame_basep);        /* dynamic link */
    push_address(0);    /* return address to be filled in later */
}

/*------------------------------------------------------------*/
/* alloc_local        Allocate a local variable on the stack. */
/*------------------------------------------------------------*/

alloc_local(tp)

    TYPE_STRUCT_PTR tp;     /* ptr to type of variable */

{
    if      (tp == integer_typep) push_integer(0);
    else if (tp == real_typep)    push_real(0.0);
    else if (tp == boolean_typep) push_byte(0);
    else if (tp == char_typep)    push_byte(0);
```

```
    else switch (tp->form) {
        case ENUM_FORM:
            push_integer(0);
            break;

        case SUBRANGE_FORM:
            alloc_local(tp->info.subrange.range_typep);
            break;

        case ARRAY_FORM: {
            char *ptr = alloc_bytes(tp->size);

            push_address((ADDRESS) ptr);
            break;
        }

        case RECORD_FORM: {
            char *ptr = alloc_bytes(tp->size);

            push_address((ADDRESS) ptr);
            break;
        }
    }
}

/*------------------------------------------------------------*/
/* free_data          Deallocate the data area of an array    */
/*                    or record local variable or value       */
/*                    parameter.                              */
/*------------------------------------------------------------*/

free_data(idp)

    SYMTAB_NODE_PTR idp;            /* parm or variable id */

{
    STACK_ITEM_PTR  itemp;          /* ptr to stack item */
    TYPE_STRUCT_PTR tp = idp->typep;  /* ptr to id's type */

    if (   ((tp->form == ARRAY_FORM) || (tp->form == RECORD_FORM))
        && (idp->defn.key != VARPARM_DEFN)) {
        itemp = stack_frame_basep + idp->defn.info.data.offset;
        free(itemp->address);
    }
}
```

FIGURE A-13   execstmt.c

```
/*****************************************************************/
/*                                                               */
/*      S T A T E M E N T   E X E C U T O R                      */
/*                                                               */
/*      Execution routines for statements.                       */
/*                                                               */
/*      FILE:     execstmt.c                                     */
/*                                                               */
/*      MODULE:   executor                                       */
/*                                                               */
/*****************************************************************/

#include <stdio.h>
#include "common.h"
```

```
#include "error.h"
#include "symtab.h"
#include "scanner.h"
#include "parser.h"
#include "exec.h"

/*------------------------------------------------------------*/
/* Externals                                                  */
/*------------------------------------------------------------*/

extern int      level;
extern int      exec_line_number;
extern long     exec_stmt_count;
```

```
extern char          *code_segmentp;
extern char          *statement_startp;
extern TOKEN_CODE    ctoken;

extern STACK_ITEM    *stack;
extern STACK_ITEM_PTR tos;
extern STACK_ITEM_PTR stack_frame_basep;

extern TYPE_STRUCT_PTR integer_typep, real_typep,
                       boolean_typep, char_typep;

/*----------------------------------------------------------*/
/* exec_statement      Execute a statement by calling the   */
/*                     appropriate execution routine.       */
/*----------------------------------------------------------*/

exec_statement()

{
    if (ctoken == STATEMENT_MARKER) {
        exec_line_number = get_statement_cmarker();
        ++exec_stmt_count;

        statement_startp = code_segmentp;
        trace_statement_execution();
        get_ctoken();
    }

    switch (ctoken) {

        case IDENTIFIER: {
            SYMTAB_NODE_PTR idp = get_symtab_cptr();

            if (idp->defn.key == PROC_DEFN)
                exec_routine_call(idp);
            else
                exec_assignment_statement(idp);

            break;
        }

        case BEGIN:   exec_compound_statement();   break;
        case CASE:    exec_case_statement();       break;
        case FOR:     exec_for_statement();        break;
        case IF:      exec_if_statement();         break;
        case REPEAT:  exec_repeat_statement();     break;
        case WHILE:   exec_while_statement();      break;

        case SEMICOLON:
        case END:
        case ELSE:
        case UNTIL:                                break;

        default:  runtime_error(UNIMPLEMENTED_RUNTIME_FEATURE);
    }

    while (ctoken == SEMICOLON) get_ctoken();
}

/*----------------------------------------------------------*/
/* exec_assignment_statement       Execute an assignment    */
/*                                 statement.               */
/*----------------------------------------------------------*/

exec_assignment_statement(idp)

    SYMTAB_NODE_PTR idp;          /* target variable id */
```

```
{
    STACK_ITEM_PTR  targetp;       /* ptr to assignment target */
    TYPE_STRUCT_PTR target_tp, base_target_tp, expr_tp;

    /*
    -- Assignment to function id:  Target is the first item of
    --                             the appropriate stack frame.
    */

    if (idp->defn.key == FUNC_DEFN) {
        STACK_FRAME_HEADER_PTR hp;
        int                    delta;  /* difference in levels */

        hp    = (STACK_FRAME_HEADER_PTR) stack_frame_basep;
        delta = level - idp->level - 1;
        while (delta-- > 0)
            hp = (STACK_FRAME_HEADER_PTR) hp->static_link.address;

        targetp  = (STACK_ITEM_PTR) hp;
        target_tp = idp->typep;
        get_ctoken();
    }

    /*
    -- Assignment to variable:  Routine exec_variable leaves the
    --                          target address on top of stack.
    */
    else {
        target_tp = exec_variable(idp, TARGET_USE);
        targetp   = (STACK_ITEM_PTR) tos->address;

        pop();          /* pop off target address */
    }

    base_target_tp = base_type(target_tp);

    /*
    -- Routine exec_expression leaves the expression value
    -- on top of stack.
    */
    get_ctoken();
    expr_tp = exec_expression();

    /*
    -- Do the assignment.
    */
    if ((target_tp == real_typep) &&
        (base_type(expr_tp) == integer_typep)) {
        /*
        -- real := integer
        */
        targetp->real = tos->integer;
    }
    else if ((target_tp->form == ARRAY_FORM) ||
             (target_tp->form == RECORD_FORM)) {
        /*
        -- array := array
        -- record := record
        */
        char *ptr1 = (char *) targetp;
        char *ptr2 = tos->address;
        int  size = target_tp->size;

        while (size--) *ptr1++ = *ptr2++;
    }
    else if ((base_target_tp == integer_typep) ||
             (target_tp->form == ENUM_FORM)) {
```

```
        /*
        -- Range check assignment to integer
        -- or enumeration subrange.
        */
        if (   (target_tp->form == SUBRANGE_FORM)
            && ((tos->integer < target_tp->info.subrange.min) ||
                (tos->integer > target_tp->info.subrange.max)))
            runtime_error(VALUE_OUT_OF_RANGE);
        /*
        -- integer     := integer
        -- enumeration := enumeration
        */
        targetp->integer = tos->integer;
    }
    else if (base_target_tp == char_typep) {
        /*
        -- Range check assigment to character subrange.
        */
        if (   (target_tp->form == SUBRANGE_FORM)
            && ((tos->byte < target_tp->info.subrange.min) ||
                (tos->byte > target_tp->info.subrange.max)))
            runtime_error(VALUE_OUT_OF_RANGE);
        /*
        -- character := character
        */
        targetp->byte = tos->byte;
    }
    else {
        /*
        -- real := real
        */
        targetp->real = tos->real;
    }

    pop();      /* pop off expression value */

    trace_data_store(idp, idp->typep, targetp, target_tp);
}

/*--------------------------------------------------------------*/
/* exec_routine_call            Execute a procedure or function */
/*                              call.  Return a pointer to the  */
/*                              type structure.                 */
/*--------------------------------------------------------------*/

    TYPE_STRUCT_PTR
exec_routine_call(rtn_idp)

    SYMTAB_NODE_PTR rtn_idp;    /* routine id */

{
    TYPE_STRUCT_PTR exec_declared_routine_call();
    TYPE_STRUCT_PTR exec_standard_routine_call();

    if (rtn_idp->defn.info.routine.key == DECLARED)
        return(exec_declared_routine_call(rtn_idp));
    else
        return(exec_standard_routine_call(rtn_idp));
}

/*--------------------------------------------------------------*/
/* exec_declared_routine_call       Execute a call to a         */
/*                                  declared procedure or       */
/*                                  function.  Return a pointer */
/*                                  to the type structure.      */
/*--------------------------------------------------------------*/

    TYPE_STRUCT_PTR
exec_declared_routine_call(rtn_idp)

    SYMTAB_NODE_PTR rtn_idp;            /* routine id */

{
    int old_level = level;                  /* level of caller */
    int new_level = rtn_idp->level + 1;     /* level of callee */
    STACK_ITEM_PTR new_stack_frame_basep;
    STACK_FRAME_HEADER_PTR hp;              /* ptr to frame header */

    /*
    -- Set up stack frame of callee.
    */
    new_stack_frame_basep = tos + 1;
    push_stack_frame_header(old_level, new_level);

    /*
    -- Push parameter values onto the stack.
    */
    get_ctoken();
    if (ctoken == LPAREN) {
        exec_actual_parms(rtn_idp);
        get_ctoken();   /* token after ) */
    }

    /*
    -- Set the return address in the new stack frame,
    -- and execute the callee.
    */
    level = new_level;
    stack_frame_basep = new_stack_frame_basep;
    hp = (STACK_FRAME_HEADER_PTR) stack_frame_basep;
    hp->return_address.address = code_segmentp - 1;
    execute(rtn_idp);

    /*
    -- Return from callee.
    */
    level = old_level;
    get_ctoken();       /* first token after return */

    return(rtn_idp->defn.key == PROC_DEFN ? NULL : rtn_idp->typep);
}

/*--------------------------------------------------------------*/
/* exec_actual_parms            Push the values of the actual   */
/*                              parameters onto the stack.      */
/*--------------------------------------------------------------*/

exec_actual_parms(rtn_idp)

    SYMTAB_NODE_PTR rtn_idp;            /* id of callee routine */

{
    SYMTAB_NODE_PTR formal_idp;         /* formal parm id */
    TYPE_STRUCT_PTR formal_tp, actual_tp;

    /*
    -- Loop to execute actual parameters.
    */
    for (formal_idp = rtn_idp->defn.info.routine.parms;
         formal_idp != NULL;
         formal_idp = formal_idp->next) {

        formal_tp = formal_idp->typep;
        get_ctoken();
```

```
        /*
        -- Value parameter.
        */
        if (formal_idp->defn.key == VALPARM_DEFN) {
            actual_tp = exec_expression();

            /*
            -- Range check for a subrange formal parameter.
            */
            if (formal_tp->form == SUBRANGE_FORM) {
                TYPE_STRUCT_PTR base_formal_tp = base_type(formal_tp);
                int             value;

                value = ((base_formal_tp == integer_typep) ||
                         (base_formal_tp->form == ENUM_FORM))
                            ? tos->integer
                            : tos->byte;

                if ((value < formal_tp->info.subrange.min) ||
                    (value > formal_tp->info.subrange.max)) {
                    runtime_error(VALUE_OUT_OF_RANGE);
                }
            }

            /*
            -- real formal := integer actual
            */
            else if ((formal_tp == real_typep) &&
                     (base_type(actual_tp) == integer_typep)) {
                tos->real = tos->integer;
            }

            /*
            -- Formal parm is array or record:  Make a copy.
            */
            if ((formal_tp->form == ARRAY_FORM) ||
                (formal_tp->form == RECORD_FORM)) {
                int size     = formal_tp->size;
                char *ptr1   = alloc_bytes(size);
                char *ptr2   = tos->address;
                char *save_ptr = ptr1;

                while (size--) *ptr1++ = *ptr2++;
                tos->address = save_ptr;
            }
        }

        /*
        -- VAR parameter.
        */
        else {
            SYMTAB_NODE_PTR idp = get_symtab_cptr();

            exec_variable(idp, VARPARM_USE);
        }
    }
}

/*-------------------------------------------------------------*/
/*  exec_compound_statement    Execute a compound statement.   */
/*-------------------------------------------------------------*/

exec_compound_statement()

{
    get_ctoken();
    while (ctoken != END) exec_statement();
```

```
    get_ctoken();
}

/*-------------------------------------------------------------*/
/*  exec_case_statement        Execute a CASE statement:       */
/*                                                             */
/*                             CASE <expr> OF                  */
/*                                 <case-branch> ;             */
/*                                 ...                         */
/*                             END                             */
/*-------------------------------------------------------------*/

exec_case_statement()

{
    int             case_expr_value;        /* CASE expr value */
    int             case_label_count;       /* CASE label count */
    int             case_label_value;       /* CASE label value */
    char            *branch_table_location; /* branch table addr */
    char            *case_branch_location;  /* CASE branch addr */
    TYPE_STRUCT_PTR case_expr_tp;           /* CASE expr type */
    BOOLEAN         done = FALSE;

    get_ctoken();        /* token after CASE */
    branch_table_location = get_address_cmarker();

    /*
    -- Evaluate the CASE expression.
    */
    get_ctoken();
    case_expr_tp = exec_expression();
    case_expr_value = (case_expr_tp == integer_typep) ||
                      (case_expr_tp->form == ENUM_FORM)
                        ? tos->integer
                        : tos->byte;
    pop();        /* expression value */

    /*
    -- Search the branch table for the expression value.
    */
    code_segmentp = branch_table_location;
    get_ctoken();
    case_label_count = get_cinteger();
    while (!done && case_label_count--) {
        case_label_value     = get_cinteger();
        case_branch_location = get_caddress();
        done = case_label_value == case_expr_value;
    }

    /*
    -- If found, go to the appropriate CASE branch.
    */
    if (case_label_count >= 0) {
        code_segmentp = case_branch_location;
        get_ctoken();
        exec_statement();

        code_segmentp = get_address_cmarker();
        get_ctoken();
    }
    else runtime_error(INVALID_CASE_VALUE);
}

/*-------------------------------------------------------------*/
/*  exec_for_statement         Execute a FOR statement:        */
/*                                                             */
/*                             FOR <id> := <expr>              */
```

```
/*                              TO|DOWNTO <expr>        */
/*                              DO <stmt>               */
/*----------------------------------------------------------*/

exec_for_statement()

{
    SYMTAB_NODE_PTR control_idp;            /* control var id */
    TYPE_STRUCT_PTR control_tp;             /* control var type */
    STACK_ITEM_PTR  targetp;                /* ptr to control target */
    char            *loop_start_location;   /* addr of start of loop */
    char            *loop_end_location;     /* addr of end of loop */
    int             control_value;          /* value of control var */
    int             initial_value, final_value, delta_value;

    get_ctoken();       /* token after FOR */
    loop_end_location = get_address_cmarker();

    /*
    -- Get the address of the control variable's stack item.
    */
    get_ctoken();
    control_idp = get_symtab_cptr();
    control_tp  = exec_variable(control_idp, TARGET_USE);
    targetp     = (STACK_ITEM_PTR) tos->address;
    pop();      /* control variable address */

    /*
    -- Evaluate the initial expression.
    */
    get_ctoken();
    exec_expression();
    initial_value = (control_tp == integer_typep)
                        ? tos->integer
                        : tos->byte;
    pop();      /* initial value */

    delta_value = (ctoken == TO) ? 1 : -1;

    /*
    -- Evaluate the final expression.
    */
    get_ctoken();
    exec_expression();
    final_value = (control_tp == integer_typep)
                        ? tos->integer
                        : tos->byte;
    pop();      /* final value */

    loop_start_location = code_segmentp;
    control_value = initial_value;

    /*
    -- Execute the FOR loop.
    */
    while (  ((delta_value == 1) &&
              (control_value <= final_value))
          || ((delta_value == -1) &&
              (control_value >= final_value))) {
        if (control_tp == integer_typep)
            targetp->integer = control_value;
        else
            targetp->byte = control_value;

        get_ctoken();           /* token after DO */
        exec_statement();

        control_value += delta_value;
```

```
        code_segmentp = loop_start_location;
    }

    code_segmentp = loop_end_location;
    get_ctoken();           /* token after FOR statement */
}

/*----------------------------------------------------------*/
/* exec_if_statement   Execute an IF statement:             */
/*                                                          */
/*                  IF <expr> THEN <stmt>                   */
/*                                                          */
/*            or:                                           */
/*                                                          */
/*                  IF <expr> THEN <stmt> ELSE <stmt>       */
/*----------------------------------------------------------*/

exec_if_statement()

{
    char            *false_location;    /* address of false branch */
    BOOLEAN         test;

    get_ctoken();           /* token after IF */
    false_location = get_address_cmarker();

    /*
    -- Evaluate the boolean expression.
    */
    get_ctoken();
    exec_expression();
    test = tos->integer == 1;
    pop();      /* boolean value */

    if (test) {
        /*
        -- True:  Execute the true branch.
        */
        get_ctoken();   /* token after THEN */
        exec_statement();

        if (ctoken == ELSE) {
            get_ctoken();                   /* token after ELSE */
            code_segmentp = get_address_cmarker();
            get_ctoken();                   /* token after false stmt */
        }
    }
    else {
        /*
        -- False:  Execute the false branch if there is one.
        */
        code_segmentp = false_location;
        get_ctoken();

        if (ctoken == ELSE) {
            get_ctoken();                   /* token after ELSE */
            get_address_cmarker();          /* skip address marker */

            get_ctoken();
            exec_statement();
        }
    }
}

/*----------------------------------------------------------*/
/* exec_repeat_statement       Execute a REPEAT statement:  */
/*                                                          */
```

```
/*                          REPEAT <stmt-list>        */
/*                          UNTIL <expr>              */
/*-----------------------------------------------------*/

exec_repeat_statement()

{
    char *loop_start_location = code_segmentp;  /* addr of
                                         loop start */

    do {
        get_ctoken();          /* token after REPEAT */

        /*
        -- Execute the statement list.
        */
        do {
            exec_statement();
        } while (ctoken != UNTIL);

        /*
        -- Evaluate the boolean expression.
        */
        get_ctoken();
        exec_expression();
        if (tos->integer == 0) code_segmentp = loop_start_location;
        pop();          /* boolean value */
    } while (code_segmentp == loop_start_location);
}

/*-----------------------------------------------------*/
/*  exec_while_statement      Process a WHILE statement:  */
/*                                                      */
/*                           WHILE <expr> DO <stmt>     */
/*-----------------------------------------------------*/
```

```
exec_while_statement()

{
    char  *loop_end_location;      /* addr of end of loop */
    char  *test_location;          /* addr of boolean expr */
    BOOLEAN loop_done = FALSE;

    get_ctoken();          /* token after WHILE */
    loop_end_location = get_address_cmarker();
    test_location     = code_segmentp;

    do {
        /*
        -- Evaluate the boolean expression.
        */
        get_ctoken();
        exec_expression();
        if (tos->integer == 0) {
            code_segmentp = loop_end_location;
            loop_done = TRUE;
        }
        pop();          /* boolean value */

        /*
        -- If true, execute the statement.
        */
        if (!loop_done) {
            get_ctoken();
            exec_statement();
            code_segmentp = test_location;
        }
    } while (!loop_done);

    get_ctoken();          /* token after WHILE statement */
}
```

FIGURE A-14   execexpr.c

```
/****************************************************************/
/*                                                              */
/*      E X P R E S S I O N   E X E C U T O R                   */
/*                                                              */
/*      Execution routines for expressions.                     */
/*                                                              */
/*      FILE:       execexpr.c                                  */
/*                                                              */
/*      MODULE:     executor                                    */
/*                                                              */
/****************************************************************/

#include <stdio.h>
#include "common.h"
#include "error.h"
#include "symtab.h"
#include "scanner.h"
#include "parser.h"
#include "exec.h"

/*-----------------------------------------------------*/
/*  Externals                                          */
/*-----------------------------------------------------*/
```

```
extern int          level;

extern char         *code_segmentp;
extern TOKEN_CODE   ctoken;

extern STACK_ITEM       *stack;
extern STACK_ITEM_PTR   tos;
extern STACK_ITEM_PTR   stack_frame_basep;

extern TYPE_STRUCT_PTR integer_typep, real_typep,
                       boolean_typep, char_typep;

/*-----------------------------------------------------*/
/*  Forwards                                           */
/*-----------------------------------------------------*/

TYPE_STRUCT_PTR exec_expression(), exec_simple_expression(),
                exec_term(), exec_factor(),
                exec_constant(), exec_variable(),
                exec_subscripts(), exec_field();

/*-----------------------------------------------------*/
/*  exec_expression    Execute an expression consisting of a  */
/*                     simple expression optionally followed  */
```

```
/*                      by a relational operator and a second    */
/*                      simple expression.  Return a pointer to  */
/*                      the type structure.                      */
/*-----------------------------------------------------------*/

    TYPE_STRUCT_PTR
exec_expression()

{
    STACK_ITEM_PTR   operandp1, operandp2;   /* ptrs to operands */
    TYPE_STRUCT_PTR  result_tp, tp2;         /* ptrs to types */
    TOKEN_CODE       op;                      /* an operator token */
    BOOLEAN          result;

    result_tp = exec_simple_expression();    /* first simple expr */

    /*
    -- If there is a relational operator, remember it and
    -- process the second simple expression.
    */
    if ((ctoken == EQUAL) || (ctoken == LT) || (ctoken == GT) ||
        (ctoken == NE)    || (ctoken == LE) || (ctoken == GE)) {
        op = ctoken;                          /* remember operator */
        result_tp = base_type(result_tp);

        get_ctoken();
        tp2 = base_type(exec_simple_expression()); /* 2nd simp expr */

        operandp1 = tos - 1;
        operandp2 = tos;

        /*
        -- Both operands are integer, boolean, or enumeration.
        */
        if (   ((result_tp == integer_typep) &&
                (tp2       == integer_typep))
            || (result_tp->form == ENUM_FORM)) {
            switch (op) {
                case EQUAL:
                    result = operandp1->integer == operandp2->integer;
                    break;

                case LT:
                    result = operandp1->integer <  operandp2->integer;
                    break;

                case GT:
                    result = operandp1->integer >  operandp2->integer;
                    break;

                case NE:
                    result = operandp1->integer != operandp2->integer;
                    break;

                case LE:
                    result = operandp1->integer <= operandp2->integer;
                    break;

                case GE:
                    result = operandp1->integer >= operandp2->integer;
                    break;
            }
        }

        /*
        -- Both operands are character.
        */
```

```
        else if (result_tp == char_typep) {
            switch (op) {
                case EQUAL:
                    result = operandp1->byte == operandp2->byte;
                    break;

                case LT:
                    result = operandp1->byte <  operandp2->byte;
                    break;

                case GT:
                    result = operandp1->byte >  operandp2->byte;
                    break;

                case NE:
                    result = operandp1->byte != operandp2->byte;
                    break;

                case LE:
                    result = operandp1->byte <= operandp2->byte;
                    break;

                case GE:
                    result = operandp1->byte >= operandp2->byte;
                    break;
            }
        }

        /*
        -- Both operands are real, or one is real and the other
        -- is integer.  Convert the integer operand to real.
        */
        else if ((result_tp == real_typep) ||
                 (tp2        == real_typep)) {
            promote_operands_to_real(operandp1, result_tp,
                                     operandp2, tp2);

            switch (op) {
                case EQUAL:
                    result = operandp1->real == operandp2->real;
                    break;

                case LT:
                    result = operandp1->real <  operandp2->real;
                    break;

                case GT:
                    result = operandp1->real >  operandp2->real;
                    break;

                case NE:
                    result = operandp1->real != operandp2->real;
                    break;

                case LE:
                    result = operandp1->real <= operandp2->real;
                    break;

                case GE:
                    result = operandp1->real >= operandp2->real;
                    break;
            }
        }

        /*
        -- Both operands are strings.
        */
```

```
        else if ((result_tp->form == ARRAY_FORM) &&
                 (result_tp->info.array.elmt_typep == char_typep)) {
            int cmp = strncmp(operandp1->address, operandp2->address,
                              result_tp->info.array.elmt_count);

            result = (  (   (cmp < 0)
                         && (   (op == NE)
                             || (op == LE)
                             || (op == LT)))
                     || (   (cmp == 0)
                         && (   (op == EQUAL)
                             || (op == LE)
                             || (op == GE)))
                     || (   (cmp > 0)
                         && (   (op == NE)
                             || (op == GE)
                             || (op == GT))));
        }

        /*
        -- Replace the two operands on the stack with the result.
        */
        operandp1->integer = result ? 1 : 0;
        pop();

        result_tp = boolean_typep;
    }

    return(result_tp);
}

/*------------------------------------------------------------*/
/*  exec_simple_expression   Execute a simple expression      */
/*                           consisting of terms separated by +, */
/*                           -, or OR operators.  There may be */
/*                           a unary + or - before the first  */
/*                           term.  Return a pointer to the   */
/*                           type structure.                  */
/*------------------------------------------------------------*/

    TYPE_STRUCT_PTR
exec_simple_expression()

{
    STACK_ITEM_PTR operandp1, operandp2;   /* ptrs to operands */
    TYPE_STRUCT_PTR result_tp, tp2;        /* ptrs to types */
    TOKEN_CODE op;                         /* an operator token */
    TOKEN_CODE unary_op = PLUS;            /* unary operator token */

    /*
    -- If there is a unary + or -, remember it.
    */
    if ((ctoken == PLUS) || (ctoken == MINUS)) {
        unary_op = ctoken;
        get_ctoken();
    }

    result_tp = exec_term();   /* first term */

    /*
    -- If there was a unary -, negate the top of stack
    */
    if (unary_op == MINUS) {
        if (result_tp == integer_typep) tos->integer = -tos->integer;
        else                            tos->real    = -tos->real;
    }

    /*
```

```
    -- Loop to process subsequent terms
    -- separated by operators.
    */
    while ((ctoken == PLUS) || (ctoken == MINUS) || (ctoken == OR)) {
        op = ctoken;                      /* remember operator */
        result_tp = base_type(result_tp);

        get_ctoken();
        tp2 = base_type(exec_term());   /* subsequent term */

        operandp1 = tos - 1;
        operandp2 = tos;

        /*
        -- OR
        */
        if (op == OR) {
            operandp1->integer = operandp1->integer ||
                                 operandp2->integer;
            result_tp = boolean_typep;
        }

        /*
        -- + or -
        --
        -- Both operands are integer.
        */
        else if ((result_tp == integer_typep) &&
                 (tp2       == integer_typep)) {
            operandp1->integer = (op == PLUS)
                ? operandp1->integer + operandp2->integer
                : operandp1->integer - operandp2->integer;
            result_tp = integer_typep;
        }

        /*
        -- Both operands are real, or one is real and the other
        -- is integer.  Convert the integer operand to real.
        */
        else {
            promote_operands_to_real(operandp1, result_tp,
                                     operandp2, tp2);

            operandp1->real = (op == PLUS)
                ? operandp1->real + operandp2->real
                : operandp1->real - operandp2->real;
            result_tp = real_typep;
        }

        pop();  /* pop off the second operand */
    }

    return(result_tp);
}

/*------------------------------------------------------------*/
/*  exec_term          Execute a term consisting of factors   */
/*                     separated by *, /, DIV, MOD, or AND     */
/*                     operators.  Return a pointer to the     */
/*                     type structure.                         */
/*------------------------------------------------------------*/

    TYPE_STRUCT_PTR
exec_term()

{
    STACK_ITEM_PTR operandp1, operandp2;   /* ptrs to operands */
    TYPE_STRUCT_PTR result_tp, tp2;        /* ptrs to types */
```

```
TOKEN_CODE op;                       /* an operator token */

result_tp = exec_factor();  /* first factor */

/*
-- Loop to process subsequent factors
-- separated by operators.
*/
while ((ctoken == STAR) || (ctoken == SLASH) || (ctoken == DIV) ||
       (ctoken == MOD)  || (ctoken == AND)) {
    op = ctoken;                     /* remember operator */
    result_tp = base_type(result_tp);

    get_ctoken();
    tp2 = base_type(exec_factor());     /* subsequent factor */

    operandp1 = tos - 1;
    operandp2 = tos;

    /*
    -- AND
    */
    if (op == AND) {
        operandp1->integer = operandp1->integer &&
                             operandp2->integer;
        result_tp = boolean_typep;
    }

    /*
    -- *, /, DIV, or MOD
    */
    else switch (op) {

        case STAR:
            /*
            -- Both operands are integer.
            */
            if (   (result_tp == integer_typep)
                && (tp2       == integer_typep)) {
                operandp1->integer =
                    operandp1->integer * operandp2->integer;
                result_tp = integer_typep;
            }

            /*
            -- Both operands are real, or one is real and the
            -- other is integer.  Convert the integer operand
            -- to real.
            */
            else {
                promote_operands_to_real(operandp1, result_tp,
                                         operandp2, tp2);

                operandp1->real =
                    operandp1->real * operandp2->real;
                result_tp = real_typep;
            }
            break;

        case SLASH:
            /*
            -- Both operands are real, or one is real and the
            -- other is integer.  Convert the integer operand
            -- to real.
            */
            promote_operands_to_real(operandp1, result_tp,
                                     operandp2, tp2);
```

```
            if (operandp2->real == 0.0)
                runtime_error(DIVISION_BY_ZERO);
            else
                operandp1->real = operandp1->real/operandp2->real;

            result_tp = real_typep;
            break;

        case DIV:
        case MOD:
            /*
            -- Both operands are integer.
            */
            if (operandp2->integer == 0)
                runtime_error(DIVISION_BY_ZERO);
            else
                operandp1->integer = (op == DIV)
                    ? operandp1->integer / operandp2->integer
                    : operandp1->integer % operandp2->integer;

            result_tp = integer_typep;
            break;
    }

    pop();  /* pop off the second operand */
}

return(result_tp);
}

/*----------------------------------------------------------*/
/* exec_factor        Execute a factor, which is a variable, */
/*                    a number, NOT followed by a factor, or */
/*                    a parenthesized subexpression.  Return */
/*                    a pointer to the type structure.       */
/*----------------------------------------------------------*/

    TYPE_STRUCT_PTR
exec_factor()

{
    TYPE_STRUCT_PTR result_tp;          /* type pointer */

    switch (ctoken) {

        case IDENTIFIER: {
            SYMTAB_NODE_PTR idp = get_symtab_cptr();

            /*
            -- Function call or constant or variable.
            */
            if (idp->defn.key == FUNC_DEFN)
                result_tp = exec_routine_call(idp);
            else if (idp->defn.key == CONST_DEFN)
                result_tp = exec_constant(idp);
            else
                result_tp = exec_variable(idp, EXPR_USE);

            break;
        }

        case NUMBER: {
            SYMTAB_NODE_PTR np = get_symtab_cptr();

            /*
            -- Obtain the integer or real value from the
            -- symbol table entry and push it onto the stack.
```

```
    */
    if (np->typep == integer_typep) {
        push_integer(np->defn.info.constant.value.integer);
        result_tp = integer_typep;
    }
    else {
        push_real(np->defn.info.constant.value.real);
        result_tp = real_typep;
    }

    get_ctoken();
    break;
}

case STRING: {
    SYMTAB_NODE_PTR np      = get_symtab_cptr();
    int             length = strlen(np->name);

    /*
    -- Obtain the character or string from the symbol
    -- table entry.  Note that the quotes were included,
    -- so the string lengths need to be decreased by 2.
    */
    if (length > 3) {
        /*
        -- String:  Push its address onto the stack.
        */
        push_address(np->info);
        result_tp = np->typep;
    }
    else {
        /*
        -- Character:  Push its value onto the stack.
        */
        push_byte(np->name[1]);
        result_tp = char_typep;
    }

    get_ctoken();
    break;
}

case NOT:
    get_ctoken();
    result_tp = exec_factor();
    tos->integer = 1 - tos->integer;    /* 0 => 1, 1 => 0 */
    break;

case LPAREN:
    get_ctoken();
    result_tp = exec_expression();
    get_ctoken();          /* token after ) */
    break;
}

return(result_tp);
}

/*------------------------------------------------------------*/
/*  exec_constant      Push the value of a non-string constant */
/*                     identifier, or the address of the value */
/*                     a string constant identifier onto the  */
/*                     stack.  Return a pointer to the type    */
/*                     structure.                              */
/*------------------------------------------------------------*/

    TYPE_STRUCT_PTR
```

```
exec_constant(idp)

    SYMTAB_NODE_PTR idp;          /* constant id */

{
    TYPE_STRUCT_PTR tp = idp->typep;

    if ((base_type(tp) == integer_typep) || (tp->form == ENUM_FORM))
        push_integer(idp->defn.info.constant.value.integer);
    else if (tp == real_typep)
        push_real(idp->defn.info.constant.value.real);
    else if (tp == char_typep)
        push_integer(idp->defn.info.constant.value.integer);
    else if (tp->form == ARRAY_FORM)
        push_address(idp->defn.info.constant.value.stringp);

    trace_data_fetch(idp, tp, tos);
    get_ctoken();

    return(tp);
}

/*------------------------------------------------------------*/
/*  exec_variable      Push either the variable's address or  */
/*                     its value onto the stack.  Return a    */
/*                     pointer to the type structure.         */
/*------------------------------------------------------------*/

    TYPE_STRUCT_PTR
exec_variable(idp, use)

    SYMTAB_NODE_PTR idp;      /* variable id */
    USE             use;      /* how variable is used */

{
    int             delta;            /* difference in levels */
    TYPE_STRUCT_PTR tp = idp->typep;
    TYPE_STRUCT_PTR base_tp;
    STACK_ITEM_PTR  datap;            /* ptr to data area */
    STACK_FRAME_HEADER_PTR hp;

    /*
    -- Point to the variable's stack item.  If the variable's level
    -- is less than the current level, follow the static links to
    -- the appropriate stack frame base.
    */
    hp = (STACK_FRAME_HEADER_PTR) stack_frame_basep;
    delta = level - idp->level;
    while (delta-- > 0)
        hp = (STACK_FRAME_HEADER_PTR) hp->static_link.address;
    datap = (STACK_ITEM_PTR) hp + idp->defn.info.data.offset;

    /*
    -- If a scalar or enumeration VAR parm, that item
    -- points to the actual item.
    */
    if ((idp->defn.key == VARPARM_DEFN) &&
        (tp->form != ARRAY_FORM) &&
        (tp->form != RECORD_FORM))
        datap = (STACK_ITEM_PTR) datap->address;

    /*
    -- Push the address of the variable's data area.
    */
    if ((tp->form == ARRAY_FORM) ||
        (tp->form == RECORD_FORM))
        push_address((ADDRESS) datap->address);
```

```
        else
            push_address((ADDRESS) datap);


        /*
        -- If there are subscripts or field designators,
        -- modify the address to point to the array element
        -- record field.
        */
        get_ctoken();
        while ((ctoken == LBRACKET) || (ctoken == PERIOD)) {
            if      (ctoken == LBRACKET) tp = exec_subscripts(tp);
            else if (ctoken == PERIOD)   tp = exec_field();
        }


        base_tp = base_type(tp);


        /*
        -- Leave the modified address on top of the stack if:
        --      it is an assignment target, or
        --      it represents a parameter passed by reference, or
        --      it is the address of an array or record.
        -- Otherwise, replace the address with the value that it
        -- points to.
        */
        if ((use != TARGET_USE) && (use != VARPARM_USE) &&
            (tp->form != ARRAY_FORM) && (tp->form != RECORD_FORM)) {

            if ((base_tp == integer_typep) || (tp->form == ENUM_FORM))
                tos->integer = *((int *) tos->address);
            else if (base_tp == char_typep)
                tos->byte = *((char *) tos->address);
            else
                tos->real = *((float *) tos->address);
        }


        if ((use != TARGET_USE) && (use != VARPARM_USE))
            trace_data_fetch(idp, tp,
                        (tp->form == ARRAY_FORM) ||
                        (tp->form == RECORD_FORM)
                            ? tos->address
                            : tos);


        return(tp);
}


/*-------------------------------------------------------------*/
/* exec_subscripts     Execute subscripts to modify the array  */
/*                     data area address on the top of stack.  */
/*                     Return a pointer to the type of the      */
/*                     array element.                           */
/*-------------------------------------------------------------*/

    TYPE_STRUCT_PTR
exec_subscripts(tp)

    TYPE_STRUCT_PTR tp;          /* ptr to type structure */

{
    int subscript_value;

    /*
    -- Loop to execute bracketed subscripts.
    */
```

```
    while (ctoken == LBRACKET) {
        /*
        -- Loop to execute a subscript list.
        */
        do {
            get_ctoken();
            exec_expression();

            subscript_value = tos->integer;
            pop();


            /*
            -- Range check.
            */
            if ((subscript_value < tp->info.array.min_index) ||
                (subscript_value > tp->info.array.max_index))
                runtime_error(VALUE_OUT_OF_RANGE);


            /*
            -- Modify the data area address.
            */
            tos->address +=
                (subscript_value - tp->info.array.min_index) *
                                    tp->info.array.elmt_typep->size;


            if (ctoken == COMMA) tp = tp->info.array.elmt_typep;
        } while (ctoken == COMMA);


        get_ctoken();
        if (ctoken == LBRACKET) tp = tp->info.array.elmt_typep;
    }


    return(tp->info.array.elmt_typep);
}


/*-------------------------------------------------------------*/
/* exec_field          Execute a field designator to modify    */
/*                     the record data area address on the     */
/*                     top of stack.  Return a pointer to the   */
/*                     type of the record field.                */
/*-------------------------------------------------------------*/

    TYPE_STRUCT_PTR
exec_field()


{
    SYMTAB_NODE_PTR field_idp;

    get_ctoken();
    field_idp = get_symtab_cptr();

    tos->address += field_idp->defn.info.data.offset;

    get_ctoken();
    return(field_idp->typep);
}


/*-------------------------------------------------------------*/
/* promote_operands_to_real    If either operand is integer,   */
/*                             convert it to real.             */
/*-------------------------------------------------------------*/
```

```
promote_operands_to_real(operandp1, tp1, operandp2, tp2)           {
                                                                       if (tp1 == integer_typep) operandp1->real = operandp1->integer;
    STACK_ITEM_PTR  operandp1, operandp2;   /* ptrs to operands */    if (tp2 == integer_typep) operandp2->real = operandp2->integer;
    TYPE_STRUCT_PTR tp1, tp2;               /* ptrs to types */    }
```

FIGURE A-15   execstd.c

```
/****************************************************************/
/*                                                              */
/*          S T A N D A R D   R O U T I N E   E X E C U T O R   */
/*                                                              */
/*          Execution routines for statements.                 */
/*                                                              */
/*          FILE:     execstd.c                                 */
/*                                                              */
/*          MODULE:   executor                                  */
/*                                                              */
/****************************************************************/

#include <stdio.h>
#include <math.h>
#include "common.h"
#include "error.h"
#include "symtab.h"
#include "scanner.h"
#include "parser.h"
#include "exec.h"

#define EOF_CHAR                    '\x7f'

#define DEFAULT_NUMERIC_FIELD_WIDTH    10
#define DEFAULT_PRECISION              2

/*--------------------------------------------------------------*/
/* Externals                                                    */
/*--------------------------------------------------------------*/

extern int          level;
extern int          exec_line_number;

extern char         *code_segmentp;
extern TOKEN_CODE   ctoken;

extern STACK_ITEM       *stack;
extern STACK_ITEM_PTR   tos;
extern STACK_ITEM_PTR   stack_frame_basep;
extern STACK_ITEM_PTR   stack_display[];

extern TYPE_STRUCT_PTR integer_typep, real_typep,
                       boolean_typep, char_typep;

/*--------------------------------------------------------------*/
/* Forwards                                                     */
/*--------------------------------------------------------------*/

TYPE_STRUCT_PTR exec_eof_eoln(), exec_abs_sqr(),
                exec_arctan_cos_exp_ln_sin_sqrt(),
                exec_pred_succ(), exec_chr(),
                exec_odd(), exec_ord(), exec_round_trunc();

/*--------------------------------------------------------------*/
/* Globals                                                      */
/*--------------------------------------------------------------*/
```

```
BOOLEAN eof_flag = FALSE;

/*--------------------------------------------------------------*/
/* exec_standard_routine_call  Execute a call to a standard     */
/*                             procedure or function.  Return   */
/*                             a pointer to the type structure  */
/*                             of the call.                     */
/*--------------------------------------------------------------*/

    TYPE_STRUCT_PTR
exec_standard_routine_call(rtn_idp)

    SYMTAB_NODE_PTR rtn_idp;            /* routine id */

{
    switch (rtn_idp->defn.info.routine.key) {

        case READ:
        case READLN:    exec_read_readln(rtn_idp);       return(NULL);

        case WRITE:
        case WRITELN:   exec_write_writeln(rtn_idp);     return(NULL);

        case EOFF:
        case EOLN:      return(exec_eof_eoln(rtn_idp));

        case ABS:
        case SQR:       return(exec_abs_sqr(rtn_idp));

        case ARCTAN:
        case COS:
        case EXP:
        case LN:
        case SIN:
        case SQRT:      return(exec_arctan_cos_exp_ln_sin_sqrt
                                    (rtn_idp));

        case PRED:
        case SUCC:      return(exec_pred_succ(rtn_idp));

        case CHR:       return(exec_chr());
        case ODD:       return(exec_odd());
        case ORD:       return(exec_ord());

        case ROUND:
        case TRUNC:     return(exec_round_trunc(rtn_idp));
    }
}

/*--------------------------------------------------------------*/
/* exec_read_readln        Execute a call to read or readln.    */
/*--------------------------------------------------------------*/

exec_read_readln(rtn_idp)
```

```
    SYMTAB_NODE_PTR rtn_idp;          /* routine id */


{

    SYMTAB_NODE_PTR parm_idp;         /* parm id */
    TYPE_STRUCT_PTR parm_tp;          /* parm type */
    STACK_ITEM_PTR  targetp;          /* ptr to read target */

    /*
    -- Parameters are optional for readln.
    */
    get_ctoken();
    if (ctoken == LPAREN) {
        /*
        -- <id-list>
        */
        do {
            get_ctoken();
            parm_idp = get_symtab_cptr();
            parm_tp  = base_type(exec_variable(parm_idp,
                                         VARPARM_USE));
            targetp  = (STACK_ITEM_PTR) tos->address;

            pop();      /* pop off address */

            if (parm_tp == integer_typep)
                scanf("%d", &targetp->integer);
            else if (parm_tp == real_typep)
                scanf("%g", &targetp->real);

            else if (parm_tp == char_typep) {
                scanf("%c", &targetp->byte);
                if (eof_flag ||
                    (targetp->byte == '\n')) targetp->byte = ' ';
            }

            trace_data_store(parm_idp, parm_idp->typep,
                             targetp, parm_tp);
        } while (ctoken == COMMA);

        get_ctoken();   /* token after ) */
    }

    if (rtn_idp->defn.info.routine.key == READLN) {
        char ch;

        do {
            ch = getchar();
        } while (!eof_flag && (ch != '\n'));
    }
}

/*------------------------------------------------------------*/
/* exec_write_writeln    Execute a call to write or writeln. */
/*                       Each actual parameter can be:       */
/*                                                           */
/*                             <expr>                        */
/*                                                           */
/*                  or:                                      */
/*                                                           */
/*                       <epxr> : <expr>                     */
/*                                                           */
/*                  or:                                      */
/*                                                           */
/*                   <expr> : <expr> : <expr>                */
/*------------------------------------------------------------*/

exec_write_writeln(rtn_idp)
```

```
    SYMTAB_NODE_PTR rtn_idp;          /* routine id */


{

    TYPE_STRUCT_PTR parm_tp;          /* parm type */
    int         field_width;
    int         precision;

    /*
    -- Parameters are optional for writeln.
    */
    get_ctoken();
    if (ctoken == LPAREN) {
        do {
            /*
            -- Push value
            */
            get_ctoken();
            parm_tp = base_type(exec_expression());

            if (parm_tp == integer_typep)
                field_width = DEFAULT_NUMERIC_FIELD_WIDTH;
            else if (parm_tp == real_typep) {
                field_width = DEFAULT_NUMERIC_FIELD_WIDTH;
                precision   = DEFAULT_PRECISION;
            }
            else field_width = 0;

            /*
            -- Optional field width <expr>
            */
            if (ctoken == COLON) {
                get_ctoken();
                exec_expression();
                field_width = tos->integer;
                pop();          /* pop off field width */

                /*
                -- Optional decimal places <expr>
                */
                if (ctoken == COLON) {
                    get_ctoken();
                    exec_expression();
                    precision = tos->integer;
                    pop();      /* pop off precision */
                }
            }

            /*
            -- Write value
            */
            if (parm_tp == integer_typep)
                printf("%*d", field_width, tos->integer);
            else if (parm_tp == real_typep)
                printf("%*.*f", field_width, precision, tos->real);
            else if (parm_tp == boolean_typep)
                printf("%*s", field_width, tos->integer == 1
                                        ? "TRUE" : "FALSE");
            else if (parm_tp == char_typep)
                printf("%*c", field_width, tos->byte);

            else if (parm_tp->form == ARRAY_FORM) {
                char buffer[MAX_SOURCE_LINE_LENGTH];

                strncpy(buffer, tos->address,
                             parm_tp->info.array.elmt_count);
                buffer[parm_tp->info.array.elmt_count] = '\0';
                printf("%*s", -field_width, buffer);
```

```
                }

            pop();          /* pop off value */
        } while (ctoken == COMMA);

        get_ctoken();      /* token after ) */
    }

    if (rtn_idp->defn.info.routine.key == WRITELN) putchar('\n');
}

/*------------------------------------------------------------*/
/* exec_eof_eoln          Execute a call to eof or to eoln.   */
/*                        No parameters => boolean result.    */
/*------------------------------------------------------------*/

    TYPE_STRUCT_PTR
exec_eof_eoln(rtn_idp)

    SYMTAB_NODE_PTR rtn_idp;            /* routine id */

{
    char ch = getchar();

    switch (rtn_idp->defn.info.routine.key) {

        case EOFF:
            if (eof_flag || feof(stdin)) {
                eof_flag = TRUE;
                push_integer(1);
            }
            else {
                push_integer(0);
                ungetc(ch, stdin);
            }
            break;

        case EOLN:
            if (eof_flag || feof(stdin)) {
                eof_flag = TRUE;
                push_integer(1);
            }
            else {
                push_integer(ch == '\n' ? 1 : 0);
                ungetc(ch, stdin);
            }
            break;
    }

    get_ctoken();      /* token after function name */
    return(boolean_typep);
}

/*------------------------------------------------------------*/
/* exec_abs_sqr           Execute a call to abs or to sqr.    */
/*                        integer parm => integer result      */
/*                        real parm    => real result         */
/*------------------------------------------------------------*/

    TYPE_STRUCT_PTR
exec_abs_sqr(rtn_idp)

    SYMTAB_NODE_PTR rtn_idp;            /* routine id */

{
    TYPE_STRUCT_PTR parm_tp;            /* actual parameter type */
    TYPE_STRUCT_PTR result_tp;          /* result type */
```

```
    get_ctoken();       /* ( */
    get_ctoken();
    parm_tp = base_type(exec_expression());

    if (parm_tp == integer_typep) {
        tos->integer = rtn_idp->defn.info.routine.key == ABS
                       ? abs(tos->integer)
                       : tos->integer * tos->integer;
        result_tp = integer_typep;
    }
    else {
        tos->real = rtn_idp->defn.info.routine.key == ABS
                    ? fabs(tos->real)
                    : tos->real * tos->real;
        result_tp = real_typep;
    }

    get_ctoken();       /* token after ) */
    return(result_tp);
}

/*------------------------------------------------------------*/
/* exec_arctan_cos_exp_ln_sin_sqrt Execute a call to arctan,  */
/*                        cos, exp, ln, sin, or sqrt.         */
/*                        integer parm => real result         */
/*                        real_parm    => real result         */
/*------------------------------------------------------------*/

    TYPE_STRUCT_PTR
exec_arctan_cos_exp_ln_sin_sqrt(rtn_idp)

    SYMTAB_NODE_PTR rtn_idp;            /* routine id */

{
    TYPE_STRUCT_PTR parm_tp;            /* actual parameter type */
    int          code = rtn_idp->defn.info.routine.key;

    get_ctoken();       /* ( */
    get_ctoken();
    parm_tp = base_type(exec_expression());
    if (parm_tp == integer_typep) tos->real = tos->integer;

    if (   ((code == LN)   && (tos->real <= 0.0))
        || ((code == SQRT) && (tos->real <  0.0)))
        runtime_error(INVALID_FUNCTION_ARGUMENT);
    else
        switch (rtn_idp->defn.info.routine.key) {
            case ARCTAN:   tos->real = atan(tos->real);   break;
            case COS:      tos->real = cos(tos->real);    break;
            case EXP:      tos->real = exp(tos->real);    break;
            case LN:       tos->real = log(tos->real);    break;
            case SIN:      tos->real = sin(tos->real);    break;
            case SQRT:     tos->real = sqrt(tos->real);   break;
        }
    }

    get_ctoken();       /* token after ) */
    return(real_typep);
}

/*------------------------------------------------------------*/
/* exec_pred_succ         Execute a call to pred or succ.     */
/*                        integer parm => integer result      */
/*                        enum parm    => enum result         */
/*------------------------------------------------------------*/

    TYPE_STRUCT_PTR
```

```
exec_pred_succ(rtn_idp)

    SYMTAB_NODE_PTR rtn_idp;         /* routine id */

{

    TYPE_STRUCT_PTR parm_tp;         /* actual parameter type */

    get_ctoken();       /* ( */
    get_ctoken();
    parm_tp = base_type(exec_expression());

    tos->integer = rtn_idp->defn.info.routine.key == PRED
                    ? --tos->integer
                    : ++tos->integer;

    get_ctoken();       /* token after ) */
    return(parm_tp);
}

/*-----------------------------------------------------------*/
/* exec_chr              Execute a call to chr.             */
/*                       integer parm => character result   */
/*-----------------------------------------------------------*/

    TYPE_STRUCT_PTR
exec_chr()

{

    get_ctoken();       /* ( */
    get_ctoken();
    exec_expression();

    tos->byte = tos->integer;

    get_ctoken();       /* token after ) */
    return(char_typep);
}

/*-----------------------------------------------------------*/
/* exec_odd              Execute a call to odd.             */
/*                       integer parm => boolean result     */
/*-----------------------------------------------------------*/

    TYPE_STRUCT_PTR
exec_odd()

{

    get_ctoken();       /* ( */
    get_ctoken();
```

```
    exec_expression();

    tos->integer &= 1;

    get_ctoken();       /* token after ) */
    return(boolean_typep);
}

/*-----------------------------------------------------------*/
/* exec_ord              Execute a call to ord.             */
/*                       enumeration parm => integer result */
/*-----------------------------------------------------------*/

    TYPE_STRUCT_PTR
exec_ord()

{

    get_ctoken();       /* ( */
    get_ctoken();
    exec_expression();

    get_ctoken();       /* token after ) */
    return(integer_typep);
}

/*-----------------------------------------------------------*/
/* exec_round_trunc      Execute a call to round or trunc.  */
/*                       real parm => integer result        */
/*-----------------------------------------------------------*/

    TYPE_STRUCT_PTR
exec_round_trunc(rtn_idp)

    SYMTAB_NODE_PTR rtn_idp;         /* routine id */

{

    get_ctoken();       /* ( */
    get_ctoken();
    exec_expression();

    if (rtn_idp->defn.info.routine.key == ROUND) {
        tos->integer = tos->real > 0.0
                        ? (int) (tos->real + 0.5)
                        : (int) (tos->real - 0.5);
    }
    else tos->integer = (int) tos->real;

    get_ctoken();       /* token after ) */
    return(integer_typep);
}
```

FIGURE A-16   debug.c

```
/*****************************************************************/
/*                                                               */
/*      I N T E R A C T I V E   D E B U G G E R                  */
/*                                                               */
/*      Interactive debugging routines.                          */
/*                                                               */
/*      FILE:       debug.c                                      */
/*                                                               */
```

```
/*      MODULE:     executor                                     */
/*                                                               */
/*****************************************************************/

#include <stdio.h>
#include "common.h"
#include "error.h"
#include "scanner.h"
```

```
#include "symtab.h"
#include "exec.h"

#define MAX_BREAKS        16
#define MAX_WATCHES       16
#define COMMAND_QUERY     "Command? "

/*----------------------------------------------------------*/
/*  Externals                                               */
/*----------------------------------------------------------*/

extern TYPE_STRUCT_PTR  integer_typep, real_typep,
                        boolean_typep, char_typep;

extern TYPE_STRUCT      dummy_type;

extern int              level;
extern SYMTAB_NODE_PTR  symtab_display[];
extern STACK_ITEM_PTR   tos;

extern int      line_number;
extern int      buffer_offset;
extern BOOLEAN  print_flag;

extern char     *code_segmentp;
extern char     *statement_startp;
extern int      ctoken;
extern int      exec_line_number;
extern int      error_count;

extern char     *bufferp;
extern char     ch;
extern char     source_buffer[];
extern char     word_string[];
extern int      token;
extern LITERAL  literal;
extern BOOLEAN  block_flag;

extern char     *code_buffer;
extern char     *code_bufferp;
extern char     *code_segmentp;

/*----------------------------------------------------------*/
/*  Globals                                                 */
/*----------------------------------------------------------*/

FILE    *console;

BOOLEAN debugger_command_flag,  /* TRUE during debug command */
        halt_flag,              /* TRUE to pause for debug command */
        trace_flag,             /* TRUE to trace statement */
        step_flag,              /* TRUE to single-step */
        entry_flag,             /* TRUE to trace routine entry */
        exit_flag;              /* TRUE to trace routine exit */

int     break_count;                   /* count of breakpoints */
int     break_list[MAX_BREAKS];        /* list of breakpoints */

int              watch_count;           /* count of watches */
SYMTAB_NODE_PTR  watch_list[MAX_WATCHES];   /* list of watches */

typedef struct {                    /* watch structure */
    SYMTAB_NODE_PTR watch_idp;      /* id node watched variable */
    BOOLEAN         store_flag;     /* TRUE to trace stores */
    BOOLEAN         fetch_flag;     /* TRUE to trace fetches */
} WATCH_STRUCT, *WATCH_STRUCT_PTR;
```

```
char *symbol_strings[] = {
    "<no token>", "<IDENTIFIER>", "<NUMBER>", "<STRING>",
    "^", "*", "(", ")", "-", "+", "=", "[", "]", ":", ".",
    "<", ">", ",", ".", "/", ":=", "<=", ">=", "<>", "..",
    "<END OF FILE>", "<ERROR>",
    "AND", "ARRAY", "BEGIN", "CASE", "CONST", "DIV", "DO", "DOWNTO",
    "ELSE", "END", "FILE", "FOR", "FUNCTION", "GOTO", "IF", "IN",
    "LABEL", "MOD", "NIL", "NOT", "OF", "OR", "PACKED", "PROCEDURE",
    "PROGRAM", "RECORD", "REPEAT", "SET", "THEN", "TO", "TYPE",
    "UNTIL", "VAR", "WHILE", "WITH",
};

/*----------------------------------------------------------*/
/*  init_debugger       Initialize the interactive debugger. */
/*----------------------------------------------------------*/

init_debugger()

{
    int i;

    /*
    -- Initialize the debugger's globals.
    */
    console = fopen("CON", "r");
    code_buffer = alloc_bytes(MAX_SOURCE_LINE_LENGTH + 1);

    print_flag = FALSE;
    halt_flag  = block_flag = TRUE;
    debugger_command_flag = trace_flag = step_flag
                          = entry_flag = exit_flag
                          = FALSE;

    break_count = 0;
    for (i = 0; i < MAX_BREAKS; ++i) break_list[i] = 0;

    watch_count = 0;
    for (i = 0; i < MAX_WATCHES; ++i) watch_list[i] = NULL;
}

/*----------------------------------------------------------*/
/*  read_debugger_command    Read and process a debugging   */
/*                           command typed in by the user.  */
/*----------------------------------------------------------*/

read_debugger_command()

{
    BOOLEAN done = FALSE;

    debugger_command_flag = TRUE;

    do {
        printf("\n%s", COMMAND_QUERY);

        /*
        -- Read in a debugging command and replace the
        -- final \n\0 with ;;\0
        */
        bufferp = fgets(source_buffer, MAX_SOURCE_LINE_LENGTH,
                        console);
        strcpy(&source_buffer[strlen(source_buffer) - 1], ";;");

        ch = *bufferp++;
        buffer_offset = sizeof(COMMAND_QUERY);
        code_bufferp  = code_buffer;
        error_count   = 0;
```

```
        get_token();

        /*
        -- Process the command.
        */
        switch (token) {
            case SEMICOLON:      done = TRUE;                    break;
            case IDENTIFIER:     execute_debugger_command(); break;
        }

        if (token != SEMICOLON) error(UNEXPECTED_TOKEN);
    } while (!done);

    debugger_command_flag = FALSE;
}

/*------------------------------------------------------------*/
/*  execute_debugger_command      Execute a debugger command. */
/*------------------------------------------------------------*/

execute_debugger_command()

{
    WATCH_STRUCT_PTR wp;
    WATCH_STRUCT_PTR allocate_watch();

    if (strcmp(word_string, "trace") == 0) {
        trace_flag = TRUE;
        step_flag = FALSE;
        get_token();
    }
    else if (strcmp(word_string, "untrace") == 0) {
        trace_flag = FALSE;
        get_token();
    }

    else if (strcmp(word_string, "step") == 0) {
        step_flag = TRUE;
        trace_flag = FALSE;
        get_token();
    }
    else if (strcmp(word_string, "unstep") == 0) {
        step_flag = FALSE;
        get_token();
    }

    else if (strcmp(word_string, "break") == 0)
        set_breakpoint();
    else if (strcmp(word_string, "unbreak") == 0)
        remove_breakpoint();

    else if (strcmp(word_string, "entry") == 0) {
        entry_flag = TRUE;
        get_token();
    }
    else if (strcmp(word_string, "unentry") == 0) {
        entry_flag = FALSE;
        get_token();
    }

    else if (strcmp(word_string, "exit") == 0) {
        exit_flag = TRUE;
        get_token();
    }
    else if (strcmp(word_string, "unexit") == 0) {
        exit_flag = FALSE;
        get_token();
    }
```

```
    }
    else if (strcmp(word_string, "watch") == 0) {
        wp = allocate_watch();
        if (wp != NULL) {
            wp->store_flag = TRUE;
            wp->fetch_flag = TRUE;
        }
    }
    else if (strcmp(word_string, "unwatch") == 0)
        remove_watch();

    else if (strcmp(word_string, "store") == 0) {
        wp = allocate_watch();
        if (wp != NULL) wp->store_flag = TRUE;
    }
    else if (strcmp(word_string, "fetch") == 0) {
        wp = allocate_watch();
        if (wp != NULL) wp->fetch_flag = TRUE;
    }

    else if (strcmp(word_string, "show") == 0)
        show_value();
    else if (strcmp(word_string, "assign") == 0)
        assign_variable();

    else if (strcmp(word_string, "where") == 0) {
        print_statement();
        get_token();
    }
    else if (strcmp(word_string, "kill") == 0) {
        printf("Program killed.\n");
        exit(0);
    }
}

                /*******************************/
                /*                             */
                /*       Tracing routines      */
                /*                             */
                /*******************************/

/*------------------------------------------------------------*/
/*  trace_statement_execution   Called just before the       */
/*                              execution of each statement.  */
/*------------------------------------------------------------*/

trace_statement_execution()

{
    if (break_count > 0) {
        int i;

        /*
        -- Check if the statement is a breakpoint.
        */
        for (i = 0; i < break_count; ++i) {
            if (exec_line_number == break_list[i]) {
                printf("\nBreakpoint");
                print_statement();
                halt_flag = TRUE;
                break;
            }
        }
    }

    /*
```

```
         --  Pause if necessary to read a debugger command.
         */
         if (halt_flag) {
             read_debugger_command();
             halt_flag = step_flag;
         }

         /*
         --  If single-stepping, print the current statement.
         --  If tracing, print the current line number.
         */
         if (step_flag)  print_statement();
         if (trace_flag) print_line_number();
}

/*-----------------------------------------------------*/
/* trace_routine_entry        Called upon entry into a  */
/*                            procedure or a function.  */
/*-----------------------------------------------------*/

trace_routine_entry(idp)

    SYMTAB_NODE_PTR idp;        /* routine id */

{
    if (entry_flag) printf("\nEntering %s\n", idp->name);
}

/*-----------------------------------------------------*/
/* trace_routine_exit         Called upon exit from a   */
/*                            procedure or a function.  */
/*-----------------------------------------------------*/

trace_routine_exit(idp)

    SYMTAB_NODE_PTR idp;        /* routine id */

{
    if (exit_flag) printf("\nExiting %s\n", idp->name);
}

/*-----------------------------------------------------*/
/* trace_data_store           Called just before a variable */
/*                            is stored into.          */
/*-----------------------------------------------------*/

trace_data_store(idp, idp_tp, targetp, target_tp)

    SYMTAB_NODE_PTR idp;             /* id of target variable */
    TYPE_STRUCT_PTR idp_tp;          /* ptr to id's type */
    STACK_ITEM_PTR  targetp;         /* ptr to target location */
    TYPE_STRUCT_PTR target_tp;       /* ptr to target's type */

{
    /*
    --  Check if the variable is being watched for stores.
    */
    if ((idp->info != NULL) &&
        ((WATCH_STRUCT_PTR) idp->info)->store_flag) {
        printf("\nAt %d: Store %s", exec_line_number, idp->name);
        if     (idp_tp->form == ARRAY_FORM)  printf("[*]");
        else if (idp_tp->form == RECORD_FORM) printf(".*");
        print_data_value(targetp, target_tp, ":=");
    }
}

/*-----------------------------------------------------*/
/* trace_data_fetch           Called just before a variable */
```

```
/*                            is fetched from.          */
/*-----------------------------------------------------*/

trace_data_fetch(idp, tp, datap)

    SYMTAB_NODE_PTR idp;             /* id of target variable */
    TYPE_STRUCT_PTR tp;              /* ptr to id's type */
    STACK_ITEM_PTR  datap;           /* ptr to data */

{
    TYPE_STRUCT_PTR idp_tp = idp->typep;

    /*
    --  Check if the variable is being watched for fetches.
    */
    if (   (idp->info != NULL)
        && ((WATCH_STRUCT_PTR) idp->info)->fetch_flag) {
        printf("\nAt %d: Fetch %s", exec_line_number, idp->name);
        if     (idp_tp-> form == ARRAY_FORM)  printf("[*]");
        else if (idp_tp->form == RECORD_FORM) printf(".*");
        print_data_value(datap, tp, "=");
    }
}

                /********************************/
                /*                              */
                /*        Printing routines     */
                /*                              */
                /********************************/

/*-----------------------------------------------------*/
/* print_statement               Uncrunch and print a statement. */
/*-----------------------------------------------------*/

print_statement()

{
    int     tk;                 /* token code */
    BOOLEAN done = FALSE;
    char    *csp = statement_startp;

    printf("\nAt %3d:", exec_line_number);

    do {
        switch (tk = *csp++) {

            case SEMICOLON:
            case END:
            case ELSE:
            case THEN:
            case UNTIL:
            case BEGIN:
            case OF:
            case STATEMENT_MARKER:    done = TRUE;
                                      break;

            default:
                done = FALSE;

                switch (tk) {

                    case ADDRESS_MARKER:
                        csp += sizeof(ADDRESS);
                        break;

                    case IDENTIFIER:
                    case NUMBER:
```

```
            case STRING: {
                SYMTAB_NODE_PTR np = *((SYMTAB_NODE_PTR *) csp);

                printf(" %s", np->name);
                csp += sizeof(SYMTAB_NODE_PTR);
                break;
            }

            default:
                printf(" %s", symbol_strings[tk]);
                break;
            }
        }
    } while (!done);

    printf("\n");
}

/*----------------------------------------------------------*/
/* print_line_number          Print the current line number. */
/*----------------------------------------------------------*/

print_line_number()

{
    printf("<%d>", exec_line_number);
}

/*----------------------------------------------------------*/
/* print_data_value            Print a data value.          */
/*----------------------------------------------------------*/

print_data_value(datap, tp, str)

    STACK_ITEM_PTR  datap;      /* ptr to data value to print */
    TYPE_STRUCT_PTR tp;         /* ptr to type of stack item */
    char           *str;        /* " = " or " := " */

{
    /*
    -- Reduce a subrange type to its range type.
    -- Convert a non-boolean enumeration type to integer.
    */
    if (tp->form == SUBRANGE_FORM)
        tp = tp->info.subrange.range_typep;
    if ((tp->form == ENUM_FORM) && (tp != boolean_typep))
        tp = integer_typep;

    if (tp == integer_typep)
        printf(" %s %d\n", str, datap->integer);
    else if (tp == real_typep)
        printf(" %s %0.6g\n", str, datap->real);
    else if (tp == boolean_typep)
        printf(" %s %s\n", str, datap->integer == 1 ? "true"
                                                    : "false");
    else if (tp == char_typep)
        printf(" %s '%c'\n", str, datap->byte);
    else if (tp->form == ARRAY_FORM) {
        if (tp->info.array.elmt_typep == char_typep) {
            char *chp = (char *) datap;
            int  size = tp->info.array.elmt_count;

            printf(" %s '", str);
            while (size--) printf("%c", *chp++);
            printf("'\n");
        }
        else printf(" %s <array>\n", str);
```

```
    }
    else if (tp->form == RECORD_FORM)
        printf(" %s <record>\n", str);
}

            /****************************************/
            /*                                      */
            /*        Breakpoints and watches       */
            /*                                      */
            /****************************************/

/*----------------------------------------------------------*/
/* set_breakpoint     Set a breakpoint, or print all        */
/*                    breakpoints in the break list.        */
/*----------------------------------------------------------*/

set_breakpoint()

{
    get_token();

    switch (token) {

        case SEMICOLON: {
            /*
            -- No line number:  List all breakpoints.
            */
            int i;

            printf("Statement breakpoints at:\n");

            for (i = 0; i < break_count; ++i)
                printf("%5d\n", break_list[i]);

            break;
        }

        case NUMBER: {
            /*
            -- Set a breakpoint by appending it to
            -- the break list.
            */
            int number;

            if (literal.type == INTEGER_LIT) {
                number = literal.value.integer;
                if ((number > 0) && (number <= line_number)) {
                    if (break_count < MAX_BREAKS) {
                        break_list[break_count] = number;
                        ++break_count;
                    }
                    else printf("Break list is full.\n");
                }
                else error(VALUE_OUT_OF_RANGE);
            }
            else error(UNEXPECTED_TOKEN);

            get_token();
            break;
        }
    }
}

/*----------------------------------------------------------*/
/* remove_breakpoint  Remove a specific breakpoint, or remove */
/*                    all breakpoints.                      */
/*----------------------------------------------------------*/
```

```
remove_breakpoint()

{
    int i, j, number;

    get_token();

    switch (token) {

        case SEMICOLON: {
            /*
            -- No line number:  Remove all breakpoints.
            */
            for (i = 0; i < break_count; ++i) break_list[i] = 0;
            break_count = 0;
            break;
        }

        case NUMBER: {
            /*
            -- Remove a breakpoint from the break list.
            -- Move the following breakpoints up one in the
            -- list to fill in the gap.
            */
            if (literal.type == INTEGER_LIT) {
                number = literal.value.integer;
                if (number > 0) {
                    for (i = 0; i < break_count; ++i) {
                        if (break_list[i] == number) {
                            break_list[i] = 0;
                            --break_count;

                            for (j = i; j < break_count; ++j)
                                break_list[j] = break_list[j+1];

                            break;
                        }
                    }
                }
                else error(VALUE_OUT_OF_RANGE);
            }

            get_token();
            break;
        }
    }
}

/*------------------------------------------------------------*/
/* allocate_watch       Return a pointer to a watch structure, */
/*                      or print all variables being watched.  */
/*------------------------------------------------------------*/

    WATCH_STRUCT_PTR
allocate_watch()

{
    int               i;
    SYMTAB_NODE_PTR   idp;
    WATCH_STRUCT_PTR  wp;

    get_token();

    switch (token) {

        case SEMICOLON: {
            /*
            -- No variable:  Print all variables being watched.
            */
            printf("Variables being watched:\n");

            for (i = 0; i < watch_count; ++i) {
                idp = watch_list[i];
                if (idp != NULL) {
                    wp = (WATCH_STRUCT_PTR) idp->info;
                    printf ("%16s  ", idp->name);
                    if (wp->store_flag) printf(" (store)");
                    if (wp->fetch_flag) printf(" (fetch)");
                    printf("\n");
                }
            }

            return(NULL);
        }

        case IDENTIFIER: {
            search_and_find_all_symtab(idp);
            get_token();

            switch (idp->defn.key) {

                case UNDEFINED:
                    return(NULL);

                case CONST_DEFN:
                case VAR_DEFN:
                case FIELD_DEFN:
                case VALPARM_DEFN:
                case VARPARM_DEFN: {
                    /*
                    -- Return a pointer to the variable's watch
                    -- structure if it is already being watched.
                    -- Otherwise, allocate and return a pointer
                    -- to a new watch structure.
                    */
                    if (idp->info != NULL)
                        return((WATCH_STRUCT_PTR) idp->info);
                    else if (watch_count < MAX_WATCHES) {
                        wp = alloc_struct(WATCH_STRUCT);
                        wp->store_flag = FALSE;
                        wp->fetch_flag = FALSE;

                        idp->info = (char *) wp;

                        watch_list[watch_count] = idp;
                        ++watch_count;

                        return(wp);
                    }
                    else {
                        printf("Watch list is full.\n");
                        return(NULL);
                    }
                }

                default: {
                    error(INVALID_IDENTIFIER_USAGE);
                    return(NULL);
                }
            }
        }
    }
}
```

```
/*------------------------------------------------*/
/*  remove_watch        Remove a specific variable from being  */
/*                      watched, or remove all variables from  */
/*                      the watch list.                        */
/*------------------------------------------------*/

remove_watch()

{
    int              i, j;
    SYMTAB_NODE_PTR  idp;
    WATCH_STRUCT_PTR wp;

    get_token();

    switch (token) {

        case SEMICOLON: {
            /*
            -- No variable:  Remove all variables from watch list.
            */
            for (i = 0; i < watch_count; ++i) {
                if ((idp = watch_list[i]) != NULL) {
                    wp = (WATCH_STRUCT_PTR) idp->info;
                    watch_list[i] = NULL;
                    idp->info = NULL;
                    free(wp);
                }
            }
            watch_count = 0;
            break;
        }

        case IDENTIFIER: {
            /*
            -- Remove a variable from the watch list.
            -- Move the following watches up one in the
            -- list to fill in the gap.
            */
            search_and_find_all_symtab(idp);
            get_token();

            if ((idp != NULL) && (idp->info != NULL)) {
                wp = (WATCH_STRUCT_PTR) idp->info;
                for (i = 0; i < watch_count; ++i) {
                    if (watch_list[i] == idp) {
                        watch_list[i] = NULL;
                        idp->info = NULL;
                        free(wp);
                        --watch_count;

                        for (j = i; j < watch_count; ++j)
                            watch_list[j] = watch_list[j+1];

                        break;
                    }
                }
            }
            break;
        }
    }
}
```

```
/********************************/
/*                              */
/*        Show and assign       */
/*                              */
```

```
/********************************/

/*------------------------------------------------*/
/*  show_value          Print the value of an expression.     */
/*------------------------------------------------*/

show_value()

{
    get_token();

    switch (token) {

        case SEMICOLON: {
            error(INVALID_EXPRESSION);
            break;
        }

        default: {
            /*
            -- First parse, then execute the expression
            -- from the code buffer.
            */
            TYPE_STRUCT_PTR expression();
            TYPE_STRUCT_PTR tp        = expression();    /* parse */
            char *save_code_segmentp = code_segmentp;
            int  save_ctoken         = ctoken;

            if (error_count > 0) break;

            /*
            -- Switch to the code buffer.
            */
            code_segmentp = code_buffer + 1;
            get_ctoken();
            exec_expression();                           /* execute */

            /*
            -- Print, then pop off the value.
            */
            if ((tp->form == ARRAY_FORM) ||
                (tp->form == RECORD_FORM))
                print_data_value(tos->address, tp, " ");
            else
                print_data_value(tos, tp, " ");

            pop();

            /*
            -- Resume the code segment.
            */
            code_segmentp = save_code_segmentp;
            ctoken = save_ctoken;
            break;
        }
    }
}

/*------------------------------------------------*/
/*  assign_variable     Execute an assignment statement.      */
/*------------------------------------------------*/

assign_variable()

{
    get_token();

    switch (token) {
```

```
case SEMICOLON: {                                  /*
    error(MISSING_VARIABLE);                       -- Switch to the code buffer.
    break;                                         */
}                                                  code_segmentp = code_buffer + 1;
                                                   get_ctoken();
case IDENTIFIER: {                                 idp = get_symtab_cptr();
    /*                                             exec_assignment_statement(idp);    /* execute */
    -- First parse, then execute the assignment statement
    -- from the code buffer.                       /*
    */                                             -- Resume the code segment.
    SYMTAB_NODE_PTR idp;                           */
    char *save_code_segmentp = code_segmentp;      code_segmentp = save_code_segmentp;
    int  save_ctoken         = ctoken;             ctoken = save_ctoken;
                                                   break;
    search_and_find_all_symtab(idp);           }

    assignment_statement(idp);        /* parse */
    if (error_count > 0) break;                }
                                               }
```

FIGURE A-17   error.h

```
/*****************************************************************/
/*                                                             */
/*       E R R O R   R O U T I N E S   (Header)               */
/*                                                             */
/*       FILE:       error.h                                   */
/*                                                             */
/*       MODULE:     error                                     */
/*                                                             */
/*****************************************************************/

#ifndef error_h
#define error_h

#define MAX_SYNTAX_ERRORS 25

/*-------------------------------------------------------------*/
/* Error codes                                                 */
/*-------------------------------------------------------------*/

typedef enum {
    NO_ERROR,
    SYNTAX_ERROR,
    TOO_MANY_SYNTAX_ERRORS,
    FAILED_SOURCE_FILE_OPEN,
    UNEXPECTED_END_OF_FILE,
    INVALID_NUMBER,
    INVALID_FRACTION,
    INVALID_EXPONENT,
    TOO_MANY_DIGITS,
    REAL_OUT_OF_RANGE,
    INTEGER_OUT_OF_RANGE,
    MISSING_RPAREN,
    INVALID_EXPRESSION,
    INVALID_ASSIGNMENT,
    MISSING_IDENTIFIER,
    MISSING_COLONEQUAL,
    UNDEFINED_IDENTIFIER,
    STACK_OVERFLOW,
    INVALID_STATEMENT,
    UNEXPECTED_TOKEN,
    MISSING_SEMICOLON,
    MISSING_DO,
    MISSING_UNTIL,
    MISSING_THEN,
    INVALID_FOR_CONTROL,
    MISSING_OF,
    INVALID_CONSTANT,
    MISSING_CONSTANT,
    MISSING_COLON,
    MISSING_END,
    MISSING_TO_OR_DOWNTO,
    REDEFINED_IDENTIFIER,
    MISSING_EQUAL,
    INVALID_TYPE,
    NOT_A_TYPE_IDENTIFIER,
    INVALID_SUBRANGE_TYPE,
    NOT_A_CONSTANT_IDENTIFIER,
    MISSING_DOTDOT,
    INCOMPATIBLE_TYPES,
    INVALID_TARGET,
    INVALID_IDENTIFIER_USAGE,
    INCOMPATIBLE_ASSIGNMENT,
    MIN_GT_MAX,
    MISSING_LBRACKET,
    MISSING_RBRACKET,
    INVALID_INDEX_TYPE,
    MISSING_BEGIN,
    MISSING_PERIOD,
    TOO_MANY_SUBSCRIPTS,
    INVALID_FIELD,
    NESTING_TOO_DEEP,
    MISSING_PROGRAM,
    ALREADY_FORWARDED,
    WRONG_NUMBER_OF_PARMS,
    INVALID_VAR_PARM,
    NOT_A_RECORD_VARIABLE,
    MISSING_VARIABLE,
    CODE_SEGMENT_OVERFLOW,
    UNIMPLEMENTED_FEATURE,
} ERROR_CODE;

typedef enum {
```

```
RUNTIME_STACK_OVERFLOW,                              UNIMPLEMENTED_RUNTIME_FEATURE,
VALUE_OUT_OF_RANGE,                               } RUNTIME_ERROR_CODE;
INVALID_CASE_VALUE,
DIVISION_BY_ZERO,
INVALID_FUNCTION_ARGUMENT,                           #endif
```

FIGURE A-18   error.c

```
/***************************************************************/
/*                                                           */
/*      E R R O R   R O U T I N E S                          */
/*                                                           */
/*      Error messages and routines to print them.           */
/*                                                           */
/*      FILE:      error.c                                   */
/*                                                           */
/*      MODULE:    error                                     */
/*                                                           */
/***************************************************************/

#include <stdio.h>
#include "common.h"
#include "error.h"


/*----------------------------------------------------------*/
/* Externals                                                */
/*----------------------------------------------------------*/

extern char     *tokenp;
extern BOOLEAN  print_flag;
extern char     source_buffer[];
extern char     *bufferp;

/*----------------------------------------------------------*/
/* Error messages      Keyed to enumeration type ERROR_CODE */
/*                     in file error.h.                     */
/*----------------------------------------------------------*/

char *error_messages[] = {
    "No error",
    "Syntax error",
    "Too many syntax errors",
    "Failed to open source file",
    "Unexpected end of file",
    "Invalid number",
    "Invalid fraction",
    "Invalid exponent",
    "Too many digits",
    "Real literal out of range",
    "Integer literal out of range",
    "Missing right parenthesis",
    "Invalid expression",
    "Invalid assignment statement",
    "Missing identifier",
    "Missing := ",
    "Undefined identifier",
    "Stack overflow",
    "Invalid statement",
    "Unexpected token",
    "Missing ; ",
    "Missing DO",
    "Missing UNTIL",
```

```
    "Missing THEN",
    "Invalid FOR control variable",
    "Missing OF",
    "Invalid constant",
    "Missing constant",
    "Missing : ",
    "Missing END",
    "Missing TO or DOWNTO",
    "Redefined identifier",
    "Missing = ",
    "Invalid type",
    "Not a type identifier",
    "Invalid subrangetype",
    "Not a constant identifier",
    "Missing .. ",
    "Incompatible types",
    "Invalid assignment target",
    "Invalid identifier usage",
    "Incompatible assignment",
    "Min limit greater than max limit",
    "Missing [ ",
    "Missing ] ",
    "Invalid index type",
    "Missing BEGIN",
    "Missing period",
    "Too many subscripts",
    "Invalid field",
    "Nesting too deep",
    "Missing PROGRAM",
    "Already specified in FORWARD",
    "Wrong number of actual parameters",
    "Invalid VAR parameter",
    "Not a record variable",
    "Missing variable",
    "Code segment overflow",
    "Unimplemented feature",
};

char *runtime_error_messages[] = {
    "Runtime stack overflow",
    "Value out of range",
    "Invalid CASE expression value",
    "Division by zero",
    "Invalid standard function argument",
    "Unimplemented runtime feature",
};

/*----------------------------------------------------------*/
/* Globals                                                  */
/*----------------------------------------------------------*/

int error_count = 0;     /* number of syntax errors */

                         /******************************/
```

```
/*                              */
/*      Error routines          */
/*                              */
/*******************************/
```

```
/*----------------------------------------------------------*/
/* error              Print an arrow under the error and then */
/*                    print the error message.               */
/*----------------------------------------------------------*/
```

```
error(code)

    ERROR_CODE code;     /* error code */

{

    extern int buffer_offset;
    char message_buffer[MAX_PRINT_LINE_LENGTH];
    char *message = error_messages[code];
    int  offset  = buffer_offset - 2;

    /*
    -- Print the arrow pointing to the token just scanned.
    */
    if (print_flag) offset += 8;
    sprintf(message_buffer, "%*s^\n", offset, " ");
    if (print_flag) print_line(message_buffer);
    else            printf(message_buffer);

    /*
    -- Print the error message.
    */
    sprintf(message_buffer, " *** ERROR: %s.\n", message);
    if (print_flag) print_line(message_buffer);
    else            printf(message_buffer);
```

```
    *tokenp = '\0';
    ++error_count;

    if (error_count > MAX_SYNTAX_ERRORS) {
        sprintf(message_buffer,
            "Too many syntax errors.  Aborted.\n");
        if (print_flag) print_line(message_buffer);
        else            printf(message_buffer);

        exit(-TOO_MANY_SYNTAX_ERRORS);
    }
}
```

```
/*----------------------------------------------------------*/
/* runtime_error      Print a runtime error message and then */
/*                    abort the program execution.           */
/*----------------------------------------------------------*/
```

```
runtime_error(code)

    ERROR_CODE code;     /* error code */

{
    char          *message = runtime_error_messages[code];
    extern int    exec_line_number;
    extern BOOLEAN debugger_command_flag;

    if (debugger_command_flag) printf("%s\n", message);
    else {
        printf("\n*** RUNTIME ERROR in line %d: %s\n",
                exec_line_number, message);
        read_debugger_command();
    }
}
```

FIGURE A-19   common.h

```
/****************************************************************/
/*                                                              */
/*      C O M M O N   R O U T I N E S   (Header)                */
/*                                                              */
/*      FILE:     common.h                                      */
/*                                                              */
/*      MODULE:   common                                        */
/*                                                              */
/****************************************************************/

#ifndef common_h
#define common_h

#define FORM_FEED_CHAR          '\f'

#define MAX_FILE_NAME_LENGTH    32
#define MAX_SOURCE_LINE_LENGTH  256
#define MAX_PRINT_LINE_LENGTH   80
```

```
#define MAX_LINES_PER_PAGE      50
#define DATE_STRING_LENGTH      26
#define MAX_TOKEN_STRING_LENGTH MAX_SOURCE_LINE_LENGTH
#define MAX_CODE_BUFFER_SIZE    4096
#define MAX_NESTING_LEVEL       16
#define MAX_STACK_SIZE          1024
#define STACK_FRAME_HEADER_SIZE 4

typedef enum {
    FALSE, TRUE,
} BOOLEAN;

typedef char *ADDRESS;
```

```
        /****************************************/
        /*                                      */
        /*      Macros for memory allocation    */
        /*                                      */
        /****************************************/
```

```
#define alloc_struct(type)          (type *) malloc(sizeof(type))       #define alloc_bytes(length)       (char *) malloc(length)
#define alloc_array(type, count)    (type *) malloc(count*sizeof(type))
                                                                        #endif
```

FIGURE A-20   run3.c

```
/******************************************************************/      /*--------------------------------------------------------*/
/*                                                              */        /* main               Initialize the scanner and call    */
/*      Program 11-1:  Interactive Pascal Debugger              */        /*                    routine program.                   */
/*                                                              */        /*--------------------------------------------------------*/
/*      Interpret a Pascal program under the control of an      */
/*      interactive debugger.                                   */        main(argc, argv)
/*                                                              */
/*      FILE:      run3.c                                       */            int  argc;
/*                                                              */            char *argv[];
/*      REQUIRES:  Modules parser, symbol table, scanner,       */
/*                      executor, error                         */        {
/*                                                              */            /*
/*      FLAGS:     Macro flag "trace" must be defined           */            -- Initialize the scanner.
/*                                                              */            */
/*      USAGE:     run3 sourcefile                              */            init_scanner(argv[1]);
/*                                                              */
/*          sourcefile      name of source file containing      */            /*
/*                          the Pascal program to interpret     */            -- Process a program.
/*                                                              */            */
/******************************************************************/        get_token();
                                                                           program();
#include <stdio.h>                                                       }
```

APPENDIX B

This appendix contains listings of all the source files of the Pascal compiler and the runtime library, as written in Chapter 14.

Parser Module

Scanner Module

Symbol Table Module

Code Module

Error Module

Miscellaneous

FIGURE B-1   parser.h

```
/***************************************************************/          /*******************************/
/*                                                           */
/*       P A R S I N G   R O U T I N E S   (Header)          */          /*-----------------------------------------------------------*/
/*                                                           */          /*  if_token_get            If token equals token_code, get */
/*    FILE:     parser.h                                     */          /*                          the next token.                 */
/*                                                           */          /*-----------------------------------------------------------*/
/*    MODULE:   parser                                       */
/*                                                           */          #define if_token_get(token_code)                      \
/***************************************************************/              if (token == token_code) get_token()

#ifndef parser_h                                                           /*-----------------------------------------------------------*/
#define parser_h                                                           /*  if_token_get_else_error    If token equals token_code, get */
                                                                           /*                             the next token, else error.    */
#include "common.h"                                                        /*-----------------------------------------------------------*/
#include "symtab.h"
                                                                           #define if_token_get_else_error(token_code, error_code) \
/*-----------------------------------------------------------*/               if (token == token_code) get_token();          \
/*  Uses of a variable                                       */               else                     error(error_code)
/*-----------------------------------------------------------*/
                                                                           /*-----------------------------------------------------------*/
typedef enum {                                                             /*  Analysis routine calls    Unless the following statements */
    EXPR_USE, TARGET_USE, VARPARM_USE,                                     /*                            are preceded by                 */
} USE;                                                                     /*                                                            */
                                                                           /*                                    #define analyze           */
/*-----------------------------------------------------------*/            /*                                                            */
/*  Functions                                                */            /*                            calls to the analysis routines  */
/*-----------------------------------------------------------*/            /*                            are not compiled.               */
                                                                           /*-----------------------------------------------------------*/
TYPE_STRUCT_PTR  expression();
TYPE_STRUCT_PTR  variable();                                               #ifndef analyze
TYPE_STRUCT_PTR  routine_call();                                           #define analyze_const_defn(idp)
TYPE_STRUCT_PTR  base_type();                                              #define analyze_var_decl(idp)
BOOLEAN          is_assign_type_compatible();                              #define analyze_type_defn(idp)
                                                                           #define analyze_routine_header(idp)
              /*******************************/                            #define analyze_block(idp)
              /*                            */                             #endif
              /*      Macros for parsing    */
              /*                            */                             #endif
```

FIGURE B-2   routine.c

```
/***************************************************************/          #include "parser.h"
/*                                                           */            #include "code.h"
/*       R O U T I N E   P A R S E R                         */
/*                                                           */            /*-----------------------------------------------------------*/
/*    Parsing routines for programs and declared             */            /*  Externals                                                */
/*    procedures and functions.                              */            /*-----------------------------------------------------------*/
/*                                                           */
/*    FILE:     routine.c                                    */            extern int            line_number;
/*                                                           */            extern int            error_count;
/*    MODULE:   parser                                       */            extern long           exec_stmt_count;
/*                                                           */
/***************************************************************/          extern TOKEN_CODE     token;
                                                                           extern char           word_string[];
#include <stdio.h>                                                         extern SYMTAB_NODE_PTR symtab_display[];
#include "common.h"                                                        extern int            level;
#include "error.h"
#include "scanner.h"                                                       extern TYPE_STRUCT_PTR integer_typep, real_typep;
#include "symtab.h"                                                        extern TYPE_STRUCT    dummy_type;
```

```
extern int            label_index;
extern char           asm_buffer[];
extern char           *asm_bufferp;
extern FILE           *code_file;

extern TOKEN_CODE     statement_start_list[],
                      statement_end_list[],
                      declaration_start_list[];

/*------------------------------------------------*/
/* Globals                                        */
/*------------------------------------------------*/

char buffer[MAX_PRINT_LINE_LENGTH];

/*------------------------------------------------*/
/* Forwards                                       */
/*------------------------------------------------*/

SYMTAB_NODE_PTR formal_parm_list();
SYMTAB_NODE_PTR program_header(), procedure_header(),
                function_header();

/*------------------------------------------------*/
/* program       Process a program:               */
/*                                                */
/*                    <program-header> ; <block> . */
/*------------------------------------------------*/

TOKEN_CODE follow_header_list[] = {SEMICOLON, END_OF_FILE, 0};

program()

{
    SYMTAB_NODE_PTR program_idp;        /* program id */

    /*
    -- Intialize the symbol table and then emit
    -- the program prologue code.
    */
    init_symtab();
    emit_program_prologue();

    /*
    -- Begin parsing with the program header.
    */
    program_idp = program_header();

    /*
    -- Error synchronization:  Should be ;
    */
    synchronize(follow_header_list,
                declaration_start_list, statement_start_list);
    if_token_get(SEMICOLON);
    else if (token_in(declaration_start_list) ||
             token_in(statement_start_list))
        error(MISSING_SEMICOLON);

    analyze_routine_header(program_idp);

    /*
    -- Parse the program's block.
    */
    program_idp->defn.info.routine.locals = NULL;
    block(program_idp);
    program_idp->defn.info.routine.local_symtab = exit_scope();

    if_token_get_else_error(PERIOD, MISSING_PERIOD);
```

```
    /*
    -- Emit the main routine's epilogue code
    -- followed by the program's epilogue code.
    */
    emit_main_epilogue();
    emit_program_epilogue(program_idp);

    /*
    -- Look for the end of file.
    */
    while (token != END_OF_FILE) {
        error(UNEXPECTED_TOKEN);
        get_token();
    }

    quit_scanner();

    /*
    -- Print the parser's summary.
    */
    print_line("\n");
    print_line("\n");
    sprintf(buffer, "%20d Source lines.\n", line_number);
    print_line(buffer);
    sprintf(buffer, "%20d Source errors.\n", error_count);
    print_line(buffer);

    if (error_count == 0) exit(0);
    else                  exit(-SYNTAX_ERROR);
}

/*------------------------------------------------------------*/
/* program_header      Process a program header:              */
/*                                                            */
/*                     PROGRAM <id> ( <id-list> )             */
/*                                                            */
/*                     Return a pointer to the program id     */
/*                     node.                                  */
/*------------------------------------------------------------*/

TOKEN_CODE follow_prog_id_list[] = {LPAREN, SEMICOLON,
                                    END_OF_FILE, 0};

TOKEN_CODE follow_parms_list[]   = {RPAREN, SEMICOLON,
                                    END_OF_FILE, 0};

    SYMTAB_NODE_PTR
program_header()

{
    SYMTAB_NODE_PTR program_idp;        /* program id */
    SYMTAB_NODE_PTR parm_idp;           /* parm id */
    SYMTAB_NODE_PTR prev_parm_idp = NULL;

    if_token_get_else_error(PROGRAM, MISSING_PROGRAM);

    if (token == IDENTIFIER) {
        search_and_enter_local_symtab(program_idp);
        program_idp->defn.key = PROG_DEFN;
        program_idp->defn.info.routine.key = DECLARED;
        program_idp->defn.info.routine.parm_count = 0;
        program_idp->defn.info.routine.total_parm_size = 0;
        program_idp->defn.info.routine.total_local_size = 0;
        program_idp->typep = &dummy_type;
        program_idp->label_index = new_label_index();
        get_token();
    }
```

```
        else error(MISSING_IDENTIFIER);

        /*
        -- Error synchronization:  Should be ( or ;
        */
        synchronize(follow_prog_id_list,
                    declaration_start_list, statement_start_list);

        enter_scope(NULL);

        /*
        -- Program parameters.
        */
        if (token == LPAREN) {
            /*
            -- <id-list>
            */
            do {
                get_token();
                if (token == IDENTIFIER) {
                    search_and_enter_local_symtab(parm_idp);
                    parm_idp->defn.key = VARPARM_DEFN;
                    parm_idp->typep = &dummy_type;
                    get_token();

                    /*
                    -- Link program parm ids together.
                    */
                    if (prev_parm_idp == NULL)
                        program_idp->defn.info.routine.parms =
                                        prev_parm_idp = parm_idp;
                    else {
                        prev_parm_idp->next = parm_idp;
                        prev_parm_idp = parm_idp;
                    }
                }
                else error(MISSING_IDENTIFIER);
            } while (token == COMMA);

            /*
            -- Error synchronization:  Should be )
            */
            synchronize(follow_parms_list,
                        declaration_start_list, statement_start_list);
            if_token_get_else_error(RPAREN, MISSING_RPAREN);
        }
        else program_idp->defn.info.routine.parms = NULL;

        return(program_idp);
}

/*------------------------------------------------------------*/
/* routine          Call the appropriate routine to process   */
/*                  a procedure or function definition:       */
/*                                                            */
/*                      <routine-header> ; <block>            */
/*------------------------------------------------------------*/

routine()

{
    SYMTAB_NODE_PTR rtn_idp;    /* routine id */

    rtn_idp = (token == PROCEDURE) ? procedure_header()
                                   : function_header();

    /*
```

```
        -- Error synchronization:  Should be ;
        */
        synchronize(follow_header_list,
                    declaration_start_list, statement_start_list);
        if_token_get(SEMICOLON);
        else if (token_in(declaration_start_list) ||
                 token_in(statement_start_list))
            error(MISSING_SEMICOLON);

        /*
        -- <block> or FORWARD.
        */
        if (strcmp(word_string, "forward") != 0) {
            rtn_idp->defn.info.routine.key = DECLARED;
            analyze_routine_header(rtn_idp);

            rtn_idp->defn.info.routine.locals = NULL;
            block(rtn_idp);
        }
        else {
            get_token();
            rtn_idp->defn.info.routine.key = FORWARD;
            analyze_routine_header(rtn_idp);
        }

        /*
        -- Exit the current scope and emit the
        -- routine's epilogue code.
        */
        rtn_idp->defn.info.routine.local_symtab = exit_scope();
        emit_routine_epilogue(rtn_idp);
}

/*------------------------------------------------------------*/
/* procedure_header     Process a procedure header:           */
/*                                                            */
/*                          PROCEDURE <id>                    */
/*                                                            */
/*                      or:                                   */
/*                                                            */
/*                          PROCEDURE <id> ( <parm-list> )    */
/*                                                            */
/*                      Return a pointer to the procedure id  */
/*                      node.                                  */
/*------------------------------------------------------------*/

TOKEN_CODE follow_proc_id_list[] = {LPAREN, SEMICOLON,
                                    END_OF_FILE, 0};

    SYMTAB_NODE_PTR
procedure_header()

{
    SYMTAB_NODE_PTR proc_idp;       /* procedure id */
    SYMTAB_NODE_PTR parm_listp;     /* formal parm list */
    int             parm_count;
    int             total_parm_size;
    BOOLEAN         forward_flag = FALSE;   /* TRUE iff forwarded */

    get_token();

    /*
    -- If the procedure identifier has already been
    -- declared in this scope, it must be a forward.
    */
    if (token == IDENTIFIER) {
        search_local_symtab(proc_idp);
```

```
        if (proc_idp == NULL) {
            enter_local_symtab(proc_idp);
            proc_idp->defn.key = PROC_DEFN;
            proc_idp->defn.info.routine.total_local_size = 0;
            proc_idp->typep = &dummy_type;
            proc_idp->label_index = new_label_index();
        }
        else if ((proc_idp->defn.key == PROC_DEFN) &&
                 (proc_idp->defn.info.routine.key == FORWARD))
            forward_flag = TRUE;
        else error(REDEFINED_IDENTIFIER);

        get_token();
    }
    else error(MISSING_IDENTIFIER);

    /*
    -- Error synchronization:  Should be ( or ;
    */
    synchronize(follow_proc_id_list,
                declaration_start_list, statement_start_list);

    enter_scope(NULL);

    /*
    -- Optional formal parameters.  If there was a forward,
    -- there must not be any parameters here (but parse them
    -- anyway for error recovery).
    */
    if (token == LPAREN) {
        parm_listp = formal_parm_list(&parm_count, &total_parm_size);

        if (forward_flag) error(ALREADY_FORWARDED);
        else {
            proc_idp->defn.info.routine.parm_count = parm_count;
            proc_idp->defn.info.routine.total_parm_size =
                                            total_parm_size;
            proc_idp->defn.info.routine.parms = parm_listp;
        }
    }
    else if (!forward_flag) {
        proc_idp->defn.info.routine.parm_count = 0;
        proc_idp->defn.info.routine.total_parm_size = 0;
        proc_idp->defn.info.routine.parms = NULL;
    }

    proc_idp->typep = NULL;
    return(proc_idp);
}

/*------------------------------------------------------------*/
/*  function_header      Process a function header:           */
/*                                                            */
/*                          FUNCTION <id> : <type-id>         */
/*                                                            */
/*                      or:                                   */
/*                                                            */
/*                          FUNCTION <id> ( <parm-list> )     */
/*                                        : <type-id>         */
/*                                                            */
/*                      Return a pointer to the function id   */
/*                      node.                                 */
/*------------------------------------------------------------*/

TOKEN_CODE follow_func_id_list[] = {LPAREN, COLON, SEMICOLON,
                                    END_OF_FILE, 0};
```

```
    SYMTAB_NODE_PTR
function_header()

{
    SYMTAB_NODE_PTR func_idp, type_idp;    /* func and type ids */
    SYMTAB_NODE_PTR parm_listp;            /* formal parm list */
    int             parm_count;
    int             total_parm_size;
    BOOLEAN         forward_flag = FALSE;  /* TRUE iff forwarded */

    get_token();

    /*
    -- If the function identifier has already been
    -- declared in this scope, it must be a forward.
    */
    if (token == IDENTIFIER) {
        search_local_symtab(func_idp);
        if (func_idp == NULL) {
            enter_local_symtab(func_idp);
            func_idp->defn.key = FUNC_DEFN;
            func_idp->defn.info.routine.total_local_size = 0;
            func_idp->typep = &dummy_type;
            func_idp->label_index = new_label_index();
        }
        else if ((func_idp->defn.key == FUNC_DEFN) &&
                 (func_idp->defn.info.routine.key == FORWARD))
            forward_flag = TRUE;
        else error(REDEFINED_IDENTIFIER);

        get_token();
    }
    else error(MISSING_IDENTIFIER);

    /*
    -- Error synchronization:  Should be ( or : or ;
    */
    synchronize(follow_func_id_list,
                declaration_start_list, statement_start_list);

    enter_scope(NULL);

    /*
    -- Optional formal parameters.  If there was a forward,
    -- there must not be any parameters here (but parse them
    -- anyway for error recovery).
    */
    if (token == LPAREN) {
        parm_listp = formal_parm_list(&parm_count, &total_parm_size);

        if (forward_flag) error(ALREADY_FORWARDED);
        else {
            func_idp->defn.info.routine.parm_count = parm_count;
            func_idp->defn.info.routine.total_parm_size =
                                            total_parm_size;
            func_idp->defn.info.routine.parms = parm_listp;
        }
    }
    else if (!forward_flag) {
        func_idp->defn.info.routine.parm_count = 0;
        func_idp->defn.info.routine.total_parm_size = 0;
        func_idp->defn.info.routine.parms = NULL;
    }

    /*
    -- Function type.  If there was a forward,
    -- there must not be a type here (but parse it
```

```
         --  anyway for error recovery).
         */
         if (!forward_flag || (token == COLON)) {
             if_token_get_else_error(COLON, MISSING_COLON);

             if (token == IDENTIFIER) {
                 search_and_find_all_symtab(type_idp);
                 if (type_idp->defn.key != TYPE_DEFN) error(INVALID_TYPE);
                 if (!forward_flag) func_idp->typep = type_idp->typep;
                 get_token();
             }
             else {
                 error(MISSING_IDENTIFIER);
                 func_idp->typep = &dummy_type;
             }

             if (forward_flag) error(ALREADY_FORWARDED);
         }

         return(func_idp);
}

/*------------------------------------------------------*/
/*  formal_parm_list      Process a formal parameter list:  */
/*                                                          */
/*                         ( VAR <id-list> : <type> ;       */
/*                           <id-list> : <type> ;           */
/*                           ... )                          */
/*                                                          */
/*                         Return a pointer to the head of the  */
/*                         parameter id list.               */
/*------------------------------------------------------*/

     SYMTAB_NODE_PTR
formal_parm_list(countp, total_sizep)

     int *countp;          /* ptr to count of parameters */
     int *total_sizep;     /* ptr to total byte size of parameters */

{
     SYMTAB_NODE_PTR  parm_idp, first_idp, last_idp;    /* parm ids */
     SYMTAB_NODE_PTR  prev_last_idp = NULL;            /* last id of list */
     SYMTAB_NODE_PTR  parm_listp = NULL;               /* parm list */
     SYMTAB_NODE_PTR  type_idp;                        /* type id */
     TYPE_STRUCT_PTR  parm_tp;                         /* parm type */
     DEFN_KEY         parm_defn;                       /* parm definition */
     int              parm_count = 0;                  /* count of parms */
     int              parm_offset = PARAMETERS_STACK_FRAME_OFFSET;

     get_token();

     /*
     --  Loop to process parameter declarations separated by ;
     */
     while ((token == IDENTIFIER) || (token == VAR)) {
         first_idp = NULL;

         /*
         --  VAR parms?
         */
         if (token == VAR) {
             parm_defn = VARPARM_DEFN;
             get_token();
         }
         else parm_defn = VALPARM_DEFN;

         /*
```

```
         --  <id list>
         */
         while (token == IDENTIFIER) {
             search_and_enter_local_symtab(parm_idp);
             parm_idp->defn.key    = parm_defn;
             parm_idp->label_index = new_label_index();
             ++parm_count;

             if (parm_listp == NULL) parm_listp = parm_idp;

             /*
             --  Link parm ids together.
             */
             if (first_idp == NULL)
                 first_idp = last_idp = parm_idp;
             else {
                 last_idp->next = parm_idp;
                 last_idp = parm_idp;
             }

             get_token();
             if_token_get(COMMA);
         }

         if_token_get_else_error(COLON, MISSING_COLON);

         if (token == IDENTIFIER) {
             search_and_find_all_symtab(type_idp);
             if (type_idp->defn.key != TYPE_DEFN) error(INVALID_TYPE);
             parm_tp = type_idp->typep;
             get_token();
         }
         else {
             error(MISSING_IDENTIFIER);
             parm_tp = &dummy_type;
         }

         /*
         --  Assign the type to all parm ids in the sublist.
         */
         for (parm_idp = first_idp;
              parm_idp != NULL;
              parm_idp = parm_idp->next) parm_idp->typep = parm_tp;

         /*
         --  Link this list to the list of all parm ids.
         */
         if (prev_last_idp != NULL) prev_last_idp->next = first_idp;
         prev_last_idp = last_idp;

         /*
         --  Error synchronization:  Should be ; or )
         */
         synchronize(follow_parms_list, NULL, NULL);
         if_token_get(SEMICOLON);
     }

     /*
     --  Assign the offset to all parm ids in reverse order.
     */
     reverse_list(&parm_listp);
     for (parm_idp = parm_listp;
          parm_idp != NULL;
          parm_idp = parm_idp->next) {
         parm_idp->defn.info.data.offset = parm_offset;
         parm_offset += parm_idp->defn.key == VALPARM_DEFN
                        ? parm_idp->typep->size
```

```
                              : sizeof(char *);
        if (parm_offset & 1) ++parm_offset;    /* round up to even */
    }
    reverse_list(&parm_listp);

    if_token_get_else_error(RPAREN, MISSING_RPAREN);
    *countp = parm_count;
    *total_sizep = parm_offset - PARAMETERS_STACK_FRAME_OFFSET;

    return(parm_listp);
}

/*------------------------------------------------------*/
/* reverse_list        Reverse a list of symbol table nodes.  */
/*------------------------------------------------------*/

reverse_list(listpp)

    SYMTAB_NODE_PTR *listpp;     /* ptr to ptr to node list head */

{
    SYMTAB_NODE_PTR prevp = NULL;
    SYMTAB_NODE_PTR thisp = *listpp;
    SYMTAB_NODE_PTR nextp;

    /*
    -- Reverse the list in place.
    */
    while (thisp != NULL) {
        nextp = thisp->next;
        thisp->next = prevp;
        prevp = thisp;
        thisp = nextp;
    }

    /*
    -- Point to the new head (former tail) of the list.
    */
    *listpp = prevp;
}

/*------------------------------------------------------*/
/* routine_call        Process a call to a declared or    */
/*                     a standard procedure or function.  */
/*                     Return a pointer to the type       */
/*                     structure of the call.             */
/*------------------------------------------------------*/

    TYPE_STRUCT_PTR
routine_call(rtn_idp, parm_check_flag)

    SYMTAB_NODE_PTR rtn_idp;            /* routine id */
    BOOLEAN        parm_check_flag;     /* if TRUE check parms */

{
    TYPE_STRUCT_PTR declared_routine_call(), standard_routine_call();

    if ((rtn_idp->defn.info.routine.key == DECLARED) ||
        (rtn_idp->defn.info.routine.key == FORWARD) ||
        !parm_check_flag)
        return(declared_routine_call(rtn_idp, parm_check_flag));
    else
        return(standard_routine_call(rtn_idp));
}

/*------------------------------------------------------*/
/* declared_routine_call   Process a call to a declared   */
```

```
/*                     procedure or function:             */
/*                                                        */
/*                         <id>                            */
/*                                                        */
/*                     or:                                */
/*                                                        */
/*                     <id> ( <parm-list> )               */
/*                                                        */
/*                     The actual parameters are checked  */
/*                     against the formal parameters for  */
/*                     type and number.  Return a pointer */
/*                     to the type structure of the call. */
/*------------------------------------------------------*/

    TYPE_STRUCT_PTR
declared_routine_call(rtn_idp, parm_check_flag)

    SYMTAB_NODE_PTR rtn_idp;            /* routine id */
    BOOLEAN        parm_check_flag;     /* if TRUE check parms */

{
    int old_level = level;              /* level of caller */
    int new_level = rtn_idp->level + 1; /* level of callee */

    actual_parm_list(rtn_idp, parm_check_flag);

    /*
    -- Push the static link onto the stack.
    */
    if (new_level == old_level + 1) {
        /*
        -- Calling a routine nested within the caller:
        -- Push pointer to caller's stack frame.
        */
        emit_1(PUSH, reg(BP));
    }
    else if (new_level == old_level) {
        /*
        -- Calling another routine at the same level:
        -- Push pointer to stack frame of common parent.
        */
        emit_1(PUSH, name_lit(STATIC_LINK));
    }
    else  /* new_level < old_level */  {
        /*
        -- Calling a routine at a lesser level (nested less deeply:
        -- Push pointer to stack frame of nearest common ancestor.
        */
        int lev;

        emit_2(MOVE, reg(BX), reg(BP));
        for (lev = old_level; lev >= new_level; --lev)
            emit_2(MOVE, reg(BP), name_lit(STATIC_LINK));
        emit_1(PUSH, reg(BP));
        emit_2(MOVE, reg(BP), reg(BX));
    }

    emit_1(CALL, tagged_name(rtn_idp));

    return(rtn_idp->defn.key == PROC_DEFN ? NULL : rtn_idp->typep);
}

/*------------------------------------------------------*/
/* actual_parm_list    Process an actual parameter list:  */
/*                                                        */
/*                         ( <expr-list> )                */
/*------------------------------------------------------*/
```

```
TOKEN_CODE follow_parm_list[] = {COMMA, RPAREN, 0};

actual_parm_list(rtn_idp, parm_check_flag)

    SYMTAB_NODE_PTR rtn_idp;            /* routine id */
    BOOLEAN         parm_check_flag;    /* if TRUE check parms */

{
    SYMTAB_NODE_PTR formal_parm_idp;
    DEFN_KEY        formal_parm_defn;
    TYPE_STRUCT_PTR formal_parm_tp, actual_parm_tp;

    if (parm_check_flag)
        formal_parm_idp = rtn_idp->defn.info.routine.parms;

    if (token == LPAREN) {
        /*
        -- Loop to process actual parameter expressions.
        */
        do {
            /*
            -- Obtain info about the corresponding formal parm.
            */
            if (parm_check_flag && (formal_parm_idp != NULL)) {
                formal_parm_defn = formal_parm_idp->defn.key;
                formal_parm_tp   = formal_parm_idp->typep;
            }

            get_token();

            /*
            -- Check the actual parm's type against the formal parm.
            -- An actual parm's type must be the same as the type of
            -- a formal VAR parm and assignment compatible with the
            -- type of a formal value parm.
            */
            if ((formal_parm_idp == NULL) ||
                (formal_parm_defn == VALPARM_DEFN) ||
                !parm_check_flag) {
                actual_parm_tp = expression();
                if (parm_check_flag && (formal_parm_idp != NULL) &&
                    (! is_assign_type_compatible(formal_parm_tp,
                                                 actual_parm_tp)))
                    error(INCOMPATIBLE_TYPES);

                /*
                -- Push the argument value onto the stack.
                */
                if (formal_parm_tp == real_typep) {
                    /*
                    -- Real formal parm.
                    */
                    if (actual_parm_tp == integer_typep) {
                        emit_1(PUSH, reg(AX));
                        emit_1(CALL, name_lit(FLOAT_CONVERT));
                        emit_2(ADD,  reg(SP), integer_lit(2));
                    }
                    emit_1(PUSH, reg(DX));
                    emit_1(PUSH, reg(AX));
                }
                else if ((actual_parm_tp->form == ARRAY_FORM) ||
                         (actual_parm_tp->form == RECORD_FORM)) {

                    /*
                    -- Block move onto the stack.
                    */
                    int size = actual_parm_tp->size;
```

```
                    int offset = size%2 == 0 ? size : size + 1;

                    emit(CLEAR_DIRECTION);
                    emit_1(POP,  reg(SI));
                    emit_2(SUBTRACT, reg(SP), integer_lit(offset));
                    emit_2(MOVE, reg(DI), reg(SP));
                    emit_2(MOVE, reg(CX), integer_lit(size));
                    emit_2(MOVE, reg(AX), reg(DS));
                    emit_2(MOVE, reg(ES), reg(AX));
                    emit(MOVE_BLOCK);
                }
                else {
                    emit_1(PUSH, reg(AX));
                }
            }
            else  /* formal_parm_defn == VARPARM_DEFN */  {
                if (token == IDENTIFIER) {
                    SYMTAB_NODE_PTR idp;

                    search_and_find_all_symtab(idp);
                    actual_parm_tp = variable(idp, VARPARM_USE);

                    if (formal_parm_tp != actual_parm_tp)
                        error(INCOMPATIBLE_TYPES);
                }
                else {
                    actual_parm_tp = expression();
                    error(INVALID_VAR_PARM);
                }
            }

            /*
            -- Check if there are more actual parms
            -- than formal parms.
            */
            if (parm_check_flag) {
                if (formal_parm_idp == NULL)
                    error(WRONG_NUMBER_OF_PARMS);
                else formal_parm_idp = formal_parm_idp->next;
            }

            /*
            -- Error synchronization:  Should be , or )
            */
            synchronize(follow_parm_list, statement_end_list, NULL);

        } while (token == COMMA);

        if_token_get_else_error(RPAREN, MISSING_RPAREN);
    }

    /*
    -- Check if there are fewer actual parms than formal parms.
    */
    if (parm_check_flag && (formal_parm_idp != NULL))
        error(WRONG_NUMBER_OF_PARMS);
}

/*------------------------------------------------------------*/
/* block              Process a block, which consists of      */
/*                    declarations followed by a compound      */
/*                    statement.                               */
/*------------------------------------------------------------*/

TOKEN_CODE follow_decls_list[] = {SEMICOLON, BEGIN, END_OF_FILE, 0};

block(rtn_idp)
```

```
SYMTAB_NODE_PTR rtn_idp;     /* id of program or routine */

{
    extern BOOLEAN block_flag;

    declarations(rtn_idp);

    /*
    -- Emit the prologue code for the main routine
    -- or for a procedure or function.
    */
    if (rtn_idp->defn.key == PROG_DEFN)
        emit_main_prologue();
```

```
    else
        emit_routine_prologue(rtn_idp);

    /*
    -- Error synchronization:  Should be ;
    */
    synchronize(follow_decls_list, NULL, NULL);
    if (token != BEGIN) error(MISSING_BEGIN);

    block_flag = TRUE;
    compound_statement();
    block_flag = FALSE;
}
```

FIGURE B-3   standard.c

```
/* Figure 14-12 */

/***************************************************************/
/*                                                             */
/*          S T A N D A R D   R O U T I N E   P A R S E R      */
/*                                                             */
/*          Parsing routines for calls to standard procedures and */
/*          functions.                                         */
/*                                                             */
/*          FILE:      standard.c                              */
/*                                                             */
/*          MODULE:    parser                                  */
/*                                                             */
/***************************************************************/

#include <stdio.h>
#include "common.h"
#include "error.h"
#include "scanner.h"
#include "symtab.h"
#include "parser.h"
#include "code.h"

#define DEFAULT_NUMERIC_FIELD_WIDTH    10
#define DEFAULT_PRECISION               2

/*------------------------------------------------------------*/
/* Externals                                                  */
/*------------------------------------------------------------*/

extern TOKEN_CODE       token;
extern char             word_string[];
extern SYMTAB_NODE_PTR  symtab_display[];
extern int              level;
extern TYPE_STRUCT      dummy_type;

extern TYPE_STRUCT_PTR  integer_typep, real_typep,
                        boolean_typep, char_typep;

extern int              label_index;
extern char             asm_buffer[];
extern char             *asm_bufferp;
extern FILE             *code_file;

extern TOKEN_CODE       follow_parm_list[];
extern TOKEN_CODE       statement_end_list[];
```

```
/*------------------------------------------------------------*/
/* Forwards                                                   */
/*------------------------------------------------------------*/

TYPE_STRUCT_PTR eof_eoln(), abs_sqr(),
                arctan_cos_exp_ln_sin_sqrt(),
                pred_succ(), chr(), odd(), ord(),
                round_trunc();

/*------------------------------------------------------------*/
/* standard_routine_call   Process a call to a standard       */
/*                         procedure or function.  Return a   */
/*                         pointer to the type structure of   */
/*                         the call.                          */
/*------------------------------------------------------------*/

    TYPE_STRUCT_PTR
standard_routine_call(rtn_idp)

    SYMTAB_NODE_PTR rtn_idp;          /* routine id */

{
    switch (rtn_idp->defn.info.routine.key) {

        case READ:
        case READLN:    read_readln(rtn_idp);        return(NULL);

        case WRITE:
        case WRITELN:   write_writeln(rtn_idp);      return(NULL);

        case EOFF:
        case EOLN:      return(eof_eoln(rtn_idp));

        case ABS:
        case SQR:       return(abs_sqr(rtn_idp));

        case ARCTAN:
        case COS:
        case EXP:
        case LN:
        case SIN:
        case SQRT:      return(arctan_cos_exp_ln_sin_sqrt(rtn_idp));

        case PRED:
        case SUCC:      return(pred_succ(rtn_idp));
```

```
        case CHR:        return(chr());
        case ODD:        return(odd());
        case ORD:        return(ord());

        case ROUND:
        case TRUNC:      return(round_trunc(rtn_idp));
    }
}

/*------------------------------------------------------------*/
/* read_readln              Process a call to read or readln.  */
/*------------------------------------------------------------*/

read_readln(rtn_idp)

    SYMTAB_NODE_PTR rtn_idp;            /* routine id */

{
    TYPE_STRUCT_PTR actual_parm_tp;     /* actual parm type */

    /*
    -- Parameters are optional for readln.
    */
    if (token == LPAREN) {
        /*
        -- <id-list>
        */
        do {
            get_token();

            /*
            -- Actual parms must be variables (but parse
            -- an expression anyway for error recovery).
            */
            if (token == IDENTIFIER) {
                SYMTAB_NODE_PTR idp;

                search_and_find_all_symtab(idp);
                actual_parm_tp = base_type(variable(idp,
                                          VARPARM_USE));

                if (actual_parm_tp->form != SCALAR_FORM)
                    error(INCOMPATIBLE_TYPES);
                else if (actual_parm_tp == integer_typep) {
                    emit_1(CALL, name_lit(READ_INTEGER));
                    emit_1(POP,  reg(BX));
                    emit_2(MOVE, word_indirect(BX), reg(AX));
                }
                else if (actual_parm_tp == real_typep) {
                    emit_1(CALL, name_lit(READ_REAL));
                    emit_1(POP,  reg(BX));
                    emit_2(MOVE, word_indirect(BX), reg(AX));
                    emit_2(MOVE, high_dword_indirect(BX), reg(DX));
                }
                else if (actual_parm_tp == char_typep) {
                    emit_1(CALL, name_lit(READ_CHAR));
                    emit_1(POP,  reg(BX));
                    emit_2(MOVE, byte_indirect(BX), reg(AL));
                }
            }
            else {
                actual_parm_tp = expression();
                error(INVALID_VAR_PARM);
            }

            /*
            -- Error synchronization:  Should be , or )
```

```
            */
            synchronize(follow_parm_list, statement_end_list, NULL);

        } while (token == COMMA);

        if_token_get_else_error(RPAREN, MISSING_RPAREN);
    }
    else if (rtn_idp->defn.info.routine.key == READ)
        error(WRONG_NUMBER_OF_PARMS);

    if (rtn_idp->defn.info.routine.key == READLN)
        emit_1(CALL, name_lit(READ_LINE));
}

/*------------------------------------------------------------*/
/* write_writeln           Process a call to write or writeln. */
/*                         Each actual parameter can be:       */
/*                                                             */
/*                             <expr>                          */
/*                                                             */
/*                         or:                                 */
/*                                                             */
/*                             <epxr> : <expr>                 */
/*                                                             */
/*                         or:                                 */
/*                                                             */
/*                             <expr> : <expr> : <expr>        */
/*------------------------------------------------------------*/

write_writeln(rtn_idp)

    SYMTAB_NODE_PTR rtn_idp;            /* routine id */

{
    TYPE_STRUCT_PTR actual_parm_tp;     /* actual parm type */
    TYPE_STRUCT_PTR field_width_tp, precision_tp;

    /*
    -- Parameters are optional for writeln.
    */
    if (token == LPAREN) {
        do {
            /*
            -- Value <expr>
            */
            get_token();
            actual_parm_tp = base_type(expression());

            /*
            -- Push the scalar value to be written onto the stack.
            -- A string value is already on the stack.
            */
            if (actual_parm_tp->form != ARRAY_FORM)
                emit_push_operand(actual_parm_tp);

            if ((actual_parm_tp->form != SCALAR_FORM) &&
                (actual_parm_tp != boolean_typep) &&
                ((actual_parm_tp->form != ARRAY_FORM) ||
                 (actual_parm_tp->info.array.elmt_typep !=
                                           char_typep)))
                error(INVALID_EXPRESSION);

            /*
            -- Optional field width <expr>
            -- Push onto the stack.
            */
            if (token == COLON) {
```

```
    get_token();
    field_width_tp = base_type(expression());
    emit_1(PUSH, reg(AX));

    if (field_width_tp != integer_typep)
        error(INCOMPATIBLE_TYPES);

    /*
    -- Optional precision <expr>
    -- Push onto the stack if the value to be printed
    -- is of type real.
    */
    if (token == COLON) {
        get_token();
        precision_tp = base_type(expression());

        if (actual_parm_tp == real_typep)
            emit_1(PUSH, reg(AX));

        if (precision_tp != integer_typep)
            error(INCOMPATIBLE_TYPES);
    }
    else if (actual_parm_tp == real_typep) {
        emit_2(MOVE, reg(AX),
               integer_lit(DEFAULT_PRECISION));
        emit_1(PUSH, reg(AX));
    }
}
else {
    if (actual_parm_tp == integer_typep) {
        emit_2(MOVE, reg(AX),
               integer_lit(DEFAULT_NUMERIC_FIELD_WIDTH));
        emit_1(PUSH, reg(AX));
    }
    else if (actual_parm_tp == real_typep) {
        emit_2(MOVE, reg(AX),
               integer_lit(DEFAULT_NUMERIC_FIELD_WIDTH));
        emit_1(PUSH, reg(AX));
        emit_2(MOVE, reg(AX),
               integer_lit(DEFAULT_PRECISION));
        emit_1(PUSH, reg(AX));
    }
    else {
        emit_2(MOVE, reg(AX), integer_lit(0));
        emit_1(PUSH, reg(AX));
    }
}

if (actual_parm_tp == integer_typep) {
    emit_1(CALL, name_lit(WRITE_INTEGER));
    emit_2(ADD, reg(SP), integer_lit(4));
}
else if (actual_parm_tp == real_typep) {
    emit_1(CALL, name_lit(WRITE_REAL));
    emit_2(ADD, reg(SP), integer_lit(8));
}
else if (actual_parm_tp == boolean_typep) {
    emit_1(CALL, name_lit(WRITE_BOOLEAN));
    emit_2(ADD, reg(SP), integer_lit(4));
}
else if (actual_parm_tp == char_typep) {
    emit_1(CALL, name_lit(WRITE_CHAR));
    emit_2(ADD, reg(SP), integer_lit(4));
}
else  /* string */ {
    /*
    -- Push the string length onto the stack.
```

```
    */
        emit_2(MOVE, reg(AX),
               integer_lit(actual_parm_tp->info.array
                                          .elmt_count));

        emit_1(PUSH, reg(AX));
        emit_1(CALL, name_lit(WRITE_STRING));
        emit_2(ADD, reg(SP), integer_lit(6));
    }

        /*
        -- Error synchronization:  Should be , or )
        */
        synchronize(follow_parm_list, statement_end_list, NULL);

    } while (token == COMMA);

    if_token_get_else_error(RPAREN, MISSING_RPAREN);
}
else if (rtn_idp->defn.info.routine.key == WRITE)
    error(WRONG_NUMBER_OF_PARMS);

if (rtn_idp->defn.info.routine.key == WRITELN)
    emit_1(CALL, name_lit(WRITE_LINE));
}

/*---------------------------------------------------------------*/
/* eof_eoln              Process a call to eof or to eoln.       */
/*                       No parameters => boolean result.        */
/*---------------------------------------------------------------*/

    TYPE_STRUCT_PTR
eof_eoln(rtn_idp)

    SYMTAB_NODE_PTR rtn_idp;            /* routine id */

{
    if (token == LPAREN) {
        error(WRONG_NUMBER_OF_PARMS);
        actual_parm_list(rtn_idp, FALSE);
    }

    emit_1(CALL, name_lit(rtn_idp->defn.info.routine.key == EOFF
                          ? STD_END_OF_FILE
                          : STD_END_OF_LINE));

    return(boolean_typep);
}

/*---------------------------------------------------------------*/
/* abs_sqr               Process a call to abs or to sqr.       */
/*                       integer parm => integer result         */
/*                       real parm    => real result            */
/*---------------------------------------------------------------*/

    TYPE_STRUCT_PTR
abs_sqr(rtn_idp)

    SYMTAB_NODE_PTR rtn_idp;            /* routine id */

{
    TYPE_STRUCT_PTR parm_tp;            /* actual parameter type */
    TYPE_STRUCT_PTR result_tp;          /* result type */

    if (token == LPAREN) {
        get_token();
        parm_tp = base_type(expression());
```

```
        if ((parm_tp != integer_typep) && (parm_tp != real_typep)) {
            error(INCOMPATIBLE_TYPES);
            result_tp = real_typep;
        }
        else result_tp = parm_tp;

        if_token_get_else_error(RPAREN, MISSING_RPAREN);
    }
    else error(WRONG_NUMBER_OF_PARMS);

    switch (rtn_idp->defn.info.routine.key) {

        case ABS:
            if (parm_tp == integer_typep) {
                int nonnegative_labelx = new_label_index();

                emit_2(COMPARE, reg(AX), integer_lit(0));
                emit_1(JUMP_GE, label(STMT_LABEL_PREFIX,
                                        nonnegative_labelx));
                emit_1(NEGATE, reg(AX));
                emit_label(STMT_LABEL_PREFIX, nonnegative_labelx);
            }
            else {
                emit_push_operand(parm_tp);
                emit_1(CALL, name_lit(STD_ABS));
                emit_2(ADD, reg(SP), integer_lit(4));
            }
            break;

        case SQR:
            if (parm_tp == integer_typep) {
                emit_2(MOVE, reg(DX), reg(AX));
                emit_1(MULTIPLY, reg(DX));
            }
            else {
                emit_push_operand(parm_tp);
                emit_push_operand(parm_tp);
                emit_1(CALL, name_lit(FLOAT_MULTIPLY));
                emit_2(ADD, reg(SP), integer_lit(8));
            }
            break;
    }

    return(result_tp);
}

/*-----------------------------------------------------------*/
/* arctan_cos_exp_ln_sin_sqrt  Process a call to arctan, cos, */
/*                             exp, ln, sin, or sqrt.         */
/*                             integer parm => real result    */
/*                             real_parm   => real result     */
/*-----------------------------------------------------------*/

    TYPE_STRUCT_PTR
arctan_cos_exp_ln_sin_sqrt(rtn_idp)

    SYMTAB_NODE_PTR rtn_idp;            /* routine id */

{
    TYPE_STRUCT_PTR parm_tp;            /* actual parameter type */
    char           *std_func_name;     /* name of standard func */

    if (token == LPAREN) {
        get_token();
        parm_tp = base_type(expression());

        if ((parm_tp != integer_typep) && (parm_tp != real_typep))
            error(INCOMPATIBLE_TYPES);
```

```
            if_token_get_else_error(RPAREN, MISSING_RPAREN);
        }
        else error(WRONG_NUMBER_OF_PARMS);

        if (parm_tp == integer_typep) {
            emit_1(PUSH, reg(AX));
            emit_1(CALL, name_lit(FLOAT_CONVERT));
            emit_2(ADD, reg(SP), integer_lit(2));
        }

        emit_push_operand(real_typep);

        switch (rtn_idp->defn.info.routine.key) {
            case ARCTAN:    std_func_name = STD_ARCTAN;   break;
            case COS:       std_func_name = STD_COS;      break;
            case EXP:       std_func_name = STD_EXP;      break;
            case LN:        std_func_name = STD_LN;       break;
            case SIN:       std_func_name = STD_SIN;      break;
            case SQRT:      std_func_name = STD_SQRT;     break;
        }

        emit_1(CALL, name_lit(std_func_name));
        emit_2(ADD, reg(SP), integer_lit(4));

        return(real_typep);
}

/*-----------------------------------------------------------*/
/* pred_succ           Process a call to pred or succ.        */
/*                     integer parm => integer result         */
/*                     enum parm    => enum result            */
/*-----------------------------------------------------------*/

    TYPE_STRUCT_PTR
pred_succ(rtn_idp)

    SYMTAB_NODE_PTR rtn_idp;            /* routine id */

{
    TYPE_STRUCT_PTR parm_tp;            /* actual parameter type */
    TYPE_STRUCT_PTR result_tp;          /* result type */

    if (token == LPAREN) {
        get_token();
        parm_tp = base_type(expression());

        if ((parm_tp != integer_typep) &&
            (parm_tp->form != ENUM_FORM)) {
            error(INCOMPATIBLE_TYPES);
            result_tp = integer_typep;
        }
        else result_tp = parm_tp;

        if_token_get_else_error(RPAREN, MISSING_RPAREN);
    }
    else error(WRONG_NUMBER_OF_PARMS);

    emit_1(rtn_idp->defn.info.routine.key == PRED
                ? DECREMENT : INCREMENT,
           reg(AX));

    return(result_tp);
}

/*-----------------------------------------------------------*/
/* chr                 Process a call to chr.                 */
```

```
/*                      integer parm => character result    */
/*----------------------------------------------------------*/

    TYPE_STRUCT_PTR
chr()

{
    TYPE_STRUCT_PTR parm_tp;            /* actual parameter type */

    if (token == LPAREN) {
        get_token();
        parm_tp = base_type(expression());

        if (parm_tp != integer_typep) error(INCOMPATIBLE_TYPES);
        if_token_get_else_error(RPAREN, MISSING_RPAREN);
    }
    else error(WRONG_NUMBER_OF_PARMS);

    return(char_typep);

}


/*----------------------------------------------------------*/
/*  odd                        Process a call to odd.       */
/*                             integer parm => boolean result */
/*----------------------------------------------------------*/

    TYPE_STRUCT_PTR
odd()

{
    TYPE_STRUCT_PTR parm_tp;            /* actual parameter type */

    if (token == LPAREN) {
        get_token();
        parm_tp = base_type(expression());

        if (parm_tp != integer_typep) error(INCOMPATIBLE_TYPES);
        if_token_get_else_error(RPAREN, MISSING_RPAREN);
    }
    else error(WRONG_NUMBER_OF_PARMS);

    emit_2(AND_BITS, reg(AX), integer_lit(1));
    return(boolean_typep);

}


/*----------------------------------------------------------*/
/*  ord                        Process a call to ord.       */
/*                             enumeration parm => integer result */
/*----------------------------------------------------------*/
```

```
    TYPE_STRUCT_PTR
ord()

{
    TYPE_STRUCT_PTR parm_tp;            /* actual parameter type */

    if (token == LPAREN) {
        get_token();
        parm_tp = base_type(expression());

        if (parm_tp->form != ENUM_FORM) error(INCOMPATIBLE_TYPES);
        if_token_get_else_error(RPAREN, MISSING_RPAREN);
    }
    else error(WRONG_NUMBER_OF_PARMS);

    return(integer_typep);

}


/*----------------------------------------------------------*/
/*  round_trunc         Process a call to round or trunc.   */
/*                             real parm => integer result  */
/*----------------------------------------------------------*/

    TYPE_STRUCT_PTR
round_trunc(rtn_idp)

    SYMTAB_NODE_PTR rtn_idp;            /* routine id */

{
    TYPE_STRUCT_PTR parm_tp;            /* actual parameter type */

    if (token == LPAREN) {
        get_token();
        parm_tp = base_type(expression());

        if (parm_tp != real_typep) error(INCOMPATIBLE_TYPES);
        if_token_get_else_error(RPAREN, MISSING_RPAREN);
    }
    else error(WRONG_NUMBER_OF_PARMS);

    emit_push_operand(parm_tp);
    emit_1(CALL, name_lit(rtn_idp->defn.info.routine.key == ROUND
                          ? STD_ROUND : STD_TRUNC));
    emit_2(ADD, reg(SP), integer_lit(4));

    return(integer_typep);

}
```

FIGURE B-4   decl.c

```
/***************************************************************/
/*                                                   */
/*      D E C L A R A T I O N   P A R S E R          */
/*                                                   */
/*      Parsing routines for delarations.            */
/*                                                   */
/*      FILE:    decl.c                               */
/*                                                   */
/*      MODULE:  parser                              */
/*                                                   */
/***************************************************************/
```

```
#include <stdio.h>
#include "common.h"
#include "error.h"
#include "scanner.h"
#include "symtab.h"
#include "parser.h"
#include "code.h"

/*----------------------------------------------------------*/
/* Externals                                                */
/*----------------------------------------------------------*/
```

```
extern TOKEN_CODE      token;
extern char            word_string[];
extern LITERAL         literal;

extern SYMTAB_NODE_PTR symtab_display[];
extern int             level;

extern TYPE_STRUCT_PTR integer_typep, real_typep,
                       boolean_typep, char_typep;

extern TYPE_STRUCT     dummy_type;

extern int             label_index;

extern TOKEN_CODE      declaration_start_list[],
                       statement_start_list[];

/*-----------------------------------------------------------*/
/* Forwards                                                  */
/*-----------------------------------------------------------*/

TYPE_STRUCT_PTR do_type(),
                identifier_type(), enumeration_type(),
                subrange_type(), array_type(), record_type();

/*-----------------------------------------------------------*/
/* delarations         Call the routines to process constant */
/*                     definitions, type definitions, variable */
/*                     declarations, procedure definitions,  */
/*                     and function definitions.             */
/*-----------------------------------------------------------*/

TOKEN_CODE follow_routine_list[] = {SEMICOLON, END_OF_FILE, 0};

declarations(rtn_idp)

    SYMTAB_NODE_PTR rtn_idp;    /* id of program or routine */

{
    if (token == CONST) {
        get_token();
        const_definitions();
    }

    if (token == TYPE) {
        get_token();
        type_definitions();
    }

    if (token == VAR) {
        get_token();
        var_declarations(rtn_idp);
    }

    /*
    -- Emit declarations for parameters and local variables.
    */
    if (rtn_idp->defn.key != PROG_DEFN) emit_declarations(rtn_idp);

    /*
    -- Loop to process routine (procedure and function)
    -- definitions.
    */
    while ((token == PROCEDURE) || (token == FUNCTION)) {
        routine();

        /*
```

```
            -- Error synchronization:  Should be ;
            */
            synchronize(follow_routine_list,
                    declaration_start_list, statement_start_list);
            if_token_get(SEMICOLON);
            else if (token_in(declaration_start_list) ||
                    token_in(statement_start_list))
                error(MISSING_SEMICOLON);
    }
}


        /************************/
        /*                      */
        /*       Constants      */
        /*                      */
        /************************/

/*-----------------------------------------------------------*/
/* const_definitions   Process constant definitions:        */
/*                                                           */
/*                     <id> = <constant>                     */
/*-----------------------------------------------------------*/

TOKEN_CODE follow_declaration_list[] = {SEMICOLON, IDENTIFIER,
                                        END_OF_FILE, 0};

const_definitions()

{
    SYMTAB_NODE_PTR const_idp;          /* constant id */

    /*
    -- Loop to process definitions separated by semicolons.
    */
    while (token == IDENTIFIER) {
        search_and_enter_local_symtab(const_idp);
        const_idp->defn.key = CONST_DEFN;

        get_token();
        if_token_get_else_error(EQUAL, MISSING_EQUAL);

        /*
        -- Process the constant.
        */
        do_const(const_idp);
        analyze_const_defn(const_idp);

        /*
        -- Error synchronization:  Should be ;
        */
        synchronize(follow_declaration_list,
                declaration_start_list, statement_start_list);
        if_token_get(SEMICOLON);
        else if (token_in(declaration_start_list) ||
                token_in(statement_start_list))
            error(MISSING_SEMICOLON);
    }
}

/*-----------------------------------------------------------*/
/* do_const            Process the constant of a constant    */
/*                     definition.                           */
/*-----------------------------------------------------------*/

do_const(const_idp)

    SYMTAB_NODE_PTR const_idp;          /* constant id */
```

```
{
    TOKEN_CODE    sign     = PLUS;    /* unary + or - sign */
    BOOLEAN       saw_sign = FALSE;   /* TRUE iff unary sign */

    /*
    -- Unary + or - sign.
    */
    if ((token == PLUS) || (token == MINUS)) {
        sign     = token;
        saw_sign = TRUE;
        get_token();
    }

    /*
    -- Numeric constant:  Integer or real type.
    */
    if (token == NUMBER) {
        if (literal.type == INTEGER_LIT) {
            const_idp->defn.info.constant.value.integer =
                sign == PLUS ?  literal.value.integer
                             : -literal.value.integer;
            const_idp->typep = integer_typep;
        }
        else {
            const_idp->defn.info.constant.value.real =
                sign == PLUS ?  literal.value.real
                             : -literal.value.real;
            const_idp->typep = real_typep;
        }
    }

    /*
    -- Identifier constant:  Integer, real, character, enumeration,
    --                       or string (character array) type.
    */
    else if (token == IDENTIFIER) {
        SYMTAB_NODE_PTR idp;

        search_all_symtab(idp);

        if (idp == NULL)
            error(UNDEFINED_IDENTIFIER);
        else if (idp->defn.key != CONST_DEFN)
            error(NOT_A_CONSTANT_IDENTIFIER);

        else if (idp->typep == integer_typep) {
            const_idp->defn.info.constant.value.integer =
                sign == PLUS ?  idp->defn.info.constant.value.integer
                             : -idp->defn.info.constant.value.integer;
            const_idp->typep = integer_typep;
        }
        else if (idp->typep == real_typep) {
            const_idp->defn.info.constant.value.real =
                sign == PLUS ?  idp->defn.info.constant.value.real
                             : -idp->defn.info.constant.value.real;
            const_idp->typep = real_typep;
        }
        else if (idp->typep == char_typep) {
            if (saw_sign) error(INVALID_CONSTANT);

            const_idp->defn.info.constant.value.character =
                            idp->defn.info.constant.value.character;
            const_idp->typep = char_typep;
        }
        else if (idp->typep->form == ENUM_FORM) {
            if (saw_sign) error(INVALID_CONSTANT);

            const_idp->defn.info.constant.value.integer =
                            idp->defn.info.constant.value.integer;
            const_idp->typep = idp->typep;
        }
        else if (idp->typep->form == ARRAY_FORM) {
            if (saw_sign) error(INVALID_CONSTANT);

            const_idp->defn.info.constant.value.stringp =
                            idp->defn.info.constant.value.stringp;
            const_idp->typep = idp->typep;
        }
    }

    /*
    -- String constant:  Character or string (character array) type.
    */
    else if (token == STRING) {
        if (saw_sign) error(INVALID_CONSTANT);

        if (strlen(literal.value.string) == 1) {
            const_idp->defn.info.constant.value.character =
                                    literal.value.string[0];
            const_idp->typep = char_typep;
        }
        else {
            int length = strlen(literal.value.string);

            const_idp->defn.info.constant.value.stringp =
                                    alloc_bytes(length + 1);
            strcpy(const_idp->defn.info.constant.value.stringp,
                   literal.value.string);
            const_idp->typep = make_string_typep(length);
        }
    }

    else {
        const_idp->typep = &dummy_type;
        error(INVALID_CONSTANT);
    }

    get_token();
}

            /***********************/
            /*                     */
            /*        Types        */
            /*                     */
            /***********************/

/*------------------------------------------------------------*/
/* type_definitions      Process type definitions:            */
/*                                                            */
/*                   <id> = <type>                             */
/*------------------------------------------------------------*/

type_definitions()

{
    SYMTAB_NODE_PTR type_idp;        /* type id */

    /*
    -- Loop to process definitions separated by semicolons.
    */
    while (token == IDENTIFIER) {
        search_and_enter_local_symtab(type_idp);
        type_idp->defn.key = TYPE_DEFN;

        get_token();
```

```
        if_token_get_else_error(EQUAL, MISSING_EQUAL);

        /*
        -- Process the type specification.
        */
        type_idp->typep = do_type();
        if (type_idp->typep->type_idp == NULL)
            type_idp->typep->type_idp = type_idp;

        analyze_type_defn(type_idp);

        /*
        -- Error synchronization:  Should be ;
        */
        synchronize(follow_declaration_list,
                declaration_start_list, statement_start_list);
        if_token_get(SEMICOLON);
        else if (token_in(declaration_start_list) ||
                token_in(statement_start_list))
            error(MISSING_SEMICOLON);
    }
}

/*------------------------------------------------------*/
/* do_type              Process a type specification.  Call the */
/*                      functions that make a type structure    */
/*                      and return a pointer to it.             */
/*------------------------------------------------------*/

    TYPE_STRUCT_PTR
do_type()

{
    switch (token) {
        case IDENTIFIER: {
            SYMTAB_NODE_PTR idp;

            search_all_symtab(idp);

            if (idp == NULL) {
                error(UNDEFINED_IDENTIFIER);
                return(&dummy_type);
            }
            else if (idp->defn.key == TYPE_DEFN)
                return(identifier_type(idp));
            else if (idp->defn.key == CONST_DEFN)
                return(subrange_type(idp));
            else {
                error(NOT_A_TYPE_IDENTIFIER);
                return(&dummy_type);
            }
        }

        case LPAREN:    return(enumeration_type());
        case ARRAY:     return(array_type());
        case RECORD:    return(record_type());

        case PLUS:
        case MINUS:
        case NUMBER:
        case STRING:    return(subrange_type(NULL));

        default:        error(INVALID_TYPE);
                        return(&dummy_type);
    }
}
```

```
/*------------------------------------------------------*/
/* identifier_type    Process an identifier type, i.e., the    */
/*                    identifier on the right side of a type    */
/*                    equate, and return a pointer to its       */
/*                    type structure.                           */
/*------------------------------------------------------*/

    TYPE_STRUCT_PTR
identifier_type(idp)

    SYMTAB_NODE_PTR idp;        /* type id */

{
    TYPE_STRUCT_PTR tp = NULL;

    tp = idp->typep;
    get_token();

    return(tp);
}

/*------------------------------------------------------*/
/* enumeration_type   Process an enumeration type:             */
/*                                                              */
/*                        ( <id1>, <id2>, ..., <idn> )          */
/*                                                              */
/*                    Make a type structure and return a        */
/*                    pointer to it.                            */
/*------------------------------------------------------*/

    TYPE_STRUCT_PTR
enumeration_type()

{
    SYMTAB_NODE_PTR const_idp;           /* constant id */
    SYMTAB_NODE_PTR last_idp   = NULL; /* last constant id */
    TYPE_STRUCT_PTR tp         = alloc_struct(TYPE_STRUCT);
    int             const_value = -1;   /* constant value */

    tp->form     = ENUM_FORM;
    tp->size     = sizeof(int);
    tp->type_idp = NULL;

    get_token();

    /*
    -- Loop to process list of identifiers.
    */
    while (token == IDENTIFIER) {
        search_and_enter_local_symtab(const_idp);
        const_idp->defn.key = CONST_DEFN;
        const_idp->defn.info.constant.value.integer = ++const_value;
        const_idp->typep = tp;

        /*
        -- Link constant ids together.
        */
        if (last_idp == NULL)
            tp->info.enumeration.const_idp = last_idp = const_idp;
        else {
            last_idp->next = const_idp;
            last_idp = const_idp;
        }

        get_token();
        if_token_get(COMMA);
    }
```

```
    if_token_get_else_error(RPAREN, MISSING_RPAREN);

    tp->info.enumeration.max = const_value;
    return(tp);
}

/*--------------------------------------------------------*/
/*  subrange_type      Process a subrange type:           */
/*                                                        */
/*                         <min-const> .. <max-const>     */
/*                                                        */
/*                      Make a type structure and return a */
/*                      pointer to it.                    */
/*--------------------------------------------------------*/

TOKEN_CODE follow_min_limit_list[] = {DOTDOT, IDENTIFIER, PLUS, MINUS,
                                      NUMBER, STRING, SEMICOLON,
                                      END_OF_FILE, 0};

    TYPE_STRUCT_PTR
subrange_type(min_idp)

    SYMTAB_NODE_PTR min_idp;     /* min limit const id */

{
    TYPE_STRUCT_PTR max_typep;   /* type of max limit */
    TYPE_STRUCT_PTR tp = alloc_struct(TYPE_STRUCT);

    tp->form     = SUBRANGE_FORM;
    tp->type_idp = NULL;

    /*
    -- Minimum constant.
    */
    get_subrange_limit(min_idp,
                       &(tp->info.subrange.min),
                       &(tp->info.subrange.range_typep));

    /*
    -- Error synchronization:  Should be ..
    */
    synchronize(follow_min_limit_list, NULL, NULL);
    if_token_get(DOTDOT);
    else if (token_in(follow_min_limit_list) ||
                token_in(declaration_start_list) ||
                token_in(statement_start_list))
        error(MISSING_DOTDOT);

    /*
    -- Maximum constant.
    */
    get_subrange_limit(NULL, &(tp->info.subrange.max), &max_typep);

    /*
    -- Check limits.
    */
    if (max_typep == tp->info.subrange.range_typep) {
        if (tp->info.subrange.min > tp->info.subrange.max)
            error(MIN_GT_MAX);
    }
    else error(INCOMPATIBLE_TYPES);

    tp->size = max_typep == char_typep ? sizeof(char) : sizeof(int);
    return(tp);
}

/*--------------------------------------------------------*/
/*  get_subrange_limit  Process the minimum and maximum limits  */
```

```
/*                         of a subrange type.            */
/*--------------------------------------------------------*/

get_subrange_limit(minmax_idp, minmaxp, typepp)

    SYMTAB_NODE_PTR minmax_idp; /* min const id */
    int             *minmaxp;   /* where to store min or max value */
    TYPE_STRUCT_PTR *typepp;    /* where to store ptr to type struct */

{
    SYMTAB_NODE_PTR idp      = minmax_idp;
    TOKEN_CODE      sign     = PLUS;    /* unary + or - sign */
    BOOLEAN         saw_sign = FALSE;   /* TRUE iff unary sign */

    /*
    -- Unary + or - sign.
    */
    if ((token == PLUS) || (token == MINUS)) {
        sign     = token;
        saw_sign = TRUE;
        get_token();
    }

    /*
    -- Numeric limit:  Integer type only.
    */
    if (token == NUMBER) {
        if (literal.type == INTEGER_LIT) {
            *typepp = integer_typep;
            *minmaxp = (sign == PLUS) ?  literal.value.integer
                                      : -literal.value.integer;
        }
        else error(INVALID_SUBRANGE_TYPE);
    }

    /*
    -- Identifier limit:  Value must be integer or character.
    */
    else if (token == IDENTIFIER) {
        if (idp == NULL) search_all_symtab(idp);

        if (idp == NULL)
            error(UNDEFINED_IDENTIFIER);
        else if (idp->typep == real_typep)
            error(INVALID_SUBRANGE_TYPE);
        else if (idp->defn.key == CONST_DEFN) {
            *typepp = idp->typep;
            if (idp->typep == char_typep) {
                if (saw_sign) error(INVALID_CONSTANT);
                *minmaxp = idp->defn.info.constant.value.character;
            }
            else if (idp->typep == integer_typep) {
                *minmaxp = idp->defn.info.constant.value.integer;
                if (sign == MINUS) *minmaxp = -(*minmaxp);
            }
            else /* enumeration constant */ {
                if (saw_sign) error(INVALID_CONSTANT);
                *minmaxp = idp->defn.info.constant.value.integer;
            }
        }
        else error(NOT_A_CONSTANT_IDENTIFIER);
    }

    /*
    -- String limit:  Character type only.
    */
    else if (token == STRING) {
```

```
        if (saw_sign) error(INVALID_CONSTANT);
        *typepp  = char_typep;
        *minmaxp = literal.value.string[0];

        if (strlen(literal.value.string) != 1)
            error(INVALID_SUBRANGE_TYPE);
    }

    else error(MISSING_CONSTANT);

    get_token();
}

/*----------------------------------------------------------*/
/*  array_type         Process an array type:              */
/*                                                          */
/*                          ARRAY [<index-type-list>]       */
/*                              OF <elmt-type>              */
/*                                                          */
/*                      Make a type structure and return a  */
/*                      pointer to it.                      */
/*----------------------------------------------------------*/

TOKEN_CODE follow_dimension_list[] = {COMMA, RBRACKET, OF,
                                      SEMICOLON, END_OF_FILE, 0};

TOKEN_CODE index_type_start_list[] = {IDENTIFIER, NUMBER, STRING,
                                      LPAREN, MINUS, PLUS, 0};

TOKEN_CODE follow_indexes_list[]   = {OF, IDENTIFIER, LPAREN, ARRAY,
                                      RECORD, PLUS, MINUS, NUMBER,
                                      STRING, SEMICOLON, END_OF_FILE,
                                      0};

    TYPE_STRUCT_PTR
array_type()

{
    TYPE_STRUCT_PTR tp       = alloc_struct(TYPE_STRUCT);
    TYPE_STRUCT_PTR index_tp;           /* index type */
    TYPE_STRUCT_PTR elmt_tp = tp;       /* element type */
    int array_size();

    get_token();
    if (token != LBRACKET) error(MISSING_LBRACKET);

    /*
    -- Loop to process index type list.  For each
    -- type in the list after the first, create an
    -- array element type.
    */
    do {
        get_token();

        if (token_in(index_type_start_list)) {
            elmt_tp->form     = ARRAY_FORM;
            elmt_tp->size     = 0;
            elmt_tp->type_idp = NULL;
            elmt_tp->info.array.index_typep = index_tp = do_type();

            switch (index_tp->form) {
                case ENUM_FORM:
                    elmt_tp->info.array.elmt_count =
                            index_tp->info.enumeration.max + 1;
                    elmt_tp->info.array.min_index = 0;
                    elmt_tp->info.array.max_index =
                            index_tp->info.enumeration.max;
```

```
                    break;

                case SUBRANGE_FORM:
                    elmt_tp->info.array.elmt_count =
                            index_tp->info.subrange.max -
                                index_tp->info.subrange.min + 1;
                    elmt_tp->info.array.min_index =
                                index_tp->info.subrange.min;
                    elmt_tp->info.array.max_index =
                                index_tp->info.subrange.max;
                    break;

                default:
                    elmt_tp->form     = NO_FORM;
                    elmt_tp->size     = 0;
                    elmt_tp->type_idp = NULL;
                    elmt_tp->info.array.index_typep = &dummy_type;
                    error(INVALID_INDEX_TYPE);
                    break;
            }
        }
        else {
            elmt_tp->form     = NO_FORM;
            elmt_tp->size     = 0;
            elmt_tp->type_idp = NULL;
            elmt_tp->info.array.index_typep = &dummy_type;
            error(INVALID_INDEX_TYPE);
        }

        /*
        -- Error synchronization:  Should be , or ]
        */
        synchronize(follow_dimension_list, NULL, NULL);

        /*
        -- Create an array element type.
        */
        if (token == COMMA) elmt_tp = elmt_tp->info.array.elmt_typep =
                            alloc_struct(TYPE_STRUCT);
    } while (token == COMMA);

    if_token_get_else_error(RBRACKET, MISSING_RBRACKET);

    /*
    -- Error synchronization:  Should be OF
    */
    synchronize(follow_indexes_list,
                declaration_start_list, statement_start_list);
    if_token_get_else_error(OF, MISSING_OF);

    /*
    -- Element type.
    */
    elmt_tp->info.array.elmt_typep = do_type();

    tp->size = array_size(tp);
    return(tp);
}

/*----------------------------------------------------------*/
/*  record_type        Process a record type:              */
/*                                                          */
/*                          RECORD                          */
/*                              <id-list> : <type> ;        */
/*                              ...                         */
/*                          END                             */
```

```
/*                                                   */
/*                  Make a type structure and return a    */
/*                  pointer to it.                    */
/*----------------------------------------------*/

    TYPE_STRUCT_PTR
record_type()

{
    TYPE_STRUCT_PTR record_tp = alloc_struct(TYPE_STRUCT);

    record_tp->form      = RECORD_FORM;
    record_tp->type_idp = NULL;
    record_tp->info.record.field_symtab = NULL;

    get_token();
    var_or_field_declarations(NULL, record_tp, 0);

    if_token_get_else_error(END, MISSING_END);
    return(record_tp);
}

/*----------------------------------------------*/
/* make_string_typep  Make a type structure for a string of */
/*                    the given length, and return a pointer */
/*                    to it.                          */
/*----------------------------------------------*/

    TYPE_STRUCT_PTR
make_string_typep(length)

    int length;               /* string length */

{
    TYPE_STRUCT_PTR string_tp = alloc_struct(TYPE_STRUCT);
    TYPE_STRUCT_PTR index_tp  = alloc_struct(TYPE_STRUCT);

    /*
    -- Array type.
    */
    string_tp->form      = ARRAY_FORM;
    string_tp->size      = length;
    string_tp->type_idp = NULL;
    string_tp->info.array.index_typep = index_tp;
    string_tp->info.array.elmt_typep  = char_typep;
    string_tp->info.array.elmt_count  = length;

    /*
    -- Subrange index type.
    */
    index_tp->form      = SUBRANGE_FORM;
    index_tp->size      = sizeof(int);
    index_tp->type_idp = NULL;
    index_tp->info.subrange.range_typep = integer_typep;
    index_tp->info.subrange.min = 1;
    index_tp->info.subrange.max = length;

    return(string_tp);
}

/*----------------------------------------------*/
/* array_size           Return the size in bytes of an array */
/*                      type by recursively calculating the  */
/*                      size of each dimension.       */
/*----------------------------------------------*/

    int
```

```
array_size(tp)

    TYPE_STRUCT_PTR tp;         /* ptr to array type structure */

{
    if (tp->info.array.elmt_typep->size == 0)
        tp->info.array.elmt_typep->size =
                            array_size(tp->info.array.elmt_typep);

    tp->size = tp->info.array.elmt_count *
               tp->info.array.elmt_typep->size;

    return(tp->size);
}

                        /************************/
                        /*                      */
                        /*      Variables       */
                        /*                      */
                        /************************/

/*----------------------------------------------*/
/* var_declarations     Process variable declarations: */
/*                                                    */
/*                      <id-list> : <type>       */
/*----------------------------------------------*/

var_declarations(rtn_idp)

    SYMTAB_NODE_PTR rtn_idp;     /* id of program or routine */

{
    var_or_field_declarations(rtn_idp, NULL,
                        rtn_idp->defn.key == PROC_DEFN
                            ? PROC_LOCALS_STACK_FRAME_OFFSET
                            : FUNC_LOCALS_STACK_FRAME_OFFSET);
}

/*----------------------------------------------*/
/* var_or_field_declarations   Process variable declarations */
/*                             or record field definitions. */
/*                             All ids declared with the same */
/*                             type are linked together into */
/*                             a sublist, and all the sublists */
/*                             are then linked together. */
/*----------------------------------------------*/

TOKEN_CODE follow_variables_list[] = {SEMICOLON, IDENTIFIER,
                        END_OF_FILE, 0};

TOKEN_CODE follow_fields_list[]    = {SEMICOLON, END, IDENTIFIER,
                        END_OF_FILE, 0};

var_or_field_declarations(rtn_idp, record_tp, offset)

    SYMTAB_NODE_PTR rtn_idp;
    TYPE_STRUCT_PTR record_tp;
    int            offset;

{
    SYMTAB_NODE_PTR idp, first_idp, last_idp;   /* variable or
                                                   field ids */
    SYMTAB_NODE_PTR prev_last_idp = NULL;        /* last id of list */
    TYPE_STRUCT_PTR tp;                          /* type */
    BOOLEAN var_flag = (rtn_idp != NULL);        /* TRUE: variables */
                                                 /* FALSE: fields */

    int size;
```

```
    int total_size = 0;

    /*
    -- Loop to process sublist, each of a type.
    */
    while (token == IDENTIFIER) {
        first_idp = NULL;

        /*
        -- Loop process each variable or field id in a sublist.
        */
        while (token == IDENTIFIER) {
            if (var_flag) {
                search_and_enter_local_symtab(idp);
                idp->defn.key = VAR_DEFN;
            }
            else {
                search_and_enter_this_symtab
                    (idp, record_tp->info.record.field_symtab);
                idp->defn.key = FIELD_DEFN;
            }
            idp->label_index = new_label_index();

            /*
            -- Link ids together into a sublist.
            */
            if (first_idp == NULL) {
                first_idp = last_idp = idp;
                if (var_flag &&
                    (rtn_idp->defn.info.routine.locals == NULL))
                    rtn_idp->defn.info.routine.locals = idp;
            }
            else {
                last_idp->next = idp;
                last_idp = idp;
            }

            get_token();
            if_token_get(COMMA);
        }

        /*
        -- Process the sublist's type.
        */
        if_token_get_else_error(COLON, MISSING_COLON);
        tp = do_type();
        size = tp->size;
        if (size & 1) ++size;     /* round up to even */

        /*
```

```
        -- Assign the offset and the type to all variable or field
        -- ids in the sublist.
        */
        for (idp = first_idp; idp != NULL; idp = idp->next) {
            idp->typep = tp;

            if (var_flag) {
                offset -= size;
                total_size += size;
                idp->defn.info.data.offset = offset;
                analyze_var_decl(idp);
            }

            else   /* record fields */ {
                idp->defn.info.data.offset = offset;
                offset += size;

                /*
                -- Emit numeric equate for the field id's
                -- name and offset.
                */
                emit_numeric_equate(idp);
            }
        }

        /*
        -- Link this sublist to the previous sublist.
        */
        if (prev_last_idp != NULL) prev_last_idp->next = first_idp;
        prev_last_idp = last_idp;

        /*
        -- Error synchronization:  Should be ; for variable
        --                         declaration, or ; or END for
        --                         record type definition.
        */
        synchronize(var_flag ? follow_variables_list
                             : follow_fields_list,
                follow_fields_list,
                declaration_start_list, statement_start_list);
        if_token_get(SEMICOLON);
        else if (var_flag && ((token_in(declaration_start_list)) ||
                              (token_in(statement_start_list))))
            error(MISSING_SEMICOLON);
    }

    if (var_flag)
        rtn_idp->defn.info.routine.total_local_size = total_size;
    else
        record_tp->size = offset;
}
```

FIGURE B-5   stmt.c

```
/* Figure 14-1 */

/****************************************************************/
/*                                                              */
/*      S T A T E M E N T   P A R S E R                         */
/*                                                              */
/*      Parsing routines for statements.                        */
/*                                                              */
/*      FILE:     stmt.c                                        */
/*                                                              */
```

```
/*      MODULE:      parser                                     */
/*                                                              */
/****************************************************************/

#include <stdio.h>
#include "common.h"
#include "error.h"
#include "scanner.h"
#include "symtab.h"
#include "parser.h"
```

```c
#include "code.h"

/*----------------------------------------------------------*/
/* Externals                                                */
/*----------------------------------------------------------*/

extern TOKEN_CODE        token;
extern char              word_string[];
extern LITERAL           literal;
extern TOKEN_CODE        statement_start_list[], statement_end_list[];

extern SYMTAB_NODE_PTR   symtab_display[];
extern int               level;

extern TYPE_STRUCT_PTR   integer_typep, real_typep,
                         boolean_typep, char_typep;

extern TYPE_STRUCT       dummy_type;

extern int               label_index;
extern char              asm_buffer[];
extern char              *asm_bufferp;
extern FILE              *code_file;

/*----------------------------------------------------------*/
/* statement            Process a statement by calling the  */
/*                      appropriate parsing routine based on */
/*                      the statement's first token.         */
/*----------------------------------------------------------*/

statement()

{
    /*
    -- Call the appropriate routine based on the first
    -- token of the statement.
    */
    switch (token) {

        case IDENTIFIER: {
            SYMTAB_NODE_PTR idp;

            /*
            -- Assignment statement or procedure call?
            */
            search_and_find_all_symtab(idp);

            if (idp->defn.key == PROC_DEFN) {
                get_token();
                routine_call(idp, TRUE);
            }
            else assignment_statement(idp);

            break;
        }

        case REPEAT:    repeat_statement();     break;
        case WHILE:     while_statement();      break;
        case IF:        if_statement();         break;
        case FOR:       for_statement();        break;
        case CASE:      case_statement();       break;
        case BEGIN:     compound_statement();   break;
    }

    /*
    -- Error synchronization:  Only a semicolon, END, ELSE, or
    --                         UNTIL may follow a statement.
```

```c
    --                         Check for a missing semicolon.
    */
    synchronize(statement_end_list, statement_start_list, NULL);
    if (token_in(statement_start_list)) error(MISSING_SEMICOLON);
}

/*----------------------------------------------------------*/
/* assignment_statement    Process an assignment statement: */
/*                                                          */
/*                      <id> := <expr>                      */
/*----------------------------------------------------------*/

assignment_statement(var_idp)

    SYMTAB_NODE_PTR var_idp;            /* target variable id */

{
    TYPE_STRUCT_PTR var_tp, expr_tp;    /* types of var and expr */
    BOOLEAN         stacked_flag;       /* TRUE iff target address
                                           was pushed on stack */

    var_tp = variable(var_idp, TARGET_USE);
    stacked_flag = (var_idp->defn.key == VARPARM_DEFN) ||
                   (var_idp->defn.key == FUNC_DEFN) ||
                   (var_idp->typep->form == ARRAY_FORM) ||
                   (var_idp->typep->form == RECORD_FORM) ||
                   ((var_idp->level > 1) && (var_idp->level < level));

    if_token_get_else_error(COLONEQUAL, MISSING_COLONEQUAL);
    expr_tp = expression();

    if (! is_assign_type_compatible(var_tp, expr_tp))
        error(INCOMPATIBLE_ASSIGNMENT);

    var_tp  = base_type(var_tp);
    expr_tp = base_type(expr_tp);

    /*
    -- Emit code to do the assignment.
    */
    if (var_tp == char_typep) {
        /*
        -- char := char
        */
        if (stacked_flag) {
            emit_1(POP, reg(BX));
            emit_2(MOVE, byte_indirect(BX), reg(AL));
        }
        else emit_2(MOVE, byte(var_idp), reg(AL));
    }
    else if (var_tp == real_typep) {
        /*
        -- real := ...
        */
        if (expr_tp == integer_typep) {
            /*
            -- ... integer
            */
            emit_1(PUSH, reg(AX));
            emit_1(CALL, name_lit(FLOAT_CONVERT));
            emit_2(ADD, reg(SP), integer_lit(2));
        }
        /*
        -- ... real
        */
        if (stacked_flag) {
            emit_1(POP, reg(BX));
```

```
                emit_2(MOVE, word_indirect(BX), reg(AX));
                emit_2(MOVE, high_dword_indirect(BX), reg(DX));
            }
            else {
                emit_2(MOVE, word(var_idp), reg(AX));
                emit_2(MOVE, high_dword(var_idp), reg(DX));
            }
        }
        else if ((var_tp->form == ARRAY_FORM) ||
                 (var_tp->form == RECORD_FORM)) {
            /*
            --   array  := array
            --   record := record
            */
            emit_2(MOVE, reg(CX), integer_lit(var_tp->size));
            emit_1(POP,  reg(SI));
            emit_1(POP,  reg(DI));
            emit_2(MOVE, reg(AX), reg(DS));
            emit_2(MOVE, reg(ES), reg(AX));
            emit(CLEAR_DIRECTION);
            emit(MOVE_BLOCK);
        }
        else {
            /*
            --   integer := integer
            --   enum    := enum
            */
            if (stacked_flag) {
                emit_1(POP, reg(BX));
                emit_2(MOVE, word_indirect(BX), reg(AX));
            }
            else emit_2(MOVE, word(var_idp), reg(AX));
        }
    }
}

/*------------------------------------------------------------*/
/*  repeat_statement    Process a REPEAT statement:           */
/*                                                            */
/*                      REPEAT <stmt-list> UNTIL <expr>       */
/*------------------------------------------------------------*/

repeat_statement()

{
    TYPE_STRUCT_PTR expr_tp;
    int            loop_begin_labelx = new_label_index();
    int            loop_exit_labelx = new_label_index();

    emit_label(STMT_LABEL_PREFIX, loop_begin_labelx);

    /*
    --  <stmt-list>
    */
    get_token();
    do {
        statement();
        while (token == SEMICOLON) get_token();
    } while (token_in(statement_start_list));

    if_token_get_else_error(UNTIL, MISSING_UNTIL);

    expr_tp = expression();
    if (expr_tp != boolean_typep) error(INCOMPATIBLE_TYPES);

    emit_2(COMPARE, reg(AX), integer_lit(1));
    emit_1(JUMP_EQ, label(STMT_LABEL_PREFIX, loop_exit_labelx));
    emit_1(JUMP, label(STMT_LABEL_PREFIX, loop_begin_labelx));
```

```
        emit_label(STMT_LABEL_PREFIX, loop_exit_labelx);
}

/*------------------------------------------------------------*/
/*  while_statement      Process a WHILE statement:           */
/*                                                            */
/*                      WHILE <expr> DO <stmt>                */
/*------------------------------------------------------------*/

while_statement()

{
    TYPE_STRUCT_PTR expr_tp;
    int            loop_test_labelx = new_label_index();
    int            loop_stmt_labelx = new_label_index();
    int            loop_exit_labelx = new_label_index();

    emit_label(STMT_LABEL_PREFIX, loop_test_labelx);

    get_token();
    expr_tp = expression();
    if (expr_tp != boolean_typep) error(INCOMPATIBLE_TYPES);

    emit_2(COMPARE, reg(AX), integer_lit(1));
    emit_1(JUMP_EQ, label(STMT_LABEL_PREFIX, loop_stmt_labelx));
    emit_1(JUMP,    label(STMT_LABEL_PREFIX, loop_exit_labelx));
    emit_label(STMT_LABEL_PREFIX, loop_stmt_labelx);

    if_token_get_else_error(DO, MISSING_DO);
    statement();

    emit_1(JUMP, label(STMT_LABEL_PREFIX, loop_test_labelx));
    emit_label(STMT_LABEL_PREFIX, loop_exit_labelx);
}

/*------------------------------------------------------------*/
/*  if_statement         Process an IF statement:             */
/*                                                            */
/*                      IF <expr> THEN <stmt>                 */
/*                                                            */
/*                      or:                                   */
/*                                                            */
/*                      IF <expr> THEN <stmt> ELSE <stmt>     */
/*------------------------------------------------------------*/

if_statement()

{
    TYPE_STRUCT_PTR expr_tp;
    int            true_labelx  = new_label_index();
    int            false_labelx = new_label_index();
    int            if_end_labelx;

    get_token();
    expr_tp = expression();
    if (expr_tp != boolean_typep) error(INCOMPATIBLE_TYPES);

    emit_2(COMPARE, reg(AX), integer_lit(1));
    emit_1(JUMP_EQ, label(STMT_LABEL_PREFIX, true_labelx));
    emit_1(JUMP,    label(STMT_LABEL_PREFIX, false_labelx));
    emit_label(STMT_LABEL_PREFIX, true_labelx);

    if_token_get_else_error(THEN, MISSING_THEN);
    statement();

    /*
    --  ELSE branch?
```

```
        */
        if (token == ELSE) {
            if_end_labelx = new_label_index();
            emit_1(JUMP, label(STMT_LABEL_PREFIX, if_end_labelx));
            emit_label(STMT_LABEL_PREFIX, false_labelx);

            get_token();
            statement();

            emit_label(STMT_LABEL_PREFIX, if_end_labelx);
        }
        else emit_label(STMT_LABEL_PREFIX, false_labelx);
}

/*-----------------------------------------------------------*/
/*  for_statement       Process a FOR statement:             */
/*                                                           */
/*                      FOR <id> := <expr> TO|DOWNTO <expr>  */
/*                      DO <stmt>                            */
/*-----------------------------------------------------------*/

for_statement()

{
    SYMTAB_NODE_PTR  for_idp;
    TYPE_STRUCT_PTR  for_tp, expr_tp;
    BOOLEAN          to_flag;
    int              loop_test_labelx = new_label_index();
    int              loop_stmt_labelx = new_label_index();
    int              loop_exit_labelx = new_label_index();

    get_token();
    if (token == IDENTIFIER) {
        search_and_find_all_symtab(for_idp);
        if ((for_idp->level != level) ||
            (for_idp->defn.key != VAR_DEFN))
            error(INVALID_FOR_CONTROL);

        for_tp = base_type(for_idp->typep);
        get_token();

        if ((for_tp != integer_typep) &&
            (for_tp != char_typep) &&
            (for_tp->form != ENUM_FORM)) error(INCOMPATIBLE_TYPES);
    }
    else {
        error(IDENTIFIER, MISSING_IDENTIFIER);
        for_tp = &dummy_type;
    }

    if_token_get_else_error(COLONEQUAL, MISSING_COLONEQUAL);

    expr_tp = expression();
    if (! is_assign_type_compatible(for_tp, expr_tp))
        error(INCOMPATIBLE_TYPES);

    if (for_tp == char_typep) emit_2(MOVE, byte(for_idp), reg(AL))
    else                      emit_2(MOVE, word(for_idp), reg(AX))

    if ((token == TO) || (token == DOWNTO)) {
        to_flag = (token == TO);
        get_token();
    }
    else error(MISSING_TO_OR_DOWNTO);

    emit_label(STMT_LABEL_PREFIX, loop_test_labelx);

    expr_tp = expression();
```

```
    if (! is_assign_type_compatible(for_tp, expr_tp))
        error(INCOMPATIBLE_TYPES);

    if (for_tp == char_typep) emit_2(COMPARE, byte(for_idp), reg(AL))
    else                      emit_2(COMPARE, word(for_idp), reg(AX))
    emit_1(to_flag ? JUMP_LE : JUMP_GE,
        label(STMT_LABEL_PREFIX, loop_stmt_labelx));
    emit_1(JUMP, label(STMT_LABEL_PREFIX, loop_exit_labelx));
    emit_label(STMT_LABEL_PREFIX, loop_stmt_labelx);

    if_token_get_else_error(DO, MISSING_DO);
    statement();

    emit_1(to_flag ? INCREMENT : DECREMENT,
        for_tp == char_typep ? byte(for_idp) : word(for_idp));
    emit_1(JUMP, label(STMT_LABEL_PREFIX, loop_test_labelx));

    emit_label(STMT_LABEL_PREFIX, loop_exit_labelx);
    emit_1(to_flag ? DECREMENT : INCREMENT,
        for_tp == char_typep ? byte(for_idp) : word(for_idp));
}

/*-----------------------------------------------------------*/
/*  case_statement      Process a CASE statement:            */
/*                                                           */
/*                      CASE <expr> OF                       */
/*                          <case-branch> ;                  */
/*                          ...                              */
/*                      END                                  */
/*-----------------------------------------------------------*/

TOKEN_CODE follow_expr_list[]       = {OF, SEMICOLON, 0};

TOKEN_CODE case_label_start_list[] = {IDENTIFIER, NUMBER, PLUS,
                                      MINUS, STRING, 0};

case_statement()

{
    BOOLEAN          another_branch;
    int              case_end_labelx = new_label_index();
    TYPE_STRUCT_PTR  expr_tp;

    get_token();
    expr_tp = expression();

    if (   ((expr_tp->form != SCALAR_FORM) &&
            (expr_tp->form != ENUM_FORM) &&
            (expr_tp->form != SUBRANGE_FORM))
        || (expr_tp == real_typep)) error(INCOMPATIBLE_TYPES);

    /*
    -- Error synchronization:  Should be OF
    */
    synchronize(follow_expr_list, case_label_start_list, NULL);
    if_token_get_else_error(OF, MISSING_OF);

    /*
    -- Loop to process CASE branches.
    */
    another_branch = token_in(case_label_start_list);
    while (another_branch) {
        if (token_in(case_label_start_list))
            case_branch(expr_tp, case_end_labelx);

        if (token == SEMICOLON) {
            get_token();
```

```
                another_branch = TRUE;
            }
        else if (token_in(case_label_start_list)) {
            error(MISSING_SEMICOLON);
            another_branch = TRUE;
            }
        else another_branch = FALSE;
        }

    if_token_get_else_error(END, MISSING_END);
    emit_label(STMT_LABEL_PREFIX, case_end_labelx);
}

/*------------------------------------------------------------*/
/* case_branch              Process a CASE branch:           */
/*                                                           */
/*                          <case-label-list> : <stmt>       */
/*------------------------------------------------------------*/

TOKEN_CODE follow_case_label_list[] = {COLON, SEMICOLON, 0};

case_branch(expr_tp, case_end_labelx)

    TYPE_STRUCT_PTR   expr_tp;          /* type of CASE expression */
    int               case_end_labelx;  /* CASE end label index */

{
    BOOLEAN           another_label;
    int               next_test_labelx;
    int               branch_stmt_labelx = new_label_index();
    TYPE_STRUCT_PTR   label_tp;
    TYPE_STRUCT_PTR   case_label();

    /*
    -- <case-label-list>
    */
    do {
        next_test_labelx = new_label_index();

        label_tp = case_label();
        if (expr_tp != label_tp) error(INCOMPATIBLE_TYPES);

        emit_1(JUMP_NE, label(STMT_LABEL_PREFIX, next_test_labelx));

        get_token();
        if (token == COMMA) {
            get_token();
            emit_1(JUMP, label(STMT_LABEL_PREFIX, branch_stmt_labelx));

            if (token_in(case_label_start_list)) {
                emit_label(STMT_LABEL_PREFIX, next_test_labelx);
                another_label = TRUE;
            }
            else {
                error(MISSING_CONSTANT);
                another_label = FALSE;
            }
        }
        else another_label = FALSE;
    } while (another_label);

    /*
    -- Error synchronization:  Should be :
    */
    synchronize(follow_case_label_list, statement_start_list, NULL);
    if_token_get_else_error(COLON, MISSING_COLON);

    emit_label(STMT_LABEL_PREFIX, branch_stmt_labelx);
```

```
        statement();

        emit_1(JUMP, label(STMT_LABEL_PREFIX, case_end_labelx));
        emit_label(STMT_LABEL_PREFIX, next_test_labelx);
}

/*------------------------------------------------------------*/
/* case_label              Process a CASE label and return a  */
/*                         pointer to its type structure.     */
/*------------------------------------------------------------*/

    TYPE_STRUCT_PTR
case_label()

{
    TOKEN_CODE sign      = PLUS;        /* unary + or - sign */
    BOOLEAN    saw_sign = FALSE;        /* TRUE iff unary sign */

    /*
    -- Unary + or - sign.
    */
    if ((token == PLUS) || (token == MINUS)) {
        sign     = token;
        saw_sign = TRUE;
        get_token();
    }

    /*
    -- Numeric constant:  Integer type only.
    */
    if (token == NUMBER) {
        if (literal.type == INTEGER_LIT)
            emit_2(COMPARE, reg(AX),
                   integer_lit(sign == PLUS
                                   ? literal.value.integer
                                   : -literal.value.integer))
        else error(INVALID_CONSTANT);

        return(integer_typep);
    }

    /*
    -- Identifier constant:  Integer, character, or enumeration
    --                       types only.
    */
    else if (token == IDENTIFIER) {
        SYMTAB_NODE_PTR idp;

        search_all_symtab(idp);

        if (idp == NULL) {
            error(UNDEFINED_IDENTIFIER);
            return(&dummy_type);
        }

        else if (idp->defn.key != CONST_DEFN) {
            error(NOT_A_CONSTANT_IDENTIFIER);
            return(&dummy_type);
        }

        else if (idp->typep == integer_typep) {
            emit_2(COMPARE, reg(AX),
                   integer_lit(sign == PLUS
                                   ? idp->defn.info.constant
                                        .value.integer
                                   : -idp->defn.info.constant
                                        .value.integer));
```

```
              return(integer_typep);                                            }
      }                                                                       }

      else if (idp->typep == char_typep) {                                else {
          if (saw_sign) error(INVALID_CONSTANT);                               error(INVALID_CONSTANT);
          emit_2(COMPARE, reg(AL),                                             return(&dummy_type);
                      char_lit(idp->defn.info.constant                     }
                                  .value.character));                   }

          return(char_typep);                                     /*-------------------------------------------------------------*/
      }                                                           /*  compound_statement      Process a compound statement:      */
                                                                  /*                                                             */
      else if (idp->typep->form == ENUM_FORM) {                  /*                      BEGIN <stmt-list> END                  */
          if (saw_sign) error(INVALID_CONSTANT);                 /*-------------------------------------------------------------*/
          emit_2(COMPARE, reg(AX),
                      integer_lit(idp->defn.info.constant         compound_statement()
                                  .value.integer));
                                                                  {
          return(idp->typep);                                         /*
      }                                                               -- <stmt-list>
                                                                      */
      else return(&dummy_type);                                       get_token();
  }                                                                   do {
                                                                          statement();
  /*                                                                      while (token == SEMICOLON) get_token();
  -- String constant:  Character type only.                               if (token == END) break;
  */
  else if (token == STRING) {                                             /*
      if (saw_sign) error(INVALID_CONSTANT);                              -- Error synchronization:  Should be at the start of the
                                                                          --                         next statement.
      if (strlen(literal.value.string) == 1) {                            */
          emit_2(COMPARE, reg(AL), char_lit(literal.value.string[0]));    synchronize(statement_start_list, NULL, NULL);
          return(char_typep);                                       } while (token_in(statement_start_list));
      }
      else {                                                          if_token_get_else_error(END, MISSING_END);
          error(INVALID_CONSTANT);                                }
          return(&dummy_type);
      }
```

FIGURE B-6   expr.c

```
/**************************************************************/     extern TOKEN_CODE token;
/*                                                          */        extern char         token_string[];
/*        E X P R E S S I O N   P A R S E R                 */        extern char         word_string[];
/*                                                          */        extern LITERAL      literal;
/*        Parsing routines for expressions.                 */
/*                                                          */        extern SYMTAB_NODE_PTR symtab_display[];
/*        FILE:     expr.c                                  */        extern int             level;
/*                                                          */
/*        MODULE:   parser                                  */        extern TYPE_STRUCT_PTR integer_typep, real_typep,
/*                                                          */                               boolean_typep, char_typep;
/**************************************************************/
                                                                     extern TYPE_STRUCT     dummy_type;
#include <stdio.h>
#include "common.h"                                                  extern SYMTAB_NODE_PTR float_literal_list;
#include "error.h"                                                   extern SYMTAB_NODE_PTR string_literal_list;
#include "scanner.h"
#include "symtab.h"                                                  extern int             label_index;
#include "parser.h"                                                  extern char            asm_buffer[];
#include "code.h"                                                    extern char            *asm_bufferp;
                                                                     extern FILE            *code_file;

/*-----------------------------------------------*/                  /*-----------------------------------------------*/
/* Externals                                     */                  /* Forwards                                      */
/*-----------------------------------------------*/                  /*-----------------------------------------------*/
```

```c
TYPE_STRUCT_PTR expression(), simple_expression(), term(), factor(),
                constant_identifier(), function_call();

TYPE_STRUCT_PTR float_literal(), string_literal();

/*----------------------------------------------------------*/
/* integer_operands    TRUE if both operands are integer,   */
/*                      else FALSE.                          */
/*----------------------------------------------------------*/

#define integer_operands(tp1, tp2)  ((tp1 == integer_typep) && \
                                     (tp2 == integer_typep))

/*----------------------------------------------------------*/
/* real_operands       TRUE if at least one or both operands */
/*                     operands are real (and the other     */
/*                     integer), else FALSE.                */
/*----------------------------------------------------------*/

#define real_operands(tp1, tp2) (((tp1 == real_typep) &&     \
                                  ((tp2 == real_typep) ||    \
                                   (tp2 == integer_typep)))  \
                                  ||                         \
                                 ((tp2 == real_typep) &&     \
                                  ((tp1 == real_typep) ||    \
                                   (tp1 == integer_typep))))

/*----------------------------------------------------------*/
/* boolean_operands    TRUE if both operands are boolean    */
/*                      else FALSE.                          */
/*----------------------------------------------------------*/

#define boolean_operands(tp1, pt2)  ((tp1 == boolean_typep) && \
                                     (tp2 == boolean_typep))

/*----------------------------------------------------------*/
/* expression          Process an expression consisting of a */
/*                     simple expression optionally followed */
/*                     by a relational operator and a second */
/*                     simple expression. Return a pointer to */
/*                     the type structure.                  */
/*----------------------------------------------------------*/

TOKEN_CODE rel_op_list[] = {LT, LE, EQUAL, NE, GE, GT, 0};

    TYPE_STRUCT_PTR
expression()

{
    TOKEN_CODE      op;              /* an operator token */
    TYPE_STRUCT_PTR result_tp, tp2;
    int             jump_label_index; /* jump target label index */
    INSTRUCTION     jump_opcode;      /* opcode for cond. jump */

    result_tp = simple_expression();  /* first simple expr */

    /*
    -- If there is a relational operator, remember it and
    -- process the second simple expression.
    */
    if (token_in(rel_op_list)) {
        op = token;                  /* remember operator */

        result_tp = base_type(result_tp);
        emit_push_operand(result_tp);

        get_token();
```

```c
        tp2 = base_type(simple_expression());   /* 2nd simple expr */

        check_rel_op_types(result_tp, tp2);

        /*
        -- Both operands are integer, character, boolean, or
        -- the same enumeration type.  Compare DX (operand 1)
        -- to AX (operand 2).
        */
        if (integer_operands(result_tp, tp2) ||
            (result_tp == char_typep) ||
            (result_tp->form == ENUM_FORM)) {
            emit_1(POP, reg(DX));
            emit_2(COMPARE, reg(DX), reg(AX));
        }

        /*
        -- Both operands are real, or one is real and the other
        -- is integer.  Convert the integer operand to real.
        -- Call FLOAT_COMPARE to do the comparison, which returns
        -- -1 (less), 0 (equal), or +1 (greater).
        */
        else if ((result_tp == real_typep) || (tp2 == real_typep)) {
            emit_push_operand(tp2);
            emit_promote_to_real(result_tp, tp2);

            emit_1(CALL, name_lit(FLOAT_COMPARE));
            emit_2(ADD, reg(SP), integer_lit(8));
            emit_2(COMPARE, reg(AX), integer_lit(0));
        }

        /*
        -- Both operands are strings.  Compare the string pointed
        -- to by SI (operand 1) to the string pointed to by DI
        -- (operand 2).
        */
        else if (result_tp->form == ARRAY_FORM) {
            emit_1(POP,  reg(DI));
            emit_1(POP,  reg(SI));
            emit_2(MOVE, reg(AX), reg(DS));
            emit_2(MOVE, reg(ES), reg(AX));
            emit(CLEAR_DIRECTION);
            emit_2(MOVE, reg(CX),
                   integer_lit(result_tp->info.array.elmt_count));
            emit(COMPARE_STRINGS);
        }

        emit_2(MOVE, reg(AX), integer_lit(1)); /* default: load 1 */

        switch (op) {
            case LT:    jump_opcode = JUMP_LT;  break;
            case LE:    jump_opcode = JUMP_LE;  break;
            case EQUAL: jump_opcode = JUMP_EQ;  break;
            case NE:    jump_opcode = JUMP_NE;  break;
            case GE:    jump_opcode = JUMP_GE;  break;
            case GT:    jump_opcode = JUMP_GT;  break;
        }

        jump_label_index = new_label_index();
        emit_1(jump_opcode, label(STMT_LABEL_PREFIX,
               jump_label_index));

        emit_2(SUBTRACT, reg(AX), reg(AX));    /* load 0 if false */
        emit_label(STMT_LABEL_PREFIX, jump_label_index);

        result_tp = boolean_typep;
    }
}
```

```
      return(result_tp);
}

/*------------------------------------------------------*/
/*  simple_expression    Process a simple expression consisting  */
/*                       of terms separated by +, -, or OR       */
/*                       operators.  There may be a unary + or - */
/*                       before the first term.  Return a        */
/*                       pointer to the type structure.          */
/*------------------------------------------------------*/

TOKEN_CODE add_op_list[] = {PLUS, MINUS, OR, 0};

    TYPE_STRUCT_PTR
simple_expression()

{
    TOKEN_CODE op;                      /* an operator token */
    BOOLEAN    saw_unary_op = FALSE;    /* TRUE iff unary operator */
    TOKEN_CODE unary_op = PLUS;         /* a unary operator token */
    TYPE_STRUCT_PTR result_tp, tp2;

    /*
    -- If there is a unary + or -, remember it.
    */
    if ((token == PLUS) || (token == MINUS)) {
        unary_op = token;
        saw_unary_op = TRUE;
        get_token();
    }

    result_tp = term();        /* first term */

    /*
    -- If there was a unary operator, check that the term
    -- is integer or real.  Negate the top of stack if it
    -- was a unary - either with the NEG instruction or by
    -- calling FLOAT_NEGATE.
    */
    if (saw_unary_op) {
        if (base_type(result_tp) == integer_typep) {
            if (unary_op == MINUS) emit_1(NEGATE, reg(AX));
        }
        else if (result_tp == real_typep) {
            if (unary_op == MINUS) {
                emit_push_operand(result_tp);
                emit_1(CALL, name_lit(FLOAT_NEGATE));
                emit_2(ADD, reg(SP), integer_lit(4));
            }
        }
        else error(INCOMPATIBLE_TYPES);
    }

    /*
    -- Loop to process subsequent terms separated by operators.
    */
    while (token_in(add_op_list)) {
        op = token;                     /* remember operator */

        result_tp = base_type(result_tp);
        emit_push_operand(result_tp);

        get_token();
        tp2 = base_type(term());        /* subsequent term */

        switch (op) {

            case PLUS:

            case MINUS: {
                /*
                -- integer <op> integer => integer
                -- AX = AX +|- DX
                */
                if (integer_operands(result_tp, tp2)) {
                    emit_1(POP, reg(DX));
                    if (op == PLUS) emit_2(ADD, reg(AX), reg(DX))
                    else {
                        emit_2(SUBTRACT, reg(DX), reg(AX));
                        emit_2(MOVE, reg(AX), reg(DX));
                    }
                    result_tp = integer_typep;
                }

                /*
                -- Both operands are real, or one is real and the
                -- other is integer.  Convert the integer operand
                -- to real.  The result is real.  Call FLOAT_ADD or
                -- FLOAT_SUBTRACT.
                */
                else if (real_operands(result_tp, tp2)) {
                    emit_push_operand(tp2);
                    emit_promote_to_real(result_tp, tp2);

                    emit_1(CALL, name_lit(op == PLUS
                                           ? FLOAT_ADD
                                           : FLOAT_SUBTRACT));
                    emit_2(ADD, reg(SP), integer_lit(8));

                    result_tp = real_typep;
                }

                else {
                    error(INCOMPATIBLE_TYPES);
                    result_tp = &dummy_type;
                }

                break;
            }

            case OR: {
                /*
                -- boolean OR boolean => boolean
                -- AX = AX OR DX
                */
                if (boolean_operands(result_tp, tp2)) {
                    emit_1(POP, reg(DX));
                    emit_2(OR_BITS, reg(AX), reg(DX));
                }
                else error(INCOMPATIBLE_TYPES);

                result_tp = boolean_typep;
                break;
            }
        }
    }

    return(result_tp);
}

/*------------------------------------------------------*/
/*  term               Process a term consisting of factors    */
/*                     separated by *, /, DIV, MOD, or AND      */
/*                     operators.  Return a pointer to the      */
/*                     type structure.                          */
/*------------------------------------------------------*/
```

```
TOKEN_CODE mult_op_list[] = {STAR, SLASH, DIV, MOD, AND, 0};

    TYPE_STRUCT_PTR
term()

{
    TOKEN_CODE op;                    /* an operator token */
    TYPE_STRUCT_PTR result_tp, tp2;

    result_tp = factor();            /* first factor */

    /*
    -- Loop to process subsequent factors
    -- separated by operators.
    */
    while (token_in(mult_op_list)) {
        op = token;                   /* remember operator */

        result_tp = base_type(result_tp);
        emit_push_operand(result_tp);

        get_token();
        tp2 = base_type(factor());    /* subsequent factor */

        switch (op) {

            case STAR: {
                /*
                -- Both operands are integer.
                -- AX = AX*DX
                */
                if (integer_operands(result_tp, tp2)) {
                    emit_1(POP, reg(DX));
                    emit_1(MULTIPLY, reg(DX));

                    result_tp = integer_typep;
                }

                /*
                -- Both operands are real, or one is real and the
                -- other is integer.  Convert the integer operand
                -- to real.  The result is real.
                -- Call FLOAT_MULTIPLY.
                */
                else if (real_operands(result_tp, tp2)) {
                    emit_push_operand(tp2);
                    emit_promote_to_real(result_tp, tp2);

                    emit_1(CALL, name_lit(FLOAT_MULTIPLY));
                    emit_2(ADD, reg(SP), integer_lit(8));

                    result_tp = real_typep;
                }

                else {
                    error(INCOMPATIBLE_TYPES);
                    result_tp = &dummy_type;
                }

                break;
            }

            case SLASH: {
                /*
                -- Both operands are real, or both are integer, or
                -- one is real and the other is integer.  Convert
                -- any integer operand to real. The result is real.
```

```
                -- Call FLOAT_DIVIDE.
                */
                if (real_operands(result_tp, tp2) ||
                    integer_operands(result_tp, tp2)) {
                    emit_push_operand(tp2);
                    emit_promote_to_real(result_tp, tp2);

                    emit_1(CALL, name_lit(FLOAT_DIVIDE));
                    emit_2(ADD, reg(SP), integer_lit(8));
                }
                else error(INCOMPATIBLE_TYPES);

                result_tp = real_typep;
                break;
            }

            case DIV:
            case MOD: {
                /*
                -- integer <op> integer => integer
                -- AX = AX IDIV CX
                */
                if (integer_operands(result_tp, tp2)) {
                    emit_2(MOVE, reg(CX), reg(AX));
                    emit_1(POP, reg(AX));
                    emit_2(SUBTRACT, reg(DX), reg(DX));
                    emit_1(DIVIDE, reg(CX));
                    if (op == MOD) emit_2(MOVE, reg(AX), reg(DX));
                }
                else error(INCOMPATIBLE_TYPES);

                result_tp = integer_typep;
                break;
            }

            case AND: {
                /*
                -- boolean AND boolean => boolean
                -- AX = AX AND DX
                */
                if (boolean_operands(result_tp, tp2)) {
                    emit_1(POP, reg(DX));
                    emit_2(AND_BITS, reg(AX), reg(DX));
                }
                else error(INCOMPATIBLE_TYPES);

                result_tp = boolean_typep;
                break;
            }
        }
    }

    return(result_tp);
}

/*------------------------------------------------------------*/
/*  factor              Process a factor, which is a variable, */
/*                      a number, NOT followed by a factor, or  */
/*                      a parenthesized subexpression.  Return  */
/*                      a pointer to the type structure.        */
/*------------------------------------------------------------*/

    TYPE_STRUCT_PTR
factor()

{
    TYPE_STRUCT_PTR tp;
```

```
switch (token) {

    case IDENTIFIER: {
        SYMTAB_NODE_PTR idp;

        search_and_find_all_symtab(idp);

        switch (idp->defn.key) {

            case FUNC_DEFN:
                get_token();
                tp = routine_call(idp, TRUE);
                break;

            case PROC_DEFN:
                error(INVALID_IDENTIFIER_USAGE);
                get_token();
                actual_parm_list(idp, FALSE);
                tp = &dummy_type;
                break;

            case CONST_DEFN:
                tp = constant_identifier(idp);
                break;

            default:
                tp = variable(idp, EXPR_USE);
                break;
        }

        break;
    }

    case NUMBER: {
        if (literal.type == INTEGER_LIT) {
            /*
            -- AX = value
            */
            emit_2(MOVE, reg(AX),
                    integer_lit(literal.value.integer));
            tp = integer_typep;
        }

        else {  /* literal.type == REAL_LIT */
            /*
            -- DX:AX = value
            */
            tp = float_literal(token_string, literal.value.real);
        }

        get_token();
        break;
    }

    case STRING: {
        int length = strlen(literal.value.string);

        if (length == 1) {
            /*
            -- AH = 0
            -- AL = value
            */
            emit_2(MOVE, reg(AX),
                    char_lit(literal.value.string[0]));
            tp = char_typep;
        }
        else {
```

```
            /*
            -- AX = address of string
            */
            tp = string_literal(literal.value.string, length);
        }

        get_token();
        break;
    }

    case NOT:
        /*
        -- AX = NOT AX
        */
        get_token();
        tp = factor();
        emit_2(XOR_BITS, reg(AX), integer_lit(1));
        break;

    case LPAREN:
        get_token();
        tp = expression();

        if_token_get_else_error(RPAREN, MISSING_RPAREN);
        break;

    default:
        error(INVALID_EXPRESSION);
        tp = &dummy_type;
        break;
    }

    return(tp);
}

/*------------------------------------------------------*/
/* float_literal        Process a floating point literal.  */
/*------------------------------------------------------*/

    TYPE_STRUCT_PTR
float_literal(string, value)

    char  string[];
    float value;

{
    SYMTAB_NODE_PTR np = search_symtab(string, symtab_display[1]);

    /*
    -- Enter the literal into the symbol table
    -- if it isn't already in there.
    */
    if (np == NULL) {
        np = enter_symtab(string, symtab_display[1]);
        np->defn.key = CONST_DEFN;
        np->defn.info.constant.value.real = value;
        np->label_index = new_label_index();
        np->next = float_literal_list;
        float_literal_list = np;
    }

    /*
    -- DX:AX = value
    */
    emit_2(MOVE, reg(AX), word_label(FLOAT_LABEL_PREFIX,
                                np->label_index));
    emit_2(MOVE, reg(DX), high_dword_label(FLOAT_LABEL_PREFIX,
```

```
                                    np->label_index));

    return(real_typep);
}


/*------------------------------------------------------*/
/* string_literal      Process a string_literal.        */
/*------------------------------------------------------*/

    TYPE_STRUCT_PTR
string_literal(string, length)

    char string[];
    int  length;

{
    SYMTAB_NODE_PTR np;
    TYPE_STRUCT_PTR tp = make_string_typep(length);
    char            buffer[MAX_SOURCE_LINE_LENGTH];

    sprintf(buffer, "'%s'", string);
    np = search_symtab(buffer, symtab_display[1]);

    /*
    -- Enter the literal into the symbol table
    -- if it isn't already in there.
    */
    if (np == NULL) {
        np = enter_symtab(buffer, symtab_display[1]);
        np->defn.key = CONST_DEFN;
        np->label_index = new_label_index();
        np->next = string_literal_list;
        string_literal_list = np;
    }

    /*
    -- AX = address of string
    */
    emit_2(LOAD_ADDRESS, reg(AX),
        word_label(STRING_LABEL_PREFIX, np->label_index));
    emit_1(PUSH, reg(AX));
    return(tp);
}


/*------------------------------------------------------*/
/* constant_identifier      Process a constant identifier. */
/*------------------------------------------------------*/

    TYPE_STRUCT_PTR
constant_identifier(idp)

    SYMTAB_NODE_PTR idp;                /* id of constant */

{
    TYPE_STRUCT_PTR tp = idp->typep;    /* type of constant */

    get_token();

    if ((tp == integer_typep) || (tp->form == ENUM_FORM)) {
        /*
        -- AX = value
        */
        emit_2(MOVE, reg(AX),
            integer_lit(idp->defn.info.constant.value.integer));
    }
    else if (tp == char_typep) {
        /*
```

```
        -- AX = value
        */
        emit_2(MOVE, reg(AX),
                char_lit(idp->defn.info.constant.value.character));
    }
    else if (tp == real_typep) {
        /*
        -- Create a literal and then call float_literal.
        */
        float value = idp->defn.info.constant.value.real;
        char  string[MAX_SOURCE_LINE_LENGTH];

        sprintf(string, "%e", value);
        float_literal(string, value);
    }
    else /* string constant */ {
        string_literal(idp->defn.info.constant.value.stringp,
                strlen(idp->defn.info.constant.value.stringp));
    }

    return(tp);
}


/*------------------------------------------------------*/
/* variable              Process a variable, which can be a  */
/*                       simple identifier, an array identifier */
/*                       with subscripts, or a record identifier */
/*                       with fields.                          */
/*------------------------------------------------------*/

    TYPE_STRUCT_PTR
variable(var_idp, use)

    SYMTAB_NODE_PTR var_idp;    /* variable id */
    USE             use;        /* how variable is used */

{
    TYPE_STRUCT_PTR tp          = var_idp->typep;
    DEFN_KEY        defn_key    = var_idp->defn.key;
    BOOLEAN         varparm_flag = defn_key == VARPARM_DEFN;
    TYPE_STRUCT_PTR array_subscript_list();
    TYPE_STRUCT_PTR record_field();

    /*
    -- Check the variable's definition.
    */
    switch (defn_key) {
        case VAR_DEFN:
        case VALPARM_DEFN:
        case VARPARM_DEFN:
        case FUNC_DEFN:
        case UNDEFINED: break;        /* OK */

        default: {                    /* error */
            tp = &dummy_type;
            error(INVALID_IDENTIFIER_USAGE);
        }
    }

    get_token();

    /*
    -- There must not be a parameter list, but if there is one,
    -- parse it anyway for error recovery.
    */
    if (token == LPAREN) {
        error(UNEXPECTED_TOKEN);
```

```
        actual_parm_list(var_idp, FALSE);
        return(tp);
}


/*
-- Subscripts and/or field designators?
*/
if ((token == LBRACKET) || (token == PERIOD)) {
    /*
    -- Push the address of the array or record onto the
    -- stack, where it is then modified by code generated
    -- in array_subscript_list and record_field.
    */
    emit_push_address(var_idp);

    while ((token == LBRACKET) || (token == PERIOD)) {
        tp = token == LBRACKET ? array_subscript_list(tp)
                               : record_field(tp);

    }

    /*
    -- Leave the modified address on top of the stack if:
    --     it is an assignment target, or
    --     it represents a parameter passed by reference, or
    --     it is the address of an array or record.
    -- Otherwise, load AX with the value that the modified
    -- address points to.
    */
    if ((use != TARGET_USE) && (use != VARPARM_USE) &&
        (tp->form != ARRAY_FORM) && (tp->form != RECORD_FORM)) {
        emit_1(POP, reg(BX));
        if (tp == char_typep) {
            emit_2(SUBTRACT, reg(AX), reg(AX));
            emit_2(MOVE, reg(AL), byte_indirect(BX));
        }
        else if (tp == real_typep) {
            emit_2(MOVE, reg(AX), word_indirect(BX));
            emit_2(MOVE, reg(DX), high_dword_indirect(BX));
        }
        else emit_2(MOVE, reg(AX), word_indirect(BX));
    }
}
else if (use == TARGET_USE) {
    /*
    -- Push the address of an assignment target onto the stack,
    -- unless it is a local or global scalar parameter or
    -- variable.
    */
    if (defn_key == FUNC_DEFN)
        emit_push_return_value_address(var_idp);
    else if (varparm_flag || (tp->form == ARRAY_FORM) ||
             (tp->form == RECORD_FORM) ||
             ((var_idp->level > 1) && (var_idp->level < level)))
        emit_push_address(var_idp);
}
else if (use == VARPARM_USE) {
    /*
    -- Push the address of a variable
    -- being passed as a VAR parameter.
    */
    emit_push_address(var_idp);
}
else if ((tp->form == ARRAY_FORM) || (tp->form == RECORD_FORM)) {
    /*
    -- Push the address of an array or record value.
    */
```

```
        emit_push_address(var_idp);
    }
    else {
        /*
        -- AX = scalar value
        */
        emit_load_value(var_idp, base_type(tp));
    }

    return(tp);
}


/*-----------------------------------------------------------*/
/* array_subscript_list    Process a list of subscripts      */
/*                         following an array identifier:     */
/*                                                            */
/*                              [ <expr> , <expr> , ... ]      */
/*-----------------------------------------------------------*/

    TYPE_STRUCT_PTR
array_subscript_list(tp)

    TYPE_STRUCT_PTR tp;

{
    TYPE_STRUCT_PTR   index_tp, elmt_tp, ss_tp;
    int               min_index, elmt_size;
    extern TOKEN_CODE statement_end_list[];

    /*
    -- Loop to process a subscript list.
    */
    do {
        if (tp->form == ARRAY_FORM) {
            index_tp = tp->info.array.index_typep;
            elmt_tp  = tp->info.array.elmt_typep;

            get_token();
            ss_tp = expression();

            /*
            -- The subscript expression must be assignment type
            -- compatible with the corresponding subscript type.
            */
            if (!is_assign_type_compatible(index_tp, ss_tp))
                error(INCOMPATIBLE_TYPES);

            min_index = tp->info.array.min_index;
            elmt_size = tp->info.array.elmt_typep->size;

            /*
            -- Convert the subscript into an offset by subracting
            -- the mininum index from it and then multiplying the
            -- result by the element size.  Add the offset to the
            -- address at the top of the stack.
            */
            if (min_index != 0) emit_2(SUBTRACT, reg(AX),
                                       integer_lit(min_index));
            if (elmt_size > 1) {
                emit_2(MOVE, reg(DX), integer_lit(elmt_size));
                emit_1(MULTIPLY, reg(DX));
            }
            emit_1(POP,  reg(DX));
            emit_2(ADD,  reg(DX), reg(AX));
            emit_1(PUSH, reg(DX));

            tp = elmt_tp;
```

```
            }
        else {
            error(TOO_MANY_SUBSCRIPTS);
            while ((token != RBRACKET) &&
                    (! token_in(statement_end_list)))
                get_token();
        }
    } while (token == COMMA);

    if_token_get_else_error(RBRACKET, MISSING_RBRACKET);
    return(tp);
}

/*------------------------------------------------------------*/
/*  record_field              Process a field designation     */
/*                            following a record identifier:  */
/*                                                            */
/*                            . <field-variable>             */
/*------------------------------------------------------------*/

    TYPE_STRUCT_PTR
record_field(tp)

    TYPE_STRUCT_PTR tp;

{
    SYMTAB_NODE_PTR field_idp;

    get_token();

    if ((token == IDENTIFIER) && (tp->form == RECORD_FORM)) {
        search_this_symtab(field_idp,
                    tp->info.record.field_symtab);
        get_token();

        /*
        -- Add the field's offset (using the numeric equate)
        -- to the address at the top of the stack.
        */
        if (field_idp != NULL) {
            emit_1(POP,  reg(AX));
            emit_2(ADD,  reg(AX), tagged_name(field_idp));
            emit_1(PUSH, reg(AX));
            return(field_idp->typep);
        }
        else {
            error(INVALID_FIELD);
            return(&dummy_type);
        }
    }
    else {
        get_token();
        error(INVALID_FIELD);
        return(&dummy_type);
    }
}

        /********************************/
        /*                              */
        /*        Type compatibility    */
        /*                              */
        /********************************/

/*------------------------------------------------------------*/
/*  check_rel_op_types  Check the operand types for a rela-   */
/*                      tional operator.                      */
/*------------------------------------------------------------*/
```

```
check_rel_op_types(tp1, tp2)

    TYPE_STRUCT_PTR tp1, tp2;           /* operand types */

{
    /*
    -- Two identical scalar or enumeration types.
    */
    if (   (tp1 == tp2)
        && ((tp1->form == SCALAR_FORM) || (tp1->form == ENUM_FORM)))
        return;

    /*
    -- One integer and one real.
    */
    if (   ((tp1 == integer_typep) && (tp2 == real_typep))
        || ((tp2 == integer_typep) && (tp1 == real_typep))) return;

    /*
    -- Two strings of the same length.
    */
    if ((tp1->form == ARRAY_FORM) &&
        (tp2->form == ARRAY_FORM) &&
        (tp1->info.array.elmt_typep == char_typep) &&
        (tp2->info.array.elmt_typep == char_typep) &&
        (tp1->info.array.elmt_count ==
                        tp2->info.array.elmt_count)) return;

    error(INCOMPATIBLE_TYPES);
}

/*------------------------------------------------------------*/
/*  is_assign_type_compatible   Return TRUE iff a value of type */
/*                              tp1 can be assigned to a vari- */
/*                              able of type tp1.             */
/*------------------------------------------------------------*/

    BOOLEAN
is_assign_type_compatible(tp1, tp2)

    TYPE_STRUCT_PTR tp1, tp2;

{
    tp1 = base_type(tp1);
    tp2 = base_type(tp2);

    if (tp1 == tp2) return(TRUE);

    /*
    -- real := integer
    */
    if ((tp1 == real_typep) && (tp2 == integer_typep)) return(TRUE);

    /*
    -- string1 := string2 of the same length
    */
    if ((tp1->form == ARRAY_FORM) &&
        (tp2->form == ARRAY_FORM) &&
        (tp1->info.array.elmt_typep == char_typep) &&
        (tp2->info.array.elmt_typep == char_typep) &&
        (tp1->info.array.elmt_count ==
                        tp2->info.array.elmt_count)) return(TRUE);

    return(FALSE);
}

/*------------------------------------------------------------*/
/*  base_type           Return the range type of a subrange   */
```

```
/*                      type.                          */
/*------------------------------------------------------*/

    TYPE_STRUCT_PTR
base_type(tp)

    TYPE_STRUCT_PTR tp;
```

```
{
    return((tp->form == SUBRANGE_FORM)
                ? tp->info.subrange.range_typep
                : tp);
}
```

FIGURE B-7   scanner.h

```
/*****************************************************/
/*                                                 */
/*      S C A N N E R    (Header)                  */
/*                                                 */
/*      FILE:      scanner.h                       */
/*                                                 */
/*      MODULE:    scanner                         */
/*                                                 */
/*****************************************************/

#ifndef scanner_h
#define scanner_h

#include "common.h"

/*------------------------------------------------------*/
/*  Token codes                                        */
/*------------------------------------------------------*/

typedef enum {
    NO_TOKEN, IDENTIFIER, NUMBER, STRING,
    UPARROW, STAR, LPAREN, RPAREN, MINUS, PLUS, EQUAL,
    LBRACKET, RBRACKET, COLON, SEMICOLON, LT, GT, COMMA, PERIOD,
    SLASH, COLONEQUAL, LE, GE, NE, DOTDOT, END_OF_FILE, ERROR,
    AND, ARRAY, BEGIN, CASE, CONST, DIV, DO, DOWNTO, ELSE, END,
    FFILE, FOR, FUNCTION, GOTO, IF, IN, LABEL, MOD, NIL, NOT,
    OF, OR, PACKED, PROCEDURE, PROGRAM, RECORD, REPEAT, SET,
    THEN, TO, TYPE, UNTIL, VAR, WHILE, WITH,
} TOKEN_CODE;

/*------------------------------------------------------*/
/*  Literal structure                                  */
/*------------------------------------------------------*/

typedef enum {
    INTEGER_LIT, REAL_LIT, STRING_LIT,
} LITERAL_TYPE;

typedef struct {
    LITERAL_TYPE type;
    union {
        int    integer;
        float  real;
        char   string[MAX_SOURCE_LINE_LENGTH];
    } value;
} LITERAL;

/*------------------------------------------------------*/
/*  Functions                                          */
/*------------------------------------------------------*/

BOOLEAN token_in();

#endif
```

FIGURE B-8   scanner.c

```
/*****************************************************/
/*                                                 */
/*      S C A N N E R                              */
/*                                                 */
/*      Scanner for Pascal tokens.                 */
/*                                                 */
/*      FILE:      scanner.c                       */
/*                                                 */
/*      MODULE:    scanner                         */
/*                                                 */
/*****************************************************/

#include <stdio.h>
#include <math.h>
#include <sys/types.h>
#include <sys/timeb.h>
#include "common.h"
#include "error.h"
```

```
#include "scanner.h"

#define EOF_CHAR        '\x7f'
#define TAB_SIZE        8

#define MAX_INTEGER     32767
#define MAX_DIGIT_COUNT 20
#define MAX_EXPONENT    37

#define MIN_RESERVED_WORD_LENGTH    2
#define MAX_RESERVED_WORD_LENGTH    9

/*------------------------------------------------------*/
/*  Character codes                                    */
/*------------------------------------------------------*/

typedef enum {
    LETTER, DIGIT, QUOTE, SPECIAL, EOF_CODE,
```

```
} CHAR_CODE;

/*------------------------------------------------------*/
/*  Reserved word tables                              */
/*------------------------------------------------------*/

typedef struct {
    char      *string;
    TOKEN_CODE token_code;
} RW_STRUCT;

RW_STRUCT rw_2[] = {
    {"do", DO}, {"if", IF}, {"in", IN}, {"of", OF}, {"or", OR},
    {"to", TO}, {NULL, 0 },
};

RW_STRUCT rw_3[] = {
    {"and", AND}, {"div", DIV}, {"end", END}, {"for", FOR},
    {"mod", MOD}, {"nil", NIL}, {"not", NOT}, {"set", SET},
    {"var", VAR}, {NULL, 0 },
};

RW_STRUCT rw_4[] = {
    {"case", CASE}, {"else", ELSE}, {"file", FFILE},
    {"goto", GOTO}, {"then", THEN}, {"type", TYPE},
    {"with", WITH}, {NULL , 0  },
};

RW_STRUCT rw_5[] = {
    {"array", ARRAY}, {"begin", BEGIN}, {"const", CONST},
    {"label", LABEL}, {"until", UNTIL}, {"while", WHILE},
    {NULL , 0  },
};

RW_STRUCT rw_6[] = {
    {"downto", DOWNTO}, {"packed", PACKED}, {"record", RECORD},
    {"repeat", REPEAT}, {NULL , 0  },
};

RW_STRUCT rw_7[] = {
    {"program", PROGRAM}, {NULL, 0},
};

RW_STRUCT rw_8[] = {
    {"function", FUNCTION}, {NULL, 0},
};

RW_STRUCT rw_9[] = {
    {"procedure", PROCEDURE}, {NULL, 0},
};

RW_STRUCT *rw_table[] = {
    NULL, NULL, rw_2, rw_3, rw_4, rw_5, rw_6, rw_7, rw_8, rw_9,
};

/*------------------------------------------------------*/
/*  Token lists                                        */
/*------------------------------------------------------*/

TOKEN_CODE statement_start_list[]  = {BEGIN, CASE, FOR, IF, REPEAT,
                                      WHILE, IDENTIFIER, 0};

TOKEN_CODE statement_end_list[]    = {SEMICOLON, END, ELSE, UNTIL,
                                      END_OF_FILE, 0};

TOKEN_CODE declaration_start_list[] = {CONST, TYPE, VAR, PROCEDURE,
                                       FUNCTION, 0};
```

```
/*------------------------------------------------------*/
/*  Globals                                            */
/*------------------------------------------------------*/

char       ch;              /* current input character */
TOKEN_CODE token;           /* code of current token */
LITERAL    literal;         /* value of literal */
int        buffer_offset;   /* char offset into source buffer */
int        level = 0;       /* current nesting level */
int        line_number = 0; /* current line number */
BOOLEAN    print_flag = TRUE;  /* TRUE to print source lines */
BOOLEAN    block_flag = FALSE; /* TRUE only when parsing a block */

char source_buffer[MAX_SOURCE_LINE_LENGTH]; /* source file buffer */
char token_string[MAX_TOKEN_STRING_LENGTH]; /* token string */
char word_string[MAX_TOKEN_STRING_LENGTH];  /* downshifted */
char *bufferp = source_buffer;    /* source buffer ptr */
char *tokenp  = token_string;     /* token string ptr */

int     digit_count;        /* total no. of digits in number */
BOOLEAN count_error;        /* too many digits in number? */

int page_number = 0;
int line_count  = MAX_LINES_PER_PAGE;   /* no. lines on current pg */

char source_name[MAX_FILE_NAME_LENGTH]; /* name of source file */
char date[DATE_STRING_LENGTH];          /* current date and time */

FILE *source_file;

CHAR_CODE char_table[256];

/*------------------------------------------------------*/
/*  char_code        Return the character code of ch.   */
/*------------------------------------------------------*/

#define char_code(ch)   char_table[ch]

           /********************************/
           /*                            */
           /*        Initialization      */
           /*                            */
           /********************************/

/*------------------------------------------------------*/
/*  init_scanner      Initialize the scanner globals    */
/*                    and open the source file.         */
/*------------------------------------------------------*/

init_scanner(name)

    char *name;        /* name of source file */

{
    int ch;

    /*
    -- Initialize character table.
    */
    for (ch = 0;   ch < 256;  ++ch) char_table[ch] = SPECIAL;
    for (ch = '0'; ch <= '9'; ++ch) char_table[ch] = DIGIT;
    for (ch = 'A'; ch <= 'Z'; ++ch) char_table[ch] = LETTER;
    for (ch = 'a'; ch <= 'z'; ++ch) char_table[ch] = LETTER;
    char_table['\''] = QUOTE;
    char_table[EOF_CHAR] = EOF_CODE;

    init_page_header(name);
```

```
        open_source_file(name);
}

/*-----------------------------------------------------*/
/*  quit_scanner      Terminate the scanner.          */
/*-----------------------------------------------------*/

quit_scanner()

{
    close_source_file();
}

            /********************************/
            /*                              */
            /*        Character routines    */
            /*                              */
            /********************************/

/*-----------------------------------------------------*/
/*  get_char          Set ch to the next character from the */
/*                    source buffer.                  */
/*-----------------------------------------------------*/

get_char()

{
    BOOLEAN get_source_line();

    /*
    -- If at end of current source line, read another line.
    -- If at end of file, set ch to the EOF character and return.
    */
    if (*bufferp == '\0') {
        if (! get_source_line()) {
            ch = EOF_CHAR;
            return;
        }
        bufferp = source_buffer;
        buffer_offset = 0;
    }

    ch = *bufferp++;    /* next character in the buffer */

    /*
    -- Special character processing:
    --
    --      tab         Increment buffer_offset up to the next
    --                  multiple of TAB_SIZE, and replace ch with
    --                  a blank.
    --
    --      new-line    Replace ch with a blank.
    --
    --      {           Start of comment:  Skip over comment and
    --                  replace it with a blank.
    */
    switch (ch) {

        case '\t':  buffer_offset += TAB_SIZE -
                                    buffer_offset%TAB_SIZE;
                    ch = ' ';
                    break;

        case '\n':  ++buffer_offset;
                    ch = ' ';
                    break;

        case '{':   ++buffer_offset;
```

```
                    skip_comment();
                    ch = ' ';
                    break;

        default:    ++buffer_offset;
    }
}

/*-----------------------------------------------------*/
/*  skip_comment      Skip over a comment.  Set ch to '}'. */
/*-----------------------------------------------------*/

skip_comment()

{
    do {
        get_char();
    } while ((ch != '}') && (ch != EOF_CHAR));
}

/*-----------------------------------------------------*/
/*  skip_blanks       Skip past any blanks at the current */
/*                    location in the source buffer.  Set */
/*                    ch to the next nonblank character.  */
/*-----------------------------------------------------*/

skip_blanks()

{
    while (ch == ' ') get_char();
}

            /********************************/
            /*                              */
            /*        Token routines        */
            /*                              */
            /********************************/

        /* Note that after a token has been extracted, */
        /* ch is the first character after the token.  */

/*-----------------------------------------------------*/
/*  get_token         Extract the next token from the source */
/*                    buffer.                         */
/*-----------------------------------------------------*/

get_token()

{
    skip_blanks();
    tokenp = token_string;

    switch (char_code(ch)) {
        case LETTER:    get_word();                 break;
        case DIGIT:     get_number();               break;
        case QUOTE:     get_string();               break;
        case EOF_CODE:  token = END_OF_FILE;        break;
        default:        get_special();              break;
    }
}

/*-----------------------------------------------------*/
/*  get_word          Extract a word token and downshift its */
/*                    characters.  Check if it's a reserved */
/*                    word.  Set token to IDENTIFIER if it's */
/*                    not.                            */
/*-----------------------------------------------------*/
```

```
get_word()

{
    BOOLEAN is_reserved_word();

    /*
    -- Extract the word.
    */
    while ((char_code(ch) == LETTER) || (char_code(ch) == DIGIT)) {
        *tokenp++ = ch;
        get_char();
    }
    *tokenp = '\0';
    downshift_word();

    if (! is_reserved_word()) token = IDENTIFIER;
}

/*------------------------------------------------------------*/
/* get_number          Extract a number token and set literal */
/*                     to its value.  Set token to NUMBER.     */
/*------------------------------------------------------------*/

get_number()

{
    int     whole_count    = 0;      /* no. digits in whole part */
    int     decimal_offset = 0;      /* no. digits to move decimal */
    char    exponent_sign  = '+';
    int     exponent       = 0;      /* value of exponent */
    float   nvalue         = 0.0;    /* value of number */
    float   evalue         = 0.0;    /* value of exponent */
    BOOLEAN saw_dotdot     = FALSE;  /* TRUE if encounter .. */

    digit_count  = 0;
    count_error  = FALSE;
    token        = NO_TOKEN;

    literal.type = INTEGER_LIT;      /* assume it's an integer */

    /*
    -- Extract the whole part of the number by accumulating
    -- the values of its digits into nvalue.  whole_count keeps
    -- track of the number of digits in this part.
    */
    accumulate_value(&nvalue, INVALID_NUMBER);
    if (token == ERROR) return;
    whole_count = digit_count;

    /*
    -- If the current character is a dot, then either we have a
    -- fraction part or we are seeing the first character of a ..
    -- token.  To find out, we must fetch the next character.
    */
    if (ch == '.') {
        get_char();

        if (ch == '.') {
            /*
            -- We have a .. token.  Back up bufferp so that the
            -- token can be extracted next.
            */
            saw_dotdot = TRUE;
            --bufferp;
        }
        else {
            literal.type = REAL_LIT;
            *tokenp++ = '.';

            /*
            -- We have a fraction part.  Accumulate it into nvalue.
            -- decimal_offset keeps track of how many digits to move
            -- the decimal point back.
            */
            accumulate_value(&nvalue, INVALID_FRACTION);
            if (token == ERROR) return;
            decimal_offset = whole_count - digit_count;
        }
    }

    /*
    -- Extract the exponent part, if any. There cannot be an
    -- exponent part if the .. token has been seen.
    */
    if (!saw_dotdot && ((ch == 'E') || (ch == 'e'))) {
        literal.type = REAL_LIT;
        *tokenp++ = ch;
        get_char();

        /*
        -- Fetch the exponent's sign, if any.
        */
        if ((ch == '+') || (ch == '-')) {
            *tokenp++ = exponent_sign = ch;
            get_char();
        }

        /*
        -- Extract the exponent.  Accumulate it into evalue.
        */
        accumulate_value(&evalue, INVALID_EXPONENT);
        if (token == ERROR) return;
        if (exponent_sign == '-') evalue = -evalue;
    }

    /*
    -- Were there too many digits?
    */
    if (count_error) {
        error(TOO_MANY_DIGITS);
        token = ERROR;
        return;
    }

    /*
    -- Adjust the number's value using
    -- decimal_offset and the exponent.
    */
    exponent = evalue + decimal_offset;
    if ((exponent + whole_count < -MAX_EXPONENT) ||
        (exponent + whole_count >  MAX_EXPONENT)) {
        error(REAL_OUT_OF_RANGE);
        token = ERROR;
        return;
    }
    if (exponent != 0) nvalue *= pow(10, exponent);

    /*
    -- Set the literal's value.
    */
    if (literal.type == INTEGER_LIT) {
        if ((nvalue < -MAX_INTEGER) || (nvalue > MAX_INTEGER)) {
            error(INTEGER_OUT_OF_RANGE);
            token = ERROR;
```

```
            return;
        }
        literal.value.integer = nvalue;
    }
    else literal.value.real = nvalue;

    *tokenp = '\0';
    token   = NUMBER;
}

/*-----------------------------------------------------*/
/* get_string          Extract a string token.  Set token to  */
/*                     STRING.  Note that the quotes are       */
/*                     stored as part of token_string but not  */
/*                     literal.value.string.                   */
/*-----------------------------------------------------*/

get_string()

{
    char *sp = literal.value.string;

    *tokenp++ = '\'';
    get_char();

    /*
    -- Extract the string.
    */
    while (ch != EOF_CHAR) {
        /*
        -- Two consecutive single quotes represent
        -- a single quote in the string.
        */
        if (ch == '\'') {
            *tokenp++ = ch;
            get_char();
            if (ch != '\'') break;
        }
        *tokenp++ = ch;
        *sp++     = ch;
        get_char();
    }

    *tokenp      = '\0';
    *sp          = '\0';
    token        = STRING;
    literal.type = STRING_LIT;
}

/*-----------------------------------------------------*/
/* get_special         Extract a special token.  Most are      */
/*                     single-character.  Some are double-      */
/*                     character.  Set token appropriately.     */
/*-----------------------------------------------------*/

get_special()

{
    *tokenp++ = ch;
    switch (ch) {
        case '^':  token = UPARROW;  get_char();  break;
        case '*':  token = STAR;     get_char();  break;
        case '(':  token = LPAREN;   get_char();  break;
        case ')':  token = RPAREN;   get_char();  break;
        case '-':  token = MINUS;    get_char();  break;
        case '+':  token = PLUS;     get_char();  break;
        case '=':  token = EQUAL;    get_char();  break;
```

```
        case '[':  token = LBRACKET;  get_char();  break;
        case ']':  token = RBRACKET;  get_char();  break;
        case ';':  token = SEMICOLON; get_char();  break;
        case ',':  token = COMMA;     get_char();  break;
        case '/':  token = SLASH;     get_char();  break;

        case ':':  get_char();          /* : or := */
                   if (ch == '=') {
                       *tokenp++ = '=';
                       token     = COLONEQUAL;
                       get_char();
                   }
                   else token = COLON;
                   break;

        case '<':  get_char();          /* < or <= or <> */
                   if (ch == '=') {
                       *tokenp++ = '=';
                       token     = LE;
                       get_char();
                   }
                   else if (ch == '>') {
                       *tokenp++ = '>';
                       token     = NE;
                       get_char();
                   }
                   else token = LT;
                   break;

        case '>':  get_char();          /* > or >= */
                   if (ch == '=') {
                       *tokenp++ = '=';
                       token     = GE;
                       get_char();
                   }
                   else token = GT;
                   break;

        case '.':  get_char();          /* . or .. */
                   if (ch == '.') {
                       *tokenp++ = '.';
                       token     = DOTDOT;
                       get_char();
                   }
                   else token = PERIOD;
                   break;

        default:   token = ERROR;
                   get_char();
                   break;
    }
    *tokenp = '\0';
}

/*-----------------------------------------------------*/
/* downshift_word      Copy a word token into word_string      */
/*                     with all letters downshifted.           */
/*-----------------------------------------------------*/

downshift_word()

{
    int  offset = 'a' - 'A';   /* offset to downshift a letter */
    char *wp    = word_string;
    char *tp    = token_string;

    /*
```

```
        -- Copy word into word_string.
    */
    do {
        *wp++ = (*tp >= 'A') && (*tp <= 'Z')    /* if a letter,   */
                    ? *tp + offset              /* then downshift */
                    : *tp;                      /* else just copy */
        ++tp;
    } while (*tp != '\0');

    *wp = '\0';
}

/*------------------------------------------------------*/
/*  accumulate_value    Extract a number part and accumulate    */
/*                      its value.  Flag the error if the first */
/*                      character is not a digit.               */
/*------------------------------------------------------*/

accumulate_value(valuep, error_code)

    float       *valuep;
    ERROR_CODE error_code;

{
    float value = *valuep;

    /*
    -- Error if the first character is not a digit.
    */
    if (char_code(ch) != DIGIT) {
        error(error_code);
        token = ERROR;
        return;
    }

    /*
    -- Accumulate the value as long as the total allowable
    -- number of digits has not been exceeded.
    */
    do {
        *tokenp++ = ch;

        if (++digit_count <= MAX_DIGIT_COUNT)
            value = 10*value + (ch - '0');
        else count_error = TRUE;

        get_char();
    } while (char_code(ch) == DIGIT);

    *valuep = value;
}

        /*******************************/
        /*                             */
        /*      Token testers          */
        /*                             */
        /*******************************/

/*------------------------------------------------------*/
/*  token_in            Return TRUE if the current token is in */
/*                      the token list, else return FALSE.     */
/*------------------------------------------------------*/

    BOOLEAN
token_in(token_list)

    TOKEN_CODE token_list[];
```

```
{
    TOKEN_CODE *tokenp;

    if (token_list == NULL) return(FALSE);

    for (tokenp = &token_list[0]; *tokenp; ++tokenp) {
        if (token == *tokenp) return(TRUE);
    }

    return(FALSE);
}

/*------------------------------------------------------*/
/*  synchronize         If the current token is not in one of  */
/*                      the token lists, flag it as an error.  */
/*                      Then skip tokens until one that is in  */
/*                      one of the token lists.                */
/*------------------------------------------------------*/

synchronize(token_list1, token_list2, token_list3)

    TOKEN_CODE token_list1[], token_list2[], token_list3[];

{
    BOOLEAN error_flag = (! token_in(token_list1)) &&
                         (! token_in(token_list2)) &&
                         (! token_in(token_list3));

    if (error_flag) {
        error(token == END_OF_FILE ? UNEXPECTED_END_OF_FILE
                                   : UNEXPECTED_TOKEN);

        /*
        -- Skip tokens to resynchronize.
        */
        while ((! token_in(token_list1)) &&
               (! token_in(token_list2)) &&
               (! token_in(token_list3)) &&
               (token != END_OF_FILE))
            get_token();
    }
}


/*------------------------------------------------------*/
/*  is_reserved_word    Check to see if a word token is a      */
/*                      reserved word.  If so, set token       */
/*                      appropriately and return TRUE.  Else,  */
/*                      return FALSE.                          */
/*------------------------------------------------------*/

    BOOLEAN
is_reserved_word()

{
    int     word_length = strlen(word_string);
    RW_STRUCT *rwp;

    /*
    -- Is it the right length?
    */
    if ((word_length >= MIN_RESERVED_WORD_LENGTH) &&
        (word_length <= MAX_RESERVED_WORD_LENGTH)) {
        /*
        -- Yes.  Pick the appropriate reserved word list
        -- and check to see if the word is in there.
        */
```

```
        for (rwp = rw_table[word_length];
             rwp->string != NULL;
             ++rwp) {
            if (strcmp(word_string, rwp->string) == 0) {
                token = rwp->token_code;
                return(TRUE);              /* yes, a reserved word */
            }
        }
    }

    return(FALSE);                         /* no, it's not */
}


              /********************************/
              /*                              */
              /*       Source file routines   */
              /*                              */
              /********************************/

/*--------------------------------------------------------------*/
/* open_source_file     Open the source file and fetch its      */
/*                      first character.                        */
/*--------------------------------------------------------------*/

open_source_file(name)

    char *name;        /* name of source file */

{
    if ((name == NULL) ||
        ((source_file = fopen(name, "r")) == NULL)) {
        error(FAILED_SOURCE_FILE_OPEN);
        exit(-FAILED_SOURCE_FILE_OPEN);
    }

    /*
    -- Fetch the first character.
    */
    bufferp = ""       ;
    get_char();
}


/*--------------------------------------------------------------*/
/* close_source_file   Close the source file.                   */
/*--------------------------------------------------------------*/

close_source_file()

{
    fclose(source_file);
}


/*--------------------------------------------------------------*/
/* get_source_line      Read the next line from the source      */
/*                      file. If there is one, print it out      */
/*                      and return TRUE. Else return FALSE       */
/*                      for the end of file.                     */
/*--------------------------------------------------------------*/

    BOOLEAN
get_source_line()

{
    char print_buffer[MAX_SOURCE_LINE_LENGTH + 9];
    extern FILE *code_file;

    if ((fgets(source_buffer, MAX_SOURCE_LINE_LENGTH,
                                   source_file)) != NULL) {
        ++line_number;

        if (print_flag) {
            sprintf(print_buffer, "%4d %d: %s",
                         line_number, level, source_buffer);
            print_line(print_buffer);
        }

        fprintf(code_file, "; %4d: %s", line_number, source_buffer);
        return(TRUE);
    }
    else return(FALSE);
}


              /********************************/
              /*                              */
              /*       Printout routines      */
              /*                              */
              /********************************/

/*--------------------------------------------------------------*/
/* print_line          Print out a line. Start a new page if    */
/*                      the current page is full.                */
/*--------------------------------------------------------------*/

print_line(line)

    char line[];        /* line to be printed */

{
    char save_ch;
    char *save_chp = NULL;

    if (++line_count > MAX_LINES_PER_PAGE) {
        print_page_header();
        line_count = 1;
    };

    if (strlen(line) > MAX_PRINT_LINE_LENGTH) {
        save_chp = &line[MAX_PRINT_LINE_LENGTH];
        save_ch  = *save_chp;
        *save_chp = '\0';
    }

    printf("%s", line);

    if (save_chp) *save_chp = save_ch;
}

/*--------------------------------------------------------------*/
/* init_page_header     Initialize the fields of the page       */
/*                      header.                                  */
/*--------------------------------------------------------------*/

init_page_header(name)

    char *name;        /* name of source file */

{
    time_t timer;

    strncpy(source_name, name, MAX_FILE_NAME_LENGTH - 1);

    /*
    -- Set the current date and time in the date string.
    */
```

```
    time(&timer);
    strcpy(date, asctime(localtime(&timer)));
}


/*------------------------------------------------*/
/* print_page_header   Print the page header at the top of   */
/*                     the next page.                        */
```

```
/*------------------------------------------------------*/
print_page_header()

{
    putchar(FORM_FEED_CHAR);
    printf("Page %d   %s   %s\n\n", ++page_number, source_name, date);
}
```

FIGURE B-9   symtab.h

```
/***************************************************************/
/*                                                             */
/*      S Y M B O L   T A B L E    (Header)                    */
/*                                                             */
/*      FILE:      symtab.h                                    */
/*                                                             */
/*      MODULE:    symbol table                                */
/*                                                             */
/***************************************************************/

#ifndef symtab_h
#define symtab_h

#include "common.h"

/*------------------------------------------------------*/
/* Value structure                                      */
/*------------------------------------------------------*/

typedef union {
    int    integer;
    float  real;
    char   character;
    char   *stringp;
} VALUE;

/*------------------------------------------------------*/
/* Definition structure                                 */
/*------------------------------------------------------*/

typedef enum {
    UNDEFINED,
    CONST_DEFN, TYPE_DEFN, VAR_DEFN, FIELD_DEFN,
    VALPARM_DEFN, VARPARM_DEFN,
    PROG_DEFN, PROC_DEFN, FUNC_DEFN,
} DEFN_KEY;

typedef enum {
    DECLARED, FORWARD,
    READ, READLN, WRITE, WRITELN,
    ABS, ARCTAN, CHR, COS, EOFF, EOLN, EXP, LN, ODD, ORD,
    PRED, ROUND, SIN, SQR, SQRT, SUCC, TRUNC,
} ROUTINE_KEY;

typedef struct {
    DEFN_KEY key;
    union {
        struct {
            VALUE value;
        } constant;

        struct {
```

```
            ROUTINE_KEY       key;
            int               parm_count;
            int               total_parm_size;
            int               total_local_size;
            struct symtab_node *parms;
            struct symtab_node *locals;
            struct symtab_node *local_symtab;
            char              *code_segment;
        } routine;

        struct {
            int               offset;
            struct symtab_node *record_idp;
        } data;
    } info;
} DEFN_STRUCT;

/*------------------------------------------------------*/
/* Type structure                                       */
/*------------------------------------------------------*/

typedef enum {
    NO_FORM,
    SCALAR_FORM, ENUM_FORM, SUBRANGE_FORM,
    ARRAY_FORM, RECORD_FORM,
} TYPE_FORM;

typedef struct type_struct {
    TYPE_FORM         form;
    int               size;
    struct symtab_node *type_idp;
    union {
        struct {
            struct symtab_node *const_idp;
            int               max;
        } enumeration;

        struct {
            struct type_struct *range_typep;
            int               min, max;
        } subrange;

        struct {
            struct type_struct *index_typep, *elmt_typep;
            int               min_index, max_index;
            int               elmt_count;
        } array;

        struct {
            struct symtab_node *field_symtab;
        } record;
    } info;
```

```
} TYPE_STRUCT, *TYPE_STRUCT_PTR;
```

```
/*----------------------------------------------*/
/*  Symbol table node                         */
/*----------------------------------------------*/
```

```
typedef struct symtab_node {
    struct symtab_node *left, *right;   /* ptrs to subtrees */
    struct symtab_node *next;           /* for chaining nodes */
    char               *name;           /* name string */
    char               *info;           /* ptr to generic info */
    DEFN_STRUCT        defn;            /* definition struct */
    TYPE_STRUCT_PTR    typep;           /* ptr to type struct */
    int                level;           /* nesting level */
    int                label_index;     /* index for code label */
} SYMTAB_NODE, *SYMTAB_NODE_PTR;
```

```
/*----------------------------------------------*/
/*  Functions                                 */
/*----------------------------------------------*/
```

```
SYMTAB_NODE_PTR search_symtab();
SYMTAB_NODE_PTR search_symtab_display();
SYMTAB_NODE_PTR enter_symtab();
SYMTAB_NODE_PTR exit_scope();
TYPE_STRUCT_PTR make_string_typep();
```

```
        /****************************************/
        /*                                      */
        /*      Macros to search symbol tables  */
        /*                                      */
        /****************************************/
```

```
/*----------------------------------------------*/
/*  search_local_symtab      Search the local symbol   */
/*                           table for the current id  */
/*                           name.  Set a pointer to the */
/*                           entry if found, else to   */
/*                           NULL.                      */
/*----------------------------------------------*/
```

```
#define search_local_symtab(idp)                          \
    idp = search_symtab(word_string, symtab_display[level])
```

```
/*----------------------------------------------*/
/*  search_this_symtab       Search the given symbol   */
/*                           table for the current id  */
/*                           name.  Set a pointer to the */
/*                           entry if found, else to   */
/*                           NULL.                      */
/*----------------------------------------------*/
```

```
#define search_this_symtab(idp, this_symtab)              \
    idp = search_symtab(word_string, this_symtab)
```

```
/*----------------------------------------------*/
/*  search_all_symtab        Search the symbol table   */
/*                           display for the current id */
/*                           name.  Set a pointer to the */
/*                           entry if found, else to   */
/*                           NULL.                      */
/*----------------------------------------------*/
```

```
#define search_all_symtab(idp)                            \
```

```
    idp = search_symtab_display(word_string)
```

```
/*----------------------------------------------*/
/*  enter_local_symtab        Enter the current id name */
/*                            into the local symbol    */
/*                            table, and set a pointer  */
/*                            to the entry.             */
/*----------------------------------------------*/
```

```
#define enter_local_symtab(idp)                           \
    idp = enter_symtab(word_string, &symtab_display[level])
```

```
/*----------------------------------------------*/
/*  enter_name_local_symtab   Enter the given name into */
/*                            the local symbol table, and */
/*                            set a pointer to the entry. */
/*----------------------------------------------*/
```

```
#define enter_name_local_symtab(idp, name)                \
    idp = enter_symtab(name, &symtab_display[level])
```

```
/*----------------------------------------------*/
/*  search_and_find_all_symtab   Search the symbol table  */
/*                               display for the current id */
/*                               name.  If not found, ID */
/*                               UNDEFINED error, and enter */
/*                               into the local symbol table. */
/*                               Set a pointer to the entry. */
/*----------------------------------------------*/
```

```
#define search_and_find_all_symtab(idp)                               \
    if ((idp = search_symtab_display(word_string)) == NULL) {         \
        error(UNDEFINED_IDENTIFIER);                                  \
        idp = enter_symtab(word_string, &symtab_display[level]);      \
        idp->defn.key = UNDEFINED;                                    \
        idp->typep = &dummy_type;                                     \
    }
```

```
/*----------------------------------------------*/
/*  search_and_enter_local_symtab   Search the local symbol */
/*                                  table for the current id */
/*                                  name.  Enter the name if */
/*                                  it is not already in there, */
/*                                  else ID REDEFINED error. */
/*                                  Set a pointer to the entry. */
/*----------------------------------------------*/
```

```
#define search_and_enter_local_symtab(idp)                            \
    if ((idp = search_symtab(word_string,                             \
                        symtab_display[level])) == NULL) {            \
        idp = enter_symtab(word_string, &symtab_display[level]);      \
    }                                                                 \
    else error(REDEFINED_IDENTIFIER)
```

```
/*----------------------------------------------*/
/*  search_and_enter_this_symtab   Search the given symbol */
/*                                 table for the current id */
/*                                 name.  Enter the name if */
/*                                 it is not already in there, */
/*                                 else ID REDEFINED error. */
/*                                 Set a pointer to the entry. */
/*----------------------------------------------*/
```

```
#define search_and_enter_this_symtab(idp, this_symtab)        \                    }                                            \
    if ((idp = search_symtab(word_string,                     \               else error(REDEFINED_IDENTIFIER)
                     this_symtab)) == NULL) {                  \
        idp = enter_symtab(word_string, &this_symtab);         \        #endif
```

FIGURE B-10   symtab.c

```
/****************************************************************/
/*                                                              */
/*        S Y M B O L   T A B L E                               */
/*                                                              */
/*        Symbol table routines.                                */
/*                                                              */
/*        FILE:       symtab.c                                  */
/*                                                              */
/*        MODULE:     symbol table                              */
/*                                                              */
/****************************************************************/

#include <stdio.h>
#include "common.h"
#include "error.h"
#include "symtab.h"

/*--------------------------------------------------------------*/
/* Externals                                                    */
/*--------------------------------------------------------------*/

extern int level;

/*--------------------------------------------------------------*/
/* Globals                                                      */
/*--------------------------------------------------------------*/

SYMTAB_NODE_PTR symtab_display[MAX_NESTING_LEVEL];

TYPE_STRUCT_PTR integer_typep, real_typep,        /* predefined types */
                boolean_typep, char_typep;

TYPE_STRUCT dummy_type = {          /* for erroneous type definitions */
    NO_FORM,        /* form */
    0,              /* size */
    NULL            /* type_idp */
};

/*--------------------------------------------------------------*/
/* search_symtab      Search for a name in the symbol table.    */
/*                    Return a pointer of the entry if found,   */
/*                    or NULL if not.                           */
/*--------------------------------------------------------------*/

    SYMTAB_NODE_PTR
search_symtab(name, np)

    char            *name;          /* name to search for */
    SYMTAB_NODE_PTR np;             /* ptr to symtab root */

{
    int cmp;

    /*
    -- Loop to check each node.  Return if the node matches,
```

```
    -- else continue search down the left or right subtree.
    */
    while (np != NULL) {
        cmp = strcmp(name, np->name);
        if (cmp == 0) return(np);                    /* found */
        np = cmp < 0 ? np->left : np->right;   /* continue search */
    }

    return(NULL);                                /* not found */
}

/*--------------------------------------------------------------*/
/* search_symtab_display   Search all the symbol tables in the  */
/*                         symbol table display for a name.     */
/*                         Return a pointer to the entry if     */
/*                         found, or NULL if not.               */
/*--------------------------------------------------------------*/

    SYMTAB_NODE_PTR
search_symtab_display(name)

    char *name;                 /* name to search for */

{
    short i;
    SYMTAB_NODE_PTR np;         /* ptr to symtab node */

    for (i = level; i >= 0; --i) {
        np = search_symtab(name, symtab_display[i]);
        if (np != NULL) return(np);
    }

    return(NULL);
}

/*--------------------------------------------------------------*/
/* enter_symtab        Enter a name into the symbol table,      */
/*                     and return a pointer to the new entry.   */
/*--------------------------------------------------------------*/

    SYMTAB_NODE_PTR
enter_symtab(name, npp)

    char            *name;      /* name to enter */
    SYMTAB_NODE_PTR *npp;       /* ptr to ptr to symtab root */

{
    int             cmp;        /* result of strcmp */
    SYMTAB_NODE_PTR new_nodep;  /* ptr to new entry */
    SYMTAB_NODE_PTR np;         /* ptr to node to test */

    /*
    -- Create the new node for the name.
    */
    new_nodep = alloc_struct(SYMTAB_NODE);
```

```
new_nodep->name = alloc_bytes(strlen(name) + 1);
strcpy(new_nodep->name, name);
new_nodep->left = new_nodep->right = new_nodep->next = NULL;
new_nodep->info = NULL;
new_nodep->defn.key = UNDEFINED;
new_nodep->typep = NULL;
new_nodep->level = level;
new_nodep->label_index = 0;

/*
-- Loop to search for the insertion point.
*/
while ((np = *npp) != NULL) {
    cmp = strcmp(name, np->name);
    npp = cmp < 0 ? &(np->left) : &(np->right);
}

*npp = new_nodep;                    /* replace */
return(new_nodep);
}

/*------------------------------------------------------------*/
/*  init_symtab         Initialize the symbol table with      */
/*                      predefined identifiers and types,     */
/*                      and routines.                         */
/*------------------------------------------------------------*/

init_symtab()

{
    SYMTAB_NODE_PTR integer_idp, real_idp, boolean_idp, char_idp,
                    false_idp, true_idp;

    /*
    -- Initialize the level-0 symbol table.
    */
    symtab_display[0] = NULL;

    enter_name_local_symtab(integer_idp, "integer");
    enter_name_local_symtab(real_idp,    "real");
    enter_name_local_symtab(boolean_idp, "boolean");
    enter_name_local_symtab(char_idp,    "char");
    enter_name_local_symtab(false_idp,   "false");
    enter_name_local_symtab(true_idp,    "true");

    integer_typep = alloc_struct(TYPE_STRUCT);
    real_typep    = alloc_struct(TYPE_STRUCT);
    boolean_typep = alloc_struct(TYPE_STRUCT);
    char_typep    = alloc_struct(TYPE_STRUCT);

    integer_idp->defn.key    = TYPE_DEFN;
    integer_idp->typep       = integer_typep;
    integer_typep->form      = SCALAR_FORM;
    integer_typep->size      = sizeof(int);
    integer_typep->type_idp  = integer_idp;

    real_idp->defn.key    = TYPE_DEFN;
    real_idp->typep       = real_typep;
    real_typep->form      = SCALAR_FORM;
    real_typep->size      = sizeof(float);
    real_typep->type_idp  = real_idp;

    boolean_idp->defn.key    = TYPE_DEFN;
    boolean_idp->typep       = boolean_typep;
    boolean_typep->form      = ENUM_FORM;
    boolean_typep->size      = sizeof(int);
    boolean_typep->type_idp  = boolean_idp;
```

```
    boolean_typep->info.enumeration.max = 1;
    boolean_idp->typep->info.enumeration.const_idp = false_idp;
    false_idp->defn.key = CONST_DEFN;
    false_idp->defn.info.constant.value.integer = 0;
    false_idp->typep = boolean_typep;

    false_idp->next = true_idp;
    true_idp->defn.key = CONST_DEFN;
    true_idp->defn.info.constant.value.integer = 1;
    true_idp->typep = boolean_typep;

    char_idp->defn.key   = TYPE_DEFN;
    char_idp->typep      = char_typep;
    char_typep->form     = SCALAR_FORM;
    char_typep->size     = sizeof(char);
    char_typep->type_idp = char_idp;

    enter_standard_routine("read",    READ,    PROC_DEFN);
    enter_standard_routine("readln",  READLN,  PROC_DEFN);
    enter_standard_routine("write",   WRITE,   PROC_DEFN);
    enter_standard_routine("writeln", WRITELN, PROC_DEFN);

    enter_standard_routine("abs",    ABS,    FUNC_DEFN);
    enter_standard_routine("arctan", ARCTAN, FUNC_DEFN);
    enter_standard_routine("chr",    CHR,    FUNC_DEFN);
    enter_standard_routine("cos",    COS,    FUNC_DEFN);
    enter_standard_routine("eof",    EOFF,   FUNC_DEFN);
    enter_standard_routine("eoln",   EOLN,   FUNC_DEFN);
    enter_standard_routine("exp",    EXP,    FUNC_DEFN);
    enter_standard_routine("ln",     LN,     FUNC_DEFN);
    enter_standard_routine("odd",    ODD,    FUNC_DEFN);
    enter_standard_routine("ord",    ORD,    FUNC_DEFN);
    enter_standard_routine("pred",   PRED,   FUNC_DEFN);
    enter_standard_routine("round",  ROUND,  FUNC_DEFN);
    enter_standard_routine("sin",    SIN,    FUNC_DEFN);
    enter_standard_routine("sqr",    SQR,    FUNC_DEFN);
    enter_standard_routine("sqrt",   SQRT,   FUNC_DEFN);
    enter_standard_routine("succ",   SUCC,   FUNC_DEFN);
    enter_standard_routine("trunc",  TRUNC,  FUNC_DEFN);
}

/*------------------------------------------------------------*/
/*  enter_standard_routine    Enter a standard procedure or   */
/*                            function identifier into the    */
/*                            symbol table.                   */
/*------------------------------------------------------------*/

enter_standard_routine(name, routine_key, defn_key)

    char       *name;          /* name string */
    ROUTINE_KEY routine_key;
    DEFN_KEY    defn_key;

{
    SYMTAB_NODE_PTR rtn_idp = enter_name_local_symtab(rtn_idp, name);

    rtn_idp->defn.key                    = defn_key;
    rtn_idp->defn.info.routine.key       = routine_key;
    rtn_idp->defn.info.routine.parms     = NULL;
    rtn_idp->defn.info.routine.local_symtab = NULL;
    rtn_idp->typep                       = NULL;
}

/*------------------------------------------------------------*/
/*  enter_scope         Enter a new nesting level by creating */
/*                      a new scope.  Push the given symbol   */
/*                      table onto the display stack.         */
/*------------------------------------------------------------*/
```

```
enter_scope(symtab_root)

    SYMTAB_NODE_PTR symtab_root;

{
    if (++level >= MAX_NESTING_LEVEL) {
        error(NESTING_TOO_DEEP);
        exit(-NESTING_TOO_DEEP);
    }

    symtab_display[level] = symtab_root;
}

/*-----------------------------------------------------*/
/*  exit_scope        Exit the current nesting level by    */
```

```
/*                          closing the current scope.  Pop the    */
/*                          current symbol table off the display    */
/*                          stack and return a pointer to it.    */
/*----------------------------------------------------------*/

    SYMTAB_NODE_PTR
exit_scope()

{
    SYMTAB_NODE_PTR symtab_root = symtab_display[level--];

    return(symtab_root);
}
```

FIGURE B-11   code.h

```
/****************************************************************/
/*                                                              */
/*       C O D E   G E N E R A T O R   (Header)                 */
/*                                                              */
/*       FILE:     code.h                                       */
/*                                                              */
/*       MODULE:   code                                         */
/*                                                              */
/****************************************************************/

#ifndef code_h
#define code_h

#include "common.h"

/*----------------------------------------------------*/
/*  Assembly label prefixes                           */
/*----------------------------------------------------*/

#define STMT_LABEL_PREFIX        "$L"
#define FLOAT_LABEL_PREFIX       "$F"
#define STRING_LABEL_PREFIX      "$S"


/*----------------------------------------------------*/
/*  Names of library routines                         */
/*----------------------------------------------------*/

#define FLOAT_NEGATE    "_float_negate"
#define FLOAT_ADD       "_float_add"
#define FLOAT_SUBTRACT  "_float_subtract"
#define FLOAT_MULTIPLY  "_float_multiply"
#define FLOAT_DIVIDE    "_float_divide"
#define FLOAT_COMPARE   "_float_compare"
#define FLOAT_CONVERT   "_float_convert"

#define WRITE_INTEGER   "_write_integer"
#define WRITE_REAL      "_write_real"
#define WRITE_BOOLEAN   "_write_boolean"
#define WRITE_CHAR      "_write_char"
#define WRITE_STRING    "_write_string"
#define WRITE_LINE      "_write_line"

#define READ_INTEGER    "_read_integer"
#define READ_REAL       "_read_real"
#define READ_CHAR       "_read_char"
```

```
#define READ_LINE       "_read_line"

#define STD_END_OF_FILE "_std_end_of_file"
#define STD_END_OF_LINE "_std_end_of_line"

#define STD_ABS         "_std_abs"

#define STD_ARCTAN      "_std_arctan"
#define STD_COS         "_std_cos"
#define STD_EXP         "_std_exp"
#define STD_LN          "_std_ln"
#define STD_SIN         "_std_sin"
#define STD_SQRT        "_std_sqrt"

#define STD_ROUND       "_std_round"
#define STD_TRUNC       "_std_trunc"


/*----------------------------------------------------*/
/*  Stack frame                                       */
/*----------------------------------------------------*/

#define PROC_LOCALS_STACK_FRAME_OFFSET   0
#define FUNC_LOCALS_STACK_FRAME_OFFSET  -4
#define PARAMETERS_STACK_FRAME_OFFSET   +6

#define STATIC_LINK         "$STATIC_LINK"         /* EQU <bp+4> */
#define RETURN_VALUE        "$RETURN_VALUE"        /* EQU <bp-4> */
#define HIGH_RETURN_VALUE   "$HIGH_RETURN_VALUE"   /* EQU <bp-2> */

/*----------------------------------------------------*/
/*  Registers and instruction op codes                */
/*----------------------------------------------------*/

typedef enum {
    AX, AH, AL, BX, BH, BL, CX, CH, CL, DX, DH, DL,
    CS, DS, ES, SS, SP, BP, SI, DI,
} REGISTER;

typedef enum {
    MOVE, MOVE_BLOCK, LOAD_ADDRESS, EXCHANGE,
    COMPARE, COMPARE_STRINGS, POP, PUSH, AND_BITS, OR_BITS, XOR_BITS,
    NEGATE, INCREMENT, DECREMENT, ADD, SUBTRACT, MULTIPLY, DIVIDE,
    CLEAR_DIRECTION, CALL, RETURN,
    JUMP, JUMP_LT, JUMP_LE, JUMP_EQ, JUMP_NE, JUMP_GE, JUMP_GT,
} INSTRUCTION;
```

```
/**********************************************/
/*                                          */
/*      Macros to emit assembly statements  */
/*                                          */
/**********************************************/


/*----------------------------------------------------*/
/* emit              Emit a no-operand instruction.   */
/*----------------------------------------------------*/


#define emit(opcode)                      \
{                                         \
    operator(opcode);                     \
    fprintf(code_file, "%s\n", asm_buffer); \
    asm_bufferp = asm_buffer;             \
}


/*----------------------------------------------------*/
/* emit_1            Emit a one-operand instruction.  */
/*----------------------------------------------------*/


#define emit_1(opcode, operand1)          \
{                                         \
    operator(opcode);                     \
    *asm_bufferp++ = '\t';                \
    operand1;                             \
    fprintf(code_file, "%s\n", asm_buffer); \
    asm_bufferp = asm_buffer;             \
}


/*----------------------------------------------------*/
/* emit_2            Emit a two-operand instruction.  */
/*----------------------------------------------------*/
```

```
#define emit_2(opcode, operand1, operand2) \
{                                         \
    operator(opcode);                     \
    *asm_bufferp++ = '\t';                \
    operand1;                             \
    *asm_bufferp++ = ',';                 \
    operand2;                             \
    fprintf(code_file, "%s\n", asm_buffer); \
    asm_bufferp = asm_buffer;             \
}


/*----------------------------------------------------*/
/* emit_label               Emit a statement label.  */
/*----------------------------------------------------*/


#define emit_label(prefix, index)   fprintf(code_file, \
                              "%s_%03d:\n",  \
                              prefix, index);


/*----------------------------------------------------*/
/* advance_asm_bufferp    Advance asm_bufferp to the end */
/*                        of the assembly statement.    */
/*----------------------------------------------------*/


#define advance_asm_bufferp()   while (*asm_bufferp != '\0') \
                              ++asm_bufferp;


/*----------------------------------------------------*/
/* new_label_index          Return a new label index. */
/*----------------------------------------------------*/


#define new_label_index()       ++label_index

#endif
```

FIGURE B-12   emitasm.c

```
/*******************************************************/
/*                                                   */
/*      E M I T   A S S E M B L Y   S T A T E M E N T S  */
/*                                                   */
/*      Routines for generating and emitting         */
/*      language statements.                         */
/*                                                   */
/*      FILE:      emitasm.c                          */
/*                                                   */
/*      MODULE:    code                               */
/*                                                   */
/*******************************************************/


#include <stdio.h>
#include "symtab.h"
#include "code.h"


/*----------------------------------------------------*/
/* Globals                                            */
/*----------------------------------------------------*/


int label_index = 0;

char asm_buffer[MAX_PRINT_LINE_LENGTH];    /* assembly stmt buffer */
char *asm_bufferp = asm_buffer;            /* ptr into asm buffer */
```

```
char *register_strings[] = {
    "ax", "ah", "al", "bx", "bh", "bl", "cx", "ch", "cl",
    "dx", "dh", "dl", "cs", "ds", "es", "ss",
    "sp", "bp", "si", "di",
};


char *instruction_strings[] = {
    "mov", "rep\tmovsb", "lea", "xchg", "cmp", "repe\tcmpsb",
    "pop", "push", "and", "or", "xor",
    "neg", "inc", "dec", "add", "sub", "imul", "idiv",
    "cld", "call", "ret",
    "jmp", "jl", "jle", "je", "jne", "jge", "jg",
};


/**********************************************/
/*                                          */
/*      Write parts of assembly statements  */
/*                                          */
/**********************************************/


/*----------------------------------------------------*/
/* label              Write a generic label constructed from */
/*                    the prefix and the label index. */
/*                                          */
```

```
/*                    Example:       $L_007                */
/*------------------------------------------------------*/

label(prefix, index)

    char *prefix;
    int  index;

{
    sprintf(asm_bufferp, "%s_%03d", prefix, index);
    advance_asm_bufferp();
}

/*------------------------------------------------------*/
/*  word_label           Write a word label constructed from  */
/*                       the prefix and the label index.      */
/*                                                            */
/*                       Example:       WORD PTR $F_007       */
/*------------------------------------------------------*/

word_label(prefix, index)

    char *prefix;
    int  index;

{
    sprintf(asm_bufferp, "WORD PTR %s_%03d", prefix, index);
    advance_asm_bufferp();
}

/*------------------------------------------------------*/
/*  high_dword_label     Write a word label constructed from  */
/*                       the prefix and the label index and   */
/*                       offset by 2 to point to the high word*/
/*                       of a double word.                    */
/*                                                            */
/*                       Example:       WORD PTR $F_007+2     */
/*------------------------------------------------------*/

high_dword_label(prefix, index)

    char *prefix;
    int  index;

{
    sprintf(asm_bufferp, "WORD PTR %s_%03d+2", prefix, index);
    advance_asm_bufferp();
}

/*------------------------------------------------------*/
/*  reg                  Write a register name.  Example: ax  */
/*------------------------------------------------------*/

reg(r)

    REGISTER r;

{
    sprintf(asm_bufferp, "%s", register_strings[r]);
    advance_asm_bufferp();
}

/*------------------------------------------------------*/
/*  operator             Write an opcode.  Example: add  */
/*------------------------------------------------------*/

operator(opcode)
```

```
    INSTRUCTION opcode;

{
    sprintf(asm_bufferp, "\t%s", instruction_strings[opcode]);
    advance_asm_bufferp();
}

/*------------------------------------------------------*/
/*  byte                 Write a byte label constructed from  */
/*                       the id name and its label index.     */
/*                                                            */
/*                       Example:       BYTE_PTR ch_007       */
/*------------------------------------------------------*/

byte(idp)

    SYMTAB_NODE_PTR idp;

{
    sprintf(asm_bufferp, "BYTE PTR %s_%03d",
                          idp->name, idp->label_index);
    advance_asm_bufferp();
}

/*------------------------------------------------------*/
/*  byte_indirect        Write an indirect reference to a byte */
/*                       via a register.                      */
/*                                                            */
/*                       Example:       BYTE PTR [bx]         */
/*------------------------------------------------------*/

byte_indirect(r)

    REGISTER r;

{
    sprintf(asm_bufferp, "BYTE PTR [%s]", register_strings[r]);
    advance_asm_bufferp();
}

/*------------------------------------------------------*/
/*  word                 Write a word label constructed from  */
/*                       the id name and its label index.     */
/*                                                            */
/*                       Example:       WORD_PTR sum_007      */
/*------------------------------------------------------*/

word(idp)

    SYMTAB_NODE_PTR idp;

{
    sprintf(asm_bufferp, "WORD PTR %s_%03d",
                          idp->name, idp->label_index);
    advance_asm_bufferp();
}

/*------------------------------------------------------*/
/*  high_dword           Write a word label constructed from  */
/*                       the id name and its label index and  */
/*                       offset by 2 to point to the high word*/
/*                       of a double word.                    */
/*                                                            */
/*                       Example:       WORD_PTR sum_007+2    */
/*------------------------------------------------------*/

high_dword(idp)
```

```
SYMTAB_NODE_PTR idp;


{
    sprintf(asm_bufferp, "WORD PTR %s_%03d+2",
                          idp->name, idp->label_index);
    advance_asm_bufferp();
}

/*-----------------------------------------------------*/
/*  word_indirect        Write an indirect reference to a word  */
/*                       via a register.                */
/*                                                      */
/*                       Example:      WORD PTR [bx]    */
/*-----------------------------------------------------*/

word_indirect(r)

    REGISTER r;


{
    sprintf(asm_bufferp, "WORD PTR [%s]", register_strings[r]);
    advance_asm_bufferp();
}

/*-----------------------------------------------------*/
/*  high_dword_indirect   Write an indirect reference to the  */
/*                        high word of a double word via a   */
/*                        register.                     */
/*                                                      */
/*                        Example:      WORD PTR [bx+2]  */
/*-----------------------------------------------------*/

high_dword_indirect(r)

    REGISTER r;


{
    sprintf(asm_bufferp, "WORD PTR [%s+2]", register_strings[r]);
    advance_asm_bufferp();
}

/*-----------------------------------------------------*/
/*  tagged_name       Write an id name tagged with the id's  */
/*                    label index.                      */
/*                                                      */
/*                    Example:      x_007              */
/*-----------------------------------------------------*/

tagged_name(idp)
```

```
SYMTAB_NODE_PTR idp;

{
    sprintf(asm_bufferp, "%s_%03d", idp->name, idp->label_index);
    advance_asm_bufferp();
}

/*-----------------------------------------------------*/
/*  name_lit          Write a literal name.            */
/*                                                      */
/*                    Example:      _float_convert     */
/*-----------------------------------------------------*/

name_lit(name)

    char *name;


{
    sprintf(asm_bufferp, "%s", name);
    advance_asm_bufferp();
}

/*-----------------------------------------------------*/
/*  integer_lit       Write an integer as a string.   */
/*-----------------------------------------------------*/

integer_lit(n)

    int n;


{
    sprintf(asm_bufferp, "%d", n);
    advance_asm_bufferp();
}

/*-----------------------------------------------------*/
/*  char_lit          Write a character surrounded by single  */
/*                    quotes.                           */
/*-----------------------------------------------------*/

char_lit(ch)

    char ch;


{
    sprintf(asm_bufferp, "'%c'", ch);
    advance_asm_bufferp();
}
```

FIGURE B-13   emitcode.c

```
/**********************************************************/
/*                                                      */
/*      E M I T   C O D E   S E Q U E N C E S           */
/*                                                      */
/*      Routines for emitting standard                 */
/*      assembly code sequences.                        */
/*                                                      */
/*      FILE:       emitcode.c                          */
/*                                                      */
/*      MODULE:     code                                */
```

```
/*                                                      */
/**********************************************************/

#include <stdio.h>
#include "symtab.h"
#include "code.h"


/*-----------------------------------------------------*/
/*  Externals                                           */
/*-----------------------------------------------------*/
```

```
extern TYPE_STRUCT_PTR   integer_typep, real_typep,
                         boolean_typep, char_typep;

extern int level;

extern char     asm_buffer[];
extern char     *asm_bufferp;
extern FILE     *code_file;

/*----------------------------------------------------------*/
/*  Globals                                                 */
/*----------------------------------------------------------*/

SYMTAB_NODE_PTR  float_literal_list = NULL;
SYMTAB_NODE_PTR  string_literal_list = NULL;

            /***************************************/
            /*                                     */
            /*        Emit prologues and epilogues */
            /*                                     */
            /***************************************/

/*----------------------------------------------------------*/
/*  emit_program_prologue      Emit the program prologue.   */
/*----------------------------------------------------------*/

emit_program_prologue()

{
    fprintf(code_file, "\tDOSSEG\n");
    fprintf(code_file, "\t.MODEL  small\n");
    fprintf(code_file, "\t.STACK  1024\n");
    fprintf(code_file, "\n");
    fprintf(code_file, "\t.CODE\n");
    fprintf(code_file, "\n");
    fprintf(code_file, "\tPUBLIC\t_pascal_main\n");
    fprintf(code_file, "\tINCLUDE\tpasextrn.inc\n");
    fprintf(code_file, "\n");

    /*
    -- Equates for stack frame components.
    */
    fprintf(code_file, "%s\t\tEQU\t<WORD PTR [bp+4]>\n",
                    STATIC_LINK);
    fprintf(code_file, "%s\t\tEQU\t<WORD PTR [bp-4]>\n",
                    RETURN_VALUE);
    fprintf(code_file, "%s\tEQU\t<WORD PTR [bp-2]>\n",
                    HIGH_RETURN_VALUE);
    fprintf(code_file, "\n");
}

/*----------------------------------------------------------*/
/*  emit_program_epilogue      Emit the program epilogue,   */
/*                             which includes the data      */
/*                             segment.                     */
/*----------------------------------------------------------*/

emit_program_epilogue(prog_idp)

    SYMTAB_NODE_PTR prog_idp;   /* id of program */

{
    SYMTAB_NODE_PTR np;
    int             i, length;

    fprintf(code_file, "\n");
    fprintf(code_file, "\t.DATA\n");
```

```
    fprintf(code_file, "\n");

    /*
    -- Emit declarations for the program's global variables.
    */
    for (np = prog_idp->defn.info.routine.locals;
         np != NULL;
         np = np->next) {
        fprintf(code_file, "%s_%03d\t", np->name, np->label_index);
        if (np->typep == char_typep)
            fprintf(code_file, "DB\t0\n");
        else if (np->typep == real_typep)
            fprintf(code_file, "DD\t0.0\n");
        else if (np->typep->form == ARRAY_FORM)
            fprintf(code_file, "DB\t%d DUP(0)\n", np->typep->size);
        else if (np->typep->form == RECORD_FORM)
            fprintf(code_file, "DB\t%d DUP(0)\n", np->typep->size);
        else
            fprintf(code_file, "DW\t0\n");
    }

    /*
    -- Emit declarations for the program's floating point literals.
    */
    for (np = float_literal_list; np != NULL; np = np->next)
        fprintf(code_file, "%s_%03d\tDD\t%e\n", FLOAT_LABEL_PREFIX,
                        np->label_index,
                        np->defn.info.constant.value.real);

    /*
    -- Emit declarations for the program's string literals.
    */
    for (np = string_literal_list; np != NULL; np = np->next) {
        fprintf(code_file, "%s_%03d\tDB\t\"", STRING_LABEL_PREFIX,
                        np->label_index);

        length = strlen(np->name) - 2;
        for (i = 1; i <= length; ++i) fputc(np->name[i], code_file);

        fprintf(code_file, "\"\n");
    }

    fprintf(code_file, "\n");
    fprintf(code_file, "\tEND\n");
}

/*----------------------------------------------------------*/
/*  emit_main_prologue          Emit the prologue for the main   */
/*                              routine _pascal_main.            */
/*----------------------------------------------------------*/

emit_main_prologue()

{
    fprintf(code_file, "\n");
    fprintf(code_file, "_pascal_main\tPROC\n");
    fprintf(code_file, "\n");

    emit_1(PUSH, reg(BP));              /* dynamic link */
    emit_2(MOVE, reg(BP), reg(SP));     /* new stack frame base */
}

/*----------------------------------------------------------*/
/*  emit_main_epilogue           Emit the epilogue for the main   */
/*                               routine _pascal_main.            */
/*----------------------------------------------------------*/

emit_main_epilogue()
```

```
{
    fprintf(code_file, "\n");

    emit_1(POP, reg(BP));           /* restore caller's stack frame */
    emit(RETURN);                   /* return */

    fprintf(code_file, "\n");
    fprintf(code_file, "_pascal_main\tENDP\n");
}

/*-----------------------------------------------------*/
/* emit_routine_prologue    Emit the prologue for a proce- */
/*                          dure or a function.        */
/*-----------------------------------------------------*/

emit_routine_prologue(rtn_idp)

    SYMTAB_NODE_PTR rtn_idp;

{
    fprintf(code_file, "\n");
    fprintf(code_file, "%s_%03d\tPROC\n",
                        rtn_idp->name, rtn_idp->label_index);
    fprintf(code_file, "\n");

    emit_1(PUSH, reg(BP));              /* dynamic link */
    emit_2(MOVE, reg(BP), reg(SP));     /* new stack frame base */

    /*
    -- Allocate stack space for a function's return value.
    */
    if (rtn_idp->defn.key == FUNC_DEFN) emit_2(SUBTRACT, reg(SP),
                                               integer_lit(4));

    /*
    -- Allocate stack space for the local variables.
    */
    if (rtn_idp->defn.info.routine.total_local_size > 0)
        emit_2(SUBTRACT, reg(SP),
                integer_lit(rtn_idp->defn.info.routine
                    .total_local_size));
}

/*-----------------------------------------------------*/
/* emit_routine_epilogue    Emit the epilogue for a proce- */
/*                          dure or a function.        */
/*-----------------------------------------------------*/

emit_routine_epilogue(rtn_idp)

    SYMTAB_NODE_PTR rtn_idp;

{
    /*
    -- Load a function's return value into the ax or dx:ax registers.
    */
    if (rtn_idp->defn.key == FUNC_DEFN) {
        emit_2(MOVE, reg(AX), name_lit(RETURN_VALUE));
        if (rtn_idp->typep == real_typep)
            emit_2(MOVE, reg(DX), name_lit(HIGH_RETURN_VALUE));
    }

    emit_2(MOVE, reg(SP), reg(BP)); /* cut back to caller's stack */
    emit_1(POP, reg(BP));            /* restore caller's stack frame */

    emit_1(RETURN, integer_lit(rtn_idp->defn.info.routine
                                .total_parm_size + 2));
```

```
                                    /* return and cut back stack */
    fprintf(code_file, "\n");
    fprintf(code_file, "%s_%03d\tENDP\n",
                        rtn_idp->name, rtn_idp->label_index);
}

/*******************************/
/*                             */
/*      Emit equates and data  */
/*                             */
/*******************************/

/*-----------------------------------------------------*/
/* emit_declarations    Emit the parameter and local variable */
/*                      declarations for a procedure or a    */
/*                      function.                       */
/*-----------------------------------------------------*/

emit_declarations(rtn_idp)

    SYMTAB_NODE_PTR rtn_idp;

{
    SYMTAB_NODE_PTR parm_idp = rtn_idp->defn.info.routine.parms;
    SYMTAB_NODE_PTR var_idp  = rtn_idp->defn.info.routine.locals;

    fprintf(code_file, "\n");

    /*
    -- Parameters.
    */
    while (parm_idp != NULL) {
        emit_text_equate(parm_idp);
        parm_idp = parm_idp->next;
    }

    /*
    -- Local variables.
    */
    while (var_idp != NULL) {
        emit_text_equate(var_idp);
        var_idp = var_idp->next;
    }
}

/*-----------------------------------------------------*/
/* emit_numeric_equate    Emit a numeric equate for a field */
/*                        id and its offset.           */
/*                                                     */
/*                        Example:   field_007 EQU 3   */
/*-----------------------------------------------------*/

emit_numeric_equate(idp)

    SYMTAB_NODE_PTR idp;

{
    fprintf(code_file, "%s_%03d\tEQU\t%d\n",
                        idp->name, idp->label_index,
                        idp->defn.info.data.offset);
}

/*-----------------------------------------------------*/
/* emit_numeric_equate    Emit a numeric equate for a para- */
/*                        meter or a local variable id and  */
/*                        its stack frame offset.      */
```

```
/*                                                    */
/*                    Examples:  parm_007    EQU <bp+6>     */
/*                               var_008     EQU <bp-10>    */
/*                               dword_010   EQU <bp-14>    */
/*                               dword_010h  EQU <bp-14+2>  */
/*----------------------------------------------------------*/

emit_text_equate(idp)

    SYMTAB_NODE_PTR idp;

{
    char *name       = idp->name;
    int  label_index = idp->label_index;
    int  offset      = idp->defn.info.data.offset;

    if (idp->typep == char_typep)
        fprintf(code_file, "%s_%03d\tEQU\t<BYTE PTR [bp%+d]>\n",
                           name, label_index, offset);
    else if (idp->typep == real_typep)
        fprintf(code_file, "%s_%03d\tEQU\t<WORD PTR [bp%+d]>\n",
                           name, label_index, offset);
    else
        fprintf(code_file, "%s_%03d\tEQU\t<WORD PTR [bp%+d]>\n",
                           name, label_index, offset);
}

            /********************************/
            /*                              */
            /*    Emit loads and pushes     */
            /*                              */
            /********************************/

/*----------------------------------------------------------*/
/*  emit_load_value      Emit code to load a scalar value   */
/*                       into AX or DX:AX.                   */
/*----------------------------------------------------------*/

emit_load_value(var_idp, var_tp)

    SYMTAB_NODE_PTR var_idp;
    TYPE_STRUCT_PTR var_tp;

{
    int     var_level    = var_idp->level;
    BOOLEAN varparm_flag = var_idp->defn.key == VARPARM_DEFN;

    if (varparm_flag) {
        /*
        -- VAR formal parameter.
        -- AX or DX:AX = value the address points to
        */
        emit_2(MOVE, reg(BX), word(var_idp));
        if (var_tp == char_typep) {
            emit_2(SUBTRACT, reg(AX), reg(AX));
            emit_2(MOVE, reg(AL), byte_indirect(BX));
        }
        else if (var_tp == real_typep) {
            emit_2(MOVE, reg(AX), word_indirect(BX));
            emit_2(MOVE, reg(AX), high_dword_indirect(BX));
        }
        else emit_2(MOVE, reg(AX), word_indirect(BX));
    }
    else if ((var_level == level) || (var_level == 1)) {
        /*
        -- Global or local parameter or variable:
        -- AX or DX:AX = value
```

```
        */
        if (var_tp == char_typep) {
            emit_2(SUBTRACT, reg(AX), reg(AX));
            emit_2(MOVE, reg(AL), byte(var_idp));
        }
        else if (var_tp == real_typep) {
            emit_2(MOVE, reg(AX), word(var_idp));
            emit_2(MOVE, reg(DX), high_dword(var_idp));
        }
        else emit_2(MOVE, reg(AX), word(var_idp));
    }
    else   /* var_level < level */ {
        /*
        -- Nonlocal parameter or variable.
        -- First locate the appropriate stack frame, then:
        -- AX or DX:AX = value
        */
        int lev = var_level;

        emit_2(MOVE, reg(BX), reg(BP));
        do {
            emit_2(MOVE, reg(BP), name_lit(STATIC_LINK));
        } while (++lev < level);

        if (var_tp == char_typep) {
            emit_2(SUBTRACT, reg(AX), reg(AX));
            emit_2(MOVE, reg(AL), byte(var_idp));
        }
        else if (var_tp == real_typep) {
            emit_2(MOVE, reg(AX), word(var_idp));
            emit_2(MOVE, reg(DX), high_dword(var_idp));
        }
        else emit_2(MOVE, reg(AX), word(var_idp));

        emit_2(MOVE, reg(BP), reg(BX));
    }
}

/*----------------------------------------------------------*/
/*  emit_push_operand   Emit code to push a scalar operand  */
/*                      value onto the stack.               */
/*----------------------------------------------------------*/

emit_push_operand(tp)

    TYPE_STRUCT_PTR tp;

{
    if ((tp->form == ARRAY_FORM) || (tp->form == RECORD_FORM)) return;

    if (tp == real_typep) emit_1(PUSH, reg(DX));
    emit_1(PUSH, reg(AX));
}

/*----------------------------------------------------------*/
/*  emit_push_address   Emit code to push an address onto the */
/*                      stack.                              */
/*----------------------------------------------------------*/

emit_push_address(var_idp)

    SYMTAB_NODE_PTR var_idp;

{
    int     var_level    = var_idp->level;
    BOOLEAN varparm_flag = var_idp->defn.key == VARPARM_DEFN;

    if ((var_level == level) || (var_level == 1))
```

```
        emit_2(varparm_flag ? MOVE : LOAD_ADDRESS,
               reg(AX), word(var_idp))

    else   /* var_level < level */  {
        int lev = var_level;

        emit_2(MOVE, reg(BX), reg(BP));
        do {
            emit_2(MOVE, reg(BP), name_lit(STATIC_LINK));
        } while (++lev < level);
        emit_2(varparm_flag ? MOVE : LOAD_ADDRESS,
               reg(AX), word(var_idp));
        emit_2(MOVE, reg(BP), reg(BX));
    }

    emit_1(PUSH, reg(AX));
}

/*----------------------------------------------------------*/
/*  emit_push_return_value_address      Emit code to push the   */
/*                                      address of the function */
/*                                      return value in the     */
/*                                      stack frame.            */
/*----------------------------------------------------------*/

emit_push_return_value_address(var_idp)

    SYMTAB_NODE_PTR var_idp;

{
    int lev = var_idp->level + 1;

    if (lev < level) {
        /*
        -- Find the appropriate stack frame.
        */
        emit_2(MOVE, reg(BX), reg(BP));
        do {
            emit_2(MOVE, reg(BP), name_lit(STATIC_LINK));
        } while (++lev < level);
        emit_2(LOAD_ADDRESS, reg(AX), name_lit(RETURN_VALUE));
        emit_2(MOVE, reg(BP), reg(BX));
    }
    else emit_2(LOAD_ADDRESS, reg(AX), name_lit(RETURN_VALUE));
}
```

```
        emit_1(PUSH, reg(AX));
}

        /***************************************/
        /*                                     */
        /*      Emit miscellaneous code        */
        /*                                     */
        /***************************************/

/*----------------------------------------------------------*/
/*  emit_promote_to_real         Emit code to convert integer   */
/*                               operands to real.             */
/*----------------------------------------------------------*/

emit_promote_to_real(tp1, tp2)

    TYPE_STRUCT_PTR tp1, tp2;

{
    if (tp2 == integer_typep) {
        emit_1(CALL, name_lit(FLOAT_CONVERT));
        emit_2(ADD, reg(SP), integer_lit(2));
        emit_1(PUSH, reg(DX));
        emit_1(PUSH, reg(AX));               /* ???_1 real_2 */
    }

    if (tp1 == integer_typep) {
        emit_1(POP,  reg(AX));
        emit_1(POP,  reg(DX));
        emit_1(POP,  reg(BX));
        emit_1(PUSH, reg(DX));
        emit_1(PUSH, reg(AX));
        emit_1(PUSH, reg(BX));               /* real_2 integer_1 */

        emit_1(CALL, name_lit(FLOAT_CONVERT));
        emit_2(ADD, reg(SP), integer_lit(2));  /* real_2 real_1 */

        emit_1(POP,  reg(BX));
        emit_1(POP,  reg(CX));
        emit_1(PUSH, reg(DX));
        emit_1(PUSH, reg(AX));
        emit_1(PUSH, reg(CX));
        emit_1(PUSH, reg(BX));               /* real_1 real_2 */
    }
}
```

FIGURE B-14   error.h

```
/*****************************************************************/
/*                                                               */
/*      E R R O R   R O U T I N E S   (Header)                   */
/*                                                               */
/*      FILE:     error.h                                        */
/*                                                               */
/*      MODULE:   error                                          */
/*                                                               */
/*****************************************************************/

#ifndef error_h
#define error_h

#define MAX_SYNTAX_ERRORS 25
```

```
/*----------------------------------------------------------*/
/*  Error codes                                              */
/*----------------------------------------------------------*/

typedef enum {
    NO_ERROR,
    SYNTAX_ERROR,
    TOO_MANY_SYNTAX_ERRORS,
    FAILED_SOURCE_FILE_OPEN,
    UNEXPECTED_END_OF_FILE,
    INVALID_NUMBER,
    INVALID_FRACTION,
    INVALID_EXPONENT,
    TOO_MANY_DIGITS,
```

```
    REAL_OUT_OF_RANGE,                              NOT_A_CONSTANT_IDENTIFIER,
    INTEGER_OUT_OF_RANGE,                           MISSING_DOTDOT,
    MISSING_RPAREN,                                 INCOMPATIBLE_TYPES,
    INVALID_EXPRESSION,                             INVALID_TARGET,
    INVALID_ASSIGNMENT,                             INVALID_IDENTIFIER_USAGE,
    MISSING_IDENTIFIER,                             INCOMPATIBLE_ASSIGNMENT,
    MISSING_COLONEQUAL,                             MIN_GT_MAX,
    UNDEFINED_IDENTIFIER,                           MISSING_LBRACKET,
    STACK_OVERFLOW,                                 MISSING_RBRACKET,
    INVALID_STATEMENT,                              INVALID_INDEX_TYPE,
    UNEXPECTED_TOKEN,                               MISSING_BEGIN,
    MISSING_SEMICOLON,                              MISSING_PERIOD,
    MISSING_DO,                                     TOO_MANY_SUBSCRIPTS,
    MISSING_UNTIL,                                  INVALID_FIELD,
    MISSING_THEN,                                   NESTING_TOO_DEEP,
    INVALID_FOR_CONTROL,                            MISSING_PROGRAM,
    MISSING_OF,                                     ALREADY_FORWARDED,
    INVALID_CONSTANT,                               WRONG_NUMBER_OF_PARMS,
    MISSING_CONSTANT,                               INVALID_VAR_PARM,
    MISSING_COLON,                                  NOT_A_RECORD_VARIABLE,
    MISSING_END,                                    MISSING_VARIABLE,
    MISSING_TO_OR_DOWNTO,                           CODE_SEGMENT_OVERFLOW,
    REDEFINED_IDENTIFIER,                           UNIMPLEMENTED_FEATURE,
    MISSING_EQUAL,                               } ERROR_CODE;
    INVALID_TYPE,
    NOT_A_TYPE_IDENTIFIER,
    INVALID_SUBRANGE_TYPE,                          #endif
```

FIGURE B-15   error.c

```
/****************************************************************/
/*                                                              */
/*        E R R O R   R O U T I N E S                           */
/*                                                              */
/*        Error messages and routines to print them.           */
/*                                                              */
/*        FILE:       error.c                                   */
/*                                                              */
/*        MODULE:     error                                     */
/*                                                              */
/****************************************************************/

#include <stdio.h>
#include "common.h"
#include "error.h"


/*------------------------------------------------------------*/
/*  Externals                                                 */
/*------------------------------------------------------------*/

extern char     *tokenp;
extern BOOLEAN  print_flag;
extern char     source_buffer[];
extern char     *bufferp;


/*------------------------------------------------------------*/
/*  Error messages      Keyed to enumeration type ERROR_CODE  */
/*                      in file error.h.                      */
/*------------------------------------------------------------*/

char *error_messages[] = {
    "No error",
    "Syntax error",
    "Too many syntax errors",
    "Failed to open source file",
    "Unexpected end of file",
    "Invalid number",
    "Invalid fraction",
    "Invalid exponent",
    "Too many digits",
    "Real literal out of range",
    "Integer literal out of range",
    "Missing right parenthesis",
    "Invalid expression",
    "Invalid assignment statement",
    "Missing identifier",
    "Missing := ",
    "Undefined identifier",
    "Stack overflow",
    "Invalid statement",
    "Unexpected token",
    "Missing ; ",
    "Missing DO",
    "Missing UNTIL",
    "Missing THEN",
    "Invalid FOR control variable",
    "Missing OF",
    "Invalid constant",
    "Missing constant",
    "Missing : ",
    "Missing END",
    "Missing TO or DOWNTO",
    "Redefined identifier",
    "Missing = ",
```

```
    "Invalid type",
    "Not a type identifier",
    "Invalid subrangetype",
    "Not a constant identifier",
    "Missing .. ",
    "Incompatible types",
    "Invalid assignment target",
    "Invalid identifier usage",
    "Incompatible assignment",
    "Min limit greater than max limit",
    "Missing [ ",
    "Missing ] ",
    "Invalid index type",
    "Missing BEGIN",
    "Missing period",
    "Too many subscripts",
    "Invalid field",
    "Nesting too deep",
    "Missing PROGRAM",
    "Already specified in FORWARD",
    "Wrong number of actual parameters",
    "Invalid VAR parameter",
    "Not a record variable",
    "Missing variable",
    "Code segment overflow",
    "Unimplemented feature",
};

/*------------------------------------------------------------*/
/* Globals                                                    */
/*------------------------------------------------------------*/

int error_count = 0;    /* number of syntax errors */

            /*******************************/
            /*                             */
            /*       Error routines        */
            /*                             */
            /*******************************/

/*------------------------------------------------------------*/
/* error            Print an arrow under the error and then   */
```

```
/*                  print the error message.                */
/*------------------------------------------------------------*/

error(code)

    ERROR_CODE code;     /* error code */

{
    extern int buffer_offset;
    char message_buffer[MAX_PRINT_LINE_LENGTH];
    char *message = error_messages[code];
    int  offset   = buffer_offset - 2;

    /*
    -- Print the arrow pointing to the token just scanned.
    */
    if (print_flag) offset += 8;
    sprintf(message_buffer, "%*s^\n", offset, " ");
    if (print_flag) print_line(message_buffer);
    else            printf(message_buffer);

    /*
    -- Print the error message.
    */
    sprintf(message_buffer, " *** ERROR: %s.\n", message);
    if (print_flag) print_line(message_buffer);
    else            printf(message_buffer);

    *tokenp = '\0';
    ++error_count;

    if (error_count > MAX_SYNTAX_ERRORS) {
        sprintf(message_buffer,
            "Too many syntax errors.  Aborted.\n");
        if (print_flag) print_line(message_buffer);
        else            printf(message_buffer);

        exit(-TOO_MANY_SYNTAX_ERRORS);
    }
}
```

FIGURE B-16   common.h

```
/****************************************************************/
/*                                                              */
/*    C O M M O N   R O U T I N E S   (Header)                  */
/*                                                              */
/*    FILE:    common.h                                         */
/*                                                              */
/*    MODULE:  common                                           */
/*                                                              */
/****************************************************************/

#ifndef common_h
#define common_h
```

```
#define FORM_FEED_CHAR          '\f'

#define MAX_FILE_NAME_LENGTH    32
#define MAX_SOURCE_LINE_LENGTH  256
#define MAX_PRINT_LINE_LENGTH   80
#define MAX_LINES_PER_PAGE      50
#define DATE_STRING_LENGTH      26
#define MAX_TOKEN_STRING_LENGTH MAX_SOURCE_LINE_LENGTH
#define MAX_CODE_BUFFER_SIZE    4096
#define MAX_NESTING_LEVEL       16

typedef enum {
```

```
        FALSE, TRUE,
} BOOLEAN;
```

```
        /*****************************************/
        /*                                       */
        /*      Macros for memory allocation     */
        /*                                       */
```

```
        /*****************************************/

#define alloc_struct(type)          (type *) malloc(sizeof(type))
#define alloc_array(type, count)     (type *) malloc(count*sizeof(type))
#define alloc_bytes(length)          (char *) malloc(length)

#endif
```

FIGURE B-17   compile2.c

```
/**********************************************************/
/*                                                        */
/*      Program 14-1:  Pascal Compiler II                 */
/*                                                        */
/*      Compile Pascal programs.                          */
/*                                                        */
/*      FILE:      compile2.c                             */
/*                                                        */
/*      REQUIRES:  Modules parser, symbol table, scanner, */
/*                      code, error                       */
/*                                                        */
/*      USAGE:     compile2 sourcefile objectfile         */
/*                                                        */
/*        sourcefile      [input] source file containing the */
/*                            the statements to compile   */
/*                                                        */
/*        objectfile      [output] object file to contain the */
/*                            generated assembly code     */
/*                                                        */
/**********************************************************/

#include <stdio.h>

/*--------------------------------------------------------*/
/* Globals                                                */
/*--------------------------------------------------------*/

FILE *code_file;    /* ASCII file for the emitted assembly code */
```

```
/*--------------------------------------------------------*/
/*  main              Initialize the scanner and call     */
/*                         routine program.               */
/*--------------------------------------------------------*/

main(argc, argv)

    int  argc;
    char *argv[];

{
    /*
    -- Open the code file.  If no code file name was given,
    -- use the standard output file.
    */
    code_file = (argc == 3) ? fopen(argv[2], "w")
                            : stdout;

    /*
    -- Initialize the scanner.
    */
    init_scanner(argv[1]);

    /*
    -- Process a program.
    */
    get_token();
    program();
}
```

FIGURE B-18   paslib.c

```
/**********************************************************/
/*                                                        */
/*       P A S C A L   R U N T I M E   L I B R A R Y      */
/*                                                        */
/*      Note that all formal parameters are reversed to   */
/*      accomodate the Pascal calling convention of the   */
/*      compiled code.                                    */
/*                                                        */
/*      All floating point parameters are passed in as longs */
/*      to bypass unwanted type conversions.  Floating point */
/*      function values are also returned as longs.       */
/*                                                        */
/**********************************************************/

#include <stdio.h>
```

```
#include <math.h>

#define MAX_SOURCE_LINE_LENGTH  256

typedef enum {
    FALSE, TRUE
} BOOLEAN;

union {
    float real;
    long  dword;
} value;

/*--------------------------------------------------------*/
/* Globals                                                */
/*--------------------------------------------------------*/
```

```
BOOLEAN eof_flag  = FALSE;
BOOLEAN eoln_flag = FALSE;

/*-------------------------------------------------*/
/*  main            The main routine, which calls      */
/*                  pascal_main, the "main" of the compiled */
/*                  program.                           */
/*-------------------------------------------------*/

main(argc, argv)

    int  argc;
    char *argv[];

{
    pascal_main();
    exit(0);
}

            /*********************************/
            /*                               */
            /*        Read routines          */
            /*                               */
            /*********************************/

/*-------------------------------------------------*/
/*  read_integer       Read an integer value.         */
/*-------------------------------------------------*/

    int
read_integer()

{
    int i;

    scanf("%d", &i);
    return(i);
}

/*-------------------------------------------------*/
/*  read_real        Read a real value.               */
/*-------------------------------------------------*/

    long
read_real()

{
    scanf("%g", &value.real);
    return(value.dword);
}

/*-------------------------------------------------*/
/*  read_char        Read a character value.          */
/*-------------------------------------------------*/

    char
read_char()

{
    char ch;

    scanf("%c", &ch);
    if (eof_flag || (ch == '\n')) ch = ' ';

    return(ch);
}
```

```
/*-------------------------------------------------*/
/*  read_line        Skip the rest of the input record.    */
/*-------------------------------------------------*/

read_line()

{
    char ch;

    do {
        ch = getchar();
    } while(!eof_flag && (ch != '\n'));
}

            /*********************************/
            /*                               */
            /*        Write routines         */
            /*                               */
            /*********************************/

/*-------------------------------------------------*/
/*  write_integer       Write an integer value.       */
/*-------------------------------------------------*/

write_integer(field_width, i)

    int i;
    int field_width;

{
    printf("%*d", field_width, i);
}

/*-------------------------------------------------*/
/*  write_real         Write an real value.           */
/*-------------------------------------------------*/

write_real(precision, field_width, i)

    long i;
    int  field_width;
    int  precision;

{
    value.dword = i;
    printf("%*.*f", field_width, precision, value.real);
}

/*-------------------------------------------------*/
/*  write_boolean       Write a boolean value.        */
/*-------------------------------------------------*/

write_boolean(field_width, b)

    int b;
    int field_width;

{
    printf("%*s", field_width, b == 0 ? "FALSE" : "TRUE");
}

/*-------------------------------------------------*/
/*  write_char          Write a character value.      */
/*-------------------------------------------------*/

write_char(field_width, ch)
```

```
    int ch;
    int field_width;

{
    printf("%*c", field_width, ch);
}
```

```
/*----------------------------------------------*/
/* write_string        Write a string value.    */
/*----------------------------------------------*/

write_string(length, field_width, value)

    char *value;
    int  field_width;
    int  length;

{
    char buffer[MAX_SOURCE_LINE_LENGTH];

    strncpy(buffer, value, length);
    buffer[length] = '\0';

    printf("%*s", -field_width, buffer);
}
```

```
/*----------------------------------------------*/
/* write_line          Write a carriage return. */
/*----------------------------------------------*/

write_line()

{
    putchar('\n');
}
```

```
            /*******************************/
            /*                             */
            /*        Other I/O routines   */
            /*                             */
            /*******************************/
```

```
/*----------------------------------------------*/
/* std_end_of_file     Return 1 if at end of file, else 0. */
/*----------------------------------------------*/

    BOOLEAN
std_end_of_file()

{
    char ch = getchar();

    if (eof_flag || feof(stdin)) eof_flag = TRUE;
    else                         ungetc(ch, stdin);

    return(eof_flag);
}
```

```
/*----------------------------------------------*/
/* std_end_of_line     Return 1 if at end of line, else 0. */
/*----------------------------------------------*/

    BOOLEAN
std_end_of_line()

{
    char ch = getchar();

    if (eof_flag || feof(stdin))
        eoln_flag = eof_flag = TRUE;
    else {
        eoln_flag = ch == '\n';
```

```
        ungetc(ch, stdin);
    }

    return(eoln_flag);
}
```

```
        /**************************************************/
        /*                                                */
        /*        Floating point arithmetic routines      */
        /*                                                */
        /**************************************************/
```

```
/*----------------------------------------------*/
/* float_negate        Return the negated value. */
/*----------------------------------------------*/

    long
float_negate(i)

    long i;

{
    value.dword = i;

    value.real = -value.real;
    return(value.dword);
}
```

```
/*----------------------------------------------*/
/* float_add           Return the sum x + y.     */
/*----------------------------------------------*/

    long
float_add(j, i)

    long i, j;

{
    float x, y;

    value.dword = i;  x = value.real;
    value.dword = j;  y = value.real;

    value.real = x + y;
    return(value.dword);
}
```

```
/*----------------------------------------------*/
/* float_subtract      Return the difference x - y. */
/*----------------------------------------------*/

    long
float_subtract(j, i)

    long i, j;

{
    float x, y;

    value.dword = i;  x = value.real;
    value.dword = j;  y = value.real;

    value.real = x - y;
    return(value.dword);
}
```

```
/*----------------------------------------------*/
/* float_multiply      Return the product x*y.   */
/*----------------------------------------------*/

    long
float_multiply(j, i)
```

```
    long i, j;

{
    float x, y;

    value.dword = i;  x = value.real;
    value.dword = j;  y = value.real;

    value.real = x*y;
    return(value.dword);
}
/*-----------------------------------------------------*/
/* float_divide       Return the quotient x/y.        */
/*-----------------------------------------------------*/

    long
float_divide(j, i)

    long i, j;

{
    float x, y;

    value.dword = i;  x = value.real;
    value.dword = j;  y = value.real;

    value.real = x/y;
    return(value.dword);
}
/*-----------------------------------------------------*/
/* float_convert      Convert an integer value to real and */
/*                    return the converted value.     */
/*-----------------------------------------------------*/

    long
float_convert(i)

    int i;

{
    value.real = i;
    return(value.dword);
}
/*-----------------------------------------------------*/
/* float_compare      Return -1 if x <  y            */
/*                            0 if x == y            */
/*                           +1 if x >  y            */
/*-----------------------------------------------------*/

float_compare(j, i)

    long i, j;

{
    int   comp;
    float x, y;

    value.dword = i;  x = value.real;
    value.dword = j;  y = value.real;

    if (x < y)        comp = -1;
    else if (x == y)  comp = 0;
    else              comp = +1;

    return(comp);
}
        /*******************************************/
        /*                                        */
```

```
    /*       Standard floating point functions   */
    /*                                           */
    /*******************************************/
/*-----------------------------------------------------*/
/* std_abs            Return abs of parameter.        */
/*-----------------------------------------------------*/

    long
std_abs(i)

    long i;

{
    value.dword = i;

    value.real = fabs(value.real);
    return(value.dword);
}
/*-----------------------------------------------------*/
/* std_arctan         Return arctan of parameter.     */
/*-----------------------------------------------------*/

    long
std_arctan(i)

    long i;

{
    value.dword = i;

    value.real = atan(value.real);
    return(value.dword);
}
/*-----------------------------------------------------*/
/* std_cos            Return cos of parameter.        */
/*-----------------------------------------------------*/

    long
std_cos(i)

    long i;

{
    value.dword = i;

    value.real = cos(value.real);
    return(value.dword);
}
/*-----------------------------------------------------*/
/* std_exp            Return exp of parameter.        */
/*-----------------------------------------------------*/

    long
std_exp(i)

    long i;

{
    value.dword = i;

    value.real = exp(value.real);
    return(value.dword);
}
/*-----------------------------------------------------*/
/* std_ln             Return ln of parameter.         */
/*-----------------------------------------------------*/
```

```
    long
std_ln(i)

    long i;

{
    value.dword = i;

    value.real = log(value.real);
    return(value.dword);
}
```

```
/*------------------------------------------------*/
/*  std_sin           Return sin of parameter.    */
/*------------------------------------------------*/

    long
std_sin(i)

    long i;

{
    value.dword = i;

    value.real = sin(value.real);
    return(value.dword);
}
```

```
/*------------------------------------------------*/
/*  std_sqrt          Return sqrt of parameter.   */
/*------------------------------------------------*/

    long
std_sqrt(i)

    long i;

{
```

```
    value.dword = i;

    value.real = sqrt(value.real);
    return(value.dword);
}
```

```
/*------------------------------------------------*/
/*  std_round          Return round of parameter.    */
/*------------------------------------------------*/

    int
std_round(i)

    long i;

{
    value.dword = i;

    value.dword = (int) (value.real + 0.5);
    return((int) value.dword);
}
```

```
/*------------------------------------------------*/
/*  std_trunc          Return trunc of parameter.    */
/*------------------------------------------------*/

    int
std_trunc(i)

    long i;

{
    value.dword = i;

    value.dword = (int) value.real;
    return((int) value.dword);
}
```

FIGURE B-19   pasextrn.inc

```
EXTRN   _float_negate:PROC
EXTRN   _float_add:PROC
EXTRN   _float_subtract:PROC
EXTRN   _float_multiply:PROC
EXTRN   _float_divide:PROC
EXTRN   _float_compare:PROC
EXTRN   _float_convert:PROC

EXTRN   _write_integer:PROC
EXTRN   _write_real:PROC
EXTRN   _write_boolean:PROC
EXTRN   _write_char:PROC
EXTRN   _write_string:PROC
EXTRN   _write_line:PROC

EXTRN   _read_integer:PROC
EXTRN   _read_real:PROC

EXTRN   _read_char:PROC
EXTRN   _read_line:PROC

EXTRN   _std_end_of_file:PROC
EXTRN   _std_end_of_line:PROC

EXTRN   _std_abs:PROC

EXTRN   _std_arctan:PROC
EXTRN   _std_cos:PROC
EXTRN   _std_exp:PROC
EXTRN   _std_ln:PROC
EXTRN   _std_sin:PROC
EXTRN   _std_sqrt:PROC

EXTRN   _std_round:PROC
EXTRN   _std_trunc:PROC
```

Index

Disk Order Form

We are making available a diskette that contains all the source code presented in this book.

 To order your disk, fill out the form below and mail it along with $25 plus $2 for shipping and handling in check or money order (California residents, please add your local sales tax) to:

Apropos Logic
4899 Bela Drive
San Jose, CA 95129

- -

Please send me _____ copies of the Writing Compilers and Interpreters Disk at $25 each plus $2 shipping and handling (California residents add your local sales tax). Please make checks payable to Apropos Logic.

_____
Name

_____
Address

_____
City   State   Zip Code

_____
Telephone